The GOLDFISH Bowl

TOM REILLY

The Goldfish Bowl
Copyright © 2022 by Tom Reilly

ISBN
978-1-957895-03-1 (Paperback)
978-1-957895-02-4 (eBook)
978-1-957895-04-8 (Hardcover)

*I dedicate this novel to my beautiful Chinese wife,
Anne who inspired me to continue writing and spent
many late nights as both my critic and editor*

Table of Contents

BLUEPRINT PRESS

Preface

You two Gauchos either have shit for brains or you have a death wish. What's it gonna be?"

"Marcos, look at it this way, what have you got to lose? It's our necks that's on the block."

"And what about the gringo?"

"We take him along, then when the time is right, we blow his friggin brains out."

"That takes intelligence, huh?" Marcos shook his head

"And the money?" Now Marcos was beginning to get interested.

"We ask for ten mill."

"Hmmm . . ." Marcos was hooked. "Well, I'm sure the old goat can afford it . . . Now for the sixty-five thousand dollar question . . . When?" *"Tonight . . ."*

PART 1

New York, August 2003

CHAPTER 1

It was a humid summer night in August 2003. The New York summer, as always, is predictable, hot, and balmy; and tonight, was no exception. The central air-conditioning unit was struggling to satisfy the large luxury villa in East Village, a highly sought-after upper-class locality overlooking the river.

The humidity was uncomfortable, and June restlessly pushed the silk top sheet down to her waist, exposing her smooth naked shoulders and spaghetti string nightdress.

June Summers was pretty, all right, her shoulder-length blonde hair filling the pillow. She had just turned forty-two, but her firm breasts and shapely figure eluded the fact that she was the mother of two teenage children, Steven, eighteen, and Sheryl, sixteen. Life is good for this suburban housewife, with her private tennis lessons and "girly" lunches at the exclusive Jetty Club.

The sandman was nowhere in sight, and she sighed and turned to stare at the digital clock, its large green numerals glowing in the dimly lit room.

"Only two forty-five. *I can't believe it!*" She spoke under her breath. As for Mike, he was lying with his back facing her, the thin sweat track between his shoulder blades staining his grey T-shirt, his breathing laborious in the muggy atmosphere. He had to catch an early flight to Chicago this morning, and June didn't wish to disturb him.

Mike was one year older than her when they met as freshmen at NYU and fell madly in love, a love that is still vibrant after twenty-two years. Sure, they had their moments like most married couples, but the kids always pulled them through. Mike had climbed the proverbial corporate ladder at Global Marketing, a highly successful marketing conglomerate, as VP for marketing, with a six-figure salary and generous stock options; but like all high-flying executives, there is always a downside. The long hours; being late for dinner; entertaining clients; not to mention the traveling and the long spells away from home, so much so that during coffee mornings, the girls would tease June about her "George Clooney" look-alike husband. Like "Do you trust him? I mean women would kill for a guy like him." June would just laugh it off, but there were times she had to admit she had her suspicions.

*   *   *

The stillness was suddenly shattered with the ear-piercing ring of the phone.

"Mike." June gave him a solid nudge. *"Mike, wake up.* Mike . . . *for Christ's sake, wake up!"*

He gave a sleepy groan then turned to face his distraught wife.

"June, what the hell?" he mumbled, still half asleep.

"The phone . . . Answer the bloody phone before it wakes the kids up." Still in a daze, Mike fumbled for the lamp switch.

"Who the hell could this be at two thirty in the morning? Hello. Summers here. *Hell,* do you know what time it is? *Can't it wait until morning?* Okay.

Okay. I'll hang up and call you on my cell phone. Just give me a few minutes." "Who is it, Mike?" June asked, now wide awake and full of concern.

"Steve Langley from our Toronto sales office. He's new on the job, and I think he's had one too many. It's nothing to worry about, honey. Go to sleep. I'll take this call downstairs, and I might just grab a glass of cold milk while I'm at it." He leaned over and gave her a kiss on the cheek. "Try and get some sleep. This won't take long." He switched off the bedside lamp then hurried toward the door.

Descending the stairs in semidarkness while half-awake is a formidable challenge, and Mike was cursing under his breath when he finally reached the kitchen and switched on the lights. He grabbed the barstool and nervously punched in the numbers.

"Laura . . . what the hell! Are you crazy or something? Listen, what we had was good, but it's over. Do you read me? It's over, and don't you ever call me at my home again. No, I don't want you to explain. No, Laura, I'm hanging up. Laura, for Christ's sake, give it away. *You're what?* Is this another one of your stupid fantasies? No, I'm not buying it. Besides, how do I know that I'm the father? You can call me whatever you like. *I'm hanging up!"*

Mike shut down his cell phone, his hand shaking with anger and fear. *Was Laura telling the truth? It doesn't bear thinking. Was this one of her devious ploys? No, she's just blowing hot air.* He tried to convince himself, shaking his head as he opened the refrigerator, placing the milk carton on the breakfast bar then filling his glass.

Nevertheless, whether Mike liked it or not, he was more than concerned. "Mike," June's voice rang out, "what's keeping you?"

"Gimme a couple of minutes, honey." He swallowed the remains of the milk, his eyes staring blankly at the wall. *This was a wake-up call. Sure, he had had extramarital affairs before but always discreet, and who wouldn't in his line of work? But this Laura Williams, she was something else. He should have spotted the early warning signs: the possessiveness, the jealousy, the stalking, the phone calls to the office. I mean this babe just wouldn't take no. Sure, the sex was great, but that was all it was. But this crazy broad had to fall in love.* "Mike."

"Yeah, I'm coming, honey." He switched off the kitchen light. *How the hell could he sleep now?*

CHAPTER 2

The room was in total darkness with the exception of the thin slivers from the street lighting streaming through the gaps in the blinds. At three in the morning, it was almost eerie to see the dark silhouette of a woman lying in bed, her chest rise and fall with each sob.

"That lousy bastard." She sobbed, her eyes swollen and red. "How could he do this to me? I might have known." She gasped for air. "Men are all the same. Once they get what they want, they'll dump you like a sack of shit. I should have learned my lesson by now, but he seemed so different. And now I'm pregnant. I've been such a fool. All the promises he made divorce his wife, start a new life with me, I can't live without you. What am I going to do now? My career? An unmarried mother, a child without a father." She burst into another bout of uncontrollable sobs, almost choking her.

* * *

Laura Williams at twenty-eight, a vivacious brunette, had had a string of disastrous affairs. Desperate not to be left on the shelf, she gave herself too freely and then always regretted it. She knew Mike Summers was married, but on the rebound from her previous live-in, she just couldn't wait for another man to enter her life. She had met Mike at a dinner presentation, instigated by Global Marketing in their pursuit to conclude a multimillion marketing contract with ABM where Laura was employed as a senior marketing analyst. Mike was suave, entertaining, and witty, the perfect gentleman. And with her looks? Well, it was only a matter of time before Laura was receiving dinner invitations. I guess the rest is history. Mike was always discreet; and they would meet at motels and have secret rendezvous, or when he was traveling, Laura would catch a flight to spend the weekend with him, be it Chicago or wherever. It was only when she told him that she loved him that she felt the temperature drop, and the calls became less frequent. And when the morning sickness began, she became desperate, dreading the writing on the wall.

*   *   *

Her mind was racing. At four months pregnant, an abortion was out of the question. Besides, she was a devout Roman Catholic. The "bump" was showing, and the office gossip was rife. All she needed now was her boss to approach her to lay her cards on the table with regard to maternity leave or, worse still, her resignation. *No, she wasn't going to sit back and let Mike Summers destroy her life and that of her unborn child. He was going to pay with whatever it takes. And he was going to pay plenty!*

CHAPTER 3

Mike was wide awake when the alarm buzzed, and he quickly stretched over to kill the culprit before that crazy music awakened June, his mind turning repeatedly to the telephone conversation he had had with Laura. He lay for a moment, staring blankly into the darkness. He needed this like a lead balloon, especially with the McDonald's contract hanging over his head. This was a key account, and there was no room for screwups. He glanced at the clock once more. It had just turned six fifteen, and if he wanted to catch the seven thirty flight from Kennedy, he had better make tracks. He slipped his feet to the carpet and headed for the shower, discarding his shorts and T-shirt. Maybe the shower would clear his mind and help him think straight.

"Mike, are you all right?" June popped her head around the bathroom door, and he wiped the steam from the shower glass.

"Go back to bed, honey. I can manage."

"Not on your life," June retaliated. "I'm going down to put the coffee pot on the stove, and by the way, I've packed your carry-on, clean underwear, socks, fresh shirt, and tie. Remember to pack your toiletries after you finish shaving."

"Thanks, honey. What would I do without you?" Mike yelled above the noise of the shower.

"What would I do without you?" he repeated the words under his breath, the reality striking home. He had been a real jerk over the years, having one sordid affair after another, and only by the grace of God had he never been exposed. But now? This was too close for comfort. The scandal would destroy him. Besides, he could never hurt June and the kids, and he had made up his mind to protect them with whatever it takes. He quickly toweled and dressed then finished packing his bag. The crisp white shirt and red striped tie lifted the conservative dark blue tailored suit, and Mike glanced in the mirror to straighten his tie. His suit hung on his muscular frame as if he was born in it, and he unashamedly admired what he saw. This guy loved himself but maybe too much, and for once, this could be payback time *"for all the girls he loved before."*

"Mike," June's voice rang, "what's keeping you? I've called a cab, and it will arrive in fifteen minutes."

"Gimme a sec, honey." He grabbed his bag and briefcase and hurried to the stairs.

"My, you look handsome," June commented as she poured the coffee. "I made some toast in case you don't want to eat on the flight."

"Thanks, honey, but you shouldn't have." He gave her a kiss on the cheek and sank his teeth into the crisp bread.

Just then, there was the sound of the cab's horn.

"You had better get going, darling. Now, do you have everything?" He nodded and grabbed the second slice of toast.

"I wish you all the best, darling. Be good and don't forget to call me."

"Bye, honey . . . I will." He gave her another kiss then held the toast between his teeth while he lifted his bags, one in each hand.

The cab driver was waiting patiently, and Mike quickly slung his bags onto the rear seat.

"Hungry, boss, are we?" The black cabbie laughed.

Mike removed the toast.

"You could say that . . . Kennedy, and don't spare the horses . . . Domestic terminal . . . American Airways."

"You got it."

CHAPTER 4

Laura was exhausted and eventually fell into a distraught sleep. She tossed and turned like a trapped animal trying to escape its inevitable fate. Then suddenly, she sat bolt upright, the daylight filling the room, and she quickly placed the back of her hand over her eyes to shield them from the glare.

"Christ! What time is it?" She panicked, searching for the bedside clock. Today is the weekly marketing and sales meeting, and she knew her boss would give her a hard time; her work over this past month had been less than satisfactory.

"Seven a.m.!" she stammered, throwing her feet to the floor. "I had better get my ass outta here. Blakely is just waiting for the chance to fire me. That bastard, ever since I gave him the bum's rush, he's been leaning on me to get me into the sack . . . *fucking pervert!"*

As Laura opened the shower screen and turned the faucet, she glanced into the vanity mirror, and the face that met her made her gasp.

"My god!" She stepped back in shock then moved her face closer to study the carnage, her nose almost touching the glass. Her eyes were swollen and red, like a prize-fighter who had taken too many shots. She quickly filled the basin and submerged her face into the cold water, holding her breath as long as she could. After a few seconds, what seemed like an eternity, she raised her head, gasping for air, then with both hands flicked her long-wet hair back over her shoulders. She stared into the mirror once more in shocked silence. The swelling had slightly subdued, but she had to reluctantly conclude it was a day for the aviator shades.

"What the hell! If Spice Posh can get away with it, so can I."

* * *

Laura was a catch, all right, with her tantalizing dark brown eyes, smooth complexion, and million-dollar smile. At five nine, she had all the credentials that said, "Come on, baby, light my fire"; and she had plenty of volunteers. However, at twenty-eight, the word on the street was she was good in the cot and generous with it; and with these references, no guy in his right mind would be interested in a serious relationship.

* * *

Time was not on her side, and Laura quickly dropped her bathrobe and stood silently in the warm invigorating spray, the water streaming down her face as she closed her eyes, enjoying the sensation. For a moment, she was in another world until she noticed her silhouette on the steamed glass door. Her once shapely figure and taught abdomen was now sporting a pronounced bump, and she quickly came down to earth.

"What the hell!" she muttered under her breath. "I'm not going to give that asshole Blakely the satisfaction of firing me. I've just got to pick myself up. Besides, I need the salary now, even more than ever."

She towelled her dark brown hair and slipped on her robe. There was no time for the blow dry as it had just turned seven, and if she wanted to meet the eight thirty deadline, she had better start getting dressed. The blue pinstriped office attire, pencil skirt, white blouse, and matching suit top would be a challenge as she frantically struggled to squeeze into her skirt. There was only one option, and that was to leave the zip down and hide it with her blouse. In no time, she was dressed, makeup on, and was scurrying to the car park.

"What would today bring?" Laura spoke under her breath as she gunned the engine of the VW bug. "So, who knows, but more to the point, *who the hell cares?"*

CHAPTER 5

As she walked to her desk, she could sense the staff watching her every move, but she wasn't going to take this shit lying down.

"Good morning. Good morning." Laura smiled sarcastically. "Bitches!" She clenched her teeth under her breath.

"Hi, honey. So, what's with the shades?" It was Terry Johnson, her best friend.

* * *

Terry was always bubbly, and in this stuffy office atmosphere, it was a breath of fresh air. Laura and she were like two peas in a pod. They both loved clubbing and the good life, but unlike her friend Laura, she knew when to draw the line, especially when it came to married men. Her shoulder length blonde hair had seen too many bottles, but it kinda suited her. She was shorter, at five eight, but with that figure who cares; and guys were all over her. Her grey blue eyes, smooth complexion, narrow face, and full lips gave her a sort of "Marilyn" look; and she knew how to flaunt it. She was the same age as Laura and unattached and determined to stay that way. When Laura became foolishly involved with her "new man," she had warned her that she was playing with fire. He was married and he played the field, leaving a string of broken hearts and "yellow ribbons" on the old oak trees. However, when it comes to affairs of the heart, common sense is a scarce commodity and now this!

* * *

"It's a long story," Laura replied, shaking her head as she sat at her desk with a heavy heart and a sigh of relief, the extra weight now taking its toll.

Terry placed her hand reassuringly on her shoulder. "Is it as bad as that, honey?"

"It doesn't get any worse. Would you believe that scum is not answering my calls? So, I rang him at home at three in the morning and laid it on the line, and do you know what that bastard said?"

"Calm down, honey. Say, why don't I get you a coffee, and you can tell me all about it later. Remember, the meeting is at eight thirty, and you had better unscramble that brain of yours or Blakely will be on your tail like a ferret after a rabbit."

* * *

"All right, settle down. We don't have all day, and I have a pile on my desk."

* * *

This was Jack Blakely at his best. Rude and ignorant, and to say he loved himself would be an understatement. He was a ladies' man, *at least he thought he was,* and it was not the first time he had made a pass at a female employee.

But if you want to keep your job, discretion is the better part of valour. To his credit, he had worked his way through the ranks from salesman to VP marketing, kissing every boss's ass on the way. So, what's new? In his early fifties and married with two teenage kids, he was still handsome in his own right: six feet, slim, one hundred and eighty pounds, rugged complexion, black greying hair, narrow nose, and piercing blue eyes. Maybe he was going through a midlife crisis. Whatever? Casanova was about to start the meeting.

* * *

"Laura, before we start with the agenda, would you mind telling us what's with the aviators? That is unless we are missing something, or is this the latest ABM fashion?"

There was a spontaneous burst of laughter, and Laura flushed; but Laura was Laura, and she had to cut this jackass down to size. It was not a good time, but then it never is.

"I didn't know that there was a dress code forbidding staff to wear sunglasses during office hours. However, Jack, now that you have raised the subject, maybe you can place it on the agenda under 'any other business.'" There was another burst of laughter, and Blakely took it head-on.

"I can see Laura is in good form this morning." He grinned, still smarting. "I sincerely hope it shows through in her presentation. Item 1 on the agenda, the update on the Delta Airways contract for four AS400s. Laura, the floor is yours."

"I had a meeting at Delta's head office last Friday with Ted Worth, their VP, IT, and I'm happy to report that after burning the midnight oil, the contract is signed, sealed, and delivered for four machines with a potential for another three. The sale is valued at 1.6 million plus commissioning costs of five hundred thousand . . ."

*   *   *

The cafeteria was full as Laura and Terry Johnson queued at the server.

"Laura honey, you have to eat something," Terry commented, concerned, while studying Laura's starvation tray. "A glass of milk isn't going to help that bump you're carrying."

"I know you mean well, Terry. You're a real friend, but the way I feel right now, if I eat something, I'll throw up."

"Say, you never finished," Terry said as they took their table. She was trying to change the subject and pick up where Laura left off prior to the marketing meeting.

"Never finished?" Laura was trying to unscramble her brain, looking puzzled.

"Like what the bastard said to you when you hit him with the early morning house call?" Terry answered, a smile on her face, trying to cheer up her best friend.

"Oh . . . Ah . . . Yeah sure . . ." Laura had connected. "You're gonna love this. *Would you believe it?* He said, 'How do I know it's mine?' I mean how could he? I tell you, Terry, how low can one get?" Laura's voice was beginning to break.

"Honey, calm down. He's not worth it." Terry patted her hand.

Laura shook her head in despair. "How the hell did I ever get myself into this mess? The next thing that lowlife will be demanding *is a DNA test!"*

"Listen, honey, that might be a blessing in disguise." Terry pressed Laura's hand again. "Think positive and use it to your advantage."

"Thanks, Terry, I never thought of it that way. You make me feel better already." She gave a half-hearted smile before glancing at her watch. *"Is it that time already?"*

* * *

Blakely could see Laura return to her desk. He was still smarting from her cocky retaliatory attitude during the meeting, and this guy wasn't about to give up easily. Ever since Laura gave him the ass, he was like a wounded bull in a China shop. He lifted the phone.

"Laura, Jack here. Do you have a minute?"

"What's up, honey?" Terry asked as Laura passed by her desk.

"Casanova called. *This guy just doesn't give up!"*

"Take it easy and keep your cool. Remember, Blakely is just biding his time. Don't give him any excuses."

"Don't worry. I can handle him." Laura grinned.

Blakely signalled through the glass partition.

"Take the load off, Laura." He pointed to the empty chair.

"So, Jack, is there a problem?"

"Well, there is and there isn't." He placed his chin on his hand, a half grin on his face before sitting back in his chair, his staring eyes purposely making Laura feel uncomfortable.

"Okay, Jack, the charade is over. Just get to the point."

"That's what I like about you, Laura, no shit, straight for the jugular. It's like this." He paused. "I gotta tell you the shades and that bump send bad vibes, like maybe you are going through a personal trauma or something. Therefore, I'm not going to beat about the bush. It's like this . . . Your work over the past couple of months has been less than satisfactory, and unless you pick up your game, I'm putting you on notice."

"So, what does that mean?" Laura retaliated, fire in her eyes.

"Laura, if the cap fits! I'm giving you one month to improve, or the next time you come to my office, Stevens from personnel will be here. I don't have to spell it out now, do I?"

"No, Jack, you have made it perfectly clear, but if you are thinking of firing me, I'll take you the whole nine. Is there anything else?" Laura asked abruptly.

"No, Laura, thank you." Blakely was being rudely polite.

"Oh, just one more thing." Laura hesitated at the door. "There's a little thing called sexual harassment, which I am sure you are familiar with, or if you aren't, you soon will be. So, if I were you, Jack, I would tread carefully." Laura slammed the door, startling the staff. Now the office gossipers would have something to really talk about. Laura grinned as she walked back to her desk.

"How did it go, honey?" Terry asked as she passed.

"What do *you* think?" Laura smiled. "Anyhow, I'll tell you about it later."

CHAPTER 6

"And that, gentlemen, wraps up Global Marketing's proposals for McDonald's new McCafé."

"Nice job, Mike." Brad Smith, VP of sales and marketing, rose to his feet and gave Mike a warm handshake. "I am sure I'm speaking on behalf of all the sales staff and, Mike, be rest assured I will recommend to the president that we run with it. It's now just a case of passing the new contract through our legal department and the financials through the CFO."

"Thanks, Brad. It's been a pleasure." Mike felt relieved; it had been a long one.

"Listen, Brad." Mike paused. "Before I go, should there be anything that perhaps needs further clarification, don't hesitate to call me at the office or at my hotel. I am staying overnight at the Downtown Hilton."

"Sure. I will give your boss a call tomorrow to congratulate Global on the excellent presentation. Just give me a minute, Mike, and I'll get Nora, my secretary, to call a cab. You must be bushed."

"Thanks, Brad. I really appreciate it." Mike was all smiles as he walked to the elevator with a spring in his step and who wouldn't, with another successful contract under his belt and Global's largest account!

"Yes." He smiled as the elevator chimed. "It doesn't get any better."

*   *   *

It was all of a thirty-minute cab ride to the Hilton, and it gave Mike a chance to relax and reflect on his marketing presentation, but somehow, he just couldn't shake off Laura's early-morning phone call. It was getting to him, and whatever, he had to nip it in the bud. *But how?*

*   *   *

The cab pulled into the busy sidewalk. "That'll be twenty-five straight, boss." The driver was becoming impatient. He had other pickups. This was his breadbasket. Mike, unfortunately, was in another world, oblivious to the fact that he had arrived at his destination.

"Hey! Man, we're here. Check it out, man. I got customers waiting." The black cabby rapped angrily on the driver's cage.

"Eh . . . Err . . . Sorry, buddy." Mike was embarrassed. "It's been a real shit of a day."

"I know the feeling, dude, but I can't hang around."

Mike passed two twenties though the slot. "Keep the change." "Thanks, buddy. You are a real gentleman. Have a good one." The young bellhop had already opened the cab door.

"Checking in, sir?" Mike nodded.

"Luggage, sir?" The bellhop asked.

"In the backseat, kid." He slipped the kid a five.

"Nice to see you again, Mr. Summers. Welcome to the Hilton Towers. I believe you are staying with us for one night?"

"That's correct, Helen." Mike smiled proudly. He loved the attention.

"And this will be charged as normal to your company account?"

Mike nodded, his mind still on a roller coaster, not really registering what Helen was saying.

"Are you all right, Mr. Summers?"

"Sure. Sure. I just need to relax. It's been one of those days." He half-heartedly smiled.

"Room 220. This is your security pass for the towers. Have a nice stay."

"Helen, I need a wake-up call for six thirty, and can you call a cab for eight to the airport? *Oh!* And should my wife phone, I will be in the cocktail bar."

"Certainly, Mr. Summers. Is there anything else?"

"No and thank you."

"My pleasure, sir." She gave a seductive smile.

Mike slotted the plastic and opened the door. It was a relief to close today's chapter, and he removed his jacket and flopped onto the bed.

"Man, do I need this!" He spoke out loud, loosening his tie, and before he knew it, he had dozed off.

The loud knock on the door startled him, and he sat bolt upright.

"Yes?" Mike barked, only half awake.

"Room service. Can I turn down your bed, sir?"

"No . . . Eh, err, no . . . I don't want to be disturbed. Thank you."

Mike hit the floor, running; he felt like shit and headed for the bathroom. He turned on the cold tap and flushed his face then briskly towelled before staring into the vanity mirror then shook his head before quickly combing back his hair.

"Hell! It's eight thirty." He was taken aback as he glanced at his watch.

"A stiff bourbon on the rocks and a club sandwich wouldn't go astray." Mike spoke aloud before removing his tie and slipping into his jacket. "Now it's time to relax." Mike hung the "Do not disturb sign" on the doorknob and briskly walked to the elevator.

The cocktail bar was reasonably quiet for a Monday, but in the "windy city," as they say, "the night is young."

The barman, upon seeing Mike, immediately stopped polishing the glasses.

"Mr. Summers, nice to see you again."

"Thanks, Dave. And nice to be back." Mike grinned, taking the barstool.

"The usual, sir?"

"You bet. And, Dave, can you get the chef to rustle up my favorite club sandwich?"

Dave smiled. This guy is a big tipper.

"Coming up, sir." He reached for the bourbon.

They say "the first cut is the deepest," and the bourbon hit the spot. The club sandwich filled the gap, and after the second hit, he was feeling no pain. "Same again, Dave. Set 'em up."

As Mike put his lips to the glass to relish the amber liquid, he suddenly felt the vibration of his cell phone. He had set it in silent mode as there's nothing worse than a noisy phone call when you are sitting at the bar, enjoying your favourite pastime.

"Who the hell can this be? Yes?" Mike answered abruptly, but in hindsight, he should have recognized the number.

CHAPTER 7

Laura walked to her car, accompanied by Terry. It had been one of these days, and she just wanted to put it all behind her.

"So, are you purposely keeping me in suspense?" Terry asked as they stopped at Laura's car.

"Oh, you mean my run in with Blakely. Let's put it this way. That asshole will think twice before putting the hard word on me again, or he will be up for sexual harassment, and believe me, I'll sing like a canary."

Terry couldn't help laughing. It couldn't happen to a better person.

"Terry, what's so funny?" Laura asked, puzzled.

"I can just imagine that asshole caught with his pants down." Terry burst into laughter again.

Laura half grinned. She wasn't in the mood.

"Terry, I'm sorry, but I'm really bushed. I just want to get home and try to relax."

"I understand, honey. *Listen,* would you like me to keep you company?" Terry asked, concerned. Laura had gone to hell and back these last few days, and in her state of mind, one can never tell. "Besides," she continued, "I've nothing better to do, and we can do the 'couch potato' thing and indulge in our own company, watching TV."

"Sounds good, Terry, but I think I'll take a rain check." Laura was really down.

"Well then, promise me that you will give me a call when you arrive at your apartment."

Laura smiled reassuringly, crushing Terry's hand. "You are a real friend. I don't know what I would do without you." She opened her car door. "Ciao, and don't worry. I'll see you tomorrow." "Bye . . . Remember to phone . . .

* * *

Laura turned the key and switched on the lights, giving a sigh of relief as she kicked off her heels. She didn't feel hungry, but a coffee wouldn't go astray. As she walked toward the kitchen, she stepped out of her skirt; it was strangling her.

"Boy, does that feel good!" she spoke aloud while rubbing her now enlarged waistline.

The coffee tasted good, and Laura relaxed on the sofa, placing her feet on the coffee table. Loneliness is a curse, and Laura could feel her anger mounting as she thought how Mike had used her then mercilessly dumped her when she needed him most. She couldn't take it any longer and lifted the phone, murder in her eyes.

* * *

"Mike . . . It's Laura here."

"Laura, for Christ's sake . . . How many times have I told you it's over? Do yourself a favour."

"Or you'll what? Listen, you asshole, you had better get it through that fucking thick head of yours that *I am* pregnant and you're the father. If you don't believe me, then maybe a simple DNA check will convince you."

"Oh, no! Not on your life. You're not pulling that shit on me."

"Then you had better listen and listen good. I will be contacting my lawyer tomorrow, and here's the bottom line. A monthly allowance of four thousand dollars until your child is twenty-one, all schooling and university fees paid. My apartment rent of two thousand dollars per month plus utilities as long as I remain single."

"In your fucking dreams. You must be fucking crazy."

"Mike, don't you dare hang up! Now you listen to me. There is an easy way and a hard way. The easy way is we meet at my lawyer's office and sign a legal and binding contract in complete confidentiality. The hard way is I start by phoning your wife then your boss. Do I need to continue? I think you get the picture?"

The phone went dead.

Laura stared at the receiver then slammed it into the cradle.

"That bastard! Who does he think he is? I'll show him." She lifted the phone.

* * *

"Hit me again, Dave." Mike was staring at the bottom of his empty glass.

"Excuse me, Mr. Summers, are you feeling all right?" The barman was concerned, as Mike had just annihilated his fourth double bourbon.

"Dave let's put it this way. I've had, shall I say, better news." Mike looked toward the barman again with his bourbon-clouded vision. Maybe this guy is sending me a message. Moreover, it really *is* time to call it a night. Mike opened his wallet and placed two big ones on the bar.

"Whatever, Dave. Keep the change. There's no point in having my own private party now, is there?" Mike rose unsteadily to his feet then turned to leave.

"If you say so, sir. But, Mr. Summers, perhaps I can get someone to assist you to your room?"

"No. I'm good, Dave, but maybe I won't be saying that in the morning." Mike gave an alcoholic grin. "Good night . . ."

Dave just shook his head and continued polishing the glasses. So, what's new? He had seen it all before.

* * *

The elevator seemed to take forever, and to say that Mike was relieved when he finally reached his room would be an understatement. In his alcoholic stupor, he wasn't thinking straight.

"Oh, what the hell!" He threw his jacket on the chair and kicked off his shoes as he hit the bed. *"That fucking bitch!* If she thinks she's going to scare me, she has another thought coming."

Mike had just finished cursing when the phone rang.

"If it's that bitch again, so help me!" He grabbed the receiver.

"Now you listen . . ."

"Mike, what's wrong, darling?" It was June on the line.

"Eh . . . Err . . ." He could have bitten his tongue. "Honey, you caught me by surprise. I just had a run in with room service. I mean half of them can't even speak fucking English."

"Now, now, darling, calm down and tell me how your day went."

"It went good, honey, but I'm missing you." He was lying to his back teeth, but it sounded like the real deal.

"I think by the tone of your voice, Mike Summers, you have had one bourbon too many." He wasn't fooling anyone. June knew him only too well.

"Awe, come on, honey, gimme a break! You know what it's like staying in boring hotel rooms."

"Yeah . . . Yeah . . . I'll give you the benefit of the doubt. Say, I almost forgot to mention that a woman rang earlier this evening, asking to speak to you. Hang a sec. I have her name here . . . a Laura Williams. She says that it is urgent that you phone her and that you know what it's about. Is it something serious, darling?"

"No, nothing to worry your pretty little head. It's probably about the ABM contract. Laura is the senior marketing manager."

"So it's Laura now, is it?"

"Come on, honey. It's just a slip of the tongue."

"So how did she get your home phone number and why is it so important that she must phone you at home? I mean why can't it wait until tomorrow?"

"Honey, I believe you are jealous."

"Mike, don't change the subject."

"Honey, if it gives you peace of mind, I will get her to ring you tomorrow to explain this whole misunderstanding."

"No, that won't be necessary, Mike. I believe you but *tell her to keep business at the office.* Now before I hang up, when should I expect you home tomorrow?"

"I'm going straight to the office, and I might be a bit late. I have to tie up the loose ends of this contract, but I'll ring you."

"I was hoping for a nice change, like you would take me out for a romantic dinner for two."

"I'll try my best, honey . . . I promise . . . Remember I love you more than anything else in this world."

"I believe you. Good night, darling."

*   *   *

Mike sat stunned. It was like from boot camp to combat, only this was no "Desert Storm." His mind was clouded between the alcohol and the "reality show." Either way, he was in serious shit, but what could he do?

"I never dreamt that bitch would phone June." He spoke out loud, as he lifted the phone. *Wait a minute!* He dropped the phone back into its cradle. He had to think straight, keep his cool. What were his options? Money? Could he buy her off? *That's it!* Everyone has their price. He dialed her number.

"Listen, Laura, I just had a phone call from June."

"Now isn't that interesting, *you smuck*? So why *this* phone call . . . *pangs of guilt?*"

"*Laura,* for Christ's sake, be sensible. Now shut your mouth and listen. I have a proposition for you."

"I'm listening." Her voice was agitated.

"I can't discuss it over the phone, but here's the deal. Take it or leave it. I'll meet you at your apartment tomorrow evening at eight. If it's a 'no go,' then I guess we go to the wire, and that's not going to do anyone any good."

Laura paused for a moment. *What the hell? I am damned if I do, and I damned if I don't,* she thought to herself.

"Eight o'clock then. Oh, Mike, a word of caution. Don't fuck with me, or you will wish you had never been born." The phone went dead.

Chapter 8

"Good morning, Mike."

"Good morning, Julie. Anything urgent?"

"Chuck wants to see you once you settle down to discuss the renewal of the McDonald's contract, and Laura Williams called from ABM about a meeting you had planned. She said you would understand."

"Thanks, Julie. Tell Chuck I'll see him in a few minutes." Mike quickly entered his office and dropped his briefcase to the floor, his hand shaking with anger as he picked up the phone.

"ABM. How can I help you?

"Good morning. My name is Mike Summers, VP of Global Marketing. It's urgent that I speak with Laura Williams." "Can you hold, Mr. Summers?"

"Certainly," Mike replied, his adrenaline now off the scale.

"I'm sorry, sir. She cannot take your call and she stresses she will be engaged for the rest of today."

"That bitch!"

"I'm sorry, sir?" The receptionist was taken aback. Surely, she hadn't heard correctly.

"I said that's a hitch," Mike stuttered in desperation.

"I'm sorry, sir. I must have misunderstood. Do you wish to leave a message?"

"Eh . . . Err . . . No . . . No, and I am sorry for the misunderstanding. Have a nice day."

Mike sat back in his chair, thinking. Somehow, he had to get rid of this broad, but it was easier said than done. The secretarial phone rang.

"Mike, Chuck is doing his proverbial, like he is on his second coffee and waiting patiently."

"Julie, tell him I will be in, in a second." Mike hung up then sat for a moment, rubbing his chin. He had better kick the cobwebs as Chuck Briggs, the CEO of Global, took no prisoners. Shall we say a likable boss or a mean SOB.

"Just go straight in, Mike. He is waiting."

"Thanks, Tracy."

"Take the load off, Mike. *Hell*, what kept you? Did Julie give you, my message?"

"Apologies, Chuck. I had a couple of urgent calls to make."

Chuck gave some kind of an animal grunt. This guy had a low attention span and a short fuse, and by the grace of God, the phone rang.

"Tracy . . . Yes, put him through. *Brad*! And good morning to you." Chuck's expression suddenly changed. "Yes, I have him right here in front of me. No, I was just about to discuss the results of Mike's presentation when you called. Yeah, you know what Mike is like. He always does a thorough job. That *is* great news, Brad! Sure, I'll tell him. Then can I expect the contract by the end of this week? *Great*! Say, why don't you and Nancy come down to the 'Big Apple' for a weekend and stay with Sherry and I, compliments of Global. Brad, I know the feeling but try to make a slot. Sherry really enjoys Nancy's company. Sure, I'll tell her. Thanks again, Brad. It's my pleasure." Chuck's sombre look had disappeared, and Mike was relieved.

Chuck smiled and rose to his feet, offering Mike his hand with the usual knuckle cruncher, making Mike wince.

"I guess you got the gist of that phone call with Brad Smith?" Chuck was all smiles. "Once again, Mike, well done. Now I guess you have a few matters to attend to and so do I. I want to pass the good news to the chairman, then we can discuss the contract in more detail over lunch at the club. Say, twelve thirty?"

*   *   *

"Honey . . . Yeah, I'm fine. I just finished the meeting with Chuck. You know what he is like when there are medals around. As usual, another boring lunch. Yes, that's why I am phoning. I'm sorry, honey, but I must attend this meeting. Say after nine. I know you are disappointed. Well, let's plan it for tomorrow night. I promise. Love you too."

CHAPTER 9

It had turned seven, and Mike had just finished clearing his desk when there was a knock on the door.

Julie popped her head around. "Is there anything else, Mike?"

"Oh, I'm sorry, Julie. No . . . and thanks for staying late."

"A pleasure. Good night, Mike."

Mike sat back and relaxed. The office was uncannily silent, as everyone had gone home for the day. He opened the bottom drawer and placed the half empty bourbon bottle on his desk, accompanied by a hazy glass, then slowly poured himself "two fingers." The bourbon bit into his throat, and he gave a slight cough, but the warm feeling was good. He pondered for a moment before opening his briefcase, searching for his check book.

"Twenty big ones!" He started to scribble. "The bitch is not worth it. I know she's going to bleed me, and it's a long shot, but I gotta start some place." Mike spoke aloud, shaking his head as he hit the signature line. He would have to explain the hole in his bank account to June, but then that was for another day.

*   *   *

Taxi . . . "Mike hailed the cab from the sidewalk. The yellow cab stopped abruptly then reversed.

"Where is it tonight, boss?" the black driver asked as Mike closed the door.

"Elm Apartments on Watts."

"Nice location overlooking the river." The cabby was trying to make light conversation.

"Not mine . . . A friend's," Mike replied rather abruptly. In his frame of mind, the last thing he wanted was a cosy chat with a black cab driver.

"Here we are, dude." The cabby's politeness now down the toilet. "That'll be forty-five straight." He grunted

Mike slipped a fifty through the slot in the security cage.

"Keep the change." Mike grabbed his briefcase. It was time to do business. "Thanks, boss." The driver smiled. "You're not such a bad dude after all."

Mike pressed the security buzzer at L. Williams, apartment 6b, then waited patiently. He had been rehearsing his speech, so to speak, and was trying desperately to keep his cool.

"*Come on . . . Come on . . .* What the fuck is keeping you, bitch?"

"Yes?"

"Laura, Mike here."

"*So what the fuck kept you?* It's nearly eight fifteen!"

"*Keep your shirt on and open the fucking door.*" Mike was losing it.

The security lock buzzed, and the door briefly opened. Mike grabbed the heavy glass panel before quickly entering the foyer. In no time, the elevator chimed, and he was pressing the bell on 6b.

*   *   *

Laura had finished early at the office and was feeling fresh, having showered after her healthy salad dinner; and she slipped into one of Mike's shirts, "leftovers" from their previous steamy encounters. The pale blue shirt barely touched her knees; and the sack like effect, although sexy, conveniently camouflaged her "bump." She rolled up the sleeves just past her elbows, purposely leaving the top four buttons open to expose the deep cleavage between her voluptuous breasts then fluffed up her shoulder-length chestnut hair. Laura knew how to use her sexy body and those long legs to her advantage, and she could read Mike like an open book. He was vulnerable like a spider caught in a web. She may be pregnant, but at sixteen weeks, sex was still exciting; and Mike was a sucker for a "free lunch."

*   *   *

Mike was solemn faced as the door opened with Laura dressed in her "combat" outfit. She was sexy all right, but at this stage, Mike wasn't falling for her usual tactics.

"Hi, Mike." She smiled. "For a spell there, I thought that you had taken cold feet. *Well?* Aren't you going to give me a big kiss?" she teased.

Mike sported a disgusted look.

"*For Christ's sake, Laura, get real!* Now do I have to stand here in the hallway or what?"

"Of course, Mike. How foolish of me." She was being more than sarcastic. "Come in." She turned and walked toward the sofa, purposely laying it on her long sexy legs disappearing below the "sacked" shirt. *This babe could tempt a saint.* "Grab a seat, Mike." She pointed to the sofa. "Coffee?"

"Laura," Mike took the sofa, "I'm not here for a coffee break, so let's get down to business."

"*Oh well,* if that's how you feel. *Pity!*" She took the soft leather chair directly facing him, her shirt rising well above her knees, exposing more thigh than Sharon Stone. Then she slowly crossed her legs, and Mike couldn't help but notice that Laura wasn't wearing panties, and she caught his eye. "*Oops! Mike!* How forgetful of me, but I'm sure you are not complaining?" She smiled as she slowly uncrossed her legs, deja vu, studying Mike's every expression. "Laura, I'm not stupid. I know you're throwing everything at me and I would be telling a lie if I said that I wasn't tempted, *but it's over!* Dead in the works. *Cappice.* Do you understand?" He slipped his hand into his inside pocket and pulled out the envelope before laying it on the coffee table.

"What the fuck is this?" It was beginning to turn ugly as Laura emptied the contents. "*Twenty thousand dollars! Are you fucking serious?*" she screamed, as she ripped the check into little pieces, throwing it into the air like wedding confetti. "*Oh no, Mr. Big Shot.* You're not getting off that easy. You've got responsibilities, *mister!*"

"Laura, for Christ's sake, be sensible. Besides, how do I know that *you* are pregnant?"

Laura jumped to her feet and pulled her shirt above her waist, leaving nothing to the imagination.

"What do you think this bump is, *a fucking gumball?*" She dropped the shirt. "Now either you divorce your wife as you promised and you make me a decent woman, or you pay through your nose. The alternative? I start by phoning that pretty wife of yours, *right now!* What's it gonna be?"

"You're a fucking psycho. You're crazy." Mike screamed. "Over my dead body." He was already on his feet, preparing for the worst.

Laura lunged at the phone. "Well, we'll soon see about that—"

Mike was fast on his feet and grabbed her hand in a vicelike grip, but Laura was determined as Mike wrestled her to the floor. She was holding the future of her unborn child in her hand.

"You fucking bitch . . . Gimme that phone!"

Laura was struggling and kicking, and with Mike's weight on top of her, she could feel her strength fading fast. But somehow, she had to do something to protect her unborn child; and in sheer desperation, she rallied all her strength, bringing her knee up hard into Mike's groin.

He screamed and rolled onto his back, cringing in pain.

"Why you—" He slapped Laura hard across the face with the back of his hand, a slight trickle of blood ebbing from her mouth. "Now let go of that fucking phone *or so help me."*

The adrenaline rush was on, and with her free hand, Laura viciously dug her nails into Mike's cheek; and he screamed again in pain as blood trickled down his chin.

Suddenly, he couldn't think straight. He was going crazy. His whole world was falling apart. He was desperate. He had murder in his eyes; and without thinking, he placed both hands around Laura's neck, his mind a blank as he kept squeezing and squeezing.

Laura's legs and arms were flaying in the air as she smashed the phone against Mike's forehead. That was the last straw, blood running into his eyes, blurring his vision; and like a madman, he squeezed even harder. Laura's eyes were now bulging from their sockets, her face turning a pale shade of blue, her brain starved of precious oxygen. Then everything was quiet, and her body went limp.

Mike staggered to his feet trying to regain his balance, but the anger and the adrenaline rush was like Daytona, and he couldn't cut his motor.

"You fucking corporate whore," he screamed, as he uncontrollably kicked her again and again in the abdomen. Then suddenly he stopped as he stared unbelievingly at Laura's half-naked limp body; blood now oozing from between her legs.

"Christ! What have I done?" He crushed his head between his hands. His world was falling apart, and reality and panic go hand in hand.

"Murder! I never meant to kill you, Laura, you stupid bitch! *Why? Why?* You could have taken the money. But no, you stubborn broad, you had to go the whole road."

For a moment, Mike stared blankly into space as if in a trance. Then just as quickly, he regained his thoughts, his mind now clearing as he absorbed the carnage. He had to get out of here, *and fast!* There was no way he was going down for murder, but he had to make sure the police couldn't connect him to Laura's death, and that meant no clues. He rushed to the bathroom and doused his face in the cold water. The deep cut on his forehead and the puncture marks from Laura's nails would be difficult to explain, but he would think of something. Then with a wet hand towel, he meticulously wiped the vanity basin and the tap to remove any blood remnants and fingerprints.

"Next the phone," he spoke out loud, carefully wiping the blood from the handset before placing it back in its cradle on the small table directly behind Laura's body. But the fragments of the torn check? That was something else. Then it came to him!

"There must be a vacuum cleaner here somewhere. The utility cupboard. Now where the hell could that be?" He rushed to the kitchen, spotting the long narrow door.

"Got it." Within minutes, the paper remnants were gone, and he removed the dust bag then returned the vacuum cleaner but not before carefully removing his prints. He scanned the room once more before wiping the door handle. He would dispose of the towel and the dust bag down the garbage chute.

Should he take the elevator? No, it was too dangerous. He must take the fire exit, and he quickly disposed of the dust bag and towel then hit the fire exit stairs.

*　*　*

Terry was lounging on the sofa, watching TV.

"I don't know why I pay for this fucking 'Fox.'" Terry griped aloud. "These fucking ads and shit repeat movies. *I tell you!*" She was shaking her head as she generously filled her empty wine glass. "What's the time?" She glanced at her watch. "Eight forty-five. And no call from Laura. That woman! *What to do?*" She lifted the receiver.

*　*　*

The loud ring of the phone echoed through the room. It kept ringing and ringing. It was as if she was dreaming, and why didn't someone answer that phone? Her eyelids flickered, and she began to cough violently. But that pain in her throat? She could hardly breathe, and she felt so cold. She began to shiver uncontrollably, slowly opening her eyes and staring blankly at the ceiling. Now it was all horribly coming back. Suddenly, she winced in excruciating pain, and she clutched her abdomen, placing one hand between her legs. That wetness? She gazed in horror at her blood-soaked hand, but the pain returned with a vengeance and made her scream. The phone kept ringing. Somehow, she had to reach that phone. She turned and crawled on her stomach, desperately grabbing the phone cable, pulling the phone to the floor with a loud crash.

"Hello . . . Hello . . . Is anyone there? Is that you, Laura?" There was a sort of a croak then a barely audible voice.

"Terry . . . Terry . . . Hurry . . . Hurry . . . He tried to kill me." Then the phone went silent as Laura slipped back into unconsciousness.

"Jesus Christ!" Terry was now a deathly pale, fearing the worst for her friend. But the line was still open. *"Laura . . .* Laura, say something . . . Speak to me."

Terry was in panic mode, not knowing what to think, but now she couldn't use her house phone. She hit the floor running and grabbed her bag, searching for her cell phone.

"Where the fucking hell is that phone?" In desperation, she emptied the contents onto the coffee table. *"At last, here it is!"* Her hands trembling as she dialed 911.

CHAPTER 10

"Mike, is that you?" June called from the TV lounge. She had been patiently waiting for him to arrive from his "after-hours" meeting.

"It's okay, honey. Don't let me disturb you," Mike answered. "I have already had something to eat."

"Not on your life. It has only been one night, but your wife still misses you, *you big heel!*" June was smiling as she rose from the sofa to greet him. As for Mike, he was dreading the thought of June's reaction when she sees his swollen cheek and cut forehead. It was ugly, and he had to think up some convincing story, *and fast!* He dropped his bag and briefcase in the hallway, purposely keeping his face out of sight.

"Aren't you going to give your wife a big kiss?" June was in her track shorts and pale blue low-cut training vest, her blonde hair tied in a ponytail. The summer temperature was still crazy, and in that outfit, June looked just as hot. She snuck up on Mike from behind to surprise him, throwing her arms around his waist just as he was about to remove his jacket.

"Now turn around and give this 'desperate housewife' a big kiss." He sheepishly turned to face her.

"My god, Mike! What happened to your face?" June stepped back in shock and horror at the sight that met her eyes and placed her hand against her lips in disbelief.

"Honey, I feel so embarrassed and ashamed." He was struggling to find the right words and quickly held her in his arms to console her. *"There . . . There*, it's only a few superficial scratches and more to the point, I'm still in one piece."

"What do you mean?" June's mind was in turmoil, and it was now becoming even more of a mystery.

Mike began. "I'll try to make it brief . . ."

"So let me get this straight . . ." June was trying to get to grips with Mike's complicated story. "You're meeting at ABM with this Laura or something was cancelled, and she telephoned to ask you to come to her apartment to sign some papers and gave you her address. When you arrived by cab and pressed the security button, there was no answer. You tried her cell phone but drew a blank then you hung around for five or ten minutes before walking down the street to call a cab. There was a couple arguing, and the man was about to assault the woman, and you stepped in as the Good Samaritan, but it was a cunning ploy to mug you?"

"In a nutshell, honey." Mike was relieved, but June was no fool, and he dreaded she would question him about the highly irregular request by a senior female ABM executive to meet him at her apartment. Somehow he had to throw her off track.

"I was lucky, honey. When I tried to separate them, the guy suddenly head-butted me on the forehead, and the woman jumped on my back and dug her a nails into my face. Luckily, I got a shot in and knocked the guy to the ground. A passing car pulled up, and they ran off."

"Did you call the police?" June asked. His tactic had worked, *at least for the moment!*

"Honey, you know what it is like. It would be a waste of time. In New York, muggings are an everyday occurrence, and the police have more to do than chase around for muggers when more serious crimes like homicides and robberies are rife." Mike paused, studying her distraught eyes. "Listen, honey." He changed the subject again, laying on the "drama queen." "If you don't mind, I'm bushed and I would really love a stiff bourbon to calm my nerves."

"I'm sorry, darling, for being so insensitive. But there's something. Oh! It doesn't matter." She kissed him on the lips. "Here, let me help you with your jacket. Now go and sit in the lounge and relax while I fetch you that drink. It must have been a terrible experience." She gave him another kiss. "I'll bathe that head of yours once you have a shower."

But June had that woman's distrustful look in her eyes. She was no fool, and Mike's amateurish "Broadway play" would come back later to bite him in the ass.

CHAPTER 11

"Emergency services?" The woman's voice was calm and collective. "Police, ambulance, or fire?"

"It's my friend. It's my friend!" Terry screamed at the pitch of her voice.

"Someone has tried to kill her . . . *Please . . . Please hurry!"*

"Now calm down, ma'am. You say someone tried to kill your friend?"

"For fuck's sake, who are you . . . *Judge Judy?* My friend is gonna die, and you want a sworn statement."

"Okay . . . Okay . . . Lady." The operator was losing her cool. "Now you listen to me. Unless you calm down, your friend *is* gonna die! *So, what's it gonna be?* Like, you start by giving me your friend's name and address or what."

"It's apartment . . ."

* * *

Terry was almost out of her mind as she dropped everything and rushed to the elevator.

"Come on . . . Come on, for Christ's sake." She was stamping her feet in frustration as she watched the numbers descend. *"What's keeping this fucking crate?"* she yelled *out loud.* "Keep it down, lady." A muffled voice echoed down the hallway.

At last, the doors chimed, and Terry crushed into the box, rudely pushing the other occupants aside.

Within minutes, the pedal was to the metal, and Terry was heading down West Street. *So who gives a shit about speeding?* With luck, she would hit Watts in around thirty minutes.

* * *

"Say, did you mention to Judy about the barbeque this Sunday?"

Detective Sergeant Bill Hayden was at the wheel of the cruiser. It had just turned eight thirty, and after a frustrating day and a well-deserved coffee at the diner, the detectives were finally heading back to the precinct to pick up Tony's car.

"Is that an order, Lieutenant?" Bill laughed. Tony Perrino and Bill had been buddies since Police College, and fate had brought them together, having both pursued careers in Homicide.

"Well?" Tony asked, grinning.

"Judy and the kids wouldn't miss these burnt steaks for anything." Bill was still laughing.

"Now you tell me!" But before Tony could continue, the red incoming call button began to flash.

"Shit! This is all we need. Perrino here. *Don't tell me, Alice!*"

"Afraid so, Tony. A 911 call has just come in. A young woman is in a serious condition after an attempted murder. Here's the lowdown. A Laura Williams, Caucasian, address Elm Apartments on Watts, apartment 6b. CSI are already on their way."

"Thanks, Alice, and no thanks." Tony laughed.

"I know the feeling, guys, but think of me. *I don't finish until six in the morning!"*

"My heart bleeds for you, Alice." Tony was being humorously sarcastic.

"Get out of it, you two! Ciao."

Perino glanced at the digital clock. It had just turned nine forty-five, and it looked like it would be a long one and, in the doghouse, once again, nothing new for a homicide cop, *but try telling that to his Italian wife Rose!*

Bill nimbly opened the window and clamped the red magnetic light to the roof of the Pontiac then hit the siren. The big car's wheels spun as Bill crashed the gas.

"At least this one is still with us," Bill commented as he straightened the car. Too often when they arrived on a 911, it was all too late.

*   *   *

Tony and his partner were the same age, both in their late thirties, married, and with two kids. The name Perino immediately conjures up an olive-skinned handsome Italian with the "Dean Martin" hair, long nose, rugged face, and dark Latino eyes; and Tony fitted the bill to a tee. And he is from Sicily. *Who would have guessed?* Italians tend to marry into their own ethnic circle, and Tony was no different. Rose, his beautiful Roma wife, had borne him two handsome sons, Mauro, seven, and Samuel, five. Needless to say, she had her hands full with two boisterous boys and with Tony's erratic work commitments one could just imagine. At times, Rose's mother, Maria, was a godsend and wouldn't hesitate to babysit to allow her daughter and Tony some quality time together for a romantic dinner or just a simple movie. Life for the Perino's was upper-class suburban, a pool, pizza nights and barbecues at the weekend, not to mention the annual pilgrimage to Disneyland with the kids. This is America. As for Bill? Tony's partner of four years is third generation Anglo Saxon, the name most likely originating from the United Kingdom. His wife, Judy, was more understanding, having met Bill during her service in the NYPD. She was Bill's partner in the early years, and you know what they say about close proximity; and they eventually fell in love and married. Judy consequently quit the force with the advent of her first pregnancy, and things were tough for a time until Bill finally reached the rank of detective sergeant. With two sons—Ian, eight, and Taylor, five— it doesn't get any better. At just over six feet and one hundred and eighty pounds with blondish hair, blue eyes, and that certain smile, Bill was a hot number in the force; and Judy, I guess, arrested him just in time.

Over the years, the two detectives had become icons in the Homicide Department as two of the most experienced detectives in the NYPD with commendations for bravery above and beyond the call of duty.

As Bill swung into Watts, the ambulance was just departing, sirens blaring, an eerie sight, as the red and blue flashing lights glared in the darkness.

The big Pontiac screeched to a halt, rocking on its shockers, and Bill cut the motor and turned to Tony with a grin. "Let's do it, partner." Perino acknowledged and hit the sidewalk only to be met with the burly cruiser sergeant blocking their paths. His shirt was showing heavy stains of perspiration, and Perino quickly put it to bed, the gold shield glistening in the street lighting.

"Homicide . . . Lieutenant Perino and Detective Sergeant Hayden."

The big cop nodded. "You can go right in, sir . . . apartment 6b." He turned and waved to the uniformed cop guarding the elevator. "Jake . . . Homicide." The officer nodded, waving the detectives through.

The elevator gave a slight jolt as it arrived at the sixth floor, and the two detectives briskly walked to the apartment, not knowing what to expect; but the quicker they got this over with, the quicker they would be heading home.

As expected, CSI were already there, actively dusting for prints with the apartment, occasionally bursting into the glaring lights from the overzealous police photographers.

"Hi, Tony . . . Bill . . . I might have known it would be you two." Lieutenant Dave Adams of CSI greeted them, a big grin on his face.

"You sadist." Bill laughed, shaking his head.

Adams, like the detectives, was in his mid-thirties; and it was not unusual for the families to get together over the "famous" Sunday barbecue at Tony's place.

"Say, are Joyce and the kids free for the barbecue this Sunday?" Tony asked.

"Wouldn't miss it for the world," Adams replied with a smile.

"What did I tell you?" Tony turned to Bill. "You and your burnt steaks!" Adams looked confused at Tony's remark.

"I'll explain it to you later, Dave." Tony shook his head. "Now getting down to why we are here, what's the take?"

"White pregnant female . . . Mid—to late twenties . . . Brutally attacked . . . Severe bruising on the neck, possibly attempted strangulation. The fetus was aborted and has been taken for blood and DNA analysis. The doc's preliminary examination . . . severe bruising to the ribs and lower abdomen from heavy blows most likely from the perpetrator going into a crazy rage and frantically kicking the victim. She is in a critical condition and unconscious, and she may not pull through. Her close friend . . ." Adams glanced at his notes again. "A Terry Johnson called 911 at approximately eight thirty-five, and the rest . . . well . . ."

"Prints . . . clues?" Bill asked.

Dave held up a sealer bag with a small piece of paper inside. "We found this on the floor. I'll pass it to forensic for tests . . . But prints? The suspect is no fool . . . *Nothing!* The place is squeaky clean. Even the vacuum cleaner was gone over."

"Hmmm . . ." Tony rubbed his chin. *This was different*, he thought. *Was the assault premeditated, and if so, what was the motive . . . And a pregnant woman? It couldn't be sexual, but then these days, there's a bunch of crazies on the street and who knows?*

"Thanks, Dave." Tony turned to Bill. "I guess we have to start with this friend of hers, Terry Johnson. Say, Dave, would you happen to have her address and phone number on hand?"

"Yeah . . . it's . . ."

CHAPTER 12

Terry was driving like a crazy woman, weaving in and out of the traffic, horns blaring.

"You crazy bitch. Do me a favour and go and kill yourself on your own fucking time!"

"Go stick your head up your lousy ass," Terry screamed back.

Just then an ambulance, its lights flashing, drove past at high speed, the draft of displaced air wafting against Terry's Mazda, making her swerve and brake.

"Could it be?" she asked herself. The car behind blasted its horn, brakes protesting, almost rear-ending the Mazda.

"You fucking maniac." The driver screamed from the open window then swung out roaring past, his tires screeching, his hand still on the horn. Terry gave him the finger. *"You fucking moron."*

Now she was in total disarray as she pressed the pedal and slowly continued. *Should she U-turn and follow that ambulance?* But maybe it was someone else and not Laura? *"No,"* she spoke out loud. *"I can't take a chance. I gotta get to Laura's apartment. Whatever!"*

As she swung hard into Watts, in the distance she could clearly see the "black and whites" and the yellow tape cordon blocking the entrance to the apartment tower; her mind was still in panic, screaming for an answer.

* * *

"I'm all wrapped up, Tony, unless there is anything else."

"No, I'm good, Dave. I think Bill and I have had enough for the day. What say you, partner?"

"I'm with you, Tony," Bill answered, a relieved smile on his face.

"What about this broad Terry Johnson?" Dave asked.

Tony glanced at his watch. *At this time of night!* I'll take a rain check. Besides, we have enough on our plate with the Davis case. I'll get Baker to pass it to Brown and Lucas. They're a couple of loose cannons at the moment. Let's hit the road, partner." He turned to Bill, relieved. Another long fruitless day had bitten the dust. "Remember Sunday," he called to Adams.

Tony was still deep in thought as he stood silently in the elevator.

"So, what's on your mind, partner?" Bill asked. It was unusual for Tony to be scarce on words.

"Something is bothering me about this whole case, and I just can't put my finger on it . . . *Oh, what the hell!*" The elevator chimed. "Besides, I need a drag." He was already flicking the Marlboro pack.

Tony stood for a moment at the entrance, still in thought, then thumbed his lighter. The bright red glow from the cigarette was conspicuous in the darkness as he filled his lungs with virgin smoke before promoting a groan of satisfaction.

"Did anyone ever tell you these things can kill?" Bill shook his head.

"*Yeah . . . Yeah . . . Yeah . . .* So, who are you, my mother? Listen—" But before Tony could continue, he was interrupted with a woman's irate voice slanging the cruiser sergeant.

"*I don't give a shit!* I want to see the guy that's in charge."

Tony turned to Bill. "*Hmmmm . . .* With a bit of luck, this just might be the mysterious Terry Johnson."

"It's okay, Sergeant. I'll take it from here." Tony stepped in. "Back off, lady. What's your problem?"

"*I'll tell you what my fucking problem is.* I want to see my friend Laura, and this fucking lump of lard won't let me pass."

"You wouldn't happen to be Terry Johnson by any chance?" Tony asked.

"*And you?*" Terry threw it back.

"Lieutenant Tony Perino, Homicide, and my partner Detective Sergeant Bill Hayden." They flashed their shields.

"*So, I'm impressed.* Now if it's not too much to ask, *can someone fucking tell me what's happened to my friend?*"

"Take it easy, lady. We'll get 'round to it once you answer some questions." Tony was losing his cool with this rude broad.

"*So, what if I am?*"

"To put it bluntly, Terry, we don't have all night to listen to a rude bastard like you. So why don't you cut to the chase, and we will all get along like a house on fire?"

Perino's comment struck the nerve. "Okay . . . Okay . . . I'm Terry Johnson, and I'm the one who dialled 911. *Now for Christ's sake, can someone tell me what happened to my friend?*"

"*Take it easy.*" Tony cut her short. "Let me put it this way. She's in a bad way, and the doc says she has only a fifty-fifty chance of making it. She took a terrible beating, and she is lucky to be alive."

"Was that her in the ambulance that just screamed past?" Terry was almost in tears at the news.

Tony nodded. "I'm afraid so."

"Where to? I must go and see her."

"It's St. Luke's, Roosevelt Memorial on Tenth, but you will be wasting your time. She is still unconscious, and no visitors are allowed to see her."

Terry just ignored Tony and turned to sprint to her car but was blocked by the next "Biggest Loser."

"Lady, you're going no place until the detectives are finished questioning you. Do you get my drift?"

"Listen, Terry." Tony grabbed her by the arm to restrain her. "Why don't you come into reception and take a seat. There's nothing you can do to help your friend at the moment except to answer our questions, and then maybe we can catch her assailant within the next 'forty-eight.'" Perino was back in it. "I guess so," Terry reluctantly answered, her sanity returning.

"Grab a seat." Tony pointed to the leather-clad sofa while Bill searched for his notepad.

"Where do you want me to start?"

*   *   *

"So, let's get this straight." Bill was reading from his notes. "Laura confided in you that she was having an affair with a married man, some high-flying executive. She never told you his name, and you have never knowingly met him. She meets this guy on the rebound from a previous disastrous relationship and falls head over heels for this corporate Casanova who promises her the world and then dumps her like a roadside bomb when she tells him she's heading for the maternity clinic. Laura got mad and threatened to call his wife and spill the beans to his company for impropriety."

Terry was finding it hard to concentrate. She kept thinking about her best friend Laura. *If only she had agreed to her suggestion that they spend the evening together.*

"Ms. Johnson, are you listening?" Hayden was getting impatient. He just wanted to get home to his wife and kids.

"And Laura never mentioned this guy's name?" Tony interrupted before she could answer.

"Eh . . . Err . . . I'm sorry detective. I'm spent . . . Sergeant, your notes are pretty accurate. And no, Lieutenant, she never mentioned his name. Now if there *is* nothing else, I'm heading for the hospital."

"Thanks for your help, Ms. Johnson. Here's my card. You can call me anytime should something come to your mind that might assist us with our inquiries. Sergeant Hayden here has your particulars, and we will get in touch with you. *Oh . . .* A word of advice, go easy on the gas pedal."

Terry shook her head and dejectedly walked toward her car, anticipating the worst when she reached Roosevelt Memorial.

Tony stepped outside and watched the taillights of Terry's car disappear into the night. He lit another cancer stick and took a deep drag then turned to his partner. "It's a crazy world we live in, and I think it's time we call it a night."

*　*　*

It was just a fifteen-minute drive to Roosevelt Memorial, and Terry had now calmed down. After all, what could she do? It was a done deed; but that sadistic bastard, whoever he is, killing an unborn child and attempting to murder the mother, *deserves to be burned.* Then she thought for a moment. *Who could he be? Maybe his name and number is stored in Laura's computer phone book at the office. She turned into the hospital car park. It was a long shot, but it was certainly worth a try; but tonight, the state of her friend's health was more important.*

*　*　*

Bill hung a right into the car park of the NYPD police headquarters in Pearl Street, lower Manhattan, a well-known city landmark, *especially for the crims!*

Hayden smiled as he cut the engine of the Pontiac 350 Bonneville, turning to Tony.

"So, what's so funny?" Tony seemed a bit irate. It was not one of his better days.

"Come on, admit it, you're dying for a smoke."

"Hayden, why do I put up with you? *You would* turn a guy to smoking. How about me with your wet farts every day?" Tony was struggling to stifle his laughter.

"Heh . . . Heh : . . Heh . . ." Bill couldn't help himself. Laughter is contagious, and before long, they were both cracking up. *"Perrino, you are a piece of work!"* Bill was struggling to speak.

"I'm outta here. Nine tomorrow. I'm taking it easy. I'm gonna have breakfast with the kids . . . Ciao."

"Get out of it. What am I gonna say to Baker?"

"Tell him to . . . No . . . You had better not." Tony was laughing. "But you gotta admit. It's a thought!" Tony opened the car door. "See yah."

Bill just shook his head and smiled as he slipped the car into drive. *Tony is one helluva guy but a better buddy you couldn't find.*

Roosevelt Memorial, like any other hospital in the Big Apple at any time of the day, is a war zone; and tonight, was no exception.

Terry stood for a moment in a daze, searching for the reception through a maze of bodies, hospital trolleys, and stretchered emergency patients whizzing by, cops and injured drunks' commonplace. Fortunately for Terry, the security guard had an eye for a good-looking broad and who could blame him in this joint?

"Can I help you, ma'am?" he politely asked.

"Eh . . . Err . . . Yes, officer. You see, my friend was admitted to emergency this evening as the result of a brutal assault, and I am desperate to find her." "No problem. Come with me, ma'am." The handsome young security guard pushed his way through the battlefield. "Jacky," he asked the sister at the desk, "can you help this young lady in distress? She is desperately trying to locate her friend who was admitted to casualty . . ."

"Laura Williams . . . Around, say, eight forty-five this evening."

The night sister punched the details into the computer. "Give me a few moments, ma'am. Ah, here we are. I remember her well, poor woman."

Terry went pale at the sister's remark, assuming the worst, her eyes filling; and it didn't go unnoticed.

"Miss . . . *Eh?*" the sister asked.

"Terry . . . Terry Johnson," she replied, her voice almost at breaking point.

"The bad news is . . . the assault left her with serious internal haemorrhaging, but she is holding her own after undergoing major surgery. She is still unconscious and in intensive care."

"Would it be possible for me to visit her?" Terry's eyes were saying it all.

"Unfortunately, no. Only her next of kin have access to intensive care. Besides, it's a serious assault case, and she is under police surveillance."

The sister could see the disappointment on Terry's face, and her heart could feel her pain. She had experienced this situation only too often.

"Now if this handsome security guard just happened to slip past my watchful eye, I mean how would I know? This place is going crazy tonight!" She gave Terry a sly wink.

"Just follow me, ma'am." The security guard got the message.

"Terry."

"Eh . . . Terry." He pressed the elevator button.

This guy was handsome, all right, but tonight Terry had more serious thoughts on her mind.

"Terry, just walk close to me. You can't stay long, and you can only look through the intensive care screen."

"I understand."

"You can call me Frank."

Terry gave a half-baked smile. If this guy was hitting on her, *his timing was way out!*

"Here we are." Frank pointed to the window.

As Terry stared through the tinted glass, she was unprepared for the grizzly sight that met her. Laura had more tubes running from her body than a plumber's yard, and she shockingly placed her hand to her mouth and burst into tears.

"There . . . There." The young security guard tried to console her, placing his hand on her shoulder.

Terry quickly searched her bag and pulled out a handkerchief, losing the battle to wipe her eyes.

"I'm sorry, but I just couldn't help myself," she sobbed.

"That's okay, Terry. You don't have to apologize. I understand, but we gotta go. You're attracting the attention of that cop."

As Terry walked toward the elevator, an elderly couple brushed past them in one helluva hurry, accompanied by what looked like a detective; and Terry turned inquisitively. They stopped and briefly spoke to the police officer who nodded and immediately opened the door of the intensive care ward.

"I guess that must have been the parents, "Terry commented as they stood in the elevator. "There was something about the middle-aged guy's face, as if I have seen him before someplace . . . Awe, maybe it's nothing."

"I guess so, Terry, but listen, why don't you go home and have a good rest?

You look all washed out." The elevator doors chimed.

"Frank, I don't know how to thank you." She squeezed his hand.

"Awe, it's nothing . . . By the way, my name is Frank Reynolds. I'm on the midshift all this week, so if you need any help . . . *Well* . . . It goes without saying."

"Thanks again, Frank. I'm sure I'll be seeing a lot more of you. I can manage from here . . ."

*   *   *

Tony dropped the Marlboro butt to the ground and stubbed it with his feet. It wasn't the best example from a cop, but at this time in the evening, *who cares?*

He turned and squeezed the remote to deactivate the car alarm and opened the door of the Jeep Cherokee. The humidity wasn't letting up; and he removed his jacket and tie, chucking them into the backseat. He closed the door and sat for a moment, watching Bill slowly drive from the car park. It had just turned ten, and he would kill for a cold Bud.

"Hell, I had better phone Rose, or I *really will* be in the doghouse." He spoke out loud, opening the cell phone and entering the numbers.

"Hi, honey . . . Yeah, I know I'm late, but something come up . . . *I know . . . I know*, but I'll see the kids at breakfast . . . I promise . . . In around thirty minutes . . . I love you too . . ." *Phew, that was easier than I thought.* He grinned as he turned the key, the Jeep's eight pots giving a low growl.

The traffic was light, but it would take him all of thirty minutes to reach the East Village Estate. As he drove through the half-deserted streets, he couldn't help reflecting back almost four years ago to when Rose's father passed away. They were doing it hard on a lowly detective's salary, and what with the added expense of two kids and renting a crummy apartment in the Bronx, it wasn't exactly what Rose's parents envisaged for their daughter and grandchildren. Giovanni Borgetti, her father, was a successful entrepreneur amassing his fortune from importing fine Italian wine and food produce from Sicily. Rose and her two sisters, Paula and Lena, were enjoying the good life, living in the wealthy suburb of Washington Heights; and Tony could still remember the shock when the will was read with his wife and her two sisters receiving four million dollars each. Life would never be the same; and subsequently, they moved to East Village, purchasing an exclusive villa. It doesn't get any better. Rose tried as she may to convince Tony to leave the force and do something better with his career, but this boy from Sicily had his mind made up: the NYPD was his life, and before he knew it, he was turning into River Street.

In the distance, Tony could see Rose sitting on the front porch, relaxing, enjoying a glass of chilled white wine, the children having gone to bed. It was one of those summer nights when you enjoy one another's company over an evening drink.

As Tony approached the driveway, he could see his neighbour, Mike and his wife June, also relaxing on their front porch. They lived in number 16, and he stopped the Jeep and rolled down the window. "Hi, Mike, how's things? Hi, June." "Late again, Tony?" Mike asked.

"Hey, don't rub it in. I get enough of that from my wife. Say, why don't you two come over and join us for a nightcap."

"Sorry, Tony, I'll have to pass. I just arrived home from Chicago, and I have a meeting first thing in the morning."

"Listen, we're having a barbecue this Sunday. How about joining us?"

Mike laughed. "With all these cops around, *are you serious? Hey,* I'm only joking. I'll let you know, Tony, as I don't know if I will be out of town."

"Sure, anyhow you know you guys and the kids are always welcome. Ciao." Tony swung the Jeep into the driveway. He liked Mike and June, although older with two teenage kids, better neighbours you couldn't find.

"Hi, honey. Sorry, I'm late." Tony locked the Jeep after collecting his stuff from the rear seat.

"So, what's new?" Rose was being sarcastic as usual.

"Gimme a sec, honey, and I'll join you. I want to hang this stuff in the closet." Tony removed his shoulder holster and opened the front door.

"Aren't you going to park the car in the garage?" Rose asked. The Jeep was only a year old, and she felt Tony didn't really appreciate the material things in life.

"Nah, it's easier for me in the morning."

Rose just shook her head. This was Tony.

"Are you hungry, darling?" she called as Tony disappeared into the hallway.

"I'm good, honey. Bill and I grabbed a bite at the diner." He reemerged. "Now how about a big kiss and tell me you are glad to see this handsome husband of yours?"

Rose had to laugh. How could she be angry with this joker? He grabbed the seat beside her and leaned over and gave her a big kiss on the lips.

"You're incorrigible, Mr. Perino, and you never noticed your favourite beer on ice."

Rose had stuffed four bottles of Bud into the ice bucket next to the table, of course including her half-empty bottle of sauvignon blanc.

"Gee, thanks, honey! What would I do without you?" Tony laughed as he twisted the top from a cold one.

"So, what kept you? You were on your way home when suddenly you changed your mind."

"A woman." Tony laughed.

"Oh yeah! You had better be joking or you will wake up in the morning with your nuts stuck to your leg with superglue."

"Ouch!" Tony winced at the thought. "But it really was a woman." He shook his head in disgust. "An attempted murder. A woman in her mid—to late twenties . . . *And pregnant!* Would you believe it?"

"And?"

"She survived but was severely beaten by her attacker and miscarried. She's unconscious with serious internal injuries and lucky to be alive." Tony shook his head in dismay. "There are some real bad asses out there, and I just hope we can put this bastard behind bars." He took another mouthful of the amber liquid. "Now this *is* good!"

CHAPTER 13

It was a humid night, and Tony was wrestling with his subconscious. Dreams often arise from an event or discussion that happened during the day and come back to haunt you. But why was the Laura Williams's case any different from the hundreds of attempted homicides he had investigated? *The taking of a life of an innocent unborn child!* He stirred and muttered something in his sleep, waking his wife Rose from her unadulterated slumber.

"Tony, what the hell!" She gave him a hard nudge to the ribs.

"Eh . . . Err . . ." His mind was still trying to jump from his tremulous dream to realty. He leaned over to the bedside table and took a paper towel from the box to wipe the perspiration from his forehead then sat up staring into the darkness. "I'm sorry, honey. I don't know what came over me . . . *What was I saying?"* He was still confused.

"For the life of me, I haven't a bloody clue!" Rose answered irately. Her beauty sleep well and truly went down the toilet.

"I'm sorry, honey." He gave her kiss on the lips.

"Now if it's not too much trouble, Mr. Detective"—she thumped the pillow with her hand, making a hollow for her head—*"can I get back to sleep?"*

Tony crashed onto his pillow, still staring hypnotically into the darkness until finally his eyes closed through sheer fatigue.

It seemed like only ten minutes when the loud buzz of the radio alarm broke his deep slumber, and he quickly killed the culprit before that crazy music disturbed the whole house. The early morning sunlight was now streaming through the gaps in the blinds, and he covered his eyes with the back of his hand.

"Six thirty already! I can't believe it." He muttered to himself. Then he smiled and turned on his side, wrapping his arm around his wife's waist.

"What's with you this morning?" Rose asked, trying to prize his arm away.

"Didn't I tell you? Well . . . for your information, my beautiful sexy wife, I want to spend breakfast with the kids. So why don't you relax, honey, and let nature take its course.

"The kids my foot! I would have to be a real bimbo not to know what's on *your mind* this morning." Rose turned on her side.

Tony snuggled into her back and gave her a sexy kiss on the nape of her neck.

"I love you, honey."

"Yeah . . . Yeah . . . Sometimes I think you only love me for the sex." She was hiding her grin. She really loved this big heel. "Well, Romeo, are you going to satisfy this 'desperate housewife' *or what?*"

*   *   *

"And she is still unconscious in intensive care? I see . . . but the surgery went well. Well, I guess that's something. Thanks again, sister, for all your help. I'll call again in the evening after work." Terry placed the receiver back in its cradle then sat back for a moment, gathering her thoughts. The prognosis was not good, but at least Laura was holding her own. *Then there was the office.* She didn't relish the thought of the gory gossip and Blakely giving her the third degree.

"Oh, what the hell!" She quickly glanced at her watch and didn't like what she saw. *"Seven forty-five!"* she spoke out loud, not believing the eyes. "Blakely will go off his fucking brain if I'm late again." She hurried to the bedroom and grabbed her sneakers. The stilettos gave her sexy legs *but in heavy traffic?* It was not the first time that had she almost rear-ended the car in front, her designer heels catching the floor mat. She would change her shoes in the company car park. Terry quickly grabbed her keys and gulped the dregs of her forgotten coffee. *"Yuk!"* She screwed up her face at the disgusting taste of stale caffeine then quickly opened the apartment door, almost sprinting to the elevator. Today she had more important things on her mind.

*   *   *

The elevator door opened, and it was just her luck! There, standing on his lonesome, was Nick Donnelly, the woman ogler. *This was all she needed!*

"Late again are we, Terry?" His eyes were already stripping her down to her panties, and Terry expediently pulled her short tight-fitting skirt down past her knees.

Donnelly gave her a cheeky grin; he knew he was getting to her. "Feeling the cold, Terry, huh?" He was being sarcastic, and she could feel her blood pressure rise. *I mean what woman needs a sexual pervert hitting on her at this time in the morning?*

"Nick"—she looked him straight in the eyes—"why don't you go crawl up your own ass?"

"Terry, that's the first positive thing you have said to me." He was trying to keep a straight face. "Now *I know* you are interested."

Fortunately, the elevator chimed; and the doors opened, a timely intervention, saving the "Midnight Cowboy" from another ear lashing.

"Bye, honey. Remember I am always available should you change your mind."

"Yeah, over my dead body." Terry retaliated as she briskly walked to the car park elevator.

"That's what they all say." This guy wasn't going to go away.

"Creep!" Terry yelled as she hit the button, relieved to get this Nick out of her face.

She quickly turned the key in the Mazda 6, its tires screeching as she hit the pedal. On a wing and a prayer, she could still reach the office by nine. The Lincoln Tunnel would be her best bet then to the ABM building in Madison Avenue. She slipped into the heavy traffic and sat back to relax. The slow drive would give her time to think.

CHAPTER 14

Tony was already at the breakfast bar, enjoying his bacon and scrambled eggs.

"Honey, did anyone ever tell you that you are the greatest cook in the world?"

"Yeah, you!" Rose answered, laughing at the same time. "I think that's a request for another cup of coffee."

"How did you guess?" Tony laughed.

"Get out of it!"

"Hi, Dad." It was Mouro, the oldest boy, still in his pyjamas, rubbing the sleep from his eyes.

"How about giving your mother a big kiss and come and join me." Tony patted the empty breakfast stool.

"And where's that brother of yours?" Tony asked as Mouro took his seat.

"He'll be down in a few minutes, Dad." He could hear the footsteps of his brother running down the stairs.

"Daaaad!" Sam rushed to his father and sprang onto his knee.

"Samuel, let your father eat his breakfast in peace."

"Awe, Mom."

"It's okay, honey. You can't blame the boys. It's not often that I get the chance to have breakfast with the family."

"Come now, Mouro, eat your flakes."

"Sure, Mom." Mouro always liked playing the big brother, showing an example.

"Dad, did you catch any bad guys yesterday?" Samuel innocently asked.

"Hundreds." Tony laughed.

"Don't listen to your father. He's just being silly." Rose was shaking her head.

The phone rang, and Rose lifted the receiver from the wall phone. "Mrs. Perino here."

"Rose, is that husband of yours free?"

"I might have guessed it would be you, Bill. Hang on, and I'll pass you to him . . . Tony . . . Bill on the line." She passed the phone.

"Yeah?"

"Tony, it's nearly nine thirty, and Baker's going into orbit. You gotta get your ass over here, *like now!"*

"Take it easy, Bill. *Hell,* I gotta spend some time with the family! Tell him I'll be there in around forty-five minutes."

"Okay, it's your ass that's on the line and don't say I didn't warn you . . . Give my love to Rose . . . Ciao."

Rose gave Tony that disgusting look that only a distraught wife can produce.

"Don't tell me you have to drop everything again and jump three feet high when that boss of yours calls."

"I got news for you, honey. For once I'm finishing my breakfast, *and Baker can go take a hike."*

"Tony, watch your language in front of the boys." When Rose is in that mood, better to say nothing at all.

"Now why don't you sit on this other stool, young man, and eat your breakfast or your mother will get crossed with us all."

Young Samuel leaped to the other stool with the agility of a chimpanzee and started to demolish his Captain Crunch. He knew how to keep in his mother's good books. This kid was smart.

"Dad"—it was Mouro's turn—"when I grow up, I would like to be a detective just like you."

"Oh, would you now." Tony grinned. "I think your mother would have something to say about that."

"I certainly would, young man. There is one too many detectives in this house with your father. No, I have bigger things planned for you two boys."

"It's all right, Mom." Young Sam gave his mother that innocent look. "I want to be a fireman."

Tony looked at his wife, and the two of them burst into laughter. *This kid was something else.*

*   *   *

Terry was trying to unscramble her thoughts as she drove through the snailing morning traffic. Who could the mystery man be? Laura was shrewd and kept her affairs to herself, with the only exception that she did tell her that he was a high-powered executive, married with two teenage kids. Now not being a mathematician, you would have to be dumb not to work out that this guy would have to be in his mid—to late forties and someone that she met in her professional capacity in marketing. *Naw . . . For the love of me, I just can't hang it together. It's probably staring me straight in the face. It'll come to me. Maybe her diary will throw some light on this lowlife grub.*

"At last!" Terry gave a sigh of relief as she signalled and hung a right into the underground car park. Terry paused as the young black security guard scanned her employee tag. He studied the picture for a moment then looked at Terry.

"Come on, Lee, don't be such a fucking horse's ass. You know who I am. *Christ,* you stop me every day and ask me that same shit!"

He laughed and pressed the control button to lift the boom gate. "Have a good day . . . *Eh?* What's your name again?" He was grinning all over.

"Fucking joker." Terry hit the gas, her tires screaming on the smooth sealed concrete. She could see in her rear mirror that Lee was laughing. *"That asshole!* Always with the jokes." She quickly parked the Mazda.

Terry strutted into the office. Okay, so she was late. *So what?* It was nothing new. With the looks on the faces of the office gossips, the news of Laura's misfortune had hit the streets and was hot copy. Terry dumped her stuff on her desk and was about to get her early morning caffeine when she was distracted by the noise coming from Blakely's "glass house." There he was frustratingly banging on the glass to attract her attention. Terry turned and acknowledged, trying to put on a half-baked smile. "Asshole!" she muttered, gritting her teeth.

*   *   *

"Take the load off, Terry." Blakely pointed to the empty chair in front of his desk.

"Listen, Jack, if this is about me being late again—"

Blakely cut her dead. "That's one thing, but I'm beginning to think that's a lost cause. *No* . . . It's about Laura."

"News travels fast." Terry was surprised.

"*Hell!* It's spread across the front page of every newspaper in town. Or haven't you read the news yet?" Blakely pushed the *Herald* in front of her.

Terry stared at the large print. U.S. SENATOR'S DAUGHTER BRUTALLY ATTACKED. POLICE CLASSIFY CASE AS ATTEMPTED MURDER . . . Laura Williams, the daughter of Senator Dave Williams . . .

"I knew I had seen that guy somewhere before when I bumped into him at the hospital, but I never suspected for one moment it was Laura's father." Terry shook her head. "The press will have a field day with this one, and they'll be looking to dig up as much dirt as they can."

"Come on, Terry, get real. That's what sells papers . . . Of course, you knew Laura was pregnant." Blakely came from nowhere.

"Did I?" Terry answered, a sarcastic tone lacing her voice

"Terry, cut the slack. Who are you trying to fool?"

"Listen, Jack, unless there's anything else, this conversation is over."

"Have it your own way, but a word of advice before you leave. Your annual appraisal is coming up next week, and you had better be wearing sunglasses to protect your eyes from the red ink."

"Can I go now?" Terry was getting frustrated and about to blow a gasket.

"One last thing . . . You know who the guy is, don't you?"

"If I knew, Jack, *I certainly wouldn't be telling you . . . Now?*"

"Yeah, you can go . . . But remember what I said, *and you had better be on time tomorrow!*"

*   *   *

"Goodbye, honey." Tony gave his wife a kiss as they stood on the porch. "Now, you kids, be good and do what your mother tells you. And, Samuel, no more bad reports from Kindy."

"Okay, Dad." Young Sam bowed his head, staring at the ground.

"So when can I expect you home tonight?" Rose asked. Tony was looking for cover.

"I'll try my best to be home for dinner, honey. Should anything come up, don't worry. I'll call you."

"Did I tell you my mother is coming 'round today? She could babysit and give us some space for a romantic dinner or even a movie."

He could see the look in Rose's eyes, and he felt pangs of guilt. "If you put it that way, honey, I promise."

Rose's face lit up. At last Tony was getting the message.

"Bye, kids." He unlocked the jeep.

"Bye, Dad" came the chorus. And for once Tony felt good as he drove down the driveway. Maybe this is what he should do every day. His cell phone rang.

"Yes, Bill." Tony gave a big sigh. "Tell him I'm on my way, and I should arrive at the office in around forty-five minutes. He's going nuts about the Williams's case. So, what's so special about this one? I'll soon find out. So, it's that way, huh? Keep my coffee warm, partner. By the sound of things, I'm going to need it."

*   *   *

The drive to Pearl Street was uneventful, with the exception of the usual frustrated crazies on the road and the occasional good-looking broad giving him the eye. It would be easy for a guy to go astray in Sin City, but this is the Big Apple, and anything goes.

"I wonder why," Tony spoke to himself, "the Laura Williams case is so important. Hell, I have enough on my plate with the Davis homicide. *We've drawn a blank at every turn.* But this Williams case, for the life of me, is bothering me and I don't know why. There's *something* odd. I guess the break will be when this broad gains consciousness." He shook his head. "*That is if she ever does!* Then that's a whole new ball game. *At last!*" he spoke aloud as he hung a right into the car park, his next challenge to find a parking slot!"

The bright warm summer's morning made Tony smile as he walked casually to the front entrance of police headquarters. "With a day like this"—he grinned—"it makes it all worthwhile."

Bill was twiddling his thumbs, anxiously waiting for his partner, and his troubled expression changed to relief as he spotted Tony emerging from the elevator.

"Christ, Tony, you took your time!"

"So what's the big deal? Listen, first things first, what do you say I buy you coffee?"

"Are you serious?" Bill looked Tony straight in the eyes. "Yeah, *I guess you are.*

"Perino." The "Paul Robeson" voice boomed across the office. *"Now . . .* in my office . . . *And that includes you, Hayden!"*

"Didn't I tell you Cassias Clay was on the warpath?" Bill shook his head.

"Cool it, Bill. I'll handle it." Tony was a veteran when it comes to the chase.

*   *   *

As for Ted Baker, the captain of detectives, at six two, black, shaven head, and weighing in at 250, he was not to be messed with. He was an ugly SOB in his early fifties, with a face like antique leather and from the old school. A beat cop climbing the ladder, and with all the discrimination that goes with a black face, you had to hand it to this guy. But now his pension was high on the agenda, and he wanted to retire in a blaze of glory, and hard asses like Perino were a pain in the butt. This morning, something was getting under his skin, and whoever was first in line was going to feel the blast from the past.

*   *   *

Baker pointed to the empty chairs. *"Sit!"*

Tony could have sworn for a moment that Baker's face had turned a pale shade of white, and he covered his mouth to stifle his laughter.

"Am I missing something, Perino? Because if there *is* something funny, don't keep I to yourself. Hayden and I can't wait."

Tony quickly reverted to the serious face. There was no point in chancing his luck further.

"Now if it's not *too* much trouble, perhaps, Perrino, you can start by telling me what kept you this morning?" Baker sarcastically looked at his watch. "Because in one hour, it will be time for lunch."

"Awe, come on, Ted, there's more to life than 24/7 police work. I like to see my family once in a while."

"And I suppose your bosom friend Hayden here agrees with you. *Well, let me tell you two jokers,* when you join the NYPD and work in Homicide, you're married to *me,* and I call the shots. This is your family, and if you don't like it, the traffic department is looking for recruits, so be my guest and pick up the transfer applications from the front desk. *Do I make myself clear?" Silence is golden, and this was the time.*

"Now here's the cut. You drop everything on the Davis case and hand over all your files to Brown and Lucas."

"*What?* These two jerks?" Tony couldn't help himself. And Bill? Well, he just cringed at Tony's outburst.

"Perino, I'll pretend I didn't hear that insubordinate remark, and one more wisecrack like that, *so help me!*" Baker paused for a moment to calm down. "Okay, here's the deal. You throw everything at the Williams case, *and I mean everything.* Would you believe that I had Murray on the phone at seven o'clock this morning, burning my ear?"

Tony was puzzled. Why would Jake Murray, the DA, have such an interest in an everyday attempted murder?

"Let's have it, Perino. What's on your mind?" Baker recognized the body language.

"Ted, you can't blame a guy for begging the question, *why?*"

"I'll tell you why. Laura Williams just happens to be the daughter of none other than Dave Williams, the U.S. senator, who happens to be the brother in-law of Jake Murray, the district attorney. How does that grab you?" *"Shit!"* Tony couldn't believe his ears. Now it all makes sense.

"You can say that again, Perino," Baker acknowledged. "Now let's get this show on the road, and I want kept up to speed every twenty-four. Any questions?"

Tony and Bill were still trying to get over the dramatic change of events.

"I gather by the ear-breaking silence that means no!" Baker pointed to the door. *"Out!"* He was a man of few words but with a clear message.

* * *

As Terry Johnson sat at her desk, she could feel the stare of the office bitches drilling into her back. Enough was enough, and she angrily rose to her feet.

"So, what's the big deal?" she screamed. "You can read the paper, can't you? What do you want, the gory details? *You bunch of fucking hypocrites."*

In the corner of her eye, she could see Blakely staring through his office window toward the commotion, and it was time to drop the curtain. She was in enough shit as it is. There again, Blakely was on the medal hunt, especially when he found out Laura was Senator Williams's daughter. Just imagine if he could pull a rabbit out the hat identifying Laura's attacker! Terry rose to her feet. An idea had just struck her.

Blakely looked up as Terry knocked on his door. He frowned for a moment then reluctantly motioned her to enter.

"Terry, this had better be good. At your peril, don't waste my time. I'm not in the mood for any more of your tantrums. *So?*" Blakely placed his chin on his hand.

"Jack, it's like this. I have a hunch that Laura knew this guy through a business contact and that there may be some clue to his identity stored in her computer diary, which is encrypted."

Now she had gotten Blakely's attention!

"That *is* interesting! I guess what you are asking is that I give you permission to crack Laura's firewall." He lifted the phone. "Nancy, put me through to DP. Neil, Blakely here. I need a favour."

"Thanks, Jack. I really appreciate it." Terry rose to leave.

"Terry." He stopped in her tracks. "You know I quite like you." Blakely's roving eyes make her feel uncomfortable. "Sure, we've had our disagreements, but there's no reason why you should dislike me. I mean I'm not all that bad!" He had that X-ray smile. "Listen, maybe we could get to know each other better over an after-office drink one evening."

Terry had to smile, get a load of this guy. "I'll keep it in mind, Jack, but at the moment, I'm sure you appreciate I can't get Laura out of my mind."

"I understand." Blakely looked her up and down, once more admiring her shapely legs. "When Neil cracks Laura's file, let me know if you find something."

"You'll be the first, Jack." Terry gave a ventriloquist smile.

When she arrived at her desk, Neil Gardener, the DP manager, was already working on Laura's computer.

*   *   *

Tony slumped into his chair with Bill sitting on the corner of his desk.

"Bill, I think it's time we had that coffee." Tony was still in shock.

"Stay put, Tony. I'll go fetch them." As Bill turned and walked toward the coffee machine, he caught Brown and Lucas, their smug black faces saying it all; and Bill guessed that Baker had already broken the news.

"Take a look at these two assholes." Bill placed the polystyrene cups on the desk.

"Yeah, I see them, Bill, but let's play it cool. We don't want accused of being in the Klu Klux Klan."

Bill almost choked on his coffee. *"Get out of it!* Tony, at times you crack me up." He hit the serious mode. "So, what's next on the cards with the Williams case?" Bill took another mouthful of coffee.

Tony pondered. "Good question, but first things first. We have to find a motive, and with what we have so far, that's going to be difficult. Bill, let's start by phoning the hospital to check if Williams has regained consciousness."

"Sure. It was?"

"Roosevelt Memorial," Tony answered, deep in thought.

"Roosevelt Memorial? Good afternoon. I'm Detective Sergeant Hayden, NYPD, Homicide. I'm checking on a Ms. Laura Williams. That's correct, the serious assault victim."

* * *

"She's all yours, Terry." Neil was feeling good with himself. Cracking a firewall is no mean fete.

"Thanks, Neil." Terry grabbed the seat in front of the desktop; she couldn't wait.

"Is there anything else, Terry?" The young computer whiz was enjoying an eyeful of Terry's thighs, her skirt well above her knees, and he wasn't in hurry to get back to his office.

"I'm good, Neil. Thanks again." Terry half smiled. *Guys! You can always read them.* "Now let's see what we got," she spoke out loud. "Almost eighty names and telephone numbers with about three quarters of them guys. But nothing stands out, like dinner dates or 'must' call. So where do we go from here? This was just a hunch, and maybe none of these guys is the one."

Suddenly, she could feel someone breathing down her neck, and she quickly turned. *"Christ, Jack,* you scared me for a moment there."

Blakely looked into her eyes and just grinned. This guy was a pro.

"The good news or the bad news, Terry?"

"It's not good, Jack. It was just a hunch, but I'm afraid I've drawn a blank. There're plenty of guy names and companies but nothing to indicate anything other than business contacts."

"Hmmm . . ." Blakely rubbed his chin. "What do you suggest now?"

"We call the detective that's handling the case. *Eh?"* Terry opened her bag and retrieved the card. "A Lieutenant Tony Perrino . . ."

Blakely studied the card. *"Good!* Leave it to me. I'll give him a call. Now enough drama for today, Terry. We all have work to do." It was Blakely's polite way of saying "the party's over."

*   *   *

Tony turned to Bill as he picked up the thick manila folder. "Let's go to these two cats and lay it on the line."

They both walked over to Brown and Lucas's desk. There was no love lost between these guys.

Brown turned to his partner and gave an ugly sneer as Tony dumped the files on his desk. "I'll be darned. Mohamed comes to the mount, huh?" "I guess Baker has spoken to you," Tony scowled, ignoring the stupid remark.

"Yeah, he told me you two snowflakes weren't up to it, and he needed two real detectives to wrap up the Davis case. Like, in the next forty-eight. Isn't that right, Bert?" He gave an ugly laugh.

"It's like the man said." The other brown bomber answered, the look on his face, like the "cat that had just swallowed the canary."

"You guys have been watching too much of that TV shit." Bill took the shot. It was too good to miss.

That comment was enough to ring the bell, and Brown jumped to his feet and eyeballed Hayden.

"Listen, white boy. If you know what's good for you, you'll button that fat lip of yours before I do it for you."

Hayden just laughed. "One of these days, *black boy,* I'm gonna rip out your fat lips and kiss my white ass with them."

"Why you!"

"What's the deal here? Have you guys got nothing else to do except behave like a bunch of fifth graders?" It was a timely intervention by Baker. *"And you two!"* He turned to Brown and Lucas. *"In my office, now!* I want to discuss the Davis file."

Tony grinned. This kinda stuff he liked. "Listen, I say we go to the cafeteria and grab a sandwich. What say you, partner?"

"That's the best suggestion I've heard this morning." Bill laughed.

"Of course, you know you're paying."

"I might have guessed." Only this time, Bill wasn't laughing.

CHAPTER 15

Mike tossed and turned the whole night. It was a nightmare that kept coming back to haunt him time and time again. He kept seeing Laura's bluing face as she kicked and screamed, fighting for dear life. *What had he done? But that stupid broad wouldn't go quietly. She was determined to destroy my family and my career. What was I to do? Then there was the pregnancy. Whether I was the father or not, she was going to bring the world down on me. I mean I had to do something."*

June nudged him. "Darling, are you all, right? You were talking in your sleep."

"Eh . . . Err . . . Was I, honey?" Mike rubbed his bagged eyes. He was bushed. *"Eh,* what was I saying?"

"Something or other about you had to do something." June glanced at the bedside clock. "Darling, do you know that it has just turned four! Why don't you just snuggle up next to me and go back to sleep."

"Sure, honey." He gave her a reassuring kiss on the lips. "I'm sorry I disturbed you."

But it was easier said than done, and Mike gave a sigh of relief when he finally heard the alarm.

*   *   *

Summers was quick to hit the floor and headed straight for the shower, dropping his pyjamas on the way.

"What's the hurry, darling? It has just turned six," June asked, only half awake. "Why don't you just come back to bed?"

Mike had to smile. The thought was more than appealing. "Honey, I'm really sorry, but I have to be in the office early this morning. I have a meeting at eight with Chuck."

"Oh well then." June gave a disgruntled sigh. "I suppose I had better rise and rustle you up some breakfast then."

"There's no need to, honey. I can stop by at the diner."

"Now enough of that! I wouldn't think of it. *Ahhhh . . ."* June yawned, covering her mouth as she placed both feet on the rug. Mike had killed her beauty sleep with his ranting, and she was now feeling somewhat tired.

*   *   *

He could hear the crackle of the frying pan, and the smell of bacon and eggs was to die for. But today Mike had more important things on his mind, and he quickly grabbed the morning edition to search the headlines.

"Darling, you seem to be up tight this morning. Why don't you relax and enjoy your breakfast? I'm sure the news can wait till later."

It was as if Mike didn't hear a word June was saying. He lifted his coffee mug and took a sip while scanning the large print. There it was in black and white. "U.S. SENATOR'S DAUGHTER BRUTALLY ATTACKED.

POLICE CLASSIFY CASE AS ATTEMPTED MURDER. Laura Williams, the daughter of Senator Dave Williams . . ." Mike almost choked, his coffee mug crashing to the breakfast bar.

"Mike!" June yelled, jumping to her feet. *"Are you all right?"* What happened?" She could sense by the shocked look on Mike's face that something had spooked him.

"It's nothing, honey. I just thought about something that I carelessly I missed on that new contract." He was searching for something to wipe the bar top and the illegible coffee-soaked *Herald*'s front page.

"Leave that to me, darling. Just make sure that your shirt is not stained." "I'm all right. I just feel so stupid." Mike was checking his shirt and tie. *"But this paper!"* He crumpled the soggy mess and stuffed it in the garbage crusher. There was no way he could take a chance on June recognizing Laura's name and recollecting that phone call. "Listen, honey, I gotta go. I'm sorry for the mess."

"But you have hardly touched your breakfast," June protested. "Listen . . ."

June stopped what she was doing and confronted him. "Mike darling, I know what you are going to say, but lately you have not been yourself, and it's about time that you took some time off. I mean you have been working so hard lately. I'm sure Chuck would understand."

"Honey, *please.*"

"Good morning, Father." It was Steven. "Hi, Mom. That smells good."

"Take a seat, young man. Yours is coming up. Where's that sister of yours?"

Steven just shook his head. "In front of the mirror as usual . . . *Father!* What the hell happened to your face?" He was shocked at the sight of his father's swollen cheeks.

Mike just let it go over his head. It was embarrassing enough. "Listen, I gotta go, Steven. I have an early meeting. Your mother can tell you all about it later."

"Must you, Father? I was hoping I could spend some time with you over breakfast to get your advice on which university I should apply for. Remember I will graduate from college in eight weeks' time."

"I'm sorry, son. I must go. I don't want to get stuck in the morning rush. Can we discuss this tonight over dinner?"

Steven's facial expression reflected his disappointment. "I guess so, Father . . . *It's just* . . . well . . . you are always so busy."

"I promise, tonight over dinner. Bye, honey." Mike gave June a kiss on the lips. "I might just speak to Chuck about your recommendation." He grinned as he picked up his briefcase.

"I'll hold you to that, Mike Summers. Drive carefully, darling."

* * *

Tony's cell phone buzzed as he was halfway through his pastrami on rye.

"Who the hell can this be now? Can't a guy get ten minutes peace to grab a sandwich and coffee." He shook his head. "Yeah? Perino here. Yeah, that's me. Jack Blakely from ABM. I see. So you are Laura Williams's boss. *Hmmm* . . . And you think that maybe one of her business contacts could be our man. I see. Well . . . *Err . . . Eh . . .* Jack, it's like this. We may have to check them all. Say, would it be possible to fax a copy of that list? Thanks, Jack. That would be really helpful and, of course, thanks again for all your help. My fax number is . . ."

"That sounded interesting," Bill commented as Tony shut the line.

"Could be . . . That was Laura's Williams's boss, and he has a hunch that . . ."

"And this guy is gonna e-mail this list. Well, I guess we have to start someplace."

"Yeah, and I'm gonna start by finishing my sandwich!" Tony sank his teeth into the moist bread and smiled before indulging in another mouthful of coffee.

* * *

Mike was still in shock; he was sure Laura was at the pearly gates. How could that be? He had checked her pulse, and there was no sign of life. But now more importantly, he had to get another paper and he hit the stock switch, the big car's tires screeching as he pulled into the sidewalk in front of the news stand amidst a hail of horns.

He fished a five from his wallet. "Make it quick, kid. The *Herald*. And keep the change." He grabbed the paper and gunned the big Lincoln just in time before some driver threatened him with violence.

"I'll stop at Charlie's Diner and grab a coffee and study the pulp fiction." He was talking to himself.

* * *

Hi, Mike. So what's new?" Charlie asked.

"The usual, all work and no play." Mike half smiled.

"Coffee?"

"Black, no sugar." Mike unfolded the paper.

"Too bad about Senator Williams's daughter, huh?"

"I haven't got to that yet." Mike was endeavoring not to be rude.

"Of course, you know that Williams is the brother-in-law of Jake Murray, the DA. I mean whoever this bastard is, I wouldn't wish to be in his shoes. The whole of the NYPD will be after his ass. With people in high places like these two guys, this will be the 'mother of all manhunts.'"

"I guess so. Charlie, can I have that coffee now? I'm in a bit of a hurry."

"Sure, Mike, no sweat. Coming up."

Mike started to read the newsprint, but it wasn't giving much away, except that Laura was still unconscious and in intensive care after major surgery and that her life was on the line.

"But at which hospital?" he spoke out loud as he ran his finger down the column. "Here we are, Roosevelt . . ."

Mike's mind was in a spin. *What if she wakes up?* He went a pale shade of grey, thinking of the consequences. *He would be done for, that's for sure. But then it would be his word against hers. He had left no clues, or the police would be knocking on his door by now. But then again, if the foetus was his and they checked the DNA? Hell! What am I thinking about?* He convinced himself. *If she doesn't regain consciousness, then they'll never hang it on me. I mean they have nothing.* The more he convinced himself, the more confident he became. He folded the paper and left a five on the bar top.

"Thanks, Charlie."

"See you, Mike."

*   *   *

The drive to the office seemed longer than normal with his mind continually churning out fresh questions on the consequences of his stupid and inhuman assault on a pregnant woman. How could he have done such a crazy thing and, more to the point, what were the police up to? Should he check with the hospital? No, *that would be stupid!* The police could easily trace the call. It was a nail-biting waiting game, and he was stuck with it.

He parked the Lincoln and dejectedly walked to the car park elevator. And what would today bring? *Who the hell knows?*

"Good morning, Mike." Julie couldn't help but stare for a moment at the state of her boss's swollen face.

"Good morning, Julie. Yeah, I know what's running through your mind.

I'll tell you all about it later. Has Chuck arrived?"

"Around ten minutes ago. Do you wish to speak with him?"

"Later, Julie. I have a few things to do first."

"Coffee?"

"No, I'm good." He disappeared into the office.

Julie shrugged. This was not like her boss. He looked as if he had all the troubles of the world resting on his shoulders.

Mike spread the paper on his desk, studying each word of the reported so-called attempted murder. *"Hell!* What am I doing? I'll drive myself crazy reading through this stuff time and time again." He folded the paper and chucked it in the wastepaper bin. *"I've got work to do!"* He took the McDonald's contract from his briefcase. There were few points he needed to revisit.

The secretarial phone rang. "Yes, Julie?"

"Chuck would like to see you when you are free." "Inform him that I'll be free in a few minutes." *"What now?"* Mike closed the file.

*   *   *

Bill swallowed the last of his coffee and turned to his partner. The sandwich had hit the spot, and it was time to get serious. "So where do we go from here partner?"

Tony pondered. "That's a good question. And there's never been a crime without a motive, and for the life of me, this one has me beat." Tony was rubbing his chin. "No sign of sexual assault. No sign of robbery. The perpetrator had murder on his mind that night or did he, and if so, why? A pregnant unmarried woman. Could it be an affair of the heart that had turned ugly? Bill, look at it this way. Romeo was having an extramarital affair, enjoying all the good things that go with it, as long as it was kept under wraps. But for this broad, she was the 'fall in love' type, and it was all or nothing. She wanted the 'family grapes' or she's going to take the lead part be in the next 'Swan Lake.' But lover boy became careless and sends his secret lover to the maternity club. This broad comes from high places, and the heat is on to make her an honest woman. When the hot sex ended and he found that he should have had a vasectomy, his world caved in. The broad refused an abortion, and over a heated 'I will tell all' argument, he flipped his lid and went ape. Blackmail. Yeah, *but sexual blackmail. But* unless we nail this guy, we'll never really know, that is, *unless 'Sleeping Beauty' finds her glass slipper."*

"Maaan . . . You have a vivid imagination. Talking from experience, huh?" Bill was laughing.

"Get outta here! Rose would kill me. Never cross an Italian woman from Roma."

Bill laughed, shaking his head. "I get the picture."

As they stood in the elevator, Tony was still pondering. His theory had something to it, but it was still naked and not enough to hang his hat on.

"I was thinking, Bill. The apartment was clean except for the woman's prints, but Adams found one tiny scrap of paper, and come to think of it, I wonder if Ken Brody, the pathologist, has finished his report." Tony grinned. "*Partner,* I think our first stop is CSI."

* * *

"Grab a seat, Mike." Chuck stared for a moment, flabbergasted at Mike's swollen cheeks. "*Christ, Mike!* What the hell happened to your face? *I hope it wasn't a domestic!*"

Mike forced a grin. He was uncomfortable with Chuck's discerning humour.

"*Naw,* nothing like that." Mike flushed. "If you must know." He paused again. "*Eh,* I'm a bit embarrassed. You see, I was mugged last night on my way home. Or should I say an attempted mugging."

"*You're serious?*"

"It doesn't get any worse. You know when I think back, I can't believe it myself. I was just standing, patiently minding my own business, waiting for a cab, when I saw this couple having an altercation, and the woman was coming off second best. So, like a good Samaritan . . ."

"So, this was just a setup, and after you managed to get a shot in, the woman jumped on your back and clawed at your face, and the arrival of the cab luckily avoided what could have become ugly?"

"*In a nutshell!*" Mike was relieved. It seemed convincing.

"You were lucky, Mike. I wouldn't wish to go through that one. But why didn't you call the cops?"

"Chuck . . . You know how it pans out. All that shit blown out of proportion in the tabloids, and besides, there was nothing stolen, and except for a few superficial wounds to my face, it's no big deal."

Chuck shook his head in disgust "*This town!* Now getting back to business. Mitch Wade, an old college friend of mine, who may I say is not short of the readies, intends to invest in a soft drink company in West Palm Springs. But before he runs the gauntlet and mercilessly throws his money into the pot, he needs a market survey report. I'm sorry, Mike, to have to lay this on you. You're the best, and I'm afraid I have no alternatives."

Mike inwardly breathed a sigh of relief. It couldn't have come at a better time. *Of course, June will be upset, and as for Steven, well, no more is said!*

"Mike, are you all, right?" Chuck was concerned at Mike's lost expression. It was as if he was somewhere else.

"*Eh* . . . Sorry, Chuck, for a moment there I was mentally trying to arrange my commitments."

"I understand, but more bad news. I need you to fly to West Palm today." *This was even better! Mike couldn't believe his luck.*

"I half expected that." He smiled, now more relaxed. "But you're not getting off that lightly, Chuck. You owe me one, and I'm holding you to buy June and I dinner one evening."

Chuck grinned. "You know, that's not such a bad idea. Jenny loves June's company, and besides, we don't do enough entertaining. You know the old saying . . . 'All work and no play.'"

"*You're preaching to the converted!* Now if you want me on that plane today, the first thing I need is a write-up on the company, its products, competitors, and annual accounts, and of course, the shareholders."

"Now isn't it a coincidence." Chuck was grinning like a Cheshire cat as he passed Mike the thick manila folder. "It just so happens I have all that stuff in front of me."

"You old dog, I can't put anything past you."

"You should know me by now, Mike. How long have we worked together?" Chuck grinned.

"*Too long!*" It was a shot too good to miss. "But listen, *seriously*, if you want to catch that plane today, I had better make tracks."

Chuck couldn't contain his laughter as he placed the Delta Airway ticket in front of him.

"*Why you* . . ." Mike was shaking his head and laughing at the same time. "You never miss a trick."

"Maybe that's why I'm the boss. Get outta here! *Oh* . . . And give me a ring tomorrow evening to bring me up to speed. Have a good flight."

* * *

"Julie, I suppose you have heard of my predicament?" Mike stopped in front of his secretary's desk. He had that cheeky inquisitive look on his face.

"Mike." She was smiling. "You should know by now that we secretaries are like the 'Band of Brothers' or should I say 'Sisters'?"

"*Whatever* . . . Now if you don't want to be fired, can I trouble you for a cup of coffee?"

"Oh . . . I'll think about it." She was being naughty, but it was all in good humour. "By the way, I have arranged for a taxi to pick you up in an hour to catch the noon flight from Kennedy, so you don't have much time. One other point, I'm afraid I couldn't get a direct flight straight to West Palm, so unfortunately, you will have to change at Fort Lauderdale with an hour between your connecting flight."

"That's not so bad. I can indulge in the first-class lounge. Now for the worst part, I have to phone June and tell her the good news." He was being sarcastic. "I promised to take her out tonight for dinner." *"Ouch!"* Julie winced at the thought.

"Christ, Julie, don't make it any worse. I feel a big-enough heel as it is. Now if it's not too much trouble?" Mike grinned. *"That coffee . . ."*

* * *

"Dave, Perino here. Listen, I was wondering if you have received Brody's report. So you heard. Boy, the drums are good in this dump. Yeah, Baker did a bunk and reassigned these to meatheads to the Davis case. Of course, you know the Williams broad is none other than the daughter of Dave Williams, the U.S. senator, and the brother-in-law of Jake Murray, the DA. Yeah, I guess it runs in the family like wooden legs. So you have Brody's report? Sure, we'll be up in about ten minutes."

Bill was listening to the phone conversation when he noticed the fax coming through on Tony's machine and he quickly picked up the sheets and studied their contents. The fax was from Jack Blakely of ABM with the list of names, dates, and telephone numbers as he promised.

Tony dropped the phone and turned to Bill. "Good news. Dave has just received Brody's report."

"And more good news." Bill passed Tony the fax. "It's from Blakely at ABM, with the list of probable suspects."

Tony grinned. "It's all happening, partner. We'll study that later, but let's hit that elevator."

* * *

"Take the load off guys." Adams already had three polystyrene cups of the hot caffeine on his desk.

Tony laughed at the sight of the coffee. "How did you know?"

"You'd do the same for me. Besides, you are only one floor down." He grinned. Dave and Tony were still the best buddies from police college, and the detectives momentarily enjoyed the dark brew.

"So, Dave, what's new?" Tony was anxious.

Bronson held up the plastic zipper bag. "Tony, do you remember this little scrap of paper I found on the carpet in Laura Williams's apartment? Well, the lab report concludes that it is special paper used by most banks for customer check books."

"Now isn't that something?" Tony turned to Bill. His theory on sexual blackmail was coming together.

"But, Tony, getting down to the forensic and medical report, you're gonna love this. We presumed, because of the skin remnants found below Laura's nails, the general assumption being that Laura Williams during her struggle for dear life, the perpetrator suffered deep lacerations to his face.

That's the first point. *But get this.* The DNA check from the miscarried foetus and that of the skin samples prove beyond reasonable doubt that our man is none other than the father of Laura Williams's aborted child."

"This is getting better by the minute," Bill commented, turning to Tony.

"Hold it, guys. That's the good news, but the bad news is we ran the DNA results through the police databank and drew a blank."

"Hmmm." Tony was disappointed. "For a moment there, Dave, you had me going, but the plot thickens, and my assumptions on the motive are getting better by the hour. Dave, you mentioned the medical report."

'Yeah, I'll be brief. Severe bruising to the neck as the result of attempted strangulation. Fractured larynx. If this babe recovers consciousness, she's going to be silent for a long time. Three broken ribs and punctured left lung, possibly from blunt trauma, e.g., heavy footwork. The aborted fetus? Approximately four months premature. But here's the crunch. Her abdomen was so badly beaten that her fallopian tubes and womb had to be surgically removed to stop the internal haemorrhaging. The bottom line is that is if she survives, unfortunately, she will never experience the joys of motherhood."

"Shit! That's a tough call," Bill interrupted, thinking about his own kids. Tony rubbed the bristle on his chin. "Where do we go from here, partner?"

"Hey, don't hang this on me. You are the lieutenant, *remember?"* Bill was laughing.

"Why do I put up with you, Hayden? Get a load of this guy, Dave. You wouldn't happen to have a vacancy for one 'past used by date,' Detective Sergeant."

Dave had to laugh. "You guys . . . you crack me up."

Tony smiled. "But to get back to your question, Bill, we start with that list of suspects Blakely faxed. I have an idea."

*   *   *

Mike lifted the phone. It was crunch time.

"Hi, honey." He laid on the "charm."

"Mike!" June was surprised. It was unusual for her husband to call midday once he was engrossed in his work.

"So why the call? I'm sure it's not 'I just called to say I love you.'"

"Well, it is, and it isn't."

"Mike don't beat about the bush. Let's have it." June could sense the inevitable. *"Don't tell me!"*

"I'm afraid so, honey. You see, I have to leave for West Palm Springs this afternoon."

"Mike, I give up! You promised to spend time with Steven tonight then take me to dinner."

"I know, honey, but in my line of work, it comes with the job. Chuck feels bad about it and has promised to treat us to dinner when I return."

"Yeah, yeah, I've heard it all before. *Chuck is full of it!* Mike, I'm really up to my teeth. We never do anything as a family these days, *and just how long will you be away this time?"*

"At least until Monday," Mike sheepishly answered.

"I might have known. So, I guess we can kiss goodbye to the family barbeque at Tony's place?"

"Honey, don't rub it in. I feel bad enough as it is. Give Rose and Tony my apologies."

"As usual, I'm left to do all the dirty work." June was becoming more and more irate. "I tell you, Mike, when you return, we're going to have a real heart to heart. We have no life at the moment, and the way we are going, *we are going to have no marriage either!"*

"Honey, calm down. I promise."

"Have you got everything you need for your trip?" As much as she was annoyed, she loved this guy.

"Honey, you know I always keep spare shirts and all that stuff in the office in case of an emergency."

"Tell me about it! For the love of me, Mike, I don't know why I put up with you . . . You *big heel* . . . I guess it's because I love you."

"I love you too, honey. I'll give you a call this evening, and please give my apologies to Steven. I'll make it up to him when I return."

"Have a safe trip, darling, and remember that call."

"Phew." Mike placed back the receiver just as Julie opened the door.

"Mike, I hope you are all packed because your cab is here."

CHAPTER 16

"Okay, so let's hear about this idea of yours." Bill was intrigued. Tony had a natural talent for thinking outside the box.

Perino sat back in his chair, studying the list of names, phone numbers, dates, etc.

"Bill, there're over sixty names on this list, and that's one helluva lot of shoe leather and phone calls. Now let's take a step back. Point 1, according to the pathologist, the aborted foetus was approximately four months premature."

"So?" Bill asked.

"So whoever was pumping Laura must have met her around five months ago. You don't have to be a mathematician to work that one out." Tony grinned, feeling prouder by the minute. "This is August, and my educated guess would make the dating session around March or April."

Bill procrastinated. "I get it, but it's a long shot."

"Yeah, but it's better than spending the next week tracking down every one of these guys. *Let me see.*" Tony spread the sheets on his desk. "*Hmmm . . .*" He was running his finger down the list. "*Ah,* here we are. Three names coincide with my theory, an R. Thomas, N. Black, and M. Summers. Now point 2, Bill. Didn't it strike you that it was odd that the apartment was squeaky clean with the exception of the Williams's woman's prints. It was as if someone had taken the time to wipe everything down and then vacuum the place. But here's the crunch. *The vacuum cleaner was empty!* Now doesn't that strike you as being strange?"

"I must admit, Tony, it did cross my mind, and looking back, the one thing that CSI missed was to search the garbage from the collection chute." "*Correct!* Bill, I want you to phone the apartment management and check when the garbage is normally collected. Meanwhile, I'll start by calling these numbers."

*   *   *

"And Mr. Summers, you say, has gone to West Palm Springs on business and won't be returning until Monday?"

"Yes, that is correct, Lieutenant." Julie was more than concerned. "Lieutenant, is there something wrong? I mean should I contact him?"

"No, nothing serious, just general routine. I just want to ask Mr. Summers some questions. By the way, would you be familiar with the name Laura Williams of ABM?"

"Yes, she has phoned my boss on a number of occasions regarding a recent contract that Global won. She is their marketing manager, and she consequently had a number of meetings with Mike to cross the 'i's' and dot the 't's,' so to speak."

"You mentioned Mike?"

"Yes, Mike Summers, our marketing VP."

"I see . . . Julie . . . *Eh,* you said your name was Julie?"

"That's correct, Lieutenant."

"Julie, can you get your boss to give me a call immediately when he returns. It's extremely urgent. My number is . . ."

Mike placed back the receiver and sat back, rubbing his chin. "It couldn't be? Naw, it couldn't be. It's just a coincidence . . . What you got, Bill?" Hayden was patiently waiting for Tony to drop the phone.

"I phoned the apartment manager, and he informed me that the garbage is collected once per week every Thursday."

"Tomorrow is Thursday, so what are we waiting for?" Tony chucked Bill the keys. "You're the wheel man."

* * *

As they sat in the car, both detectives were deep in thought.

"How did the calls pan out?" Bill asked.

"Drew a blank." Tony sighed. "With the exception of one guy that could be interesting. One moved to Toronto, and the other was transferred to Los Angeles. So, they couldn't have been at the crime scene on Tuesday evening.

Watertight alibis, as they say, tighter than a duck's ass."

Bill laughed. "Christ, Tony, where do you get that stuff.?"

"But this other guy, a Mike Summers? The name bothers me, but maybe it's just a coincidence. Anyhow, he is at West Palm Springs, on business, and he will contact me on Monday when he returns."

"Here we are, Elm Apartments!" Bill pulled into the sidewalk and cut the engine.

The warm summer weather was still humid and uncomfortable, and the detectives reluctantly slipped into their jackets to conceal their "hardware."

Bill quickly placed the yellow NYPD cover over the parking meter and followed Tony to the reception. The apartment manager looked up, studying the new traffic, and decided to divert his concentration from the "sports page" to the two heavies approaching him at speed.

"Eh . . . Err, gentleman, how can I help you?" He looked rather nervous. Maybe he had a rap sheet or something.

Tony flashed his shield. "Perino and Hayden, NYPD, Homicide."

The apartment manager still looked uneasy. "Detective Hayden, you must be the one that phoned?"

Bill nodded and passed him his cards.

"I'm Chris Benson, the duty manager. Now . . . *Eh* . . . Detective Hayden . . ."

He quickly glanced at Bill's card.

"Bill and Tony is okay."

"*Err* . . . Bill, you're the one that phoned me this afternoon about the apartment garbage collection roster?"

"That's correct," Bill answered abruptly, anxious to cut to the chase.

"As I told you, the garbage is not collected until tomorrow. Now the problem is, three apartments on each floor use their own chute but going into one garbage collecting bin in order to avoid blockages with too much stuff coming down at the same time. Would you believe that some moron chucked an umbrella down . . ."

"Chris, I appreciate the histrionics, but we don't have all day. So, if you don't mind?" Hayden cut him short.

"*Eh* . . . Sure, I'll show you to the basement."

"Chris, just before we go"—Tony stopped him in his tracks—"I'd like to ask you a few questions."

"I told everything to the lieutenant yesterday."

"Well, you can tell me again, unless that's a problem?" It was Tony's turn to lay on the heat.

"It's no problem." Brown was now feeling more than uncomfortable.

"*Um* . . . *Eh* . . . Am I a suspect, Detective?" he asked nervously.

"Not unless you think you are." Bill grinned, adding to the duty manager's discomfort.

"Relax, Chris. Let's start from basics. Bill, can you take Chris's statement?"

"Sure." Bill searched for his notepad.

"Okay, where do we start?" Chris was more than nervous.

"Chris, relax, take a seat. There's no point in all of us standing." Benson retrieved his seat at the front desk, but now he felt even more intimidated with the detective's stand-over tactics.

"So, Chris, tell me how long you have worked at Elm Apartments?" Tony asked.

"Just over three years."

"And before?"

"Uncle Sam . . . Gunnery Sergeant, U.S. Marine Corp. Twenty-five-year vet, retired."

"Now that's interesting. So, you've—"

"Yeah, been there, done that, from Vietnam to Desert Storm."

"Married?"

"Was . . . Somehow holy matrimony and army life never seem to jive." He paused. "Fortunate or unfortunate, no kids. This job pays well, and I'm sort of my own boss, nine to six, five days a week, and no worries."

"*Hmmm* . . . So, there is no one on the front desk after six?"

"That's the deal." Chris seemed more relaxed. "But here's the drop. There's no CCTV either, although the owner is thinking about it and who can blame him after Tuesday's episode . . . *Security?* Each owner or tenant is issued with a security card to open the front door and the entrance from the underground car park." He pointed to the steel door next to the lift.

Tony turned to Bill, shaking his head. *"Well, that's a good start!"* He was being sarcastic. "Now Laura Williams, how well did you know her?"

"I didn't! She is normally gone before I start at nine and arrives after I finish. The only time we cross paths is if she comes back from the office early or on holidays. She's a good-looking chick, and I'm sure she gets her share, but I've never seen her with any men friends. She's a cool bird and keeps to herself. I didn't know that she is the daughter of Dave Williams, the U.S. senator, but maybe that explains it."

"Chris, is there anything, I mean even the littlest anything, that crosses your mind that may help us to catch this lowlife?" Tony was drawing a blank in his frustration.

Benson moved his head dejectedly from side to side. "Sorry, detectives, that's the take."

"Christ, Bill, this is a stack of cards with no ace." Tony paused again. "Okay, Chris, let's go garbage hunting. Bill, did you fetch the coveralls, plastic gloves, and overshoes?" Bill nodded, displaying the carry bag. "What would I do without you?" Tony laughed. *"Christ, Tony,* you sound like my bloody wife!"

"Is that a bad or good thing?" Tony was still laughing. "I take the fifth . . ."

* * *

The basement was dark and airless, with the pungent smell of rotting garbage overpowering the humid atmosphere.

"Man, this is something else. From detective to garbage scrounger."

"Stop bitching, Bill. Think of it as another profession when you retire." Tony laughed.

"Get a load of this guy." Bill turned to Benson, but the duty manager was more interested in what they might find and kept a deadpan.

"Here we are, garbage bins 4,5, and 6B." Chris pointed to the oversized container on wheels, its methane gas edging on a fire hazard.

"Let's get into this stuff." Tony removed his jacket and slipped into the white coveralls, plastic hat, mask, and all.

Bill burst into laughter. "If only I had a camera."

"Get out of it, and no more of the wise cracks." Tony turned to Chris. "Listen, this is going to take some time, so I suggest you best go back to the front desk."

"Sure," Chris agreed. "If you need anything, just give me a call. I'll take your jackets and hang them in the utility room. *Oh,* and don't worry about the mess. I'll get the day cleaners onto it."

"Thanks, Chris, appreciate it," Tony answered.

Bill stood for a moment, studying the large garbage bin resting on its cradle.

"My suggestion, Tony, would be to just pull the bin over on its fulcrum shaft and empty the whole caboose to the floor."

"I agree, Bill. Let's face it. It's better than you standing inside up to your waist in shit."

"I'm one step ahead of you, partner. That's why I am a detective, remember?"

"Now you tell me! I should be so lucky." Tony just had to take the last shot.

"Well, aren't you going to give me a hand to tip over this crate?" Bill was standing with his hands on his hips." "Move over, 'drama queen,'"

* * *

Terry was about to finish for the day, but as far as her work was concerned, it was a train wreck waiting to happen. She just couldn't stop thinking about her best friend. Her mind was churning repeatedly like flour being sifted through a sieve, trying to find the slightest clue to the identity of Laura's cold-hearted attacker. She paused for a moment at the thought, tears ebbing into her eyes, then gave a futile sigh as she opened the top drawer of her desk using her other arm in a circular motion to recklessly scoop everything into the drawer.

"What the hell, *I'm outta here!"* She had had enough.

"Finishing early are we, Terry?"

"*Christ, Jack*, you scared the crap out of me sneaking up on me like that." Blakely sat relaxed on the edge of Terry's desk with one leg dangling. "Terry, I know how you must feel about your best friend, and I feel for her to, but going into your shell won't change a thing. *You gotta lighten up.*" He placed his hand sympathetically upon Terry's shoulder, which she rudely rebuffed.

"Jack, keep your hands off the merchandise."

"Terry, lighten up." Blakely smiled, trying to camouflage his annoyance at being rejected. He had to be compassionate and understanding if he wanted to get Terry in the sack. "I was thinking, Terry, why don't you join me for a cocktail and maybe a light supper? It would do you the world of good, and we could get to know one another a little better. I'm not all that bad, you know."

"Jack, to quote Napoleon . . . 'Not tonight, Josephine.' Now if you don't mind, I've a date at Roosevelt Memorial."

"It's your loss, Terry. Should you have a change your mind, my offer is still open."

"Thanks, and no thanks. Good night, Jack, and sweet dreams."

* * *

"Tony, I'm suffocating in this compost dump." Bill gripped, repositioning his face mask tightly over his nose.

"*Stop being a fucking wimp.* The quicker you stop moaning, the quicker we get our asses out of here."

"What's this?" Bill held up a knotted plastic shopping bag. "*I think we've struck gold, buddy!*" He was frantically trying to untie the knot.

Tony stopped sifting the pungent heap and stood up straight. "I hope this is not your usual stupid macabre humor. *My back is fucking killing me!*" He groaned as he stretched.

"Who's the woos now?" Bill retaliated.

"*Listen,* just open the fucking bag, huh." Tony was reaching the end of his tether.

"*Ah!* What have we got here?"

"Well?"

"*Pay dirt, Tony!* A blood-soaked hand towel and guess what? A vacuum garbage bag full of what looks like bits of paper." Bill was grinning from ear to ear.

"So what do you want . . . the fucking police medal?"

"Awe, come on, Tony, give a guy some credit."

"Okay . . . Okay, but first things first. I need some air, so let's get out of this cesspit and maybe . . . just maybe, I'll shout you a beer."

"That's the best suggestion I've heard today, partner." Bill laughed while in the process of discarding his garbage outfit as he headed for the utility room.

The twosome quickly grabbed their jackets and waded through the garbage to the elevator. The quicker they passed this newfound evidence to CSI, the better. It might just be the break they needed to crack this case.

"All finished detectives?" Chris rose to his feet, curious as to the contents of the mysterious plastic bag.

"For the moment," Tony answered. "Remember, Chris, should something come to your mind . . . Ciao."

Bill glance at his watch as they walked to the car. It had just turned five thirty.

"Tony, looking at the time, I suggest we get Adams on the blower to tell him to hold it until we arrive at headquarters. It's crucial that we get the lab working on this new evidence tonight."

"Yeah, I agree. I'll call him from the car."

Bill gunned the big V8 and slipped the Pontiac into the heavy evening traffic. In this stuff, it would take about an hour to reach Pearl Street in Lower Manhattan.

"Dave . . . Tony here . . . Listen, new evidence has just come up on the Williams's case, and I need . . ."

CHAPTER 17

Terry Johnson was in a trance as she drove through the office traffic. *Maybe she should have called the hospital. No, it's better I arrive unexpectedly. Besides, the way Frank, the security guard, was giving me the eye, I'm sure I'll have no problem. I think he's kind of cute.* It was a diversion, and she half smiled. *But a security guard? A bit below my league, but then maybe I'm missing something.* The sudden blast of a car horn made her jump. *"Shit,"* she spoke out loud, her concentration returning with a jolt. "I had better pay attention to my driving or else *I'll* be in the next bed to Laura."

Time passed quickly; her mind occupied on what to expect when she reached the hospital. "Will Laura recover? If she did, would she be a vegetable?" The more she thought about it, the more frightening it became. She pulled into the car park and gave a sigh of relief. Her journey was over, but Laura's was just beginning.

*   *   *

Hospitals always look surreal. What with the pristine lighting, the overpowering odour of disinfectants, the highly polished floors, and the constant arrival and departure of ambulances screaming to the emergency, it was the last place you would want to be. The reception as normal was milling with relatives and visitors, their troubled expressions and stress-filled eyes painting a morbid picture. Life is temporary, and its prolongation as such is part of the journey, we all have to eventually face.

*   *   *

As Terry nervously entered the reception, she had a bad feeling, but then it's always normal to think the worst. The light tap on her shoulder startled her, and she quickly turned only to find her "knight in shining armor" smiling, standing by her side.

"*Frank*, am I glad to see you!" Terry's face was a picture of relief.

"I had a feeling I would see you tonight." He smiled warmly.

"Is that wishful thinking or are you just being nice?"

The tall handsome guy looked into her eyes. There was no doubt he had a thing for her.

"Let's just say a bit of both." He grinned, flashing his straight white teeth.

This guy was a hunk, all right, at over six foot, a hundred and eighty pounds, muscular frame, blue eyes, and blondish hair. His smooth tanned complexion, long narrow face, and deep dimpled chin gave him a sort of young Michael Douglas look; and Terry reluctantly had to admit he was a piece of work, but for the moment, her mind was more occupied with the health of her best friend, Laura.

"Stick close to me, Terry, and I'll escort you to you to the intensive care unit."

"Frank, I can't thank you enough. I don't know what to say."

"*Then don't.*" He gave her that "certain smile." "But then on the other hand, maybe I can buy you a coffee." He grinned.

"*Deal.*" *Now Terry* was returning *that* smile.

The desk sister recognized the twosome and turned a blind eye. In her job, it's rare to see happy people in the emergency reception.

Frank pressed 4, and the elevator ascended to the intensive care wing. As they walked silently down the immaculate, white-walled corridor, it's vinyl floor almost like glass, Terry couldn't help but think that this is the nearest you can get to death's door; and a strange shiver rippled through her spine.

"Terry, are you all right?" Frank had noticed the sudden paleness in her complexion, and he quickly held her arm in case of sudden vertigo. In Terry's case, it was highly implausible because of her strong character, but he was taking no chances.

"I'm sorry, Frank. For a moment there, I . . ."

He held her arm even firmer. "Terry, stop . . . You don't have to explain.

Anyhow here we are." He stopped in front of the observation window. "I'm all right now." She gently prized Frank's hand away.

*　　*　　*

Laura unfortunately was showing no change, her face a shocking deathly gray. The catheters and the tracheotomy tube visibly protruding from her windpipe was scary. Now it was Terry's turn to grab Frank's arm for support as she struggled to hold back her tears. Somehow the comfort of a man by her side gave her a warm feeling, and she appreciably looked up and glanced into his eyes. It was a sort of "don't leave me" look, and Frank got the message. *Maybe she was not the only one that was getting that warm feeling!*

The elderly couple, it appeared, were about to leave; and Terry assumed it was Laura's parents as she recognized them from her previous visit and their pictures in the tabloids. Laura's father leaned over and gently kissed his daughter on the forehead then said something to his wife and gave her a reassuring hug. *If only she could hold Laura's hand to comfort her,* Terry thought. The cop on duty wasn't an option, and her only hope was to try and speak to Laura's parents. It is a medical fact that the comatosed patient can hear and recognize voices, often jolting the brain back to consciousness.

"Excuse me, Mr. Williams, please accept my deepest apologies for intruding." Laura blocked their paths as they were walking toward the elevator.

Dave Williams was taken aback. He was in no mood for what he suspected was a cheap shot by the paparazzi.

"This is a trying time for my wife and I, and I humbly request that if you have any conscience at all, you will respect our privacy. Now if you don't mind?" He was about to brush Terry aside.

"Mr. Williams . . . *Please* . . . Let me explain!"

"Young lady . . ." He turned toward the officer, anxious to request his intervention.

"Please, Mr. Williams, just give me a moment. I'm Terry Johnson, your daughter is my best friend. We both work together at ABM."

Laura's mother grabbed her husband's arm. "David, I have heard that name from Laura. Give her a moment."

"Young lady, this had better be good!" The young police officer was now on his feet, concerned that there may be an altercation; and Williams turned, raising his arm. "It's all right, Officer. We know this young lady."

"I'm asking your permission . . . *Please."* Terry pleaded almost in tears. "Just to let me spend some time with Laura, to speak to her and hold her hand. It's a medical fact that sometimes this therapy can return a comatosed patient back to consciousness."

"Dave." Margaret squeezed her husband's arm, the anguish reflecting in her eyes. "What have we got to lose?"

"I guess so." He sighed in his reluctance to agree. *"Officer"*—he turned— "you can let this young lady through."

"Thanks, Mr. Williams. I promise I won't stay too long."

"Hmmm." Williams grunted, whereas Margaret warmly grabbed Terry's hand.

"Thank you for your genuine concern. Come, David, there's not much more we can do here except pray." The elevator chimed.

*   *   *

Hayden pulled into the Pearl Streetcar park. It had taken him an hour to get through the evening traffic.

"I wonder if that broad is still unconscious," Tony commented as they left the car.

"Yeah, I wonder," Bill replied, deep in thought. "Maybe we should check it out personally before you shout me that beer." He grinned.

It was a cheap reminder, and Tony just shook his head laughing. "I'm sure you have Scottish blood in your veins."

"Get out of it, Mussolini."

"Hey, now you *are* hurting my feelings."

"What with your skin? *That would have to be a first!"*

"Cut the slack and hit that elevator button, and maybe I'll cancel your transfer request."

They were both laughing as they walked to Adams's office.

Dave was patiently waiting and promptly rose to his feet, signalling the two jokers to come straight in.

"I hope you guys appreciate I'm in the doghouse again."

"Awe, come on, Dave, you got good company."

"Tony, you can tell that to my wife when you see her on Sunday. Now in the interests of avoiding the divorce court, what's new?" Bill proudly displayed the grubby plastic shopping bag.

"And this is it!" Dave was being prematurely sarcastic.

"You know what they say about sarcasm, Dave?" Tony retaliated.

'Yeah, but I'm ignoring it until I see the evidence."

"That's why you're in CSI," Bill interjected, slightly deflated.

"Okay . . . Okay . . . You win, wise guys. Let's have it!"

Bill thrashed inside the plastic then placed a dusty brown paper disposable vacuum bag on Adams's desk. "Now before you look inside exhibit A, besides the normal carpet dust, there is a handful of torn paper fragments that by sheer coincidence bear a remarkable resemblance to the piece of paper your boys found on the floor of Laura Williams's apartment." Bill's statement immediately brought Adams's unequivocal attention. "Also . . ." Bill was on a roll. "Exhibit B." He placed the bloodstained hand towel on the desk.

"Now *this is* something!"

"How soon, Dave?" Tony was overanxious.

Adams paused for a moment then dejectedly shook his head. "Tomorrow afternoon at the earliest . . . Now *can I go home?*"

"What do you think, Bill?" Tony turned to Hayden.

Bill grinned. "Better still, how about joining Tony and me over a beer? Tony's buying."

"*Not on your life!* I've joined you guys for a beer before and ended up getting a cab home."

"Your loss, buddy." Bill shook his head jokingly. "Too bad, especially when Tony's on the tab."

"This guy . . . Tomorrow then . . . Ciao." The detectives left for the elevator.

"So, what's the bottom line, partner?" Bill asked before hitting the button.

"My educated guess is that the bloodstains on the face towel will match the DNA from the aborted foetus and the skin remnants from under the Laura Williams's nails. It's like . . . we are getting someplace but going nowhere fast. If only this broad would regain consciousness. Changing the subject, let's take two cars, then we can split after leaving Jakes."

"Sure," Bill replied as they crossed the car park. "Then I'll meet you at the hospital?"

* * *

As Terry entered the intensive care unit, she felt intimidated by the glaring white pristine walls and the pungent odour of disinfectant. It was expected without question that Laura would have the luxury of a private room, *if one could call it that,* and the undying attention of a dedicated nurse. I suppose money talks, and to be ill and wealthy certainly helps.

The nurse rose to her feet. She looked a bit of a battle-axe, possibly in her mid-forties. Her starched uniform and the crazy hat didn't do her lined face any favours, but then maybe she is all heart, and first impressions can be deceiving.

She dropped the magazine and rose to meet Terry with "*a be careful, you're on my patch look."*

"I assume that you have been given clearance by Mr. Williams to spend some time with his daughter." She looked toward the sergeant who gave her an assuring nod.

Terry nodded in silence, staring at the pitiful sight of her friend. She was in no mood for lengthy assurances.

"My name is Nancy, and my shift finishes at ten, at which time another nurse will take over. It's . . ." She glanced at her watch. "Time for my break. I'll be back in around fifteen minutes. The golden rule is don't touch anything and immediately press that red emergency button should the patient become stressed or have difficulty breathing." She pointed to the switch dangling on the cord at the side of Laura's bed.

Again, Terry acknowledged in silence and took her seat on the opposite side of the bed.

"*Remember the emergency switch"* was Nancy's passing broadside as she left.

Terry stared for a moment in partial shock at the array of intravenous drips, oxygen tubes, catheter bag, and the constant bleep from the heart monitoring screen. But the scariest of all was the air rush from the tracheotomy, almost like a whale as it surfaces, exhaling and inhaling huge bursts or air.

Although in a coma, Laura looked as if she was in a peaceful sleep. Her eyes closed, her chest rising and falling in perfect rhythm, and Terry took Laura's hand and placed it between hers, gently massaging her skin.

"Laura honey, it's Terry. Can you hear me? I spoke to your mother and father this evening, and they told me to tell you that they missed you and to get better soon and that they love you very much. The guys at the office are also missing you. The place is not the same without you, except for Blakely, that sex maniac. Would you believe that lowlife? Of course, I told him to get on his bike. The gall of that guy. The doctors tell me you're a fighter, and before you know it, you will be back on your feet and your old self and *boy are we gonna* have a party." Terry kept rubbing Laura's limp hand. "Honey, I know you can hear me. Just give me a signal. Flick your eyelids or squeeze my hand."

Terry suddenly raised her left hand to her mouth in disbelief. "I could have sworn I felt her fingers move. *There it is again!*" She spoke out loud. "Laura honey, can you do that again?" Laura's fingers moved again, only this time a little stronger; and Terry, in her anxiety without thinking, hit the emergency switch. And within seconds, Nancy was on the doorstep.

"What the hell?" The warhorse was in no mood for trivialities, Terry having cut her precious coffee break short.

"Her fingers moved . . . I swear to God."

"Is that all?" Nancy was relieved. "Cool it, honey. It's normal for nerves to react. When a person is in a coma, the brain does strange things."

"But I tell you, when I asked Laura to move her fingers if she can hear me, she did precisely that. Here let me show you. Laura honey, can you move your fingers again?"

Terry held Laura's hand in the palm of hers to make sure Florence Nightingale had a clear view.

"Did you see that?" Terry was so excited.

"I sure did." Nancy lifted the phone. "Dr. Nathan, Nurse Simpson here from intensive care. That's correct, the Williams woman. I just wanted to report that . . ."

Nancy turned and gave Terry a warm smile as she hung up. "The duty doctor is on his way. In this hospital, miracles happen every day."

*   *   *

The tall young doctor entered the intensive care room, his white coat flaying, his stethoscope dangling around his neck. He was, as they say, "tall, dark, and handsome"; and Terry had to give him a second look.

He immediately pulled out a small torch from his top pocket and opened Laura's eyes one at a time shining the light into each pupil.

"Hmmm . . . Good. Her brain is in recovery mode, and the pupils are responding to the light." He turned to Terry. "And you are?"

"Terry Johnson, Laura's friend."

"Well, whatever . . . You did a great job . . . Nurse, continue with the intravenous antibiotic drip and saline, and measure her fluid intake and output. She's not out of the woods just yet."

The question was begging, and Terry couldn't help herself. "Doctor?"

"Dr. Nathan . . . Paul Nathan."

"Doctor, what does this mean?" Terry asked, praying for good news.

"The prognosis is positive, and unless she goes into relapse, I am confident she will fully recover consciousness in another twenty-four hours." He turned to Nancy. "I'll leave you, nurse. I'm on call until eight tomorrow morning. And you, young lady, I think it's time that you leave and allow the patient to rest. It would be beneficial if you could come back tomorrow evening and continue talking to your friend."

"Thank you, Doctor, and don't worry. Wild horses couldn't keep me away."

* * *

"Frank, you're still here!" Terry was surprised.

"I finished my last round and came back just to make sure you are all right."

"That's so sweet, but I bet you do that with all the girls."

"How did you guess?" Frank burst into laughter. "Only joking."

"You had me going there for a moment, *mister!*" Terry was now also laughing; and for some reason, she looked so different and more relaxed, the sparkle returning to her eyes.

"You look different, Terry," Frank commented, looking into her eyes.

"It's like a miracle." Terry was so excited and desperate to unload her experience. "Have you ever heard that when a person is in a coma and a friend . . ."

"Terry"—Frank placed his hand gently on her shoulder—"why don't you relax. My shift is over, and I have only to change. Meet me at reception in five minutes, then you can tell me all about it over a coffee or a glass of wine?" "I would really like that." Terry had now calmed.

"Then reception in five minutes, and don't *you* change your mind!" Frank winked.

"Don't worry. I won't." She gave a reassuring smile as she walked to the elevator. This could be the beginning of something special.

CHAPTER 18

June was busy preparing dinner when Steven arrived home from college.

"Hi, Mom." He greeted his mother with a kiss on the cheek. "So what's for dinner? It smells so good."

June smiled. "Pumpkin soup, southern fried chicken, and mash. The dessert is a secret. Now, young man, *can I continue?* And where is that sister of yours, may I ask?"

"The last I saw of her, she was hanging out with some friends at the bus depot."

"I hope girlfriends." Mothers are always concerned when it comes to daughters.

"Mother, Sis can look after herself. You worry too much." Suddenly, there was the sound of the front door opening.

"What did I tell you?" Steven shook his head.

"Hi, Mom. I'm going upstairs to change. Call me when dinner is ready." Sheryl had her cell phone glued to her ear. *"That girl!"* June shook her head.

*   *   *

Young Steven Summers at eighteen was a tall good-looking kid with plenty of friends, especially the opposite sex. He loved football and was a kicker for the college team. At six feet and one hundred and fifty pounds, with that unruly crop of blond hair and those blue eyes, to say, he was popular. *Well? You can fill in the rest.* Whereas his sixteen-year-old sister, Sheryl, was a cheerleader and loved the "boy attention" that went with it. She was trim with all the curves in the right places and the same genetic blonde hair and blue eyes as her mother, but she was also bright and excelled in her studies with "A" grades her norm. Of course, they both looked up to their father as the pinnacle of success with undying admiration. He provided them with a comfortable life, private schooling, and above all took good care of their mother; but the one thing they missed most was their father's closeness and love. They envied the simple holidays they enjoyed as a happy family when they were much younger before their father became a slave of corporate Wall Street, now only a memory. The disconcerting wealth-seeking shareholders, concerned only with their franked dividends, called the shots; and once you reach the six-figure salary with all the perks, values change and unfortunately the family more than often suffers.

*   *   *

"Mom, I'm going up to change before Father comes home."

It was the moment that June dreaded, and she swallowed nervously. "Steven . . . I know you are going to be disappointed when I tell you that your father has been unexpectedly called away on business to West Palm Springs this afternoon and will not be returning until at least Monday. *He really is sorry, son."* She placed her hand affectionately on his shoulder. "He promised me he will ring you this evening."

The look on Steven's face said it all as he shrugged, struggling to find words to express his disappointment at this all-too-often sad story.

"Well, I suppose I should be thankful for small mercies," he answered sarcastically.

"Steven *don't say that about your father!* He loves you very much." "He has a strange way of showing it, Mother." Steven shot back.

"One day you will understand what it is to be the breadwinner of the family and the pressures of corporate life. You'll reach a stage when the company virtually owns you, and because of financial and family commitments, there's no turning back."

Steven gave a big sigh as if to say, "I've heard it all before."

"I think it's best that I go to my room, Mother. Can you call me when dinner is ready?"

"Of course, son, but try and understand what you father is going through. I mean do you think he enjoys being away from his family?" I'm sure he would rather be joining us for dinner than sitting in a lonely stuffy hotel room."

"I guess so, Mother. I'm sorry, but . . ."

"Steven, enough! I'll call you and your sis when dinner is ready." With not another word, he turned tail and left.

*   *   *

Mike was more than bored as he sat in the first-class lounge at Fort Lauderdale, making love to his bourbon on the rocks, as he waited for his connecting flight, his mind still clouded with the disastrous events over the last two days. *How could he concentrate on his work?* he thought to himself as he impatiently waited for the latest CNN news bulletin.

"Would you like a sandwich or something, sir?" the pretty hostess inquired.

"No." Mike smiled. "I'm good." Just then, he heard the news announcement on the flat screened TV.

"This is Trevor McDonald with the latest news from the CNN front . . ."

Mike waited patiently, only half listening to all the boring crap about Bush, the Gulf War, and politics on Capitol Hill but no mention of U.S. Senator Dave Williams's daughter. Was it a good sign or bad? "No news is good news," as they say, but Mike was gaining little comfort from that cliche.

"Delta flight 017 to West Palm Springs is departing from gate 6. Boarding will commence in approximately fifteen minutes."

Mike finished the last of his bourbon and picked up his briefcase. He was now even less enlightened, and the feeling of uncertainty was driving him crazy. The only thing he was looking forward to now was another double bourbon on flight 017.

CHAPTER 19

"Frank, you look so different out of uniform."

"So it's the uniform that gets you, huh?" He was laughing.

"Get out of it, you male chauvinist. But then again?" Terry liked to tease.

*   *   *

The New York summer was at it its worst, hot and humid; and Frank, our "Dar Tania," was dressed to suit. His tight-fitting T-shirt silhouetted his firm pecks and biceps. The stone washed Levi's and Nike sneakers were "babe catchers," and Terry was proud to stake her claim, hanging on to his arm.

"So where to?" Terry asked the question, begging.

"Giovanni's Wine Bar in Little Italy, just a block from Canal Street."

"I wouldn't have read that you're a wine freak."

"I'm not! But somehow, I guessed . . . *Well* . . . You being a lady and all, you would enjoy a glass of say . . . chilled Pinot Grigio accompanied with a crispy bruschetta, and besides, you'll love the atmosphere."

"I can't wait. I'm so hungry I could eat a horse. So hit the road, Jack, or should I say, Frank."

"Terry! What a coincidence." Tony was smiling cheekily. There was something about this broad you couldn't help but like, *that is, besides her good looks.*

"Well, if it aint New York's finest! Frank, these are the two detectives I mentioned." Terry was returning the "friendly fire."

"Bill and I were just about to call it quits before relaxing over a cold Bud when I decided to call into the hospital to check on your friend Laura."

"You'll be pleased to hear . . . *Eh?* Detective?"

"Tony . . . Tony Perino."

"Of course . . . *Tony!* That Laura showed positive signs by squeezing my hand when I asked her some questions. She is on the mend, all right, although not fully conscious, and the doc says she could open her eyes in the next twenty-four."

Tony turned to Bill; his brow furrowed. "This just might be the break we are looking for."

"Hold it!" Terry cut him short. "Don't run away with yourself. The doc says she is not to be disturbed, and in fact, he politely showed me the door. If I were you, guys, take my advice and call back tomorrow evening, but if you don't believe me, be my guest?" Terry pointed to the desk phone. "Dr. Nathan . . . Dr. Paul Nathan."

"Nah, I'll take your word for it, Terry." Tony grinned. "Gimme a call if something breaks. You have my card. Bill . . ." Tony turned to his partner. "Let's hit Jakes Bar and Bistro on Canal, and that cold Bud . . ."

*   *   *

"Guys, dinner's ready," June called from the kitchen, emptying her lungs.

"Do you hear me?"

"Coming, Mother," Steven replied. "Sis, are you coming?"

"Yeah . . . Yeah . . . Don't be so pushy. Can't you see I'm on the phone?"

Steven just shook his head as he walked to the stairs. He had changed into his board shorts and T-shirt. In this "Indian summer," that's the uniform. "Sis will be down in a moment, Mom. That's if she can get surgery to remove that phone from her ear."

"You two!" June sighed. "Never mind. Take your place at the table. We'll start without her . . ."

"Hi, Mom." This was Sheryl at her best, all smiles.

"You took your time, young lady. Your brother and I have almost finished. Now one more show of disrespect like that, and I will confiscate that phone for a week."

"Hmmm . . . This chicken is good, Mother." Sheryl purposely ignored her mother's comment.

This was all June needed, what with Mike being out of town on business again and Steven showing his resentment at his father's absence and now Sheryl being purposely rebellious. It was just too much.

"Did you hear what I said?" June retaliated.

Sheryl gave a big sigh and threw her napkin on the table.

"I'm going to my room. I can see I'm not wanted here."

"Young lady don't throw your tantrums here. You're lucky that your father isn't home."

"So what's new? He's never home," Sheryl shot back.

"Now whether you like it or not, you're going to apologize to me right now and sit right back at that table and finish your dinner." June's eyes were blazing. *"I'm waiting."*

Sheryl stared blankly at her plate; her head bowed. She knew she had crossed the line.

"I'm sorry, Mother, for being so selfish. I apologize." She rose from the table and gave her mother a kiss on the cheek. *She knew how to play the game.*

"Okay, enough. Now sit down and finish your dinner."

"Drama queen," Steven muttered under his breath."

"I heard that! *Mother . . .*"

"Steven, that's enou—" Before June could finish, the phone rang.

"That must be your father now." June reached for the wall phone.

"Hi, honey. I've just had a light snack and thought I would give you a call. Besides, I've gotta 'smoke the pipe' with Steven."

"You had better. He's pretty upset. I'll pass you to him now. Steven, it's your father on the line . . ."

"Hi, Dad."

"Listen, son, what can I say?"

"Awe, it's okay, Dad. I understand . . . It's just that . . . Awe, it doesn't matter . . ."

Mike could hear Steven sigh as if it was a lost cause and a lump swelled in his throat. His whole world was crumbling around him. Even his kids were sending him bad jibes.

"You wanted to discuss your university tickets?"

"Dad, I'm in bit of a quandary. I've been offered a place in Harvard in the Law Faculty and in Cornel in medicine . . . but I'm really at a loss."

"I know the feeling. Two excellent universities that students would die for, and you have the luxury of choice. I wish I could make it easy for you. All I can say is whichever one you feel you would get the greatest reward from and contribution to society, then follow your heart."

There was a long pause. "Thanks, Dad. Now I know what I want to study."

"Steven, we can still discus it when I return on Monday."

"It's all right, Dad. You have given me the kicker, and my mind is made up."

"Aren't you going to let me in on the secret?"

"No, not yet Dad." Mike could hear Steven laugh. "I want to pass it by Mom first. Love you, Dad. Bye"

"Son, can you pass me to your mother?"

"Sure."

"Hi, honey. Is everything all right?"

"Yes, but I miss you."

"I know how you feel. I miss you too. Listen, the reason I also phoned was to tell you that I checked into the Sheraton West Palm. I'm in room 1621, and the phone number is 03-9333 . . ."

"So, what are you going to do now?" June asked.

"Maybe I'll have a nightcap at the cocktail bar then shack down and watch some TV."

"Okay, darling, but don't drink too much. Love you. Gimme a call tomorrow."

"I will, honey. Good night." Mike hung up, relieved that his chat with Steven had gone so well. "Now for that bourbon," he spoke to himself as he slipped on his jacket. Maybe the TV at the bar will be more enlightening with CNN's late evening news.

*   *   *

Jake was boringly polishing the oak bar when the detectives arrived; Thursday night is always quiet.

"So, what'll it be, guys? I'm always glad to serve New York's finest." Jake, as always, is a joker. *In his line of work, I guess it's an essential part of the credentials.*

Tony grinned as he grabbed the barstool. "Cut the bullshit, Jake, and sling up two cold Buds."

"What, no beer nuts?" Bill interrupted.

"You guys, always with the freebies. You should be arrested for daylight robbery."

Jake was always glad to see the faces of the law after recently experiencing an armed robbery. The hooded perpetrator pistol whipped him unconscious before emptying the cash register and making off with an expensive bottle of Cognac. *Whoever this guy was, he certainly knew his liquor.*

The cold beers hardly touched the sides. This was beer-drinking weather.

"Again?" Jake asked, smiling at the empty glasses.

Tony turned to Bill. "One more?"

"Yeah, *but only one!* I don't want to be picked up for DUI."

"Now wouldn't that be something!" Jake was in earshot and couldn't help himself. It was too good to miss.

"Set 'em, Jake, and no more of the wisecracks," Tony joked.

"Coming up."

Just then, Tony felt the buzz on his cell phone. *"Awe . . . Awe . . .* I know who this . . . Yes, honey?"

Bill covered his mouth to muffle his laughter.

"Don't honey me! What's the excuse tonight?" came the blast.

"Bill and I . . . Well, we had to make a last-minute call to the hospital . . . You remember that woman I told you . . ."

"Yeah . . . Yeah . . . You and that partner of yours, you're like two peas in a pod. And may I ask where you are now?"

"I'm just about to head for home."

"Just don't go to confession on Sunday, or I'll have to send in food for the priest . . . Tony Perino, *I can smell the beer from here!"*

"Awe, honey, give me a . . ." The phone went dead.

Tony just shook his head and took another sip of his beer then gave a big sigh.

Bill turned to his partner, grinning. "It's like that, is it?"

"Worse! You're lucky being married to a wife that's an ex-cop."

"Don't let that fool you. We still have our problems. Like why I am still only a detective sergeant when I passed my lieutenant exam nearly a year ago?"

"Bill, you know that it takes time. Hell, I waited two years before I got my bars."

"Yeah, well try and tell that to Judy! Kindergarten, mortgage, you name it!" Bill placed the empty beer mug on the bar and glanced at his watch. "It's time I hit the road, partner."

"Listen, Bill, the good news is Brady is retiring next month, and the grapevine tells me you're up for that slot. Besides, if we crack the Laura Williams case, the DA will be smelling of roses, and being the daughter of a U.S. senator, you might even get a commendation." Tony was being serious for a change.

"I'll believe it when it happens, but thanks for the motivation talk." He slapped Tony on the shoulder. "Listen, partner, I gotta go."

Tony glanced at his empty beer mug as Bill rose to leave, sensing what was coming.

"Don't even think about it! I'm outta here. Besides, you're on the tab, remember?" He was half smiling.

"Boy, I'll be glad when you get promoted, then maybe you can afford to buy me a beer. *Now* wouldn't that be something!"

Bill just laughed it off. "Ciao, partner. Gimme five. Tomorrow then and drive carefully. Give my love to Rose"

"Jake . . . The damage . . ."

CHAPTER 20

"So will I follow you in my car?" Terry asked.

"Naw, that's too complicated. Besides, you might lose me in the traffic and then what? Don't worry. I'll bring you back safely." Frank grinned.

"The perfect gentleman, huh?" Terry joked as they crossed the car park.

"Hey, don't jump to conclusions. You don't know me yet." Frank laughed as he took Terry's hand. She was now more than enjoying her newfound male companion.

"Nice car," Terry commented, admiring the pale metallic blue Ford Thunderbird.

"I like it!" Frank smiled.

"It smells of bachelorhood to me." Terry laughed with a touch of sarcasm as he opened the passenger door of the coupe.

"Madame, s'il vous plait." He motioned, offering his hand.

"French! You never cease to amaze me." Terry held his hand for support as she maneuverer into the low-slung seat awkwardly, trying to control her micro denim skirt, giving "Young Lochinvar" the best view, he had seen all day.

He gunned the big V8 and rolled down the windows. In a humid night like this, there was more ways than one to let your hair down.

It would take all of twenty minutes to arrive at Giovanni's Wine Bar and what better opportunity for Terry to go "fishing."

*   *   *

"So, tell me a bit about yourself." It was a good opening but nothing new.

"Like . . . Where do you want me to start?" Frank asked.

"Only where it's interesting," Terry replied, a cheeky grin on her face.

"Well, to start with, I never went to university. My parents couldn't afford it. I have another two teenage brothers, and now that things are financially easier for the family, I'm sure they will be the first to graduate. My father works at the Boeing Plant, and my poor mother still does part-time work. *God bless her.* We still live in a rented apartment in the Bronx, and if I ever strike it rich, my first priority is to buy my mother her own home. As for me? Went from job to job before enlisting in the Marine Corp. After three years and Desert Storm behind me, I had had enough and ended up doing security work. I rent my own apartment. It's a bit far from my parents' place, but I make a point of visiting them every week. I'm not attached, and more to the point, here I am with a beautiful woman and looking forward to a pleasant evening over a glass of wine. *Now how does that grab you? Ah*, here we are," Frank interrupted as he pulled into the sidewalk. "And not a moment too soon before, shall I say, *this gets too heavy!*"

"Ha . . . Ha . . . Ha . . ." Terry was laughing aloud. *"I like that."*

* * *

The wine bar's facade was a typical Italian with simulated Roman stonework supposedly from the Coliseum. The half-circled synthetic sunshades displaying the Italian colours red, white, and green. The heavy wooden framed colourful leaded glass windows added to the Italian flavour.

Frank pushed open the heavy studded oak door. "Please." He motioned. "Thank you," Terry proudly answered. *This was getting better all the time!*

* * *

The first thing to strike you as you entered the dimly lit restaurant with the candled tables is the long heavy oak bar with the larger-than-life highly polished copper coffee machine at the far end, adorned with the unmistakable brass eagle. Paintings of Saint Peter's Square, the Vatican, and Leonardo's Sistine Chapel hang on the walls; and, of course, no Italian restaurant would be seen dead without a painting of the pontiff himself. The small tables with red-checked tables and Chianti bottles coated with multi-coloured candle wax added to the authenticity of the Pastina Pasteria. Behind the bar, the glass shelves displayed an array of liquor bottles reflecting sparkling colours from the low voltage down lights. On the opposite rough brick wall was a large dust-coated wine rack with a selection of the finest Italian, French, and German vintages. Giovanni's in Little Italy was the "I'll Solito Posto" or, in English, "the place to be."

* * *

"Frank, I just love this place," Terry commented as she took the stool at the bar.

"I knew you would." Frank smiled as he sat next to Terry. "You don't mind sitting at the bar?"

"Naw, I like it. It's better than staring at one another's face across the table."

Frank had to laugh. This babe was piece of work, but a pretty one at that!

"Hi, Vince. Where's Giovanni tonight?" Frank was scanning the dimly lit restaurant for the familiar face.

"Thursday night is the 'no action night,' so the boss makes it his 'night off.' Me? When you have a wife and three bambinos, every night is pay dirt. So, what'll it be, Frank?" Mario glanced admiringly at Terry.

"Crispy brochettes and one glass of Penfold's Cab Sav and?" He turned to Terry.

"That chilled Pinot Grigio you were boasting about." She smiled.

"The wine is coming up but give the chef ten on the brochettes." Mario disappeared into the kitchen.

"So?" Frank turned and looked into Terry's eyes.

"I told you I'm impressed."

"Ah, thanks, Mario." The wine had arrived. "Cheers, Terry. I hope we can do this more often." Somehow, he couldn't mask his feelings, and his eyes said it all.

"Who knows?" She smiled, taking a dainty sip from her glass. It was a polite way of saying, "Don't break the speed limit." "But I gotta hand it to you. This wine is delicious."

"What did I tell you?"

Just then, Mario appeared with the "crostini" brochettes. "Bon Appetit."

"Thanks, Mario," Frank answered. "Go ahead, Terry."

Terry sank her teeth into the "Italian experience." *"Hmmm* . . . Boy, am I hungry! But I'm watching my figure, so no pasta, mister. This will see me through until breakfast."

Frank smiled at Terry's remark. "Isn't it funny . . . Fat people think they are thin, and thin people think they are fat."

Terry had to laugh. "I never thought of it that way, but come to think of it, I guess it's true. *But I still think that I'm fat!"* She held her hand to her mouth to avoid the overspill as she took another bite of the crostini.

"It's your turn now."

"What do you mean it's my turn?" Terry raised her brows.

"Well, isn't it only natural that I want to know more about you."

"Like 'true confessions of the third kind,' huh?" Terry gave her a naughty look; she loved teasing.

"Come on. Don't keep me in suspense."

"So where do you want me to start? Like am I a virgin?"

Frank's face flushed. Terry had a reputation for being outrageous.

"Listen, you've heard 'Old Blue Eyes' . . . 'Mistakes, I've made a few but then again not too many.'" She sang the words.

"Terry, *you're some lady!*"

"But, Frank, what you really want to know is, am I in a relationship?" *"I couldn't have put it better myself."*

"Well, you'll be pleased to know the answer is no. Of course, I'm not a virgin, and I am sure that applies to you as well, but we are two consenting adults so why don't we let nature take its course?"

"Yeah, I guess you're right, Terry, *but you can't blame a guy for trying!"* "So, what's next? I have my own apartment and I enjoy my own company. I enjoy entertaining and good restaurants, and like most unmarried women of my age, one day I hope to settle down with the right guy and do all the family stuff. My parents live in Chicago, and I have one younger sister still at university. I came to New York in search of fame and fortune five years ago after I graduated in computer science from the University of Chicago, and I have worked at ABM for three years as a senior analyst. I like my job, and my best friend is Laura Williams. Now *how does that grab you?* Deja vu."

"Wow, that was like an express train!"

Terry smiled as she lifted her glass. "Cheers. Now I think it's about time you drove me to my car. I have an early morning meeting at the office." She could see the disappointing look on Frank's face, as if he is getting the "big elbow." "Cross my heart." Terry made the motion.

Frank half smiled. "I believe you . . . Mario . . . The tab . . ."

* * *

"A double bourbon on the rocks." Mike took the barstool. He was feeling like shit. *Another double on Delta 017, and he would arrive before the plane!*

The young barman nodded and went about his business. Some customers are talkative and some are not. In this job, you wait for the Q line. He placed the coaster on the bar, complete with the bourbon. "Enjoy your drink, sir."

Mike glanced at his watch. It was just coming to eight and the CNN News.

"Do me a favor, kid, and switch the television to CNN. I want to catch the news at eight."

The young barman wasn't impressed at the "kid" insult, but tips are important and silence is golden.

"Sure." He forced a smile.

"This is CNN with the latest breaking news. John Thomson reporting . . . The attempted murder of Laura Williams, the daughter of U.S. Senator Dave Williams, is still unsolved. Captain Ted Baker of NYPD Homicide was approached this morning by our reporter Connie Brown . . ."

"Captain Baker, can you give us a statement on the progress on the Laura Williams case?

"Ah, hem." Baker paused, carefully selecting his words. Whatever he said would, as usual, be exaggerated by the paparazzi. "Two of my best detectives have been assigned to the case and are evaluating new evidence that has just come to light that may result in an arrest in the next forty-eight . . ."

"Can you expand on that, Captain?"

"No further comment."

"Well, that was brief and to the point. Thanks, Connie. Now to move on to the latest from Capitol Hill."

Mike took another sip of the amber liquid. He had turned remarkably pale at hearing Baker's statement. *Just what did he mean by new evidence? Had Laura recovered and was she doing her opera thing? Naw. She couldn't have or the cops would be knocking on his door right now! Baker's full of shit. He's just doing his usual spin.*

Just then, the loud ring of the bar phone shattered his thoughts.

"Yes . . . I see . . . Just a moment . . . Excuse me, sir. Are you a Mr. Mike Summers?"

Mike went ashen grey. *"Eh . . . Err . . .* Yes . . ." He stumbled, not knowing what to expect.

"It's your wife on the line, sir."

Mike was relieved as he placed the receiver to his ear, his hands still visibly shaking. "Hi, honey."

"Mike, I just switched-on CNN, and I can't believe my ears!"

"I'm sorry, honey. I'm not with you."

"Mike, it's that woman who phoned me that night. *You remember,* a Laura Williams from ABM. You were supposed to meet at her apartment to sign some papers or something, but when you arrived and pressed the security button, there was no answer. You tried to call her on her cell phone, remember, but drew a blank."

"That's true, honey, but what's the big deal?"

"Haven't you seen the news?"

Mike gave a pronounced sigh over the phone. *"Honey, do you mind?* I'm completely in the dark here."

"Someone tried to kill her."

"Christ, June! Are you serious?" Mike was laying it on.

"Yes . . . And on the same night that you were supposed to meet with her!"

"I wondered why she never contacted me, but I guess I was so tied up at the office it slipped my mind. *But someone trying to kill her?* It doesn't bear thinking."

"Mike, I think you should go to the police and tell them your story."

"Christ, honey! I have enough problems without getting roped into an attempted murder wrap. The mugging and all that stuff would have to come out, and you know what the police are like, and before you know it, I'll be a suspect."

"But you could speak to Tony, our neighbour. He could advise you on what to do."

"No, June, I don't need it and I don't want it. *You don't think that I had anything to do with it, do you?"*

"Of course not, but I just feel that you should do what's right."

"Honey, let sleeping dogs lie. It will all come out in the washing when she recovers."

"I guess you're right." June seemed more relaxed. "There's no point in looking for trouble when we don't need it."

"I love you, honey, and don't you worry that pretty little head of yours. I can't wait to get home. Good night, honey. I'll give you a call tomorrow evening."

"Love you too."

Mike handed the receiver back to the kid. "Thanks, and . . ." He pointed to the empty glass. "Hit me."

*   *   *

June placed back the phone and relaxed on the sofa. There was something not right about this whole deal. Then suddenly something struck her. *"How did Mike know that Laura Williams was in hospital when he denied all knowledge of her attempted murder?* She spoke out loud, *"Did I mention it to him? I can't remember . . . Maybe I did."* She was becoming totally confused, but for sure, June was no dummy, and little did Mike know his comment would come back to haunt him.

*   *   *

"Rose . . . June here . . . Come over for a coffee? I wish I could, but I am still in the midst of washing up after dinner. Yeah, teenage kids. You're lucky, but your turn will come. I'm sorry, Rose. I'll have to take a rain check on that coffee. The reason I phoned? The usual. Yeah, Mike is out of town. He's gone to West Palm Springs on business and won't be back until Monday evening. The barbeque? You guessed right. I'm afraid it's off. Thanks, Rose, but without Mike, it wouldn't be the same. Listen. I'll give you call on Monday afternoon, and the coffee is on me. Sure, I will. Ciao."

CHAPTER 21

He gunned the Pontiac, anxious to get home to pacify Judy. *"Once again!"* He shook his head. He would miss the kids before the sandman.

Bill always felt that he was lucky having married Judy, an ex—cop, who understood the harrowing problems of detective work and the toll it has on family life; but sometimes enough is enough! It was a problem that continually haunted him, but police work is all he knew; and besides if nothing else, it was secure. In the Big Apple, the one thing that you can predict is that crime is like a cottage industry that continues to grow every day.

The traffic was light, being Thursday evening, and he would take East River Drive then cross the Queensbury Bridge. From there it was only a twenty-minute drive to New Rochelle and Jackson Street, his final abode. Unlike Tony, Bill and Judy lived in a modest two-storey house in a new estate where one could be forgiven for thinking that the houses fell off an assembly line; each and every one is the same on a postage-size lot with a miniscule lawn and a garage that overpowered the facade. Still, it was better than the rundown apartment that they were renting in the Bronx when they first married. On a detective sergeant's salary, it was still tough, but he was lucky to have two lovely boys and, for his eyes only, the most beautiful woman in the world. It just doesn't get any better.

*   *   *

"At last!" He slowed down and hung a right into the driveway. He cut the engine and collected his jacket from the rear seat, his short-sleeved white shirt and shoulder holster prominent in the porch lighting. The temperature was still in the eighties, and he was looking forward to another cold Bud. Judy had heard the car approach and opened the front door as Bill was about to place his key into the lock.

"Hi, honey. You beat me to it." Judy gave him that look. "Come, gimme a big kiss." He gently brushed her lips.

"*Bill Hayden*, you're incorrigible, and as for that partner of yours . . . Just wait till I see him on Sunday. *That guy could lead an angel astray!*"

"*Awe, come now, honey.* Tony's okay. You couldn't get a better friend and partner, and you gotta admit his heart's in the right place."

"Here, let me take your jacket." Judy was cooling down. "I don't know why I put up with you, *mister!*" She half smiled, shaking her head.

"Come on admit it . . . It's because you love me and can't resist this handsome detective?" Bill was getting to her.

"*Get out of it!*" She hung his jacket on the coat stand. "And get that horrible shoulder rig off, then maybe I'll fetch you a cold Bud from the icebox." Judy gave him a kiss on the lips. "*I love you, you big twit!*" "Why the hurry?" Bill tried to slip his arms around her waist. "*Oh no you don't!* There's plenty of time for that later." "Is that a promise?" Bill was teasing.

"That depends." Now it was Judy's turn . . . *Touché.*

Bill undid his shoulder holster and hung it on the top rung of the coat stand. Kids are inquisitive when it comes to firearms, and you can't blame them with all that stuff they see on TV.

The air-con was doing its job, and Bill gave a satisfying sigh as he sank onto the sofa. Judy appeared from the kitchen, a bit out of sorts, holding the Bud in one hand and a glass of chilled sauvignon blanc in her other.

"Your wish is my command . . . Oh, master." She was laughing aloud as she handed him the popular brew then sat down heavily beside him. "*Oops . . .* Almost spilled my wine!"

"Okay, 'Jeannie,' now what else can I wish for? Let me see." Bill was making a face.

"Whatever is in that pornographic mind of yours . . . *It's no!* This is not 'I dream of Judy.'" She was making fun of the TV sitcom. "Cheers!" She held up her wine glass.

"Cheers, honey." Bill took a sip from the bottle then affectionately placed his arm around her shoulder and gave her a hug and big kiss on the cheek.

"Honey, thanks for being so understanding."

Judy took another sip of her wine then looked into his eyes.

"I'm beginning to like this. We should do this more often."

"Well, it's better than you joining the book club and frustrating me, rubbing myself against old ladies in the grocery store."

Judy almost chocked on her wine. "*Bill Hayden*, you're something else! I don't know where you get that stuff. It must be from that joker Perrino.

He's always with the wisecracks, which reminds me . . . now that we are on the subject of *Lieutenant* Perino, when is that overdue promotion coming?"

"Honey don't start that again! I was just beginning to relax. *Listen,* to answer your question, for what it's worth, I passed it by Tony tonight, and he more or less assured me that I'm first in line for Brady's job when he retires at the end of this month. He'll even speak to Baker on my behalf. Honey don't worry. I assure you; you will be proud of me when I'm presented with my lieutenant bars."

Judy gave a big sigh. "Wishful thinking . . . But"—she emphasized, raising her empty glass in front of her—*"Detective Hayden*, I'm going to have a refill . . ."

Maybe Bill would be lucky tonight after all.

*   *   *

CHAPTER 22

The drive to Roosevelt Memorial was boring; and the silence was stressful to say the least, with Frank still smarting from the friendly fire. In hindsight, he couldn't blame Terry for thinking that he might be some kind of gigolo pushing his luck too far on their so-called first date, and more so, how could he convince her that his feelings were entirely honourable. There was something about this woman that was refreshing and different from all the others, and he just couldn't help himself.

"Terry," he broke the silence, "I'm sorry if I pushed the boat out too far . . ."

She stopped him in his tracks. "Frank,"—she turned, placing her hand reassuringly on his arm—"you were there for me when I needed a shoulder and *I really* do enjoy your company, but I've only met you twice. So why don't you change to first gear and ease on the brakes, then we can take it from there? After all, this is not the last time that I'm likely to see you, that is, unless my friend experiences another miracle."

"Thanks, Terry. You've made my day. It's just that . . ."

"Frank, we're here."

It was a timely interruption as the car park came into sight. Terry had too much on her mind to get roped into another affair, but she had to admit maybe it was for another day.

The car park was full, and Frank parked as near as he could to Terry's car.

"Hang on, Terry. Let me escort you to your car. You never can tell." He kept the motor running and hit the tarmac to open the passenger door. *"Here, take my hand."*

"Thanks, Frank. I can make it from here." Terry turned and looked into his eyes. Then suddenly on impulse, she stood on her toes and gave him a surprise kiss on the lips. "Thanks for the lovely evening. I'll see you tomorrow then."

Frank didn't know what to think, but he wasn't complaining, and tomorrow was another day. When the chips are down, they always have a habit of stacking back.

Terry hit the horn as she drove past and waved. For Frank, it wasn't such a fruitless night after all.

*   *   *

"Honey, I'm home." Tony hung his jacket in the closet and removed his shoulder holster. He was glad to be home, although he didn't relish Rose's "tsunami."

"I'll be down in a moment. I'm just tucking the kids in." *She sounded okay, but with Rose, you never can tell!*

*   *   *

He loosened his tie and walked toward the kitchen to the refrigerator. In this humid summer evening, there was nothing like a cold one. For a moment, his memory flashed back to "Hell's Kitchen" in the Bronx when he was a young kid, standing in front of the illegally opened fire hydrant, being drenched with the powerful water spray to keep cool. He was the tough Italian kid on the block, and nobody messed with the Perrinos from Cicely. He smiled to himself as he opened his beer. Life is so different now, but he will never forget where he came from.

*   *   *

"I thought you would have had enough at Jake's." Rose had just entered the kitchen only to catch Tony in the act, and you could have cut the air with a knife.

"Honey don't be like that. You know what like it is after a trying day and the 'guy' thing. A little relaxation over a beer, I mean is it asking too much? You know what they say about all work and no play?"

"Yeah, I know, *but try telling that to the kids.* Tony, I get so depressed. It's the same old thing day in and day out. We never seem to do anything. It's about time you gave some serious thought about me and the kids."

Tony knew what Rose was pushing, and it was the real deal. If he wanted to save his marriage, he had to do something to convince her to give him another chance to change his ways.

Tony took a deep breath. "Honey, why don't you ask your mother if she could babysit on Saturday, and I'll take you to dinner at Framesaw's on Canal. I know how much you love that restaurant."

Rose's facial expression suddenly changed. The thought of getting her hair done, a manicure and pedicure, and maybe buying a new dress, *and, of course, her favourite restaurant!*

"Are you serious?" she joked.

"Honey, of course, I am!"

"But we have the barbecue on Sunday?"

"That's no big thing. Besides, I'll be doing all the cooking. I mean what can go wrong? Burgers, steaks, and dogs." At last, Rose had that smile.

"You promise?"

"Of course, honey. Come give me a big kiss."

"Tony Perino . . ." She shook her head and placed her arms around his neck and gave him a full frontal. "Tony, if only you could be like this all the time."

"I know, honey, and I feel a real heel, and I apologize for neglecting you and the kids. I'm lucky that you have put up with me this long."

"You can say that again! Listen, changing the subject. I just received a call from June, our next-door neighbour, telling me that the family can't make it on Sunday, Mike has had to go to West Palm Springs on urgent business or something, and won't return until Monday. He's almost as bad as you." She was being sarcastic but in a jovial mood.

"I'm sorry?" Tony's mind seemed to go blank, and he sat down heavily on the barstool. *Was he hearing correctly? Was this the same Mike Summers from Global Marketing? It can't be! It just can't be! Naw, it's just a knee-jerk reaction.*

His mind racing ten to the dozen.

"Rose, I didn't quite catch that."

"What's with you? You look as if you have seen a ghost." Rose shook her head and gave a big sigh at having to repeat herself. *"Mister*! You've had one too many. I said Judy can't make it on Sunday because Mike—"

"Yeah . . . Yeah . . . I thought that's what you said." Tony cut her short.

"So why the silence all of a sudden?" Rose was concerned. This was not like Tony.

"I'm sorry, honey, but there is something bothering me. It's this case I'm working on."

"*What*, the Laura Williams case?" Now Rose was really concerned.

"Honey, just bear with me for a few more seconds. Listen, has June ever mentioned the work that Mike does, I mean like what company he is with?"

"*For Christ's sake, Tony,* how the hell do I know? From what little June tells me, he is a marketing big shot with a company." She paused for a moment. "With a company name like Global or something. Yeah, that's it. I'm sure it's Global."

Tony sat for a moment, deep in thought. It was all coming together: the name in Laura's phone book; Mike Summers, the Marketing VP with Global Marketing; the business trip to West Palm Springs. All the pieces fell into place. It was no coincidence, but it didn't mean he was the assailant. "Honey, I need to make a phone call." *Now Rose was really concerned!*

"I'll explain it to you later." He dialled. "Bill, Tony here. Something has come up on the Williams case, and I want to pass it by you."

CHAPTER 23

Bill arrived sharp and was sitting at his desk, sipping his coffee, when Tony entered the office.

"You're early this morning," Tony commented as he stood at the coffee machine. "What happened? Did Judy kick you out of bed or something?" He was laughing.

"*Naw*, I just couldn't sleep thinking about your call. That's one helluva story. It's hard to believe, but looking at the facts, it's a bit more than a coincidence, wouldn't you say?" Bill shook his head. "I know Mike well. I've met him at your house over dinner and barbecues, and a nicer family you couldn't meet."

Tony took a sip of his coffee and screwed up his face.

"*Yuk* . . . This is ugly." He threw the half-full polystyrene cup into the trash can before sitting at his desk then paused for a moment to digest Bill's comment.

"I know what you mean, Bill, and that's what makes it so difficult. And let's face it, we could be on a runaway train for all we know. I mean what have we really got? *One,* Mike Summers was one of the three names that came up from Laura's diary. *Two,* Terry Johnson stated that Laura confided to her that her boyfriend was married and was a high-level executive. *Three,* our inquiries led to a company named Global Marketing, of which our Mike Summers is a

VP. *Four,* he is on urgent business and has flown down to West Palm Springs and won't return until late Monday. *Five,* Rose receives a call from June, our next-door neighbour, informing her that her husband Mike is in West Palm Springs on urgent business, and they can't make the barbecue." Tony rubbed his chin. "If we jump too fast, and it was just a one-in-a-million coincidence, it doesn't bear thinking. To sum it up, Bill, we really have nothing. I mean Mike could just be negotiating, say, a contract with ABM, and Laura was a key player, and subsequently his contact number was in her diary purely as a business contact. No, we need something more concrete."

"You could get Rose to ask Judy where Mike worked. It's only a suggestion," Bill volunteered.

"Yeah, that did cross my mind. But can you just imagine Rose phoning? *June, a thought has just crossed my mind. What company is your husband with?*'"

"Yeah, I know what you mean, Tony. Then what do you recommend?"

"We hit CSI and see what Adams and pathology have come up with." He lifted the phone. "Dave, Tony here. I thought you would say that. So when do you think. *Monday at the earliest!* Okay. Okay. Keep your shirt on. Yeah, I understand pathology and all that stuff. Okay. Then as soon as you get the report. Thanks, Dave."

Tony looked to Bill. "I'm sure you got the gist of that."

"Yeah." Bill shook his head but stopped in his tracks. *"Awe . . . Awe,* look who's heading our way." Bill motioned with his eyes. It was Ted Baker, and he looked like a wounded bull.

"You two, in my office. Now!"

Tony Turned to Bill. "I think that's a sign that we are being promoted."

Bill covered his mouth to hide his laughter as Baker impatiently stared through his office window, not impressed.

"Christ, Tony, one of these days, you're gonna get us both fired with that kinda shit."

"Never fear, my trusted friend. Let *me* do the talking, and you do the walking."

This was Tony at his nonchalant best, and Bill was more than happy for his partner to hold the floor.

Baker rudely pointed to the empty chairs. *"Sit."* His black double-chinned face distinctly turning a lighter shade of brown. He opened his desk drawer and chucked two Alka-Seltzers into a glass of water then poured the foaming liquid down his throat in one gulp, pausing only for a few seconds to produce a repulsive burp. *"Ah, that's better! So, what's with the looks, Hayden? Has my manners offended you?"*

Bill just shrugged. "Discretion is the better part of valour."

Baker placed the glass down heavily on the desktop and gave a steely stare. "This is one of the benefits that come with this fucking job. *Ulcers!* So, if you are thinking of filling my shoes when I get pensioned off, take my advice and invest in Bayer Pharmaceuticals. You'll do better there. Now let's cut the chase. We've got work to do. For your information, I've just had my friend Murray, the DA, on the phone. And I can't repeat his ultimatum. But the good news is"—he was only being sarcastic—"like if I don't close the Williams case within the next forty-eight, you, 'Sherlock Holmes,' and 'Dr. Watson' here"—he turned to Bill—"will be joining me washing cruisers in the motor pool. *Do you get my drift? Now* if it's not too much trouble, perhaps my two 'so-called' best detectives can tell me *what the hell is happening?"* Baker emptied his lungs; his hot air rattling the office windows.

There was a pregnant pause after Baker's onslaught; and Tony being Tony, as usual, treaded where angels feared. After all, there was no point in disappointing his boss; he might as well live up to his reputation.

"So? Don't keep me in suspense, Perino. I'm only the captain of detectives who is being hounded every day by the paparazzi who for some reason assume I have a hearing impairment when I'm asked for a statement. Now whatever it is you're gonna report, for your sake, *it had better be good!"*

"Ted, it's not all bad news. Let me explain. Here's what we got."

"Let's get this straight. We have one half-baked suspect and a bag of shredded paper and a bloodstained hand towel. Not bad for two days' work. The next thing you'll be asking for is a pay rise. *Now you two listen and listen good!* I'm giving you until Monday to have a lead on my desk or both your names will be on the transfer list to beat cops. Now get your pathetic asses out of my face. Nine o'clock Monday, in my office. *Go!"* Baker pointed to the door.

As the two detectives walked to their desk, Brown and Lucas were laughing their asses off.

"Well, lookee here, Brad, the two sopranos. Only they ain't singing now." Brown burst into laughter with Lucas following suit.

Tony grabbed Bill's arm. *"Cool it.* These two numbnuts ain't worth it." But before Hayden could retaliate, Baker was back on the warpath.

"Lucas, Brown, in my office. I want to hear some music on the Davis case."

That wiped the smugness from their faces.

Tony couldn't miss the shot. "You know what they say, Lucas, 'he who laughs first laughs last.'" Perino and Hayden were now bursting their sides.

Baker turned at the hilarity. He was not impressed. "What's this, a rehearsal for a new episode for Seinfeld? Have you two got nothing better to do than make with the comedy. *What the hell is happening to this place?*" He walked to his office, shaking his head, with Lucas and Brown following like two obedient lap dogs, before Baker slammed the door, almost dislodging it from its hinges.

It seemed like Baker had taken a piece of everyone today.

* * *

Terry was awake bright and early. She had had a more than peaceful sleep after her productive visit to her friend in hospital. *Then there was Frank,* she thought, smiling to herself as she placed her feet onto the rug then gave a satisfying groan as she stretched her arms above her head. *He's nice and refreshing, but I'm only twenty-eight, and as they say, "I still have a lot of liven' to do." Besides, a security guard? It's not really my scene. What the hell am I thinking about? I don't want to be late again, or Blakely will have an orgasm.* She smiled at the thought as she stepped out of her silk pyjamas and walked unashamedly naked to the en-suite.

The warm spray from the shower was invigorating, and she turned, placing her face directly into the stimulating experience. She could easily stay there for another fifteen minutes, but time was not on her side, and she quickly squeezed the water from her shoulder-length blonde hair and closed the faucet. Her thick terry towel bathrobe adsorbed the wetness of her body as she briskly began to towel her hair.

Terry wasn't relishing the interrogation from Blakely when she arrived at the office. She hang her robe on the door peg and stood naked for a moment, admiring her slim taught body in the full-length wall mirror.

She frowned for a moment as she lifted each of her breasts with each hand in an upward motion. "My breasts seem to be sagging slightly," she spoke out loud. "At twenty-eight, am I getting the dreaded 'old women's' sagging tits? *Nah.*" She stepped back, dropping her hands. "My imagination." She stared again, a little unsure of her statement, then touched her firm flat abdomen with her hand. "I had better go easy on the carbs and the Vino." She smiled as she walked naked to the walk-in robe, glancing at the bedside clock on the way. *"Christ,* that time already! I had better 'hit the road, Jack.' You can never tell with this shit New York traffic."

* * *

As Terry stopped at the boom gate to ABM's underground car park, Lee, the security guard, was at his stupid best.

"Identity tag, ma'am." He held out his leathery hand.

"*Lee, for Christ's sake*! Don't fuck with me. I'm in a hurry. Now open that fucking boom gate before I get out of this car and kick you in the nuts."

Lee burst into laughter. "That's what I love about you, Terry. Always the lady."

"Cut the shit, Lee, and open that fucking gate. *Thaaaank . . . you.*" Terry lashed out before finally driving down the ramp. As for Lee? When she looked into her rear mirror, he was laughing his ass off. *"Jerk!"* She couldn't help herself. *This had the beginnings of a day to forget.*

She quickly glanced at her watch as she entered the main lobby. *"Shit!* It just turned nine. I can still make it. *That elevator!"* She rushed to jam the elevator door with her foot to stop it from closing. "Sorry, guys." She sensed the "annoyance" of the occupants.

"Just made it, Terry, huh?" It was Neil Gardner, the DP manager.

Terry just nodded. This guy was a player, and the last thing he needed was encouragement. The twelfth floor was forever, and she could feel this moron's warm breath purposely breathing down her neck, not to mention the body contact of the "third kind."

Enough was enough, and Terry was about to blow a gasket when fortunately for Neil, the elevator chimed, and the doors opened. As she accelerated down the corridor, Neil was hard on her heels but just far enough to "get off" on Terry's tight ass.

Christ, this guy just won't take the hint. Terry shook her head, her adrenaline now rising. She had had enough, and she hit the brakes and did a 180 to face Gardener head-on. This was "showdown time," and Casanova was taken by surprise, almost colliding with her shapely breasts.

"What the hell, Terry?"

"You know, Neil, you wouldn't be such a bad guy if you weren't such a fucking pervert. So be a good boy and go home to your wife or do me a favour and buy the latest Playboy. *Now . . . get outta my fucking face,* or so help me I'll report you to personnel for sexual harassment."

Terry's outburst was enough to send lover boy packing, his face in full bloom. He would think twice before hitting on Terry again.

* * *

As Terry walked toward her desk, she was visibly pissed off, and it showed.

"*Christ* can't a girl wear a short skirt in this office without causing an international incident?" she spoke out loud for everyone to hear before finally sitting down hard at her desk.

"I might as well get myself a coffee. I need the caffeine to keep me sane in this fucking morgue," she muttered below her breath before switching on her computer. The next she heard was a knock-on glass, and she turned toward its direction.

"I might have guessed." She could see Blakely signalling for her to come to his office. "This is all I fucking need." Terry shook her head as she dejectedly rose to her feet. "*What the fuck now?*"

"Good morning, Terry." Blakely was all smiles. *When this guy is nice, there's gotta be a hidden agenda.* "Grab a seat." He pointed. "First things first, how's Laura?"

"It's good news, Jack. Laura is responding to voice messages by making motions with her hand, but she still hasn't regained all her faculties and full consciousness. But as they say, 'where there's life, there's hope.' The doc? He estimates it might take another two to three days, but with a crushed larynx and voice box to boot, talking is going to be something else."

"Yeah, I can just imagine." For once, Jack looked genuinely concerned. "And the two detectives?" he asked.

"I think they've drawn a blank. At least that's what I've assumed, as they haven't contacted me again."

"In this case, 'no news is bad news,' huh?" He gave a stupid smile at his even more stupid remark.

"Jack, if you don't mind, I'm desperate for a coffee," Terry interrupted.

Blakely smiled. "Sure, Terry, take five and would it be rude of me to ask you for a refill?" He held up the empty polystyrene cup before chucking it into the trash can.

"No sweat, but you owe me one." She closed the door and walked toward the vending machine but not before stopping at her desk to raid her coin box.

"I just can't read this guy. He's up to some no good, that's for sure." She slotted the coins and hit the "short black" button, speaking to herself.

"Thanks, Terry. You're a gem and you know exactly how I like it." Blakely took a sip of the caffeine.

Things were going too well; and she was becoming, shall we say, more than slightly uncomfortable. And Terry? Well, she calls a spade a spade.

"Jack, at the thought of being way out of line, just what have you got in mind?" She was adding two and two, and it didn't make four!

"Calm down, Terry." He paused and sat back in his chair. "Terry, it's like this. I was discussing with Gerry Theder, you know, the human resources manager, over an after-office drink last night regarding Laura Williams. It's unfortunate, but you and I are realists, and the bottom line is it is highly unlikely that we will see Laura back to work again this side of 2003."

"So, what has this gotta do with me?"

"Terry, you're so bloody impatient. Let me finish, *please!* The bottom line is we are short of one senior marketing manager, and that leaves a big hole in the department."

Terry frowned. She was intrigued, not knowing what to expect next.

"Jack, you've lost me."

"Terry, for a moment, think outside the box. I feel, and Theder agrees with me, that you have talent, and in the right circumstances, you're the perfect candidate to replace Laura."

Terry was taken aback. *"Christ, Jack,* one minute I'm in the firing line, and the next minute I'm getting promoted."

"Terry, we all know you're a bit of a loose cannon at times, but you're hardnosed and you're not scared to call the shots, and that's exactly what I need. Now look at me. *Admit it!* You know you can hold down Laura's job. You have the experience, the talent, and the confidence. So, what do you say? Is it a deal?

"I . . . I'm still in shock, and besides, I feel so bad, like I'm stealing my friend's job when she's on deaths door."

"Well?"

Terry gave a reluctant nod.

"Is that a yes?" Blakely was becoming impatient.

"Yes, but what about the rest of the staff. There'll be a few noses put out of joint."

"Leave that to me. I'll get Theder to place the announcement on the notice board effective from Monday of next week at which point in time you will receive your new job description and salary structure. You can take over Laura's desk on Monday and go through her files. There're a few contracts still in orbit and need urgent attention. Is there anything else you would like to ask?"

"No, I'm still trying to grapple with my promotion and new responsibilities." Terry looked drawn.

"I can understand. Anyhow, we'll be seeing a lot more of each other in the future, and I have every confidence that you will do an excellent job." Blakely rose to his feet, offering his hand.

"Congratulations, Terry."

CHAPTER 24

"Einstein, what next?"

Tony was still smarting from Baker's dressing down, and Bill was pushing his luck with the wisecrack.

"You know what they say about sarcasm, so cut the shit and let me think." Tony placed his elbow on his desk to support his chin, resembling the bust of "the Thinker."

"Now to answer your 'no-brainer' question, somehow we gotta light a fire under Adams's ass and get some closure on the paper fragments and that blood-soaked towel. But how? The elephant takes its time." "I'm sorry, Tony." Bill felt a bit of a heel. "I was way outta line." *There's a time and place for everything, and this was not the time.*

"No sweat. Forget it. It's gone over my head. Now any other sensible suggestions? Deja vu." There was still a sting in his voice.

Tony's phone rang. "Yeah, Perino here. *Dave, I was just talking about you. Your ears must be burning. So, you heard. News travels fast in this dump. You know Baker, all fire and brimstone. Yeah, his bark is worse than his bite, but why the call? I'm on my way.*"

Tony dropped the receiver and turned to Bill, a big grin on his face, his grumpiness history.

"So, what's with the face?" Bill was relieved but inquisitive.

"Hayden, my friend, it's manna from heaven. Someone up there likes me." Tony made the sign of the cross.

"So?" Bill was still lost.

"So, we hit the elevator and Avanti to CSI. For your information, Adams has come to the party."

"And the Italian?"

"It means move your ass!"

* * *

"And the DNA matches the skin fragments from below Laura's nails? Dave was all smiles. "*Yep.* And not only that, the blood on the face towel."

"Well, I'll be darned!" Tony smirked. "Although, Dave, I must confess, I half expected this. That's at least one thing for sure. We now know the father of the unborn child is one and the same who attempted to ice Laura Williams."

"But I'm not finished yet, Tony. *Get this!*" Adams proudly produced what looked like a "pieced-together" bank check, placing it in front of the detectives. "We carefully put the pieces together, and bingo, we have our man! The check was made out to Laura Williams for twenty big ones to the account of a Michael Summers, Citibank, 309 Canal Street . . ."

*   *   *

Tony and Bill were patiently waiting outside Baker's office, trying to stifle their laughter upon seeing Brown and Lucas getting a strip torn off and Baker's hands flaying in the air. Suddenly, he stopped in his tracks at the sight of the two detectives and stared angrily through the glass. *A stare that only a mother could give.* All he needed now was Perino and Hayden to "make his day." He paused to get a breath then pointed to the door, to the relief of the two "boneheads."

"Out. And don't let me see your miserable faces until you have something positive!"

"Hi, guys." Tony couldn't contain himself as Lucas and Brown rudely brushed by. "Coffee break with the boss, huh?" "Fuck off, wop!" Lucas retaliated.

"Guys, don't be that way." It was Bill's turn to shellac.

"Fucking snow drops!" Lucas stopped for a second then decided to change his mind. There's always another day.

"What's this, a family reunion? If it's not too much trouble?" Baker was impatiently tapping his fingers on his desk, and the situation was becoming ugly.

"Well? What gives me this pleasure?" He pointed to the chairs.

Tony opened his case. "Ted." He smiled. "We bring tidings of good will." Tony never learns, and Bill screwed up his eyes at the thought of what was coming next.

"What the fuck's this, 'the last comic standing'? Perino, if you were as good with the detective work as you are with the jokes, you would be in my fucking job. Now cut the fucking comedy. *And a word of warning, this had better be good!*"

Tony took a deep breath. He knew there was no pleasing this guy.

"Ted, we just came down from CSI and . . ."

"Now we're getting somewhere. We have a name and a possible motive."

"Yeah, but, Ted, we need to make sure who this guy is. It may not be the same man that we were investigating earlier."

"So?"

"So, we need legal clearance to go to 'Citibank' and retrieve information on the suspect's account."

For the first time today, Baker's leathery face showed signs of cracking. He lifted the phone.

"It's Ted Baker here. I need to speak to Jake urgently. Jake, listen. We've had a break on the Williams case, and I need . . ."

The two detectives listened to Baker's conversation with the DA. Things were now hotting up.

Baker placed back the receiver and sat back in his chair, a relieved expression on his face.

"I think you got the gist of that conversation. Murray will get legal clearance to investigate this guy Summers's account through the Freedom of Information Act, via a legal warrant. Judge Donnelly will do the needful within, say, a couple of hours." Baker looked at his watch. "It's one thirty. You can still make it before the banks close at four thirty. Now if you don't mind, I'm busy."

*   *   *

It was lunchtime, and Terry patiently stood in line at the cafeteria counter, her mind not really concentrating on the display of refrigerated salads or the "get fat" section. Whatever? The lunch ritual was a must, and with only "bedsides" over the last few days, the calories were dropping; and she opted for the Caesar, a slice of cheesecake, and a cappuccino.

"That'll be fifteen straight, ma'am."

"Eh . . . Err . . . I'm sorry. For a moment, I wasn't paying attention.

The checkout lady kept a solemn face. "Like I got troubles of my own, honey, so don't lay them on me." She repeated again, "Fifteen straight," as Terry searched her bag for her wallet. She then rudely threw the then spot and the five onto the counter.

"You impatient bitch! I'm sorry for your fucking husband, that is, if you are lucky enough to be married!" Terry lifted the tray and "walked the walk" to the echoing abuse of the irate "broomstick test pilot."

Terry stood for a moment, searching for a table before spotting the raised hand. *It was Blakely!*

"Oh, what the hell!" she spoke under her breath. "I might as well give the office something to talk about."

"Grab a chair, Terry. You were standing there like a lost sheep."

"Thanks, Jack."

"On a diet, are we?" It was a throwaway line to start the conversation.

"You should know what it's like, Jack. I'm sure your wife's the same. We women are always on a diet." She was subtlety sending a reminder to Blakely of his marital status.

"Yeah, and don't I know it!"

Terry half-heartedly attacked her salad, still feeling uncomfortable at just where this conversation was going.

"I'm sure you'll be visiting Laura this evening?"

"Yes, I'm going straight from the office."

"You know, Terry, it's strange, Laura being your best friend and all that she never confided in you about her friend."

"Laura is Laura, Jack, when it comes to men friends. It's personal and private. Sure we went clubbing together, but she kept her special nights. That's why I told the detectives that all I know was that he is a married man and held an executive position with some company or other."

"So he was the father?"

Terry cut him short. "Jack, I really don't know, and I would really like to enjoy my lunch. Please don't think I'm being rude. It's just . . ."

"Don't worry. I know, Terry, what you must be going through, and I understand." He glanced uncomfortably at his watch. "I best get going. I have a meeting with the CEO of Target, and I need their business badly. I'll keep you up to speed on Monday as I want you to take the reins on this one, after of course, I soften Collins with the financials. And oh, Terry!" He rose to his feet. "If there is any good news on Laura, give me a call anytime. My cell number is on my card."

* * *

The lunch was average, and the afternoon was boring. Terry had more than enough on her mind what with Laura and Frank. This promotion was all she needed, and five o'clock couldn't come quick enough.

"At last!" she spoke out loud she opened her desk drawer for her car keys.

* * *

The evening was humid, and she chucked her jacket into the rear seat of the car. She would have dinner later after her visit with Laura and hopefully her newfound man Frank. She turned the key in the Mazda and slowly left the car park.

The drive to Roosevelt Memorial was not the most appealing. The five o'clock office "charge" hit the roads with the usual abominable driving and repulsive road rage, not to mention the foul language. But this is the Big Apple, where hustling's the name of the game and life is cheap.

As for Terry, what would this evening bring? *God only knows.*

* * *

The warrant hit Tony's desk like the "space shuttle." When it comes to the DA's niece, there's no holds barred, and Baker's expression said it all "like hit the gas, Jack, and don't spare the horses."

"It's three forty-five." Ted glanced at his watch. "That gives you approximately forty minutes before the bank closes its doors. *Need I say any more?"*

"Don't worry, Ted. We'll make it in time." Tony was already on his feet.

"You had better!" Baker mumbled something under his breath then turned to go to his office.

Tony threw the car keys. "You're on the wheel, partner."

"Why me?"

"Because I'm your boss." Tony grinned. "Cappice?"

* * *

Bill gunned the Pontiac and swung onto Pearl Street, the big car's rear end fishtailing before he oversteered and straightened up. He dropped the driver's window and placed the red magnetic light onto the roof, the familiar police siren echoing in the afternoon traffic. In New York, this was an everyday event, and the cars quickly moved aside to give the "boys in blue" free passage.

"Easy, 'Schumacher.' *We want to get there in one piece!* I hope you have the address?" Tony asked, his knuckles white as he precariously grabbed the hand restraint above the door.

"Of course, I do! Citibank, 309 Canal Street . . . *Gimme a break!* We just slip onto Centre Road, and it's all the way. I guarantee we'll be there in twenty."

"Yeah, but I have a wife and kids. *Remember!"*

"Stop being a woos. Listen, how long have I been your wheelman?"

"Too long," Tony shot back, half laughing; it was a take too good to miss.

"Okay . . . Okay . . . But let's get serious. What do you think, Tony?"

"To be honest, Bill, I don't know what to think. It's too close to home for comfort. *It just doesn't bear thinking!"*

"Yeah, like you, I keep convincing myself that it can't be the Mike Summers *we* know."

105

"Well, there's one thing for sure. We'll soon find out," Tony answered, his mind still grappling with the morbid prospect.

*   *   *

With speeds exceeding eighty, Canal Street was on their doorstep before they knew it, and Bill hung a right and braked in the "No Parking" zone directly in front of the bank. It was only four ten, and they still had plenty of slack.

The armed security guard at the front entrance suddenly awoke from his standing slumber as the Pontiac screamed to a halt, and he quickly undid his safety clip, placing his hand nervously on the grip of the 45-caliber Beretta.

Tony was first to hit the sidewalk. "Cool it," he yelled to the guard as Bill cut the siren. "It's not a holdup, so keep your itchy finger off that trigger."

The overweight guard in his mid-fifties, with the "McDonald's overhang," was more than relieved when he saw the gold shields.

"Lieutenant Perino and my partner Sergeant Hayden."

"How can I help you, Lieutenant?" Suddenly, the "would be" cop wanted a piece of the action.

"We need to see the bank manager urgently." Tony was striding to the entrance.

"I'll escort you personally to his office." The guard pushed in front.

A small group of onlookers had quickly gathered at the entrance to the bank, hoping to catch a real-life drama of "cops and robbers" or better still a take from *Die Hard II*.

Tony flashed his shield. "NYPD . . . Break it up, everybody. It's nothing serious, and you're blocking the sidewalk."

There were the usual looks of disappointment as the oglers dispersed.

Being Friday, the bank was "jam-packed" with customers drawing cash for the weekend or queuing with check deposits from the day's takings.

"*Move aside please. Move aside please.*" The guard was doing a good job. "Here we are, detectives." He knocked on the heavy wood-panelled door. "Mr. Jenkins . . ."

"Yes?"

"It's Greg, the security guard, sir."

"Come in," the commanding voice bellowed.

Greg opened the door slightly and popped his head around.

"Mr. Simmons, I have two detectives here to see you. They say it's extremely urgent."

The word "detective" was enough, and the manager didn't need a second introduction. Simmons quickly rose to his feet to greet the "officers of the law," his face already draining. *Maybe this guy was cooking the books or something, but for sure he was displaying a visual bout of nerves.*

"Come in, detectives. Come in." He motioned with his hand. "Please take a seat. That will be all, Greg. Thank you. Can I see your credentials please? These days, one can never tell, especially in my business."

"We understand," Tony replied, the detectives placing their cards on his desk.

"Eh . . . Lieutenant"—he studied the card—"Perino . . . How can I be of service?" *This guy was typical banking material. He would most likely confront bank robbers with the same protocol.*

Tony placed the pink slip on his desk.

"It's like this, Mr. Simmons. We have legal clearance from Judge Donnelly under 'The Freedom of Information Act' given in special circumstances to assist the police in solving serious crimes."

"I see . . ." Simmons was still struggling. *Was he being investigated?*

Bill could tell from the anguish on his face that this guy was in turmoil, and he decided to quickly put the situation to bed.

"We are not investigating you, Mr. Simmons, so you can relax. Here's our problem."

Tony placed the photocopy of the "pieced together" check in front of Simmons. The bank manager carefully studied the patched check then looked up.

"We suspect this man of a serious crime, and it's essential we see a copy of his bank account and any other services he has with the bank, such as a safety deposit box."

"I see . . . Of course, your request is highly irregularly, but as you have legal clearance, I have no alternative." *This guy was a bank manger to die for.*

Simmons picked up the phone. "Aileen, can you come in for a moment, please?" He placed back the receiver then sat in silence.

The door suddenly opened, and a young shapely brunette appeared. *At least this stuffy bank manger had taste!*

"Yes, Mr. Simmons?" She glanced nervously at the detectives.

"Aileen, I require a copy of Mr. Summers's account and his safety deposit box key. This is a photocopy of one of his checks." He passed her the paper.

She glanced at it to check the account number.

"This will take about ten minutes, Mr. Jenkins. Is that all right?" "Of course . . ." She quickly turned and left.

"Can I entice you with some coffee, gentlemen?" Jenkins asked at a loss for a better conversation.

Tony turned to Bill, who shook his head.

"No, we're good, Mr. Simmons."

It was begging the question, and Jenkins just had to run the gauntlet.

"I suppose it would not be prudent to ask you—"

Tony cut him short. "I'm sorry, Mr. Simmons, but it's confidential. I'm sure you understand."

There was a timely gentle knock on the door, and Jenkins looked up.

"That must be Aileen now. Come in."

"Excuse me." She smiled to the detectives. "Here is a print of Mr. Summers's account and the keys you requested, sir."

"Thanks, Aileen. That will be all."

Simmons quickly checked the printout before passing it to Tony, who studied it for a moment then turned to Bill.

"Mr. M. Summers, 16 River Street, East Village . . ."

CHAPTER 25

As Terry crawled through the evening traffic on her way to the hospital, she couldn't help but reflect on the events of today. *I mean is this guy Blakely really on the level. Was she really being promoted for her ability or was there another ulterior motive?* She sighed. *Only time will tell.*

It had just turned six when she finally arrived and swung into the hospital's crowded car park. It would be difficult to find a slot, but patience is a virtue.

"Ah, here we are." She spotted the reversing lights of the SUV and pulled in then signalled. You have to mark your spot in this world, or some cowboy will beat you to the punch.

"Boy, that was a piece of luck," Terry spoke aloud as she cut the engine. "Now my next challenge is to gain access to my dear friend in IC . . ."

As she entered the crowed reception, she momentarily scanned the horizon in search of the now-familiar face of Frank, her newfound beau. The sister at reception immediately recognized Terry and waved. The Williams case was hot copy, and Terry's so-called healing skills were the "talk of the town," so much so that senator Williams and his wife had instructed the IC staff to allow her immediate access to their daughter any time of the day.

"You can go straight to IC, Miss Johnson. Mr. and Mrs. Williams have given you security clearance."

"Thank you, sister." Terry was relieved. She didn't need the hassle.

The sister could see the anguish on Terry's face as she paused, continuing to search through the crowded reception for the familiar face.

"I'm afraid he's not here tonight." The sister looked up.

"Not here tonight, sister?" Terry had a good idea what was coming but was playing the innocent.

"Frank . . . Frank Reynolds, the security guard. He's been transferred to another facility."

"Transferred?" Terry was taken aback.

"Yes, it's not unusual," she replied. "Unfortunately, I can't help you other than it's a large company, and he could be on duty at any of their security facilities. Your best bet would be to phone. I can help you there. It's 'Security Guard.'" She glanced at the card. "New York, 8777 . . . They're well known, but I don't know if they will provide information on their staff to the public."

"Oh, well." Terry half sighed as if to say, "That's that." "Thank you again, sister." She was more than disappointed as she disconsolately walked toward the elevator, but for now she had more important things on her mind, like the health of her best friend Laura.

* * *

The cop sitting at the door of the IC unit recognized Terry from the evening before and nodded his approval as she hesitated to enter. In fact, he didn't even unfold his paper. *The ponies were more important.*

Terry stood over Laura's bed, studying her friend's peaceful expression, and was just about to take a seat when her thoughts were interrupted by none other than Nancy, the duty nurse.

"Well, you're a stayer, I must admit." Nancy pleasantly smiled for a change. "I don't want to seem rude but having been in this job for almost fifteen years, most grieving relatives and so-called do-gooders don't stay the course, especially with comatosed patients."

Terry could understand the nurse's sentiments; a prime example was her office colleagues and the disappointment that none of them had even attempted to visit Laura. *Not even a "get well" card from Blakely!* She shook her head at the depressing thought. The world has become a selfish place, with compassion at the bottom of the heap.

"Listen, honey, it always seems that you arrive when I am about to take my break, but it also has its good points." She smiled again. "Can you keep an eye on my patient for . . . say fifteen minutes?" "I'm only too happy to assist." Terry smiled.

"Good. Now remember and hit that button if anything changes, like her breathing and heart rate. The monitor will automatically sound, but I still need you to press that emergency button, like there's no tomorrow."

"Don't worry, Nancy. She's in good hands."

"Fifteen minutes then." She turned and quickly left. *Maybe it was the thought of the coffee or was it the smokes?*

Terry took her seat as close as possible to Laura and gently massaged her hand.

"Laura, honey, it's me Terry. Can you try and move your fingers if you hear me?"

Terry waited anxiously, but there was no reaction, the disappointment reflecting on her face.

"Honey, did I tell you that I met this gorgeous guy . . ."

* * *

"Ted, it's Tony here. We've just come from the bank. Yeah, he's our man all right, but we still need to seal it with a DNA check. I checked his workplace, and his secretary confirmed he is in West Palm Springs on business and won't return to New York until sometime Monday. Sure, I'll check it out, but secretaries, you never can trust. I don't want her to call and spook him. For sure we'll put the hard word on her. A warrant for his arrest? Monday at the earliest! *That's cutting it a bit fine, Ted.* I want to arrest him at the airport. Why? That's a long story. I'll give you the lowdown when I see you on Monday morning. Sure. Sure." Tony closed his cell.

* * *

As Bill weaved through the evening traffic, there was an uncanny silence. Both men were still in shock and almost lost for words.

Tony broke the silence. "I guess we both knew that there was something uncanny about this case when we first came across the name. I mean how many Mike Summers can there be?"

"I guess so." Bill was as deflated as Tony.

Tony gave a huge sigh. "You know, Bill, my biggest problem is how do I break it to June, his wife, not to mention Rose? Christ, all hell will be let loose, and that's why we gotta arrest Mike as he arrives at the airport. Can you imagine me cuffing Mike in front of his kids?" Bill didn't reply. Tony had nailed it.

"I know what I'm gonna do, partner. I'm going to Jakes to participate in the government's alcohol tax. It's called Budweiser."

"Christ, Tony, gimme a break. If I'm late again and smelling of booze, my nuts will be on the organ donor register."

"It's only for one beer."

"Yeah, and all the rest! I'm sorry, partner. It's absolutely a 'no-no.'"

"Not even if I'm paying?"

"Why didn't you say so . . ."

* * *

Suddenly, Laura's hand moved. Terry's story must have rekindled her brain.

"Now you're interested, huh? So why don't you open those lovely eyes of yours and let me see that beautiful smile?"

Terry stared for a moment in absolute disbelief. There, staring straight into her eyes, was Laura.

"Laura . . . Laura . . . I can't believe it."

Her facial muscles were still frozen, but those eyes had the sparkle of life, and Terry burst into uncontrollable tears of happiness and almost stumbled as she hit the emergency button.

* * *

Nancy was relaxing, having had her cancer stick and her caffeine hype, when she was startled with the sound of the emergency signal flashing on her wristband.

"Not again! What's that broad up to now? Probably the patient's eyelashes moved, but I had better check it out. You never can tell." She sprightly walked to the elevator, not knowing just what to expect.

* * *

"Nancy . . . Nancy." Terry was jumping up and down like an Irish dancer. *"She has opened her eyes. She has opened her eyes."*

"Calm down . . . Calm down for goodness's sake, or you'll have that cop slap the cuffs on you."

Nancy quickly shone the pocket torch into Laura's eyes one at a time to check her pupil's reaction to the light then stepped back and turned to address Terry.

"Whatever you did, honey, your friend is back in the land of the living.

I must call the duty doctor." She lifted the phone. "Dr. Nathan, Nancy here from IC. Can you come right away? It's urgent . . ."

* * *

Nathan was there in a shake and quickly examined the patient, stepping through the same procedure with the torchlight as Nancy. He liked what he saw and smiled to Terry.

"Nice job," he commented before turning to his patient.

"Now, Laura, I know you can't speak and don't even try, but what I need you to do is to squeeze both my hands as hard as you can." He gently held her hands. "Good. Now I want you to press each foot against my hands." He folded back the bedsheets. "Good. Well done, young lady."

"Nancy,"—he turned to the nurse—"you can remove the feeding tube from her nose and give her some ice balls to suck to relieve the dryness in her mouth. I'll come back in an hour to do another check. Now, Laura, I want you to close your eyes once if you understand me. That's good. You have a severely damaged larynx, and you won't be able to talk for some time. Do you understand? Good. Tomorrow the nurse will remove the tracheotomy or breathing tube from your throat to allow you to breath as normal through your mouth. But you must rest now and above all don't get excited. You're on the road to recovery, and before you know it, you will be back on your feet." He reassured her then turned to Terry. "I'm sorry, but Laura now needs absolute rest. She has had had enough excitement for one day."

"I understand, Doctor." Terry was disappointed at getting the "gentle push."

Terry leaned over and gave Laura a kiss on the forehead then squeezed her hand reassuringly.

"Don't worry, honey. I'll be back tomorrow . . ."

* * *

Terry had a spring in her step as she walked to the hospital car park. Suddenly, life seemed all worthwhile, and she could just imagine the reaction of Laura's parents. It had just turned nine, and her stomach was sending her signals.

"I was sure I would catch you here tonight."

That voice sounded familiar, but in a car park. She turned nervously.

"*Frank!* For a moment there, you scared me. Are you in the habit of accosting unaccompanied females in car parks?" She was laughing but also relieved.

"No, but if they look like you, I might change my mind."

"Get out of it, and I might just believe you."

"You know you never gave me your phone number?" He changed the subject on a more serious note.

"You never asked." Terry was being naughty.

"Then do you think we could exchange phone numbers over a light snack and a glass of wine?"

"I'll Solito Posto?"

"No other."

"Then what are we waiting for? Your car or mine?

* * *

"Set 'em up, Jake."

Jake was inspecting the cleaned glasses, holding them up to the light, and immediately ceased his boring chore when he heard that familiar Bronx accent.

"Hi, Tony. You guys are early tonight. So, what's new?"

"The usual.," Tony grinned. "Crime always pays, and everyone in the can is innocent and you can buy an AK-47 for less than a PlayStation."

"You guys . . ." Jake was shaking his head, laughing, but then Tony's comment was not so stupid on the streets of the Big Apple.

"Jake, two cold Buds and don't spare the horses." Bill was not only anxious to quench his thirst in this "Indian summer" but also to get home at a respectable time. *On a Friday evening, Judy was not to be messed with.*

"Two Buds coming up . . ."

"Boy, is that good?" Bill wiped the froth his lips with the back of his hand. "What would the government do without us, huh? Can you believe that the tax on alcohol is more than gasoline?"

"So . . . Let's support Uncle Sam . . . Set 'em up, Jake."

"Oh no, you don't, Perino. Any excuse! *I said one and one only!"* Bill seemed adamant, but Tony knew his partner well, and he wouldn't take much convincing.

"Lighten up, Bill. I have an idea to kill two birds with one stone." "I'm listening."

Tony opened his cell phone and punched in the numbers then gave Bill a sly wink and held his finger to his lips.

"Hi, honey. I know, but I promise I'll be home by around"—he glanced at his watch—"Seven . . . Is your mother still there? She is? *Good!* Listen, I was thinking of making a reservation at Brunettis in Little Italy, your favourite restaurant. Sure, I know it's Friday, but I'll convince Mario to squeeze us in somehow. Hold it, honey, for a second . . ." He turned to Bill while placing his hand over the receiver. "How are you and Judy fixed for tonight?"

Bill paused for a moment. "To join you and Rose for dinner?"

"What else and the treats on me, *so?*"

"I'm sure Judy would love to but babysitting?"

Tony removed his hand from the mouthpiece. "Honey, are you still there? Listen, Bill and Judy would love to join us, but babysitting at such notice? Are you sure your mother wouldn't mind? That's great. Then it's a done deal, and I know the kids would love it. I'll call you back, honey, once Bill gets the green light from Judy. Me too. Ciao." Tony turned to Bill. "You can use my phone. I'm sure you got that conversation. Jake, I'm getting thirsty."

"Coming up, Tony."

Bill shook his head; he was in a bind, but it was a nice one. He dialed the number then took a sip of his second Bud while waiting for a response. Tony was right; he knew his partner only too well.

"It's Daddy here. Go and fetch Mummy. Hi, honey. Listen, I have a pleasant surprise. Tony and June have invited us out to dinner. Yes, this evening at Brunettis. Don't worry about the babysitting. June's mother . . ."

"Done deal." Bill was now really enjoying his second one. "So what brought this out of the blue?"

"You'll soon know, partner." Tony had that crafty look on his face.

"Brunettis . . . can I speak to Mario?"

PART 2

The Not-So-Perfect Storm

CHAPTER 1

"Maria . . . Dio sera come stai' . . ."

"Ciao, Molto Benny."

Tony's mother-in-law, Maria, was standing in the hallway, having heard the front door open, the dishtowel still in her hand.

"Si, Tony. For a change tonight, you are home early."

Tony let Maria's comment go over his head. He had had enough of that from her daughter.

"Maria, you are looking as beautiful as ever." He changed the subject. "And where may I ask is that lovely daughter of yours?"

"She is in her room, making herself even more beautiful for that crazy husband of hers." Maria was laughing, but the shot was there.

"The boys?" Tony asked.

"I'm happy to say they are already bathed and in their pyjamas, and of course they just can't wait for Bill's boys to arrive."

"I can imagine!" Tony commented. "Where are they now?"

"Need you ask?" Maria was shaking her head. "In the TV room, *where else?"*

"Maria." Tony gave her the traditional kiss on both cheeks. "What would I do without you?"

"Be off with you." She motioned with her hand. "Now if you don't mind, I have some unfinished business in the kitchen."

"Seriously, Maria, I really appreciate you babysitting tonight, especially with Bill's kids and all."

"Si, it's a no problem." She shrugged her shoulders. "I'm an old lady. What else is there for me to do? And besides, I love my two beautiful grandchildren.

Now . . ." She pointed to the stairway. "Go and attend to that lovely wife of yours."

"Ciao . . . Bella." Tony was laughing. His mother-in-law was the salt of the earth.

In passing, he decided to pop his head into the TV room.

"Hi, guys."

"Daaaad!" Sam, the youngest, rushed to his father, grabbing him round the legs.

"Hi, Dad." Mouro was more subdued, always playing the big brother.

"Guys, I'm sorry, but I have to leave you or your mother will be scolding me."

Mouro interrupted. "Dad, what time is Ian and Taylor coming over?" he asked, keeping one eye on the Disney Channel.

Tony glanced at his watch. "In about another half hour."

"Are they going to stay over, Dad?" Young Sam asked; his big brother wasn't any fun.

"Oh, I'll think about it." Tony put on a face. He could see the disappointment on young Sam's face, and he ruffled his hair with his hand. "Your grandma has agreed, but I want no nonsense tonight. Do you both hear me?"

"Yes, Dad" came the subdued chorus.

"Okay, back to the TV, young man."

As Tony climbed the stairs, he could hear the exciting chatter of the boys discussing the sleeping arrangements, with young Sam calling the shots, much to his older brother's annoyance. "Taylor's going to sleep in my room and . . ."

Tony smiled. *Boys will be boys.* He quietly opened the bedroom door and peeked in. Rose was already dressed, sitting in front of the dressing table, putting the finishing touches to her makeup; and he snuck up behind her and gently kissed her on the nape of her neck. She had already seen him in the mirror, and two can play at that game!

"Hmmm, is that you, Giovanni? That's so nice. My husband should take a leaf from your book. But you had better hurry before he arrives home." She was finding it hard to stifle her laughter, gauging Tony's expression.

"Oh, so it's Giovanni, is it now?"

Rose turned to face him and burst into laughter.

"I had you going there for a moment, didn't I? *You big heel!"* "Oh, did *you?"* Tony was now seeing the funny side.

"Now give me a big kiss before I put my lipstick on, *Giovanni."* Rose couldn't control herself.

"Maybe, if you would stop laughing."

The kiss was long and sensuous. Suddenly, the doorbell chimed and not a moment too soon.

"Down, boy!" Rose pushed him away. "Now go and answer the door. That must be Bill and Judy."

"How about giving *Giovanni* another kiss?"

"Get out of it, Romeo . . ."

* * *

Terry, although reluctant to admit it, was relieved when Frank approached her in the car park. She was not in the habit of showing her emotions early in the game, so to speak; but for some reason, this guy was different. Maybe it was all too much, what with Laura and the pressures at the office and that SOB Blakely; she just needed a shoulder to lean on, but was Frank becoming somewhat more than that? *Only time will tell.*

* * *

The drive to Giovanni's was with the normal chitchat about Frank's temporary transfer and Terry's forthcoming promotion with ABM and of course the elusive telephone numbers. Terry was still in "Grand Prix" mode and continued to talk at breakneck speed all about her friend's "miracle recovery."

"Ah, here we are at last! I hate to tell you, Terry, Friday evening's traffic, is 'night-out' stuff, and something tells me Giovanni's will be jumping. Now where can I find a parking space in this jungle?" He shook his head at the dismal thought.

"Better you than me," Terry commented, smiling." I'm glad you suggested your car. I always have this problem."

"I wonder if that guy is leaving?" Frank noticed the car's reversing lights, and he quickly hit the stock switch and pulled over. *"Yep,* we are in luck."

He was more than relieved. On a Friday night in Canal Street, to find a parking space was scarcer than a "hen's teeth."

It was only a five-minute walk to the venue, and Frank protectively held Terry's hand. This "macho guy" was doing all the right things, and she was becoming more and more comfortable by the minute. *After all, a woman without a man is like a fish without a bicycle.*

"Here, let me." He pushed open the heavy wood-panelled door.

* * *

As expected, the place was jam-packed, and secondary smoke was part of the ambience. The "wine crowd" was vigorously indulging in vintages they had never heard of, let alone understood, but then life is for the living; and in the end, who really cares? Tomorrow is another day and another hangover, so what's new? *We know little about conscience except that it is soluble in alcohol.*

The bar was really congested, and the decibel meter was off the scale.

"Maybe this wasn't such a good suggestion after all," Frank commented as he crushed his way through the homogenous mass, desperate to find some free wood at the bar.

"I see what you mean, but do you have a better suggestion?"

"Terry, I know this may sound corny and you wouldn't be wrong in thinking it's the oldest ploy in the world, but I swear I have only the best inten—"

"Frank." She cut him short. "The next thing I know, you'll be swearing on the Bible. Do me a favour and cut the run. *I don't bite, you know!"*

Frank had to laugh seeing the funny side, but the best was still to come.

"Now . . ." He started where he had left off. "That is if you can hear me above this racket. It's like this. My place is only about a fifteen-minute drive from here. We can catch a pizza from Domino's, and oddly enough, would you believe it, I just happen to have a bottle of chardonnay waiting in the icebox." He was putting on the innocent face, but that half grin said it all.

"If I didn't know you better, Mr. Reynolds, I would say this is a setup."

"Terry, I don't blame you, but what do you say?"

"I must admit it has its merits, but a word of warning. *Don't get any fresh ideas.* There's a line in the sand, and I would hate to see our friendly relationship disappear down the toilet . . ."

The tone in Terry's voice said it all, and Frank would have to be a fool to try his luck tonight.

*   *   *

Maria answered the door just as Bill arrived.

"Judy, so nice to see you again and, of course, your handsome husband."

"Maria, you are looking younger than ever." Bill was the charmer and gave her a kiss on both cheeks.

"And, Bill Hayden"—she laughed—"you keep telling more and more white lies."

Everyone laughed at Maria's remark.

Judy stepped forward and greeted Maria with the same Italian warmth.

"Hi, Judy. You look ravishing. Where have you been hiding this woman, Hayden?" It was Tony.

"Get a load of this guy, Bill. Is this what you have to put up with every day?" Judy was only joking, and Tony new it. The two families were as close as it gets.

"Hi, Uncle Tony. Where is Mouro and Sam?" Ian asked, desperate to see his buddies.

"They are waiting for you guys in the TV room," Tony answered.

Ian turned to his father, seeking his approval.

"Never mind him, Mouro. I'm the lieutenant here," Tony said, being, as always, the joker. "Off you go."

"Be careful, Lieutenant. I might just let you keep them," Bill joked.

"You two!" Judy shook her head. "Maria, here are the kids' pyjamas. They have already bathed, and don't take any nonsense from them."

"It's a no problem. Don't worry," Maria replied in her broken English.

"Rose! At last the 'Lady of the Manor.'" Bill was teasing. "And looking stunning, if I may say so."

"You may," Rose joked as Bill gave her a kiss on the cheek. "Hi, Judy. Say what are we going to do with these two jokers.?"

"Let them treat us to an expensive dinner at Brochities."

* * *

Frank cut the gas at the underground car park of Grovner Apartments.

"A pretty fancy location," Terry commented. *"Different from the Bronx, I must say!"*

"Yes, it's a bit pricy, but these days, you only get what you pay for. It's only a one-bedroom studio, but it's enough for a bachelor. Like you, I do my own thing and enjoy my own company, but don't be too impressed. You might get a shock when you see my interior decor."

"Deja vu." Terry laughed. "It looks like we have a lot in common."

Frank grinned. "Except I'm a man, and you're a beautiful woman."

"Are you sending me message?"

"I'm not in the closet if that's what you mean, but you can never tell these days."

"Well, that's a relief, and I don't think! *He . . . He . . . He . . .*" Terry was bursting a gut. "I'm stoked."

Frank parked the car in his designated slot then cut the engine before turning to face her, staring straight into her eyes.

"They must haves broken the mould when they made you." He had that serious expression.

"So, what gives you that impression?"

"Well . . ." He smiled with an impish look. "You're witty, highly intelligent, and above all, your personality is genuinely warm."

"My god, is this a proposal or something?" Terry teased.

"Now do you see what I mean?" He was laughing. "Listen, beautiful, I think we had best get out of this car or that pizza will be past its 'use by date.'"

*   *   *

"Bye, Mother." Rose gave her mother a kiss on the cheek. "We should be home by say . . . eleven thirty." She glanced at her watch. "What do you think, Tony?"

"Yeah, we shouldn't be much later."

"Now, Mother, you have my cell number, and if there are any problems, don't hesitate to call me." Rose gave her mother that stern look, fully knowing her words were going in one ear and out the other.

"Thanks again, Mrs. Borgetti, for babysitting the kids," Judy called as she was leaving.

"I'm only too happy to give the young ones a chance to enjoy themselves and get a break from the children. *You deserve it!*"

"Nevertheless, thanks again, Maria."

"The young ones, huh?" Bill liked the sound of that. "That reminds me of that Cliff Richard song."

"Who the hell is Cliff Richard? Any ideas, Tony?" Judy was being jovially sarcastic.

"Some Brit that's probably on the aged pension by now."

As always, Tony brought the house down; and everyone burst into laughter, except, of course, our friend Bill.

"Come now, darling. Don't take it to heart." Judy felt a bit guilty at belittling her husband and gave him a hug and a reassuring peck on the cheek.

"Are you two love birds finished?" Tony was being politely impatient. "I told Mario we would be there by eight thirty, and if we want to make it on time, it looks like we might have to use the siren." Of course, he was only joking.

"Oh no, you don't! Not tonight, buddy." Bill dived in. "I have enough driving you around all day, every day!"

"Judy, where did you find this guy?"

"Come on, you two. We'll use the Jeep, and that's it, settled." Rose dropped the final curtain.

"Bye, Mother."

* * *

As the party walked to the Cherokee, Tony couldn't help but think how lucky Bill and he was having married these two beautiful creatures.

* * *

Rose, was absolutely stunning in her black fitted knee-length dress, emphasizing her slim shapely figure as the result of yoga classes and "easy" on the pasta, which for Italian women is a real challenge. Somehow heels seem to add to the female beauty, and Rose's four-inch black open-toed shoes ticked all the boxes. Her shoulder-length back hair, olive skin, and large brown eyes complemented her narrow facial features and high cheekbones. Tonight, *she was absolutely stunning!*

As for Judy, she had a slightly fuller figure that suited her being tall, but her dark blue dress blended well with her Anglo-Saxon complexion and natural blonde hair cut in a sort of Posh Beckham style. Of course, it was competition time for "the heels," and Judy's five-inch beauties sent her past the post by a "short nose." As for her olive-shaped pale blue eyes, sharpish nose, and full lips, *well,* they say a picture paints thousand words; and Judy filled the tab completely.

As Bertrand Russell said, *"Everyman wherever he goes is encompassed by a cloud of comforting convictions which move with him like flies on a summer' day."*

* * *

The pizza aroma was to die for, and Terry couldn't wait to sink her teeth into that crusty thin pastry. What with today's events and skimping on her lunch, she could literally eat a horse. They quickly stepped it out to the elevator, with Terry almost dragging Frank by the hand.

"Either you must be hungry or I'm in big trouble." Frank laughed as they stood in the elevator.

"Well?"

"Well, what?" He turned to Terry inquisitively. *"Aren't you going to press the button?"*

"What am I thinking about?" Frank answered embarrassingly.

"I can just imagine!" Terry gave a naughty smile.

The elevator chimed. "Here we are and not before time. The next problem is my apartment key."

Frank gingerly passed Terry the pizza box while he searched his Levis.

"6C, here we are." He opened the door and switched on the lights. "Just put the pizza on the breakfast bar. I might have to fire it up in the micro."

* * *

Terry was taken aback at the sparsely furnished apartment. The loungecum-kitchen was small, with a sliding glass wood partition door separating the bedroom. It was open, and Terry could see the neatly made double bed with one side table and bedside lamp. The walls were bare, and the double sofa and one chair to match in the so-called lounge had all the hallmarks of an unimaginative bachelor pad. But there was one thing for sure. This guy didn't have a live-in partner. *No woman would suffer this prison cell!*

* * *

"Make yourself at home, Terry, while I reheat the pizza. Say, do me a favour and grab two glasses from the kitchen cupboard, the one above the stove."

"And the wine?"

"In the refrigerator." Frank was busy setting the microwave.

"I'm sorry we will have to stand and eat at the breakfast bar as I haven't gotten round yet to buying chairs or even a coffee table." He poured the wine then offered a slice of the artery-blocking Margarita.

"Hmmm, this is good." Terry sank her teeth into Italy's finest. "Boy, was I hungry!"

"Have another one." He pushed the plate toward her.

"I'll get there. Don't worry." Terry took a sip of her wine.

"So, what do you think of the place?" Frank asked.

Terry burst into laughter.

"That bad, huh?"

"Let's just say it's different."

"Maybe . . . That is, if you don't mind. You can help me to go shopping and pick some stuff to make it more homely. I don't have a clue, as you have already assessed, and I would really appreciate the 'woman touch.'" "Yeah, in more ways than one." It was too good to miss.

"I deserved that." Frank grinned. "But seriously . . ."

"Frank," Terry interrupted, "why don't we grab a seat on that sofa. I'm sure you would agree it would be more comfortable than standing here getting cramps."

"Oh, I'm sorry, Terry." He looked toward the half-eaten pizza.

"No, I'm good."

"Now isn't that more comfortable?" Terry commented as she sank onto the soft cushion.

They were both awkwardly holding their wine glasses, and Terry began to laugh.

"I see what you mean, Terry, and what would I do for a coffee table right now!"

"Don't worry. It's not all that bad." Terry finished the last of her wine and rose to place her empty glass on the breakfast bar.

"You're not leaving already, are you?" Disappointment was reflecting through Frank's voice. "Tomorrow is Saturday and no work, remember?" It was his last-ditch stand.

"Darling, I would love to stay longer, but it's been one of these days, and I'm absolutely bushed."

"I understand." Frank reluctantly agreed. "Then how about tomorrow night?"

"A better suggestion. Why don't we discuss it in the car? At the moment, all I can think about is bed. And no smartass remarks please."

*   *   *

Frank drove into the hospital car park and pulled up next to Terry's Mazda. There were plenty of places at this time of night. The car park was almost empty.

For a moment, there was a pregnant silence as they both searched uncomfortably for the right words.

Terry began, "Frank, I really enjoyed tonight." "Did you really?" he answered, feeling uneasy.

"Of course, I did!"

"Then is that 'a have' that I pick you up tomorrow?"

"I tell you what. You have my phone number. Why don't you give me call?"

Then out of the blue, she leaned over and gave him an unexpected kiss on the cheek.

"Listen, I gotta go and thanks again for the lovely evening." She squeezed his hand reassuringly and opened the car door. "Ciao."

Frank waited patiently until Terry reversed her car then followed her to the car park exit. *I guess once a security guard, always a security guard.* He could see her wave through her rear windscreen and acknowledged it, flashing his headlights as she disappeared into the evening traffic. Then he sat for a moment, his train of thought still with Terry. Was she really interested in him or was he just another casual acquaintance that she met under unusual circumstances when she needed a shoulder to cry on? But there was one thing for sure. He wasn't going to hang up the gloves just yet.

* * *

The ride to Brochities was more than noisy with the two "mothers" sitting in the rear talking about kids, unfaithful husbands, and any other juicy gossip they could conjure, not to mention "the bitchy" cooking classes. Tony turned to Bill and made one of his faces and was about to make a comment when he felt the vibration of his cell phone, and with one hand on the wheel, he gingerly searched inside his jacket; and when he opened his phone, he immediately recognized the number. *It was the captain of detectives, Ted Baker.*

"Perino here . . . Yes, Ted?"

"Tony, I have some good news on the Williams woman, and I thought I would fetch you in from the cold. It's like this. The DA has just phoned to inform me that his niece has regained consciousness." "When did this happen?" Tony interrupted.

"According to the hospital, about an hour ago. Now that's the good news, but the bad news is that she is not allowed any visitors except for the parents. She is too frail, and stress or excitement could easily send her back into relapse."

"Is there an indication from the doctor when we can interview her?"

"Probably Monday or Tuesday of next week. But a further complication has arisen in that she can't speak as the result of the damage to her larynx. The doc, according to Murray, informed him that with special vocal training, she could partially regain her voice in probably six to seven months."

"Boy, that's rich. Is there any more *good* news?" Tony was being sarcastic. "No, that's as bad as it gets."

"Then I guess it will have to be the old pencil-and-paper routine. One more thing, Ted, before you hang up. Did you get that warrant for Summers's arrest?"

"Yeah, it's on your desk. You can move on that first thing Monday."

"Say, Ted, I almost forgot. I'm throwing a barbecue at my place on Sunday, and I wondered if you and Ruth could make it? Sorry for the short notice, but with the Williams case and all, it just slipped my mind."

"So who else is on your hit list?" Baker joked. The memory of Tony's last barbecue is still fresh in his mind.

Tony laughed at Ted's comment. He could well remember his boss having "one too many."

"Oh, the usual gang."

"Listen, I'll have to come back to you. I don't know if Ruth has anything on this weekend, but as for me? No more said."

"Bring your board shorts. The weather bureau forecasts it's going to be hot one."

"What with my figure!" He could hear Baker laughing. "Ciao." "Baker on the line, huh?" Bill asked.

"I hope you two are not talking shop," Rose protested.

"I'll tell you later, Bill." Tony spoke under his breath, purposely making sure his voice was inaudible to the rear. "Naw, just a friendly call from my boss. *And guess what?* We have just arrived at your favourite restaurant."

* * *

Tony pulled into the "Loading Only" and "No Parking Zone." *Being a cop, there had to be some benefits.* He opened the glove compartment and took out the large yellow NYPD sign and placed it against the windshield.

Rose shook her head. *This Tony . . .*

"You know you are breaking the law, don't you?" Rose yelled from the back.

"Yeah, but we are legally breaking it!" Bill beat Tony to the punch.

"That's ma man." Tony laughed. "Now, my lovely wife, more importantly, are we going to eat or are you going to call the traffic cops?" Bill was trying to control his laughter. "Tony Perino, *you're incorrigible!"*

* * *

Brochities on Broome in the Canal district is known for its fine Italian fare and Pasteria, with profiteroles to die for; and Friday evening, as usual, was bustling with diners enjoying the street experience in true European style. As the Perino party danced their way through the tables to the entrance, the two beautiful signorias were turning a few heads, and why not? Married mothers with children rarely get a second glace, even from their husbands, but tonight was their night; and they were basking in the sun.

Mario Ambrosino, the manager, had already spotted Tony and was there to greet them at the entrance.

"Hey, Tony! Bonasera, come stai." He gave Tony the usual bear hug and the double cheek job.

"Benny Gratsi," Tony replied with a warm smile.

"And, Rose, che Bella Donna. Tony, where have you been hiding this beautiful wife of yours?" He gave Rose the Italian treatment.

"Mario, you remember Bill and his wife?" Tony asked.

"Si, of course. It's so nice to see you both again. Now more important, where would you prefer a table . . . inside in the air-conditioning or the alfresco gardenia?"

Rose was first past the post. "In this humidity?" She shook her head and turned to Judy, making a face.

"*The air-conditioning!*" Judy laughed.

"Ciao, Bella. This way." Mario got the message. A woman's makeup is everything, and in this humidity, it's not to be messed with.

* * *

The restaurant was jam-packed, but for "the long arm of the law," Mario knew his priorities. In Little Italy, the Mafioso is a feared household name, and to have contacts in the NYPD was as good an insurance policy as it gets.

The restaurant was typical Italian. You know? Traditional checked red and-white tablecloths, the candle-laden Chianti bottles, portraits of the pontiff and Mussolini Square, the waiters scurrying around in their black aprons and white short-sleeved shirts. And Mario snapped his fingers as the party took their seats.

"Aldo will be your waiter tonight, and, Tony, should you need anything, anything at all, just holler."

"Thanks, Mario." Ambrosino smiled then hastily disappeared toward the kitchen.

"Signor, would you wish to start with an aperitif?" Aldo was attentively waiting for his instructions.

"Bill, as tonight is a special occasion, I mean when was the last time we did this?"

"You're right, Tony. So?"

"Something cold and sparkling, darling," Rose interrupted as usual. "Like Prosecco Di Valdobbiadene."

"Get a load of this gal, Bill. She even tells me the wine to order."

"Then that's it, settled, darling." She gave Judy a cheeky wink. "And, Aldo, make sure it's nice and chilled."

"Si, signorina."

Roma women take no prisoners, and Tony? Well, he knew when to surrender.

"Si, signor, here are the menus. I will return shortly with the wine."

"Hell, Rose, I don't know how you could even pronounce that." Bill couldn't help himself, and the laughter was spontaneous.

*   *   *

The antipasti, rock melon, and prosciutto, not to mention the veal and the excellent pasta, the "Italian experience," between good friends was a roaring success, especially for "the neglected housewives."

"So, what's for dessert?" Tony asked as the clock was ticking, and the way things were going, they would be the last to switch off the lights. But his protest appeared to fall on deaf ears, especially with the ladies yakking ten to the dozen. It was like they had everything in the world to talk about and not enough time to say it. Of course, not forgetting "the good, the bad, and the ugly" detective husbands; and it appeared it was a lost cause until Tony lifted his empty wine glass and struck it with his spoon, it's ringing noise infusing immanent silence

"Guys, I apologize for being a giant pain in the butt, but it's after twelve and the kitchen will be closing in around thirty minutes. So, if you still want to destroy your lovely figures and that includes you, Bill, how about placing your orders for dessert?" The women burst into laughter.

"Speak for yourself, Perino. That waist of yours is taking a bit of a beating."

"It's all that diner junk food, Bill, but do you think he listens?" Rose just had to take the shot. But like a well-trained Italian husband, Tony knew "when to fold them and knew when to hold them."

"Aldo." Tony wasn't going to let it go. "Ladies, last call. What's it gonna be?"

"Si, signor." Aldo was there in a heartbeat.

"Rose honey?"

"Cassata and a cappuccino . . .

"Judy?"

"I'll have . . ."

*   *   *

"Ladies." Tony took the last sip of his double espresso; he was about to unleash his well-rehearsed speech. "I'm sure we all agree that we have had a very enjoyable evening. How can I put it? Good food, excellent wine, and above all great company and of course two beautiful signorinas. I mean what more can a two sinful handsome guys ask for?"

Rose knew her husband like the back of her hand, and she gave a pronounced impatient sigh. This guy was up to something.

"Tony, cut the drama. I know you have something up your sleeve, so please, please take us out of our misery."

"Honey, as always, you have an annoying habit of stealing my thunder." Tony was showing his colours, but then he should have known better. *"A leopard can never change its spots."* And he took a deep breath.

'Okay . . . Where do I start?"

"Honey." Rose sighed again impatiently. "I hope this not another of your sick jokes?"

"Rose, believe me, it's not. This is the call." He sighed again. "It's like this. I have some bad news that relates to one of our close friends, and dare I say that it's extremely important that it's kept confidential, at least until the shit hits the fan."

Tony's "call" put the cat among the pigeons, and there was immediate silence.

Rose gave Judy "that look" and shrugged her shoulders.

"It's our neighbour, Mike Summers."

"So, is it a parking ticket or something?"

"Rose, *for Christ's sake, be serious!"* Now Tony was really losing it. "Can I? He shook his head. "I am sure you have read the news headlines and the media hype on TV about the attempted murder of U.S. Senator Dave Williams's daughter."

Now he had the audience in the palm of his hand, and for a change, even Rose was quiet

"The bottom line is we have a warrant for his arrest for the attempted murder of Laura Williams."

"Jesus Christ, Tony!"

*   *   *

"Now you know the whole saga. June and the kids will be devastated. Make no mistake about it. This guy is gonna go down and go down hard with a long stretch in the can, and by the time he hits the streets, we will all be at least ten years older."

Rose was devastated. *"My god!* What will Judy do? Financially, she will be vaporized. What with the kids' schooling, the mortgage, and all that stuff, not to mention the paparazzi wolves? Can you just imagine the effect on these kids?"

"Yeah." Tony nodded in agreement. "And, ladies, that's where you come in. There's no telling what June will do, and she is going to need your support.

Believe me, this his is serious shit, and Bill and I can confirm that it's not unusual for suicidal tendencies to creep in as the result of extreme depression, and the paparazzi will dig up any shit they can find to sell newsprint. You know the stuff. The unfaithful husband, not to mention the string of lovers who will jump on the bandwagon for fame and fortune with Dr. Phil and even Oprah to get in on the act. This is a big bang when it comes to a U.S. senator and the niece of the DA."

*   *   *

"*Maria,* you are still up." Tony greeted his mother-in-law, dressed in her housecoat, as she met him at the door. "Do you know what time it is?" He was shaking his head in disbelief.

"Mamma Mia . . . Non sei stanco . . . I no tired." Maria brushed Tony's comment aside. "Of course, I know the time, but I wait for my daughter to come home safely or cannot sleep."

"Bill, can you believe this mother-in-law of mine? Her daughter is married to a cop, and she still worries."

"Just ignore him, Maria," Bill's wife interrupted "But seriously, Maria, Bill and I want to thank you for babysitting the boys tonight. It was a really nice gesture."

"Gratsi . . . It's a no problem. The boys, they were good, but now I must leave you young ones . . . Devo andare a dormire . . . How you say in English . . . I must go to bed?" She turned and left for the stairs. "Buona notte."

Tony had to laugh. "I tell you, Bill, if you visit us often enough, you will be speaking fluid Italian in no time."

Rose smiled at her husband's remark. "Would you believe it, Judy? My mother arrived here from Italy over thirty years ago, and she still has trouble with her English. But listen, would you guys like to stay for a nightcap before you hit the road?"

"Thanks, Rose, but I think it's time to call it a night. Besides, with no kids, who knows this could be our second honeymoon." Bill gave Judy a sly wink, which she purposely ignored. "You wouldn't wish to adopt two more kids, would you?" Bill laughed.

"Get out of it, Hayden. I have enough when I adopted their father."

Bill couldn't control himself and was laughing all the way to the car.

"Get a load of this guy!" He was shaking his head. "Tony, I'll pick up the kids around ten, if that's okay?"

"No sweat."

"Ciao, Rose. Ciao, Tony." Bill waved as he walked to the Pontiac, smiling as he opened the car door for Judy, then broke into Rodger Millers lyric. "I'm a man of means by no means. King of the Road."

* * *

The drive home was laced with the usual chitchat. You know? The food, the restaurant, Tony's crazy jokes; but below the facade, there was a hidden tension, the reality striking home that one of their close friends was about to be arrested for attempted murder.

* * *

Bill stretched over and reassuringly grasped his wife's hand.

"Honey, I know what's going through that mind of yours, but that's how it is. Look at it this way. We have had a fantastic evening with Rose and Tony, and what more can we ask for and more to the point, getting a break from the kids and some badly needed 'chill-out time'? Honey, you know how much I love you?"

Judy gave a half-hearted smile and squeezed his hand in return.

"I know, darling. It's just that I wish Tony had never—"

"Honey," he interrupted, *"please let it go!* It was Tony's call, and under the circumstances, it was a good time after dinner to unload, and besides he *genuinely* is concerned for June and the children. Now how about 'come on baby light my fire'?"

"Bill Hayden, you're incorrigible. But then again." A cheeky smile crossed her face. "*Hmmmm*, and no kids tonight, huh?"

"That's more like the woman I married." Bill signalled and pulled into the drive. "Madam, we have arrived, and please don't leave your glass slipper on the doorstep."

Judy leaned over and pressed her lips hard against his. "Bill Hayden, did I ever tell you how much *I love you?*"

"Yes, but you can tell me again in bed." Bill was stifling his laughter.

"Why you!"

* * *

He turned the Yale and quickly switched on the lights. The house seemed so empty without the kids around. When they are home, they can be a pain in the butt, but when there not, you really miss them. But tonight, as Judy jokingly mentioned, was a chance, although brief, for a second, shall we say, "honeymoon"; and Bill wasn't going to waste it, and he gingerly closed the door. Then out of the blue, a sudden urge of passion made him grab Judy's arm, stopping his lovely wife in her tracks while at the same time turning her around to face him. Then for some reason, he paused for a moment and stared straight into her pale blue eyes and kissed her. As they passionately brushed their lips, the testosterone was off the scale, and Judy could feel the warmth of his love flowing through her veins and the moistness between her loins.

"God, I love this beautiful woman!" Bill blurted out, unable to control his emotions as he pressed ever harder against her firm abdomen. Judy couldn't help but feel his erection through her flimsy dress, and she gently levered him apart. This was not the time or place for a married couple to get all hot and bothered when there was a perfectly good bed in the matrimonial room.

"Why, Bill Hayden, you young buck!" Judy was shaking her head, laughing. "This brings back memories of our wild college days."

"Oh, is that so!" Bill smiled, with a touch of "macho pride."

"Save it for bed, *mister!*" Judy teased as she turned toward the stairs. "I'm in the shower first, so why don't you cool it and give me fifteen? You'll be surprised what I have in store for you."

Bill laid on the "disappointed" face. "Well, if that's the case, I might as well have a cold one." He commented miserably as she climbed the stairs, and he just couldn't help staring at her sexy bottom. "Honey, did I ever tell you that you have a beautiful butt?"

"Oh, no, you're not pulling that old one again. Go cool it and have your beer, *and only one!* You know alcohol gives you ED, don't you?"

"'Not tonight, Josephine.'" He quoted the famous Napoleon cliche, a cheeky smile on his face as he disappeared into the kitchen. That cold beer was getting more attractive by the minute, *but then so was the tantalizing, Judy!*

*   *   *

Bill opened the refrigerator and collected his favourite brew, but as he was about to close the door, he happened to notice the lonely bottle of Italian sparkling Prosecco that Tony had given him for his last birthday. He had been saving it for a special occasion, and what better occasion than tonight, in reminiscence of his and Judy's first night together.

"Now where's that ice bucket?" he muttered in frustration as he searched the cupboards. *"Ah, here we are!"* He breathed a sigh of relief as he placed the pewter container on the breakfast bar. *After all, without an ice bucket, Italy's finest just wouldn't be the same!* The bottle was cold but not chilled, and Bill held the bucket below the ice machine and pressed the lever, the cubes rattling into the empty container. He winced and made a face then listened for a moment to hear if Judy had heard that unearthly racket. *"Good!"* He grinned as he forced the bottle into the bucket, continually swiveling it until it submerged into a jacket of ice. *"Now that that's done, it will take around ten minutes to chill, and it's about time I had that cold beer."* He grinned as he popped the tab then gulped a mouthful, wiping the overspill froth from his mouth.

"Bill, *what's taking you so long?"* Judy was getting frustrated. Her biological clock wasn't going to last forever.

"Coming, honey." He yelled at the top of his lungs then swallowed the last of his precious Bud before opening the garbage compressor, tossing in the empty can. Judy was a stickler for keeping the kitchen pristine, and that means *no empty beer cans!*

"Wow, this ice bucket is cold," he spoke out loud as he switched off the kitchen lights. "God damn it!" He stopped in his tracks. *"I almost forgot the glasses!"* He shook his head in frustration and quickly switched back the lights before rushing to the overhead kitchen cabinet to collect the elusive champagne flutes.

"Bill, *what's keeping you?"*

"I'm on my way, honey . . . I'm on my way . . ." He yelled, almost stumbling in his haste to climb the stairs. "Shit, that would be all I need, dropping this fucking champagne bucket! "Now for the next balancing act, to open this bloody door!"

"Bill . . ."

"For Christ's sake . . . Gimme a break!"

"Darling, what was that? I couldn't quite hear you."

"Maybe just as well, huh?" He spoke under his breath as he held the glasses below his the arm, precariously grasping the frozen ice bucket. *"If I don't open this door soon, I'll be getting fucking frostbite."*

At last, he turned the doorknob and pranced into the bedroom, proud as punch, sporting the champagne flutes in one hand and the ice bucket in the other. *"Ta da ta . . ."* He sang.

Judy was lying in bed on her side in the "Angelina Jolie pose." You know, the naked sexy leg exposed up to her thigh, just stopping short before the ultimate prize. She was resting on her elbow, half sitting up, her hand supporting her chin, the bedsheet had fallen to her waist, exposing her voluptuous breasts, her large pink nipples silhouetting through her black see through nightdress. The fragrance of her Chanel was delicate and sensuous, and Bill just stood there for a moment as if frozen in time in sheer awe at this beautiful creature he had married and had taken for granted in the haze of everyday marriage.

Judy tried not to laugh at this big guy standing there like a little kid waiting for an encore.

"Christ, honey, you *are* gorgeous!" He couldn't control himself

"And you are an absolute darling, champagne and all, you big heel." Judy was finding it hard to keep a straight face. "Now drop that bucket and hit that shower or else . . ."

CHAPTER 2

Terry yawned and covered her mouth with her hand then stretched full out, giving a satisfying *"Mmmm . . ."* before turning toward the sliver of sunlight from the gap in the blind as it caught her face and she screwed up her eyes, quickly shading them.

"I wonder what time it is?" she spoke aloud. *"By the looks of that sun, I might just get a shock."* She turned to glance at the bedside clock. *"I thought so."* She threw her feet to the carpeted floor. *"Almost eleven thirty. But what the hell! I have no work today. It's Saturday, and boy, am I looking forward to a lazy weekend in my own company."* She stretched both arms above her head, clasping her hands before pulling them sideways. *"Hmmm and does that feel good! Boy, I could easily roll over and slip below these sheets . . . But?*

There again that freshly brewed coffee, and a slice of crispy full grain toast is too tempting."* She gave a satisfied smile as she rose to her feet and left for the open lounge and kitchen. She was a woman on a mission, dressed in her loose white silk pyjamas, the top three buttons undone as if on purpose, just revealing enough breast to make it interesting and with that unruly shoulder length blonde hair, Terry would look sexy in no matter what. She is just one of these lucky broads that has it all.

It was heading for another hot and humid balmy New York summer's day, but the air-conditioned apartment was a pleasant sixty-five; and she opened the blinds to let the bright sunlight stream through the hazed glass.

"I must get that window cleaner a call. It's embarrassing. I've seen cleaner windows on the subway trains, and that's saying something!"

She was still shaking her head as she poured a half cup of Costa Rico beans from the Tupperware and opened the coffee grinder, it's annoying high-pitched noise disturbing the solitude as it assassinated the beans to powder.

"Now where did I put that coffee perk? Of course, what am I thinking about?" She was talking to herself as she swung the stainless-steel front of the dishwasher open. *"Ah, here we are!"* She held the glass container to the light to ensure it was clean then emptied the contents of the grinder. The tantalizing aroma of freshly ground beans was clouding the air, and within seconds, the water was on the boil.

The coffee, the toast, all that was missing now was the morning paper; and she quickly removed it from under the door. *After all, breakfast wouldn't be the same without the "full house," so to speak.* But now it was time to relax, and she slipped onto the barstool and opened the *Times* before sinking her teeth into the crispy bread chased by a mouthful of coffee.

"Hmmm . . . This *is* good . . . Now what's front-page news today?" She unfolded the "ink rag," and there in triple print was the eye catcher:

U.S. SENATOR'S DAUGHTER REGAINS CONSCIOUSNESS . . . Laura Williams, the daughter of Senator Dave Williams, the often-outspoken Republican from Capitol Hill, and the niece of District Attorney Jake Murray, received some good news yesterday from Roosevelt Memorial . . .

Terry almost dropped her coffee mug, choking on her mouthful of toast.

"I can't believe my eyes!" She spluttered out, trying to clear her throat. "How the hell can these news dogs get this information? There must be some cops on 'the take.' It's just gotta be." She was furious to the point that her hands were trembling. "So much for catching the bastard that did this. He'll be long gone, heading for Tijuana and Enchiladas. Are these news nuts for fucking real?" She swallowed another sip of her now tepid coffee to calm down. "How to sell papers?" She was still shaking her head in disbelief.

The loud ring of the phone momentarily subdued her anger and maybe just as well.

"Now who the hell can this be? *Can't a gal get some chill-out time?*" She threw the newsprint aside and snatched the phone from its cradle. Whoever was on the other end of the line was about to get an earful.

"Terry Johnson . . ." she barked.

"Is that a Ms. Terry Johnson?" It was a woman's voice, cool, calm, and subdued, with a soft and gentle tone. Whoever it is wasn't rising to the bait.

"Yes, and at the thought of being rude, may I ask who the hell is calling?"

There was a longer-than-normal pause as if the recipient of Terry's verbal abuse had taken the wind from their sails.

"Listen, if this is some lowlife news reporter looking for a scoop, you can go and take a hike!"

"Err hmmm . . ." There was an apprehensive reply. "I am sorry to trouble you, Ms. Johnson, and I can well understand your sentiment and antipathy at being disturbed at home. From your hostile reaction, I can only assume that you are being pestered by the tabloids for confidential information as regards my daughter's private life."

The penny dropped and the old saying "Who speaks in haste bites his tongue" was so timely; and Terry was literally looking for a place to crawl.

"Mrs. Williams . . . *Ummm . . . Err* . . . What can I say . . ." Terry was searching for the right words, which, as always, are never availed? She nervously began, "Words can't express how embarrassed I feel. Please accept my deepest apologies for my inexcusable rudeness?"

"Terry, you don't have anything to be remorseful about. It's a small thing. In fact, it is I who should apologize to you for not contacting you earlier to thank you for your perseverance and support you gave our daughter in her time of need in what was diagnosed as an unpromising outcome."

"It was nothing, Mrs. Williams. I always knew she would pull through."

"The good news is that although she is still in recovery, she has a strong will and high in spirit, but above all, even though she can't speak, she keeps writing on paper that she dearly wants to see her best friend."

"Mrs. Williams . . ."

"Please call me Margaret."

"Eh . . . Margaret . . . Inform her that I'll be their mid-afternoon."

"Thanks, Terry, for everything. Dave and I would love to have you over for dinner one evening, when you are free. It's the least we can do . . ."

"Thanks, Margaret, but for the moment, I'll have to take a rain check."

"I understand, and our thanks again. Bye."

Terry placed back the phone and thought quietly for a moment. Of course, she would visit her friend today; but she was looking forward to a "lazy slob day," throwing diet to the wind and just indulging in her own company, cheesy lasagne, and a bottle of French sauvignon blanc. *But if Laura needs me?* she spoke out loud. *Don't worry, honey. I'm here for you.* The phone rang again.

"What the hell now?" But this time, she was keeping her cool, "once bitten, twice shy," as they say.

"Yes, Terry speaking?"

"So formal" came the reply.

"And who may I ask is on the line?"

"Don't tell me that you don't recognize my voice? I am mortally wounded."

Terry screwed up her face and furrowed her eyebrows. "Who is this joker?" She covered the mouthpiece, there was no answer. "Okay . . . Okay, I give in. But this had better be good, *mister.*"

"Boy, I wouldn't wish to get on your bad side! It's Frank, Frank Reynolds, your friendly security guard. *Remember?*" He could hear Terry suddenly burst into laughter.

*   *   *

The phone rang, and Mike awkwardly stretched over to switch on the bedside lamp before fumbling for the receiver and in the process almost dropping it to the floor.

"Yes?" he answered abruptly.

"Mr. Summers, your wake-up call."

"Err . . . Thank you." Mike glanced at the digital clock; it was 7:00 a.m. "Will that be all, sir?"

"Yes, thank you." He hung up.

Mike felt as if a horse had kicked him in the head, and he grimaced as he lay back on the pillow. It was the morning after the night before, and it felt as if his brain was bouncing around in his skull.

"Maaan . . . Do I feel like shit!" Mike was having a conversation with himself. "I can't even remember falling into bed last night. In fact, I'm surprised that I am even in my pyjamas. But . . ." He winced again as he raised his "eggshell" head, struggling to place his feet to the floor. "Now for 'the hair of the dog' as they say." His tongue felt like used sandpaper as he licked his parched lips and half staggered to the bar fridge, opening the door in search of the "rip-off" miniatures and his elusive bourbon. His hand trembled as he quickly broke the seal and emptied the precious contents into the short liquor glass then opened the ice container, digging his hand into the frozen cubes before chucking them into his favourite alcohol, its contents splashing in the air. He cringed again and placed the palm of his left hand over his forehead as he emptied the contents into his mouth in one throw then poured a second shot in honour of "alcoholic anonymous."

He coughed and spluttered. *"A . . . hi a hi."* As the raw bourbon bit his throat. "Who the fuck dreamt up that one . . . The hair of the dog, *my ass!* I feel *even* worse." Mike staggered on his "sea legs" and flopped onto the bed then lay staring blankly at the ceiling, his head still pounding and his mind still spinning.

*   *   *

He could hear a distant ring echoing in his ears. *It just wouldn't go away.* He screwed up his face as his clouded brain started to clear and his eyes fluttered and opening wide as he stared blankly at the ceiling.

Rrrrrring . . . Rrrrrring . . . "For Christ's sake, go away," he yelled. Then as if awaking from a dream, he suddenly sat bolt upright. "Hell, I must have dozed off." He leaned over and angrily grabbed the phone. *"Hello. Summers here."*

"Mike, when you didn't answer, I was getting worried. It's Mitch Wade here. I'm sitting in the hotel lounge. We had a meeting planned for nine thirty."

"I'm so sorry, Mitch. I just came back from my workout and had just finished showering when I received a call from a client in New York regarding a contract we signed last week. *And, man, could he talk! You know,* the usual legal questions after the event. But listen, Mitch, gimme ten, and I'll meet you in the coffee lounge. You'll be holding a large manila folder. Apologies again."
"Phew." Mike kicked off his pajamas and rushed to the shower.

*   *   *

He stared in the mirror to straighten his tie. Surprisingly, he didn't look all that bad, his liver as usual coping well with the alcohol abuse; and in record time, he was standing at the elevator.

The coffee lounge was busy at this time in the morning with tourists and the local retirees taking advantage of "half price" for seniors, not to mention the odd workaholic sipping his coffee, nose buried in complicated papers. "Can I help you, sir?" The maître d' sensed that Mike was searching for someone. But before he could reply, he spotted Mitch two tables in front with the conspicuous large manila folder under his arm.

"It's okay. I can see my friend." Mike didn't waste any time and briskly walked over to Wade's table. He could sense by the look on Mitch's face that this guy was uneasy.

"Mitch Wade? Mike Summers." Mike offered his hand as Wade rose to greet him.

This guy was tall at six two and heavy built, but in the right proportions. Mike's educated guess was that he was in his early fifties, the tell-tale shades of gray creeping through the temples of his dark brown unruly hair. He had these piercing grey eyes, the kind that immediately make you feel uncomfortable, but an advantage when you are negotiating. His face was narrow with a long jawline and nose to match. The tanned complexion was a giveaway that this guy enjoyed the good life and, as Chuck had mentioned, had the "readies" to back it up. He was dressed casually in a rather loud checked sports coat and white open-neck shirt and the "wouldn't be seen dead without" a solid gold Rolex.

"Coffee, Mike?" Mitch asked.

"Here, let me put it on my tab." Mike felt that it was only right as Mitch had been twiddling his thumbs for a least almost half an hour.

The maître d' spotted Mike's gesture and rushed to the table.

"Can I get you something, Mr. Wade?" *Money talks.*

"No, it's my call," Mike interjected. "Mitch?"

"A coffee is fine, and you, Mike?"

Mike smiled. "Make that coffees for two."

"Certainly, sir."

"Mike, I must say at such short notice the proposal you e-mailed from the flight is really creative. You must have worked nonstop."

"Not quite." Mike grinned, reflecting back to his bourbon score. "You seem to be well known here the way that maître d' reacted."

Mitch smiled. "Jack knows I'm a big tipper, but he also knows that I am a major shareholder in the Sheraton chain."

"I didn't know that." Mike was taken aback.

"Not many in the business fraternity know either. I purposely try to keep my dealings private. But down to the line, that's why the acquisition of this soft drink company is so interesting."

"Now I get it, the perfect distribution chain using Sheraton's worldwide outlets."

"You nailed it." Mitch had that larger-than-life "ten gallon" smile.

"I'll be darned. But getting back to the revenue statement and the company's balance sheet . . ."

*   *   *

"You certainly know your business. Chuck was spot on when he said you are the best."

Mike grinned. "It's early days, Mitch. As they say, 'the proof of the pudding is in the tasting.'"

"Digressing for a moment." Mitch changed the subject. "I see big mouth Senator Dave Williams is get getting plenty of print with the attempted murder of his daughter and will *he* use it to his advantage. *Bloody Democrat!* Hell, Mike, I hope you are a Republican!" Mitch felt a touch embarrassed, but it was out before he could bite his tongue."

Mike smiled, a forced smile; he had more things on his mind than politics.

"So?" Mitch was waiting for a reaction.

"Politics, religion, and good friends don't mix. At least that's what my father preached."

"A smart man and tactful with it."

"But I didn't catch the news this morning?"

"It's plastered all over the front page of the *New York Times.*'"

"Really?" Mike felt sick to his stomach, not knowing what to expect.

"Yeah, it seems that the daughter has miraculously recovered from death's door, and I guess she'll be doing the confession thing and spilling the beans on her assailant. With the father a senator and the uncle the DA, I wouldn't wish to be in that poor bastard's shoes when they arrest him. He'll be incarcerated for a hundred years after they throw the book at him . . . Are you all right, Mike? You look rather pale." Mitch could sense the sudden silence.

"No, I'm good. I should have ordered some breakfast. I guess I just overworked in the gym."

"Mike, *why didn't you say?* Listen, I'll leave you alone to enjoy the buffet. But before I go, what's your agenda for the rest of today?"

"Nothing much, I guess, except polishing up this proposal." He was not himself.

"A better suggestion . . . I'll get the chauffer to pick you up around seven, and you can relax and join Charlotte and me for dinner. There will be few business friends and their wives joining us, and it might be to your advantage."

"That's really hospitable of you, Mitch, but I'll feel like the third wheel. Are you sure I won't be intruding?"

"Not at all . . . Seven then . . ." Mitch rose to leave. "Don't overindulge. Remember, you have this evening . . ."

As soon as Mitch was out of sight, Mike raised his hand to draw the attention of the maître d'.

"Sir, how can I help?"

"Would it be possible to fetch me a copy of the *New York Times*?"

*   *   *

Tony had just finished breakfast with the kids and was about to call Bill when the phone rang."

"I'll get it, darling," Rose called from the lounge. She was having coffee with her mother and enjoying all the local gossip. After all, Maria, having lost her soul mate, had nothing better to do with her time. Loneliness is a scourge, and she just adored her grandkids.

"Perino residence . . . *Judy!* You must be practicing telepathy. I was just having a chat with Mother over coffee, and I mentioned that I was going to call you, then I had second thoughts. I didn't want to disturb you guys on your second honeymoon . . . *Ha . . . ha . . . ha . . .* Well, how was it without the kids? You take the fifth . . . *That good*, huh? What are you feeding that man of yours? Don't worry. Take your time. The kids have had their breakfast, and they are heading for the pool. *Hey,* no sweat. My mother loves to be wanted. Bill would like to speak to Tony. Sure, we can talk about it later. Ciao. *Tony* . . . it's Bill on the line."

"Coming. Hi, partner. So what's new? Yeah, it had crossed my mind. Judy can spend the afternoon with Rose and Maria. You know how these women love to yak, and besides, the boys are having a ball. Great minds think alike. That thought did cross my mind to go to the office and pick up that warrant, just in case Mike decides to do a runner. You can't trust secretaries, and besides, it gives us a chance to grab a beer 'away from the maddening crowd.' Okay, in about an hour then. Don't do anything I wouldn't do. Yeah, I believe you. Millions wouldn't. Ciao."

*   *   *

Judy was sitting at the breakfast bar, enjoying the last of her coffee, her sheer black nightdress leaving little to the imagination, her legs crossed, showing more thigh than Tina Turner.

"Honey, I told Tony that we would be over in around an hour."

"*Mm . . . Mm.*" She was engrossed in the front page of the *New York Times*.

"Are you listening, honey? Like we still have an hour." Bill had that look that Judy knew only too well.

"Oh no, you don't, *mister!* I know what's in that perverted mind of yours, and besides, I can hardly sit on my fanny after last night." She was both laughing and shaking her head at the same time. "Why don't you give your poor wife a break and go and take a cold shower."

"Okay. That's it! We go and see a divorce lawyer on Monday for failing to consummate our marriage on our second honeymoon and mental torture or, better still, sexual torture." Bill was cracking up, holding his sides.

Judy rose to her feet, trying to ignore his crazy remarks, and hide the smile from her face before throwing her arms around his neck and crushing his lips with a full frontal.

"I really love you, you big heel, and I wouldn't trade you for the world." Then she stood on her tiptoes and whispered in his ear, "Do you think you are up to it?"

"*Up to it!* Why you . . ."

She placed her fingers over is lips. "Cool it, big boy, and hit that cot. *We only have an hour!*"

*   *   *

"Well, Mr. Friendly Security Guard, why the call?"

"If you must know . . ." He burst into song. "*You are always on my mind . . . You are always on my mind . . .*" Terry just had to laugh. *This guy?*

"You aint no Willy Nelson, but I get the message." Now they were both laughing.

"Listen, gorgeous, I am finishing at two, if you are interested?" "And if I am?" Terry was just teasing.

"I thought I could come over and pick you up."

"I beg your pardon . . . *pick me up?*"

"*You know what I mean!*"

"*Oh, do I now?*" Terry was playing it to the fullest.

"Awe, come on, honey. Give this love-forlorn guy a break."

"Well, if you put it that way." He could hear her laugh again.

"So when can I expect you?"

"I can't tell you."

"Stop fooling around. Why can't you tell me?"

Now it was Frank's turn. "*Because you never gave me your address!*"

The thought made Terry burst into uncontrollable laughter, almost losing her breath.

"*Touché.* Do you have a pen and paper handy?"

"Gimme a sec. Okay, shoot."

"You Take West Street to just past the Holland Tunnel, and it's on the corner of Clarkson, overlooking the river. It's Brickfield Apartments 10A. If you happen to get lost, you have my number."

"Don't worry. I'm a born and bred New Yorker. *Remember?*"

"Yeah, I've heard that one before. So when?"

"Say around four. That will give me time to check out and get changed."

"Frank, before you hang up, I must visit Laura today. Her mother just phoned. Would you mind?"

"Of course not. No sweat. I'll drive you to the hospital. Besides, I want to see your friend as well."

"Frank, just bear with me, one other small thing. I'm stoked, and tonight I would rather stay at home and relax and watch some Fox. I bake a mean lasagne and with bottle of chilled Frascati, need I say more?" "I'm feeling hungry already. Can I fetch something?"

"Yes, yourself."

"I like the sound of that." Frank laughed.

"Four then, and don't be late . . ."

Terry hung up and placed the receiver against her temple, that certain smile on her face.

"I'm beginning to really like young Lochinvar." She smiled as she hitched the receiver back onto the kitchen wall phone then sat for a moment in silence, digesting her comment. "Enough of that. It's about time that I stop dreaming and get that lasagne going."

But whether Terry liked it or not, she was falling like a stone into a deep pool, *maybe too deep for comfort.*

*   *   *

The "honeymoon" reluctantly over, the mature love birds showered and dressed. There's nothing like rekindling the spark that everyday family life had placed on the back burner, for kids and career.

"You know, honey?" Bill smiled as he slipped into his slacks and tucked in his shirt before fastening his belt. "We have to do this more often." Then for a moment, the smile suddenly disappeared, and a more sombre-faced Bill continued, "I know that's a much-abused cliche with most married couples, but before we know it, if we don't do something about it now, we will find ourselves going our different ways. You, with nothing else on your mind but the kids, and me with my career. I know the kids are a handful, and I'm anything but guilt-free, what with the unruly hours that a detective's job demands. But, honey, I love you and I miss you. I miss the intimacy and warmth that we cherished before the kids came along, and there's nothing to stop us making a special effort to find that space again. It's so easy to say, 'I'm tired, honey. I've had a trying day with the kids.' Or inwardly think, 'It's just too much of an effort. I just want to relax and hit the sack.'"

Judy didn't let him finish, her eyes already tearing up, and she rushed over half dressed and threw her arms around his neck and gave him a more than passionate kiss.

"Darling." She gasped for air, pangs of guilt straining through her voice. "Please don't. We've had a beautiful night together. Please don't spoil it. I too feel the sadness in my heart. I've have been neglecting you, but last night made me realize what I have been missing, and I promise—" She never got to finish as Bill kissed her again. It was a long passionate kiss, that kiss that you gave your sweetheart before you were married and now almost forgotten.

"I love you, honey. Let's make this the first new day of our married lives." Judy gave him anther passionate kiss. "*You bet!*"

*   *   *

Bill was at the breakfast bar, pouring himself a mug of coffee while waiting for Judy to finish dressing and the "makeup" saga. The *New York Times* was sitting in front of him, and he casually unfolded it to read the front page.

"*Shiiit!* What the hell is this? 'U.S. SENATOR'S DAUGHTER REGAINS CONSCIOUSNESS. Laura Williams, the daughter of Senator Dave Williams, the often-outspoken Republican . . .' *I don't believe this!*" He grabbed the phone and dialled.

"Rose . . . Bill here. Can I speak to Tony?" He could hear Rose call in the background.

"*Tony . . . It's Bill on the line.* He'll just be a minute, Bill. He has his nose stuck the *Times*."

CHAPTER 3

Mike was stunned as he read the bold print.

I can't believe it! He was thinking to himself, his face now an ashen grey. *Laura recovered! And just how much has she told the police? Strange. There's not a mention from the DA's office. Like . . . "We have the name of the suspect who will be apprehended for questioning within the next twenty-four hours . . ." But then again?* He was trying to convince himself. *Maybe, just maybe, the coma has affected Laura's memory or she is just too fragile to be questioned by the police.*

But . . . No . . . I can't take the chance.

"*Is there anything else, sir? Is there anything else, sir?*"

The voice kept echoing in his ears as if someone was shouting down a tunnel.

"Sir, *is there something wrong? Are you feeling all right?*" There it was again.

It was as if he was looking through a thick blanket of fog that was slowly dispersing, and his brain began to clear as if he was walking from a smoke-filled room into the fresh air; and for a brief moment, he felt completely disoriented.

"Sir, would you wish me to call a doctor?" The maitre d' was now seriously concerned.

"Eh . . . Err . . . no. I take blood pressure pills, and stupidly this morning I forgot to take them." Mike was searching for a plausible excuse, somewhat embarrassed at his impromptu blackout. "I do apologize, and to make things worse, I've have just received some very discerning news about a very close friend."

Mike's forehead is now oozing droplets of nervous perspiration. He just had to get out of this restaurant. "Je veux sortir," as they say in French for, *I'm outta here!* In his haste to leave, he almost forgot Pierre, the maître d'. He turned around, much to Jack's relief and crushed a twenty into the palm of his hand.

"Thank *you*, Mr. Summers. Should there be anything you need . . .

Anything at all . . . Please don't hesitate to call."

"I'll keep that in mind, Pierre." Mike forced a smile then hurriedly left for the elevator, his mind racing ten to the dozen.

He fumbled for the key card, his hands still shaking. The aftershock still vibrating through his nervous system, and he quickly opened the door and crashed onto the bed, staring blankly at the ceiling. Somehow, he had to find a way to get out of this God-forsaken mess. But how? Then suddenly it came to him, and he sprang to his feet and rushed to the writing table to open his notepad computer.

"Let me see." He was talking to himself as he punched in an Internet search question. "Which Latin American countries have no extradition treaty with the United States?"

"Come on. Come on." He was scolding the computer. "At last! *Hmmm . . . Let me see . . .* Chile, Brazil, Argentina, and of course Cuba." He paused for a moment, his natural computer searching for a solution as he stared at himself in the mirror above the writing table and was taken aback at what he saw. *"Christ, Mike! You gotta calm down and think straight. You look like a fucking train wreck."* He was talking to himself again while running his fingers nervously through his hair. *"Get a grip, man!* First things first. I have to reschedule my return flight to New York." He grabbed the phone. "Let me see . . . Travel Services." He pressed the button.

"Front desk. How can I help you, Mr. Summers?" the gentleman asked.

"I'm sorry. I must have dialled the wrong number. But perhaps you can connect me to Travel Services?"

"Certainly, sir. Just bear with me for a few seconds while I transfer your call."

"Sheraton Travel Services . . . How can I help you, sir?" The lady with the soft voice politely inquired.

"My name is Mr. Mike Summers, room 1623. I have a flight confirmed with Delta Airways . . . Flight D17 to Kennedy at 1800hours on Monday,16. Unfortunately, due to unforeseen circumstances, I must now return to New York today."

"Can you give me your ticket number, sir?"

"I'm flying first class. My ticket number is D76500 . . ."

"Mr. Summers, this might take some time. I suggest that you hang up and I will return your call as soon as I can check out all flights that have vacant-seat capacity leaving West Palm for Kennedy today."

"Thank you, but please be as expedient as possible. Your name is?"
"Angie."

"Thanks, Angie."

"I understand, sir. Be assured I will do my very best . . ."

*   *   *

"Ruth, it's Tony here. I'm sorry to disturb you on a 'day of rest,' but it's important that I speak to that husband of yours."

"Not to worry, Tony. It's all part of the job. Just gimme a sec. He's in the garden, reading the morning news."

"*Tony don't tell me!* I know why the call. I've just read the headlines in the *Times and* believe me I'm as mad as hell."

"Ted, you gotta to get to Murray to stitch up his brother-in-law's big mouth. I know he is a senator, but is this guy crazy or something or just desperate for an Oscar? I mean, Ted, Summers will be already planning his 'escape from Alcatraz.'"

"For Christ's sake, Tony, *cool it!* When you drop this phone, I'll be on the blower to Murray, and believe me he'll get an earful."

"Well, I guess what's done is done. Bill's picking me up in around half an hour, and we are going to the office to get that warrant. You never know.

This guy might just be stupid enough to return to New York." "When is he originally scheduled to return?" Baker asked.

"His secretary confirmed he was on Delta 17 to arrive at Kennedy at 2100hours, Monday evening."

"Listen, I'll leave you with it, and I agree it's a good idea to have that warrant handy. Phone me should anything change. Ciao." The phone went dead.

Tony had just replaced the receiver and walked to the kitchen to finish his coffee when the phone rang again.

"I'll get it, honey," Rose called from the lounge. *"Tony . . . It's Bill on the line . . .* He'll just be a minute, Bill."

"Hold it, Bill. I know what you are calling about, and I've just been on the phone with Baker. You're on your way . . . In about thirty minutes . . . Yeah, he agrees that we should pick up the warrant as a contingency measure. Listen, we'll talk about it when you get here." Tony placed back the receiver, his face grim.

"What's up, darling? You look uptight."

"It's a long story, honey. I'll fill you in later." He glanced at his watch. "Listen, I had better get showered and dressed. Bill and Judy will be on our doorstep before we know it!"

*   *   *

Mike was feeling like a bear with a sore head. Only a few minutes had passed since he made the call, but it seemed like hours, and he impatiently stared at his watch as if counting every minute.

"Christ, I can't sit here and do nothing!" he spoke out loud. "It's now after ten, and the way things are going, I'll be lucky if I get a fucking flight before Christmas!" He was blowing air. "Take your time, Mike, and think!" he uttered to himself. "Money! *Of course, I need cash!"*

He lifted the phone again and pressed concierge.

"Mr. Summers, it's Bert here. How can I be of service, sir?"

"You *do* have a Citibank in West Palm, don't you?"

Bert was taken aback by the throwback rudeness. "Of course, sir, but only one," he replied with a touch of sarcasm in his voice . . . *touche.* "It's downtown on Lantana Road just before you arrive at Palm Beach Central Park Airport. It's around a twenty-minute taxi ride from the hotel. You can't miss it."

"Now the next question is, is the bank open for business on a Saturday?"

"Yes, but only until 1:00 p.m."

"Good! For once, I'm in luck. Bert, perhaps you can call a taxi for me?"

"A better suggestion, sir. Why don't you use the hotel limo, sir?" Bert wasn't slow when it comes to greenbacks.

"Even better . . . Can you arrange that?"

"Certainly, sir. I'll call you back." Bert had a large grin on his face. *"This has got to be worth at least a twenty."*

Mike gave a sigh of relief; his plan was beginning to take shape. Suddenly, the ear-piercing ring of the desk phone shattered his thoughts, and he made a grab at the receiver.

"Come on, honey. Let this be good news. Summers here."

"It's Angie from Travel. You're in luck, sir. I can transfer your first-class ticket to Delta 18 departing from West Palm Springs at thirteen hundred, arriving at Kennedy at eighteen hundred. Shall I give confirmation?"

"You certainly can, Angie. Nice Job, but that's only the start. I need you to check all flights departing from Kennedy this evening to Latin America, the later the better."

Angie was momentarily lost for words. *What kind of crazy request was that?* she thought.

"I'm sorry, Mr. Summers, and I do apologize, but could your repeat that request again?"

"I need you to check all flights . . ."

"I thought that was what you said, sir. It's just that it's a little bit unusual, if you don't mind me saying so."

"Angie, you don't have to apologize. I understand, but I would really appreciate your help. It's extremely important."

"Just give me some time, sir. And it must be this evening?" She still sounded unsure.

"Yes, it must be, and thanks again."

Within seconds of placing back the receiver, our friend Bert, the ingenious concierge, was on the line.

"Mr. Summers, your limo is ready, sir."

"Thanks, Bert. Give me around five minutes."

Mike opened his briefcase to double-check his check book and credit cards. Fortunately, he always carried his passport for identification purposes in case of emergencies.

"Okay, now let me see. Do I have everything?" He stopped short before opening the door. "Yep, I'm good."

He was feeling more relaxed as he stood in the elevator. With a wing and a prayer, he would be out of the country before midnight. How he would explain it all to June would be another nightmare, but he had made his bed. *Well, you know the rest.*

Bert was waiting patiently at the entrance, the rear door to the limo already open.

"I have instructed the driver, sir."

"Thanks, Bert." True to form, Mike slipped him a twenty."

"Thank you, sir." It disappeared faster than the eye could see. *Maybe Bert's was a "stand-in" for Breaking the Magician's Code.*

The West Palm Citibank branch was small, and being a Saturday, it was almost "sleepy valley," and Mike couldn't have asked for more. He just had to catch that 1:00 p.m. flight, and time was of the essence

"What can I do for you today, sir?" the pretty young teller asked with a smile that would make the Osmond's weep.

"I wish to make a cash withdrawal." Mike slipped the check under the security grill.

The teller studied the check thoroughly. "I see . . . Twenty thousand in cash, sir. That's quite a large sum of money. I will require a few minutes to check with the manager for security purposes as you are not a customer of this branch and, more so, from out of town."

Mike nodded in agreement. "I understand, but I would really appreciate if you can speed things up, as I have a New York flight to catch at 1;00 p.m."

The teller smiled and disappeared toward the manager's office. Jenkins agitatedly stopped what he was doing and looked up when herd the knock. It was getting near time, and he promised Jill, he would take her to lunch.

"Come in."

"I'm sorry to bother you, Mr. Jenkins, but I have a gentleman here from New York, requesting to cash a large check."

"*Yes . . . Yes . . . Yes . . .*" Jenkins rudely interrupted. "I don't have all day, Ms. Brown. Let me see the check. *Hmmm . . . It is* a rather large sum in cash. I'll ring up the New York branch, but . . . checking his account on the screen." He had entered Mike's branch and account number. "He has sufficient funds, but only just." He lifted the phone and dialled the operator. "Can you connect me to New York . . ."

Mike was getting impatient. *"Christ!* Why is it taking so long?"

"Hi, Les. It's Jenkins here from West Palm Springs. I have one of your customers here with an unusual request to withdraw a large . . .' The young teller returned to her desk, a smile on her face.

"I'm pleased to inform you, Mr. Summers, that your check has been cleared, but I need to see two forms of identification."

Mike reluctantly smiled and opened his briefcase and placed his passport under the grill. Then he fumbled into his wallet to produce his New York driving license.

The girl studied the documents for a moment then produced a satisfied smile.

"That's fine, Mr. Summers. Everything is in order." She returned the documents. "Now which denominations would you wish the withdrawal?"

"Five hundred in fifties and the rest . . ."

* * *

When Mike arrived back at the Sheraton, his first priority was to pack. The time on the digital clock read eleven thirty, and planes don't wait. He made sure the cash was safe in his briefcase then snapped the locks and turned the combination wheels. He would carry his passport and ticket on his person. Opening a briefcase with that cash stash could raise some awkward questions. Engrossed with his packing and the time deadline, he had failed to notice the red message button flashing. Then a slight knock on the door further distracted him for a moment, and he turned to investigate only to notice a white envelope being slipped below.

"Probably the damn bill! Now let's see." He pushed his index finger below the glued fold-over. "What's this? 'Please call Angie at Travel. Urgent. Dial 9. Not answering your message call.'" Mike turned to the desk phone and killed the flashing message light.

"Damn it! I fucked up there." He picked up the phone and hit 9.

"Angie here."

"Angie, its Mr. Summers. I hope it's good news."

"Good and bad. All flights to Latina America's capital cities leaving J. F. Kennedy this evening are fully booked, but with one exception. There is one first-class seat available on Argentinean Airways Flight A12 to Buenos Aires, departing from JF at 2300 hours, arriving at 0900. There's a time difference of plus three hours. I placed a reserve on the seat. I hope I did the right thing."

"You certainly did, Angie." Mike was impressed.

"I also took the liberty of inquiring about visa requirements."

"Angie, *you are* a darling."

"There's no pre-entry visa required for U.S. citizens on vacation, but a tourist visa will be granted at immigration after you pass through customs. The visa is for a duration of ninety days and costs thirty-five U.S. dollars. You can extend the stay for a further thirty-five dollars or cross the border to

Argentina and get an entry stamp as many times as you require or . . . better still overstay your visa, and you only get a fifty-dollar fine for visa expirers when you leave the country."

For Mike, this was getting better all the time, but the best plans in the world have a bad habit of going astray.

"Angie, you are a lifesaver. Book me on the Buenos Aires flight. Hang on a sec, and I'll give you my credit card details. Are you there? It's American Express . . ."

"Thanks, Mr. Summers. I'll get the bellhop to deliver both flight confirmations to your room. It will take about fifteen minutes. One other point, can I make a reservation for you at the Sheraton, Buenos Aires?"

"No, I'm good, Angie. I'll take care of that myself, and again, I can't thank you enough."

"That's what I am here for, Mr. Summers. Glad to be of service. Have a safe journey, and I hope you enjoyed your stay at the Sheraton." "Thanks, Angie."

* * *

"Welcome to Delta flight 18, Mr. Summers. I'll show you to your seat, sir. It's 3A."

"Thank you . . . *Eh?*"

"Janet." The pretty blonde gave Mike one of her "Delta smiles." *Not bad,* Mike thought to himself.

I guess *you really* can't change a leopard's spots.

"I'll be looking after you today in first class. Here we are, sir. Let me take your garment bag. Perhaps I can get you a refreshment before departure?"

Mike smiled. "A double bourbon on the rocks wouldn't go astray."

CHAPTER 4

Frank Reynolds couldn't wait to hang up his uniform. There was just something special about Terry that he couldn't explain, and it was driving him crazy. Most guys are too macho to utter the words "I love you," and Frank was no exception. But then there's the old saying, *"You'll soon know when you find the right one."*

"That's it, guys." He clocked his card as he headed for the locker room. *"I'm outta here!"*

"So we have a date, Frankie boy, have we?" Ken Brody, his buddy, was always making with the wisecracks; and he opened the locker next to Frank.

* * *

Frank and Ken had been buddies since their stint in the Marine Corp. It's hard to say exactly why people click, but maybe it was because these two had a lot in common. Both are the same age at twenty-seven, liked the wildlife, and enjoyed the company of good-looking broads with "no obligation" sex. They were both body-building freaks and had the physiques to prove it. Ken was slightly taller than Frank at six two, but maybe that's why the chicks were attracted to him. Tall guys with "Armey's" biceps made them feel safe, at least that's one theory. His black unkempt curly hair gave him a sort of rugged look. With the "six o'clock" shadow, dark blue eyes, and white even teeth and that crazy smile, he was certainly a head turner; and his cot was never empty. They joined the security company together almost three years back, having difficulty finding jobs after military life, but they are two better friends you couldn't get.

* * *

"Don't be so fucking nosy, Ken. Anyhow, what makes you think that?" Frank was now down to his skin and heading for the shower.

"*Man,* after you have your shower the way you splash on that faggot cologne, it's either that or you've crossed over."

"Don't gimme that shit." Frank shook his head as he turned the faucet then jumped back as the cold spray hit his credentials.

Ken laughed as he stood naked beside him. "You gotta watch that, man. That cold spray shrinks parts of your body that may never come back again." "Ken, you're something else." Frank was already laying on the lather.

"Listen, buddy, if you're interested, I'm meeting these two hot chicks tonight at the 'Tin Mine' to shoot some tequilas. You know the club on Canal Street?"

"Sure, I've heard of the joint."

"Listen, two's company, but three's a crowd if you get my drift."

"Ken, buddy . . ." Frank began to towel himself. "I would really like to, but I'm locked in another situation. So, I'll reluctantly take a rain check."

"Since when are you getting so polite, using all these fancy words? It must be that blonde-haired broad that I saw you hitting on in the car park?" Frank just laughed and didn't reply.

"I tell you, man, I wouldn't mind a piece of that. If you're in there for the whole nine, why don't you fetch her along tonight? We can all have a blast."

"Yeah, I've been to your blasts before, and it took me a day to regain consciousness."

"I tell you. You don't know what you're missing, *man . . .*"

Frank slipped into his Levi's, splashed on his Chanel for men, then squeezed into his skin-tight T, purposely silhouetting his muscled physique.

"Ahhea . . . Ahhea." Ken was purposely coughing, hitting on the cologne. *"Man, I can't breathe!"*

"Ken, did I ever tell you you're a fucking 'drama queen'?"

"Now that's more like the buddy I know!"

Frank glanced at his watch, Terry's last words echoing in his ears. *"And don't be late."*

"Ken, I gotta go."

"Aren't we going to have our usual 'end shift' beer?"

"Sorry, Ken buddy, not today."

"Maaan! You must really have this chick bad."

* * *

"Bill, Judy! Come in." Rose gave Judy a sly wink. Judy just smiled. She knew where Rose was coming from.

"Judy, why don't you join me by the pool? I've just opened a bottle of chilled Frascati, and I'm looking for a partner."

"Now . . . *that's an offer I can't refuse."* Judy loved Rose's company. She was fun. "And the boys?" she asked.

"Don't worry about them. They're having a grand time splashing around in the pool. Maria is keeping an eye on them." She turned to Bill. "Tony is sitting outside in the alfresco, having a cold Bud. Go grab one from the icebox on your way and join him."

"Thanks, Rose." Bill disappeared. He knew his way around, and he couldn't wait to meet his partner to chew out this asshole Williams.

"Bill! Take the load off." Tony pointed to the basket chair. "I see you're locked and loaded." Tony laughed, gesturing at Bill's beer.

"Well, you always tell me to make myself at home when I visit," Bill answered, grinning.

"Spoken like a true gentleman. Cheers." Tony raised the dark green bottle. "So what's with Baker?"

"Bill, he can only go so far. Taking a congressman head-on is no joke. You're treading on big toes. The only positive side to this mess is that the media didn't report anything like the usual. 'A suspect has been named and will be taken into custody for questioning.' Besides, Laura is still in IC, and with a 'dumb larynx,' Summers might just think he has time on his side. Besides, some of these 'lovesick broads' have second thoughts and drop the case."

"Yeah, we've had that before and ended up with aggravated assault and a good behaviour bond."

"Drink up, Bill, and let's head for the office to pick up that warrant." Tony paused, a thought crossing his mind. "Say, why don't you, Judy, and the kids stay for dinner?"

"Are you serious?" Bill was laughing. "What, with the barbecue tomorrow, I'll be moving in."

"Better still." Tony was on the comedian trail asexual. "Why don't I move in with you and leave our two wives to their own devices. Just imagine . . . No more nagging . . . guys' nights . . . *and the hell with weight watchers!*"

"Yeah, but who's going to do the cooking?"

The thought of Rose's lasagne was too much. *"Good point, partner.* On second thoughts, maybe we should let the status quo prevail, huh?" Bill grinned. "Well, it *was* a thought . . ."

*   *   *

Frank had a spring in his step as he walked to the car park. It had just turned three, and he still had plenty of time. The Holland Tunnel might be a problem with the Saturday shoppers, but he was in good shape.

His red vintage 65 Mustang cabriolet had just been given an executive valet and *"she was lookin' good!"* Frank opened the door and sank into the firm leather bucket seats then switched the ignition key. The three-fifty block burst into a low growl, and Frank pressed the hood switch. This was a day to let the breeze run through your hair. He switched on the audio system, *"Love Is in the Air."* The melody burst through the speakers, and he couldn't help but laugh. *Maybe someone was sending him a message.*

The temperature was reaching ninety, and the natural air-conditioning was perfect. Life for Frank was taking a turn for the better, but it was early days, and Terry was still playing hard to get.

The tunnel, as predicted, was busy with three lanes at a snail's pace; and he breathed a sigh of relief as he saw daylight and the Hudson in all its glory.

"Got it." He dropped a couple of gears and turned into West Street. "Now let me see . . . Brickfield Apartments . . . *Nice* . . . And overlooking the river too!"

He didn't waste much time and quickly signalled before pulling into the sidewalk.

*   *   *

Brickfield's low-rise condominium with its stylish brick facade sent a dollar message. The building was a converted customs house from the late nineteen twenties, when New York was a major sea-faring port. Some smart entrepreneurs had recognized its potential and purchased the dilapidated warehouse for a song. But under the city's stringent waterfront conservation, the structure and ambience had to be retained. The result was a stunning refurbished antique brick and heavy oak beamed building displaying Gothic curved windows with cement-rendered edging finished in beige-coloured Graffiada. It was definitely yuppie territory; but then Terry, the young, up and coming single female exec, certainly looked the part.

*   *   *

"I gotta hand it to you, Terry. You got style," Frank spoke out loud as he searched for the parking sign.

In the Big Apple, you never take parking for granted.

FREE PARKING: 2:00 TO 6:00 p.m.

"This is getting better all the time." He cut the engine and lowered the hood then hit the sidewalk, but not before locking his "baby."

"Let me see . . . Here we are." He was searching the occupancy listing.

"Terry Johnson, 10A." He smiled and pressed the security button.

There was a loud buzzing noise then a click.

"Yes?"

"Terry, it's Frank here."

"And on time too. I'm impressed." He could hear her laugh. "Come straight up." There was a pronounced clank as the security lock disengaged and the hammer fell, and the heavy wood-panelled security door was suddenly ajar.

"Wow! This is some joint," Frank exclaimed as he entered the reception. "The polished beach front desk stood empty, but I guess the concierge has a life like everyone else, and being the weekend . . . *Well?*"

*   *   *

The antique ambience with the brick interior and cobbled floor was emphasized throughout. The congested walls adorned with a variety of framed black-and-white photography of New York's docklands and bonnet wearing moustached mole-skinned stevedores posing in "classroom" style, not a smile on their faces. The late twenties Great Depression was a tough period, and to be lucky enough to become a stevedore was even tougher, what with the under the table extortion money and Mafiosi union dues. If only this building could talk, it would undoubtedly be a "best seller."

*   *   *

"*Boy!* Now isn't this some elevator?" Frank stared at the ancient-looking Michelangelo contraption, and he could almost envisage the workers crammed into this animal cage.

The large steel-meshed box looked intimidating as Frank searched for the lift controls then pressed the up arrow.

At least the controls are modern, he thought, feeling more assured. But the noise was even more scary as the cage doors clanked open like an old iron gate followed by a loud buzzing alarm, which almost scared the crap out of him. "*Christ,* I hope this fucking contraption doesn't freeze halfway," he muttered under his breath.

He pressed 10 and crossed his fingers as the ear-piercing buzz repeated itself.

"This is like the countdown for the space shuttle." He began to smile then burst into laughter at seeing the funny side. The elevator suddenly bounced to a stop then moved slowly to level with the floor. Terry was waiting to greet him with that cheeky smile of hers, her memory still fresh at her first nerve-racking experience with "Old Betsy."

The wire door slid back on its rollers as it finally came to a stop.

"Scary, huh?" Terry laughed.

"Let's put this way, I'm glad to see a friendly face."

"And you're an ex-marine! What would 'Uncle Sam' think?" She gave him a warm hug and a peck on the cheek. Then she stepped a back and jovially put both arms in the air, like the gesture at the end of a stage show. "*Ta . . . Da . . . Daaa . . .* Welcome to Brickfield."

*   *   *

Terry, as usual, was looking gorgeous, what with her white almost see-through sleeveless off-the-shoulder blouse, dark blue sneakers, and stonewashed jean shorts. You know the ones, chopped off just below the crotch line with the torn frayed edges and the pocket linings showing. And with those legs that just won't quit, Frank was getting messages below his belt. Like Marilyn didn't have a patch on this "blonde bombshell." All that was missing was the subway vents and the parachute dress.

*   *   *

"Come on in, mister. I'll show you, my pad." She partially turned to walk away, but Frank gently caught her by the arm and turned her to face him. For a moment, their eyes met in a surprise stare. A stare that sends a message in anticipation of a gesture of love; and Frank didn't hesitate and pressed his lips against Terry squeezing the air from her lungs. He could taste the sweetness of her saliva as he explored her inner cavity, and she felt the bulge in his jeans pressing into her abdomen and the moisture flowing to her loins. It was time to stop before it went too far, and besides, having sex in the hallway was not Terry's style. *She had more class than that!*

"Frank, stop. *Please!*" She gently prized him away. "Besides, I need some air." She gasped.

There was a sort of pregnant pause as both a parties recovered their senses. "Terry, I just couldn't help myself . . ."

She stopped him in his tracks. "Frank don't apologize. I don't like men that apologize. It's a sign of weakness. Besides, am *I* complaining?" She stood on her toes and gave him a gentle kiss on the lips. "Now, mister, perhaps now I can show you, my apartment?" She grabbed his hand.

*   *   *

"Boy, this *is* some joint." Frank was momentarily taken aback with the spacious so-called one-bedroom studio apartment. "It must be all of twelve hundred square feet."

"You're getting close," Terry remarked.

"It makes my apartment look like a matchbox!"

"Frank darling, you have to remember this is an old, converted customs house, and I guess it was difficult for the architect to design the units on each floor without changing the exterior structure of the building. So some apartments are smaller or larger than others. I'm one of the lucky ones. But remember the old saying, everything has a price, and this apartment is no exception."

"So, I won't ask?"

"Let's just say that I can afford it, and with my new promotion, it's gotta be better."

"Well, whatever, honey. This place is something else." "So, you like it?" Terry proudly asked.

"Do I? You go it made."

"Yeah, and don't get any fancy ideas about moving in. This is strictly 'Tea House of the August Moon.' One woman only, and two's a crowd."

"That's what I love about you, honey. You call it as you see it. But seriously, this place is fabulous, and whoever your ID was, he or she did a beautiful job."

"It was a 'he,' for your information, young and good-looking with it, but don't worry. I'm not into 'toy boys.'"

Frank laughed. "Is that meant to make me feel better?"

"If the cap fits, big boy."

*   *   *

The beige thick-piled shag wine-coloured hide sofa set, glass carpet, the matching drapes, the dark coffee table, and breakfast bar with red matching stools fell together like what you see in the *House and Garden* magazine. This guy, whoever he was, knew his business, and the scattered table lamps and artificial flower arrangements in large terracotta pots and that European kitchen to die for added to the "Piece De Resistance."

*   *   *

"Listen, I have to put on my makeup. So give me ten. There's a cold one in the icebox. Help yourself," Terry called as she disappeared into the bedroom.

"No, I'm good. Besides, I'm driving." There was no reply.

Within minutes, Terry was ready and looking smoking hot. She could see the look on Frank's face and could just imagine what was running through his mind. But this was Terry, and she knew how to flaunt it.

"Let's get this ship on the rails. It's nearly five, and Laura will be wondering what's keeping me."

"*Hmmm* . . . Say, what's that smell. It's making me hungry?" Frank was overzealously sniffing.

"My lasagne, remember?"

CHAPTER 5

"Is everything all right, sir?"

"I'm good, Janet. Thanks to your excellent service," Mike replied with a warm smile.

"It's a pleasure, sir, to have you on board, but you never had any lunch, Mr. Summers."

Mike sighed. He had more on his mind than lunch, but the stewardess was just trying to be pleasant, and he returned her warm smile.

157

"When you are always traveling on business, the waistline becomes a problem, and my wife has given me the ultimatum." He winked.

Janet smiled at Mike's comment. "It's like that, is it?" *She was a looker; and Mike, well, no more said.* "Mr. Summers, we will be arriving at Kennedy in approximately fifteen minutes, so would you wish me to freshen your drink?"

"That's the best suggestion I've heard all day."

"No problem, sir. On the rocks?"

Mike nodded. But he was getting near his limit after four doubles, and the last thing he wanted was to screw up as a result of an alcohol binge.

"Thanks, Janet. One more and *I'll* be flying," he casually joked.

The bourbon drenched his tongue, and he felt no pain. His brain dulled by the alcohol, the realism of his predicament didn't seem to matter that much anymore, and it gave him a warm feeling that "all's well, it ends well."

"This is your captain speaking . . . Will the crew please prepare for landing? We will touchdown on time at 6:00 p.m., New York time. Please fasten your safety belts . . . On behalf of Delta Airlines, it has been a pleasure . . ."

The descent seemed to take forever before there was a sudden bump and the screaming of jet engines as the pilot hit reverse. The plane braked in a jerked motion, throwing the passengers slightly forward as the ABS kicked in.

"Now for the worst part." Mike sighed. *The slow taxiing to the deplaning bay and the mad scramble to disembark like cattle from a truck.*

Fortunately, in first class for the privileged few, there was no such problem; and Mike had to admit the feeling was special.

"Goodbye, Mr. Summers. We look forward to seeing you again."

"Thanks, Janet. The pleasure is all mine. Bye."

Garment bags are a time saver, and Mike headed straight to the taxi stance. He opened the rear door of the yellow cab and threw his bag onto the seat.

"Where to, buddy?" the bonneted driver asked in his distinctive Brooklyn accent.

Mike smiled to himself. *It was good to be back.*

"16 River Street, East Village," Mike answered.

"Nice part of the city," the cabbie commented as he slowly slipped into the busy airport traffic. This was the kind of fare that was worth waiting for.

As Terry stood in the antiquated elevator, she had a sort of smile on her face that was begging the question, and it didn't go unnoticed.

"So?" Frank asked as the "Alcatraz" cage buzzed again as it commenced the groaning descent.

Terry gave a cheeky laugh that had a kinda undertone.

"I was just thinking about how we met only a few days ago, and here we are dating. It must be fate, huh? I'm a great believer in fate. How about you?"

Frank shrugged. "Never really thought about it."

"My mother used to believe in fate, bless her soul." Terry paused again, but this time, there was a pronounced sadness in her eyes. "Frank, I can't explain it, but I feel sort of all messed up at the moment. I know it may sound silly, but with Laura almost on death's door and worse still, now I have her job, then I met you under devastating circumstances. *I just don't know what to expect next.*"

Terry's voice was beginning to crack, and Frank could see the glaze in her eyes.

"Come here, honey, and let me give you a big hug."

She threw herself against his chest and roped her arms around his neck. "I wish tomorrow never comes."

"Honey, you gotta snap out of this." He gave her a reassuring kiss on the nape of her neck and gently stroked her long blonde hair. "You can cry on these shoulders anytime."

Terry took a step back and looked into his eyes, the large crocodile tears blurring her vision.

"Frank darling, I'm so fucked up."

"Here, honey, take my handkerchief and wipe those 'baby blue' eyes." Frank was trying to console her.

"Thanks, darling. You came along at the right time. *It's gotta be fate!* Now I don't know what I would do without you. I guess someone up there likes me."

"*Now* that's the kinda stuff I want to hear!"

The elevator bounced to a halt, a distraction that was more than timely, and Frank pulled the heavy meshed slider open; and before he could utter another word, Terry grabbed his hand in an almost "don't leave me hold" as they walked to reception.

Frank opened the door, now even more confused.

"Terry." He looked into her troubled eyes. "I want you to love me for who I am, not as a comfort zone and a shoulder to cry on."

She squeezed his hand reassuringly as she embarrassingly wiped the tears from her cheeks.

"Don't worry, darling. I love you for all the right reasons."

"I just love this car," Terry commented, the smile blooming on her face as she proudly sat in the white leather bucket seat, the hood slowly retracting.

"So do I." Frank smiled as he turned the key.

"As much as me?" Terry was now being her usual naughty self.

"Well, that depends?" He gave an awry smile.

"Why you . . ."

* * *

The hospital car park was full, as usual, being a Saturday, with families visiting their loved ones, sick relatives, and unfortunately bereavements.

At that thought, Frank reflected back to his late father's advice. He would say, "Son, the three things to avoid in life are funerals, public toilets, and dinner with the in-laws."

Terry caught the flicker of a smile on his face.

"So, aren't you going to tell me?"

"Awe, it's nothing. Honey, it was just something funny that crossed my mind."

Fortunately, the congested car park took priority, and Terry changed the subject.

"Oops! I think we're going to have a problem," Terry commented, concerned at the saturated car park.

"Somehow or another, I don't think so." Frank grinned.

"Oh, this I must see, Mr. Smartass!"

"Oh, is that so . . . Well, how about this?"

Frank signalled just as he passed the front entrance and pulled into the slot marked "SECURITY ONLY."

"Frank Reynolds, you never cease to amaze me." Terry was being pleasantly sarcastic, *if there is such a thing.*

"I that good or bad?"

"Well, we'll see when you taste my lasagne." Frank burst into laughter. "I can't wait . . ."

* * *

As usual, the hospital reception was more than congested, and the pungent odour of hospital hygiene annihilated any trace of expensive perfume and good cologne.

"I hate hospitals," Terry commented as she entered the affray. Poor Martha the midshift sister on the front desk, was looking rather worse than the wear.

Frank grabbed Terry's hand and crushed to the front desk. Hospital receptions on the weekend are not for the faint of heart.

"Hi, sister." Martha turned fire in her eyes at the "wise guy" comment, then a smile crossed her face as she recognized Frank.

"I thought I recognized that voice, and maybe just as well or you would have received the wrong side of my tongue. So, what brings you here? I heard that you were transferred to St. Francis."

"I just miss you, Martha." Frank was always with the wise cracks.

"Yeah, just like I miss my ex . . . Like a hole in the head."

*   *   *

Martha, in her late forties, was busty with the accelerated "grandma" look. She was normally pleasant and understanding, but like everyone else, she had her moments; and this was her day. Her grey bagged eyes, deep laugh lines, and sagging turkey neck was a giveaway that she had given up the chase. But then again, she still had something dressed in her white crisp uniform and "Nightingale" cap; but the grey tights and white sneakers were most certainly a turn off.

*   *   *

"Martha, don't be like that!" Frank was teasing, as usual.

"Don't push your luck, Frankie boy. I'm over the top today and short-fused."

"Sister, I've been waiting here for . . ."

"I'll be with you in a moment, sir. Now, Frank, how can I help you?" Her patience was wearing thin.

"My friend is here to visit Laura Williams in IC."

She studied Terry's face for a moment. "By chance, you wouldn't happen to be . . ." She studied the computer terminal for a few seconds. "I thought so . . . A Ms. Terry Johnson?" Yes," Terry replied.

I recognize you from yesterday. The Williams have given you priority clearance to visit their daughter anytime. In fact, you have just missed them."

"Sister, I'm still waiting . . ."

"Be with you in a moment, sir. Listen, I gotta go. Just go straight to the IC wards. I'm sure you know the way by now."

"Good to see you, Martha. Maybe Terry and I can shout you a coffee during your break."

"What break?" She broke a smile. "Now, sir, what can I do for you?"

As they walked to the elevator hand in hand, Terry turned for a moment to look back at Martha. Like most complainers, they actually love their job, and Terry wished that she could say the same.

"I really admire her, Frank. I'm sure she is a lovely person."

"Yeah, she's really special," Frank answered in a serious tone.

The elevator chimed, and the doors opened, and it took a few moments to empty the packed "sardine can." That momentary delay is never good when you feel nervous, and it further adds to the tension at just what to expect when you finally see your friend again.

*   *   *

It was after seven when the taxi swung into River Street.

"You said number 16, buddy?" the cabbie asked.

"Yeah, but there's another twenty in it for you if you just drive slowly to the end of the street then turn back again."

"For an extra twenty, bud, you're on the wheel."

As the taxi slowly passed Mike's house, he could see June's red BMW parked in the driveway, but that was not what was catching his eye. It was the Grand Cherokee and the Pontiac G8, the NYPD pursuit car, sitting in Tony's drive. Mike put two and two together and guessed the detectives were probably having a social evening over dinner with their families, but with his flight to Buenos Aires departing at twenty-three hundred, time was not on his side; but *"who dares wins?"*

Mike knocked on the security partition.

"Driver, I've changed my mind. Just drop me off in front of my house. Don't worry. The extra twenty is still good."

"Whatever you say, buddy." He studied the digital red numbers on the meter. "The fare is eighty-five straight."

"It's your day." Mike unfolded two fifties and a twenty from his billfold and passed it through the teller slot.

"Thanks, buddy, for you anytime. Here's my number. Just ask for Dino." He smiled. "No relation . . ."

Mike didn't waste any time and grabbed the garment bag from the rear seat, slamming the door behind him then sprinting across the road and up the driveway.

The cab driver was intrigued. *"So maybe he's screwing someone's wife or worse still someone's husband. You never can tell these days, but with that kinda tip, who the hell cares?"* He shook his head and smiled before stuffing the "extras" into his wallet then did a U-turn. "Now I might just call it a night."

Mike slipped the key into the lock and opened the door. He could hear the TV blaring in the lounge. "Honey," he called at the top of his voice. *"It's me. I'm home."*

June turned the volume down; she was sure she heard a man's voice call.

"Honey, are you there?" Mike called again, hanging his jacket on the coat stand.

June smiled, recognizing the familiar voice, and quickly rose to her feet and rushed to the hallway.

"Mike!" She threw her arms around his neck, pressing her moist lips hard against his in a long, sensuous kiss then stepped back and looked into his eyes with anguish.

"Darling, I miss you so much, but why didn't you phone to tell me that you had decided to cut your trip short?"

Mike gave her a reassuring gentle kiss upon the lips. "Because I wanted to give you a surprise. *Silly!"*

She took his hand. "Undo your tie and come and sit beside me in the lounge and tell me all about your trip. The kids are both upstairs in their rooms. They will be so glad to see you, especially Steven, but that can wait until later. Can I fetch you your favourite poison?"

"No, I'm good." Mike forced a smile. "I had enough on the plane." He sank into the plush leather sofa and put his arms around June and looked sadly into her eyes.

"I just want to tell you, honey, that I really love you, no matter what."

"I feel uncomfortable when you speak like that, Mike. Is there something wrong, darling? Something you want to tell me?"

"It's nothing, honey. What with my work and all this traveling, I just wanted to assure you, that's all."

"You silly thing! Of course, I know you love me. Now give me another big kiss and no more of this nonsense! Do you hear me?"

Her kiss was warm and reassuring, and Mike knew how much she really loved him. *He had been such a fool, and now he was on "the river of no return." What a mess! But he had to come up with something plausible . . . and fast!*

"Honey, I know you're not going to like this, but I must go into the office to tie up some papers as unfortunately I'll be flying out on Monday again, first thing, after I report to Chuck. I should have stayed on, but I just wanted to come home and spend the weekend with you and the kids."

"Hush, darling. No more . . . I understand, and besides, you are home now, and that's all that's matters. Even better, we can all go to Tony's barbecue on Sunday. I'll give Rose a call." June motioned to lift the phone on the side table.

"No, honey, don't." Mike stopped her in her tracks. "I want to make it a surprise." He noticed the disappointed look on her face. "You're not angry, are you?"

"No, it's a small thing. *You and your surprises, Mike!"* She smiled, shaking her head. "I'll call the kids and tell them you are home." She left for the hallway. *"Steven . . . Sheryl . . . Your father's home."* Within minutes, Steven appeared.

"Father!" He gave his father a bear hug. "I didn't expect you home until next week."

"The bottom line is I just missed you guys." His eyes were glazing over at the thought of possibly never seeing his family again.

It didn't go unnoticed, and Steven was taken aback; he had never seen his father so emotional before.

"Are you all right, Father?" he asked, concerned.

"Ughhh . . ." Mike swallowed. "It's just me. I'm being silly. It's just that . . . Say, you never told me about your choice of university." Mike had to do something to stop the "Niagara."

"Cornell, Father . . . in the medicine faculty," Steven answered proudly.

"That's fantastic, son. A noble profession and I'm so proud. You will make a great doctor." "Hi, Dad."

"Sheryl honey, you're looking like your mother every day, *as beautiful as ever.*

"Awe, come on, Dad. Don't get all woozy on me."

"Well, aren't you going to give your father a kiss?"

She gave a pathetic sigh and reluctantly kissed her father on the cheek. The daughter and father were never close, and today it was more prominent than ever; and Mike just brushed it aside. It was a sensitive issue, and there was no point in making it a federal case.

"Guys, unfortunately, I have to go back to the office to clear up some unfinished business, but I should only be a couple of hours."

"Great!" Sheryl had suddenly changed her tune. "Then you can fetch back some pizzas."

"I might have guessed." Mike laughed. "Give your mother your orders while I go and pack some clothes as I will be leaving for West Palm straight from the office on Monday. I always keep a change of clothing at the office for emergencies."

"I'll come and help you, darling," June volunteered.

"It's okay, honey. Just unpack the dirty laundry from my garment bag, and I'll do the rest." He didn't want June to see the clothes he was taking, or she would twig it wasn't just an overnight stay.

Mike quickly went upstairs and laid out some shirts, a suit, underwear, a couple of pairs of shorts, deck shoes, and dress shoes. Then he sprinted down the stairs to collect his empty garment back. Fortunately, June was in the laundry room, loading the clothes washer. He glanced at his watch. Eight ten, he couldn't waste any more time and who knows what the traffic would be like.

"Honey, I've got to be on my way," he called.

June appeared from the laundry room. *"Such a hurry?"* "Yeah, I want to get back early and enjoy some pizza." "Only pizza?" June was teasing.

"Now you've got me going." Mike laughed and gave her a big kiss. Little did she know it was a "sayonara" kiss, and as he looked into her beautiful blue eyes, he could feel his heart almost tear apart. "I'll use the Town Car." He was desperate for something to say as he opened the adjoining garage door.

"Haven't you forgotten something?" June was standing, hands on her hips.

"Forgotten something?" Mike didn't know what to expect. *"The pizza order."*

*   *   *

Nancy, the IC nurse, was just leaving for her break when she walked straight into Terry and Frank.

"Again! We have to stop meeting like this." She smiled, recognizing the two love birds. "You two can take over my watch while I grab a cuppa." "Nancy, before you go, how is she?" Terry asked.

"Your friend never ceases to amaze me. She's one helluva battler. But I gotta hand it to you. You're the one that brought her home. You had best waste no more time as visiting closes in one hour, and Laura can't wait to see you guys." Nancy turned her attention to the cop sitting with his face in the newsprint. "Ted, they have clearance from the Williams family. Just let them through."

NYPD's finest nodded and went back to the *Playboy. With the kinda study time he had on his hands, maybe he was on "the Streetcar Named Desire."*

"Terry, you do remember my instructions from the time you were here last?"

"Don't worry, Nancy. She's in good hands."

"I'll be back in fifteen. Ciao."

The officer impatiently opened the door. "Just go straight in." He had more important things on his mind, and policing wasn't one of them.

As Terry and Frank approached her bed, Laura's eyes said it all when she recognized her best friend, and the tears began to flow.

"There . . . there, honey. No more of that." Terry gave a teary smile. "Or before you know it, I'll be crying too." She took a paper napkin from the side table and gently wiped away Laura's tears then gave her a reassuring kiss on the forehead. *"Honey, you look great!"*

* * *

There's a time for lying and a time for telling the truth, just like eulogies at a funeral, and this was one of these times.

* * *

Laura's shining locks of shoulder-length brown hair had lost their glisten and lay lifeless and straggled on her pillow, and her dark olive-shaped brown eyes were fast following suite. He face was pale and drawn, with the tell-tale fatigued dark shadows beneath her eyes. The tracheotomy tube had gone, but the large plaster covering the surgical opening to her windpipe was frightening, but the good news was she is breathing on her own. The oxygen tubes inserted into her nostrils and the intravenous drip snaking to the plastic bag filled with clear fluid on the elevated stand was a further indication that she was not out of the woods just yet, and the constant bleep from the heart monitoring machine connected to her right index finger was both disturbing and distracting; and Terry was having putting it all together.

* * *

Laura pointed anxiously to her larynx as Terry took her seat. She was signalling in frustration with her free hand constantly, placing her other hand over her mouth as if trying to tell Terry something.

Then it donned on Terry that Laura was trying desperately to tell her that she couldn't speak.

"You can't speak, honey?"

Laura nodded and put up her thumb. It was almost like a game of charades. Then she pointed to Frank who was standing by her bedside, looking kinda lost.

"Oh, I forgot to introduce you to my friend Frank . . . Frank Reynolds." Laura gave an approving smile.

"By the way, the office staff wish you well, including Blakely." That made Laura smile.

From there on, it was a one-way chat with Terry telling Laura how she met Frank.

*   *   *

Nancy had popped in and out to check Laura's temperature and blood pressure, each time giving a nod of approval. Then she returned and tapped her watch.

"I'm sorry, guys, but visiting time is over."

Terry could see Laura's eyes swell again at the thought of her friend leaving.

"Don't cry, sweetheart. I'll be back to visit you every day. I promise." Terry gave a parting smile to hide the pain.

That seemed to cheer Laura up, and she returned the smile, nodding her head.

"Ciao. I'll see you tomorrow. Be good." Terry squeezed her hand then gave a final wave as Frank and she left for the elevator.

For Laura, the bad news was still to come, but that was for another day.

*   *   *

As they stood hand in hand in the elevator, Terry's dead-pan expression said it all.

"I know how you feel, honey." Frank was trying his best. "It's like you really want to see your friend, but you're glad when the ordeal is over."

"I guess I never thought of it that way, but you're right, Frank. I'm really glad that's over." Then she hesitated, reflecting on her words. "Not in a bad sense, but seeing my friend so helpless lying there, it scares the living daylights out of me."

The elevator chimed. "Come on, honey. Let's get out of here before I start crying as well." Frank was doing his best to bring a smile to Terry's face.

"*You big ape,* stop fooling around and let these people into the lift." Terry was smiling on the surface, but below the facade, there was a pending train wreck.

*   *   *

"See you, Martha. Have a good shift and don't do anything I wouldn't do."

The night sister shook her head. She was in the middle of World War III. The queue at the front desk wasn't getting any smaller. "That gives me plenty of scope," she shot back. "Anyhow, I'm sure I'll be seeing you guys again tomorrow. Have a good one. Ciao. Now, sir, how can I help you?"

*   *   *

Frank's Mustang was conveniently parked right in front of reception; and although they both had been sitting for the past hour, it was a relief to relax in the car, away from the stark reality of life.

Frank turned the key and gunned the eight pots. The sky was beautiful and clear, and he opened the hood.

"Just look at these stars, Terry. *Isn't that something?*"

She snuggled up close to him as he gassed the engine.

"It really *is* surreal, but to tell you the truth, darling, it's been a long day, and I'll be glad to get home and put my feet up."

He turned and gave her a gentle kiss on the forehead.

"Hey! Keep your eyes on road, big boy, or we might both end up in the next bed to Laura."

*   *   *

Mike drove through the New York traffic like a man on a mission as he kept looking at the dash clock. It was now eight fifty, and check-in time for international flights was two hours before departure; but fortunately, Angie had reserved the only seat left on flight A12, and it was first class.

"But this fucking traffic!" Mike cussed out loud, shaking his head. *"Where the hell is everyone going at this time of night?"* He shook his head again and horned the geriatric driver on the left to move over. "What's this fucking guy doing, going to awake?"

The driver in his mid-fifties just ignored Mike and stuck to his lane. In the Big Apple, it doesn't pay to get into a "road rage" altercation. *Too many shooters and not enough targets.*

The traffic was banking up, and Mike was getting hot below the collar. Somehow, he had to hit the Staten Island Expressway then cross the toll bridge and slip onto Ericson Drive, then it was the Southern Expressway straight to Kennedy.

"Somehow I gotta out of this shit." *And there it was!* The "in your face" big blue sign on the right in bold letters: "STATEN ISLAND EXPRESSWAY. EXIT HWY 278."

Mike was more than relieved as he as signalled, slipping off the New Jersey Turnpike. The traffic was now light, but it would take at least another thirty minutes, and he still had JF to contend with!

168

After a nail-biting forty minutes, he could finally see the runway lights and he slipped onto J. F. Kennedy Road and slowed down to look at the departure guide.

"Let me see . . . Terminal 1 departures . . . Aero Mexico . . . Air France . . . Argentine Airlines . . . *Good.* Now for the long-stay car park."

Mike had flown many times from Kennedy, but each of the terminals has its own car park; hence, the confusion continues. Then he spotted the sign: TERMINAL 1 LONG-STAY CAR PARK. The sigh of relief on his face was worth taking a snapshot for the album as he screeched to a halt in front of the ticket machine and gingerly snatched the card activating the boom gate.

"Now for a parking slot! *This shit is never ending.*" He was having a running conversation with himself. The clock was ticking; first class or no first class, he only had an hour and fifteen minutes before the final bell.

Much to his relief, he finally saw a slot. It was a bit too narrow for the big Buick as some inconsiderate meathead had overparked.

"*What the hell!* I won't be driving this baby again," he commented as he scraped the left-hand side of the culprit Mercedes. The screeching noise of metal to metal was bone chilling, and Mike screwed his face. But he had no alternative; he had to get out of the car, and this was the ugly solution. He cut the engine and squeezed open the driver's door with barely enough gap to exit, producing a pronounced dent in the door of the BMW.

"Boy, won't this guy be happy." Mike grinned as he grabbed his briefcase and garment bag. Then he paused for a moment as if having second thoughts before finally chucking the car keys onto the driver's seat and slamming the door. There was no turning back now. He had made his bed.

*   *   *

"The courtesy bus! *Where the hell is it?*" Then a thought occurred to him. "Maybe it has departed as it's every fifteen minutes. That means ten o'clock . . . *Fuck!*" He sprinted to the car park entrance. For a guy in his mid-forties, he was no slouch. *It's amazing the power of adrenaline.* His only hope now was to hail a cab, having dropped off passengers at departures and now heading for arrivals. It was against the cab drivers' so-called "code of ethics," but money talks. I mean who wouldn't wish to pocket a few extras before joining that "ass end" queue at arrivals?

It looked like catching his flight was fast diminishing as the yellow cabs kept whizzing by. He had to do something desperate. There was only one solution left. It was fraught with danger, but when "the going gets tough" . . . He stood in the centre of the left lane and virtually closed his eyes.

"What the fuck?" The oversized "burger eating" black man stomped on the brakes, the cab screeching to halt only a couple yards from the fugitive.

"This fucking . . ." The big guy opened the door of the cab and approached Mike, the whites of his eyes brighter than his headlamps.

"What the hell you doing, dude? You got a death wish or something?" He was plenty mad.

"Cool it, man, and just gimme five to explain."

"And there's a fifty in it for me to drive you to Departures? Man, that's only five minutes!"

"You heard right." Mike already had the face of Grant in his hand.

"Move that fucking crate, you asshole." One of his buddies screamed as he overtook.

The big guy just ignored the other cab driver. With his build, he was in safe territory.

"Okay, buddy, jump in." He grabbed the greenback. After all, "a bird in the hand" . . .

* * *

Mike lifted his gear and rushed from the cab, not even giving a "thanks" to the driver.

The black man shook his head as he slipped into the traffic. *"Crazy bastard!"*

Mike glanced at his watch as he sprinted to Argentine Airways, first class ticketing counter. It was now ten after ten, and it looked as if they were closing shop.

"Sir, how can I help you?" the pretty young Latino hostess asked, startled at the sight of this middle-aged guy almost falling on his face as he stumbled to the ticketing counter.

Mike panted. "Gimme a second to catch my breath, and I'll explain . . ."

"I see, sir. But the doors are most likely closed as the Buenos Aires's flight is due to depart in thirty-five minutes."

Mike protested. "Honey, it's life or death. You gotta help me."

"Calm down, sir, and give me your passport, and I'll see what I can do, but I can't promise." She quickly entered Mike's details into the computer then nodded as she checked the passenger listing. *"Hmmm . . . Pedro . . ."* She turned to the attendant on the next desk. This guy had gold braids on his epaulettes and looked important, but in Argentina, you get that stuff in Captain Crunch packets.

"Yes, Rita?" God's answer to women inquired.

"Pedro, I have a big problem here. I have this first-class passenger booked on A12 for . . ."

"Hmmm, and you have no check-in bags?" "You got it," Mike answered.

"Don Guan" lifted the phone and spoke in Spanish, and after a what seemed a long-heated conversation, he smiled and placed back the phone.

"It eez okay, Mr. Summers. You are lucky. The doors of the flight are not closed as yet. The first officer is still checking the manifest and fuel. Give me a second, and I'll instruct our man to escort you through immigration and straight to the departure gate."

"Wow!" Mike was still breathing heavily, *but what a relief!*

As the officer predicted, a staff member suddenly appeared. "Please follow me, senor."

As for Mike, his journey was only beginning.

*   *   *

Terry had been extremely quiet during their drive home; and Frank, *well, he was just playing it cool.*

"Are you feeling hungry, Terry?" he casually asked as he hung a left into West Street.

Terry smiled and reached over, affectionately squeezing his hand. She knew where Frank was coming from, and she appreciated what he was trying to do.

Frank gently braked and pulled into the sidewalk in front of Terry's apartment.

"In case you haven't noticed, we're here, honey."

"Already! It's like for the last half hour I've have been in another world." Her eyes still glazed, thinking of her friend.

Frank closed the hood and cut the engine then turned and gave her a gentle, sort-of-understanding kiss on the lips.

She smiled. "Now that you mention it, *I am,* feeling hungry." Within minutes, she was turning the key in the lock.

"Home at last!" She opened the heavy security door and switched on the scattered soft lighting, giving the apartment a cozy romantic ambience.

"This is really something," Frank commented.

"Yeah, I just love soft lighting. It makes the apartment look larger than it really is." She turned and looked into his eyes. "Besides, it's romantic, don't you think?" Then she paused. "Listen, why don't you grab a seat on the sofa and make yourself at home while I play the nickelodeon?" Terry kicked off her shoes and walked over to the music centre to select a CD.

The music from Robbie William's *Eternity* filled the room. *You were there for summer dreamin', and you gave me what I need . . .*

Terry was humming the tune as she walked to the kitchen and placed the lasagne into the oven then set the time and the temperature. Her mood had changed, and she seemed more relaxed. Maybe it was the music or maybe it was "love is in the air."

"Frank darling, would you like a cold beer or a glass of wine?" she called from the kitchen.

"A beer's fine, honey. I'll save the wine for the Italian experience." He laughed.

"A Michelob?" "Whatever."

Terry opened the bottle and slipped it into a beer sleeve.

"Thanks, honey. Aren't you going to join me on the sofa?" Frank took a swig of the chilled liquid. *"Hmmm,* that *is* good!"

"Not on your life," Terry answered, a cheeky smile on her face. "Put that bottle on the coffee table, big guy, and let's trip the 'light fantastic.'"

"Only if your feet can take the punishment." Frank joked as he rose from the sofa.

"Kick off these size tens, dude, to avoid collateral damage." She snuggled into Frank's chest as he cautiously took the lead.

"Not bad!" Terry strained her neck, looking into his eyes. "A bit of a dark horse, huh?" At five eight, it was no mean task hanging on to Frank's sixfoot-one frame.

Terry had the sort of smile and clear blue eyes that made a guy's heart melt, and Frank couldn't help himself and passionately crushed her lips. It was a long "no air" kiss, and Terry finally pushed him away to inhale.

She could now feel the large bulge in his jeans against her abdomen and gently parted their bodies. She needed some space to clear her mind. It was too early, but what did she expect? The body contact, the music, and an invitation back to her apartment. I mean any red-blooded guy would react in the same way. Just then, the timely bell from the oven timer broke the heat, and Terry was relieved. It gave her a genuine excuse to "put out that fire" or was she just "dancing in the dark"?

"Darling, why don't you help me set the table? The cutlery is in the middle drawer, and the plates and wine glasses are in the right-hand cupboard."

"I gotta hand it to you, honey." Frank had a big grin on his face. "There's no fire without a spark that's for sure, but I think you're just scared to let your hair down when you think about what happened to your friend Laura. But you gotta trust me, darling. I wouldn't harm a hair on that pretty little head of yours."

"The table, remember?"

*   *   *

"You are seated in 1A, Mr. Summers. Let me show you to your seat. My name is Rosetta, and I'll be looking after you in first class. Please let me take your bag. Here we are, sir." She pointed to the seat at the nose of the plane next to the window. "We will be departing in around ten minutes, so please fasten your seat belt. Once we are airborne, I will fetch you an aperitif. Do you prefer champagne, Mr. Summers, or wine or maybe something stronger?"

"For a change, Rosetta, I'll take my chances with the champagne. Thank you."

"This is Captain Arizpe, your first officer. We will be departing on time at 2300hours. Will all passengers please fasten their safety belts and crew take their flight seats? The weather is forecast as clear all the way to Buenos Aires. Ground temperature on arrival will be approximately twenty-six degrees centigrade. Our flight this evening will take ten hours and forty-five minutes. There is a three-hour time difference, so please set your watches to 0200hours or 2:00 a.m. Argentinean time. ETA is 1215hours. Enjoy your flight and thank you for flying Argentinean Airways."

Mike at last was able to relax in the comfort of the first-class cabin.

I might as well make the best of it, he thought to himself. *It could be a long time before I indulge in this kind of luxury again.*

As the big bird rumbled down the runway, Mike stared sadly from the port window at the New York skyline. There is something about New York that's unique to the world, and the nostalgia sent a lump to his throat.

How would June and the kids survive? What had they done to deserve this? I've been such a fool. The questions kept running through is mind, and he shook his head in sheer dismay. *What a price to pay for a piece of adulterated skirt. Now I have nothing but memories, and as for the chances of seeing my wife and family again, it is scarcer than sighting Big Foot.* "Maaaan . . ." He spoke aloud, his voice cracking.

"Excuse me, sir?" the lady in the aisle seat asked, concerned.

Mike turned, slightly embarrassed. "I beg your pardon and I do apologize if I rudely disturbed you. It's just that I will be out of the country for some time on this assignment and I was just thinking how much I will miss my family."

"I understand. Don't worry. You didn't disturb me." The pretty Latina smiled then buried her nose in her magazine.

Mike casually glanced at her again while endeavouring to be inconspicuous. She was pretty to say the least, probably in her early thirties, with beautiful smooth olive skin, narrow face line with nose to match, full lips, and straight white teeth. And as for those dark brown eyes and that shoulder-length tightly curled black hair, they say a picture paints a thousand words.

The thrust of the four pods made the giant shudder as it climbed to cruising height, then suddenly, the cabin went quiet.

"I am Cleo, your chief purser this evening. Cabin service will commence as soon as the seat belt sign is switched off. Thank you for your patience."

Mike was feeling the penitence and a sense of hopelessness when the seat belt sign chimed, and he unbuckled the uncomfortable harness and reclined his seat.

Hmmmm, that feels much more comfortable, he thought to himself as he bedded into to the plush leather seat. It had been a more than hectic day, both physically and mentally, and he could have easily closed his eyes; but he had to remain alert and think about his next move once his feet hits the tarmac. Twenty thousand U.S. dollars sounds a lot; but when there's nothing coming in, well, *you don't have to be an accountant.*

"Your champagne, Mr. Murray, Dom, accompanied with some fine black Russian caviar."

Mike smiled. "Thanks, Rosetta. *Am I going to enjoy this!*"

The lady in the adjoining seat smiled at Mike's remark then returned to her magazine.

"Senorita Menzel, perhaps I can entice you with the same as this gentleman?" Rosetta politely inquired.

Senorita, Mike thought to himself. *Well, there's one thing for sure. She' not married.*

"I think I might try the same. It looks enticing." She turned her head slightly and gave Mike a smile.

"Certainly, senorita. Good choice." Rosetta went about her business, and within minutes, the mystique senorita was enjoying the taste of France's finest; and Mike could gauge the pleasure in her expression as she enjoyed the gastronomic experience.

"Nice, huh?" *This was Mike at his best when it comes to a piece of skirt and especially with those legs.*

She acknowledged with a smile. "Yes, it certainly is different."

"I hope you don't think I'm being forward, but since we have a long boring flight in front of us, let me introduce myself . . . Mike Summers."

She smiled again. "No, it's all right, but I have to warn you. If I drink too much champagne, I tend to talk too much."

"That's a woman's privilege." Mike laughed, laying on the charm.

"I'm Monalita Menzel. You can call me Mona for short. It's my pleasure, Mike, and like you, I agree. At least when you have an interesting person to talk to, the flight seems to pass a lot quicker. As they say, 'Great minds think alike.'" Her smile was catching.

"I'll drink to that." Mike raised the champagne flute.

Mona happily followed suit. "Cheers, as you say in America."

This had the makings of "where angels fear to tread." "So your wife and family, Mike—" *"Ex-wife."* He cut her short.

"Oh, I'm sorry. I didn't mean to pry."

"It's okay. No harm done. Just one of those things. You know, my work, always away from home, entertaining clients. You've heard it all before. I guess she just got bored and, with the kids grown up, met someone else that made her feel wanted. It's strange. You never see it coming, although it's staring you in the face. Fortunately, my two teenage kids are more like adults so there was no custody battle. As far as finances and property, there is no problem as long as you agree that your ex-wife gets everything."

Mona had to laugh at Mike's summation. "You seem to be well and truly over it."

Mike thought for a moment before replying; he had to sound convincing.

"To answer your question, Mona, I guess it's a part of my life that I will never *really* get over. We're still friends and behave like mature adults when we meet, because of the children."

"That's a commendable attitude," Mona answered. "And you mentioned you miss the kids and your wife?"

"Not really. Time heals everything." He almost dropped the ball and had to think of something. "But sometimes I wish things could have been different. I guess at times it's just loneliness."

"I understand." Mona nodded. "As the same happened to me . . . divorced almost three years ago today. Fortunately, we had no children. I caught him cheating on me and I never forgave him. Argentinean men have this so-called

Latin blood in their veins, and they think it's their God-given right to lay every pretty girl they see. Excuse my language, Mike, but I'm still bitter. Don't worry. I'm not going to cry on your shoulder." She smiled.

"I would be my pleasure." Mike was now full on.

"And are you from New York?" Mona switched the subject, feeling slightly uncomfortable with Mike's remark. But then, she thought, *he is handsome in a mature sort of way; and sometimes a lady needs to be flattered or otherwise this was going to be a long boring flight.*

"Yes, born and bred in the Big Apple. And yourself?"

"I was born in Rio de Janeiro, but my father's business took us to the capital. I have two sisters, both married each with two kids. Of course, my mother just adores the grandchildren, and it gets to me sometimes, being the oldest and, worse still, divorced with no children and devout Roman Catholics. Latin American families have Spanish blood, and big families are an important part of life."

"Can I interrupt for a moment?" Rosetta asked politely.

Mike smiled. "Of course, I assume that's the dinner menu?"

"Yes, Mr. Summers. Dinner will be served in one hour. Would you wish me to refill your champagne?"

"Yes," Mike and Mona answered in tandem then looked at one another before spontaneously bursting into laughter.

"What did you say about great minds thinking alike?" Mike was laughing through his words.

Rosetta poured the sparkling wine. "Take your time with your menu choices and just press the call button when you have decided. Perhaps another refill?" She smiled

"I'll drink to that." Mona touched Mike's glass.

Maybe she was partaking on an empty stomach. Whatever. She was lightening up, and as for Mike, he was back to his normal "ladies" man self.

* * *

"I gotta hand it to you, honey. That lasagne was something else . . . and those brochettes and that salsa?"

"*Now* what's in that evil mind of yours?" Terry gave him that look.

"You can't blame a guy for trying?" Frank was laughing at Terry's underlying comment.

"Have another piece." Terry pointed to the remaining lasagne.

"Honey, I would love to, but I have had two portions already, and if I take another, I'm going to burst at the seams. Come to think of it"—Frank had a cheeky grin on his face—"maybe that's your intension. To get me so full I won't be able tie my laces, let alone undo my belt."

"That's wishful thinking." Terry was fast on the take.

"Well, a guy can think, can't he?"

Terry purposely ignored Frank's remark and left the table for the kitchen.

"Why don't you finish your wine while I brew the coffee?"

"What, no dessert?"

"Why you . . ." Terry threw the dishtowel at him. "The next time, mister, *you're in the kitchen!"* She was laughing.

The dishes stacked in the washer, the table cleared, Frank had taken the liberty to retreat to the sofa and relax with another cold beer.

"Well, aren't you going to join me?" Frank patted the sofa.

"Gimme a sec, darling, while I switch on the washer, but no more wine for me or I'll fall asleep on you."

"That's the last thing I want." Frank was quick on his feet.

"That's what I like about you, darling. You never take no for answer, but . . . There again . . . Your suggestion has some merit." She smiled.

Terry turned and slowly walked toward the sofa, purposely taking her time while moving her hips in a sexy catwalk fashion before crashing heavily onto the soft leather. She turned and placed the cushion behind her back then swung her legs onto Frank's lap. There's something sexy about a woman's feet with those manicured, red-painted toenails, and Frank did the only thing he could think of and began to gently massage Terry's feet.

"Hmmmm . . ." Terry groaned in pleasure. "That feels *so* good. I gotta hand it to you, darling. You know how to get to a gal." But Frank had other thoughts on his mind as he struggled to keep his eyes from those sexy thighs, Terry's micro denim shorts raising the mercury.

Is this a "come on" or I am dicing with fire? Frank thought to himself as he planned his next move. Whatever? This babe is smoking hot, and he cautiously slipped his hand inside the right leg of her shorts.

"Frank!" Terry protested, restraining his wandering extremity, then without another word, she threw her feet to the floor and walked angrily to the breakfast bar before pouring herself the remainder of the wine. She took a large sip in desperation, her troubled eyes staring blankly at her empty wineglass.

Frank just sat in confused silence, his eyes frowned, and brow furrowed, not really knowing what to do next, wondering why the sudden mood change, especially when they were having such an enjoyable evening.

"Terry." He rose to his feet. "What's wrong, honey? Is it me? Have I done something to upset you? If I have, please tell me, and we can work it out."

"No, it's not you, darling. It's me." She turned to face him, tears trickling down her cheeks.

Frank gently removed the glass from her hand and placed it on the breakfast bar.

"Honey, whatever it is, alcohol is not the solution. Now let me wipe these beautiful eyes of yours." He tried to make her smile as he unfolded the white handkerchief from his pocket.

"You're so sweet, darling, and you don't deserve my problems. It's just I feel so insecure." She looked into his eyes again with that "sad song" look. "Can you just hold me for a few moments?" She placed her arms around his waist and snuggled her head against his chest. "I'm just so mixed up and confused. I know what my heart tells me, but I'm scared that I'm falling into another relationship too soon, only to be hurt again."

Frank put his hand below her chin, forcing her to look into his eyes.

"Honey, I love you. I *really* do love you. Don't ask me why. I know that I have only known you for only four days, but you are so different, and I just can't get you out of my mind. You must think I'm crazy?"

Terry stood on her toes, and their lips met. It was a hungry kiss that exposed her warmest feelings, her soft wet sensuous lips gently massaging his, the kind of kiss that sends tingles from the back of your spine to your toes.

Frank could feel both her warmth and sadness as he stared into those glazed blue eyes, and his heart almost melted.

"Honey, *now do you believe me?*"

"Yes, darling," she whispered, her moist lips again searching for his.

As Frank gently parted their bodies, Terry felt her heart miss a beat as she looked at his confused eyes.

"Honey, I have told you that I love you. What more can I do to convince you?"

A smile crossed her face. "*Take me to bed!*"

*   *   *

June was engrossed with Wimbledon and her favorite tennis player Rodger Federer, ignorant of the time, when suddenly her concentration was disturbed with Steven entering the TV lounge.

"Mother . . . do you realize what time it is? It's nearly eleven thirty. What's happened to Father and our pizzas?"

"My god, you're right, Steven." She glanced at the digital wall clock. "That's strange. He should have been well home by now. I wonder what could have kept him? I'll call him on his cell phone." She stretched over to the coffee table and lifted the phone then dialled then placed the phone to her ear. "That's strange. I'm getting his voice mail, asking to leave a message. Darling, it's getting late, and I'm worried. Please call me as soon as you can. Love you."

June momentarily sat in salience, her mind now totally confused, when Steven suddenly interrupted her thoughts.

"How about Father's office, Mother? Remember he said that he was going there first." He was trying to console her, but June was now seriously concerned and was barely paying attention. Nevertheless, Steven's recommendation bore some merit, and she nervously dialled again waiting patiently as Mike's office phone monotonously kept ringing.

"No luck, son." She looked at the floor in consternation.

"How about security?" Steven asked, searching his mind. "They're round the clock."

"Good idea!" June looked slightly relieved. "You're right, son. Although the office is closed, your father must clear security to enter." She dialed again, her hand shaking.

"Good evening. Wilburn House, security speaking. Please call back during working hours as the office is closed for the weekend."

"Karl, is that you on the line?"

"Err, yes." June could sense his apprehension.

"It's June Summers here."

"Oh, Mrs. Summers! I didn't recognize your voice. How can I help you?"

"Karl, did Bill arrive at the office this evening?"

"No, Mrs. Summers, and my shift started at six. I'm sorry. Is there a problem?"

"Don't worry, Karl. He's probably met a business colleague and stopped off for a drink. Can you call me when he arrives?"

"For sure, Mrs. Summers. I have your home number. Good night."

Now June was really worried. *Mike had never reached the office, and in New York, anything can happen!*

"Steven, I'm now really worried about your father's safety. I didn't tell you . . . but only a few days ago, your father was almost mugged." *"Mother!* You never said." Steven was shocked.

"You know your father . . . but more importantly, what do we do now?" "Mother, can I make another suggestion?"

June nodded reluctantly; she had had enough.

"Why don't you go next door and speak to Mr. Perino? He'll know what to do."

June screwed up her face. "I know where you are coming from, but I saw Bill's car in the drive, and I assume that the families must be having dinner and I wouldn't want to disturb them. It's so embarrassing." She was shaking her head.

"Mother, this is serious. You have to do something. I tell you what . . . why don't I come with you?"

June smiled; she needed support.

"Okay, but how about Sheryl?" She turned to Steven.

"Mom, forget it! She probably has her cell phone glued her ear and is dead to the world."

June shook her head. *"You two!"*

*   *   *

June stood apprehensively on Tony's porch, still lacking the courage to ring the bell.

"Mother!" Steven squeezed past her and pressed the button.

The two—to three-minute delay before the latch unlocked was like forever, only to be met by the smiling Maria, Rose's mother.

"Si, June . . . *Eh,* Steven. Bonasera, come stai . . . Si, *come in . . . Come in."* "Who is it, Mother?" Rose's voice echoed from the dining room.

"It's a June and a Steven from a next door," Maria called at the top of her lungs.

Tony turned to Bill. They say both minds think alike.

Maria escorted the distraught Summers into the dining room, June's face now an ashen white.

"June, honey!" Rose was taken aback at June's sickly appearance. "You look pale. Here take a seat." She pointed to the vacant chair at the dining table. "Is there something wrong, honey?"

"Rose." June burst into tears. "I'm worried out of my mind."

"Come now, honey. Why don't I fetch you a cup of coffee, then you can unload?"

June nodded in acceptance between sobs then wearily slumped into the vacant chair at the dining table.

June turned, looking sheepishly at the family gathering, in total humiliation.

"What can I say? I'm really sorry for interrupting your family dinner." She was wiping her eyes.

"Don't be silly, June!" Bill's wife stopped her in her tracks. "We've been friends for so long. It's no sweat. Now why don't you tell me what's wrong?"

June took a sip of the espresso. It tasted good, the caffeine helping her to relax.

"It's Mike." She placed her cup on the table, her eyes twitching nervously. "He arrived home this evening, two days early from his business trip and . . ."

Tony turned to Bill and gave an "I don't believe it sigh." This was the kinda stuff he hated in his job, a grim look on his face.

"June, I want you to brace yourself as I have some really bad news." June turned as pale as ghost, not knowing what to expect.

"It's like this. I can only presume that Mike has done 'a runner' as we say in the NYPD, and believe me, June, if there was another way. I'm sorry to tell you that I have a warrant for Mike's arrest for the attempted murder of Laura Williams . . ."

*   *   *

Frank placed his arm under Terry's shoulders, the other below the calves of her legs, before lifting her up into his arms and doing the "wedding threshold."

"Is this a rehearsal?" Terry laughed as she leaned over and switched on the bedside lights in passing before Frank kicked the door closed with his heel and gently laid her on top of the bed.

As she lay in anticipation, she looked so beautiful; and Frank snuggled beside her and kissed her passionately on the lips, a kiss that was tender and loving. But for Terry, it was the slow boat to China. *She had to put some fire into this guy's butt.* The niceties long gone, she swung her feet to the floor and grabbed his hand, pulling him upright, then without a word began to literally rip the shirt from his back and undo his jeans like a woman possessed. She was smokin' hot, and now there was no turning back as she feverishly worked her way down his naked body, her moist lips caressing his chest and his taught "six pack" before finally dropping his briefs around his ankles. As for Frank, I guess you could say he was in another world as she enveloped her lips around the tip of his rock-hard penis.

It was too much, and Frank tensed up, quickly pulling her to her feet. The look of disappointment on her face said it all. *I mean who is this guy?*

Terry thought in bewilderment. *He is either one cool dude or I don't want to think of the other . . .*

"What's wrong, darling?" Terry protested in dismay, searching his eyes.

Frank grinned, a cheeky grin. *"It's my turn*! Now are you gonna take off that blouse and these shorts or is clumsy Frank here gonna have an accident?"

Terry laughed. "Now I get you, darling." She feverishly began to unbutton her blouse, the half-bra followed suit, and they hit the floor in record time.

Frank was now a man possessed as he gawked at this adorable creature. Her naked unashamed nudity could proudly adorn the front page of *Playboy* any day. Those firm white breast, the large pink nipples, the smooth skin and firm abdomen, and that blonde mystique patch between her legs. He was now like a 747 coming in to land as he roughly pushed her back onto the bed, her legs automatically splaying apart.

"Now you're talking, big boy!" She groaned as Frank worked his tongue in a circular motion, stimulating her now protruding nipples. It was time, and he gently entered the moist crevasse between her legs, the ultimate prize, the sensation invigorating as Terry gasped and entwined her legs around his waist, their bodies moving in tandem in the ultimate act of love.

"Take it slowly, darling," she whispered in his ear. "Remember, we have the whole night . . ."

* * *

"Bill, you lift her below the arms, and I'll take her legs. Rose honey, remove these cushions from the sofa."

"That's it!" Tony was relieved as he and his partner placed the limp body of June on the leather couch.

"Judy"—Tony turned to Bill's wife—"grab a couple of these cushions and place them below her ankles to elevate her legs. She'll come round in a couple minutes."

Tony could see the anguish on Steven's face at the sad and helpless sight of his unconscious mother, and he placed his hand reassuringly on Steven's shoulder.

"Don't worry, kid. Your mother has only gone into a faint. It's not uncommon when people get bad news, *believe me.* I experience this all the time in my job. Ah, she's coming round now." Tony pointed relieved.

Bill turned to his partner, shaking his head. "So what's new, Detective Sergeant?"

"You know the answer better than I do. I guess we both saw it coming, Bill, after big mouth Williams blabbed to the media."

Tony turned his wife. "Rose, take care of June. Bill and I have to make an urgent call."

Tony lifted the receiver and dialed then waited for a moment before the call was finally answered. After all, it was now twelve fifteen in the morning, and he wasn't looking forward to the anticipated hostile reception.

The sleepy voice of a woman answered, *"Yes . . . Eh . . . Err . . . Yes . . . A . . . Hmmm . . ."* It was as if she was taking a moment to clear her throat. "May I ask who is on the line?"

"Ruth, it's Tony . . . Tony Perino. Listen, I really apologize for phoning at this time in the morning, but it's crucially important that I speak to Ted."

"Hang a sec, Tony, but I gotta tell you he's not gonna be too happy."

There was a long pause, and Tony could clearly hear Ruth's agitated voice in the background.

"Ted . . . Ted . . . Wake up . . . Wake up, darling!"

"What the bloody hell is it now?"

Ruth switched on the bedside lamp and held up the phone, and Ted quickly covered his eyes, squinting from the sudden brightness.

"I'm not that blind, but I should be! Whoever it is tell him to get lost. It can wait until morning." He thumped the pillow and sunk his head into the hollow. *"Can't a guy get some sleep in this godforsaken world?"*

"Tony . . ."

"Ruth, I heard Ted, but it's really important. Tell him it's regarding the Williams case."

"I heard that. Gimme that phone . . ." Baker rudely wrenched the receiver from his wife's hand. "This had better be good, Perrino, or so help me, you and that partner of yours will be washing dishes in the police cafeteria . . . *Cappice?"*

"Brace yourself, boss. The news is not good." Tony sighed.

"Don't tell me!"

"I'm afraid so. The bird has flown. His wife June is here with me now. For what it's worth, my guess is that . . ."

"*Christ,* this is all I need. And you say he arrived home from his business trip two days early? I could kick my own ass for not telling you guys to fly down to West Palm and pick him up. Well, Perrino, what's on your radar now?"

"According to his wife, he packed some clothes and headed for his office to tie up some paperwork. The clothes were a standby in case of emergencies as he often had to fly at a moment's notice."

"This guy is no dummy, and boy has he made us look like a bunch of amateurs. I can just imagine my phone tomorrow with Murray and Williams roasting my ear, not to mention the paparazzi."

"Ted, you never let me finish . . ."

"*I'm waitin'.*"

"You start by calling the commissioner to put out an APB covering all airports, domestic, international, private, you name it . . . bus depots, car parks . . ."

"Okay . . . Okay, I get the picture, but I also need a photo of this guy and not from his high school yearbook."

"Don't worry, boss. I'll get one from his wife and fax it to HQ with his car make and registration number for the attention of the desk sergeant to wait for further instructions."

Then something suddenly struck Baker.

"How come Summers's wife is at your place?"

"Ted, are you serious? You remember Mike from our last barbecue? Mike . . . Mike Summers, my next-door neighbour . . ." "*Shiiiiit!*"

*   *   *

"I guess it's bad news, darling?"

"The worst. Listen, honey, why don't you try and get some sleep? I have another phone call to make, and at this time in the morning, I'm sure the commissioner will love to hear my sweet voice." Baker had that cocky grin on his face as he dialled.

"If I can be pulled out my bed at this time in the morning, then why not?" He was grinning at the thought.

The phone rang for a few seconds, then a man's voice answered.

"Yeah . . . Evans here."

"Nev, it's Ted Baker from Homicide."

"You're lucky you caught me. Jean and I were about to retire, having just arrived home from a late dinner party. But enough of my private life. Why the call? I'm sure it's not social?"

"Nev, it's like this . . ."

"Hmmmm . . . I see. Okay, I'll issue an APB to all stations to use whatever it takes to pull this guy in."

"Thanks, Nev. I owe you one. Hopefully, tomorrow will bring some better news." Baker hung up.

"Is everything all right, darling?" Ruth asked as she switched off the bedside lamp.

"As right as it can be, honey. Now how about getting some sleep? I think we have had enough drama for one night."

*   *   *

"June, are you sure you will be all right?"

"Yes, Rose, and thanks for everything." She was standing on the porch, about to leave, Steven grasping her hand to support his mother. "The kids will keep me company tonight. Don't worry. I won't do anything stupid."

Bill's wife interrupted. "June, if you need anything, and I mean anything, don't hesitate to call."

"Thanks, Judy, and I know you mean well, but this is something we will have to overcome and face as a family." Her eyes were puffed from the aftermath of constant tearing.

"Let's go, Mother. Sheryl will be wondering what's happened to us." Steven gently tugged his mother's hand.

"Bye and thanks again."

"June"—Tony knew it was a bad time, but he had no alternative—"I'm sorry to lay this on you before you leave, but I'm sure you appreciate that I will require to ask you some questions as part of our ongoing investigation. Of course, when you feel up to it."

"I understand, Tony. Just give me some space. You have my assurance that I will cooperate in any way I can to bring a close to this horrible mess. *I still can't believe it.*"

"June, remember, Mike is innocent until proven guilty."

"Tony, I wish I had your optimism, but unfortunately, no one knows my husband better than me." She turned, walking unsteadily toward the driveway, but her next hurdle was Sheryl; and the balloon was sure to go up. She and her father had little in common.

*   *   *

As June turned the key in the lock, her mind was racing in all directions. *Has something terrible happened to Mike, and if so, what would become of her and the children? Mike took care of everything: the mortgage, the kids, the private schooling, the car payments. I didn't bear thinking. My god, what would she do? And if the police arrest him for attempted murder, there is the scandal, the media, her friends at the club, and worse still the kids.*

"Come, Mother." Steven escorted his mother into the house, concerned that she might have another bout of fainting as she still looked pale and drawn.

"Listen, why don't you relax on the sofa while I go and fetch Sis?"

"Thanks, son. That would be good." June wearily walked toward to the lounge with Steven in close pursuit. He wasn't taking any chances.

"Here, Mother, let me help you." He offered his hand as she unsteadily approached the sofa.

"Don't worry, son. I'll be all right," she assured him as she sat down heavily, sinking into the soft cushions, relief on her face.

"I'll be down in a second, Mother." Steven disappeared up the stairs at a great rate of knots and barged straight into his sister's room without knocking.

Sheryl, as predicted, was glued to her cell phone; and she turned, startled at her brother's rudeness and inconsideration.

"I'll call you back. My ignorant brother has just burst into my room without knocking. *There's nothing sacred in this fucking house!*" She snapped her phone closed, her eyes like the eyes of a tiger.

"*You ignorant pig!* There's such a thing as knocking."

"Sis, cut the drama. It doesn't wash with me."

"Well?"

"It's Father!"

"What do you mean . . . *it's Father?*"

"*Christ, sis!* Why don't you shut up for a moment and listen? Mother is in the lounge in one helluva state, and all she needs is your ranting and raving."

Sheryl's mood suddenly changed at the thought of her mother being sick or something; and she threw her feet to the floor, brushing past Steven, sprinting toward the stairs.

"Mother, are you all, right?" Sheryl could sense that her mother was distressed as she sat beside her on the sofa, her eyes bloodshot and puffed from crying.

"I'm bearing up, honey, and I know I have to be strong for the sake of you and your brother."

"*Mother,* I am totally confused. Can someone please tell me what's going on?"

"It's your father, honey . . ."

"I keep hearing . . . *'It's my father,'* but I'm none the wiser."

"There is warrant for your father's arrest for the attempted murder of Laura Williams. I'm sure you have seen the news bulletins over the past week."

"Senator Williams's daughter?'

Steven interrupted, "The same."

"If you don't mind, I'm asking Mother," she hit back. *"Mother*, there must be some mistake. This is like a bad dream."

"I wish there was, honey, but worst of all, your father has just disappeared into thin air, and I'm more worried that he may be the victim of foul play. The streets of New York are a jungle of crime." It was too much, and she put her head between her hands and started to sob again. "I don't know what to do and I don't know who to turn too. I feel so lost"

"There, there, Mother. Steven, get some paper napkins from the kitchen." Sheryl was comforting her mother, resting her head on her shoulder.

Suddenly, Sheryl's mood changed to that of frustration and anger. "How could that sick bastard do this to us . . . *I hate him . . ."*

"Honey don't say that. Remember, whatever, he is still your father."

"Mother, how can you be so forgiving? *I don't believe it!* And what's going to happen to us?"

"Kids let's not jump to conclusions. There are two sides to every story, and as Mr. Perino said, 'your father is innocent until proven guilty.'"

"Would you like some coffee, Mother, or something a little stronger to calm your nerves?" Steven asked, trying to change the subject.

June gave a half-hearted smile.

"I know that you both mean well, but common sense tells me there's nothing we can do tonight. So, I'm going to shower and retire." She rose to her feet.

"Mother, I'll sleep with you tonight," Sheryl volunteered.

"I think that's a good idea, Mother." Steven agreed.

June turned to her daughter and nodded.

"It's going to be a long night . . ."

CHAPTER 6

Tony stirred restlessly. It was as if daylight would never come, his mind like a runaway train heading for the brake barrier. For some reason, this case was getting to him, and he turned wearily to glance at the bright green numerals on the digital clock; it read 00:60.

"*Christ!* Is that all the time it is?" he muttered under his breath, trying not to disturb Rose.

"This bloody case, *I don't need it and I don't want it!*" The old cliche was running through his mind. "Never get involved personally with the family of the accused."

"*Maaan,* is this one big headache!" he spoke out loud.

Rose gave a sleepy groan and turned to face her husband.

"What was that you were saying, darling?"

"Nothing, honey. I'm just dehydrated from last night's dinner. Why don't you turn over and go to sleep? It's only six ten. I know where I'm heading and that's to the refrigerator to get a cold beer."

"It's no surprise, after the amount of booze you and your buddy consumed last night. Luckily, we have a couple of spare rooms as Bill was in no state for driving, and Judy wasn't far behind him."

"Rose honey don't start. I have a big-enough headache as it is."

Rose just ignored the comment and turned over on her side. When Tony is in his mood, it's a waste of time; but then Rose, like most wives, always has the last word.

"Don't switch on the lights or I'll never get to sleep again, and I have to be up early for the barbecue, or have you conveniently forgotten?" Rose was getting more and more irate, and it was time to hit the floor running and throw in the towel. "*Those who run away live to fight another day.*"

Tony made a quacking motion with his hand behind her back, impersonating a duck's bill, and it was just as well that Rose never saw him. Italian women are known for their hot temper.

As Tony stumbled blindly toward the door in pitch darkness, he let out an ugly oath as he stubbed his small toe on the dressing table chair then cussed all the way to door

"Fucking women!"

"*I heard that!*"

"Honey, do me favour and go count sheep."

There was a barrage of Italian swear words in retaliation, and Tony didn't need a translator; he hurriedly opened the bedroom door, trying not to disturb the household before switching on the hallway lights.

"There's was no way I'm going to brave these fucking stairs in this darkness, especially with this fucking hangover." He touched the top of his head and cringed before searching for the elusive saliva to satisfy his parched tongue. *"Boy, am I looking forward to the hair of the dog,"* he spoke under his breath.

Then as he walked barefooted toward the kitchen, stopping every couple of steps to balance on one leg and sooth his stubbed toe, he noticed the kitchen light.

"That's interesting. I wonder . . ."

There, perched on the kitchen barstool, with a cold beer in his hand, was none other than Dr. Watson himself.

"Hayden, I might have known it was you raiding the icebox! But as they say, 'man can't live on bread alone.' Move over and get your partner a cold one."

They both burst into laughter.

"Ouch!" Bill screwed up his face, holding his head. "It was that bloody grappa you were feeding me last night, Perino."

"Hey, no one was twisting your arm. Now are you going to get me that fucking beer?"

* * *

"Buddy . . . cheers." They touched bottles, and Tony almost drained his in the first gulp.

"Boy, did I need that!"

"Tony, thanks again for letting Judy and the kids stay over."

"Don't thank me. Just wait till you get the bill." Tony laughed then cringed, screwing up his eyes. His headache wasn't letting up.

"I got news for you, partner. With the way I feel now, I'm not looking forward to tomorrow's barbecue standing over that hot Webber. So you'll have to don your apron and help me with the steaks and the 'snags,' as they say in Australia."

Bill laughed. "As long as the beer keeps a coming', I'm your man. Cheers." He popped the cap of another cold one.

At this rate, neither would be capable of cooking anything on the barbecue tomorrow unless charred burned steak has suddenly become popular!

* * *

"Ten green bottles sitting on the wall. And if one green bottle . . ." Bill was serenading the empties stacked in a line on the breakfast bar.

"Hayden, you're pissed!" Tony's voice was slurred. But between the two of them, it was hard to tell who was the most intoxicated.

"Paaarttneeer . . . the party's over. It's time to call it a night." The karaoke was in full swing.

"Bill, did anyone ever tell you that you have a tin ear? Your fucking singing would turn Simon Cowell's hair grey."

"Oh, is *thaaat sooo* . . . Well, let me tell you, Detective Sergeant . . . *Eh . . . Eh?*"

"Perino."

"That's it . . . *Perino.* I never told that I once thought about being a professional singer before I joined the NYPD."

"*Maaaan* . . . you're something else." Tony was shaking his head, almost losing his balance and falling off the barstool as he struggled to stand up straight.

"*Saaay . . . Dooo* you *knoooow* what time it is?" Bill was now really having trouble, his words now almost completely inaudible. *"It's four thirty. Would you believe it?"*

Tony stood unsteadily on his feet then turned to face his buddy.

"I know what I'm gonna do, and that's hit this fucking sofa and my . . . *and my . . . suge . . . suggestion.*" Tony paused blankly for a moment, trying to recollect what he was about to say. "Is . . . You take the other and remember to switch the off the lights."

He crashed onto the soft leather then stuffed a cushion below his head. He was heading for in the "Lost Horizon"; and when daylight comes, fortunately, he won't remember a thing.

"*Sooo* much for my best buddy. But I'm not finished yet." Bill held the green bottle up to the light to study what was left of its contents as he staggered to his feet. Then he gulped the last dregs of the Bud and proudly placed the empty bottle next in line before wobbling over to the other sofa. "*Ooooops*, the lights. Awe, what the hell." He stood over the other sofa for a few seconds then almost in slow motion fell like a logged pine.

For these two sleeping beauties, "hell hath no fury like a woman's scorn."

CHAPTER 7

Frank stirred then opened his eyes before turning to caress his part-time lover. The bird had flown; but the smell of crackling bacon, scrambled eggs, toasted rye, and freshly brewed coffee is the way to man's heart. And he wasn't about to complain.

"Wake up, sleepyhead. Your breakfast is about hit the plate, and I don't want it to get cold."

Terry was standing over him, dressed only in the top of her pyjamas. Those sexy legs could drive a man crazy, and that dark shadow just showing enough . . .

"*Here* . . ." Terry chucked Frank his jeans. "Get dressed, dude."

"And how about you?"

"Well, if you want me to put on my pyjama bottoms?" She lifted her right leg on top of the bed. "Do like what you see or what?"

"Stay as you are honey. I'm not complaining. I believe in miracles . . . you sexy thing.'" Frank burst into a song.

"You're not getting to me with that stuff. Now get out of that bed or else." Terry pulled back the bedclothes and threw them onto the floor, leaving Frank as naked as a jaybird.

"Now, *do you* like what *you* see?" Frank laughed as he threw the question back.

"Deja vu. I deserve that, I have to admit. *Now, mister?'* She stood with her hands on her hips.

"Okay . . . Okay, I surrender, but you don't know what you're missing." Frank was laughing as he slipped on his jocks then squeezed into his stonewashed Levi's, trying to keep his balance as he stood on one leg.

"Grab a seat at the bar, big boy, while I pour the coffee." Terry seemed to like the domestics.

"Big boy? Are you referring to my height or something else?"

"Don't flatter yourself. Now stop fooling around." She poured the coffee then bent over to take the warm plates from the oven.

"Can you do that again, honey?"

"Get out of it, you pervert! Didn't you get enough last night?" "No."

"Ask a silly question, huh?" She placed the "full house" in front of him. "Don't wait for me."

Frank tucked into the crispy bacon and scrambled egg while Tracy emptied the pan and sat beside him.

"I tell you, honey, you are a really good cook."

"You're full of it, Reynolds. I mean who can spoil bacon and eggs?"

He placed his hand on the top of her naked thigh then leaned over and kissed her on the cheek.

"I really love you, honey."

Terry gently removed the wandering hand.

"Concentrate on your breakfast and not the dessert." She gave him a naughty grin, but she was enjoying the attention. It had been a long time.

"So, after breakfast, what have you got planned for today?" Frank asked between mouthfuls.

"Didn't your mother tell you no to speak with your mouth full?" Terry was teasing.

"That's it!" Without another word, he lifted her from the barstool then threw her onto the bed. *To hell with the main course. I want my dessert now!"*

* * *

Rose had just put the coffeepot on the stove when Judy arrived, dressed in her borrowed housecoat. She looked different without her makeup or was she still feeling a bit hangover from last night's dinner and too much Frascati?

"Boy, I could do with a cuppa." She sighed as she grabbed a barstool.

"Should I say good morning, or will the noise of my voice make you wince?" Rose was being both sarcastic and humorous.

"Good morning, Rose, but do me favor and keep the decibels down till I get my injection of caffeine." She rested her head between her hands.

"That bad?" Rose asked.

"Worse . . . Ah, *now that tastes good!"* She cautiously sipped from the coffee mug.

"Would you like me to cook you something before the kids come down?"

"Naw, I'm good. Coffee is fine."

Rose pointed to the lounge and the two lifeless bodies.

"Get a load of these two. Wasted . . . drunk as skunks. I ask you . . . What did we do to deserve these losers?" Rose was shaking her head, laughing.

With Judy's hangover, she was in no mood for hilarity. Lately, Bill had been overindulging, and she was not impressed and turned to Rose as she joined her at the breakfast bar.

"Rose, I envy you."

"Are you serious? Why would you say that?" Rose was intrigued.

"It's not often I get a chance to unload, especially with a friend that has an understanding ear."

"Judy, I don't know where you are coming from. I mean is your marriage going through a problem or something?"

"I look at you in envy. You have a lovely house, kids at private schools, a lady of leisure . . . *Me?* After ten years of marriage, a miserable box of a house. I have to take a part-time job to pay for the kids' schooling, a lousy used car, and by the look of things, no light at the end of the tunnel. *That is, not on a detective's salary!* And Bill . . . I hardly see him. Most weeks he works 24/7 and for what? I tell you, Rose, it's getting to me. Staying at your place for a couple of nights has been a relief bender."

Rose could see the swell in her eyes, and she could well understand Judy's frustration.

"Judy, it hasn't been all milk and honey for Tony and I. Unfortunately, if it hadn't been for demise of my dear father, bless his soul, Tony and I would have been in the same boat. Look at it this way. We both knew what we were getting into when we married these two apes." Rose was trying to add some humour. "Bill's a really nice guy, and you should think yourself lucky. Tony and I, we have our ups and downs, but we always find a way. Try and make space for a cup of coffee one day, and I'll meet you at Macy's. Their black forest cheesecake is to die for."

Judy gave a dejected sigh. "That is, if I can ever find the time. They say love is blind, and boy was I fooled by that one."

"Do me a favor, honey, and stir this pancake mixture. In a few minutes, there will be four hungry kids converging on this kitchen."

* * *

"Signorina Menzel." Rosetta gently touched her shoulder to wake her.

"*Ah . . . hmmm.*" Mona gave an enjoyable groan as she stretched her arms above her head.

Even in first class, although the seats are comfortable, there is nothing like your own bed.

Rosetta smiled. "Breakfast will be served in one hour. I'll leave the menu. Mr. Summers . . ." She turned to Mike.

"It's all right, Rosetta," Mona volunteered, as she studied Mike who was sleeping like a baby. "I'll wake him."

"As you wish, senorita." Rosetta gave one of her smiles as if to suggest that the "cosy twosome" had now more in common than meets the eye.

"*Mike . . . Mike . . .*" Mona gently prodded his shoulder.

"*Yes . . . Eh . . . Yes?*" Mike stirred, having trouble opening his sleepy eyes, then turned embarrassingly to face Mona.

"For a moment there, I didn't know where I was." He pressed the seat adjuster to raise his seat to semi upright.

"I hope it wasn't a bad dream," Mona teased, a cheeky smile on her face.

"There're bad dreams and bad dreams, and in the company of a beautiful lady such as you, I think I'll settle for the second one."

"Heh . . . Heh . . ." Mona laughed at Mike's comment, getting the picture. "You Americans! Changing the subject, breakfast will be served in less than an hour." She passed Mike the menu.

"I'm not feeling too hungry." He licked his parched lips. "But I would enjoy a champagne, orange juice." He pressed the call button.

"Si, Signor Summers?" Rosetta was there in seconds with her encapsulating smile.

"Rosetta, I hate to be a pain, but would it be possible to mix me a champagne and orange juice?"

"Si, senor . . . a Buck's Fizz, as they say in England."

"Make that two," Mona interrupted. "I like the sound of that."

* * *

"Hmmm, *this is* good, Mike." Mona took a sip from the champagne flute.

"It doesn't get any better." Mike smiled, holding up his empty glass before pressing the call button once again.

"Can you please?" He smiled to Rosetta.

"Certainly, sir. I'll fetch you a fresh glass."

"And oh, Rosetta, I'll skip breakfast."

"And Signorina Menzel?"

Mona studied the menu for a moment.

"Eggs Benedict, fresh fruit, and Argentinean coffee."

"Certainly, senorita." Rosetta took note then disappeared toward the galley.

"Hungry?" Mike asked.

"Not really, but I am a great believer in having breakfast as it sets you up for the rest of the day."

"I must remember that" Mike commented. "Like a double-edged sword." Mona smiled. "Is that a pun?"

"I'm just being a bit naughty, but seriously, Mona, I do enjoy your company, and I *would be* extremely disappointed should we part not to see one another ever again."

"That's a nice compliment, and the feeling is mutual, dare I say?" Her eyes were saying it all.

"Your breakfast, senorita."

The interruption was untimely, just when Mike was making his play.

"Changing the subject"—Mona was studying her breakfast tray—"where are you staying in Buenos Aires?"

"The Downtown Sheraton." The question took Mike by surprise, and it was the first hotel that came to his mind.

"Which one?" Mona asked.

"Eh . . . What the hell is that address again?" He screwed up his face. "It must be the one on V. San Martin. It's the best, but expensive." "That's the one! Of course." Mike breathed a sigh of relief.

"Reserve a room facing the bay or Rio de La Plata to the locals. It's nice." Then something crossed her mind. "Come to think of it, how are you getting there? Is the hotel limo picking you up?"

"Not that I know of." Mike was struggling.

"Well then, that's it, settled! My father's chauffeur will be waiting for me, and I can drop you off on the way." "Are you sure it's no problem?" The plan was working.

*   *   *

Frank's body was vacuumed against Terry's, and he was panting slightly.

"Am I too much for you, big boy?" Terry laughed as she gently prized their sweat-laden bodies apart.

Frank rolled over onto his back, partially relieved, and stared momentarily at the ceiling. He felt like "Apollo 13" re-entering the atmosphere, trying to avoid a "burn out." That last climax was out of this world, and he inwardly had to admit that he had *really* been to the moon and back.

"What, no more dessert?" Terry joked, purposely trying to embarrass him as he rolled on his side to face her, her milky naked body resembling a Michelangelo painting from the Sistine Chapel, and he kissed her passionately on the lips.

"I've said it before, and I'll say it again . . . *I love you, honey,"* he blurted out between breaths.

"You mean you love the sex," Terry teased.

"And that too." It was too good to miss.

"Why you! Get out of my bed, you ungrateful . . ." Terry was teasing as she pushed him toward the edge of the bed with both her feet. "Besides, I need to shower, and for your information, dude, you've ruined my sheets!" She outrageously laughed as she swung her feet to the floor.

"And oh, Frank, darling, do me a favour and warm up that coffee before you join me in the shower." She gave him a naughty smile. "I'm gonna need that caffeine after I'm finished with you, dude."

Frank had to admit she was a real teaser, and he couldn't help but admire her shapely naked butt as she disappeared into the bathroom, purposely doing the Hawaiian swing, only without the grass skirt! *This broad was a piece of work, but he wouldn't change her for the world.*

* * *

"Judy, can you help me with the salada?"

"Sure. You know, Rose, it's great to see our kids so happy splashing around in the pool together."

"Yeah, it brings back memories, doesn't it? We were kids once, although it seems a million years ago." She passed Judy the supermarket lettuce pack.

"The cherry tomatoes are in the fridge."

"What are we gonna do with these two?" Judy pointed to the cadavers.

"I know what I would like to do!" Rose retaliated. "Leave it to me." She winked as she filled a glass with ice-cold water.

"Rose, I don't want to know!" Judy winced at the thought.

As for Rose, she was enjoying the brutal reaction as she poured half the glass on Frank's forehead before quickly passing it to Judy. "Go for it, honey!" Rose was on roll, and she was loving it.

"Shiiiiiit, what the fuck?" Bill half rose, wiping the iced water from his face with his hand. *"You crazy woman!"*

Judy couldn't stop laughing at Bill's outburst, and the shocked look on his face as she poured the remainder of the "lethal weapon2" on Bill's forehead. "For fuck's sake . . . *You fucking crazy bitch!" That did it!* Judy's anger hit the roof.

"Don't you ever . . . ever call me a bitch! Now get your perverted ass off that sofa and go shower. *You smell like a cesspool!"*

The two buddies sat up and stared at one another, trying to find their bearings. They knew that they were a couple of assholes, *but why admit it?*

"Rose?" Tony was looking for cover.

"Oh no you don't, mister! I'm not in the mood for apologies. Remember . . . *barbecue* . . . Does that ring a bell in your alcoholic brain? Now get real and shower. You still have to marinate the steaks and sausages. It's after ten thirty, and before you know it, the gang will be on our doorstep." "And take that lazy lump with you." Judy couldn't resist it.

As for Bill? Well, his head was just clearing. He was in "no-man's land," his booze-lined face resembling an overripe mandarin orange on the "bruised fruit" supermarket shelf.

"Rose . . ."

"Tony, take my advice. The less said the better. Now get out of my face and go shower. Judy, did you find these tomatoes?"

*   *   *

"This is your First Officer Captain Arizpe speaking. I hope you have enjoyed the flight. We are about to commence our descent to Minitro Pitarini, Buenos Aires International Airport. We will arrive on time at 0930 hours, Argentinean time. The temperature on the ground is approximately twenty-six degrees centigrade with clear blue skies. The airport is close to Porto Madero and is approximately twenty kilometres from the city. A taxi will cost around one hundred and eighty pesos. Our airport ground staff will assist you in any way possible. Please fasten your safety belts and ensure your seat is in the upright position. Crew, please ensure all safety exits are clear and occupy your flight seats. The audio system will now be closed. On behalf of the crew and Second Officer Delgado, we thank you for flying Aerolineas Airways and hope to see you again in the near future. Thank you."

Mike was pressing the wrong button on his seat, and it inadvertently went backwards instead of upright, and Mona laughed at his predicament.

"I think it was that second Buck's Fizz that did it, huh?" She was teasing. "Here let me help you." She pressed the button, and the seat rose slowly to the upright position.

Mike laughed. "I guess it needs a woman's touch. Thanks, Mona. I think I'm still on New York time. Don't worry. I can manage the safety belt." He was searching for the elusive buckle.

Mona smiled again as she passed him the clip.

"Maybe you are right . . . *that second Buck's Fizz!*" Mike laughed.

"And no breakfast!" Mono scolded him.

There was a pronounced shudder as the "eagle landed" then came the loud, almost ear-piercing, noise as the jets were switched into reverse thrust, coupled with the ABS snatching and releasing, throwing them both back and forward for a few seconds until the big bird went into taxi mode.

"I hate these landings." Mona's hand touched Mike's, her tension momentarily.

Mike enjoyed the touch, and he smoothly removed his hand and placed it on top of Mona's, gently squeezing it in reciprocation.

"That feels good. Your hand is so strong and comforting." Mike knew how to play the field, and it works every time.

"Please remain in your seats until the fasten seat belt sign is switched off and the plane comes to halt. Thank you."

"I hope you enjoyed the flight, Senorita Menzel and Mr. Summers."

"Yes, and it was an absolute pleasure to meet you." Mike was quick to answer. When it comes to "pretty woman, don't walk on by." He never misses a trick.

Rosetta smiled. She had seen it all before, but it was her job. However, there was also a line in the sand.

"I'll fetch your garment bag, Mr. Summers."

*   *   *

The airport was bustling as Mike escorted Mona to immigration.

"Do you have a business visa, Mike? I forgot to ask." Mona was concerned.

"No, I decided that it was easier just to get a tourist visa for three months at the desk. Its only thirty-five American dollars, and then I can keep renewing it, depending on my length of stay."

"I agree. It's less hassle. I'll wait for you at the baggage claim before customs. Don't get lost." Mona gave him that smile then went on her way to the Argentinean Citizen counter.

The female immigration officer studied Mike's face for a moment then his passport picture. She was pretty but in a manly sort of way.

"Please step back to the line, senor, and place your feet on the imprints then face the camera. Gracias. Now place each finger on the print scanner. Gracias."

She studied Mike again, her face expressionless.

"And you require a tourist visa, senor?"

"Yes, that is correct." Mike was feeling a bit nervous. Maybe the cops were onto him. *Naw, it's impossible,* he reassured himself.

"That will be thirty-five U. S. dollars." Frozen Face stamped the passport. "Pay at the next counter." She pointed dryly.

Mike gave a sigh of relief as he finally approached customs clearance, and he could see Mona patiently waiting in the distance and gave her a wave.

"Is everything all right, Mike?" Mona asked.

"Yes, no problem." Then something struck him. He hadn't completed a customs declaration form. "Hell, I haven't compl—" Mona was one step ahead of him.

"A customs declaration form? I knew what you were thinking. But Argentina has its own system. There is one button in front of each desk. You press once, and if the light turns green, you walk through. If it turns red, they will search your luggage. I guess it's kinda like a lottery, but it works. They stole the idea from Costa Rica, and it makes the drug mules think twice."

Now Mike was really sweating. The twenty thousand dollars in his briefcase would raise some questions with customs. He pressed the button with bated breath. *Green!* The customs officer waved him through, much to Mike's relief.

"Boy . . . this *is* different!" Mike turned to Mona. "Let me go get a trolley." But before he knew it, they were swamped with young kids tugging each other to carry their bags.

"Buenas tardes, senorita. Comestai?" The tallest kid on the block pushed the mob back. This guy was not to be messed with.

Then he turned his attention to Mona laying on the Oliver Twist look with the "missing-tooth smile" that tugs on the heartstrings. He was no more than twelve years old; and at just under five feet and with that scraggly thin body, he looked like he couldn't lift a bowling ball, let alone Mona's overweight baggage. His black unkempt hair hadn't seen water from the day he was born; but the olive skin and those dark brown appealing eyes, the ripped jeans, and white T-shirt, its colours resembling a camouflage vest and thongs that were barely holding together, was a sucker punch for the tourists. And Mona was no different. This kid must have been taking acting lessons because for him it was Oscar time and his next tortilla.

Mona gave a sad look, turning to Mike. "I'm afraid poverty is a part of life here in Argentina, and these kids, would you believe it, don't even go to school. And unfortunately, they end up as professional beggars and more often part of a beggar's cartel."

She turned to the young rag tag; twelve years old. "Estoy bien. Gracias. No." No means the same the world over, and she pushed him aside like a wooden stick as she scanned the crowd, searching for the driver.

But this kid wasn't giving up easily, and he turned his attention to Mike. "Signor, Americano?"

Mike reluctantly answered in the only Spanish word he knew. "Si."

"Bagaje?" The kid pointed to the baggage and grabbed the handle of Mona's Samsonite.

Mike laughed. "Come on, Mona, give the kid a break."

"You Americans . . ." She sighed, opening her handbag then her wallet.

"Como te llamas?" she asked.

"Pino."

"Dies pesos." She passed Pino the ten "Adios . . ." She pointed rudely and gestured with her feet to kick him in the butt. He got the message. "Prego, senorita."

"De nada," Mona replied, shaking her head.

Happy with the ten spot, Pino was on his way to his next sucker.

"Ah, there's the driver." Mona waved to the chauffer-suited man standing by the large black stretched Chevy limo.

Mike was impressed. *Life was getting better by the minute!*

"Buenas tardes, Senorita Menzel." He touched his cap and took Mona's bag to the waiting limo and opened the trunk then turned to look at Mike. He was not only the chauffeur but also the bodyguard. In Buenos Aires, kidnapping is rife.

"Aldo"—she drew his attention to Mike—"Americano, no hablo Espanol . . . Engle's . . ." The muscle-bound moustached chauffeur nodded and opened the rear door.

"Now what was all that about?" Mike asked intrigued.

"I just told him that you can't speak Spanish, and his English, which may I say is not the best, should be spoken when you are in my company."

"Now I get it!" Mike smiled as he slipped into the spacious interior beside her, unable to avoid glancing at her smooth olive thighs.

"Aldo . . ." Monalita spoke to the chauffer as he drove cautiously into the airport midday traffic.

"Si?" he asked.

"Senor Summers is staying at the Sheraton on Via San Martine. Please stop there first."

"Si, Senorita Menzel . . . Encantadola, Senor Summers."

Mona shook her head. "He says welcome. How is my father, Aldo?"

Aldo thought for a moment before replying, his brain trying to translate English into Spanish and vice versa.

"Senor Menzel . . . is a good and is a missing . . . *Eh . . . Ah . . .* You muchos."

* * *

Tony and Bill arrived downstairs, looking like two new recruits from Alcoholics Anonymous who had just come from a "tell all" session. Dressed in their colourful Hawaiian shirts, checked shorts, and sneakers, they could easily be mistaken for twins.

"Get load of these two." Rose nudged Judy as the two "heroes" hurriedly passed the kitchen on their way to supposedly examine the barbecue, and both women had to laugh.

"What are we gonna do with them?" Rose was still laughing, shaking her head.

"Bill must have borrowed Tony's stuff."

"How did you guess?" They both burst into laughter again.

*   *   *

Tony pulled the hood from the barbecue.

"Fold this up, Bill, while I take a look at the damage. You know, we haven't used the griller since last summer."

"Yeah, and *do I* remember *that* barbecue! I think this hangover I'm having is a 'carryover.' But do you know what I would kill for?"

"If you have the courage, buddy, to walk into that kitchen, then fetch me one as well."

"Are you serious, dude? Here, let me help you clean the grill. As they say, 'if you do the crime, you do the time.'"

"Spoken like a true cop. *Now* . . . who's going to get the steaks and stuff from the icebox? I need a volunteer for this dangerous mission."

"Hey, don't look at me. Who do you think you are . . . George Bush?"

Tony gave a big put-on sigh. "Okay then, we'll toss a coin." He fished a ten-cent piece from his pocket.

"Wait a minute! Wait a minute! Let me see that coin. I don't trust you." "Now would I break the law with a double-headed coin, being a proud officer of New York's finest?"

"Don't make me answer that. *The coin!"* Bill put his hand out impatiently.

"Okay, what's it gonna be . . . heads or tails?" Bill balanced the coin on his two fingers.

Tony thought for a moment as if it was life threatening, but then again, *maybe it was.* "Heads."

Bill flipped the coin then caught in the palm of his other hand. He studied it for a moment then shook his head, carrying a big grin on his face.

"Too bad, buddy, it's tails, and don't try and pull rank on me. We're off duty, *remember?"* Bill was like a dog with two tails.

"A better idea . . . why don't we call in the Navy Seals?" Tony put on that serious face.

"*Get out of it!* Just think of it this way. You can get another commendation for bravery above and beyond the call of duty."

"*And I thought you were my buddy!* Okay, wish me luck. Here goes."

Tony casually walked into the kitchen, humming "Don't Worry, Be Happy."

"Here's a little song I wrote . . ."

Rose covered her mouth with her hand to stifle her laughter.

"Just ignore him, Judy." She was almost choking.

Tony cautiously opened the refrigerator door, looking over his shoulder before slipping a cold Bud in each pocket. Then he took out the plate of steaks, burgers, and sausages; and as he was, he was just about to exit the kitchen, Rose called to him.

Awe . . . Awe, he thought.

"The marinade. It's on the second shelf."

"*Eh . . . err,* thanks, honey . . ." He wasn't going to hang around, lightning doesn't strike twice in the same place.

"Bill, for Christ's sake, grab these plates. My nuts are 'frozen over' with these cold beers."

* * *

Terry was relaxing, stretched out on the sofa, her head on Frank's lap. She felt so peaceful after her shower and kinda lazy, and who wouldn't be after that hot session with lover boy?

"Gosh, darling, I'm almost falling asleep." She yawned, covering her mouth with her hand to hide her fillings.

"Too much for you, huh?" Frank joked.

"Don't flatter yourself, dude!" Terry threw it back at him, but in good humour.

"So what do you have in mind for the rest of the day?" Frank asked.

"I'm sorry, darling, but I but I must go and visit Laura."

"Don't worry. I understand."

"Are you sure? You're not just saying that to please me?"

"Of course not. Your problems are mine. Besides, it's my day off, and I want to spend it with you, whatever."

"Darling, I really appreciate it."

She leaned her head back and pulled down Frank's, grabbing his neck to give him a long sexy kiss.

"And that's how much I love you."

"Is that all?" Frank teased, laughing.

"If you don't want to be grounded, mister, you had better apologize with another kiss."

"Your word is my command."

"Well, what's keeping you?" Terry laughed.

* * *

Terry was enjoying the cool breeze streaming through her hair.

"Frank, I really love this car. You know, I never thought of buying a soft top because of the pollution in New York, but today I'm really enjoying the experience."

Frank turned to her and smiled. He could see from the sparkle in her eyes that she was really happy, and it gave him a warm feeling.

"You know, darling, what keeps bothering me? Laura has never told me her lover's name."

"Remember, honey, she's still recovering, and worse still, she can't speak, and her father still hasn't given the police clearance to question his daughter."

"I guess you're right." Terry smiled satisfyingly then leaned over and squeezed Frank's hand.

"We're here, honey." Frank signalled and turned into the hospital car park. *"So quick?"*

"They say time fly when you're having fun . . ."

* * *

"Hi, gorgeous."

Martha, distracted, took her eyes from the computer screen.

"I might have known!" She gave Frank that look. "How do you put up with this Casanova, honey?"

"Now you tell me!" Terry laughed.

"Listen, I've got news for you, gorgeous. You'll be seeing my ugly face again as of Monday morning."

"It didn't take them long to find you out at St. Francis, huh?" she teased, checking the register again. "Now, as usual, as you can see, I'm over the top and you, mister, are jumping the queue, *but.*" She paused, a smile on her face. "I'll make an exception for your lovely lady friend. You can go straight up to IC, but I should warn you that Laura's parents have just arrived."

"Thanks, Martha. I really appreciate it." Terry gave her a warm smile then grabbed Frank's hand. "Well?"

Frank couldn't help himself. "Have a good day, gorgeous."

Martha just shook her head then looked up, the smile on her face gone. "Next please."

*   *   *

The drive down Av. Leopoldo Lugones was interesting for Mike as it was his first time in Argentina. The modern highway from the airport was like any other U.S. six-lane expressway built to impress visitors and potential investors.

Buenos Aires is a thriving modern metropolis of twelve million people and the second largest city in South America; but poverty and unemployment go hand in hand, and Argentina was no different from its Latin neighbors. The unsuccessful Falklands conflict with the United Kingdom and its subsequent humiliating defeat still left a bad taste with little palate for the United States, Reagan having given support to Margaret Thatcher to facilitate the use of U.S. airbases.

But for Mike, it was a depressing picture as he stared out the window of the speeding limo, fascinated with the continual change of scenery, from modern freight facilities feeding the airport to shanty towns and squatters. The contrast was mind-boggling, and the poverty was rife.

He could see small food and fruit stalls lining the roadways just off the feeder roads to the expressway and airport, and wondered how these people survived, let alone these kids running around barefooted. But strangely, everyone seemed happy. Maybe there was a lesson to be learned for the developed countries where obesity and material wealth is god.

*   *   *

"I know what you are thinking, Mike, and for me it is also depressing, but Argentina is progressing slowly, and with attractive government incentives, we have seen the influx of foreign manufactures, from automobiles to oil exploration and refineries bringing badly needed employment to the population. Of course, the wealthy are wealthy, and the poor are poor with nothing in between, and corruption is part of everyday life here, but let's not get depressed. As they say, 'you can't change the world.'"

"I guess you're right, Mona." He smiled. "Changing the subject, are we far from my hotel?"

"About another five minutes. Why, are you feeling hungry? *Remember, no breakfast!*"

"You're not going to let me forget that, are you?" "You deserve it!" Mona smiled cheekily.

"Is that so? Well, how about I make it up to you by taking you out to dinner this evening?"

"*Hmmm* . . . Let me see . . . Do I have another date with an attractive unattached Americano this evening?" Mona pouted her lips, putting on a special show; but inwardly, she couldn't wait to say yes.

"Well . . . I'm waiting." Mike was laying on the charm as he purposely stared into her large brown eyes. "Senorita Menzel."

Aldo just had to interrupt!

"Si, Aldo?" Mona was now distracted.

"Hotel, here now." He signalled and swung the big limo into the hotel entrance, its shockers bouncing on the slope from the roadway.

As the big car drew to a halt, Mona had still not answered Mike's question.

"Aldo, bagaje."

"Si, senorita." He pressed the trunk release as the concierge approached the car, sensing that it was someone important and of course the proverbial "palm grease."

Mona turned to Mike and smiled. "Bad timing, but in Spanish, as we say, 'Yo era trieso. I was being mischievous, and my answer is, I would be delighted."

"What time?" Mike was relieved. He had a good feeling.

"Say, seven thirty."

"Seven thirty then." He leaned over and kissed her on the cheek. "How do I say thank you, senorita?"

"Gracias, senorita."

"Of course . . . How could I forget that one? Bye, Mona. I'll be waiting at the reception." He closed the limo door and waved.

"Buenas tardes, senor." The concierge turned and snapped his fingers at the young bellhop who appeared to be daydreaming.

"Senor's bagaje!"

"It's all right. It's just a garment bag." Mike felt sorry for the kid.

"No, senor, Carlos will take it. Let me escort you to the front desk."

"You speak excellent English," Mike commented as they entered reception.

"In my job, it's a must, senor. Is this your first visit to Argentina?"

CHAPTER 8

As she stood in the lift with Frank, Terry didn't know what to expect, with Laura's parents here and all. Maybe it is just a normal visit or, worse still, something more serious. Whatever! Terry breathed a sigh. She was glad she had Frank by her side.

The elevator doors opened, and Frank reassuringly took Terry's hand. She turned and smiled; it was a good feeling.

As they walked hand in hand down the hallway toward the IC unit, they could see the police sergeant sitting bored out of his mind, his nose buried in the morning edition. Maybe he was a punter, but for sure today, security was the last thing on his mind.

Looking through the glass partitions of the IC unit, Terry recognized Laura's parents, her mother seated beside her bed, her father standing. They had that serious look on their faces that wasn't encouraging.

The big cop folded is paper as the pair approached then paused for a moment like a dinosaur with the tail sending the message to the brain before he finally recognized Terry.

"It's okay, Ms. Johnson. You have clearance to go straight in." He politely opened the door.

Dave Williams was the first to greet them.

"Terry! It's good to see you again, and I'm sure that goes for Laura. And this is?"

"Frank, my boyfriend."

"Of course . . . Of course . . . I recognize you from the last time we met."

"Good afternoon, Terry." It was Laura's mother. "We can't thank you enough for the support you have given our daughter. We owe you a lot."

"Don't say that Margaret. Laura's my best friend." She could see Laura smile at her remark, sitting up in bed, propped up by a couple of pillows.

The door of the IC opened with a slight squeal, making the party turn in response. It was Dr. Paul Nathan doing his rounds.

"Ah, here's the doctor now, Margaret." Williams glanced at his watch. "And right on time. He said two thirty."

"Mr. Williams . . . Mrs. Williams." Nathan shook Dave's hand. "And of course, this is Laura's friend, Terry, the miracle worker." He grinned.

Terry smiled, with a slight bloom on her face.

"And how's my patient today?" He turned to Laura.

Laura smiled and gave him the thumbs-up.

"Now I'm sure you are wondering why I called you. First, Laura's recovery is excellent, and she will be transferred from intensive care tomorrow to a private room. And I must say, when considering the beating she took and her internal injuries, she is lucky to be alive. But with the good news, there is always the bad."

He walked to Laura and held her hand, her eyes now wide with concern.

"Laura, with the exception of your crushed larynx, which will take time to recover, you will lead a normal life, but unfortunately, your uterus and fallopian tubes had to be removed to stop the internal bleeding as they were severely damaged." He paused for a few seconds to allow the collateral damage to sink in. "Which." He paused again. "Unfortunately, means you will never enjoy the pleasures of motherhood."

He increased his grip on Laura's hand in anticipation of a severe nervous reaction, which in some cases require an immediate intravenous sedative.

Laura snatched her hand away and covered both eyes with her hands, immediately bursting into tears followed by uncontrollable sobs.

Her mother went an ashen white on hearing the news, and her eyes immediately overflowed.

Then suddenly, out of the blue, Laura's sorrow turned to violent anger; and she grabbed the sheets to wipe her eyes and pointed frantically to the doctor's notepad, making a signing motion with her hand that she desperately wanted to write something. Her eyes were now ablaze.

The doctor was taken aback but quickly recognized her request and passed her the notepad and pen. Her hand was shaking violently as she scribbled something on the paper before passing it to her father.

Dave Williams studied the bold scribble.

"What does it say, darling?" Margaret was in sheer desperation.

"It says . . . MIKE SUMMERS . . . GLOBAL MARKETING . . ."

*   *   *

"I'll be glad when this shift is over. What do they say about 'Never on a Sunday'?"

"Sunday or no Sunday, I don't know about you, but my stomach is sending me messages."

"Hell, Neil, you're always thinking of your stomach. You're about twenty pounds overweight, and remember you've got your physical and fitness test coming this month."

"Tell me about it! But it's in two weeks' time, and Jill will kick-start me on the salads."

"Yeah, I can just imagine you on that rabbit food!"

"Christ, Rob, are you my mother or something?"

"Listen, buddy, we've been sittin' in this cruiser now for two years, and I've put up with all your crazy colognes and smelly farts, and I don't want to start over again. Besides, I might get a sexy broad next time, and you know where that leads to."

"You wish! *Now what's it gonna be?"*

"Burger King?"

"Listen to you. You never put on weight and you'll be ordering that double whopper and fries. Oh, and don't forget the diet Coke." He had to laugh.

"Neil, you crack me up at times. Now where's the nearest one?" Rob studied the GPS.

"Let me see . . . We are now on Rockway Boulevard. We could slip off at the Medowmere Park exit using the underpass. I know there's one there as I've taken the kids to it on our way to the airport."

*   *   *

"I gotta hand it to you, Rob. You've got a good memory." Neil was at the wheel of the cruiser and parked straight in front of the entrance.

As the "boys in blue" entered the fast-food outlet, they were met with the usual uncomfortable stares. *And let's face it, New York's finest are famous for their intimidating size, not to mention the large forty-five Browning, ammo pouches, cuffs, baton, shoulder phone, sunshades, you name it. It would scare the crap out of any felon!*

The cops removed their caps and sat at the bar.

"What'll it be, officers?" the pretty young college student asked.

Rob turned to Neil and burst into laughter.

"Get out of Taggart! You're a piece of work. I'll have the double whopper combo with a diet Coke."

"I thought that was my order." Rob was cracking his sides. "Just ignore him, kid. Make that for two."

*   *   *

"The burgers are better at Burger King." At least that's what the ad preaches, and by the looks of these empty wrappers, the "boys in blue" were not complaining.

"Maaan . . . was that good?" Neil wiped his mouth with the napkin after demolishing the last bite of the famous whopper.

Rob looked at the empty tray and laughed.

"I'm only halfway through, and you're finished already?"

"No, I'm not!" Neil pointed to his diet Coke, a smirk o his face.

"Listen . . ." The buzz and flashing light on Neil's shoulder radio stopped him in his tracks, and he put on a face. "Christ, what now? Car 17, Sergeant Taggart here?"

"Sergeant . . . central have had a call from the Airport Police at Kennedy regarding the APB on a Mike Summers for attempted murder and the whereabouts of a Buick Town car registration NY18, presumed to be the property of the accused. As your cruiser is nearest to JFK, the captain wants you to check it out immediately and report back."

"Will do. Message received, over and out."

"What was that all about?"

"We have to call in at Kennedy, *like now!* This is a hot potato. It's regarding that APB we just received this morning on some guy named Summers. The airport cops think they may have found his car in the 'Long Stay' car park."

Rob shook his head then wiped his mouth with the paper napkin, pushing his tray aside with the half-eaten whopper.

"Man, you're not leaving that, are you?"

Rob laughed. "So why don't you ask for a doggy bag?"

"I'll treat that remark with the contempt it deserves, but on second thoughts . . ."

They both burst into laughter. These two guys were the best of friends. "Okay, Benson, *let's leg it!*"

*   *   *

It had just turned noon when the first of the gang arrived for the famous Perino barbecue. As usual, it was an all-police function, with the exception of Tony's parents and his mother-in-law, Maria. Today would be a typical get-together, with the guys talking shop and, as usual, the women doing all the work like setting the tables, not to mention slaving in the kitchen, plating the antipasti, melon with prosciutto, and how about the famous Sicilian salada and tiramisu?

*   *   *

The column of smoke from the barbecue grill filled the air with the gastronomic aroma of char-grilled steaks and the occasional burst of flames as the fat ignited just to add the spark for the occasion.

"Hi, Dave, Ann. There's chilled wine, beer, and Coke in the Eski box." Tony pointed to the large, insulated container stacked to the brim with ice.

"Just help yourselves."

Ann turned to her husband. "Dave, be a darling and pour me a glass of Bianca before I disappear to the kitchen to help Rose and Judy."

"Hi, Ken." Tony waved to the police pathologist and his wife Senga as they meandered into the garden.

"You know your way around, Ken. Just help yourself to some drinks. The food will be ready in around half an hour."

"No sweat, Tony," Brody answered. "But don't take too long. The smell of these steaks is making me hungry."

"Listen to this guy, Tony." Senga prodded Ken's stomach with her finger.

"With his waistline, he should be strictly on the salads!" Tony just laughed, waving the aromatic smoke from his eyes.

"Boy, this is hot work, partner!" Bill exclaimed as he expertly tossed the steaks and burgers.

Rose had buttered a stack of buns on a large plate on the table next to the barbecue.

Tony's eyes were smarting from the onions sizzling on the hotplate, and the tears began filling his bloodshot eyes.

"Man *are your* eyes red! Is that from the booze or the onions?" As usual, Bill always put his big foot where his mouth is.

"Any more wisecracks from you, Hayden, and I'll put the cuffs on," Tony joked.

"Hi, Ted, Ruth." Tony greeted his boss.

"We'll not disturb the chef. We can help ourselves." Ted gave Tony a wink.

"Rose and Judy are in the kitchen, Ruth, if you are wondering where they are."

"I'll pop in and say hello, once I fill my glass." Ruth gestured, holding up the empty wineglass. "Your mother-in-law is doing a great job as concierge extraordinaire at the front door."

Tony grabbed a napkin to wipe his eyes. "Yeah, that's Maria. She's one of a kind. She loves to be busy"

"Hayden, I thought you were on the bar." Tony wiped the sweat from his brow before turning to Bill.

"Christ, Tony, I feel like Tom Cruise in *Cocktails,* juggling the beer and flipping the steaks at the same time."

"I thought you guys looked thirsty, standing over that hot grill." The voice came from behind them. It was Dave Adams holding two cold Buds. "Thanks, Dave. You saved my life." Tony took a long one.

*   *   *

"Maria! Buona pomeriggio. Come stai." Tony's father Giovanni gave the usual Italian welcome, kissing Maria on both cheeks."

"Giovanni!" Maria was delighted to see Tony's parents arrive. At least now she could speak her native tongue.

"Molto bene grazia," she replied before turning to greet Tony's mother Lena.

"Eh, Tony?" Lena was searching for her son.

"Gardena." Maria pointed to the garden. Suddenly, another couple arrived at the front door. "Mi scusi, Lena, a presto."

*   *   *

"Hi, Dad, Mother. I'm really glad you could both make it." Tony hugged his father and gave his mother a welcome kiss.

Giovanni studied the steaks on the grill then gave a cough as the smoke bit his throat.

"Va bene?" he pointed.

"It's going well, Father, but you must speak English. My friends might think it's rude if you speak in Italian as you may be saying something behind their backs."

Giovanni nodded and just smiled. "I understand. I go and fetch your mother a glass of Frascati."

*   *   *

Tony's father immigrated to the United States in 1935 with his mother Lena. Two naive eighteen-year-old sweethearts, eloping in their search for happiness and a new life in the land of "opportunity" to ultimately get married and start a family. Needless to say, as Italian immigrants, they were made less than welcome, often being ridiculed as wops and dagos for stealing American jobs at lower than the labour rates.

Understandably, the few meager dollars they possessed when they landed on American soil quickly evaporated on food and lodgings at ten dollars a week in a lousy "one roomer" in Brooklyn, the "bowels of the earth."

Italians are enterprising people, and nothing was too degrading when it came to making a buck, working 24/7, taking any work they could find, from dishwashing to scrubbing floors, even doing runners for illegal bookmakers. It was survival against adversity, but nothing could dampen their spirit in the pursuit of the almighty dollar and the American way of life.

In 1939, after two years of struggle, Giovanni and Lena had finally saved enough to open a small deli specializing in Italian delicacies, from pastrami to fresh cannelloni, and consequently decided to take the big step and make it legal. It was hard work and heartbreak, and there were times when returning to Sicily was more than an option; but perseverance paid off, and they managed to purchase a small apartment not far from the deli. And suddenly, life was good, in fact good enough to start a family, and they decided to apply for U.S. citizenship. But France and Britain declared war on Nazi Germany after Hitler invaded Poland, with President Roosevelt stressing U.S. neutrality, although he would later commit to the supply of arms to the United Kingdom and his good friend and ally Winston Churchill.

Giovanni and Lena were uneasy at the thought that the United States could be drawn into the European conflict and more so Benito Mussolini declaring Italy's support for Adolph Hitler; and the writing was on the wall when Germany and Italy declared war on the United States on December 11, 1941.

Suddenly, their motherland was at war. It was a frightening thought with their parents and brothers taking up arms against the country they called home, and to start a family was now inconceivable and was sensibly placed on the back burner.

But Roosevelt had further problems when on December 7, 1941, with Japan's cowardly attacked on the U.S. Sixth Fleet anchored in Pearl Harbor and the catastrophic loss of three hundred aircraft, eight battleships severely damaged, four sunk and ten other navy vessels destroyed, not to mention the tragic loss of two thousand four hundred service personnel. December 1941 would be the "mother of all months," and with the United Sates declaring war on Japan on December 8, it would be inscribed in the history books forever.

But they say things always happen in threes, and the war in the Atlantic was in full swing with Hitler's U Boat "wolf packs" raining terror on U.S. merchant shipping en route to deliver vital supplies to the United Kingdom. The cost was tremendous, with the loss of 3,500 merchant ships and 175 warships. It was time for Roosevelt to get serious, and millions of young American men were called to arms. As for Giovanni Perrino, he suddenly found himself in front of the draft board, and in 1943, he landed on the beaches at Salerno and Amalfi and eventually the ultimate battle for Monte Casino.

With the end of the war in Europe, Germany signed the instrument of surrender at Reims, France, on May 7, 1945; and Giovanni suddenly found himself on a troopship heading for State side and demobilization.

The war had taken its toll; and when he finally walked down the gangway at the Port of New Jersey, Lena was in shock, hardly recognizing this tall lean troubled marine who now looked ten years older.

The advent of the GI Bill for returning veterans, providing one-year free fulltime training plus time equal to their military service to a maximum of forty-eight months and free college education, put the country back on its feet. But most importantly, for the Perino family, there were the housing benefits and almost-zero interest loans for small businesses. It was a godsend, and before long, they purchased the adjoining shop and expanded the deli into a full-blown Italian restaurant specializing in Sicilian food. Of course, what better name than plain and simple "Giovanni's."

In 1947, the baby boom period was in full swing with Tony's sister Annette arriving in 1952, Rita in 1955, and Tony in 1958, not a planned addition as Lena had just turned thirty-nine and childbirth at her age was a major health concern; but as they say, "all's well that ends well," and the rest is history.

Tony's two sisters always returned for Christmas. Annette, the oldest, moved to Toronto with her Canadian husband who is the senior editor with the *Ottawa Times* and Rita to West Palm Springs, her husband a golf pro and tutor at the country club. The three siblings produced six grandchildren, the pride of the Perino family.

Tony's parents finally decided to sell the restaurant and the Giovanni's franchise businesses, with fifteen outlets throughout the United States, to retire and enjoy their "twilight years" and leave their native Brooklyn and its many nostalgic memories.

They now lived in a modest four-roomed villa in Rochdale Village, a gated community just off the Belt Parkway Highway and a forty-minute drive from Brooklyn.

Giovanni enjoys his modest garden and Lena her vegetable patch. Life is good for Tony's parents; and after the traumatic life experiences they had gone through, without question, they deserved it!

*　　*　　*

Within minutes, cruiser 17 was speeding down the Van Wyck Expressway, only a few miles from terminal 1, "International Departures." Neil was at the wheel of the cruiser, and it was pedal to the metal all the way.

"So what's with you today, man?" Rob commented, his knuckles white from hanging onto the overhead handgrip, the deafening siren blazing in his ear.

"It's like this, partner. We need some spice in our lives. Besides . . ." Neil grinned. "I've always wanted to know what this baby could do."

"Save it! I'm happy with my lot, and more importantly, I want us to arrive in one piece." Rob was shaking his head, a sly grin on his face. He was secretly enjoying the chase.

"Here we are. *So, what's the gripe?"* Neil was still laughing as he pulled into the curb, the oversize airport cop striding toward them, having spotted the black and white.

"Hi, Sergeant Neil Taggart and Corporal Rob Benet." Neil greeted the lieutenant.

"Lieutenant Vince Russo., I guess you're here to check out the Town Car my men reported abandoned in the 'Long Stay' car park." "On the nail," Taggart replied, smiling.

*　　*　　*

New York's finest didn't think much of airport cops. They had a cushy number compared with real policing, *at least that was the gist!* The lieutenant sensed it and gave a sort of annoying grunt.

The big man was agitated as he spoke into his radio phone. "It's Russo here. Listen, I have a couple of cops from NYPD to take stock on that abandoned car with the registration that matches that from the APB. Yeah, we're outside departures terminal 1. *Like now!* We have a lot on our plate today. I'll jog your memory. King Abdullah of Saudi Arabia arrives here at 1400 to be met by President Bush and the First Lady. *Listen, just move it!"* Russo turned to Neil. "I apologize, Sergeant, but I must leave. As you can imagine, I have my hands full. This is a security nightmare." He shook his head in disgust. "Here's my card. Call me should you have any problems.

Sergeant Nickels will be here in around five minutes." The big man abruptly turned then left.

*   *   *

"I'm Nickels." The heavy girthed cop introduced himself. Maybe working in the airport in close proximity to all the fast-food outlets was too much of a temptation; but from a positive aspect, who knows? This guy might be the favourite for the next episode of the *Biggest Looser*!

"Taggart and Benet," Neil replied, minus the need for formalities.

"Say, can you guys do me favour and gimme a lift? It's a bit of a hike, and my boss is burning my ass. He's in one of his crazies today."

"Sure, but it will cost you. Stace, switch on the meter." Neil loved taking the "Michel."

Nickels just laughed; he knew they were ribbing him. *"You guys!"*

*   *   *

Neil slumped into the driver's seat and switched the radio phone.

"HQ . . . Car 17 reporting on the car found abandoned at the airport. Yeah, Lucy, my partner and I checked the vehicle, and the registration matches the one on red alert. It's owned by a company named Global Marketing. Don't worry. I've instructed the airport police to cordon off the vehicle until Forensic arrives No sweat. Is there anything else? No, we haven't.

That's Homicide Department. I don't want to stand on their toes. Yeah, you too. Over and out."

Neil turned to his partner. "Well, what's it gonna be? You or me on the wheel?"

"Gimme that key!"

*   *   *

Laura's father was beside himself with rage; but as for her mother, the thought of never having grandchildren by her only daughter was just too much, and she burst into uncontrollable tears.

"There, there, honey. Take my handkerchief and wipe your eyes. Don't worry. The police will find this scum, and he will feel the full force of the law." He was rubbing her shoulders, trying to console her, while Terry and Frank would have gladly hid in the closet. They felt so embarrassed and useless.

"Excuse me." Williams turned to both Terry and Frank. "I have an urgent call to make." He already had his cell phone in his hand. "I'll go to the hallway. I don't want to disturb Laura and her mother any more than necessary. She's been to hell and back."

*   *   *

"Jake, Dave here."

"Where are you phoning from and, more to the point, why the urgency? Has anyone told you it's Sunday?"

"Jake, cut the humour. This is serious. I'm phoning from the hospital."

"Well, I guess it must be important, so put me out my of misery."

"It's Laura. We've just received the surgeon's prognosis and were told that because of the nature of Laura's internal injuries, he had to remove her fallopian tubes and uterus. The bottom line is Laura can never bear children. *Can you imagine how her mother feels,* not mention my poor daughter?"

"Dave, it was always on the cards."

"Yeah, but 'while there's life, there's hope,'" Williams shot back at his brother-in-law

Murray gave a muffled sigh. This was the senator at his best, obnoxious and demanding.

"Dave, *I really am sorry.* Be rest assured I'll pass on the bad news to Stephanie, I'm sure she will give my sister a visit once the dust has settled."

"*Whoa! Whoa!* Wait a minute, there's more. Laura wrote down the scumbag's name. *It's a Mike Summers.*"

"Dave . . . *listen.* We have already a warrant out for this guy's arrest."

"You never told me! What's with you? Doesn't family count?"

The DA could feel his blood pressure hike the scale, and it was about time he told the senator a few home truths.

"Okay, Dave, I'm not gonna pull any punches. The bottom line is Baker's boys would have had this guy behind bars if you hadn't spooked him with your statement on TV, and now for you information, *we don't know where the hell he is!*"

"But I only mentioned . . ."

"Dave, drop the ball. What's been said has been said. My big headache now is to catch this bastard. Listen, why don't you meet me on Monday for a coffee when you are in a better frame of mind?" The phone went dead.

Murray stared into the receiver, as if to say, "What the hell?" But in his job, nothing is a surprise, even when to comes to family.

*   *   *

"Okay, Bill, *hit that triangle.*"

Bill grinned as he held up the old "Chuck Wagon" cymbal and rattled it with the barbecue poker.

Ding . . . Ding . . . Ding. The bell-like sound echoed throughout the garden.

"Come and get it."

All Bill needed to set the scene was the ten-gallon Stetson, and the sight of Bill and Tony adorned in their aprons with Bill clanging the triangle almost brought the house down, especially with the cloned Hawaiian shirts and board shorts; they were a sight for sore eyes.

Within seconds, the queue had grown in front of the smoking barbeque, their taste buds savouring the smell of char-grilled steaks. You could say it was "license to grill."

Before long, the steaks and snags were being demolished like it was going out of fashion. Everyone was now seated at the long table Rose had set in the garden to seat at least sixteen people. It was a typical Italian family gathering with good wine, good food, and good friends. Unexpectedly, Ted Baker rattled his wineglass with his spoon, an old Italian custom to capture the guest's attention.

"Ahh . . . hmmm." Ted was on his feet. "Please charge your glasses and be upstanding to propose a toast to the perfect hosts. Rose and Tony Perino, 'salutey.'"

"*Hear, hear*" came the chorus.

"And . . . I almost forgot . . . a toast to the assistant chef . . . Bill Hayden . . . salutey."

Bill rose to his feet and gave a crazy bow as if meeting the queen or after the final curtain.

"Grazie . . . eh, signor's and signorinas . . . Those are the only words in Italian I know." He burst into laughter.

"Sit down, Hayden, or the next thing, you will be hitting the high notes." It was Dave Adams taking a cheap shot.

"I'll have you know I almost entered *American Idol*."

"Yeah, yeah, yeah . . . Boo." Everyone was joining in the fun.

Tony is Tony, and he was letting loose on the vino, and Rose being Rose knew the danger signs and quickly sat beside him and whispered inconspicuously into his ear.

"Go easy, darling. It's early days."

"Awe, come on, honey. I'm enjoying myself. Don't worry. I promise I won't embarrass you."

"Now where have I heard that before? Besides, there's something I want to pass by you."

"Honey, not today. Can't you save it until later?"

"How can you say that when you don't even know what I'm going to ask you?"

Tony gave a big sigh, emphasizing his annoyance, exhaling a large burst of spent breath, kinda like a "*phew.*"

"*Go on*, take me out of my misery."

"Tony buddy, you're falling behind," Bill interrupted with his now slurred words as he topped up Tony's glass, much to Rose's disgust, followed by her special "look that could kill."

"I was just thinking about June next door and the trauma the poor soul must be going through, and I wanted your approval to knock on her door and invite her and the kids to the barbecue."

"Since when did you ask my approval?" Tony was grinning from ear to ear.

"Okay, big shot, I'll take Judy with me. Hold the fort until I return. I shouldn't be long, and easy on the grape juice. *Judy . . .*"

* * *

As Terry and Frank stood in the elevator, you could have cut the air with a knife, and someone just had to break the ice.

"Honey, you've got to let it go. Our visit to Laura today was scarier than Friday the thirteenth"

Terry gave a half smile at Frank's crazy remark.

"There you are. Isn't that a lot better than crying in your beer?"

"Now that you mention it, and come to think of it, I wouldn't mind a cold jug of Stella and some delicious pub food. Remember it's been a while since we had breakfast, and after all these calories I burned, well?" Terry gave Frank a cheeky smile.

"I couldn't have put it better myself." Frank couldn't help but laugh at Terry's innuendo. "So, where's it gonna be?" he asked still smiling. *There was that something about Terry.*

"You choose big boy."

"Pub food . . . *Hmmmm?*"

The elevator chimed, and the doors opened.

"*I'm waiting!*"

"Stop being such a pain. I'm thinking." Frank grabbed her hand as they walked toward the reception.

"Bye, Martha."

But Martha didn't acknowledge. On a Sunday, visiting is hectic, and she had her hands full.

"Oh well, there's always another time." Frank shrugged.

"Okay, how does this grab you?" Frank stopped in front of the car and turned to face Terry. "We hang a right onto Seventh Avenue. It's only five minutes from here, then it's straight all the way to Soho. It should take me around fifteen minutes."

"Yeah, but where are we going?" Terry was intrigued.

"Where every day is Friday," Frank replied, a grin on his face. "None other than TGI Friday's. There's one on Watt's Street, and being Sunday, parking should be a breeze."

* * *

True to form, Frank arrived on time outside TGI Friday's, the household name in pub restaurants. Luck was on his side, and he parked in the empty slot directly opposite the familiar large red-and-white sign.

"I gotta hand it you, darling." Terry had lightened up. "This is a good choice, and I just can't wait to relax over a cold beer and messy finger food."

* * *

The place was bustling; and all the tables, it seemed, were taken. The young kid dressed in the red apron, white shirt, and white-and-red striped bonnet was quick to attend the two lost souls.

"I'm afraid there are no tables free at the moment, sir, but if you care to sit at the bar . . ."

Frank looked to Terry for her opinion, and she smiled in agreement.

The high cushioned red coved stools at the bar were comfortable and even though they hadn't been on their feet for long it felt good just to relax.

"The menus, sir." The young college kid placed the large menus on the bar top. This kid had a cocky smile, and his black complexion made his teeth stand out, whiter than white.

* * *

TGI Friday's is an international chain renowned the world over for its scrumptious American classics served in a warm and casual dining environment.

The long dark wooden polished bar top, the high, red-covered barstools, and the colourfully lit beer fonts is the modern pub scene. Adorning the wall immediately behind the bar was an array of glass shelving sporting a huge variety of liquor bottles in all shapes and sizes, the low-voltage spotlights bouncing off the glass, reflecting against the dark red rustic brick wall, adding to its pleasant and unique ambience. The performance of the cocktail barman was something else, locking in the patron's attention as he performed his juggler act tossing the shaker over his shoulder then doing a three sixty to catch the stainless missile on its way down. It was the movie *Cocktails* all over again.

* * *

"Drinks for you and the lady, sir?"

"Two pints of Stella." Frank turned to Terry. "I got that right, didn't I?"

"You sure did, dude." Terry was relaxing.

"Coming up." The barman held each of the pint pots up to the lights to make sure they were pristine clean before placing them under the Stella font and the long-awaited stream of golden liquid.

"Cheers." They touched glasses and consumed the first mouthful.

They say the first cut's the deepest, and it couldn't be more true as Terry and Frank gave a satisfied *wow!*

"Now isn't that good?" Terry wiped the froth from her lips with her paper napkin.

"You can say that again," Frank replied. "But now the serious stuff . . . the food." He opened the menu.

"You do the ordering, darling. I'm enjoying my beer." "Waiter." Frank raised his arm to catch his attention.

"With you in a minute, sir," the "Teeth" replied. "Okay, sir, have you decided?" He was now standing, pencil at the ready.

"*Hmmm* . . . Let me see . . . to start with, we'll have the 'three for all' platter, with fully loaded potato skins, fried mozzarella, buffalo wings, and crusty fried parmesan chicken quesadillas. For the main course, the fire grilled chicken and steak fajita combo. And dessert . . . chocolate brownies with vanilla ice cream, caramel sauce, and pecans. How's that?" He proudly turned to Terry.

"I'm impressed, but you can't fool me. You've been here before." "Good try." Frank grinned.

"It will probably be around twenty minutes, sir." "That's okay. We're relaxing here, enjoying our beer." It was time, and Frank turned to Terry.

"Honey, I know how you feel about Laura and the dreadful news she received today." He squeezed Terry's hand.

Terry frowned. "The thing that gets me, Frank, is Laura's secrecy. I mean we're so close, yet she didn't trust me enough to confide in me who the father was even when she fell pregnant. And this vulture . . . Mike Summers . . .

I know the guy. Typical marketing VP hates himself. Tall dark hair, suave, blue eyes that strips you naked . . . Christ, I can't believe Laura fell for this addicted womanizer. His reputation is second to none. I think he has hit on every female at our head office, *including me*! *Can you believe it?*" Terry's hand trembled with anger as she indulged in another sip of beer, her eyes tearing over.

"There, there, honey. Calm down. I know how you must feel,"

"Do you, Frank, *do you really?*"

"Your order, sir . . . Enjoy your lunch. The main course and dessert will be served once you finish the entree."

"Thanks . . . *Eh?*"

The Teeth pointed to the plastic nametag on his shirt.

"Eh, Eric . . . I apologize I'm not with it today. Terry honey, don't let the food get cold."

*   *   *

"Frank, I'm bursting at the seams. Why don't we just order one brownie and share?"

"I agree, honey. I'm stuffed, but it was really enjoyable, and of course, the company was . . . well, it goes without saying . . . *Eric* . . ." "Sir?"

"We will share the dessert and one cappuccino and one double short black."

"So where on the cards after lunch, honey? It's only just turned three forty-five."

"Darling would you mind if you just drop me off at my apartment? I feel bushed, and worse still, tomorrow I have to start my new job and I can just imagine the 'shop talk' and the bad mouthing . . . like . . . 'We all know how she got that promotion.'"

"Come on, honey, I'm sure it's not as bad as all that."

"Worse . . . You don't know these bitches. Honey, I just want to get my feet up and be a couch potato for this evening. You *do* understand?"

"Of course, I do, but remember, I'm there if you need me. I'll give you call on Monday."

*   *   *

Rose and Judy are a formidable pair when together. and Rose boldly knocked on June Summers's front door. There was a delay of at least five minutes, and Rose gave sigh of relief as she heard the lock unlatch. June had the security chain hooked for safety, and she opened the door just enough to peer through.

"June, it's me Rose . . . Tony's wife."

Rose heard the chain drop, and the door cautiously opened.

The face that met them was a pretty sad sight, and to see this normally bubbly forty-two-year-old blonde beauty in such a distraught state was more than concerning.

"Are you all right, honey?" Bill's wife, Judy, asked.

"Yeah, I'm holding up. Thank God for the kids," June replied, her eyes puffed up and bloodshot.

"Listen," Rose began, "Judy and I are really concerned about your state of mind, locked away like this and worrying yourself to death. So why don't you clean yourself up and join us at the barbecue? Sitting at home brooding won't change anything."

"I know, Ruth, but I feel so embarrassed. I don't want to face the world."

"Don't be silly," Judy interrupted her. "We are all behind you. After all, it's not your fault, honey."

"June, have you had anything to eat?" Rose asked, but before she could reply, "Silly question. Don't answer that."

"Now, June, Judy and I are gonna wait here until you freshen up, and we're not taking no for an answer."

June reluctantly smiled. "Well, in that case, you had best come in. Gimme fifteen while I have a shower. *I must look awful!* Grab a seat. There's some chilled chardonnay in the fridge. Help yourselves . . . Steven. .

Cheryl," she shouted at the pitch of her voice as she disappeared up the stairs.

Rose smiled, turning to Judy. "Gimme a high five."

*   *   *

"Ah, June." Maria rose from the table to greet her. "Make a room for June, Rose's next-door neighbour. Tony, move the chairs to give her seat at the table." Tony smiled. When his mother issued an order . . .

"Hi, June, welcome to the 'feast of the Passover.'" Tony's bent humour brought a flicker of laughter. "Move over, guys, and make room for this beautiful blonde."

June was slightly embarrassed by Tony's comment, but then that's Tony. But whatever, he means well.

"Thanks, Tony." June laid on a lame smile, knowing full well that the predicament with her husband was now New York's worst-kept secret, and who could blame her with half of the detective bureau were sitting at the table. "Here, squeeze in beside Judy and I." "Thanks." June forced a smiled.

"Come now, honey. What can I get you to eat?" Tony had already placed the glass of Frascati in front of her.

"Salad is fine, Tony."

"What? I can't entice you with a Perino burger or one of my chili dogs with onions and American . . ."

"*Well* . . . if you insist . . . the chili dog, but not too much mustard." June took a sip of her wine for fortitude.

"Where are the kids, honey?" Bill's wife asked.

"I tried to convince them, but they are both pretty upset. Besides, there's plenty of food in the fridge. Don't worry. They'll be all right. They are grownups now and can take care of themselves."

Judy sighed. "I wish mine were that age."

"Don't worry. You will be surprised how time flies and . . ." Suddenly, the loud ring of Baker's cell phone distracted her.

Ted just shook his head and flipped open the phone.

"Baker here. Nev! I guess it's important. What's the deal? Summers's car has been found abandoned at Kennedy's International Terminal. It's definite. Okay, I'll tell Adams to send his team there first thing tomorrow morning. Yeah, I can just imagine Murray on your tail. Thanks, Nev. Ciao. Sure, I'll phone you first thing."

Judy could hear every word. Her face went a deathly grey.

"Tony," Baker beckoned him, assuming June had absorbed his every word to the commissioner, and he whispered into Tony's ear. Tony nodded and made a motion with his eyes to attract Rose, but June was no dummy, and she faced Baker full on.

"It's my husband's car. It's been found, isn't it?" The tone of her voice momentarily stopping the overindulgence.

"Honey, let's retreat to the kitchen." Rose endeavoured to console June. "Tony, I'm sure, will be able to give you the latest on Mike . . ."

* * *

"I wish to check in please."

223

The young lady behind the desk, dressed in the smart, white-collared blouse and black fitted skirt, rose to her feet to greet Mike.

These Latino women are really pretty, Mike thought to himself as he admired this olive-skinned beauty with her shoulder-length curled black hair and olive-shaped dark brown eyes. And when she smiled with those white even teeth and full lips, no more was said.

"Senor . . . Excuse me. You were saying?" the "looker" asked.

Mike quickly returned to his senses, studying her nametag.

"Eh . . . Err . . . Lolita, I'm so sorry. It has been a long flight . . . I wish to check in."

"Certainly, senor. I understand." She gave Mike a warm smile and returned to her seat. "Please." She pointed to the plush chair in front of her desk then passed Mike the registration document.

"Please complete this, senor."

Mike quickly scanned the document and completed the information but not before entering a fictitious New York address.

"I see, Senor Summers." She was studying the computer screen. "That you don't have a reservation."

"That is correct. I thought at this time of the year it would not be necessary."

Lolita smiled. "Don't be fooled, senor. Buenos Aires is always busy no matter what time of the year. But . . . let me see . . . Ah! You are in luck." She smiled, relieved. "A guest has just checked out, and the room is still vacant. It's a business suite at three fifty U.S. dollars per night and includes full breakfast." She hesitated, waiting for Mike's agreement.

Mike pondered for a moment. It was above his budget when considering his nest egg, but then again, he had to impress Mona.

"I'll take it."

"For how long, senor?"

Again, Mike was caught short. "Eh . . . let's say three weeks, but that depends upon my business negotiations."

"Senor, I understand, but I need to know as the hotel at the moment is fully occupied."

Mike sighed and shrugged it was all or nothing.

"Then three weeks it is."

Lolita quickly entered the confirmation into the computer.

"How do you wish to pay, senor?"

"Cash," Mike replied, knowing full well that cards are traceable.

Lolita looked up. *This was unusual.*

"I'm sorry, sir, but you must provide a credit card for security reasons. I will take a copy of your card and destroy the payment slip when you check out and you settle your account in full by cash. Of course, as usual, the hotel must check your card details to ensure your credit is good."

Mike hadn't expected this twist, but in his line of work, he should have known better, Besides, he was in a corner.

"American Express." He passed her the platinum card.

After a few minutes on the phone, Lolita smiled, placing back the receiver. "Everything is good, Senor Summers. Here is your key card for suite 202.

Carlos . . ." She called the bellhop. "Bagaje . . . el cuarto, doscientos dos." The young bellhop didn't hang around, especially when it comes to Americana's. They are always heavy on the tips.

He was about to leave when something crossed his mind, and he suddenly stopped in his tracks.

"Lolita, now that I remember, I need some U.S. dollars changed to pesos"

"That's no problem, senor. Go to the cashier's desk on your left, and you will be attended to." She pointed to the counter.

"Gracias," Mike replied, his Spanish exhausted.

"How much, senor?" the male cashier asked.

"Three thousand U.S. dollars to pesos. *And oh!* Can you give me some small bills?"

The cashier acknowledged with a smile.

The bellhop, while carrying the garment bag, took Mike's keycard and motioned to follow him toward the elevator.

Within minutes, the elevator chimed; and as the doors opened, Mike was partially relieved. The kid had that permanent "locked in" smile, and it was making Mike feel uncomfortable. He was trying hard for a ten spot, and who could blame him, with the kind of poverty Mike had seen with his own eyes.

"Just leave the bag there, kid." Mike pointed, assuming that "laughing gas's" command of English was little or non-existent, but whatever, he slipped him a ten anyway.

"Gracias, senor." The kid disappeared quicker than the ten.

Mike had to smile as he removed his jacket and tie before kicking off his shoes, wearily walking to the bedroom. He placed his precious briefcase on the bed before opening the wardrobe's sliding door in search for the room safe.

"Ah, here we are!" He quickly read the instructions on the safe door.

"No sweat," he commented then returned to his briefcase and removed the remaining swag of U.S. bank notes. Seventeen grand was all he had between "walking the streets alone" and finding a job. He stuffed the notes into the miniature safe then the barrels using the first three numbers of his birthdate as the combination.

"Boy, *does this feel good!*" Mike spoke out loud as he finally flopped onto the king-size bed. "I just want to close my eyes and sleep. That flight was like forever. But first things first." He stretched over and grabbed the phone.

"Yes, Senor Summers?" It sounded like Lolita's voice.

"Lolita, I would like a 'wake up' call for five thirty this evening."

"Certainly, senor. Five thirty for room 202."

Mike was now more than relieved. After all, he didn't want to be late for his latest conquest; and within minutes, he was dead to the world, a world that would be vastly different when he woke up.

*   *   *

The forced siesta seemed like an eternity, with Mike tossing and turning, sweat saturating his shirt, his troubled mind tearing his subconscious apart. *June . . . the kids . . . Laura . . . the police . . .* It was all too much. Now he was another Richard Kimberly on the run in a foreign country, and where would it end?

The perpetual ring of the phone kept echoing inside a tunnel. Why did that phone keep ringing and ringing? "Please make it stop. *Please!*" he screamed, clamping both hands over his ears. But it wouldn't go away. Then something jolted his troubled mind, and he sat bolt upright; and for a brief moment, he was disoriented as he studied the unfamiliar surroundings of the dimly lit hotel room. Then he noticed the red flashing light on the bedside phone, and everything suddenly fell into place.

"*Yes?*"

"Your wake-up call, senor . . . five thirty."

"*Eh . . . Err,* thank you." Mike placed the receiver back and thumped his head back into the hollow of the sweat-laden pillow before again staring blankly at the ceiling.

This whole catastrophic mess was scarily coming back; but now, more importantly, he had to pull himself together before his date with Mona. If he played his cards right, she could be his lifeline, and there was no way he was going to blow it.

*   *   *

He showered, shaved, and cologned before slipping into his bathrobe. He not only had to look good; he had to smell good too. And he quickly checked the time on the bedside clock.

"Six twenty-five," Mike spoke out loud.

The timing was perfect, and he quickly unpacked the blazer and hung it in the wardrobe with his beige white slacks then picked up the phone.

"Front desk. Senor Summers, how can I help you?"

"Can you put me through to housekeeping?"

"Housekeeping?"

"This is room 202. I need a shirt pressed urgently."

"Si, I will send someone up immediately."

No sooner had he placed the phone back than the doorbell chimed.

The white sharply pressed shirt was returned in fifteen minutes, with Mike already dressed in his slacks and shoes, patiently waiting when the chambermaid arrived; and he palmed her a ten for the nice job.

Time was running out as he gingerly slipped into his shirt and looped the blue spotted bow tie, tightening it to perfection. His smart dark blue double-breasted blazer sporting the familiar brass buttons was the "Arc de Triomphe," and when he finally fluffed the matching handkerchief into his top pocket, he certainly looked the part. He studied himself in the mirror for few more seconds and straightened his bow tie. He was back to his old self again, and tonight the beautiful divorcee would be an easy prey.

*   *   *

As Mike paced the reception, continually glancing at his watch, the lovely Lolita caught his eye as she watched his every move.

So why miss an opportunity? Mike thought to himself. After all, he still had a few minutes before Mona arrived; and there's nothing wrong with getting familiar with one of the hotel's receptionists, especially a doll like Lolita. Receptionists are a great source of information, and Mike was about to test the water.

"Buenas tardes, Senor Summers. You look so handsome tonight. Who is the lucky lady, may I ask?"

"I shouldn't tell you, but her name is Senorita Monalita Menzel." "She is a beautiful Argentinean lady. You have good taste." "Do you know her?" Mike asked, now intrigued.

"Everyone knows the Monzel family, one of the oldest and richest in Argentina, but I won't keep you as I see a large black limousine at the front entrance."

"Thanks, Lolita." Mike gave her a sly wink. He might as well keep the door open.

Aldo, the chauffeur, was waiting with the rear door of the limo ajar; and he touched his peak his cap as Mike took the backseat next to Mona, her perfume filling the car with a fresh floral bouquet.

Mona was tastefully dressed in a sheer black sleeveless dress, with just enough cleavage to torture a lesser man and showing enough thigh to keep one guessing. Her subtle fine gold-chained necklace carried a one-carat pale blue Sri Lankan sapphire encrusted with a fine circular border of small diamonds.

Although she is wealthy, she was by no means flaunting it.

"Mona, from what I see in this dim lighting, you look absolutely stunning."

Mona politely smiled. "Muchas gracias. And *you too*, if I may say, are looking handsome tonight. *Aldo, un momento.*" She knocked on the separation screen.

"Now, Senor Summers?"

"Why so formal?" Mike joked.

"You don't know me yet. It's early days." She had that smile. "Now getting back to food, as I can sense Aldo is getting impatient. Buenos Aires is dangerous at night, and Aldo gets nervous when we park too long in one spot. I suggest good meat and where better than our own Gaucho Grill Steak House."

"My taste buds are already being tortured. I love steak, and more to the point, I am really hungry."

"Then that's it, settled. *Aldo . . .*"

*   *   *

(Speaking in Spanish)

"Fuck it! Who is this macho guy accompanying her?"

"Sergio, gimme these fucking binoculars and stay out of sight behind this tree just in case that little shit Aldo spots us. That Gaucho is trigger-happy. Yeah, you're right, Sergio, but he doesn't look Argentine. His skin is too white. My guess, Americana. *It's just our fucking luck!*"

"Carlos, don't just stand there. They are moving off. *You got the fucking car keys!*"

"Si."

"Then let's get going. We don't want to lose them."

"What about Marcos? He's gonna be very pissed. We were supposed to do the job tonight."

"You just fucking drive, let *me* deal with Marcos."

*   *   *

"It's quite early for dinner," Mona commented as Mike settled into the plush leather seating. "I thought, as this is your first time to Buenos Aires, it might be of interest to get Aldo to give you a brief tour of the city by night on the way to the restaurant."

"That would be really interesting." But Mike couldn't leave it there. "And what more can a guy ask for with a beautiful tour guide named Mona?" She just smiled. *I mean what woman doesn't enjoy flattery.*

Mona knocked on the glass partition.

"Aldo, me gestaria, senor, para ver la ciudad por la noche. Lon plesae tome la routa hacia el restaurante."

Aldo didn't seem too happy. "Si, senorita, eh padra pasar La Plaza San Martin premero?

"Si, Aldo, sugerenenci es buena." Mona shook her head.

As the limo slowly slipped into the evening traffic, Mike wondered what the hell that was all about, and Mona could see the confused look on his face.

"I've almost given up on Aldo speaking English. That Gaucho is just too lazy. To be brief, I asked him to give you a tour of the city, but Aldo is Aldo, and he is always concerned for my safety. And you guessed right, he wasn't too happy."

"I gathered that from the facial expression," Mike answered.

"Then Aldo recommended the Plaza San Martin as the first stop, and would I agree? I told him it was a good suggestion."

Mike grinned, absorbing the truncated explanation, but the message was coming loud and clear. If he means to hang around Buenos Aires for any length of time, he had better start getting his tongue around the el Espanola.

*   *   *

Downtown Buenos Aires is no different from any other budding metropolis with its brightly lit streets and the array of multicolored neon signs advertising everything from food to liquor and the usual girly bars.

Mike was intrigued. Somehow it was not what he expected, but then in the real world, nothing ever is.

229

Suddenly, Aldo hung a left without signalling, irate drivers blasting a chorus of ugly horns. Aldo grunted and opened the window, retaliating with a barrage of abuse in Spanish before pulling the car into the curb, oblivious of the road hazard he was causing. *This was one time Mike wasn't going to ask Mona for the translation!*

The brightly lit full-size bronze of an officer on horseback in full military regalia around four meters tall, perched on an unusual stepped black marble base, stood majestically in the centre of a magnificent landscaped square.

Mona smiled, turning to Mike. "At the thought of boring you, I'll be brief."

"Not at all, Mona. I'm genuinely interested."

"I believe you." Mona gave him that "*Yeah . . . yeah . . . look.*"

"Now let me see, where do I start? Well, this is the very famous patriotic square situated between Avenue Santa Fe and Avenue del Liberator and San Martin Street, known as the 'Campo de la Gloria,' or the battlefield of glory. And do you know that this was the actual place in the early eighteen hundreds where the people of Buenos Aires defended themselves against the British Invasion and hence the famous bronze of General Jose San Martin, who commanded the Argentinean army? The base of the monument is made up of twenty-five large black marble plaques inscribed with each of the names of the soldiers, sailors, and airmen who died during the Malvinas or Falkland Isles war against the British. And you are still not bored, huh?" Mona asked, a smile crossing her face.

"Mona, honestly, I *really am* enjoying myself."

She smiled again before tapping the glass partition, signalling Aldo to continue.

"What is that big pink building on the right, Mona?" Mike asked again.

As for Mona, her mind was on other things . . . like what was so intriguing about this American that she enjoyed his company so much? She had been burned before, but then Argentinean men have that kind of reputation.

"Sorry, Mike?" Her mind was momentarily confused.

Most people have difficulty thinking of two things at the same time, and Mona was no exception.

"*That building on the right?*" Mike repeated.

"Of course, what am I thinking about? That's Government House, better known to the locals as the Casa Rosado or 'Pink House,' built in 1580. However, in the nineteenth century, during the presidency of Domingo

Faustino Sarmiento and with the cooperation of the Italian architect Francisco Tamaberini, the facade was reconstructed and was given a French

Italian look. You may ask why the colour pink? It's the combined colours of the two political parties, red for the federals and white for the Unitaries, hence combined, the colour pink. These colourful uniformed guards. *Aldo, lento!"* Mona shook her head. *"This guy!"*

"Si, senorita." Aldo took his foot off the gas pedal.

"Are the Granaderos an elite army group who guard the building day and night? The current president, Nestor Kirchner, has just been elected and is extremely popular and of course promises to transform the nation into a first world industrialized country . . . with the usual . . . jobs, foreign investment, and improved standard of living, and so on."

Mike grinned. "Politicians promise you the moon and at the thought of being pessimistic . . . I wish you all the best."

Mona looked concerned and didn't comment, her mind only half on what Mike was peddling.

"Mona, is there something wrong?" Mike was now also concerned.

"It's Aldo. His driving is erratic. *Aldo . . .*"She pressed the button to lower the glass separating partition. "Aldo, es algo malo?"

"Si, senorita—"

Mona rudely interrupted before Aldo could continue stating his case.

"Aldo, *habla Ingle."*

"Si, Me . . . eh thinka car follow."

Mona turned to peer out the rear screen. There was certainly an old rust bucket 1952 green Chevy Belair about fifty meters or so behind them.

*   *   *

(Speaking in Spanish)

"Carlos, I think that junk yard dog has spotted us. If he takes that sharp turn immediately on the left, he's onto us. I might have guessed. Don't follow, pull in, and find a place to park. We have to throw that bastard."

"And where the fuck do I park here?"

"Just do as I say!"

*   *   *

Aldo studied his rear mirror.

"Senorita, car now gone. No trust . . . still I keep look."

"I apologize, Mike, for my rudeness, but in Buenos Aires, one can never be too careful. *At last, . . . Florida Street!* The restaurant is only five minutes

231

from here. This street is the most famous pedestrian street in the city. As you can see, the many restaurants and cafes light the street day and night, and depending on the time of day, there are lots of street artists entertaining the tourists with the famous Argentinean tango dancing. Now enough of the night tour. It's time to sample a delicious Argentinean char-grilled steak . . ."

"Can't wait . . ."

For a change, Aldo signalled and stopped in front of the brightly lit restaurant. It's large neon circular sign with a ruby red background and a stand-out border of bright yellow emphasized the white silhouette of a long horn placed in the centre. The red neon sign below flashed every five seconds, lighting the side walk in a haze of bright red. "Gaucho Restaurante Azador. Especializado en Bistics." The facade, portrayed as an old ranch house with replicating logs and rough-cut windows, was most unusual.

"I tell you, Mona, I love the look of this place," Mike commented as he escorted Mona to the entrance, the oversize doorman-cum-bouncer greeted Mona as he politely opened the heavy wooden door.

"Well, as they say in English, 'the proof is in the tasting.' Did I get that right?" Mona teased.

"Near enough." Mike gave her a warm smile. He was getting to like this broad more and more by the minute.

"Buenas noches, Senorita Menzel. Es buena verte de Nuevo." The big man smiled.

"Gracias, Bruno."

"You seem to be well known. You must be a regular patron, huh?" Mike commented as they entered the dimly lit interior.

"In Buenos Aires, Mike, everyone knows the Monzel family." Mona smiled.

"I get the picture," Mike acknowledged with a grin.

The head waiter was more than attentive as he recognized Mona and immediately gave her the VIP treatment, personally escorting her to an exclusive table at the far corner of the restaurant and politely assisted her with her chair.

"Por favor, habla Engles, Vincento, me amigo de este pais."

"Si, senorita, excuse my English. No good . . . I leave you with menus. Gracias."

"So how do you like the place?" Mona asked as they settled down, and Mike immediately responded without hesitation.

"When I first walked inside, I instantly liked the decor. It's very cavernous with low lighting, brick-lined arches, and lots of mirrors. While the place looks full, it's an illusion because everyone is seated near the mirrors, and I just love these stand-out framed pictures in black and white, and color depicting the large Argentinean plains and these small wiry men on horseback as they herd the beef steers across the grasslands. But the final 'piece de resistance' is the waiters dressed in traditional Argentinean costume. I gather from the pictures on the wall this is how the Gauchos dressed?"

"Mike, you are absolutely spot on, but let's order first . . . *Vincento . . .*"

"Si, senorita."

"Vino tinto, por favor."

Vince quickly returned with the wine list.

Mona scanned the listing then turned to Mike.

"Since we are about to experience excellent Argentinean beef, what better than our own Cabernet Sauvignon to accompany the prime char-grilled cuts." Mike nodded in agreement, pouting his lips.

"Hmmm . . . Let me see . . ." Mona was running her finger down the cellar list.

"Ah! Ben Marco Expresivo Cab Sav."

Vince was patiently waiting for the order. Mona pointed to her choice, tapping the wine list with her index finger.

"Si, excelente." Vince took note and disappeared to the cellar.

"Now where was I?"

"The Gaucho getup that the staff are wearing!"

"First, let me tell you a little about the famous Gauchos of Argentina. The theories as to the origin of the Gaucho vary. The term is derived, the Mapuche or *Cauchu,* meaning vagabond. The first recorded use of the term dated from the Argentinean independence in 1816, and at one time, Gauchos made up most of the rural population in Argentina, herding cattle and practicing hunting in addition to serving as gorilla-fighting forces. They were hardworking, good-humoured, but historically prone to violence and carried a large knife called a "Facing" tucked into the rear of their Gaucho sash. But unfortunately, just as the disappearance of the "Wild West" altered the character and employment of "cowboys" so did the nature of the Gauchos changed but their image still suggests adventure and romance.

"Senorita." Vincento had already uncorked the wine and was about to pour a sample glass for tasting when Mona intervened. "Vincento, you must allow the wine to breath." "Si, senorita." He didn't look too happy.

"Now getting back to the dress . . . the traditional dark brown hat with the colourful band is called the campero, and the loose cotton grey baggy pants are called bombachas supported by the famous "capybara," a heavily stitched leather belt. The bombacha is especially suitable for horse riding and is normally tucked into the Gaucho's high leather boots. Of course, no Gouache would be seen dead without his colourful poncho covering his loose-fitting "pampera" shirt. Yes, you can pour now, Vincento. Mike, would you wish to sample?"

"As tonight I am the host, I would be delighted."

Mike inhaled the bouquet then held the half-filled glass to the light before finally taking a sip.

"Hmmm, excellent choice."

"Vincento, please proceed to fill Mona's glass."

Then out of the blue, Mike raised his glass to propose a toast. "To a wonderful evening and the most pleasurable company." "Thank you." Mona took a sip of the ruby liquid.

"Tell me, Mona, where did you learn all that stuff?"

"Argentinean history is a compulsory subject at school and university. We are a proud nation, and it was a subject, as you can imagine, in which I excelled."

*   *   *

Mike wiped his mouth with the napkin then took another sip of wine.

"How did you find it?" Mona asked, studying the satisfied expression on Mike's face.

"What can I say, Mona? My empty plate says it all."

"Shall I order another bottle of wine?"

"No, I'm . . . Unless?"

"No, I've had enough, Mike. I have to be in the office early tomorrow to catch up. After all, I have been away for over a week."

"Yeah, I know the feeling." Then Mike turned serious. "Mona, can you please ask the waiter for the check?"

"Vincento, cuenta por favor."

"Si, senorita."

Mike quickly glanced at the bill and paid in cash, including a generous tip for the more-than-happy Vincento.

"Mona, I forgot to ask you if you would like dessert and coffee."

"*Please* . . . no dessert." Mona touched her waistline. "I have to watch my figure. But coffee! *Yes,* but in a very special part of town. I'm sure you will be impressed."

*　*　*

(Speaking in Spanish)

"Carlos, pull over. That's her limo in front of the restaurant. For a moment there, I thought you had lost them."

"Yes, but now what?"

"Carlos, *keep your fucking cool.* You worry me!" Sergio flicked open his cell phone.

"Marcos . . . just button your lip and let me fucking speak! Yeah, we tracked them down, and they are just leaving the restaurant. I know, but if we don't have the money, *then we don't!* Listen, all I'm asking for is more time. *What are you fucking worrying about?* Carlos and me are taking all the risks. Don't worry. If we pull this off, we'll all be rich, and Francesco will get paid in full. Just get the bastard off my back. *That's all I'm asking!* You don't have to remind me . . . So, the deal went bad and we are into him for a hundred grand . . . I know. *Don't you think I'm worried?* He's only given me another five days before he breaks every bone in my body. So you gotta take the heat off. *Christ,* I said I would give you 10 percent. What more do you fucking want for sitting on your fat ass doing nothing? Yeah, I'm calling it off for tonight. If the Americana gets involved, who knows? We could risk the FBI on our tails. Yeah, I'll meet you tomorrow at the same place . . . say around ten. Adios." "So?" Carlos asked, having picked up only half of the phone conversation. "We call it off and head for some tapas and cold Quilmes." "Now you're talking." Carlos turned the key.

*　*　*

Aldo hit the sidewalk and opened the rear door of the limo.

"Por favor . . . Eh, senorita. Eh, senor." Aldo seemed more occupied, scanning the pedestrian jungle than attending to his passengers, his right hand tucked nervously inside the left side of his jacket. He stood for a few more seconds until Mona and Mike were safely seated before closing the rear door. Then one more scan up and down the sidewalk before finally taking his seat. He glanced into the rear and side mirrors, turned the key and slipped discreetly into the evening traffic.

"What was all that about?" Mike asked, the cloak-and-dagger stuff like something from *The Godfather.*

"Mike, I think I mentioned to you before that Aldo is not only my father's chauffeur but also his bodyguard."

"Is it that bad in Buenos Aires?"

"As bad as it gets," Mona replied.

"I guessed that from the bulge on the left side of Aldo's jacket that he's packing a piece."

"In this city, one can never be too complacent."

Mike gathered from the way Mona cut him short that it was a no-go to pursue the subject further.

"Aldo." She knocked on the partition. "Avenida de Mayo . . . Edificio de estilo art Nouveau."

"Si."

As they approached the brightly lit avenue, Mike could hear the sound of what sounded like the popular jazz music like you find in the French Quarter of New Orleans.

"Mona, that music?"

She smiled. "I love it, don't you? It's my favourite place for coffee."

Aldo was already slowing down, finally stopping in front of the brightly lit arcadia, the jazz music having an acoustic holiday as it bounced from the high colorful lead light glass-domed ceiling. This was the place to be, all right, and Mike was looking forward to another unique experience.

As they walked toward the arcade entrance, Mike protectively grasped Mona's hand, and to his enchantment, Mona didn't complain.

Then suddenly, Mona stopped in front of a brightly lit cafe.

"Here we are at the Cafe Tortoni, the most famous coffeehouse in town. This coffeehouse goes back to 1858 as you can read from the antique typed sign above the door: **Centos cienuento Ants can la cultuturo Argentina 1858.**" "That's a bit of a mouthful, but I get the gist." Mike laughed.

*　*　*

The interior was just amazing: dark red walls, soft lighting, plush studded leather wooden seats and Spanish-type low coffee tables, bronze busts of famous people, and beautiful large paintings of landscapes adorning the walls. It was absolutely stunning. To the far end of the extra-large room was a small stage with a guy tapping the ivories, an oversized double-bass player and a hot tenor sax, not to mention the black guy at the mike, blasting Ella Fitzgerald's classics in broken English. *This place was smokin' hot!*

*　*　*

"Mona, I had a fantastic evening," Mike commented, looking into her eyes as Aldo parked in front of the hotel.

"It was my pleasure, Mike, and I truly enjoyed your company."

"Does that mean I can see you again?"

Mona smiled. She sort of anticipated Mike's "come on." He wasn't the type to let the grass grow.

"I tell you what, here's my card. I have a heavy schedule this week. Why don't you give me a call say . . . Wednesday?"

"Thanks again, Mona, for a lovely evening."

He would have loved to crush her lips, but only "fools and horses" would venture down that path prematurely.

"Bye, Mike." She warmly squeezed his hand.

PART 3

The Deadliest Catch

CHAPTER 1

Tony and Bill had just filled the polystyrene cups from the vending machine when Baker stormed past.

"You two, in my office!"

"Tony, I think Ted's going to thank you for the barbecue."

"Hayden, you crazy bastard, I don't know how I put up with you."

"Look who's calling the kettle black."

"Drink your coffee. *You gimme a fucking headache!*"

"With the booze you put away yesterday, *I can just imagine!*" Bill retaliated.

"Listen to 'Goody Two-shoes,'" Tony shot back.

The loud bang on Baker's office window shook the glass like an earthquake shattering the silence.

"Tony, I think Baker is sending us a message."

"I give up on you, Hayden. *Move your ass.*"

Baker pointed to the empty chairs. "I've just had the DA on the phone." He lifted the receiver and pointed to the mouthpiece. "Can't you see the burn marks?" He smashed the phone back in its cradle. "Of course, what could I tell him? My two best detectives have just arrived at"—he pointed to the face of his watch—"nine thirty . . . Not unlike some people I know. Dave Adams is already at the crime scene with CSI. Thank God! Now . . . here's the bottom line. Are you listening, Hayden? Get your booze-soaked brains over to that airport and investigate where Summers has so conveniently disappeared to. *And I mean like now! Cappice. Out!*"

As Tony and Bill walked toward their unfinished coffees, Bill turned to Tony, a smirk on his face.

"Tony, do you think Ted was telling you in a subtle way that he enjoyed the barbeque?" Bill was covering his mouth, trying to control his laughter.

"*Hayden*, you fucking moron." But Tony couldn't stop himself from laughing either.

"*Well, lookee here, Dan!* It looks like them two snowflakes have just received another commendation from the captain himself."

"Now what could that be for? Let me think, Bert. *I got it! For the two biggest jerks in Homicide!*"

"Yeah, and they just got the 'golden arch' medal for the McDonald's discount burgers. *Maaan . . . now aint that something?*" Tony grabbed Bill's arm to restrain him.

"Play it cool, Bill. The secret is to turn out the lights, then we won't see two 'shoeshine' boys."

"Why you!" Brown jumped to his feet. He had had enough of Peron's shit.

"Tony, I'm glad you understand what these apes are saying! I mean what kind of manglish shit is that they talk?" Bill was slicing into the bone.

Tony gave that "let me think look." "Hell, I forgot, Bill. How stupid of me. Of course, they're not like us. They are *African Americans!*"

"Why you fucking greasy wop! Anytime you want to put the gloves on."

It was Lucas's turn to pour it on, his eyes protruding from their sockets like cue balls against his black complexion.

Tony burst into uncontrollable laughter. "*Bill, listen to 'Sugar Ray' here!*"

"What the hell is going on?" It was Baker. He had unnoticeably walked up behind them, catching the ugly scene.

"Now listen to me, you airheads! I want no more of this shit. What's this, a busman's holiday? Haven't you got work to do instead of behaving like a bunch of 'no brain' adults? Now you two, get you asses out of here. Russo is waiting to meet you at Kennedy. And as for you two knuckleheads . . . *my office!* I want an update on the Davis homicide. *And it had better be good!*" Tony gave Brown a cheeky wink but couldn't resist a parting shot.

"See you, Lucas, at Madison Square! Who's your manager, Don King?"

"You fucking . . ."

"*I said my office . . . And you two . . . hit the road . . .*"

CHAPTER 2

It was Terry's big day at the office, so to speak, and she wasn't looking forward to taking up her new position; but more to the point, she hadn't had the courage to tell Laura yesterday during her visit to the hospital, and it was playing on her conscience. She had struggled to convince herself it wasn't the right time, but then somehow it never is.

Terry had risen early, showered, and settled down in her bathrobe at the breakfast bar over fresh coffee and a slice of toast. She wasn't into big breakfasts and unfolded the *Times*, placing it next to her, taking a much needed sip of her coffee before scanning the headlines.

"Hmmm, that tastes good! Now let's see what's news."

There it was in bold letters: SUSPECT IN SENATOR'S DAUGHTER ATTEMPTED MURDER ON THE RUN. Captain Ted Baker of Homicide . . .

"Christ! Have these people nothing better to write about?" Terry turned in disgust to the sports section. "Now let's see how the Lakers did? *I guess it will be more bad news!"* She shook her head.

As she finally swallowed the last of her coffee, unaware of the time, she casually glanced at the kitchen wall clock.

"God, is it that time already? Being late today is the last thing I need!" she spoke out loud. "I had better get my skates on."

She quickly dressed, slipping into a dark blue fitted knee-length skirt and white open-necked short-sleeved blouse. The blue stilettos finished the painting as with the simple gold-chained necklace sporting a dainty sapphire pendant encrusted with diamond dust. As a final check, she ran the comb through her shoulder-length blonde hair before studying herself for a moment in the full-length mirror.

"It'll have to be." She sighed, slipping on the matching suit jacket then grabbing her briefcase before legging it to the elevator, impatiently pressing the descend button, the doors finally opening with the familiar chime.

"Christ! It would have to be you! *What have I done to deserve this?"* Terry was exasperated and looked toward the ceiling in disgust.

It was none other than "Mr. Lady Killer" himself, Nick Donnelly.

"Now, Terry, don't be like that. I know you're secretly glad to see me. Come on, honey. 'Make my day.' Admit it." He was grinning from ear to ear like a Cheshire cat.

"Yeah, *in your dreams!*" Terry shook her head. "But I gotta to hand it to you, Nick. You never take no for an answer. So full marks for trying." She gave him that look.

"How about tonight for dinner? I'm free." He had that silly grin on his face.

At last the elevator chimed, and the doors opened, with Terry exiting, giving an Oscar sigh.

"Thank goodness." She brushed past Nick then turned with a parting shot. "Listen, Nick, you're not a bad-looking guy. So, hang in there. You never know!"

"*I knew it!* Tonight then, say around seven?"

Terry had to smile, shaking her head as she walked to the car park elevator.

"*That guy!*" she muttered under her breath, but Terry had far bigger problems on her mind than Nick Donnelly.

*   *   *

Terry's heels echoed with a distinctive *click . . . click . . . click* on the sealed car park concrete. Car parks for some reason are always eerie, and this morning was no different, and it was a welcome relief when she finally slipped into the front seat of her Mazda 6 and hit the lock button. She glanced at the dash clock as she gunned the engine and slipped the stick into drive, the tires screeching as she climbed the steep ramp to the security boom. It had just turned seven forty-five, and she still had sufficient time to reach the office before nine.

The traffic this morning seemed heavier than normal as she slipped onto West Street by the river and followed the large green sign to the Holland Tunnel. It was the shortest route to Madison Avenue, but the next "*I don't want to think about it*" would be none other than the Lincoln Tunnel!

"*Awe, what the hell now?*" Her voice was almost at scream pitch as the traffic slowed down to a snail's pace before entering the tunnel.

"*Christ!* What the hell is happening this morning with all this traffic? Is Bush visiting Wall Street or something? Somebody up there must hate me. *I just can't believe my fucking luck!*" She was shaking her head in semi disbelief, but this was not the first time she had experienced this shit traffic en route to the office, and it most probably won't be the last.

Terry could cuss with the best of them when she is in a foul mood, and she ferociously switched on the radio for the latest traffic update.

"Good morning to all you happy drivers. This is Marilyn, your favourite traffic ranger, reporting from the CNBC helicopter at approximately eight twenty New York time with the latest traffic update. For those of you heading for the Lincoln Tunnel, be prepared for a long wait. An eight-wheeler has tipped on its side, spilling the contents of its gas tank onto the freeway. Fire crews have just arrived and are foaming the roadway, and traffic is now reduced to a one-lane trickle for safety precautions. Now moving on to . . ."

Terry shook her head and groaned in dismay as she looked ahead. Before she had even approached the slip off, the traffic was banking up, and she could see it stretching for at least a couple miles toward the tunnel entrance.

"This is all I fucking need to start the week," she cursed as she boldly squeezed the Mazda into some semblance of organized chaos moving from three lanes into one. Suddenly, the large black Cadillac Deville on her left gave her a horn blast.

"What the hell now? Who is this smut? I mean . . . *just who the hell does he think he is?"* Terry angrily pressed the window switch to give whomever it was an earful, but before her window was fully retracted, there was another irate blast.

"Listen you ignorant son of a bit—" Terry screamed.

"Terry, hold your fire . . ." The Cadillac's passenger window now fully open.

Terry was suddenly taken aback. "Terry? How does he know my name? And that voice?"

"It's your boss. Remember me, Jack Blakely." His voice was bellowing above the traffic congestion.

Terry stared for a moment, trying to put it together. She could now clearly see the driver smiling and frantically waving as he held his up cell phone before closing the window.

"Blakely . . . I'll be darned . . ." *Now!* She recognized him.

The cell phone suddenly buzzed, and she searched frantically in her bag to find the culprit.

"Yeah, Terry here?" she breathlessly voiced.

"It's me . . . Jack Blakely . . ."

"Hell, Jack, you had me going there. I didn't recognize you. I thought some dude was getting fresh."

"Still the same, Terry, huh?"

"Can you blame a gal?" Terry could hear Jack laugh.

"When you put it that way, I guess not." He was still laughing. "But listen, Terry, and more to the point, God only knows when we will both reach the office this morning."

"Jack, the same thought had occurred to me," Terry answered with a touch of sarcasm. "But the good news is at least I don't have to make up some crazy excuse about being late." She could hear Jack laugh.

"Say, maybe when we get out of this mess, we can stop someplace, and I'll shout you a coffee?"

"For once, Jack, you are talking my language."

*   *   *

For June Summers, morning couldn't come fast enough. The barbecue yesterday at Tony's was both humiliating and embarrassing and a day in her life that she would never forget, *or rather forget!* But life goes on, and besides, she had to be there for Steven and Sheryl in their hour of need. Sure, they are no longer children, but teenagers are the most vulnerable; and in this so-called affluent society of drugs alcohol and consensual sex and with the traumatic break up of a family and loss of their father, let alone a fugitive, their world could invariably fall apart with devastating physiological and sociological consequences.

"I have to be strong. *I can get through this!* I *must* get through this for the sake of the children." June was babbling to herself, partially incoherent of what she was saying.

The morning sun was now filling the room with bright sunlight. It was the start of a new day, and *it was time to stop feeling sorry for herself and get out of bed!* There was a million things she had to think about as she swung her feet to the floor and walked unsteadily to the en suite, switching on the light. Her eyes were smarting from a night of crying, and she opened the faucet of the wash basin and soaked her face in the cold refreshing water. It was such a relief, the water cooling her eyes, but the sight that met her when she towelled and stared into the vanity mirror was that of shock. *Who was this woman with the sixty-year-old face?* The bagged swollen red eyes, the cracked lips, the deeply laugh-lined cheeks, and that straggled lustreless blonde hair, now looking like a scare crow's. Her pale white makeup less complexion made her grab the towel rail for support.

"*My god!*" June gasped. "*I've really got to snap out of it before the kids see me like this.*"

There was a loud knock on the bedroom door.

"Mother, it's Steven here. Are you all right?"

'Eh . . . Err, yes . . . Steven. I'm all right, son. I'm just about to have a shower. I'll be down in a while once I get dressed. Can you do me a favor and put on the coffee?"

"Sure, Mum. I'll go wake up Sis." She heard the footsteps disappear down the hallway then the loud crack of knuckles on wood. "Sis, are you up yet?"

*   *   *

The warm shower felt like heaven as the water flushed through her hair, her firm tanned body glistening in the spray. She felt good within herself that even in her midforties she was still something to look at. *Why had she been so naive?* She had to ask herself. She had always felt that Mike was playing around, but it was easier to avoid conflict. And besides, she had no proof. But now this? *How could he?* She held back the tears. *"I gotta get out of this shower and pull myself together."*

She quickly towelled and dried her shoulder-length hair, vigorously running the brush through her scalp, the tingling sensation invigorating.

"Hmmmm . . . That looks better." She was doing a good job of convincing herself as she began to apply her makeup. She had to look good for the children's sake; it was depressing enough without seeing their mother a debouched nervous wreck

She dropped her bathrobe and slipped into her panties and bra and a casual loose-fitting low-cut mauve short-sleeved dress. Mike always said she suited that colour. One more look in the mirror and she was ready to face the world. She remained in her house shoes and proceeded downstairs to the kitchen.

"I made some toast, Mother." For once in her life, Sheryl was showing signs of domestication.

"Thanks, honey."

"Mother, can I pour your coffee?"

"Thanks, Steven . . . And yourselves?" June asked, turning to the kids.

"We're good, Mother. Sis and I have had something already," Steven sombrely replied.

June grabbed a stool at the breakfast bar and took a sip of the warm coffee, trying desperately to equivocate her trembling hand. "Hmmmm . . . That tastes good."

Steven and Sheryl both sat pokerfaced.

Sheryl broke the ice, "Mother, *what are we going to do? I mean . . ."*

"Sis, give Mother a break. *Can't you see she's terribly upset?"*

"Steven don't scold your sister. We're all upset. There's no point arguing about it. We have to think positive. After all, we don't know what's happened to your father, and remember, he's innocent until proven guilty. So, my suggestion is you both attend college today as normal. There has been nothing on the TV or in the media mentioning your father's name."

"What are you going to do next, Mother?" Steven was displaying more stability than his sister.

"First of all, I need to check on our financial status. Your father handled all that, and now I wish I had taken more interest."

"Mother, *what are you trying to tell us?*" Suddenly, it dawned on Sheryl that the good life she had been accustomed to was under threat.

"Honey don't jump to conclusions. I'll give the bank manager a call as soon you both leave . . . which reminds me . . ." She glanced at the wall clock.

"It's almost eight fifteen. Isn't it time you make roads?"

Before they could answer, there was the double blast of a car horn.

"That must be Brendan. Come on, sis, let's get going. Mother, will you be all right?" Steven gave his mother a kiss on the cheek.

"I'll try my best." June half joked on the threshold of tears.

"Mother, promise me to call me on my cell if you get any word on Father."

"Of course . . . Now you two, off you go. Don't keep Brendan waiting."

Sheryl stood for a moment in hesitation then rushed toward her mother, giving her a big hug.

"I love you, Mom."

*   *   *

Tony chucked Bill the keys to the Pontiac. "You're at the wheel, partner. I need time to think."

"You mean to snooze." Bill laughed, catching the keys.

"Less of the insubordination and just drive. That remark is gonna cost you a double whopper at Burger King."

"I might have known it . . . bloody freeloader."

*   *   *

Bill gunned the V8 then stretched out the driver's window to clamp the red magnetic flashing light onto the roof before switching on the siren to create a gap in the midday traffic. From Pearl Street, Lower Manhattan, to J. F. Kennedy was at least a forty-five-minute drive; and time was not on their side, especially after that blasting from Baker.

Tony opened his cell phone. "Dave, Perino here. Yeah, we're on our way . . . How long? At least half an hour . . . *You're finished already?* I was hoping to catch you before you left. Yeah, I agree . . . You dusted some good prints and the parking ticket with the time . . . At least that's something. And the car is going to the pound. Dave, what was the time on that parking ticket? 2215 . . . hmmm . . . Okay, we'll take it from there. Thanks, Dave. I'll call you. The barbecue? No sweat, we all had a great day. Yeah, sure . . . ciao." "That was Dave Adams?" Bill asked.

"Yeah, Dave's crew are done. The usual prints and all that stuff, but the parking ticket found on the seat read 2215 hours . . . International Departures."

"So?"

"So, Watson, for international flights, you are required to be at the check-in desk at least two hours before departure except for first class, which is one and half hours. We cut the slack and check all flights departing at around fifteen past midnight."

"That's what I like about you, Tony. *You're so fucking tactful.*"

*   *   *

As Bill powered down the Van Wyck Expressway, the traffic obediently pulled over to make way for the law upon hearing the wail of the siren.

"I gotta hand it to you, partner. Thirty minutes flat, and we are almost there," Tony commented, now more relaxed.

"Yeah, but just let me take this loop onto the access road first . . . *eh* . . . Tony, do me a favor and keep your eyes peeled for Terminal 1 International Departures."

"*There it is, Bill!* Slow down then hang a left, and it's straight ahead."

"These fucking airports, you need a GPS to find your way around," Hayden moaned.

"Stop fucking griping and pull in, in front of that airport cop, and for Christ's sake, *switch off that siren!*"

The oversized boy in blue suddenly awoke from the "big sleep" and legged it toward the Pontiac, anticipating something in hot pursuit.

Hayden hit the brakes, and the big V8 screeched to a halt, turning the heads of the inquisitive travellers.

Tony shook his head. "*Bill,* cut the theatrics. I almost went through the fucking windshield. Now more to the point, what was that lieutenant's name we're supposed to get in touch with?"

Bill just ignored him, while sporting a silent grin. Tony's sarcastic humour can sometimes be over the top.

"Dude, are you with me?" Tony was becoming agitated.

"The cop's name. How the hell do I know?" Bill shot back. *"You're the lieutenant . . . remember!* Like the one that's getting paid for all that brainwork."

"I give up on you, Hayden." Tony shook his head and hit the sidewalk.

"Can I help you guys?" The young cop was no slouch.

"Tony Perino, Homicide, and my partner Bill Hayden." Tony flashed the gold shield. "Listen . . . *Eh . . .*"

"Officer Manalo . . . Victor Manalo . . . I normally just get Vic."

"Okay, Vic. Listen, I'm supposed to meet a lieutenant . . . *Eh?"* "That'll be Lieutenant Russo . . . Vince Russo." "On the button, Vic." Tony smiled.

The young cop proudly grinned. He wasn't used to getting compliments, but Tony knew how to play the cards to get this kid on his side.

"Just gimme a second, and I'll call him," Vic spoke into the radio phone.

"Lieutenant, I have two detectives here from NYPD, Homicide Division. Yeah, that's right, a Lieutenant Perino and his partner. Sure, I'll pass on the message."

Vic switched off the phone then turned to the detectives.

"He sends his apologies. He'll be with you in around five minutes."

*   *   *

"Lieutenant Russo . . . And?" The big guy was short of breath.

"Perino and Hayden," Tony replied, cutting the formalities.

"How can I help you guys?" Russo asked, impatiently looking at his watch as if he had a monkey on his back.

"We need to check the passenger manifest of all international flights that departed on Saturday, August 15, after midnight."

"Gimme a sec while I call the airport manager. Sandy . . . Russo here.

Listen, I have two detectives here from NYPD, and they need . . ." Russo turned to the young cop.

"Manalo here will escort you to the airport manager's office. As you heard, I've explained the situation, and he stressed he will give you guys his full cooperation. Now the bad news is I have to leave you. I'm over the top today with airport security. First it was Bush on Sunday, and now it's his running mate Blair from the UK. Must be some big meeting to discuss another war or something. This shit gives me a fucking headache. I gotta leave you guys. Manalo . . . give me a call if there are any problems. Ciao."

For a big guy, he could move, and he hastily disappeared into the crowded departure lounge.

Tony looked at Bill and smiled. "And we thought we had problems. Okay, Vic, lead the way."

*   *   *

As the saying goes, "You can't see light at the end of the tunnel," only this time it was the reverse as Terry emerged from the Lincoln. After an hour stuck in semidarkness with not to mention the suffocating exhaust fumes, it was heaven to see the thing we all take for granted . . . *daylight! But where the hell was Blakely?* she thought.

Terry's cell rang again.

"Jack?"

"Ah . . . ha! So now I know . . . the boyfriend you have been hiding in the closet."

"Frank! Yooou! So, you've been checking upon me, huh? *Listen, dude,* for your information, my boss called earlier, and I thought that was him on the phone."

"Yeah . . . yeah . . . yeah . . . I believe you . . . Millions wouldn't." She could hear Frank laughing.

"Okay . . . Okay . . . So why the call?"

"I just called to say I love you . . ." Frank was singing into the phone.

"You big ape . . ." Terry couldn't stop laughing either. "Okay, Stevie Wonder, so?"

"I'll be free tonight after six, and I was wondering if I could take a beautiful woman named Terry to dinner? That is . . . not unless the phantom 'Jack' has beaten me to it?"

"Now listen, you big heel, you be at my place by seven or else!" "Is that a yes?" Frank was still laughing.

"I'm hanging up . . ." She was shaking her head, smiling. "And you had better not be late or you'll be speaking with a high voice." Terry hung up, the smile still on her face. She really liked this guy.

No sooner had she closed the phone than it rang again.

"Terry . . . I've been trying to call you, but your phone was engaged. It's Jack here."

"I had another call on the line. Say, listen, where are you?"

"There's a diner about two miles on your right. There's parking at the rear . . . The Last Chance Diner sounds ugly, but the coffee's good. I'm talking from experience."

249

"I'll be there in five. Make mine a coffee latte. Ciao."

June gave a big sigh as the front door finally closed. With the kids gone, the house suddenly felt empty, and she crashed the sofa to sit and think. Where would she start and what has happened to Mike? When you love someone that's been a part of your life for twenty years, you refuse to believe the truth, but in the end, it all boils down to money; and in hard cash, she only had four hundred dollars to her name. Mike handled all the financials, and now the thought of being penniless suddenly had become a real possibility. But Mike wouldn't do such a thing. She was trying to convince herself. Or would he? He loved his kids and he had always been a good provider.

"No . . . he wouldn't do that," she spoke out loud. "But where do I start? It has to be the bank manager. *Yes, that's it!* I must go and change."

*   *   *

All sorts of things were running through June's mind as she sat outside the bank manager's office. It was strange that she had never been inside the central branch of Citibank before. She had her driving license ready for identity purposes, just in case. June was deep in thought when the secretary broke the silence.

"Mr. Simmons will see you now, Mrs. Summers. Please go straight in." "Thank you," June nervously replied.

*   *   *

Simmons was typical bank manager material. The dark blue expensive tailored pinstriped suit, the crisp white shirt and poker dot dark tie to match, the gold Rolex, and Mont Blanc cufflinks all hung together to spell money. His thinning black hair combed in a side shade and the round rimless glasses gave him a sort of Glenn Miller look, on the other side of fifty, especially with the long narrow cheekbones sharp nose and grey blue eyes. From the sitting position, Simmons looked slim, but for some reason, bank managers are always short; and there was no reason to think Simmons was any different. His friendly face a front for the real deal when it came to money talk and keep your hand on your wallet.

*   *   *

"I'm Mr. Simmons." He shook June's hand. "I apologize for the wait. Please take a seat and make yourself comfortable." He pointed to the chair in front of his desk.

"Not at all. I know you are a busy man," June nervously replied.

Simmons gave an artificial smile as if to say *"Get to it and don't waste my fucking time!"*

"Mrs. Summers, I have never had the pleasure. Of course, I know your husband well, but more to the point, how can I be of assistance?" June froze. Where should she begin? The embarrassment . . .

"Mrs. Summers?"

"I apologize. This is extremely embarrassing. I wish to check the status of our liquidity."

Simmons was puzzled. It was strange that a wife was unaware of the contents of the family's bank account.

Simmons frowned. "Does your husband know you are here?" He looked puzzled.

"Mr. Simmons . . ." June began then suddenly burst into tears, her nerves getting the better.

This was different. Simmons had experienced many failed businessman bursting into tears, pleading for a second chance before foreclosure, but never a woman asking to check the family bank account!

"There . . . there, Mrs. Summers." He pressed the secretarial button. "Aileen, can you fetch Mrs. Summers a coffee. She's not feeling well."

June wiped her eyes and took a sip of the soothing liquid. She could crawl under Simmons's desk, being so embarrassed.

"Now, Mrs. Summers, can we start again?"

*   *   *

Mike stretched and gave a loud groan, like "Ah, that feels better," then sat up in bed and ruffled his hair. He could see the daylight streaming through the drapes and wondered what time it was. After that long tiring flight and then the impromptu dinner with Mona, when he hit the cot last night, that was the last thing he remembered.

"Now the time?" He turned to the bedside clock. *"Shit!"* he spoke out loud. *"Ten fifteen!* I don't believe it! I must have slept like a log, but if I want some breakfast, for sure I had better get my ass out of this bed." He swung his feet to the floor and made a "bee line" for the bathroom.

Mike didn't hang around and quickly shaved and showered before slipping into his casual slacks, white open-necked short-sleeved shirt, and board shoes.

The elevator doors opened, and to Mike's surprise, it was "standing room only"; and he squeezed into the "sardine can." *The women certainly dress well here,* he thought to himself. *I guess it's the olive complexion and the long black shiny hair contrasting against their white dresses. I'm beginning to like Argentina if this is what I have to face every day.* He smiled to himself. *Of course! This is Monday! Workday. That's why the congestion.* But before he could think further, the elevator opened, and he was politely exited by the anxious crowd.

"Now where the hell's this restaurant?" he muttered to himself as he walked toward the marbled reception hall.

Lolita looked up from her desk and spotted the lost soul.

"Buenos Dias, Senor Summers. I think you are in need of some help . . . no?" Her Spanish accent was difficult to hide.

Mike turned to face the pretty receptionist, putting on the "sham surprised look."

"*Lolita!* Buenas Dias. Como estas, Senorita Lolita. You are looking lovely today."

"Estoy bien. Gracias. Your Spanish is improving, Mr. Summers." She smiled. Lolita was used to middle-aged foreign businessmen throwing their hat into the ring, but this guy was no matador.

"But I'm sure you are getting a tutorial from Senorita Monzel." She smiled cheekily.

Was that a "come on" or is she just being friendly? Mike as usual was thinking from below his belt.

"Mona is a lovely lady, but just an acquaintance," Mike replied, less than convincing.

Lolita got the message, but she was not taking the bait. She had been there before.

"*Now, Senor Summers!*" She cut to the chase. "How can I be of service?" Mike had to smile to himself. "*Is this broad serious?*

"It's a small thing. Can you point me in the direction of the restaurant?" Lolita burst into laughter. "Of course . . . straight down . . ."

* * *

"Buenos Dias, senor. Can I have your name and room number?" the tall slim maître d' asked.

"Mr. Summers, room 202."

"This way, senor. Would you prefer a table at the window overlooking the bay or in smoking?"

"The bay would be fine."

Mike settled down at the table and studied at the magnificent view.

"*Hmmmm,* this *is* pleasant," Mike commented.

"Here is the menu, Mr. Summers, or should you prefer." The maître d'
pointed to the long table lined with copper coated food trays. "The buffet
breakfast?"

"I tell you what *I would* like . . . some coffee to start with and if possible,
the *New York Times*!"

"Si, senor. I will instruct the waiter to fetch your coffee. Please accept
the hotel's apologies. I'm afraid the international papers we have are at least
three days old."

"In that case, don't bother," Mike replied, disappointed.

"My name is Renaldo, and I am the maître d' this morning. Please don't
hesitate if there is anything you need. Gracias, senor."

Mike was more than disappointed at the "no newspapers," but then
sometimes no news is good news; and he diverted his attention to the menu
that fortunately was printed in Spanish, with English subtitles.

"Huevos divorcados . . . Divorced eggs! Well, that *is* different!" He almost
burst into laughter.

"Your coffee, senor."

"Eh . . . Manu . . . What is this dish?" Mike asked the waiter.

"Eh . . . It's difficult to explain, senor. I get Renaldo . . . Lo siento." Renaldo
suddenly appeared out of nowhere. "Senor, how can I help?" Mike smiled. This
was going to be something else. I mean divorced eggs! *What a hoot.*

"I wish to order this for my breakfast . . . Huevos Divorciados. Excuse my
Spanish." Mike was having trouble keeping a straight face.

Rolando had to smile; he also could see the funny side.

"I'll try explain, senor. Just like Mark Anthony and Cleopatra decided to
go their separate way, so have the chef's eggs in the special version of Spanish
breakfast dish Huevos Divorciados or dos., I mean two fried eggs on tortillas
with two different salsas, one green and the other red. So like divorce partners,
better to keep apart. You must a try. It's a very, as you say, tasty, and of course
chef's specialty." Rolando smiled proudly.

"*Renaldo* . . . you've sold me, buddy." Mike laughed. "Say, can I also have
some traditional Spanish bread?"

"Si, traditional pan with olive oil and balsamic dip . . . it's as we say in
Spanish . . . delicioso."

*   *   *

The breakfast was certainly different and, as Renaldo put it, delicioso;
and Mike was finally relaxing, enjoying his coffee and the beautiful view over

the bay. It was a pristine summer's morning, and he couldn't help but think to himself what would he give to start a new life in Argentina? *But a life lived is irreversible, and what you have is what you've got!*

Mike's thought train was abruptly interrupted.

"Senor Summers, phone call for you." Renaldo passed Mike the cordless receiver.

Mike's heart missed a beat. *Who could this be?*

"Yes, Summers here?"

"Why so formal? It's Mona."

*   *   *

The young cop made a short work of the stairs and knocked on the glass door with the gold-leaf lettering: "Airport Manager." "Come in." A voice boomed.

"Sandy, these are the two detectives Russo phoned about."

"Thanks, Officer. I'll take it from here." The big man smiled.

Tony turned to Manalo as he was about to leave. "Thanks, kid, for all your help."

"No sweat." Vic grinned. "Anytime for the NYPD."

"Sandy Baden." The big guy rose to his feet and gave a "knuckle cruncher."

*   *   *

This guy was tall at least six two and probably on the other side of fifty. His full head of unruly gray black hair, bushy eyebrows, dark blue eyes, and rugged complexion gave him a disorderly sloppy look; the loosened tie image and curled-up collared second-day shirt didn't help. His half rolled-up sleeves and the burger stomach overhang could make him a double for Brian Dennehy, the cop in *Rambo*.

*   *   *

"Take the load off, guys." He pointed to the empty chairs in front of his desk. "Say, can I get you some coffee?"

Tony turned to Bill who shook his head.

"Thanks, Sandy, but we're good," Tony replied, a half grin on his face. "Okay, then let's get down to business. Now . . . let's see . . . international flights departing at 2400 . . ." He was tapping away on the keyboard while studying the computer screen. "And the name of the passenger again?" "A Michael Summers," Tony answered.

"Hmmm . . ." Baden was putting it together. "There were three flights that departed at midnight on Saturday, the seventeenth, or just after midnight.

Air France, bound for Paris. Nope your boy wasn't on that flight. Let me see
. . . Qantas bound for Sydney Australia . . . Another blank and Lufthansa for
Frankfurt . . . Nothing doing, guys."

"Are you absolutely sure, Sandy?" Tony was taken aback. He felt sure he
had nailed it.

"As sure as 'God made little apples.'" Baden shook his head. "Sorry, guys.
I wish it was better news."

"Yeah, so do we, Sandy. *But hey,* thanks for your time. I know you're busy
with Bush's mate arriving today."

"You heard, huh?" Sandy laughed, shaking his head. "Boy, news travels!"

"Yeah, so we won't keep you. Thanks again." Tony warmly shook his
hand.

"Anytime . . ."

*   *   *

"I'll be darned." Tony turned to Bill as they descended the stairs.

"Yeah, that's a real curver. I was with you. I thought this would be a
walkover."

"Let's grab a coffee and mull this over," Tony pondered.

"I thought you didn't want a coffee?"

"I don't, but I need some peace and quiet to think."

"And I suppose I'm on the tab?" Bill could sense it coming as always.

"No, *remember, I'm the lieutenant paid for all the brainwork!*" "Now you're
talking, Perino."

*   *   *

Tony took a sip of his double espresso then sat for a moment, deep in
thought.

"Hell, Tony, I don't know how you can drink that black shit. You
Italians . . ." Bill was shaking his head.

"For Christ's sake, Bill, I'm trying to think. *How about something more
constructive?*"

Tony took another sip of his coffee as if waiting for something from up
above.

"Look at it this way. The way I see it, this guy Summers is no bimbo. He's
smart. So to throw us to the wolves, he abandons his car in the airport car
park and takes a taxi back to town and goes to ground. What do you think,
Bill?" Tony was desperate for answers.

"It makes sense. I mean there's no way this guy could catch an international flight before midnight if he arrived at the car park at ten fifteen." Tony took a deep breath and sat back.

"*Shit!* This is all we need." Tony was feeling sick. "Now where do we go from here? In this city, if he has the greenbacks, he'll go to ground."

"If he took a cab, Tony, from the airport, maybe some driver would recognize his picture." Bill threw in his "double six."

"You're right, Bill, and besides, what have we got to lose? Let's head for the entrance and check each cab that arrives. You have a copy of Mike's picture, don't you?"

"Of course! What do you take me for?" "I'll take the fifth on that one."

*   *   *

An hour had passed with no luck, with Tony taking one cab as it arrived and Bill the other.

As Tony was just about to call it off, he heard Bill's conversation with the black cab driver in front.

"Yeah, I remember this crazy dude. I almost ran him down, standing in the middle of the road, waving his arms like a crazy man. He asked me to take him to the departure terminal and offered me a big one. He was like out of his mind, screaming that he had to catch some flight leaving at eleven o'clock. It was a life-or-death situation, and for a hundred for a five-minute ride . . . *I ask you, am I* gonna complain?" "Tony, over here," Bill shouted.

"Yeah, I heard it all . . . *And is this sweet music?* Get the driver's name and cab number in case we need him to make a statement." "Sure, Tony." Bill was pretty happy.

*   *   *

"Now let's take a step back and recap." Tony was rubbing his six o'clock shadow. "So, he takes a cab to the terminal . . . as the cabby says five minutes. That makes it around eleven twenty to eleven twenty-five. And let's just say he has no check-in baggage. He gets to the check-in counter at ten thirty. The plane hasn't closed its doors as yet, and Mike is traveling first class. Yes, he might, just might, convince the airline staff that it's an emergency, and could they bend the rules as the flight still had another twenty-five to thirty minutes before departure clearance?"

"I think you've solved it, Tony."

"Don't be too sure, Bill. But there *is* one thing for sure. We need to pay another visit to Sandy Baden."

*   *   *

"Ted . . . Perino here. Yeah, it's good news. We tracked Summers down. He left on flight A12 to Buenos Aires on Argentine Airlines at 2300 hours on Saturday evening. I'll tell you more about it when I arrive at the office. Yeah, we are on our way now."

CHAPTER 3

Although Terry didn't have a bag for Blakely, after that stressful drive, the coffee was more than tempting.

The traffic was still thick; and Terry kept a wary eye on the highway, searching for the so-called "Last Chance Diner" as she signalled, switching to the right lane in preparation for the slip off.

"Ah, there it is!" she spoke out loud. "Funny I never noticed that diner before . . . probably because I wasn't looking, huh?"

Blakely was on the money. There was plenty of parking at the rear of the diner, and Terry swung into the nearest slot.

As she entered the crowded diner, she was surprised it was so popular. *Maybe true to form, it was the "Last Chance" after all!* She grinned.

It's strange, when you're searching for someone, it always appears that everyone is staring at you; but then Terry was a dish, and who could blame the masculine audience?

Blakely had captured a table at the far end of the diner and was frantically waving to draw Terry's attention.

"Terry . . . Terry, over here," he called.

Terry spotted Blakely's "arm wrestle" above the noisy diners and gave a relieved wave in return.

"Excuse me. Excuse me . . ." She crushed her way through the crowded tables and the "ogling" eyes. *"Thank God!"* Terry commented as she hit the chair. *"This place is a jungle!"*

Blakely just laughed. "When someone as sexy as you passes through . . . can you blame the guys?"

"Jack, I'm sure you didn't invite me for a coffee just to discuss my figure." Blakely began to laugh then cut it short; he knew Terry only too well.

"Terry, I gotta admit the thought had crossed my mind . . . Your latte . . ."

She gave him one of her looks. "Jack, *get real!* Now what do *you really* want to discuss with me?"

"It's about Laura."

"So?"

"Listen, it's no secret that you visit her every day, and the way the media is touting, Laura has spilled the beans and they now know the guy, and more to the point, *I am sure you do too!*"

"Now we're getting to it! And if I do, so what's the big deal?"

"Come on, Terry, in *our* business, I need to know. I mean is he a customer or what?"

Terry thought for a moment. *So, what! It's probably the worst-kept secret on the block.*

"Oh, what the hell, you know this guy, Jack. It's Mike Summers, Global's Marketing VP."

Blakely almost choked on his coffee. *"Summers! I'll be . . .* It's no secret this guy is a chaser. But Laura? I thought she had more sense, and a married man at that!"

"You're talking from experience?" Terry couldn't help herself. *I mean Blakely calling the kettle black!*

"Terry, give it a miss. You know where I'm coming from. But isn't it gonna be interesting when I speak to Briggs?" Blakely had that cunning smile. "We still have three months to run on the contract."

"Well, whatever, Jack. The important thing is that Laura is on the road to recovery."

"And Summers?"

"Christ, Jack! How the hell do I know? You read the papers."

"And she never mentioned this guy to you?"

"I knew Laura was having an affair with a married man, but that was far as it went . . . Jack, do you know what time it is?" Terry just had to kill this conversation.

"Hell . . . eleven thirty! We had better get going." Blakely drank the last of coffee and rose to leave.

Terry stopped him in his tracks. "Jack, just one thing. Let's make sure we arrive at least half an hour apart. There's enough office gossip on how I was promoted without adding fuel to the fire."

Blakely laughed. "I can just imagine. Pity it isn't true."

"Get out of it! I'll be there at one. I am sure you can make up some colorful excuse for me."

"I could think of a few . . . *pity.*"

"In your dreams, Jack . . . in your dreams . . ."

*   *   *

Simmons listened intently to June's tale of woe and could only unfortunately pity this poor woman. Banking is banking, and "benevolence" is a dirty word.

"And you say Mr. Summers is still missing?" Simmons was playing the "memory loss," clearly recollecting his discussion with the detectives.

"Yes." June's voice again on the verge of breaking.

"Hmmmm . . ." Simmons rubbed his chin. "Would you happen to know your account details?"

"No, I'm sorry, Mr. Simmons."

"That's understandable. It's not a problem. If you have your ATM card, it would certainly help."

June fumbled nervously in her bag before producing the colored plastic.

"Would you like another coffee, Mrs. Summers?" Simmons was trying to calm her.

"No, I'm good, but thanks for the kind thought."

Simmons punched the numbers on the keyboard then waited to study the flickering screen. He paused then inhaled deeply, unhappy with what he saw.

"I'm afraid it's not good news. Your fixed deposit account has only five hundred dollars, and your check account has just been withdrawn to the tune of twenty thousand, leaving a positive balance of only five. Our records show that Mr. Summers withdrew the amount from our West Palm Springs Branch on Saturday. There is also a four thousand negative balance on your credit card. Now the only bright spot on the horizon is that Mr. Summers's salary will be credited at the end of this month."

June was now really nervous. *What does all this mean?* she thought. *Is Simmons politely telling me that we are broke?*

"So, what other liabilities do we have other than my credit card?" June nervously asked.

Simmons gave a sort of sigh then exhaled, pouting his slips.

"For a start, your BMW is on lease with the bank at fifteen hundred a month, and then there's the mortgage of four thousand and house insurance, car insurance, school fees, health insurance . . . Do you want me to continue?"

With the catastrophic expression on June's face, Simmons felt she had had enough punishment for one day and discontinued the tale of woe. It was enough to make anyone grab the letter knife.

"My god! I foolishly left it all to Mike, and now this . . . And Mike's salary?"

"Sixteen thousand credited per month," Simmons answered. "I'm afraid, Mrs. Summers, most people of your standing live to the maximum of their income. The good life doesn't come without a price."

"And the mortgage?" It was getting worse by the second.

"There is an outstanding of approximately seven hundred and fifty thousand."

June rubbed her forehead. It was coming toward her like an express train. *It was just too much to comprehend.*

"What happens if we default on the mortgage repayments?"

"The bank forecloses on your mortgage contract and repossesses the property to place it on the market for sale, but however, there is one major problem. We are only interested in recovering the outstanding, which of course determines the selling price. In short, the mortgagee loses everything and is still required to pay the legal costs incurred by the bank."

"And if I decide to sell?"

"That's your prerogative, Mrs. Summers, but there *is* still one problem. You need the consent of your husband as the property is owned in both names."

It was "the river of no return" and the final death knell, and June just kept shaking her head in disbelief. There was nowhere to run. She was trapped in a financial tsunami beyond the boundaries of sanity.

Simmons was the typical bank manager who lends you an umbrella and asks it back when it rains.

"I'm sorry, Mrs. Summers, for all your troubles. Please don't hesitate to inform me if your situation changes and be assured the bank will do everything in its power to allow you time to explore all avenues to meet your liabilities. If you, please . . ."

"Thank you, Mr. Simmons, for your time." June was absolutely shattered.

"Not at all." Simmons opened the door.

*   *   *

June was in a daze as she walked from the bank to her parked car. If only she knew what has happened to Mike. Sure, they found his car, but that doesn't mean anything.

"Shit!" She just noticed the parking infringement placed below the wiper. *"Is this my day or what?"* This was the "straw that broke the camel," and she desperately held back the tears, refraining from kicking the car door.

Suddenly, the vibration of her cell phone distracted her for the moment, and she searched frantically in her bag.

"It could be Mike *or worse still the police!* But whatever, any news is better than none." It was a frightening thought, the uncertainty almost driving her to the wall.

She settled into the front seat of the BMW, pushing the crumpled citation into the side pocket before flipping open her phone.

"June Summers, here." She didn't recognize the caller's number.

"June . . . It's Tony . . . Tony Perino."

"Tony!" She was relieved and yet not relieved, sensing the worst. In June's case, "no news is bad news."

There was a pregnant pause as Tony struggled to find a soft landing, but being a friend, it was all but wishful thinking.

"Ehh . . . Err, June . . ."

"Just tell me, Tony. It's about Mike, isn't it?"

"June, according to the evidence, we have uncovered Mike is in good health and by the looks of it is basking in the sun in Buenos Aires." Now she was even more confused. *Mike, in Argentina?*

"Tony . . ."

"June, it's a long story and best not discussed over the phone. To cut it short, we would like to interview you and take a statement at the police headquarters."

"When?"

"Like yesterday!"

June gave a big sigh. With all the problems she had on her plate, now *this* was all she needed. She glanced at her watch; it had just turned twelve. "Three o'clock is the best I can muster. I have so much to do, Tony."

"I understand . . . Then three o'clock it is . . . *Oh,* do you know the address?"

"No, I'm afraid I have never had the pleasure." Her tongue had that bite.

"It's in Pearl Street, lower Manhattan. You can't miss it. When you arrive, just ask the sergeant at the front desk for me."

* * *

Terry was in no hurry and took her time over another latte before glancing at her watch. One thirty had come and gone, and there was no point in "swinging the lead" further. It was time to face the "office music" and the year of the cat.

She squeezed through the crowded tables, and the "oops, sorry, honey" fresh asses, before finally reaching the door with a sigh of relief. The overzealous cologne and secondary tobacco smoke for once made her appreciate the fresh air as she briskly walked to her car.

"Boy, am I glad to get out of that joint!" she spoke aloud, unlocking the Mazda.

The traffic was now much lighter, and she hung a right and slipped onto the freeway. In another fifteen minutes, she would reach Madison Avenue and the famous ABM building.

As she sat back in the orderly traffic, trying to relax, Laura was still on her mind. *And as for that bastard Mike Summers,* she shook her head. Her vivid memory of Laura lying in a coma in intensive care was still fresh. The only bright spot on the horizon was her new beau Frank, and she smiled to herself at the thought. He was there for her at the right time, but it's so easy to confuse friendship with love, and Terry was still playing it close to her chest. Sure, she had feelings for the guy, probably more than she would wish to admit; but as they say, "the day is young" and best let nature take its course.

Before she knew it, she had come to a halt in the underground car park in front of the security checkpoint. She hit the electric window and held her hand out, holding her security tag.

"Good morning . . . *Eh* . . . I mean good afternoon, Lee."

Lee, the young black security guard, studied her picture for a moment then looked at Terry again.

"Lee, this is getting boring. Stop fucking screwing around. *For Christ's sake, you see me every day!"*

"That language is unbecoming of the new marketing manager." He had a stupid grin on his face.

"News travels fast in this place. It must be the jungle drums, huh?"

Lee's smile suddenly disappeared. Terry had crossed the line, and he didn't like it.

"You are clear to go, Ms. Johnson." His abruptness was sending a message, making Terry feel a real heel.

"Lee . . . listen . . . *Eh*, I didn't mean it that way . . ." He just ignored her and opened the boom gate.

"Miss, there's another car waiting behind you. Please *move on!"*

"Damn it!" Terry hit the gas. "Me and my big mouth again!"

Terry found her slot and cut the engine then sat for a moment to reflect. For Terry, it was a new day and a new challenge, a challenge that she was not particularly looking forward to.

*   *   *

She could feel the heat of the penetrating eyes as she walked to Laura's desk. Office gossip is lethal and so is the proverbial "grapevine." She knew that by now the "cat was out of the bag," and noses would be out of joint regarding her unexpected promotion, which was to "the dogs of war" suspiciously sexually orientated. *So Blakely is a player. So what?* But there's a line in the sand; and Terry was not about to follow in Laura's footsteps, becoming emotionally involved with a married man, especially her boss!

She stopped in front of Laura's desk and stood for a moment in indecision. On second thoughts, it would be better that Blakely made the announcement before taking Laura's seat. The noise of shaking glass made her turn abruptly, only to see Blakely signalling her to come to his office.

"Take the load off, Terry. You took your time. I was getting worried there for a moment."

"And so you should, leaving me in that bloody dive of a diner! I must have been stripped naked ten times before I got to the car park."

Blakely smiled at the thought. "Maybe that's why it's named 'The Last Chance Diner,' huh?"

"Jack, only you could think of that shit." *Does this guy ever give up!* The thought was running through Terry's mind.

"Can you blame a guy?"

"Let's not start that again. Listen, Jack, if you're going to keep the wolves from your door, let's get this over with and satisfy the Moguls."

"I admire your style, Terry, and of course you are on the money!" A touch of sarcasm was ringing through. "I'll get Rita to inform *your* staff to gather in the conference room. *How does that grab you?*" Blakely grinned.

"Jack, at the thought of being rude, *let's get this over with!*"

Suddenly, his expression changed from joker to seriousness, the original "Jekyll and Hyde."

"Meet me there in say"—he held his hand up to glance at his watch—"in fifteen minutes. I have an important call to make."

"Not Chuck Briggs!"

Blakely was sporting that mischievous grin again. "How did you guess?"

*   *   *

Jack smiled as he dialled Briggs's private line.

"Chuck . . . Blakely here."

Briggs was surprised at Blakely's impromptu call.

"So why the call, Jack?" He didn't give Blakely time to answer. "Listen, if it's about the BM2000 marketing contract, I'm afraid Summers is not available as he is out of town. But I'll get his second in command to give you a call ASAP. Or if you want to meet over lunch, check your diary and give me call."

It was a brush off, and Blakely wasn't going to be pushed over the cliff.

"Come on, Chuck! I'm sure the police have contacted you by now regarding Mike. *Look* . . . I can understand. I mean who needs the bad publicity and all the media hype once the news hits the streets, but we're in business, and I need to see value for ABM's buck and beat the competition by hitting the market first with an aggressive and creative marketing campaign . . . So?"

Chuck could feel the steam coming from his ears. Sure, ABM is a key account, but to have to listen to this ideas Blakely was over the top.

"Jack, I know where you are coming from. Okay, so Mike is wanted by the police, and you know as much as me. So, let's load buckshot and line up the ducks. As far as the contract is concerned and because ABM is one of Global's major accounts, I will take the responsibility for the marketing program myself."

Jack grinned; he had nailed Briggs to the wall.

"Chuck, that's all I want to hear. Now, about that lunch? Say, why don't I give you a call tomorrow?"

"I'll look forward to that," Briggs answered dryly.

"Then tomorrow." Blakely hung up; mission complete.

* * *

"Jack, the staff have congregated in the lecture room." Rita stuck her head around the door.

"Thanks, Rita. I'm on my way." Blakely placed the receiver back, an evil smile on his face. Jack is that kind of guy who enjoys twisting the knife.

* * *

"I'm sure I have fully explained the reason for Terry's promotion, and I am sure you will support her in her new role as marketing manager. Of course, it goes without saying we all wish Laura a full and speedy recovery. And may I stress that there will always be a position for Laura Williams with ABM should she wish to return to full-time employment." Blakely paused for a moment, searching the faces for some reaction. "Are there any questions? *Good!* Then let's get back to work."

Jaycee Donnelly, the office mouth, intentionally brushed past Terry, raising her voice, the cheap shot too good to miss.

"Mildred"—she nudged her partner in crime—"we all know how she got that promotion, don't we?"

"Yeah, it's called 'pillow talk.'"

"You got that one right, honey, but she'll never fill Laura's shoes, huh?"

Terry was fuming and could easily have retaliated, but then there's the old saying, "Still water runs deep."

"Terry, stay for a minute. How do you think that went down?" Blakely loved admiration.

"Jack, do you want me to be brutally honest? *Like a lead balloon!* But it's my problem now, and don't worry. I'm quite capable of sorting out that bitch Donnelly and her cronies."

"That's what I admire about you, Terry. You call a spade a spade. And for the record, I spoke to Briggs, and I'm planning to have lunch with him tomorrow, and I want you to join me."

"Just let me know. Sorry, Jack, but I've got work to do."

CHAPTER 4

Marcos pumped the horn twice, tapping his finger impatiently on the steering wheel of the "used by date" '52 Pontiac Chieftain Coupe deluxe. The old antique had all but seen its day, but the eight-pot forty-one twenty-cubic-inch still rose to the occasion when the pedal hit the metal. This apple green "tank" was losing its luster, and the red primer undercoat after decades in the sun was showing through like a patchwork quilt. But this baby in its heyday had class, with the large shark mouth chrome grill and heavy gauge bumper complete with overriders and the custom triple-chrome strip down the centre of its large hood, and who could forget the familiar two-piece windshield?

(Speaking in Spanish)

Sergio, where the fuck are you? Carlos spoke to himself. *It's almost nine, and we have to meet Marcos at ten, and Avenida de Mayo is at least a thirty-minute drive depending on the traffic.* "Where *is* that dago?" He thumped the horn again, this time shouting aloud.

The broken-down wooden shutters slammed open, crashing against the faded white concrete of the rundown second-floor apartment house, flaking paint falling like snowflakes. Then a moustached unshaven bleary-eyed head appeared.

"Sergio, *what the fuck?* You woke up the whole neighbourhood, you crazy bastard."

"Carlos, come back to bed." The half-naked senorita was tugging on his shoulder, showing more breast than Pamela Anderson.

* * *

Once upon a time, this babe had been pretty with her shoulder-length crinkly black hair and the typical Latino features, but booze and drugs had taken their toll; and this thirty years old now looked on the other side of forty. The olive brown eyes that once sparkled were overshadowed with the premature eye bags. Her full lips now looked parched and lined, and her once youthful complexion was fast following suit. The strap of the so-called nightdress had fallen from her shoulder, exposing her full breast and dark brown nipple. The needle marks on both arms was a dead giveaway of her heroin addiction, but there was still something that could make a man think twice.

* * *

"Eva, for Christ's sake, give it a miss. Can't you see I have important business?" He wrenched her hand from his naked shoulder.

"Then go fuck yourself. I have plenty of dagos who would love to sleep with me."

"Don't bother me, bitch." Sergio roughly pushed her away. "Carlos, I'll be down in ten minutes." He bawled from the window.

Carlos just gave a grunt and shook his head. *"Why do I put up with this stupido?"*

True to form, Sergio appeared from the front door, half running, half walking, tripping over his own two feet while trying to tuck his crumpled shirt into his jeans.

"Move over. I'll drive." He opened the heavy rusted door, it's croaking noise like a guy on his death knell, only these hinges *were really dying* from the lack of oil.

"Carlos, you drive like an old vieja. You want to be there on time, no? I know this rust bucket like my own mother."

Sergio gunned the eight pots and opened the clutch, the back wheels spinning raising a huge cloud of dust.

Carlos shook his head and grabbed the overhead handgrip.

"I've said it before, Sergio, and I'll say it again. *You're one crazy son of a bitch!"*

* * *

True to form, Sergio was burning the rubber. At this rate, for sure he would make it in time.

"Sergio, easy on the gas. We don't want no trouble from the policia."

As for Sergio, he wasn't giving a shit; it was going in one ear and out the other. For him, it was Cafe Tortoni or bust! But the traffic cop at the junction to Avenida de Mayo made him think twice; and he sobered up and pressed on the brake pedal with all his strength, closing his eyes, hoping for the best as he almost rear-ended the heap in front.

"That *was* close!" He gasped. "These fucking brakes . . . *American shit.*" He screamed, thumping the steering wheel.

"Sergio, keep your fucking cool and don't draw attention. That cop may look stupido, but he's no dummy."

"Carlos, you worry too much. I can handle it."

After a few minutes and acrobatics from the traffic cop, they were finally on their way, much to the relief of Carlos.

Sergio's luck was in finding the parking slot directly in front of the Cafe Tortoni, but his expression suddenly changed having recognized the 1968 metallic brown Cadillac Eldorado Coupe with the stand-out white leather roof; and he nervously nudged Carlos.

"Yeah, I see it. It's Marcos's car. So, we're late! Is he our fucking keeper or something?"

"With that 45 Rugger he packs, something tells me, *yes!*" Carlos answered.

"Cut the shit and let's hit the dirt." Sergio was first on the sidewalk.

Marcos could see the two ragtag hombres hurrying toward him as he sat outside in the arcadia, sipping his coffee, his deadpan facial expression hard to read.

*   *   *

Marcos Perez is a well-known figure in the drug world, a middleman that sets up the deals with third parties for the drug lords. He gets not only a piece of the action but also a piece of the risk should the deals go feral, and the meeting this morning was to find a way to save his hide as the result of this giant fuckup by Mendez and Garcia to the tune of a hundred grand; and Francesco Gomez's enforcers were getting itchy trigger fingers. Gomez is *the* drug lord in Buenos Aires, and nobody double-crosses Francesco and lives to tell the tale.

*   *   *

Perez was in his late fifties, five foot eight; and at two hundred and fifty pounds, boy, was he an excellent candidate for abdominoplasty. The white Panama hat and suit to match, the leathery skinned clean-shaven round face, the turkey neck, grey blue eyes, and bushed eyebrows could easily mistake him for Sydney Greenstreet from the famous movie *The Maltese Falcon*. But under those calculative penetrating eyes was a man with no conscience, a man that would stop at nothing, even murder, to get what he wants, as Carlos and Sergio were soon to experience.

*   *   *

Perez pointed to the empty chairs, being a man of few words, then dramatically tapped the crystal of his wristwatch.

"Marcos, I know we are late, but let me explain. The traffic on Avenida . . ."

Marcos raised his hand as if to say, *cut it!*

"This kind of shit, I don't want to hear. Save it for the confession box." He was in an ugly mood.

"Now since you have wasted my fucking precious time, you can order me another coffee." He raised his hand once again to attract the waiter. "Saonero . . ."

"Si, senor."

"Tres cafes, por favor."

"Si, me dan dies minutos. Gracias."

"Now"—he looked straight at Carlos—"I have a message from Gomez. Listen, and listen good. Francesco has asked me to tell you that he's an understanding and generous man, and to show you just how sincere he is, he is going to give you one week from today to payback the hundred grand you fucked up on. But here's the scoop. For every day you're late, it will cost you an extra ten grand in interest, but only for another seven days." *"And if we run out of time?"* Sergio just had to ask.

"Don't even think about it . . . *comprende?*"

"El Senor cafes." The waiter interrupted just in time before the situation became ugly.

"Si. Gracias," Marcos replied, pointing to the table.

"But, Marcos, we were double-crossed by the gringos. They pulled a fast one and—"

"Cut the slack. I'm not interested in history. I want to know the future, like how are you are going to get the money? And to cheer you up, my cut has increased from 10 to 20 percent as my reputation has been severely damaged, and Francesco is very upset with me. Do you get the message?" "Marcos, *give us a fucking break!*" Carlos blasted out.

"You got yourselves in this fucking hole. You get yourself out. You should have checked out the gringos before the swap. *Big mistake!*"

"Marcos, if you would let me fucking explain. Sergio and me we have this sure-fire plan that will make us all rich, but we need time . . ." "I'm listening . . ."

*   *   *

Bill parked the car in the Pearl Street lot and cut the engine then gave a sigh as he turned to Tony. The events of this morning had left two highly respected detectives' reputations down the toilet, and they both knew that they should have moved earlier to bag Summers; but in hindsight, we can all be smart.

"I gotta say, Tony, I'm not looking forward to facing Baker. I'm sure the shit has hit the fan by now, and everyman and his dog will be on the blower, including the DA and the famous senator. With Williams's pull on 'Capitol Hill,' who knows? Ted might even get a call from George."

"Bill, *get serious for Christ's sake!* Come on. Let's get this over with." Tony opened the car door.

*   *   *

As they stood silently in the elevator, Tony was still smarting.

"You know, Bill, you gotta hand it to Mike. He really made us look like a couple of amateurs with that taxi stunt."

"Yeah, but what really gets me, Tony, is we're right next door having a 'knees up' when this guy, as bold as brass, calmly comes home right under our noses, picks up his car, then does a bolt to the airport." "Don't remind me." The elevator chimed.

"Well, lookee here, Dan, isn't that them two detectives that couldn't even arrest a neighbour?"

"But, Brad, didn't you hear that they are up for a commendation for the two biggest idiots above and beyond the call of duty?"

"*Ha . . . Ha . . . Ha . . . Ha . . .* Dan, you're gonna crack my ribs. Gimme a high five."

Bill abruptly stopped in front of Lucas's desk, almost skidding to a halt like Kramer in *Seinfeld.*

"Why you half-baked pieces of shit! Go pick some cotton."

"Come on, Bill." Tony grabbed Bill's arm, almost pulling it from its socket.

The two boneheads were cracking up. They knew they had hit the spot, but it was too good to "walk on by."

"Say, Dan, I heard that, that TV show *The Next 48* is looking for a couple of detectives. Maybe Perino and Hayden should go for a screen test . . ." "You mean *The Next 348!*" There was another howl of laughter.

"What's this . . . the *Last Comic Standing*? Have you guys got nothing better to do than screw around cracking jokes? *Perino . . . Hayden . . . my office . . .*"

*   *   *

Baker looked over his half glasses. He was in a foul mood. With the shelling he had received this morning, *he would rather be wearing a flak jacket in Iraq!*

He rudely pointed to the empty chairs. "Now perhaps you two dimwits can explain to me why my department has been nominated for the next remake of *The Key Stone Cops?*"

Bill turned and looked toward Tony.

"So, what's with you, Hayden? Is Perino the Messiah or something?"

"Ted, we flunked it, so what else do you want me to say?" Tony knew when to fold them.

"Perino, don't think *True Confessions* is gonna get you mileage? It's just one giant fuckup, so let's start from the beginning. Why your next door neighbour did a number on you?"

"Ted, the information we received from his secretary, his wife, and his boss was that Summers would be returning from West Palm on Monday evening. Remember you yourself went along with the plan to . . ."

Baker threw his hands in the air. *"Hold it! Hold it!* That's history. I want to know how this guy managed to get under the radar and is now basking in the sun in Buenos Aires, hitting the margaritas and the tapas. *Do you get my drift?"*

Tony took a deep breath then exhaled, trying to find the right spot where to start.

"Ted, it was like this. Summers is no dummy, and he purposely threw us off track, knowing that we would check the time on the airport parking ticket."

Baker rubbed his chin as he listened to "the never-ending story," but inwardly, he had to admit he felt some compassion for the duo and "comedy of errors."

"Enough . . . Enough! I've heard all I want to hear. Now you say Summers's wife has agreed to come in from the 'cold' to provide a statement?" "Yeah,"

Bill interrupted. "She'll be here around three." Baker nodded in approval. *At least it was something!*

Ted just stared straight in front deep in thought as he rested his chin on his hand.

"Guys, for what it's worth, the message from above is"—he gestured sarcastically at the ceiling, raising his eyes—"we bring in Summers at any cost. So, I've given it some thought and have come up with a plan that I passed by the DA. Presumably, he spoken to the commissioner and, of course, Congressman Williams for their approval, and surprisingly, I've been given the green light." Baker had that Sherlock Holmes look on his face that invariably spelled trouble. "Now here's where I'm coming from . . ."

* * *

Terry Johnson was not the kind to run away from a fight, but once you go down that road, you had better make it stick. She lifted the phone.

"Rita, Terry here. Listen, I want to meet with the marketing staff in the lecture room in about ten minutes. Can you arrange that for me?"

"Yes, that's no problem. I'll give them a call right now." Rita, Jack's secretary, smiled. She could just imagine.

"Thanks, Rita." *Terry sported that "war cry" look as she laid down the phone. It was either going to be a "Little Big Horn" or a win for "Custard."*

* * *

"Grab a seat, everyone. I know you are all busy, so I'll try to be as expedient as possible. As your new boss, I want to clear the air so you and I both know where we stand. Like you, I admired Laura Williams as my superior and a personal friend. But as a boss, if everyone loves you, then you are doing something wrong, and I don't want to go down that same path. So where is this leading to you, may ask? Common sense. Punctuality. Meeting deadlines. Creative thinking. And above all, *respect.* Now you may say respect has to be earned. Well, have I got news for you? That's old hat, and it doesn't cut with me. I'm the boss, and what I say goes, and above all I don't make decisions by consensus. I'm willing to listen, and if I feel I'm going down the wrong path, then I'm not too big to change. Now the next sensitive point is disrespect and bad mouthing, which I will not tolerate under any circumstances in my department."

Terry stopped dead and turned to stare directly at Jaycee Davis and Mildred Pitt.

"Now in case you haven't noticed, I'm looking directly at you, Jaycee, and your easily led friend Mildred. I and everyone in this room heard your derogative comments at the close of Mr. Blakely's communication meeting, specifically directed at me, and I will not tolerate that kind of gross insubordination and character assignation under any circumstances from you or any other member of the staff. *Do I make myself clear?* Well, I'm waiting, that is unless suddenly you are dumbstruck."

Davis and Pit's faces could not be described. They *were* dumbfounded and for once speechless.

"Well?" Terry was breathing fire.

"Apologies."

"Apologies accepted. Now unless there is any other business, this meeting is closed, but before you go, tomorrow I intend to go through each of your workloads and projects one by one. My advice is you had better be prepared as I am known to have a short concentration span and a fuse to match, and I don't treat fools lightly. Thank you for your attention."

There was a rumble of feet as the staff dispersed, not another word spoken, much to Terry's satisfaction. But for Davis and Pitt, they weren't going to go down easily as Terry would soon find out, much to her determent.

*   *   *

Terry felt, shall we say, "more than relieved at getting that huge burden off her chest." She knew as the Chinese say, "one maintain his higher than the other," and she was under no allusions that her problems were just beginning. As she walked to her new cubicle, she could still feel the tension in the air, "how you start is how you finish"; and she casually glanced at her watch.

"My god, five o'clock already! Where has the time gone?" She was talking under her breath. *"Boy, has this been one day!"* She sat down hard in her chair like she had been on her feet all day. *"Now where do I start?"* She lifted the phone.

"Rita, can I speak to Jack for a moment?"

"Just a sec."

"Yes, Terry?

"Jack, I think a good start would be to go through any outstanding projects that Laura was working on."

"I agree. I'll get Rita to pass all the files to you first thing in the morning. Terry, I think I'm going to call it day and so should you. It's after five, and there's little you can achieve at this time in the day that can't wait until tomorrow."

"Thanks, Jack. I appreciate it. I'm bushed. Ciao."

Terry placed back the receiver and smiled. *Jack, maybe I've misread you. You're not such a bad ass after all.*

The phone rang. "Yes?"

"Lucy from reception, Ms. Johnson. I have a Mr. Reynolds on the phone. Shall I put him through?"

"Yes."

"Ms. Johnson, just a reminder, the reception will close at five thirty."

"That's all right, Lucy. Put him through."

"Can I speak to the marketing manager?" Frank was talking in a deep voice, trying to throw Terry.

"Stop fooling around, you jerk. You know dam well who you are speaking to."

"Then may I presume that I'm speaking to the beautiful Terry Johnson?"

Terry *had to* laugh. The way she was feeling Frank was a breath of fresh air.

"Okay, Charles Boyar, why the call?"

"I just called to say I love you." Frank sang over the phone."

"So, it's Stevie now? Okay, Stevie, now get serious. Why the call?"

"Because I want to take the woman I love to dinner, to celebrate her new job."

Frank could hear Terry laugh, and a smile crossed his face. *"Well?"*

"Pick me up at eight. I have a few things to tidy up. And don't be late!"

CHAPTER 5

"Mona! Isn't this a coincidence? I was just thinking about you when you called."

"I must have made a lasting impression or was it just the food?"

"Both!" Mike laughed. "No, I'm only joking. Of *course,* it was you I was thinking of. Mona, life is strange. I come all the way to Argentina on business, only to meet a complete stranger, and may I say *a beautiful stranger,* that for some reason I can't get you out of my mind."

"Is that good or bad?"

"For me, Mona, after going through an ugly divorce and feeling lower than low then to meet a lovely person such as you . . . the only words I can find is that I am still pinching myself in disbelief."

Mona laughed aloud. "Mike, you say the craziest things, but I must admit I do enjoy your company. It's been a long time since, shall I say, I 'ventured' after my divorce. But I suppose we do have something in common. We both married unfaithful partners."

"Mona honey, let's change the subject and move to happier thoughts . . . like are you free this evening?"

Mike neatly side-stepped any further questions. He was feeling uncomfortable riding on the streetcar named Desire. When you tell lies, you had better have a good memory, and after too many cocktails on the plane, well, it goes without saying.

"You must be practicing telepathy as I was about to ask you the same question," Mona answered.

"Now isn't hat something?" Mike could hear her laugh.

"When will you be finished today?" Mona asked.

"You'll probably scold me when I tell you that I have decided to relax today, and I have cancelled all my appointments."

"No, I can understand, and I feel like joining you, but after being away from the office for nearly two weeks, well, *you know* what it's like, Mike." *"Do I ever!"*

"So, what are your plans?"

"Simple! Laze around the pool, get some sun, and read my business papers."

"So, Mr. Lazy Man, can I pick you up around seven then?" *"Can't wait."*

"I'll call you when I'm on my way."

"Anyplace special?" Mike was inquisitive.

"It's a secret. Adios, and don't get too much sun."

* * *

Rafa, the front desk attendant, had the phone glued to his ear, nervously looking over his shoulder. He had placed Mona's call through to Mike in the restaurant and was secretly eavesdropping on the conversation.

(Speaking in Spanish)

"Rafa." It was Lolita. *"What's keeping you?* I have a guest here waiting to check in."

"Coming." He gently replaced the receiver back on the switchboard. "Buenas dias, senor. Welcome to the Sheraton."

* * *

"Lolita, can you manage at the front desk while I go to the restroom?" She shrugged her shoulders. "And what if I say no?" She was very mad. The morning had been extra busy with an influx of guests attending this week's International Trade Conference at the Exhibition Centre.

"Lolita *don't be that way!* You know how I feel about you. Have mercy." He laughed. "I'm desperate for a cigarette. I promise I'll make it up to you after work."

"Like?"

"I'll buy you dinner at Pedro's."

"Hmmm, I'll think about it."

Rafa was always trying his hand, and Lolita knew she had him like a puppet on a string; and like most women, she used it to her full advantage.

"I'll be back in five . . ."

Rafa cautiously touched each of the closet doors in the staff restroom to make sure none were occupied. Satisfied, he opened his cell phone and entered the name.

"Si, Sergio here?"

"Sergio, Rafa here."

"So do you have anything?"

"Si, Senorita Menzel is meeting with the . . ."

* * *

June's insides were churning up. She felt she could easily throw up, but having had no breakfast, her empty stomach saved the day. Her discussion with the bank manager was a "slash the wrist" finale, and the thought of a "financial meltdown" was now more worrying than the loss of her unfaithful and heartless spouse. But somehow, she had to find a way to get enough liquidity to tide her over and pursue legal advice. There was one final avenue left . . . *Chuck Briggs, Mike's boss!* In desperation, she plucked up the courage and nervously opened her cell phone.

"Global Marketing, Mr. Briggs's office. Elizabeth speaking."

"Good morning, Elizabeth. It's June Summers here. Would it be possible to see Chuck today? It's extremely urgent and personal." She was biting her lip.

"Bear with me for a moment, June. I understand. Chuck, I have June Summers on the line. She seems very upset and wishes to meet with you today, if possible?"

"Hmmm . . . I see . . . Tracy, have I any appointments for this afternoon?"

"One at three thirty with Grant Wilson, the CEO of Sun Valley Health Drinks."

"*Hell*, I almost forgot about Wilson! Thanks, Tracy. Tell June I'll see her, but it must be before two thirty. I need to prepare for my meeting with Grant. *Oh,* and, Elizabeth, fetch me the Sun Valley file."

"I have it ready, Chuck. I'll fetch it in once I close this call. Eh . . . June, sorry for the delay, but as you can appreciate, Mr. Briggs has a very heavy schedule."

June's jaw dropped at the thought of rejection; it was her last hope.

"*However,* . . . he understands your predicament and will see you today, but it must be . . ."

June gave a giant sigh of relief. "Thanks, Elizabeth. I'm on my way."

*   *   *

The drive to Twelfth Avenue from Wall Street was straightforward. She would hang a left onto 9A West Street and straight all the way to Twelfth Avenue. At eleven thirty in the morning, the traffic should be light; and "on a wing and a prayer," hopefully, she would be there by noon. Suddenly for June, things were looking better, and she gave a cynical smile as she switched the ignition. *It was all or nothing!*

*   *   *

As she sat in the car robotically driving through the traffic, her mind was running through how she would approach Briggs, in fact almost rehearsing it word by word. Sherry, Chuck's wife, always enjoyed June's company at business dinners and functions, and they were good friends; but when the chips are down, "so-called" friends have short memories.

Time seemed to pass so quickly, and before June knew it, she could see the traffic lights ahead at the T junction of West Thirty-Fourth Street and Grovner Towers, the prominent high-rise located directly on the corner. Global's office on the twentieth floor said it all, plush, modern, and "marketing" written all over.

She would have to use the underground car park, but Mike was well known as she had visited the office on many occasions, and she knew she would have no problems.

*   *   *

"Can I help you, ma'am?" the young security guard in the smart blue uniform inquired.

"I have an appointment with Mr. Briggs, Global Marketing, floor 20."

"And your name, ma'am?"

"Mrs. June Summers."

"Mrs. Summers! My apologies, ma'am. I didn't recognize you."

"That's all right, Victor. It's been a while." June gave him a warm smile.

He pressed the switch to lift the boom gate. "You know where to park, ma'am."

"Basement 2."

Victor smiled. "On the button, ma'am. Have a nice day."

*　　*　　*

The car park elevator opened into a plush beige marbled reception area sporting a larger-than-life curved polished oak and stainless-steel reception counter, overshadowed with the large prominent letters in gold plate, "Grovner Towers." *This place had class and no doubt the rentals to match.* June knew the drill and quickly walked to the reception to sign the visitor's book and collect her security pass. She impatiently slipped the pass into the security slot and pressed 20.

When you are both nervous and impatient, for some reason, the elevator seems to take forever; and June breathed a sigh of relief as the doors finally opened. She pressed the security button on the large plate glass doors, the overzealous buzz startling the bored receptionist who embarrassingly came to life and quickly pressed the unlock button. The heavy security glass door opened with a loud click, and with one mighty shove, June pushed it ajar.

"Mrs. Summers, nice to see you again." The young peroxide blonde receptionist flashed the artificial smile that comes with the job.

"Thanks, Evan. I have an appointment with Mr. Briggs."

"Yes, he is expecting you. I'll call his secretary. Elizabeth, I have Mrs. Summers here in reception. Certainly." Evan replaced the receiver. "You can go straight in, Mrs. Summers."

*　　*　　*

"Here's the scoop." Baker threw the two airline tickets in front of the detectives.

"I hope you can 'puede nablor en Espanol,' which when translated means 'I hope you can speak some Spanish.' You both have reservations on flight A12 to Buenos Aires on Argentine Airlines tonight at 2300hours."

Tony turned to Bill in disbelief then to Baker. *Was he hearing right?*

"Yes, you heard right, Perino . . . the same flight as your friend Summers took . . . *Coincidence, huh?"* Baker was rubbing salt into the wound, a touch of self-indulgence. "Any questions?"

"First class, Ted?" Bill had a habit of putting his big foot in his big mouth.

"Hayden, I'll pretend I didn't hear that stupid remark. Now for your information, this directive has come all the way down from the top, but let's not get carried away. This is not a 'dead or alive' wild west movie. You bring him back in one piece to stand trial. Cappice, Perino?"

Tony could bite his lip no longer; he just had to cut a wisecrack.

"Ted, you amaze me!" He was trying to contain his laugher. "First you speak Spanish and now Italian. I gotta hand it to you."

"Cut the wisecracks, Perino. It's not a good time. Now *you* listen! I have been in touch with the Argentinean police commissioner, a General Salvador Cerise, and the good news, from what the FBI can tell us, he's as crooked as a bent nail and not to be trusted." *"Nice!"* Tony interrupted.

Baker turned to Tony. "Can I continue?" You could hear a pin drop. "Thank you. Now can we start again if it's not too much trouble? You will be dealing with Cerise's second in command, a Captain Juan Avalos, who is a mean son of a bitch and has a huge chip on his shoulder about Americans since the Regan incident, and the good news is he will be meeting you on your arrival. Now I don't want any heroics or an international incident, and remember you have no jurisdiction in Argentina, and if you step out of line, this guy Avalos will have no hesitation in throwing in the slammer, and I don't have to tell you what that means! Even Bush would have to throw in the towel on that one. Your hotel reservations? They are attached to your air tickets, and no, Hayden, before you ask another dumb question, *it's not five star!"* "How long for, Ted?" Bill cautiously inquired.

"Christ, Hayden, for as long as it takes, but then that's up you two guys. Cash? Stace will organize 'drawdowns' and a bank account in Buenos Aires for telegraphic transfers as you require."

Baker's expression suddenly changed. "Listen, guys, for what it's worth, you are two of my best detectives, and I know you will bring home the bacon. But more important, this is a dangerous mission, and I don't want any posthumous heroes. So, take care." Baker rose to his feet. "Unfortunately, I won't see you before you leave as I have an appointment this afternoon with the commissioner. So good luck and safe return."

"Thanks, Ted. We won't let you down."

Baker laughed. "That's what I'm worried about, Perrino. *Get out of here!"*

* * *

"Elizabeth, thanks for your help."

"Don't mention it. I fully understand. Just go straight in. Mr. Briggs is waiting."

"Take a seat, June. Believe me, I really wish we were meeting under different circumstances."

"So you know all the gory details?"

"June, before we get down to it, I suggest you calm your nerves with a hot cup of coffee. If you don't mind me saying so, you look washed out."

"Chuck, I think I'll take you up on that." June half smiled. She was feeling worse than a "begging letter."

"Elizabeth, can you do me a favor and fetch June a cup of coffee?" Chuck placed back the secretarial phone. "Now, June, where do you want to start? Your coffee shouldn't take long."

Almost before he could finish, there was a knock on the door, and Elizabeth popped her head around.

"Thanks, Elizabeth. Just place the cup on my desk." He pointed to the place mat on his precious polished walnut top.

June took a long sip of the warm "pick me up," the caffeine surge calming her nerves.

"Chuck, I have got to admit the coffee was a good suggestion. Now where do I start and why am I here? How much do you know about Mike's predicament?"

"Only what the police have told me, but I guess that's enough."

"Then, of course, you know that Mike has been charged with the attempted murder of Laura Williams, Senator Dave Williams's daughter."

"Something like that." Briggs sort of shrugged. He wasn't giving too much away. He rested his chin on his hand as if preparing for the "long wait." He had a good idea what was coming, and he wasn't looking forward to it. June took a deep breath. "Well, it gets worse. Mike has absconded to Argentina and of course left me, and the kids desolate. Chuck, I don't need to spell it out why I am here as a last resort, and I feel lower than low. You see, Mike has emptied the . . ."

"June, I can understand the bank manager's predicament. He has a set of rules, and it's called money. As for Mike, he was more than an employee. He was a good friend, but now . . . is this the Mike I knew? I still can't believe it!" Chuck was shaking his head. "June, I fully understand your quandary and I had given it some thought before you arrived. Mike's monthly salary before tax is 20K. His contract of employment legally demands six months' termination notice by either party or payment in lieu. I have therefore decided, in 'layman's terms,' to sack Mike on the basis of insubordination and gross misconduct, threatening the reputation of Global. Now what does this mean to you, you may ask? The bottom line is that Global will settle Mike's termination entitlements, being six months' salary in lieu, and I have informed payroll to ensure the money is deposited in your joint account no later than the end of this week."

June almost burst into tears. It was better than she had dared expect.

"Chuck, how can I ever thank you?"

"Don't! It's the least I can do. June, I apologize, but I have a heavy meeting with a client at three, and I need to be prepared. I wish you well, and my sympathy goes to you and the children. I'll get Sherry to give you a call. Tracy will see you out."

* * *

June stood in the elevator, still smarting from the "bum's rush" she had politely received from Briggs; but the bottom line was a 100k hitting the bank account, *and this week!* Although a drop in the bucket, it was a lifeline that would carry the family over for at least three months. Of course, the BMW would have to go, then there was the private school fees and the fancy Jetty Club. Of course, there was no way she could keep up the mortgage repayments.

"Excuse me, ma'am. This is the ground floor," the tall young gentleman in the business suit reminded her.

June was in oblivion and hadn't heard the elevator chime.

"I apologize. I must have been dreaming." She gave an embarrassing smile then quickly exited. She had to be at Pearl Street before three, a meeting she would rather abort. She glanced at her watch as she walked to the car. It had just turned one forty-five, and for once, time was on her side.

* * *

(Speaking in Spanish)

"You two Gauchos either have shit for brains or you have a death wish. What's it gonna be?"

"Marcos, look at it this way. What have you got to lose? It's our necks that's on the block."

"And what about the gringo?"

"We take him along, then when the time is right, we blow his fucking brains out."

"That takes intelligence, huh?" Marcos shook his head.

"And the money?" Now Marcos was beginning to get interested.

"We ask for ten mill."

"*Hmmm . . .*" Marcos was hooked. "*Well*, I'm sure the old goat can afford it. Now for the sixty-five-thousand-dollar question . . . *when?*"

"*Tonight.*"

CHAPTER 6

Tony sat at his desk, a pronounced smirk on his face before turning to face Bill who was now struggling to stifle his laughter. But Hayden, as always, couldn't hold it to save himself; and he almost brought the house down.

"Just look at these two fucking jerks." Brown swung his chair around to attract Lucas, his so-called "partner in crime."

"Yeah, I see them. As if we didn't have enough clowns in the office without these two fucking boneheads."

Stace's, Baker's PA, voice echoed across the office to attract Perrino and Hayden's attention.

"Ted, forgot to ask you guys if your passports are current."

"No worries in that department, Stace, and I also speak for Bill," Tony purposely answered at the top of his lungs.

Brown shrugged his shoulders, screwing up his eyes before turning again to Lucas. "*What the fuck?*"

"Well, you had best come over and sign for this cash," Stace called again.

Tony rose from his desk and gave Brown a cheeky wink in the passing. It was all in the game.

"So, what's it gonna be tomorrow, Bill? Tapas for breakfast and maybe an early morning swim in the hotel pool, huh?"

"Yeah, somebody has to do it." Hayden was purposely adding fuel to the fire.

"One thousand U.S. each and don't spend it all in the one bar." Stace grinned. "Sign on the dotted line. Tomorrow I'll e-mail to your hotel the name and address of your bank in Buenos Aires and your account confirmation. Now . . . I have here authorization from the DA stating you are NYPD Homicide detectives and licensed to carry firearms. You will have to show this to Argentine Airways who may decide to commandeer your weapons until you arrive. Now is there anything else that may require further clarification?"

"Naw, we're good, Stace," Tony answered. "And thanks, buddy"

"No sweat, and come back in one piece." Stace grinned. "This place wouldn't be the same without your two ugly mugs."

"*You see how popular we are!* What did I tell you?" Bill laughed.

"Get out of it, Hayden. You're a piece of work."

Not content, Tony turned the "friendly fire" on Lucas and Brown; he just couldn't "walk on by."

"How forgetful of me, not telling you two guys that Bill and I are shipping out tonight on a special assignment to Buenos Aires. *Don't cry for me Argentina . . .*"Tony was half singing the famous ballad and half laughing at the same time.

Just then, Tony's phone rang and maybe just in time before there was, "in police terms," an aggravated assault. Brown and Lucas had had enough ribbing for one day.

"Perino here."

"Tony, it's Ben from the front desk. I have a Mrs. Summers who says she has an appointment to see you."

"Send her up, Ben."

"Floor 2, ma'am. The elevator is straight ahead."

*   *   *

June looked tired and haggard as she entered the office. On spotting her, Tony quickly rose to his feet and waved to June's relief upon recognizing the familiar face in the hostile police environment.

"June, are you all, right?" Tony offered his hand. "You don't look too good," he commented as he and Bill escorted her to the "interview room."

"To be honest, Tony, *I've had a day of it!*" She was shaking her head in utter despair. "I feel like a train wreck waiting to happen."

"Listen, June, I'm sorry to have to drag you here, but—"

She stopped him in his tracks. "Tony don't apologize. Just do me a favor *and get this over with!*"

"*Eh . . . Err . . .* Sure, I understand . . ." Tony was taken aback at June's bluntness. "*Eh,* this won't take long. Bill, why don't you fetch June a coffee?"

"I'll take a rain check on that, Bill. I know you mean well, but I think I've had enough coffee today to last me a week!"

"Why don't you take a seat, June, and try and relax. This is not an interrogation but just a simple factual statement on the events leading up to

Mike's disappearance." "I see." June frowned.

"Bill, you're on the keyboard."

Hayden opened the laptop and gave his usual disgruntled reply. *"Gee thanks!"* But Tony just ignored him.

"June, think back over last week, and try and recall to the best of your memory anything, anything at all, that struck you as being strange and/or out of the ordinary regarding Mike's behavior . . ."

"And you say Mike received this call at approximately two thirty in the morning on August 12?"

"Yes."

"Was this unusual, I mean considering his position with Global?"

"Mike receives lots of calls at home but never at two thirty in the morning," June bluntly answered.

"Did you ask him to give you a reason?"

"Of course! What wife wouldn't? And to make it worse, he quickly hung up like almost in panic and took the call on his phone downstairs in the kitchen, on the pretext that he didn't want to disturb me. When I challenged him, he gave a sort of lame duck story about some new salesman in Canada . . . *I mean* . . ."

Tony rubbed his chin, trying to understand June's comment. Maybe there was something more than meets the eye. Was he missing something?

June could sense from Tony's puzzled expression, and it was now the "whole nine" or nothing, and she took a deep breath.

"Okay, I'll lay it on the line. Mike is suave, handsome, and distinguished and has an eye for the ladies, and in his job, he could sell refrigerators to Eskimos. I've always felt he was playing around behind my back, but I could never prove it. He either covered his tracks well or I just didn't want to admit my husband was being unfaithful. He is a good provider, loves the kids, and our matrimonial relationship is good, if you know what I mean?"

Tony nodded. "I get the message, but you seem to be holding back something."

"Whatever . . . Mike is still my husband and the father of my two children, and no matter what, I still love him dearly."

"June, before you continue further, I can't overemphasize how serious it is to withhold information that could assist the police in their investigation of a serious crime. I short you can be charged with perverting the course of justice, being an 'accessory after the fact.' June, as friend, my advice is to take a step back, think carefully, and start again."

*   *   *

"Now let's recap. On the evening of the twelfth, around eleven thirty, you received a call from a Laura Williams, requesting that you contact Mike as she wished to speak with him about an urgent matter and that he knew what it was about. It was late, and you hadn't heard from him, so you decided to call him at his hotel in Chicago to see how his business went and also to pass on the message. Now you mentioned that when he answered the phone, he seemed angry, almost like he was being harassed by someone. Can you recollect his exact words?"

"It was like . . . *'Now you listen'* or something to that effect. I was taken aback, and he apologized, his excuse being that he had just had a run in with room service."

"And how did he react when you passed the message from Laura Williams?"

"Hmmm . . . I see. So, his answer seemed plausible."

"Mike always has meetings at strange times."

Tony just looked at Bill, who gave a sort of "this adds up."

"Okay, let's move on to the night of August 13, where you say Mike returned home late." Tony was reading from his notes. "Can you remember the time?"

"Not really, but it was certainly after nine."

"Now he told you that he never had that meeting with Laura because . . ."

"That's correct."

"And the scratches on his face . . ."

*   *   *

"June, I think we've buttoned it up. Bill will give you a copy of your statement in a few minutes. Read it carefully, and if you wish to make any changes, you are free to do so."

Bill removed the memory stick and left the room.

"Can I fetch you anything, water or something?" Tony asked. He could almost sense her ordeal.

"No, I just want to get home to see the kids."

"Listen, Rose said she will pop in to see you tonight, if it's convenient?"

"Tell her thanks, Tony, but some other time."

"I understand, June." Tony was feeling uncomfortable. This was a new experience . . . *I mean a neighbour and a friend!*

The door opened, and Bill handed June her statement.

"Stace, this is June Summers's signed statement. Make sure Ted gets it when he returns."

*   *   *

"Sure. You guys are still here, huh? I thought you would have gone by now, considering you have a long flight in front of you and at midnight."

Tony just grinned. "A coffee and then we're off, Stace. Hayden, you're on the bell."

"I might have guessed!" Bill shook his head and dejectedly walked to the coffee machine, fumbling in his pocket for the coins. Within minutes, he returned with the polystyrene cups, placing them on Mike's desk. He was not impressed.

"Hey, partner, it's only a couple of bucks. Never mind. I'll by you coffee at the airport."

"Perino, you're a piece of work." Bill was shaking his head as he took his chair. *"I give up on you."*

"Touché. No, let's get serious. What do you think, Bill?" Tony took a sip of the "Diesel."

"You mean Summers's statement?"

"What else?"

"It certainly adds up, but, partner, we have more important things on our mind."

"Like what?"

"Tell our wives we're leaving tonight for Argentina."

CHAPTER 7

Laura was so happy to see her friend again when Terry unexpectedly opened the door to her room.

"I hope I'm not disturbing you." Terry laughed as she placed the bunch of flowers on the bedside table.

"Gladiolas . . . Terry, *you shouldn't have!"* She croaked, her voice barely a rasp. "But they smell so nice. I'll get the nurse to place them in a jug of water when she comes to check my pressure." Laura's face was beaming all over at the sight of her friend. "I just knew you would come."

"Enough! Enough! You're not meant to be talking. If you damage your larynx for good, then what? We'll not be able to talk about anyone." Terry laughed. *"Now no more talking.* Use that pen and paper on your bedside table."

Laura nodded in agreement and leaned over to pick up her communication tools.

"This is a nice room. You got class, honey."

Terry's comment made Laura laugh again. Still the same old Terry! She scribbled on the notepad. I'm so glad to see you. *I'm so bored in this bloody place. The doctors tell me I will be in here for at least another three to four weeks. Can you believe it?*

"I'm not surprised. You've been to hell and back, and I'm amazed at how resilient you are. But the bottom line is you have got to rest to let your wounds heal, and I was thinking . . . *it's only a suggestion . . .* When you are discharged from hospital, you can come and stay at my place for a while and let me look after you. You can't live in that apartment by yourself, and no disrespect, I don't think you want to go back home and live with your parents." *You got that right! But are you sure I wouldn't be burden?*

"What do *you* think? We're best buddies, aren't we?" That made Laura smile again.

"But what about your love life?" Laura was teasing.

"You mean Frank? Listen, we're not at the 'live in' stage just yet! In fact, I'm meeting him tonight for drinks, but . . ." Terry glanced at her watch. *"That time already.* I had better call to say I'll be late."

You shouldn't had come, Terry, if you had a date. "Don't be silly. Besides, Frank is very understanding." *How do you feel about him?*

"Serious . . . is that what you are asking?" Laura nodded.

"Well." Terry paused before answering. It was a good question. It's like you store it in your mind until someone presses the button.

"Laura honey, I would be telling a lie if I didn't say he was special. I mean after some of the jerks I've been with! I ask you? Listen, I know he's just a

security guard, but he's ambitious and who knows?" *So, you have slept with him. Come on, be honest!*

Terry just laughed.

Well, aren't you going to phone poor guy?

"Thanks for reminding me." Terry opened her phone and dialled; the ring tone seemed to go on forever.

"Come on. Come on. Answer the bloody phone, Frank. It's nearly eight fifteen!" She shook her head in dismay before closing the phone then turned to Laura. *"I'm in trouble now,* but I'm sure Frank will recognize the 'missed call' and ring me."

She no sooner had she made the comment than her phone buzzed.

Terry put her finger to her lips and whispered. *"It's Frank!"*

"I'm sorry I missed your call, honey, but something has come up. One of the guards at the Bank of America has called in sick, and the company is flat strap with no spare bods, and they have asked me to stand in at short notice."

"So you're politely standing me up?" Terry gave Laura a cheeky wink. "Awe, come, honey, I really apologize. I mean what could I do?"

"Oh well then, I'll just have to phone one of my old boy friends"—Terry was covering her mouth to hide her laughter—"since I've been stood up."

"You *are* joking, aren't you?" Frank was biting the hook line and sinker.

"Of course, I am, *you big jerk!* But then how do I know that you are telling the truth. Maybe you're two timing me?" She couldn't stifle her laughter any longer.

"Why you . . . For a moment, you had me going. Honey, I'm really sorry, believe me."

"I forgive you. Millions wouldn't."

"I'll make it up to you, I promise."

"Now *that* sounds interesting! Then I'll forgive you. Poor me, I'll just have to sit here all on my lonesome like a couch potato with a lousy TV dinner and watch some boring television."

Now Laura was trying to stifle *her* laughter.

"Honey, don't make me feel any worse. I love you and I wouldn't hurt you for the world."

"I know, darling. I'm just ribbing you. Why don't you call me tomorrow?"

"For sure. I'm sorry, honey, but I must hang up. Tomorrow then." The phone went dead.

You are something else, Terry. That poor guy. You were just stringing him along, letting him think it was all his fault when in fact you haven't even left the hospital.

"Actually." Terry had that naughty grin on her face. "I was really looking forward to my own company tonight and just chilling out. You can get too much of the dating scene, and it's good to get some space."

Laura's expression suddenly changed. Terry's remark had struck a nerve. The memory of Mike was flashing back in her mind. She really loved that guy, and what she wouldn't do to be in Terry's shoes. "I'm sorry, Laura . . . I didn't . . ." She raised her hand to stop her.

It's not his fault. It's just that I loved him so much, and how could he do this to me and his unborn child?

The tears began to flow freely, ad Terry reached for the box of paper napkins.

Thanks, Terry. I'm sorry. I keep making a fool of myself.

"*I know, honey . . . I know.*" Terry squeezed Laura's hand to comfort her.

"Listen, changing the subject, I've been dreading telling you this, but Blakely has given me your position. I feel so bad. It's as if I am benefiting from my best friend's dilemma."

Now it was Laura's turn to squeeze Terry's hand.

Don't worry. I'm happy for you. Blakely made the right choice.

"Laura, Blakely's not all bad. He told me that if I was seeing you tonight to tell you that once you fully recover, there will always be position for you at ABM."

Laura gave Terry a warm smile. She knew where she was coming from.

A word of advice. Don't turn your back on Jaycee Donnelly or that other bitch Mildred Pitt.

"Don't worry, honey. I've already zeroed in on these two kamikazes!"

"Ms. Williams, it's time to check your pressure and to change your dressings." Then the nurse turned to Terry. "I'm sorry but visiting hours are over."

"I understand." Terry smiled and rose to leave. "Bye, honey." She gave Laura a kiss on the cheek. She could see her eyes fill. "Remember my offer . . . Ciao."

As Terry sat in her car, she couldn't help but dread Laura's reaction when her doctor informs her she can never have children. She shook her head and turned the key. "*Let's take one step at a time.*"

*   *   *

June was all washed out as she turned in the key in the lock.

"*Boy,* am I glad to be home!" She entered the security code to disable the alarm then kicked off her heels and rubbed the sole of her right foot while trying to keep her balance.

"These bloody heels are killing me, and it seems it's always the right foot. They say you have one foot larger than the other. *To hell with vanity!* I should try a bigger size." She gave a big sigh. "What a woman will do for fashion." June was talking to herself. If nothing else, it was a timely distraction from her larger-than-life problems.

"*Gosh,* it's now after five, and the kids will be home soon." She shook her head as she walked barefooted to the kitchen. "And what the hell I'm gonna tell them? God only knows. But first things first. *Dinner!* And believe me the last thing I feel like is cooking."

She stood for a moment as most mothers do from habit, scratching her head. Then she smiled. *"A simple frittata.* Hell, it's only eggs, bacon, milk, and cheese baked in the oven! *Simple and foolproof."* She opened the refrigerator.

"Mom, we're home." It was Sheryl calling from the hallway.

"I'm in the kitchen, honey. Is Steven with you?"

"Yes, we caught the school bus together."

"Hi, Mom." Steven suddenly appeared and helped himself to a Coke from the icebox. "Sis has gone upstairs probably to phone some of her weirdo friends."

"Steven, don't talk about your sister like that!" June changed the subject. "So how did college go?"

"If you mean did someone twig that my father is the fugitive wanted by the police?"

"Hardly. His name has not been released to the media."

"Yes, but walls have ears, and there're no secrets in this world. Mother, when it comes to making a buck, someone will break the 'code of silence' and phone the media."

"And who might that be, may I ask?"

"The police, of course, Mother."

He took a mouthful of coke and gave a rude burp, the gas entering his nostrils.

"Steven, don't be so rude!"

"Sorry, Mother." He hugged her and gave her a peck on the cheek.

"That's more like it." June placed the frittata in the oven. "Dinner will be ready in about twenty-five minutes so why don't you go and watch some television?"

"Na, I'll keep you company, Mother." "Hi, Mom." Sheryl grabbed a stool.

"Now suddenly I have two to keep me company." June gave a forced a smile as she laid the cutlery and plates on the breakfast bar.

"Steve, can you get me a Coke?" Sheryl as usual was being naughty.

"Are you legless? Go get it yourself!"

"Steven! What have I just told you?" June turned to face him, standing with both hands on her hips with that look he knew so well.

"Oh, all right." Steven reluctantly walked to the refrigerator.

"Thanks, bro." Sheryl was rubbing it in as she popped the tab.

Kids have an intrinsic nature for putting problems aside and living for the moment and maybe just as well.

* * *

"Kids, dinner is ready. Grab your seat at the bar." June took the pan from the stove and laid in on the wooden chopping board. "This baby is hot," she commented as she removed her gloves. "We'll grab a coffee later. You guys just go ahead and start without me."

"*Mmmm* . . . You always make great frittata, Mom." Sheryl was indulging. "I thought you were on a diet." Steven just had to throw his "double six."

"*You two!*" June was shaking her head as she lit the stove before taking her seat.

"Now I don't want to spoil your appetite, but this an opportune time when we are all together over dinner to . . ."

* * *

"*Mother, are you serious?*" Steven was first cab off the rank. As for Sheryl, she was almost in tears.

"And the bank manager says Father cleaned out the account?"

"I'm afraid so, son."

"*Twenty-five thousand*! What the hell is Father up to? If he's innocent, he should come back and face the music."

"*I'll tell you what he's up to.*" June was trying to keep her cool, but now it was time to open the valve. "He's absconded and according to the police is now in Argentina."

There was a deathly silence as Steven and his sister turned to each other in utter disbelief.

"*I don't believe it!* Father running away to save his lousy hide and leaving his family destitute." Steven was on a hate trip.

"Mother, what are we going to do?" Sheryl was now in full flow.

"I met with Mike's boss, Chuck Briggs. You remember, he and his wife have been here her for dinner. Well, a long story cut short. He has agreed technically to fire your father and deposit six months' salary in lieu of notice into our account. It's less than a hundred thousand after tax, but it's a godsend. Of course, unless there is a miracle, we are well and truly broke."

"*Mother*, what's going to happen to us?"

"Sheryl, stop crying and let Mother finish."

"It means we have to cut our cloth to suit. The BMW will be the first casualty, and the house may be repossessed unless we can find a legal loophole to sell it as the bank is holding the title as collateral for the mortgage, and worse still the deed is in your father's name. Fortunately, your schools fees are paid until the end of this semester, but after that . . . well, I don't have to spell it out."

"I'll never forgive him, Mother, and if I ever get the chance, so help me I'll . . ."

*   *   *

Mike was feeling relaxed after a day of nothingness loafing around the pool and reading the dated *Financial Times*. Of course, it wouldn't be the same without his favourite poison on the rocks. But Mike was no fool. Too much booze can send the wrong message, and he needed to keep Mona on the back burner. The rich and powerful Mendoza family, and with his marketing experience, could provide him with a wealth of opportunity; and of course, should he eventually become one of the family, the world is his oyster. Mike felt pretty good with himself. Who would have thought? Even better, Mona was a looker. He had the best of both worlds.

"Yes." He smiled at the thought as he relaxed on top of the bed, staring at the ceiling, his hands behind his head. "I might as well start getting dressed or Mona will be on my doorstep before I know it."

*   *   *

(Speaking in Spanish)

Mona checked the time and finished the last of her coffee. It had been another hectic day. Since returning from her business trip, her "in tray" was still in trouble, and she hadn't even finished her overseas report as yet. Worse still, she had to meet Mike at seven, and time was not on her side. She lifted the phone.

"Lucia, is the chairman free?"

"Senorita Menzel, the chairman had a lunch appointment with Senor Delgado, Presidente de Banko Argentina, and will not be returning to the office."

"Thanks, Lucia. Should anyone want me, I'll be leaving in around five minutes. *Oh*, and tell Aldo to fetch the car and meet me at reception."

"Gracias, senorita. I will let the staff know and inform Aldo. Buenas noches."

Mona bundled her unfinished report into her ostrich-hide briefcase and briskly walked to her office door, but then something crossed her mind, and she dropped her case, returning to her desk to pick up the phone. She dialled and waited. Lorena, the maid, finally lifted the receiver.

"Si, Menzel residence?"

"Lorena, Senorita Menzel speaking. Is Mother home?"

"Si, I go call her. *Senora . . .* Senorita Mendoza is on the telephone," Lorena yelled unceremoniously.

Mona held the phone away from her ear and screwed up her face as Lorena's voice broke the sound barrier.

"That woman! I don't know why Mother puts up with her?" Mona was talking to herself.

"I'm coming, Lorena." Carla grabbed the phone. "Is everything all right, dear?"

Carla, her mother, was always worried. What with the ever-escalating drug-related crimes in Buenos Aires, one can never tell. The wealthy Mendoza family had been targeted on a number of occasions, but with the police on the payroll, what better security?

"Of course, Mother. I'm still in the office. It's just that I forgot to tell you that I won't be joining you and Father this evening for dinner. I have another pressing appointment."

"Don't tell me you have forgotten your brother and his wife are joining us?"

"Mother, *I completely forgot!"*

"Your father won't be impressed. After all, it's not often that the whole family get together over dinner."

"Mother, I really do apologize. It's unforgivable of me to forget, but it's too late for me to cancel at this late hour. I'll explain to Father when I arrive home to change. I'm sorry, Mother. I must hang up as I'm running late." "I understand, honey . . ."

* * *

At just before five in the evening, Mona walked past the executive suites on the thirtieth floor, and she felt slightly conspicuously embarrassed at her early exit. But then why should she? She had well and truly earned her stripes as marketing director and a position on the main board of Menzel International, working her way up the ladder upon joining the company after graduating with honours in computer science from the prestigious University of Buenos Aires.

* * *

At last she arrived finally at reception; and as usual, Aldo was there, waiting patiently, ready to shadow Mona to the limo.

"Buenas noches, Senorita Menzel." The security guard saluted and pushed opened the large plate glass door.

"Gracias, Enrique. Tener una buena noche."

The elderly guard smiled. "Gracias, Prego, senorita." It was unusual to get a compliment, especially from the boss's daughter.

Aldo quickly squeezed past Mona and held her back with his hand.

"Un momento, por favor, debo comprobar."

"Aldo, hablar ingles!" Mona expressed her annoyance.

"Me a sorry but must check street dangerous."

"Aldo, how are you ever going to learn English unless you try?"

"Lo sentimos, boss."

(Speaking in Spanish)

"I give up. Let's get moving. I'm running late."

Aldo and Mona were inseparable as he escorted her to the limo, his right hand never far away from the bulge on the left side of his jacket. He wasn't to too happy at getting a dressing down, but he and his family have to eat, and he hurriedly opened the rear door of the Cadillac.

Mona settled into the plush leather seating. The drive to Recoleta is about fifteen minutes from Menzel Towers, depending on the traffic. It was short, but it gave her time to recollect and think about Mike. As she looked in the rear mirror, she could see the thirty-floor office block, now a famous landmark on the Plaza San Martine in the CBD, disappear in the distance.

*   *   *

Recoleta is one of the most exclusive districts in Buenos Aires, populated with the rich and famous. In 1871, due to the yellow fever epidemic, many wealthy families lost loved ones only to be buried in the famous Cemetery of Recoleta, the burial place of many dignitaries and famous people, including none other than one of the most famous, *Eva Peron.*

Eva was a simple country girl who came to Buenos Aires to make her fortune and met Juan Peron at a charity function, and they eventually married. Juan Peron later was elected to vice president of the Republic and minster of War. Eva consequently became famous in films and radio with her most famous song "Don't Cry for Me Argentina." Unfortunately, she passed away in 1952 at the young age of thirty-three as the result of terminal cancer, and Argentina lost the people's most beloved sweetheart.

*   *   *

As Aldo slipped into the evening traffic, Mona suddenly noticed another man in the passenger seat next to the driver, and she angrily knocked on the glass partition; and Aldo quickly lowered the screen.

"Si, senorita?" Aldo nervously glanced in the rear mirror. Mona took no prisoners, and she looked anything but happy.

"Aldo, who is this?" She raised her voice.

"This is Jose, security guard from company. I have okay from big boss to take holiday with family next week, and Jose take my place. So I train him what to do."

"Why wasn't I told?" Mona was furious. In Buenos Aires, you never take chances.

"I'm sorry, boss, but your father approve Jose after security check." *"Huhh?* Next time, Aldo, you tell *me first. Entiendes?"*

"Si, I understand." Aldo flushed. To be dressed down in front of a colleague was an insult to the Gaucho culture, and he boiled in silence.

Mona finally calmed down and tried to relax, her mind drifting back to Mike.

It felt good to be in the company of a handsome man again after so long, but am I being too naive? she pondered. *I have been married once and against my father's advice to a gigolo who's only motive was money and the luxuries life that the Mendoza family could provide. The fast cars, the expensive Italian suites, and a fat wallet to go with it, and who wants to work for a living?* Her eyes teared over at the thought. *How could I have been so foolish? That unfaithful bastard broke my heart, and I vowed I would never get involved with another man again. But here I am going down the same path, and I've only known Mike for two days! Yet I feel he is special and has no ulterior motive. But there is a lot I still don't know about him. Sure, he's some years older than me, but does that really matter?* She was trying to convince herself. *Divorced and grown-up kids? Hey! What am I thinking about? As the saying goes, "it's early days."*

Time passes so quickly when your mind takes over your thoughts and you self-diagnose, but the loud blast of the horn and Aldo's curses quickly brought Mona back to her senses.

"Usted bastardo loco," Aldo screamed at the offending motorist as he signalled and hung a right into Av. Callino.

Mona gave a disgusted sigh and shook her head. "What am I to do with this crazy Gaucho?"

* * *

Avenue Callino is one of the wealthiest streets in Recoleta. Only the rich can afford to live here in their grand mansions and manicured gardens, but like most things in life, there is always a downside; and this place was no different: their large three-story mansions heavily walled and fortified with security cameras at every point imaginable, their owners all but living in a self-imposed prison. The Menzel mansion was no different with its three-meter wrought iron gates and round-the-clock security with armed guards patrolling the parameter walls and gardens 24/7. But then this is Argentina, with one of the highest crimes statistics in Latin America from drug lords to organized crime with kidnappings commonplace. As for the police, they had enough problems fighting corruption in their own backyard. And the politicians? *What's new? It's the same the world over.*

* * *

The stunning large white-pillared Menzel mansion stood out from the rest of the grotesque avenue, and Aldo came to a halt in front of the four-meter-high black enamelled security gate with its leafy wrought iron design and large arched curves on either side. This electric gate was a work of art standing prominent against the towering white security walls.

The armed guard raised his hand to stop the limo. Even though he recognized Aldo, he still had to check the car thoroughly. It's commonplace for armed robbers to hide lying on the floor while threatening the passenger at gunpoint to remain silent in order to gain entry.

(Speaking in Spanish)

The guard in the military-style uniform carbine at the ready cautiously approached Aldo, who had wound down the car window.

"Saul, *for god's sake,* you go through this shit every night. It's me, Aldo, *remember!*"

The young black moustached guard gave a cheeky grin. He loved to annoy Aldo. Besides, he had to put on a show for the boss's daughter.

"You may be Aldo, but who is this man?" He pointed to the co-driver.

"Jose," Aldo annoyingly replied. "He is standing in for me next week when I go on vacation. He is office security guard from head office."

Saul walked round to the front passenger window and loudly tapped on the glass.

"Open please."

Aldo pressed the auto button. This was becoming getting out of hand.

"Papers please?" Saul asked. Jose obliged. Saul studied the ID for a second then nodded.

"Aldo, open the rear door and trunk."

Now even Mona was becoming, shall we say, *pissed off.* But then again, the guard was only doing his job, and she suffered in silence, nervously checking her watch.

"Senorita Menzel, please excuse me, but I must check the floor."

Mona nodded in approval.

The trunk finally checked, the guard saluted then waved to the security camera, giving the all clear to open the gates, then saluted once more as Aldo finally drove past but not before shouting all sorts of abuse at Saul, who just kept grinning.

The long winding drive to the mansion's entrance was a welcome sight, but Mona still had to face the family, and she was anything but looking forward to it.

CHAPTER 8

It had just turned nine thirty when the yellow cab pulled up in front of the Perino residence and gave two loud blasts of the horn.

"*Tony . . .* That must be Bill's cab," Rose called from the kitchen.

"*Honey,* tell him to come in for a moment as I haven't quite finished packing."

"*Tuuut.*" Rose inhaled as she walked to the front door, complaining under her breath. "*I told him to start earlier and not horse around with the kids!*"

At seeing Rose appear on the front porch, Bill gave her a wave from the open window, the summer humidity still unpleasant.

"Bill, come in for few minutes. I tell you . . . that lazy oaf hasn't finished packing yet. Tell the cab driver to keep the meter running."

"Make yourself comfortable and grab a seat in the lounge. Tony shouldn't be too long. Would you like a cold beer?" Rose asked as Bill sank into the leather sofa.

"As I'm not driving, I wouldn't say no." He grinned.

Bill, it appeared, was on vacation, dressed in his short-sleeved Hawaiian shirt, light-coloured slacks, and deck shoes like "*I'm going on a summer holiday.*" "You really look the part, Bill." Rose smiled.

"Thanks, Rose." He popped the can and took a long sip of the cold one. "Boy, *that hits the spot!*"

Rose turned as she heard the heavy footsteps coming down the stairs.

"This will be your buddy now, *and not before time.*" She put on a face.

"Well, look at you!" Tony laughed as he dropped his garment bag. "All you need now, Hayden, *is the Panama hat!"*

"Get out of it! You're not doing so bad yourself with that outrage beach shirt, and all *you need* is the Bermuda shorts."

Rose couldn't help herself and burst into laughter, listening to these two comedians, one as bad as the other.

"Listen, you two. Get serious. That cab is sitting waiting outside with the meter running."

Rose was more than anxious to see the back of them, picturing herself lounging on the sofa, a glass of chilled sauvignon blanc, indulging in some Pringles, watching TV. It had been one of these days with Tony's last-minute bombshell regarding his out-of-the-blue assignment and, to top it all, *departing tonight for Buenos Aires!*

"Bye, honey." Tony gave Rose a kiss on the lips. "I'll give you a ring when we arrive at our hotel."

Rose gave Bill the "Italian job." "Look after him. I want him back in one piece. *And you two, behave yourselves!"*

"Yes, Mother," Tony replied, trying to control his laughter.

"Why you . . . Tony Perino, you had better bring me back a nice present," Rose called as they were walking to the cab.

"Yeah, *myself!* Bye, honey. I love you."

Rose stood on the porch, watching the cab disappear.

"I wouldn't have that big heel any other way . . . I really love that guy." She closed the door and walked to the refrigerator.

"Now for that well-deserved glass of wine . . ."

*   *   *

Tony turned to Bill and laughed. "Well, partner, we're on our way. So how did Judy take it?"

Bill just shook his head. He looked really down.

"That bad?"

"Worse . . . I mean that woman . . . I don't know what to do to please her, Tony."

"I'm sorry, partner. I can't help you in that department," Tony answered, but he couldn't help feeling sad for his buddy. Bill is a regular guy and a hardworking honest cop who doesn't deserve this crap.

"She's always complaining and always about money. I'm running out of patience, and I've almost given up trying."

"Awe, come on, Bill. It can't be all bad?"

"She wants me to resign from the force and get a better-paying job. I ask you? Police work is my life. She complains about having to take a part-time job to help support the family and always benchmarks the life that you and Rose have."

"Bill, I have already recommend you for lieutenant when Wilson retires."

"I know, Tony, and don't think that I don't appreciate it."

"Bill, marriage is a wonderful invention and—" Bill cut him short. *"And so is the bicycle pump!"* At that comment, they both burst into hysterics. *"Hayden."* Tony was lost for words.

"We're here. Which terminal, guys?"

"International departures, terminal 1, Argentine Airways."

* * *

At ten in the evening, Kennedy was surprisingly busy; long haul night flights must be in fashion, or was it the price?

Tony had flown back to Sicily some eight years ago for his grandfather's birthday and a family reunion, fortunately, before Papa Perino passed away one year later. As Rose was from Rome, it was like killing two birds with one stone and a grand family bash. That was Tony's first time out of the United States and his first long international flight.

Sure, Bill had flown domestically like the time they flew to Chicago and Detroit on police business, but he had never been out of his own patch, and this overnight flight to Latin America was proving to be a real adventure. But Argentina is no United States, as Tony and Bill would soon find out.

* * *

The female attendant at the check-in studied the document.

"I would appreciate your patience, sirs, while I go and find my supervisor." The pretty olive-skinned young Latino gave her trained smile.

Bill turned to Tony, grinning. "Eat your heart out, buddy. Did you see the smile *I* got?"

"Hayden, there's nothing like dreaming. It was the Italian stallion that attracted her."

"Your full of it, Perino."

"Good evening." The tall moustached immaculately groomed gentleman in the blue airline uniform, sporting more gold braid than a Christmas tree, studied the two detectives. He was holding the document.

"Seniors, this document." He glanced at it again. "From a?" He checked the name. "Mr. Murray, the New York district attorney, and endorsed by the Argentinean Consulate General, explaining your need to carry firearms, is in order. However, the airline has strict safety procedures and regulations regarding the transportation of ordinance on passenger aircrafts."

"So, what are you trying to tell me?" Tony asked aggressively, expecting the worst.

The officer held up his hand in a "hold it" gesture: don't be so impatient.

"Please, senor, excuse. One moment. Have you packed any live ammunition in your baggage?" "No," Tony answered.

"And you, Mr. Hayden?"

"Same."

"Good. Then I suggest you check-in first and meet with me at the fragile freight counter."

* * *

"Only carry-on baggage, seniors?" "Yes," Tony replied.

"Your passports and reservations, please. That's a window and an aisle, 11A and 11B. Boarding is at ten thirty. The business-class lounge is immediately to the right after you clear immigration. There are clear directions on the back of your boarding pass. Have a good flight. Next please."

CHAPTER 9

(Speaking in Spanish)

The guard on the front door quickly stepped aside and gave Mona a smart salute before assisting her to open the large oak-paneled door.

"Buenas noches, Senorita Monzel."

"Muchas gracias, Pedro." Mona smiled. The young security guard was a bit of a dish.

* * *

The first thing to strike you when you enter the Monzel mansion is the larger-than-life entrance hall with its black and white marble tiles, not to mention the *Gone with the Wind* staircase and its highly lacquered balustrade with ornamental wrought iron slats. Its plush carpeted stairs in a dark blue sapphire colour arching in a half circle sweeping up to the first floor was absolutely spectacular. But in Buenos Aires, a mansion wouldn't be the same without the trademark crystal chandelier, and the Menzel's wouldn't be outdone. This complicated glass masterpiece must have at least weighed half a ton dangling on a gold-plated chain that could hold a liner in dock. This was money at its ugliest, but some people are born to be rich and then there's the others . . . *And unfortunately, in Argentina, it's mostly the others!*

* * *

"Senorita Menzel, buenas noches." It was Lorena, the head maid.

Mona handed Lorena her briefcase. "Lorena, put this in my study, gracias. Is my father home yet?"

"Si, he his is resting in the lounge with your mother and your brother and his wife, enjoying a glass of champagne. Will you be staying for dinner, as I must let the chef know?"

"No, Lorena, apologize and inform him that I have another appointment."

"Gracias." Lorena turned around and left for the study.

Mona opened the French doors and popped her head around.

"Am I interrupting something?" It was a throwaway line.

"Sis." Felipe, her brother, rose to his feet to give his little sister a big hug. "I haven't seen you since you went on that business trip to the States. Aren't you going to join us for dinner?"

"I'm sorry, Felipe, but I have another appointment, and it's too late to cancel."

"That's disappointing, sis, because we have something special to celebrate tonight."

"Something special to celebrate?" Mona repeated, intrigued by her brother's remark. *Now come to think of it,* Mona thought. *It seemed that everyone had a smile on their face.*

Rosita, her sister-in-law, rose from the sofa and gave Mona a warm hug then stepped back . . . "Da . . . Da." She raised her arms shoulder high. "Anything different?"

Mona stared for a moment. What could be different? This was becoming like a "who done it" mystery.

Then Rosita proudly rubbed the small bulge on her abdomen.

"Rosita, you're pregnant!"

"As pregnant as could be." She was smiling all over.

"Would you like a glass of champagne, senorita," the maid interrupted.

"You bet! This *really* calls for a celebration . . ."

* * *

Mona greeted her parents with the usual kiss before taking her seat next to her brother.

"Gracias." She took the champagne flute from the maid then raised her glass. "A toast to Felipe and Rosita and their forthcoming addition to our family . . . Health and happiness and a trouble-free pregnancy . . . *Salutey'* . . ."

*   *   *

"So, brother, how's business?"

"It's good. Our beef exports to the United States continue to grow, and our franchise outlets have never looked back." He grinned. "Thanks to my little sister's marketing skills."

"Felipe, now you're embarrassing me."

"But tell me about *your* trip to the U.S.?"

"I was good but tiring, but I have a few proposals to pass by Father on some exciting business opportunities."

Salvador just gave a grunt. "Not tonight, Mona, I just want to relax . . . Tomorrow at the office."

"I understand, Papa," she replied disappointed.

"Now tell me why this appointment of yours is *so* important that my only daughter can't join the family this evening for dinner?" The tone of her father's voice was sharp.

"*Eh . . . Hmmm . . .*" Mona knew the question was coming, but it was just a matter of when . . .

*   *   *

Salvador, Mona's father, is a Gaucho from the old school and a self-made man with traditional values, and above all, family comes first, especially when it comes to his only daughter . . . a true Argentinean, small in stature around five nine with not a sliver of fat on his wiry frame. Having just turned eighty-five, his full head of bushy grey hair and eyebrows to match made him look like a Chinese warrior from *Crouching Tiger* except for his leathery olive complexion. His deep laugh lines and slightly bagged eyes gave him a boorish but distinguished look, a look that was not to be messed with. The grey searching eyes and narrow lips portrayed a man who had experienced the hardships of working on the pampas as a drover with little or no education and the memories of the half yearly muster and the exhausting hot and dusty weather, returning to the bunkhouse exhausted, only to be ridiculed by his father and the other Gauchos. When his father finally passed away at the ripe old age of ninety, the hacienda was willed between him and his elder brother,

Antoine. Salvador subsequently decided to sell his share and bought his own cattle station, and as they say, "the rest is history."

But Mona's mother was from the other "side of the fence." Her father was a wealthy exporter of prime Argentinean beef stock and hence her by-chance meeting with Salvador at their home during export contract negotiations. Carla was a pretty young thing with shoulder-length jet-black hair, dark brown eyes, and a pearly smile that could knock you cold and a figure that would make Marilyn Monroe take a backseat. The Gaucho fell like a stone, and a long courtship followed, much to the dislike of Carla's father, who, like all fathers, "no one is good enough for his daughter." But then who listens to their parents' advice, and contrary to beliefs, their marriage has lasted fifty years. Sure there had been trials and tribulations, but Carla knew how to handle her husband, and now they were looking forward to their golden anniversary to be held in December this year. The good thing that comes of a true marriage is that although faces age, the heart stays the same . . .

*   *   *

"Well . . ." Mona paused. "I met this American on the flight and . . ." She didn't get a chance to finish, her father rudely interrupting. "I assume this gringo is a man?"

"*Father* . . ." Mona gave a loud tut-tut.

"Come on, sis, don't keep us in suspense." Now it was Felipe's turn to pour it on.

"Yes, of course, it's a man and handsome with it. He is from New York and is here to attend the Trade Conference at the Exhibition Center representing a large U.S. company as VP for marketing. Now, *is everyone happy?*" Mona was laughing, but her father wasn't going to hang up his guns just yet . . .

"Mona, I know you are old enough and I hope wise enough to look after yourself and make no mistake. Your mother and I would love to see you settle down with the right man . . ."

"*Father* . . . Please don't lecture me. Mike is just an acquaintance, and I really enjoy his company. It's his first time in Argentina, and I promised to show him the sights and experience our excellent food and hospitality. *And .* . . That's all there is to it!"

Felipe could feel the hot air and hastily stepped into the breach to change the subject and save another family "incident."

"When are Rosita and I going to enjoy your company at the hacienda? Of course, Mother and Father included."

Carla, her mother, loved the family thing and was quick to reply.

"I think that's a wonderful suggestion, Felipe. What do *you* think, Salvador darling?"

He sort of half nodded and mumbled under his breath.

"I assume that's yes?" Carla concluded; she could handle this old dog.

"Yes," Salvador reluctantly replied, his mind saying the opposite, like he would much rather stay at home than take a boring two-hour dusty drive to the Pampas.

Then before anyone could comment further, Mona's mother wrapped it up.

"That's it, settled. We'll travel down on Friday and stay over the weekend . . . Mona honey . . . *Eh* . . . Why don't you invite your newfound boyfriend?"

"Mother . . ." Mona shook her head. The trap was set, and now she had no alternative but to agree.

"I'll ask Mike if he is free . . . But . . ." She finished the last of her champagne. "I have go, I'm running late . . ."

*   *   *

(Speaking in Spanish)

The "beat up" blue Volkswagen bug pulled in behind the vintage '52 Pontiac, its brakes squealing as it drew precariously to a stop, and Carlos nervously glanced into the rear mirror waiting for the inevitable bumper nudge.

"What the fuck?" he yelled as Sergio reversed the bug, its rear engine rattling like bag of nails with the exhaust belching burnt oil fumes. As for the Pontiac, it took the knock like a mothballed battleship sitting in dry dock and hardly moved an inch.

Sergio leaped into the front seat of the Pontiac before Carlos could even open the passenger door.

"Carlos, *take it easy!* So, the brakes are a bit dodgy! But that's the best I could do at short notice. *Hey,* look on the bright side. The streets are full of these Mexican 'cookie' cans, and who's gonna spot us? The police have more important things to do than put out an APB for a clapped-out stolen beetle."

"If this piece of garbage lets us down, *so help me!* Now would it be stupid of me by chance to ask where you found it?"

Sergio grinned. "Some kids on the bay beach were more interested in sex and rolling in the sand, leaving the keys in the dash. I mean who in their right mind would steal this piece of shit?"

"*Okay . . . Okay . . .* No more, were getting fucking tight for time. Follow me in the bug while I hide this tank below these trees next to the park."

"No sweat." Sergio left the car and jumped into the Volkswagen with Carlos giving a "*wow*" of relief as the bug burst into life.

Maybe Sergio has something after all. Carlos grinned, speaking to himself as he gunned the engine . . .

* * *

The drive to the Sheraton on V San Martin would take around thirty minutes, but it had just turned six, and they were making good time. Sergio was crunching the gears now and again, but the trusty bug was not complaining.

"I gotta hand it to you, Sergio, steeling this heap isn't such a bad idea after all, and what I like about it is the two doors."

"Yeah, it's perfect for the job. Have you got the hardware?"

"What do *you* think? I had to pay that lowlife bastard Bruno three hundred each and another hundred for the silencers and the two additional clips."

"*Eight hundred, you're shitting me!* Where did you get the readies?"

"I gave Lena a sob story that my mother was in the hospital, and I needed the money to pay the medicine bills."

"*Santa Maria!* Sergio, how can you sleep at night? If Lena finds out, she'll fucking castrate you. You had better hit that confession box like *tomorrow!*"

"Stop fucking acting like an old superstitious fishwife. I got the pieces, didn't I, and keep your eyes on the road. The last thing we want is pulled over by a traffic cop . . ."

His cell phone rang . . .

* * *

Mike was dressed in a short-sleeved wrinkled Panama cotton white shirt and lightweight slacks to match. He had picked up some sun at the pool while exercising his arm, and in this getup, he could almost be mistaken for a local. His sparse wardrobe was boring and old hat, and he didn't want to meet Mona again with the same boring outfit. The hotel boutique was limited and expensive, but the male assistant who was a bit overzealous when measuring Mike's inside leg did a good job, and he now felt more comfortable and relaxed in his new garb. As they say, "When in Rome, do as the Romans do."

* * *

Mike glanced at his watch again as he impatiently walked the walk in the hotel lobby.

"Hmmmm . . . Seven fifteen, it's not like Mona to be late. I wonder if she's had second thoughts. *Naw,* she wouldn't do that," he half-heartedly convinced himself.

Rafa, the front desk attendant, answered the phone.

"Hotel Sheraton, Rafa speaking. Senorita Menzel, Senor Summers is standing right here in front of me. I'll transfer you to one of the house phones. My pleasure. Gracias. *Senor Summers," Rafa* called. "Yes?"

"Phone number 2. You have an incoming call."

For a second, Mike was taken aback. It could only be Mona, he convinced himself, as he nervously lifted the receiver.

"Yes, Mike Summers here?"

"So formal again!"

"Mona! *Eh . . . Err . . .* I thought it was my boss phoning from the States." Mike quickly changed the subject. "You're not standing me up, are you?" She could hear him laugh.

"What do *you* think?" Mona was throwing it back just to be naughty.

"You wouldn't do that to Romeo now, would you, Juliet?"

"I think that smacks a bit from Shakespeare, if I'm not mistaken."

"You can't blame a guy for trying."

"We'll talk about that later. Now getting serious, I was delayed at home as my brother and his wife . . . *Hey,* why am I telling you all this boring stuff? The bottom line is I'm running at least another half an hour late, so don't get bored and hit the bourbon, Jack!"

Mike had to laugh at Mona's Americanisms.

"So where are you now?" Mike was intrigued.

"I've just finished showering and about to dress."

"Can I be a devil and ask you what you are wearing right now?" Mike whispered in a low sexy voice.

"Only Chanel," Mona answered cheekily, but she could feel the moisture between her loins, and she couldn't help but wonder what this guy had that was so special. Maybe she was just "man starved." *Whatever.* She had to nip it in the bud or she would never get dressed.

"Listen, Mr. Summers, I have told you enough. You will have to leave the rest to your imagination . . . *Entiendes?"*

"I think I get the translation." Mike laughed.

"Half an hour then. Adios."

"Maybe I can have just one." Mike smiled to himself as he walked to the cocktail bar. After all, he still had half an hour.

* * *

(Speaking in Spanish)

"Si, Carlos here."

"Listen, it's Rafa from the front desk."

"Yeah, so what's the scoop?"

"It's no big deal except that the Menzel chick is running late by at least half an hour. She has just called the Americano."

"Gracias, Rafa. You did well but remember and keep your mouth shut."
"Don't worry, Carlos."

"Rafa, let me put it this way. If you want to see your next birthday, you had better." Carlos abruptly closed the call.

"So, what's the deal?" Sergio asked.

"The Menzel woman is running late, but that's good news as it buys us more time to walk through the plan. We can't afford any fuckups this time."

CHAPTER 10

The detectives felt naked as they cleared customs after losing their "best friends." Their police specials were an everyday part of their garb and a necessity in New York, *that's if you want to stay healthy!* But for Tony and Bill, this would be only the first of many hurdles that would challenge them in their quest to arrest a U.S. citizen outside the jurisdiction of the United States.

* * *

"Now let's see where this business-class lounge is. We still have plenty of time before boarding." Tony was studying the instructions on the back of his boarding pass.

"It's right in front of you, *dee-tective.*" The cheap shot was too good to miss.

"Don't be such a fucking jerk, Hayden! *Of course, I see it.*" Tony just shook his head at the joker's sarcasm.

"Good evening, sirs." The pretty receptionist greeted the detectives with a warm smile. "Can I have your boarding passes, please?" The Italian stallion returned the smile. "Certainly." Now it was Hayden's turn to shake his head.

"Everything is in order. I will call you when it's time to board flight 12 for Buenos Aires."

She was a looker, all right: the olive skin, the characteristic shoulder length black shiny hair, the large brown eyes, the pearly ivories, and the smooth Latino complexion. She had it all, and at around twenty-three, the guys must be stacked up.

"Thanks, eh?" Tony couldn't let it go.

She pointed to the nametag on her blouse.

"Annette. Nice name," Tony replied, overemphasizing.

She smiled again. "Please help yourself to the drinks and refreshments. Excuse me. Sir, welcome to the our business-class lounge. Can I have your . . ." *If this wasn't the bum's rush, it was the nearest thing to it!*

"Perrino, get wise to yourself. That broad is almost half your age." "So a guy can dream, can't he?" Tony irately returned the fire.

"If you say so." When Tony gets his backup, it's best to take the easy road.

"Changing the subject"—Bill was searching for a suitable resting place—"this place has class. I'm getting to like this. Say, there's an empty sofa over there, Tony, in front of that coffee table." Bill pointed.

"Go for it. I'm looking forward to planking my ass. It's been a long one."

"Boy, isn't this something! Now I know how the other half lives," Bill commented as he sank into the plush leather.

"Yeah, you can say that again." Tony gave a grunt of satisfaction, relaxing in the air-conditioned opulence. "I guess we had better make the best of it, as they say, 'we ain't gonna pass this way again.'"

"Lighten up, partner. How about a drink?"

"Bill, that's the best suggestion I've heard all day." "I'll have a grappa and a double espresso . . ."

*   *   *

The pretty stewardess checked their boarding passes.

"To the aisle on the left, Mr. Perino and Mr. Hayden. Seats 11A and 11B. Welcome to Argentina Airways. Our business-class purser will attend to you shortly."

"These seats have class, better than that domestic economy shit we usually get lumbered with." Bill was enjoying the roller coaster.

"My name is Lulu, and I'll be looking after you during this flight." The tall blonde with the million-dollar smile and the figure to match stopped at their seats while pushing the refreshment trolley. "As we have another half an hour before take-off, perhaps you would like to indulge in some fine French champagne."

Tony turned to Bill, and they smiled simultaneously. "This is getting better all the time . . ."

*   *   *

The evening meal over and a few more nightcaps, the guys settled down to the long flight.

"We'll be hitting the tarmac at nine thirty tomorrow. Remember, there's a two-hour time difference."

"Yeah, two hours ahead. I'm already setting my watch." Bill was in the process.

"I wonder what our man is doing now, and more to the point, why Buenos Aires?" Tony turned to Bill.

"The same thought crossed my mind. But it might boil down to the simple fact that it was the only international flight not fully booked."

"You're most probably right, Bill. Sometimes we think in complicated circles. I guess when you're a fugitive on the run-in desperation, anything goes."

"So where do we start?" Bill asked.

"Good point, and I would be telling you a lie, Bill, if I had the solution. From what I gathered from our conversation with Baker, this General Cerise or whatever his name is, is a piece of work and as bent as they come and ugly with it. In short, we watch our backs and keep our hands on our wallets. The word on the street is his sidekick a Captain?" "Avalos." Bill filled the gap.

"You have a good memory, partner . . . A Captain Avalos"—Tony picked up his train of thought—"is running a close second in the corruption race."

"So, we are at the mercy of these two banditos?"

"You nailed it, and the way I see it, to get their cooperation, we're going to have to dig deep, if you get my drift."

"Then I guess the first stop is immigration."

"That was my thought too, Bill. They must have a record of Summers's passport and entry documents stating his address during his stay in Buenos Aires. Of course, he could name any hotel. Who the hell is gonna check?"

"Well, we gotta start someplace, Tony."

"Yeah, and I'm gonna start by getting my head down. I'm bushed. Don't wake me for breakfast . . ."

*   *   *

(Speaking in Spanish)

"Park the bug over there below these trees where we can get a clear view of the hotel front but still keep out of sight." Carlos did as he was told.

308

In every walk of life, we have leaders and followers, and you guessed right.

The beetle parked, and the engine cut it was suddenly so quiet. Avenue V San Martin is one of the busiest thoroughfares in the city but at seven in the evening the traffic dies abruptly for "siesta time," then at around ten it's back to "party time" and "tapas bars," and the city bursts into life once again.

Sergio pulled the miniature opera binoculars from his bag. He had picked them up at the local flea market for a few pesetas. They were pretty low powered but sufficient for the job, and it was now a waiting game.

Sergio opened the beat-up sports bag and removed the Glock 38s, passing one to Carlos.

"Nice." He fondled the handgun for a moment. "I like it, Sergio. This baby has a good feel to it . . . And the ammo?"

Sergio handed Carlos the two eight-round clips.

"You haven't forgotten how to handle a semiautomatic, have you? It's been a while."

"Are you shittin' me?" Carlos proudly pushed the magazine clip home and pulled back the slider, sending one round into the chamber, then flicked on the safety catch before stuffing the other magazine into his back pocket.

"Locked and loaded, boss." He gave Sergio a "don't mess with me" smile. "Have you got the silencers?"

"Of course, I have, stupido."

Sergio didn't like Carlos's smug, overconfident attitude, that's how "fuckups" happen. He passed him the four-inch-long tube. "Be careful how you screw the silencer to the muzzle, and don't run the fucking thread. If you fuck that up, we got big problems. Without the silencer, that baby will sound like a fucking cannon!"

"For Christ's sake, Sergio, what do you think I am, a Dumbo or something?"

"Just cut the shit and pay attention, that's all I'm asking. Here." Sergio handed him the black ski mask and gloves. "When I give you the signal, you slip these on at the same time as me."

"Yeah, yeah, I know the drill. I can almost do it in my fucking sleep. You've gone through the plan so many times."

"Better to be safe than sorry," Sergio shot back.

There was a couple of minutes' silence before Carlos burst into laughter. "Hombre, how long have we known one another?"

Sergio slapped Carlos on the shoulder and pushed a cigarette into his mouth.

"Since we were kids." He flicked his lighter, and Carlos inhaled the tobacco stick like it was his last breath. "Gracias, Compadre." Sergio lit another for himself then sat back to relax.

"You remember, Carlos, when we were slum dogs in Villamisseria and didn't have a shoe on our feet."

"Yeah, and your father was always pissed out of his mind with illegal hooch, and when he was drunk, we would sneak up on him and steel a few pesetas from his pocket to buy a couple of cigarettes."

"*Hey,* and what about your father when he threw you out and you had to come and stay with us."

"That bastardo, don't remind me . . . and how he used to treat my mother. He deserved to die in that cantina fight over a prostitute when some hombre sliced him up with a machete. It was good riddance, but my poor mother died soon afterward. Her heart just gave up."

"But your bright idea to rob that gas station sent us to the La Plata Caseros high-security prison for ten years. Luckily, we were released from that hellhole after doing six. But we stuck together, comrade . . ."

"We had to, with these fucking queers, rapists, and murderers and the crazy Mexicans fighting the Argentineans. Boy, was I glad when *that gate* was unlocked."

Sergio suddenly gave Carlos a sharp dig to the ribs.

"*Hey,* easy, amigo!"

"*The limo!* It has just arrived." Sergio made a motion with his head.

*   *   *

Aldo drew the stretched Cadillac to a gentle stop outside the entrance to the Sheraton. The elderly overdressed doorman in the red gold braded "long coat" and crazy top hat resting on his ears was fast on his feet to attend the dignitaries. Can you blame this guy, on the pittance he is paid? His lifeline hung on the generosity of the guests, but with Aldo at the wheel, unfortunately this was not his day.

Aldo rolled down the window and said something to the anxious doorman who stood for a moment absorbing the message then immediately retreated to the inner lobby. Whatever the Gaucho said, the message was loud and clear . . . "*Get lost.*"

The limo's rear door open, Aldo stood back, scanning the dense tropical foliage surrounding the hotel driveway, his right hand close to the bulge on his chauffeur's jacket. This guy didn't take any chances. Satisfied, he signalled the all clear to Mona and took her hand to assist her from the car.

"Es Seguro, Senorita Menzel."

Mona acknowledged and briskly walked to the reception searching for Mike.

*   *   *

(Speaking in Spanish)

"Shit, Sergio, do you see what I see?"

"I can see all right." He was peering through the opera glasses. "Tonight, of all nights, *would you believe it,* a second security guard. *It's just our fucking luck!"*

"What now?" Carlos asked.

"We stick to the plan . . . So we waste one more bullet, huh?" He shrugged his shoulders. "So what?"

*   *   *

Mona approached the front desk.

"Lolita, have you by chance seen Mr. Summers?"

"Si, Senorita Menzel. He is in the Drover's Bar. It's to your left just past the Labordega Tapas Restaurant."

"Gracias."

Mike was about to "set 'em up Joe" when he felt a light tap on his shoulder.

"Enough, mister! Remember what I said?" Mona was teasing as Mike was caught in the act, so to speak.

"Mona!" Mike gave her a peck on the cheek. "You look as lovely as ever."

"I apologize for being late, Mike, but let's not waste any more time. I don't know about you, but I'm famished."

"The beer nuts kept the wolves away, but what do you have in mind for tonight?"

"Tapas, with a selection of fine Argentinean wine. How does that grab you?"

"It's the company that counts." Mike flashed his teeth.

Mona just smiled as she walked to the limo; this guy was a pro.

Aldo obediently opened the rear door.

"Hacer el favor."

"Aldo!"

"Excusa . . . senorita, ingles eh a speak a no so good."

Mona shook her head as she settled into the plush leather for the twenty-minute drive. All of a sudden, the stretched limo seemed so empty, and she patted the cushion next to her as Aldo slipped into the traffic.

"Why so far away, Mike . . . I'm not gonna bite."

Mike smiled and moved closer. He could feel the warmth of her leg through her loose white chiffon dress, and it felt better than good.

"Now isn't that better?"

If this was a "come on," it doesn't get any better, and for Mike, it was all or nothing, and he gently placed his hand behind the nape of her neck and pressed his lips hard against hers. The kiss was long and sensual, the moisture flowing freely between lips and tongue.

Mona gently put her hands on his shoulder to prize him apart.

Mike could have gone further, but the gamble was too risky. He would have to wait for another signal. Until then, the perfect gentleman . . .

"Do you always kiss like that?" Mona stared into his eyes.

"Only for someone special." Mike smiled.

"Senorita, que restaurant?" Aldo broke the air without turning his head, not knowing what to expect with the two lovers.

"Restaurant Olson on V Gorrito."

"Si, senorita."

"Mona, I've just noticed that we have two chauffeurs tonight."

"It's a long story . . . Now where were we?" She gave Mike her special smile.

Maybe it was time after all . . .

* * *

(Speaking in Spanish)

"Don't just sit there, *move it!*"

Carlos turned the key. *Put . . . Put . . . Put . . . Chig . . . Chig . . . Chig.* The cabin of the bug rattled like it was about to fall apart. Then . . . Hrrrummm. The sixteen hundred rear engine burst into life with a backfire like a cannon followed by a cloud of dense black exhaust fumes.

"Hell, Carlos, for a moment there . . ."

"You worry too much, Sergio." Carlos slipped into first gear and released the clutch, the beetle almost standing on its rear wheels.

"So I'm used to driving an automatic." Carlos shrugged and pressed the pedal to the metal, blindly swinging into the traffic to a hail of abuse and horn blowing.

"For Christ's sake, Carlos, everyone knows we are here now. Pull back and keep your distance. That Aldo has eyes like a bat . . ."

*   *   *

Aldo hung a left and swung the limo into this monstrous street, making the Santa Monica Highway look like a line in the sand.

"My god!" Mike exclaimed as Aldo steered into the maze of traffic. Driving in downtown Buenos Aires is not for the faint of heart.

"Ha . . . Ha . . ." Mona couldn't help laugh at Mike's astonished expression. "Don't worry, Mike, I can understand your amazement. For your information, this is not just any street. It's the largest street in the world with nine lanes on either side separated with gardened medians between the opposing flow of traffic.

Mona began laughing again as a thought crossed her mind.

"You know, Mike, just digressing. Those with long legs would be lucky if they got to the other side during the changing of two traffic lights that are placed at every intersection. A pedestrian crossing usually requires a few extra minutes and a few green lights. Luckily the inevitable stop in the center provides a great perspective of the magnitude of the street as well as the city. At the thought of boring you, I'll give you a bit of background and the history to V 9 De Julio. On July 1816, Argentina gained its independence, and in commemoration of this big event, the Argentines named Main Street in down town Buenos Aires, 9 De Julio. And if you look straight in front, you can see the magnificently lit Obelisk, a Washington Monument—like structure built in 1936 that sits in the median strip."

"Yes, I can just see it now."

On impulse, Mike gently held her cheek and turned her face toward him.

"Thanks for the history lesson, honey, but I'm more interested in you." He pressed her lips again. The feeling was mutual, but this time Mona didn't hesitate to respond . . .

*   *   *

"Carlos, it looks like they are stopping in front of that restaurant. Pull over, the parking is free on this side."

Olson, the ritzy downtown restaurant on V Gorrito, was smack on the main sidewalk, and Carlos looked uncomfortable.

"Sergio, I don't like the look of this." He was moving his head from side to side like a Pakistani.

"Why do you say this, amigo?" Sergio didn't like the tone in Carlos's voice.

"There's no cover, and it's right on the main road and worse still right next to another restaurant. We have to think of a change of plan."

"Hombre, *you listen to me!*" Sergio was losing his cool. "The bottom line is, *there's no turning back.* That is unless you want to end up on a slab in the city morgue, and just to refresh your memory, we only have another three days before Francesco lets the 'dogs of war' loose."

Carlos knew Sergio was right, but he still had a bad feeling, like skydiving without a safety chute. But then that pot of gold at the end of the rainbow was more than convincing.

"Si." Carlos gave a half-convincing smile then grasped Sergio's hand. "Camarada."

"Siempre, amigos . . ."

* * *

Aldo quickly walked the sidewalk and approached the security heavyweight. This guy at six three was a least two hundred and fifty pounds with muscles in his neck like a tree trunk larger than his black bowling ball head. He looked a mean son of bitch, but then everyone has a price. After a few words and a palm grease, the big gorilla nodded then attended to other patrons waiting to enter.

Aldo returned to the limo, a smug grin on his face.

"Non problema, senorita . . . *Eh* . . . can apar el cache." He assisted Mona from the backseat.

Mike took Mona's hand as they approached the restaurant. "I assume Aldo is telling us there's no problem parking there?"

"*Hmmmm* . . . I'm impressed. Another few weeks and you'll be speaking fluent Spanish."

"Now isn't that a thought, but as they say, the easiest way to learn another language is called 'pillow talk.'"

"*Why, Mike Summers!* You should be ashamed of yourself trying to take advantage of a gullible divorcee."

Mike laughed heartily as they entered the restaurant.

"That makes two of us . . ."

* * *

Restaurant Olson is arguably one of the hottest restaurants in town, with creative Spanish cuisine and a polished earthy atmosphere. The understated wooden entrance leads to an outdoor garden with a series of waterfalls and eventually to the spacious wide-open restaurant. During the summer months, it is an ideal hangout to sip on martinis and sample delicious tapas appetizers. The scene is Buenos Aires chic with the beautiful well-dressed people at almost every table. The dining room is unique with tables spaciously spread around a large woodstove, the long wooden bar displaying a myriad of vodkas. The head chef, German Martitegui, is famous for his long plates of appetizers including the delicious beef carpaccio, setting the stage for an evening of slow sips of wine, good conversation, and of course fabulous cuisine.

*   *   *

"Mona, I just love this place. What a great choice. You've done it again. How do you find these places?"

"Good evening, Senorita Menzel. It's nice to see you back again. Your usual table?" Ramon, the head waiter, was all smiles; and Mona loved the attention, indulging in her own importance.

"Buenos noches, Ramon, it's good to be back. Yes, my usual table beside the waterfall."

"Gracias." He escorted them.

"This *is* nice!" Mike commented as he took his seat, many of the diners recognizing his beautiful host.

"It appears you are well known in this restaurant. It must be your favourite 'hideaway.'" Mike was naturally inquisitive.

"As they say in the States, 'I'll take the fifth on that one.'"

"Memories from your dark past, huh?"

"Don't be so inquisitive, Mike . . ." Mona gave him a sexy smile. "Marcos, I'll start with my favourite."

"Si, senorita. I'll make sure it's nice and chilled."

*   *   *

"Carlos, this Americana must be *eating* the fucking restaurant out." Sergio was cursing as he crushed the empty Marlboro pack and chucked it out the car window. "It's almost twelve thirty. Do you have any more smokes?"

Carlos fished inside his shirt pocket and pulled out the crumpled packet. "Only two sticks left." He passed one to Sergio and flicked the gas lighter.

Sergio took a deep drag then exhaled. "Gracias."

He had just put down the opera glasses when suddenly Mike and Mona unexpectedly appeared, hand in hand, deep in conversation, as they walked toward the open rear door of the limo.

"*Carlos!*" Sergio screamed in panic at the thought of another unholy fuckup.

"*A change of plans!* Hit that fucking gas pedal. We gotta stop that limo."

The trusty bug burst into life; and Carlos crunched the gears as he put the pedal to the floor, at the same time pulling hard on the hand brake to perform an almighty one eighty, creating a huge trail of smoke from the burning tires, the stench of molten rubber filling the air.

"Close your eyes and hang on to that safety belt," Sergio screamed. "We gotta ram that limo head-on."

CHAPTER 11

The kids gone to their rooms; June relaxed stretched out on the lounge sofa. She had poured a glass of chilled chardonnay and was about to take time to herself. For her, today was one day she would never forget for the rest of her life.

The TV was blaring in the background, but June was oblivious to the sound her mind occupied with more important things, such as her new responsibility to become the family breadwinner and the almost-insurmountable challenge to finance the children's university.

She took a sip of her wine. *My god where do I start?* she was thinking out loud. *My first priority tomorrow is to consult a lawyer to seek legal advice on the sale of the family home. There was no way she could meet the mortgage payments except in the short term with the help of Mike's severance pay. She had to get a sale before the bank foreclosed and repossessed. If that happened, it was most likely she would receive nothing. But worse still, if the property sold below the outstanding balance, Mike could be sued for the gap, and where would that leave her? It didn't bear thinking.*

But it was Steven's final comment, "I'll never forgive him, Mother, and if I ever get the chance, so help me . . ." That was emblazoned in her mind. *Just what did he mean by that?* Little did she know that comment would come back to her.

Her glass now empty, June was becoming more relaxed, and she stretched over and extracted the bottle from the Pewter chiller sleeve and filled her glass once again.

"*Hmmmm . . .* I'm beginning to enjoy this . . . maybe too much." She was speaking aloud. "Come to think of it, I used to work with Burt & Stevens Attorneys at Law, as a legal assistant before I met Mike, and now *I really* regret not carrying on with my studies to become a lawyer. But then again, I was swept off my feet by this handsome executive and gave up a promising career to become a stay-at-home mother and a loyal wife. *And look where it got me! Yes,* I'll phone them first thing in the morning. *Why not?"*

June stared at her empty glass once more. "Time for a refill?" She poured another. "That's better." She proceeded to half empty the rather generous pour. "I wonder what Mike is doing now?" She was becoming nostalgic as the effects of the alcohol clouded her brain.

"*Mike,* how could do this to me? I love you so much. Mike, how could you do . . ."

Her now empty wine glass bounced on the carpet. At last June was at peace with herself, but tomorrow is another day, and she would need "the hair of the dog."

Steven came down to the kitchen to raid the fridge and indulge in the leftover Frittata and a glass of milk. As he was leaving for his room with the swag, he turned and noticed the lounge lights, and he went to investigate.

His mother was lying on the sofa fast asleep, and he noticed the wine bottle and the empty glass lying on the carpet; and it made him sad to see her in such a state.

"Poor Mother." His eyes filled with tears. "I won't disturb you." He went to the linen cupboard and removed a blanket, placing it gently over her sprawled posture.

Then suddenly, his eyes changed to unadulterated anger. "I'll never forgive him, Mother, and if I ever get the chance, so help me . . ."

*   *   *

Terry switched on the soft lighting and dropped her briefcase to the floor.

"Boy, am I glad to be home!" she commented as she turned on the television then walked to the percolator, emptying the stale coffee down the waste disposal.

"It's been a shit of a day," she complained as she spooned the ground coffee and added the water before turning on the stove. "And are my dogs *killing me?*"

Terry kicked off her heels and half staggered to the sofa as she tried to massage the soles of her aching feet.

"So, am I a contortionist or something?" She was laughing at her own predicament.

"Once I have that caffeine injection, I know where I'm headed . . . *straight to the shower!*"

When you are all alone, talking to yourself is more gratifying, and there's no need for justification to other so-called interested parties.

The coffee hit the spot as she relaxed on the sofa just in time for the nine o'clock local news.

"The police are still mystified at the disappearance of the prime suspect in the attempted murder case of Laura Williams, the daughter of . . ." Terry grabbed the remote and switched the channel.

"I'm fed up listening to this shit every night. *Have they nothing better to report?"*

She walked to the bedroom and stepped out of her skirt, dropping it around her ankles. Terry is normally an organized freak, but tonight she couldn't give a damn. The bra, the panties, all ended up in the same heap as she walked stark naked to the bathroom. The feeling of absolute freedom to do as you please in your own "castle" is invigorating. She stopped and stared into the vanity mirror for a moment as most women do.

"My god, am I seeing things? I can't believe it! *My breasts!* They're sagging like an old woman's." Terry cupped her breasts in each hand and lifted them up. "Maybe it's that stupid new bra I bought. *I'm getting worried.* Well, there's one thing." She cupped her breasts again. "I don't need any fucking implants, and I haven't heard Frank complaining!"

She turned the faucet and held the back of her hand below the spray to test the temperature.

"Nice!"

The warm water glistened on her lean body, streaming through her blonde hair, falling across her breasts. "Solitude's the name of the game," and she stood for a moment her like a beehive swarming back to the challenges that faced her: her new job, then there's Laura, and now Frank. She gave a big sigh. But she had to reluctantly admit she was glad when Frank phoned to tell her that because of work problems he would have to take a rain check.

But now she wished he was here. If nothing else but to console her, to feel his strong arms squeeze her close, and the warmth of his muscular frame.

"Frank, *where are you when I need you?"* She teared up.

It was too much, and the river started to flow. Then suddenly she felt claustrophobic and just had to get out of that shower, and she quickly turned off the spray and slipped into her bathrobe before running the brush through her wet hair, glancing once more into the vanity mirror.

"I'm such a mess. *What the hell!*" She walked to the door, almost slipping on the wet tiled floor. The lounge carpet felt more secure, and that second cup of coffee was enticing.

"It's strange I don't feel like eating." Terry took another sip from the oversize coffee mug then rested both feet on the coffee table, her bathrobe falling open, exposing her smooth silky thighs.

The phone rang.

"Now *who* can this be? Terry Johnson here."

"I was wondering how you are coping, honey, new job and all, and I had a minute, so I thought I'd give you a call."

"*Frank!* Am *I* glad to hear your voice?" Then she laughed. "Checking up on me, huh?" She was fast returning to her old cheeky self.

"Now whatever gave you that idea?" She could hear Frank laugh.

"Why you . . ."

"Listen, I'll be finishing my shift around midnight, and I . . ."

"Cut the chase, big boy. I thought you would never ask. I'll be waiting."

"Yeah, *and don't be late?*"

"You took the words right out of my mouth . . ."

*   *   *

The stretched Caddy took the crunching impact full on, it's heavy chromed bumper now a U shape as the pointed nose of Germany's people's car bounced off the two-ton limo.

"*What the—*" Mike grabbed Mona's arm to shield her from the impact.

"*Siento en el piso . . . Siento en el piso,*" Aldo screamed at the top of his lungs as he flicked the safety catch on his Makaron 9m Russian-made semiautomatic.

Mike was in turmoil, completely confused and scared.

"*What the hell's he saying?*" Everything was happening so fast.

"Get down on the floor, Mike. *Get down.*" Mona grabbed Mike's hand, pulling him in a heap beside her.

"Bastardo." Aldo opened the limo and crouched behind its heavy door to use it as a shield as the two hooded men opened fire, the spats from their silencers almost unnoticeable in the noisy street, the thirty-eight-ordnance shattering the windshield before going clean through the rear window, showering Mona and Mike with fragmented glass and plastic.

"*Jose. Jose,'*" Aldo screamed again, turning to his partner.

319

Jose lay slumped on the dash, his ears leaking a dark crimson sticky fluid. For Jose, his siesta had come too early.

Aldo snuck his head around the limo door and squeezed off two shots at the banditos, with Sergio crouching for cover.

"Shit." Sergio grabbed his neck as the 9mm copper nose cut a groove through his skin, and he grabbed at the wound then studied his blood-soaked hand. It was only a flesh wound, but Sergio was a bleeder, and his shirt now looked like that of the San Francisco Demons. As for Carlos, he had already opened the front passenger door, pushing Jose's bullet-ridden body onto the roadway.

The heavy on the door of Olson's restaurant heard the shots and rushed toward the limo. But the big boy was in the wrong place at the wrong time, and Sergio stopped with clean slug to the head, dropping him like sack on the sidewalk.

Aldo was now in a spot and turned his automatic on Carlos, but before he could squeeze off another round, the silencer of Sergio's Glock 38 dug into the back of his neck. *Splat.* The bullet shattered Aldo's spinal cord, passing clean through his mouth, broken teeth, tongue fragments, and blood splattering the seats and dash.

"Why you!" Mike made a threatening gesture as he rose from the floor.

Carlos pointed the Glock at Mona's head, the index finger of his other hand moving back and forth in a "don't even think about" it motion.

"American, no estupido . . . entiendes?"

Mike may not speak Spanish, but he sure got that message.

Sergio turned the key and reversed, taking the bumper of the bug with him. He pressed accelerator to the floor and screeched into the traffic, clipping a car in the process, while Carlos threw the modified potato sacks at Mike and Mona.

"*Rapido . . .* eh over head," he screamed in broken English, the threatening tone in his voice meaning business.

"Do as he says, Mike. In Buenos Aires, life is cheap, and it's me they want, and you are just excess baggage."

"You lowlife bastards," Mike retaliated. But words are only words, and in a life-or-death situation, it's best to play dumb.

Suddenly, they were both in darkness, scared out of their minds, not being able to see where they were being taken and even more frightening not seeing their captors.

"*Hands.*" Carlos was losing his patience and shattering the decibels.

Mike and Mona held their arms out straight, wrists together, and Mona cringed with pain as Carlos overtightened the plastic zip ties.

For the two hostages, their nightmare had just begun.

Chapter 12

The shudder of the 747 touching the tarmac awoke Tony, and he gave a weary yawn and a futile stretch. Long haul flights for the nontraveling public are not what they are made out to be, boring and tiring, to say the least. The stewardess had briefly wakened Tony, instructing him to buckle his safety belt and raise his seat upright, but he had dosed off again. The sight of Bill tucking into his breakfast after the booze he had consumed during the flight almost turned his stomach, but now even he would die for a beer.

"How are you feeling, partner?" Bill asked, a smug look on his face as if to say, "*So what happened to you?*"

"Please remain in your seats until the safety belt sign is switched off and the plane has come to stop. Thank you for flying Aerolineas Airways. For those who . . ."

"Don't rub it in. It must have been that last grappa." Tony was looking paler than pale.

"Christ, Tony, I don't know how you can drink that shit. You should have stuck to the beer. Look at me. I feel great. Man, have *I* really enjoyed this flight!"

"Yeah, you look it." Tony sighed.

The plane seemed to taxi forever, and Tony's tongue felt like grade 60 sandpaper.

"Bill, as soon my feet are on the ground, I'm heading for the first 'watering hole.'"

Bill couldn't help but laugh to himself at his partner's predicament.

"Well, you'll be happy to know we have arrived."

The plane came to a halt, rocking on its shock absorbers, the passengers swaying back and forth.

"Come on, Tony. Let's get our bags we have a big day ahead of us." Bill was in good form.

As for Tony, he felt like shit, but he had to put on a show if nothing else to put Hayden in his place or he would never hear the last of it.

"Okay then, let's move it. I'm feeling better already."

"Yeah, *and you look it!*"

* * *

Immigration and customs cleared, the detectives merged into the arrival hall amidst a mass of screaming bodies waving and hugging relatives and brushing Tony and Bill aside like blockers in an AFL game.

"This is *one* crazy place," Tony commented as he hung on to his garment bag, shouldering his way through the crowd.

"Bill, do you see anyone in the crowd that looks like a cop?" Tony was anxiously scanning the horizon.

"Over there, Tony." Bill pointed to a uniformed guy holding a crudely written cardboard sign: Senor PERRINO. Senor HAYDEN. "That must be our man." Tony waved.

* * *

"Lieutenant Medina. And you are?" He folded the makeshift sign and dumped it in the nearby garbage bin.

Tony shook his hand. "Lieutenant Perino and Detective Sergeant Hayden . . . NYPD."

"Gentlemen, welcome to Argentina." He gave a warm smile. "Captain Avalos sends his apologies. He is very busy. There was a serious incident yesterday evening. The daughter of one of the wealthiest businessmen in Argentina was kidnapped, a bad business." He shook his head. "I will accompany you during your stay in Buenos Aires, and I have authority to give you any assistance you require, of course, within the law." He smiled. "Shall we, gentlemen? Oh, I almost forgot . . . your hotel?" Tony nudged Bill who was fumbling in his passport.

"*Eh err* . . . Marriott Plaza." Bill was reading from the confirmation slips.

"Nice hotel on Av. Florida overlooking the Plaza San Martin, an excellent location. Most five-star hotels are located there like the Sheraton, Hyatt, and so on. Of course, you must try the famous Puerto Madera Restaurants. But, gentlemen, enough of the tourist talk. We have work to do. I have a patrol car with a driver at our disposal parked outside the main plaza."

"One small thing, Lieutenant Medina . . ."

"Please, eh?"

"Tony and Bill."

"Call me Victor. There's no need for formalities if we are going to work together. You were saying?"

Tony passed Victor the slip to collect their firearms from customs. Victor studied the official receipt and frowned. "*Hmmmm . . .*" "Is there something wrong?" Tony had a bad feeling.

"The receipt is correct for two Browning 9mm semiautomatics plus forty rounds of ammunition."

"So?" Now Tony was getting really concerned.

"Please, Tony, let's keep cool heads. I am a policeman and have no jurisdiction over customs and excise. Although my boss has given approval that you can carry firearms during your stay in Buenos Aires, customs are a law unto themselves. But . . ." He smiled. "Let's not jump to premature conclusions."

"I must say, Victor, you speak excellent English." Bill was fishing.

"And so I should! I spent three years in New York, studying at your famous university, NYU."

"That makes sense." Bill smiled. *This cop is not just any Argentinean cop. He is educated and smart with it. Maybe too smart,* Bill thought.

"Come, gentlemen, I'll speak to the comandante.'"

The group walked toward the large sign: "Las Advanas Nad Policia Fiscal."

*   *   *

The lieutenant was probably in his mid-thirties, around five eleven, and not a layer of fat on his body. *Maybe this guy works out. Who knows?* If the food here is like the stuff you get in the States, Tony and Bill would certainly wish to know his secret. He looked smart in his immaculately pressed dark blue uniform, braided peaked cap, and the row of brightly coloured ribbons pinned to his tunic. In Argentina, you get this stuff for courage above and beyond the call of duty at the tapas bars! The heavily black moustached upper lip, the eyebrows to match, and the dark brown eyes gave him a sort of young Cesar Romero look; but the deep pock marks on his tanned face spoiled his good looks, most probably reflecting a bad case of acne when he was a kid. But all in all, this guy looked the part.

*   *   *

Victor knocked on the half glass door marked "Comandante." "Tome entrar." The heavily accented guy commanded.

Victor turned to the detectives and put his forefinger to his lips as he opened the door. "Understand?" Tony and Bill nodded.

The oversized comandante was sitting slovenly at his desk, a half-eaten tortilla resting on the greaseproof paper, the food morsels still clinging to his moustache.

(Speaking in Spanish)

"Lieutenant Medina." He grinned and took a sip from his disgustingly brown-stained coffee mug then wiped his moustache with his napkin. This guy was not only ugly. He was a rude bastard with it as he stared down the detectives.

"Buenas Dias, Comandante.'"

The fat man stared again at the detectives, sizing them up.

"Americanos?"

"Si, Comandante."

"So?"

Victor gestured to Tony and Bill. "Detectives from New York on official police business to extradite a criminal back to the United States. I have here a receipt for two pistolas and ammunition to be collected upon their arrival. General Cerise has given clearance to allow the detectives to carry firearms for their own protection during their stay in Argentina."

Big Daddy studied the paperwork then gave a grunt of displeasure, or was it pleasure?

"Franco"—he turned to the officer on the next desk—"go fetch the pistolas."

"Si, Comandante.'"

The guy was back in seconds with the zip bags containing the firearms and clips.

"Lieutenant, tell the Americanos they can only have their pistolas cleared in twenty-four hours as we have to register them and enter the firearm numbers in our data bank. This takes time and is very expensive." He had that look that spelled trouble. "Which means the Americanos will have to pay duty of two thousand U.S. dollars for clearance. Or if they are unhappy, one thousand U.S. dollars is the alternative, and they can collect their guns in fourteen days."

The puffed-faced comandante sat back in his swivel chair, the ugly grin on his face, as fake as a three-dollar bill.

"But Comandante," Victor protested vigorously.

Jacky Gleeson raised his hand to signal his decision was final.

Tony and Bill turned to face one another, sensing all was not well, but they were not prepared for what was coming. "Victor, trouble?" Tony asked.

"Yes, the comandante says you must . . ."

"Are you serious?" Tony was stunned at the blatant outright corruption.

"Tony don't make the situation worse by raising your voice. Remember you are guests in our country, and if you upset the comandante, you'll be on the next plane back to New York. *Entiendes?*"

Tony shook his head his eyes full of anger as he looked at the smug fat bastard with the stupid grin on his face. He knew he had them by the shorts, and a two-grand payoff was an easy day's work.

"Christ, Tony, we only have two grand between us!" Bill protested.

"Well, unless you have any other bright ideas, partner, it looks like we're down two G's." He turned to Victor who just shrugged his shoulders. There was no point; it was a done deal.

The detectives reluctantly placed the twenty big ones in front of the Alan Greenspan who quickly counted the greenbacks, folded them, then slipped the wad into his shirt tunic pocket.

"Don't we get a receipt?" Tony asked angrily.

The comandante may not be able to speak English, but he sure got the body language and rose to his feet and slowly walked around his desk, eyeballing Tony and Bill, his nose only six inches from their faces. Then he screamed at the top of his voice to intimidate the New Yorkers.

"*Que hasar estos Americanos estadounidenses piensan que estan en preguntarme?*"

"Victor, what the hell is he saying?"

"Tony, keep calm and keep your voice down. He says you Americans . . . who do you think you are? My advice is to offer your hand and then vamoose out of here, *pronto.*"

Against his better judgment, Tony offered his hand and gave a forced smile.

The lump laughed then heartily slapped Tony on the back. Maybe there's honor among thieves after all.

"Muchas gracias alto funcionario de stardoms unidos, puede disfrutar de su estnacia en Buenos Aires."

Victor caught Tony's eye. "Shake his hand again and say gracias."

Tony performed the "two faced" ritual and was escorted to the door by one happy comandante now two grand richer.

"So, what did the big boy finally say?" Tony knew it was a lost cause, but he was still interested.

"Simple . . . He said thank you and enjoy your stay in Buenos Aires. Looks like you have made a friend," Victor joked.

"Yeah, but an expensive one!"

"Now where's that driver of mine?"

* * *

June stirred on the sofa, the bright sunlight streaming through the partially opened drapes.

"Hell, what time is it?" She raised her head from the cushion. "*Ouch!*" She cringed. It was as if her head belonged to someone else. *She wished!*

"*My god*, I feel like shit, and my mouth!" She wet her parched lips. "I just gotta get something to drink. I feel so dehydrated." She walked unsteadily to the kitchen to open the refrigerator. "*Coke!*" She unscrewed the cap and guzzled the cold liquid as if she had just come across an oasis in the Sahara; she gave an ugly burp. "*That feels better!*" She took another long swig. "Now the time?" She spoke out loud, turning to the wall clock then breathed a sigh of relief. "I was worried there for a moment. It has just turned seven thirty. Still time for a shower and change into something more casual before the kids wake. I don't want them to see me like this. But then again, who placed that blanket over me?" She paused for amount then shrugged there was no time to procrastinate, and she made for the stairs.

June didn't waste much time before streaking from the shower, toweling her wet lean body before the slipping into her bathrobe and running the wide plastic-toothed comb through her bedraggled blonde hair.

"That's better." She took a final look in the vanity mirror. "Now where's my slippers?"

It was time for the kid's breakfast.

* * *

There's nothing like the aroma of bacon and eggs crackling in the frying pan.

"Sis, are you ready?" Steven knocked on his sister's bedroom door. "Mum's already cooking breakfast."

"Gimme another five." Sheryl's voice rang out.

"Good morning, Mother." Steven snuck up on his mother who was bent over the stove.

June turned startled, her hand across her heart.

"*Steven*, you scared the hell out of me!"

"I'm sorry, Mother." He was trying to keep a straight face.

"*Steven* . . . It's not funny! Now make yourself useful and bring me the plates and place the cutlery on the breakfast bar."

"Mother, that's Sheryl's job." Steven grumbled.

"Well, I've got news for you. *It's yours today!* Now hurry or you'll be late for college. What's keeping that sister of yours?"

"She said she will be down in five minutes," Steven answered while placing the plates beside the stove.

"That girl." June shook her head and pressed the button to spring the toast.

"Hi, Mom. Sorry I can't take breakfast this morning as Dave will be here to pick me up any minute now."

"Young lady, *just hold it there!* Dave, or whatever his name is, can just wait until you have finished your breakfast." June placed the filled plates on the breakfast bar. "Which I have cooked with TLC? Steven, can you pour the juice please?"

"Sure thing, Mom." He just loved that look on his sister's face.

Two short blasts from a car horn broke the tension.

"Awe, *Mom.*"

"You heard me, young lady."

"Then can I at least go and tell him to wait?"

June nodded. "But don't take too long. I didn't cook you breakfast for it just to get cold."

"These eggs are really good, Mom." Steven was putting it away.

"I'm glad someone enjoys my cooking."

Steven's plate was clean, and he was about to finish his juice and still no sign of his sister.

"Where *is* that girl? Steven, go and see what's keeping her."

Steven tutted, reluctantly rising to his feet walking to the front window to pull back the curtain.

"Damn it, Mother. She's gone!"

"I don't believe this girl. She'll be grounded for sure when she arrives home tonight. *What am I gonna do with this sister of yours? This is all I need." June sat down heavily on the barstool. "What with your father and now this rebellious kid, I'm at my wit's end." She burst into uncontrollable tears.

"There . . . there, Mother." Steven put his arms around his mother's shoulder to console her. He hated to see her in such a state. "Don't worry, Mother. I'll speak to her."

June warmly rubbed the back of her son's hand.

"Son, now that your father's gone, you're the man of the house, and I'm depending on you."

"Don't worry, Mother. I'll look after you." He passed her the napkin to wipe her eyes, but inside his anger was tearing him apart. The more he thought about it, the more he hated his father. It was a matter now of biding his time.

*   *   *

Steven gone; June rested on the sofa. She could easily turn to the bottle, but that wouldn't solve anything. If nothing else, she had to be strong for the sake of the kids, and she glanced at the time then lifted the phonebook. "I wonder?"

"Good morning, Burt & Stevens, Attorneys at Law . . ."

*   *   *

Frank gently withdrew his arm from around Terry's naked waist. He didn't want to disturb her. It was after three this morning when they finally dozed off, exhausted or worn out or both. Whatever, he knew he really loved this woman. His shift begins at two, and the least he could do was to make her a nice breakfast. Today would be her first full day in her new job, and according to Terry's outpouring over a couple of wines last night, the battle lines were already drawn.

He pulled the sheet back and quietly swung his feet to the floor. The bedside clock read six thirty. He would wake her at seven when breakfast was ready. He slipped on his jocks and squeezed into his stonewashed Levis and white T-shirt then paused for a moment in the dimly lit room to admire his sleeping beauty, but it was "chef time," and he would have to skip the kiss to awaken his princess.

Terry gave a groan and a stretch then turned to face her lover only to be disappointed with the empty pillow.

"Now where is that that man of mine?" The sheets falling around her naked body as she sat upright, her firm nipples standing proud in the cool room temperature. Then she smiled as she heard the noise from the kitchen and the tantalizing smell of toasted bread and scrambled eggs. *And oh, for that coffee!*

Terry slipped into her flimsy housecoat and opened the curtains, the pristine sunlight filling the room.

"Oh, what a beautiful morning. Oh, what a beautiful day." She sang the chorus from the musical *Oklahoma*, all be it slightly off key, but then Terry was never a fan of karaoke. For her, today was special, in that she had finally found the right partner. What with Frank's undying love and support, *not to mention the fabulous sex,* today she was ready to go out and face the world.

Frank was busy over the frying pan, fluffing the eggs, and didn't notice Terry sneak up behind him. She put her arms around his waist and stood on her toes to kiss the nape of his neck.

Frank smiled. "Honey, can you do that again?"

"Why, Frank Reynolds!" She swung him around. "Now for that remark, you owe me a proper kiss."

She closed her eyes and stood on her toes her lips pouted in anticipation and Frank didn't disappoint her as he gently pressed his lips against hers, the moisture flowing freely between the soft flesh. This was a kiss that would arouse any full-blooded male and Terry could feel the hardness through his jeans biting into her abdomen and as for Frank? Well, he just couldn't resist the impulse to run his hand up the front of her silk housecoat searching for the "Holy Grail," her rough moist hair the ultimate prize, his fingers exploring the soft crevasse.

"Terry, I love you." Frank whispered in her ear before placing his arm below her legs and lifting her from the floor. He was about to walk to the bedroom when Terry suddenly stopped him in his tracks. *"Frank . . . Wait!"*

"What's wrong, honey?" He was taken aback.

"Move back a little, huh." Terry stretched her arm out. "I gotta turn off that stove or you'll burn the eggs . . ."

* * *

"Have you got everything . . . Cell phone, briefcase?" Frank asked as she was applying the finishing touches to her makeup.

"Yeah . . . Yeah . . ."

Terry was struggling to slip into her heels while balancing on one foot and munch on a piece of cold toast.

"Frank Reynolds, I could kill you!"

"I just love when you're angry." Frank was bursting his sides at Terry's predicament.

"Well, don't just stand there looking like a laughing hyena! Go fetch my jacket from the sofa."

"Thanks, honey . . . I forgive you. Now give me a big kiss before I leave." Terry was holding the door open with her foot.

"Hmmm, I'll think about it." Frank was putting on the "hard to get" face.

Terry's eyes flashed. *"Mister,* you're treading on thin ice." "Okay . . . Okay . . ." Frank raised his arms "I surrender." Their lips met again . . .

"Oh *no* you don't." Terry pushed him away. *"I'm outta here. .*

Remember and lock up when you leave and set the alarm. When will I expect you tonight?"

"I'll give you a call, honey, but it will be after ten . . . And knock 'em dead."

"Don't worry, I will . . . Love you." She was gone . . .

* * *

Terry stood anxiously at the elevator her eyes continually glancing at her timepiece.

"If I'm late today, that's all I fucking need," she mumbled under her breath.

The elevator chimed, and the doors thankfully opened.

"And not before time." Terry cussed as she squeezed into the crowded box. "Late again, are we, Terry?"

"*Christ, Nick,* of all the people I least want to meet at this time in the morning it has to be you."

"Terry, I know you don't mean that. Have you thought about my offer for dinner?"

Suddenly a man's voice echoed from behind.

"*For Christ's sake, Terry, say yes!* We're sick and tired listening to this scrap every morning."

Nick burst out laughing. "Thanks, Bob, for your support . . . Did you hear that, Terry? Even the neighbors know we are meant for each other."

The timely chime of the elevator saved Nick from a torrent of abuse, and Terry squeezed out of the sardine can.

"Get yourself a life, Nick, or better still, *ask Bob for a date!*" Terry was at her best.

"You got my number, Terry." She could hear Nick's "last post."

"Yeah, I got your number all right . . . *Number 2!*"

She pressed the elevator button to the car park, a cheeky smirk on her face. She had brought the house down . . .

* * *

The Mazda 6 screeched up the ramp almost demolishing the auto boom gate, the security guard shaking his head.

"That Terry . . . One day . . . Well, at least she breaks the monotony." The old man shook his head once more before burying his nose in the *Times.* It was the same old route. West Street . . . The Holland Tunnel, then to Madison.

Terry switched on the radio to take her mind off the tedious journey and the usual hoon drivers.

The traffic for a change was not as bad as she anticipated, and for all intents and purposes she would make it before nine. She relaxed and listened to Gold 104.3 "Light and Easy"; it was her favourite radio station.

At last Madison Avenue. She hung a left at the lights toward the towering ABM building.

Lee, the black guard, raised his hand for the usual security check with Terry rolling down the driver's window.

"Good morning, Lee . . . Say, I must apologize for yesterday. I opened my big mouth without thinking."

Lee smiled. "It's history, no sweat. I guess we both had a bad day. Now your name and ID, please."

"Christ, Lee, I give up on you!" Terry had to laugh.

"Get outta here! It's good to see that smile of yours again. Have a good one, Terry . . ."

* * *

Terry breezed into the office, the distinct floral fragrance of her Chanel filling the air. Most of the staff had already started work but stopped, momentarily distracted by their new boss's "walk the walk."

"Good morning, everyone." Terry smiled with an air of confidence the staff hadn't experienced for a long time. Maybe this was the change they all needed, like the coming of the "Messiah" . . .

"Good morning," came the belated replies, the girls glancing toward Davis and Pitt, the "bitches and witches," for some reaction. But as with all office shit stirrers, they kept their heads down.

Terry grabbed a coffee while reading some of Laura's outstanding mail.

She had to start someplace, and this was as good a place as any.

The ring of her internal phone shattered her thought process, and she annoyingly lifted the receiver.

"Johnson here."

"Terry, sorry to disturb you, but I need to speak to you about our prearranged lunch with Chuck Briggs. Why don't you drop everything and come to my office right away. It's important."

"I'm on my way."

"Grab a seat . . . Coffee?"

"No, I'm good, Jack. Now what's this all about?"

"I'm about to phone Chuck to arrange lunch, and I want you to meet with him in your new capacity as marketing manager, Laura's replacement."

"I see." Terry was trying to put the pieces together and more so the hidden agenda.

"You'll be handling the Global contract and signing off the progress payments, so it's important you get acquainted with Briggs who assures me he will take the full responsibility for the launch of the BM400/2000 in Summers's absence. Shall we say permanent absence?" Jack gave a childish grin.

"Ah. Hmmmm." Terry cleared her throat. "Jack, since I'll be on Briggs's case, so to speak, can you fill me in on this guy."

"Sure." Blakely sat back in his chair. "Firstly, you are well aware he is the CEO of Global Marketing, a private consortium owned by three shareholders . . . Namely, his wife her father and her mother."

"Poor guy."

"Exactly! But when you marry into money, there's gotta be a downside, but fortunately salary ain't one of them. He's kinda laid back and leans heavily on Summers, his VP for marketing, whom, may I say, is damn good at his job, and that's what worries me. The BM400/2000 are compact powerful new business machines that are taking the market by storm. But the domestic market is one thing, and the global market is another, such as China, Asia, and the EEC, and that's where you come in, Terry. You have to make sure we're getting the best bang for our buck. Here's a copy of the contract. You can go through it when you find the time."

"I get the picture . . . So?"

"Hang on while I make the call."

Blakely dialed Briggs's private line.

*   *   *

"Good morning, would it possible to speak to Philip Stevens please. I'm sure he is busy, but perhaps if you tell him, it's an old friend . . ."

"Can you give me your name please."

"June Summers."

"Just a moment."

"Philip Stevens here, how can I help you." The was voice commanding and assertive.

"Phil, it's June . . . June Mathers . . . Remember me from the gang at NYU?"

"June Mathers, after all these years. *Well, I'll be darned!* When the receptionist mentioned June Summers, an old friend, the name didn't ring a bell."

"Summers is my married name."

There was a pregnant pause. "So, you're married?"

"If you can call it that!"

"So, is that why you called me?"

"Partly . . . And the other, to see what happened to that young handsome college kid I had a crazy crush on."

"June, I never knew. I felt the same about you, but you never gave me even the smallest hint, and I eventually closed the door."

"You big heel, guys have to take the initiative, didn't anyone tell you?" June could hear Phil laugh. "And as for you, young Casanova?" The question was loud and clear.

Phil laughed again. "I've been called lots of names but never that one. But if you're asking what I think you are . . . No, divorced. Now no more true confessions, how can I help you?"

"It's a long story, Phil, but it's extremely urgent that we meet, and I wonder if you could possibly see me today."

"For an old friend, how can I refuse? Better still, are you free for lunch?"

"That's the best offer I've had in a long time."

"Then that settles it . . . Twelve thirty at Arrivederci on Baxter. It's Italian, and the food is to die for."

"Baxter Street?" There was an unsure ring in June's voice.

"You take Canal Street and head toward the Bowery, then it's the first left past Center Street. You can't miss it. I'll get my secretary to make a reservation as getting a table at lunchtime is scarcer than 'hen's teeth.'"

"Same old Phil, always with the cliches." June laughed.

"Hey, less of the old stuff! But seriously, June, I'm really looking forward to seeing you again. It's been such a long time. Twelve thirty then . . . Ciao."

June sat back and relaxed on the sofa, her thoughts reflecting back to her NYU days and the handsome Philip Stevens. "I wonder what he looks like now." She was having a conversation with herself; a cunning look on her face. *"That reminds me, what time is it? . . . Ten thirty . . . So late! It will take me at least forty-five minutes to get to Canal, and I still have to shower and get dressed. I had better get a move on as the last thing I want is to arrive late . . . On my first date."* June had that twinkle in her eyes.

She showered and brushed her shoulder-length blonde hair, the shine for some reason returning to its old self as if a new lease of life. Suddenly the horizon had changed from storm to sunshine, and instead of a problem, there was now an opportunity. She slipped on her panties and awkwardly fastened the bra clip.

"Now the next question is, *'what shall I wear, that is the question'?"* She impersonated the deep tone of a man's voice. "Sounds like I'm rehearsing Shakespeare." She laughed aloud. *"Mmmm,* how about the purple sleeveless dress?" She held it in front of her. *"Mmmm,* maybe too low cut. I don't want to scare him off. But then again?" That cunning smile was back again. *"Yes, that's the one."* She changed her mind. *"Now a simple gold chain and no earrings, a sort of plain Jane look but with class. The shoes? The purple ones to match my dress. Medium heels and a simplistic black handbag."*

Within minutes she was dressed and admiring herself in the full robe mirror.

"Not bad, even if I say so myself. *Now my makeup . . ."* She had that cunning look again . . .

CHAPTER 13

The limo's tires were burning rubber as the stretched Caddy swayed from side to side with Sergio sideswiping a few innocent cars in the process. It had all gone to plan with the exception of icing the second guard and Sergio being creased by that crazy Gaucho, Aldo. Although only a flesh wound, he was bleeding like a blood bank, and he had to get medical attention soon. But first things first, they had to dump the limo before the police woke up.

* * *

(Speaking in Spanish)

Carlos rolled down the partition.

"Bitch Monzel, I have a gun pointed directly at the Americano's head. If you dare scream, I'll blow his fucking brains out. We don't need the gringo. He's excess baggage. *But then maybe you like him.* Maybe you like him mucho, huh? So, if you want to keep him healthy, you do as I say . . . Comprender? *I said comprender!"*

"Si!" Mona screamed. "I heard you the first time, you bastardo. *You'll never get away with this."*

"Carlos, make that bitch shut her face. I have a big-enough headache as it is without her emptying her lungs. If I don't get this crease in my neck stitched up soon, I'll fucking bleed to death. *That bastardo Aldo . . ."* He was cursing and shaking his head.

"Don't worry, Sergio. I'll shut her up." Out of the blue, without warning, Carlos held his pistol by the muzzle and crashed the grip down hard on Mike's skull. Summers gave a short, muffled moan before falling semiconscious against Mona, the red stain seeping onto his white shirt from the stream of blood trickling down his neck below the makeshift hood.

"You fucking creeps! What have you done to him?" Mona was struggling to support Mike's limp body from falling like a sack of potatoes to the floor, but her hands were tied, and she was searching in the dark. The best she could do was to forcefully push him to the other side of the backseat only to add insult to injury as Mike's head smashed against the rear door window pillar.

As for Mike, he felt no pain.

"You rich bitch . . . You don't fucking listen. The next time you decide to scream, I will put a bullet through the dude's kneecap. *Comprender?"*

The limo, like a wounded elephant, suddenly swerved out of control as it took the corner throwing everyone to one side as the front left wheel crunched against the curb with an ear-piercing screeching noise as the alloy rim disintegrated and buckled under the impact, the wrecked front bumper bar clanging onto the road and jamming below the undercarriage, rupturing the oil sump.

"What the fuck, Sergio?" Carlos grabbed the courtesy handle above the front door to stop from smashing his face against the dash as the limo died.

Luckily the airbags exploded in a millisecond, saving them both, especially Sergio who was now semiconscious from the severe blood loss.

Sergio slowly came to. "Carlos, I'm okay. Help me get these two to the Pontiac. It's just over the street."

"I can see it, Compadre." Carlos kicked open the front passenger door. Already there was a small crowd of oglers gathering, and that was the last thing they needed as the next thing some "do gooders" will be calling the cops.

"Carlos, gimme your gun, I'll cover the bitch and the gringo. My head's a bit clearer now. *But that fucking crowd!* I don't like the look of it, but you did good with the false number plates."

Carlos ran to the Pontiac and unlocked the large door of the coupe. The crowd was now even more intrigued, thinking maybe this was an American movie playing out.

Sergio, although still unsure on his feet, staggered to the rear door of the limo.

"Out . . . Out . . . Out!" he shouted, dragging Mona out by the wrists, making her fall heavily onto the rough bitumen, and she screamed in pain as her knees scraped the roadway, her arms outstretched like a blind woman trying to feel her way in the hooded darkness.

Carlos had sprinted back to the limo to help Sergio.

"It's okay, I've got her. You go and get the Americano."

Sergio grabbed Mona under her arms. *"On your feet . . . On your feet, bitch!"* he screamed.

"You fucking bastardo, you'll pay for this." Mona's knees were grazed and bleeding as she was dragged to the Pontiac.

"Shut your face or so help me, when I'm finished with you, even a dog wouldn't look at you." Sergio pushed her into the back of the coupe, with Mona tripping over the car sill, feeling her way on her hands and knees to the backseat, her dress dishevelled above her waist.

"Nice ass you got there, honey. Now what could I do with that?" "You are fucking pervert," Mona screamed again.

"I like a woman with fire in her blood." Sergio laughed then grabbed his neck in pain. *"That fucking Gaucho!"*

Carlos was just behind him, carrying Mike over his shoulder like a fireman.

"Move the bitch over. This dude is fucking heavy." Carlos poured Mike into the backseat next to Mona.

"Sergio, we should dump this fucking freeloader."

"No, let's keep this hombre. He might be worth selling."

"I hope you're right." Carlos was far from convinced. "The last thing we need is the FBI on our tails."

"Muchacho, let's get this heap on the move. Carlos, you'll have to drive." Sergio passed him the keys. "I'm wasted."

Carlos turned the key then suddenly changed his mind as he stared out of the open window, a worried look on his face at what he saw.

"Sergio, we gotta get rid of this crowd."

"So, what do you fucking suggest?" Sergio hit back. The way he was feeling, he just wanted to get the hell out of there.

Carlos smiled, a crazy look on his face as he pulled the Glock from behind his belt.

"Easy!"

He hit the road and waved his pistol openly in the air to scare the crowd then cracked one shot into the sky.

"Vamoose . . . Vamoose," he screamed, waving the gun in a circular motion. The Glock cracked a second time, but this time, the crowd had gotten the message and scattered like a bunch of scared rabbits."

"What the fuck are you doing, Carlos? You crazy hombre."

"I got rid of them, didn't I?" He was laughing as he gunned the Pontiac and hit the gas. "Sergio, get your head down and rest. You worry too much."

Carlos could hear the police siren in the distance, but by the time they arrived, all they would find is a trail of burned rubber.

*   *   *

Mike's listless body was thrown from side to side as Carlos practiced for the Grand Prix. The vintage '52 Pontiac Chieftain Coupe was holding her own, the proud old lady answering the call. "Carlos, check to see if we are being followed." He glanced in the rear and side mirrors.

"Clear . . ."

"Good, then pull over and change the plates."

As the Pontiac came to a screaming halt, the abrupt change in acceleration brought Mike back to consciousness.

"My head!" he moaned in pain as he struggled to touch the egg on his head with his zip-tied wrists while throwing his elbows out in front of him to avoid smashing his face against the back of the driver's seat.

Where am I? Where am I? His mind was slowly unclouding in the "iron mask."

"Shut the fuck up, hombre, if you know what's good for you," Sergio barked. *"Carlos, what the fuck's keeping you?"* he screamed.

No sooner had he commented than Carlos appeared back in the driver's seat.

"Done! Now let's get this crate out of here." Carlos pulled down on the stock lever and released the hand break. The drive to Villa Miseria, "the slum dog" part of the city, would take at least another twenty minutes; but it was home sweet home to the two banditos, where drugs, prostitution, murder, and rape are commonplace. The Villa Miseria became famous for the unsolved murder of "Adams Ledesma," the founder of the community TV channel Mundo Villa, while filming a documentary.

"Mona, are you there?" Mike was grabbing air as he moved his hands blindly to the right.

"I'm here, Mike, but more to the point, how are you?" She touched his hand.

"Let's put it this way. I have *one* helluva headache."

"At least you're getting your sense of humour back. That's something." Mona forced a hidden grin.

"I said keep quiet or so help me!" Sergio was losing it, and when this guy goes wacko, he gets ugly.

Mona squeezed Mike's hand hard to signal him to keep his mouth shut. Besides, she was desperately trying to listen to anything, anything at all, that might give her a clue to where they were in the city: railway stations, bus stations, airports, *anything.*

* * *

Sergio was staggering like a "drunken sailor" as he thumped his fist on the rough planked door.

"Lena . . . Lena. For Christ's sake, open this fucking door. Carlos, you stay in the car."

"Santa Maria!" Lena sat bolt upright, her eyes reflecting a crazy scare look. In "slum land," life is cheap. She swung her feet to the floor in panic, the sweat stains prominent in the dim light on her white flimsy nightdress. Air-conditioning is on the "bucket list," but with stolen electricity for lighting, there was precious little hope; and consequently, the corrugated roofed breezeblock shack was worse than a sauna.

"Where is that fucking 'no good' Sergio when I need him?"

Lena was scared, all right; and who could blame her, living in this hellhole of a place.

"Lena, it's me," Sergio screamed again. *"Open the fucking door, for Christ's sake!"*

Having now recognized Sergio's voice, Lena ran barefooted toward the door, in the process banging her leg on a rickety wooden chair.

"Bastardo!" she screamed in pain as she skipped and hopped, trying to keep her balance.

"The light? Where the hell's that fucking globe?" She stood on her toes to twist the lightbulb dangling from its solitary electric cable, the 40 watts barely breaking the darkness.

Lena ran her fingers along the dust-coated door beam, searching for the padlock key. Door locks in this part of town are a joke. At last, she found the elusive metal but, in her panic, dropped it to the earthen floor.

"Fuck it! Now where the hell is that key?" She groped around on her hands and knees. "Found it!" She jumped to her feet and nervously opened the padlock, ensuring the heavy-duty chain was still intact as she peered through the four-inch gap. It was Sergio, all right, but the sight of his blood-soaked shirt almost scared her to death.

"My god!" She raised her hand to her mouth in panic, dropping the safety chain, the door almost smashing into her face from Sergio's deadweight as he fell flat on his face.

"Sergio . . . Sergio!" Lena screamed as she tried to pull him to his feet. "You stupid hombre, what trouble have you gotten yourself into this time? For a moment there, I thought you were dead."

"Shut your mouth, woman, and get out of my way. Can't you see I need to lie down? Go fetch Senorita Teresa, you know, the old woman from up the road. She knows how to stitch up bullet wounds. Tell her I'll make it worth her while. *Well, don't just stand there, woman,* unless you want to visit your husband in the mortuorio!"

"I should be so fucking lucky!" Lena scorned, shaking her head in disgust. "For the life of me, I don't know why I have put up with your shit all these years. I must be out of my fucking mind, but then who wants to see a dog die a slow death?" She turned to leave, morally pissed off, Sergio now sprawled on the solitary bed, pressing a blood-soaked cloth to his neck. As for Lena, she had seen it all before.

"Tell Carlos the coast is clear."

"Tell him your fucking self," Lena bawled.

"That fucking woman! Carlos, Carlos, do you hear me?" Sergio shouted.

"Yeah, I hear you."

"Bring the prisoners in, and hurry. This place has eyes and ears."

Carlos didn't waste much time in dragging Mike from the backseat and marching him around to the other side of the Pontiac.

"Stay put," he bawled in Mike's ear. "I'll tell you when to move." Carlos quickly opened the other door. *"Menzel, out."* He supported her by the arms until she regained her balance. "Now hang on to your boyfriend's belt and follow him." Carlos frog-marched them into the house like elephants in a circus ring.

Lena was stunned at the sight of the two handcuffed hooded prisoners staggering like the disabled blind, being pushed and prodded into the shack under the watchful eye of Carlos's semiautomatic.

"My god what is happening here?" Lena blocked Carlos's path, who roughly brushed her aside, ignoring her protests.

"Out of my way, Lena. This is no business of yours. Do as your husband says if you don't want trouble. *Move it. Move it.*" He gave Mona a vicious dig with the Glock to the lower part of her back, and she flinched in pain but kept her cool; her time would come.

Lena was suddenly gone. She knew her husband only too well. It wouldn't be the first time she had suffered domestic violence.

"Where do I dump these two, Sergio?" Carlos closed the door.

Sergio groaned, pointing to the curtained doorway. He was feeling worse than shit.

* * *

The shanty shack was better than most in Villa Miseria; its corrugated roof sheeting nailed to the old wooden timber supports stolen goods from the freight yard. Although rusted, at least it didn't leak!

The main room, *if you could call it that,* at around ten by six, miraculously squeezed in a bed and a table, and a variety of scattered stolen cantina chairs. The radio in the far corner rested on an empty wooden orange crate, giving the room a contemporary look. *Who knows?* This rustic interior decoration with the lime-coated rough cast walls and the large wooden cross above the bed *might just catch on!* As for a TV, when you struggle to buy a tortilla, *that's definitely on the bucket list!* The phone? *Are you serious?* Just steal a cell phone from the gullible tourists.

The shack had another small room for cooking and the storage of large plastic water bottles and the all-important "thunder box" complete with a removable galvanized pale. *It is not the most hygienic place to have a dump while cooking in the makeshift kitchen!* Neither room had any windows with the exception of two rectangular slats at roof level, doubling as air vents and an ingenious security system. *Windows attract robbers.* But all in all, this place was a palace compared with the other cardboard huts.

On a number of occasions, the government had taken a heavy hand, using bulldozers and police in a last-ditch operation to clear the squatters; but they received more than they bargained, with the body bag count of over twenty police.

For sure there wouldn't be a second assault on "Gangster City"!

* * *

Carlos grabbed two chairs in the toilet-cum-kitchen. *"Sit."* He forced Mona and Mike. *"And I don't want one fucking murmur from either of you . . . Comprender?* Now, let's see what we got here." He rummaged through

Mona's bag. *"Not baaad!* Four thousand pesos, cell phone, ATM, American Express and Visa cards. *This is a pot of gold . . ."* Carlos couldn't believe his luck. "And the American dude?" He searched through Mike's pockets. "A wallet containing . . . *Let me see."* He counted the notes. "This is our night dude . . . Twelve thousand pesos in five hundred notes . . . A Citibank card and Amex and . . ." He undid the solid gold Rolex Oyster from Mike's wrist, almost taking the skin with it.

"Nice watch," Carlos commented, grinning from ear to ear, flashing his tobacco-stained teeth before slipping it over his wrist.

"Why you . . ." Mike gritted his teeth, trying to control his anger.

"I don't know what the Americano is saying, senorita, but you had better tell him that I am a compassionate hombre, but my partner? You don't want to know. He has more notches on his gun than the famous gangster Al Capone."

"Go fuck yourself, whoever you are. My father will hunt you down like rabid dogs. I tell you, there's in no place in Argentina where you can hide, and when you are caught, your miserable bodies will be hung from the gallows to rot in the sun."

"You fucking rich bitch, you think you're special but you feel pain the same as we peasants." Carlos lashed out with the back of his hand crashing against Mona's cheek, the blow so forceful she toppled from her chair, landing heavily to the floor in an unlady-like posture, her clothes dishevelled showing more underwear than "Target."

"Help me, you fucking coward." She was on her knees searching for the chair in the forced darkness.

"Help your fucking self, I've got better things to do. Maybe that will teach you a lesson to keep your mouth shut."

Carlos pulled the makeshift curtain aside to attend to his ailing partner but not before stuffing a bundle of pesos into his back pocket and admiring his watch.

As they say, *"there's no honour among thieves."*

*   *   *

As Lena stumbled up the dirt roadway in her flimsy sandals, her eyes trying to focus in the semidarkness, she couldn't help but think back to when she met Sergio almost twenty years ago. She was young and foolish, a pretty farm girl that had run away to the "big smoke" in search of fame and fortune and a wealthy husband. No way did she intend to end up like her mother, working her fingers to the bone, married to a drunken no-good farmer and down at the heels and out at the front with two siblings. Now when she stares in the mirror every day, she wonders what happened to that pretty innocent foolish farm girl. The dark shadows below her eyes, the aged brown leathery texture of her skin, the troubled dark brown eyes, and the sagging breasts and lifeless black hair. She pondered for a moment, her thoughts sadly focusing on her two children, Susana, eighteen, and Edu, nineteen. Where are they now? A solitary tear filled her eyes. They had left home just after Susana turned sixteen, and she had never heard from them since. But in Argentina, this situation is not unusual. She had heard from a friend that they had crossed the border into Brazil, but that was almost two years ago, and every night before she closes her eyes she would say a prayer hoping that one day they will return. As for Sergio, the good-looking Casanova who coaxed her into the cot and the inevitable, being a practicing Roman Catholic, there was only one thing she could do, and that was go to the altar. *Big mistake!* Sergio was a no-good bum and a petty criminal into the bargain in and out of prison, searching for an easy buck, and like a faithful wife, she always waited for him, but now this! *But kidnapping . . . ?* He had gone too far this time, and she could easily be classed as an accomplice and go to prison herself. What can she do? *But if push comes to shove . . . Life is precious . . .*

*   *   *

Lena banged on the door of the ramshackle dwelling, the shock waves almost sending it to Mother Earth.

"What the fuck!" Jario leaped from his bamboo and rattan laced bed and searched below his pillow for the Sig Mosquito 22. The small-calibre double action pistol wouldn't stop a full-grown man, but it makes holes. He pulled back the hammer then stood sideways behind the doorjamb just in case the shooter sent a couple through the wooden planks.

"Jario, who is it?" Lucia shouted, about to struggle from her bed.

"Don't worry, Mother, stay where you are. I'll handle it . . . *Who the fuck's there?"* Jario screamed.

"Jario, it's me, Sergio's wife, Lena. I must speak to your mother. It's a matter of life and death. Sergio has been wounded."

On hearing Lena's pleas, the old lady hit the floor in a hurry. She was the "local surgeon"; what she didn't know about gunshot and stab wounds was no one's business. Mistakes, she'd had a few, but then again not too many. Besides, the money is good.

"Open the door, Jario, I recognize Lena's voice . . . It will be that no-good husband of hers . . ."

* * *

Carlos opened his cell phone.

"Si?" the almost-inaudible voice answered.

"*Eva*, fucking wake up. It's Carlos."

"So, where the hell are you? *Let me guess!* In some brothel or some cantina getting pissed with that no-good Sergio."

"*Watch your tongue, hembra.* For your information, I'm at Sergio's. He's had an accident."

"So, what am I supposed to do, *cry in my Quilmes?*"

"Listen, you no good . . . Go to the mini mercado and buy two packs of Quilmes and dos botellas of tequila."

"*You stupido!*" Eva screamed. "*The mercado is closed.*" She was getting tired of taking Carlos's shit.

"Well, you'll just have to fucking waken Eduardo and tell him it's for Sergio. If he knows what's good for him, he'll get the stuff accelerando."

"And how do I pay?"

"Tell him he'll get his fucking money later." Carlos was becoming agitated . . . *This woman?* "Sergio is good for it."

"*That'll be the first time!*" Eva just couldn't hold her tongue.

"*Just do it!*" Carlos closed his phone, muttering all sorts of obscenities under his breath . . .

* * *

"Boil some water pronto," Lucia ordered Lena. The old woman's wizened face was studying Sergio's gaping neck wound.

* * *

Lucia's grey lifeless straw hair was tied in a bun, her sunken cheeks the aftermath of nonexciting dental care, and with her crinkled, aged, leatherlike complexion, with more creases than a crumpled bedsheet and the dried orange peel lips, she could have easily been a "stand-in" for Norman Bates's mother in *Psycho*.

* * *

"I need a needle and thread . . . and hurry." "How bad is it, Lucia?" Sergio asked.

"You'll live, but not for long if you can't pay me my three hundred pesos." Carlos fished inside his pocket and pulled out the wad of stolen notes.

"Here." He passed her the six fifties.

"Since when did *you* become so rich?" Lucia asked, stuffing the money into the pocket of her "sack" frock.

"Si, where did you get that money?" Sergio, although out of it, was compos mentis when it came to money.

"Relax, hombre, and let the old lady do her job. I'll tell you about it later."

No sooner had Carlos made the comment than Eva opened the door laden down with the beer and tequila.

"Well, don't just stand there looking like a spare prick at a wedding." She was shooting at Carlos. "For Christ's sake, gimme a hand."

"Good!" Lucia commented on seeing the tequila. "Just what the doctor ordered." She gave an ornery smile as she unscrewed the stop then took a couple of large hits. *This old babe knew how to put it away.*

"I thought the tequila was for Sergio?" Carlos laughed.

"It is! But the doctor first." Lucia gave a toothless grin.

"Lena, the hot water . . . Good! Now a needle and some strong thread . . . Lena, you do the needful. My eyes are not so good anymore."

Lucia threaded the needle and placed them into the boiling water then unscrewed the cork on the tequila, studied the bottle for a moment, and grinned once more before taking another swig.

"Now, Sergio, this is going to hurt." Old Lucia gave an orny laugh. She was enjoying her fifteen minutes, and "for all the guys she'd loved before," this was payback time.

Lucia drenched the open wound with the raw liquor, and Sergio let out an ear-piercing scream as the alcohol killed all known germs. But for Sergio, this was just the beginning . . .

CHAPTER 14

June felt good as she turned the key in the BMW. She might as well enjoy her "baby" before the bank repossession. She glanced in the visor mirror for a final check on her makeup then smiled with that same mischievous smile. As the French say, "Il n'y pas libre fromage dans le piege a souris" (There's no free cheese in the mousetrap).

She smiled again as she pouted her lips. *"Not bad,* even though I say so myself." Then she sort of flicked her blonde hair back with her fingers to give it a more rugged look. "I think I'll pass." She grinned as she reversed down the driveway. *"Now how the hell do I get to Canal from here?"*

* * *

The drive through the city would take at least forty-five minutes, but June had given herself plenty of slack; it had just turned eleven.

It's strange, when you are driving, it's like second nature and your mind can concentrate on other things at the same time, like Phil Stevens, that handsome quarterback on the college football team. *He was a catch, all right.* June smiled, thinking to herself. *And the word on the campus was he wasn't short of bedfellows either . . . Whatever . . .* She sighed. *But that was a long time ago . . . in fact a lifetime ago, at least that's what it felt like! I can just picture him then . . . tall, lean, and muscular, diving around in that supped-up open-topped yellow hot rod.* June smiled again. *Yeah, he was a catch, all right, but I wonder what he looks like now?*

Before she knew it, the time had passed so quickly, and she signalled turning left into Center Street; and sure enough, as Phil directed, Baxter was straight ahead. She glanced at the digital clock, twelve twenty. And there, just to the right, was Arrivederci and unmistakably Italian.

June parked the BMW in the nearby car park, only five minutes' walk from the restaurant. She checked her makeup again then straightened her tight-fitting dress as she stood by the car. She was gonna "knock 'em cold."

Walking past the sidewalk tables situated under the red, white, and green canvas awnings, you could have sworn you were actually in Italy. The aroma of charcoaled oven pizza and smiling couples enjoying the delicious antipasti, fish soups, and spaghetti with the famous bologna sauce and a glass of fine Italian wine, *it just doesn't get any better!*

Of course, there will always be the so-called business lunch or the worst kept "secretary affair," but whatever, everyone seemed to be enjoying the Italian experience; and much to June's delight, she drew a few interested stares. It made her feel good that at the ripe old age of forty-two, she could still turn heads. But then again, guys will be guys, and the grass is always greener. As Rose, Tony's wife, used to say, "All men are the same. They just have different faces." And June couldn't help but smile at the thought as she entered the restaurant.

"Senorita, how can I be of assistance?" the smooth Latino maître d' inquired, the smile that of a typical Italian stallion.

"I'm meeting a Mr. Phillip Stevens for lunch. I believe he has a reservation." "Certainly, and you are?" He was checking the reservation list.

"June Summers."

"*Of course.*" He snapped his fingers. "Francisco, escort Senorita Summers to table 20. Have a pleasant lunch." The "stallion" gave June his special smile.

"Please." Francisco was the typical "type cast" Italian waiter, dressed in an open-necked white shirt rolled up at the sleeves and a black apron tied at the waist. The crinkly hair, the olive complexion, and dark brown eyes and the "ladies" smile fitted the bill to a tee.

June, for some reason, suddenly felt butterflies in her stomach; the moment of truth had arrived. What could she expect and, more to the point, what would Phil expect?

As she followed Francisco through the crowded tables, a tall slim man suddenly rose to his feet and waved, a huge grin on his face.

Could this be Phil Stevens? June thought. *If it is, he may be a lot older, but boy does he still have that something.*

"June, I must say you look fabulous. You haven't aged one bit." Phil gave her a kiss on the cheek. "Please." The waiter withdrew the chair to assist her.

June smiled as she made herself comfortable.

"*Phil Stevens,* you're either lying to your back teeth or should go and see your optician."

Phil burst into laughter at June's comment. "June, I really mean it. You look fabulous."

* * *

June monetarily studied Phil. He looked really fit, not like most successful businessmen over age forty with the "lunch overhang," having settled down to the boredom of married life and the trials and tribulations of children and sex only on special occasions. For some reason, Phil didn't seem to fit into that category. His full head of blond hair hadn't really changed, but his lightly tanned face had lined some, especially around those pale blue eyes. He had that sort of smile that was fresh and contagious, sporting his even white teeth and dimpled chin. His long narrow face line and six-one stature gave him a distinguished look that surely was an advantage in the legal profession.

* * *

"June, I was really surprised when I received your call. Of course, your married the name threw me." Phil was looking straight into her eyes, but June wasn't complaining. In fact, it was a breath of fresh air.

"Don't remind me." She sighed.

"That bad, huh?"

"Worse than worse! Phil, please excuse me for unintentionally being rude, but perhaps we should order first then enjoy each other's belated company before I explain my tale of woe and spoil our lunch date."

He looked into her eyes again with that serious look. "June, as my memory recollects, you were never the one to be rude out of all the NYU gang."

June gave s sort of immature giggle. "Phil, you're embarrassing me. You say the nicest things, but then you were always a ladies' man, if *my* memory serves me right!"

"Ouch! I deserved that one. You're right. We should concentrate on the menu." They both laughed in tandem.

"I'm going to enjoy this lunch. Now what should I order? Any suggestions?"

* * *

"Global Marketing, Mr. Briggs's office, Elizabeth speaking."

"Liz, it's Blakely here from ABM. Is that boss of yours free?" Briggs's secretary was less than impressed with the Liz familiarity.

"Give me a second, Mr. Blakely." Her reply was frigid and ice-cold.

Blakely drummed his fingers impatiently on the desk.

"Mr. Blakely?"

"Yes?"

"I'll put you through. Mr. Briggs is expecting your call."

"Chuck . . . And the top of the morning to you. I'm calling to set up that lunch appointment we discussed and of course to meet our new marketing manager, Terry Johnson."

"Can't wait," Chuck replied dryly.

"Chuck, I'm glad you see it that way," Blakely answered with a touch of sarcasm. "So time and place?"

"Twelve thirty at the New York Business Club on Madison."

"Yeah, I know the place. And, Chuck, please bring with you the latest progress report on Bowing's status on the AB400/2000. We need that contract like tomorrow and leave Hewlett-Packard on their proverbial asses. And, Chuck, it goes without saying that if you need technical support, I'll send my best team across to Bowing."

"Maybe we can discuss that before lunch to get the hack work done before we eat?"

"Agree. Then twelve thirty it is." Blakely hung up. He had that cunning smile on his face. As usual, this guy was up to something no good.

Terry was intrigued with Blakely's style. *How can this guy sleep at night?*

"Now let's, see?" Blakely glanced at his timepiece. "It's almost eleven thirty. I suggest we leave in around fifteen minutes. You can never tell with the lunchtime traffic. How does that grab you?" "I'm good," Terry replied.

"Oh, and while I remember, bring these papers with you." He pointed to the manila folder he had passed to Terry. "Sure, no sweat. I'll be ready."

* * *

Terry stood at her desk for a moment, deep in thought. On her first day in her new job, she would rather have spent the whole day in the office. Standing in silence, she could feel eyes burning a hole in her back, and she quickly turned to face the foe; but as usual, everyone had their heads down.

"Can I have your attention please?"

The staff stopped what they were doing momentarily and looked up.

"And that means you, Jaycee, that is unless you think you are something special?" Terry was furious at Jaycee Davis's continuing insubordination. "*Ehh . . . Hum . . . Heh . . .*" She spluttered, taken aback at the Terry's direct challenge, and her face went a pale shade of red. "Eh, I'm sorry. I wasn't paying attention."

"Next time then," Terry answered abruptly. "I have a luncheon appointment today, and depending upon the discussions, it may be too late for me to return to the office. However, before I go, I need to get something straight. I intend to start by having a one-on-one discussion with each of you tomorrow, commencing at nine thirty. Bring whatever you are working on, and I'm open to any suggestions that will make the marketing department more efficient, even though it means criticizing the system and work ethics. But let me be clear. Under no circumstances will I tolerate badmouthing. I want you all to be happy and to enjoy the challenge of working at ABM. Any questions?" There was no response. "Good, and thank you."

"Terry, we gotta make tracks." "With you in a minute, Jack."

* * *

The drive to Madison was rather tense as she sat in her boss's car for the first time.

"You seem a bit nervous, Terry. Are you all, right?" Jack briefly turned.

"I guess this is a bit different from being just a number in the marketing department and, more to the point, to be promoted like overnight. It feels a bit surreal."

"Regrets?"

Terry shook her head. "No, in fact, I'm enjoying the challenge. And for what it's worth, Jack, you won't regret it."

"Now *that's* what I like to hear!" Blakely smiled.

"So how do we play this meeting?" Terry asked, feeling rather left in the dark.

"You let me do most of the talking, and I'll bring you in when I need your opinion."

"I understand." Terry nodded. "But what's the scoop?"

"Terry, I'll be as straight to the point as I can. Briggs is swinging the lead and, in my opinion, ripping off ABM with budget overruns and living the fat life."

"So?" Terry was becoming more and more intrigued. *Just what was Blakely up to?*

"You see, Ian Simpson, my boss, is 'buddy' with Briggs. Now I'm not saying there's collusion or under-the-table stuff, but I would be telling you a lie if I said that it hasn't crossed my mind." "I'm still at a loss, Jack?" Terry frowned.

"The contract dictates that Global, with their expertise and advertising campaign, would jack our sales up of the ABM2000 to fifty machines per month. Target markets would be the big boys: Bowing, Coca Cola, Ford, GM. Need I go on? Well, you know what our sales have been, not even ten units this months, and our contract with Global is watertight. I know. I helped to put it together."

"I'm still at a loss, Jack."

"Let me put it this way. Simpson and I have always been at loggerheads regarding sales and marketing. He's pig-headed and feels it would be less expensive to outsource, but then we are not in control of our own destiny, so to speak. Now listen to what I am about to say and never repeat it to anyone."

"Christ, Jack, you scare the crap out of me," Terry answered, now even more confused.

"Simpson is screwing Chuck's wife. It's the worst-kept secret, and why Chuck hasn't twigged beats me. But the grapevine says he and his wife are estranged, and to get this multimillion-dollar contract, Briggs was willing to turn a blind eye."

"Jesus Christ, Jack, are you serious?" "As sure as God made little apples."

"So, what's the bottom line?" Terry asked.

"I force him into a corner and cancel the contract for incompetence and sue for recompense. Then I've got Simpson by the shorts, and he will have to agree with my plans to bring sales and marketing back in-house."

"What if he doesn't agree?"

"He will, or a ghost e-mail will be sent to his wife."

"Jack, you're incorrigible!"

"That's why I'm the boss." Blakely laughed aloud. This meeting was going to be interesting.

*   *   *

A black Ford Falcon police cruiser, with its large blue stripes and Polinzonte in bold white letters, was sitting at the curb, its engine running. This baby looked all of twenty years old and covered in dust, its tires as bald as Telly Savalas. The young moustached police driver in the crumpled uniform was casually smoking what looked like a joint; but then again, in Argentina, there're no surprises.

"I'll be darned, the old Ford Falcon!" Bill exclaimed as Victor walked toward the cruiser.

The lieutenant couldn't help but overhear Bill's comment and turned to Hayden, a broad smile on his face.

"Bill, at the thought of boring my U.S. compatriots from the Big Apple with a piece of useless history . . . For your information, Ford Argentina in 1962, at the request of the then government, was given the tasks of producing a Falcon specifically designed for the needs of the police force, and with the exception of technological changes and an improved transmission, we still use the same car to this very day. The design was, of course, the 1960 Falcon built by Ford, USA, the only difference being the grill and the twin head lamps. I am sure standing here at the taxi stance, you have noticed the same model is as popular as the yellow and black cabs, of course, with less powerful engines." Victor smiled, feeling good with himself.

Bill laughed. *"But of course!* And, Victor, thanks for the history lesson. You've made my day."

On seeing the funny side, everyone burst into laughter, including Tony who was feeling like the "fish that drank too much."

Victor knocked annoyingly on the front side widow, startling the driver whom by the glaze in his eyes should have been ticketed for DUI. The young cop quickly stubbed the joint then blew on the dog before saving it in his tunic pocket for another "twilight zone."

"Please." Victor opened the rear door. "I will accompany the driver, but first place your bags in the trunk.

The lieutenant slipped into the front seat then turned to the young cop. "Driver, Marriott Plaza, San Martin, ando no cintura mas tiempo."

"Si, Lieutenant." He quickly slipped the cruiser into gear, the transmission giving a protesting thud.

"You, hombres, must be feeling tired and jetlagged so I've told the driver to step on it."

"Thanks, Victor. Although we had some shuteye on the flight, we're both feeling pretty stoked."

"Your hotel is a good forty-five minutes' drive from the airport, so if you want get your heads down, feel free," Victor answered.

"Maybe Tony would, but for me, I want to see the sights." Bill turned to Tony, but there was no reply. "Our friend was already in another world . . ."

* * *

As Bill studied the ever-changing scenery, the contrast between rags to riches was apparent and overpowering. The highway was a death trap for the hundreds of crazy motorcyclist who had little concern for life or limb or anyone else for that matter! Street vendors lined either side of the socalled freeway, plying their wares from fruit to exhaust tainted hawker food with crazy taxi drivers pulling in without warning to grab their Salmonella infested morning snack. Soon they were passing by congested shantytowns and squatter camps, *the squalor unbelievable!* Rusty makeshift corrugated roofs, tarpaulin-draped walls, old timber, and discarded bricks was "home sweet home" to the thousands of Argentineans. As for sanitation, it's best not mentioned.

* * *

"At last, gentlemen, here we are," Victor commented as the driver slowed down at the entrance to the Marriott Plaza, a five-star hotel, and it seemed the lieutenant was as relieved as Bill. A policeman's job is not to chaperon two cops from New York; he had much better things to do, like arresting the kidnappers of Monalita Menzel.

"Tony." Bill was embarrassed at "Sleeping Beauty" who was lying with his mouth open, producing the inevitable sound of a bull elephant in heat.

"Tony, come on, buddy." It was time for the "rib" awakening, and Bill gave him the proverbial elbow.

351

"*What . . . eh?* Christ, for a moment there, I thought that was Rose doing her wakeup thing."

"*Well, it's me,* your buddy, and for your information, we have just arrived at our hotel."

"Awe, I'm okay. *Don't worry!*" Tony could see the concerned expression on Bill's face. "*But do I need a drink!*" He sat straight up as he came to his senses and quickly opened the car door for some fresh air to clear his head to avoid throwing up.

"Victor, please excuse my partner. This is completely out of character."

"Don't worry." Victor smiled. "In the American movies, New York cops are always portrayed as being tough and hard drinkers. Come, I'll assist you to check in just in case there is a language problem."

"Thanks, Victor, but you don't have to. I'm sure you have other more important things on your plate."

"It's no problem. Besides, I need to discuss a few points with you both before I leave."

*   *   *

The check-in complete and the bags delivered to their rooms, Victor suggested that they retire for a coffee in the hotel lounge.

"How are you feeling now, Tony?" Victor asked, concerned at Tony's "hang over" look.

"I'm just a bit sensitive, *but what I wouldn't do for a beer!*"

Victor raised his hand to attract the waiter as they took their seats at the coffee table.

'Si, senor?"

"Dos cafe's y una Quilmes cervesa, por favor."

"Si, senor. Gracias."

"Whatever you asked for, Victor, it sounded good." Tony forced a desperate smile.

"So, gentlemen, I'm sure you have some ideas as to where you wish to start?"

"You're right, Victor. Tony and I have given this some thought, and we have both come to the same conclusion that we start with immigration."

Tony just grunted in agreement. Normally, it would be his show, but with how he was feeling, he was only too happy for Bill to raise the curtain for the first act.

"*Hmmmm.*" Victor was listening.

"I'm sure you will agree that there must be a record of Summers's passport number and entry visa and the address where he intends to stay in Buenos Aires. That should be our first port of call."

"Ah, here's our coffees and Tony's transfusion." Victor joked as the waiter placed the coffees on the table and began pouring Tony's Quilmes, the local beer.

"Salutey." Tony raised his glass and demolished the amber liquid. "Boy, does *that* feel good!"

Victor just smiled and took a sip of his coffee, but he was deep in thought about Bill's suggestion.

"I hear what you say, Bill, and I tend to agree, but it is easier said than done. I will need special dispensation to get clearance, even just to approach immigration, as it's not under the jurisdiction of the police."

"So how do we do this?" Bill could sense a train wreck on its way.

"First of all, I will have to approach my superior, Captain Avalos, then he will have to get final approval from General Ceres, and of course, that will take time."

"Man, this is getting messy." Tony was now back in the affray.

"I understand how you must feel, Tony, but in Argentina, we take protocol very seriously."

"So how long will this take?" Tony was being a touch rude.

"Maybe two or three days." Victor could see the disappointment on their faces. Like *not another roadblock*. "But you have my assurance that I will do my very best, but please be patient and understand with the Menzel kidnapping, the general has more important things on his mind than arresting an American fugitive."

"Victor, at the thought of being rude, once we have the green light, *whenever that will be,* I assume we still have to get agreement from the same comandante?"

"The one and only." Victor grinned. "If it wasn't so serious, Tony, it would be funny."

"I wish I had your sense of humor," Tony replied sarcastically before turning to Bill. "It's looks like we'll be out of pocket for another two grand." Then he turned to Victor again. "I think your comandante should be the host on the American game show *Who wants to be a Millionaire?*" "You got that one right, Tony!" Bill was fast on his feet.

Victor was taking all the crossfire. As having lived in New York for three years, this guy had been there.

Now Victor was getting anxious. The American humor was not to his taste, and the quicker he left the two detectives to do their "own thing," *the better!*

"Gentlemen, thanks for the coffee, but I must be on my way. I suggest you have a good night's rest, and I will pick you up at nine tomorrow morning."

"Why don't you join us for breakfast?" Tony asked.

"As how you say in America . . . 'Sorry, but I will have to take a rain check.'" He grinned again. So much so that Tony felt like patting him on the head. *Good boy . . . Good boy . . .*

"Tomorrow then at nine. We will be waiting in the coffee shop. And as they say in the American movies, 'Adios muchas gracias, hombre.'"

"Touché." Victor shook his head then abruptly left. He wasn't relishing another day with these two smart-assed American cops.

* * *

Tony sat for a moment in silence then turned to Bill. "So what do you make of all that shit?"

"The same as you, partner. Round and round the merry go round and then some more."

"I couldn't have put it better myself. Let's sign the check and head to our rooms. I can do with a good shower."

"I'm glad you've noticed." Bill burst into laughter.

"Get out of it, Hayden! I'll meet you in the bar at seven."

* * *

The New York Business Club is as stuffy as it sounds. The three-story building in blocked granite with the four-pillared entrance looked like something from Caesar's palace, and I don't mean the one in Las Vegas! Its large oak-panelled door complete with a uniformed guard almost seemed like an institution, but then maybe that's the idea. I mean who wants to be institutionalized? The two floors of five-star rooms for overnight business stays, I'm sure, could tell some stories; but the library and well-stocked bar complete with its dark brown Moran leather sofas gave it the old colonial look, and when you add the cigar room, well, you get the picture. As for the annual fees, even Bush couldn't afford the membership. But the one saving grace is it's fine-dining restaurant, and today Jack Blakely was looking forward to that free lunch.

* * *

"Boy, this is some joint, and it scares the shit out of me," Terry commented as the Caddy came to a stop in front of the "mausoleum" entrance.

"Don't worry, Terry. It looks stuffy, but you would be surprised at the number of business deals that are done here over a drop of aged bourbon and an expensive Cuban."

"I can just imagine!" Terry smiled.

Terry opened the car door, exposing more thigh than Angelina Jolie, and it didn't go unnoticed. The young car jockey, hoping for a better show, rushed to her aid.

"Let me help you, ma'am." He held Terry's arm. "My name is Tom."

The braided hat and the dark "one size fits all" blue uniform adorned with old-fashioned brass buttons didn't do the kid any favours. But when you are a UNI student trying to earn an extra buck, *who gives a damn?*

"Can I park the car, sir?"

Jack chucked him the keys. "Make sure, kid, it comes back in one piece."

"Certainly, sir." The "kid" gave Terry his special smile, the memory of her sexy thighs still vivid.

"Excuse me, sir." The uniformed security guard blocked their paths. "Hold it there, kid, till I get clearance. I'm sorry, sir, but you require a member to sign you in. You are the guest of?" "Mr. Briggs," Jack replied.

"Of?"

"Global Marketing."

The oversized "no-brainer" stepped aside and cupped his hand over the wireless phone and mumbled a few words out of ear reach.

Jack shook his head, turning to Terry. *"Christ! This is like being a fucking member of the Klu Klux Klan."*

Terry just grinned. Whatever! As they say, *"there's no point in getting your knickers in a twist."*

"If you can just hang on, sir, Mr. Briggs will be here in a few minutes. Tom, you can park the car now." The kid nodded and slipped into the driver's seat but not before giving Terry an adoring smile.

The heavy planked door suddenly opened. Chuck could have easily been mistaken for a look-alike Teddy Kennedy waiting to be interviewed. For sure he certainly fitted the bill.

"Jack, *good to see you again!"* He offered his hand. "Please." He motioned. "And this is?"

"Terry Johnson."

"Of course, the lady you mentioned on the phone. I knew your predecessor . . . nice lady . . . Tragedy what happened . . . Excuse me one moment while I sign the register."

Briggs entered their names under the watchful eye of security.

"I suggest we go to the lounge and enjoy an aperitif before lunch. It's quiet, and hopefully we can have an uninterrupted discussion. I have switched off my cell phone just in case." Briggs gave a phony smile.

"Whatever, Chuck," Jack replied with a straight face.

This was going to be a game of cat and mouse, and by the size of Chuck, there's no guessing who was going to be the mouse. But mice are cunning, and Briggs would soon find Blakely was no pushover. For sure there was no love between these two.

*   *   *

The plush leather chairs were comfortable, but the room was dark and stuffy. The large portraits of past presidents with heavy gilded dust collecting frames added to the sobriety as with the dark wood-panelled walls. As for the heavy oak bar, *the barman looked older than the establishment!* But maybe he is the secret weapon for the rocket-fuelled cocktails and the "done deals." The room was filled with low voices and pinstriped suits, grey hair, crisp white shirts, and floral bow ties. Maybe this fashion will come back. Who knows? But whatever, the smell of money was unmistakable, and as Jack put it, "over" or "under the table" deals will most certainly be sealed this day.

*   *   *

"Drinks?" Briggs asked.

"I think I'll start with a single malt." Jack turned to face Terry, waiting for her decision.

"I never knew you were a 'scotch' man," Briggs interrupted. "And you, Terry?"

"A flute of chilled French champagne would be nice."

"You got style, lady." Briggs smiled as he raised his hand to attract the waiter.

"Sir?"

"Eh?" Chuck looked at the nametag. "David . . . a bottle of my favourite Cab Sav, Chateau St. Michelle, and a double Scotch . . . single malt. Any preference, Jack?"

"Glenmorangie." The waiter noted the name.

"And one flute of fine French champagne."

"Certainly, sir. It will only take a few minutes. In the meantime, I suggest if you are staying for lunch, perhaps your guests may wish to study the menu?"

Briggs just nodded as if to say, *"Just get on with it, man!"*

"So, Jack, where do you wish to start?" Briggs placed the folder he was carrying under his arm on the coffee table. "I have here an update on the BM2000's marketing and sales strategy and technical material for your approval. The first overlays of the TV ads, target markets, 'big hit' customers, and our costs versus budget to date, with some unfortunate overruns, which I will explain in due course. *Ah!* Here's our drinks."

The waiter placed Terry and Jack's orders on the glass-topped coffee table then showed the label of the 1996 Cab Sav to Briggs, who nodded his approval. The bottle uncorked; Chuck interrupted the wine-tasting process. "David, there's no need to go through the rigmarole. It's my favourite poison. Just pour."

"Certainly, sir." David was unimpressed with Briggs's rudeness, but in this club, one of the attributes you must have is thick skin. "Call me, sir, when you are ready to order."

"Cheers." Jack led the way.

Terry daintily took a sip from her crystal champagne flute then smiled in satisfaction.

"*Hmmmm*, this is excellent."

"It's my pleasure," Briggs returned the compliment.

"Chuck, before we start getting hot and heavy, may I inquire if you are up to speed on Mike Summers?"

"As a matter of fact, I had his wife here yesterday, explaining all the gory details . . . sad case. Consequently, I've terminated Summers's contract. The publicity is bad for business. Of course, I did my best with his severance entitlements and then some."

"That's noble of you, Chuck."

Briggs's eyes flashed. Was that a compliment or the height of sarcasm?

Briggs continued, "The latest I heard, he is a fugitive on the run, and police are confident that he will be apprehended soon. But you know." He paused. "I never knew Laura Williams is Senator Williams's daughter and the niece of Jake Murray, our very own district attorney!"

"Yeah, it's a small world," Jack answered. "And you never suspected there was anything between Summers and Williams?"

"*Listen,* the guy is good at his job. As for his private life, outside of office hours, that's his own business."

"I suppose we all have skeletons in the closet. Isn't that true, Chuck?"

Briggs's eyes flashed again. What was Blakely insinuating? Did he know about his wife's adultery with Simpson?

"Just what do you mean by that comment, Jack?" The tone in Briggs's voice was ugly.

Blakely grinned. He knew he had struck a nerve, but he also knew there was a limit, and he had to draw the line.

"Just a throwaway line, Chuck, nothing personal."

Terry was just sitting, quietly watching the gladiators' "face-off" and wondering just *what the hell* Jack was up to.

Jack took a slow sip of his scotch, indulging in the "water of life." He had that cunning glint in his eyes, and it was just a case of when.

"Chuck, before we get into stormy weather, it's no secret that I was totally against outsourcing the marketing responsibilities for the launch of the BM2000 series."

"So?" Chuck rudely shot back.

"The contract is quite specific regarding key performance indicators linked to progress payments, of course, sales and potential orders. I know, because I set the targets, and you, Chuck, signed the dotted line. Now where does that leave me, you may ask?"

"Jack, *just what the hell are you getting at or more so insinuating?*"

"What I'm getting at, Chuck, is if we tick the boxes, the launch, being the single most important market communication for any new product, was sloppy and abysmal, not to mention the absorbent cost. Then there's the technical literature. *Well, you know my comment on that front!* Finally, sales or more to the point what sales? And where's the man that's responsible for all this? *I'll tell you!* Doing the Richard Kimble somewhere in Buenos Aires! So, Chuck, where does that leave ABM? And now to add insult to injury, you're firing shots across my bow, warning me there's more bad news on the way with a further expenditure 'blowout' and a new begging bowl in the pipeline. *Not good enough, Chuck. Not good enough!*"

"I think what you are telling me, and correct me if I'm wrong, is that you're invoking the termination clause for breach of contract."

"Chuck, you don't have be a lawyer to pull that one outta the hat. Not only am I going to tell Simpson that I'm terminating the contract for noncompliance. I'm also recommending that ABM sue for recompense."

Briggs slammed his glass on the coffee table, almost breaking the stem.

"You'll never get away with it! Besides, what makes you think Simpson will agree?"

"*Oh, he will, Chuck!*" Blakely grinned sarcastically. "As I mentioned before, everyone has a skeleton in their closet, and Simpson is no exception."

"Be careful what you say, Blakely, or I'll have you up for liable."

"Chuck, whatever has been said around this table today, I will irrefutably deny, and besides, there are no witnesses. Isn't that true, Terry?"

"*Eh,* err yes, of course, Jack." Terry was completely mesmerized.

"*Why you jumped-up—*"

"*Say it, Chuck,* let it all hang out."

"Fortunately for you, Blakely, there's a lady in the company. Besides, I wouldn't lower myself to your level."

"Excuse me, Mr. Briggs. Are your guests ready to order?"

There's never a good time, but then there's always an exception.

"Thank you, David, but unfortunately, my guests are just about to leave."

* * *

June wiped her mouth with her napkin then took a final sip of the Frascati. She gave a satisfied sigh and pouted her mouth as if to say "Boy, am I full!"

"Phil, you certainly know how to order, but I must say the food was to die for. I haven't eaten so much since Thanksgiving. I think you're purposely trying to ruin my figure."

"At the thought of boringly repeating myself, June, *you* look absolutely fabulous."

"Keep 'em coming, Jack." June laughed. "I can't remember the last time I had a compliment like that, especially from a handsome young man."

Phil burst into laughter. "This keeps getting better all the time." He took a deep breath then paused. "On a more serious note . . ." He had that solemn look on his face that only a lawyer could have.

June went quiet, not knowing what to expect.

"Dessert?"

"*Why you!*" She burst into relieved laughter.

"You had me going there. But are you serious, after that ravioli?" They both laughed again, having seen the funny side.

"Well then, can I entice you with a cappuccino?"

"*Phil Stevens . . .*"

* * *

"Hmmm, this coffee is good." June took a sip of the milky brew as Phil gave a sort of nervous cough. It was time to face the enemy.

"June, I'm not naive to think this an NYU reunion. I have broad shoulders, and I'm a good listener, and more to the point, I am a qualified attorney."

June rested her chin on her hand, her elbow on the table, not the most ladylike position. Then she gave an overzealous sigh. *It's so sad,* she thought.

To end such a lovely lunch with the "fall out" that is inevitable. June looked into Phil's eyes. "Where do I begin?"

* * *

"*My god, June,* I feel so bad for you. Of course, I'll take your case. Divorce is not my specialty, but I'll speak to Glen Jacobs when I return to the office. As for your joint property deed, I'm afraid you need your husband's consent before proceeding with a sale, which becomes messy, as the bank could foreclose on your mortgage for failure to meet the instalments as they have the title deeds. As far as a missing person is concerned, it takes seven years before a missing person can be legally proclaimed deceased. I'm sorry, June." Phil placed his hand warmly on hers. The gesture felt supportive and genuine, and June returned the touch, placing her other hand on top of his.

"I wish I had better news, but listen, don't worry about the fees. We can talk about that later."

"Phil, you're so sweet. At least you have given me some hope."

"Now your children?"

"Sheryl, sixteen, and Steven, eighteen. Both still studying. And you, Phil?

"No children. My wife just couldn't conceive no matter how hard we tried. The best gynaecologists and so on. I wanted children desperately, and that put a terrible stress on our relationship and in hindsight probably the straw that broke the camel. Anyhow, the bottom line is she was having an extramarital with some 'toy boy,' and after some good 'gum shoe' with pictures and all that ugly stuff, we finally divorced. That was two years ago. And before you ask . . . no . . . I'm not seeing anyone. I'm still enjoying, as they say, 'the bachelor life.'"

That was sweet music to June's ears, but was she being too forward and was Phil something more than just a shoulder to cry on?

* * *

Phil glanced at his watch then raised his hand to attract the waiter.

"Check please. I apologize, June, for cutting it short, but I have another appointment at four, and it's getting tight."

He took the bill, glanced at the details for a few seconds, nodded, then passed the waiter the gold Amex Card.

"You don't have to apologize. It should be *me* for upsetting your busy schedule."

"Not at all." Phil touched her hand. "It is *my* pleasure. Now more to the point, why don't you come to my office tomorrow? I'll ask my secretary to squeeze you in somehow. I suggest that you give her a call first thing in the morning, and maybe, that is if you are free tomorrow evening, you can join me for dinner."

"I would love that," June replied, full off enthusiasm.

"Come, I'll see you to your car."

"There's no need, Phil. You have a prearranged appointment, and lawyers shouldn't be late." June grinned.

"Good advice."

They left the restaurant then stood for a moment on the sidewalk, looking into each other's eyes.

"Eh . . . Um . . . That's my car parked over there." June pointed precariously. "I can manage from here." She smiled. "I can't thank you enough, Phil." She stood on her toes to kiss him on the cheek. "Till morrow then. Ciao." "Bye, June." He turned and left.

For June, it had been a more than interesting lunch.

CHAPTER 15

(Speaking in Spanish)

"Nice job, Lucia." Carlos was admiring the embroidery on Sergio's neck.

"He's lucky this time." She gave a toothless grin. "But you two banditos as usual, are up to no good. The policia are not stupido, and you'll end up once again behind bars." The "would be surgeon" was shaking her head.

But "curiosity killed the cat." Her inquisitiveness was getting the better of her, and Lucia stupidly pulled back the curtain to the "everything room."

"Santa Maria!" she gasped, raising the back of her hand to her mouth, her eyes bulging at the sight of the hooded captives.

Carlos hadn't been paying attention, more interested in the health of his wounded friend.

"Why you stupid old bitch!" He grabbed Lucia by her scrawny arm, almost breaking her fleshless wrist, the Glock already in his hand, pressed against the old woman's temple. "I should blow your fucking brains out, you crazy old bitch."

Eva rushed at Carlos, fearful for Lucia's safety, and grabbed his arm, trying to restrain him from hurting the old lady, or worse still pulling the trigger.

"Carlos . . . Carlos!" she screamed. "Leave her alone. You can trust her to keep her mouth shut."

He pushed Eva back with such force she almost lost her balance only to be caught by Lena from crashing to the floor.

"You try that again, Eva. *And so help me!*" Carlos yelled at the top of his voice as he roughly swung the old lady round to face him, still pointing the gun menacingly at her head. "You listen to me, old witch, and listen good. Your memory is bad, and you will forget everything you seen or done here tonight should the policia come asking. Comprender? *I said comprender?*" "Si." Lucia nodded petrified.

Carlos released her then shoved her toward the door.

"Now get the hell out of here! And remember, old lady, what I said, or you'll be making an appointment with the 'Virgen Del Lujan.'"

Lucia quickly did an about-face. She didn't need a second prompt but not before making a grab for the half-empty tequila bottle. If she was leaving, she wasn't going empty-handed.

"Why you old . . ."

"Let her be, Carlos. She knows how police informers are treated in Villamisseria."

* * *

Sergio was now in a deep sleep. The "tequila aesthetic" had killed the pain, and the two exhausted women crashed down at the table. It had been one helluva night.

Eva passed Lena a can of Quilmes and pulled the tab. "I don't know about you, but I'm gutted."

"Are you forgetting something, femenino?" Carlos was in a foul mood. "Where is *my* beer?"

In Argentina, the women must obey "until death do us part."

"Get it your fucking self, you despicable bastardo," Eva ferociously retaliated. *Hell has no fury like a woman's scorn.*

For Carlos, enough was enough. It was time to teach his wife a lesson or lose face, for the Gaucho an insufferable embarrassment. The anger in his bloodshot eyes was murderous, and without warning, the back of his hand crashed against Eva's cheek, spurting warm blood from her lips as her gums smashed against her teeth, the blow so hard she toppled from her chair semiconscious, sprawling onto the earthen floor, her eyes glazed over. Lena rushed to her friend's aid, cradling her broken face on her lap, gently trying to stop the flow of blood from Eva's swollen lips with the only cloth she had available, *the hem of her dress!*

"Now get me that fucking beer!" Carlos screamed again, ignoring his injured wife.

Lena stretched over and grabbed a can with her free hand and threw it with all her might at Carlos's head. He saw the missile coming and weaved to one side like a prize-fighter, avoiding a right hook.

"You fucking bitch!" Carlos stood over Lena; his hand raised ready to dish out the same medicine.

"Go on do it, *you fucking coward!"* Lena held her hand up, cowering to protect her face. "If you dare touch me, Sergio will fucking kill you."

"Awe . . . you're not fucking worth it." Carlos didn't want to tangle with Sergio, Lena's threat making him have second thoughts, and he smugly walked to the table and pulled the tab on another Quilmes.

"Buena Saluda." Carlos gave a crazy laugh, mocking the two women while raising his arm above his head in a repulsive gesture before placing the can to his lips, making a disgusting swallowing gurgle as he demolished half of its contents, the frothed beer streaming down his chin. Then he stopped for a moment to regain his breath, staring at the half-empty can for a moment, as if admiring it before erupting a revolting burp.

"Ah, that's better." He wiped his mouth with the back of his hand, ready to start again. *This Carlos was an ugly son of a bitch!*

"I need water and I must go to the bathroom" came Mona's barely audible voice and just in time to break the Mexican standoff.

"What the fuck now? Lena, take care of that fucking wife of mine and keep that big mouth of yours shut." Carlos pulled the black ski mask over his head while Lena unsteadily assisted poor Eva to a chair.

"Listen, when I pull aside this curtain, keep out of sight. I don't want them to see your faces."

Carlos muttered a variety of new swear words as he went to investigate, the solitary electric globe barely lighting the cell-like room. Mona and Mike were sitting on the earthen floor with their knees together pointing up toward their chins, their backs resting against the rough cast wall, not the most comfortable position, what with the cold dampness from the earthen floor getting to places best not to mention.

"I know you are there, *you fucking scumbag."* Mona let loose.

"You watch your fucking mouth if you know what's good for you, you rich bitch." Carlos was taking no shit; he had had enough for one night from Eva.

"We need some water and more urgently I need to take a piss." Mona's etiquette was taking a hit. "And you had better get a doctor for my campanero or you're gonna have one dead Americano on your hands."

"Americans have thick skulls and no brains, so what's the problem?"

Carlos walked toward Mona and Mike to remove the crudely stitched jute sacks from their heads. For a moment, Mona screwed up her eyes, trying to shield them from the light with her tied hands before turning to Mike who had a large open wound and a lump the size of an egg, crusted with congealed blood, on the side of his forehead.

"Christ, Mike, are you all, right?" Mona was shocked. *"You look terrible!"*

"It could be better, but I'll live. But, Mona, we gotta find a way outta here and fast. I don't trust these assholes. Once they don't need us, it's sayonara."

"Eh . . . sayonara?" Mona didn't understand.

"It's Japanese for goodbye."

"Eh, I still don't . . ."

"Shut up, you two!" Carlos had drawn the Glock and was pointing it straight at Mike's head. "What did the hombre say?"

Carlos, having no English, was suspicious of Summers. As a kid, he was taught to never trust Americans, and he was taking no chances.

"He said he needed water and some food," Mona answered, scorn lacing her voice.

"Be careful, senorita. I'm being nice to you, but don't try my patience."

Then Carlos turned and pointed to the fruit crate with the broken-down toilet seat covering the hole to the galvanized bucket.

"If you want to piss, you had better hurry before I change my mind."

Mona leaned forward, resting on her knees, then cautiously struggled to her feet, trying to keep her balance.

"If you don't mind!" Mona held her wrists forward, gesturing at the zip ties.

"Hembra, you don't need your hands free to drop your pants. Now move it before I change my mind." Carlos wasn't biting.

Nature calling, Mona hurried to the crude toilet then turned to face Carlos.

"Do you mind?"

"No . . . *I* don't mind." He grinned. "I never thought I would see the famous Senorita Menzel taking a leak."

"Fucking pervert!" Mona let loose, but her bladder was calling, and her modesty was long gone. She fumbled up her dress to pull down her panties.

"I hope you are enjoying yourself!" She scowled, but the relief was all over her face.

The deed done, Mona quickly rose to her feet and lifted her dress to pull up her underwear.

"Well, I hope you enjoyed the show, you bastardo."

(Speaking in English)

"Mike, I suggest you go as well. Don't worry. I was married once."

She gave Mike a helping hand to get to his feet.

"Thanks, Mona. I think I can manage the rest on my own." Mike put on a pained smile.

(Speaking in Spanish)

"*Sit down*. Both of you sit down. *Do you hear me?* Do it! *Do it now.*" Carlos was waving his pistol in a threatening manner. This guy was in an ugly mood, and to test his patience would be a big mistake.

Carlos quickly placed their hoods back, and the less he saw of their faces, the better.

As he was about to leave, something crossed his mind. If Sergio and he were not around, the gringo might make a break for it, and more to the point could the two woman handle it? he thought. No, he had no option but to tie their legs. His mind made up, he removed the ski mask and drew the curtain.

"Lena, I need some rope or something to tie the Americano and Senorita Menzel's legs."

"How the fuck should I know?" Lena was busy pressing a wet compress against Eva's jaw to reduce the swelling and avoid the inevitable black eye.

"There must be something I can use." Carlos stood frustrated, scratching his head. Then his eyes suddenly brightened as he noticed a bundle of old electric cable stacked in the corner next a large bag of rice.

"*Santa Maria!* This is just what I need." He pulled the large flick knife from pocket and pressed the release, the vicious serrated blade glistened in the dim lighting. The relieved Carlos began to cut the cable into relatively similar lengths before returning to the hostages.

"I've got some bad news for you and your boyfriend." He had a sadistic grin on his face. "Just in case you get any funny ideas about escaping . . . don't! Now do as I say and put your ankles together."

Securely tied and under a barrage of curses from Mona, Carlos stood back to admire his work before double-checking the knots just to be sure before looping another length of cable between their wrists and ankles.

"Just another precaution to prevent you from removing your hoods. Good. Now that that's done, maybe I can indulge in another beer." He left the storeroom feeling pretty proud with himself.

The second beer gone; Carlos yawned. It was after four in the morning; he was fatigued and desperate for sleep.

"Eva, stop feeling sorry for yourself and get your ass out of here. I have a busy day tomorrow."

Eva rose unsteadily to her feet; she wasn't going to protest a second time. "You didn't have to go, Eva." Lena grabbed her arm. "You can stay here tonight."

Eva just shook her head and walked toward the door; her fate sealed.

"Lena, make sure they have some water and ask Sergio to give me a call when he wakens. Come on, woman, don't just stand there!"

PART 4

Revenge Is Sweet

CHAPTER 1

Sergio stirred from his comatosed "tequila sleep" then winced in pain as he was reminded of the gunshot wound to his neck. He stared at the dimly lit room for a few seconds, trying to get his bearings and uncloud his alcohol-soaked brain. Lena, dressed in her flimsy nightdress, was lying next him fast asleep, the humidity almost unbearable, her moist sweat lines clearly visible.

(Speaking in Spanish)

Sergio gave Lena an elbow to the ribs. *"Woman, wake up.* Do you know what time it is?" He glanced at the stolen Rolex.

"I don't know, and I don't fucking care. Go back to sleep and do us both a favor."

"I'll tell you what time it is. *It's nine thirty!* Now get your ass out of bed, you lazy bitch, and get me some breakfast."

Lena uttered another oath then rolled over on her side, her back to him. She was bushed and she was taking no shit from this looser.

"Well, there's one way to get you out of bed." He grinned as he pulled up her nightdress; his tobacco-stained teeth would embarrass a camel.

"Keep your dirty hands to yourself." Lena pushed him away. "Go and wash. I've smelled pigs that are better than you."

But Lena was no fool, and the last thing she wanted was this greasy slob lying on top of her, and she hit the dirt floor.

"Well now, isn't that something?" Sergio laughed as he sat on the edge of the bed.

"That's not even fucking remotely funny. You fucking brainless ape. And what do I cook for breakfast, may I ask . . . *thin air?"* Lena walked barefooted to the large, galvanized water container and soaked her face in the semi cold water.

"Get dressed. I need you to go to the mercado to buy some tortillas, beans, and Quilmes."

Lena slipped out of her nightdress, standing naked before filling the large water jug and pouring it over her head. She could see Sergio taking it all in, and she knew that look on his face spelled trouble.

"Don't even think about it! Keep you dirty thoughts to yourself, and if I were you, I wouldn't try anything with that neck of yours . . . *Comprender?"*

Sergio touched his neck at the thought and decided "every dog has its day."

"And just what do I do for money?" Lena asked, now fully dressed.

Sergio fumbled in his trouser pocket and fished out a few crumpled notes.

"That should be enough, *woman."*

"You're fucking serious?" Lena yelled as she counted the crumple notes. "There's only one hundred pesos here!"

'So, tell Eduardo to put it on my slate and make sure you buy enough food to feed our guests." He gave another ugly grin as Lena slipped into her sandals.

"Before you go, did Carlos leave a message?"

"No, just to call him when you waken." Lena slammed the ramshackle door.

*   *   *

Sergio opened his cell phone.

"Carlos . . . Si, I'm okay. Lena? She's gone to buy some food. Si, that's why I'm calling. Here's the take. You call Marcos and tell him we will meet him at Cafe Tortoni at eleven this morning. Once he gets the lowdown on the Menzel Kidnapping, that is if he doesn't already know, we will need Marcos to convince Gomez to give us more time to collect the ransom. It's now nine thirty so pick me up at ten and give me a call once you set up the meeting. Gracias."

Sergio washed his face and doused himself from the a same makeshift tub then searched through the clothes piled on the chair for a change of shirt and trousers, but no matter how this guy was dressed, he would still look like a sack of shit.

"Now I wonder how my guests are behaving?" Sergio spoke to himself as he pulled the ski mask over his head and opened the makeshift curtain.

"Buenas Dias, Senorita Menzel and your American friend. I apologize for our modest five-star hotel, and I warn you I don't take credit cards."

Sergio gave a silly laugh; there's nothing like laughing at your own stupid humour.

"I see my compadre has done a fine job with that electric cable." Sergio removed their hoods.

Mona and Mike were in poor shape, having sat cramped in the same position the whole night, their legs and knees screaming for circulation as if not part of their extremities.

Mona had had enough. "Whoever you are, please I beg you to at least untie our ankles and wrists to allow us to stretch our legs and go to the toilet."

Sergio pondered for a moment, considering Mona's request. She had something in what she said. After all, she was "their ticket to ride," and how well she was treated spelt money.

"Si, *but don't try anything stupid."* Sergio pulled the gun from the waist of his trousers and pointed it at Mona and Mike. *"Comprender?"*

"Si!" Mona replied, gritting her teeth. *"Now untie my fucking ankles before gangrene sets in."*

Sergio kneeled and untied Mona's ankles but not her wrists and quickly stepped back taking no chances.

"Senorita Menzel, use your hands to untie the Americano. I will see to it that you get water and food shortly."

But before Sergio could continue, he was distracted by the sound of a door slamming.

That must be Lena returning with the food, he thought. And with not another word, he turned and disappeared into the front room, leaving Mona and Mike to do their thing.

* * *

"My legs . . . Christ, I can hardly feel them!" Mona staggered as she tried to take a few steps, but then her expression changed. "Mike, I gotta go." She had that urgent look on her face.

"Mona don't be embarrassed. Remember, we're in this together, and we need to depend on one another if we want to get out of shit hole alive."

"I agree, Mike, but can you please turn your back." Mona forced a grin.

* * *

"Mona, do you have any idea where we might be?" Mike asked, more relaxed.

369

"It's a long shot, Mike, but when we were being driven through the town, although I couldn't see anything, if I'm not mistaken, I could clearly hear the mooing and groaning sound of cattle. Which could only come from one place . . . the only cattle market in Buenos Aires . . . Liniers Market." "So, what's the significance?" Mike asked.

"It's only a few kilometres from the largest squatter slum in town . . . the Villamisseria, a notorious crime area, and I would stake my reputation that we are holed up somewhere inside the maze of broken-down shanty huts. *If I just had my cell phone.*"

"At least that's something, but more to the point, how the hell are we gonna get out of here?"

"*Shhhuus!* Someone's just come in. Keep quiet, Mike, while I try and listen to what they are saying."

*   *   *

(Speaking in Spanish)

"You took your fucking time. So did you get everything?"

"Eduardo is not happy. He told me to tell you this is the last time."

"*That fucking old woman!* He'll get paid once we close the deal. He's not so fussy when he fences our stolen goods and rips us off with the price. I have a long memory, and he had better be careful."

"Sergio, there's an old saying, and you're full of it."

"I've had enough of your crap. Now do what you're good at and get that food on the table. I'm fucking starved."

"At least you admit I'm good at something but only when it comes to your lousy stomach."

Sergio ran his fingers through his hair using both his hands. *"You give me a fucking headache, woman."*

*   *   *

"It sounds like we are near a small sundry shop as the woman has just returned with some food, and I picked up the name Sergio, although it's pretty common, but at least it's something."

"Hold it, Mona. They're coming." Mike signalled.

Lena suddenly appeared, ski mask and all, holding two plates with tortillas and beans.

"Gracias." Mona couldn't wait, sitting on the floor, both her legs outstretched, the plate on her lap. She folded the tortilla and scooped up the beans. This was peasant food at its best.

"Don't thank me. It's because of you two I have to do without. Make the best of it. It may be your last for a long time." As Lena left, Mona just shrugged.

"What was all that about?" Mike asked.

"It's not important. I'll tell you later. Looks like we got company." Mona heard the noise of a car stopping directly outside the shack, its brakes making a cringing squeal. Then there was a loud bang on the front door.

"Lena, that must be Carlos. Check it out and let him in."

Lena gave Sergio a look as if to say, "*I'm not your fucking servant*" but had second thoughts, the vivid memory of Eva's damaged face still fresh in her memory.

"Carlos, how is Eva?" Lena asked as he rudely pushed her aside, ignoring her question, and took the chair next to Sergio who was just finishing his breakfast.

"Buenas dias, Compadre. How is the neck?" he asked.

Sergio didn't reply, his mouth full of half-chewed tortilla; he pointed to the Quilmes. Carlos nodded and popped the tag on the beer before taking a repulsive gulp.

"The meeting is set. No tequila, huh?" Carlos was hoping for something stronger.

"This morning, that old bitch stole what was left," Sergio answered, shaking his head. "Which reminds me, where did you get the money to pay her? And that fancy watch you're wearing, huh?"

"The Americano had six thousand pesos in his wallet, and of course, this lovely gold Omega watch." Carlos suddenly looked uncomfortable. When you tell lies, you had better have a good memory. "Sergio, we go back a long ways. We are best friends, and we always share."

Carlos placed his hand in his pocket and hastily forked out three thousand in notes.

Sergio stared directly into Carlos's eyes, a chilling stare that would send fear into the hardest criminal. He had a reputation for violence then asking questions later.

"I'll ask you one more time." Sergio placed the Glock on the table, his finger resting on the trigger.

"*Sergio, gimme a break!* I have expenses and I had to give Eva some money. Christ, Sergio, be reasonable. *We have to live.*"

"One last time?" Sergio picked up the pistol and pulled back the hammer, pointing it straight at Carlos's "family jewels."

"All right! All right!" He raised both hands. "I was going to give you the rest, *I swear."* Sweat beads are now prominent on his brow.

"Place your pistola on the table, *like now!"* Sergio screamed.

Carlos nervously obeyed.

"Now tell me again, before my patience runs out, how much was the Americano carrying?"

"Eh . . . Eh . . ." Carlos nervously began to stutter. *"Eh . . .* twelve thousand pesos." He poured it out, almost relieved with his "true confession."

"The rest . . . on the table, darse prisa."

Carlos gingerly extracted another three thousand from his pocket.

"Sergio, I swear, that that's exactly half."

"Don't you ever . . . *ever* . . . double-cross me again or so help me, the next time you'll be carried out feet first. Now go and tie up our guests. I had to release them temporarily to relieve themselves."

As for Lena, she was quietly taking it all in. This kinda stuff was nothing new to her, but on seeing so much cash, well, she just had to get a piece of the action.

"And how about me? What do I live on? I can't even afford my fucking breakfast," she blurted.

Sergio leaned forward and picked up the bundle of notes, quickly counting the contraband.

"Here, woman, and for Christ's sake, give me some peace." Sergio counted two thousand pesos and laid them in front of her.

"Is that it?" Lena complained but didn't hesitate to grab the cash. Sergio's temper is erratic.

Sergio was pissed, like there's no pleasing this woman, and he turned and looked Lena straight in the yes without saying another word. That was enough.

*   *   *

Sergio checked his watch. "Carlos, make it snappy. We gotta go. It will take us at least half an hour to get there."

Carlos appeared from the behind curtain and removed the ski mask.

"Okay, let's go. Don't worry. They'll give us no problems. But, Lena, you must continually keep an eye on them and don't let your guard down, feeling sorry for their sob story. Give them water if they need it, and as for going to the toilet, they'll just have to manage. Remember and don't let anyone in or you leave the house until Sergio, and I return."

"So are you my father? Do you think I'm fucking stupid or something?"

"This woman!" Sergio shook his head. "Let's go, Carlos, before I change my mind and do something I might regret."

"And good riddance!" Lena shouted as they slammed the door.

She counted the money again then smiled before stuffing it between her sagging breasts.

"Now it's my turn for a beer." Lena smiled, speaking aloud.

* * *

Carlos searched up and down the dirt road. In this neighbourhood, there's no "honor among thieves"; and when there's a heist, a kidnapping, or a major drug deal, the "drums" alert whole of Villamisseria and the "dogs of crime" come barking.

"The coast is clear, Sergio. Let's get going." Carlos slipped into the driver's seat of the "old lady" and hit the gas pedal, a cloud of dust like a sandstorm rising from its spinning rear wheels.

"Which way are we taking?" Sergio asked.

"It's easier to use the highway then slip off onto Via Florida. Don't worry. We'll get there in time and maybe some."

"So how did Marcos react?"

"He didn't say much, and I didn't tell him much either. I went straight to the point and said, 'If you want to see the hundred grand, then you had better meet me and Sergio at Cafe Tortoni at eleven this morning.'"

"What was his reaction?"

"Nothing much. I think he has a good idea what's it's about. Let's face it. It's either begging or paying. But you know, Sergio, I really don't trust that bastardo and even worse Francisco Gomez. That Gaucho thinks he can walk on water."

"I have that same feeling, Carlos, that we are being taken for a ride. *Hey! Keep your eyes on the fucking road!"*

* * *

"Well, lookee here!" Sergio recognized Marcos Perez's car, the metallic brown '68 Cadillac Eldorado Coupe, a rare sight in Buenos Aires, and low and behold the Jaguar Sovereign XJ12 belonging to none other than Francisco Gomez himself.

Sergio laughed. "We should be honoured, Carlos. The big boss is here to pay us homage."

"*I wonder*, Sergio. I'm not so sure. We are twenty minutes early, and I don't like the look of this."

"Compadre, maybe *you* have something. Carlos, pull in here. I know it's about a hundred meters from the cafe, but I don't want these two hombres to know that we have arrived."

Carlos parked out of sight and cut the engine.

Sergio checked the magazine on his Glock and sent one to the breach then turned to his partner.

"Carlos, I suggest you do the same. I'm sure Perez and Gomez are armed, and I don't trust them. This could be a setup to rescue the Monzel woman and claim a fat reward for themselves."

"What you suggest is not stupid, Sergio." Carlos double-checked the semiautomatic.

"*Let's go.*"

The two men stealthed the sidewalk, keeping out of sight, shadowing the heavy tropical foliage along the footpath leading to the Arcadia and Cafe Tortoni.

As they drew nearer, Sergio could clearly see both men sitting outside under the shade, deep in conversation, and he quickly held Carlos back with his hand, putting his finger to his lips, signalling him to keep quiet.

"I want to hear what they're saying," Sergio whispered as he crouched in the short palms, using the large leaves as camouflage.

Gomez glanced at his watch. "We need to watch our time. They'll be here soon, and I don't want them to see me with you or they may suspect something."

"Si, Marcos, I'm surprised these two losers had the brains to pull off the kidnapping. Do you think that's what they want to talk to you about?"

"I guess so," Marcos replied. "But look at it his way, Francesco. Whatever happens, we win both ways. Don't forget we set them up with the cocaine sale using our own men for the heist and ending up with both the dope and the hundred grand." He grinned again. "And the irony is they are going to pay us back another hundred grand." He couldn't stop laughing. "*Idiots.* It doesn't get any better!"

Gomez laughed heartily. "But, Marcos, my suggestion is we use 'standover tactics' *not for the hundred grand* but for 80 percent of the ransom payment as interest overdue."

"I like that, Francesco. You have a wicked sense of humour. Listen, I think it's time you should go."

Sergio turned to Carlos; his eyes bloodshot with anger. He had heard it all.

"Bastardos! They will soon find out who are the losers." Sergio signalled to Carlos with his pistol. "Come, let's teach these fat slobs a lesson they will never forget."

Seething in anger, they crashed through the undergrowth like two wounded elephants, pistols flaying.

"You're going no fucking place, you double-crossing bastardos," Sergio screamed at the surprised duo. *"We heard it all."*

At the sight of the semiautomatics, Gomez went whiter than white.

"You got it all wrong, Sergio. We were just discussing—" He didn't get time to finish his sentence as Marcos made a stupid move and put his hand inside his jacket.

Sergio's gun barked twice, the 38's passing clean through Marcos's forehead, the back of his skull disintegrating like a young coconut, splattering Gomez's face with blood fragments and warm sticky brain matter, his chair crashing to the floor, the sound of gunshots panicking the other diners who were now turning tables on their sides and ducking for cover.

Francesco was shivering in fright as he stared down the muzzle of Carlos's gun and the crumpled lifeless body of his dead friend lying in an ever-expanding pool of blood.

"Please . . . please . . . Carlos, I'll give you anything. You can forget the money and—"

Sergio motioned to Carlos to take this now pitiful "big time drug boss" out of his misery.

"It's too late, you cowardly lowlife." Carlos gave a crazy laugh as he squeezed the trigger twice.

One copper nose fracturing Gomez's windpipe, making a gurgling sound like a unblocked drain as he grabbed his throat, the blood oozing between his fingers like futilely trying to plug a leak in a submarine. The second slug severed his aorta, spurting the thick fluid in bursts from the gaping hole in his heart, resembling an erupting volcano. In desperation, as his life ebbed away, Gomez grabbed at the tablecloth as he fell to his knees, dragging it on top of him, the coffee cups smashing to the floor in a hundred pieces, the linen now covering his lifeless body like a white shroud, the huge crimson stain getting larger and larger. As for Gomez, he was already knocking on Satan's door.

* * *

Carlos fired two shots into the air in rapid succession as a warning to the onlookers, sending them scurrying in all directions.

"You trigger-happy idiot! ?" Sergio screamed in the heat of battle. "Just what the fuck are you trying to prove?"

"To scare them from calling the cops. We need time to vamoose."

The two were now sprinting down the sidewalk like Olympic runners.

"Carlos." Sergio panted out of breath upon reaching the car. "Get in that fucking car and hit the gas."

Carlos turned the key. *Chug . . . Err . . . Chug.* The big V8 wasn't happy.

"Oh no!" Sergio yelled at Carlos. "This is all we fucking need! You *did* fill her up this morning, *didn't you?"*

"Of course, I fucking did. Just keep calm. I know this old lady like she's my mother."

He turned the key again.

Errr . . . Errr . . . Errr. The starter motor whined then *barroom*, the old faithful Eldorado burst into life.

"Thank God!" Sergio made the sign of the cross. "Someone up there likes me. *Now get your ass out of here!"*

Carlos swung into a U-turn, smoke spiralling from the rear tires as he straightened up and pressed the pedal.

He turned to Sergio as he sped down Via Florida, blending in with the congested traffic in the busiest street in Downtown Buenos Aires.

"Gimme a high five."

Sergio burst into laughter. "You crazy hombre, but we pulled it off and in broad daylight, *didn't we?"*

"Si, Sergio, but now *we* are the hunted like wild boar with a price on our heads."

CHAPTER 2

"Are you hungry, Terry?" Blakely asked, fracturing the pregnant silence as they drove down Madison.

"To be honest, Jack, I don't know whether I'm hungry or half pissed after these two glasses of champagne on an empty stomach."

Blakely laughed at Terry's comment. "I tell you what, why don't I make the decision that we take timeout and enjoy a light lunch?" He glanced at his watch. "We still have time. Besides, I think we both deserve some R&R after *that* meeting . . . *don't you?*"

Terry just smiled. "Whatever you say, Jack. *You're the boss.*"

"Then it's a done deal. Now the next question is, *where?* Any suggestions?"

"I know a small place in Watts Street just off Sixth Avenue. It's only a half hour from here, Gatsby's. It's Italian, and I know the owner and his wife. They're a lovely couple, originally from Rome. It's wholesome Italian fare, and the place is delightful."

"You've sold me. Now I guess I have to hang a left here at the lights and swing onto Canal."

"I'm impressed." Terry smiled.

"Remember, I am a born and bred New Yorker, and I know this city like the back of my hand," Blackly boasted.

As for the meeting with Briggs, Terry was just playing dumb, but there was no doubt in her mind that it would raise its ugly head over lunch. Blakely was a cool customer, all right, and devious with it; but how would Simpson take it? And was Jack serious about his threat? For sure it will all come out in the washing, and as for the lunch, it's anyone's guess.

*   *   *

"This *is* nice, Terry," Blakely commented as the waiter escorted the "odd couple" to their table.

Gatsby's is traditional Italian in every aspect, a small family restaurant with recipes passed down from generation to generation. The blackboard menu was "keep it simple, simple": antipasti, a choice of three traditional homemade pasta dishes and Italian seafood soup. Desserts? It wouldn't be Italian without the famous tiramisu, panna cotta, and ricotta cheesecake.

The red checkered tablecloths, the candle-waxed crusted Chianti bottles, the heavy wooden oak bar with the highly polished copper and brass, larger-than-life coffee machine; it had it all, including the boring paintings and prints of famous landmarks in Rome and of course the gold-framed portrait of Pope Benedict XVI in full regalia. On a warm summer's day, this is as good as it gets, and what better than enjoying the view of the "Spanish Steps"?

"Terry! Buona pomeriggio . . ." Mario had spotted Terry and her companion, taking their table as he was frothing the cappuccinos. "I'll be with you in a minute, Terry, once I serve this customer." Mario was all smiles.

"Nessun problema . . . Come lei e ed, Anna?" Terry asked.

"Siamo buoni."

"I didn't know you can speak Italian." Blakely was impressed.

"I can't." Terry laughed. "Had an Italian boyfriend once, picked up a few words."

"Pillow talk, huh?" Blakely couldn't let it pass.

"As they say, Jack, 'when in Rome . . .'"

"You never cease to amaze me, Terry."

"Deja vu."

"I'll take that as a compliment." Blakely was in good form.

"Terry, it's been so long. I must tell Anna you are here." Mario gave an inquisitive look at Blakely.

"Mario, this is my boss, Jack Blakely. We just finished a meeting, and I enticed him to experience Anna's cooking."

"Bonjiorno." Mario offered his hand. "I must go, Terry, as you can see we are busy today, and one of my staff called in sick. Ricardo here will look after you."

* * *

"Terry, I don't know how you found this place, but for sure I'm going to bring Margo here one evening. The food is exceptional." Blakely took another sip of the Prosecco.

"I'm glad. Dessert?"

"I'd love to, Terry." Jack made a rubbing gesture to his stomach. "But that seafood soup saw the boots of me."

"You must have coffee!" Terry raised her hand to attract the waiter. "Cappuccino or short black?"

"I'll go for the low calorie . . . short black."

* * *

"Hmmm . . . this coffee *is* good!" Terry commented, taking a second sip.

"Changing the subject, Jack, I'm sure Briggs is hot on the line to Simpson by now. Are your ears burning?" Terry was trying to keep it light.

Blakely just laughed in a nonchalant attitude. "The deal is done. I don't anticipate any heat from Simpson. I've done my homework, and he knows I'm holding all the cards. He would be stupid to test me. The only worry I have is the legal kickback, but once I reach the office, I'll phone Stevens & Stevens, our company lawyers, and get Phil onto it right away."

"And the BM2000 launch, where do we go from here?" Terry asked.

"That's your baby now, Terry. I am putting you totally in charge."

* * *

At four thirty, there was little point in returning to the office, and Terry leaped at Blakely's suggestion to call it a day. As she picked up her car and slipped into the busy evening traffic, she had to admit that her new job was not only challenging but also life—changing. Was she comfortable with it? *Well,* only time will tell.

*   *   *

Terry felt more than fatigued. The lunch with Briggs had been stressful, and she breathed a sigh of relief as she finally swiped her security card to the apartment underground car park. What she would do is just to kick off these heels and do the couch potato thing with a glass of chilled white wine and a pack of fries.

"Yes?" she spoke aloud as she cut the engine, her mind made up.

Within minutes, Terry had arrived at her apartment, turning her key in the Yale, the relief on her face abundantly visible. She opened the door and disabled the alarm, smiling to herself, remembering her last words to Frank this morning before leaving for the office. Her heels kicked to one side, her suit jacket strewn over the chair, she flopped onto the sofa, legs outstretched, wiggling her cramped toes. *The price of vanity.* It felt good to finally relax in her "castle" and for a change enjoy her own company. Frank is a great guy, but there are times . . . The phone rang.

"Yes?"

"Terry, it's Margaret . . . Margaret Williams, Laura's mother. I apologize for disturbing you at home, but I phoned the office and was informed that you had gone for the day."

Terry's heart missed a beat. *Was it Laura? Did she have a relapse?*

"I hope it's not bad news," Terry nervously inquired.

"It is and it isn't. Don't worry. Laura is well. I apologize if I gave you a fright, but you see, I need your help . . ."

Terry listened to Margaret's truncated explanation.

"I see. Don't worry. Anything I can do to help, I'm only too happy. I'll be there by seven thirty."

"Thanks, Terry. I really appreciate it."

Terry sighed and hung up. *So much for her "couch potato" night!* But then Laura was her best friend. Then something crossed her mind. *Frank!* She gave an aggravated sigh and picked up the phone again.

"Come on, Frank, answer the bloody phone! Yes, it's me. Listen, something's come up. Laura's mother asked me to meet her at the hospital tonight at seven thirty. No. Laura's all right. Don't worry. I'll tell you about it later. Yes, that's the reason I'm calling. You have your own key. I'll call you when I'm on my way home. Would you like me to fetch a pizza or something? Sounds good. You'll give me a surprise. I'll look forward to that. Love you too."

*   *   *

"*Steven . . . Cheryl,*" June hollered. "Dinner is ready. *Don't let it get cold.*"

Having arrived home reasonably early from her "secret lunch," June had decided to make Steven's favorite, meatloaf and potato mash, as a special treat. She pondered over the stove for a moment, reflecting on her freshman days at NYU and more so the crush she had on that handsome quarterback and still as handsome as ever. Age had been kind to Phil, but more to the point, a divorcee with no children, now that *is* something! Today, even with her bag full, for a change, June felt radiant, like a new woman. She had long forgotten what it was like to receive a compliment from the opposite sex. But was she self-indulging in her own fantasies or was it premature love on the rebound and a car wreck waiting to happen?

"Mother, that smells good . . . *meatloaf* . . . my favorite, and with mash!" Steven gave his mother a kiss on the cheek. "Thanks, Mom."

"Awe, be off with you. It's time we had something to cheer us up. Grab a seat at the bar while I serve . . . Coke?"

"I'll get it, Mother, and one for sis. That is, as and when she decides to come down to dinner."

"Go easy on her, son. We're all feeling the pain, and more so your sister being so close to your father. She misses him without saying."

Steven just shook his head as he took his seat at the breakfast bar. They were all feeling the pain of insecurity. June sliced a generous portion of the meatloaf and passed it to Steven, the aroma attacking his taste buds.

"*Hmmm,* this is really good, Mother." "Hi, Mother." It was Sheryl.

"So, you finally decided to come down." Steven just couldn't let it be.

"*Steven, enough!*" June retaliated. "Let's just enjoy our dinner together as a family for a change."

"Just as small portion for me, Mother. I'm trying to lose weight." Cheryl took a sip of her diet coke.

"Changing the subject, Mother, how did your day go?" Steven asked.

June continued to serve in silence, at last taking her seat at the breakfast bar, having poured herself a glass of white wine. Coke was not her thing.

380

"How did my day go? *Good question!* To start with, I decided to phone an old friend of mine from my NYU days."

Sheryl butted in, "A male friend, I presume, by that smile on your face?"

"Hell, Sheryl, don't be so rude, interrupting Mother like that."

"Of course," June continued, smiling. "And a lawyer into the bargain."

"Mother, are you divorcing Father?" Sheryl went straight to the point.

"Sis, give it a miss and stop interrupting."

"It's all right, son. We are all a bit uptight. The reason I contacted Phil Stevens was first as an old friend and second to get legal advice to try and find some way to stop the bank foreclosing on our mortgage. We are not at that stage yet, but we *will* be in five to six months, once your father's severance pay is exhausted."

"As serious as that, Mother?" Sheryl had calmed down.

"I'm afraid so. But don't be dejected. All we have to do is stick together as a family, and more so, *I* need your support."

Steven stretched over and reassuringly touched his mother's hand.

"Don't worry, Mother. We are all in this together. I've already started to look for a job after school to help with my university fees."

June was touched with Steven's remark, and she almost cried. But on the brighter side, her appointment with Phil Stevens tomorrow would be more than interesting.

CHAPTER 3

Tony showered and shaved, then slipped into his bathrobe. To say he felt like a new man would be an understatement. He had already phoned the office and spoken to Stace, instructing him to urgently TT cash to the local bank after explaining his experience with the crooked customs officer. He could still remember Stacey's laugh. *"So, the two best detectives in New York were ripped off in Buenos Aires. That's one for the book."* Tony had to smile. I mean that was the last he remembered after his head hit the pillow.

The annoying ring of the phone kept echoing in Tony's ear.

Why won't that irritating sound go away and leave me in peace? Tony was talking in his subconscious. Then suddenly, he came to his senses as his clouded brain defogged.

Of course, the bloody phone! he groaned, still half-asleep.

"Yeah?"

"Tony, for Christ's sake, wake up! I've been sitting at the bar here for at least half an hour." Hayden was pissed off.

"I'm sorry, dude. Gimme fifteen, I'll hit the floor now. It must be the jetlag. I should have stayed up as I feel worse than shit now."

"Jetlag my ass! It was all that booze you whacked on the plane."

"Yeah yeah . . . Well, are you gonna stay on the phone all day?"

*   *   *

Tony slipped into his white short-sleeved cotton shirt and light beige slacks. Rose had made sure he had the correct attire for the South American climate, and as he slipped into his deck shoes, he smiled. *What would I do without you, Rose honey?*

Bill was sitting, sipping a beer on the wood of the Falklands Bar.

"Nice name! I'm sure the British would appreciate it. Set 'em, Joe, or should I say, Bill." Tony tried to break the ice.

"Christ, *you* took your time." Bill raised his hand to catch the barman's eye.

"Same again."

Tony took a sip of his beer then peered at the contents of the glass.

"Not bad, but not as good as a Bud, huh?" Bill didn't comment.

"I gave Rose a call. and she asked for you." Tony tried once again to lighten it up.

"That was nice of her," Bill answered dryly, only half interested. He had more on his mind than meets the eye.

"Come on, partner. What's your problem? So, *I* was late, *no big deal!"*

"It's that fucking wife of mine." Bill let loose, shaking his head in despair, like *"I give up"* sort of thing.

"So, what does *that* mean?" Tony knew that Bill was having marital problems, but it was no big deal. *But now?*

"Do *you really* want to know, Tony?" Bill asked depressingly.

"Bill, if you really need to get something off your chest"—Tony reassuringly touched Bill's shoulder—"then seriously, I'm willing to listen."

"All she does is fucking complain, and I tell you, Tony, it's wearing me thin. It's money this and money that. Like why don't I quit the force and start my own security business? Then there's the mortgage, and I dread going to your place because when I get home, I never hear the end of it. *Maaan . . . am I pissed off!"*

Tony was shocked at Bill's outburst. "Buddy, I didn't think it was so bad."

"I doesn't get any worse, I tell you." Bill drained the last of his beer and raised his hand again. "Same again."

"Si, senor. Let me get some fresh glasses."

"Take it easy, partner. We have all night," Tony interrupted, his booze binge on the flight still painfully fresh in his memory. "Bill, remember when Holden retires in two weeks' time, you have it in the bag. I told you that I've already spoken to Baker, and it's more or less a done deal. Lieutenant means more pay, and more to the point, Bill, *you deserve it.*"

"Yeah, *and more long hours.* I mean I don't know how to please this broad!"

The beers came up, and Bill almost half-emptied his schooner in one go, as if drinking was going out of fashion.

Tony grabbed Bill's arm. *"Easy, partner!* Looking down the bottom of an empty glass isn't going to solve anything. *And on an empty stomach . . .* Well, I don't have to tell *you.* I think we both need something in our stomachs." Tony signalled to the barman.

"Si, senor?" the tall slim grey-haired barman inquired. *"Eh?"*

"Eric, senor."

"Parla degli ingles?" Tony asked, throwing in his Italian . . . like well it's sort of near enough to Spanish.

The elderly barman laughed. "Si, senor. Of course, I speak English, but only piccolo Italian." Eric laughed again, seeing the funny side. "Now how can I help you, senor?"

Bill, for a change, was laughing as well. "You Italians!" He shook his head.

"Eric, Argentinean beef is the best. Is that so?"

"But of course, senor!"

"Then can I order a steak sandwich, medium rare, with fries on the side?"

"Si . . . and?" He turned to Bill.

"Make that for two." Bill smiled.

"Your orders will be ready in about twenty minutes, seniors. Gracias." He scribbled the order on the pad then hailed the pretty waitress serving the tables."

"Eric?"

"Tome esta orden a la cocina ye el apuro." Eric handed her the slip of paper.

"Si. Gracias." She turned and gave a cheeky smile to the Americans before scurrying toward the kitchen.

"While we are waiting for our food, Tony, how do we play it tomorrow?"

"Bill, for the life of me, I don't how it's going to pan out. For a start, we need to get our firearms back from this crazy bastard at customs, and the way things are going, it would be cheaper to buy a couple of pieces here on the black market."

"What's your thoughts on Victor?" Bill was interested in Tony's opinion.

"Like, *can we trust him?*" Tony replied.

"Something like that."

"He's a bit of a dark horse, and I would like to think so, but when it comes to money, just who in this Godforsaken country *can you trust?*"

"Yeah, I get the feeling like we're the meat in the sandwich."

Tony laughed. "You got something there, partner. But this Menzel woman." Tony paused. "That was the name, wasn't it?"

"Something like that."

"She's like more important than the president. In my opinion, with all this shit going on, it looks like we'll be taking the backseat until all this has blown over." Tony paused again. "But I have an even bigger concern that we are going to be given the run around from immigration, that is unless we fork out some more pictures of Benjamin Franklin."

"Your orders, seniors." Eric placed the overladen plates in front of the detectives, complete with napkins and cutlery.

"*Wow!* This is some sandwich!" Bill commented, studying the Dagwood. "And I thought New Yorkers are gluttons!"

Tony had to laugh. "Whatever. I'm so hungry I could eat a horse. Bon appetite." Tony sank his steak knife into the crispy baguette. "*Hmmmm*, this steak just melts in your mouth." The barman was taking it all in.

"Eric." Tony drew his attention. "Barmen are a wealth of information.

"Si, senor?"

"This . . . eh, kidnapping of the daughter of some famous rich man—" Before Tony could finish, the barman interrupted.

"Senorita Menzel, the daughter of Salvador Menzel, one of the richest men in Argentina. It's a bad business, but in Argentina, well? But now I hear from the customers that she was with an Americana, and he unfortunately ended up with the same fate."

"You mean they were *both* kidnapped." Bill couldn't help himself.

"Yes, at least that's what the drums say. It seems they were enjoying dinner at the restaurant when the kidnappers struck." He smiled as he continued to polish the glasses.

Tony turned to Bill. "I wonder . . . Now *wouldn't that* be a coincidence?"

* * *

(Speaking in Spanish)

Carlos pushed the old lady to the max, weaving in and out of the midday traffic, the horns of irate drivers painting a colourful picture.

"Carlos, slow down for Christ's sake." Sergio made the sign of the cross.

"Forgive us, Lady of Lujan, for the deed we have done this day."

"I'm not repentant, Sergio. I hope these two lowlifes rot in hell."

"I said slow down! That cop directing traffic at the crossroads is already looking at us with suspicion."

"Sergio, you worry too much. We pulled it off, didn't we, and iced these two bastardos? And we're still in the clear. Gimme a high-five."

"You watch too many American movies. Now do as I say and slowdown and signal to hang a left at the intersection and put on your best smile."

The cop raised his hand to stop the oncoming cars then cleared the traffic coming from the right. It was a nail-biting few minutes before he finally signalled to continue.

Sergio gave a wave and a thank you smile as he turned left. The traffic cop was deadpan and uninterested, concentrating on the congestion, his carbon monoxide-filled lungs in the early stages of emphysema.

"Boy, that was fucking close!" Carlos breathed a sigh of relief as he slipped off the freeway onto the dirt roads of Villamisseria and the maze of shanty huts and shacks draped with a rainbow of tarpaulin covers.

* * *

"It looks like they are back, Mike." Mona recognized the familiar squeal of the worn breaks.

Then there was a loud bang on the door as Sergio impatiently waited for Lena to answer.

"Who is it?" Lena was a sack of nerves. With the two prisoners in the back, it didn't bear thinking.

"It's me, Sergio, *for Christ's sake!"*

* * *

Mona whispered to Mike; her voice muffled under the canvas hood. "Now I know that one of them is Sergio, and the woman's name is Lena. My guess is these people are a bunch of amateurs, and they will inevitably slip up."

"Mona, I wish I had your confidence. But in saying that, I've given it some thought, and our best bet is to work on the woman. She's the most vulnerable."

"Quiet, Mike. They're coming."

*   *   *

"Where the hell have you two been?" Lena screamed. "I've been worried out of my fucking mind, and I need to go buy some food. *I haven't even had breakfast yet.* Not that *you* would care!" Lena just couldn't wait to spend the stash hidden between her breasts. Bras are for the rich.

"For Christ's sake, is that all you think about, *woman?* Get out of my fucking sight and keep your mouth shut. *Comprender?*"

Lena shrugged her shoulders, ignoring Sergio's ranting. She was more interested in contacting Eva and heading to the nearest cantina.

"Good riddance." Sergio turned to Carlos as Lena slammed the door.

Carlos had already pulled the tab on a beer while sitting at the table.

"Gimme one as well." Sergio pointed.

Carlos slid the can across the table.

"So where do we go from here?" Carlos asked, slovenly wiping his mouth with the back of his hand.

"I say we let the cops take the heat from the Menzel Family, and we lie low for at least another day before we make contact with the ransom demand." "And just how do you intend to do that?" Carlos sneered.

"It's like this." Sergio pointed the cell phone lying on the table, but before he could explain, Carlos crashed in.

"And just what he fuck does that mean?"

"Dumbo, we use the woman's phone. That way, the police can't trace our calls."

Carlos kept quiet for a moment, the anger reflecting in his eyes at Sergio's belittling remark.

"Well?"

"Whatever you say, *Mr. Brains!*"

From the tone in Carlo's voice, Sergio got the message loud and clear. He would think twice the next time. When thieves fall out, there's no telling.

*   *   *

"What are they saying, Mona?" Mike could sense through her silence that she was concentrating on anything she could pick up.

"Now we have another name . . . Carlos. These guys are either stupid or dumb or both."

"Is that a good thing?" Mike half laughed.

"It could be, and it's a weakness we can exploit, but then again, being stupid and dumb is dangerous. Many kidnappings in Argentina end up with their victims in the morgue or their bodies never found. For the poor and uneducated, life is cheap."

"Thanks for the self-assurance." Mike gave a muffled laugh.

Mona's voice unexpectedly changed its tone.

"You know, Mike, I feel so sad that I got you into this mess."

"Mona don't be silly. I love your company and I felt we had something special, and maybe this is not the right time, but I confess I had even considered permanently staying in Argentina and finding work."

Mona didn't reply. She had also felt the same way, but now was not the time for Romeo and Juliet, and she changed the subject.

"On what I have picked up, these two mongrels only intend to contact my parents tomorrow."

Mike was disillusioned at Mona's diversion, but inwardly, he was more perturbed that his devious plan may now be down the toilet.

"Then I guess it's a waiting game," Mike answered dismally. "But do you think your father will meet their demands?"

"Mike, you live in New York. You've seen the movies. Once the ransom is paid, our lives are not worth a shot of Izarra Jaune."

"Izarra Jaune?"

Mona had to laugh. "I apologize, Mike. I inversely switch back to Spanish when I can't find the English words. Izarra Jaune is a cheap local hooch originally from the Basque district of Spain."

"I get the picture."

*   *   *

"I must say, Victor, that bank manager was pretty helpful," Tony commented as they sat in the dated Ford Falcon heading for the airport and the dreaded meeting with the famous comandante.

"Banco Argentine is the largest and most powerful." Victor seemed pleased, but deep down, his mind was on other things.

"Well, at least we are liquid again, but for how long, that's anyone's guess." Bill just couldn't miss the opportunity.

"Mike, when we meet with the comandante, let me do all the talking."

"Whatever you say, Victor. *And immigration?"*

"As they say in America . . . we'll cross that bridge when it comes."

"Let's hope it's not a 'bridge too far.'" As usual, Bill put his foot in his big mouth; but fortunately, Victor just frowned not, catching the bullet.

"Here we are, hombres, at the Minitro Pitarini Airport and please remember what I said." Victor was taking a shot at Hayden, *and who could blame him?*

The airport, as usual, was "organized chaos," with kids begging everywhere and taxi drivers tugging at passenger's bags in the arrival hall with the airport police conspicuous by their absence.

As the threesome pushed through the "bullfight," Mike turned to Victor.

"Is it *always* like this?" he asked.

"Ask a silly question." Victor just grinned as he knocked on the commandant's glass door

(Speaking in Spanish)

"Tome entrar" came the gruff response.

"Buenas dias, Comandante Alverez."

"Si," the fat man with the double chin acknowledged and pointed to the empty chairs, his piercing dark brown eyes sizing up the detectives. He slurped a mouthful of coffee from his stained mug then leaned back in his president's chair, his chin resting on his hand after placing the disgusting drinking utensil on his desk

"Victor, you look down today. It must be the Menzel kidnapping or is it the murder of Perez and Gomez?" Alverez gave an ugly grin.

"Whoever burned these two scums of the earth did Argentina a favor, but the Menzel kidnapping, now *that's* a headache! But, Comandante, if I dare to refresh your memory, I am here with the Americanos to collect their firearms."

"I'm not suffering from dementia, Lieutenant. Watch your tongue!" He leaned over and pressed the red button on his internal phone then lifted the receiver. Alverez mumbled a few words then returned the phone followed by another supercilious grin and the loud knock on the glass door.

"Tome entrar." The door opened, and a young customs officer appeared with a small cloth sack and placed it on the table.

"Gracias." Alverez waved his hand to disperse the young man. He undid the string and emptied the contents onto his desk.

"The detectives' pistolas and ammunition. Victor, as I mentioned yesterday, there is a further administration fee, and that is two hundred and fifty U.S. dollars for each firearm payable now. Convey this to you Americano friends. Gracias."

Victor turned to Mike and Bill and sort of shrugged his shoulders.

"I don't know if you read the body language and put two and two together that here nothing is for free, and only money talks." Victor embarrassingly shook his head. "You'll have to dig deep guys to cover the socalled administration costs to release your guns and ammunition?"

"Victor, cut to the chase and tell us what we have to pay." Mike being Italian could understand most of it, but he just needed confirmation of the hit.

"Five hundred covers it." Victor made a "what can I do" face.

Tony forked out the five hundred. "Do I get a receipt? I need it to justify our expenses."

"Take my advice, Tony, and just pay the money and get the hell out of here before Alverez ups the ante."

"What was that the Americano said?" Alverez had a nasty look on his face.

"He said thank you for your understanding and wishes you a good day." Victor turned to the detectives. "*Smile.*"

"Gracias." The five big ones went the same way as the others into Alverez's top pocket, and the fat man with the elephant waistline rose from his desk to escort his benefactors to the door.

Tony quickly looked at the serial numbers of the Browning semiautomatics. In the NYPD, you must memorize your firearm number much the same as the military. "2355. This is mine, Bill."

"Thanks, partner." Bill clipped the magazine home then slipped the Browning into his shoulder holster. "Now *I* feel dressed!"

"Gracias, senors." Alverez smiled, flashing his tobacco-stained teeth. "Buenas tardes."

As they left the customs office, Tony turned to Victor who anticipated what was coming.

"*Don't say it, Tony.* Remember, this is Argentina. It could have been worse. Now the next mountain is immigration."

"*I'm looking forward to that,*" Tony answered sarcastically.

CHAPTER 4

Terry could easily have laid her head on the sofa cushion and snoozed for a while, but time was not on her side. It had already turned six, and to be at Roosevelt Memorial on West 59 by seven thirty was a tall order, and she would have to get her skates on to beat the evening traffic and the after-office drink brigade.

She swung her feet to the floor then stretched her arms above her head and gave a big yawn.

"Why the hell do I get myself involved? I have to ask myself." She was speaking out loud. "Late or not late, I'm going to have *that* coffee."

Terry walked determinedly to the kitchen, switching on the TV as she passed; the six o'clock news on CNN was in its final throws.

"And now for the latest on the Laura Williams case, we have here Captain Ted Baker from NYPD Homicide. Captain Baker, first, thank you for your time. I know you are a busy man, but my question is and that of the public. Are the police any nearer to apprehending Laura Williams's assailant?"

Hudson looked uncomfortable for a few seconds before slowly responding, carefully choosing his words.

"We do have a suspect, but the information we have gathered on his whereabouts confirms that he has left the country. Two of our finest detectives have been assigned to the case, and we are receiving maximum cooperation from the overseas government concerned."

"Captain, can you please be more explicate?"

"No, that's as much information as I can give you at this point in time. I'm sure you appreciate the confidential nature of our investigation in order to arrest the perpetrator as soon as possible. I have no further comments. Thank you."

"It seems that the NYPD is no further forward in arresting the suspect. I hope the district attorney is listening. Now moving on to . . ."

Terry had already poured her coffee and was locked in on the newscaster's interview. Of course, she knew who the suspect was, but why wouldn't the police release the information to the public? She shrugged and finished the last sip of her caffeine.

"Now more importantly, *what shall I wear?*"

*   *   *

Terry dropped her dark blue fitted skirt to her ankles then undid her white sleeveless blouse, chucking it onto the bed. Neatness was not Terry's forte, especially when she was late for a date or was behind on a deadline. Standing in her black bra and panties, at twenty-eight, she still had a figure that Madonna would kill for. She rummaged through the walk-in and finally emerged with a pair of stonewashed and a white woollen polo neck. Even though summer was still on our doorstep, it was now becoming chilly in the evening. She squeezed into the Levi's and slipped the polo over her head then flicked her long blonde hair back over her shoulders and walked barefooted to challenge the full-length mirror. Terry stared at her refection for a few seconds, like "mirror, mirror on the wall." She pushed the sleeves of the polo neck up to her elbows, producing a rugged sexy casual look, then flicked her hair back once more and smiled.

"Not bad, Terry. Even though I say so myself!"

*   *   *

The drive to Roosevelt in the unforgiving New York traffic, as usual, was boring and laborious. Terry had no idea what the crisis was, but whatever, she had to be there for her friend. *Then there was Frank, and what will happen to their relationship when Laura moves in to convalesce?* Terry was deep in thought. *It could take months, but she had made a compassionate commitment, and there was no turning back.* She shook her head again then almost jumped out of her skin as an irate driver gave her the horn.

"Are you on a death wish, lady?" he screamed from his open window. *"Do me a favor and stay in your own fucking lane!"*

"Why that! *You fucking moron."* Terry let loose. *"Stevie Wonder is a better driver than you."*

The irate driver retaliated and gave Terry the bird.

"I hope your fucking dog dies." Terry retuned the fire. "Get a load of that guy. Can you imagine? What the hell is this world coming to?" She was still cursing under her breath. But within minutes, she had settled down, and Frank was once again back on the agenda; his handsome physique was clouding her brain, and she began again where she had left off.

That guy . . . he is already under the assumption because we both admitted we love one another, which is easy under the sheets. I'm just moving too fast. Am I ready to give up my freedom? Not yet, that's for sure! I still have a lot of living to do before I hang up my dancing shoes. Then another thought crossed her mind. *Frank is twenty-five, and I'm twenty-eight. I know it's not a big difference, but then who wants a toy boy? So what? I have enough on my plate at the moment. Besides, the sex is out of this world!*

*   *   *

"Here already and in good time." Terry glanced at the dash clock, speaking to herself as she swung into the congested hospital car park.

"Hell, when I see all these cars, it's depressing to think there are so many poor souls with serious illnesses requiring surgery or worse still terminally ill." Terry shook her head again as she reversed into a vacant slot.

391

The two-minute walk to reception seemed longer than normal, and what lay ahead was anyone's guess.

"Hi, Terry." Martha, the sister manning the front desk, recognized her. "Just go straight up. You know the floor. The Williams have already arrived and are expecting you."

"Thanks, Martha." Terry gave her a warm smile.

"And how's that man of yours?"

"Eh . . . Frank?" Terry was playing it cool.

"There's no other." Martha gave a naughty smile.

"Awe, Frank is Frank," Terry answered awkwardly.

"Hang on to him, honey. He's a catch."

"I'll give him your regards, Martha." What else could she say?

It seems everyone is playing matchmaker, and where do I come in? Terry was less than impressed as she walked to the elevator.

The door to Laura's private ward was slightly ajar; and Terry could see the parents seated by her bedside, deep in conversation, Laura frantically scribbling on her pad.

Terry gently knocked on the door then popped her head around.

"Terry!" Margaret rose to her feet to greet her. "We're so glad you could make it."

Terry just smiled. She was more interested in Laura, whose face immediately burst into life, glowing like Ronald McDonald's nose at the sight of her best friend. Terry could just imagine the usual boring conversations that parents normally bring to the table. No wonder Laura was glad to see her, and she couldn't wait to hold Terry's hand.

"Honey, you look as beautiful as ever." Terry leaned over and gave Laura a kiss on the cheek and a warm hug before taking her seat. "In fact, I'm downright jealous." Terry laughed, teasing her.

Laura had to restrain her laughter, touching her throat, a painful reminder of her crushed larynx; and she smiled and eagerly grabbed her pen and pad.

The nurse helped with my makeup. After all, a girl has to look her best, but where's that handsome beau of yours?

"I'm glad to get rid of him for one night. *I'm only joking.* He finishes his shift a ten and couldn't make it, but he sends you his love and a get-well kiss."

I'll take him up on that. You're so lucky, Terry. He looks like a really nice guy.

Terry couldn't help but see Laura's brightness slightly fade.

"Hey! Why so morbid? You'll be out of here before you know it, and boy are we gonna have a blast, just like old times."

That comment seemed to cheer Laura, and once again, that warm glow ebbed into her smile.

"Of course, it could be some time before you do your karaoke thing," Terry teased her. "But with that tin ear of yours, it might be a blessing in disguise, huh?"

Terry was trying her best to make with the humour. So much for the parents, what with that look on their faces; one could be forgiven for thinking that they were waiting for the priest.

Just then, Nancy, the IC nurse, entered the room.

"Terry, it's so nice to see you again . . . *Mr. and Mrs. Williams* . . . Excuse me but this is temperature and blood pressure time." Nancy smiled. As for the humour?

The Williams gave a polite acknowledgment then remained silent.

Nancy wrapped the armband around Laura's bicep and pressed the start button on the Panasonic blood pressure machine. "Hmmm . . . Good . . . And your temperature is fine. Now just look straight ahead while I shine this light into your eyes. Good." Then Nancy lifted the bedsheet to expose Laura's feet. "Press hard against my hand. Now the other one. Good." She entered the data on her clipboard and hung it at the bottom of the bed. "I'll leave you for now. Dr. Nathan is on his rounds and will be here to see you in around five to ten minutes. Doesn't she look well, Mrs. Williams?"

"She certainly does." Margaret finally broke her silence, but as for the senator, once a politician, always a politician; and his mind is somewhere else.

* * *

There was a gentle knock on the door; and the distinguished-looking gentleman in a long white coat, stethoscope dangling, entered the private ward.

Most probably in his mid forties, tall and lean, his greying sideboards and shaded black hair gave him a sort of Peter Lawford look; and to say he was handsome, well . . . He flashed the bedside smile then turned to the Williams. "Mr. and Mrs. Williams," he acknowledged. "Dr. Paul Nathan. I'm glad you could make it, Senator. And I remember this young lady. Terry, if I'm correct?" Nathan smiled again.

Terry retuned the smile. *This guy was a dish, but then again maybe a bit on the old side.* But this was Terry.

Laura's smile abruptly disappeared; she didn't like the look of this. first her parents, then Terry. It had all the makings of a setup. *But why?*

"And how's my favourite patient?" Nathan turned again to Laura as he took the clipboard from the bed frame and glanced at the information.

"Everything looks good, I'm pleased to say. And if there's no unforeseen problems, then there's nothing to stop you from being discharged in about two weeks' time. Now how does that sound?"

Laura's expressions said it all. *It was like great news, but was that what all this was about?*

"Isn't that good, darling?" Margaret broke her silence.

Then Nathan's smile changed as he sat beside his favourite patient and held her hand, looking straight into her eyes with a sort of sad but reassuring look.

"Laura, it's time that I explain a few things now that you are strong enough. First, your body has gone through tremendous trauma and life-threatening surgery. Three broken ribs, a punctured lung, and a fractured larynx. But the good news is, physically, everything is healing beautifully, and the strapping around your waist will be removed next week. However, in saying that, your damaged larynx will take much longer to recover, possibly ten to twelve months and unfortunately you will be left with a rather husky voice." Nathan gave another reassuring smile. "Of course, Laura, you are well aware that sadly the foetus or in layman's terms, your unborn child, was aborted. It's the body's normal reaction to protect the mother and child. But regrettably, this led to other complications as the result of your severe beating, causing internal haemorrhaging that required immediate surgery. In saying that, nothing is clear-cut when it comes to surgery, and there were further complications. In short, to save your life, Laura, I had to remove your uterus and fallopian tubes." Nathan was trying desperately to find a soft landing. "Laura, believe me. It was a life-or-death situation, and I had no alternative, or you would have bled to death. I can't say how sorry I am, and the bad news is unfortunately you will never experience motherhood."

Laura burst into tears, sobbing uncontrollably, covering her eyes with the back of her hand.

For Laura, life would never be the same again.

* * *

"I'm home, darling. Where are you?" Terry could smell the food but no chef.

Frank's head popped up from behind the breakfast bar as he closed the oven door while wiping the sweat from his forehead with a paper towel.

"Honey, you're home earlier than I thought. When you called, I had just arrived. I'm sorry to disappoint you, mademoiselle." Frank bowed, placing his arm at his waist. "But dinner will be served in another thirty minutes." Terry tried to hide her laughter as she kicked off her sneakers.

"Yeah, the traffic was pretty obliging." She stifled her smile. "But more to the point *measure,* Reynolds, what has zee chef in store for the lovely mademoiselle tonight? *And I mean food!*"

Frank burst into laughter. "That's for dessert."

"Is that so? *Well, now* that depends on the main course. Now, Master Chef, whatever you're cooking, it smells good, so put me out of my misery." "It's Shepherd's pie, an old English recipe that my mother used to cook. It's pretty simple, and I hope I don't disappoint you."

"The proof is in the tasting, darling." Terry purposely left him guessing. "But aren't you going to give me the *I miss you, honey kiss?*"

Frank dropped the dishtowel and almost leaped from the breakfast bar; he didn't need a second "come on."

Terry stood on her toes in anticipation of the onslaught, and she wasn't disappointed as Frank wrapped his arms around her, almost crushing her ribs as he bruised her lips with a hungry kiss.

The kiss was penetrating and sensual as their tongues explored the warmth of their mouths. It was becoming too much, and Terry pressed her hands against Frank's chest, forcing them apart.

"Down, boy. Down, boy! Cool it, darling. We have all night. Why don't you do me a big favor and pour me a glass of that chilled sauvignon blanc you'll find in the refrigerator?"

Frank looked into Terry's eyes for a moment, like it's hard to stop a runaway train.

"I love you, honey."

"Frank . . . the wine!"

*　*　*

"Well, your mother must have been a good cook because this pie is delicious." Terry raised her glass. *"Cheers."*

"I'm glad you like it, honey." Frank had that "little boy pleased" look on his face. "But you have yet to tell me . . ." Frank almost choked, his mouth full, coughing to clear his windpipe. *"Excuse me! Eh* . . . How did your visit go with Laura and why the cloak-and-dagger stuff with the parents?"

"Your mother may have taught you the recipe for this pie, Frank, but she forgot to tell you never to speak with your mouth full," Terry scolded him, a cheeky grin on her face.

"Oh, is that so . . . And I'll treat that remark with the contempt it deserves." It was light barter, and the fun mode between the two lovers was full on.

"You still haven't answered my question!" Frank was determined.

Terry just smiled as she began to clear the empty plates.

"Let's keep it until after the coffee and perhaps another glass of wine . . . *or two . . . or three."* She laughed.

"At least let me give you a hand."

"This is woman's work. Besides, the chef doesn't clean up, but you can do me a big favor and place the percolator on the stove. The coffee's on the top shelf."

"For you, honey, *anything."*

"Heh . . . Heh . . ." Terry laughed, holding her sides. *"*Now *you have* got me worried."

*   *   *

"Frank, I just feel like relaxing. I've had a very unusual day to say the least and stressful with it." Terry searched the disc stacker. "Ah, here we are, my favourite CD." She slipped the disc into the player and pressed play. "I just love this guy . . . Enrique Iglesias. 'Let me be your hero.' And he's a looker with it." "That should be my line!" Frank interrupted, laughing.

The stereo burst into life, and Terry hit the karaoke.

"Would you dance if I asked you to dance? Would you run and never look back? Would you cry if you saw me crying?

Would you save my soul tonight?"

Terry grabbed Frank's hand. "Come on, big boy. Take your wine and come and join me on the sofa."

"I didn't know you could sing?"

"I can't." Terry laughed as she sat down heavily. "Now are you going to sit beside me or what?" She patted the soft leather cushion.

Frank didn't need a second offer, grabbing his wineglass and placing it on the coffee table.

"Now, isn't that more comfortable?" Terry swung her feet and placed her legs on Frank's lap, her head on the large cushion, still humming the music.

It was Frank's turn. *"I can be your hero, baby . . . I can kiss away the pain."*

"Listen to this guy!" Terry was amazed. "The next American Idol, huh?" But Frank had other thoughts on his mind.

"Can you massage my feet, darling?" Terry wiggled her toes. *"Mmmm, that feels nice."*

"And you're sexy." Frank couldn't help himself.

"Can you pass me my wine, darling?" The voice of the handsome Enrique had stopped, and Terry was purposely ignoring Frank's heavy weather.

"Thanks, darling." Terry took a sip and rested her head again.

"Now that lover boy Enrique has croaked." Frank was being critical of his mythical competitor. "Can you please tell me what happened tonight at the hospital?"

"Do you really want to know?"

"It would help, that is, not unless your double-dating?"

"Why, Frank Reynolds! You just take that back, *right now!"*

"I'm sorry, honey. I was only joking. Gimme a kiss." "Listen, do you want to hear about Laura or what?"

*   *   *

"My god, Terry! And how did she take it?"

"Like a lead balloon. That bastard Summers. *I hope he rots in hell . . .* Poor Laura. She doesn't deserve this."

Terry swung her feet to the floor and snuggled against Frank's chest, her arm around his neck, her cheeks now wet with tears.

"I feel so safe when I'm with you, darling."

"There . . . there, honey." He kissed her on the forehead. "Come now and wipe away these tears." He took the napkin from the side table.

"You look tired, honey. You've had a day of it, and I'm not going to ask you about the office. In fact, I think it's time we grab a shower and hit the cot. Don't you?" Terry just nodded and snuggled closer.

Frank slipped his arm below her legs. "Just keep your arm around my neck, and I'll carry you to the bedroom."

"Darling, what would I do without you?"

*   *   *

Frank gently placed Terry on top of the bed and sat beside her, her pale blue eyes reflecting her inner sadness, and he stroked her now unruly hair to one side.

"Relax, honey. I know that's easier said than done, but there's nothing you or I can do to change the world." Frank pressed his lips against Terry's soft moist mouth; the sensation of her return sent his testosterone off the scale, and he frantically searched below her white polo to release her bra.

Terry, in her state of mind, was powerless to resist his warm strong hands as he cupped her breasts, her nipples protruding like under-ripe cherries, firm to the touch but sweet to the lips.

It was too much, and Frank just had to taste the warmth of her breasts, and he lifted her sweater to expose the treasures that have been captured on canvass by countless artists.

"Wait, darling." Terry gently prized Frank back as she endeavored to sit up. "Let me take off my sweater and bra, but everything else is all yours . . . *Well?*"

Frank buried his head between Terry's firm breasts like a newborn baby searching for food. The gentle sucking of her nipples sent her crazy, and she gabbed Frank's shirt, almost tearing the buttons from their threads. There was no turning back, and their bodies were soon locked in the unadulterated nakedness of two people madly in love, searching for their ultimate fulfillment. The panting, the pushing, the breathlessness, the explosion, and the final *"I love you, honey"* was the ending to a perfect evening.

CHAPTER 5

June had a restless night, her sleep continually interrupted with flashes of her old flame and her forthcoming appointment this morning at his office. It was a godsend that they had met again after almost twenty years and just when she most needed a shoulder to cry on.

Breakfast over and the kids gone to college, she stacked the dishwasher and poured herself another coffee before retreating to the lounge to relax on the sofa. She was still in her housecoat, and at eight thirty, she still had plenty of time to shower and dress. The kids seemed to be coping well; but you never can tell, especially Steven, who is venomously nursing his hate for his father.

She sipped the warm brew, her mind reflecting back to her NYU days. She had taken a job between semesters at Burt & Stevens, a downtown law firm, to help subsidize her university fees and also gain on-the-job training as a practical insight to her law degree; and she could still remember her shock upon finding that Phil's father was one of the partners.

I often wonder what would have happened, she thought, if I had finished my law degree. It was my own silly fault, having given up on Phil and falling for that handsome Mike Summers who had just graduated with honours in commerce. He was suave, good looking, and from a wealthy upper-crust background, and the inevitable happened after the graduation prom, and I foolishly fell pregnant. Mike did the honourable thing, and we were married, but as a consequence, my NYU days went out the window. I was heartbroken after a gruelling and painful birth only to be informed the baby was stillborn. Both our parents supported me in my hour of need, but life goes on. Mike achieved a successful career and was a good provider, and I loved him dearly, and when the two children arrived, that was the icing on the cake.

She glanced at her cell phone. *My god, how time flies! Nine already. I had better make that phone call.*

"Thank you, Ethel. Please tell Mr. Stevens eleven thirty is fine."

June closed her phone and gave a big sigh. "That's one worry off my chest, and I think that calls for another coffee. Now the next problem is what should I wear?" She pondered, a cunning smile crossing her face.

* * *

June studied her face one last time in the sun visor mirror.

"Just a little more gloss on the lips, huh?" She hurriedly searched in her bag for the stick. *"Hmmmm,* that's much better." She rubbed her forefinger over the final coating. "And sexy too." She grinned as she turned the key, the series three bursting into life. "I love this baby, but unfortunately, I won't have you for much longer, honey. But as the French say, *'C'est la vie.'"*

The South Street Viaduct was the easiest route from East River, and with luck on her side at this time in the morning, it would be a free flow to the Wall Street turn off. For a change, she felt a glow of confidence and spring in her step, but how she played her hand depended on the cards.

It had just turned eleven twenty as she slipped off the freeway; she had cut it fine, but Pine Street was now only five minutes away.

"Christ, these bloody lights always seem to be against me, but then this is Wall Street." She gripped, while simultaneously breathing a sigh of relief as she signaled to take a right into Broad Street past Federal Hall then one more into Pine.

"So, I'll be about ten minutes late! *So what the heck?* It's good to keep a guy waiting." She smiled at the thought as she drove down the ramp into the underground car park of Carter Towers, a twenty-five-story building dwarfed in towering Manhattan.

Having worked here during her NYU days at Burt & Stevens, she knew the building well. The marbled reception hall still looked the same, bringing back fond memories. Of course, it had had a facelift with its fancy new reception desk and all, not to mention the handpicked young females with their beaming smiles, but for June, she didn't hang around. Being slightly late is one thing, *but overdoing it is another!* She knew the ropes and went straight to the elevator, avoiding the "sausage machine."

Now if my memory serves me right. She pressed 20.

*   *   *

The office had changed so much, looking like cubicles in a beehive, but I guess this is progress, or so they say! But what's happened to the friendliness? It's so cold and unappealing. June shrugged at the thought as she approached the young receptionist.

"Can I help you, ma'am?" For a change, the smile seemed genuine.

"I have an appointment with Mr. Stevens."

"And your name?"

"June Summers."

"If you can bear with me for one moment, Ms. Summers?" She picked up the phone. "Ethel, I have a . . ."

June quickly interrupted, a thought crossing her mind, "Excuse me but make that June Mathers."

The receptionist looked puzzled. "*Eh . . . Ah . . .* Ethel . . . A June Mathers . . ." She replaced the phone. "Mr. Stevens's secretary will be here in a few seconds to escort you to his office."

"Thank you . . . Eh?"

"Beatrice."

*   *   *

"Ethel, I do apologize. I underestimated the traffic."

"Don't worry, Ms. Mathers. You are only a few minutes late. Besides, Mr. Stevens has had a rather hectic morning. You can go straight in. He is free."

"Thank you, Ethel." June gave her a warm smile. Secretaries must be treated with respect as they are usually very protective and loyal to their bosses; and their opinion, although discretionary, carries more weight than often predicted.

*   *   *

"June, take a seat." Phil was all smiles. "*My,* you *are* looking well this morning."

"I think it was that enjoyable lunch yesterday that lifted my spirits."

Phil smiled. "That's a nice compliment, but the feeling is mutual."

"Phil, I must apologize for being late—"

He held up his hand. "Please, there's no need. Besides, I've had one of these mornings. A corporate client has a major legal problem, and it's like '*drop everything now,*' so to speak."

June laughed. "I can well remember."

The loud ring of the phone interrupted June's "lay it on" plan.

"Ethel, put Blakely through." Phil put his hand over the receiver and made a "what can I say" motion with his eyes." "Shall I leave?" June felt uncomfortable.

Phil put his finger to his lips and moved his head from side to side in a no gesture.

"Jack . . . Yeah, I'm getting Stan to go through the contract with a fine-tooth comb. How do I see it? From the facts you have provided, and I've no reason to disbelieve them, I think you are on solid ground to terminate ABM's contract with Global. I could understand Chuck's reaction, but not having his VP for marketing to back him up, he'll have to do the 'hard yard.' Jack, give me at least until two. Yeah, leave it with me. *Of course, I'll get back to you!"*

You could have knocked June over with a feather. *Was she hearing right? Chuck Briggs from Global! It could only be him, and the VP for marketing! It didn't bear thinking. I just can't believe it. But should I play ignorant or come clean?* June's mind was racing. There was only one way if she wanted to catch the spider in her web, and that was to . . .

"June . . ." Phil placed back the phone. "I'm sorry about that but getting back to your problem. I've had a word with Glen Jacobs, our litigation and divorce lawyer, and I arranged a meeting with him before you leave, and you will be relieved to hear, after explaining your predicament, he feels confident that to protect your property from foreclosure in the short term and the subsequent loss of your matrimonial home, he could legally apply for a caveat." June couldn't hide her disillusionment, and it didn't go unnoticed.

"June, have I said something wrong?"

"Phil, I'm sorry, but I couldn't help eavesdropping." Now Phil was disillusioned.

"I know Chuck Briggs. Listen, why don't I start from the beginning?"

Phil shook his head. "Now I believe lightning can strike twice in the same place . . . And the marketing VP, of course, is none other than your husband Mike Summers. *I'll be darned!* Talk about fate. But worse still, Laura Williams is an employee with ABM, reporting to Jack Blakely. *This is like an Agatha Christie!* June, what can I say?"

"It's not your fault, Phil. You have helped me enough already, but—"

Phil stopped her dead in the water. *"June,* it's not a conflict of interest, if that's what you are worrying about."

"Are you sure?"

CHAPTER 6

As they crashed through the mass of unruly bodies, manners were prominent by their absence, with taxi drivers shouting their fares and baggage kids tugging and pulling at the bemused tourist's luggage. It was everyman for themselves with the almighty dollar being king. The detectives now felt more relaxed, packing their forty-fives. Victor was leading the way, his uniform making not the slightest difference, a blatant reflection of the disrespect the locals show toward the police.

At last the battle of the fittest was almost over, and the larger-than-life sign in meter-size red letters loomed in the distance. It appears they don't do anything in half measures in Argentina when it comes to the government.

*"Seniors. "*Victor pointed. "Departmento Masculino De Immagracion." And within minutes, he was knocking on the door marked "CAPITAN VARGAS."

"Entre, por favor."

As a last shot, Victor turned to Tony and Bill. "Remember—"

But before he could finish, came the chorus *"Keep quiet and let you do all the talking."* The detectives were bursting at their sides.

Victor had to laugh as well while shaking his head.

"You Americans never take anything seriously."

(Speaking in Spanish)

"Good morning, Capitan Vargas. Capitan Juan Avalos sends you, his regards."

"He must be very busy at the moment,." Vargas replied in a sarcastic tone. "What's with the Menzel Kidnapping and the icing of drug scums Gomez and Perez? *I say good riddance!* Victor, do you think there is a connection?" Vargas was curious; it was the talk of the underworld.

"Who knows, but whoever burned these two lowlifes, I wouldn't wish to be in *their* shoes. They have double-crossed their own, and every hit man and his dog will be chasing the syndicate's reward, *'dead or alive.'"*

Vargas just grinned. "Si, maybe I should take up that challenge, huh? But why the Americanos?" He changed the subject, staring rudely at the detectives.

* * *

"So let me get this straight. You want me to authorize a computer search for this Americano fugitive, a"—he looked at his notes—"Senor Summers who arrived in Buenos Aires two days ago?"

"Yes, the commissioner himself, General Salvador Cerise, has given his approval," Victor replied.

"That may be so, Lieutenant, but may I remind you that the police have no jurisdiction over Immigration, but I am an understanding a man and I admire your boss." He gave an orny smile.

Bill turned to Tony. He didn't know what this joker was up to, but he could certainly read the body language. And no surprises here; *it spelled dollars!*

Vargas turned to the keyboard of the ancient-looking monitor and proceeded with his one finger typing.

"This will take only a few minutes." He grinned. "Of course, we don't have the fancy computers like the Americanos."

The screen continued to flicker, then Vargas hit the key.

"Ah, here we are! But, Lieutenant Medina, before I pass you this confidential information, there is an administration fee of three hundred U.S. dollars. It is normally five hundred, but as a special favor to your boss, I have reduced the cost."

Victor turned to Tony and Bill. "I'm sure you got the gist of *that* conversation."

Tony grinned. He already had the three big ones ready and handed them to Victor.

The Capitan smiled, another bonus for a hard day's work. He counted the greenbacks. *It must have been difficult since there are only three!* Then he nodded his approval before slipping the lettuce into his top pocket.

"It will take a few minutes to print the information." He touched the keypad, and the laser printer began to buzz, churning out a ream of paper. Vargas smiled, a job well done, then passed the printout to Victor.

Medina studied the contents for a few moments then nodded. The information was correct.

"Gracias, Capitan. Buenas Dias." Victor saluted then motioned for Tony and Bill to vamoose.

"Don't keep us in suspense, Victor. What's the lowdown?" Tony was showing his frustration as they squeezed through the masses in the arrival hall.

"Listen, why don't we have a coffee, and we can sit in comfort to discuss this and then jointly decide a course of action?" Victor folded the sheets of A4.

"It sits okay with me," Tony answered. "But where?" He shrugged his shoulders, staring at the sea of bodies.

"There is a cantina not far from here just off the freeway, a pit stop for truck drivers and travellers."

* * *

"Boy, am I glad to get in this car!" Tony commented as he sat in the backseat of the cruiser.

Victor woke up the half-sleeping driver. *"Corporal . . . Parade en la cantina freeway Av Leopoldo Lugones . . . Entiendes?"*

"Si, Teniente." His face flushed as he crunched the gear shift and prematurely released the clutch, kangarooing into the four-lane traffic. Tony and Bill cringed their eyes and made a grab for the overhead passenger grips.

Victor remained silent while still studying the printout, much to the annoyance of the NYPD boys.

There is something not right here, Tony thought to himself. *And why the cloak-and-dagger stuff?*

Then Victor, out of the blue while still digesting the information, glued his cell phone to his ear.

"Si tengo la informacion Lo esperara de las instrucciones de su, Capitan." He closed his phone, not uttering another word.

Bill whispered in Tony's ear, "Can you make out what he said?"

"He said something like, 'I have the information and will wait for your instructions, Captain.' Most Italians can speak Spanish, but I gotta be frank,

Bill, mine is pretty hairy."

"Well, it's better than mine, *that's for sure!* So what do you make of it?"

"I don't know, but there's one thing for certain. If we're gonna catch Summers, we gotta give Victor the slip."

"Yeah, I'm beginning to agree with you, Tony, but first let's see how it plays out. That's a tall order. Instead, maybe we should consider using this guy to our advantage."

"You could be right, Bill, but I still have a bad feeling."

"You are discussing the case . . . No?" Victor asked, suspicious at the low tone conversation out of ear's reach.

"Yeah, we were just planning our next step once we see the immigration report. I heard you calling your boss, and Bill and I are curious."

"You can speak Spanish, Tony?" Victor was surprised, feeling uncomfortable.

"I speak fluent Italian, Victor, but let's put it this way. I can just get by with my Spanish."

Tony was purposely sending a message.

Victor would be more careful in future, and he didn't reply, his mind now deep in thought.

The driver slipped off the freeway and drove into the congested car park of the rest stop and parked in the slot marked "POLICIA." "Come, gentlemen, I'll buy you that coffee."

*   *   *

"Yes, that's our man, all right." Tony studied the photocopy of Mike's passport. "And you say his address during his stay in Buenos Aires is given as the Sheraton Hotel?"

"Yes," Victor replied. "And only five minutes from where you are staying at the Marriott Plaza on Av. Florida."

"Now *isn't that* a coincidence?" Tony turned to Bill, giving him a sly wink. "Then if I may suggest, Victor, that's our first port of call?"

The lieutenant was less than enthusiastic at Tony's suggestion, but he was in a bind and how could he refuse?

"I'll instruct the driver, but first let me pay for this."

"Thanks, Victor. I owe you one." Tony rose from the table.

"Our friend didn't seem that excited, huh?" Bill commented as Victor was busy at the checkout.

Within minutes, they were back in the cruiser, screaming down Av. Leopoldo. Medina was giving the driver instructions.

"El cabo, el Hotel de Sheraton, V. San Martin y apura." "Si, Teniente."

*   *   *

Lolita, the receptionist, was more than nervous when she was approached by the police lieutenant and the two burly New Yorkers.

"Buenas despues del medioda, Capitan."

"Lolita, estos hombres son Americanos asi que por favor habla ingles."

"Si, Capitan. I apologize."

"And thank you, Lolita, for my promotion." Victor smiled. As for Lolita, the puzzled look on her face said it all.

"Now, Lolita, *calm down.*" Victor was playing the good cop. "I know it's against hotel security, but we need to question one of your guests."

"Si, Capitan." Victor just shook his head in an "I give up" gesture. "We want to interview an American, a Mr. Michael Summers."

"Ah yes, Mr. Summers of room 202. He checked in two days ago." Victor placed the photocopy of Mike's passport in front of her.

"Now think carefully, Lolita. Is this the same man?"

"Si, Capitan, but I have not seen him since yesterday, and he is not answering house calls."

Victor frowned. "Lolita, can you contact housekeeping now and check if his room has been disturbed."

"Si." She picked up the phone and pressed the button. "Lolita, impieza de reception romm dos cero dos tiene el Senor Summers. Veranos devuelven todavia . . ." "Si."

She placed back the phone and turned to Victor.

"Capitan, he has not slept in his room."

"Then can you remember the last time you saw him?"

"Si, yesterday evening, around eight, I think. He was picked up by Senorita Menzel's chauffer."

"Victor, isn't that the woman that was kidnapped?" Tony interrupted, the name ringing a bell.

"Unfortunately, yes, Tony."

Tony turned to look at Bill, shocked. *I don't believe this. This adds up, but now we have an even bigger headache!* he thought to himself.

"Victor, at the thought of being rude, *where do we go from here?* Worse still, by the sound of it, you have a double kidnapping on your hands and, more to the point, *a U.S. citizen!*"

* * *

"Would you like a coffee, June? I know *I* would!" Phil was trying to brighten the atmosphere.

"I you say so," June replied, still down; it was hard to grasp the circle of events.

Phil pressed the buzzer. "Ethel, can you do me a big favor and fetch a coffee for me and Ms. Mathers? Thanks, Ethel. You're a gem."

Within minutes, Ethel returned and placed the cups on Phil's desk.

"Is there anything else, Mr. Stevens?"

"No, Ethel, we're good. Thanks." She closed the door.

Phil took a sip of his then leaned back lazily in his swivel chair, a relaxed smile on his face.

"June, do you remember when you worked for my father? This pretty blonde undergraduate who was going to take the legal world by surprise?" That brought a smile to June's face.

"A trainee paralegal, if my memory serves me right. But I really enjoyed working for your father. He was a hard task master but had a heart of gold."

"Try telling that to my mother!" Phil laughed. "But I do miss him." He paused for a moment as if saying, "Thanks for the memories."

"I'm sorry, Phil, but I didn't—"

He raised his hand. "June, how were you to know? Sadly, he passed away almost six years ago to the month . . . My mother . . . she is still going strong at eighty-five, but she really misses her soul mate. Life can be so cruel."

"But whatever happened to Mr. Burt?" June's curiosity is killing the cat.

Phil smiled. "You mean old Peter? Now wasn't *he* a character! He took a position on the bench and decided to retire from the company and offered his share of the business to my father. Of course, when I graduated and took the Bar Exam, it was inevitable that I join the company, hence the name Stevens & Stevens. As for Peter, he's fully retired now and in his late eighties, but you would never know it. He comes in every so often and keeps everyone off their work then barges into my office for a coffee." Phil laughed. "But he's the salt of the earth, and I wouldn't have it any other way."

June was smiling at the thought. She could still see old Peter as if it were yesterday.

"Yes, I gotta admit he is a character and with an eye for the ladies."

"I missed that side of him, maybe for the better." Phil grinned. "But, June, getting back to your problems. The crucial question is financially how much lead time do you have before you are in serious trouble?"

"Approximately six months, Phil, which equates to Mike's severance pay, and I could probably stretch it a bit further by returning my leased BMW."

"Yes, that would be a sensible move to reserve your cash." Phil glanced at his watch. "June, I have a few urgent things to attend to, so if you don't mind, I'll phone Glen to check if he is free."

"No, not at all."

"Glen, I have June Summers with me, and I wondered if you are free . . . Good, I'll get Ethel to escort her to your office." He pressed the button. "Ethel . . ."

June rose to her feet, about to leave, feeling more than disappointed that Phil hadn't popped the question about this evening's dinner.

"Oh, June . . ." He tutted. "I almost forgot. Are you free for dinner this evening?"

*   *   *

The tall slim man with the receding hairline and the David Niven moustache offered his hand.

"Glen Jacobs . . . *Please.*" He pointed to the empty chair, his piercing brown eyes giving June a thorough going-over. "Mrs. Summers, would you like a coffee?"

"No, I'm good." June appeared slightly nervous; this was something different. *It's not every day you file for divorce, especially against a husband that has disappeared and is a fugitive from the law.*

"Then perhaps you can take your time and start from the beginning . . ."

*   *   *

Terry was back at her desk to "face the foe," so to speak. The meeting with Chuck Briggs, still fresh in her mind and even Frank's performance last night, couldn't eradicate "the clash of the gladiators." But now the onus was on her, and the only way to launch the BM2000 all over again was to wipe the slate clean. It would be messy but necessary.

The thick manila folder marked BM400/2000 was right next to her, and it looked frightening. Blakely had passed it to her the day before that eventful meeting, and she had intended to take it home and do the "red eye." But the best-intended plans are destined to go astray; what with Laura's predicament and "lover boy" Frank, it was a foregone conclusion. Her phone rang.

"Terry, can I see you for a moment before you settle down?"

"Sure, Jack, I'll be right there." Terry started to "walk the walk" to Blakely's office then suddenly did an about-face.

"I had better take this with me." She picked up the manila folder.

Blakely could see Terry approach through the glass partition and waved her to come straight in.

"Is it serious, Jack?"

"Yes and no. Grab a seat and let me explain. I haven't called Simpson yet, but I'm sure Briggs will be bleeding all over him by now. So, I got to get the jump on them both before the shit hits the fan, and, Terry, that's where you come in."

"So, what's the deal?" Terry didn't know what to expect, and with this guy, *anything goes.*

"I contacted our legal eagle early this morning and laid the case at his feet. He wants as much info as I can give him before he cuts Global loose. On the bright side, he says that our case is strong, but the chase is never over until it ends. His name is Phil Stevens of Stevens & Stevens. Here's his card and the address. Phil has agreed to see you at twelve, so take all the papers with you and call a cab. That will give you sufficient time to go through the slush bucket and note down the salient points for your meeting."

"Hell, Jack, you're not giving me much slack!"

"You can do it, Terry. You've got the 'right stuff,' that's why I promoted you."

* * *

"Stevens & Stevens, floor 20, and your name is?" the pretty receptionist inquired.

"Terry Johnson from ABM. I have an appointment with Mr. Stevens at noon. I'm slightly early."

She smiled again and pressed the button on the exchange. "Ethel, I have a . . ."

Terry stood patiently in the elevator, the folder under her arm.

Christ, what have I got myself into? she thought. *A couple of weeks ago, I was happy and carefree and not a care in the world and now this!*

The elevator chimed. *"Your floor, miss."* The young good-looking guy in the suit gestured.

Normally, Terry would have spotted this catch a mile away, but her mind was more absorbed with her forthcoming meeting.

"Oh, I'm sorry. For a moment there, I was just dreaming. Thank you." Terry laid on her special.

"I hope it was a good one." He smiled.

"That's a lady's privilege. You should try it sometime." Terry left the elevator, carrying a big smile with "Mr. Macho" wondering what the hell that was all about!

Terry informed the receptionist then waited patiently for Ethel to appear.

"Thanks, Mrs. Summers. I think we have covered everything, but I may have to contact your husband's ex-boss at Global Marketing . . . you know, for character references and so on during his time of employment. I'll see you to the elevator. Excuse me." He stopped in front of Terry who was blocking their passage.

"Eh, I'm sorry." Terry stepped aside dumbfounded. Was she hearing right? *Mrs. Summers . . . Global Marketing . . .* It could only be?'

"Ms. Johnson, I'm Ethel, Mr. Stevens's secretary. This way please."

* * *

The red light on the secretarial phone kept flashing.

"What the hell is it now?" Blakely disgustingly threw down his pen. *"Christ,* I'll never get this bloody three-year plan out on time. Yes, Rita?" He sighed.

"I have Mr. Simpson on the line, and he is in a ugly mood, demanding to speak to you immediately and downright rude with it!"

"Don't worry, Rita. I've been waiting for this call. Put him through."

"Ian, if it's the three-year plan, inform the chairman it will be completed on time for the budget meetings next Monday."

"Nice try, Jack, but you know what I'm phoning about, and this time, you've really crossed the line. It seems protocol is a word that's not in your fucking vocabulary."

"Ian, cut the shit and get to the point!"

"Watch your mouth, Jack, *or you'll be joining the unemployed.*"

"So lay it on the line. I'm getting bored listening to your threats. If you're gonna fire me, then do it now, but if I were you, I would think twice." *"You listen to me . . . you . . . you . . ."*

"Come on say it, Ian."

"I'm ordering you to get on that blower to Phil Stevens and instruct him to abort legal proceedings against Global Marketing, *and I mean right now!*"

"Ian, blowing your top doesn't scare me. You know that contract is way over budget and what have we got to show for it, and as for sales . . . *you don't want to know.* Think carefully. If it goes all the way to the top, there'll be a lot of people with blood on their hands, and the buck stops with the boss and you're 'numero uno' on the shit parade."

"Are *you* threatening me? *Why you jumped-up—*" Blakely cut him short.

"Ian, we all know why Briggs got that contract. Do you want me to spell it out? If I were you, to avoid collateral damage, I would sit back and let me do my job and you collect the glory?"

There was a deathly silence. The bullet had struck its target, and the phone went dead.

Blakely smiled. He had won this round, but Simpson is no pushover and he'll be back again for the second bout.

*   *   *

Rafa inconspicuously lifted the external phone and dialled nervously, his voice a mere whisper.

(Speaking in Spanish)

"Sergio?"

"Si?"

"Rafa here."

"Rafa, drop the phone now! Your landline can easily be traced through the hotel phone records. Take note of this new number and use your cell phone in future. Hang up and call me back."

"Si . . ." Before Rafa could continue, there was only the buzzing sound. He quickly opened his cell and began to redial as instructed, reading from his notepad. "0-6-1 . . ."

"Si, Sergio here?"

"Sergio, I'm reporting to tell you that we had a police lieutenant and two American detectives looking to interview one of our guests, a Mr. Mike Summers. This guy must be important, and from what I could put together, he is the Menzel woman's boyfriend."

"You're shitting me?" Sergio was taken aback.

"It's true, and maybe there is a reward on this guy's head, huh?"

"Gracias, Rafa. You did good, and it won't go unrewarded once we get the ransom money."

"Sergio, the word on the street is that Perez and Gomez were iced last night."

"Si, I heard that. Have you heard who might be the hit man?"

"I heard there were two, but that's as far as know."

"If you hear anything, call me again pronto. Gracias, Rafa."

*   *   *

It was as if the lieutenant was under fire as he digested Tony's comment. At all costs, he must get back to headquarters to report the bad news to Capitan Avalos.

"Gentlemen, I must apologize, but I urgently must get back to police headquarters to report to my superior, Capitan Avalos. This new development on the kidnapping is important as we now have the American's name, and we will have to officially notify your embassy. Will it be a problem if you return to your hotel by taxi?"

"No, not at all, Victor. You do what you have to do. You've been a great help," Tony replied, more relieved than sincere.

"The front desk will help you. I will call you later in the day. Your cell phone is activated?"

"Yes, I purchased a sim card at the hotel. *But wait a minute, you need my number. It's . . .*"

*   *   *

"It looks like someone up there likes us." Tony turned to Bill, a cunning smile on his face.

"So why the smile, Perino? What's in that head of yours?"

"Can't you see, Bill? We've gotten rid of Medina with not a shot fired."

"I get that part, but—"

"Bill, I'll explain to you in a minute, but first—" Tony walked to the front desk. "Lolita."

"Si, senor?"

"You speak excellent English."

"Senor, that is a prerequisite of the job."

"Do you like working in hospitality?" Bill remained mute as the puzzle was still in the first act.

"Si, I love it."

"But the hours must be long and disruptive to your private life."

"Not so much. We work eight-hour shifts unless there is absenteeism. For instance, Rafa and me finish tonight at six, so it's not all bad news, and besides, there are plenty of perks."

"Rafa."

"Si, senor?"

"Can you call us a cab? We are going to the Marriott Plaza."

"Certainly. I will immediately inform the concierge. Your cab should be here in no more than five minutes."

"Now would you mind?" Bill was losing it.

"Wait till we get back to hotel, and I'll explain it over that beer you're buying."

"Smart ass!"

CHAPTER 7

(Speaking in Spanish)

"Carlos, it's time we make our move." The two six-packs gone; Dutch courage prevailed. Sergio opened Mona's phone and dialled.

"Mona honey, at last! Where are you and are you all right?" It was Mona's mother's number that Sergio had dialled by mistake, his boozed mind alcohol clouded, and he quickly covered his mouth to muffle his voice.

"Listen bitch, I want to speak to the old man and don't get any smart ideas like calling the cops or you can kiss goodbye to that pretty daughter of yours. *Comprender?"*

"Who is it, Carla?" Salvador, Mona's father, had heard the commotion.

"I don't know who is on the phone, Sal, but they want to speak to you. It's about Mona." Carla's voice was on the verge of hysteria.

"Gimme that fucking phone." Salvador grabbed it from her hand, ignoring the state of his wife, in the process almost dropping it to the floor.

"Carla, get a grip of yourself!" This was Gaucho, not giving Sergio a chance to speak as he screamed down the phone.

"Now you listen to me, *you jumped-up piece of shit.* If you return my daughter with not hair on her head harmed, I will not press charges. *If you don't,* I will hunt you down like a rabid dog with a reward on your head, dead or alive. There will be no place on this earth that you can hide, and I will not rest until I see your miserable body hanging from the gallows."

"Why you!" Sergio took a step back and counted to five. There was no point in a slanging match. He had to remain cool and think smart.

"Old man, you watch your fucking tongue. You're in no position to threaten me. Now shut that big mouth of yours. *I'm* not one of your fucking lackeys."

"You fucking bastardo," Salvador screamed. He couldn't hold back, the veins on the side of his temple almost rupturing.

"Shut up, old man. Shut up! Or I'll drop the phone *now. Good!* Now you're being sensible. Now here's the deal and listen carefully. I have your daughter here, and she has not been harmed, and that will continue as long as you cooperate and don't contact the policia."

"How do I know that she is alive? I need proof of life."

"Old man, why don't you give that big mouth of yours a rest and let me fucking finish? That's better. Now the next time I phone, you can speak to your daughter, but everyone has a price, and that price is twelve million U.S. dollars."

"Are you fucking crazy?"

"Old man . . . old man . . . I'm tired of your shit . . ." The phone went dead.

Salvador stared at the phone as if it was human.

"Hello? Hello?" he screamed.

"Sal, *what's happened?"* Carla was now competing with Niagara. As for Sal, he was still stunned, having his own self to blame for having blown it. And now what?

He lifted the phone. "Si, General Manuel Cerise . . . Senor Menzel speaking. It's urgent."

*   *   *

"Two beers. Gracias."

"Si, senor." The young barman smiled and stopped polishing the glasses. At this time in the day, the action was still in first gear. Within minutes, the chilled receptacles filled with the local brew came sliding down the bar like something from the Clint Eastwood movie *A Fist Full of Dollars.*

"You're wasting your time, kid. You should have been in *Cocktail.*"

"Next time, senor."

Bill took a sip of the lager beer then turned to Tony.

"Since *I* am buying, would you mind explaining to me what's in that devious mind of yours?"

"Not devious, Bill, *smart!*" Tony gave a toothy grin before taking another sip of the "Argentinean special."

"When we were discussing the situation at the desk in the Sheraton with the beautiful Lolita, did you notice the clerk Rafa eating our every word?"

"No, I didn't, Tony."

"But get this. As soon as we decided to leave, he quickly grabbed the phone and dialled, and after speaking for only a few seconds, he sort of panicked then looked around and hung up. Then he phoned again, only his time using his cell phone, like someone leaned on him."

"Interesting, but I still don't get it."

"Bill, can't you see the kid was reporting in to someone, and my gut tells me it's the kidnappers."

"Tony, even if you are right, how can we prove it?"

"I purposely asked Lolita when her shift finishes."

Bill rudely interrupted and as usual wrongly putting two and two together. *"Christ, Tony,* you're not hitting on that young chick to get information!"

"Bill, you're always jumping the gun. For fuck's sake, let me finish! Now can I continue?" Hayden didn't answer.

"Her shift and that of Rafa, the desk clerk, finishes at six. Now I also purposely asked her if part of the job requirements for the front desk staff was that they must speak fluent English, and she confirmed it's a 'have.'"

"Why did you ask that?"

"Because when we speak to Rafa after he finishes his shift, I don't want a cock and bull story that he doesn't understand English."

"I get it, but just how do you intend to get Rafa to pour his heart out?" Tony had that crazy smile again that invariably spells trouble. "I'll tell you later, but first we must hire a car." *"Hire a car!"* Bill almost choked on his beer.

"*You heard me!* But only after you shout another round." Tony couldn't stop laughing.

*   *   *

"Mona, what was all that about?" Mike asked.

"I think they called my father, and if I heard correctly, they are demanding twelve million dollars for my release."

"You're shitting me?"

"No. My father, he can afford it, but I know him better than anyone, and he's as stubborn as a mule when it comes to money, and that's what scares the shit out of me. *Excuse my French.*"

Mike gave a muffled laugh. This woman has class.

"Any ideas?" Mike asked, changing the subject.

"I still feel the weak link in the chain are the wives. We gotta find a way to work on the women when these two apes are not around. Women tend to feel sorry for their own sex, and the way these mongrels treat them, I'm sure we can swing them on our side."

"Well, *you should know, Mona!*"

*   *   *

(Speaking in Spanish)

"So what the fuck do we do now?" Carlos was not impressed at the way his partner in crime had handled the ransom demand.

"Calm down, Carlos. We are in no hurry. The longer we take, the more desperate they'll become fearing for their daughter's safety, and that's when we get the payoff."

"I hope you're fucking right. That's all I can say!"

"You worry too much. We have come this far, haven't we?"

Carlos didn't answer, then something crossed *his* mind. "What about the Americano?"

"Good question! From being a worthless piece of shit, it now appears from Raffa's call that this hombre has a price on his head, and he could be worth selling."

"So, who's gonna buy?"

"The American government. They always look after their own. So, we give the embassy a discreet call."

"I don't like it, Sergio. We could be getting ourselves into even deeper shit. The last thing we need is the FBI breathing down our necks."

"Leave it to me. I know what I'm doing." Sergio was becoming irate at Carlos's continued whining.

"We need a toilet break," Mona screamed. It was the start of her psychological warfare.

Sergio turned to Carlos. *"What the fuck now?"*

* * *

It had just turned one thirty when Tony and Bill approached the front desk.

"I didn't think much of the beer, but that steak sandwich was something else."

"Well, they say Argentinean beef is the best." Tony smiled.

"How can I be of service, sir?"

Tony glanced at the young guy's nametag.

"Eh, Salva, two things. I need to rent a car, and can you check when the American Embassy closes today?"

"Si, senor. It will take a few minutes." He immediately dialled the business centre. "Marcia, a que hora carrer la embajada estadounidense?"

"Un momento, Salva. Se cierra a las cinco pm."

"It closes at 5:00 p.m., senor."

"Yeah, I got the message. And the rented car?"

"Give me one more moment, senor, but before I organize the car, for how long?"

"What do you think, Bill?"

"At least I'm good for something!" Bill was being sarcastic.

"Well?" Tony gave him that look.

"A week at least."

"It looks like you like this place, huh?"

"Get out of it, you Italian immigrant!" Tony let the remark go over his head. He knew Bill only too well.

"Salva, we need the car for at least seven days. Oh, and I need it today before four thirty."

"Si, senor." Salvo conveyed the message. "Marcia, los estadounidenses necesitan el carf o al menos uno semana y estar disponibles por cuarto trienta?"

"Tratare de llamanda nad que volvor en treinta minutos. Gracias."

"Marcia says she will try and call me back in around thirty minutes"

"Thanks, Salva, but we must leave like now. If . . . eh?"

"Marcia."

"If Marcia calls, ring me on my cell. Give me a piece of paper, and I'll jot down the number. Remember, Salva, it's very important."

"Si, senor."

Tony slipped the kid fifty pesos. Salva grinned. Tips like this don't come every day.

"Muchas gracias, senor."

"Now the next thing, Bill, is to get the concierge to call a cab."

"Where to, sir?"

"The American Embassy."

The concierge gave a blast on his whistle.

*   *   *

Although the traffic was congested, the cab driver made good time. Americans are always generous with the tips.

He counted the pesos then flashed his tobacco-stained teeth.

"Gracias, seniors." *Another two gullible Americans; it doesn't get any better.*

The U.S. Marine sentry in full-dress blues, complete with white gloves, blocked their paths at the heavily guarded embassy gate.

"I'm sorry, sir. You can't cross the line." He pointed to the ground. The two heavily armed sentries behind the two-meter wrought iron gate were not to be messed with.

"Sergeant, we have an appointment with the consulate general. We were supposed to meet with him this morning, but unfortunately, something urgent came up."

The marine sergeant showed no emotion. He had heard it all before.

"Identification please."

Tony and Bill, already short of time, quickly obeyed handing over their passports and IDs.

The stone-faced sergeant checked the documents thoroughly in complete silence before returning them. Then he abruptly turned around and walked smartly to the security phone. He spoke for a few moments then hung up, nodding to the sentries.

"The consulate general, Mr. Bradley Mason, will see you now. You must go through the normal security checks." The electric gates slowly opened.

"Boy, *was that guy* a laugher!" Bill remarked, commenting on the sergeant at arms.

Tony just grinned. He had more important things on his mind.

The security tunnel gone, and their weapons secured, they were soon in front of the CG's secretary.

"Mr. Mason will be with you in few minutes, gentlemen. Why don't you take a seat?" The pretty Latino flashed the "boys in blue" her special sexy smile.

Bill spoke to Tony in a whisper as they took to the comfortable leather chairs.

"Boy, these Argentinean broads are something else." Bill couldn't help himself.

"Down, boy, and don't speak so loud. I'm getting worried about you. You must be missing Judy."

"Yeah, *that'll be right!*"

The secretary smiled to herself. She either spoke good English or was a lip reader.

Her secretarial phone broke the silence. The looker listened for a second then smiled again before placing the phone back.

"Mr. Mason is free now." She pointed to the heavy wood-panelled door.

* * *

Mason looked the part: the expensive Italian dark blue suit, the red-and blue striped tie with pocket handkerchief to match, the well-groomed grey hair, lean face, and blue eyes. He was most likely in his late fifties. Young guys never get these plum jobs, but his smile was warm and businesslike as he greeted the two detectives.

* * *

"Take a seat, gentlemen. I wondered when you would make contact. Mr. Murray, your New York district attorney, phoned. I know Jake well. Whenever I'm in the Apple on business, we always make a point to meet over lunch. Although I'm not familiar with the case, he has explained to me your assignment."

Tony smiled. "At least that saves us going through the 'never-ending story.'"

"Not at all." Murray smiled.

"Listen, I forgot to introduce ourselves." Tony was apologetic.

"Don't worry. I have all your details complete with pictures in front of me. Technology is a wonderful thing." He smiled while glancing at the computer monitor.

Suddenly, Mason's phone rang. "Excuse me, gentlemen, while I take this call. Yes, Lola. *Hmmm.* What does security think? I see. Get an interpreter up here right away, and I'll take the call direct." Mason had that puzzled look.

Whoever was on the line was causing waves, *big time!*

"Shall we leave?" Tony asked.

"No, somehow I think you both will be interested in this call."

* * *

"The caller made it clear he wanted three million U.S. for Summers hide or he would be posted in bits to the embassy. He would call back in twenty-four hours with further instructions."

"Well, what do you make of that, detectives?" Mason was shaking his head. They had only just been discussing the missing fugitive.

"Mr. Mason?"

"Brad . . ."

"Eh, Brad, it's definitely authentic. Let me explain why. Our first port of call was with immigration and . . ."

"I see." Mason was resting his chin on his hand, his elbow on his desk, listening to the detective's progress on their investigation.

"Now isn't that phone call a coincidence. But what's your next lead?" Mason was intrigued.

"There was this . . ."

"Bill—" Tony cut Bill short. "That was a wild hunch, and I've given up on it already as a dead-end lead. Besides, Brad is busy, and we shouldn't take up much more of his time."

Bill gave Tony an ugly look, as if to say, *"What the hell was that all about?"* "Detectives, a word of advice. General Cerise and his side kicks, Avalos and Medina, are not to be trusted. Therefore, to be safe, any breakthrough you have, contact me first so that if anything does go wrong, I can protect you diplomatically as American citizens. *Oh!* One further and very important point. If by chance or necessity you discharge your firearms, even in self-defence, and as a result an Argentinean citizen is wounded or worse still dies, it is an extremely serious offense, especially for a foreigner, and I can't protect you from the heavy hand of the law. Corrupt or otherwise, you will both be locked up, and you don't want to know what prison is like here! The Bangkok Hilton is a holiday camp compared with the dreaded Caseros Prison. Of course, as usual, money will come into play for your release, and you know

419

what Uncle Sam thinks about paying 'under the table' kickbacks to corrupt government officials. A big *no-no!*"

Tony gave a "thanks for the memories" and nodded his understanding.

"Thanks again, Brad, and be assured that we will certainly take your advice. Don't worry. We can find our own way out."

*   *   *

The detectives collected their firearms then hailed a cab. It was just after four, and they still had plenty of time.

"Marriott Plaza Hotel . . . Av. Florida. Gracias."

As they drove through the afternoon traffic, Bill was still smarting from Tony's rudeness, cutting him short in front of the consulate general. *It was as if Tony was holding all the cards and the glory to go with it.* "Bill, I know you're pissed off at me, but let me explain." *"I'm waitin',"* Bill shot back angrily.

"When the kidnapper phoned and Mason asked for an interpreter, the guy that arrived seemed confused. Mason made eye contact, and the guy played out the part."

"Played out the part? What do you mean?"

"Get this. As the interpreter was translating the phone conversation, Mason was almost answering before he was finished. Which, if my hunch is right, Mason speaks fluent Spanish. And for some reason, he didn't want us to know and hence the charade. That's why I stopped you, Bill, from telling him about Rafa. Bill, I don't trust the guy. Like 'phone me first . . .' *My ass!"*

"Hmmm . . ." Bill was taking it all in. Then he laughed. "Who said Sherlock Holmes was dead.?"

*   *   *

(Speaking in Spanish)

Mason lifted the secretarial phone.

"Lola, have the detectives gone? Good. Get me General Cerise on the phone at police headquarters. Gracias."

"Si, General, I had a visit from the two detectives today. Si, they know something, but their keeping it off the radar. What do I suggest? Get your boy Medina to stick to them like glue, 24/7. I'm trusting you to keep your end of the bargain. Don't worry. *I* will . . ."

CHAPTER 8

"Mr. Stevens . . ."

"And you are?"

"Terry Johnson . . ."

"Please take a seat, Terry. Jack has told me a lot about you."

"All good, I hope?" Terry smiled and placed the thick folder on Phil's desk. "Do you mind? These papers are becoming rather heavy."

"No not at all." Phil smiled warmly. "A coffee?"

"Please." Terry smiled. "I promised myself that I would stay off the caffeine, but the way this morning is going, *bring it on!*"

Phil smiled as he lifted the secretarial phone. There was something about this young woman's raw humour that was vigorously refreshing and, of course, pretty into the bargain. "Ethel . . ."

Phil sat back. "So, tell me a bit about yourself. Jack *did* inform me that you have just been promoted to group marketing manager. Congratulations!"

"Thank you, and yes, but I must say not under the best of circumstances . . ."

"Thanks, Ethel. Just place them on my desk. Your coffee. Now you were saying?"

"It's a long-complicated saga, Phil. You don't want to know." Phil just smiled. He knew when to pull the rug.

Terry took a sip of the warm coffee. "I needed this."

Phil just smiled. "As a matter of interest, how do you get along with Jack?"

"How does anyone?" Terry grinned. "He is certainly a rough diamond and at times a wild card not frightened to call a spade a spade, but he is smart and knows the business, and I admire him for that."

Phil laughed. "I couldn't have described him better myself!" He opened the thick folder in front of him then moved his finger, tracing the salient points.

"Terry, I suggest we start by going through the progress payments in detail and the continued cost overruns and Chuck Briggs's monthly updates."

"I guess that's as good a place to start as any," Terry answered. She felt comfortable with Stevens. He was not the typical stuffy lawyer.

*   *   *

"Well, I guess that wraps it up, Terry. You've covered everything that I need. I'll get Ethel to make photocopies of the documents, and I will return them by courier to your office."

"How does it look, Phil?"

"On the surface, I would say it looks pretty positive, but I'm sure Briggs by now would have sought legal counsel, and there are always 'rabbits in the hat.' But don't worry. I have a few of my own. *My god,* that time already? How time flies." A typical derivative to hint "the party's over."

"Phil"—Terry was hesitant—"before I leave, there is something I must ask you." She just had to get it off her chest.

"If I can help"—Phil was intrigued—"*fire away!*"

"You see, when I was waiting at reception . . ."

"And Laura Williams is you best friend? *I see.* It certainly is a coincidence. Normally, I couldn't provide you with that kind of information, breaching the client's privacy, but since you have explained the heinous circumstances, yes, that *was* June Summers, but, Terry, that's as far as it goes."

"I understand, Phil. I suppose it was a shock to the system to meet her in the flesh. Actually, she's somewhat more than pretty. I don't know what she's ever seen in that bum, but as they say, 'beauty is in the eyes of the beholder.' Thanks again, Phil, for the coffee. I'm sure this will not be my last encounter with June Summers."

* * *

With June still fresh in his mind, Phil dialled her number. "I hope she has arrived home," he spoke to himself. "*Ah, June,* I wondered if you had arrived. Listen, I've been thinking, it seems a bit silly to drive two cars to dinner, so why don't I drop by and pick you up?"

* * *

At last Terry arrived at the office, another day almost gone and nothing to show for it. But more to point, "when the cat's away, the mice will play." She had hoped to kick the goals and lay out a work schedule for the new product line, but at this time of the day, it was a lost cause. Terry dumped her stuff on her desk and headed to Blakely's office to report on her meeting with Phil Stevens. He hadn't noticed Terry approach, his head down, preoccupied in a mound of paper, and was momentarily startled with the knock on his door.

"*Come in, Terry. Come in.*" He waved, pointing to the empty chair in front of his desk. "So how did it go?"

"It's hard to say, Jack, but Stevens seemed confident, and I suppose that's the bottom line."

"You know, I just had Simpson on the blower, sounding his strumpet and acting like a killjoy, threatening all sorts of repercussions and ordering me to immediately discontinue any legal action against Global or I would join the ranks of the unemployed."

"Jack . . . you're serious?" Terry was shocked. The last thing she wanted was her boss to be fired. *Hell, she had just taken up her new position only a couple of days ago!*

"Terry don't worry that pretty little head of yours. Simpson is full of it. If he has the balls to raise it with the president, his blood will be all over that contract. Naw, he's not that stupid. He's running scared. I know too much, like why Global was awarded the contract, even though they were the highest bidders. For sure I haven't heard the last of it, but I have a few trump cards still up my sleeves, and I'm not afraid to show my hand."

"I believe you, Jack, but I don't know how you can sleep at night!"

"You will, Terry, and *you'll* get used to it. This is just the beginning."

*   *   *

Tony paid the cab, both detectives glad to be back at their hotel.

"I wonder if Salva managed to get that rented car? I was hoping that broad from the business centre would phone, so it may be bad news," Tony commented as they walked to the front desk

"Well, we'll soon find out, partner. I see the kid is there." *But Bill was still in the dark as to why Tony wanted that car.*

"Ah, Senor Perino, I've been trying to call you." Salva was apologetic.

"Strange. I didn't receive the call." Tony frowned.

"It's a common problem here, senor, as the reception is poor. But I have good news. Marcia managed to get you a car. It was extremely difficult because of the International Trade Exhibition being held this week, with lots of foreigners in town."

"That adds up," Tony replied.

"But, senor, it is not a big limo like you have in the United States, so I apologize."

"That doesn't matter, kid. Now what else do you need?"

"Passport, driving license, and credit card. I will just be a minute as I need to photocopy your documents, and then you will be required to sign the contract and the insurance agreement."

Tony glanced at his watch. He was getting concerned about the time.

"Salva, just one more thing."

"Si, senor?"

"How long will it take me to drive to the Sheraton Hotel from here?"

"It's only around five kilometre's, at the worst around fifteen minutes, depending on the traffic."

Tony just nodded. He still had plenty of time; it had just turned five ten.

"Time for a beer?" Bill grinned.

"Get out of it, Hayden! You're just trying to get me on the bar tab. I'll meet you in the lobby in say . . . fifteen minutes. I need to wash up and a change of shirt. This place is really humid, and I suggest you do the same."

"Just what the hell does that mean?"

"You either change your shirt or use as stronger cologne. Cappice?"

"Smart ass. I suppose you want me to take a different elevator?"

"I thought you would never ask."

"Why you . . ."

Even Bill saw the funny side, and they both burst into laughter as they walked to the elevator, best of friends

"I don't know why I put up with your shit, Perino."

* * *

Bill was pacing the lobby when Tony finally arrived.

"You took your time. You said fifteen minutes. *Remember?"* He was anything but happy.

"I'm sorry, buddy, but I got stuck on the phone with Rose, and then the kids came on. *You know what it's like, Bill.* Come on, lighten up. Besides, I'm on the tab tonight." Tony was trying to cool it.

Bill just shook his head, like it's a lost cause. *"I fucking give up on you."*

* * *

It was now five thirty, and Tony needed that car like now! If his plan was going to work, timing was critical.

"Salva."

"Si, senor?"

"The car?" Tony was showing his impatience."

"It's parked at the entrance, senor. Here are the keys and a street map of the city. The registration is . . ."

"Thanks, Salva." Tony slipped the kid a fifty.

"Listen, you still haven't told me what I'm getting myself into." Bill was frustrated at the cloak-and-dagger stuff. "And if my hunch is right, it's probably another one of your crazy ideas and dare I say breaking the law."

"How did you guess?" Tony laughed. "Awe, come on, Bill. Calm down. I'll explain it to you on the way."

"And who's driving, or is that a stupid question?" Bill gave Tony that look.

"Have a guess?" Tony laughed and chucked him the keys.

"I might have known, Perino. I'm always the fucking fall guy!"

*   *   *

The concierge was occupied with some guests that had just arrived.

"Seniors, I will be with you once I attend to these guests." He spoke perfect English.

"Don't worry. Just point to the car." There was no time for formalities.

"That blue car over there, senor."

Bill turned to Tony. *"Is this guy for real?* A fucking clapped-out Volkswagen rust bucket that they captured in World War II? *Even Hitler would disown that heap!"*

"Fucking hell!" Tony was also lost for words, then he laughed. "Well, at least we won't get a speeding ticket, huh?"

"It's all right for you. *I'm the one driving this piece of shit!"*

Bill unlocked the bug, still muttering obscenities, the concierge and bellhops standing at the hotel entrance, patiently waiting for the "big show." *"A fucking shift stick!* I haven't driven one of these since I was in college."

Bill was still complaining as he crushed into the driver's seat, trying to unfold his legs. As for Tony, he was almost choking, trying to hide his slaughter.

"I don't think it's fucking funny," Bill growled as he turned the key. It was now or never. The rear engine chugged a couple of turns then gave two repeated misfires resembling an M1 carbine before finally bursting into life, rattling like a bag of old nails.

"What have I done to deserve this?" Bill shook his head as he stomped the clutch to the floor then crunched the stick into first gear, almost stripping the transmission before bouncing down the hotel driveway to the hilarity of the hotel staff.

"Come on, you fucking piece of shit, *make my day,"* Bill yelled.

"You're doing a good job, partner. Hang a left, and it's straight all the way to the Hilton."

"Thanks for the compliment, *and I don't think!"* Bill was still bitching.

"Bill, pull in over there just below these trees. Good."

He cut the engine that had a mind of its own running for a few more minutes before finally spluttering to a halt.

"This fucking thing!" Bill was becoming more and more pissed off.

"Here's the deal, partner." Tony glanced at the time. "In about five minutes, our friend Rafa, the front desk clerk, will be knocking off work. My educated guess is that he doesn't have any transport and will be legging it to the subway, which is about a mile down the road. I am banking that he will be alone. If not, then we'll have to abort the mission to another night. Now here's the plan. Bill, you take . . ."

"For Christ's sake, Tony, are you serious?"

"Bill, if ever there was a time to think outside the box, *it's now!*"

* * *

Terry stepped out of her office attire and walked naked to the shower. She needed to relax and what better than a warm spray tingling your body. The faucet turned on and the steam building up she wiped the vanity mirror with her hand and stared for a moment. A woman will always sacrifice herself if you give her the opportunity. It's her favorite form of self-indulgence, and Terry was no different. She flicked back her long blonde hair and for a moment studied her olive-shaped blue eyes, searching for the dreaded "crow's feet" and premature eye bags. Satisfied she half mooned her lips admiring, the whiteness of her teeth.

"I feel like a fugitive from the law of averages." She laughed, speaking to herself. *"What the hell!* Let me in that shower."

Her hair blow dried, she felt refreshed as she slipped into her track suit bottoms and NYU sweatshirt. Walking barefooted on the deep piled carpet felt good, and her first pit stop was the icebox and that chilled bottle of Bianca Napa Valley.

Frank would be home around ten thirty when he finished his shift, and Fettuccini Marinara was simple and only a thirty-minute cookout, so there was plenty of time. With more than two hours to spare, it was time to enjoy her own company and deliberate where she was going in life as before she knew it the big thirty would be on her doorstep.

She lay back on the comfortable leather sofa and lifted her legs while balancing her precious glass of chardonnay. The glass now half empty she leaned over and placed it on the coffee table her memory, reflecting back to her brief encounter with Judy Summers.

"I can just imagine what that woman is going through. A two-timing lowlife is bad enough, but what he did to Laura, I hope he rots in hell. Her life will never be the same, and where the hell is that bastard? He's probably lying on some beach, conning another gullible woman with his charms and sweet talk."

Terry gave a big sigh, the wineglass now empty. "Life is so unfair. But loneliness is a scourge, and I suppose I don't blame Laura after so many disastrous affairs. In fact, I'm getting kinda worried myself. I've nothing to sing a song about." Her mind now drifting back to Frank.

At the moment, things are good. Frank most definitely loved her and had hinted on a number of occasions that he wanted to "move in." "I'm just not ready for a trial marriage. Sex is one thing, and in small doses, it's great, but to live with a guy permanently . . . *That's something else!* Then I promised Laura she could come and bunk with me until she felt she had the confidence to return to her own apartment, and now how would Frank take it? This is the problem I always have when I throw myself at someone. *Hell, I'm* the pot calling the kettle black!"

It was becoming all too much, and she swung her feet to the floor, another chardonnay was more than tempting.

With the couch potato scene, chips and another glass of wine, and *Desperate Housewives* what could be better? But time was passing, and Frank would be bouncing in that door soon, full of energy and unused testosterone, which would lead to only one thing; and for a change, Terry was not looking forward to it. Maybe it was the wine; maybe it was her mood. Whatever! She felt lethargic and lacklustre, and cooking was the last thing on her mind.

"I'll give Pizza Hut a call just before Frank arrives. In fact, I'll ring him now."

*   *   *

"So, what's on the cards tonight, buddy?" Jack asked.

Frank grinned. He and his best friend Jack Brody were doing their rounds at the Westgate Shopping Mall. They had been in the Marine Corp together and all through Desert Storm, and it was more than a coincidence they had both ended up as security guards but having been in the military for three years it seemed the next best thing. They had often talked about forming their own security company, which was Frank's ultimate ambition, and what better partner than his mate, Jack Brody.

"Don't tell me it's that broad again? *Maaan* . . . She's got you by the shorts, buddy. It's like 'I dream of Jeanie' or should I say Terry?" Brody was pushing the line.

"Brody, you're something else! So what happened to the beautiful Kate?" Frank retaliated.

"Love 'em and leave 'em, that's my motto, dude."

"You mean she gave you a 'Dear John'?" Frank was on the defensive.

"We're not in the military now, buddy, but I look back and laugh at the 'Dear Johns' posted on the notice board when we were in Iraq. *Women . . .* You can never trust them. *'I'll wait for you . . .'"* Jack sang, impersonating a woman's high-pitched voice.

"Brody, you're wasting your time in the security business . . . You would make a top ventriloquist. Why don't you go get an audition for the next season of *America's got Talent?"*

"Smart ass! But seriously, Frank, what's the deal tonight? I'm meeting Bruce and Eddie at the Stetson to sink a few beers and some pool. *We miss you, man.* Give the broad a rain check."

Brody was getting to Frank, and he had to admit he was missing the "guy's night." Then he smiled to himself. Why not? It's not healthy to become domesticated at his age. Sure, the sex is great, but it's not everything. *Or is it?*

"So, what's with the joke?"

"Let's say 'the joke's on me.' So, what's the stakes?"

"Now you're talking . . . Ten- spot a game, that's if you are up to it?" Jack was laying it on.

"Just to show you . . . You mongrel . . ." Frank opened his cell phone, but before he could enter the number, his phone rang.

"Hi, honey. Would you believe it? I was just about to call you."

"Yeah, and cows can fly. Listen, I was thinking. About dinner tonight, I've had a shit of day, and I don't feel like cooking, so I thought." Frank didn't give Terry a chance to finish.

"I'll save you the apology, honey. I have decided to join the boys at the Stetson to shoot some pool so I won't be staying over tonight."

Terry was more than relieved, but she had to play the wounded heart.

"Okay, so I'm second best when it comes to your buddies, huh? And I was looking forward to a romantic evening over a home-cooked dinner and bottle of Frascati."

"Awe, honey. Come on. It's not often that I—" It was now Terry's turn to cut him short.

"Don't sin your soul. Give me a call tomorrow evening, *that's if you're free!"*

"But, honey—" The phone went dead. *"Women!"* Frank was shaking his head.

"Now you're getting the message, buddy. *What did I tell ya?*" "*So, when are we meeting the boys?*"

*   *   *

Terry couldn't control her laughter. She had read the script well.

"Now for another glass of that wine and tonight a bed all to myself . . ."

*   *   *

June was in another world. She had almost given up on Phil asking her to dinner tonight, and now he was even picking her up at home. Her meeting with Jacobs was encouraging in that although the bank held the title deeds to the property, he would apply to the court for a caveat injunction as the result of special circumstance, consequently placing the property in dispute of ownership although being in joint names. She still had some "meat on the bone" with Mike's severance pay, and she could probably hold out for at least six months provided she returned her precious "Beamer." But the cancellation of the lease car still entailed penalty costs, but that was another problem for another day. Tonight, she felt like Cinderella, *only without the glass slippers!*

Phil was picking her up at seven, and time was running away. She had been stuck in the traffic for the last hour on her way home, and as yet she still hadn't prepared the kid's dinner. The thought was no sooner in her mind than she heard the school bus squeal to a stop, and she could hear the students yelling and carrying on before the bus finally drove off. "See you tomorrow, Sheryl . . . Steven . . ."

"Hi, Mom." Steven gave his mother a big kiss on the cheek. "How did your day go?"

"Nothing is ever straightforward, Steven, but I'll tell you about it later."

"Hi, Mom." It was Sheryl. "Excuse me, but I'm going straight up to my room as I have some prep to do for tomorrow."

Steven just shook his head he knew his sister only too well.

"Just hang on a second, young lady. I want to ask you both something." June looked serious.

Sheryl and Steven looked to one another, not knowing what to expect. What with all the stuff that was going on, what now?

"It's like this. I have an appointment at seven, and I'm running late. Would you mind if I ordered you pizzas for dinner?"

A smile crossed their faces in part relief, and Sheryl couldn't help herself. *"Would we mind, Mom?* That's the best suggestion I've heard all week! Now for my order, a thin crust with . . ."

Sheryl having now disappeared upstairs, Steven held back to speak to his mother. Like most sons, he was protective and wondered what the mysterious seven o'clock appointment was all about.

"Mother, it's Phil Stevens, the lawyer, isn't it?"

The tone in Steven's voice was concerning, but it was only natural.

"As a matter of fact, it is, Steven, but don't worry. As I explained before, he is nothing more than a good friend. In fact, he is picking me up at seven, and you will get chance to meet him in person."

Steven didn't respond. Even though he hated his father, his mother going on a date, *and so soon,* was not a picture that enthused him.

"I'll get on the phone, Mother, and order the pizzas."

It was a polite snub, but June understood. It would take some time for the kids to understand that parents are no different from anyone else when it comes to loneliness.

"Thanks, Steven, but I must go shower and get changed. Here's a fifty that should cover it, but I might not be down before Domino's arrive." "Leave it to me, Mom. You go ahead. You don't have much time."

Steven crashed on the sofa and hit the remote. The pizzas' on their way. It was time to relax, and he had just begun watching his favourite program *Two and a Half Men* when the doorbell rang. He screwed up his face as he quickly swung his feet to the floor. *"It can't be the pizzas already!"*

He walked to the window and pulled the drapes aside; a black Cadillac Deville was parked in the driveway.

"Steven, answer the door. If that's Phil, apologize on my behalf and tell him I'll be down in about ten minutes," June shouted, having heard the chimes.

The tall handsome man was patiently waiting on the porch, a bunch of roses precariously held in his hand.

"And you must be Steven?" Phil greeted him with a warm handshake. "I'm Phil Stevens. I'm sure your mother has told you I'm an old friend from our NYU days?"

Steven was lost for words. Somehow, he had pictured Phil as much older. This guy was slim, tall, good-looking, and immaculately dressed in his Italian cut suit. *Well, I gotta to hand it to you, Mother. You got taste,* he thought.

"Eh, err, can I come in?" Phil smiled jokingly."

"Gosh, I'm sorry, Mr. Stevens. I apologize for being inhospitable. *Please . . . Please* come in. Mother will be down in a few minutes. *Eh,* would you wish to come through to the lounge?"

"Thanks, Steven." Phil took a seat in the armchair while Steven joined him sitting the sofa.

"Can I take these roses?" Steven could sense Phil's awkwardness, sitting holding a bunch of red roses like a young student on prom night.

"Thanks, Steven, but I'll hang on to them. I want to give your mother a pleasant surprise."

"Mr. Stevens, can I get you something?"

"Call me Phil. No, I'm good."

"Steven, have the pizzas arrived? I heard the doorbell . . ."

"Sorry to disappoint you, sis. This is Mr. Stevens. Err, I mean Phil. He's here to pick up Mum. This is my sister Sheryl."

"Nice to meet you, Sheryl. You look so much like your mother."

"Thanks, Mr. Stevens. Listen, I'll leave you two. My computer is open. I'm working on something for school tomorrow. Steven, give me a holler when these pizzas arrive. I'm starved." Sheryl disappeared up the stairs.

As she passed her mother's bedroom, she couldn't help herself and knocked on the door.

"Can I come in, Mother?"

"Yes, I'm decent."

Sheryl popped her head around. "Your date is waiting in the lounge, and I gotta say, Mother, *he's a dish!*"

"Is that so?" June had to smile. "I haven't put on my makeup yet, but how do I look?"

"You look absolutely stunning, but don't keep Mr. Handsome waiting too long or he might change his mind and stay and join us for the pizzas. Enjoy yourself, Mother. You can tell me all about it at breakfast."

"Your mother mentioned this is your final year at college?"

Steven seemed more relaxed now. In fact, he kinda admired this successful lawyer.

"Yes, and I can't wait. I've been offered a scholarship at Cornell." *"That's really something!* In what faculty?" Phil was really interested.

"Medicine," Steven replied with a touch of pride.

"That *is* fantastic! Your mother must be very proud."

"Did I hear someone mention my name?" June suddenly appeared.

Phil looked up and was taken aback; she looked absolutely stunning.

"June, what can I say? You look beautiful. I'm gonna be the envy of the restaurant this evening." Phil rose awkwardly to his feet feeling, a bit embarrassed; it had been a long time since he offered a beautiful woman a dozen red roses.

June flushed in front of Steven.

"Thank you, Phil. That's so sweet of you."

"Don't worry, Mother. I'll put them in a vase of water."

"Thanks, Steven." June passed her son the flowers. "Phil, I think we had better be on our way."

"It was nice meeting you, Steven, and give my regards to your sister." As Phil was about to open the front door, the doorbell chimed.

"This must be our pizzas," Steven interrupted.

"Pizzas for Summers?" the kid in the outrageous Domino uniform asked.

"Yes, that's correct." Steven was about to put his hand in his pocket when Phil stopped him.

"Please, this is my treat." He gave the kid two twenties. "I'm sure that will cover it. Keep the change."

"Thank *you,* sir." The kid was smiling all the way to his motorcycle.

"Phil, you shouldn't have," June protested, but inwardly, she felt good.

Phil is a real gentleman.

"Bye, Mr. Stevens. Have a nice evening, Mother. *Sis, the pizzas have arrived."*

CHAPTER 9

Tony checked his watch. "It has just turned five fifty. Remember what I said, the plan is to scare the crap out of him, *so keep your finger off that trigger!* I don't fancy spending the next twenty years in an Argentinean prison." *"Now you tell me!"* Bill loved to gripe.

"I kept the best to the last, partner." Tony almost choked.

"Cut the crap, Tony. *This is serious shit!"*

"Have I ever let you down?" Tony just had to keep it going.

"There's always a first time!" Bill hit back as he pulled the slider on the Browning sending a shell into the chamber then locked the safety before slipping the "piece" into his shoulder holster. "I'm all set."

"Now listen, when Rafa walks toward the subway, I'll be out of sight behind these palms." Tony pointed. "You stay at the wheel and slowly drive behind him, trying not to draw suspicion that he is being followed. *You know the rest."*

"Good luck, buddy." Bill slapped Tony on the shoulder. "I'll be there as your backup."

"How many times have I heard that one?" Tony joked.

"Have I ever let you down?" Bill was getting annoyed.

"Fuck you. "Tony couldn't stop laughing.

"Maaan, when are you ever serious?"

Tony hit the sidewalk, still laughing as he briskly walked to the planned rendezvous.

Darkness was falling, the perfect camouflage for the "heist." His adrenaline like Mount Everest, and Tony flicked a stick from the Marlboro pack and took a deep drag to calm his nerves.

"I'm trying to give up the cancer habit, but there are times . . ." He was arguing with himself as he stood impatiently out of sight while casing the street. Then suddenly he spotted Bill slowly driving the bug, a sure signal that Rafa was on his way, and he hastily stubbed his smoke and moved into position.

As for Rafa, he was too busy yakking on his cell phone to notice anything unusual, let alone the ugly sound from the clapped-out Volkswagen; and Tony used the opportunity to its fullest emerging from his cover to block Raffa's path.

"Buenas noches, Rafa. Remember me, the American detective you were so interested in at the hotel . . . Hagale comprende?"

Rafa went as pale as driven snow, quickly closing his phone and slipping it into his pocket as if he had something to hide.

"Phoning someone interesting like the kidnappers."

"Dispenseme pero hago no speaka ingles." Raffa's eyes were bulging like two quail eggs. He was scared, all right.

"Don't gimme that shit, Rafa. You speak perfect English."

Rafa froze for a moment; he knew the game was up. There was only one way to get out of this, and that was to do a runner, and Tony could sense it.

"Don't even think about it, kid." Bill pressed the nose of the semiautomatic hard into Rafa's ribs while Tony blocked his path and opened his jacket, flashing the grip of the holstered Browning.

"You got the message, kid? Now if you know what's good for you, you don't make a sound. *Comprende?"* Rafa nodded.

"That's more like it. Now slowly walk to that Volkswagen and get into the backseat. Easy does it." Bill grabbed Raffa's left arm just to make sure and thrust it behind his back in an arm lock. The kid winced in pain.

"Okay . . . Okay, I'll do what you want, but please don't hurt me."

"Suddenly, we can speak English. *Nice!"* Tony grabbed him by the neck of his shirt. *"Move it!"*

Bill frog marched the kid to the bug; he was taking no chances.

"In!" He forced Raffa's head down and pushed him into the backseat. Tony quickly jumped in beside him, pushing the muzzle of the pistol hard into Raffa's jugular.

"Close the door, Bill, and hit the gas."

*   *   *

(Speaking in Spanish)

Sergio turned at the sound of the door being unlocked; it could only be Lena returning.

"Sergio don't worry. It's only me and Eva." Lena's voice slightly slurred. It looked like the senoritas had had a blast at the cantina, and the two thousand pesos had taken a serious hit.

The two women entered unsteady on their feet, with Eva carrying a full canvas shopping bag filled with tortillas, beans, onions, corn, and tequila while Lena struggled with a slab of Quilmes.

"It's about fucking time." Sergio shot at Lena. "Now get us some food, *pronto!"*

Lena dumped the slab of beer on the rickety table, while Eva unpacked the canvas bag.

"You pair of ungrateful bastardos," Lena screamed. As for Eva, she was playing it dumb, the black eye she was sporting a remembrance trophy of the night before.

Carlos ripped open the slab and chucked Sergio a beer.

"Gracias, hombre." Sergio popped the tab and took an ugly mouthful, the froth running down his chin and neck, then turned to Carlos. "Get Eva to see what that woman is bitching about. If it's toilet time, the last thing I want to see is some whore having a piss."

"Eva, you heard Sergio. Put this over your head." He handed her the ski mask.

"Why me?" Eva protested.

"Because I fucking say so! Lena is doing the cooking, so move your ass or I'll lose my fucking patience."

In the boozed-up state Carlos was in, "discretion is the better part of valour," and Eva didn't relish going down that road again.

Lena was high and just ignored the two assholes as she lit the stove, pouring the beans onions and corn into the oiled pan, but not before she took a big swig of the tequila.

Carlos was getting impatient; things were going too slow and getting pissed wasn't the answer.

"Sergio, I'm getting nervous. We haven't been contacted by either the Menzel's or the American Consulate. They have the phone number, and by now, they will have worked out the phone belongs to Menzel's daughter."

"*Santa Maria!* Carlos, you're so fucking impatient. If we show our hand too fast, we will make stupid mistakes."

Carlos gave a grunt and a curse; he still wasn't happy. "Pass me another fucking beer."

* * *

"What the fuck do you want, bitch?" Eva was desperate to get this over with. She didn't want a bag of this kidnapping shit.

"Toilet break," Mona blasted. "Unless you want us pissing all over the floor? So, untie my fucking legs. Have you ever tried to piss with your legs closed? And I need to see, or I'll be missing that shithouse bucket."

Eva was both confused and scared, but it was either doing what she was told or getting the crap beat out of her, and she nervously began to untie their legs and remove the hoods. Mona and Mike winced at the light, having been in continual darkness for hours on end, but it was a relief to get the circulation going.

"Make it quick. I don't have all day." Eva was flaunting her authority.

"Here, grab my hand, Mona, till you stretch your muscles." Mike had already staggered to his feet and could sense that Mona was in trouble. "Thanks, Mike. I'll be all right, but I must ask you to do the gentlemanly." The toilet escapade over, it was time to work on Eva.

"Eva," Mona began.

"How do you know my name?" She panicked.

"We know all your names." Mona was purposely antagonizing her.

Eva was now scared shitless, and she showed it. *How could they possibly know her name?*

"Sit down on the floor *now!*" Eva screamed, quickly covering their faces; she was running scared and couldn't bear to look into their eyes.

"Keep your feet together, or so help me I'll be not be responsible." She nervously began to retie their legs with the electrical wire.

"You know you're going to be caught, don't you?"

"Shut up, bitch!" Eva was fumbling with the knot, her nerves getting the better of her.

"Eva, you know they are going to kill us once you get the ransom, *don't you?* Then it won't only be kidnapping. It will be murder, and even though you didn't pull the trigger, you'll be as guilty as the rest. And remember what I said when you hang from the gallows, kicking and screaming, struggling for air, your eyes bulging from their sockets as the noose eventually separates your spinal column, because make no mistake about it, Eva, you're going down." *"Shut your fucking mouth!"* Mona was really getting under her skin.

"But here's the deal, Eva. If you help us to escape, I'll make sure the police drop all charges, and on top of that, I promise you you'll be one million U.S.

dollars richer. Just think of it, Eva. You'll be rich and a hero into the bargain."

"I don't want to listen to any more of your shit." Eva turned and left, but Mona had gotten to her, and now it was just a waiting game.

"What did you say to her, Mona?" Mike asked.

"I offered her a deal to set us free and become an instant millionaire."

Mike laughed. "I like it but what do you think?"

"She's thinking about it, all right. It's just whether she has the guts or not, but I'm not writing her off just yet. There's an elephant in the room."

* * *

Lena had just finished cooking a typical peasant meal, and she placed the pan in the centre of the table with some wooden spoons and tortillas. *With this kind of food, who needs plates?*

"Well?" She stood brazenly both hands on her hips. "I thought you hombres said you are hungry."

"It's about fucking time. Carlos, pass me that tequila."

"You ungrateful bastardo. Who would sit beside you two? Eva and I will wait until you have stuffed your ugly faces. Besides, we've had some food at the cantina. Sergio, give me that bottle before you fucking finish it."

Sergio grunted before passing Lena the "fire water," and she grabbed the two cups and poured a generous two fingers.

"Come, Eva, join me in the corner and fetch a couple of beers. Let these two assholes enjoy each other's company. *They deserve one another!"* Carlos was stuffing his face with a half-eaten tortilla wrap.

"I don't know how you put up with that shit, Sergio. She must have something going for her. Maybe she's a terror in bed, huh?" He burst into laughter, spraying a shower of corn and half-eaten beans over Sergio.

"You fucking pig!" Sergio was on his feet, wiping the debris from his shirt and face.

"What did you call me?" Carlos jumped to his feet, both men grabbing their pistolas in a Mexican standoff.

"Cool it, you two. If you're going to kill one another, do me a favor and go outside. I've just cleaned this place" Lena as usual treads where angels fear.

Fortunately, her crazy comment was enough to break the ice, and the banditos couldn't help laughing, seeing the funny side. The drama over, Sergio passed Carlos another beer.

"Friends?"

"Si, friends," Carlos answered, touching their beer cans. For the moment, it seemed there *is* "honour among thieves" after all, but for how long?

Eva was whispering to Lena.

"You know what? That Menzel woman offered me a deal . . ."

"No shit. You say one million U.S. dollars. And she won't press charges? All she is asking is for you to screw up and forget to tie the cords then turn a blind eye."

"Don't tell me, Lena, you?" Eva was running scared.

"I gotta admit, Eva, it's a thought."

"Sergio let's give that kid at the Sheraton a call. What's his name?"

"Rafa."

"You said he called about the two American detectives sniffing around?"

*   *   *

"Bill, pull in under these trees. Now listen, kid. There're two ways we can do this. I have a hunch that you know the kidnappers and that in fact you phoned them at the hotel to tell them about the Americans. That number will be stored in your phone, including the time of the call. Now you either practice your karaoke or I turn you over to the police for the rubber hose treatment. Comprender?"

Before Rafa could answer, his cell phone rang.

"Now I wonder who that could be? *Answer it!* And don't do anything stupid or you'll be on crutches for the next six months. Savvy" Tony had his piece pressed hard against Raffa's kneecap, the hammer cocked.

Rafa got the message and hurriedly fished his phone from his inside pocket.

"One more thing, kid . . . Puedo hablar Espanol . . . I can speak Spanish." (Speaking in Spanish)

"Si, Sergio. The Americanos have gone. Yes, I think they know something as they have hired a car. No, the police have not been back, but if they do, I will phone you immediately. You have my word. Si, adios."

*   *   *

"Gimme that phone." Tony wrenched the phone from Raffa's hand. "Take note of this number, Bill . . . 503 . . . Now, Rafa, I can easily phone that number and inform this dude Sergio that you're singing like a canary, or you can tell me who the kidnappers are and where I can find them, and guess what? *You can make a thousand pesos and who's to know!"*

Rafa was no dummy. For one thing, he didn't trust Sergio as far as he could throw him, and as for Carlos, he would rob his own mother.

"Si, if I tell you, can I go free and I get the thousand pesos?"

"Kid, you sing the right song, and I'll make it two thousand pesos." Tony was playing the full hand.

"The two hombres are Sergio Garcia and Carlos Mendez. The word on the street is that they iced Marcos Perez and Francisco Gomez over a drug deal gone wrong."

Bill interrupted. "That must be the two dudes that Medina was raving about."

"Si, senor. Garcia and Mendez are two mean hombres always in trouble with the policia and have served hard time in the famous Caseros Maximum Security Prison where many criminals are incarcerated for life."

"Okay, kid, cut the history lesson and let's get down to business. Sergio and this guy Carlos, are they the kidnappers?"

Rafa looked scared; going the whole nine was something else.

"Answer me, you son of a bitch!" Tony was losing it, and all that was left now was the shock treatment.

"Eh . . . ah . . . si." Rafa finally blurted it out.

"And do they have this Menzel woman and the American?"

"Si, senor." Rafa now seemed more relaxed having gone to the confession box.

Tony turned to his partner in high hopes. *"Now we're getting someplace!"*

"Yeah, and not before time. But more to the point, *where?"*

"You heard him, kid. *Where?*"

"Somewhere in Villamisseria, the largest and most dangerous shantytown in Buenos Aires. I'm sorry, senor, but even I don't know where they live. I swear on the Bible."

"Somehow, kid, I believe you, but I need a knockdown on what these two dudes look like."

Rafa was getting flustered. The detectives were putting the hard word, and now he couldn't think straight.

"Rafa, take a deep breath and think hard." Tony tried to calm him.

"Carlos, is about my height, probably in his late forties, bushy greying hair, kinda round fat face with dimpled chin, overweight with a bit of a paunch."

"Anything else? Think hard, Rafa."

Rafa was quiet for a few seconds then smiled. *"Of course!* Now I remember.

He has a tattoo of the crucifixion on his left forearm." "Good boy. And Sergio?" Bill was taking notes.

"He is slightly taller than Carlos and is the brains rather than the brawn." "I get the picture. *Go on!*"

"He is quite thin and is easily recognizable with his long black hair combed back tightly in a pigtail. I think he and Carlos are the same age. As the story goes, they went to school together. Narrow face heavily lined with the sun, giving him a sort of leathery look. *Oh*, and he has a deep ugly scar about four centimetres long under his right eye. That's about all I can remember. *Now do I get my two thousand pesos?*"

Tony opened his wallet and counted the money; it was cheap at the price. "One more thing, Rafa." He held back the notes. "Wheels." *"Wheels?"*

"The car, *they must have a car!*"

"Si." It came to him. "It's Sergio's pride and joy."

"What is it?"

"I don't know much about American cars, but Sergio says it's a '52 Pontiac. Is that correct, senor?"

"If it is the famous '52 Pontiac Chieftain Coupe, that's one helluva antique car, and it's a collector's piece in the States," Bill interrupted.

"But this one does not look so good, senor. It has a mucho rusto."

"And the colour?"

"Green."

"Here, kid." Tony handed him the swag and opened the car door.

"Gracias, senor." Rafa smiled, much relieved and two thousand pesos richer.

"Kid, just one thing. If you're full of shit, we will be back, but the next time, it will be ugly."

June was feeling on top of the world. She couldn't recollect the last time she was taken to dinner by Mike, the memory now long gone. This was exciting and what better than dining with her old flame and handsome to boot.

Phil turned the key and reversed the Caddy down the drive; Steven and Sheryl were taking a sneaky peak from behind the drapes. "I like him, Steve. He's nice and really good looking."

"Yeah, I'm with *you,* sis, but it's just great to see Mother so happy. Come on, these pizzas are getting cold . . ."

June laughed. "Did you see the nosy parkers?"

"June, kids are kids, and you can't blame them. I mean with their mother being taken to dinner by a complete stranger."

"You're not a stranger to me, Phil." June warmly smiled.

"Yes, we go back a long ways. But tonight, let's not get morbid and just enjoy ourselves. June, in hindsight, we all make mistakes, but unfortunately, we can't turn the clock back. You know, June, I'm really looking forward to tonight. I can't remember the last time I took a beautiful woman to dinner."

June leaned over and gently touched Phil's hand. "That's so sweet."

"And I mean it! And that perfume . . . it's so feminine and enchanting, and it suits you to a T."

"I confess I spoiled myself today. I know I shouldn't have, but I couldn't resist. Chanel Number 5, do you like it?"

"Do I? It's you, June, and don't ever deprive yourself. You deserve better . . ."

*   *   *

The drive through downtown, although long and tedious, passed unnoticed with the lively conversation; June and Phil were reminiscing on their NYU days and the different characters that were their friends. And where are they now?

Phil finally signalled and turned into Manhattan Avenue.

"It's been a bit of a drive, June, but we'll be at the restaurant in another few minutes."

"I didn't notice." June smiled. "I was enjoying myself so much, just talking."

Phil signalled and pulled up in front of the famous Manhattan Grill.

"This *is* going to be an experience. What a lovely surprise. I've heard so much about this restaurant, and now it's hard to believe that I'm about to dine here."

The young car jockey was polite and attentive, assisting June from the car, and Phil handed the young man the keys to the Deville. To find parking on Manhattan Avenue is almost impossible.

"Good evening, sir, and I wish you an enjoyable evening. Welcome to the Manhattan Grill. Be assured, sir, I will take good care of your car." He took the keys and slipped into the driver's seat.

The young man's comment was a pleasant start to the start of evening, and Phil smiled, turning to June and taking her hand. "Shall we?"

*   *   *

The Manhattan Grill is located in Downtown Ocean Springs and is known coast-wide for its award-winning prime steaks and fresh Gulf seafood.

Locals and tourists alike gather for a relaxing cocktail at the famous Martini Bar to enjoy the romantic ambience of a dining room that feels like a chic New York bistro yet welcomes guests with traditional casual elegance.

Menu favourites include fried oysters and lump crab meat with the famous crab cakes made from the "catch of the day."

*   *   *

The doorman, dressed in a smart tuxedo complete with bow tie, was more than muscular in his obvious dual role. At around two hundred pounds and six one, he had all the credentials to maintain law and order, but his shaved polished head spoiled the image. It seems that bowling balls are all the fashion. *Maybe it's a macho thing. Who knows?*

"Good evening, sir. If I can trouble you to wait a second while I fetch the maître d'. I gather you have reservations?" "Yes," Phil replied.

The tuxedo athlete lifted the phone, and within seconds, the large glass and chrome-panelled doors opened.

"Good evening. Welcome to the Manhattan Grill. Please." The tall slim man with a matching tuxedo held the door before walking to the podium.

"Your name, sir?"

"Mr. Stevens, for 8:00 p.m."

"Ah, here we are." The maître d' placed his finger on the reservation list. "My name is Charles. I'm the maître d'. Would you wish to enjoy an aperitif at our famous Martini Bar?"

Phil turned to his date with an inquisitive smile.

"Would love to." June didn't wait for the question.

Charles snapped his finger to attract the inattentive waiter dressed in the traditional white shirt and black apron.

"Vince, escort Mr. and Mrs. Stevens to the Martini Bar. They have reservation for table 16.

"This way, please. I'm Vince, your waiter for this evening. Don't hesitate to call once you are ready to be seated."

Phil and June were both trying to control their laughter as they took the simulated glass barstools.

"Mr. and Mrs. Stevens, it could have been worse." Phil laughed. *"It could have been Mr. and Mrs. Smith!"* Phil was beyond himself."

"So, is this the matrimonial dinner? If it is, it's the shortest engagement I've ever known." June was also in stitches.

"But, June, listen, on a more serious note, don't you just love these barstools?"

The soft blue lighting's reflection from the glass bar made the chairs glow.

"And the bar, I've never seen anything like it," June interpolated.

The bar was virtually glowing from the hidden internal blue lighting reflecting through its glass-panelled front and the shelving supporting an array of coloured liquor bottles haloing a unique display of color reflecting up through the heavy glass bar top.

"Isn't this something?" Phil commented as the barman approached.

"What can I get you and the lady, sir?" the handsome Latino barman with the dashing smile asked. Somehow the dark suave hair, the olive skin, and brown eyes are a catalyst for a round of martinis, and how can one refuse?

"Well, after all, this *is* the famous Martini Bar!" Phil turned to June with an endearing smile. "What say you, lovely lady?"

"A twist poured through ice and a black olive."

"Not bad. That sounds good. Make that for two."

"Certainly, sir." The barman smiled as he opened the shaker. "Excellent choice."

"Cheers, June. Here's to a lovely dinner and, most important of all, to my lovely companion."

"That's so nice of you, Phil." They touched glasses.

*   *   *

"Vince." Phil raised his hand to attract the waiter.

"Yes, Mr. Stevens?"

"Can you escort us to our table please?"

"Certainly, sir. Please follow me. Your table is overlooking our large alfresco garden. I'm sure you will enjoy the scenery."

"Thank you, Vince. This *is* a nice table."

The waiter assisted June with her chair then unfolded the white starched napkin.

"I'll leave you with the menu, sir, and the wine list. Just call me when you are ready to order."

"Phil, this dining room is absolutely stunning, and I just adore the blue leather seats piped with some sort of lacquered wood."

"Yes, I think it's mahogany, and the deep blue carpet to match gives the place a conservative but yet modern ambience, and those pale blue walls with the multitude of pictures of the rich and the famous who over the years have patronized the grill certainly adds a touch of class."

"I agree, and yet it's so cosy."

"And how about the music?" Phil turned to look at the quartet located in the far corner in front of a small highly polished wooden dance floor.

The pianist, saxophonist, double bass player, and electric guitarist were chomping out "Blue Moon." Maybe it had something to do with the ambience. Whatever. They were good!

"It's an oldie but romantic," June answered with a hidden tone. "But the next challenge is what to order." She was scanning the menu.

Phil signalled to Vince. "Sir?"

"We are ready to order. June?"

"I'll stick with the seafood, peppered calamari for entree, and for the main course, I'll have the lump crab with a simple side salad."

"Certainly, madam, and for you, sir?"

"I'll have the salt and pepper fish to start and the medium to rare rib eye." "Wine, sir?"

"Vince, why don't I just trust your judgment? I'm never good at selecting wines. My suggestion . . . to accompany the seafood, a nicely chilled sauvignon blanc and for me a full-bodied Cab Sav." "I have just the wines in mind, sir."

* * *

"And do you remember that Bill Shorten?"

"*Do I?*" June answered. "He was a real crazy, always chasing the girls." June laughed, reflecting back to when the "gang" used to meet at the tavern and crash the jukebox.

"You know he married Susan Taylor, don't you?"

"Naw, I don't believe it!"

"And guess what? He ended up in the military."

"What a waste. He was really talented."

"How was the food, sir?" Vince interrupted while clearing the table.

"Compliments to the chef," Phil replied. "The food was just excellent."

"I'll pass your comments, sir. Coffee?"

"I think we will take a breather, Vince. Besides, I want to trip the light fantastic with my beautiful partner."

Vince smiled. He knew where Phil was coming from. And who could blame him?

"Take your time, sir." He smiled as he precariously balanced the plates and cutlery after clearing the table.

"Now listen, Phil Stevens. You're not going to drag me onto that dance floor, are you?"

"Not unless you want me to ask someone else?" Phil teased, a glint in his eyes. "And listen to that music, a beautiful slow foxtrot perfect for two oldies."

"Speak for yourself, *Mister.*" June laughed. She was really enjoying herself.

"See the pyramids along the Nile . . . Watch the sunrise on a tropic isle." The quartet were excelling themselves with the revived hit by the Canadian artist, Ann Murray.

"I just love this one." June hummed to the music.

"Who's the oldie now?" Phil laughed.

"Touché. Okay, you win. Now aren't you going to ask me?"

"Can I have the pleasure of this dance, madam?" Phil grinned as he rose to his feet and held June's hand.

"I'll think about it." June was laughing.

"Why you!" Phil pulled June to her feet. "Come on, Jeanette McDonald."

"So, you think you're Fred Astaire, huh?"

"You'll soon find out."

The happy couple couldn't stop laughing as they took to the dance floor.

"Not bad!" June commented as Phil strutted his steps, pulling June closer and closer, her cheek now pressing against his.

Phil hummed the tune then sang in her ear the title to the famous lyric.

"Just remember, darling, all the while . . . You belong to me . . ."

June couldn't help herself and squeezed closer, with Phil reciprocating in a more than zealous manner. The quartet finally wrapped it up to the applause from the remaining dinners.

Phil looked down into June's eyes as the music stopped.

"I wish that was true, June."

"Eh . . . err . . . the coffee . . ."

*   *   *

"I've had a wonderful evening, June. I hope the feeling is mutual."

"Phil, what can I say? Married life with growing kids . . . I had forgotten what it feels like to be appreciated, and tonight you have shown me that life is all about living. Thank you, Phil, for the lovely evening."

"Can I entice you to do it again?"

"Just try me!" June answered, looking into his eyes, and Phil reached over and gently squeezed her hand. The body language was saying it all.

"June, at the thought of dulling an enjoyable evening, getting back to your problem, I spoke to Glen Jacobs after your meeting, and he stresses that filing for divorce will be difficult with the absence of Mike. But there are a number of avenues you can pursue. The first is desertion, and the second is mental cruelty, and the third is infidelity. Jacobs recommends that you go for all three."

"More coffee, sir?" Vince was more than attentive. He had to make a killing tonight.

"Yes, Vince, another double short black for me."

"And the madam?"

"No, I'm good, Vince. Thank you. One more coffee and I won't be able to sleep tonight. Phil, you were saying?"

"The difficulty is serving divorce papers when we can't find your husband, but we could exploit the extenuating circumstances of the criminal investigation and consequentially a fugitive from the law."

June pondered for a few seconds. "It makes sense, Phil, and the quicker I file for divorce, the quicker I get rid of this adulterous cheater and attempted murderer."

"I know how you must feel, June." Phil held her hand again.

"But what worries me, Phil, is the legal fees."

"Let's not worry about that for now. We'll cross that bridge when it comes But I have a proposition I want you to consider."

June's heart missed a beat. *Naw, it couldn't be?*

"You worked for my father as a paralegal to assist with your law degree, and as far as I recollect, according to him, you had exceptional potential. Unfortunately, you never fished your degree due to extenuating circumstance.

Now here's the deal. I would like to offer you the same position, only fulltime. The salary is not that special at around 40k, but here's the scoop. It's on the condition that you to go back to 'UNI' and finish your degree. Of course, Stevens & Stevens will meet all expenses."

June sat for a moment, lost for words. *Where had this man been all her life?*

Tears began to ebb as her emotions captivated, and she quickly wiped them with her fingers, endeavouring not to run her mascara. Now totally embarrassed and fortunately, Phil, like a true gentleman, came to the rescue, removing his handkerchief from his jacket pocket.

"Please."

"Thanks, Phil. I don't know what came over me. It's just that you are . . ."

"June, please, I really want to do this. Listen, let's change the subject. How about another dance?"

"Are you serious?"

*   *   *

"Hi, guys, gimme five." Frank disrupted their conversation. "Well, lookee here, Bruce. Can you remember this guy?"

"What's his name, Jack?" Eddie was clowning as usual.

"Eh, what's your name again?"

"Cool it, Jack. It's my shout." Frank raised his hand to attract the cute blonde with the Pamela Anderson's and the micro-Levi shorts wearing the Roy Rodger head gear. *All this babe needed was Trigger.*

"What can I do for you. big boy?" the peroxide blonde with the tomato lips and blue eyes asked, but then who would notice with that Hoover Dam cleavage?

"Buds all round, and whatever is your poison, honey."

"Thanks, big boy. I'll be back in five. My name is Jill. Don't go away." Jill hit Frank with the full frontal.

"It's looks like you scored there . . . *big boy."* Jack was impersonating the "blonde bombshell."

"Get out of it, you pervert. *Is anyone here still interested in a game of pool?"*

*   *   *

The Stetson is a popular pool joint off Spring Street in central Soho. The bar food is cheap and good, and the country and western music from the popular Dallas Cowboys was a crowd puller. Needless to say, the name attracted the New York cowboys who wouldn't know the difference between a horse's ass and its main. The Stetsons, checked shirts, high-heeled chisel toed boots, and stonewashed Levi's were the order of the day; but the cow gals stole the show with their poured-in jeans and miniskirts. *I mean who needs a horse with this muster!* Most nights, the place is jumping; and tonight, was no different, the long wooden bar, congested bar flies, and good time gals looking for another sucker to feed them free booze, then when the "heavies" start, cry foul, and move to the next "my wife doesn't understand me" cowhand. But all in all, it is the place to be; and Clarence Clearwater's revival, "The Midnight Special," was crowding the small dance floor with the shoe shufflers and cheek to cheek B-rated porn and *"will you still love me tomorrow?"*

*   *   *

"Table number 2. I took the trouble to reserve it for 8:00 p.m." Eddie pointed to the empty pool table; the balls already stacked.

"Your drinks, guys." Jill was doing a balancing act. "That'll be twenty-eight straight, including one tequila shooter." She gave Frank a cheeky wink.

"Keep the change, honey." Frank folded three tens.

"Guys, if you need anything else, just holler. *I'm talking about drinks!*" Jill turned as a customer had just hollered. "Coming."

"Cheers, guys. Now what's the stake? I say a ten spot a game." Frank was grinning.

"Listen to this guy, Jack. He's a burglar."

"Come on, guys, you overrate me." Frank lifted his cue. "Which end do I chalk?"

"Get out of it, you shyster!" Bruce was shaking his head. It was not the first time he has gone down for a fifty to Frank.

"Hi, Jack." The brunette with the "off the shoulder" sleeveless white blouse and super-shrunk Levis was giving Brody the "long lost boyfriend look."

"Maggie, you look great, and your friend?"

"We've met before, Jack. I remember the big boy here. Frank, isn't it?"

"You got that right, honey!" The peroxide blonde was a looker and with all the right credentials.

"I'm Teana, guys, and I'm looking for some dude to teach me how to play pool."

She leaned over the table as low she could, purposely holding the pool cue in an awkward pose. Her low-cut see-through blouse about to "shoot" a few buttons.

"We can't play pool with six, honey, but why don't I buy you two gals a drink then I can admire the scenery between shots?" Jack was a sucker for the chicks.

"Didn't I tell you, Teana, that these guys are cool?"

*　*　*

Maggie, well she looked like she was in her mid-twenties, but with her overzealous makeup, she was most likely a couple of years younger. Nevertheless, her brown olive eyes, almost matching the colour of her shoulder length hair, highlighted her pale smooth complexion and ruby lips. She had that certain smile when she flashed her whitened teeth, and you could say she was a dish that spelled serious caution. But as for her friend, Teana, she was a different kettle of fish. She was brassy with her short peroxide blonde hair and pale blue eyes and that contagious smile. The wet look lipstick and the low-cut blouse . . . like teaching her to hold a pool cue would a challenge for any red-blooded guy.

*　*　*

"Jill." Jack raised his arm. "Over here, Jill."

"What'll it be, guys?"

"Ladies?" Jack was laying on the charm and the "hey big spender." "Two tequila shooters with beer chasers." Maggie was first past the post.

"And one for yourself, Jill." Jack was playing the part.

"Sure thing, honey. I'll be back in five." Jill was shaking her head, a smile on her face as she walked to the bar to place the order. *"Guys . . ."* She shrugged.

The tequilas were hitting the spot, and the "pool girls" were cheering the guys on and where it was all gonna end was anyone's guess, but I'm sure the guys were not short of suggestions.

*　*　*

Terry had done her "couch potato" thing and was now getting rather bored. Maybe she should have convinced Frank to come to her apartment after all.

"I know." She had that cheeky smile. "I'll give him a surprise phone call and drop the hint. It's not good for a lady to show her hand . . . But . . ." Terry was trying to convince herself before taking the final plunge.

"What the hell!" She opened her cell.

Teana was wrapped around Frank like a wild tropical vine when his phone rang.

"Terry honey!" Frank exclaimed, more than surprised.

"Oh, it's Terry honey, huh?" Teana was impersonating Frank. "Listen, Terry or whoever you are," Teana bawled into the phone, "Frankie boy has his hands full with me at the moment, so do him a big favor and get lost."

"You crazy woman . . . Terry, let me explain . . . Terry, are you there? *Terry* . . .

"What's the matter, dude?" Jack could sense by the look on his buddy's face that all was not well.

"*A giant fucking screwup!* That was Terry on the phone."

"Awe, come on, man. Enjoy yourself. It's like old times." Brody was three sheets to the wind.

"Your friend is right, Frank. Gimme a dance, and I'll make it up to you." Frank sighed as he looked into the eyes of the beautiful sexy Teana. "Honey, that's an offer I can't refuse . . ."

*   *   *

"Why that two-timing son of a bitch. A guy's night out, huh? *Just wait till that no-good shows his face on my doorstep!* Still . . . better now than later!"

Terry was in hate mode, and you know what they say about a woman's anger.

*   *   *

The long drive home was so quiet you could have heard a pin drop.

"Have I said something to upset you, June?"

"No, to the contrary, Phil . . . It's just that I don't know where to start and what to say. I have to keep pinching myself. Like only yesterday from down in the dumps and feeling the whole world was against me, a 'knight in shining armour' suddenly appears out of nowhere." Her voice was breaking.

"Now *enough of that!* June, believe me, there's no greater reward than giving. I haven't done enough of it in my lifetime, and who better to start with than someone I genuinely have feelings for?"

"*Phil,* do you really mean that?"

He stretched his right hand over, searching for June's.

"June, you're like a breath of fresh air that's stormed into my life from nowhere, and I don't want to ever lose you." Phil squeezed her hand again.

"You say the sweetest things, but are you sure it's not just because you are feeling sorry for me?"

"You have my word, *honey.*"

"That sounds nice, *darling.*" They both began to laugh like a couple of young teenagers on their first date.

"*Ah,* here we are!" Phil swung the Caddy into June's driveway.

"My god, is it that time already?" June glanced at the digital clock. It read one twenty-five. "Phil, I would ask you in for a nightcap, but at this . . ."

"Shussss, honey. You don't have to explain. I understand. Besides, I'll make sure there will be other nights."

"Oh, is that so?" June was teasing him. "But Phil . . . *err,* I mean *darling,* I really must go or Steven, the new man of the house, will be rushing down to protect his mother from her amorous lover."

"I wish!" Phil was laughing at the thought.

"Darling, I really had the most wonderful evening." Then out of the blue, June leaned over and kissed him full on the lips. *"Phil, for the life of me, I don't know what came over me.* I don't know what you must—"

June didn't get a chance to finish as Phil crushed her lips.

It was both passionate and clumsy, but the feeling was exhilarating.

"Phil darling—"

Another long passionate kiss killed the messenger.

"June, I agree, I really must go."

It was getting hot and heavy, and Phil didn't want to spoil an enjoyable evening as he took a deep breath and looked into her eyes. "Now do you believe me. Come. I'll see you to the door."

"Phil, what can I say?"

"Just say you'll call me tomorrow."

Chapter 10

The general was in an ugly mood. President Carlos Menem himself was on the phone, concerned about the latest crime spree. The assassination of two drug lords was bad enough, but then there was the kidnapping of Monalita Menzel, the daughter of one of the wealthiest men in Argentina and, to add fuel to the fire, *an American citizen!* It was just too much for one day.

"Si . . . Si . . . Mr. Presidente." Cerise's ear was burning; he had already received a call from Salvador Menzel, and it was getting worse by the minute. "I am placing every man I have on the case 24/7. *Si,* you have my word, Mr. Presidente . . . I will call you as soon as . . ." The commissioner was rudely cut short. *"Bloody* bastardo!" Manuel stared at the phone for a second, holding it high above his head before smashing it down in its cradle. *"Ay yah!"* But as Manuel was about to scream, there was a knock on his door, and maybe just as well.

"Si, enter."

Cerise was still foaming at the mouth, and whoever was on the other side of that door had better be singing from the same hymn sheet. The growl from Cerise made Avalos and Medina turn and stare at one another as if to say, "So what's new?"

Manual stared in silence at the two unfortunates, his penetrating eyes full of fire and anger. *Menem may be the presidente, but I'm not his fucking lapdog!* He was cursing to himself.

The general pointed to the empty chairs, then, like a crazy man out of the blue, with one sweep of his arm, cleared his desk, sending papers and phones crashing to the floor.

"*That fucking* bastardo!" Cerise just had to release.

Medina made a feeble gesture and half rose to collect the debris.

"*Sit, Lieutenant!*" Cerise bawled. "Lola can clean up the mess. It will give her something useful to do for a change . . . *Well, are you both dumbstruck or what?*"

Captain Avalos held the senior rank, and for once, Victor was relieved. If someone's nuts were on the line, *at least it wasn't his!*

"Si, General, I came to report Lieutenant Medina's news that an American was also . . ."

"*Stop!*" Cerise sighed, raising his hand. "*Capitan* Avalos, for your information, *even the presidente knows that!* So, what other yesterday's news do you have? And I'm waiting to hear from *you*, Lieutenant!"

"I have nothing more to report, Generali," Victor nervously replied.

"I might have known." Cerise looked up to the ceiling, playing the drama out. "*Santa Maria*, what have I done to deserve this? I'm surrounded by a bunch of incompetents! Now, you listen to me, Capitan, *and listen good!* I just received a call from Mason, the U.S. consulate general and . . ."

Avalos rubbed his chin. "Three million U.S. for the American, and Mason has a hunch that the detectives are on to something?"

"You heard right, Capitan. And you had better start getting your act together or you'll will be back directing traffic on Avenida Corrientes . . . *Comprender?*"

"Si, General, I will instruct Lieutenant Medina to stick to the American detectives closer than his own shadow."

"*Out!*" Cerise screamed, flailing his arms "And I don't want to see your ugly faces again unless you have something worthwhile to report."

Avalos turned to Medina as they walked the corridor. "You had better come to my office, Lieutenant. We can discuss over a coffee what best to do next . . ."

*   *   *

"Victor, let's go back to when the detectives accompanied you to the Hilton." Juan took a sip of the local coffee. "*Shit!*" he spluttered, almost choking on the first mouthful. "We are famous for our coffee all over the world, *and I have to suffer this fucking poison!*" Avalos growled as he disposed of the remainder into the trash bucket.

Victor paused for second before answering the Capitan's question to let him calm down. *After all, what's the big deal about the coffee when "Rome is burning"?*

"Nothing unusual. As I recollect, the detectives spent most of their time questioning the female receptionist." Victor was searching his "browser" for even the slightest clue.

"*And?*" Avalos was becoming impatient.

"Lolita is her name, most likely around twenty to twenty-five . . . Really pretty . . ."

"*Santa Maria!*" Juan was at a loss, slamming his hand on the desk. "*Victor,* I'm not looking for extramarital. I'm looking for clues, *something, anything* that the detectives may have latched on to."

Avalos was running his fingers through his hair in sheer frustration, and his dumb lieutenant wasn't helping.

Suddenly, Victor broke loose. "But there was one thing I did notice . . . The senior detective . . . Perino . . . was paying attention to everything except what the receptionist was saying."

"*Hmmm* . . . And was there anyone else at the front desk during this time?"

"A young kid named Rafa."

The Capitan's interrogation was now making Victor think.

"And what was this Rafa doing during 'question time'?" Avalos was being sarcastic.

"He was on the phone."

"*And is that something that strikes you as being unusual?*"

"Not really, Capitan, but come to think of it, the kid suddenly hung up and then, for some reason, made another call, but this time from his cell phone."

"Now *that is* interesting! Maybe we should have a word with this Rafa after all. But first, call the detectives and find out what hell they have been up to. I know they have visited the American embassy, but that was this afternoon. My suggestion is that you meet with them first thing in the morning and don't let them out of your sight, and that means even joining them for a piss. You know . . ." Avalos paused. "I'm thinking that maybe *we should* pull this Rafa kid in for questioning. Anyhow, call me tomorrow first thing . . . Now I have work to do." It was a polite way of telling the lieutenant to get lost.

"Si, Capitan. Gracias . . ."

*   *   *

It was an easy ride back to the Marriott, being only ten minutes from the Hilton on San Martin. As Bill finally pulled into the hotel car park, he was more relieved than happy. Driving this "Made in Mexico" heap was a challenge that even "Shoemaker" would renege upon, and Bill groaned as he turned the wheel using both hands like a bus driver, finally parking the bug in the empty slot. The "original" power steering was something else!

"Boy, am I glad to park *this* baby!" Bill complained as he cut the engine, the preignition continuing for a few more seconds before Old Betsy finally surrendered.

Bill wiped the sweat beads from his brow with his handkerchief. "I guess in Hitler's time, air conditioning was only for the wealthy, huh?"

"Come on, Bill, let's leg it. You deserve a cold one." "Now you're talking *my language*, partner!"

*   *   *

"Good evening, signor's. I trust the car was acceptable?" Salva, a smile on his face greeted the two detectives as they approached the front desk to pick up their room keys. Maybe the kid was genuinely concerned or inwardly laughing his ass off or whatever; the Gaucho Bar was high on the agenda.

The young barman gave a warm smile as he approached the detectives. He just loved speaking to American guests as they were always friendly, and he could only but dream what it would be like to live in the United States. "Good evening, signor's. I trust you are guests of the hotel?" "Yes," Tony replied as he took his stool.

"I apologize, signor's, but I need your room numbers for security.

The detectives understood and placed their room keys on the bar top.

The kid took note, then checked the computer screen.

"Thank you, Signor Perino and Signor Hayden . . . My name is Arturo. In English, it means Arthur. Now what can I get you?"

"Two cold draughts, and don't hang around."

"*Eh, signor?*" Tony's remark had Arturo completely confused. Maybe it was some kind of beer chaser?

Tony laughed. "It means 'pronto.'"

"Ah, now I understand, signor." He laughed. "As we say in Spanish, '*muy rapidamente*,' which means 'I be very fast.'"

Tony suddenly felt the vibration of his cell, and he fished it from his inside pocket.

"*Fuck,* it's Victor! And would you believe it! I have four missed calls. This guy must be in heat." "So?" Bill asked.

"So, I'm just going to ignore him. Don't worry. If he's desperate, he'll send me an SMS . . . *Ah,* what did I tell you? *'Will pick you up at your hotel tomorrow morning at nine thirty. Lieutenant Medina'* . . . Boy, is *he* gonna be disappointed!" Tony laughed. "Salutey." He touched Bill's glass. "The first cut is the deepest."

"You got *that* right, partner." Bill raised his hand to attract Arturo. "Same again, kid . . ."

*   *   *

"What's on the cards for tomorrow?" Bill asked while enjoying his beer.

"Somehow . . .," Tony pondered. "We gotta track down these kidnappers, but then that may be easier said than done."

"We have their names, phone number, and a description of the car." Bill replied, then thought for a second. "But you're right, Tony. Finding them in that shanty town or whatever it's called would be like finding a needle in a haystack."

Tony had to laugh at Bill's remark. "Yeah, but I'm thinking, maybe the talkative kid behind the bar can help."

"It's your show, buddy." Bill drained the schooner and raised his hand. "Arturo . . .," Tony called.

"Si, signor?"

"Maybe you can help me. It's like this . . ." Tony reluctantly flashed his NYPD gold shield, and at the sight of the lacquered badge, Arturo's eyes almost popped out from his head . . . *Two real American detectives, just like you see in the movies!* He was all ears.

"Arturo, firstly I must have your word that you will tell no one, even your priest, what we are about to discuss."

"Si, signor, you have my word. I won't even tell my mother." Arturo was just loving the chase.

"It's like this kid," Tony began. "We need to question two slum dogs whom we believe are holed up in Villamisseria, some kind of shanty town here in Buenos Aires."

Arturo was visibly taken aback at the name Villamisseria. That place was trouble by any other name, and he shook his head, unsure of what was coming next, but the least he could was to tell it as he saw it.

"I have to warn you, detectives, as you say in America . . . This is a cowboy town. even the policia are scared to go there." "Sounds like the Bronx." Bill laughed.

"Thanks for the advice, Arturo, but most importantly, how do we get there?"

"You need a car, signor, as no taxi will ever take you to Villamisseria."

"Don't worry, we have wheels."

"Good, but you need a city map so I can explain."

Bill searched in his jacket pocket for the map that came with the rented car.

"Here we are, just what the doctor ordered." Bill placed the folded map on the bar top.

"This is good. *Uno minuto* while I serve this customer."

"*Maybe you have something, Tony,* and this kid just might be the answer." Bill now seemed more convinced.

"We'll soon find out, partner, but more importantly, can we trust him?" Arturo was fast on his feet and returned holding a black felt pen.

"Now let me see." Arturo was studying the map. "Now we are here." He ringed the hotel. "And Villamisseria is there . . . I suggest you take this route." He marked the roads with a thick black-ink trail. "It's not that far from the hotel, and if you stick to the freeway as I have marked, you won't get lost." "*Hmmm.*" Bill studied the ink track. "Tony, it doesn't look that difficult . . . Thanks, Arturo." Bill was satisfied.

"One more thing, Arturo," Tony interrupted. "Can you tell me anything about this place, like . . ."

"Signor, it's a maze of dirt streets with no names. The houses are made from all sorts of recycled bricks with tarpaulin roofs and even cardboard walls. But I believe that there are a few buildings that were built many years ago which are now owned by the drug lords. Some have been turned into upper apartments and brothels with the lower level into cantinas. You can easily recognize them as the local fruit and vegetable markets, and food stalls are always located in front of the bars. It just goes to prove that drunks are always hungry." Arturo's wisecrack fell on deaf ears.

"But signor's . . ." Arturo shook his head as he looked at the detectives' attire. "If you want to stay healthy, you cannot go into Villamisseria dressed like that!"

"I get the picture, kid. So, what's the bottom line?" Bill was more interested in his third beer, and it annoyed Tony. "Pay attention, Hayden." Tony gave Bill a rude nudge. "And go easy on the booze. *Remember, we have an early start in the morning!*"

"Give a guy a break, Tony . . . Have I ever let you down?"

"*Don't start that shit again!* Arturo, just ignore my partner . . . So what is it you suggest?"

"Un momento, Signor." Arturo lifted the phone. "Salva, Arturo aqui . . . Son liberta para venire al a barra . . . Si entonses le vere en cinco minutos." Arturo placed the phone back, seemingly happy with the call. "Excuse, signor's, I asked Salvo from the front desk if he was free, and he said he will meet us at the bar in ten *minutos.*"

Tony just shrugged, turning to Bill. "The plot thickens, huh?"

*   *   *

Salva arrived on time at the Gaucho Bar, but he seemed to be in rather a hurry.

"*Buenas noches, signor's.* Arturo, I only have about ten *minutos* to spare, as I have left Anna on the front desk by herself. Now how can I be of assistance?"

Arturo interjected before the detectives could attempt to offer their confused answer.

"Salva, don't ask any questions, but the detectives need to be dressed like locals, so I thought you could accompany them to the hotel boutique and ask Carlito to fit them with local attire. When does he close?" "At nine o'clock," Salva answered.

"It's just after eight thirty, signor's, so you don't have much time."

"*Gracias*, Arturo, we owe you one." Tony opened his wallet. "Here's my card, kid. If you ever get to the United States, call me. I'm sure I can offer you a cot . . . And here's a little something to help with your expenses." Tony slipped him a big one.

"*A hundred U.S. dollars,* signor! Perhaps you have made a mistake." Arturo couldn't believe his eyes as he stared at greenback.

"No mistake, kid. Just don't spend it on the first broad you hit the cot with." Tony laughed. "And remember what you promised."

"Si, signor . . . *Gracias . . . Gracias.*"

Salva didn't waste much time; he had to get back to the front desk, *pronto*!

*   *   *

"Carlito, the two Americans need to look like locals, as they are working on a special tourist project for the government." The less Carlito knew the better.

"Si, Salva, you can go. I will look after the guests." "Gracias, adios." Salva was gone in a heartbeat.

"Now your sizes." Carlito stepped back, sizing up the big guys. Then he puckered his lips to sort of reassure himself. "*Hmmm,* first of all, the Panama hats. I think yours, signor, will be a seven and a half." He looked to Bill. "And yours an eight."

"*You got that one right Carlito!* A ten-gallon hat for a twelve-gallon head."

"Don't pay attention to him, Carlito, he's always fooling around."

"I have two hats in the storeroom that have seen their day, old and frayed around the brim. You can try them for size. If they fit, I give you good discount."

"Not bad!" Tony and Bill studied themselves in the mirrors.

"That really suits you, Bill. You look like a Caribbean sugarcane cutter. *All you need is the rum!*"

"Yeah . . . Yeah, so what's new . . . Carlito?"

"Next, the loose, short-sleeved cotton shirts and the crumpled gaucho baggy pants to match. But firstly, signor's, I must close the boutique to ensure we are not disturbed." Carlito hastily locked up and hung the "Closed" sign on the door.

The detectives disappeared into the changing closets.

Tony appeared first. "I gotta hand it to you, Carlito, I hardly recognize myself in this getup. And just look at my buddy!" Tony was trying to contain his laughter. "But Carlos, we look like twins!"

"You are right, signor. I need to change the colour of your friend's shirt and maybe his slacks instead of white."

Carlito returned with a pinkish-coloured shirt. "I think we keep the trousers the same . . . Now shoes."

"I take a U.S. size . . ."

"I suggest these deck shoes. I only have white but take some dirt from the plant pot in your room and rub it onto the canvas. Try these for size."

The detectives studied one another for few seconds before bursting into spontaneous laughter.

"*Bill . . .*" Tony couldn't help himself. "You look like Bill Clinton on his first visit to Hawaii!"

"Yeah, and you look like Hillary . . ."

Even Carlito had to laugh at these two jokers.

"One last thing, signor's." Carlos handed them each a spray can of fake tan.

"You're gonna need this to cover your white skin . . ."

"Thanks, Carlito. What's the damage?"

CHAPTER 11

Terry felt kind of drained as she entered the office. She had had a restless night, what with Frank continually disturbing her "beauty sleep" with his persistent text messages, so much so that she eventually stuffed her cell phone below the mattress. Then there's the challenge of her promotion and the project to revitalize the company's new range of business machines, but more to the point, her "hand-me-down" marketing crew, where even Mother Teresa couldn't pull a rabbit from the hat.

"*Good morning . . . Good morning.*" Terry didn't enjoy being two faced but in the marketing field, it was all part of the "reality show."

She stopped at her desk and removed her jacket and hung it on the back of her chair, then sat in silence for another few moments, blankly staring at the cubicle partition. She had to quickly get a new marketing plan together and consolidate the KPIs, but to achieve the best and most expedient results, the key to any plan is the quality and support of the staff.

"*Hmmmm . . .*" Terry scribbled some notes on her phone pad and gave a cunning smile as she boldly walked down the office thoroughfare.

"Can I have your attention please?" Terry's voice boomed. The office went silent.

"I'm calling a meeting in conference room B in . . ." Terry glanced at her Rolex. "In thirty minutes, relating to the relaunch of the company's new business machines, which needless to say, you are all familiar with. Please fetch any information that you may deem relevant . . ." Terry glanced at her watch once more. "*Ten thirty sharp it is!*"

*   *   *

"I feel like I need a caffeine injection." Terry was talking to herself as she walked to the vending machine, slipping two one-dollar coins into the slot, then pressing "Espresso." Within seconds, the small polystyrene cup was serviced, and Terry took a sip. "*Not bad!*" She commented as she returned to her desk.

"Now for the nitty-gritty . . . Let me see." Terry booted her desktop.

"So, if I promote . . . And." She smiled to herself. "There's an old saying, 'If you can't beat 'em, join 'em.'" She finished her coffee, more than pleased with her intuition, whispering below her breath. "There are many ways to skin a cat . . ."

*   *   *

Terry was purposely five minutes late as planned to allow the staff to have their normal gossip and "two plus two makes three." It was the old "get it off your chest" and see "who has the guts" approach.

As Terry entered the room, as expected, it went suddenly quiet, the badmouthing coming to an abrupt silence.

"Apologize for my lateness," Terry began. "But I had an irate customer on the line." A white lie, but it suited the occasion, and Terry took her seat in front of the whiteboard.

"Now without further ado, let's get down to business . . . Firstly, I'm sure that the grapevine is excellent and that by now you all aware that the market launch of our new business machines, having been outsourced, will now no longer be the responsibility of Global Marketing, as their contract has been terminated due to non-performance. Litigation is in the hands of our legal department for breach of contract and damages. *But what does this mean for us?* It means, unfortunately, that we, as the marketing team, have to start again, *and this time from scratch! A problem or opportunity?* I'll let you dot the i's and cross the t's on that one! Of course, as the new marketing manager, I will be leading the team, but as always, a boss needs good subordinates, and that's where you people come in. It will mean lots of 'working smart' and late nights, but I'm confident that with Jaycee Donnelly as the new project leader and with Mildred Pitt as her second in command, we will do an excellent job."

Davis and Pitt turned to look at one another in absolute shock and partial embarrassment. It was the last thing they had envisaged. From being the office "shit stirrers" to project leaders and, worse still, appointed by the woman they continually slagged was more than "one for the books." But then what would the rest of the staff think? Turncoats if they accept or sent to the wilderness if they rejected. As they say, "you can't turn back the clock, but you can wind it up again."

"I assume by your silence that you are either thinking of accepting the promotion or rejecting?" Terry's stare was cold and calculating.

Davis turned and whispered something in Pit's ear, who returned a reluctant nod, followed by a nervous smile.

"Mildred and I appreciate your confidence in our ability and be assured that we will give you our utmost support."

"Thank you, Jaycee. I will discuss with you tomorrow your new job descriptions and remuneration packages.

"Now let's talk turkey."

Terry rose to her feet, turning to the whiteboard and uncapped the marker pen.

"Here's where I want you to start . . ."

*   *   *

Blakely was knee deep in paperwork when his phone rang.

"*What the fuck now!* Yes, Rita?" Jack gave a mammoth sigh.

"I'm sorry to disturb you, but I've just had a call from Bill Hall, the president . . ."

"*Christ, Rita, why didn't you put him through?*" Jack rudely interrupted.

"Because, Jack, *he didn't give me chance.* His message is simple . . . He and Simpson will arrive at your office today at twelve sharp."

"Did he say what it was about?"

"No. That was the message, and then he just hung up. For what it's worth, by the tone of his voice, it's going to be ugly."

Jack as usual gave a subtle laugh. "I have a good idea what this is all about . . . Rita, before I hang up, get Terry Johnson in my office ASAP . . ."

*   *   *

There was a loud knock on the glass door.

"Come in, Terry . . . Grab a seat . . . Before you ask, the shit has just hit the fan, and Hall and his sidekick, Simpson, are heading for a *High Noon* at my office at twelve today."

"Christ, Jack, this *is* serious!"

"Terry, let me be the judge of that. but here's where you come in . . ."

"Don't worry, Jack, I'll have all the information by . . ." Terry glanced at the time. "Say, eleven thirty."

"A bit tight, but I guess at such short notice, it's a tall order . . ."

*   *   *

June was up bright and early, already in the kitchen preparing breakfast for the kids. The flapjacks smelled good, and the tantalizing aroma was enough to awaken the taste buds of the doubting few.

Steven banged on his sister's door.

"Are you awake, sis?"

"With the smell of those fresh pancakes . . . Are you kidding? Hang on, and I'll be down in a second."

"Good morning, Mother." June was caught by surprise at the sound of Steven's voice.

"Hi, Mom." This time it was Sheryl. "These flapjacks smell absolutely delicious."

June laughed, shaking her head. "Now I know what to do in future to get you two out of bed. Grab a seat at the bar, Sheryl. Steven, go fetch the juice from the fridge and pour the glasses."

There was subtle period of quietness until the overindulgence finally subsided.

"Aren't you having any, Mother?" Steven asked surprised at his mother's empty plate.

"Steven are you serious! After that dinner I had last night, I could give up food for a week!"

"Watching your figure, Mom, huh?" Sheryl laughed, giving a sly look to her brother.

"And just what does that look mean?" June put on her serious face.

"Aw, come on, Mother, don't keep us in suspense. How did your date go with the handsome Phil Stevens?" Sheryl asked.

"Oh, so that's what this is all about?" June couldn't hide her smile. "For your information, it wasn't a date, just two old uni friends having a pleasant reunion dinner."

"It didn't look like that to me, Mother . . . And the way he looked at you . . ."

Sheryl, that's enough. Behave yourself!"

So where did Phil take you to dinner?" It was now Steven's turn for the third degree.

"God . . . *You two!*" Then June smiled. "Well, if you must know, Phil reserved a table at the Manhattan Grill in Downtown Ocean Springs."

"Wow! He certainly has style. But I really like him, Mother, and he is handsome into the bargain." Sheryl was treading on thin ice.

"*Now enough of that!* Do you hear me? Now changing the subject, who's for more pancakes?"

June's diversion as expected, fell on deaf ears.

"Sis, never mind Phil . . . How about Mother? Didn't she look absolutely stunning last night?"

June was touched at Steven's comment, and there was a hint of sadness in her voice before composing herself.

"Steven, Sheryl, you don't know how much I appreciate your love and support. It has been a terrible journey for us all and where it's all going to end for the love of me, I don't know. But as they say, every cloud has a silver lining, and Phil Stevens is just that, to the point that he has offered me a fulltime position in his law firm as a paralegal. *Can you believe it?* The salary is not exceptional at 40K but it's a start and get this! The company is going to send me back to NYU part time, all expenses paid, to continue my studies in the law faculty."

"*Mother!*" Steven and Sheryl rushed over and hugged her. "We're so happy for you."

"Thank you both for all the love you have shown me, I don't know how I would have gotten through this mess without you, but there is also some bad news. I have filed for divorce from your father on the basis of desertion and mental cruelty . . ."

PART 5

Who Dares Wins

CHAPTER 1

The loud ring of the phone startled Tony as he searched in the darkness for the receiver, almost knocking the bedside light over.

"Where's that bloody phone!" He managed to hit the light switch. "Yes, room 1021?"

"Your wake-up call, signor. It's six thirty."

"Thank you . . . Oh . . . Have you also called Mr. Hayden in room 1022?"

"Si, Signor Perino . . . Is there anything else?"

"No, gracias."

"Muy buenos Dias, signor."

But Tony, knowing Bill, decided to be on the safe side and dialled the operator.

"*Muy buenos Dias*, Mr. Perino."

"Can you put me through to room 1022?" "Si, un momento."

The phone rang and rang.

"*I hope this jerk hasn't hit the pillow again!*" Tony was getting irate. "*Come on. Come on,* answer it!"

"Yeah, who's on the line?"

"Christ, Bill, what the hell took you so long?"

"Can't a guy get some peace sitting on the can?"

"*Okay . . . Okay.* Cool it! I just wanted to make sure you were awake after 'Play it again, Sam' last night."

"*Now* can I get some peace in my little private room?" Bill grumbled.

"Just cut the slack, Bill, and be ready not later than eight. I'll knock on your door in the passing. And Bill, as we are leaving straight from the hotel, bring your passport, firearm, and a spare clip and keep them out of sight, and don't forget the shades!"

"Christ, what's this, World War III?"

"Just finish what you're doing and be ready at eight." Tony gave a big sigh, then hung up. "*That guy!* Now *I* had better get in that bloody shower myself. I still have to dress up for the fucking Mardi Gras."

*   *   *

Tony put the final touches to his "tanned" face and arms, then slipped on the scruffy Panama hat. It was a bit too large and rested on his ears. He studied himself one last time in the full mirror and gave a sort of "*hmmmm.*" "*Not bad!*"

Tony certainly looked like a local, with the baggy pants and crumpled cotton shirt and those scruffy deck shoes. If he stood long enough in one spot on the sidewalk, someone was sure to throw him a peso. Before leaving, he double-checked everything one more time, then slipped a pair of cuffs into his baggy trouser pocket. The "shades" were next, and he gave one last look.

"Christ, even my mother wouldn't recognize me in this getup!" Tony was still laughing as he finally closed the door and walked briskly down the hallway, passing a group of what looked like businessmen on their way toward the lift.

"Buenos Dias."

"Gracias tanto," Tony replied with a smile.

"Si, Quario, debe ser alguna clase de desfile e gala de facy?" *(Must be some kind of fancy dress parade, huh?)* They continued laughing as they entered the elevator.

Tony banged on Bill's door. "Come on, remove the digit."

"*Keep your fucking shirt on, I'm coming,*" Bill's voice erupted.

Tony took one look at Bill as he stood in the doorway and doubled up.

"*Heh . . . ha . . . ha . . . ha . . . ha . . .* For Christ's sake, Bill . . . *I'm gonna piss myself.*"

Laughter is contagious, and Bill had to grab the wall and take deep breaths between bursts of choking.

"Christ, Tony, we look like the fucking Beach Boys . . . *Aruba, Jamaica, oooh, I wanna take yah . . . Bermuda, Bahama, come on, pretty mamma . . .*" Bill was fooling around, singing the lyrics of "Kokomo," and by the time they got to the elevator, they were holding their sides in pain.

It was a hilarious start to a dangerous mission . . .

*　*　*

"Do you think we have time for a coffee?" Bill asked as the elevator doors opened.

"Get out of it, Hayden! Hell, it's nearly eight forty-five and our friend Victor, I'm sure, will be here any minute now. "We'll grab a bite on *Mission Impossible.*"

"That's what I like about you, Tony. You got a weird sense of humour." Bill was searching for the car keys.

"You got the map?"

"Have I got dementia or something?" Bill was still in a fragile state from the night before and desperate for the hair of the dog.

"Buenos Dias." The doorman touched his cap. "Can I get someone to fetch your car, signor?"

"No, gracias." Tony replied, his Spanish improving by the minute.

Bill turned the key in the bug. It gave a sort of an early-morning cough to clear its throat, then shook a couple times before spluttering into life, the large cloud of black smoke spewing from the exhaust resembling a miniature atomic bomb.

"*Maaan*, isn't this something?" Bill crunched the gears and drove down the driveway at the breakneck speed of five miles an hour.

"Can't you get Adolf here to go any faster?"

"Listen, you want to get there in one piece, *you do it my way.*" Bill signalled and swung onto Vi San Martin, "the Mexican Express," finally picking up speed.

At this time in the morning, the highway was busy as usual, and Bill's driving blended in beautifully with the locals. What with their new identities and the heap they were driving, who would ever guess?

*　*　*

(Speaking in Spanish)

Sergio stirred, then winced as he tenderly touched the wound to his neck; it still hurt like hell, and he threw his arm over to one side of the bed, searching for Lena.

"It's about time, you lazy hombre. Get out of that bed and give yourself a wash. You stink like hell." Lena was boiling some water on the bottled gas stove.

"Stop fucking complaining, and get me some coffee, woman. You're always fucking bitching. What time is it anyway?" Sergio yawned, flashing his uneven, tobacco-stained teeth, the powerful waft of his booze-soaked breath made Lena turn her head. Sergio finally sat up and threw his legs over the side of the bed and began scratching his back like a domesticated ape. His neck was still swollen and looked ugly and what with that with the six o'clock shadow; he wasn't the prettiest sight first thing in the morning.

"For your information, it's after nine, and I'm sure that fucking no-good Carlos will be here any minute to scrounge some breakfast. *But have I got news for him!*"

"What happened to the money I gave you yesterday?" Sergio growled.

"Who do you think? I can't produce miracles on a thousand pesos, so you had better dig deep, mister, *if you like eating!*" Lena wasn't letting up, determined to cross the line.

Sergio dropped his feet to the floor, then sat for a moment just staring into space before finally rubbing his forehead and then walking naked to the makeshift shower.

Lena quickly chucked him a towel. "For Christ's sake, cover yourself. Who do you think you are, *Mr. Argentina?*"

Sergio just ignored her remark and threw the towel onto the chair. If she didn't like what she saw, *tough shit!* He lifted the ladle from the water pail and doused himself.

"*Brrrrrr,* that's *fucking* cold!"

"Serves you right, you 'no hoper,' and look at the shit you've got us into. You and your easy money. I tell you; I don't want any part of this."

"*Man,* what did I do to deserve you?" Sergio was busy washing his eyes to clear the alcohol haze.

"And use some soap!" Lena barked. "Between your BO and that fucking breath of yours, it's enough to make a camel commit suicide."

"Did you check on the Menzel woman and the Americano this morning?" Sergio just had to stop the runaway train.

"Who do you think I am, a fucking prison warden or something? I'm sick of emptying that shit pail. *Go check on them your fucking self.*"

*   *   *

"What was that all about, Mona?" Mike cringed as he tried to get rid of the cramp in his legs.

"The usual husband and wife screaming match, but the good thing that came out of this is, Lena doesn't want a bag of this kidnapping deal. Somehow, we gotta keep working on her. I don't know about you, Mike, but I need a drink. My tongue feels like sandpaper, and I have to go to the bathroom."

(Speaking in Spanish)

"Lena, we need some water!" Mona roared like a wounded lion.

Sergio turned to his wife as he slipped into his pants. "*Shit*, how do they know your name?"

"The way you scream and bawl at me, the whole of fucking Villamisseria knows!"

"Well, don't just stand there! Go and see what they want. The last thing I need is to see a woman having a piss, no matter how good looking she is!"

"Christ, it's down to me again! You want this done . . . Then you better have some money on that table when I get back." Lena filled the empty plastic juice bottles, then covered her face with the ski mask before opening the curtain.

"*Buenos Dias*, Lena. Can you take these hoods off and gimme a drink of water? *I'm desperate!*"

Lena just kept mum and obliged, passing Mona and Mike the tepid water. There was no way she was getting drawn into a conversation.

"I'll untie your legs. The pail is just beside you and tell the gringo to don't even think about being a hero. He is extra baggage, and Sergio wouldn't think twice."

Mona grabbed the bottle with both hands and literally emptied it down her throat, the overflow drenching her chin and blouse. Then she poured what remained over her head.

"Does *that* feel good!" Mike was too busy indulging to answer. "Mike, do the gentlemanly thing . . ."

*   *   *

"Bill, according to Arturo's directions, take the first on the right and slip off the freeway."

"Yeah, I got you." Bill was concentrating on his driving.

"*Man*, from a distance, get a load of this place." Tony couldn't get over it. "It's like a fucking Angolan refugee camp, only here the shacks are upper class."

Mike was more interested in the makeshift dirt road that entered Villamisseria, the bug almost out of control as it bounced violently on its shocks through the deep potholes.

"Where to now, partner . . . Any suggestions?"

"Pull up in front of that guy . . ."

*   *   *

(Speaking in Spanish)

"Lena, remember what I said. You just forget to tie us up, and you're an instant millionaire. Whenever you are ready, fetch me a piece of paper and a pen, and I will sign a statement agreeing to pay you a reward of one million U.S. dollars, also exonerating you from conviction and dropping all charges."

"Do you think I'm crazy? Sergio would kill me."

"Lena, it's your call . . . The rope or one million in cash and you walk the walk."

"I don't want to hear any more of your shit. Besides, how do I know I can trust you?"

"You don't!"

"Shut up and put your legs together." Lena tied the cords tightly, then replaced the hoods before leaving, visibly disturbed. "How did it go?" Mike asked.

"She's biting. It's early days . . ."

*   *   *

(Speaking in Spanish)

The loud squeal of the brakes alerted Sergio, and he slipped on his shirt and brushed back his black scraggly hair, then tied it in a ponytail.

"That must be Carlos and Eva. Now you and your friend can get together and join the hate club."

"*Christ, Sergio!* Have you nothing good to say about anyone?" Lena was very protective of her best friend.

There was a loud bang on the door. "Sergio . . . Carlos here . . . Open up, the coast is clear."

Lena greeted her friend. "Eva, your face looks a lot better today, the swelling has gone down. I have some coffee on the stove, come and join me . . . Sergio, I'm still waiting!"

Sergio turned to Carlos. "Fucking women!" He reluctantly passed Lena another thousand, the proceeds from Mona's wallet getting thin by the hour.

The crumpled notes, like an illusionist trick, disappeared down Lena's crevasse.

"Carlos, why don't we leave these two witches and head for the cantina and the mini mercado for some fresh tortillas and a cold Quilmes . . ."

*   *   *

"Pardon, signor, im buscando la Markado?" Tony asked the shoeless, down-and-out hombre, his drug-crazed eyes lost in the wilderness. The middle-aged man cupped his right hand and held it to his mouth. This guy was either hungry or he was Oscar material. Tony reached out of the car window and slapped a ten in his palm.

"Gracias . . . Gracias, signor . . . El Markado y la Cantina esta unos decina kilometros de esta camino." He pointed straight ahead.

"What did he say, Tony?"

"The market is about ten kilometre's down the road."

Bill slipped the bug into first and continued the obstacle course . . . Little did he know that fate is not all it's cracked up to be . . .

*   *   *

(Speaking in Spanish)

"Corporal, park in the hotel car park but be ready to leave at a moment's notice."

"Si, Lieutenant."

Victor felt a shade uneasy as he strode to the front desk. He had left numerous messages on Tony's cell phone to return his calls but had no reply. Either he had forgotten to switch on his phone, or there is something more sinister in the pipeline.

"*Buenos Dias*, Salva. I'm trying to contact the two Americans. Can you please connect me to Signor Perino's room?"

Salva felt uneasy. To mess with the Buenos Aires Policia spelled big trouble, and whatever the call, it had to be convincing.

"Lieutenant, I'm afraid the two Americans left early this morning and didn't leave any messages."

"*Hmmmm* . . . That's unusual. Can you contact the concierge to see if he remembers their request for a taxi?"

"A taxi, Lieutenant?" Salva was playing the innocent.

"*You heard me!*" Victor was no dummy.

"They hired a car, sir."

"*A car!*" That was the last thing Victor expected. "Then can you give me the make and registration number?"

"It's a . . ." Salva paused and shuffled some papers. "A blue 1964 Volkswagen, registration BA 172 . . . Is there anything else I can help you with, Lieutenant?"

"Did they say where they were going?"

"Not to my knowledge, sir."

"*Hmmm* . . . Strange. Then perhaps as and when they return, you can call me on this number. It's urgent."

Salva studied the card and nodded. "You can count on me, Lieutenant . . ."

* * *

(Speaking Spanish)

Victor opened his phone and dialled and anxiously waited for a few seconds before the Capitan finally answered his call.

"Si, Capitan? Avalos speaking.

"Capitan, I have some disturbing news . . . The Americans . . ."

"I see, and I just wonder what they are up to. I'll put out an APB to hold the car until we investigate their motives."

"Capitan, with respect, it is not a crime for a foreigner to rent a car."

"Lieutenant, I'm fully aware of the law, and I'll cross that bridge when I come to it. I can trump up any charge I want . . . *Comprender?*"

"Si, Capitan."

"Lieutenant, just imagine how embarrassing it would be if the Americans find the kidnappers before us."

"Then what do you suggest, Capitan?"

"Since you haven't a clue where they have gone, I'm at a loss. Let's hope for *your sake* we pick up that car . . ."

* * *

Blakely was clock watching. "Christ, where the hell is Terry?"

No sooner had he made the comment than there was a knock on the door, and he could clearly see Terry's silhouette through the frosted glass.

"Come in, Terry, you had me worried there! Now let's see what you got." Terry spread the documents on Blakely's desk one at a time. "Jack, I suggest we start from here . . ."

* * *

"Nice job. I couldn't have done better myself." The phone rang. "Yes, Rita?"

"They're here in reception."

"Rita, go and greet them on my behalf and escort them to my office . . . Oh . . . And, Rita, do me a big favor and fetch some coffee . . . *The good kind.*"

Blakely stacked the reports in order of importance, then placed them in a neat bundle, ready for the jousting match.

"Terry, you had better go, or you'll run smack into them. Stand by in case I need you."

No sooner had Terry gone than there was knock on the glass door.

"Come in." Blakely's voice was cool and commanding. He knew this would be the mother of all meetings, but he held the trump card, and if cornered, make no mistake, he would use it at whatever the cost.

"Bill . . . Ian . . . Take a seat. Rita will be in shortly with some coffee. Now why the visit at such short notice?"

Jack had that plausible look, but as for Simpson, he looked like at tiger at feeding time—he was after blood, preferably Blakely's!

"Jack, I'm not going to beat about the bush, I've laid it in on the line to Bill that this time you have gone too far for the last time and . . ."

"And what?"

Hall raised his hand. *"Jack*, you'll have your say. Let him finish." "Now where was I?" Simpson for a moment had lost his train of thought.

"Bill, this guy is completely out of control. He's a loose cannon, and 'protocol' is a word that's not in his vocabulary. *Can you believe it!* Without any consultation, he suddenly decides, on his own accord, to cancel the marketing contract with Global and commence litigation for non-performance and breach of contract. I mean this guy is a law unto himself. Sure, we need good copy on our new product launch, but not this kind of publicity. I've had enough of this guy, Bill, and I'm calling for his resignation."

"I'll be the one to decide on that!" Hall was uncomfortable. A bunfight between senior executives gets messy, and the company loses.

"Now, can I?" Jack asked, sarcasm streaming through his voice.

Hall gave a uneasy nod.

"Brad, I joined American Business Machines straight from university twenty years ago as a management cadet. I've been with the company through the good, the bad, and the ugly. I worked my way up the executive ladder from mail boy to marketing and sales manager . . . ABM is my lifeblood, and the last thing I want is to harm the company. Once, we were market leaders in computer technology, and now we are number four. It has taken the company five years to develop this new product, and I must compliment you, Bill, with your foresight and leadership injecting new life into the business. Now finally, we have a product we can be proud of. One that's not only technologically superior than that of IBM or Hewlett-Packard, but a true global product."

"Bill . . . What's this, an autobiography?" Simpson was chomping at the bit.

"Ian, you've had your say . . . *Jack* . . ."

"Thanks . . . Bill, there's only one window of opportunity when a company launches a new product, especially in the ever-changing field of technology, and as the result of an entirely biased decision to go externally and award the contract to Global Marketing, I'm afraid to say that we may now have missed the boat."

"*That is absolute hogwash!* Bill don't listen to his crap. It's openly known that Blakely has always been flying his own kite with a personal vendetta to undermine me."

"Bill, *please*!" Jack interrupted, appealing to Hall, exasperated at Simpson's continued rudeness.

"Jack, I'm listening, but this had better be good!" Arbitration is not an envious modus operandi and Mason was becoming more and more uncomfortable.

There was a timely knock on the door.

"That will be Rita with the coffee," Jack commented as he turned to Terry's report for the next round. Now all that was missing was the Marquis of Queensbury rules.

Rita poured the coffee amid a wall of silence, and you could have cut the air with a knife.

"Let's not waste any more time." Hall rattled his cup back onto the saucer. He was more than anxious to close this chapter.

"Bill, I have here copies of the expenditures, re: progress payments versus the budget and cost overruns . . . The abysmal sales results and technical literature that you would have to be an engineering graduate to even read! And all that comes from Global is the never-ending begging bowl and more flimsy excuses. *And* . . . Just take a look at these abysmal sales figures. It would have been cheaper to give the product away for free. And now to add salt to the wounds, on top of that, Chuck Briggs is taking responsibility over the project himself . . . Why? Because Mike Summers, his VP for marketing is wanted by the police for attempted murder of none other than Laura Williams."

Jack could see the shocked expression on Hall's face as he struggled to absorb Blakely's swan song.

"You mean Laura Williams, the one that . . . ?"

"The same, Bill, and none other than the daughter of Senator Dave Williams."

This was a whole new ballgame, and Hall was getting more frustrated by the minute.

"*Hell*, is there any more good news?" Bill was shaking his head.

"But, Bill, it doesn't end there. Take a look at these quotes for the contract from a number of reputable marketing companies, and surprise, surprise,

Global is the most expensive by a long shot. But then I'm sure Ian can enlighten us on why the contract was awarded to the highest bidder."

"Ian, were you aware of this? And if you were, why didn't you take action?" The tone in Hall's voice was like the hangman's last supper request.

"*Eh . . . Err . . .* This is a typical Blakely smear campaign. He makes the bullets but never fires the gun."

"I'm asking you once more, Ian, why was the contract given to the highest bidder?"

Simpson was lost for words. He was trapped by his own doing, and desperation was now clouding his mind.

"Bill, can't you see that Blakely's setting me up because he wants my job?"

"Not good enough, Ian. I want some answers."

"Bill, be assured, everything is above board . . . It's just that . . ."

Blakely had had enough, and it was time to humanely put down the bleeding man. He opened his desk drawer and pulled out a large envelope.

"I've had enough of this fiasco." Blakely emptied the photographs onto his desk.

"I know it's unethical, but I had no alternative and, furthermore, make no apologies."

Simpson's face went white as Hall scanned the snapshots.

"In case you don't know, Bill, that's Simpson in a lip-lock with Briggs's wife, and from what I heard, Briggs knew of his wife's affair but was willing to keep it secret, but at a price—namely, the contract."

"Bill, *let me explain!*"

"Ian, there's no need. Just make sure you have your resignation on my desk tomorrow first thing. Jack, can you kindly get your secretary to call me cab? I'll find my own way out. And, Jack, be at my office by ten tomorrow."

Jack had won the day, but now he was in the driver's seat. He had better deliver!

Blakely wasted no time and lifted the phone. "Rita, can you get Phil Stevens on the line?"

Simpson rose to his feet to leave.

If looks could kill. "It's not over yet, Jack . . ."

*   *   *

June had finished the breakfast dishes and was still in her housecoat. It had just turned one, and she was feeling rather lazy after last night's dinner when the loud ring of the phone shattered the silence.

"Now who could this be, and just when I was about to rustle up a sandwich for my lunch?" She spoke out loud.

"Yes?"

"June, Phil here."

"*Phil!* I was kinda hoping it was you."

"*Oh, is that so!*" June could hear him laugh.

"Coincidently, Phil, I was just about to call *you*."

"June, a couple of things. Firstly, and I shouldn't be telling you this, but I've just had a call from Jack Blakely at ABM to inform me to continue with the litigation against Global Marketing, your husband's ex-employer." "But how does that affect me, Phil?" June was confused.

"On the surface, it's an open-and-shut case that could cost Global millions in reimbursement, and after studying their last audited report, this could send them to the wall. My question is, have you received Mike's severance entitlements?"

"No, not as yet."

"Then you should contact Chuck Briggs immediately and give him some sort of sob story on how you need the monies banked into your account urgently. You've got bills to pay, etc., just in case they file for chapter 11. If they do, as an inconspicuous creditor, you'll get nothing."

"Thanks, Phil. I'll pick up the phone immediately after this call. And the second thing?"

"Can you meet me for dinner this evening?"

CHAPTER 2

(Speaking in Spanish)

Carlos turned the key in the '52 Pontiac, the forty-one twenty cubic block burst into life, its nostalgic roar a sucker for the classic car hunters. But then this is Argentina, where American classics are commonplace, but to repatriate these works of art is easier said than done.

The morning was pleasant and sunny, with the temperature just breaking twenty-seven. It was one of these days meant for relaxing in the shade, enjoying good food, and chasing it with a cold beer, but the kidnappers were running low on cash, and they had to do something soon to collect the ransom.

The open quarter lights provided natural air conditioning, and the breeze was refreshing as the "old lady" lumbered down the potholed ridden dirt road.

Suddenly, a blue Volkswagen came from nowhere, almost sideswiping the Pontiac, and Carlos was forced to take evasive action at the same time, with his free hand furiously rolling down the window before he thrashed the brakes.

"*You fucking crazy hombres!* Who are you? Stevie Wonder's fucking brother!" Carlos screamed; the Glock pointed straight at Bill's forehead.

"The next time, I blow your fucking head off. Vamoose before I change my mind. *Fucking idiots!*" Carlos's ranting still echoing as they disappeared from sight.

"Did you see the look on that hombre's face, Sergio?" Carlos laughed, regaining his composure.

"Si, for sure he was scared shitless, but go easy on the ordnance. If you upset the drug gangs, your crazy play could come back to bite us in the ass."

"No one messes with Carlos if they know what's good for them . . . Sergio, *enough*! Let's go get that beer . . ."

*   *   *

Bill hit the brakes hard, the bug's rear end snaking before finally coming to a stop in a cloud of dust. Tony already had his kerchief covering his mouth while coughing his lungs out.

"*Eh . . . keh . . . keh*, Bill," Tony spluttered trying to clear his throat. "Are you all, right?"

"Yeah." Bill coughed, sending dry spit out the window. "But that was a close call." He cleared his throat. "*Man,* that's better . . . You know, Tony, that kid at the hotel was right. This place *is worse* than fucking Dodge City!"

As Bill spoke, he could see the cloud of dust from the apple-green '52 Pontiac disappear in his rear mirror.

"Tony, did you notice the guy with the finger on the trigger and then that car?"

"You mean the tattoo of the crucifixion on his forearm? Unless there's a fire sale at Miami Ink, that's our man . . . And as for the car? It fits the bill to a tee."

Bill was already doing a three-sixty; he didn't need a second prompting.

"Just follow that dust cloud, partner, something tells me we are about to get lucky . . ."

*   *   *

(Speaking in Spanish)

"Now that these two bastardos are out of our faces." Lena gave Eva a cheeky wink as she rose and placed the two beat-up steel mugs on the rickety table. "I have a nice surprise." She continued laughing as she walked to the corner of the bed, then kneeled on all fours, groping below in the darkness before a big grin crossed her face as she proudly held up the bottle of tequila.

"Magic, huh?"

Eva burst into laughter. "*Why you . . .*"

"Don't say it!" Lena was already loading the mugs.

"Too bad you don't have the ice." Eva was poking fun at her.

"*Aplausos.*" Lena touched Eva's mug. "*Now,* I'm going to relax, si."

Eva took a deep breath and sighed. "You are lucky, Lena, as least you have some money. That Carlos of mine is lower than a snake's belly . . . Why do we suffer these two losers? I ask myself this question every day."

Lena generously topped up Eva's mug. As they say in France, *ll n'y a ni libre-fromage dans le piege . . .* (There's no free cheese in the mousetrap)

"Listen, Eva, *we don't have to be poor!*" She moved her head in the direction of the curtained room where Mona and Mike were "incarcerated."

"What do you mean?" The tequila was hitting the spot, and Eva was changeably all ears. "So, tell me, what is this magical solution, like you rub Aladdin's lamp, huh?"

"I'll tell you what it is . . . *One million U.S. dollars!*"

"*Are you fucking serious?* Not the 'we let them loose' deal again." Eva's joviality had suddenly gone down the toilet.

"Eva, bite your tongue, and just let me finish . . . *Santa Maria!*" She made the sign of the cross. "The deal is this, *and don't interrupt!* The Menzel woman is willing to . . ."

"So let's get this straight." Eva was trying to punch a hole in the "get rich" plan. "This Menzel broad is willing to put it in writing that she will pay us a bounty of one million dollars in American money if we have a memory lapse and forget to tie them up properly after their toilet break?"

"That's it in a nutshell, honey . . . Easy as pie." Lena was even more convincing.

"Lena, *are you really serious?* Carlos, never mind Sergio, will hunt us down like wild boar, and how can we spend the money from the graveyard?"

"I've given it a lot of thought Eva, and as part of the deal, the Menzel family must agree to smuggle us out of the country, preferably to Brazil."

"*Hmmmm . . .*" Eva was now taking the bait. "And you say one million in American money? *Hmmmm.*"

"Just think of it, Eva . . . We'd be rich . . . Over two million pesos each."

"I'm thinking, but, like, when does this all happen?" "Before these two losers return . . ."

* * *

Bill was having trouble keeping the Pontiac in his sights through the never-ending dust cloud, the dirt road converging through a myriad of coloured tarpaulins supported by old railway sleepers and shoeless kids oblivious to the poverty, laughing and screaming as they kicked a rag ball around in the name of slum soccer.

"Don't worry, Tony, I can see them. *Hang on!* They have just taken a left off the main track, and I see a kind of marketplace ahead and an old dilapidated whitewashed building like something from the movie *Dodge City*."

"Yeah, I got yah . . . Pull over here, Bill, we can leg the rest. The two 'uglies' might just recognize the Volkswagen. The one good thing is, our disguises went unnoticed for the time being, but I gotta tell yah . . . As for my Spanish, *the least said, the better!*" Tony grinned.

Bill laughed. "For sure, it's a lot better than mine." He pulled over and cut the reluctant engine. *Maybe this was Hitler's revenge.*

Tony lifted his Panama hat and wiped the sweat beads from his forehead as they began to walk the five hundred meters to the mercado and the now prominent cantina. They say, "Only mad dogs and Englishmen walk in the midday sun."

The detectives, as expected, drew inquisitive looks from the locals at their twin getups, resembling something out of *The Blues Brothers* as they entered the bar-cum-cantina. The nauseating smell of body odor and hand-rolled cancer sticks with horses' dung was enough to make you turn tail and leave, but the detectives had a job to do, and there was no way that they were going to go home empty handed.

As they leaned on the rough-cut wooden bar, there was like a moment's silence as the locals studied the intruders. Anyone new in this part of town was treated with suspicion and contempt. The congested tables taken by mostly unshaved male patrons, the word "shower" obviously not in their vocabulary. Their loose-fitting cotton pants and shirts, wide-brimmed straw hats, and dusty sandaled feet depicted that of farmhands whose meager income from fruit and vegetables evaporated daily on alcohol and painted prostitutes.

* * *

"Si?" the barman asked, resentment in his voice.

"Dos Quilmes, gracias."

The barman promptly slid the uncapped bottles down the bar top.

"Veinte pesos." The ugly dude tapped the bar impatiently, as if saying, "Pay up or ship out."

Tony gave Mr. Ugly the "don't mess with me" look, then threw the crumpled twenty on the bar.

The big guy in the sweat-ridden shirt studied the twenty for a minute, then gave a grunt as he turned his attention to an irate customer, presumably dying of thirst.

"*Mantenga su* fucking *camisa*!" he barked, showing his temper.

"It looks like the gorilla is annoyed." Bill grinned.

But as Tony was about to sample his lukewarm Quilmes, Carlos rudely crashed against him, almost knocking the bottle from his hand.

(Speaking in Spanish)

"What the . . . ?" Tony turned to face Carlos, fire in his eyes.

"You have problem, *signor*?" Carlos stared him down.

Tony felt like bringing his knee up into Carlos's groin, but it was neither the time nor the place.

"No, no problem," Tony answered in Spanish through gritted teeth.

"I thought so . . . Si, Pedro, two Quilmes, pronto." Carlos leaned over the bar to get a better look at Bill. "Have we met before, *signor*? You look familiar." Bill just ignored him and kept sipping his beer.

Carlos turned and spit on the floor. "Maybe your friend is a transvestite, eh?" He laughed out loud, the rest of the bar flies joining in. "I pay you later, Pedro." Carlos turned and left holding the beers, still laughing at his own joke.

"Keep your cool, Bill," Tony whispered. "That's our man, but first let's make sure the other guy, the one with the ponytail, is his accomplice."

Tony snuck his cell phone from his pocket to below the bar top and dialled the number they had got from Rafa.

"Bill, keep a wary eye on these dudes to see if their phone rings," Tony whispered.

Sure enough, Sergio cut his discussion for a moment before searching for the culprit.

"Si?" Sergio asked.

Tony quickly hung up as Sergio could trace the number, but he would draw a blank as Tony had purchased a local SIM card.

Carlos gulped the last of his beer, then turned to Sergio. "Who was that on the line?"

Sergio shrugged and made a face. *"No one!"* Then he pondered, *"Strange. I'm using Monalita Menzel's phone. It could be a setup, Carlos, and I don't like the look of these two hombres standing at the bar. I've never seen them here before. They could be undercover policia."*

Carlos sighed. "The trouble with you, Sergio, is you're scared of your own fucking shadow, and you think too much. Come, drink up, and let's get back. I don't trust those two women. They're too soft and might do something stupid."

"Si, I agree, let's go."

Tony nudged Bill. He could see the two uglies preparing to leave. *"Bill."*

"Yeah, don't worry, I see them. As soon as the Pontiac's exhaust fumes darken the skies, we hit the road . . ."

*   *   *

Lena slipped on the ski mask and pulled back the curtain, then stared for a moment at the pitiful sight of two human beings trussed up like wild animals ready for the slaughter. She knew only too well that their lives would be worth nothing once the ransom is paid, and she didn't want a bag of a double homicide, and the more she stared, the more she was scared.

"Is that you, Lena?" Mona was playing the game.

"Eh . . . Err . . . Si, signorina." Lena was trying to conceal her nervousness. "Have you and Eva given my proposition some thought?"

Lena plucked up the tequila courage and unsteadily walked over to the two jack-knifed bodies and removed their hoods.

"Well?" Mona asked, encouraged at Lena's positive reaction. As they say, everyone has a price.

"There is one more condition that you must agree to before I loosen the cords."

"And that is?"

"You must also put in writing that your father will ensure we get to Sao Paulo in Brazil. It's all or nothing because once we set you free, we're dead meat."

"I understand." Mona hadn't thought of that. "But smuggling you across the border is a tall order and something that I can't guarantee."

"Well, *have I got news for you!*" Lena walked over and began to place the hood back on Mike's head. *"No deal!"*

"*Hold it, Lena,* don't be too hasty." Mona was losing the plot. "*Listen*, I'm sure my father has got contacts in the border police. Go get me paper and a pen, and I'll prove it to you in writing."

"*Are you fucking serious?* I can barely write my own fucking name, never mind have a paper and pen!"

Mike was completely confused but glad to be back in daylight, his hood once more removed.

"Lena, go get my handbag. I'm sure it has been thoroughly thrashed, but my diary may be still intact, complete with a pen hidden in the spine."

"I'll go, but don't get smart with me and try to pull a fast one. I may be illiterate, but Eva, my friend, has gone to school, and she can read."

Time was of the essence as their two husbands could appear anytime soon, and Lena quickly did an about-face without uttering another word and left the room.

Eva was still hitting the tequila while Lena was searching for the elusive handbag.

"It has to be here somewhere," Lena was talking to herself.

"I think that's it over there." Eva pointed.

"At last!"

Lena quickly turned the bag upside down, its remaining contents scattering over the table.

"This must be it!" Lena flicked over the pages of the small book.

"Lena, are you sure you want to go through with this?" Eva asked, her voice now slurred.

"For Christ's sake, Eva, lay off the booze. I need you to read the bounty agreement. We gotta move our asses before the losers return."

Lena's comment shut her up, the reality blues a sobering thought.

Lena handed Mona the miniature daybook. "Is this what you're looking for?"

"Yes, *and am I relieved!* Listen, Lena, why the mask now? There's no point."

"I guess so." Lena pulled the ski mask from her head, then chucked it to the corner. "Signorina Menzel, you had better be quick before Sergio and Carlos return or you may have to wait for another day."

"Can you untie my hands?" Mona asked, holding her wrists above her head.

"Oh no, I'm not falling for that one!"

Mona didn't need another prompt and began awkwardly scribbling on the miniature pages.

Father, I have agreed to . . .

Mona finally finished, then signed it before passing the two-page article to Lena, each page initialled.

"*Hmmmm.*" Lena studied the pages as if she understood every word. "One moment." She put on an educated look. "I want Eva to double-check this . . ."

*　*　*

"Keep your distance, Bill, I don't want these dudes to suspect they have a tail."

"I'm doing my best, Tony. I can hardly see them in this dust cloud, and driving this fucking German cement mixer is no joke."

"They've taken the next right, Bill. Easy on the corner, just in case they are waiting."

Bill slowly took the corner and just as the Pontiac had come to a stop outside the breeze-block shack.

"Shit!" Bill hit the brakes, the bug sliding another three meters before it came to halt in a cloud of dust. They had just blown their cover . . .

Lena stopped in her tracks as she heard the familiar brake squeal of the Pontiac as it stopped outside the door.

"*Santa Maria*, Eva, *they're here!*" She had already cut the zip ties on Mona and Mike's wrists. "Put these fucking hoods back on. Carlos and Sergio have just returned, and they'll be here any minute. You'll have to bide your time until the coast is clear."

"Put that over your head again, Mike, and pretend as if nothing has changed." Mona handed him the hood.

"Mona, I'm totally confused." Having not understood a word of Spanish, Mike was dancing in the dark.

"I don't have time to explain, Mike, just trust me, and do as I say."

Lena almost sprinted back to her seat at the table and faced Eva, putting her finger to her lips and pointing to the door.

"No more booze, and keep your fucking mouth shut, the losers have returned . . ."

*　*　*

Carlos glanced in the rear mirror, the noise of Bill dropping the anchor and the familiar sight of the blue Volkswagen kicking his memory. "*Sergio!*

It's these two hombres. They must have been following us!" Carlos already had the Glock locked and loaded.

"Don't worry, we can take them. Just stay where you are and let them show their hand."

"Aw . . . Aw . . . I don't like the look of this, Bill, I think they are on to us . . . It's showtime or no time."

As the detectives cautiously walked toward the Pontiac, guns drawn, it was a scene they had enacted many times in the Big Apple, but as always, you can never tell what's round the corner.

"I knew it . . . *Policia!*" Sergio screamed as both men leaped from the car, with Carlos squeezing off two rounds like a gunfighter from *The Alamo.* Sergio was not so stupid, having rolled down the window, crouching behind the heavy door of the coupe, using it as a shield.

As the first slug cracked past Bill's ear, the other sliced through the skin on his left bicep, leaving a neat crimson groove, and he threw himself almost horizontally at Tony as Sergio squeezed the trigger again. The two rounds flew over Tony's head, with Bill grimacing in pain as both men hit the dirt like sacks of potatoes.

With no cover, it was fast reaction time, and Tony's copper heads bounced off the Pontiac's armour, with Bill lying on his side, squeezing off round after round, the heavy forty-fives thudding into Carlos's chest, lifting him off his feet as they ripped through his rib cage, puncturing his lung with the sickly gurgling sound of escaping air. For Carlos, it was *hasta la vista,* the ruby-red liquid oozing from his mouth as he wriggled and jerked, choking on his own blood.

Carlos's violent demise distracted Sergio for a moment.

"Carlos . . . Carlos, are you all right?" Sergio screamed, fearing the worst.

It was Tony's moment of truth. He had no cover, and the next shot from Sergio was *sayonara,* and he emptied the magazine at Sergio's exposed ankles, tearing them into ground meat. Sergio screamed in pain like a wounded elephant as he rolled on his side, his severed feet dangling on the few slivers of raw flesh remaining. But this hombre wasn't going down easily, and he shakily raised his gun, pointing it at Tony, whose magazine was spent.

Bill's forty-five kicked once as the Browning emptied the copper nose. The neat red hole in the middle of Sergio's forehead would have made a Hindu proud. The gunfight at Villamisseria was suddenly over.

* * *

"Stevens and Stevens, good afternoon, Mr. Stevens's office."

"Ethel, it's Jack Blakely here from ABM . . . Is Phil free?"

"Just give me one second, Mr. Blakely . . . Yes, I'll put you through."

"*Jack,* so what's new?"

"All good. Firstly, I'm pleased to say Simpson got the axe, and it couldn't happen to a better guy. It's a long story, Phil, and we'll touch base on that when we meet just in case, I'm facing a law suit. But here's the deal: it's 'open sesame' on Global all the way. Hall has given me the green light."

"That *is* good news! You must have had some heavy artillery."

"You know me, Phil. But listen, my new marketing manager, Terry Johnson . . ."

"Yeah, I've met her . . . *Nice!*"

"*Of course,* she was over at your office yesterday. So you have noticed. I thought lawyers were immune to that kinda stuff."

"We're human like everyone else, but you were saying?"

"She compiled the heavy-gauge package with all the financials, launch shortfalls, overruns, the whole shooting match. I'll courier it you."

"That would be really helpful. So when can we meet? I have a number of points I need to clarify before I can proceed with legal action."

"How about tomorrow, say around twelve, and maybe we can continue over lunch?"

"Just a sec . . . Yeah, I'm free, so it's twelve then."

"I'm bringing Terry with me."

"*I'll look forward to that!*"

*   *   *

"Rita." Blakely lifted the phone. "Ask Terry to come in right away, there's something I need to discuss with her . . ."

"Well, wasn't that a quick meeting!" Terry was joking, a touch of sarcasm in her tone.

Blakely smiled. "I guess so. Take a seat. I just want to congratulate you on your report. It made my case so much easier."

"And?" Terry's inquisitiveness was getting the better of her.

"To cross the red line, Simpson has been fired, effective immediately." Blakely leaned back in his chair, a smug grin on his face.

"*Jack, you never . . . !*"

"It had to get down and dirty, Terry, I had no option." Jack pushed the photographs toward her.

Terry glanced through the pictures, shaking her head as she looked at each one.

"*Hell, Jack,* I'm glad you're on my side! But what about Simpson? He could sue for breach of privacy and the possible ruination of his marriage. That's if these pictures ever go viral."

"I'll cross that bridge, Terry, but more to the point, Hall wants to see me at head office first thing in the morning, and my educated guess is, he's going to offer me Simpson's position."

"*Wow!* Congratulations, Jack. You deserve it."

"Not just yet, Terry, but that gives me another problem—like who replaces me?" He gave Terry that smile that spelled trouble.

"Oh, no you don't. *Don't look at me.*"

"Why not, Terry? It's a great opportunity, and the kind that only comes once in a lifetime. I tell you what. Why don't you finish early and go home and sleep on it?"

Terry went quiet for a few seconds.

"Terry?"

"Eh, err, yes."

"Are you all, right?"

"Jack, I promise I'll think about it, *but that doesn't mean yes . . .*"

* * *

June appreciated Phil's call, but the thought of Briggs reneging on Mike's severance pay was more than a wake-up call. She slumped on the sofa for a moment, her mind trying to get to grips with yet another problem, as if she didn't have enough already! That money would have seen her through for another six months before trying to sell the house, and with the job offer from Phil, everything was falling into place, *and now this!*

June picked up the phone. "There's only one way to find out," she spoke aloud as she dialled the number.

"Global Marketing . . . Good afternoon."

"Can you put me through to Elizabeth, Mr. Briggs's secretary please?"

"Whom shall I say is calling?"

"June Summers."

"I'm sorry, Mrs. Summers, I didn't recognize your voice. I'll put you straight through."

"Elizabeth, it's me, June Summers."

"Good afternoon, Mrs. Summers, how can I help you?"

"I need to speak to Chuck. It's urgent."

"If you can bear with me for a moment, I'll check to see if he is free . . . Mr. Briggs, I have June Summers on the line, she says . . ."

"That's all I need . . . Tell her I'm busy and to call back some other time," he snubbed Elizabeth.

"I'm sorry, June, but he is busy and can't take your call."

"Elizabeth, I need to speak to him . . ."

"*June,* I'm sorry! Why don't you call again tomorrow? I'll leave a note on his desk."

"Well, thanks anyway." June hung up, feeling even more depressed.

"That bastard is trying to give me the run-around. Phil was right. But if he thinks I'm going to give up that easily, he's got another think coming."

June dialled again. "Ethel, can you put me through to Phil please? . . . Phil, you were right. Briggs wouldn't take my call . . . Sure, I'll discuss it with you over dinner . . . You'll pick me up? Seven thirty Phil, I can't tell you how much . . ."

*   *   *

"Bill, are you all, right?" Tony could clearly see the crimson patch on Bill's shirt, an overspill from the bullet crease to his left arm.

"Yeah, I'm okay, nothing that a few stitches wouldn't cure." Bill had already ripped a strip from his shirt and was wrapping it tightly around his bicep to stem the flow of the now-congealing blood.

Tony released the spent clip, then slammed home a full magazine. What was behind this door was anyone's guess, and he was taking no chances.

"This has gotta be the place, Bill. How are you for ammo?"

"I'm good. Stand aside, Tony." Bill banged on the door using the grip of his pistol.

*   *   *

"*Mike,* that sounded like gunfire!"

"Do you think it's the police?"

"Police or no police, let's get these fucking hoods off and finish untying ourselves . . ."

*   *   *

(Speaking in Spanish)

"*Lena,* what was that? I'm scared. I think something terrible has happened to Carlos and Sergio. Something really bad, and I fear the worst." Eva made the sign of the cross.

"Eva, for Christ's sake, calm down. It *could be* the policia, but don't worry, we are in the clear." Lena held up the paper that Mona had signed before stuffing it down her dress.

Bill signalled to Tony as he banged on the door for a second time.

"Now's your chance, partner, to test your Spanish." Bill forced a laugh. Typical Bill.

"Arbe le puerta a la policia!" Tony shouted.

A hostile crowd had now gathered to watch the drama. With two of their buddies heading for the city morgue, what's with two cops keeping them company?

"Volvor a policia!" Tony shouted, flashing his gold shield. *So it's NYPD . . . Who cares?* In Villamisseria, nobody gives a shit for the policia or anything that smells of the law, and the crowd weren't having a bag of it. Tony raised the Browning and squeezed off two shots in the air. The crowd immediately scattered like scared rabbits, but make no mistake, they would be back and with a vengeance.

*   *   *

(Speaking in Spanish)

"Lena, I'm shit scared, what shall we do?" Eva was suddenly sober.

"*I'll tell you what you do!*" Mona screamed as she brushed them aside.

"You open that fucking door . . . *Now!*"

But it was too late, and Tony was back to pigeon Spanish.

"*Move away from the door . . . Do you hear me?* Move away from the door."

Collateral damage was all they needed, and in Argentina, with two corpses already in the dust, it would be lock-up time and a "throw away the key" scenario.

Mona hit Eva and Lena with a quarterback tackle, landing in a heap on the floor as the two heavy-calibre forty-fives splintered the door like matchwood, almost blowing it clean off its crude hinges.

Bill kicked the door open as Tony rushed in, both arms outstretched, gripping the loaded police special with both hands, the hammer cocked.

"*Down on the floor . . . Down on the floor . . . Hands behind your back . . . Hands behind your back!*"

Mona immediately spotted Tony's accent.

"Hold it, Officer . . . Hold it, I can speak English."

"You can explain later, sister. In the meantime, *you do as your fucking told* . . . Bill, slip these plastic zip ties on each of them."

Mike was lying face down, and the sound of an American accent was music to his ears but this was no Mozart's third symphony, it was "New York, New York," and he turned to look up at his captors.

"*Tony . . . Bill . . .* I don't believe it!"

"Well, *what do you know?* On your feet, buster, and a word of advice, Mike, *don't even think about it!*"

"Mike Summers, you are under arrest for the attempted murder of Laura Williams. I must warn you that anything you say may be taken down and used as evidence in a court of law."

Mona turned to Mike in disbelief, her eyes glowing red like a mad bull before the matador's sword trick. "Why you low down . . ."

"Save it for later, lady. There's a lynch mob in the street plenty mad at the sight of the two *amigos* heading for Boot Hill." Tony studied Mona again. "I gather you are Mona Menzel, the babe who was kidnapped? And these two?" Tony turned to Lena and Eva, the "five-minute" widows.

"Let them go. If it wasn't for them, we might both be getting measured for pine boxes. Now if you want outta here in one piece, then you untie me pronto, before that mob starts searching for a rope."

"Okay, lady, we're on your side . . . Bill, cut the plastics except for our friend here." He turned to Mike.

Eva burst into tears at the sight of Carlos's lifeless body leaking like a sieve. (Speaking in Spanish)

"*My poor Carlos . . . My poor husband!*" she screamed, kissing the cross around her neck before trying to dash forward, but Bill was fast on his feet, grabbing her and throwing her back.

"Mona, tell your new friend that if she knows what's good for her, she'll stay put until we've gone, and tell her friend to keep quiet!"

"*Lena, we're free!* Why the Niagara? And rich into the bargain." Eva was beside herself.

*　*　*

"Do you have wheels?" Mona asked, completely ignoring Mike.

"Sort of." Bill laughed, with his usual bad timing.

"It's no time for fun, signor. Give me your key, I will drive."

Bill passed Mona the keys to the dragster. "It's all yours, honey."

"Bill, keep a grip of wonder boy here." Tony was referring to Mike. "I'll go first, and you, lady." He motioned to Mona. "Stay close to me."

Tony crashed out, pointing the Browning at the crowd, menacingly waiving it from side to side with both arms outstretched; he meant business, and he wasn't afraid to use it.

"*Moverio . . . Moverio . . . Fuera de me camino . . .* Move it . . . Move it . . . Outta my way . . ."

The crowd immediately obeyed and let them through; it was not the day for heroes.

"Bill, cover our backs!" Tony shouted as they ran to the car.

"*Santa Maria!*" Mona yelled at the sight of the Mexican "Italian Job." You guys must be on a fucking budget!" She unlocked the door. "And locked too! *You gotta be kidding me!*"

Tony joined Mona in front after Bill bundled Mike into the back.

"*Come on . . . Come on!*" Mona yelled as she turned the key, the mob now more confident, running toward the car.

Ahey . . . Ahey . . . Burt . . . Burt . . . "*Start, you son of a bitch!*" she screamed.

Tony had already rolled down the front window, his left arm outstretched, his finger on the trigger.

Brrummm! The engine finally burst into life. "*Thank God!*"

Mona crunched the gears, then hit the pedal to the metal, the bug responding, snaking from side to side as its rear wheels searched for traction. At last, they were on their way, leaving a cloud of dust and the screams from the disappointed lynch mob.

"Where to, Mona?" Mike asked.

"To Recoleta, my father's house . . . That's if I'm lucky enough to find my way out of this dump."

The bug was bouncing like a rubber ball as its shocks bottomed out, hitting pothole after pothole, throwing everyone from side to side.

Mike just sat in silence. He knew the game was up, but he never once thought the cops would follow him to Argentina. His plan to stay here now in tatters, but worst of all, he would lose Mona and the "good life" dream.

And what was he going back to? A long prison stretch if found guilty, and a wife and family who now probably hated the ground he walked on. *What a mess!* He sighed, his eyes teared.

"I hear the noise from the cattle market, so we must be near the freeway. Hang on while I take this corner."

Mona swung the wheel hard to the left. She was used to driving an automatic, and fortunately the Volkswagen, with its low ground clearance and center of gravity, took the three sixty in its stride, creating a huge cloud of dust resembling a mini twister. Forgetting to use the clutch was a big mistake, and the inevitable happened: the bug protested, then stalled.

"Hell, this is all we need," Mona cursed as she slipped the stick in neutral and turned the key again.

Chug . . . chug . . . chug . . . They were in a standoff with the "Mexican." Mona hit the ignition again. *Chug . . .*

"That's it *everyone out!*" Tony shouted. "We'll have to push this fucking heap, or we'll never get it started."

The car emptied like lightning. There was no time for delay. The police by now would have been called to investigate the murders of Carlos and Sergio, and the last thing the New Yorkers needed was to be locked up in an Argentinean prison.

"That means you as well, Summers . . . *Out!*" Tony didn't mince his words, his one-time good friend now history.

"Mona, you stay at the wheel while we push. Once we turn the car around, then we'll give it all. I'll give you the signal to slip into first, and when we gather enough speed, I'll scream to release the clutch. Have you got that?"

Tony was already at the rear of the car, both hands on the engine hood, ready for the assault on "das auto."

"Yes, I hear you . . . *Now just fucking push!*" Mona could mix it when she wanted. This was not time for femininity.

Just as Bill put his shoulder to the wheel, Mike, although his hands were tied, suddenly saw an opportunity to do a runner and decided to do a Ben Johnson.

"*Why that fucking, no-good . . . !*" Bill dropped him like a stone with a rugby tackle, rolling Mike over and over in the dirt until he finally put his knee in Mike's back, with both hands below his chin in a "Hulk Hogan" hold. "Freeze it, Mike, or so help me, I'll break your fucking neck," Bill panted.

"Okay . . . Okay!" Mike screamed in pain, almost choking, and Bill applied even more pressure just to show he meant business.

"I said okay . . . *I said okay, for Christ's sake!*"

"On your feet and get in the back of that car." Bill grabbed Mike by the scruff of the neck and bundled him into the back of the Volkswagen, smashing his head on the door pillar for good measure.

"Come on, partner, push . . . *Push* . . . Steer it, Mona!" Tony yelled.

"What do think I'm trying to do? This crate has no power steering. Do you think I'm a fucking truck driver?"

"Mona, you're doing a great job." Bill was now using the gentle touch.

"That's it now, Mona, you're facing the right direction," Tony bawled.

"Now clutch in and stick to first."

Bill suddenly straightened up and motioned to Tony to keep quiet.

"Do you here that . . . *Cops!*"

There in the distance, loud and clear and heading straight toward them was the familiar sound of police sirens.

"*You're right, I hear it.*" Tony shook his head. "Bill, we gotta get this crate up to speed and crank that engine first time or we're dead in the water."

Bill looked toward the kids standing at the side of the road, intrigued with the road runner circus.

Tony fished inside his pocket and unfolded the crumpled notes. "Push . . . Push . . ." He handed the kids ten pesos each, then demonstrated with his hands on the back of the bug.

"Si." The oldest one smiled. He got the message, all right, flashing his white teeth. He couldn't be older than twelve, but it looked like he was the boss as he ordered his younger companions. "*Perisa . . . Perisa . . . de que la policia.*"

"Even I understood that." Bill laughed. "Come on, kids, push . . . again, push . . . *Come on, harder!*" The wail of the siren was getting closer and closer.

"Okay, Mona, it's time!" Tony yelled.

The Volkswagen gave a sickly shudder before it stalled again.

"*Fuck it!* Bill, you grab the wheel from Mona."

"Mona move over, this is *my* specialty . . . Okay, Tony, pour it on."

"Come on kids . . . *Push . . . Push.*"

Bill bade his time until he reached take-off speed, then released the clutch. "Old Betsy" was reluctant and coughed a couple of times before Bill caught the right timing and gassed the pistons, sending the car off like a rocket before Bill gently touched the brakes and slipped the stick into neutral. If he stalled the rear engine "primadonna" one more, it was the Buenos Aires "Watch House."

"Mona, I'll drive. Just point me in the right direction."

The flashing lights of the cruisers could be clearly seen through the dust cloud, now only five kilometre's away.

Mona leaped from the front seat and folded the seat back for Mike to get in the back.

"Let's get outta of here . . . Straight ahead, Bill. With luck, these bimbos will be too preoccupied with the police drama and won't even notice us."

Bill didn't wait for an encore and hit the gas, and as Mona rightly predicted, the cruisers screamed past, lights flashing, sirens blaring, oblivious to the dust-covered Volkswagen and Buenos Aires's most wanted.

CHAPTER 3

"Come on, Frank, wakey, wakey, rise and shine." Brody placed his bare foot on Frank's ass and gave him a mighty shove, almost pushing him from the bed.

"Maaaan . . . My head." Frank turned to face Jack, who was standing naked at the side of the bed, except for the towel wrapped around his waist.

"Listen, buddy, if you want to get to Woolworth Towers to start our shift at two, you had better get your lazy ass out of that cot."

Frank immediately sat up and ran his fingers through his unruly hair.

"What time is it?"

"For your information, it's twelve thirty-five, and it will take us at least thirty minutes to get to Fifth Avenue, and I don't want another run in with Buckley for being late again.

Frank didn't waste any more time and hit the floor running when he heard the supervisor's name. He already had a couple reprimands on record over his timekeeping, and with three strikes, you join the ranks of the unemployed.

"Have *you* already showered?" Frank asked.

"Do you think I'm standing here like this as an extra for Shakespeare's *Julius Caesar?*"

"Okay . . . Okay, I get your point, don't make me feel more the worse . . . *. My poor fucking head."* He walked naked to the bathroom. *"And keep your voice down!"*

Frank purposely left the bathroom door open to carry on the conversation from the shower box. He turned the faucet, then stood for a moment, adjusting the hot spray.

"So how did I end up in your apartment?" Frank yelled above the sound of the shower.

"Man, you were wasted, *I couldn't let you drive."*

"So where's my car?"

"Down in the visitors' car park. Teana drove the car . . . *You do remember Teana, don't you?"*

"Yeah, *don't remind me!"*

"*Man,* she was smoking hot, and you blew it. After you spoke to the mysterious Terry, you began hitting the tequila shots like they you were born in Mexico."

"And . . . ?"

"*Well,* when you arrived at my apartment, you were legless and kept hitting that cell phone of yours every ten minutes . . ." Brody shook his head. "You pissed off the best lay in town and she give you the ass and I don't blame her. I tell you, buddy, she looked hotter than Helen of Troy."

"And Maggie?"

"I had to make up for you *maaan,* to save our honour. In fact, Maggie only left about an hour ago."

"Thanks . . . That makes me feel worse still. Don't rub it in."

"So what's with this broad Terry anyhow? I mean why is she so special? I've never seen you hung up like this before on a chick."

Frank appeared, a towel round his waist while vigorously drying his hair, whereas Jack was already in his jeans and white T-shirt.

"Come on, Frank, move it."

"Have you seen my cell phone?"

"*Oh, no you don't . . .*"

*   *   *

Terry was still recovering from the "shock meeting" with Blakely. The last thing she expected was Simpson getting the axe. Jack had the deck stacked in his favor, and it was the Last Supper for Simpson. But now she saw a different side to her boss, an ambitious, cutthroat individual who would stop at nothing to climb the proverbial ladder. *But to hire a private detective?* That was something else! And the writing was on the wall. People who crossed his path would inevitably end up on "death row." But there again, Jack's offer was certainly attractive: the extra salary, the perks and the company car being the icing on the cake. She glanced at her watch; there was no point becoming depressed about a situation that hadn't materialized.

"*Four thirty-five . . .* That time already!" Terry was surprised. Where had the time gone? "Jack, I'm gonna take your advice and call it a day. It'll take me only five minutes to clean up my desk, and I'm outta here." The message signal on her cell phone chimed.

"Frank, go away and leave me in peace." Terry didn't even read it. She knew whom it was from. "*That guy!*" She was talking to herself as she slipped into her jacket. "I'm sorry, Frank, but once bitten, twice shy. I've been there and done that." Terry packed her notebook and headed for the elevator.

"Good night, Mildred, don't stay too late. I'll catch up with you tomorrow on what we discussed."

"Good night, Terry, I'll take you up on your offer."

Terry had won the day with the office witches and bitches, and she had to smile to herself . . . As they say, "those who live in glass houses . . ."

The elevator seemed to take forever before Terry finally reached the underground car park. As She finally slipped into the seat of the Mazda, her mind went back to poor Laura still in hospital, and she wondered what her friend would make of today's events.

Terry gunned the motor, the tires making a loud squealing noise on the sealed concrete as it climbed the ramp.

"Finishing early tonight, Terry?" Lee, the security guard smiled as he activated the exit barrier.

"Yeah, a girl's gotta have a life, Lee. Take it easy and don't do anything I wouldn't do." Terry laughed as she slipped into the evening traffic . . . But for her, what was on the cards tonight would be another story.

*   *   *

June was still concerned over Chuck Briggs's brush-off. She needed that money like there was no tomorrow. Sure, Phil had thrown her a lifeline with the job and all, but without Mike's severance pay and the sale of the property, she wouldn't last the month. There was only one road, and that was to take Briggs head-on, and she was just the lady to do it.

"But then I'm sure Phil will advise me," she spoke to herself in a half convincing tone before giving a demonstrative sigh. "What would I do without him?"

With so many problems coming at her like a driverless *Abraham* heading for the sand break, she had to get a grip of herself, not only for the sake of the children's future, but for her own pride and well-being.

Still in her housecoat, she rose from the sofa and glanced in the hallway mirror.

"*God*, I'm such a mess!" June ran her fingers through her unkempt hair, trying to place it in some sort of order. "If Phil could see me now, I'm sure he would be unimpressed . . . *God*, I feel so lazy, and there's nothing to do except prepare dinner for the kids, and it's only just turned one thirty." June was having a heated conversation with herself when the phone rang.

"This could be Phil!" June's depressed facial lines suddenly vanished.

"Yes, 7650 . . . June Summers here.'

"Mom, you sound so formal, it's Steven."

"There's nothing wrong, is there?" June couldn't help herself. It was unusual for the children to phone from college.

"No, there's nothing wrong, Mother, I'm sorry if I gave you a scare."

"You *did*, young man." June breathed a sigh of relief. "So?"

"Sis and I have been invited to an impromptu birthday bash . . . You remember Neil Davies? He came round to the house a couple of times. I think he has a crush on Sheryl."

"*Oh, do you now!* So I gather you and your sister will be skipping dinner tonight?"

"You're not annoyed are you, Mother?"

"No, not at all . . . But don't drink too much and look after your sister and remember you have college tomorrow."

"Will you be all right by yourself?" Steven sounded concerned.

"Sure, I'll be all right. Besides I have a dinner appointment tonight." June gave a muffled laugh.

"*Another one!* Let me guess . . . ?"

"Enough of that . . . *And remember, don't be late!*"

"Bye, Mom, and have a nice evening . . . Love you."

June grinned as she hung up. "*Oh, to be young again . . .*" She shook her head. "Now what am I gonna do until seven? First things first . . . *That coffee . . .*"

As June walked toward the kitchen, the phone rang again.

"Now *who could this be?*" She lifted the receiver.

"Yes?" June's voice sounded rattled.

"Have I caught you at a bad time? Phil here."

"*Phil!* I apologize. It's been one phone call after another, and I guess you know what that's like?"

"No bad news, I hope?"

"Naw, the kids and all that stuff."

"June, I was thinking about tonight's dinner. Why don't we go to Taco Bell for touch of Mexico? Nothing formal, and we can just relax. Slip on a pair of Levi's, a T-shirt, and sneakers like our old NYU days . . . How does that grab you?"

"*Love it!*"

"Then I'll pick you up at seven."

"That is, if I can still squeeze into my jeans . . ."

* * *

As Terry swung into the Roosevelt Memorial car park, she felt lower than low. She needed a lift, and who better to cheer her up than best friend, Laura.

She parked the Mazda and cut the engine. Tonight, for some reason, the car park was half empty, but then it had just turned five thirty, and most people were still at work. As Terry walked to the front desk, she could hear the familiar voice of Martha, as always, completely in charge, issuing directives over the phone, most probably to some poor trainee nurse. She hung up, then cussed a few times under her breath before looking up.

"*Terry!*" she exclaimed; her expression now completely changed. "It's nice to see you again, and where's my boyfriend tonight?"

"Frank? *Ah* . . . He's on the midshift and doesn't finish until ten."

"We miss having him around. Too bad he was transferred, but I'm sure we'll see him again, huh?" Martha was hinting at their relationship, which made Terry feel even more uncomfortable after the ugly events of yesterday evening.

"You can go straight up, honey . . . Eighth floor, room 22. Your good friend Laura requested a room with a view. I guess she was getting bored staring at four walls and square eyes watching Fox."

The phone rang. "Martha Warring . . . Duty sister . . ."

Terry gave her a sort of "thank you" wave as she walked to the elevator. Martha was still preoccupied on the phone.

"A room with a view," Terry spoke to herself, half smiling as she pressed 8. "Sounds good."

As Terry stood patiently in the elevator, her empty stomach gave a low rumble resembling that of distant thunder.

"Boy, *am I hungry!*" The elevator chimed. "Floor 8 . . . Thank you."

"Between cell phones and talking elevators." Terry shrugged. "What's the world coming to? And they call this progress?" She stopped to study the signboard in the corridor.

"Let me see . . . Straight ahead, follow the blue line, then turn left at the bottom of the hallway . . . *Huuum,*" Terry sort of grunted as she stepped it out.

"*At last,* room 22." Terry stood on her toes and peered through the small rectangular window; unaware Laura was engrossed in some pulp fiction.

Terry quietly opened the door without knocking; there's nothing like the element of surprise.

"Ta-da! Surprise . . . Surprise." Terry stepped into the room, her arms waving above her head.

The look of surprise and happiness on Laura's face was priceless—they say a picture paints a thousand words. Laura protested, touching her bandaged throat as if to say, "If only I could speak."

Terry gave her a gentle hug, then a kiss on the cheek before taking the chair.

"My poor feet." Terry moaned, having slipped out of her five-inch-heels, vigorously massaging her toes.

"Laura, I hate to tell you, but I am seriously hungry. I know it sounds terrible, but when is dinner served?"

Laura couldn't contain her laughter and motioned with her hand as if to say "Don't be embarrassed" before she stretched over to grab her notepad and pen and began to scribble.

Terry, what a nice surprise . . . You can share my dinner.

Not on your life! I mean how would it look? Your best friend coming to visit you in hospital to scrounge a free meal?

Laura burst into laughter again at Terry's comment.

Don't be silly, just look at me! With three meals a day and supper into the bargain . . . when I get discharged, I'll have to join Jenny Craig.

They both burst into laughter at the thought.

"Maybe we can join together." Terry was on a roll when the door suddenly opened, and the dinner cart rumbled into the room.

"Your dinner, Laura." The young trainee nurse in the pink Florence Nightingale cap gave a warm smile. "As you have a visitor, I'll return after you finish eating to check your temperature and pressure." She gave another smile, then left.

"Wow, this looks good." Terry admired the overladen food cart.

Go ahead, honey, be my guest. Just leave me that tub of yogurt. I'm still recovering from my lunch.

"If you say so . . ."

*   *   *

"My, someone must have been hungry." The young nurse pushed the cart aside, the stacked empty plates making an annoying rattling sound.

"This won't take long, Laura. I'll get out of your hair as quick as I can. I'm sure you and your visitor have lots to talk about."

She quickly took Laura's temperature and blood pressure, then flashed the miniature torch into each of her eyes.

"*Hmmm,* it's all good." She took the clipboard from the bottom of the bed and entered the readings. "Just one more check." She lifted the bedclothes. "Good, I'll leave you now. If you need anything, just press that buzzer. I'll be back at ten before I finish my shift. *Ciao . . .*"

*   *   *

And Simpson was fired! That's one for the books. But Blakely . . . I can't believe it. For fame and fortune, he'll stop at nothing.

"But, Laura, *the gumshoe!*" Terry interrupted. "That's something else . . . And even more scary, Jack is almost certain that Hall will offer him Simpson's position, and more to the point, where does that leave me?"

That's pretty obvious, but would you accept? It's a great opportunity, but don't count your chickens before they're hatched. "I'm looking for your advice, Laura." *My advice? Jump at it.*

"I knew you would say that, but I'm just scared. Anyhow, I told him I would sleep on it."

So, are you seeing Frank after you leave from here?

"That's another problem for another day," Terry glumly replied.

Don't tell me!

"Afraid so . . . I caught the bastard cheating on me last night. *Pool night with the boys, my ass!* And as for that broad that gave me an earful on the phone, believe me, the last thing she was there for was playing pool . . . Laura, I've been burned before, and now I won't take any of this crap. I've made up my mind . . . It's *sayonara.*"

Too bad. He was a hunk.

"Yeah, but a two-timing hunk."

Just as Terry was about to expand on her hate campaign, her phone buzzed.

"*Not again . . .*"

*   *   *

June had finished showering and was sitting in front of the dressing table clad only in her G-string and sexy half-cupped bra, putting the final touches to her makeup.

"It's been a long time since I've felt good about myself, and I still can't believe that at forty-two I'm still in the market." June was in a conversation with herself as she ran the brush through her hair. "And up until to now, no sign of the dreaded grey . . . Now the real deal . . ." She walked over to the bed to challenge the Levi's. *"Here goes."*

She slipped into the legs and jumped up and down, squeezing into the elusive space that was left. *"Ughhh,* just about there." She screwed up her face in pain before taking another deep breath and sucking in her abdomen, and finally much to her liberation, the top button popped home. *"Is that a relief?* Not bad!" June studied herself again in the full-length mirror. "Thank God I decided to wear a G-string, otherwise the world would see my panty lines . . . *Now the T-shirt.* Sheryl, it looks like I'll have to raid your wardrobe.

"Hell, I had better watch my time." She glanced at her watch. "Or before I know it, Phil will be ringing the doorbell."

June quickly stepped it up. Sheryl's room was only a stone's throw away, and before she knew it, she had selected a simple white cotton T-shirt complete with the red heart and the famous slogan, "I Love New York," and she eagerly slipped it over her head.

"Nice . . . But there's something not right! *Hmmmm* . . . Of course, *the bra.* It makes me look like a hump-front camel. The bra has to go." She stretched her arms behind her back and undid the hooks. *"Now* that's more like it! And sexy too. It's full house tonight, Phil . . . Now where's my Nikes?"

* * *

No sooner had June slipped into her sneakers then, as predicted, the doorbell rang.

"Just in time, that must be Phil." She bounded down the stairs like a two-year-old.

"Coming!" she yelled at the top of her voice before finally opening the front door.

"June, you're panting." Phil was sporting his usual warm smile.

"I was worried," June teased. "In case you thought I had stood you up and no one was home."

Phil just laughed, treating June's comment as a throwaway. "Changing the subject . . . June, you look like a young college grad." Phil had that serious look as he stared into her eyes. "Where have you been all my life?"

"You're not doing so bad yourself, *young man.* Now aren't you going to give a damsel in distress a big kiss?

Phil grinned. "This is the best part." He stooped and gently brushed her lips. It was short but passionate and respectful.

"I like your shirt . . . NYU. And these muscles . . ." June jokingly felt Phil's biceps. *"Not bad!"*

"Cut it out, you're embarrassing me." Phil slipped his arms around June's waist and kissed her again.

"Do you want to come in for a few minutes? The kids have gone to a birthday bash."

"Not on your life. I don't trust myself."

"In that case, you had better escort me to your car or the neighbours will have a ball, and that's the last thing I need."

"Madame, s'il vous plait." Phil offered his arm.

"Merci, monsieur." June laughed as she looped her arm through Phil's.

"If we keep this up"—Phil was laughing—"maybe we should go to a French restaurant."

* * *

June made herself comfortable, sinking into the plush leather of the Cadillac Deville.

"Taco Bell, it brings back memories. Phil. Do you remember the outlet the gang used to go on Green Street, not from O'Malley's, the Irish pub?"

The big grin on Phil's face was a dead giveaway. "I'll let you take a guess where I'm taking you tonight."

"Naw . . . I don't believe you!"

* * *

From East River to Manhattan is a good forty-five minutes' drive, and what better opportunity to reminisce on bygone days and the events that led them to meet again after almost two decades.

"My, how time flies." June commented, now fully relaxed and, for a change, not at the wheel. "You know, Phil, it's been almost twenty years since we left NYU, and to this day I still regret dropping out of law school."

"June, darling," Phil reassuringly touched her hand. "In hindsight, we can all be smart. The secret is not to make the same mistake twice, huh?"

"You're throwing me a curver. Anyhow, it's all your fault. If you had only noticed that I had a serious crush on you . . . *Well* . . . Things might have been a lot different."

"So *that's* it!" Phil couldn't control his laughter. "Just like a woman, after twenty years, still nursing a grudge."

"You deserve it, you big heel, leaving me in the lurch like that." June was teasing him, but beneath the charade of joviality, she was smarting at the thought of what could have been.

"June, believe me, I *wish* I could turn the clock back."

"Do you really mean that?"

"If I weren't driving, I would kiss you right now!" "Do you want to pull over?" June teased.

"*What,* in this traffic?" Phil laughed.

"Everything is possible . . ."

* * *

"We're not far off now," Phil commented as he hung a right into West Houston. He would take a right at McDougal Street and pass NYU.

"Doesn't the old building with its unmistakable facade and fort-like battlements do something to you?"

"And these lights add the nostalgic touch, don't you think?" June asked.

"Yeah, I can almost feel a lump in my throat."

"Why, you sentimentalist! Now I see another side of Phil Stevens."

"Lawyers, much to the public's negative impression, are human too, you know."

"I know you are, darling, I was just teasing. Now it's my turn . . . Deja vu. If you weren't driving, I would kiss you right now!"

"Well, now's your opportunity." Phil grinned as he drove into Taco Bell's car park.

* * *

The restaurant chain is famous for Mexican fast food on the run. The spacious car park was starved of cars, but then, being a Wednesday evening, TV dinners, "square eyes," and PlayStations are now the new American dream.

* * *

The famous Taco Bell logo was prominent on the large neon sign standing on a pole at least fifteen feet tall, its gold brightly lit bell reflecting shadows on the sidewalk. The facade, as always, is standard red brick, and the red tiled roof was emphasized with rows of low-voltage lighting giving it a sort of Christmas look, its arched doorways a desperate attempt to add the Mexican touch. But it wouldn't be Taco Bell without the brightly painted fibre glass hombre about five foot tall, complete with the large coloured sombrero and blue-and-white poncho, flashing his outrageous teeth with the banana smile and the heavy black *amigo* moustache; his arm outstretched pointing the way to the entrance.

* * *

Once Phil had pulled into the parking slot and cut the engine, it was an opportunity he couldn't miss.

"What did you say . . . Everything is possible?" he teased. But before June could answer, Phil smothered her lips with a long, passionate kiss.

"*Why, Phil Stevens!*" she gasped. "You're not only a sentimentalist, but a hopeless romantic as well. *But* . . . Between you and me, the Taco Bell car park is not my scene."

"*Oh,* for our NYU days!" Phil laughingly sighed. "Car parks, discos, anyplace was right at that time when you were in love. But then I suppose you could say we are mature adults and now appreciate the better things in life." "*Like a dinner at Taco Bell!*" June couldn't miss the cheap shot.

"Now *you're* teasing me! It was my idea to turn the clock back and . . ." Phil was now laughing between his words. "We look like the oldest students in town trying to recapture our 'ill spent' youths. But June, you gotta admit, it's different . . . *Viva Mexicana.*"

"Si, signor. Now give me another kiss before the chillies ruin my taste buds . . ."

* * *

The decor in the restaurant was still outrageously unchanged. Large, illuminated, brightly coloured plastic-ballooned pictures of the various dishes and the chef's specials, which never look the same once they hit the plate. The red simulated leather bench seated booths, and the white Formica-topped tables gave the place a characterless look. But then, what do you expect with a fast-food chain where all the fixtures and fittings appeared to have fallen of an assembly line . . . *Unfortunately, much like the food!* The dark-blue service counter with the large pink Taco Bell on the front encircled with a ring of pale blue looked different; maybe it was a new marketing ploy to project a high-tech image and attract the younger clientele. Who knows? But for sure, the Mexican counterfeit menu was still the same.

* * *

The restaurant was almost empty, so the seating choice was a personal preference.

"Let's take that booth in the far corner. It's quiet and inconspicuous." June didn't reply as Phil took her hand and escorted her to the table.

They had just taken their seats when the young kid, presumably in college, approached, dressed in the Taco Bell uniform. The red baseball cap with the gold threaded logo and yellow bell, supposedly complementing the short-sleeved red shirt with dark-blue cuffs and collar, loosely hanging over a pair of black slacks and red sneakers, could easily be mistaken for a competition between McDonald's and Pizza Hut for the ugliest outfit, and Taco Bell was way ahead.

* * *

"Here are the menus, sir." The hard-backed menus displayed the Taco Bell Chihuahua embossed on the cover, with the caption "I *Yo Quiero* Taco Bell." As for the kid? He was polite and good looking into the bargain.

"Eh . . . Err, John," Phil read his name tag. "Two frozen margaritas to start with, *eh*, if that's all right with you, June?"

"How could I forget."

"John, something tells me that you are a university student."

"Your intuition is correct, sir . . . NYU." John dished out the proud smile.

"Now isn't that a coincidence," Phil joked.

John was no dummy, having noticed Phil's NYU T-shirt as the couple entered the restaurant and had put two and two together.

"John, do you eat here often?" Phil asked.

The kid smiled. "Only when it's free."

"*Ha-ha* . . ." Phil laughed. "Then can you recommend what's best on the menu?"

"Let me see. First of all, are you hungry?"

"June?"

"I only had sandwich for lunch. Yeah, I'm feeling a bit peckish." June made a face.

"Okay, fire away. You heard the lady."

"To start with . . . Volcano Nachos . . . Then two grilled steak taquitos . . . A crunchy Taco Supreme and a Fiesta Salad on the side."

"Phil, I hope it's not too much!"

"Aw, we can always take a doggie bag home for the kids."

"Then I'm with you." June smiled. This had the makings of an unforgettable evening.

"We'll take your advice, kid, and remember the margaritas. I don't know about you, June, but my throat is parched."

"I'll be back in five, sir . . . The food will take a little longer. Would you wish me to serve the salad first?" Phil turned to look at June.

* * *

The food only half finished, Phil sat back and wiped his mouth with his napkin, then took another satisfying sip from the outrageously large margarita glass.

"So, June, what's your opinion of the food?" "It was not that bad." June frowned.

"That means it wasn't that good either."

"The salad was good."

Phil burst into laughter. "How does that song go . . . ? 'You say it best when you say nothing at all.'"

"I didn't mean it that way, darling. Your company is the most important thing, and *I'm really enjoying myself.*"

Phil stared across the table into June's eyes and gently squeezed her hand.

"Honey, you say the nicest things . . ."

"Phil, while we have a moment and I apologize for raising this over dinner . . . I'm worried . . . It's . . ." June paused. "It's just that, if Briggs reneges on Mike's severance entitlement . . . I feel really terrible saddling you with all my baggage."

"Don't you worry your pretty little head, that's what I'm here for. Listen, I've given it some thought, and what I suggest is . . . Number 1, you search for Mike's contract of employment. Then you have a legal document to pursue litigation. *But* . . . The problem might arise that Mike may have filed it in his office. Of course, if Global goes under and Briggs files for chapter 11 as a small creditor, the chances of getting Mike's entitlement is very slim, to say the least."

Phil could have bitten his tongue at his insensitiveness, noticing June's eyes.

"Honey, don't worry." Phil reassuringly held her hand again. "If it makes you feel more comfortable, I can always instruct the accounts department to give you a salary advance."

June half cried and half laughed. *"And I haven't even started my job yet!"* They both burst into laughter at seeing the funny side.

"There's no substitute for laughter, honey. Now doesn't that make you feel better?" Phil kept it going.

"I gotta hand it to you, darling, I feel much better. But at the thought of being a party pooper, Phil, I'm legally worried for you."

"Legally for me?" Phil was amused. "Now tell me what's bothering you now?"

"Like . . . A lawyer having an affair with his client. You know, like the doctor-patient taboo."

Phil laughed again.

"Now you're making fun of me." June put on a face.

"I'm sorry, honey. I know you have the best intentions, but to put your mind at ease, *firstly, you are not my client.* You are an employee of Stevens & Stevens, but you are the client of Glen Jacobs, who is processing papers for your divorce. *Now,* if you were having an affair with *him,* that *would* be extremely serious . . ." Phil was trying hard to control his laughter. "Anyhow, who said we are having an affair?"

"*Well, aren't we?*"

Phil couldn't stop laughing.

"Yes, but don't tell everyone . . . *Check please . . .*"

*　　*　　*

The drive to East River was both witty and funny, but June couldn't help feel that this is too good to be true and, as they say, "the lull before the storm." "*Ah,* here we are!" Phil steered the Buick into the driveway.

As the two long-distance lovers sat in awkward silence, June decided to break the ice.

"Phil, would it be unladylike to entice you in for a nightcap or a coffee?"

"A coffee *would* be enticing after that margarita and that poor excuse for Mexican delicacies salted up to the hilt. My mouth is parched, but I promise I won't stay long."

"Have you forgotten the kids are at a birthday bash?"

"No, and that's what's bothering me." Phil gave a cheeky grin.

"I trust you, millions wouldn't. Now gimme a big kiss, and let's get outta this car."

"Your wish is my command."

"Stop fooling around, and gimme that kiss, you big heel . . ."

*　　*　　*

June unlocked the door and switched the lounge lights on.

"Phil, why don't you take a seat in the lounge and make yourself comfortable on the sofa. I'll be back in a moment once I coffee up . . . You did say coffee, didn't you?"

"Yes, but I would kill for a glass of ice water."

"Then come join me in the kitchen and help yourself from the icebox."

As June opened the kitchen cupboard while standing on her toes to retrieve the container of ground coffee, she suddenly felt Phil's arms around her waist.

"Something tells me the ice water was just an excuse?" June joked.

But she was no fool and quickly restrained Phil's hands to prevent them moving upward, but before she could protest Phil spun her round to face him. There was no holding him back, and he pressed hard against June's mouth, exploring her open lips and the inner depths of the moist cavity. It was sudden and unexpected but also invigorating, and as for June, she was enjoying every moment of it, an experience she had long forgotten, and she reciprocated by standing on her toes and wrapping her arms around Phil's neck. She wasn't going to let this guy go easily. But breathing is important, and she had to break the deadlock to surface for the essential oxygen. But it was time for "mission abort," and she gently pressed her hands against Phil's chest to separate their bodies as she could feel the rock-hard lump against her abdomen. It was too early for the sex thing; besides she had never experienced another man other than Mike. And what would Phil think if she jumped between the sheets on their second date? No, it was time to ring the bell and return to their separate corners.

"Now, mister, are you going to let me brew this coffee?"

Phil knew where June was coming from, and he couldn't blame her. In fact, he felt somewhat embarrassed at coming on so strong. "June, I . . ."

She pressed her two fingers against his lips.

"*Shush,* it's as much my fault as yours. It's just . . ."

"I understand, honey, and *I* really apologize."

"Please, Phil . . . *don't.* It's just that I'm scared to fall hard again and so soon."

"June don't be scared. I feel the same away about you. Since you have come back into my life, it has given the word *living* a new meaning, and now I never want to let you go."

Fortunately, or unfortunately, the lovers could hear the voices of the children as the front door unlocked.

Phil looked into June's eyes. "Can I kiss you once more?" he asked sheepishly.

"Of course, you can, darling, but make it quick." June had that twinkle in her eyes.

"Mother, are you home?" It was Steven's voice.

"I'm in the kitchen with Phil, putting on the percolator."

"Hi, Phil."

"*Eh, err* . . . Steven . . . Sheryl. How did the party go?" Phil had a slight bloom on his cheeks, and June squeezed his hand as if to say, "*Yeah, we almost got caught.*"

Sheryl half turned to catch her brother's eye, a cheeky grin on her face.

"Eh . . . The usual," Steven replied. "You know, the disco thing, and kids getting smashed . . ."

"Well, you were doing all right with that dish Samantha Norton, like she couldn't get enough of you."

"Now, sis, don't get me started, I seem to remember . . ."

"I'm off to bed, Mom." Sheryl didn't cherish the thought of mixing it. "Good night, Mr. Stevens."

"Yeah, I'm off as well, Mom. Say, I like the young getup." Steven just couldn't let it go. "You look as if you are both dressed for a college reunion."

"That was supposed to be the idea . . ."

Steven had to laugh at his mother's remark; she could be very witty at times.

"So how was the dinner?"

"I'll tell you about it over breakfast," June replied, getting slightly agitated.

"I gotta be going June, it's past my bedtime. If you don't mind, I'll take a rain check on that coffee."

"Steven, *bed!* Come, Phil, I'll see you to the door."

"Good night, Mr. Stevens."

"Good night, Steven."

"I'm sorry about the coffee, Phil, but you know how inquisitive teenagers are."

Phil smiled and gave her a gentle good-night kiss. "It's a small thing . . . Oh, June, before I go, I think it would be prudent that you visit the office tomorrow so that I can introduce you to the staff . . . Say . . . around ten thirty?"

"As they say, the sooner the better."

June stood on her toes and returned the gesture. "Drive carefully, darling."

PART 6

The Great Escape

CHAPTER 1

The "antique" police cruisers screamed to a halt in a cloud of dust, almost shunting the '52 Pontiac Chieftain. On either side of the coupe lay the crumpled bodies of Carlos and Sergio, bloating in the midday sun, the buzz of large blue flies, attracted by the dead-body aroma, already actively laying their eggs in the cadaver's facial cavities.

As always, the crowd of onlookers were enjoying the real-life MGM drama of cops and robbers and the gory sight of blood-soaked corpses sprawled in the dust where they had been ruthlessly gunned down. Death has no dignity.

As for Eva and Lena, they were standing as if frozen in time, like two lost sheep, confused and bewildered, their tearless eyes expressing their relief at finally being free from the two "biggest losers" but, then again, laced with uncertainty as to what to expect from the corrupt Argentine police whose reputation in this field is second to none.

*   *   *

(Speaking in Spanish)

The doors of the Falcon violently swung open, overriding their restraint rods and buckling the front bodywork as the police drama unfolded.

"*Benito* . . ." The sergeant barked, hitting the ground running, *pistola* drawn.

"Control the crowd and see if you can get statements on what happened here and who phoned."

"Si, Sergeant." Benito pulled out his pristine notepad, its first page still virgin.

507

"*Celino,* check the bodies for signs of life." The sergeant was on a run before finally turning his attention toward the two bereaved *casadas,* his gun pointing menacingly at the so-called widows.

"Do you know these *hombres?*" he asked, finally placing the *pistola* back in the holster, showtime over.

The sound of the sergeant's voice was enough to trigger the "Niagara," and Eva turned on the waterworks for her first "audition." She had to dramatize the loss of her beloved, gunned down in cold blood in front of her very eyes, so to speak.

"Yes, this one is my boyfriend." Eva nervously stooped over, gently closing Carlos's eyes. Even though she had had a terrible life with this drunken, out-of-work petty criminal, for a moment she felt heartbroken at the sight of the man she once loved, now ashen grey, lying motionless in the dirt in his humiliating hour of death.

"I'm asking you a question, signora . . . *Do you hear me?*"

"Who do you think you are? *Fucking God?* Of course, I hear you," Eva shot back, her hatred for the cops opening old wounds. "His name is Carlos Mendez, and for what it's worth, we live on the other side of Villamisseria."

"And *your* name?"

"Eva Alfaro . . . Now are you fucking happy?"

"You watch your mouth, bitch . . . *Say* . . ." The sergeant wrinkled his brow, trying to recollect. "Haven't I seen you before? *Yeah,* now I remember . . . Prostitution and using drug paraphernalia . . . A 'two-time loser' coming up for the big one."

"*Maybe.*" Eva shrugged in a "so what" attitude.

"Don't worry, honey, be assured, I'll check you out at the station."

The sergeant had that evil glint in his eyes. So why not use it to his advantage?

"You still look good, babe. If you would like to come inside and do as I tell you, I could have a severe memory lapse."

"Over my dead body, *you fucking pervert.*" Eva was no pushover. For money, yes, but for this ugly *bastardo,* with his bad breath and body odor, she would rather face the judge in the morning.

"Have it you own way, honey, but the offer still stands if you change your mind . . . And . . ." Flavio suddenly stopped in his tracks, turning his attention to Lena. "Who are you?"

"My name is Lena Garcia. That's my husband, Sergio, lying at the other side of the car."

"Hmmm." The sergeant was noting the names when something struck him, and he nervously fumbled for his cell phone.

"Si, Sergeant Flavio Muro here. I need to speak to Lieutenant Medina, it's urgent . . ."

*   *   *

"And you say their names are Carlos Mendez and Sergio Garcia?" "Si, Lieutenant," Flavio nervously replied.

"There's an APB for their arrest for the suspected murders of Francisco Gomez and Marcos Perez . . . Unfortunately, now posthumously. Get the bodies to the city morgue for an autopsy, and phone me immediately after you get the statements on how they were murdered . . . I have a hunch, but it might be premature."

"Si, Lieutenant." Muro closed the line, then turned his attention again to Lena.

"Sergeant . . ."

"What the fuck is it now, Diego? Can't you see I'm questioning the suspects?"

"But, Sergeant, you must come with me and see this." He pointed to the doorway of Lena's shack.

Muro gave a disgusted sigh before following the corporal.

"And you two." He turned to Eva and Lena as he crossed the doorway.

"I'm not finished with you yet, so don't get any fucking crazy ideas."

Eva turned to Lena; she was running scared. Only a dummy couldn't guess what was about to hit the fan.

"Now *we have* big problems."

"Shut your mouth, Eva, and let me do the talking . . ."

*   *   *

"Are you all right, Bill?" Mona asked, concerned at the sight of Bill's blood-soaked shirt.

"*For Christ's sake, Mona!* It's only a scratch." Hayden was a guy that didn't like to be fussed over.

"*Turn left . . . Quickly, Bill . . . Turn left!*" Mona screamed. "We almost missed the exit to Av Leopoldo Lugones, the main highway that takes us directly into town."

The bug slew from side to side as Bill turned the wheel hard to the right, then tried to correct the oversteer, almost overshooting the exit.

"*Thanks, Mona, for the early warning!*" Bill was being more than sarcastic.

As for Tony and Mike, one can imagine, they were being thrown from side to side as the bug struggled to climb the steep dirt ramp, momentarily becoming airborne before crashing down hard on the tarmac, showering sparks like the Fourth of July from its rear exhaust, almost ripping it from its mountings in the process as the VW's shocks bottomed out. The blare of car horns and screaming rubber was deafening as the stream of heavy traffic swerved to avoid the "German" intruder.

"That was close." Bill gave a sigh of relief as he straightened the bug.

"Guys, I gotta tell you, we're gonna have big problems when we hit the city. Every man and his dog will be looking for ARG 6018."

"Thanks, Mona, for your reassurances. That's all we fucking need." This was Bill at his best.

"So?" Tony's voice echoed from the rear.

"So, Bill keeps the pedal to the metal until we reach the central roundabout, and then we take it from there. Guys, I'm sorry for the good news, but there's no other route we can take to Recoleta." Now it was Mona's turn to be sarcastic, the stress getting to her.

As normal the traffic began to congest, slowing the stream of irate drivers to a halt as the central roundabout came into sight, connecting to the famous Nueve de Julio, the widest street in the world.

"*Awe . . . Awe . . .* This doesn't look good." Mona pointed toward the three traffic cops on duty standing rigidly on their customized pedestals, frantically making all sorts of contortioned motions to direct the oncoming six-lane traffic.

As for Bill, he could only slowly weave in and out of the congestion until finally stopping only fifty meters from "D-day."

"Which exit, Mona?" he yelled, preparing to hit the floor. But before she could answer, one of the traffic cops stared at the blue Volkswagen as if memorizing the number plate. Then suddenly he ceased his traffic antics and opened his cell phone, said a few words, then nodded before unfastening the safety lug on his holster while keeping the bug in his sights.

Bill, who was inadvertently waiting for Mona's reply, wasn't paying attention to the car immediately in front that had suddenly braked, and the inevitable happened.

"*Fuck it!*" Bill yelled as their bumpers crunched, stalling the engine, and he automatically reacted by slipping the stick into neutral and trying to restart.

Chug . . . chug . . . chug . . .

"Aw, no . . . Don't fucking tell me!" Bill yelled in frustration.

The driver in front had already hit the tarmac, screaming all sorts of abuse in Spanish.

"I tell you, Mona. Who needs shit like this?" Bill just couldn't believe his bloody luck.

The traffic cop was now at full speed, gun drawn, running toward the commotion, leaping between the bumper-to-bumper traffic. This guy was running faster than a South African buck.

"Bill, gimme your gun . . . *Come on . . . Come on!*" Mona screamed, impatiently holding out her hand out.

"My gun?" Bill exploded.

"Don't ask fucking questions, *just do as I say!*"

Mona grabbed the Browning and swung open the passenger door; the vocal motorists spotting the semiautomatic went suddenly quiet and crouched for cover below their dashboards. In Buenos Aires, no one argues with a *pistola*.

Mona's mind was racing. They were in a desperate situation; the gun toting cop getting nearer and nearer. Then she spotted the green-and-white taxi to her right. It was their only hope.

"*Out . . . Out!*" she screamed at the driver, through his open window, the muzzle of the Browning only six inches from his forehead.

"Si . . . Si . . . signorina." He raised his hands above his head as Mona opened the car door and dragged the pear-shaped driver onto the roadway on his knees.

"Don't fucking move, do you hear me?"

"*Si . . . Si . . . Si.*" The cab driver was now a nervous wreck, thinking that he might be robbed.

"Bill . . . Tony . . . Get into the taxi . . . *Hurry . . . Hurry* and bring that scum Mike with you. That cop's getting too close for comfort."

The four-door Ford was a blessing in disguise, and they all piled into the Falcon.

"*Bill,* you're the wheel man. Do your thing and get us out of this shit.

Take the first exit on the right . . . *Comprender?*" Mona screamed.

"Loud and clear."

Bill shunted the car behind, then swiped the car on the right using the heavy-gauge Falcon like a competitor in a demolition derby. But the agile cop was now only meters away and well within range.

Bill hit the gas pedal and went straight for the cop; it was his only chance to shake him off. The young policeman was taken off guard, throwing himself onto the hood of another taxi to avoid being hit, but as the taxi sped past, the cop somehow managed to squeeze off three rounds, sparks flying as the snub-nosed thirty-eights pierced the heavy gauge of the taxi. But this guy was going for broke, squeezing another three rounds in quick succession at the rear of the taxi, smashing the window and the left side mirror, sending the high tensile glass into a hundred fragments before the car was finally out of range.

"Come on, Bill, hit the gas. Another fifteen minutes and we'll be home.

Is everyone all right?" Mona asked now that the commotion had died. "Yeah, I'm okay," Bill answered. "But that was close . . . Tony . . . Mike?" "I'm all right," Mike answered.

"*Pity . . .,*" Bill replied. "*Tony?*"

"*Yeah . . . Err . . .* Yeah, I'm all right."

Tony could feel this strange burning sensation in his right side, and he pressed the wound with his hand, the warm liquid oozing through his fingers leaking like a sieve, and he momentarily studied his blood-soaked hand. Having seen many gunshot wounds in the Big Apple, he knew he was in big trouble, and it didn't go unnoticed.

Knowing how popular he was, Mike was reluctant to convey Tony's predicament to his captors but having noticed Tony's crimson hand and from the colour of his complexion, he knew it was life threatening. "Bill."

"Yeah, what do *you* want?" There was no love lost between these two.

"It's Tony. He's bleeding badly and needs a doctor immediately or he'll go into shock . . ."

* * *

(Speaking Spanish)

"*Santa Laura Vicuna.*" Flavio made the sign of the cross. "What do you make of this, *Corporal?*" Flavio was studying the "dungeon room" where the captors were imprisoned.

"It has all the hallmarks of a kidnapping . . . The empty plastic water bottles, the electric tie cables, ropes, hoods, and the makeshift toilet. Unless I'm wrong, Sergeant, my guess is this place could be where Mona Menzel was held captive by her kidnappers."

"Corporal, I think we're on to something that's bigger than big. Go get these two broads. I think they know a lot more than they are saying."

"Si, Sergeant." The corporal seemed pleased with his postulation, another stripe flashing before his eyes.

* * *

"You two, inside. Sergeant Flavio wants to ask you some questions."

"What did I tell you?" Eva was now in panic mode.

"Shut your fucking mouth . . . Do you hear me?" Lena whispered. "You two stop talking and move it."

* * *

Flavio was sitting at the rickety table.

"Take a seat, *signoras*." An evil smile on his face. "I'm sure you are in familiar territory since Signora Garcia confirmed that this is where you both were at the time of the shootings."

The two women reluctantly took their chairs; they had an uneasy hunch that the game was up.

"*Now listen to me.* Kidnapping is a federal offense, punishable by death or life imprisonment if found guilty . . ."

"But, Sergeant." Eva was the weak link in the chain, and by the "scared shitless" look on her face, the sergeant knew he had struck gold.

"*Shut up*, you stupid bitch, or you'll get us both hanged!" Lena emptied her lungs.

"*You* . . ." Flavio pointed to Lena. "*Shut up!* Don't worry, *signora*, your turn will come . . ." He turned again to Eva. "Carry on, I'm listening." The sergeant was playing the good cop.

"It was all Sergio's idea to kidnap Mona Menzel," she blurted out. "To get the ransom money to pay for a drug bust that went wrong. They were being threatened by Francisco Gomez and Marcos Perez, the big boys. If they didn't pay up, they would find themselves on a slab in the city morgue, and Carlos went along with Sergio's suggestion. Me and Lena had nothing to do with it, you gotta believe me. In fact, I convinced Lena to let Menzel and the American free after the men left on some kind of business this morning. Why if it wasn't for me . . ."

"You lying *bastarda* . . . You low-down snake . . . How can you tell such lies?" Lena went into orbit.

"I'm telling you for the last time, Garcia . . . *Shut up!* Continue, *signora* . . ."

"It was like this . . . Against Lena's protests, I had just finished untying the Menzel woman and the Americano when I heard Carlos and Sergio return.

I was scared out of my mind because if I was caught in the act, Carlos would kill me, and I knew Lena would rat on me."

"*You bastard,* I don't believe my ears. *How could you, Eva . . . How could you?*" Lena was in tears; her best friend had betrayed her. "Corporal, escort Signora Garcia outside. I've had enough." The corporal grabbed Lena's arm.

"Come now, and don't give me hard time."

"Keep your fucking filthy hands off me." Lena pushed him away. "*I'm not a fucking invalid!*" Lena turned to her so-called friend before leaving. "I'm coming back for you, and wherever you are, I'll find you. You will never be able to sleep at night, you fucking lowlife . . ."

* * *

"I see, and you say there was a firefight with the two Americanos, and Carlos and Sergio were shot dead after which they took Mona Menzel and the other Americano and drove off in a blue Volkswagen?"

"That is correct, Sergeant."

"And are you willing to come to the station and make a statement to that effect?"

"Of course, Sergeant!" Eva replied, feeling good with herself. Self-preservation was obligatory, so who needed a friend like Lena? But little did Eva know that her lies would come back to bite her in the ass.

* * *

"Corporal . . . Handcuff *Signoras* Garcia and Alfaro."

"*Sergeant?*" Eva was astounded; she had confessed in the box. *What the hell was going on?*

"You are both under the arrest for aiding and abetting the kidnapping of one Mona Menzel and an unknown Americano. Furthermore, you are both being charged with accessory after the fact, knowingly and willingly concealing evidence and subsequently perverting the course of justice. I must warn you that anything you say may be taken down and used in evidence against you in a court of law. Take them away, Corporal."

Eva struggled to push the corporal away. "But, Sergeant, you promised me . . . *You promised me . . .*" Eva was sobbing, unable to stand up straight. She had been tricked by the smooth-talking sergeant.

"*I promised nothing, bitch!* You had your chance, but you refused my offer, and I know I have a good memory. You blew it, honey. *Pity,* but it's too late now . . . Corporal, keep them apart, or there will be another murder . . ."

* * *

The siren was still blaring when the ambulance finally arrived, the so called paramedics examining the bloated bodies, with Lena and Eva now handcuffed in the back of each police cruiser, awaiting their fate. It was time to call HQ, and Flavio was back on his cell phone, feeling pretty good with his day's work.

"Si, Lieutenant, I have arrested both *signoras* and read them their rights . . . As you instruct, I will take them back to police headquarters . . . That is exactly what Signorina Alfaro confessed . . . And the Americanos? They sped off in a blue Volkswagen toward the city . . . Probably around forty-five minutes . . . Si, Lieutenant . . . *Gracias.*"

*   *   *

Medina sat at his desk . . . *I mean how many things can go wrong in one day in a policeman's life?* The murder of the two drug barons, the shootout at Villamisseria, killing two "most wanted," the solving of the Menzel kidnapping, and all under the noses of Argentina's finest. *Worse still*, by two NYPD cops! Victor kept shaking his head. Why did he ever become a policeman? But his next challenge was yet to come, and he loathingly lifted the phone.

"Lieutenant Medina here . . . Is Capitan Avalos free? I'll be right in."

*   *   *

Avalos was probably in his late forties, slim, fit, and lean with a facial expression that spelled "mean." His reputation as a no-shit taker and an SOB was Oscar material. He fit the part with his neatly pressed uniform, the traditional thin moustache, and the black centre-parted hair brushed straight back, and with his brown beady eyes, olive complexion and narrow jaw line, he could have easily auditioned for *Evita.*

*   *   *

The Capitan was leisurely sipping his "local brew" when the knock on the door disturbed him, and he looked up.

"Enter." He took another sip of his coffee.

"Buenas tardes, Capitan."

"I wouldn't know. I haven't seen the light of day since I arrived at the office this morning. Take a seat, and don't waste my time."

"Si, Capitan." The lieutenant was searching for a soft landing.

"*Well?*"

"I have just received a report from . . ."

Avalos sat back in his chair; his eyes narrowed like a leopard about to attack its prey.

"*What the fuck are you telling me, Lieutenant?* That I'm surrounded by incompetence and my most senior officers cannot do a simple task like tailing two American cops? I'll be the laughingstock of the department, and now with four murders on my hands and one of the richest men in Argentina's daughter freed from the kidnappers . . . *And by two American detectives . . . I fucking ask you?*"

Avalos ran his fingers through his immaculately groomed hair, then crashed his fist hard on the desk and stared up at the ceiling as if searching for a miracle.

"Father, what have I done to deserve this?"

Medina was also searching . . . *But for a place to hide!*

"Lieutenant, I should demote you to traffic duty, but because you are one of my most intelligent officers, *probably the only one,* treasure my benevolence this day . . ."

Avalos sat for a moment in sheer silence, just staring at Medina.

"So what bright ideas do you have now, Lieutenant?" Avalos was being sarcastic.

"With respect, Capitan, there is an APB out for the blue Volkswagen, and all my men including the traffic division are working twenty-four to pick up that car, which, from my latest report, is somewhere between Villamisseria and Av Leopoldo Lugones, heading for Nueve de Julio, and we have immediately set up roadblocks."

"I suppose I should be thankful for small mercies, and for your sake, I hope someone up there likes you."

The shakedown to Medina was thankfully interrupted by the loud ring of the phone.

The Capitan lifted the receiver. "It's for you." He passed the phone. "You had better pray that it's good news . . ."

"Si, Medina here . . . When? Around fifteen minutes ago . . . Are you sure? You did well . . . And no one else was injured . . . Well, that's something . . . No, you carry on. I'll handle it from this end . . . *Gracias,* and well done. Leave your name with my assistant."

"Well?" The Capitan could sense from Medina's body language that it spelled big trouble.

"That was the traffic sergeant manning the roundabout to Av Nueve de Julio."

"And . . ."

Medina took a deep breath. "Capitan, I'm afraid it's more bad news . . ."

*   *   *

Chapter 2

June undressed and showered; it had been a somewhat different but enjoyable evening. Phil was showing his true character, and the more she was getting to know this man, the more she liked him.

June vigorously towelled her shiny body, then coarsely dried her long blonde locks before slipping into her bathrobe. She felt fresh and glowing as she took the stool in front of her dressing table to blow her hair dry before bed.

"*Hmmm,*" June was speaking aloud, thinking of Phil. "He is compassionate, understanding, and intelligent, with an enjoyable sense of humour, and most importantly, the kids seem to like him, which surprises me, with them having only met him twice. Sheryl is Sheryl, always a bit of a show-off in front of the opposite sex, and of course, Phil is handsome to boot. But Steven . . . It's as if he is almost encouraging me to get his father out of our lives as quickly as possible." She shook her head again and pondered for a moment. "Of course, Phil is a charmer, good looking, well heeled, a respected lawyer, and the owner of a very successful law firm. I guess in Steven's eyes, if his mother is looking to start a new life, Phil has all the credentials. But what puzzles me is that he worshipped the ground his father walked on, and now this ugly hate campaign. But below his nonchalant attitude and stiff upper lip, I'm sure he is hurting just as much as me, and I guess only time will heal. As for Mike? Until the day I die, I can never find it in my heart to forgive him. If he had faced the charges like a man instead of fleeing the country and deserting the people that love him, leaving them to face the scandal, desolate and poverty stricken . . . What kind of a man is he?" June glanced at the bedside clock.

"My god is it that time already! I have a busy day tomorrow, but what's new? Hell, I almost forgot my appointment at three with that scrooge Simmons at the bank. Tomorrow is the last day to cancel the lease on the Beamer, and worse still, I need wheels."

June thumped the pillow with her hand, making a hollow, then switched of the bedside lamp.

"Somehow I have a good feeling about tomorrow . . . But there again? Oh, whatever . . . I had better get some sleep. the kids are up at seven thirty . . . Did I set that alarm?"

*   *   *

"*Frank,* I'm telling you for the last time . . . No, I don't want to hear your excuses . . . *Frank,* get real . . . Sure we had something going, but I could never trust you again . . . *Frank,* for the last time, it's over, and don't even think about coming to my apartment . . . *It's no, Frank!*" Terry hung up, steam pouring from her ears.

Laura was surprised at Terry's reaction, but then again, was she? It brought back old memories. She had been burned so many times, but then there's that famous quote from Saint Augustine: "Better to have loved and lost, than to have never loved at all."

Laura gave a half-hearted laugh as she scribbled on her pad.

Terry, you're fooling no one! You love this guy, and you are scared to admit it.

"Oh no you don't. You're not puling that one on me! No, Laura, it's well and truly over. I mean do you really expect me to take him back and all is forgiven?"

Far from me to give you advice, I've got a track record that would make even Danielle Steel cringe.

Terry had to laugh. "Well, as they say, 'All's fair in love and war,' huh, if you get my drift?" She was still laughing.

Terry, I hope it's nothing to do with me coming to stay at your apartment after I am discharged?

"Don't be silly. And while we are on that subject, when is the big day?" *Believe it or not, it could be as early as next week . . . Can you believe it!*

"And what about your parents? Remember their reaction when you broke the news that you were coming to stay at my place?"

Mother is all right. It's father that's the problem, but give it time, and he'll come round.

"I certainly hope so for both our sakes." Terry's face was sombre.

Well, whatever, I can't wait to get out of here. Is there any news on that bastard Summers?

"I'm surprised you asked, Laura. As for me, I cringe at the mention of his name. But to answer your question . . . No."

The duty nurse cut Terry's reply short as she entered Laura's room, wheeling the blood pressure machine.

"It' s that time again, Laura. I hope I'm not disturbing your visitor."

"Not at all," Terry replied. "In fact, I was just about to leave . . . Laura, honey, I'll see you again tomorrow after I finish at the office."

I can't wait to hear about Blakely . . . Ciao . . . Remember the tomorrow . . .

Terry turned and gave a parting wave as she left the room. It had been one helluva day, and now she was looking forward to that glass of chardonnay and some chill-out time.

CHAPTER 3

(Speaking in Spanish)

Bradley's hotline buzzed. "Lola, we can continue with this report later." Lola knew when the red phone rang, it was exit time.

"Certainly, Mr. Mason, just buzz when you are free. Would you wish me to fetch a coffee?"

"Later, Lola, not now . . ." Mason nimbly lifted the phone. Who knows, this may even be Bush.

"You took your time."

"So why the urgency."

"We got big trouble . . . Or should I say *you* got big trouble!"

"Don't fuck with me, General. Get to the point, I'm busy." Mason could cut it when the occasion arose.

"It's these two fucking detectives that you assured me were in your pocket. You would keep your boys on their tail to lead us to the Menzel woman and this guy Summers, then my men would move in and arrest the Americanos and we split the reward."

"Yeah . . . So?"

"*So, you blew it!*"

"What do you mean *I* blew it?" Mason was starting to boil, general or no general he wasn't taking his shit.

"I just had Capitan Avalos in my office, and you had better listen and listen good . . ."

Mason was getting paler by the second; the news was not good. Two American citizens wanted for murder and on the run from the Argentine police after having hijacked a taxi at gunpoint. Nightmares like this are only in James Bond movies.

"Okay . . . Okay . . . Manuel, cool it, for Christ's sake. Screaming at each other is not the solution. So, what the fuck do *you* suggest?"

"You contact them by phone and tell them to turn themselves in, and you will give them diplomatic protection at the embassy under the flag of American citizenship. They meet you undercover at a planned rendezvous where my men will be waiting."

"These guys are not fucking stupid, but then again, it might just work if I guarantee them a flight to Brazil."

"Mason, you had better be convincing. I don't want the presidente on my back if this fuckup hits the media. Remember, I can send you down for corruption in the visa racket."

"*Don't you fucking threaten me!* You get a fifty-fifty cut from the proceeds of the under-the-table payments, and you better believe it, I aint going down alone . . . *Comprender?*"

"Do you think *your* word will be taken against mine? *The commissioner of police, General Manuel Cerise, appointed by the presidente himself!* No, my friend, you got that one wrong."

"So what the fuck are you doing about it instead of shooting off your big mouth?" Mason didn't want to mix it; Cerise is a devious bastard and not to be trusted.

"One of my best men is on his way to the Menzel house, as that's where I am sure the fugitives are heading. It will take me at least twenty-four hours to get a search warrant, but then that's my problem."

"Well, the quicker we get off this phone, the quicker I can do something about it. I'll call you later if anything breaks." Mason was getting impatient.

"You had better make sure it's good new—"

Mason hung up before Cerise could finish. He had more than enough on his mind without listening to more of his crap.

*   *   *

"*Tony . . . Tony . . .* Do you hear me?" Mona yelled at the top of her voice, trying to keep him from slipping into unconsciousness.

"*Eh . . . Heh . . . Keh . . . Keh.*" Tony was coughing his lungs out, searching for a breath, the tell-tale trickle of blood from the side of mouth getting worse by the second.

"Just keep . . . *eh* . . . going, Bill . . . Don't worry about me . . . *Keh . . . I'll* be all right." His voice was now all but a faint rasp as he coughed and spluttered blood between words.

Mona turned to Bill. "I don't like the look of this, Bill. Tony's in bad shape and needs urgent medical attention. I'm really worried and can't help thinking the worst."

Bill didn't answer; he didn't want to face the reality.

"How far now?" Bill asked driving like a crazy man, breaking all the rules.

"About another fifteen."

"Shit, *that far!*"

"*Bill, gimme your cell phone.*" Mona was on a mission.

"My cell pho—"

Mona cut him short; she was in no mood for explanations. "Don't ask fucking questions . . . *You heard me! And just concentrate on the fucking road!*"

Bill fumbled for a few seconds in his baggy pants, precariously hanging on to the wheel with his other hand.

"Here., I hope you know what you're doing!" Bill yelled above the screaming engine. "We're not out of the woods yet, and the cops can trace that call."

Mona ignored Bill's advice and punched in the numbers.

When the going gets tough the tough get going.

(Speaking in Spanish)

"Father . . . It's me . . . Never mind, I'll explain it all later . . . I'm in a stolen taxi, and the police are hot on our tail . . . *Father . . . I said I would explain it later!* Two American police officers risked their lives to set me free. Yes, you heard me right! Both are suffering from gunshot wounds, with one serious, and he's needing urgent medical attention . . . *Father . . . For god's sake, let me finish!* Here's what I need you to do . . . Fetch our neighbour, Dr. Quario, who is the director of surgery at Hospital Britanico, to come over to the house and briefly explain the urgency that an American policeman is critically wounded . . . Have you got that? *Good!* Now I need one more thing . . . Get the driver to bring the station wagon and wait at the bend where that vacant lot is that leads down to the gully. I'll meet him there in say . . . Another five minutes . . . *Just do it, Father!* I'll give him his instructions when we meet . . . *Oh and* keep the front gate open."

*   *   *

Bill listened intently to Mona's conversation, and now it was all coming together.

"What do you think, Mona?" Bill asked.

"I wish I knew, Bill. It all depends on Dr. Quario if he's willing to help. You know what like doctors are when it comes to aiding and abetting a fugitive from the law."

"Tell me about it! I've been there before," Bill answered, his memory kicking in.

"Bill, do you see that sign on your left?"

"I see it . . . Avenue Celino."

"*Good!* Slow down and hang that left. That's where I live."

"*Thank God!*" Bill swung the taxi hard to the left, almost doing a burnout before straightening the Falcon, much to Mona's relief.

"*Christ, Bill,* for a moment there, you almost scared the crap out of me." "Stop griping, Mona, I said I would get you there in one piece, didn't I?" Mona shook her head. "*And by the grace of God!*" Then she suddenly stopped in her tracks. "*Bill* . . . Pull up in front of that station wagon parked on the bend."

Bill screeched to a halt with Mona halfway out of the door before the car finally came to a standstill.

(Speaking in Spanish)

"Franco . . . Hurry . . . Hurry . . . Open the tailgate." "Si, signora." The chauffeur didn't hang around.

"Now come and help us carry the Americano onto the rear platform . . ."

* * *

"Bill, how is he?"

Bill was already struggling with Tony's deadweight, trying to lift him from the rear seat, the car door wide open.

"If you take these cuffs off, I can help," Summers volunteered from "out of the wilderness," his hands locked behind his back.

"*You've fucking helped us enough!* The cuffs are staying unless you need a piss . . . *Savvy* . . . He's unconscious, Mona," Billy finally answered as the driver came to the rescue, supporting Tony's limp legs.

"*Easy . . . Easy, man!*" Bill bawled as he laid Tony flat on the cargo trunk of the wagon. The driver acknowledged having not a clue what Bill had said, but the body language said it all.

"Out of the car . . ." Mona motioned to Summers, Bill's forty-five sending a message.

"*Fucking cops!*" Summers growled under his breath as he struggled to stand on his own two feet, his handcuffed wrists affecting his balance. "Go easy with that thing, Mona, accidents can happen!" Mike yelled, staring down the barrel of the Browning.

"Keep your mouth shut and get in the back of that wagon . . . *Pronto!* And don't try any shit. It would give me the greatest pleasure to blow your fucking brains out, *you fucking gigolo.*"

"Come on, Mona, we gotta hit the road," Bill called as he closed the tailgate.

"Yeah, but first we gotta get rid of the evidence, *and that means that taxi!"* (Speaking in Spanish)

"Franco, drive the taxi to that empty lot, then keep the engine running and the car in drive, and then get the hell out and let it roll down into the gulley. The undergrowth is so thick, it will be difficult for the cops to find . . . *Hurry . . . Hurry . . .* I can hear the sound of the sirens only about twenty minutes away."

"Si, Signora."

Franco started the engine of the Falcon and steered it toward the steep incline, then leaped for dear life. The car crunched and bumped as it bounced its way through the heavy undergrowth, heading for the car graveyard.

*   *   *

"Nice touch, Mona." Bill grinned as he ran toward the station wagon. "You're wasting your time on the right side of the law."

"I watch CSI New York, remember?" Mona could still squeeze out that cheeky smile. "Franco . . . *Moverio . . . Moverio.*"

Bill leaped into the backseat to keep an eye on Tony, who was now completely out of it.

As he leaned over to check Tony's pulse, he was almost thrown onto the cargo flatbed as Franco hit the floor, the big Ford's wheels spinning with the stench of burning rubber.

"Easy, Schumacher." Bill yelled, grabbing the safety harness.

"How is he? Mona looked into the rear mirror.

The large crimson stain on Tony's shirt now resembled the map of Africa.

"His pulse is hardly feel-able, but it's there." "Another five minutes, Bill . . ."

*   *   *

The corporal was driving like a hellcat. Dusk had fallen, and the glare from the oncoming headlights was making it difficult to weave in and out the traffic even with the siren and flashing lights. In Buenos Aires, who cares, it's an everyday occurrence.

Victor tapped the corporal on the shoulder, pointing to the barely visible street sign.

"Avenue Celino . . ."

"Si, Lieutenant." The driver signalled and hung a left.

"Casa numero veinte seis." Victor was peering at the address under the dim courtesy light.

"*Si . . . Si . . .* Lieutenant." The corporal was praying he didn't fuck up.

Victor opened his cell phone and dialled; it was worth a try.

Mona had Bill's phone and answered the call-in silence.

"Whoever is on the line . . . Tony or Bill . . . This is Lieutenant Victor Medina here. You can make it easy on yourselves if you turn yourselves in to the police. I will make sure that you are given a fair hearing regarding the shooting of Sergio Garcia and Carlos Mendez. I have witnesses that will testify that it was self-defence. The longer you are on the run, the more serious it becomes, and make no mistake, whatever it takes, I will bring you both into custody to face the charges of manslaughter. I know you are heading to the Menzel mansion and are most probably there right now, but all it requires is a search warrant, and your game is up. And remember . . . I can lay charges on the Menzel family for harbouring suspected criminals and perverting the course of justice. This is my last offe—"

Mona closed the phone, cutting him short; she had heard enough. "Did you hear that crap, Bill?" Mona asked.

"Yeah, but I don't want you and your family dragged into this."

"Here we are and thank God the gate's open." Mona politely ignored Bill as if she had never heard one word.

* * *

(Speaking in Spanish)

Cerise was still in "tsunami" mode as he smashed the phone back into its cradle.

"*Fucking Mason, American smart-ass!* Who does he think he is, challenging my authority? *The gall of the guy!*"

Cerise sat for a moment in silence, gathering his thoughts. He had to plan his next move or lose the plot. He lifted the internal phone.

"Si, Generale."

"Corporal, fetch me a coffee and get Capitan Avalos. I want to have a word with him, it's urgent."

"Si, Generale."

Within minutes, there was a loud knock on the door.

"*Enter!*" Cerise barked.

"You want to see me, Generale?"

"Si, Juan, take a seat."

"Your coffee, sir," the corporal interrupted.

Cerise rudely pointed to his desk. The corporal knew it was not a good time and quickly laid the coffee cup in front of his boss, then left the room in fourth gear.

"*Have you had any news from Lieutenant Medina?*" Cerise was in a foul mood.

"No, not as yet" Avalos replied, keeping it brief. There was no need to truncate the situation.

"I've just been on the phone with the American embassy, and Mason is trying to contract the American cops by phone to offer them diplomatic sanctuary."

"Sanctuary at the embassy?" Juan was lost.

"Don't worry, I'll explain it to you later . . . Listen, Juan, I've been thinking about the Menzel woman, and the conclusion I have reached is that she is protecting the Americans because she feels she owes them a debt for risking their lives to set her free from the kidnappers, even though their real agenda was to arrest the American fugitive to face criminal charges in the United States."

"So?"

"So, I expedite a warrant for their arrests and a search warrant to enter the Menzel mansion, where I am sure they are holed up."

"But if Bradley . . ."

"Never mind Bradley. His plan may or may not work, and we will lose valuable time. No, I have to get these warrants at all costs." Cerise lifted the phone once again.

"Is that all, Generale?" Juan half rose to leave.

"No, I want you to stay and listen . . . Corporal, get me state judge Benito Ortego on the line. Tell him it's urgent . . ." Cerise placed back the receiver, then suddenly remembered his coffee and proceeded to take a mouthful. "*Ugggh!*" Cerise screwed his face up, almost choking on the foul taste. "*Why do I drink this shit for coffee?*" The phone rang.

CHAPTER 4

The security gate wide open, Franco swung the oversize Plymouth Valiant onto the driveway and hit the brakes. Mona's father and mother were nervously waiting at the front door, not knowing just what to expect. The sketchy phone conversation Mona had had with her father left a lot to be desired, but the important thing was that their daughter was home safe and sound.

(Speaking in Spanish)

"Close the gates!" Mona yelled at the security guards as she leaped from the semi stationary Plymouth. "Hurry, the police will be here any minute . . .

Franco, drive the wagon into the garage, out of sight."

Mona's mother rushed to meet her daughter, tears streaming down her cheeks as she threw her arms around her neck.

"Mother, don't worry. I'm all right, and Father, I don't have time to explain. We must get urgent medical attention for the wounded American . . . *Has Dr. Quario arrived?"*

"Yes, fortunately he is not on call this evening, and he is patiently waiting inside with what medical equipment and drugs he could muster at such short notice. I briefly explained our predicament, and being an old friend, he didn't hesitate to offer his services."

Quario, on hearing the stressed-out conversation, was already on his way, stethoscope dangling from his neck.

"Dr. Quario, *am I* glad to see you," Mona greeted him. Bill was hot on her tail, his blood-soaked shirt sending shock waves.

"It's only a scratch, Doc, don't worry about me, I'll live. It's my partner. He's unconscious in the back of the wagon and losing blood in buckets. *Doc, you gotta do something!"*

"Firstly, let's get your friend into the house to keep him warm as I suspect he has already gone into shock." Quario spoke perfect English. "And, Mona, clear a table in the dining room or whatever. I need to examine the detective's wounds."

"Come with me, Doctor . . ." Bill escorted Quario toward the garage. "Mona, I need the guards to help me carry Bill into the house . . . *Hurry . . . Mona, hurry."*

"Muro, Arellano . . . Ayudar American co el detective herido . . . Prisa!" Mona didn't mince her words; she had to get these lazy-assed guards moving. "Padre, Madre, debe habla Ingles." Mona ordered her parents to at least *try* and speak English.

Quario glanced at Tony's limp body as the guards frog-marched past him to the dining room where the large, majestic twelve-seat walnut table had been cleared and covered with a crisp white bedsheet. It was near as you could get to an operating table.

"Mona, I need your help." The doctor handed her a pair of scissors. "Cut his shirt apart while I take his pressure . . . *Hmmm* . . . Not good." He shone the small torch into Tony's pupils, then shook his head. "Before I can examine his wounds, he urgently needs a blood transfusion . . . I can perform the procedure here, but the problem is I need a donor with the same blood group, *and just how do I get that?*" Quario was in a predicament.

"Don't worry, Doc, all police officers in the United States must show their blood group on their warrant card in case of injury in the line of duty." Bill fumbled in Tony's hip pocket and fished out the crumpled wallet.

"Here we are . . . Blood group O RhD positive." Bill read from the photo ID.

Quario's expression brightened. "*We're in luck* . . . Forty percent of the population have that blood group, it's the most common. Now for the donor?"

"*That's my blood group, Doctor!*" Mona jumped in. "I know for sure from my birth certificate."

"I can't take a chance, Mona, can you show me?"

"Give me a couple of minutes, Doctor, I also have it on my passport, which is on the desk in the study."

Mona was back in a heartbeat.

"*Good*, then let's get started . . . Mona roll up your sleeve and lie next to . . . eh?"

"Tony," Bill interrupted.

"Tony . . . Now I have to find a good vein . . ."

*   *   *

"Just keep pumping your hand, Mona . . . Now for these wounds . . ." Quario quickly removed the pads of cotton wool covering Tony's right side, he previously performed a temporary plug to try and reduce the bleeding, and he gently cleaned the congealed blood to study Tony's wounds more clearly. "Hmmm . . ." He unzipped Tony's slacks and began to tap different parts of his abdomen using his two fingers.

"*Hmmmm . . .*" Quario went quiet again, the expression on his face was less than encouraging. As for Bill? He just couldn't control himself.

"Doc, give it to me straight, how bad is it?"

"I'm afraid it's very serious. Tony has internal bleeding, most likely from a damaged liver and bleeding from the right kidney. My preliminary diagnosis is that one or maybe two bullets fragmented, entering his right-side lodging in his kidney and liver. Once the liver begins to fail, the kidneys quickly follow. His bladder is most likely now full of blood, which I will have to drain using a catheter. I'm afraid I can only do so much under these circumstance and without x-rays . . . To answer you, Bill . . . If your friend doesn't not receive immediate surgery, he won't last till morning. I have given him intravenous antibiotics to reduce the possibility of infection. Other than that, my hands are tied."

The news was devastating, and for a moment there was a deathly silence as the bad news, although not unexpected, still came as a shock.

The guard interrupted.

"La policia esta en la puerta principal exigiendo verte, jefe."

"What's he saying, Mona?" Bill had the jitters; the day was getting shorter.

"The police are at the front gate demanding to speak with my father . . ."

*   *   *

(Speaking Spanish)

"Si, Benito, *buonasera*. Manuel Cerise here."

"Commissary, it's been a while, but why the call? I'm sure you're not checking on my health."

Manuel gave a sort of hollow laugh. The judge was no fool, and although there was no love lost between them, sometimes you have to turn the other cheek.

"Same old Benito, once a judge always a judge, huh?"

"Get to the point, Commissary, I'm just about to have dinner."

"Benito, I need your help. I'm sure you have read in the media about the kidnapping of Salvador Menzel's daughter."

"*Hasn't everyone?* Bad business but unless . . ."

"Benito, let me explain . . ."

*   *   *

"But how do you know for certain that the American fugitives are in hiding in Salvador Menzel's home? Did one of your officers see them go in?

"You're not listening, Benito."

"Listen, Manuel . . . *You're not listening!* Even though you have witnesses who will testify that one Carlos Mendez and one Sergio Garcia, the presumed kidnappers, were shot and killed in a firefight with the two American police officers, remember, they are American citizens. And for all intents and purposes, in the eyes of the Menzel family, *heroes*. No, Cerise, it's not good enough, and I'm sorry, but I must refuse . . . Salvador Menzel is one of my personal friends and, don't forget, a close friend of the presidente. No, I don't want egg on my face by issuing a warrant on a hunch. If something more concrete turns up, give me a call. Now if you don't mind, I have guests for dinner . . . *Gracias* . . ."

"*Bastardo, that Benito has his head up his ass!*" Manuel slammed the phone down.

"I gather from that conversation that he refused to issue the warrants?" Avalos, as they say, asked a stupid question, and Cerise befittingly gave him the appropriate look.

"*No . . . I'm not giving up.*" Cerise was shaking his head. "I know Menzel is protecting these Americans." Cerise lifted the phone once again. "Corporal, get me the attorney generalie, Marco Delgado."

"Generale, are you sure you want to do this?" Avalos was getting worried; his boss wasn't thinking straight. Besides in the legal fraternity protocol is God, and Cerise was crossing the line.

"*Don't question me, I know what I'm doing! Ah . . . Eh . . . Signor* Attorney Generale . . . Manuel Cerise here . . . I'm sorry to disturb you at home, but something important has come up regarding the kidnapping of Signorina Menzel . . . Yes, that's correct . . . I'll be as brief as I can . . ."

*   *   *

"And you have already spoken to Judge Ortego? Then why are you phoning me?"

"Franco, you don't understand, it's a matter of national security."

Cerise was getting desperate; he could sense his case was about to go down the toilet.

"Are you questioning me? Do you expect me to overrule one of my most respected judges? Generale, I'll pretend that you never made this call, so please hang up, and I bid you . . . *Buenas noches* . . ."

Manuel crashed the phone back again and sat in silence for a few moments as if counting to ten. *This was not his day.*

Then out of the blue, he suddenly let loose. "Everyone is on fucking Salvador Menzel's payroll, *I might have known! But I'll get these two* Americanos *if it's the last thing I do!*"

The phone rang again, the distraction a welcome relief for Avalos.

"Yes?"

"Lieutenant Medina on the line."

"Put him through, Corporal . . . Yes? *That's all I fucking need . . .* Lieutenant, be prepared for a long night. I want 24/7 surveillance on the Menzel home. They have to come out sometime and keep out of sight . . . A warrant for their arrest? That's my problem, Lieutenant, just you concentrate on doing your job and keep me informed . . ."

Cerise once again placed back the receiver; it had been one helluva day.

"Generale, if you don't mind me asking, what are you going to do about the warrant?"

"If I must, I'll issue the fucking warrant myself, *and don't tell me I'm breaking the law, Lieutenant . . .*"

*   *   *

Salvador returned after the heated discussion with the police.

"What happened, Father?" Mona was worried; Argentine police were famous for taking the law into their own hands.

"A lieutenant demanded to search the premises, but without a warrant. Of course, I refused. However, when he threatened to enter by force, I stopped him in his tracks by opening my cell phone, pretending to contact my personal friend, the attorney generale, Franco Delgado . . ."

"And?"

"He hurriedly made a phone call, then quickly turned tail and left, but my gut feeling tells me we haven't seen the last of the lieutenant. Before he left, Mona, I also informed him that I would make a statement tomorrow once you have had a chance to recover from your ordeal."

"I'm worried, Salvador, the Americans condition is deteriorating." Quario wasn't helping the situation.

Mona's father was searching for space. He was no fool and understood the gravity of the situation, but the deck was stacked.

Salvador turned his attention to Bill. *A New York detective . . . Who knows . . . He just might bring something to the table.*

"Detective, I'm at a loss, and I fear for your friend's life. If we take him to the local hospital, he will most certainly be arrested, and even then, I can't guarantee that he will get the best medical treatment."

Mona interrupted, "Father, if we could create a diversion . . ." *"A diversion? Carry on, Mona!"* She caught Bill's attention.

"Like if we storm out the gates in two cars, each traveling in different directions to confuse the cops, we might just be able to get Tony to the American embassy."

"Naw. too dangerous." Bill was in retreat and didn't want a bag of it. "Besides, Mona, I don't trust that bastard, Mason. I'm sure he and the generale are in cahoots."

"Just a second, honey." Salvador seemed to have something going. "That idea of yours has some merit. Bear with me while I make a call." Salvador lifted the house phone.

* * *

"Capitan, are you certain the flight time to Sao Paulo is two hours and thirty minutes? Get the helicopter ready, we don't have time to waste . . . Who is on call at the airport? Capitan Martinez . . . He's a good man. Contact him and tell him to stand by with the Lear jet and get flight clearance. We should arrive at the airport within thirty minutes. I'll give him his flight schedule when I arrive."

Mona's father for once was speaking in English, and the pieces from the telecon were falling into place, and there was a pregnant pause before Salvador was bombarded with questions, his daughter leading the onslaught.

"Father?"

"Yes, you heard correctly . . . And, Bill, for your information, I have a helicopter pad at the rear of the house. I keep a pilot on standby twenty-four hours. Sometimes I require to fly to the Pampas to tie up cattle deals, and what better way than by helicopter. The pilots rotate every week and stay in the servant's quarters."

"*Now you've got my attention!*" Bill was all ears.

"Here's the plan . . ."

* * *

"That's not a problem, I'll phone the captain right now . . . Mona, my phone."

Bill listened impatiently to the irritating tones from the international line, a sleepy disgruntled voice answering.

"Yes . . . *Eh* . . . Baker here."

"Ted, it's Bill on the line . . ."

"Bill?"

"*Bill Hayden.*"

"Christ, Hayden, do you know what time it is? This had better be good."

"It's the good and the bad, Ted. The good news is we nailed Mike Summers, but the bad news is . . ."

*　*　*

"Bill, how serious is it?"

"Ted, it doesn't get any worse. The doc says Tony may not last the night if we don't get him to a hospital for immediate surgery."

"So, let's touch base again. You want me to phone the DA, and Senator Williams if necessary, to get the American consulate general in Sao Paulo, Brazil, to meet this guy . . . ?"

"Salvador Menzel . . ."

"Whoever's Lear Jets' at Guarulhos International Airport and whisk Tony under the veil of diplomatic immunity to the nearest hospital."

"Something like that."

"That's a tall order. But I'm not going anyplace hanging on this phone. Hang up, and I'll call the DA. I'm sure Jake has contacts in the right places . . . Bill, I'll move heaven and earth or whatever it takes to get Tony back in one piece . . . You say fifteen minutes . . . I'll call you back, but gimme some slack . . ."

*　*　*

"What's wrong, honey?" Ruth was now sitting up in bed, the bright light from the bedside lamp making her cover her eyes.

"One of our detectives in Buenos Aires has been seriously wounded." *"Buenos Aires?"* Was she hearing right?

"Honey it's too complicated to explain. Why don't you go back to sleep, and I'll go downstairs and use the phone in the kitchen?"

"Are you sure? I can join you and make you a cup of coffee." "Is there any of that cheesecake left?"

*　*　*

"You look nervous, darling." Ruth had rarely seen her husband in such a state. There was no point in going back to bed now, what with him prowling up and down the kitchen floor like a pregnant father. She too was worried. Ruth knew the Perino family well and couldn't bear to bring herself to fear the worst.

"What's happened to Murray? I thought he would have called back by now." Ted was staring at the kitchen wall clock, counting the seconds.

Suddenly the ring of the phone startled him, and he grabbed for the receiver, almost dropping it to the floor.

"Take it easy, darling," Ruth tried to console him. "*Hell, Jake*, I had almost given up!"

*   *   *

"Bill . . . Yeah we've received the clearance from the American embassy in Brazil and also the Sao Paulo Immigration Department . . . Don't worry about the diplomatic fallout, there's no love lost between Brazil and Argentina . . . Yes . . . You have my assurance that there will be an ambulance waiting on the tarmac when your plane arrives . . . *Don't ask me!* Murray did it. His brother-in-law, Senator Williams, has direct access to Bush. *Need I say more?* Don't thank me, just make sure there's no more fuckups . . . You *better* call . . . Oh, before you hang up, the consulate general's name is Stanley Broaden." "Come on, Bill, we gotta go!" Mona shouted in the background. "Yeah, Bill, I heard . . . Gimme a call from Sao Paulo."

*   *   *

Baker placed back the phone, the color returning to his cheeks.

"There, there, darling. Now don't you feel much better now?" Ruth gave him a big hug. "Are you coming back to bed?"

"Yes, but I'm dammed if I'll be able to sleep." "*I told you* not to eat that cheesecake . . ."

*   *   *

"Father let's go through this again. We dress two of the guards in white shirts and slacks as decoys to fool the police into thinking that they are the Americans. They take the backseat in the Buick town car with Franco at the wheel in his chauffeur's uniform. We open the gates in a mad scramble and pour on the gas as if the Americans are making a break for it. The undercover police cruiser takes up the chase in hot pursuit . . ."

"Yes, so far so good. Your idea was not so silly after all, Mona. You see, we need that diversion to distract the police until we get the helicopter airborne, which when by the time they finally catch our "Grand Prix" driver Franco, we will be well and truly on our way to the airport, with the generale committing suicide."

"I gotta hand it to you, Salvador, that's neat." Bill was laughing heartily at the thought.

"Thanks for your vote of confidence, Bill, but we're not clear yet. Mona, get the guards and Franco organized.

We gotta get this show on the road . . ."

533

* * *

The pilot was already unfolding the large blades on the twin-engine Westland AW169 six-passenger helicopter, sporting the corporate logo in large blue-and-white lettering against a white background: *Menzel Empresas Limitado.*

(Speaking in Spanish)

"Capitan, how long will it take to be ready for takeoff?" Salvador asked anxiously, with Bill and Quario in tow.

"About another fifteen minutes, boss." "*Good,* that will give us enough time."

* * *

"Boy, this is some machine." Bill was awed by the wealth of it all.

Salvador turned to Bill and the doctor. "I suggest we don't waste any more time. Let's make Tony comfortable in the back row . . . Eh, *Mona* . . ."

Getting Tony to the helicopter was one thing, but the journey to the airport was another, then the two-and-a-half-hour flight to Sao Paulo, Brazil . . . Bill was shaking his head; he was really concerned for his partner, and he turned to Quario.

"Doctor, will you be accompanying us?"

"Only in transit to the airport, that's as far as I can go. I have my responsibilities at the hospital, with surgeries scheduled for tomorrow. I'm sorry, but I'll make sure your friend is as comfortable as permitted with a saline drip and more intravenous antibiotics. I will also provide a medical report for the hospital at Sao Paulo to save time."

"Thanks, Doc, you've done more than enough." Bill felt more relaxed, but the chase had just begun.

* * *

It resembled a military exercise. Mona, her father, the doc, Bill, and now most hated of all, *Summers,* are all accompanying Tony by helicopter to the airport.

"Capitan, as soon as you hear the police siren, you turn these blades . . . Is everyone aboard?"

"*Summers* . . . Where's Summers?" Bill leaped out of the helicopter; Summers was pitifully standing there, the forgotten fugitive.

"Can someone remove these cuffs . . . *I need to piss.*"

CHAPTER 5

(Speaking Spanish)

"What would I do for a cup of hot coffee?" Avalos sighed, moving his cramped legs to stimulate the circulation.

"Si, Lieutenant, and the temperature is dropping. It's forecast to be a bad one tonight."

"Do you have any children, Corporal?" Avalos digressed. "I can see from the ring that you are married."

"Yes, fifteen years." Alano smiled proudly. He never knew his boss was so observant, let alone interested. "Three girls . . . *Would you believe it?* Can you imagine what it's like with four women to contend with?" Avalos had to smile; the thought intrigued him.

"No, Corporal, I'm afraid I can't . . . You see, I'm not married . . . Just haven't found the right one."

The corporal smiled; his boss was human after all.

"Take my advice, Capitan . . . There's plenty of fish in th—"

Before he could finish, the large wrought-iron gates in the Menzel mansion unexpectedly swung open, catching the cops by surprise. Then a Buick town car appeared from nowhere, slewing from side to side as it maneuvered a right turn at speed, its tires screeching as Franco straightened and hit the gas. The nauseating stench of burning rubber contaminated the air as the big car's wheels spun.

"*Corporal!*" The Capitan didn't have to repeat himself twice.

Alano turned the key; the Falcon seemed to be asleep for a few seconds before finally turning the six pot three fifty with four on the floor; it gave a low growl as Alano slipped into first.

"*Corporal,* unless I'm half blind, I can clearly see the two gringos sitting in the back of the limo, and I don't have to tell you that we must catch that car *at any cost!*"

"Si, Capitan." The corporal had more on his mind than a conversation with his boss as he gripped the wheel, his knuckles white, as he raced down the badly lit winding road at speeds exceeding eighty miles an hour.

"*Faster, Corporal . . . Faster . . .* We're losing them."

The cruiser was swaying from side to side as Alano took the corners. But Franco . . . Well, he's a pro. An ex-con bank robber whom Salvador had given a second chance, and he knew how to outrun the cops.

Avalos was struggling to pick up the radio phone to call HQ when suddenly the cruiser became airborne as its four wheels left the road after hitting the unseen speed hump.

"*Watch it, Alano!*" Avalos screamed as the Falcon returned to earth, crunching down hard, sending the Capitan's stomach into his mouth.

The cruiser was now completely out of control and heading straight for the large maple, and Alano, in desperation, swung the wheel hard to the left to take evasive action. He should have spent another month at the police driving school to master the skills of high-speed police pursuits; unfortunately, now he was paying the ultimate price as the Ford flipped over and over again, smashing side on against the large mature tree before finally coming to rest, its crumpled monocoque shell severed into two.

*   *   *

"Franco, the police car has crashed into a tree, and it looks bad." Andres, one of the masquerading guards, was staring out of the rear screen of the Buick.

"We gotta turn back before what's left of that police car bursts into flame. These cops must be badly injured."

Franco hit the brakes, and the big car skidded for at least fifteen meters before finally coming to a stop.

"*Santa Maria!* You are right, Andres, no matter what, we must turn back . . ."

*   *   *

Putt . . . Putt . . . Putt . . . The eggbeater slowly became airborne. Mona's parents and the doctor were standing at the perimeter of the helipad, the turbulence from the big blades blasting against their bodies as they waved farewell and God bless. The fugitives were now on their way and without a hitch.

"Boy, is that a relief." Mona sighed. She was holding the saline drip high above Tony's head to ensure gravity did its job. Then she smiled, turning to Bill. "We will be on the tarmac before the dumb police find that they have been left with their shirttails hanging out. I'd love to be a fly on the wall when the generale is told that 'the birds have flown.' But for this poor guy." Mona shook her head as she looked at the unconscious Tony who was in a peaceful comatose sleep. "Bill, I'm worried," she said, her voice almost breaking.

"Mona, I know how you and, for that matter, how we all feel, but my partner . . . He's a fighter . . . He won't give up." Then he turned to Summers, who had concluded that silence is golden. "Should anything happen to Tony, Mike . . . So, help me, I'll gladly do a one to ten for grievous bodily harm."

"Easy, Bill . . . That lousy bastard's not worth it." Mona gave Summers a death scowl.

The distant runway lights of Minitro Pitarini Airport were now clearly in view, and Mona gave another sigh.

"Thank God, we are just about there . . . Capitan, you know where the Learjet is parked?"

"Si, signora . . . Another ten minutes to touchdown." "Gracias . . ."

*   *   *

"Honey, try and get some sleep."

"I just can't seem to close my eyes. I have so many things running through my mind at the same time. It's beyond me, Ruth, why I ever agreed to send two of my best men to Argentina to arrest Summers. It's the old story— Senator Williams pressures Murray the DA, Jack pressures the commissioner, and it comes down all the way and lands on my fucking desk."

"Don't blame yourself, darling. For Tony and Bill, policing is their life, just like you."

Baker sighed again. Ruth was right, but it doesn't make it any easier.

"Now what's in that mind of yours?" Ted was staring into space.

"Ruth, something has just come to me." Ted turned and once again switched on the bedside lamp, much to Ruth's disgruntlement, while purposely ignoring her question.

"Now where's my telephone list?"

Ruth sighed, shaking her head; this was Ted at his best. As usual, he can never find where he places anything.

"It's in the bedside table drawer where you left it."

Ted quickly opened the drawer, then smiled. "I don't know what I would do without you, honey. Now let me see . . . *B . . . B . . .* Ah, here we are . . . *673.*"

*   *   *

"*Shit!*" The phone was blasting in Brown's ear.

"Who can that be, darling?"

"Go to sleep, honey, it's either someone crazy or the wrong number." Dan switched on the light while shaking his head. "*Fucking creeps at this time in the morning . . .* Yeah?"

"Brown . . . *Baker here.*"

"*Captain Ted Baker . . . Homicide?*" Was he hearing right?

"*Who the fuck else do you think it is?* Am I disturbing something?" Baker was being rude.

"*Who is it . . . Who is it ?*"

Dan covered the mouthpiece with his hand.

"For Christ's sake, Pat, *cool it* . . . It's Captain Baker . . . Eh, err, yes, Ted?"

"Something has come up. I'll explain it to you and your partner Lucas tomorrow. Be at my office sharp at nine, prepared to fly to Sao Paulo, Brazil, on the first flight. Make sure you got your toothbrushes packed . . . Sharp at nine then."

"Shit! He's hung up!"

"What do you mean *he's hung up?*"

"Bert and I have to fly to Brazil first thing tomorrow . . ."

"*Brazil!*"

"*You heard me!* Now for Christ's sake, Pat, go to sleep and gimme a break. I have enough on my mind.

"Bert, it's me, Dan . . . Listen, I just had a call . . ."

* * *

(Speaking in Spanish)

Franco rushed from the Buick in his haste, almost tripping over his own two feet. He knew there was not a moment to spare as the gasoline from the cruiser's ruptured tank was snaking across the roadway, creating a small, pungent stream. A spark or even a drip from the carburettor onto the hot block would send a fireball into the sky, negating any hope of saving the injured police officers.

"*My god!*" Franco was stunned at the carnage. The Ford was unrecognizable, like two balls of crumpled aluminium foil, and even worse, there were human beings in there somewhere.

"Andres . . . *Hurry* . . . Go get the fire extinguisher from the trunk of the Buick while I phone 000 . . . Hello, emergency? Yes, all three, police, fire, and ambulance. The address is Recoleta, Avenue Celino . . . A police car has crashed, and the occupants are still trapped in the wreckage . . ."

"Here's the fire extinguisher, Franco."

"*What the fuck are you handing it to me for?* Foam the engine then the ruptured gas tank."

"How do you get this thing to work?" Andres was hopelessly trying under the dim street lights to read the instructions.

"Gimme the fucking thing!" Franco wrenched the red tube from Andres's hand, then smashed the trigger on the ground to break the seal. "Christ, where is the engine?"

The front was just a mangled lump of twisted steel, mag rims, and smouldering tires. *Whatever* . . . Franco frantically began to foam the homogeneous mess.

"That ought do it, but I need to save some for that leaking gas tank . . . Andres, check the front to see if there is any sign of life, and, Demetrio, you check the rear."

Franco kept spraying the foam until the extinguisher was empty.

"Man, I feel my stomach turning. The driver is unrecognizable, and there's no way I can get to him. We need the Jaws of Life, Franco."

"Andres!" Franco yelled as he chucked the empty foam bottle aside.

Andres just shook his head. He could see the lieutenant crushed between the rear door pillars, blood everywhere. No one could survive this mess, it was "a car too far."

"My gut feeling tells me it's a lost cause . . ."

CHAPTER 6

The helicopter gently touched down on the runway about fifty meters from the Menzel Company Learjet. Capitan Martinez was waiting patiently, the door open and the stairs down. Salvador had briefed him on the mission, and he knew the stakes and the quicker he was airborne the better.

"Signorina Menzel." Martinez gave a polite salute.

"Forget the protocol, Capitan, and prepare for take-off. We need to get the wounded man on board as quickly as possible."

"Si."

The Capitan wasn't impressed at Mona's rudeness, but he had to get this crate in the air before anything untoward happened, and he disappeared into the cockpit to ignite the jets.

"Capitan." Mona turned to the helicopter pilot. "Keep these blades moving. Once we transfer the wounded police officer to the Learjet, there had better be a vapor trail. I have a bad feeling the cops will be here any minute."

"Si, signorina, I understand."

"*Our first, Summers*, and no fucking heroics. Mona has my forty-five, and the way she feels about you . . . Well, let's just say, *if I were you, I wouldn't chance it.*"

Summers scowled at Bill's remark as he unsteadily made his way to the door of the helicopter, and just as Hayden predicted, Mona was standing there, the Browning pointing precariously at Summers's forehead.

"Get your ass on that plane . . . *Comprender?*" Mona yelled above the noise of the jet engines.

Summers gave Mona an ugly stare, then stood in defiance. "*I said move it, you fucking loser.*"

Mona waved the semiautomatic in a threatening gesture but whatever . . . Summers would rather stay in Argentina than return to New York to face his fate.

"*Bill!*" Mona yelled. "*We got trouble!*"

On hearing Mona's plea, Bill didn't waste a second and leaped from the copter.

"We got Mr. Stubborn here."

"*Oh, is that so . . .*" Bill rushed Summers from behind, grabbing his shirt collar and handcuffed wrists, literally lifting him off his feet, half marching and half dragging him onto the stairs of the jet.

"You bastard, you're breaking my fucking wrists!" Summers screamed in pain.

"I'll break more than your fucking neck, *if you don't climb these fucking steps.*"

They say it's "pain for gain," and Summers suddenly had a change of heart.

"Thanks, Bill. Now let's get Tony on board . . ."

* * *

"Please, *signor*, we must go." Capitan Martinez was standing at the door of the jet.

"Well, I guess this is it, Mona. I know that you can't fly with us to Brazil and . . ."

"*Don't, Bill . . .* Save it until the next time we meet. There *will* be a next time, won't there?"

Bill gave her a gentle kiss on the lips, then smiled. "*You bet!*"

* * *

In the short period he had known Mona, something had sparked. If only things could be different.

Mona could feel the body language, and the look in Bill's eyes said it all.

"Mona . . ."

"Bill, don't, or you'll have me crying. Besides, I must smell awful. I haven't showered in two days."

"Mona, you'll always smell beautiful to me."

"*Bill Hayden,* get on that plane, or so help me . . . !"

"Goodbye, Mona . . ."

* * *

June felt a strange relief when she finally heard the buzz of the alarm at six thirty. She always liked to set the time early so that she could relax for at least half an hour before showering and cooking breakfast for the kids. Every day without Mike was another challenge, and today would be no different. The thought made her sigh.

"*Hell!* I almost forgot," June spoke out loud. "I have an appointment with that creep Simmons, the bank manager, to cancel the lease on the Beamer and return it to the leasing company, and this morning Phil asked me to come to office, as he wanted to introduce me to the staff. *Shit!* What time was that bloody appointment with Simmons?"

Without hesitation, she switched on the beside lamp and swung her feet to the floor.

"Where the hell's that diary of mine?" June opened the side drawer to search.

"Ah, here we are . . . *Would you believe it? Ten thirty this morning!* That's all I need. I'll phone Phil as soon as the kids leave for school . . . But then there's the other problem . . . *What the hell am I going to do for a car?*"

* * *

"Come on, sis, the bus will be here any minute." Steven was getting impatient; his sister was always the same . . . *late!*

"I'm coming, keep your shirt on!" Sheryl yelled as she came bounding down the stairs two at a time. The bus had already arrived, with the driver leaning on the horn.

"*Sheryl,* you haven't even touched your breakfast!" June scolded her as she grabbed a slice of toast before running to the door, her schoolbag dangling from her shoulder.

"*Bye, Mom.*"

"*That girl!*" June shook her head as the front door slammed. Then she smiled. "I was young once."

With the breakfast dishes rinsed and the washer stacked, it was time to relax over a coffee, and June topped up her mug before strolling into the lounge. It had just turned eight thirty, and it was too early to start making calls.

Then something crossed her mind, making her stop in her tracks and go to the study.

"I may as well do the dreaded sums." She opened the desk drawer and laid out some foolscap. "Now where do I start? *Coffee first.*" June smiled as she sipped the dark brew.

"Let me see . . . I've transferred the cash from my fixed deposit to my check account, and after drawing money from the ATM, I have a credit balance of four five. That's gonna get me far, *and I don't think!* The Beamer goes back today, but I might face cancellation charges. The mortgage is due on Friday, but if Mike's salary is deposited on time, then I'll have some breathing space and get to clear my credit card."

Hmmmm, June was pondering. "I could probably buy a used car for, say, four grand. I know . . . I'll ask Phil if he has time to come and help me choose. Men are better at that than a woman . . . *Yep!* I can get through this month, but only just!" She paused again and frowned. "If only I can get Mike's termination settlement . . . I've been through the whole house for that bloody contract with no avail . . . *It's just gotta be in his office! And . . .* That's my first call."

*   *   *

"Good morning, Elizabeth, is Chuck free?"

"I'm sorry, he is not taking any calls today."

"I see . . . Perhaps, Elizabeth, then you can help me?"

"If I can."

"I need the original . . . Or a photocopy of Mike's contract of employment. I'm sure it's on file."

"I'm sorry, Mrs. Summers, but that would have to be cleared by Mr. Briggs."

"I thought as much . . . Well, maybe you can confirm if Mike's salary for this month has been deposited with the bank?" There was a moment's silence.

"Mrs. Summers, I wish I could help, but I don't have access to the payroll. I shouldn't, but I'll put you through to accounts. I'm sure you have met our chief accountant at some of the company functions . . . To refresh your memory, his name is Jim McGill . . . Give me a moment. "Thanks, Elizabeth, I really appreciate it."

"McGill here."

"Jim, it's Mrs. Summers. I wonder if you can help me . . .

"And it will be deposited today . . . Thanks, Jim, for your help." "No problem, Mrs. Summers, glad to help."

* * *

June placed back the receiver, then sat for a moment. The news was good; at least Briggs had kept his word.

"Let's see the time . . . Just after nine thirty. I'll phone Phil, I have his direct line . . ."

"Hi, honey, I was just about to phone you."

"You don't sound very happy. I hope it's not bad news."

It's Global Marketing . . . Briggs has filled chapter 11, declaring insolvency . . ."

CHAPTER 7

Terry was up bright and early, showered and dressed, ready for the office. She sipped the last of her coffee and straightened her blue pencil skirt as she descended from the high barstool.

"Now just a touch of lipstick, and I'm outta here." She wiped her lips with napkin.

After the needful in front of the hall mirror, she slipped into her heels, then grabbed her jacket and briefcase. It would be an interesting day ahead, what with Jack's meeting with Hall, the president of ABM, and then Phil Stevens, the lawyer, to discuss the company's legal action against Global . . . *It was going to be one helluva day!*

* * *

The drive to the office as usual was stressful and boring. In New York, the traffic never changes, and the drivers get ruder and ruder by the minute, *but what's new?*

Terry's mind was preoccupied reflecting on Laura's words: "*My advice . . . jump at it!*" It's easy for Laura to say. She's been there and done that. But to be appointed to sales and marketing manager, *like overnight,* was something else.

543

Terry signalled and turned left, halting at the boom gate to the office tower. As usual, Lee was on duty and flashed his "Osmond" smile.

"Good morning, ma'am, can I see your ID please?"

"Christ, Lee, try a new line."

Lee just laughed; he loved to tease Terry.

"Seriously, Terry, I'm always glad to see you. You make my day. Not like these other bitches that work here."

"The feeling is mutual, Lee, and you are a really nice guy." She winked with a smile.

"Have a good day, Terry." Lee triggered the boom.

Terry parked the Mazda and walked sprightly to the elevator; her mind preoccupied with the marketing meeting with the staff at nine thirty. She had laid the ground rules and the KPIs, and it was going to be interesting how the "barrack room lawyers" had approached their new responsibilities.

"*Good morning . . . Good morning,*" Terry addressed the staff as she approached her desk. There seemed to be a change of atmosphere in the office, and Terry was pleasantly surprised. They say, "a change is as good as a holiday."

Terry settled in and read her mail. It had just turned eight forty-five, and she still had another fifteen minutes before "D-day."

I wonder how Blakely's meeting is going with the president. Terry was thinking to herself as she sipped the last of her coffee. Well, I'll soon know when we meet at the lawyers. "*Hmmmm . . .* It's that time already. I had better get my skates on." The staff were already walking toward the lecture room.

* * *

"*Good morning . . .* Can I have your attention please . . . Yesterday I specified the parameters for our revamped marketing and sales plan for the ABM 2000 range of new business machines. Unfortunately, the window of opportunity is small, and the timing and stock availability is crucial to satisfy that window. To create the demand and be unable to supply what is the result . . . Jaycee?"

"Our competitors fill the demand with their products and thank us for it."

"Did you all hear that . . . Jaycee has hit the nail on the head. So where do we start?"

"With a sales forecast for the first six months of the launch."

"Correct, Mildred . . . But first of all, we need to test the market. And how do we that? With an extensive marketing campaign through the media, mail drops, technical brochures, and seminars, inviting all our ex and potential new customers. In short, we make a list of our competitors and explore new opportunities through target marketing. Jaycee, would you wish to elaborate on your ideas based on what we covered at our last meeting . . ."

"*Sure.* I've given it some thought, and Mildred and I have decided a good start point would be a product comparison with our major comp . . ."

*   *   *

"Thank you and keep up the good work. We'll meet on Friday morning same time. same place . . . *Well done!*"

*   *   *

As Terry returned to her desk, she had a warm feeling that her strategy was working. The team now seemed to have a purpose and, for a change, were working together as a team.

"And that reminds me." Terry lifted the phone. "Angela, Terry here.

Listen, I need new job descriptions and salary grades for . . ." Terry had just placed her phone back when it rang again.

"Johnson here."

"Terry, I have a Frank Reynolds on the line. He says it's important. Shall I put him through?"

"*Christ, I don't believe my ears.*"

"I'm sorry, Terry, I missed that," the receptionist queried.

"Tell that creep I'm not taking any calls, and if he rings again, just hang up!"

Terry couldn't believe it. "This guy is either crazily in love *or just plain hard of hearing!*"

*   *   *

"Just go in, Mr. Blakely, Mr. Hall is waiting."

"Thanks, Lola. Is the boss in a good mood?" Jack gave her that special smile.

Lola gave one in return. Confidential secretary means "confidential," even with her spouse.

Jack knocked on the door; he was sticking to protocol.

"Come in, Jack." Hall knew who it was.

As Blakely opened the door, he was surprised to see another smartly dressed gentleman sitting in front of the president, enjoying a coffee.

*   *   *

545

He was around Jack's age, lean, immaculately dressed. He was clean shaven, had dark-brown hair swept straight back, and had penetrating blue eyes that were sizing up Blakely's facial expression toward the "intruder." This guy's face seemed familiar, but where had Jack seen him before?

*   *   *

"Take a load off, Jack." Hall pointed. "Coffee?"

"No, I'm good."

"Jack, I would like you to meet your new boss, Fred Morris, who is replacing Simpson, who submitted his resignation this morning as I requested. Fred has joined us from Hewlett-Packard, having resigned as VP of marketing. I called you here this morning for you to personally meet him. You know, Jack, you did me a big favor, although I don't approve of your methods, as I was about to fire Simpson anyhow, and you gave me the perfect excuse."

"*Eh, err* . . . I'm sorry, Bill, and I apologize if I seem rather confused." For once in his life, Jack was lost for words.

"Confused? About what, Jack?" Hall frowned. "Unknown to you, I have been head hunting for a replacement for Simpson for months."

"It's just that . . ."

Hall could see the disappointment on Blakely's face, and it was all coming home.

"Jack, I know you must feel disappointed, and be assured, I seriously considered you, but in the end and after discussions with human resources, we felt you needed more experience and that to promote you prematurely would damage your career."

Blakely sat dumbfounded. *How can this be?* He had given his loyalty and dedication to the company all those years, and now this slap in the face! *Maaan* . . . It's hard to swallow.

"I see," Jack replied, almost in whisper. "So, is that all?"

"Jack don't do anything silly. We need you at ABM."

Blakely rose from his chair. "Congratulations, Mr. Jackson, I wish you well. Now if I can be excused, I have an appointment with the lawyers at noon."

"Jack, if it's the Global case, there's no need. Briggs has filed for chapter 11."

"*Well, I'll be darned!*" Jack couldn't contain his sentiment. It was all a waste of time after all.

Blakely was still shaking his head in disbelief as he left Hall's office, but another chapter in his life was about to begin.

*   *   *

Terry had just filled her second coffee and was walking back to her desk when her phone rang.

"Yes, Johnson here."

"Terry, it's Rita. Jack's been trying to contact you for the last fifteen minutes. His tone is pretty ugly."

"*Hmmmm?* Put him through."

"Jack, I'm sorry I miss—"

Blakely just talked over her.

"Terry, there's now no need to meet with the lawyers, Global has filed chapter 11, insolvency."

"That's a curver I didn't expect."

"Yeah, and here's something else that *I* didn't expect . . ."

*   *   *

Bill cringed as the eighteenth stitch finally closed the wound.

"Is that it, Doc?"

"Yes, and you are one very lucky guy. There's no damage to the nerves or major blood vessels. Just a clean flesh wound. I'll raise your arm with a sling to improve the circulation."

The nurse handed Bill a glass of water and a brightly coloured two-toned capsule.

"These antibiotics will stop any infection. Take two now and then twice daily until the course is finished."

"I understand, Doc, but any news about my buddy?"

"He's in good hands, Mr. Hayden. Two of our finest surgeons are operating *right now*. Other than that, I'm afraid it's a waiting game."

"I understand, Doc." Bill forced a smile. "Say . . . Is there a chance that I could perhaps get a coffee? Something tells me this is going to be a long night."

"Sure." The doctor smiled, turning to the nurse. "I think I can persuade this young lady to do the needful. Now why don't you get some rest and make yourself comfortable in the waiting room? A Mr. Broaden from the American embassy is patiently waiting to speak with you."

"Thanks, Doc, I like the embroidery." Bill glanced at the wound and gave the doctor a cheeky wink.

*   *   *

As Bill emerged from the "patch up" room in his one-sleeved, blood spattered shirt, arm in a sling, all he needed was a bandage around his forehead to look like a casualty from Gettysburg.

"*Mr. Broaden!* I'm surprised that you are still here. It's nearly four in the morning. Listen, I can't begin to thank you . . ."

"Bill, there's no need to. That's what the embassy is here for, to take care of our U.S. citizens abroad, and there's no need for formalities. Call me Stan . . . Now I know what you are going to ask. *Summers?* He's in the lockup under the watchful eyes of the embassy marines, so don't worry."

"That was my second, but more importantly, my buddy, Lieutenant Perino?"

"He is undergoing extensive surgery, and we can only hope and pray that he pulls through . . . Bill . . . I'm afraid it's a waiting game."

"Your coffee, sir?"

"Thank you, young lady. Please place it on the coffee table." Bill gave the young nurse a warm thank-you smile.

"And you, sir?" She turned to Broaden.

"No but thank you." Broaden smiled. "I've had one too many already . . . Bill, try and relax. I know it's easier said than done, but you look bushed."

Bill gave a weary sigh as he sat down hard on plastic chair. *What he would do for some shut eye.*

"So what's on your mind, Stan?" Being a detective, Bill could sense that Broadens niceties had an ulterior motive.

"Bill, it's like this. I'm sure, being a police officer, you are familiar with reports, and I'm afraid the civil service is no different. This whole episode is, shall I say, like a something from a TV series, only played out in real life. I know how you must feel physically and mentally, but I need some answers."

Broaden could see that weary look in Bill's eyes as if to say, *"Any other time but not now!"*

"Listen, Bill, if you feel you are not up to it, I fully understand. I'll take a rain check, and we can meet at the embassy tomorrow once you've had a good night's sleep to recuperate."

"No, Stan, it's all right. I might as well get it over with. It's something to kill time, or else I'll go outta my mind. Where do you want me to start?"

* * *

"*That's one helluva story!*" Broaden was shaking his head as he wrapped up his notes.

"Before you say anything further, Stan . . ."

Bill rose to his feet at the sight of the two surgeons in their plastic-covered shoes and green operating attire, talking to one another, their voices inaudible as they approached the two men.

"Are you Mr. Hayden?" the taller of the surgeons inquired.

"*Eh, err, yes!*" Bill's nerves were shot; he didn't know what to expect.

"Mr. Hayden, we did everything possible, but I'm afraid it was just too late . . ."

* * *

Baker had just finished counting sheep when the phone blasted in his ear again.

"Ted, darling . . . *Wake up* . . . *Wake up* . . . It's the phone again." Ruth gently shook her husband's shoulders. "Come, darling, it could be something important!"

"*Eh . . . Eggg . . . Err.*" Baker cleared his throat. "*Eh* . . . the phone?" He was still half asleep. He fumbled, then placed the phone to his ear.

"Baker here."

"Ted, it's Hayden. I have some really bad news . . . Tony passed away this morning at four thirty-five Brazil time . . ."

CHAPTER 8

Thanks, darling . . . At least I have once piece of good news." "*You have!* And what's that?" Phil was puzzled.

"Brigg's conscience must have plagued him, and he credited Mike's salary into the bank today. Sixteen thousand . . . It won't take me far, but it will cover another month."

"Now that *is* something!"

"Darling, there's one more thing. I forgot I had an appointment with 'Scrooge' the bank manager." She could hear Phil laugh in the background at her remark. "I have to return my BMW today."

"No sweat, you can come into the office in the afternoon. *But of course.* What am I thinking about, *you have no car! Hmmm* . . . Listen, just call a cab when you're finished with . . . 'Scrooge.'" Phil laughed again. "You can use the spare car here at the office until you get a set of wheels."

"Are you sure, darling? It won't look good with the staff."

"Honey, let me be the judge of that."

"Thanks, darling, I'll give you a call once I'm free . . . Ciao."

* * *

"Good morning, Hewlett-Packard, how can I be of assistance?"

"Would it be possible to put me through to Alan Beazley, your VP of human resources? Just mention Jack Blakely from ABM."

"If you don't mind waiting, sir, I'll contact his secretary."

"Not at all."

"*Jack!* I'll be darned, what's the occasion?"

"You still owe me that drink."

"*Get out of it!* But be serious, you're not phoning me to check on my health."

"*You got that right!* I'm phoning because you need someone to fill the slot left by Fred Morris, your ex-VP of sales and marketing, and I'm just the man you're looking for."

"Same old Jack, not slow in coming forward. But that's not to say I'm not interested. You have the experience, and there's no doubt you know the market and you kept ABM together through their worst downturn. Yeah, Jack I'm interested. Why don't you come over and see me and bring your CV."

"No sweat. What would be a convenient time?"

"There's no time like the present. Let me see . . . How does two today grab you?"

"I'll be there. Thanks again, Alan, and I'll forget that beer." He could hear Beazley laughing.

Jack closed his phone, then gave a wry smile. If he pulled this off it would be the coup d'etat of the decade.

* * *

"Ted, what is it, darling? You've gone as white as sheet." Baker was now wide awake.

"It's Tony Perino. He never made it."

"My god! *Tony* . . . I can't believe it. What happened?"

"Not now, honey, my mind is in a daze. I'll have to phone the commissioner, then the DA, and worst of all, go see Tony's wife. It doesn't bear thinking."

"Darling, if there's anything I can do to help . . ."

"It's all right, honey, there's nothing anyone can do now . . ."

* * *

To say Terry was shell-shocked . . . *Well?* It was a done deal that Blakely would fill Simpson's shoes, but in her heart, there was now a sense of relief and no decision to make. But then again, Blakely was not the type to take this lying down, and as for that crafty bastard Hall? It was as if he anticipated Blakely's every move setting up Simpson for the big fall, having already recruited Morris from Hewlett-Packard.

"I gotta hand it to that bastard." Terry was reflecting on Hall's shifty footwork as she spoke to herself. Then she turned her attention to the thick folder she had compiled for the twelve-noon meeting with the lawyers.

"What a fucking waste of time! Well, I guess I won't be needing this shit anymore." Terry pushed the folder aside, still brooding, amazed at the turn of events and how things can change at the blink of an eye.

"I can just imagine Laura's reaction." She half smiled, retaining a cheeky grin on her face and turning to her computer screen.

"I have plenty of work, but that call from Blakely just blew me away, and now I feel claustrophobic, like I need some space."

Terry checked the time on the computer screen.

"Hmmm, that time already. Another hour before lunch . . . I can't wait."

*   *   *

Baker had less than two hours sleep when the alarm kicked in. He had done his round robin with the phone calls, and most importantly, before the word hits the street, he had to break the sad news to Tony's wife. Ted had contacted Lieutenant Linda Perkins from the psychological trauma department, who had agreed to accompany him and collect Ted at his home at nine this morning.

"Darling, you've hardly touched your breakfast." Ruth poured another cup. *"You must eat something."*

"Honey, I know you mean well, but I still can't get over losing one of my best detectives and, most of all, one of my best friends. Tony and I, we go a long way back . . . Why I can remember when he first . . ." The front doorbell rang.

"That must be Lieutenant Perkins . . . Honey, do me favor and answer the doorbell while I finish the last of my coffee."

"You just sit where you are." Ruth disappeared.

*   *   *

Linda Perkins was qualified from Cornell University as a psychologist with the highest grades. After some time in private practice, she decided that

551

she needed some drama in her life, and what better than to join the Trauma Unit of the NYPD. Of course, her father and brother both being police officers made her decision even easier and made her proud to follow in the family tradition. After a number of major crime incidents where hostages and police fatalities occurred because of her dedication and excellent results, she was promoted to captain and was highly respected by her superiors. Unmarried at twenty-nine, she is still a catch, what with her trim figure, swept-back auburn hair, and dark brown eyes; she could still turn the heads, and many an officer had fantasies about the mysterious Linda. Unlike most female officers, she liked wearing her dark-blue uniform, sporting her two-bar captain epaulette. The uniform gave her status in the macho world of the NYPD.

*   *   *

"Come in, Linda, Ted's just finishing his coffee. Go straight through to the kitchen."

"Thanks, Ruth . . . Good morning, Ted."

"*Wish it was.* Grab a seat . . . Coffee?"

"I've already poured one, darling."

"Thanks, Ruth, that was thoughtful of you . . . Ted, I know how you must feel. I knew Tony as well, you know."

"*Who didn't!*" Baker dejectedly answered.

"Ted, don't blame yourself. You were being pressured from all quarters, and it was the only decision."

"*Was it?*" Baker retaliated. "Two of my best men wounded, one fatal, and for what? A piece of shit like Summers, whom if found guilty will most probably get a light smack on the wrist by a goody-two-shoes judge and, with good behaviour, will be back on the streets in a couple years . . ." Baker shook his head. "And how do I tell his wife and kids that her husband and their father will never be coming home again? Linda, I should have been strong enough to tell the commissioner and the DA to go and take a hike."

"Ted, get over it . . . You're too hard on yourself . . . It's in the past . . . It's done, and all the regrets in the world won't bring Tony back." Baker didn't react to Linda's advice.

"Linda, if you don't mind, I don't feel like driving."

"Of course, Ted, that's not a problem. I'm only too happy to oblige."

"Thanks, I'll get a cruiser to drive me home." "What's Tony's address again . . . ?"

*   *   *

It was the nearest thing to a wake as the two police officers sat in silence during the hour drive to East Village, each thinking along the same lines as the other. *What would be the right words to break the unthinkable news?*

"Linda, I don't know if you have ever experienced this before, but this is way out of my league. Sure, I've had detectives wounded in the line of duty, *but never fatal!*"

"Ted, it's an important part of my job. Leave the woman thing to me. It's not my first time."

Baker looked more relieved in that he had backup, so to speak, but he was still feeling washed out.

"Linda, before I retire, I hope I never go through this again."

"Ted, the way the gun laws are in this country, I wouldn't bank on it . . . What was that street again?"

"River Street, number 16 . . ."

*   *   *

June had finished dressing and was just putting the finishing touches to her makeup when she heard the noise of a car as it turned into the Perrino driveway, and she pulled the curtains aside out of curiosity.

"*Hmmm . . .*" she studied the young policewoman and the tall gentleman as they left the car.

"*That man!* I'm sure I recognize him . . . That's Captain Baker, *of course,* Tony's boss. I met him a couple of times at Tony's barbecues. *Hmmm . . . Strange.*" June dropped the curtains; she had other things on her mind, and it was getting near nine thirty. "*So if I'm late, I'm late!*"

Baker rang the bell. He could hear Rose in the background, scolding the kids and telling them to finish their breakfast while she answered the door, and Ted looked toward Linda and shrugged.

Rose opened the door, then stood for a moment in shock. *Why would Captain Baker be standing at my door, and who is this uniformed policewoman?*

"*Ted?*" Rose looked as if she had been turned into salt. "*Ted . . . Eh . . .* Is something wrong? It's Tony, *isn't it?*"

"Rose, can we come in please?"

"Tell me, Ted, *I want to know, here and now!*"

"Please, Rose, let's go inside."

Rose reluctantly stepped aside.

"Can we go through to the lounge?" Baker asked sheepishly.

Although still distraught, Rose agreed and pointed to the sofa.

"Mom, who are these people?" Mauro, the oldest boy, was holding his glass of juice.

"*Mauro,* what did I tell you? Go and finish your breakfast and look after your brother."

Rose sank into the armchair, and Linda could sense that she was about to go into shock . . . It was time, and she turned to Ted, giving him that look.

"Rose," Ted began, his voice shaky. "There's no easy way to express my sadness that I have to inform you that Tony sadly lost his life in the performance of his duty."

Rose sat for a second in absolute silence as Baker's words rang in her ears. It was as if she was digesting each syllable before bursting into hysterical tears.

"*Tell me it's not true . . .,*" Rose sobbed almost choking. "Please, Ted, tell me it's all a horrible dream, a mistake . . . *Please . . . Please . . .*"

"Mommy, is something wrong?" Mauro and Sam, his younger brother, were standing at the entrance to the kitchen, and when Baker looked at these two innocent kids, his eyes filled.

"What am I going to do, Ted? How can I tell these kids? My god, Tony, why did you leave me?" Rose sobbed uncontrollably. "*I can't live without you.*"

Young Samuel began to cry at seeing his mother in such a state, and his big brother, although only seven, rushed over and threw his arms around his mother.

"Don't worry, Mom, I'll protect you."

"I know you will, son." Rose held him close, her words slurred through her sobs.

"Rose, Linda is here, from our Trauma Unit, to give you support, and she can stay the whole day with you if you wish. We are worried you might harm yourself or the children in your distraught state of mind, which is not uncommon in these situations."

"Rose." Linda held her hand reassuringly. "Let me fetch you a coffee . . . Do you happen to have some Panadol?"

*　*　*

Within thirty minutes, her mother, Maria, arrived, then minutes later, Tony's parents, their cars stacked in the driveway. They had come over immediately upon hearing the tragic news over the phone from Lieutenant Perkins, who had convinced Rose to give her their phone numbers.

"Rose, darling, why don't you take a sedative and go upstairs and lie down for a while? We'll look after Mauro and Sam."

"Mother, *what am I going to do?*" Rose continued to sob.

"There, there, darling." Maria cradled her daughter's head in her arms to comfort her as she sat beside her. It reminded her of the day she lost Rose's father.

"Darling, why don't I came upstairs with you, and we can rest together. The kids are not going to kindergarten or school today, Tony's parents will take care of them." Maria turned to Linda in despair, her eyes now resembling two bloodshot balloons.

The kids were back in the kitchen, being comforted by their other grandmother. They were both scared and crying at the commotion, wondering what was wrong and why everyone was crying, but the time was not right to break the news.

"Ted, I'm not happy leaving Rose like this." Linda turned to Baker as Maria supported her daughter's limp body up the stairs to her bedroom. "I'll write a prescription for a strong sedative to make her sleep." She scribbled on a notepad, then detached the page. "Mr. Perino, can I trouble you to go to the nearest drugstore?"

* * *

"I agree, Linda, I'll call the office . . . Captain Baker here . . . Yeah, put me through to Stace . . . It's 16 River Street, East Village . . . I'll explain it to you when I arrive . . . For Christ's sake . . . *I know I had a meeting at nine! So it will just have to wait . . . Well, call the nearest one!*"

Within ten minutes, a cruiser had arrived at the Perrino house; the doorbell rang.

"That'll be my lift, Linda. Call me once things have settled down."

"Sure, Ted."

"*Oh,* and, Linda, thanks again for your support." Linda acknowledged in silence.

Ted proceeded to the front door. This day will be emblazoned in his mind for the rest of his life.

"Sergeant, take me direct to Pearl Street."

"Certainly, Captain."

As Baker escorted the sergeant to the black and white, by sheer coincidence, June Summers was leaving at the same time.

"*My god, the cars!* And that police car . . . It must be something serious." June stood for a moment, taking in the scenery.

Her inquisitiveness getting the better of her, she couldn't resist the temptation and called to Baker.

"*Captain Baker.*"

Baker turned at the sound of the woman's voice.

"*Fuck,* this is all I need! Summers's *goddamn* wife. The timing couldn't be worse."

"Sir?" The sergeant was confused at Baker's outburst.

"It's all right, Sergeant, I'm just talking to myself."

"Is something wrong, Captain?" June called again in persistence.

Baker cursed below his breath. "*Mrs. Summers*, take my advice . . . If I were you, I would make myself scarce?"

June was taken aback at Baker's rudeness.

"For your information, your husband was arrested in Buenos Aires yesterday and will be escorted to New York tomorrow to face the charge of attempted murder. Tragically, in the apprehension of the fugitive, two of my best officers received gunshot wounds, and sadly your neighbour and friend, Lieutenant Perino, died of his wounds at 4:15 a.m. this morning."

"*My god!*" June raised her fingers to her lips, flabbergasted at the heartbreaking news.

"I will be contacting you later, Mrs. Summers . . . Make sure you are still in town."

June was still standing in the driveway as the black and white disappeared out of sight. She was confused, disorientated, lonely, and brutally angry. What had she done to deserve this? Rose . . . Those poor kids . . .

"*Mike Summers, I hope you rot in hell!*"

*   *   *

June turned tail and walked back to the house; she needed something strong to calm her nerves as she slammed the front door and made a beeline for the liquor cabinet.

The bourbon bottle, Mike's favourite poison, seemed as good as any, and June poured herself a more than generous measure. Her hand was shaking as the neck of the dark-green bottle rattled against the crystal glass, making a pinging sound as she sat down heavily on the sofa, almost spilling the contents before overindulging in a larger-than-life mouthful. The raw bourbon stung the back of her throat, almost choking her, and she gasped for breath.

"*Heh, ahem . . . Ahhh.*" June continued to cough.

"I still can't get over it . . . *Tony.*" She was shaking her head in disbelief before finally gaining her calm and placing the half-consumed "fire water" on the coffee table.

June stretched over and lifted the phone.

"Phil, I'm sorry, darling, but I just had to phone." The tears now in full flow.

"Honey, are you crying?"

"Phil, I've just heard the most terrible news . . ."

CHAPTER 9

"So, what happens now, Stan?" Bill turned to Broaden.

Broaden thought for a moment before answering. He had been through similar traumas where U.S. citizens visiting Brazil, either on business or vacation, had met their deaths through accident or health problems. It was always a headache for the embassy, but thankfully there are strict procedures laid down for emergencies, and it's simply a case of going by the book.

"To answer your question, Bill. Firstly, I need clearance from customs and immigration to ship the body back to the United States. But in this case, it's only a formality. When I return to the embassy, I'll arrange the paperwork. The casket will be placed in a refrigerated compartment on the flight and, upon reaching New York, will be taken to the city morgue for an autopsy to determine the cause of death. It's standard procedure. Of course all costs will be met by the embassy."

"Stan, can you make sure I'm on the same flight as my friend?"

"Of course, that goes without saying, and you'll be staying at the embassy tonight and tomorrow." Stan stepped back, taking in the state of Bill's ragged, bloodstained shirt and slacks. "And . . . I *must* get you a change of clothing! Shall we go?"

Broaden seemed calm and collected; it was all part of his job.

Bill shook his head. He was really down. He would miss that partner of his and his crazy Italian humour. *Police work would never be the same again without him.*

You big heel, I hope you're listening, you inconsiderate wop, leaving me like this. Bill could just imagine Tony up there laughing his ass off.

"Are you all right, Bill?" Broaden could see that hazy look in Bill's eyes.

"Yeah, I was just thinking to myself that it's highly unlikely I'll get some shut-eye tonight."

"Well, shall we?" Broaden was becoming impatient. "I have an embassy car on standby."

"Stan, give me ten. I have a personal call to make." "Then I'll meet you at the front door." "Thanks." Bill opened his cell phone.

"Yes?"

"Mona . . . Bill here."

"*At last!* I'm almost out of my mind waiting for your call . . . How are you?"

"I'll live, but Tony . . . Well . . ." Bill paused, finding it hard to say the words. "He never made it."

A pin dropping would have been ear piercing, the silence scary as Mona's shock system kicked in, and Bill could identify a faint sobbing in the background.

"Are you okay, Mona?" Still more silence.

"Mona, answer me!" Bill was worried; she could easily have fainted.

"Yes, I'm all right . . . It's . . . It's just hard to take," Mona sobbed.

"And how about you, honey?" Bill asked.

"You called me honey!"

"Eh, err, a slip of the tongue."

"It may be, but it was so sweet . . . But Bill, we have another tragedy on our hands this morning . . . When we created the diversion and with Franco pedalling the Buick at high speeds, the police gave chase just as we planned, and from what I gather, the cruiser appeared to hit a speed bump, and the driver lost control, smashing sideways into a tree, slicing the vehicle in two, killing both officers . . ."

"*My god . . . I don't believe it!* And the police?"

"They can't prove anything, but that bastardo Cerise won't let it go easily. Don't worry, Bill, my father has contacts in high places and is a personal friend of the presidente, but in the end it all boils down to money, and fortunately my father is not short."

"Mona, honey, I'll most likely be flying back to the States tomorrow . . . *Eh* . . . Bill paused. "*Eh* . . . And I just want to say . . . Well, you know what I mean?"

"Do I, Bill?"

Bill could sense her doubt by the tone in her voice.

"Mona, I'll never forget you."

"And I'll never forget *you*, Bill, but only time will tell . . . Bye, Bill . . ."

*   *   *

"June, try and calm down. It's a horrible turn of events with the death of a police officer, especially your neighbour and a friend, it doesn't get any worse. But June, above all, don't go on a guilt trip. It's not your fault, you're just a victim of circumstances. Now I know I shouldn't be saying this, but being a lawyer, with every problem there's always an opportunity."

"*Opportunity!*"

"June, don't you see? Now that Mike is in custody, he will be returning to New York to face charges, and we can now serve your divorce papers in person. Furthermore, we can commence legal action to sell your property should he refuse to sign the title deed, which the bank currently possesses as collateral for the mortgage."

"I see . . . *My god, it's so confusing.* So, what do you advise, darling?" "*Make sure you keep that appointment with Scrooge!*"

*   *   *

"Ted, it's the commissioner on the line."

"Put him through, Stace . . . Nev?"

"I've just had Murray on the phone to discuss a press interview, and I agree with him. now that Tony's family and next of kin have been informed, we need to move fast before the media get a whiff of it. I gather you have conveyed the bad news to your staff?"

"Yeah . . . I had to, Nev."

"Well, you can't keep it under wraps now. I'm sure the lines will be running hot. There's always one bad apple chasing a buck."

"I'll get Stace on it right away. What time would be convenient? You'll be attending?"

"*Of course*, as with the DA and Senator Williams . . . Let's make it twelve noon . . . Oh, and, Ted, I've discussed it with Murray and the mayor, and we have unanimously agreed that Lieutenant Perino posthumously receive the Police Medal for Valour, the highest recognition for bravery above and beyond the call of duty. Sergeant Hayden will also receive a commendation for bravery and promotion to lieutenant."

"I wholly agree . . . Do you want me to put something together and pass it by you? You know what these reporters are like. You say one thing and report another."

"You've been there before, Ted, I'll leave it up to you."

"It's twelve noon then."

Baker knocked on the glass partition to attract Stace's attention.

"Yes, Captain?"

"Stace, I need you to arrange a media conference for . . ."

* * *

"Here's your flight tickets . . . Delta Airways, departing at eleven from Kennedy. Check with Stace and sign for a cash drawdown. For your information, the flight to Sao Paulo, Brazil, is nine hours plus one hour ahead time difference. So, you should arrive at Guarulhos International Airport at nine tonight. American embassy staff will be at the airport to meet you." Baker looked up at Brown and Lucas as they stood in silence. "You *do* have passports, don't you?"

"Yes, Captain." Lucas answered.

"I gather that means both of you?"

"Captain, before we leave, we would just like to say . . ."

Baker raised his hand. "Please, I know what you are going to say, and I appreciate it, but I've had enough this morning to last me a lifetime . . ." Baker pointed to the door.

"Just make sure you bring Summers back in one piece . . ."

CHAPTER 10

Laura was relaxing after finishing her lunch. The hospital food was getting to her, she had been though the menu so many times during her sixteen days in hospital, but then I guess there is only so much a chef can do cooking healthy food. Laura smiled to herself. The sixteen days she had been in care was a drama in her life that she would never forget, but life goes on. It had just turned two, and it was time to relax and read today's news or, better still, switch on the television to the 2:00 p.m. news. She pressed the remote.

"Welcome to CNN, bringing you the latest in world breaking news, with your host, Helen Frost.

"Good afternoon. My name is Helen Frost. But let's start with the latest news on the home front . . .

"The elusive fugitive, Michael Summers, wanted for questioning for the attempted murder of Laura Williams, the daughter of Senator Dave Williams, has been arrested in Buenos Aires, Argentina, and is now in custody, awaiting deportation from Sao Paulo, Brazil.

"Captain Ted Baker of the New York Homicide Department made this statement to the press at twelve noon today:

'A SPECIAL POLICE OPERATION INVOLVING TWO OF OUR MOST EXPERIENCED DETECTIVES AND WITH THE COOPERATION OF THE ARGENTINE POLICE, THE FUGITIVE MICHAEL SUMMERS WAS ARRESTED YESTERDAY AT 3:00 P.M. ARGENTINE TIME. HOWEVER, AS THE RESULT OF LOCAL POLICE COMPLICATIONS AND DEPORTATION IMMIGRATION LAWS, SUMMERS WAS CONSEQUENTLY FLOWN TO BRAZIL . . . MAY I STRESS THAT FOREIGN POLICE OPERATIONS REQUESTED BY THE UNITED STATES, EVEN WITH THE AGREEMENT OF LOCAL GOVERNMENTS, IS FRAUGHT WITH DANGER, AND IT GIVES ME THE DEEPEST REGRET TO INFORM YOU THAT ONE OF OUR BRAVE OFFICERS LOST HIS LIFE IN THE OPERATION. TO EXPAND ON THIS FURTHER, THE DEPARTMENT OF FOREIGN AFFAIRS WILL MAKE A STATEMENT TO THE PRESS IN DUE COURSE . . . OUR DEEPEST CONDOLENCES GOES TO THE OFFICER'S FAMILY.'

"WELL, THAT LEAVES US HANGING, DOESN'T IT! I'LL COME BACK TO YOU ON THAT STORY LATER IN THE PROGRAM AS SOON AS ANYTHING BREAKS.

"NOW LET'S TURN TO IRAQ AND PRESIDENT BUSH'S SO-CALLED SURGE . . ."

Laura couldn't believe her ears. *Mike arrested and in Brazil! It's just too much to comprehend . . . And that poor detective . . . I can't imagine what his family is going through, and all because of my stupid affair with someone else's husband. My god, what have I done?* She pressed the call button.

The duty nurse was there in seconds. When the buzzer sounds, you can never tell.

"Laura, is everything all right?"

Laura grabbed her notepad and pen; she looked paler than driven snow.

Nancy, I need a sedative. I just watched the news on CNN.

Nancy immediately got the picture; she had also watched the news during her break and was already on her way to Laura's room, fearing the worst, when the buzzer sounded.

"Laura, honey, now calm down. Let me take your pulse . . . *Hmmm,* it's racing like a clockwork orange. Now take a deep breath and count to five.

You're just upset. Stay calm. I'll be back in five minutes with a cup of sweet tea, but no sedatives! You hear me?"

Laura didn't answer, her mind still in a daze.

*　*　*

"There now, how do you feel?"

Laura was reluctantly sipping the sweet tea. Coffee would have been more to her liking.

I feel a lot better, Nancy, thanks.

"Then I'll leave you. But you just press that buzzer if you feel faint or giddy . . . *You hear me!*"

Laura silently acknowledged. If only she could speak in her hour of need, she would phone her best friend Terry.

*　*　*

"Have you flown overseas before?" Brown asked Lucas as they sat at the airport bar.

"Same again?"

"Yeah, another Bud . . . So?"

"So why the mystery?" Lucas gave a shrug.

"*The passports!*"

"Well, if you must know, I took a trip to Toronto. Not exactly overseas, but then Canadians are different."

"Wow . . . You're treading on dangerous ground, buddy, I hope there's no Canucks at the bar."

Lucas just laughed and took a sip of the fresh Bud.

"And you, Dan?"

"I took a trip to South Africa a couple of years back to try and track my ancestors."

"No shit! And how did it go?"

"What, with a name like Brown!" Dan laughed. It seems some Englishman got my great-grandmother pregnant, and whites and blacks didn't mix in those days with the apartheid, and like all English gentlemen, he ate the fruit and left the seeds."

"And?"

"My mother is third-generation African American, and don't ask me how my father got the name Brown. Hell, I was watching the BBC News on Fox, and the reporter's name is Trevor McDonald, and he's blacker than the ace of spades!"

Lucas couldn't stop laughing. "*Maaan,* this *is* a crazy world!"

"*This is the last and final call for all passengers on Delta Airlines 12 to Sao Paulo, Brazil. Please proceed to gate 15 for immediate boarding.*" "Drink up, Bert, that's us . . ."

* * *

June's mind was choking with all sorts of scenarios after hearing the news from Baker. *But Phil was right!* Mike was now under arrest, but that was only the beginning. There was the service of the divorce papers, then the joint agreement for the sale of the property . . . Her dreams of getting together with Phil, her law degree . . . It was what she wanted, but was it? Only too often, reasons turn into excuses, and when push comes to shove, the reality of it all kicks in with the consequential insecurity and doubt, and June was heading down that path. And to add fuel to the fire, there was the terrible tragedy of the death of Tony Perino, a neighbour and friend. *The media would have a field day, and what about Steven and Sheryl? They've gone through enough already . . .*

As Citibank's towering building came into view, June desperately tried to unravel her thoughts in order to face her next major challenge . . . *Simmons, the bank manager!*

* * *

"*Cab!*" June called, standing on the busy sidewalk, waving her arm outside the German automaker's central office and showroom. Her eyes were still moist after seeing her precious red BMW 3.1i being driven away.

The yellow cab pulled into the curb, and June quickly opened the rear door and leaped in. In New York, "he who hesitates is lost."

"Where to, lady?" The cab driver with the Brooklyn accent asked.

"Carlton Towers, Manhattan."

"Sure thing, lady . . ."

"Driver, how long do think it will take?" June asked, worried about the time, as it was almost noon.

"Your guess is as good as mine, honey. This is lunchtime, and the dogs are hungry." June could see him grinning in the rear mirror.

She was thinking that she could easily phone Phil to tell him she was on her way, but she didn't want to disturb him. He could be with a client, and she had already phoned once this morning already; his secretary, Ethel, may start putting two and two together.

Twelve thirty had come and gone, and finally the cab pulled over.

"That'll be fifteen straight."

June fished out a twenty. "Keep the change."

"For you, honey, anytime." The cab driver smiled. *Some broads are generous, some are . . . Well?* "Have a good one." He slipped into the busy traffic in his search for another fare.

Within minutes, June was in the elevator, pressing 20. She was looking forward to seeing Phil to tell him about her meeting with Simmons.

"Good afternoon, Beatrice. Can you inform Ethel that I have finally arrived? Mr. Stevens is expecting me."

"Certainly, Mrs. Summers . . . Ethel, I have . . ." Ethel arrived at the front desk within seconds.

"Good afternoon, June. Mr. Stevens is free and will see you now. Please go straight in."

June gently knocked on the heavy wood-panelled door.

"Come in."

Phil was standing at the door like a tiger stalking its prey, waiting to greet her and roughly pulling her toward him while pushing the door closed with his foot, their bodies crashing against the heavy panelling, his arms crushing her in a bear hug, squeezing the air from her lungs, his lips searching for the moistness of her mouth and the sweetness of her lips.

"Phil." June gasped for breath as she gently separated their bodies. "Phil, what's come over you . . . *And in the office!*"

"June, I can't get you out of my mind." He buried his mouth into her neck, his hands pressing her buttocks into his crotch, and she could feel his rock-hard erection.

"*Phil please!* There's a time and place, and it's not on your office desk!"

"I'm sorry, honey." He squeezed her closer, pulling her skirt up from behind, his hands now fondling the soft flesh of her cheeks, and June gave a feeble groan, the moistness in her loins sending messages.

"Please, Phil, please don . . ." She never finished. "*Oh . . . Ohhh . . .*" She moaned as she felt the thrust of Phil's large erection enter deep into her moist vagina. The feeling was ecstatic as he thrust time and time again, deeper and deeper. "Phil, darling, I love you . . . I love you . . ."

*   *   *

Blakely had grabbed a cup of coffee and a sandwich at Joe's Diner on his way to Brooklyn and Hewlett-Packard's corporate office on Atlantic Avenue. His stomach was satisfied with a greasy dog and black coffee; it wasn't the healthiest of lunches, but it hit the spot. Beazley had mentioned that he bring his CV, but there was no time, and he would have to use his selling skills to turn the tables. It had just turned one fifteen. It would be tight, but if he took the Brooklyn-Queens Expressway, he would bypass the city and, with luck, arrive on time.

The large blue sign at the slip off was a welcome relief, and Jack pressed the stock switch and hung a left off the expressway. He could now clearly see Carlton Towers and the large HP letters in the distance, only five minutes away.

"This is going to be a new experience." Blakely grinned, speaking to himself. "Being interviewed for a job with our major competitor, huh? *Maaan . . .* That's one for the books!" Blakely grinned again. He kinda liked the thought. As they say, "revenge is sweet." *"Hell,* I've been with ABM since I graduated from Cornell, but loyalty and dedication is not worth a dime in today's business world. But then again, there's two sides to every coin. *Oops!* I almost missed the turn!"

"Can I help you, sir?" The security guard at the entrance to the underground car park inquired, blocking Blakely's car.

"I have an appointment with Mr. Beazley at 2:00 p.m."

"Just a second, sir." He lifted the security phone and spoke a few words. "Level 2 for visitors, sir, floor 15 for Mr. Beazley."

Blakely nodded and gunned the Chevy and poured down the ramp.

He was surprised that security was light as he approached the front desk from the car park elevator.

"Please sign the visitor's book, sir, and state the name of the person you are visiting." The young blonde receptionist flashed her sexy smile.

"It's okay, I have a pen." Jack returned the compliment; he was never one to miss an opportunity.

"And you are seeing?" She turned the book toward her. "Mr. Beazley . . . Of course . . . I will phone his secretary to inform her that you are on your way . . . It's floor . . ."

"I know, honey . . . 15. Have a nice day." Jack was still grinning as he entered the elevator. "If I have to see her every day, I won't be complaining. Something tells me I'm gonna like the change . . ."

*   *   *

"Please come this way, Mr. Blakely . . . Mr. Beazley is expecting you. My name is Lilly. I'm Mr. Beazley's private secretary."

"Jack, you old dog, grab a seat. *You're* looking pretty fit."

"You're not doing so bad yourself, Alan."

"Coffee?"

"No, I'm good. Say, thanks for seeing me at such short notice."

"Jack, when I do something, there's always a motive. And that motive, as you well know, is I urgently need to fill the VP for marketing position."

"Alan, before we continue, I haven't put together my CV. It's not as if I keep one handy, like I'm always searching the job market."

Beazley laughed at Jack's comment. That was something to be said.

"No worries. Hell, you're an icon in the computer world."

Blakely grinned. "Thanks for the compliment, Alan, I didn't know I was so famous."

"Listen, Jack, off the record, your boss did us a big favor by taking that useless piece of shit, Morris, off our hands. We've been trying to find a way to fire him without suing us for unfair dismissal. Hewlett has a number of new products under test for release in the next month, and we need a good man to spearhead the launch. I hate to say it, Jack, but Simpson really screwed up the launch of your ABM2000, which I must say is a good product. But you missed the boat, and we're gonna pick up the slack. But enough of that, let's get down to business."

"Alan, whatever . . ."

* * *

"I've heard enough, Jack, and I feel pretty comfortable that you are the man for the job, and I want to pass you by our president." Beazley lifted the phone. "Lilly, can you check if Ron is free?"

* * *

"Well, you certainly made an impression with Hutchison, and it's all stations go . . . Grab a seat."

"Alan, I wouldn't refuse that coffee now."

Beazley grinned. "No sweat, I'll call Lilly. I could do with one myself. Now let's get down to the nitty-gritty."

* * *

"Your contract of employment will be in the post tomorrow. Now when can you join us?"

"I'll resign as soon as I get back to the office. My contract with ABM is three months termination notice by either party. But as soon as Hall learns I'm jumping ship, I'll be asked to clean up my desk and leave immediately. It could be as soon as Monday."

"That's great, welcome aboard." Beazley warmly shook Jack's hand.

"Alan, there's one more thing. I have an excellent marketing team, and it would be . . ."

* * *

There was a gentle knock on the door.

"*Christ, Phil*, that must be Ethel!"

"Mr. Stevens, I wondered if you would wish for some coffee?"

"Thank you, Ethel, for the kind thought. Can you also fetch one for Mrs. Summers?"

Phil quickly made himself respectable while June stepped out of her soiled panties and stuffed them into her handbag.

"Use this, honey." Phil quickly removed his pocket handkerchief and passed it to her to do the needful.

"Phil Stevens, I could murder you!" June pulled down her crumpled skirt, feverishly trying to decrease it. "And now I have to sit wearing no panties."

"June, honey, don't turn me on again . . . *Please!*"

There was another knock on the door.

"Can I come in, Mr. Stevens?"

June made a beeline for the chair in front of Phil's desk and tried to look composed while Phil almost leaped over his desk to his executive chair.

"I'm sorry to disturb you, Mr. Stevens."

"That's all right, Ethel, we had just finished, and the coffees will be most welcome."

Ethel placed the cups on Phil's desk and turned to leave.

"Ethel before you go, can you check when Mr. Jacobs is free?"

"Certainly, Mr. Stevens." The door closed with June's mighty sigh of relief.

"*Why you big heel,* we were almost caught with our pants down . . . And you and your '*We have just finished, Ethel.*'"

It was too much, and they both burst into laughter.

"And now me with no panties."

Phil was grinning all over. "Well, you know the solution . . ." "*And what might that be?*" June answered sarcastically.

"Bring a second pair next time."

"*Why you.*" June hit him smack in the face with the rolled-up soiled handkerchief.

"*Ouch!*"

"*Serves you right, taking advantage of me!*" The phone rang.

"Stevens . . . *Glen* . . . Listen, I have Mrs. Summers here, and she has just had some good news regarding her 'long-lost' spouse . . . Two o'clock, you're free . . . Yes . . . She is nodding . . . Thanks, Glen."

Phil turned to June and smiled. "It has just turned one so we have a bit of time to spare, and I was thinking . . ."

"*Oh no you don't!*"

"Honey, let me finish, although *that* had also crossed my mind." Phil laughed aloud. "No, the free time would be an ideal opportunity to introduce you to the staff . . ."

*   *   *

Terry had just finished her lunch and was walking back to the office from the cafeteria when Jaycee Davis stopped her.

"Terry, I'm sorry to bother you, but I wondered if you had watched the CNN two o'clock news?"

Terry shrugged. "No . . . Why, should I have?"

"Because Mike Summers has been arrested and is now in Brazil awaiting deportation to the States to face criminal charges."

"*Are you serious, Jaycee?*"

"I heard it with my own ears."

"*Well, I'll be* . . . Thanks, Jaycee, it's time I made a special phone call . . ."

*   *   *

Blakely breezed into the office. He looked cocky and full of it, *but then this was Jack!* He's like a prizefighter with a cut eye when the referee stops the fight. The word "defeat" was not in his vocabulary. "Terry," he called as he passed her desk. "*My office.*" Terry was still on the phone with Laura.

"I gotta hang up, honey, the 'Messiah' is calling. Now don't you dare try and speak. I'll see tonight around seven thirty."

"Rita, can you fetch two coffees from the machine?" Blakely placed a ten on Rita's desk. "Terry will be joining me." He had a grin on his face like Ronald McDonald.

"Your boss seems like he's just won the lottery." Terry commented to Rita as she knocked on Blakely's door.

"With Jack, you never can tell. How do you like your coffee, Terry?"

"Latte, no sugar."

Terry knocked on the glass door.

"Come in, Terry . . . Come in." Jack seemed to be in a jovial mood.

"*My*, you're in a good mood this afternoon. I would have thought this morning, being the bearer of bad news, that you might be taking the rest of the day off."

"*Terry . . . Terry*!" Blakely sighed. "You should know me by now! When have I ever run away in the face of adversity?" There was a knock on the door.

"Come in, Rita . . . Thanks . . . Just place the cups on my desk. Listen, Rita, come to think of it, grab a seat. You can have my coffee. I want you both to listen to this phone conversation."

Rita turned to Terry as she took her seat and gave a shrug. Jack didn't notice; he was busy dialling.

* * *

"Lola, Jack Blakeley. I need to speak to Bill, it's urgent."

"He's busy at the moment. He's in a meeting with Mr. Morris, and he doesn't want to be disturbed."

"*Tough shit, Lola*, excuse my French, but he better pick up that phone and listen to what I have to say, than get a shock when he reads the *Financial Review* tomorrow."

"If you put it that way . . ."

Jack turned to Terry and Rita and gave them gave a cheeky wink. Blakely was up to something, *but what?*

"So your plan is to . . ." The secretarial phone rang. "What is it now? Excuse me, Fred . . . Lola, *I told you that I don't want to be disturbed!*"

"I have Jack Blakely on the line. He's determined to speak with you, and he won't take no for an answer. I told him you were not to be disturbed, but he mentioned something about the *Financial Times*, and furthermore, he is being *downright rude.*"

Hall covered the mouthpiece and shook his head.

"*It's Blakely* . . . He's a pain in the butt . . ." He removed his hand and spoke into the receiver.

"I'm busy with your boss, Fred Morris, so don't waste my fucking time, Jack."

"I couldn't have gotten you at a better time, Bill, what with Morris there . . . It's like killing two birds with one stone."

"Jack, *I'm warning you* . . . If it it's about being bypassed over for the VP position, *get over it!* Now unless there is anything else?"

"There is, Bill, and I hope your listening. It gives the me greatest pleasure to inform you that you will receive my resignation letter on your desk first thing in the morning. I'm not good enough for ABM, but it seems that I'm certainly good enough for Hewlett-Packard, as their new VP for marketing. Now listen, Bill, and listen good! At my interview, according to Alan Beazley, whom I'm sure you know, you did HP a big favor by taking Morris off their hands. They have been trying to find a way to fire that freeloader for months. You blew it Bill . . . *big time!* And get this! I can recruit my own staff, and that means you're going to be left naked and *sayonara* to the new product launch. And Bill . . . At every opportunity, I'll kick ABM's ass . . . And pass my thanks to your new boy Morris, he did me a big favor. *Oh,* and, Bill, before I hang up . . . Once the shareholders are finished with you, should I need an office cleaner, I'll put in a good word."

"*Why you jumped up . . .*"

"Before you finish your foul-mouthed abuse, instruct the accounts department to have my entitlements ready in full tomorrow. I'll be out of the office by ten, and also prepare the chief accountant for at least another three resignations." The phone went dead.

Terry and Rita were speechless.

"Well, ladies." Blakely gave a big grin. "Are you going to join me?"

CHAPTER 11

"Darling, how do you think that went?"

June and Phil had returned to his office after making the announcement about the new staffer.

"It's hard to say. Employees in legal firms show little emotion. It's the kinda business we're in, but, honey, did *you* feel uncomfortable?"

"*Are you serious!* Standing there with no panties."

Phil had to laugh, but the thought was a real turn on.

"I must admit, honey, when you said your 'thank you' to the staff, my mind was on other things."

"I can just imagine, *you sex maniac!*"

Phil glanced at his watch. "It's just gone two, and Glen, if I know Glen, will be waiting patiently. Gimme a sec, and I'll give him a call."

"So will I see you tonight?"

"Wild horses couldn't keep me. Here's the keys to the office car. It's parked in basement 1. It's a pale-blue metallic Ford Fiesta, registration NY 67 . . . A bit of a letdown from the Beamer, but it's the best I could do honey."

"It's a lot better than taking the subway. Now I'll ask you again . . . What time tonight?"

"Say, seven thirty. I have a desk full." Phil gestured to the stack of folders. "I had best be going . . . But before I leave, here's a souvenir for you."

June opened her handbag and chucked Phil her soiled white panties, and he caught them like a professional catcher.

"Thanks, honey, I'll stack them with the rest." He had to stifle his laughter.

"*Phil Stevens!* Now I know you really are *a sex maniac!*"

* * *

Glen Jacobs was rather short at around five eight but had that look that made you immediately feel at ease. He had a roundish face with a fresh complexion and slightly greying swept-back hair. His pale-blue eyes complemented his blondish hair and that warm friendly smile. The immaculately tailored blue pinstriped suit had "lawyer" written all over it and with no sign of a wedding ring and most probably in his mid-thirties, he had that affluent look of the "well healed." A good catch for the right woman . . . That is, *provided he's not in the closet!*

* * *

"Take a seat, June. I've just heard the news on CNN. A bad situation regarding the deceased detective."

"Tell me about it . . . *He's my neighbour!*"

"*Wow!* That *is* tough. But then again, June, as far as your divorce is concerned, when Mike returns to New York, we can serve him personally with the subpoena."

"Yeah, *behind bars!* Glen, I'm sacred to think what's in front of me. If Mike pleads not guilty to attempted murder, there will inevitably be a trial and all the media hype." June was shaking her head at the thought.

"Yes, I don't envy you. But, June, I need you to sign these papers."

"I suppose I can kiss any alimony goodbye?"

"I'm afraid so, should Mike get a prison sentence if he's found guilty, and it's not looking good. But on the brighter side, you are entitled to half the sale of your house, being in joint names."

"It sounds good, but with a mortgage of 750,000, I'll be lucky if we can break even."

"I agree, but even though the net amount after legal fees and real estate commissions is say, fifty K, we can contra Mike's half for the alimony."

"I'll leave that in your good hands. Glen, is there anything else?" June had finished the signing.

"No, I'll give you a call once your husband is back in New York."

"Glen, in case you are worrying about your fees, to put your mind at ease, I have sufficient funds."

"*I'm not, June.* You're a dear friend of my boss, and that's good enough for me."

"Thanks, Glen, for everything . . . I'll wait for your call."

* * *

The small low-cost Ford was certainly a change, but then beggars can't be choosers.

"Phil is coming around tonight at seven thirty and considering I haven't had dinner with the kids for almost a week, they must be bored with pizzas. And to be honest, I'm getting fed up with restaurant food. I'll pop into the supermarket and pick up some groceries. Besides, it would be good for the children to get to know Phil better." June was talking aloud as she weaved through the late afternoon traffic. "Say, this car isn't so bad after all . . ."

* * *

The loud ring of the "school's out" bell echoed throughout the classroom, the students giving a sigh of relief. The works of William Shakespeare is not the most exciting subject.

"*Hold it . . . Hold it!* Before you run." Mr. McNaughton, the arts teacher, bawled. "For homework, I want you to compile a three-hundred-word essay giving your opinion of *Romeo and Juliet* and how it relates today to our modern society. Reference 'True love never runs smoothly.' On my desk by Friday! You can go now . . . *Remember, Friday!*"

Steven dejectedly shook his head as he picked up his books.

"I'll be glad when I graduate in a month's time. Boy, am I looking forward to Cornell and reading medicine?" Steven was talking aloud.

"You were saying, Summers?"

"*Eh . . . Err . . .* Nothing, sir, I was just talking aloud saying to myself how much I love Shakespeare."

"Then I'll be looking forward to read your essay." McNaughton gave a sarcastic grin. After twenty years in teaching, he had seen and heard it all.

"Hi, sis, how did it go?"

"The usual . . . *Boring.*"

"I know the feeling. Let's go catch the bus."

"Hey, Summers . . ."

"That rude bastard could only be Dennis Millar," Steven spoke to his sister.

"How does it feel to be the son of a 'woman beater'? Did you hear that they caught your old man in South America? It was on CNN's two o'clock news."

Steven went pale, and he turned to Sheryl, who shrugged embarrassedly.

"I heard it on the grapevine, but I couldn't catch you in the cafeteria."

"Don't worry, sis, it's not your fault, but Mother? She must have heard most likely from the police . . . *Shit!*"

"You had better watch out, Sheryl . . . You know what they say . . . Like father like son."

Dennis Millar was the local turd stirrer and self-proclaimed "hard man." He and his two cronies ruled the roost, so to speak, with a few of the other students willing to put their name on the line.

"Millar, why don't you climb up your own ass? That shouldn't be a problem. It's as big as your mouth."

Sheryl grabbed her brother's arm. "Steven, don't, it's not worth it."

"And who's gonna make me, *pussycat?*"

"Without your two strong-arm buddies, you're a yellow piece of shit."

Millar signalled to his henchmen. "Taylor . . . Wilson . . . Stay back, I'm gonna enjoy whopping Summers's ass."

"Bring it on, Millar baby." Steven pushed his sister aside.

Millar rushed at Steven like a bull in a China shop, throwing a clumsy fresh-air punch, and Steven nimbly stepped aside. Millar was now off balance, having spent his useless energy, and Steven grabbed the advantage, kicking him hard in the groin. Millar stood like a moment in time before clutching his family jewels, his face contorted in excruciating pain as he staggered forward. It was an opportunity too good to miss, and Steven took two steps forward, grabbing Millar by the neck of his shirt, using both hands to pull his semi limp body toward him. The crack of disintegrating cartilage from the bridge of Millar's nose made his two buddies cringe as Steven head butted him for the second time, with Millar's nose searching for a place to go and Dennis raising his hand, throwing in the towel.

"*No more. No more!*" He screamed as he crumpled in a heap sitting on the floor, blood spouting from his nostrils and mouth as he desperately clutched his disintegrated airway, coughing and choking in his own blood.

"You broke my fucking nose, you bastard."

A crowd of students had gathered to watch the "prize-fight," and it was time to leg it.

"Let's get out of here, sis, before the dean appears."

"I'm with you." Sheryl felt so proud. "Where did you learn to fight like that?"

"I didn't . . ."

* * *

June's cell phone rang as she was walking from Safeway's car park.

"*Steven!*"

"*Mother*, did you know that Father was arrested in South America?"

"Steven, calm down . . . Captain Baker informed me this morning when he was visiting our next-door neighbour's house."

"*Our next-door neighbour's house!*"

"Yes, you see Tony . . ."

* * *

Terry was still getting over the shock of Blakely's phone call and of course the job offer.

"I've gotta hand it to you, Jack, you don't let the grass grow. And *boy,* this is one for the books, I must say. *Hell,* I've only been in my new job a couple of weeks and now I'm been promoted again and, more to the point, recruited by Hewlett-Packard, the number 2 in the market. But I'm not gonna burn my bridges just yet until I see that salary package and prerequisites . . ."

"*Where the hell are you going?* You dickhead!"

Terry screamed from the open window at the driver who had just cut into her lane.

A man's hand emerged with the one-finger salute as the black Porsche accelerated and slipped off the Queensbury Exit.

Terry's adrenaline was off the scale, and she had to have the last say.

"*You fucking moron.*" She let loose again.

The young man laughed and gave Terry a friendly wave.

"See you tomorrow, honey . . . Maybe we can have dinner, I have your car number."

"*The gall of that guy . . .*" Terry had to laugh. "But then again, he's not bad looking." She had that glint in her eyes that spelled trouble.

* * *

It had taken her almost one hour to arrive at Roosevelt Memorial, and it was a welcome relief to finally park the car.

As Terry walked to the reception desk, she had to admit that she missed Frank's friendly smile.

"Hi, Martha, can I go straight up?"

"Sure . . . Say, where's that handsome boyfriend of yours?"

"I don't want to bore you."

"It's like that, is it?"

"Worse! See you later, Martha."

"Take it easy, honey . . . I wish I was your age. *Next . . .*"

Terry knocked on Laura's door, then breezed in to give her a surprise.

"*Teeh . . . Tah.*" Laura burst into laughter, her face beaming. She was so glad to see her friend.

"I hope you haven't had dinner yet because I'm starved." Laura grabbed her pen and paper.

No, I was hoping you would join me. It'll be served in a few minutes.

I so depressed using this writing stuff, but the doc says I can begin to say a few words in a couple days . . . But I have to take it easy.

"That's great news, honey, I'm so glad for you."

The door opened with a bang as the dinner cart bounced off the protective stainless-steel guard.

"Dinnertime." Nancy the IC nurse announced with a cheery smile. She really liked Laura.

"Terry, I'm sure you planned this. I think she's saving on her dinners, Laura."

Laura acknowledged with a big grin. She and Nancy had struck a real friendship.

"Sit up straight, honey, while I place your tray . . . There, that's done. I'll leave you guys to do your thing."

"She's really nice, Laura . . . So can you spare a beggar that chicken leg?"

Of course, I'm only too glad. Would you believe that I have gained five pounds?

Terry smiled. "That makes me feel a lot better. *Mmmm*, this *is* good. Ask Nancy if she can find me a spare bed, I'm moving in."

Laura laughed again. Terry was a hoot and always made you feel good even when the chips were down. But as Laura half-heartedly picked at her food, Terry could see the troubled look in her eyes.

"Laura, honey, I know what's bothering you. It was difficult to speak on the phone, and I just want to stress that I'm with you all the way."

Thanks, Terry. I knew I could depend on you. But I'm scared and if I know Mike, he will plead not guilty, and you know what that means. The media, the trial, all the gory details. Terry, I don't think I can take it. "Laura you have to get over it, and don't go on a guilt trip." *But a police officer lost his life.*

"I know, honey, but it's not your fault, so don't crucify yourself. You've got to be strong. Summers is in deep trouble with the law and he will go down and I hope it's for a long time. The bastard deserves it after what he did to you." Laura was still depressed, and Terry somehow had to change her mood.

"You'll never guess what happened today at the office. Remember I told you about Blakely being passed over? Well . . ."

*   *   *

The kids had arrived home before their mother and were sitting in the lounge, glued to the television, waiting for CNN's next news bulletin.

"That must be Mother now." Sheryl turned to her brother as she heard the front door close.

"*Steven . . . Sheryl,* I'm home." June went straight to the kitchen to unload the groceries. "I'm having dinner at home tonight. I hope you don't mind, but I asked Phil to join us."

Steven just shrugged. He was engrossed watching the box.

June had decided to cook lamb shank, and it would take at least three hours to roast in the oven, so she didn't have much time.

"Mother, aren't you coming through?" Steven was agitated. "We've so much to discuss."

"Give me another twenty minutes, darling."

"Rome's burning, and all Mother can think about is dinner with Phil." Steven was pissed off.

"Come on, Steven, give her a break. After what she's been through, *do you blame her?*"

Steven seemed to mellow at his sister's remark. "Yeah, I guess you're right, sis . . ."

*   *   *

The CNN news had come and gone, and the kids were none the wiser. Foreign affairs had yet to clarify what led to the death of Lieutenant Perrino, citing diplomacy as being essential for U.S.-Argentina relations.

"*What the hell does that mean?* They tell you all and tell you nothing, not even when they expect Father to return to the States and why is he now under arrest in Brazil instead of Argentina?'

"Steven, let it go." Sheryl was getting fed up with it all, and besides, she was feeling hungry.

"Hi, kids." June was still wearing her apron and looked dishevelled. She too had had a stressful day, of course with one exception . . . which reminded her.

"Kids, I'll be with you in a sec. There's something that I must do." June chucked the apron onto the lounge chair and almost sprinted up the stairs.

She was a woman on a mission. Once in her bedroom, she wasted no time and went straight the shower, kicking off her clothes on the way. Within minutes, she was under the warm spray, washing what comes naturally. She towelled and went to the walk-in to select her gray tracksuit; she would dress casual tonight for dinner. But first things first. June opened her lingerie drawer and slipped into a pair of white lace panties.

"Now I feel much better . . . That Phil!"

*   *   *

"Mother, have you been contacted by the police again?"

"No, Steven, I'm as wise as you. But I think all hell will break loose tomorrow once the paparazzi get our address. Come to think of it, it might be wise that you both skip school tomorrow and stay at home."

"I don't think that's a good idea, Mother," Steven precariously replied.

"You see, Mother, what Steven is failing to tell you . . ."

"Sis!" Steven cut her short. He knew where she was coming from with her usual big mouth.

"And what, may I ask, is Steven failing to tell me?" June had risen to her feet on her way to the kitchen. She had that look that only a mother can give, standing defiantly with both hands on her hips. *"Well?"*

"He had, shall I say," Sheryl nervously began. "An altercation with Dennis Millar and his henchmen, who were mocking him about Father and saying really rude things about me. I don't know where my brother learned the art of self-defence, but he really kicked Millar's ass, and he'll be calling Michael Jackson's surgeon for a nose job. *Mom,* I was so proud of him." *"Is what your sister saying true?"* June barked.

Steven gave a dejected nod.

June was furious. "This is all I need. No doubt the dean will most likely penalize you and just before your final exams. Worse, still this kid's parents may call the police and charge you with assault causing bodily harm. *Christ,* Steven, what were you thinking? His parents can even sue for medical expenses through a civil action." June took a deep breath. "I need a drink."

"Mother, it was self-defence. I saw it with my own eyes. It was either Steven ending up in hospital or breaking Millar's nose."

"Don't tell me anymore. I'm going to the kitchen and a glass of chardonnay and *boy do I need it!* No college tomorrow, *that's for sure!*"

Steven looked really depressed, staring aimlessly into space, his chin resting on his hand.

Sheryl felt a real heel for dropping her brother down the toilet, but if it didn't come out now, it would be worse later, and she placed her arm around Steven's shoulders to console him.

"I'm sorry, bro, it's my big mouth again."

"It's not your fault, sis, maybe *I am* like Father . . ."

* * *

"Sheryl, help me to set the table, Phil will be here any minute. Now don't look at me that way, I have to prepare the food."

No sooner had June made that comment than the doorbell rang.

"God, that must be Phil. He would have to be early, tonight of all nights . . . Steven, go answer the door."

"Mom, it's Rose, our next-door neighbour . . ."

* * *

Terry glanced at her watch.

"Listen, it's after ten, and I think it's about time I hit the road. You gotta get your beauty sleep if you want discharged next week. I have your room all ready for you."

I'm liking forward to that. My mother is still giving me a hard time, but I'm determined to manage my own life. If I agree to go back home, I'll be locked in a prison for the rest of my life. Are you sure you can't stay a little longer?

"As much as I would like to, I've had a very trying day, and I dread to think about tomorrow."

The door suddenly opened.

"Laura, it's that time again." Nancy was wheeling the blood pressure cart.

"It's all right, Nancy, I was just about to leave."

"*Listen*, this won't take long . . . You can stay if you want."

"No, I'm on my way . . . Bye, honey." Terry gave Laura a peck on the cheek. "I'll visit you again tomorrow around the same time . . . *Ciao.*"

* * *

Terry felt exhausted as she turned the key to her apartment. It was chillout time, a hot shower, tracksuit, and feet up on the sofa with her favourite sauvignon blanc.

The shower was heaven, and Terry felt fresh and relaxed as she slipped into her grey woollen pants and top.

"Boy, is it good to kick off that bra," she spoke to herself as she barefooted it to the fridge. "Now the glass." She stood on her toes to get the wineglass from the kitchen cabinet. "Who put these glasses on the top shelf, may I ask? It must have been Frank."

When Terry mentioned Frank's name, it brought back memories of what could have been.

"Oh well." She sighed. "Memories."

Terry poured herself a generous measure of the lemon liquid, then carted the wine bottle and glass to the coffee table.

"I don't want to watch the box tonight, the stuff you see on TV is depressing." She walked to the CD stack and selected a disc. "Something nostalgic . . . *Hmmm* . . . Ann Murray, 'See the Pyramids along the Nile' . . . *Nice!*"

The music was dreamy, and the wine was just what the doctor ordered, but it was not to be as her cell phone agitatedly continued to buzz.

"*What now!* Can't a gal get some peace? If it's Frank, so help me, I'll go berserk."

Terry looked at the number. Now who could this be at this time of night? "Terry Johnson speaking."

"You must have been on a date, coming back so late, I've been trying to call you for ages."

"For your information . . . *No!* But then, *mister*, whom might I be talking to?"

"I'm the poor guy you scolded on the freeway today. *Don't say you've forgotten me already!* Remember the black Porsche? I asked you out to dinner, but you never replied, so I'm giving you a second chance to meet a handsome young man who would just love to meet you . . . That is, if you are not already spoken for."

Terry burst into laughter. "Whatever your name is, you have some gall, mister . . . But how did you get my phone number?"

"Friends in the vehicle registration office, but don't tell anyone." Terry could hear his laughter. "My name is Brent Kennedy . . . No relation . . . And when I heard your sexy voice over the phone, I'm already madly in love with you."

Terry had to smile. This guy is a breath of fresh air and downright cheeky with it.

"I tell you what, Brent, why don't you let me sleep on it and give me a ring tomorrow at my office . . . Who knows, you might get lucky. The number is . . . 261-91 . . . Good night, lover boy . . ."

Terry took another sip of her wine, that dreamy look in her eyes spelled trouble.

"*Hmmmm* . . . Interesting . . ." Terry reached for the wine bottle.

*   *   *

Rose looked like death, her eyes puffed and bloodshot.

"I just came over to tell you and the kids not to blame yourselves over Tony's death and that I bear no malice or grudges." June put her arms around Rose and hugged her.

"Rose, I can't stress how sorry I am for your loss. My problems are insignificant compared to yours. If it's not too sensitive and rude, can I ask you when the funeral will be, as the kids and I wish to pay our respects? But we don't want to give you and your parents any problems. Bigoted people can be so cruel."

"Don't worry about that, June, but I still don't know. From what Captain Baker indicates, it will most likely be in two or three days' time."

The black Caddy parked in the driveway diverted their attention. It was Phil, and he couldn't have arrived at a more awkward time.

"I'm sorry, June, I didn't know you are expecting a guest."

"That's not a problem . . . Phil, let me introduce you to my next-door neighbour, Rose Perino."

"Mrs. Perino, what can I say? June has informed me about your loss. I heard it on the news, but no names were mentioned. Please take my card. Should you ever need any legal services and or advice, don't hesitate to give me a call."

"Thank you . . . Mr. Stevens, that's so kind."

"Listen, Rose, we are about to have dinner and I would love for you to join us."

"Thank you, June, for your kind offer, but I would be bad company. Besides, Tony's parents and my mother are here to help me with the kids . . . Nice meeting you, Mr. Stevens. June, I'll call you when I have more news . . . Good night."

"Thanks, Rose. Remember, if you need anything . . ."

* * *

"Phil, I have decided to eat at home tonight, as it will be a good opportunity to become more acquainted the kids and, of course, my cooking." June smiled.

Phil gave her a kiss on the lips, out of sight from the kids.

"I like you in that tracksuit, honey, it makes you look sexy, and am I looking forward to some home cooking! For the love of me, I couldn't take any more restaurant food."

"*Touché!* Well, don't just stand there! Come in, and I'll fetch you a predinner drink."

"Hi, Steven, Sheryl . . . Can I join you?"

"Of course, Phil," Steven replied, rising from the sofa.

"It's all right, Steven, I'll grab one of the lounge chairs. So how did school go today?" Phil asked, breaking the awkwardness.

"I'll be happy when my final exams are over and begin my scholarship at Cornell." Steven replied. "Would you believe it! I have a three=hundred-word essay on William Shakespeare's *Romeo and Juliet* to complete by Thursday."
"That should be a challenge." Phil smiled.

"And what are you guys discussing?" June had just checked the oven and was now the barman.

"Steven was just talking about school today."

June turned to Sheryl and gave her that look.

"Steven was discussing *Romeo and Juliet*, Mother."

"*I'm sure that was interesting!* Phil, would you like something to drink before dinner?"

"Some red wine?"

"Of course. Any preference?"

"Not really."

"Then I'll be back in a minute to join you."

* * *

"June, this lamb shank is delicious. The meat just falls off the bone. What do you think, Steven?"

"It's really good, Mother . . . *Phil . . .*"

"Yes, Steven?"

"If you don't mind me asking, being a lawyer, what will happen to my father now?"

"*Steven*, this is not the time nor place for that kind of discussion. Let's enjoy our dinner." June was really annoyed.

"It's all right. It's only natural that Steven is inquisitive."

"Phil, would you wish some more lamb?" June was intentionally creating a diversion.

"No, I'm good."

"Then can I offer you more wine?"

"Just a little, honey . . . *Eh, err, June* . . . Remember, I'm driving." Phil smiled. He had put his big foot in it.

"Then I'll serve the desert." June had to smile. It was an innocent slip of the tongue, and Sheryl looked at her mother and grinned.

"Going back to your question, Steven. When your father returns to New York, he will be read his rights and formally charged and held in custody pending his plea. Should he plead not guilty, then the district attorney will request trial by jury."

"I see." Steven looked pretty down. "And how long will the trial take?"

"Let me put it this way. There's a lot of big names involved. Laura Williams is the daughter of Senator Dave Williams and the niece of the Jake Murray, the district attorney. Of course, the jury has to be selected and so on, but with the media hype, events will move pretty fast . . . June, you are exceeding yourself tonight. This Creme Brulee is absolutely delicious." "I'm glad you like it . . ."

* * *

"How do you think I went with the kids tonight?" Phil had retired to the lounge after dinner to enjoy June's company, the kids having gone to their rooms.

June was stretched out on the sofa, making herself comfortable with her legs up and her head resting on Phil's lap.

"I think the kids are really impressed, especially Steven. But I feel so sorry for him, Phil, because he and his father were so close, and now he looks to you as a father figure."

"Honey, I never thought of it that way." Phil leaned over and gave her a kiss on the forehead. "I do miss you, honey!"

June pressed his hand. "Me too . . . *Now, mister*, it's nearly twelve, and no funny business with the kids upstairs."

"I'm disappointed." Phil laughed. "But you're right, honey, it's time I get on my way."

June swung her feet to the floor. "Come, I'll see you to the door."

Phil stood on the porch, looking into June's blue eyes. His kiss was long and invigorating, the intimate moistness of their lips passing between their bodies as they locked together in a passionate embrace.

"*God*, I love you honey . . ."

BLUEPRINT PRESS

PART 7

The Argentine Identity

CHAPTER 1

"Bert, I'm beginning to like this flying business class. It's really something."

"Yeah, I wonder what the peasants are doing in steerage, huh?" Dan laughed as he adjusted the oversize seat.

"*Man*, this is luxury. It's just a pity that it wasn't for a better cause. I still can't believe that Perino is gone. He was a real pain in the butt, but Homicide will never be the same without that crazy bastard."

"Can I fetch you gentlemen a refreshment before take-off?"

Lucas turned to Brown. "This is getting better all the time."

"Eh, err . . . Marcy." Dan was checking out her name tag. "Eh . . . I'll have a scotch on the rocks. Would you happen to have a Johnny blue?"

"Most certainly, Mr. Brown. And for you, Mr. Lucas?"

"I'll stick to beer. Do you have Brazilian beer? I might as well get acclimatized." Bert laughed. He had a bad habit of laughing at his own jokes.

"We sure do." Marcy smiled. "Cervejas Brazileiras. It's the most popular beer with the locals. It's a lager type with a high alcohol content."

"That's for me." Lucas turned to Dan. "*You can keep your scotch!*"

"I'll be back in a few minutes with your orders."

"*Hmmm*, nice-looking broad."

"Keep your mind on your beer, Bert . . . What was the name of that beer again?"

"Are you serious?"

* * *

The food was excellent, and the alcohol was even better and the detectives were enjoying the new experience at the taxpayers' expense.

"Now let's go through this again, Bert."

"Can I clear your tray, gentlemen?" Marcy interrupted.

"Yes, thanks, Marcy."

"Another drink perhaps?" She smiled, anticipating the answer.

"Bert?"

"Last one, huh?"

"Yeah, make that the same again. Now where was I?"

"The embassy staff will meet us at the airport. They will fast track us through customs and immigration. Then it's straight to the American embassy. We stay over one night, then catch the same return flight to Kennedy the next day, of course with Summers."

"I hope this broad is on the return flight."

"*Get out of it, Lucas!* Can't you be serious for a change?"

"Talking about serious . . . I feel naked without my nine mill."

"Yeah, that worries me as well, Bert. You just never know."

"I guess after the Perino and Hayden catastrophe, Baker must be scared shitless to risk another international incident."

"Cheers, Bert, I'm getting my head down after this, *and this is definitely the last round!*"

There was no answer. Bert was counting sheep.

*   *   *

The nine-hour flight to Sao Paulo, Brazil, was well into its eighth hour, and breakfast was about to be served.

"Excuse me, Mr. Brown, I'm sorry to disturb you. I wondered if you studied the breakfast menu. There are three choices. Omelette . . ."

"I'll take a rain check, Marcy, but just a sec." Dan nudged Lucas. "Bert, wake up, would you like some breakfast?"

"No chance. The way I'm feeling, I need the hair of the dog."

"Then can I entice you to a cup of hot coffee?" Marcy smiled, looking at "the morning after." Alcohol and flying don't mix, but guys . . . Well, they never learn.

"That's a good idea, the caffeine will wake me up."

"Make that for two." Bert was back in the real world.

*   *   *

"This is Captain Muller speaking. Please fasten your safety belts, as we are about to make our descent. The local time is 9:30 p.m., and the ground temperature is a pleasant twenty-three degrees Centigrade.

"We will be arriving on time at 9:40 p.m. local time at Guarulhos International Airport . . .

"The airport is approximately sixteen kilometre's from downtown Sao Paulo, and a taxi will cost approximately twenty U.S. dollars. The Brazilian currency is the real, and one real is fifty cents U.S.

"For those passengers who are visiting Brazil for the first time, Portuguese is the spoken language, but English is widely used . . .

"I hope you have had an enjoyable flight, and from myself and on behalf of the crew, thank you for flying Delta . . ."

* * *

The big bird shuddered as its main undercarriage touched the runway, its sixteen tires puffed smoke, making a screeching sound with the smell of burning rubber. The four Pratt & Whitney's roared into reverse thrust to assist the ABS braking system. The nose gear finally touched the runway with the brakes snatching momentarily, and the plane shuddered, throwing the passengers forward before finally reaching its taxiing speed.

* * *

"Please keep your safety belts fastened until Delta 12 has finally docked for deplaning . . ."

* * *

"That was a bit scary. Thank God we're back on terra firma." Lucas didn't look too happy. Maybe it was the hangover effect from the Cervejas Brazileiras local hooch.

"Do you know what your problem is, Bert?" Dan was shaking his head. "You watch that *Air Crash Investigation* shit on Fox."

"You're full of it, Lucas . . . Let's get our asses out of here. I want to feel Mother Earth."

"I hope you have had an enjoyable flight, gentlemen. Have a pleasant stay in Brazil."

"Thanks, Marcy . . .," Lucas replied with the "banana smile." "Eh, Marcy, as a matter of interest, will you by chance be on . . ."

Dan grabbed Lucas by the arm. "*Come on, man!* Give it a miss. We've more important priorities on our plate than hittin' on the air hostess . . ."

* * *

The guys were traveling light with only carry-on baggage, so there was no need for the long wait at the baggage carousels, and they went straight to immigration and passport clearance.

The young female Latino officer in that dark blue uniform that didn't do her any favours looked as if she loved everything except her job as she rudely pointed to the four-inch yellow line painted on the floor about a meter from the immigration counter.

"Stand on that yellow line until I call you," she barked.

"She's a good-looking chick, but she has an attitude problem. I wouldn't like to be her old man when she arrives home tonight."

"*Bert*. Keep your fucking voice down . . . *Well, go on, she's calling you!*"

She stared Lucas straight in the eyes, comparing the picture on his passport before finally stamping it with what looked like a piece of tread from a car tire glued to a clumsy wooden handle.

"Stay." She pointed from behind the counter.

"My passport?"

"Later . . . Next."

As Bert stood patiently waiting for his partner, he couldn't help but notice the two well-built guys dressed in dark-blue business suits, standing about five meters behind the immigration counter. Their eyes were glued on the detectives.

"My guess is that they are from the embassy." Bert tried to convince himself, but being a cop, something just didn't jive.

"So why are we standing here, and what's happening to our passports? I don't like it, Bert." Dan was getting nervy.

The two heavies made their move.

"Sergeants Brown and Lucas?" The slightly taller of the two asked with a heavy accent.

"Yeah, you got that right. Listen, what's happening to our passports?"

"Don't worry, you'll get them when the time is right. We don't have much time. Our car is parked out of sight for security reasons, so please accompany us without delay."

"Just a second, big boy, let's see some ID." Dan met the guy head-on.

"This is my ID." He opened his jacket, revealing his leather shoulder holster complete with a Glock 9 mm semiautomatic. "Do you get the picture?"

"That's what you think, buddy." Lucas made his move but was stopped in his tracks as the snub nose of the Glock dug into his spine. The other dude was taking no shit.

"Now listen, Made in America. I don't give a shit whether you walk or get carried to the car. My orders are to bring you in. *Comprender?*"

"Spanish, huh?"

"You're too smart for your own health, detective. If you know what's good for you, my advice is don't try anything you'll live to regret because I won't hesitate to blow your fucking brains out. That is you have any . . . *Now move it!*" The big guy turned and nodded to the female immigration officer.

With two guns trained on their backs, the detectives knew they meant business, and who wants to join Tony in the freezer hold?

The black stretched limo with the dark tinted windows was parked in the staff car park. Whatever is going on, there's a lot of people on the payroll.

The big guy with the olive complexion and the black, tightly swept-back Mafiosi hair style, complete with the signature ponytail, waved the Glock menacingly.

"You heard me, *move it.*" He gave Bert a push with the muzzle, and Lucas cringed with pain as the steel dug into his back.

Dan grabbed him by the arm. "Don't even think about it . . . Our turn will come . . ."

*   *   *

The two men in black sat opposite the detectives, their handguns now openly displayed.

"Place these hoods over your heads . . . *I said do it!* My patience is running thin."

Dan had synchronized the time on his watch when the pilot communicated the local time to the passengers. He would check the time again when he arrived at wherever they were being taken. Was this a kidnapping or something more sinister?

*   *   *

Broaden had reluctantly agreed to Bill's request to accompany the FBI agents to the airport.

"I don't need this stupid sling." Bill chucked it aside on the car seat. "I feel like a volunteer in a Boy Scout's first aid demonstration. "How long to the airport, guys?"

"Around fifteen to twenty, depending on the traffic," the younger of the two agents answered.

As for the driver? He just kept his eyes on the road, like "hear no evil, speak no evil."

He's probably local, Bill thought, half smiling. *I guess he would have to be to drive in this crazy traffic.*

*   *   *

The Ayrton Senna Highway was the brainchild of Presidente Dutra and connects the city direct to the airport, and before long, they were snailing through the usual congestion at arrivals.

*   *   *

As Bill stared silently stared through the rear window, narrowing his eyes from the glare of headlights and bright red stoplights in never-ending streams as the traffic snaked down the highway. His thoughts drifted back to when he and Tony first touched down in Buenos Aires. Within four days, their worlds were completely shattered, and life would never be the same again. An exciting adventure turned into a horror story, and a young family lost their loving father. How this drama is going is going to pan out, who knows. Bill shook his head his mind congested, confused and bewildered. As for Judy? *I just can't believe her cold and callous attitude. All she thinks about is money and status. Imagine, she hardly asked how I was and was more interested in my possible promotion to lieutenant to fill Tony's shoes. I can still hear her words ring in my eras . . . "Bill, if you get promoted to lieutenant, what will the salary be? I'm sick and tired of living in this box you call a house mortgaged up to our eyeballs. And I want the kids to go to a better school like all my friends." I wonder if she has even phoned Rose, Tony's wife? They say you never know a person until you live with them, and how true that is. Now take Mona, for instance . . .*

"Are you with us? We have just arrived at the arrival terminal."

"Eh, err, sorry. I missed that."

"I said, *we have just arrived at the arrival terminal!*"

"Apologize, I was lost there for a moment."

The agent didn't reply; he was concentrating on the driver finding a parking place.

"Anton, try and find a decent parking place as close to the arrival hall as possible. Remember, there are no parking restrictions for embassy plates . . . *Comprender?*"

"Sim." The driver nodded.

"You speak Portuguese?" Bill asked the younger guy.

"Some . . . Say . . . My name is Chet, and my partner is Nick . . . And you?"

"Bill . . . Bill Hayden . . ." Bill tapped the face of his watch; he was back to his old self. "Chet, we had better get going. It's just after nine thirty."

*   *   *

"Boy, *is this* an experience! I thought the airport in Buenos Aires was a battleground, but this one gets the prize. These kids holding the taxi placards must only be about twelve years old."

"Don't worry, they're not the drivers." Chet laughed. "They get a few cents commission if they nail a fare. *It's a tough life here, Bill,*" Chet commented as he pushed his way through the crowd blocking the arrival exit.

"What do you think, Nick?" Chet asked his partner. He was worried about the time, the last thing he wanted was to miss the detectives.

"The guys, I assume, are traveling light, so I estimate fifteen minutes to clear immigration and customs."

"Yeah, I'm with you. They should be coming out just about now. There's the Delta crew." Chet pointed. "Give them another few minutes."

Thirty minutes had passed, and with no sign of Brown and Lucas, Bill was becoming seriously concerned.

"I wonder what's keeping them, Chet? This is taking far too long."

"You can never tell, but it's concerning, I must admit. Just a sec. I'll approach this passenger . . . *Descuple-me voce* speak *ingles*?"

"Yes, I speak English." The grey-haired elderly gentleman smiled. "How can I help you?"

"Were you a passenger on Delta flight 12 from new York?"

"Yes, and I think I'm about the last passenger to clear customs. At my age, I'm in no hurry." He smiled again.

"By chance, did you happen to notice two black American men on the flight?"

"As matter of fact, I did. They were seated in the business class cabin and, of course, received priority clearance when we landed. Strange . . ." He frowned. "As I was waiting in line, I saw them leave with two gentlemen in business suits."

"Are you sure?"

"I may be old, son, but I'm not at the dementia stage just yet!"

"I'm sorry, sir, I wasn't trying to be rude . . . It's just that . . . Listen, thanks anyhow, you've been a great help."

"I hope you find them . . ." The elderly gentleman smiled before going on his way.

Bill was now totally confused. *What the hell was going on?* How could they possibly miss Brown and Lucas . . . *I mean those two dudes stand out like sore thumbs.*

"So, what's the take, Chet?" Bill shrugged his shoulders.

"I know it's no consolation, Bill, but I'm afraid your guess is as good as mine. Nick." Chet turned to his wingman. "We have no authority to check immigration, but we *can* check with the airline."

*   *   *

"And you're absolutely sure they were definitely on that flight?"

"*Absolutely!*" the chief purser replied. "Just a sec, there's Marcy. She was attending the passengers in the business class cabin . . ."

"Yes, I remember the two black Americans well. A Mr. Brown and a Mr. Lucas. They were a jovial pair and well-mannered with it. They were traveling light, with only carry-on bags. They collected their stuff from the overhead bins and left. From what I gather from their comments, they were catching our return flight to New York tomorrow. I hope that helps." She eyed the handsome young agent.

"Thanks, Marcy, sorry to keep you. You must be bushed after that long flight."

"Glad to be of help . . . Bye, guys." She gave her "fly the friendly skies" smile. "I hope I see you on Delta one day . . ."

Nick opened his cell phone. "Stan, it's Nick Stanford here. I'm sorry to disturb you, but we have a situation . . ."

Broaden listened in silence; this was something new. Two U.S. citizens disappearing into thin air and cops into the bargain. *What the hell is going on!*

"There's not much more you can do, Nick. Tell Chet I'm calling off the wait and to return to the embassy. I'll meet you there within the hour . . ." Broaden hung up, still pondering on what to do next.

*   *   *

The drive seemed forever, the unknown inducing nervous silence as the limousine finally reached its destination, coming to a sudden stop, its brakes squealing.

As Dan listened intently, he could distinctly hear one of the captors issuing orders in Spanish, *which was strange*, as in Brazil, the spoken word is Portuguese. With the never-ending illegal immigrants from "south of the border," Dan could certainly recognize Spanish when he heard it.

(Speaking in Spanish)

"*Berto,* open the gates, and Arran go inform the boss we have arrived with the goods."

"Si, Alano."

Although Dan didn't understand a word of Spanish, the one noise he did recognize was the squealing sound of poorly maintained gate hinges. It was either a large well-guarded estate house of some important person or a hacienda, which would be unusual in the city. Dan could see the time on his watch through the gap at the bottom of the sack hood, and from the time he left the airport until now, it had taken over twenty-five minutes. Which means that they had to be somewhere downtown.

"Hands!" Alana barked. "*I said hands out, wrists together.* I'm taking no chances with two smart-assed cops." He put the zip tie on Dan and wrenched it tight. "*That means you as well, big boy.*" He kicked Lucas hard in the shin as an incentive.

"You bastard." Lucas cringed in pain. "I've have a long memory, Alana, and your name is number 1 on my shit parade."

"So now you know my name, *huh!* That's a shortcut to the city morgue . . . What's *your* name again? It's hard to distinguish between you and your buddy here, as you are both the same colour and both . Of course! You in the Mr. Ugly competition and in my books, it looks like a draw.

are Lucas!" Alana was studying Bert's passport. And you are?" He turned to Dan, checking the "blue book" again. "*Brown!*" Alano burst into laughter. "*Man,* that says it all. Your father didn't do you any favours, dude . . . *Now listen.*" Alano was serious again. "Fortunately, my boss wants you both alive and kicking, but that doesn't mean I won't do the 'rubber hose job' if you step outta line. Like you fell over or something. Now there's the easy way and the hard way. Remember, there's lots of dead heroes, and there's plenty room for two more. *Now get your asses out of this fucking car.*"

"Brown, grab your buddy's belt from the back of his waist . . . Carilla, guide them downstairs to the empty storeroom."

Dan was taking note of every word, down to even counting the steps.

"Watch these steps, Carilla, I don't want them falling on their face and breaking bones. *They are a big enough liability as it is!*"

"Place your foot out, and step down one at a time," Carilla ordered.

Dan took note once again. They had now gone down two flights of stairs to most probably the basement.

"Okay, in." Alano gave Bert a mighty push, and he staggered like a blind man, his arms outstretched, almost losing his balance.

"Carilla, you can cut their wrist ties and remove the hoods."

The detectives covered their eyes at the sudden bright light from the florescent tubes, then stood for a moment to collect their bearings before quickly weighing up their new prison. The room had no windows, for a start, but strangely enough there was a door leading to a toilet and washbasin.

Most likely for the cleaners, Dan thought, recollecting Alano's comment about the storeroom.

*   *   *

The room was approximately eight by eight feet, with flaking, faded white walls and a nauseating musty smell, most likely as the result of the dampness and humidity associated with the Brazilian climate. On the floor lay two mouldy, stained blue-and-white-striped mattresses that had certainly seen their day. Then there were the ragged towels hanging over the bathroom door, the "Bangkok Hilton" a close second. Whatever, this would be home until "someone up their likes us."

*   *   *

"Make yourself comfortable, guys, it's not exactly five star, but it's the best we could do at such short notice." Alano sniggered. He was getting off at the thought. "If you want water, you can drink from the tap in the toilet. I wouldn't, but I guess you African boys are used to it . . . . Oh, and one other thing . . . Dario here will make sure you don't get into any stupid heroics."

Dario was around six one, muscle bound and dressed in a blue military uniform two sizes too small. But the Kalashnikov with its thirty-round magazine strung over his shoulder meant business. He gave an ugly smile, then left the room to stand guard in the corridor.

"Enjoy your stay, guys. *Adios.*"

The door slammed shut with the loud click of the double lock, and suddenly the detectives were on their own. But then, knowing Brown and Lucas, they weren't about to take this lying down.

Chapter 2

Broaden had already arrived at the consulate and was nervously pacing the floor of his office when security rang.

"Broaden here. Yes, they have security clearance. Escort them up to my office immediately."

A few minutes passed before there was a loud knock on the door.

"Come in."

The FBI agents and Hayden entered, their expressions reflecting their embarrassment at screwing up a simple security pickup. *I mean how could this happen?*

"Take a load off." Broaden took his seat at his desk, the depressed look on his face saying it all.

"Now perhaps if it's not too much trouble, can you just explain to me why this giant fuckup happened?"

"There's nothing to explain, Stan." Nick was first past the post. "We arrived on time and . . ."

"*Hmmm* . . . And you say, according to an eyewitness, that Brown and Lucas were escorted from immigration to the staff car park by two unknown men dressed in dark business suits." Broaden rubbed his chin, then sighed again, shaking his head. "I don't know what to make of it. First of all, let's look at who would know that Brown and Lucas were arriving on Delta 12 this evening. *My secretary. You guys.*" Broaden shrugged. "It has to be someone in the embassy. *But why*, and what's their motive?"

"Stan, we are as much in the dark as you," Bill answered. "But let's look at some scenarios . . . Kidnapping for ransom? Two New York cops? *Are we serious?* No, it just doesn't jive. There has to be some other . . ."

Broadens private line burst into life, interrupting Bill's detective work.

"*Now who the hell can this be?*" Broaden thundered. "This number is unlisted." Then something crossed his mind, and he grabbed the phone.

Could it be?

"*Who is this?*" Broaden yelled into the receiver.

"Never mind who it is, *just fucking listen.*" The male voice had a distinct Spanish accent. "We have your two boys here unharmed, but if want to see them again in the same condition, you do as I say, and do it within the next forty-eight, or I'll post their bodies back to the embassy one piece at a time . . ."

"*Who the hell do you thi—*"

"*Fuckhead.* Don't interrupt. *Now listen carefully* . . . You immediately extradite Perino and Hayden on the first flight back to Buenos Aires to stand trial for the murder of two Argentine citizens. Whenever you confirm their flight details, my men will be at the airport to meet them and escort the detectives to Argentina. My advice to you, Broaden . . . Don't be a smart-ass and do anything foolish like calling the cops. *Remember, forty-eight . . .*" "Just a second, *whoever you are!* How do I know I can trust you? "*You don't.*"

"Then what proof do I have that Brown and Lucas are alive?" The phone went dead.

*   *   *

Dan flopped down on the wafer-thin mattress, his back resting against the wall while Lucas was busily examining the lock. He always carried a lock pick in his wallet, an essential tool for illegal entries in the so-called pursuit of justice, and for some reason, their captors had not confiscated their personal possessions, with the exception of course, of their cell phones.

"I could easily pick this lock." Lucas had already removed the burglar's tiny piece of flat, serrated steel from his wallet. "But with that ape guarding the door?" Bert was talking to himself. As for Dan? He was deep in thought and not listening to one word Lucas was saying.

Suddenly the door was thrown open with a vengeance, just missing Bert getting a face full as he staggered back, just barely keeping his balance and dropping his illegal lock pick to the floor.

The "Hulk" was standing menacingly with his AK-47, trigger finger at the ready, and Alano rudely pushed the 'no-brainer' aside. He was carrying what looked like peasant clothing and rubber thongs.

Alano threw the cotton clothes onto the mattress. "Change into these and place your personal belongings and clothes into these bags." Alano threw the canvas sacks to the floor.

The detectives looked to one another. Lucas didn't expect this, but more importantly, he was concerned about his lock pick! It lay about six inches left of the Hulk's big foot. *If this guy just happens to look down . . .*

"I don't have all day, *you heard me!*" Alano signalled to the guard, who immediately lifted his AK-47 and smashed the steel-inlaid plastic butt down hard on Lucas's right shoulder.

Bert yelled in pain. "You bastard." As he staggered under the blow, purposely falling forward onto his knees, his right hand grasping the lock pick out of sight between his fingers. His collarbone felt like it belonged to someone else, and he played the drama to its fullest, dramatically rolling over and grabbing the mattress before finally staggering unsteadily to his feet.

Alano grinned. He had that sadistic look on his face, like he was enjoying himself. *Maybe the leather whip was next . . .*

"*You!*" Alano yelled at Brown. "Start getting undressed, or you'll get the same medicine."

"Are you all right, Bert?" Dan asked.

"Yeah, I'm okay, but you had better do as he says." Lucas gave Brown a sly wink, then started to get down to his birthday suit.

Alano turned to the guard, laughing as he spoke in Spanish.

"Quien digo que los hombres negros tienen penes grandes?" *Who said black men have big dicks?*

The guard immediately burst into laughter, almost choking in the process. Dan turned to Lucas. "Must be one helluva joke, *huh?*"

"Maybe it's these fucking pyjama suits. *We look like stand-ins for* Alcatraz!" Alano picked up the sack with the clothing and passed it to the guard, then took the detectives' watches from the other bag, admiring the timepieces for a moment before they disappeared, presumably into his pocket. *Maybe he has been watching* Breaking the Magician's Code. Then, not unexpectedly, he rummaged through the detectives' wallets.

"American money." Alano's face glowed as he counted the "lucky strike" before passing the guard a fifty for his special skills.

"Si, gracias, Aldo." The Hulk was happy . . . *Probably a week's salary.*

Alano signalled again to the guard. The deed done, they turned and left, slamming the door behind them.

"Bert, that was a real whack you got. Are you sure you're okay?" Dan asked.

"I'm better than okay . . ." Bert kneeled and searched below the mattress.

"Look what I got."

Lucas proudly held up his pride and joy . . . *The lock pick!* "Why you crafty son of a gun . . ."

*   *   *

Broaden was as white as a sheet. Was it anger or shock? It was hard to tell, but the way he smashed that receiver into its cradle . . . *No more said!*

"What's the take, Stan? You look as if you have seen a ghost."

"Worse than that, Bill. I just received an ultimatum. Some guy just phoned to tell me . . ."

"Are you serious, Stan?" Chet interrupted. *"I don't believe my ears!"*

"Well, you had better fucking start! We have a real situation on or hands, and I'm looking for some creative thinking—*starting with the FBI!*"

"Stan," Bill began. "I have a good idea who is behind this, but first, let me make a call."

Broaden pushed the external line toward Bill.

"Be my guest."

"You wouldn't happen to know the country code for Argentina would you, Stan?"

"It's 0064 followed by the number . . . Nick, while Bill is on the line, how about doing me a favor and shouting coffees from the machine? It might wake us all up."

"Sure, gimme ten." Nick disappeared down the corridor.

Bill dialled the stretched number, almost getting finger cramp, then agitatedly waited as the dialling tone seemed forever.

"*Hell,* I never thought to check the time difference, and it's now after twelve. I hope she isn't fast asleep . . . *It will just be my fucking luck!*" Mona rubbed her eyes, then switched on the bedside lamp.

"Hello, *who is this?*" She gave a big yawn, covering her mouth with her other hand.

"It's me, Bill . . . Bill Hayden. Don't tell me you have forgotten the sound of my voice already?"

A man's voice cut into the line. "Who is on the line?"

"It's all right, Father, it's a personal call for me. Go to sleep. *Bill!* Of course, I haven't forgotten your voice, you big heel . . . But why the call? Is it because you are missing me?"

"That's one thing, but the other is I need your help."

"You disappoint me . . . *I'm only teasing.* How can I help you, darling?"

"Now who's doing the teasing?" Bill laughed. "Mona, do you remember I informed you that two detectives were flying into Sao Paulo from New York to escort Summers back to the United States?"

"Yes . . . *So?*"

"So you're not gonna believe this. It's like a double-take from Buenos Aires."

"I'm not with you, Bill."

"It's like this . . . The detectives arrived all right, but then disappeared into thin air."

"You're shittin' me."

"We just received a call at the embassy from their kidnapers . . ."

"*Kidnappers!* I don't believe this."

"Yeah, and here's the buzz . . ."

"*Shit* . . . So, your hunch is that the Generale Manuel Cerise is behind this?"

"What do you think, Mona?"

"I wouldn't write him off, that's for sure. The press has been hounding him for allowing two foreigners who are wanted for the murders of Carlos Mendez and Sergio Garcia to slip through his fingers. Then there's the small case of the loss of two policemen in a botched-up car pursuit. His job is on the line all right, and of course, if he can extradite the two U.S. citizens back to Argentina to face justice by whatever means, it's all shit and sugar . . ." There was a long silence.

"Are you still there, Mona?"

"Yeah, I'm just thinking . . . Listen, my father has a lots of contacts in the policia, and as always, money talks. But it's too late now, Bill . . . You said you had forty-eight hours . . . It'll be tight . . . Wait for my call tomorrow before you do anything. Will you be at the embassy?"

"Yeah."

"Then I'll call around 10:00 a.m. What's your number there?"

"It's . . ."

"I gotta get some shut-eye, Bill, if I you want me to be in good form tomorrow morning . . . Bye, darling . . . I miss you . . ."

Bill placed back the phone and looked up at the "three wise men."

"*Eh . . . Errr . . .* Um, that was my friend, Mona, in Buenos Aires."

"So we gathered." Broaden gave a sarcastic grin, and the smirks on the faces of the agents didn't help. Bill slightly flushed.

"Here's the scoop. Tomorrow at 10:00 a.m., I'm expecting a call that hopefully will inform me who is behind this and, more importantly, where Brown and Lucas are being held captive."

"What makes you so sure, Bill?" Broaden asked in part disbelief.

"*I'm sure.*" Bill smiled. "But there *is* one thing that I am sure of. There's not much we can do at this late hour, and boy, do I need some shut-eye. But I have to make one more call, and believe me, I'm not looking forward to this one."

Bill lifted the phone and dialled.

"Ruth, Bill Hayden here. Listen, my apologies for interrupting your sleep, but I must speak to Ted . . . *It's really urgent . . .*"

CHAPTER 3

Terry was feeling good as she stopped at security.

"Good morning, Lee." She gave him one of her specials.

"You look bright and breezy this morning, Terry." He quickly glanced at her security tab.

"Yep, I feel good. I visited Laura yesterday evening, and the good news is, she will be discharged before the end of the week with a clean bill of health."

"That *is* really good news." Lee seemed genuine. "Terry, if you don't mind me saying, you are one of the nicest people in that crazy office of yours."

"Thanks, Lee, I'm impressed, *but don't tell everyone.*" She laughed.

"Did I tell you my wife is pregnant with our first child?"

"No. *Congratulations*! I'm really happy for you both. So when's the big day?"

The blast of a car horn interrupted their conversation.

"Some people . . . *What did I tell yah!* Just a second, sir, I'm busy." Lee called, giving the driver a hostile look. "Terry, that's what I was about to ask you . . . If all goes well, the date is six weeks from now, and I was wondering if you would do me and my wife the honour of attending the christening?" The frustrated driver hit the horn once again.

"Just gimme one sec, Terry." Lee shook his head as he walked menacingly to the "buffoon's" open window.

"Sir, can I request you to be patient for just a few more seconds while I continue checking this lady's security pass. Now if you don't mind, sir, *don't be rude.*"

"As I was saying, Terry."

Terry had to smile at Lee's coolness. Whatever he said to "Mr. Rude," it certainly had the right effect, but with Lee's size and prize-fighter physique, who's brave enough to argue?

"Lee, that's so sweet of you. *Of course!* I'm more than happy to attend."

"Have a good one, Terry." Lee smiled and opened the boom. As for the other driver? *One can imagine . . .*

* * *

As Terry stood in the elevator, she smiled to herself, recollecting the phone call last night from that "cheeky fellow." *What was his name again? Was is Brent or Bert . . . Whatever . . . I wonder if he will phone, and more to the point, what does he look like? Still, the guy has something. Hmmm . . .* The elevator chimed. "*Good morning, everyone!*" Terry was really on a high. She dumped her briefcase at her workstation and headed for the caffeine injection before returning again to boot her computer.

The office seemed overly quiet, and why was everyone looking toward Blakely's office? And Terry turned out of curiosity. There, to her surprise, was a security guard using standover tactics as Jack packed his personal belongings into cardboard boxes. It was too much to take. Terry had a lot of respect for Blakely, and she quickly abandoned her coffee and barged into his office.

Guard or no guard, this looked ugly.

"Jack, what's up?" Terry interrupted.

"Lady, if you don't mind, I have a job to do, so would you mind leaving, or I may have to escort you from Mr. Blakely's office."

"*Oh, is that so!* Well, I do mind." When Terry raised her hackles, she's not to be messed with.

"Terry, it's all right." Jack made a gesture. "Don't worry, but I appreciate your concern. This is Hall's way of trying to humiliate me. I'll contact you as soon as the dust settles."

"Ma'am, if you don't mind?"

"Cool it, big boy, I'm leaving under my own steam, and let me tell you, you'll be standing at my desk next because I am just about to present *my* resignation."

"Terry, you've made my day . . ."

*   *   *

Rita, Blakely's secretary, was in tears. Seeing her boss of fourteen years being escorted from the premises like a criminal, carrying his few possessions in cheap cardboard containers, was a shock to the system. The reality that loyalty means squat when it's down to the line.

"Rita, wipe your eyes, it's not the end of the world. Meet me in conference room 1 in ten minutes."

"But . . ." Rita was confused. With her boss now gone, what was she to do? "Jaycee . . . Mildred . . . Conference room 1 in ten minutes." Terry sat at her desk and took a sip of her coffee.

"*Ahhhh,* this tastes ugly, *and worse still, it's cold!* Now for that resignation letter." Terry hit the keyboard. *It is with the deepest regret that I resign . . .*

*   *   *

"Settle down, this won't take long." Terry could see from the expressions on the staff's faces that they knew what was coming, but when push comes to shove, heroes are scarcer than hen's teeth.

"You have all seen this morning what loyalty means in this company. No one deserves to be treated like a criminal just because they resign. Remember, Blakely began his career with ABM straight from university. Management could have at least given him some dignity in recognition for his loyal and dedicated service. Now why are you here, you may ask? Firstly, I have tendered my resignation, and most likely, no doubt, tomorrow morning I'll face the same inhumane fate as Jack."

The desk phone rang, interrupting Terry's swan song.

"Yes?"

"It's Lily from reception. I told the gentleman that you are in a meeting, but he insisted, stressing he was phoning at your request. His name is Mr. Brent Kennedy. Do you want to take the call, Terry?"

"*Well, I'll be darned,* young Casanova himself!" Terry was speaking aloud. "Lily, tell him I'm sorry that I can't take his call at the moment but to phone back in say . . . thirty minutes."

"Now where was I? Yes . . . Blakely has asked me to join him at Hewlett, and I have agreed and will most likely receive my new contract of employment within the next few days."

"Yes, Jaycee?"

"Will you be employed in the same capacity as with ABM, namely, marketing manager?"

"According to Jack, the job title will remain the same but in a much bigger department, and furthermore, he has given me the green light to take two of my best staff with me. And that means you, Jaycee, and you, Mildred. As for you, Rita? Jack has already offered you the position as his confidential secretary."

Mildred and Jaycee turned to one another; they had already put two and two together and knew the reasons of the meeting.

"Don't get us wrong, Terry . . . Aaahem . . ." Jaycee nervously cleared her throat. "It's like this, and I'm sure I'm speaking on behalf of Mildred. We really appreciate the confidence you have in our abilities . . . But you see, we are in a secure job, and the market is not that buoyant. Therefore, it would be silly and bordering on stupidity to resign based on a verbal promise. Hewlett-Packard is an excellent company, but without a firm job offer on the company's letterhead and a contract of employment, it's a roadblock that needs to be breached before we both resign."

"But . . . Let me put it this way. Do I get the nod that you'll jump ship and come with me provided you receive your official job offers with better conditions and better remuneration?"

Jaycee smiled. "Let *me* put it this way. It would be like a breath of fresh air to face new challenges and get as far away from ABM as possible. *Have I answered your question?*"

"Affirmative," Terry replied. "And you, Rita?"

"I have already written my resignation letter . . ."

* * *

This was June's first day in her new job, and she arrived at the law firm bright and early. Dressed in her navy-blue jacketed suit, white open-necked blouse, and simple gold chain, complete with pencil skirt and modest heels, she certainly looked the part.

"Good morning, Ethel," June greeted Phil's secretary.

If you want to make friends in the office, you start with the boss's secretary.

"Has Mr. Stevens arrived?"

"No not yet." Ethel glanced at her watch. "It's not like him to be so late. It must be the traffic due to that heavy downpour. June, if you feel like having a coffee, the machine is just down the hallway next to the staff restroom."

"Thanks, Ethel, but I'm good."

"Then why don't I show you to your workstation so you can take the load off these heels until Mr. Stevens arrives? He shouldn't be too long."

* * *

The workstation was typically small and compact, surrounded by the *"Berlin Wall."* It had all the commonplace stuff—desktop computer, phone, filing cabinet, and, of course, the uncomfortable low-cost office chair in the name of productivity. But the stack of manila folders neatly piled on one side of Jones's desk intrigued her.

"Ethel, before you leave . . . These folders?"

"Mr. Stevens wishes to familiarize you with the type of cases and clients he handles."

June acknowledged in silence. It was too much too early. She frowned before hanging her jacket on the stand. She hadn't expected a ready-made workload waiting for her. June had been introduced to the other two legal assistants during yesterday's staff meeting, and she was eager to make friends, and the morning coffee break, she thought, would be as good as any.

"Good morning, June." Phil gave her a special smile but not too conspicuous. "I see you have settled in already. That heavy downpour really caught me, and the traffic was nose to tail. *June,* can you come to my office in say . . . ten minutes, once I've gone through my mail with Ethel." Phil smiled again. *"Ethel . . ."*

"I'm Marjorie Cooper, and this is Nora Taylor." The two women introduced themselves. "The first day in a new job is always frightening, and we just wanted to say welcome and anything you need or are unsure of, just holler."

"Thank you both, that's so nice."

"By the way, coffee break is at ten." Marjorie commented as she left for her desk

"Thanks, Marjorie."

"Call me Marj. Everyone else does."

"*Eh,* thanks, Marj . . ."

*   *   *

As June glanced through the outstanding cases, she soon settled down, the work bringing back memories of when she was a young freshman working for Phil's father.

"*So much for the ten minutes!*" June glanced at her watch. No sooner was the thought in her mind than Ethel called.

"He's free now, June, just go straight in."

"Thanks, Ethel." She knocked on Phil's door.

"Come in, June." Phil was cunningly waiting behind the door, out of sight.

"*Phil,* are you there?" Not seeing him, she looked toward his private john.

The door suddenly closed behind her with the click of the latch.

"*Why Phil Stevens!* I might have . . ."

June didn't get a chance to finish her protest as Phil's lips pressed against hers, crushing her body against him in a passionate embrace. The kiss seemed to last forever, and June had to pry their bodies apart.

"*Wow!*" She inhaled. "*You are wild this morning.*" But as June looked into his eyes, she could sense what was really in his mind.

"Honey, I really miss you."

"*You mean you miss the sex.*"

"*Well* . . . Now that you mention it!" Phil laughed. He loved to tease, and he pulled her closer using both his hands to squeeze her firm buttocks into his groin and the rock-hard bulge in his slacks.

"*No, Phil . . . No!* I want you as much as you want me, but not in the office . . . This is not the place. Besides, Ethel is not stupid, and the last thing I want is to spend the whole day without my panties."

"You certainly know how to turn me on, honey, just the very thought . . ."

"Phil, a better idea. Why don't you come over this evening? I'll try and coax the kids to go to a movie or something."

"Better still, I'll drive my Porsche to your house and hand the keys to Steven."

"Now I know why you are such a successful lawyer." June gave Phil that look.

"You win." He sighed as he reached behind her and released the latch.

"I'm sure Ethel heard that."

"She's not married. Maybe the thought will turn her on."

"Phil, you're incorrigible. In fact, you're downright wicked. Now what did you really want to see me about?"

"Are you serious!"

*   *   *

"So, your advice, Phil, is that I continue to use my maiden name, and that's the reason that you introduced me to the staff as June Mathers."

"Exactly . . . June, you know how destructive office gossip is, and when the story cuts loose in the press, your so-called office colleagues will be talking about it in their sleep."

"I guess you're right, darling. But I feel so awful bringing all this upon you. I mean you have more important things on your plate rather than I burden you with my problems."

"Honey." Phil reached over his desk to hold June's hand. "I love you, and that's what matters most. Now why don't you grab that coffee with the staff.

It's just gone ten, and I'm sure they can't wait to meet you."

"Thanks, darling, for your support, and you're right, I need that coffee." June smiled and rose to leave.

"Hey, what happened to my kiss?"

"Too bad, big boy. I'm afraid you'll just have to wait until tonight."

As June closed the door, she was still smiling at the thought, but tonight will be a different story.

*   *   *

Ten o'clock had come and gone, and the empty polystyrene coffee cups told the story. The FBI agents and Bill were on edge as they sat in Broadens office, waiting for the call.

"Bill, while we are waiting, I thought I would take this opportunity to inform you that we will be shipping Tony's body back to the States this morning. It's important that the coroner completes the autopsy as soon as possible to release the body to the family for burial and closure. I took it upon myself to cancel your ticket, as I was sure you wanted to see this kidnapping escapade through to the end.”

“Thanks, Stan, I really appreciate it.”

“Are you sure, Bill, that your contact will ring . . . I mean . . .” Broaden was sceptical.

The red phone burst into life, and Bill leaped from his seat.

“Yes, Hayden here.” Everyone was on edge.

“Bill, it’s Mona . . . *And boy*, do I have some news for you! Your hunch was spot on.”

“Honey, don’t keep me in suspense.”

“It’s the Generale all right. That low-down snake Manuel Cerise is behind this, trying to save his lousy hide.”

“How did you find out?”

“There’s always squealers for the right price, but get this . . . Your two friends are held captive in the Argentine embassy.”

“I’ll be darned!”

“Unfortunately, I couldn’t find out which part, but my suggestion would be to go to city Hall and get a copy of the building plan. I’m sorry, darling, that’s the best I could do.”

“Don’t *be* sorry. You did a great job and give my thanks to your father. Honey, I gotta go, as time is running out. I’ll phone you again whenever something breaks.”

“I’ll be waiting . . .”

“It seems you are pretty cosy with this friend of yours,” Broaden commented, smiling.

Bill grinned. “That’s for another coffee break . . . Now here’s the lowdown . . .”

*   *   *

“And your friend, can she be trusted?” Broaden asked.

“Stan, how do you know it’s a she?”

“It’s highly unlikely that you would address a guy as ‘honey.’ Not unless . . . *Eh* . . . We’ll skip that one.”

Nick and Chet burst into laughter at Broadens one liner.

“*Okay . . . Okay . . .* The joke’s over. Now let’s get down to business, and the ball is now in your court, Stan, to get a copy of the architect’s plan.”

"Just a sec." Broaden lifted the phone and spoke in Portuguese. Although Bill didn't understand a word he was saying, he could certainly recognize "*Embajada* Argentina."

"I'll have the architect's plans in my office before two. How does that grab you?" Broaden was looking for the compliment that never came.

"Somehow, we have to get into the embassy, but how?" Bill was shaking his head.

"I have an idea." Broaden lifted the phone. "Carlota, can you get me the chief of police on the line?"

"Certainly, sir . . ."

"*The chief of police, Stan?*"

That was something Bill hadn't anticipated. Bringing in the police could make things even more complicated.

The phone rang, and Stan raised his hand for Bill to keep it for later.

(Portuguese translated to English)

"Stan, what's the occasion?"

"Rodrigo, I have bad situation on my hands, and I need your help."

"I was hoping you were calling for a barbecue this weekend." Broaden could hear Rodrigo laugh. "How's my sister . . . Hey, it's not personal, is it?"

"No, Rodrigo, nothing like that . . . Paula is fine, Rodrigo. I don't want to discuss it over the phone. Walls have ears. Can you be here within the hour?"

"For you, my brother, *anything.*"

"Thanks, Rodrigo, and give my love to Elvira and the kids . . ."

"I don't know what that was all about, but I can put two and two together," Bill interrupted.

"For your information, if we want to get into the Argentine Embassy, we need to bring in the police."

"I understand, Stan, but can you trust the commissioner? Like, how well do you know him?" Bill asked.

"*How well do I know him?*" Broaden burst into laughter. "*He's, my brother-in-law!*"

*   *   *

The clock was ticking, and no further contact had been made by the kidnappers.

"Stan, a thought has just crossed my mind. Shouldn't you bring the ambassador in on this?

"Bill, *for Christ's sake,* I have enough problems without getting McGovern involved. He couldn't make a decision even if it were staring him in the face. No, let sleeping dogs lie."

"Then how about your counterpart in Buenos Aires?" Bill questioned. "I mean, Stan, would you get any mileage by contacting him?"

"*Are you serious, Bill?* He's as bent as a two-dollar coin. He and Cerise are joined at the hip. I know for a fact that he's involved in the visa racket, getting under-the-table money, and his boss, the ambassador, I'm sure gets his cut.

When in Rome . . . Well, you can finish that one." The secretarial phone rang.

"Yes, Carlota?"

"The police commissioner is here, sir." "*Good.* Send him straight in."

*   *   *

The commissioner was immaculately dressed in his dark-blue pleated police uniform, the epaulettes encrusted with gold braid. He was capless, and with that jet-black hair combed straight back in a middle shade and not the least sign of gray . . . He was either dying it or had a face lift, looking far too young to hold such a high position. The straight white teeth the dark-brown eyes *and with that hair!* You could easily mistake him for Valentino himself. For sure he was a piece of work, but then this is Brazil and the famous Mardi Gras country.

*   *   *

"Stanley, vim tao rapido quanto poderia . . . O que esta o grande problema."

Rodrigo greeted Broaden with a bear hug.

These two are certainly buddies, Bill thought to himself.

Having turned at seeing the Americans, Rodrigo immediately switched to English.

"My apologies, gentlemen. I was just telling Stanley that I got here as fast as I could but what's the big problem?"

Broaden broke in. "Rodrigo, first of all let me introduce you. This is . . ." "This must be serious, Stanley. Two agents from the FBI and a New York detective!"

"It doesn't get any more serious, Rodrogo. Grab a chair, and I'll give you the lowdown . . ."

*   *   *

"I can believe this. I know Cerise well, and believe me, he is worse than scum . . . But the problem is how do we get into the embassy? I can't just raid the place with my TOC team . . . I'm sorry gentleman, in layman's terms, my tactical operation commandos . . . The embassy technically is on Argentine soil and enjoys diplomatic immunity. It would be crazy for me to order such an operation. Brazil has bad enough relations with Argentina as it is without aggravating it further and more so if we are wrong." There was a knock on the door.

"Come in, Carlota . . . That must be the architect's plans . . . Thanks, Carlota, just place them on my desk."

"Okay, let's see what we got." Rodrigo spread the prints on the large coffee table.

"*Hmmm* . . . I have visited the embassy on a number of occasions on official business, and my guess is your people are being held right here."

Rodrigo circled the spot with his pen. "The cleaner's storeroom." "*The cleaner's storeroom?*" Broaden reacted.

"It's the only place, Stanley . . . The basement . . . With no windows and complete with toilet facilities."

"*Hmmm* . . . You may be right, but now the big question is *how?*"

Bill and the FBI agents could only listen in silence; they were guests, so to speak, in a foreign country.

Ricardo looked up from the plans and gave a sly grin.

"Stanley, I think I have the perfect solution . . . You see, I received information this morning that tonight . . ."

* * *

Terry was feeling better already having all but the nod from Mildred and Jaycee. The saying "There's nothing like winning" was true.

"I'll phone Jack on his cell and tell him the good news . . ."

"Blakely here."

"Jack, it's Terry . . . Here's the scoop . . ."

"So, you want me to get personnel to post these job offers a soon as possible before Bill Hall gets to them? *Hmmm.*" Jack's mind was like a runaway train, heading for the stop buffers, and Terry was asking the impracticable at such short notice.

"Something like that," Terry answered. "And, Jack, the salaries have to be attractive, or it's a no-go. It's not as if you don't know these people."

"Gimme some slack, Terry. It will take at best a couple of days, including your own job offer."

"As I see it Jack, the drums are beating right now, and I'll be joining the ranks of the unemployed as early as tomorrow."

"Terry, I understand your anxiety, *believe me,* and I've had a verbal agreement from Alan Beazley, but I haven't even got my own feet below the table. I take up my new position on Monday. Once I settle in, give me a day or two, then I'll give you a call and you can come over to HP and meet with Beazley himself."

"Okay, but don't let me down. I've gone way out on a limb for you. I'll give you a call on your cell whenever the shit hits the fan."

"Terry, it's not a case that I won't let you down—it's case that I need your expertise and that of the staff."

"By the way, before you cut to the chase, Rita has also tendered her resignation. *There's a lot on the line here, Jack.*"

"Terry, call me tomorrow evening after six. I'll be at home . . . Ciao."

*   *   *

Terry felt somewhat uncomfortable after the phone call with Blakely, but then he had plenty on his plate with his new job and all. She was not the one to burn her bridges prematurely, but after experiencing the humiliation of her boss, she couldn't wait to get out of this hellhole. Anyhow, with the exception of Rita, Jaycee and Mildred are sitting safely on the sidelines. Terry took a sip of her stale coffee and pondered for a moment. Her life had changed so much in the last month, and it just goes to prove that life is so unpredictable. The phone rang. She gave a dejected sigh, then picked up the receiver.

"*Yes?*"

"Terry, its Lily again from reception. I have this Brent Kennedy on the line. What do you want me to do?"

"Boy, this guy doesn't give up . . . Put him through, Lily."

"Terry, it's Brent here, your knight in shining armour."

Terry laughed. "I gotta hand it you, Brent, I give you full marks for persistence."

"Then Terry, how about a date as a reward?"

"*Ha . . . Ha . . . Ha.*" Terry laughed aloud. "Brent, you've made my day. You caught me at a bad time, but you succeeded in making me laugh."

"Does that mean . . ."

"Yes, I'll make an exception. But don't run away with yourself and get any ideas. I'm not in the habit of going on blind dates . . . Besides how do I know you're not a rapist or, worse still, a serial killer?" She could hear Brent laugh his ass off.

"Terry, you crack me up."

"Well, I'm waiting."

"How does seven thirty grab you?"

"Can you make that eight? I have to visit my friend in the hospital."

"No sweat. Meet me at the Stetson in Spring Street, Central Soho. It's a smoking-hot country and Western watering hole, with the Midnight Cowboys chomping out the best of Creedence Clearwater Revival."

"Sounds cool, but how will I recognize you?"

"I'm just over six feet, handsome, black hair . . ."

"Brent, cut the crap and get real." Terry could hear him laugh again.

"I'll be wearing a pale-blue V-neck sweater, collared, open-neck white shirt, and stonewashed Levi's. How does that grab you?"

"You'll pass."

"And you?"

"I'll keep you guessing, and don't be late . . . Ciao." Terry had that dangerous grin on her face.

"*What the hell am I doing here?*" she spoke to herself. "I might as well pack up and hit the road early . . . *I've got a date tonight.*"

*   *   *

The office coffee break was a welcome diversion; besides, June wanted to become acquainted with her new colleges.

"Another cookie, June?" Marj asked.

"Not a chance. Even just looking at food, I gain weight."

"Your figure is to die for," Nora interrupted. "Just look at me. No matter how much I try, I just can't seem to drop the pounds." June just smiled. They looked a nice bunch.

"I heard that you used to work for Phil's father?" Marj asked.

"Yes." June smiled. "A long time ago, when I was a freshman at NYU studying law. In fact, Phil and I were in the same year and same faculty." "Are you married, June?"

"Yes, but in the process of 'not being.' I have two grown-up children, a boy and a girl, still studying."

Office walls have flies and June could only guess how much the staff knew already and there was no point in pulling the wool. Besides, Nora is Glen Jackson's legal assistant, and she would have access to June's divorce file.

"That must be tough," Nora commented.

"It depends." June cut the slack. "Say, I had better get back to my desk. I'm reviewing an import case for Mr. Stevens, and I don't want to screw up on my first day."

"You're right, June, it's about time *we all* went back to work."

Marj finished the dregs of her coffee and rose to leave. "I hope everything goes well for you, June. I'm talking from firsthand experience." She smiled. "You see, I've been there and done that."

*   *   *

It had just turned four, and June was patiently waiting to discuss her first case with Phil, but he had been so busy, and it looked like the clock would win the day.

"*June,*" Ethel called. "Mr. Stevens is free and will see you now." "Thanks, Ethel." June knocked on the door.

"Come in, June." Phil smiled. "Grab a chair."

June pulled her pencil skirt up slightly and crossed her legs, flashing a milky thigh.

"June, *don't torture me!*" Phil couldn't keep his eyes from those long sexy legs and that dark crevasse that triggered the imagination.

The phone rang and just as well.

"Ethel, *I said no calls!*" Phil was enjoying the show.

"I know, Mr. Stevens, but it's Mr. Hall, the President of ABM, and he says he must speak with you urgently.

Phil inhaled in frustration. "Oh, all right then, put him through . . . Bill, good afternoon. Now how can be of assistance?"

"I'm in a bit of a bind, Phil, and I need your legal advice."

"Fire away."

"I appointed a new vice president of marketing and sales, having terminated Simpson for the botch up of the launch of our new product range."

"Yeah, I heard," Phil replied. "*So?*"

"My decision put Blakely's nose out of joint, and he consequently resigned, having been offered a VP's position with our major competitor . . . HP."

"I can understand Jack's reaction. He's a hothead, Bill, but I was impressed with him. Let me put it this way: he was no slouch when it came to the business of marketing, and a more loyal employee you couldn't find. You certainly rubbed Blakely up the wrong way, Bill, but what's your problem? He resigned of his own accord, and if he's going to a competitor, remove him from the premises as quickly as possible. If it's intellectual property that worries you, *forget it!* There's no legal recourse to remove technical information from someone's brain."

"Phil, that's not what I am phoning you about. You see, he's trying to convince my best marketing people to join him, and two have resigned already."

"I'm sorry Bill but there's no law that states it's an offense for competitor companies to poach staff. A civil suit? I wouldn't go down that road. It will cost the company money in legal fees, and besides what's your case?"

"So, I just have to stand by and let this . . . *this . . . maverick . . .* ruin my career?"

"Bill, we can all be smart in hindsight. When an employee's pride is hurt . . . What can I say?"

"I'm disappointed, Phil, but I appreciate your honesty. I'll contact you if something comes to my mind. I'm not gonna take this lying down, you know."

Phil shrugged. "Bill, call me anytime. That's what I'm here for . . ." Phil turned to June as he put down the phone. "*Phew* . . . Some people, they never learn."

"Was that Bill Hall from ABM?" June asked.

"As a matter of fact, it was, June. Why are you asking?"

"Because Laura Williams is the marketing manager with ABM, and she was Mike's extramarital."

"*Of course,* now that you mention it! What with Global, your ex's employer, going into bankruptcy and with ABM being Laura Williams employer, it's a real conundrum, as they are all my clients. But where was I with your legs? *Eh . . . I mean the Cooper case . . .*"

*   *   *

"Rodrigo, let me get this straight . . ." Broaden was rubbing his chin. "This evening, there will be a demonstration outside the Argentinean embassy by the Muslim brotherhood to protest against their government's proposed law to ban the head scarf, or hijab, used by children at schools instead of the school uniform. The Argentine government is also refusing to build mosques and considering banning the abaya, or full woman's body dress, citing that it's intimidating and is destroying the country's culture and the very fabric of their Catholic religion."

"That's the take!" Rodrigo answered. "But, Stanley, it's no different here in Brazil. We have the same problem with Islamization, and tonight the mujahideen will be out in force outside the Argentine embassy, screaming and chanting, burning flags, throwing Molotov cocktails, the whole shooting match . . . *Can't you see it, guys?* It's our perfect cover!"

"I'm listening, Rodrigo." Broaden was taking the bait.

"Okay, let's be more specific . . . First of all, as commissioner, it's my responsibility to send a platoon of riot police to protect the embassy. *However,* they will be briefed in advance to look out for four Muslim men wearing traditional skull caps, or kufis in Arabic, that have a yellow patch sewn onto the front and back to distinguish our TOC team from the fanatics and avoid friendly fire."

"But the yellow patches . . . *Wouldn't it draw attention?"* Chet asked.

"Yellow in the Muslim world means *bersih,* or justice, and is commonly used in countries such as Malaysia and Indonesia in government protests."
"Then what?" It was Hayden's turn to butt in.

"Here's the drill . . . I select a small, handpicked team of police commandos comprising of four highly trained personnel. They will be inconspicuous in their thawbs, the long sack-like white robe that Muslim men wear, and will each be armed with the Glock 9 mm semiautomatic, complete with silencer and four clips of eight rounds . . .

"As soon as the turmoil starts, the police will use tear gas and rubber bullets, and that's the signal for the commandos to remain out of sight and scale the fifteen-foot sidewall using a rope ladder. Once my men are inside, they will dispose of the guards in anyway necessary and open the front gate to allow the crazy mujahideen to breach the ranks of the riot police and storm the building." Ricardo paused.

Fatalities, or badly injured embassy guards will automatically be blamed on the fanatics . . . *Perfect!*

"Now here's how I see it . . . Time is of the essence. Two special forces personnel will stand guard outside the main door while the other two search and destroy until they ultimately find and release the hostages. An unmarked Land Rover will be standing by as the getaway car, hidden about a hundred meters down the tree-lined avenue and out of sight, ready to push the pedal back to the embassy."

"Phew . . . Rodrigo, that's one helluva plan." Broaden was still sceptical.

"It may be one helluva plan, Stanley," Ricardo shot back. *"But it's the only one!"*

Broaden turned to the now-silent audience. "Are there any questions or points you wish to raise with the commissioner?" Bill gave a slight cough to draw attention.

"As you rightly stress, Commissioner, timing is everything, so to ask a silly question . . . When do we start to put the pieces together?"

"Good point, Detective! The ball is in my court, and I have plenty to organize in a short space of time." Rodrigo glanced at his watch. "It's just turned twelve noon . . . Stanley, I'll give you a call to come to my office once the dust has settled, to listen in on the briefing."

"What do you think that timing will be?" Broaden asked.

"Probably just after two . . . Now, gentlemen, please excuse me, I must leave."

"Before you leave, Commissioner, and I know this is a big ask. I want to be commando number 5 if it's possible. It's personal . . . You see, I lost my buddy and best friend in Buenos Aires, and I have a score to settle."

Rodrigo turned to Broaden, an uncomfortable look on his face. Although he could sympathize with Bill, it would be highly unusual to allow a civilian to take part on such a dangerous mission and possibly place the lives of his men in danger. It was too big a risk.

"Sergeant, I sympathize with you, and I understand your feelings, but . . ."

Bill rudely cut the commissioner short; he knew what was coming, and somehow, he had to convince him with whatever it takes.

"It's just too big a risk, Sergeant." Rodrigo was shaking his head.

"Commissioner, I know what you are thinking, and I can't blame you. But if I can just try and put your mind at ease . . . I am a highly trained NYPD officer with two commendations for bravery under fire."

Ricardo was in a tough position; there was now no doubt in his mind that Bill was a highly trained operative, and he frowned, rubbing his chin.

"Against my better judgment, this time I'll make an exception."

"Thanks, Commissioner. You don't know how much this means . . ."

Rodrigo raised his hand. "Save it, Detective, until after the sting . . . One other point—under no circumstance do we leave any of our men behind, either wounded or fatal. Do I make myself clear?"

"I understand, Commissioner." Bill's chest heaved. He was relieved.

"Well, Sergeant, you had better accompany me to police headquarters, and to put your mind at rest, my men all speak fluent English. They spent six months in the United States training with your Navy SEALs . . ."

*   *   *

The four commandos were fit; it was like looking at four Arnold Schwarzenegger's. Maybe the code name *should be* "Operation Collateral Damage."

Broaden had arrived just before the briefing, and he was frozen to every word Rodrigo was instructing.

"Capitano, you seem rather uncomfortable. What's biting you?" Ricardo had noticed his key man's expression. "Is it the New York police officer.?"

"Sim, Commissioner. The Americano . . . Err . . . Well, I don't know how to say this . . . The colour of his skin, shall I say, *is too white.*"

Rodrigo burst into laughter. "Capitano, you had me concerned there for a moment. If that's all that's bothering you, fake tan can solve the problem . . . Sim?"

The captain turned to Bill and shrugged as if to say, "I feel like a right idiot" and offered his hand in embarrassment.

"My apologies, Sergeant, but in my business, I can't be too careful. This operation is extremely dangerous."

Bill smiled. It was a small thing, and he quickly changed the subject to take the heat off.

"Captain, I can assume from your excellent English that you've spent some time in the United States." "Yes." He smiled proudly.

"*Say listen,* don't worry. I understand your concerns after all I'm an unknown variable in your eyes, and the colour of my skin doesn't help. But let me stress this. I'm under your command, and I'll obey your orders to the letter."

"That's good, Sergeant, now I feel more comfortable."

"How about you, Stanley?" Rodrigo turned to his brother in-law.

"I'm comfortable with the deal, Rodrigo."

"*Good,* then let's get Bill tanned up and dressed up." Ricardo laughed. We still have another hour to go, and I want to go through every detail again. *Oh,* and, Capitano, make sure the driver of the Range Rover attends the next briefing . . ."

Rodrigo turned to check the wall clock. "Which will be in another thirty minutes . . . Now I think it's time for that coffee break . . ."

*   *   *

"Laura, I'm sorry, honey, but I gotta go. It's nearly seven fifteen, and I have to drive to Soho and arrive there before eight."

"I wish I could join you." Laura flashed that sad expression.

"*Hey!* No more talking. You heard what the doctor said . . . You have the green light, but that doesn't mean you can start singing like a canary. Your larynx is still in the healing process . . . *Remember!*"

"*I know, Terry . . . I know.*" Laura's voice was all but a rasp.

"Remember, you have only two more days to go, and you'll be discharged, *don't blow it!*"

"I can't wait." Laura's voice was now a whisper.

"Tomorrow then." Terry gave Laura a kiss on the cheek. "Once again, bye, honey."

"Give my regards to your new conquest." Lara waved. "I could think of a better description . . . Ciao."

*   *   *

As Terry drove through the heavy evening traffic to Central Soho, she knew she was sailing into uncharted waters, but then the thrill of a blind date was an adrenaline buster.

"*The Stetson?*" She spoke out loud. "That rings a bell . . . Now where have I heard that name before? Aw, it will come to me."

"*At last!*" Terry sighed, spotting the large sign, "Spring Street."

"*Now to find that bloody bar!*"

Terry didn't have long to search before the large neon sign of the famous western icon was staring her in her face like a sore thumb.

"*Hmmmm.* Funny, I've been here many times before, but I've never noticed this joint." Terry pulled over and braked as a parked car signaled and reversed.

"Must be my night." She drove forward, then reversed the Mazda 6 into the tight space like a pro.

As she crossed the road, she could clearly hear the country and Western music echoing through the bar's open front entrance strategically blocked by the oversize bouncer. *Maybe you have to be black, overweight, and muscle bound as the criteria to bag this job.* Terry smiled again.

What the hell . . . Who cares as long as "Mike Tyson" does his thing.

The big guy in the rented tuxedo nodded his approval and gave Terry a toothy grin, then moved to one side.

"Good evening, miss, the cloakroom is to the left."

"Thanks, big guy." Terry laid it on, and "Mr. Universe" seemed to like the gesture.

As Terry entered the second-hand smoke, she scanned the crowded bar. It wouldn't be difficult to spot Brent dressed in a pale-blue sweater in the "OK Corral."

*   *   *

The place was jumping with DIY cowboys, and the music was hot, the Midnight Cowboys chomping out Creedence Clearwater Revival songs like they were the next act on *American Idol*. A few couples had taken to the small dance floor doing their "Siamese twin" shuffle while in the background, the distinctive crack of cue balls could be clearly heard from the dimly lit poolroom.

*   *   *

"*Boy*, this is some joint." Terry spoke under her breath. "Now where's that man of mine."

Terry was nailing a few horny glances and felt uncomfortable, most likely giving the wrong impression to the "wolves" before the "full moon."

"Can I buy you a drink, beautiful?"

"No, I'm already spoken for."

"Have it your own way, honey, but you don't know what you're missin'." Terry suddenly felt a slight tap on her shoulder and nervously turned.

"She's with me, buddy."

The dude touched his Stetson. "Sorry, lady, but can you blame a guy?"

"*Terry,* I've finally met you in the flesh, and you're everything I expected."

*   *   *

Boy this guy is a dish! Terry looked up into Brent's pale crystal-blue eyes. His unruly wavy brown hair, the chiselled jaw line, the narrow nose the straight whites, and the bronzed complexion, not to mention the Michael Douglas cleft chin. *But being over six feet tall and lean and mean . . . I mean where did this guy come from. But good lookers are normally not starved of female company, and this dude has probably been "round the world" more times than Errol Flynn!*

*   *   *

"I'm intrigued, how did you know it was me?"

"How could I ever forget that beautiful blonde hair and those baby blue eyes?"

"Yeah, and how can I forget your one finger salute, huh? I tell you . . . *You're a piece of work.*"

Terry and Brent couldn't hold their laughter. They were certainly two of a kind.

"More to the point, what can I get you?" Brent was still smiling at the thought.

"*Hmm* . . . Let me see." Terry was thinking. "Something different . . . *I know.* How about a Tequila Sunrise to quench my thirst . . . *At least to start with!*"

Brent smiled. "Don't go away. I'll be back in a few minutes." He disappeared into the crowded bar.

* * *

"Cheers." Brent clicked the Michelob bottle against Terry's long cocktail glass with its brightly colourful contents.

"*Hmmm*, this *is* good!" Terry smiled as sampled the first sip.

"Terry, I hate to say this, but I'm relieved you came dressed in your jeans and white T-shirt, I forgot to tell you it's a western bar, and I was worried in case you came in some . . ."

"*Evening dress?*"

Brent burst into laughter again.

"*I just love the humour.*"

"I knew when you told me you would be in a blue woollen sweater that it wasn't formal." A touch of sarcasm. "Now, mister."

Terry took another sip of the hyped-up tequila.

"It's 'true confession' time, so tell me something about yourself."

"*Simple* . . . I'm into money laundering, drugs, and prostitution. How does that grab you?"

Brent almost choked with laughter upon seeing Terry's expression.

"*Hey* . . . Only joking! But you gotta admit, I had you going there."

"I don't know whether to kick you in the shin or in the nuts—whichever would cause the most pain."

"*Ouch!* I can almost feel it."

"Serves you right, you joker . . . Now are you going to be serious or what?"

"*Spoilsport* . . . Now where do I start? I'm an unattached bachelor, twenty-seven years old, and a senior architect with Grollo Construction. I graduated from Harvard with honour's, and I love my job and my adorable date."

"I'm impressed, but you forgot your other love . . . fast cars and being rude to innocent young lady drivers."

"*Innocent young lady drivers!* If my memory serves me right, your French would scare the pants off any driver."

"*Touché . . . Okay,* let's call it a draw. Now are you gonna make me look like a wallflower, or are you going to ask me to trip the light fantastic?"

"*Madam,* can you give me the pleasure of this dance?"

"Oui, Monsieur . . . Merci."

"Say, your French is not bad."

"Don't kid yourself. I've already spent three of the only five words I know."

"*Heh . . . heh.*" Bret laughed. "But listen, my lovely, you haven't told me anything about *yourself.*"

"Well, firstly, I'm a woman . . ."

"*Terry, you crack me up.*" Bret was shaking his head at Terry's dry humour.

"Darling, it's a long story and for another time . . . But I'm not married, if that puts your mind to rest. Now how about that dance?"

*   *   *

Frank stared, momentarily engrossed with the dance floor, then suddenly placed his cue stick against the table.

"Frank, for Christ's sake, take your shot." Brody was on a run. "You look as if you've seen a ghost."

"Do me a favor and take my shot, Eddie, I've just seen someone I know."

"I hope it's not this broad you've been breaking your heart over." Jack was scanning the sea of bodies trying to spot the elusive "Marilyn."

"Gimme a break guys, I've been trying to get in touch with Terry all week."

"Oh, so it's Terry now, is it?" Jack was being sarcastic. "Well, I hope you know what you're doing, dude. I thought you had gotten over that chick."
"Eddie, don't piss around . . . Take the shot, I'm smokin' hot . . ."

*   *   *

Frank squeezed through the "feet stompers" and rudely tapped Brent on the shoulder.

"I'm butting in, buddy."

"*You're what?*" Bret eyeballed Frank. "I got news for you, dude . . . Like do yourself a favor and get outta my face. *The lady says no!*"

"I want to hear it from her own lips."

Terry pushed Brent aside to stare at the intruder.

"*Frank Reynolds!* I'll be darned . . . *You have some gall, buster.* Ah, now it's all falling into place . . . The Stetson . . . The guys' pool night . . . You two-timing bastard. So what's happened to Jill and Teana? Have they given you the ass already?"

Terry, gimme a brea—

"Terry, who is this guy?" Brent was in total confusion.

"Someone I don't want to know . . . Frank, go crawl up your own ass, and don't cause any trouble. *Cappice?*"

"Terry, what the . . . ?"

"*Brent,* I'll explain it to you later. Just stay out of it and let *me* handle this."

"Terry." Frank wasn't going to go easily. Jealousy has no boundaries, and he roughly grabbed Terry by the shoulder.

That was the flashpoint, and all hell was let loose, with Brent grabbing Frank by the shirt collar and giving him one mighty shove, sending Frank staggering backward, almost losing his balance.

"Why you jumped-up faggot." Frank was ready to square off, his fists raised like a prize fighter.

"Frank, if you don't fuck off, I'll call Mr. Muscles." Terry motioned with her head toward the door. "Now what's it gonna be?" Terry held Brent back.

"I told you already, Brent, stay out of it. *I can handle this.*"

As for Frank . . . Well . . . He could only see red and was coming on heavy.

"Listen, Frank." Terry stepped between them like a referee about to shout "*Break.*" Her anger suddenly changed from aggression to peacemaking. "Don't do anything silly . . . Calm down, darling, all is forgiven." Terry opened her arms to give Frank a hug.

"That's more like it. Eat your heart out, dude." Frank felt like a returned vet.

But Terry had that cunning look on her face as if she had something up her sleeve, and she wrapped her arms around Frank's neck affectionately, pulling him closer and closer. Then in a flash and out of the blue, she lifted her right knee and drove it hard into Frank's groin. His pain could even be heard above the music as he grasped with both hands his screaming testicles while yelling in excruciating pain, desperately trying to stop his nuts from lodging in his throat as he fell flat on his face onto the wooden dance floor.

He was now moaning and writhing in pain, finally rolling over onto his side in the foetal position with his knees up to his chin.

"Mike Tyson" had spotted the commotion and was barging his sway through the crowded dance floor.

"What's going on here, lady?" He looked down at the crumpled heap.

Terry poured on the innocent face.

"For the life of me, I haven't a clue. I just heard this scream and looked down and there was this dude lying on the floor writhing in pain. Maybe he's having a heart attack or something . . . Or maybe he just fell over having drank too many shooters . . . Brent, I think it's time we made a move."

The bouncer was already on his knees trying to bring poor Frank around in the process, not paying attention to Brent and Terry's "stealth" exit.

"Are you all right, buddy? Can you hear me?"

"Terry, something tells me that we had better vamoose." Brent half smiled but still in disillusionment. After what he just experienced, there was no way he was going to disagree with "Terry Lee."

Terry grabbed Brent's hand pulling him toward the door. The quicker they got the hell of here, the better.

As they hit the sidewalk and breathed the fresh air, Brent stopped Terry in her tracks and spun her around to look into her eyes.

"*Terry,* where the hell have you been all my life?" And before she could utter a word, he smashed her moist lips with a long, passionate kiss.

"*Wow,* what brought that on?" Terry gasped.

"I've been wanting to do that since I first laid eyes on you."

Terry stood on her tiptoes and gave Brent a gentle peck on the lips.

"That's so sweet, darling, but the night is young, and I suggest we go to a little joint I know. It's only a couple of blocks from here, the Rendezvous. It has a cosy atmosphere and, dare I say, romantic ambience, and the guy on the ivories is Elton John in disguise and the cocktails . . . *to die for.* So, what do you say, big guy?"

"I'm scared to say no." Brent burst into laughter.

"Don't fool around, Brent, that moron had it coming, and the last thing I wanted was for you to get involved. And just to ease your mind." Terry grinned. "I recently took self-defences classes and just couldn't resist the opportunity."

Brent had to smile. This babe was an unknown quantity, but she had something special.

"Shall we walk?" Brent asked. "Normally I wouldn't, but I feel pretty safe with you on my arm." Brent gave a cheeky grin.

"*Get out of it!* Aren't you gonna give a lady a ride in that flashy open topped Porsche of yours?"

* * *

"Terry, this is a really cool place. It's funny I never noticed it before, but I'll be back again for sure if the present company allows."

"I'm glad you like it Brent, but as they say, let's take it one step at a time, huh?"

Brent raised his hand to attract the waiter, having noticed Terry's empty shooter glass.

"No, Brent." Terry covered it with her hand. "It's late, and I have a busy day at the office tomorrow. Besides, have you noticed the time?"

"*That time already!* Where has the night gone, it's nearly twelve thirty! But you are right, Terry, to remind me. Listen, tomorrow is Friday and one of the hottest nights of the week, and I really would love to do this again . . . Of course, minus the 'kickboxing.'" Brent smiled, staring into Terry's eyes for some positive reaction.

"Terry has anyone ever told you that you have such beautiful eyes?"

"Yes."

"*Really?*" Bret was taken aback.

"*You have* on at least three occasions tonight!"

Brent burst into laughter. "You had me there for a moment."

Terry returned the intimate eye contact with her "teaser" smile.

"Now if where I think you're coming from is to ask me out another date . . . Give me call at the office, and tonight I'll . . ." "I know, *you'll sleep on it.*"

Terry had to laugh. This guy was smart and humorous with it.

"You're getting to know me better already." Terry affectionately squeezed his hand.

"I like that," Bret replied, still staring into Terry's eyes as he moved closer and closer to her lips.

"*Brent.*" Terry held him back. "Let's not get hot and heavy. I'm not a girl who throws herself at someone on a blind date."

"*Eh, hmmm.*" Bret gave as sort of embarrassing cough, then cut it. "I apologize, Terry."

"Apology accepted." Terry lifted her handbag to make a move. "It's about time . . ."

The pianist drew her attention before she could finish.

"And now for the next request . . ." He had trouble reading in the soft lighting the handwritten slip of paper. "Eh . . . It's from a Terry Johnson . . . 'Candle in the Wind.'"

Terry's face lit up. She had almost given up hope, and she clapped her hands loudly in applause.

"Thank you." The black pianist who could have been mistaken for the late Nat King Cole gave Terry a warm smile as he began to play Elton John's masterpiece.

"I just love this song, but it makes me feel so sad when I think of Princess Diana . . ."

"And it seemed to me you lived your life like a candle in the wind never knowing who to cling to when the rain sets in . . ."

"Terry . . . Do I see a tear?"

*   *   *

"Brent, I've really enjoyed your company, and I too must apologize for that ugly scene at the Stetson."

Terry had just opened the door of her car and was standing on the sidewalk.

"You know, you never really explained . . ."

"Brent don't spoil this enjoyable evening. I told you, that's for another time."

"So *you will* see me tomorrow?"

Terry gave him that look of half annoyance and half laughter.

"Okay . . . Okay. I'll call . . ." Brent knew when not to push the envelope. "Bye. Drive carefully . . ." He waited patiently, the perfect gentleman, until Terry's car was out of sight.

Brent unlocked the Porsche, a smile still crossing his face. "I really would *love* to see her again . . . C'est la vie." He shrugged.

*   *   *

The school bus stopped at the door.

"See you, Steve. How about catching up for bowling night tomorrow? Bring your sis along."

"I'll think about it, Benny."

"Bye, Sheryl . . ."

"That creep . . . He's always hitting on any female that he fancies. Who does he think he is . . . *God's answer to women?"* Sheryl muttered under her breath as she gladly stepped from the bus.

"Give over, Sheryl! Benny's not that bad. Besides, I think he has a crush on you."

"Oh, do you now! Can we talk about something else, *please?"*

"Mother's car isn't here . . . *Of course!* She's a working woman now, so I guess we had better get used to her being late." Steven slipped the key into the lock.

The house seemed different without their mother, who was always there to greet them.

"It's strange without Mom." Steven dropped his overladen school backpack to the floor.

"I guess we had better get used to it," Sheryl commented as she began to climb the stairs. "I've got some heavy stuff to prep for Monday, so I'm going straight to my room."

"Okay, sis, I'll call you when Mom arrives. I want to watch the box for a while to see if there is any more depressing news about Father." "I don't want to know . . . See ya." Sheryl disappeared.

Steven pressed the remote. The five o'clock CNN news bulletin would adorn the screen in a couple of minutes.

Steven heard the front door open, then close.

'That must be mother now, I was hoping she would arrive after the news.'

Steven was sure that tonight's CNN bulletin would cover his father's return to New York, and the last thing he wanted was more grief for his mother. No news is sometimes an antidote for depression.

"Steven . . . Sheryl . . . I'm home." June hung her coat on the stand.

"Hi, Mother, you're late tonight. I guess it's part of the new job, huh?" Steven rose from the sofa and greeted his mother with his usual welcome kiss on the cheek.

June kicked off her heels and flopped down onto the lounge chair.

"Boy, does that feels good. Where's your sister?"

"She had some prep to complete for school on Monday, and she's gone straight to her room . . ."

The timing of the newscaster's voice couldn't have come at a worse moment.

*   *   *

"WELCOME TO CNN, BRINGING YOU THE LATEST IN WORLD NEWS WITH YOUR HOST, HELEN FROST."

"GOOD EVENING . . . MY NAME IS HELEN FROST . . . LET'S START WITH THE LATEST NEWS AT HOME.

"TODAY OUR CNN REPORTER TREVOR SMITH FINALLY GOT A BREAK ON THE MICHAEL SUMMERS CASE . . . AND HERE IS

TREVOR REPORTING LIVE FROM THE PEARL STREET POLICE HEADQUARTERS IN LOWER MANHATTAN. CAPTAIN TED BAKER HAS GRACIOUSLY AGREED TO GIVE A STATEMENT AND WILL BE WITH US IN JUST A FEW MINUTES . . ."

"CAPTAIN . . . TREVOR SMITH FROM CNN . . . FIRST OF ALL, CNN WISHES TO THANK YOU FOR TAKING TIME OUT FROM YOUR BUSY SCHEDULE TO UPDATE THE PUBLIC WITH THE LATEST ON THE MIKE SUMMERS CASE.

"CAPTAIN BAKER, THE QUESTION ON EVERYONE'S LIPS IS WHEN WILL SUMMERS BE RETURNED TO THE UNITED STATES TO FACE CRIMINAL CHARGES, AND WHY IS HE UNDER ARREST IN BRAZIL WHEN HE WAS APPREHENDED IN ARGENTINA?"

AS I STATED BEFORE . . . AND I QUOTE: 'AS THE RESULT OF LOCAL POLICE COMPLICATIONS AND DEPORTATION IMMIGRATION LAWS, SUMMERS WAS CONSEQUENTLY FLOWN TO BRAZIL,' UNQUOTE.

"CAN YOU EXPAND ON THAT, CAPTAIN?"

"NO FURTHER STATEMENT . . . BUT TO ANSWER YOUR FIRST POINT . . . SUMMERS WILL BE RETURNED TO THE UNITED STATES WITHIN THE NEXT TWENTY-FOUR HOURS."

"CAPTAIN, WHY THE DELAY?"

"NO FURTHER COMMENT."

"WITH RESPECT, CAPTAIN, RECOLLECTING YOUR FIRST STATEMENT, AND I QUOTE . . . 'FOREIGN POLICE OPERATIONS REQUESTED BY THE UNITED STATES, EVEN WITH THE AGREEMENT OF LOCAL GOVERNMENTS, IS FRAUGHT WITH DANGER, AND IT GIVES ME THE DEEPEST REGRET TO INFORM YOU THAT ONE OF OUR BRAVE OFFICERS LOST HIS LIFE IN THE PERFORMANCE OF HIS DUTY . . .' THEN CAN YOU EXPAND ON THAT?

"YES . . . AS THE NEXT OF KIN HAS BEEN NOTIFIED . . . THE OFFICER IS DETECTIVE LIEUTENANT ANTHONY PERRINO, A VETERAN POLICE OFFICER WITH TWO COMMENDATIONS FOR BRAVERY AND OVER TWENTY YEARS SERVICE WITH THE NYPD. FOR BRAVERY ABOVE AND BEYOND THE CALL OF DUTY, HE WILL BE AWARDED POSTHUMOUSLY THE HIGHEST RECOGNITION FOR HIS SACRIFICE—THE POLICE MEDAL FOR VALOR. HIS BODY IS BEING RETURNED TO THE UNITED STATES TOMORROW FOR AUTOPSY TO CONFIRM THE CAUSE OF DEATH, AND AN ANNOUNCEMENT

WILL BE MADE AS TO THE DATE OF THE FUNERAL UPON FINAL CONSULTATION WITH THE FAMILY . . . LIEUTENANT PERRINO WILL BE BURIED WITH FULL MILITARY HONORS."

"CAPTAIN, ON ANOTHER POINT, CAN YOU—"

"I HAVE ANOTHER PRESSING APPOINTMENT . . . THIS INTERVIEW IS OVER. THANK YOU . . ."

"HELEN, AT LEAST WE ARE ONE STAGE FURTHER ON THE SUMMERS DRAMA, AND ON BEHALF OF ALL AT CNN, WE WISH TO CONVEY OUR DEEPEST CONDOLENCES TO THE FAMILY OF THE BRAVE OFFICER . . ."

"WELL, WE'LL LEAVE TREVOR FOR THE MOMENT AS MORE GROUNDBREAKING NEWS HAS JUST COME TO MY ATTENTION . . ."

June sat for moment in abstract silence, Baker's words now in the distance, her thoughts with the Perino family and Tony's two sons, Mauro and Samuel, the youngest, who just adored his father. If only she could change the world or just turn back the clock, but it was not to be, and June gave a monumental sigh, a tear trickling down her cheek.

"Mother, don't get upset, *he's not worth it.*"

"I know, Steven, how you must feel, but I married your father over twenty years ago, and the good times will always remain in my memory. Like when you and your sister were born and our trip to Coney Island and . . ." June burst into full flow.

Steven rose from the sofa and sat on the arm of the lounge chair, placing his arms around his mother's shoulders.

"*There . . . There . . .* Mother, don't let it get to you. Listen, can I get you something?"

June fondly held Steven's hand; he was a great comfort.

"I feel like a glass of white wine, but it's too early in the day, and I don't want to turn to alcohol for comfort. It would be so easy to stare down the bottom of an empty bourbon bottle. No, Steven . . . I'll settle for the sensible choice, a black coffee."

"Mother, just you sit there and place your feet up while I go to the kitchen . . ."

* * *

"*Hmmm* . . . I feel better already." June commented as she finished the last of the short black.

"Changing the subject, Mother. How does it feel to be back in the workforce?" The question was a crafty diversion.

"It's strange." June thought for a moment. "From a housewife to a working mother and breadwinner . . . *Well* . . . It's hard to explain, but the office staff gave me a warm welcome, but then again, it's early days, and excuse my French, but the shit hasn't hit the fan as yet. But you know, son." She pondered again. "What I'm really looking forward to is returning to study for my law degree.

Phil has given me a new lease of life, and I can't thank him enough."

"I really like him, Mother. I know I'm treading on thin ice and shouldn't ask . . ."

"*Then don't!*" June knew what was coming, and it was far too early to pour her heart.

"I hope you don't mind, son, but I invited Phil to join us tonight. He may be a successful lawyer, but he's also a lonely man, and being Friday, who wants to stay at home and watch the box?"

Steven just smiled. It was a plausible reason but a poor excuse.

"Do and your sister have anything planned for this evening?" June casually asked, and Steven got the message.

"Benny asked me and sis to go bowling with the gang on Saturday, but I feel like going tonight. I'll give him a call later. Mother, I think I'll go upstairs and relax in my room . . . *Oh,* are you cooking tonight?"

"I feel a bit lazy, so I might just rustle some sandwiches and salad. There's cold turkey breast in the icebox."

"Anything, Mother. I know sis will be happy. She's back on her never-ending diet."

"*Steven* don't be so nasty to your sister! You know how sensitive she is about her weight. I'll give you and your sister a call when dinner is ready."

"What time is Phil coming?"

"I forgot to tell him, but I guess it will before seven . . ."

*   *   *

June had just spun the lettuce when the doorbell rang.

"That must be Phil now." She rushed to the hallway mirror and fluffed up her hair, then touched up her eyes to camouflage the weep damage. "Hmmm." She stood back. "That looks a lot better . . . *Coming* . . ." Phil was standing on the porch. "Apologies, darling, I was just finish . . . *Roses!* What a lovely surprise. I can't remember the last time I received red roses." June's face was beaming.

"Don't I deserve a kiss?"

June pushed Phil back onto the porch out of sight, pulling the door closed with her other hand.

"Let me show you." She threw her arms around his neck and pressed her lips hard against his. The saliva flowing as they explored their inner oral cavities in a sex-starved display of love, and Phil feverishly drew her closer, crushing her abdomen against his instant erection as he squeezed her tight buttocks in each of his hands.

"*June . . . June.*" Phil gasped.

"Save it for later, darling. Neighbours have eyes." June pulled him by the lapel of his jacket.

"Honey haven't you noticed?"

"*Noticed?*"

"On the driveway."

June turned. "*Wow . . .* It's a beauty!" June exploded, admiring the shiny black Porsche convertible.

"Are you sure you want to trust Steven with a two-hundred-thousand-dollar car?"

"He's a sensible kid, and besides I don't have any children, let alone a son, and it makes me feel good."

June stood on her toes and gave Phil another brief kiss.

*   *   *

"Mr. Stevens, *are you really serious?*"

"As serious as I can ever be. Relax, go for a drive, take in a movie, or whatever. It's yours for the evening."

"Sis, are you gonna join me? I can call Bernie, and we could move the bowling night forward to tonight. Come on, sis, what do you say?" Sheryl made an ugly gesture, screwing up her face.

"*That Bernie . . .* I don't know. He's a real creep."

"Aw come on, sis, I'm not going without you." Steven was laying it on.

"I suppose you're gonna ask Michelle to join us?"

"Michelle . . . Who's this Michelle.?" June was intrigued.

"A student Steven had a crush o—"

"Sis . . . *Give it a miss . . .* Mother doesn't want to know. Now are you gonna join us or what?"

"Oh, well then." Sheryl gave a "drama queen" sigh. "Only because I'll look good sitting in a Porsche convertible with the top down."

Her comment brought the house down, much to her annoyance.

"Sheryl, you crack me up," Steven commented, still laughing as he left the table. "I gotta make some calls . . ."

*   *   *

"June, do me favor."

"If I can." June was puzzled.

Phil produced his wallet and flaked out three big ones.

"Give this to the kids. I know when I was student, I didn't have a dollar to my name and if *I* give it to them personally, they will be embarrassed, and I don't want them to think I'm buying their friendship."

"Darling, that's so nice of you. *I promise*, I'll make it up to you later."

Phil laughed. "Well, if that's the case, I should have made it five."

"Why, *Phil Stevens*, I said it before, and I'll say it again . . . *You're incorrigible!*"

*   *   *

"Bye, kids." June and Phil waved as Steven reversed the Porsche down the driveway, hood down.

"Well, how did go?" Phil asked.

"Steven was sceptical about receiving the cash, but I eventually convinced him it was from me. Now give me a kiss, lover boy. Remember, we have the rest of the night to ourselves . . ."

PART 8

Jihad Islamophobia

CHAPTER 1

"Gather round people, the coffee break is over." The commissioner was anxiously checking his timepiece.

"Synchronize your watches . . . It's exactly . . ."

There was a loud knock on the conference room door.

"Digit," Ricardo barked in his native tongue, annoyed at the sudden diversion.

A smartly dressed young policewoman entered, carrying a neat bundle of clothes and footwear.

"Comisserio a roupa voce requesred."

"Obrigado, Corporal." Rodrigo pointed to the table. The corporal unloaded and gave a warm smile before leaving.

"Your Muslim attire gentlemen . . ." The commissioner turned to the neatly stacked bundle. "One size fits all.

There was a burst of laughter at the commissioner's comment, but the tension in the room was clearly visible.

"Your ordnance and shoulder holsters are on the other table." Rodrigo checked his watch again.

"I need you dressed and back here in fifteen minutes . . . *Oh*, before you go, the thawbs have a long slit on the right side instead of the normal deep pocket. This modification will provide easy and fast access to your firearms . . . Capitano, I'll leave it to you to decide which of your men will conceal the rope ladder and the necessary precautions to overcome the broken glass on top of the embassy perimeter wall."

"Sim, Comisario . . . Erico . . . Flavio," the commandos acknowledged and picked up their Muslim attire and equipment.

"*Captain*, English please," Rodrigo ordered.

"My apologies, Commissioner," Benito replied. "It's just . . ."

"*Fifteen minutes then!*" Ricardo purposely ignored his excuse. "Sergeant Hayden, not you . . . Grab a seat." The conference room door was open.

"Louisa, o Americano precisa alguns voce ar drak compeom a aperencia de um homen de Portuguese," Ricardo called to his secretary.

* * *

Louisa gave Bill the "hot smile" treatment. She was certainly a head turner, trim and pretty, at around five six. Her stiletto heels emphasized her shapely legs and firm thighs, and she was not doing too bad either in the upper quartile, her firm breasts protesting in her two-sizes-too-small bra. Most probably in her mid-thirties, her complexion was standing the test of time, the dreaded eye bags still in their infancy. Her tightly curled shoulder-length black hair, dark-brown eyes, and the chestnut complexion with that smile to bowl you over . . . So who cares about her secretarial skills with a package like that? As for that tight-fitting light-purple dress? She must have shoehorned herself into that baby!

* * *

"Sim, Comisario." Louisa turned it on, motioning Bill to follow her next door.

Bill couldn't keep his eyes off the rear of the Latina beauty and clumsily stumbled over one of the chairs with his size tens.

"Don't look so worried, Detective, Louisa isn't gonna bite you. I only asked her to give your white complexion a makeover to look more like a local."

Bill kind of smiled, still embarrassed knowing full well that the delectable Louisa's hourglass figure had blown his concentration, but Bill always had an eye for the ladies.

"*Detective?*"

"*Eh,* Commissioner?"

"Your change of clothes . . . *Remember?*" Rodrigo was laughing.

Bill quickly grabbed the remaining bundle, a bloom on his face.

Ricardo flashed an oversize grin.

"Don't be embarrassed, Sergeant, you're not the first one to admire my secretary . . ."

* * *

On time, the commandos and Hayden returned to the conference room, Bill sporting his instant tan.

"Stand in the line," Rodrigo ordered. "Let's take a look at how good your disguises are. We cannot afford to overlook the slightest detail that may blow your cover."

The "valiant five" certainly looked the part in their long white thawbs and the white embroidered kufis with their yellow insignia patches, their Roman sandals the creme de la creme.

"Excellent . . ." Benito, the officer in charge, was following closely behind the commissioner.

The commissioner laughed. "Erico, pull that cushion below your thawb tighter, you look like a pregnant woman, or should I say man?"

"*Yes, Captain!*"

"*Then do it now!*" Benito barked.

The commissioner suddenly stopped his inspection and eyeballed Hayden. "As-salamu Alaikum."

Bill shrugged. "What the hell does that mean, Commissioner?"

"It's an Arabic greeting. I suggest you try and remember it. It might save your life."

"*Stanley . . .*" Rodrigo turned to his brother-in-law. "What's your opinion?"

"For the life of me, I can't tell the difference . . . *Nice job!*"

"It's . . ." Rodrigo paused, checking the time once again. "Nearly five and the protest starts around six. So, we had better make tracks, as the traffic at this time in the evening is unpredictable. *One more thing* . . . This is not a 'butter knife' operation, and there will be casualties." Rodrigo made the sign of the cross.

"*God be with you . . .*"

CHAPTER 2

Humid New York summer nights were now on the decline, the trees already dropping their leaves, and Terry gave a slight shiver as she locked the Mazda. Her thin white T-shirt was doing nothing to keep her warm.

"I hate these car parks. At this time of night, they're so fucking scary." Terry was speaking aloud as she briskly walked to the elevator.

"So where's the fucking security? I don't know what I'm paying for . . . *Body corporate, my ass!*"

As Terry stood nervously looking at the illuminated floor numbers, she gave an impatient sigh.

"Floor 21 . . . *Just my fucking luck!*"

"Out late tonight, Terry?" a man's voice startled her.

"*Nick!* You scared the living daylights out of me. You buffoon, sneaking up on me like that."

"I'm here for you, Terry, anytime." Donnelly was pouring it on, but then he had a thing for Terry.

"So *you are* glad to see me then, huh?"

"*Ha-ha*," Terry laughed. "Don't flatter yourself, Nick . . . *I'm just bloody scared.* You can never tell with all these crazies on the loose."

The elevator chimed and the doors opened and, for Terry, not too soon.

"Boyfriend trouble tonight, Terry?" Nick never learned.

"*Nick . . .*" Terry turned and gave him an eyeful. "Did anyone ever tell you that you are a nosy son of a bitch?"

The doors closed, and Terry pressed 10. She would only have to suffer Donnelly for another eight floors, *thank God*!

Nick just laughed it off; he was used to Terry's verbal abuse, and tonight was no exception.

"How's that friend of yours, Terry . . . *Eh . . . Err . . .* Laura, isn't it?" Nick knew when to fold 'em.

"She'll be home this weekend."

"*Say*, that's really something after what she has been through. I'm glad for her."

The elevator chimed.

"*Oops . . .* This is my floor, Terry."

Terry gave Nick that look. "I'll try and remember."

"Good night, Terry." Nick gave a dejected smile as he left.

Terry didn't answer. She had plenty on her plate for the moment.

* * *

"*At last!*" She stepped into the carpeted hallway, glad to be home, but as Terry slipped the key into 10A, she could clearly hear the loud ring of the phone.

"*Christ!* Who the hell can this be now? *Come on . . . Come on . . .*" Terry was struggling to turn the key. "*At last!*" She switched on the lights and kicked off her sneakers and rushed to the phone.

"Terry Johnson here."

"*Terry*, I hope I haven't caught you at a bad time. It's Laura."

"*Laura!* Listen . . . Now what did the doctor advise you about speaking too much?"

"I know, Terry, don't scold me. I just couldn't sleep, and besides, I'm dying to hear about your blind date . . . Are you free to talk?" "*Of course I'm free to talk!* I left 'Mr. Wonderful' at his car." Terry could hear Laura laugh.

"Mr. Wonderful, huh?"

"At least that's what he thinks he is!" Terry was now also laughing.

"So, what's 'Mr. Mystery' like?" Laura was dying to get the lowdown.

"Just a sec while I hit the sofa . . . Now where was I? Eh . . . Tall, at around six one, thick black hair that . . ."

"*Wow!* He sounds like a real catch and well healed with it."

"But, Laura, you'll never guess what happened . . ."

Laura couldn't stop laughing at Terry's colorful account of her altercation with Frank, her ex.

"And you say he's still searching for his nuts? Terry, you are one helluva lady. I can't imagine what your date thought. What's his name again?"

"Brent . . . Brent Kennedy."

"Brent . . . When you left Frank speaking like a soprano."

Laura's laughter was contagious, and now Terry couldn't help herself.

"Listen, honey, I gotta go." Laura could hear Terry give a big yawn.

"I'll love you and leave you. I know you have another hectic day ahead of you tomorrow . . . *Good luck* . . ."

"Thanks, Laura . . . I'm certainly gonna need it!"

CHAPTER 3

Bill had to admit that, for once in his life, he felt the dreaded butterflies and the adrenaline kick. This was different from any sting he had ever experienced during his twenty years of service in the NYPD. Now in a foreign country with no jurisdiction and no guarantees that he would see his family again or return to his beloved United States was even more frightening, and he placed his hand nervously inside his thawb for one final check on the holstered Glock, locked and loaded, complete with silencer.

Bill grinned and gave a "thank God" sigh as he momentarily fondled his "best friend."

* * *

"Are you with us, Detective?" Benito asked as the Muslim impersonators walked to the black police Range Rover. He had noticed Hayden's distant look and distinct lack of concentration . . . *Weak links in the chain spell disaster!*

"Don't worry, Captain, I'll be there when the call arises."

Benito turned to the wheel man as they settled into their seats. "All present and accounted for . . . You know the drill?"

"Yes, Capitan, I'll be waiting. Don't worry." He pointed to the AR10/44 carbine automatic assault rifle securely clipped above the driver's door. "I know how to use this baby."

"Then let's party . . ."

As dusk was falling, the police four-wheel drive was given a wide berth as it sped through the evening traffic. The oncoming darkness would provide the commandos with the perfect cover, and as they neared Ave Paulista in the Sobreloja district, famous for foreign embassies, they could distinctly hear the chants in the distance. *"Jihad . . . Jihad . . . Death to the Argentine infidels."*

"Sounds like quite a party," Bill commented as the driver pulled over parking under a clump of heavy foliaged trees.

The captain was first to hit the street.

"Now pay attention . . . The Avenue Paulista, where the embassy is, is located about a five-hundred-meter walk from here. *So let's move it, we don't have time to spare!* Stick together, and start chanting at the top of your lungs as we mix with the crazies . . ."

* * *

The embassy building looked a formidable fortress with its four-meter glass-topped security wall, its large ornamental access and egress electric gates to the 180-degree driveway, each gate manned by two heavily armed security guards. The two-floor mansion was a mixed orange-pink colour with grilled arched windows and a huge gothic-type entrance, the architecture and facade having a distinct Portuguese influence, most likely constructed around the turn of the twentieth century.

* * *

The street protest was immense, bodies pressing like a human shield toward the security gates. A breakaway group chanting *"Down with Argentina"* were stomping on a burning flag . . . Screaming women in their black abaya full-body coverings, their eyes glistening through the "bunker" slots from the bright parameter lights, drumming their chests with their hands, fanatically shouting like fans at an Argentine soccer match. *"Jihad . . . Jihad . . . Jihad . . . Down . . ."*

"*What the fuck?*" Bill was shocked at this crazy scene, almost on the verge of lunacy. "*These people are fanatics.*"

"They may be fanatics, Bill," Benito replied. "But their beliefs are dangerous. They believe they are rightfully waging a holy war on behalf of Islam as their religious duty . . . Enough of that shit, let it loose . . . *Jihad . . . Jihad . . . Jihad . . .*" Benito was into it. "*For fuck's sakes, look as if you mean it, guys . . . Jihad . . . Jihad . . .*"

Suddenly the captain turned, yelling above the screaming chants and signalling to the crew.

"Keep to the outer circle of the demonstrators . . . Remember, we have to get to that parameter wall unobserved. *Jihad . . . Jihad . . .*"

The police's thin blue line with their riot shields and helmeted face masks was showing the strain under the sheer mass of people, and it was obvious their ranks would be breached any moment.

A Molotov cocktail suddenly came from nowhere, scattering the crowd as it burst into flames at the feet of the traumatized riot police. That was the last straw, and the officer in charge gave the order the commandos were waiting for.

"Abir foga com gas lacrimoginio e balas de borrocga." *Open fire with tear gas and rubber bullets.*

No sooner had the command been given than the thunder of riot guns discharging rubber bullets and tear gas almost burst the eardrums of the team.

As the mob scattered in panic, it was the perfect opportunity, and Benito raised his hand and signalled, pointing to the parameter wall now only a hundred meters to the right and out of sight of the religious riot.

"*Go . . . Go . . . Go!*" Benito screamed. He didn't need a second call as the commandos hit the wall in force.

Erico, Flavio, and Mateus acknowledged, tapping Bill on the shoulder and pointing to Benito, who was thrashing his way through the homogeneous mass.

"*The wall . . . The wall!*" Benito screamed again at the top of his voice to overcome the sound of gunfire.

CHAPTER 4

June breathed a sigh of relief as she stood on the porch holding Phil's hand as they watched the Porsche disappear from sight.

"Now aren't you going to give me another kiss?"

"Of course, honey, but shouldn't we step inside? Remember the eyes and ears of the neighbours?"

"*Nope,* I want it now!" June demanded, closing her eyes and standing on her toes, her arms now around Phil's neck. "Well, I'm waiting . . ." June was trying to keep her eyes closed without smiling.

Phil didn't disappoint her. His lips gently touching hers for a moment, then like a thunder burst, he pulled her closer their lips, now apart in an oral orgasm, the moistness and ecstasy of this special intimacy mind blowing.

As their bodies separated, June stared into Phil's eyes. She was at a loss how to express herself, and she did the only thing that came to her and stood on her toes and gave Phil a gentle kiss on the lips while grabbing his hand.

"I think we have given the neighbours enough for one night."

Phil smiled as he was meekly lead into the house. As for what was next . . . The mind boggles.

*   *   *

"Phil, go relax in the lounge. We have the place to ourselves tonight. Remove your jacket and tie, and don't look so stuffy . . . *You lawyers!*" June shook her head. "*Now* can I fetch you a drink?"

"Not before you give me another kiss," Phil teased.

"Oh no you don't, mister . . . I *know* you! One kiss leads to another and then . . . ?"

"Spoilsport . . . A glass of wine, honey, is fine."

"I'll be with you in a jiffy . . . But first . . ." June went to the audio centre and placed a disc into the player. The melody of the late Nat King Cole's "Unforgettable" duet with his daughter gently flowing throughout the room.

"I just love that song, don't you, Phil?"

"If nothing else, it's so appropriate when I look at you."

"*Oh no you don't, I'm not falling for that line* . . . The lounge!" June pointed.

*   *   *

Phil was relaxing on the sofa, enjoying a drop from the Napa Valley, the music enveloping the atmosphere of being together at last.

June had thrown her legs up onto the sofa, resting her head on Phil's lap as she enjoyed her favourite vocalist.

"Isn't this relaxing, darling?"

"It certainly is," Phil replied, taking another sip of the wine, but he couldn't keep his eyes off June's low-cut blouse and the bulge of her more than-generous breasts. His mind conjured the picture of the real thing and the opportunity to bury his face between that soft pink flesh.

June suddenly threw her feet to the floor; she could feel the bulge in the back of her neck, and sex on the sofa was not her forte. If you're going to be intimate, you do it in comfort.

June grabbed Phil's hand. "Shall we dance?"

CHAPTER 5

Flavio dropped the rope ladder at his feet; he knew the drill and threw the grappling hook over the top of wall, then gave a firm tug to make sure it was secure before signalling to his comrades.

Erico opened the slit on his thawb and, after some persuasion, pulled out a thick felt pad the size of a cushion and immediately scaled the rope rungs and placed the protective shield over the jagged glass, and then gave the "all clear" before disappearing over the wall, landing in the soft plant bed of the embassy's tropical garden.

Benito motioned frantically for the rest to follow, but it was too late. They had been spotted.

"*Go . . . Go . . . Go!*" Benito screamed as each of his men scrambled over the wall.

But as the captain bade his turn, two Muslim men suddenly grabbed him in a bear hug, forcibly trying to restrain him.

It most likely was a misunderstanding, or was it that they too also wanted to find a way to open the gates? And what better way than to scale the wall in commando fashion.

Benito was now in deep trouble, but dressed in his Muslim attire, it was highly unlikely he would be suspected as an impostor. Somehow he had to convince them he was one of the brothers fighting for the same cause, and the only thing that came to his mind was to communicate in Arabic.

"As-salamu alaycum," he struggled, trying to offer his hand.

The Muslim men seemed shocked and immediately backed off, releasing him.

"Walaikum salaam," the tall one answered.

Benito quickly slipped his hand into the loose-fitting thawb and produced the Glock. The men immediately leaped back, fearing for their safety, but

Benito put his fingers to his lips to signal to keep quiet, then in sign language he motioned not to worry; once he climbed the wall, he would open the gate.

His assailants got the message, believing that Benito and his men were prophets of Allah.

"May Allah be with you and reward you," the tall man spoke in Arabic.

The taller of two shook the captain's hand, then touched his heart, the Muslim gesture of respect, before turning to the others who had now gathered, sensing some conflict.

(Speaking in Arabic)

"Mohammad . . . Azri . . . Zabba, back off he is one of us. Can't you see from his kufi that he has completed the holy pilgrimage to Mecca and the Haj? He is risking his life in the name of Allah to open the gates. Get back to your posts, we have work to do."

As for Benito? He didn't waste any time and disappeared over the wall before his newly made friends could finish their gesture of thanks. Once on the other side, Benito made haste to retrieve the rope ladder using the long rope attached to the grappling hooks, giving it a severe jerk to release it. They just might need that ladder again, and besides it wasn't "open sesame" for the Muslims to use and create organized havoc. Too many cooks . . .

"*Keep down . . . Keep down,*" Benito whispered. "Erico, you take the guards on the gate . . . Hayden, you stay with me."

* * *

Erico crawled through the thick foliage in the shadow of the house. The guards were oblivious to their surroundings, their own safety under threat as the large gates swayed back and forth, pushing the wrought iron to its limits. So much so, the guards were using the butts of their AK-47s to smash the fingers of the thugs who had broken through the police cordon.

(Speaking in Spanish)

"Berto, are you all right?"

"I'm okay, Arran, but I'm scared what will happen if these gates give way."

"You bastardo," Arran interrupted as he smashed the butt of his AK47 on the knuckles of a hand that was grasping and tugging menacingly on his uniform. There was a loud, ear-piercing scream as the faceless hand disappeared, leaving a trail of blood on the steel work.

Erico took aim; the Glock kicked twice. *Splat . . . Splat.* The silencer muffled the noise of the gunshots. Berto the guard clasped his neck, unable to speak as the forty-fives tore a gaping hole in his larynx, and for a fleeting moment, he stood in a motionless trance, his eyes reflecting disbelief as he desperately clutched his neck to stem the wound, the warm blood oozing between his fingers. Then like a pillar of salt, he crumpled to the ground, dropping his firearm with a pronounced clatter, his body jerking in spasms for a few more seconds before rigor mortis.

Arran, his compadre, turned at hearing the noise, his eyes scanning the garden, searching for possible intruders. Then as an afterthought, he wondered, *Berto, where is he?*

The sight of Berto's motionless body soaked in blood, lying at his feet, was enough to scare the shit out of anyone, and Arran turned an ashen gray, and in sheer panic, not knowing where the shots had come from, he recklessly discharged a burst of automatic fire from his Russian carbine, the bullets thudding aimlessly into the wall of the embassy, sending concrete chips soaring into the air in a cloud of white dust. They say you never hear the shot that kills you, and his crumpled motionless body now lying on the driveway was a testament to that, blood spurting from his chest cavity like the Trevi Fountain as his heart pumped aimlessly through its ruptured walls.

Erico rose from his cover and waved the "all clear." It was time to open the gates . . .

CHAPTER 6

"Phil, I want this night to be special." June stopped the "bear hug" foxtrot. "I'm going up to my room now, and I want you to relax over another glass of wine until I call you. I promise you that I won't be long . . . *And not too much wine!* You know what they say about alcohol affecting libido?" "I can guess, but, honey, you don't have to worry about me." June just had to take a parting shot.

"Famous last words . . . Be patient, I'll call you." She gave a tormenting smile before turning and disappearing up the stairs.

It was now a waiting game, and Phil's imaginative mind was playing havoc, metamorphosis setting in. (The profound change from one stage to the next in the life history of an orgasm.)

As Phil sipped his wine, his mind reflected back to when he first met June as a freshman at NYU. She was stunning, but as an up-and-coming quarterback, female temptation was too much, and his cot was always full. *I mean can you blame a guy?*

"*Phil* . . . I'm ready."

"*Eh . . . Err . . .* Coming, honey . . ."

"It's the last door on the left in the hallway," June called again before closing her door; she was going to keep him guessing to the last moment . . .

*   *   *

June, had showered, dried her hair, and applied her makeup, and it wouldn't be the same without the tantalizing man killer Chanel No. 1. She was determined to go the whole nine yards as she slipped into the scantiest of see-through blue lace Gs with matching floral, white-edged half-cupped bra, barely holding her nipples below the cup line. June was as sexy as she would ever be for her second "first night."

Phil walked the hallway and gently knocked on the "bridal suite." "June, are you there? Can I come in?" No answer.

Phil was puzzled, but as they say, "curiosity killed the cat," and he slowly turned the brass doorknob. The room was dimly lit, the bedside lamps giving a warm glow. But what met Phil's eyes outshone the best *Playboy* centrefold.

June was lying in bed on her right side, her chin resting cheekily on her hand, her long, smooth, sexy legs exposed, one knee bent, the other just showing enough of the narrowest of G-string, disappearing into the natural crease of her ultimate prize.

"June . . ." Phil was lost for words. "I don't know what to say. *You . . . You . . . You are beautiful . . . Stunningly beautiful.*"

"Okay, enough of the poetry." June laughed as she pointed to the en suite. "As this is our 'first night,' I want it to be perfect. There's a bathrobe behind the door. Don't take too long."

"Then can I get one kiss before I shower as an incentive?"

"*Nope,* you can't touch the merchandise until you are 'virgin' clean." June bent her right knee higher. "Do you get my message, darling?" The en suite door closed behind him, no more said.

*   *   *

"*What the hell was that?*" Brown turned to Lucas.

"If I'm not mistaken, it sounds like gunshots."

"Yeah, I'm with you . . . But what the hell could it be?"

Out of the blue, there was the sound of screaming voices in the hallway, and the detectives recognized Alano voice bellowing orders in Spanish. Then there was the mad scramble of feet running toward the stairs.

(Speaking in Spanish)

"Carilla . . . Dario, drop everything and follow me."

* * *

"Whatever it is, Dan, *it's fucking serious!*"

"Dario . . . Wasn't that the meathead's name?" Bert asked.

Dan laughed. "You mean that 'no-brainer' guard?"

"Yeah, but it's no time for jokes, Dan. If my hunch is right, our man Dario has flown and is legging it up the stairway."

"If that's the case, Bert, there is only one way to find out." Dan took four steps back, then ran at full speed, leaping into the air and giving the door one almighty kick.

There was no response from outside.

"It looks like we are all alone, Bert . . . *Get that fucking lock pick working . . .*"

* * *

The "out gate" now guard free, the plan was on target to unlock the gate and allow the mob to run amok and overrun the compound, eventually entering the main building to ransack at their pleasure. It was the ideal cover for the commandos to complete the second part of their plan.

Benito gave Erico the signal while Flavio, Mateus, and Bill ran to secure the main entrance, pressing their bodies hard against the wall for cover. Benito and Flavio were at one side and Mateus and Bill on the other. Their arms were outstretched, holding their semiautomatics to cover the entrance and one another. They would blow the heavily fortified door when the timing was right.

But inside, Alano had plans of his own. Anticipating a frontal attack, he and his honchos had barricaded the hallway entrance with a large heavy oak table placed on its side to give them cover. Locked and loaded, the "three *caballeros*" were armed to the teeth with AK-47s and enough clips to turn the tables at the Alamo.

Erico rushed to the heavy wrought-iron gate unopposed and opened the electric control box.

Now which switch is it? he pondered, touching his chin, unaware that the two guards at the "in gate" had spotted the lifeless bodies of their fallen comrades.

"Siento . . . *Look!*" One of the guards pointed.

His partner didn't second-guess and, at seeing the two bodies, flicked the automatic switch on his Kalashnikov. The burst of deadly fire was followed quickly by Dario, his compadre, bullets sipping through the air like black rain.

Erico crumpled to his knees as a one bullet shot through his thigh muscle, the other clean through his buttocks. Although in excruciating pain, he rolled over onto his face to reduce his exposure and squeezed off five rounds in quick succession. *Blap . . . Blap . . . Blap . . .* The silencer barked, making a peculiar sound.

"Benito, I'm hit," he beckoned to the captain as he released the empty clip.

"Mateus, Bill . . . We must get that gate open . . . *Go . . .* Flavio and I will cover you."

The captain opened fire, but the guards' AK-47s were pouring lead on them like the summer monsoon.

"Mateus . . . Bill!" Benito yelled. *"Hold it.* I'll tell you when."

There was a brief lull in the gunfire as the guards changed clips.

"Now!" Benito screamed. *"Run . . . Run . . . Flavio, hit them with everything we got."*

The two commandos gave a barrage of fire, emptying their magazines.

Mateus and Bill didn't need a second prompt and broke the "one-minute mile."

The hail of fire was enough to allow the runners to get to Erico and drag him out of the line of fire, resting his back against the perimeter wall, Bill squeezing off three rounds to cover Erico.

"Mateus, don't worry. I'll look after Erico. Just you concentrate on the control panel and get that fucking gate open, or were all done for!"

The Glocks were no match for the Kalashnikovs, and Benito and Flavio were pinned down and, worse still, running out of ammo. If something wasn't done soon, Operation "Kidnap" would end up down the toilet.

The commandos somehow had to get more artillery, and Bill triggered the obvious. *Of course . . . The guards' AK-47s!* They were lying about two meters from Bill's feet and, even better, with full clips taped to the magazines.

Bill waited until he heard the empty clips hit the ground before making his move, grabbing the weapons.

"Benito . . . Flavio . . ." He slid the two AK-47s across the U-shaped driveway.

"Thanks, Bill." Benito chucked one of the carbines to Flavio, who, without hesitation placed it to shoulder and dropped one of the remaining guards.

"Nice shot, Flavio . . . One down, and one to go." Benito grinned.

The other guard was keeping Benito and Flavio occupied, firing randomly from behind the gate pillar, making it difficult for them to waste him.

"Mateus, *what the fuck's keeping you?*" Bill yelled. He had torn a strip from the bottom of his thawb, tying it tightly around Erico's thigh to stem the flow of blood.

"*Got it!*" Mateus yelled as the heavy wrought-iron gates began too slowly open. The loud squeal from the greaseless hinges was drowned by the cry of jubilation as the rioters swept the police aside like matchsticks and surged into the compound. The remaining guard was now in total disarray, recklessly and indiscriminately discharging his weapon into the mass of bodies. As the wounded and dead fell like flies, the lynch mob went into a frenzy. No amount of bullets could stop them now; they were after blood, and the guard did the only thing possible and tried to make a run for it. That was the last Hayden saw of him. His screams sending a shiver down his spine as he was brutally beaten to death, his skull disintegrated with the butt of his own Kalashnikov.

But now the commandos faced an even bigger problem. The rioters in a crazy frenzy were pounding and screaming as they kicked the main door to the embassy and the sudden *crack, crack, crack* of gunfire meant only one thing . . . *They had commandeered the guards' AK-47s!*

"*Fuck it, Flavio!*" There was now no need for cover, and Benito rose to his feet. Somehow, he had to blow that door and avoid collateral damage.

Bill panted as he ran across the driveway, carrying Erico over his shoulders.

Benito looked down at Erico as he sat there in excruciating pain, his thawb now saturated in blood as he rested his back against the wall.

"You're out of it, Erico, *and that's an order.* Stay here, out of sight, until we return. *Do you hear me?*" Benito paused for a second. "*That is . . .* If we can ever blow this fucking door open."

Benito had stashed a grenade inside the long deep pocket of his thawb unknown to Rodrigo. Better to be safe than sorry, but what could he do? With the uncontrollable mob now in a frenzy, screaming and shouting all sorts of abuse, *he couldn't even hear himself thinking!*

"You three stay here and keep me covered. Remember, these crazies now have the guard's weapons, but by the way, they are expending their shells . . . . Let's hope they run out . . . *And soon!*"

"*Bill . . . Flavio . . .* Keep me covered while I try and make some sense of all this."

Benito ran from his cover into the centre of the mass of bodies, pushing and kicking his way to the door. Somehow, he had to get these people out of harm's way. He had a full clip, and he squeezed the trigger of the Kalashnikov in short bursts, riddling the ceiling of the entrance with bullets, dust and mortar choking the air. That did the trick. and the mob stopped as if in slow motion.

*   *   *

Benito held the AK-47 above his head, supporting it with both his arms. *"Stop . . . Stop!"* he yelled, using one of the few Arabic words he could remember.

Then suddenly out of the blue, he recognized one of the men that tried to stop him from climbing the perimeter wall, who yelled something to the crowd in his native tongue. There was ugly protests, but the crazies obeyed, stopping for a few minutes, giving Benito just enough time to gain some form of semblance.

Benito stepped forward and shook the guy's hand in a "thank you" gesture, then produced the grenade from his thawb. The noise from the crowd was now deafening, and in sign language, Benito motioned to clear the entrance and force the crowd as far back as possible. The tall Muslim man quickly put two and two together and began to physically push the crowd back with the additional help of his two honchos.

"Zabba . . . Muhammad, help me get the crowd back to allow our brother to blow open the door."

Azri was doing good on crowd control, and Benito didn't waste any more time and pulled the pin of the Russian-made Vasicka antipersonnel grenade, making doubly sure to keep the spring-loaded release grip intact as he cautiously placed the canister against the center of the heavy entrance doors.

"Fire in the hole." Benito released the grip, sprinting for cover behind the two support pillars. The crowd had already retreated to a safe distance, anticipating damage control.

Barroom! The shock wave of the explosion triggered another scream of jubilation, and once again the frenzied rioters surged forward, trampling and falling over one another as they ignorantly rushed the shattered doorway.

Tec . . . tec . . . tec. The familiar sound of the AK-47s cut down the first wave of rioters, the dead and wounded piled like a human dam, some screaming in pain, the others silent in death. Alano and his men showed no quarter in this callous massacre.

"Fuck it!" Benito was dumbfounded; he had never anticipated "a door too far," and he looked up, studying the double-story fortress, its windows heavily grilled. *Was there another way?* he asked himself. *One man wounded and a stockade in the making and with no more grenades, I'm fucking screwed . . .*

646

CHAPTER 7

The shower was rejuvenating, and Phil's taut, muscular body had taken on a slightly pink tinge, his skin tingling from the steaming hot spray.

"This is an orgasm in itself." Phil grinned as he placed his head below the faucet for the finale.

A brisk towel and gargle with Plax, a vigorous brush through his wet hair, and he was ready for "S" day. He took a final glance in the vanity mirror and flashed his teeth before running his fingers through his hair.

"*Hmmm.* Not bad for an old forty-five-year-old . . . But I wish I had some cologne . . . *What the hell!*" He shook his head.

"*Phil what's keeping you?* June's voice rang out loud and clear. "We're running out of sex time."

Phil smiled at June's comment. "Gimme a sec, honey . . . Now where's that fucking bathrobe?

"Ah, here we are!"

He spotted the robe on the hanger behind the door and quickly slipped his arm into the sleeve.

"You gotta be fucking joking! This either belongs to a midget or it must be June's?"

Having nothing else to wear, he squeezed into the micro robe and pulled the belt tight, the remaining gap leaving nothing to the imagination, and he glanced one more time into the mirror.

He laughed at the sight. "So, I can hold my own anytime in the locker room, huh?" He opened the door.

The ex-college footballer in his mini bathrobe would bring the house down, and June couldn't resist.

"*Ha . . . Ha . . . Ha . . .* God, I am about to choke." June kept laughing.

"I think you purposely set me up."

"Aw, poor darling." June was mocking him. "Now that you have nothing to hide, why don't you disrobe?" June covered her mouth again. "*Eh . . . Err . . .* I'm sorry, honey, I promise I'll stop laughing . . . Now come and lie beside me." She patted the bed with her hand.

Phil didn't need a second prompt and stretched out beside her, lying on his side, his eyes staring into hers before their lips met.

It was a kiss that started in first gear, then went off the road in seconds. Phil's mouth searched deep into her neck, and June was holding her hand behind his head, forcing his mouth deeper into her soft flesh.

"Phil, darling . . . *Don't stop.* You're torturing me."

His lips were now searching the canyon between her breast, his hand reaching around her back to release her bra clasp.

"Darling . . . *Darling, stop!*"

Phil was knocked out of his socks. *It can't be. I've only just started!* He panicked.

"What's wrong, honey?" Phil sheepishly asked.

"My bra clasp is in the front." They both burst into laughter.

"It just shows my inexperience."

"Get out of it . . . *Pants on fire.*"

The hilarity quickly ceased as Phil glanced at June's full frontal, her aroused pink nipples standing proudly on her soft creamy flesh. It was too much, and Phil swallowed each of them in turn with a gentle sucking motion.

"*Phil . . . Phil . . .* Don't stop." June groaned in elation.

Phil knew he couldn't hold on much longer and gently slid his hand between June's open thighs, her moistness telling him what they both knew was inevitable, and he slowly but gently moved his body on top, his entry smooth and deep.

June gave a shudder then a gasp as Phil's erection went even deeper.

"My god, darling, be gentle."

"I will, darling . . . I will . . ."

*   *   *

"There's a fucking war going on out there, Dan." Bert stopped in his tracks as they snuck along the hallway leading to the stairs.

"*I don't give a fuck, Bert!* I'm only interested in getting the hell out of here in one piece."

"I'm with you on that front, but there's something crazy going on, and it may not be as easy as we think."

As they turned the corner at the top of the stairs, Bert suddenly held Dan back and placed his finger to his lips. The gunfire had momentarily ceased, and he could now clearly hear voices.

(Speaking in Spanish)

"That's stopped the bastards, but these guys believe that if they give their lives in the name of Allah, they'll go to heaven. They've retreated to the compound gates to regroup, but make no mistake about it, they'll be back in force, and this time I don't think we can hold . . . Carilla, how's your ammo?"

"Only four clips left, Alano."

"And you, Dario?"

"Three clips, then I'm down to my *pistola*."

"*That's not good . . . I can't fucking believe this!*" Alano burst into a rage. "Where the fuck are the policia? The cowardly bastardos have most likely made a run for it . . . Whatever . . . We must preserve our ammunition. Don't fire until I give the order."

*   *   *

The Muslim brotherhood was retrieving the wounded and the dead while taking advantage of the momentary ceasefire.

"Christ, Dan, we can't just stand by and do nothing. This is worse than the fucking Holocaust!"

"Buddy, if you don't mind me asking, what's in that mind of yours?"

"We take them head-on. There's only three of them, and the element of surprise gives us the advantage."

"And just how do we do that?"

"*Come on, Dan!* What the fuck's come over you? I've never seen you running from a fight."

"I just don't want to end up in a pine box for some crazies that don't give a shit for guy's like us . . . But then again . . ." Dan had that mischievous grin on his face that spelled trouble.

"*Listen*, didn't we both play quarterback in college football?"

"So?"

"Have you forgotten how hard we can tackle? And now even better—we are about twenty pounds heavier . . ."

*   *   *

"Benito, *we're fucked if we don't do something!*" Bill stared down the captain.

"If we try to take them now, Bill, we'll be cut down like lambs at the slaughter . . . I can't take that chance. It would be a reckless decision."

The thunderous bangs and puffs of white smoke of a few rubber bullets being discharged by the Muslims from the confiscated police riot guns were falling futilely short of the main entrance.

"You have to admire them, Benito. It's not for the want of trying."

"Is that the sound of an ambulance, or is it police sirens, Benito?" Erico interrupted Flavio.

"It could be police reinforcements and, as usual, too little too late. We have do something . . . *Like now!*"

*   *   *

Phil lay on his back, panting slightly, June's head resting on his chest, the ultimate gesture of intimate love temporarily over for the moment.

"Am I in Shangri-La or what? Pinch me to see if this is real, honey," Phil joked.

"It's real, darling, but do you still love me?"

"Do I still love you? *Honey, I adore you!*" Phil stroked June's hair and gently kissed her forehead.

*   *   *

Steven was on a high after having three strikes in a row, trying to make an impression on Michelle. He had had a crush on her for the last couple of months and had almost given up trying. Bernie is Michelle's brother, and what better way to get to his sister than through his best friend. But Bernie was also in heat, and he had the same idea about Sheryl.

"What a great bowl." Michelle ran over and hugged him.

Michelle was a highly sought-after blonde beauty on campus being, nominated as the "Prom's Beauty Queen" and Steven was now momentarily basking in the sun. But as for Bernie, he was unfortunately not having much luck with Sheryl, who was playing hard to get. She loved the attention, but she was her own woman.

"I'm getting bored, Steven, don't you think that we have had enough of the bowling thing for one night?"

"Sis, stop acting like a spoiled brat."

"Steve, maybe Sheryl is right. My father gets upset if I stay out after ten," Michelle interrupted.

"But you're with your brother, Michelle," Steven protested, desperately trying to save his date. Then a last-ditch thought crossed his mind. "*I know . . .* Why don't we check out and drop by Burger King? The burgers are on me."

"Sounds good to me, Steve." Bernie was on the same wavelength and turned to Sheryl, who gave him an ugly scowl.

Steven grabbed Michelle's hand as they left the bowling alley.

"You sit in the front with me and Bernie in the back with my sis. It's a bit crushed in the back, Bernie. Do you mind?" Steven winked.

Bernie gave a big "thank you" smile. It was his chance to get up close and comfy with Sheryl.

"I don't mind, Steve." He grinned.

"It's a bit chilly, shall I keep the hood down?" Steven asked as they walked to the car park.

"*Of course!*" Michelle squeezed his hand.

This was getting better by the minute, and Steven returned the gesture.

The Porsche drove like a dream, the cold air blowing through their hair but Bernie was not having much luck in the Porsche's cramped backseat as he awkwardly tried to protect Sheryl from the so-called breeze, putting his arm around her and pulling her close.

"Do you mind?" Sheryl pried him away.

"Aw, come on, Sheryl, you know how I feel about you."

"*Yeah, and you know how I feel about you!*" She gave Bernie that look.

Steven hit the stock switch and hung a left into HJ's car park, the black Porsche drawing more attention than Michael Jackson . . .

* * *

"I had a great night, Steven." Michelle affectionately held his hand, then unexpectedly leaned over and gave him a "virgin kiss" on the lips.

Steven was taken aback. "*Eh . . . Err . . .* I'm glad. *Eh . . .* Can we do this again, Michelle?" It was go for broke.

"I would love to. I'll see you in class on Monday. Bernie, are you coming?"

"With you in minute, sis." He leaned over to give Sheryl a kiss on the lips, but it was an air job, as Sheryl had seen it coming and moved her head to the side like a prize fighter dodging a right hook.

"Sheryl, can I date you again?" Bernie timidly asked.

"I'll see. Now do you mind? I want to sit beside my brother."

* * *

As Steven drove through the night traffic, his mind was still on Michelle and that special kiss.

"Well, you were laying it on tonight, huh?"

"Sheryl, lighten up. You know how Bernie feels about you. Actually, sis, when you get to know him, he's a really nice guy."

"*Yeah . . . Yeah . . .* Anyhow, we're home. The best thing I enjoyed tonight was the burgers."

"I give up." Steven just shook his head as he closed the hood.

* * *

June sat bolt upright.

"What's wrong, honey?" Phil was startled.

"I'm sure I heard a car door slam . . . *It can't be!*"

June threw her feet to the floor and rushed to the window like Lady Godiva, only without the horse!

And as for Phil . . . Well, who could blame him? I mean how often does a guy get to admire his girlfriend as naked as a jaybird.

"Honey, calm down."

"It's the kids, Phil, *they have returned early!*" That wiped the smile from Phil's face.

"What are we going to do, darling?"

"Don't panic, that's number 1. And number 2, get dressed and go down and face the foe looking innocent, as if nothing happened . . . June, the kids are no dummies. Do you honestly think they can't put two and two together? I mean the car, the pocket money for the bowling night, and the 'Don't hurry home, enjoy yourselves.'"

"I guess you're right, Phil, making all sorts of excuses means you are as guilty as hell."

The game was up, and Phil walked in his nakedness and crushed his body against June's. The firmness of her breasts and the feel of her soft velvety skin was sending messages, and Phil gently separated their nakedness, then sucked each of pink nipples in turn.

"Darling, please stop . . ." June groaned. "You're driving me crazy, and with that pressing against me, I'm never going to let you go."

June grabbed Phil's arms and dragged him on top of her onto the bed. "So let the kids wait . . ."

* * *

"Sheryl, where's Mother and Phil? There's no one in the lounge, and they are not in the kitchen. There's no sign of them."

"Then there's only one place they can be." Sheryl was enjoying the chase.

"Smart-ass, and where can that be, may I ask?"

"In Mother's bedroom, *you big heel!*"

Steven, although he had the inclination, found it hard to think that his mother was sexually active . . . *At the ripe old age of forty-four, do couples still have sex?*

"Hi, guys, you are home early. Have you had supper?" June asked unashamed as she and Phil came down the stairs, of course *fully dressed!*

Sheryl was more receptive and just smiled. After all, what's the big deal?

"Yeah, we had Burger King. Mother, I think I'll hit the sack and watch some TV in my room . . . Good night, Phil, thanks for the joyride. I hope you and Mother enjoyed yourselves."

"Sheryl, *that's enough of that!* And wipe that silly grin from your face."

June was furious, but Phil took it all in good humour. After all, who could blame her?

"Good night, Phil. Good night, Mother." Sheryl smiled once more to Phil, then disappeared up the stairs.

What was in her head, God only knows. June tried to hide her anger.

Steven, well, he was still lost for words, and he did the honourable thing and thanked Phil for the use of the car, then gave his good nights.

"So, the cat's out the bag, honey. How do you feel now?"

"Like a kept woman!"

* * *

"Here's the deal . . . Dan, you take the Hulk with one hit, and I'll wrestle with the other two in the confusion."

"And their guns?"

"Ask a silly question . . . Wait for it . . . *Now!*" Bert gave the command.

Dan hit the Hulk with a bull charge, low and hard, smashing him into Carilla and Alano bowling them over like ten pins, and Bert didn't hesitate to take advantage of the confusion, thudding down on their backs like a ton of bricks. There was punching and kicking as the two detectives fought for their lives in hand-to-hand combat.

"Bert, grab that fucking gun . . ."

"Am I hearing things?" Bill turned to Benito his eyebrows furled. "If I'm not mistaken, I hear American voices . . ."

"By god, you're right, Bill . . . *Let's move it.*"

There was the sudden *crack, crack, crack* of a semiautomatic as Bert took Carilla down as the commandos leaped the barricade.

Alano was still struggling with Bert but somehow managed to grab his Kalashnikov and recklessly squeeze a burst of fire, luckily only riddling the ceiling full of holes before he was dropped by a single shot to the head from Benito. But Dan was wrestling for his life with the Hulk, whose brute strength was getting the better of him.

Suddenly there was an ear-piercing explosion with the splatter of warm blood spraying into Dan's eyes as Bill pressed the Glock to the side of Dario's forehead and released the trigger. The big man dropped like a stone, his strong-arm days for the history books.

"Bert . . . Dan . . . Well. I'll be a monkey's uncle! I didn't recognize the two if you in that getup." Bill was shaking their hands like there was no tomorrow.

"Are you serious, Hayden? *Man,* the way you guys are dressed, it's one for the album."

The Muslim brotherhood were licking their wounds, ready for the second onslaught, but on seeing the blockade now overrun, they surged forward, flooding through the main door, shouting and cheering their new heroes.

"Let's get outta here, guys . . . *Mission successful.*"

PART 9

Face the Music

CHAPTER 1

"Move it, Summers. You take the seat between Dan and Bert, and no fucking theatrics . . . *You heard me!"*

"Keep your fucking shirt on, Hayden, I need to go for a piss." Summers was being difficult.

"You can piss once we're off the ground. In the meantime, cross your fucking legs." Bill was taking no shit.

"Are you gentlemen all right?" The stewardess noticed the steel glint from the handcuffed wrist. She had been alerted by the captain that there was a fugitive on board being escorted back to the United States.

"Yeah, we're all right, miss." Bill replied as they settled into taking the middle row of seats.

"Then can I fetch you gentlemen a refreshment before take-off?" "We're good miss, maybe later." Dan answered politely.

"Hey!" Summers rudely interrupted. "Speak for yourselves . . . Miss, if it's not *too* much trouble, can you fetch me a double bourbon please?" The stewardess was confused and looked to the detectives for guidance. "Miss . . . *eh*?" Bert queried.

"Linda."

"Linda, Mr. Summers is the guest of the New York Police Department, and due to his unusual circumstances, alcohol is forbidden." "Well said, black boy," Summers scorned.

Mike was being a regular asshole, and his racial slur touched a nerve with Lucas, who physically and viciously yanked his cuffed hands, making Summers cringe in pain.

"Summers, so help me, if you open that big fucking mouth of yours once more . . ."

"You'll what? Arrest me!" Summers gave a crazy laugh. "I'm a loser, so what?"

"You'll lose your fucking teeth for a start!" Bert stared him down.

* * *

"Welcome to the friendly skies. This is Captain Morgan, your first officer, speaking. The flight to New York will take approximately nine hours and fifteen minutes. We will be touching down at JF at 7:15 p.m. U.S. time. There is a time difference of two hours behind. The weather forecast is fine, with clear skies expected all the way. The cabin crew will shortly demonstrate the safety procedures, so please fasten your belts and sit back, relax, and enjoy Delta's latest addition to our fleet, the Boeing 737. The audio system will be switched on once we reach our cruising altitude."

* * *

"Fucking friendly skies . . . Who *is* this fucking joker?"

Summers just wasn't going to go away. He was hell-bent on creating as much havoc as possible, and some of the passengers were already complaining to the staff about Mike's loudness and foul language. This was going to be a long flight.

* * *

The "Unfasten Safety Belt" sign flashed, and Bill quickly undid the uncomfortable webbing and beckoned the beautiful Linda as she passed with the refreshment cart.

"Mr. Hayden, sir?"

"Linda, can I make an international call now?"

"Certainly . . . The phone is in the armrest right next to you, and we accept most credit cards."

"Thanks, Linda." Bill gave her a warm smile as he quickly unlatched the phone and swiped his AMEX. He punched in the numbers and waited patiently. As usual, the dialling tone was forever.

"Yes, Mona Menzel speaking."

"Mona, honey! Bill here . . . I've been trying to contact you since yesterday."

"Thank God, Bill! I was worried out of my mind after seeing the attack on the Argentine embassy on CNN. The international lines have been hot between our two presidents, and that's most likely the cause. But more importantly, are you safe and sound, and where are you calling from?"

"Unfortunately, honey, from Delta flight 12 on my way to New York . . . And I can't stop thinking about you."

"And me about you, darling . . . Even though there was never anything physical between us, that's why it's so beautiful."

"I know the feeling, honey, and you haven't seen the last of me."

"*Bill*, are you sure you know what you're saying?"

"I've never felt more sure, believe me. But, honey, I have to hang up. Take care of yourself, I'll phone you again from New York."

"I'll be waiting . . . Bye, darling . . ."

Dan was sitting next to Bill and couldn't help hearing the phone conversation, as people tend to speak louder to drown out the noise in the cabin.

"Phoning home, Mike?" Dan casually asked.

"*Eh . . . Em . . .*" Mike was like everyone else when it came to telling white lies.

"Err . . . Yes."

"I thought your wife's name is Judy." Dan had a sardonic grin on his face.

"*So, you heard wrong!*" Bill shot back.

"Lighten up, Mike. Your personal life is none of my business. We all have skeletons in the closet, huh?"

"I need a piss, sambo." Summers was at it again.

"Bill, it's okay." Bert purposely rose to his feet, yanking Summers up by the wrist.

"*You fucking sadist.* When I see my lawyer, I'm gonna sue for police brutality."

"Shut your mouth and do us all a favor."

Bert dragged Summers down the aisle to the horror of the other passengers, who could be forgiven for mistaking the drama for a real-life movie.

Bert purposely walked to the toilet between cabins separated with a black curtain on each side.

"Hold it, Summers, while I unlock this cuff."

"So why are you pulling the curtains closed?" Mike was getting nervous. He didn't like that look on Lucas's face

"Because I'll show you why, you fucking loser."

In an instant, Lucas grabbed Summers by the shirt collar with both hands and head butted him hard on the bridge of his nose. There was a loud cracking noise as bone and cartilage disintegrated with nowhere to go.

"You fucking bastard, you've broken my nose." Mike was coughing and choking in his own blood.

Bert grabbed a towel from the galley. "Go clean yourself up, and if you give me any more fucking shit, you'll be searching for your teeth next time . . . *Cappice?* And don't take too long in that toilet . . . *Asshole.*"

* * *

Linda pulled the curtain back to fetch more refreshments from the galley just as Mike staggered from the toilet, his shirt covered in blood and pressing the saturated towel against the collateral damage.

"*My god!* What happened to Mr. Summers?" Linda was flabbergasted at the carnage.

"Don't worry, Linda, he's gonna be all right. He had one too many before he boarded the flight and fell over in the toilet. Isn't that right, Mike?" "Yes," came the almost-clouded reply.

"Stay here while I fetch you a fresh shirt from your garment bag . . . *And don't you dare move!*"

"What's up, Bert?" Dan asked as Bert retrieved the bag from the overhead locker.

"Mike needs a fresh shirt. He stumbled and fell . . ."

"Here, put this on. Linda, do you have a fresh towel and some ice?"

Needless to say, Mike was "the Quiet Man" for the rest of the flight!

* * *

The shudder and screech of rubber tearing up the tarmac was the nostalgic sound of home. It had been a trying flight and a trying mission, but at last now it was over.

"Please retain your safety belts until the plane has completely come to a halt outside the deplaning gate." Linda was speaking through the intercom.

"This is Captain Morgan, your first officer, wishing you farewell and bon voyage, and I hope to see you once again flying the friendly skies . . ."

"Stay where you are, Summers, until the plane is fully disembarked," Lucas ordered the now-dishevelled Mike, both his eyes sporting a distinct blueness.

The detectives had been informed by Captain Baker to sit tight until a police escort boarded the plane to take Summers to the watch house.

* * *

"We'll take responsibility of the prisoner from here on, Detectives." The two uniformed officers had boarded the plane.

Thank God for that! The detectives could finally relax, their charge now someone else's responsibility.

"Mike Summers, you're under arrest for the . . . Anything you say . . . Place your hands behind your back."

*　*　*

As the three detectives wearily cleared customs and immigration, walking to the departure lounge, they were surprised to see Baker himself waiting to greet them.

I just want to say . . ." Ted warmly shook their hands. "Well done . . . A cruiser will take each of you home. Have a good night's sleep, and report to my office at ten thirty tomorrow morning, as I need to make an urgent report to the commissioner. Again, guys . . . Well done."

*　*　*

"Thanks, Sergeant, for the ride."

"Anytime, Bill, it's good to have you back . . . Say, Bill, I know you haven't had time to catch your breath, but do you know that it's Tony's funeral tomorrow?"

"*The funeral is tomorrow!* I hadn't heard."

"Yeah, it's at two o'clock at the Calvary Police Cemetery in Queens."

"I know the one, Dex, unfortunately it's not the first time . . . You say two o'clock?"

The sergeant acknowledged, looking rather depressed. *When it's one of New York's finest, the department loses one of their own.*

"Bill, I know you and Tony were close, and it must be hard to accept that he's gone. He was a regular guy . . . They broke the mould when they made him."

"Thanks, Dex, for that . . . I'll most likely see you tomorrow then?"

"Wish you could, but my shift starts at two, and understandably I can't get a stand-in."

The cruiser's radio crackled. "Car 36, come in, please."

"Sorry, Bill, I gotta go . . ."

*　*　*

Bill wearily climbed the stairs to the porch after having almost tripped in the darkness over a kid's bicycles.

"*Fucking kids . . . What the hell!* I'm wasting my breath." He slipped the key into the lock, glad to be home.

"*Is that you, darling?*" It was Judy's voice echoing from the kitchen.

"*Well, I hope it's me!* Who did you think it was?"

"My boy toy with the same name." Judy could give as good as she got. "I thought you would have phoned when you touched down, but that's probably asking too much."

"My phone is out of battery." Bill answered, annoyed. *He was back home again, all right!*

Judy finally came through to the lounge, carrying two oversize margaritas.

"I made your favourite poison." She was looking rather dishy.

"Thanks, honey." Bill expression changed. "I really needed this." He took a sip from the salt-encrusted glass and gave a satisfying sigh, but usually when Judy was nice, there's always a catch.

"Well, aren't you going to give me a 'glad to see you' kiss?" Judy put on a face.

"I'm sorry . . ." Now *Bill* was feeling embarrassed. "It's just that I've had one helluva a week . . . A week that I wish never happened, and this arm of mine feels like shit."

Bill moved his arm in a circular motion, the pain reflecting in his eyes as he sat down heavily on the sofa. He was bushed, but the margarita was hitting the spot, and he knew Judy only too well. You can't change a leopard's spots.

"The boys?" Bill queried.

"Aw, they got tired waiting to see their father and are now both fast asleep." Judy sat down next to Bill, showing a bit more thigh than usual. "*Now how about that kiss?*"

Bill placed the demolished margarita glass on the coffee table, then turned and gave Judy a paltry peck on the lips.

"Well, that was a 'starver,' *I must say!*" Judy's eyes blazed.

"Honey, gimme some slack. I just can't wait to shower and hit the cot. *You should understand.*"

"*Do I*? It's nothing new . . . I'm used to it . . . I often ask myself . . . *Why did I ever marry a fucking cop?*"

"*Don't start that again.*" Bill rose to leave; he had heard it all before.

"Before you run, do you know it's Tony's funeral tomorrow?

"Yeah, the cruiser sergeant informed me."

"Bill, this may not be the time or place, but then when is there ever a right time with you?"

"*Judy.* Don't screw around and get to the point. You're never usually short of words."

"With Tony gone, will you be promoted to lieutenant?" She blurted it out, relieved.

"*You mean, will I be chasing a dead man's shoes?*"

"*Christ, Bill, Can you blame me?* Living in this dump on a measly sergeant's salary? We could do with the extra income, or haven't you noticed?" Bill shook his head, trying not to believe his ears.

"*I don't believe this shit I'm hearing . . . Money . . . Money . . . Money.* Is that all you think about? *Hell,* Tony isn't even cold yet, and you can't wait for me to get his job, and more so, you haven't even asked if I'm all right." Bill disgustedly turned to leave. "I'm off to bed . . ."

*   *   *

Bill screwed up his face as he turned in bed, the sharp pain that shot up his right arm a rude reminder of the bullet he took at Villamisseria on that fateful day. The wound was healing fine; after all, it had only been less than a week and the police surgeon had already contacted him to make an appointment. There was no point checking on Judy. Her space was already empty. Bill moved his stiff arm once more, then ruffled his unruly hair, stretching his jaws in a shark-like yawn. He could clearly hear the kids' voices in the kitchen, and he leaned over to look at the time.

Seven fifteen . . . It's about time I got my lazy ass out of bed. I have a busy day in front of me, what with that meeting with Baker and Tony's funeral, I'm not looking forward to it. He swung his feet to the floor.

Autumn was in full swing, and there was a distinct chill in the air. The warm shower would be a pick me up, and Bill dropped his pajamas to his ankles and streaked to the en suite. As the hot spray tingled down his neck and back and the shower box steamed up, for a moment it felt like heaven, and Bill had not a care in the world.

"What the hell's keeping you, Bill? The kids are patiently waiting for you to join them at breakfast."

Does this woman ever give up! Bill shook his head.

"I'm in the shower, for Christ's sake. I'll be down in fifteen."

"Sometimes I wonder what you do in that bloody shower box." The door slammed.

"*And good riddance to you!*" Bill began towelling while talking to himself. "*Mona . . . She is so different from the bitch I married. If only things were different, and now with Tony gone police life will never be the same . . .*"

Bill stared into the mirror as he gently peeled the waterproof plaster from his wound. The stitch work was pretty neat, but like it or not, they had to be removed, but the police doc will see to that. Within minutes, he was shaved and into his grey woollen NYPD tracksuit. It had just turned eight, and he had plenty of time before his meeting with Baker.

*   *   *

"*Dad!*" Ian, the oldest, jumped from his barstool and wrapped himself around his father's legs. "Are you all right, Dad?" "Of course, I am." Bill ruffled Ian's hair.

"Mom said you were wounded, like with a real bullet." "Oh, did she now?" Bill grinned proudly.

"Dad, can I see your wound?" It was young Taylor's turn; he wanted a piece of the action.

"Only if you eat your Captain Crunch and drink your juice." No more said, both boys trying to outdo one another.

"What would you like for breakfast?" Judy finally broke the ice.

"I'm not really into the breakfast thing, especially this morning. Black coffee is fine, honey."

"You're a bit late with the honey stuff. If you had played your cards last night, you might have gotten lucky."

"Judy . . . *Please*, not in front of the kids . . . The coffee or shall I make it myself?"

"*Dad*, I was first."

"No, he wasn't, Dad, he was cheating."

"Okay . . . Okay . . . I tell you what. I think it was a draw. What do you think, honey?"

There was no answer. "That means your mother agrees . . . Okay, wait for it, guys. *Ta . . . da . . .*" Bill slipped his left arm out of his tracksuit top.

"*Wow.*" The "Brothers Grim" stood in awe.

"Dad, that must have been sore?" Ian was captivated. "*A real bullet wound.*" "Can I touch it, Dad?" Taylor, the five-year-old, was so innocent.

"*Enough . . . Enough . . .* Let your father enjoy his coffee and read his paper in peace. Now be off with you to the shower. You have to get ready for kindergarten and school."

"*Aw, Mom,* can't we just skip school today and spend some time with Dad?"

"*No, you can't!* Now what did I tell you?"

"Hey, guys, it's not so bad. Gimme some high fives . . ."

*   *   *

Bill took a sip of his belated coffee and unfolded the *New York Times*. Peaceful Demonstration at the Brazil Embassy Ends in Violence

662

The Argentine government has protested in the strongest terms to Brazil's president Getulio Vargas for the inadequate police protection resulting in the death of seven embassy staff and the wanton pillaging and destruction of the property amounting to more than five million U.S. dollars. Fortunately, the ambassador and consulate general were both absent on overseas business.

The Muslim brothers are claiming responsibility in retaliation for the death of fifteen unarmed demonstrators and as many wounded. The protest was intended to highlight the plight of the Muslim refugees in Argentina . . .

Bill was engrossed in the news when Judy returned with the boys, ready for school and kindergarten.

"Say goodbye to your father."

"Bye, Dad," came the chorus.

"I'll be back within the hour; will you still be here?" Judy asked.

"Should be. Say, have you contacted Rose about the funeral?"

"No, she has enough on her plate today without me bothering her. After all, I'll see her there . . . Bye." The door slammed.

Bill glanced at the time. *I guess I had better get dressed. I'll take my dress uniform to headquarters, then, after finishing with Baker, go straight to the cemetery . . .*

CHAPTER 2

Rose's mother Maria had been staying at the house ever since the news of Tony's death, and today was the day that everyone was dreading.

Lena, Giovanni, Annette, Rita, and their husbands had all arrived, dressed respectfully in black, making the grieving atmosphere even bleaker.

After the funeral, a wake will be held in the function room at the Sheraton Hotel in Downtown Manhattan. A dinner in honour of the dearly departed has long been a tradition in the Italian community, and knowing Tony, he would wish to do it in style.

Tony's two boys, Mauro and Samuel, looked confused and lost as they resembled tailor's dummies dressed in miniature suits, like two Lord Fauntleroy's holding hands in fortitude while staring at the adults who looked more perturbed than them.

"Will you be all right, honey?" Maria asked her daughter, who looked pale and drawn; she could still remember how *she* felt when Rose's father, her beloved husband, passed away and the day of the dreaded funeral.

"I'm all right, Mother but I still can't erase from my mind how Tony looked when I went to identify him in the police mortuary." Her eyes glazed over.

Maria firmly gripped her daughter's hand. "Honey, you have to be strong for the sake of the boys. They are both confused and lost as it is, and if they see their mother fall apart . . . *Well* . . . Listen, why don't you take your mother's advice and join me in the kitchen over a small cognac *to calm both our nerves?* We still have thirty minutes before the funeral cortege arrives."

Rose nodded in a sort of zombie trance, following her mother's advice.

"There now, how does that feel?" Maria had finished the small shot in the brandy goblet and was pouring a second hit.

As for Rose, the colour was now returning to her cheeks.

"I feel a bit better now, Mother," Rose answered, but that look in her eyes was an absolute betrayal.

"The cars are here. Rose, finish your cognac while I go and fetch the boys . . ."

* * *

"That's one helluva report!" Baker was fast getting writer's cramp as he glanced though the final documents for typing.

"Stace is gonna have one helluva job deciphering my scribble." Baker half laughed. "Once it's complete, guys, I need you to walk through it again and make any changes necessary, then sign the bottom line. Changing the subject, I'm sure you read the headlines this morning. Fortunately there was nothing to implicate the NYPD. But knowing the media, they will not let it go so easily. There is always a whistle-blower willing to sell his mother."

The three detectives absorbed Baker's comment in silence; they were just glad to be back in one piece. They would all receive commendations for bravery, but with the loss of Tony, it was small comfort.

"*Ahhh . . . hem.*" Bill cleared his throat to draw attention as he glanced at his watch.

"Ted, if that's all, I'm sure I'm speaking on behalf of Dan and Bert, it's now twelve forty-five, and we have to grab a bite and change into our 'number ones' and get to the cemetery before two!"

"*Hell is it that time already!* I had better get moving as well. I have to meet with the commissioner, the mayor, and the DA. Guys, don't hang around."

"Thanks, Captain." Brown rose to leave.

* * *

"Boy, that was some session!" Lucas commented on his way out. Say, we still have time for a sandwich and a coffee. Who's game?"

"Yeah, why not Bert," Bill agreed. "I'm feeling really hungry. I don't know about you guys, but I just couldn't stomach breakfast this morning before I left."

"That's good of you, Bill, to offer." Brown laughed.

"*Oh no you don't*, I'm not falling for that old gag."

"Hey, Bill, I'm only joking, don't take it so serious." Brown grabbed Hayden around the shoulders in a friendly gesture.

"And I'm only joking as well." Bill grinned. "Guys, after what we have been through, *it's my pleasure . . .*"

PART 10

The Funeral

CHAPTER 1

It was a pleasant autumn afternoon, with bright sunshine and a nip in the air. The family cortege, a column of black limousines, slowly stacked up back-to-back on the tree-lined cemetery driveway, the hearse with Tony's flag-draped casket leading the funeral procession. The white-gloved police pallbearers in full dress blues stood stone like to attention in column of twos, waiting for the command.

The sea of blue uniforms and white-gloved officers in symmetrical rows resembled toy soldiers as they lined in uniformity behind the taped enclave, the inner circle reserved for dignitaries and the immediate family of the fallen officer.

Rose nervously turned to her mother and gripped her hand. The last few days had been a nightmare, her subconscious clouding reality from disbelief to rejection, but now the final curtain had arrived, and no matter how much she refused to accept Tony's death, the finality of it all was like "Seasons in the Sun."

* * *

Goodbye, my friend, it's hard to die When all the birds are singing in the sky . . .

* * *

Rose's large Sophia Loren hat with the traditional spotted black veil complemented her tailored black suit and matching modest heels.

"Mrs. Perino, please." The limo driver offered his hand.

"Thank you." Rose stepped shakily onto the frigid concrete, taking a second or so to gain her balance.

"Mother . . ." She turned.

"Don't worry, honey, I've got the boys . . ."

* * *

For a moment Rose, took in the sight of the manicured police cemetery, with its columns of white crosses in remembrance to each of the police officers who gave their lives in the line of duty, their sacrifice remembered by their loved ones but forgotten by the American public in their selfish materialistic world and insensitivity to the protectors of the law.

* * *

"Here, honey, hold my hand and just take it slowly. Come, Mauro, take your mother's and your brother's hands."

The five-minute walk to the graveside was like that of death row, the dignitaries making way for the family, each expressing their long-winded condolences.

With Mauro on one side holding his mother's hand and Samuel on the other, the black-veiled widow could have easily been mistaken for a Deja vu of the Kennedy funeral.

The police chaplain was solemnly waiting at the podium, his Bible open, the slight wind catching the pages and ruffling his thinning hair.

Rose was now composed; her only wish was to get the ceremony and the nauseating but necessary pomp and pageantry over with.

"Pallbearers," the sergeant's command echoed in the still air.

The highly lacquered coffin with brass ornamentals was slowly rolled from the hearse. "Old Glory" ceremoniously draping the casket, with Tony's police cap and a blue suede medal box precariously perched in the middle.

As the pallbearers robotically marched in step, straining with the heavy casket, uncomfortably wresting on their shoulders, the squeal of the bagpipes suddenly pierced the solitude, a solitary piper in full regalia eerily playing the funeral march "The Floo'ers o' the Forest."

The green mantle neatly placed around the eight-by-three grave was both serene and eerie, its two heavy wooden support batons spanning the neatly dug six-foot pit.

At last, the pallbearers gently placed the casket to rest on the batons, waiting for the priest to perform the last rites, the strain of the pipes gently echoing in the distance as the piper marched out of sight.

* * *

The Goldfish Bowl

"We are gathered here today to mourn the loss of Lieutenant Anthony Perino, an ordinary man with exceptional courage . . . A man with a young family who had everything to live for . . . A man who had the highest integrity in upholding the law. A man for all reasons . . . A man to be proud of . . . A man that is the very fabric of our great nation . . .

"Greater love has no man than to lay down his life for his fellow citizens. Anthony Perino was such a man. Life is a gamble of terrible odds, and Lieutenant Perino paid the ultimate price . . . Our thoughts this day go to Rose, who has lost a loving husband, and Mauro and Samuel, who lost their dearly beloved father. Please join me in Psalm 23 . . .

"*The Lord is my shepherd . . . He makes me lie down in green pastures . . . Even though I walk through the valley of death, I fear no evil, for you are with n me . . .*

"Pallbearers, lower the casket," the sergeant commanded.

The pallbearers removed Old Glory and Tony's cap and medal box, folding the flag into the traditional triangle to be given to Rose before finally taking the strain on the casket straps, gently lowering the coffin into the grave.

Suddenly the reality hit Rose that never seeing Tony again was forever, and she burst into hysterical tears.

"*Why, oh why . . . Please someone . . . Please someone tell me. Why . . . Why . . . Why?*" Rose sobbed, the boys now crying too, clinging to their mother's legs, more scared than confused.

"The Lord acts in mysterious ways . . . The Lord giveth and the Lord taketh . . . Ashes to ashes, dust to dust . . ."

The police chaplain sprinkled a handful of earth onto the casket, making a hollow drumming noise.

"Please join me in the Lord's prayer."

"Our father who art in heaven, hallowed be thy name . . ."

"*Honour guard*, take your stations." The captain's command was loud and clear.

"Lock and load."

The seven-member honour guard, each exactly the same height, stood in a thin blue line, M1s to port.

"When I give the command, fire in three volleys . . . Shoulder arms . . . *Fire . . . Load . . . Fire . . . Load . . . Fire!*"

The crack of the rifles shattered the silence, and a large flock of pigeons took to the sky in fright, their wings beating loudly as they circled the cemetery.

As the mourners faded for another day, suddenly it was all over as quick as it started, with Rose left holding the folded stars and stripes, Tony's hat, and the Police Medal of Honor.

"*Christ*, is this it after ten years of marriage?" Rose slowly walked toward the funeral limo.

"*Rose.*" The voice made her stop and turn.

"*Bill* . . . I thought that voice sounded familiar!"

"I tried to see you earlier." Bill put his arms around her and gave her a kiss on the cheek. "Words can't describe how I feel." Even this tough cop's voice was breaking. "I haven't spotted Judy yet, but let's catch up at the reception."

"Bill, before you go, I would like to sit down with you in private. I need to know the real circumstances of Tony's death, as I am still in the dark as to what really happened."

"Are you sure, Rose?"

"Yes, never been surer."

"Why don't I give you call next week?"

"Would really appreciate that, Bill . . . There's Judy now. Thanks, Bill, I knew I could depend on you."

As Rose sat in the limo, she was not looking forward to the long-winded eulogies from hypocritical so-called friends and colleagues who would immediately have to go the confession box to be forgiven for their lies.

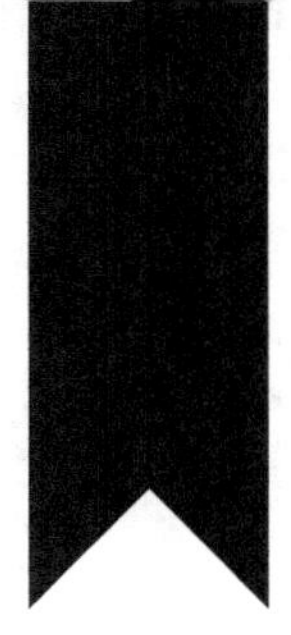

PART 11

Poetic Justice

CHAPTER 1

"When do I see my lawyer?" Summers screamed at the lockup guard.

"You'll see him when you see him. Now do us all a fucking favor and belt up. Do you want this food or what?" The corporal was waiting with the food cart.

"The Jews had better food than this in Auschwitz."

"You watch your mouth, Summers. Another crack like that, and I'll move you in with Dempsey."

"Yeah, Corp, send him over. I would just love a piece of white ass."

"Shut up, Dempsey, no one's asking you! Now do you want this shit or what?"

"I've no fucking choice."

The oversize cop pushed the stainless-steel food tray below the cell bars.

"If you don't want it, Summers, pass it across to me."

"Why don't you fucking shut that ugly mug of yours, black boy?"

"*Why you fucking . . . !* I'll be waiting for you, snowdrop, be it in the pen or when you hit the streets. I've got your number."

"I didn't know you can count in Harlem . . . *Wonders never cease.*"

"Fucking smart-ass, *woman beater.*"

"Listen, you two, *eat up or shut up.* I don't want any shit on my watch." Summers grimaced at the food tray as he placed it on his cot.

The curled-up burger bun with a piece of ground meat that you could sole your boots with, and second-day coffee was a big change from the fanciest restaurants in Manhattan and on a fat expense account to boot.

Summers could hear Dempsey bursting his sides.

"You had better get used to that, pretty boy. You're gonna be eating that dog food for a long time to come, and you know how the cons treat woman beaters in the big house. *Maaaan,* I'd be taking lots of Vaseline if I were you. I wouldn't like to be in your shoes when the 'sisters' get to you."

Summers just ignored Dempsey, but the morbid thought of prison life was fast becoming a reality.

*   *   *

"June, I think we have enough on the McCauley case to pursue a civil action. I suggest you put it together and get Ethel to type it for my review. I'll be interested in your conclusions."

"My first case as a paralegal, huh?" Phil grinned, but he had something else on his mind.

"June, don't go just yet."

"If it's about last night, Phil, I have no regrets."

"No, it's not, and *I* certainly have no regrets either! No, honey, if you had read the local rag this morning, you would have seen that your neighbour Mr. Perino's funeral is today."

"I wondered why all the commotion and the cars parked on the driveway. I haven't had a chance to read the papers as yet, but Tony's death still haunts me. I knew him so well, and if it hadn't been for Mike, he would be alive to—"

"*June, stop there!* It's not your fault in anyway, *so kick the guilt trip!*" Phil's voice was forceful, and June kept quiet. It was a wake-up call.

"Listen, honey, here's where I'm coming from. I'm sure you will be contacted by the Homicide Department anytime now to inform you that Mike is being held in custody at the central court lockup, awaiting a plea hearing in front of state judge Randal Phillips, which the grapevine informs me is at ten thirty tomorrow. The court is closed to the public with the exception of the paparazzi."

"I was dreading this day." June's deep facial lines were showing.

"*Honey, don't you see?* It's the break we've both been waiting for. Firstly, I'll get legal clearance for you to visit Mike today if possible. I know Philips well. Secondly, you serve the divorce papers on Mike and get him to sign. Glen already has the papers drawn up . . . And thirdly, I have spoken to your bank manager as your lawyer, requesting a change of title agreement, transferring the deed of the property to your name in order to liquidate the asset. Which will make the bank happy, instead of a messy mortgage foreclosure. Of course, it goes without saying that Mike will have to sign on the dotted line!"

"*Wow!* This is coming at me like a bullet train." June was trying to absorb the explosion.

"June, honey, if we want to be together, we have to strike when the iron's hot." Phil lifted the phone. "Glen, can you fetch Mrs. Summers's divorce papers . . ."

* * *

"*Summers, get your lazy ass outta that cot . . .* You have a visitor. *Do you hear me?*"

Mike gave a disgruntled sigh as he threw his feet to the floor.

"Keep your fucking shirt on . . . *I heard you.*"

"Put your wrists together and come close to the cell bars while I clip these cuffs on, and no funny business, or you'll be eating through a straw for the next six months . . . Savvy?"

Mike put his wrists together to allow the corporal to close the hardware.

"So, who's the visitor?" Mike asked.

"*How the fuck do I know!*" The watch cop unlocked the cell door.

"Just walk in front of me straight to the end of the cell block, then turn right."

"Summers is it?" the sergeant asked, blocking the door to the visiting room.

"Yeah, Sarge."

"Then I'll take it from here." The sergeant unlocked the steel door with the reinforced three-quarter-thick glass window. "Just sit at that table." He pointed. "Your visitor will be here in a couple of minutes. He's going through security."

Mike sat on the hard plastic chair, waiting patiently while drumming his fingers on the table. The entrance door suddenly opened, and a tall, slim gentleman probably in his early forties, dressed in a blue pinstriped business suit, a crisp white shirt, and a red-and-white-striped tie offered his hand.

"I'm Tim Matheson from legal aid."

Mike accepted the handshake under the wary eye of the sergeant, and Tim took the seat opposite.

Matheson was around six one, handsome in his own sort of way. The wavy greying black hair, steely blue eyes, a longish narrow jaw line and nose to match, looking every inch the lawyer.

He opened his briefcase and removed a stack of papers.

"Mike, unless you have appointed a lawyer, I will be representing you under the state's legal aid provision. In short, at no cost to you." "Am I meant to be pleased?" Summers sneered.

"Listen, Summers." Mike's attitude had ruffled Matheson's feathers, *not a good idea!* "In my job, I meet smart-asses like you every day. *Now listen and listen good!* I don't give a shit for you personally, but as a defence lawyer I have job to do, and that is to defend you to the best of my professional ability. Now don't give me a hard time and open your ears and listen . . . *Cappice?* The bottom line is that you have been charged with the attempted murder of a senator's daughter and the niece of the district attorney . . . A capital offense, which, if found guilty, carries a minimum twenty-five to thirty . . .

And with heavyweights like these, I don't have to tell you, you don't have jack shit of a chance unless you accept me as your defence lawyer . . . Now *what's it gonna be?*" Tim glanced at his watch. "I have better things to do than listen to your crap, so shape up or ship out!"

Tim passed Summers the papers agreeing to appoint him as his defence attorney.

Summers thought for a moment. What this guy was saying made good sense; besides what was the alternative?

"*Gimme that fucking paper!*"

"Read each page carefully, then if you agree, initial it, then date and sign the last one."

Summers gave a grunt, which supposedly meant yes, then went about the business of digesting the legal jargon.

"I'm good." Mike passed the papers to Matheson fully signed.

"*Good.* I'm glad you've come to your senses. Now what I need from you is a complete and unabridged account of what happened on that fateful night."

"It all started with a call from Laura Williams at around one o'clock on the morning of the . . ."

* * *

Terry Johnson had had a shit of a day. The office was in reverse gear with negative waves and with no sign of a call from Blakely, Mildred Pitt and Jaycee Davis had already accepted the inevitable. As for Terry's credibility? *You guessed right.* Down the toilet!

"*That fucking Blakely!*" Terry was nursing her wrath. "What the hell's keeping him?" She was cursing below her breath when he loud ring of the phone broke her thought train. "*It's about fucking time!*" She grabbed the receiver in anticipation.

"Johnson here."

"Terry, it's Lily from reception. I have that guy on the line again . . . Brent Kennedy. Shall I put him through?"

"Fuck, this is all I need!"

"I'm sorry, Terry, I didn't catch that."

"It's okay, Lily, put him through."

"So how's 'Bruce Lee' today?" The comment brought a smile to Terry's face; maybe this was the pick me up she needed.

"And how's Romeo?" Terry threw it back, laughing.

"Thinking about you, of course, and hoping I can entice you out on another date, like make my day?"

Terry laughed again. "You're something else, dude!"

"I hear you laughing. Does that mean a yes?"

"It's nothing to do with you, Brent . . . It's just . . ." Terry gave a sigh. "It's just that I've had one helluva day at the office."

"Nothing that some hot music and a tequila wouldn't cure . . . Come on, Terry, chill out."

"Aw, all right then, but I may not be the best company . . . So what time?"

"I'll pick you up at your apartment . . . At say . . . seven?"

"Do you have my address."

"Yeah, remember?"

"Okay, smart-ass . . . Seven, and don't be late!"

Terry placed the receiver back, then leaned back in her chair a smile on her face. Maybe it wouldn't be such a bad day after all.

The phone rang again.

"Now who the hell this time?"

"Terry, it's Lilly again. I have Laura on the line."

"Laura, what a coincidence I was just thinking about you. I thought about wrapping up early and coming to visit you as I have a date at this evening." There was pregnant pause.

"Laura, are you still there?"

"I'm being discharged early, in fact today, and I thought I would tell you the good news, hoping you could pick me up, but now that you have other plans . . ."

"Laura . . . Laura . . . Don't be silly. You're coming home with me, that's what we agreed. Don't worry about my date. That's not important."

"Are you sure?"

"No more said. I'll pick you up around six. Honey, that's great news, and I'm gonna look after you. Now drop this phone and save your voice . . . *Ciao.*"

"*Hell*, I had better phone Brent and tell him the change of plan . . . *Christ,* I just remembered . . . *I don't have his fucking number!*"

* * *

Tim sat back and puffed his lips.

"I gotta lay it in on the line, Mike, you don't have a lot going for you. The jury's going to be tainted with the death of Perino splashed across the tabloids . . . A respected cop leaving a young family while doing his duty arresting a fugitive on the run. *Christ, Mike!* Why didn't you turn yourself in?"

"You said it yourself—Senator Williams . . . Jake Murray, the DA. Hell, I'm hung, drawn, and quartered before I even open my mouth."

Matheson sighed again, Summers was right, but whatever, he was going to go down and go down hard, but by how much would depend on a creative defence lawyer.

"Mike, somehow I have to nullify in the jury's eyes the attempted murder charge and you must plead not guilty at the session's court tomorrow. I'll be attending that hearing with you. Clean yourself up and look like a respectable businessman and, above all, put on that remorseful face. Do you think you can contact your wife to fetch a suit and stuff?"

"That's one helluva ask, considering."

"Well, you had better try. I'm leaving now, I have everything I need, but if you think of something that might be I important, here's a pen and paper, jot it down. I'll see you at nine tomorrow to discuss your defence."

Tim turned to the sergeant. "I'm done." "Stay there, Summers, you have another visitor." Mike looked at Tim and shrugged.

"This must be my day . . . I didn't know I'm so popular . . ."

* * *

"Mrs. Summers, you must walk through the metal detector first for security purposes. Place anything that's metal into this plastic tray, including your bag."

June nodded and began to unload.

As Tim was about to leave, he couldn't but help hear the guard mention "Mrs. Summers."

"Excuse me, Mrs. Summers." He turned to catch June before she left for the visitor's room.

"*Eh . . . Err.* Yes?" *Who can this be?* the thought immediately crossed her mind.

"Sergeant, can I speak with Mrs. Summers? It will only take a moment." The sergeant nodded, a man of few words.

"I'm sorry. How can I help you?" June asked somewhat agitated, she had plenty of other things on her mind and didn't need another distraction.

"Let me introduce myself." Tim passed June his card. "My name is Tim Matheson, your husband's defence lawyer."

"Listen." June stopped Matheson in his tracks. "If it's question time about my husband's case, you got the wrong person. I've given the police a signed statement which, I'm sure, under the freedom of disclosure, you have legal access to. Now if you don't mind?"

"Mrs. Summers, you've got it all wrong. If you could just let me explain."
"I don't have all day." June gave him the full facial.

"Your husband has to appear in court tomorrow, and I wondered if it would be possible for you to fetch him a change of clothing and toiletries?"

"*Why should I?*" June shot back, hostility in her voice. "After what he's done to me and his children, *let alone the Perino family?*"

Tim shrugged dejectedly; he could understand June's sentiments.

"I'll leave it you, Mrs. Summers, but it's a small thing I'm asking."

June paused for a moment in thought. "I'll think about it . . . Now do you mind?" She rudely brushed him aside.

"I'm finished, Sergeant." Tim sported a wry smile; he knew he had nailed it.

*   *   *

"Well, lookee here, I didn't expect to see my loving wife."
"Keep it down, Summers," the sergeant barked. "*And no touching.*"
"Yeah . . . Yeah, *I heard you!*"

As June took the plastic seat, she knew this wasn't going to be easy, but her strategy was to play it cool and not to start a war. She had to play on Mike's conscience, the faithful wife, the deserted family left destitute by an unfaithful and cruel husband.

"Mike, you look terrible!" she began.

"Wouldn't you be in this hellhole?"

"Listen, I'll send a change of clothing and toiletries by courier when I return home."

Mike didn't expect the loyal wife treatment, and he immediately calmed down.

"Thanks." His expression didn't change, and June had to start again somewhere.

"*Mike.*" She paused. "There's no point asking you why you got into this mess. I guess over the years, I always suspected that you were unfaithful. The lipstick on your collar, the perfume, the late nights when you were supposed to be at the office and when I phoned you were never there. *Mike, why?* I was a good wife, looking after you and the children. *I mean am I ugly or something?*"

The pain was getting to Mike, and it showed in the lines on his face as he listened in silence. June looked as radiant as ever, and he had to ask himself the question.

"Should I ask how the children are coping?" Mike was dancing with wolves.

"Sheryl is Sheryl." June shook her head. "But Steven, he really hates you."

"*Hmmm . . . And you?*"

"Mike, it's over. It's nonnegotiable."

"I guess I don't blame you." Mike reached over and touched her hand.

"Summers . . . *I said no touching!*"

Mike gave a disgusted look and promptly removed his hand.

"June, if only I could turn the clock back. I've been such a jerk, but she was going to expose me if I didn't leave you, and I couldn't bear to see you and the kids get hurt. It may sound a bit corny now, *but it's the truth!*"

June sighed. "Whatever, Mike, the damage is done, and all the remorse in the world won't change a damn thing."

"I guess I deserve that. If that's the case, then why are you here?"

June gingerly removed the papers from her computer bag and placed them on the table. There's never a good time.

"Mike, let me put it this way. Firstly, you emptied the joint bank account and left me and the kids with virtually nothing. In fact, if it wasn't for the generosity of your boss, Chuck Briggs, agreeing to pay your severance entitlements, we would be on skid row, and to add fuel to the fire, the bank is going to foreclose on the mortgage and auction off the property. I have already returned the Beamer, and there will be cancellation charges as stipulated in the lease agreement. Mike, don't you understand . . . *I am stone broke!*" "So, what's with the stationery?"

June passed the transfer title deed.

"Mike, if you have any conscience at all, you will sign the transfer to allow me to sell. With some luck, I might get more than the outstanding mortgage to help me pay for the first year of Steven's university and a deposit to rent a small apartment."

Mike listened to June's plea in silence, his eyes reflecting his regret and sadness.

"I guess it's the least I can do for the kids," he grumbled. "Gimme a pen . . . Where do I sign?"

June breathed a sigh of relief, but the worst was still to come.

"Thanks, Mike, but it doesn't stop there." June slid the papers in front of him.

"I might have guessed." Mike read the large, printed heading. "Application for divorce nisi."

"It's the only way, Mike . . . *It's over.*" June blurted out, relieved it was finally out in the open.

"And the lawyers . . . Stevens & Stevens. *Now doesn't that ring a bell? Phil Stevens*, I remember him well. The handsome NYU quarterback that had all the chicks dropping their panties, and if my memory serves me right, you were in the queue. You had him bad until I laid you on the night of the prom, huh?" "Mike, don't be so fucking crude." June was losing it.

"*Cosy* . . . The old flame helping you out at no charge or maybe a roll in the cot is more like it. *So why should I sign this?*"

"It's either that, Mike, or I divorce you for desertion and mental torture, which will take two years. You and I both know you're not going to walk the walk. You're going to prison for a long-time whichever way you look at it. Mike, I am still young, and I want to start a new life. If you have any feelings left for me, you will sign these divorce papers . . . Mike, I'm asking you *please . . .*"

Mike leaned forward on his elbow, placing his chin in his hand. He was brooding at the thought that you can't have your cake and eat it too. *But doesn't everyone want that?*

"Mike, are you listening?" June was at the desperation stage.

Without saying another word, Mike suddenly picked up the pen and scribbled his signature.

"Sergeant, *I'm finished here.*" He rose to his feet, turning to stare at June one last time. "It's too bad. I wish things could have been different, but I've made my bed . . ."

For a fleeting moment, June felt pity and remorse, looking at this once successful executive, now a broken man, and all because of the forbidden fruit. *What a waste!*

"Goodbye, Mike." June turned and left, a solitary tear trickling down her cheek. A new chapter in her life was about to begin.

CHAPTER 2

"Hi, Judy."

"*Captain Baker*... And Ruth, how have you been?" Judy was being polite, although there was no love lost between her and Baker's wife.

"I'm good, we must get together one of these days but most certainly under better circumstances. It's been a very sad day, and I really feel for Rose and the boys."

"We were just about to leave, Ted." Bill grabbed Judy's hand. She had a big mouth, and it was not the first time she had embarrassed him.

"This was a befitting reception for a fine cop," Baker commented. "Rose did a nice job under the circumstances . . . Bill, I'm glad I grabbed you before you left. I need to discuss something important with you first thing in the morning. When are you seeing Doc Nelson?"

"If my memory serves me right, two in the afternoon at his surgery. I have some embroidery to be removed."

Baker grinned. Same old Bill.

"I know you are still on sick leave, but I would appreciate it if you can you make it at ten in my office?"

"*What sick leave?* I can't wait to get back. Sure, I'll make it, no sweat . . . We had best get going, Judy, or your mother won't be too happy."

"Bye, Judy."

"Bye, Ruth." Judy gave a ventriloquist smile, gritting her teeth.

As they left the Sheraton for the car park, as usual Judy couldn't wait to beg the question.

"So what was all the cloak-and-dagger stuff about?" Bill unlocked the Pontiac without replying.

"Did you hear me?"

"I heard you, for Christ's sake! Get in the bloody car."

"Hey, who do you think you are you bossing around? I'm not one of your kowtow detectives."

"Judy, give it away. I saw how you looked at Baker's wife . . . You fucking embarrass me."

"Who does she think she is anyway? *Mrs. High and Mighty.* That should be your job. You are every bit as good as Baker!"

"Judy, are you going to get in this fucking car or what? I'm losing my fucking patience. You know what your problem is? *You are just downright fucking jealous!*"

Judy scowled as she finally opened the passenger door and slipped into the front seat, her tight black fitted skirt sliding up past her thigh, and Bill couldn't help but take in the view. *Is Judy doing this on purpose or what?* he had to ask himself.

"Do you like what you see? Because that's all you're gonna get tonight." Judy slammed the door and struggled to pull her skirt down.

Bill turned the key and slipped the stick into drive.

"You're a piece of work . . ."

* * *

"I need to go home and change first and get out of these office clothes."

She glanced at her watch. *"It's just turned four fifteen and I might . . ."* Terry was speaking to herself. *"Might just be able to pick up Laura and return to the apartment before seven."*

Terry grabbed her briefcase and began to stuff some papers between the dividers, then suddenly stopped.

What the hell am I doing? I don't need this stuff anymore.

She threw the papers back on the desk, grabbing her jacket and almost sprinting down the passageway past reception toward the elevator.

"You're leaving early tonight?" Lily the receptionist commented. "Is it Brent?" She grinned.

"Don't be so nosy." Terry joked. "No, I'm going to pick up Laura. She is being discharged from the hospital today."

"Give her my regards . . ."

Terry didn't answer as she barely squeezed between the elevator's closing doors.

* * *

Terry's drive to West Street through the Holland Tunnel to Clarkson, overlooking the river, was surprisingly smooth. For whatever reason, tonight the traffic was light. Brickfield's apartment building came into view, and Terry grinned as she checked the dash clock. She was making good time.

At last, she turned the key in the lock and switched on the lights. In no time, her heels kicked off and skirt at her ankles, she was squeezing into her Levi's. The white woollen polo, sneakers, and a jacket would keep the autumn chill away. One last glance in the mirror and a final hair ruffle and she was gone.

"Tonight's the night . . . Everything is gonna be all right . . . Ain't nobody gonna stop us now . . ." Terry sang Rod Stewart's famous hit. She was really on a high after a disappointing "no call" day from Blakely. This was just the diversion she needed.

*   *   *

"Hi, Martha." Terry smiled as she arrived at reception. "Can I go straight up?"

"Yeah, she's waiting for you . . . You know the room."

"*Do I!* I've been here often enough. How is she?" Terry asked.

"*Waiting patiently* . . . Say, listen before you go." A thought crossed Martha's mind. "'Meet the Parents' are here. You get my drift? I'm just giving you a friendly warning."

"Thanks, Martha, you're a gem. Don't worry, I'm prepared."

"Good luck to you, honey . . . *You're gonna need it!*"

Martha's parting words were still echoing in Terry's ears as she stood in the elevator.

Tonight's the night. Terry hummed the tune again as she knocked on the door of Laura's private room, as matter of courtesy. And sure enough, seated in doom and gloom were Laura's parents, almost like a wake; the look on their faces were anything but happy. The battle lines already drawn.

Laura was seated on the side of her bed fully dressed; her small carry-on parked at her feet.

"Hi, honey, you look great." Terry was laying it on. In fact, Laura looked anything *but* happy!

"Terry," Senator Williams interjected. "I know you have nothing but the best intentions, but even though the hospital has discharged our daughter, she is still an outpatient requiring constant monitoring and medication with weekly check-ups at the hospital. And with you in full-time employment, should the unthinkable happen, *God forbid,* and Laura had a relapse, who is going to be on hand to call the emergency services?"

Terry took a deep breath. She had to be tactful if she was going to win the parents over for Laura's sake.

"First of all, Mr. Williams, to put your mind at rest, I'm taking my outstanding annual leave, meaning I'll be at home for at least three weeks to look after Laura 24/7 and help her settle in. I have a comfortable apartment and Laura will have her own room and most importantly, you are welcome to visit Laura at your pleasure."

"*David,* you are visibly upsetting Laura." Margaret had had enough. "Now please, for your daughter's sake, don't continue. If this is what Laura wants, and as long as she is happy, you should be grateful for her speedy recovery."

The senator was not used to being the loser, and the anger in his expression was clearly visible.

"Margaret, I've said my piece, *be it on your head.*"

"Father, please don't spoil my day. I love you both, and I appreciate your concerns, but with respect, at twenty-eight, I can make my own decisions."

"Just like you did before and look at the mess it got you into!" Her father scowled, rubbing salt into her wounds.

"David, if you are hell-bent on continuing this . . . *Then I'm leaving.*"

"Maybe we should both leave. I've said my piece. Remember, Laura, if you should change your mind, you are always welcome to come home, twenty-eight years old or not."

"Goodbye, darling, it's time your father and I left. Now you look after yourself . . . You hear me? And promise to ring me tonight."

"I will, Mother."

Margaret gave Laura a kiss on the cheek; she was visibly upset and on the verge of tears.

"Goodbye, Father."

"Come, Margaret." The senator turned and left without another word.

Terry turned and gave a big smile. "Let's go, honey, we got a lotta livin' to do . . ."

* * *

"Honey, that's great news. Listen, it's too late for you to return to the office, so why don't I drop by your place, then we can discuss your meeting with Mike?"

"What time?" June asked.

"Looking at my desk, it'll be pretty late. Look, why don't I call you when I'm about to leave?"

"I understand, darling, but don't stay too late. I'll keep you some dinner. I'm sure you'll be starved. Love you . . ."

* * *

"Would you like more meatloaf, Steven?" June asked.

"No thanks, Mother, I'm good. But I really enjoyed it. It's been so long since you cooked meatloaf, it was Fathe—" Steven stopped abruptly in the middle of his sentence, the painful memory of his father and how things used to be inducing an awkward silence.

"*Your father's favourite, Steve?* Son, I know how you must feel, but somehow we all have to get over this and move on."

"*But, Mother,*" Sheryl interrupted. "The TV, the newspapers, they are always in our face." She was almost in tears. "I wish we could go someplace . . . Someplace as far away as possible from New York and start again." She threw her napkin on the table and rose to leave.

"*Sheryl,* just sit where you are for a few minutes . . . *Sheryl* . . . You heard me!"

"Mother, if it's about . . ."

"Yes, it's about your father, and for your information, I went to visit him today."

"Mother, *must we?*" Steven protested.

"*Yes, we must!* Your father will appear in court tomorrow in front of a state judge where he will hear the charges laid against him to enter a plea of guilty or not guilty. If he pleads not guilty, then he will go to trial. Which means the media will be knocking on our doorstep, so be prepared. The good things that came out of our stressful meeting, to say the least, was your father has agreed to a divorce and has transferred the title deeds of the house to me. Which means I can now sell and retain the proceeds if in excess of the outstanding mortgage and expenses. It may not be much because of the market downturn, but it will give us breathing space to rent a new place and move away and, more importantly, Steven, help with your university fees."

"At least he has a conscience, which surprises me," Steven reacted.

"Mother, does this mean you're going to divorce Father?" Sheryl came to life.

"Yes, *and the sooner the better!*"

"And how about Phil?" Sheryl was Sheryl.

"*Sheryl!*"

"It's all right Steven, it's a perfectly normal reaction . . . Phil has been really good to me at a time when I was destitute and lost and, in reality, I admit, a shoulder to cry on. But to answer your question, Sheryl, I'm not going to rush into marriage. Of course, as you have surmised, Phil and I are close, but still waters run deep. I've been burned once, and it will be a long time before I trust a man enough to marry him."

"Is Phil coming over this evening?"

"Yes, honey, but he's held up at the office. He'll be here around eight. Now how about helping your mother clear the table and stack the dishwasher?"

* * *

The drive to Queens with Judy in her usual hostile mood was the norm.

"Well, are you going to sit there like a dummy? What the hell is getting into you, Judy?" Bill was showing his frustration.

"It's you and this lousy 'cop's wife' thing. I'm fed up with it! I want a life where I don't have to scrape and scrounge and look after two kids every day, the 'Desperate Housewife.'"

"So, what do you want to do . . . Put on your heels and go dancing?"

"Don't be so fucking ridiculous . . . Well . . . I might as well tell you I've taken a job."

"*You've what!*"

"*You heard me!*"

"And if it's not too much to ask, who's fucking looking after the kids?"

"My mother . . . Since my father, died she has had plenty of time on her hands and I've phoned her, and she has volunteered."

"*Nice* . . . The mother-and-daughter conspiracy . . . I might have known. Your mother and I have never seen eye to eye. So where's this job of yours?"

"Do you remember Adam Scott . . ."

"Adam Scott?"

"You met him on a couple of occasions at Tony's barbecues. He's a friend of Tony's brother."

"Go on."

"It just so happened I bumped into him today at Tony's funeral and then at the reception. We got to talking, and he offered me a job as his personal secretary."

"*Just like that!*"

"*So what are you insinuating?*"

"Christ, Judy, it's been years since you worked as a secretary."

"Is that such a big deal? Anyhow I'm taking the job. I start with a salary of forty-five K, and now at last I'll have my own money."

"So what does this . . . this . . . whatever his name is do?"

"He has a GM Auto franchise, if you must know, and for your information, I start my new job on Monday."

Bill shook his head in disgust. "You might have at least discussed it with me first."

"*What* . . . Only to have cold water poured on it?" "*I should have stayed in fucking Argentina . . .*"

*　*　*

"So how do you feel now?" Terry asked as she drove through the traffic. In another twenty minutes, they would arrive home.

"*Free as a bird.* I just couldn't stay in that house with my father. I don't know how my mother has put up with him all these years."

"Whatever, Laura, you're coming home with me, and you can stay at my apartment as long as you like. I've had your room ready since yesterday."

"But how about your work? You mentioned to my parents you were taking accumulated leave?"

"You *know* how I have resigned?"

"Yes."

"So, I'll phone personnel tomorrow and tell them I'm taking leave. The company will be happy, as it will reduce my severance pay . . . Or they may even tell me to come in and clear up my desk, huh?" Terry laughed.

"I gotta hand it to you, Terry, you handled my parents like a pro . . . *Or should I say my father!*"

"Lighten up. We'll soon be home, and I have a nice bottle of chardonnay in the icebox . . . *Say,* maybe you can't indulge if you're on medication!"
"Who says?"

Both girls burst into laughter; it was like old times.

*　*　*

Terry pressed the stock switch and hung a right into Clarkson.

"Home at last!" she commented as she drove toward the underground car park.

"Say, I thought you had a date tonight with the handsome Brent?" It suddenly struck Laura.

"I did, but would you believe it, I don't have his phone number and I couldn't tell him of my change of plan . . . And it's seven twenty-five now, so unless he is madly in love with me, he'll be nowhere to be seen." Terry slowed down to turn into the ramp.

"There's a guy sitting over there in a black Porsche. It wouldn't happen to be him, would it?" Laura pointed.

"I'll be darned!" Terry rolled down the window and waved. "Come up to the apartment . . . 10A . . . I'll explain it to you later." Brent smiled. At least he wasn't stood up.

"He looks a hunk," Laura commented, a smile on her face as they walked to the car park elevator.

"Oh, does he now?"

"Well, at least I'll get a chance to meet him."

"Gimme that bag and get to that lift before I change my mind." Terry burst into laughter.

"Competition, huh?"

"Get out of it!"

*   *   *

"Honey, I'll take your bag to your room. You take the load off on the sofa. You must be bushed after the helluva day *you've* had!"

"Thanks, Terry." Laura kicked off her shoes. "Ah, that feels better." The bell rang.

"That must be Brent. Stay where you are, Laura, I'll get it." "Hi, Brent." Terry gave him a peck on the cheek.

"Well, don't stand just there, *come in.*" Terry could be tactless at times.

"Listen, I'm sorry about tonight, but let's not cry in our beer. I want to introduce you to my best friend, Laura."

Laura . . . Brent Kennedy." He offered his hand.

"Brent, while I unpack Laura's stuff you can entertain her until I'm free, and you can start by going to the refrigerator and opening that bottle of chardonnay. The glasses are on the second shelf in the first kitchen cupboard."

"So, tell me, Brent, what line of work are you in?" Laura took a sip from her glass. "*Hmmm*, this *is* good. After weeks in the hospital, I almost forgot what good wine tastes like."

"I'm an architect."

"That must be interesting." It was light banter.

"And you were in the hospital?"

"Yes, I was just discharged today, and you don't want to know. I have my own apartment, but Terry has volunteered to look after me until I get back on my feet. She's a true friend."

"So I gather."

"You two seem to be getting along fine, I'm jealous . . . Big boy, where's my drink?"

*   *   *

"And that's the reason why I almost stood you up."

"*Now I understand!* But first things first. Here's my cell number, it's on my business card." Bret handed Terry his card.

"Laura, you must be tired, and I have an early appointment tomorrow, so I think I had better call it a night."

"Are you sure you don't want another refill?"

"No, I'm driving."

"Then if you'll excuse me, Laura, I'll see Brent to the elevator."

"No sweat, honey." Laura smiled. She couldn't blame Terry; this guy is a piece of work.

Terry pressed the button.

"I really feel a real heel almost standing you up tonight."

"It's no big deal, honey. Besides, I enjoyed your friend's company. However, I would really enjoy taking you both to dinner tomorrow evening, if that's possible."

"Anything is possible." Terry grinned.

The elevator doors opened.

"I gotta go, honey." Brent brushed Terry's lips with his. "I'll pick you both up at seven thirty. You have my number, in case of, as you say, a change of plan." Brent gave a cheeky grin.

"Don't worry. I can't pull that one twice in a row. Good night, darling."

*   *   *

"I'm off to my room, Mother, it's after nine." Steven was keeping his mother company watching television. Sheryl had retreated to her room immediately after dinner.

"I wonder what's keeping Phil? *Eh . . . err*, yes, Steven . . . Good night, son."

No sooner had Steven disappeared upstairs than the doorbell rang.

"That must be Phil now." June hurried to the window and pulled back the drapes. "I thought as much." She smiled as she went to the door.

"Hi, honey, I'm sorry I'm late, but I couldn't face that desk again tomorrow. Gimme a big kiss." Phil placed his arms around June in a bear hug and savagely crushed her lips.

"*Now the neighbours really have something to talk about!*" June pulled him inside and hurriedly closed the door.

"Have the kids gone to their rooms?" Phil was laughing at June's antics.

"Yes, only just. Here, gimme your jacket, and go into the kitchen, I've kept aside some meatloaf and mash. It'll only take a few minutes to heat in the micro . . . I assume you are starved?"

"*Am I!*"

"Would you like a beer? Go help yourself from the refrigerator and grab a seat at the breakfast bar."

Phil unscrewed the cap and took a swig from the cold Bud.

"Isn't *that* good! You spoil me, honey."

"Away with you." June was busy "Glad Wrapping" his supper for the microwave, and Phil couldn't help feasting his eyes on June's sexy bottom as she bent to open the door. Her tracksuit, although loose, when she stooped, outlined the lines of her panties. It was a real turn on.

"God, June, you're so sexy!"

"Mister! Concentrate on your beer. Your supper will be on the bar in a few minutes."

"If you say so." Phil gave a big smile, but his mind was on something else.

*   *   *

"Hmmm, *is this good!* I'm not a fan of meatloaf, but this doesn't get any better."

"Darling, you'll have to do better than that to get me into bed." June teased, taking her stool.

"I'll touch that subject later." Phil laughed. "So how did it go with Mike today?

"As I told you, he's done the honourable thing, and for that, I am grateful. It wasn't easy and when he read your company name . . . *Well, you can just imagine.* He put two and two together and almost reneged on the signing."

"But it's great news, honey. I'll get Glen to proceed with the divorce papers first thing in the morning." "Darling, once my divorce is final . . ." Phil interrupted, like he couldn't wait.

"I want to marry you . . .," he blurted. *"That's if you'll have me?"* Phil waited somewhat sheepishly.

"Honey, I really love you, but do you know the baggage I'm carrying? I have two teenage kids. I'm all but broke and looking to go back and continue my law degree . . . My husband has been arrested and charged with attempted murder. Any man in his right senses would leave a vapor trail."

"Does that mean no?"

"Phil, you would make me the happiest woman in the world . . . Of course, it's yes, but time can change everything. What I'm saying is let's wait until the decree nisi is final, which will take around three months, and then if you still feel the same . . ."

"*Is that all!*" Phil gave a sigh of relief. "For a moment, you had me worried there. Honey, nothing will change. I want to spend the rest of my life with you."

"That's so sweet, darling . . . I think that deserves a very special kiss. Uh-uh . . . Not tonight, Napoleon."

CHAPTER 3

Summers was awake bright and early; this was decision day and certainly the most important day in his life except for the day his mother gave birth, and after a scrape with the razor, he looked a new man. A shower would have been the icing on the cake, but Mike would have to make do with the tiny stainless-steel sink and water that would freeze the nuts off an Eskimo.

"*Breakfast, Summers,*" the "new face" barked.

"*For Christ's sake . . .* Can't you see I'm on the can? Slip that pig swill below the bars."

"You watch your mouth, pretty boy, I'm the new cop on this watch, and I don't take any shit from snowdrops. I'm not Morris. He's too fucking soft with you lowlifes. *Now,* if you don't want city hall's food, *personally I don't give a shit!*"

The black mountain with the grotesque overhang pushed the food below the bars, the second-day coffee swill, spilling into the steel divider, floating what looked like a stomped-on hamburger.

"You tell 'em, Sarge."

"Dempsey." Jackson turned to face "the mouth," his hands on his hips, giving the "don't mess with me" stare. "If you don't shut that that fucking big mouth of yours, I'll put you in with that ape Corry."

"Bring it on, Sarge, I forget what having a piece of black ass feels like."

Jackson shrugged. "Do you see what I mean, Summers?" I'm surrounded by queers and steers . . . *Maaan . . .*"

The sergeant turned and viciously kicked the empty food cart down the cell block, crashing and rattling against the cell bars.

"I feel like a fucking waitress cow towing to these fucking losers. I'll be glad when my shift is done."

Jackson's grumblings followed him all the way to the watch house, and he had just sat on his fat ass and unfolded the race rag when the phone rang.

"Sergeant Jackson here."

"Jackson, it's Captain Norris."

"Yes, Captain."

"Summers is due for a court appearance in front of Phillips at ten. Make sure he's ready. His lawyer Tim Matheson will be interviewing him at nine. I'll call you when he arrives." The phone went dead.

Jackson slammed the phone back. *"Fucking asshole!"*

He poured a coffee from his flask and returned to study the form.

*   *   *

Mike looked at his neatly pressed shirt and the garment bag containing his suit and office apparel and sighed. From a successful marketing executive to a broken-down wreck about to face the "hanging judge." For a moment, he just stared blankly, his mind confused in a vacuum of reality and disbelief. But there was no way out. He was caged like a wild animal destined to be behind bars or set free by twelve people who would decide his fate: guilty or not guilty.

He sighed again; it was a lost cause. *I suppose I had better get dressed. Matheson will be here shortly, and I had better look my best. If I'm gonna go down, I might as well go in style.*

Mike slipped on his shirt and fastened his cuff links, then unzipped the garment bag. His dark-grey Italian tailored suit with the fine pinstripes was his favourite, and his mind flashed back to June. *Still the good wife.* He shook head in dismay as he stepped into his slacks.

"Dempsey, do you want this shit they call food? If I stare at it much longer, *so help me*, I'll throw up."

"Man, why the change? You're not hitting on me are yah, Summers?"

For a fleeting moment, Mike saw the funny side, and a smile crossed his face.

"You never know . . ." Mike slid the tray across to Dempsey's cell. "Bon Appetit."

"What the fuck does that mean?"

"I'll tell you later." Mike grinned and continued getting dressed.

*   *   *

The phone rang.

"What the fuck now?" Jackson was in the process of making big financials on the "three thirty." "I can't concentrate with this shit going on." He crumpled the notepaper and chucked it into the garbage bucket.

"Yeah, Jackson here."

"It's Delaney from the front desk. I have a Tim Matheson here from legal to see Summers, and he has clearance from Norris."

"Send him in. Tell him I'll meet him at the cell block entrance."

* * *

Jackson escorted Matheson to Summers's cell.

"*Summers,* your lawyer's here. Place both your wrists together through the food slot."

"Tim, is this necessary? It's not as if I'm going to leg it!" Summers protested.

"You had better get used to it Mike, it's going to be part of your life from now on."

"Thanks for the words of comfort . . . I had better slip on my suit jacket, if that's the case."

Jackson clipped the cuffs.

"*Go easy, fat man.*" Mike grimaced as the steel pinched his skin.

"What did you call me, white boy?"

"You heard me, shit face."

"*Why you . . .*"

"Hold it, Sergeant . . . *Mike, cool it!* This kinda stuff will get you nowhere."

Jackson had drawn his billy club ready to crack it over Mike's skull when he unlocked the cell.

"Don't do something you'll regret, Sergeant. Remember, I'm a legal witness." Matheson eyeballed him.

"I've got your number, Summers." Jackson scowled and backed off. He would wait until the time was right.

"Mike, you certainly look the part . . . *All businessmen.* I knew your wife would come to the party."

"*Shortly to be my ex-wife,* I'm sad to say. So, how's this getup gonna help me?"

Matheson took the load off and sat on Mike's cot.

"It's not gonna get you off, if that's where you're coming from, but it shows Philips that you respect the court and more so, Philips himself."

"How long have we got before Phillips dons the black hood?"

Tim had to laugh. "At least, Mike, you've retained your sense of humour, but to answer your question . . ." Tim glanced at his watch. "Fifteen minutes to be precise, so let's get down to business. We don't have much time . . ."

* * *

"So, I plead not guilty and throw myself at the mercy of the court?"

"Not so dramatic, Mike, but you've got the right idea . . . It's time to go . . . *Sergeant* . . ."

*   *   *

The armed guard escorted Mike through the side door of the courtroom accompanied by Matheson.

"He's all yours, Dave."

The security guard acknowledged and pointed the desk. "Over there, Summers. *Easy does it.* Don't get any ideas."

*   *   *

The courtroom looked like a courtroom, that is, if there is such a thing! Like the overpowering, dark, dismal oak paneling; the low-pillared wooden barrier separating the audience from the lawyers; the judge's elevated bench next to the witness stand; and the intimidating jury box to the right with its two-tier seating, the rear seats slightly higher than the front, just like the movie house, and with "Old Glory" proudly poled on either side of the judge's throne, adding a touch of class. *All that was missing was Richard Burr in his wheelchair!*

*   *   *

The grey-haired lady stenographer took her seat in front of the bench while the short, pear-shaped bailiff with the seriously thinning hair and the ridiculous parting above his left ear, endeavouring to camouflage his bald cranium, was standing at attention outside the door leading to the judge's quarters.

The door suddenly opened, with Philips storming into the courtroom full of energy, sprightly stepping up the three stairs to the bench.

"Please be upstanding for the Right Honourable Judge Randall Phillips." The bailiff's voice echoed throughout the empty courtroom.

Phillips donned his half glasses, taking a few moments to sort out his paperwork, then looking over the top to stare for a few moments at Summers and Matheson.

The crack of the gavel was like gunfire, either purposely to waken up the sleepers or scare the shit out of the jurors. Whatever . . . It would awaken the dead.

"Be seated. This court this now in session."

*   *   *

Phillips was recognized in the legal fraternity as a fair but firm New York state judge, with over fifteen years on the criminal bench. So much so, it was inevitable his nomination for the Supreme Court was overdue. In his mid-fifties, his thinning grey hair; fresh, rounded complexion; and grey eyes produced a pleasant amicable intuition, but under that human veneer was a tough, no-nonsense individual that suffers fools lightly and criminals even less. Around five nine, he was still in good shape, witty and sharp, with many a counsellor misjudging his temperament, albeit at their folly.

* * *

Phillips was about to begin when the sound of the heavy oak doors closing distracted his attention, reflecting the anger in his eyes as he looked up, and to his further annoyance, the annoying click, click of stiletto heels pierced his precious oak floor.

* * *

The tall hourglass figure of Lesley Collins performed the catwalk to the legal section dressed in her fitted dark-blue pinstriped suit, her jet-black hair tightly swept back in a coxcomb. As she was about to take her seat at the prosecution's desk on the opposite side of the courtroom, she momentarily turned to face Matheson a smirk on her face. They had met before. Her dark blue eyes and blemish less complexion placed her probably in her mid-thirties and to say she was a looker would be an understatement. Jake Murray, the DA, could certainly pick them.

* * *

"Counsellor Collins, please approach the bench."

"Your Honour?"

"Lesley, I don't care whether you had a heavy night last night or your alarm clock failed, or your boyfriend slept on your tail. When I say ten o'clock for the plea hearing . . . *I mean ten o'clock* . . . Do I make myself clear?"

"Yes, Your Honour."

"Then return to your desk. Now perhaps, Counsellor Collins, if I can have your undivided attention, I will continue . . ."

Summers whispered into Matheson's ear. "So, who's the good-looking broad?"

"*Shush.*" Matheson put his finger to his lips. "*Later.*" Phillips gave a "pay attention" cough.

"The State of New York versus Michael Summers in that on the evening of August 12, 2003, at approximately 8:30 p.m., you assaulted one Laura

Williams at apartment 6B Elm Apartments on Watt Street, inflicting serious bodily harm to the detriment of her life, with criminal intent to murder. How does the accused plead?"

"Not guilty, Your Honour." Matheson answered.

"Counsellor Matheson, unless *you a*re hard of hearing, I asked the accused the question. *What is happening to this court today?*" Phillips gave an "I give up" sigh. "Shall I repeat the question?"

"My apologies, Your Honour . . . Mr. Summers, please enter your plea."

"Not guilty, Your Honour."

"Stenographer, please enter in the records the accused plea of not guilty." "This court is in recess until Monday August 20, at 10:00 a.m. Mr. Matheson, on behalf of the defence, please ensure jury selection is completed before then. A word of advice to both counsellors . . . Make sure your material and witnesses are well versed. Because of the high profile of this case, the media will be in a feeding frenzy, and the last thing I need is a paparazzi circus . . . Guard, please escort the accused to the cells . . . This court is now in recess." Phillips slammed the gavel.

"Please be upstanding for the . . ."

* * *

"Mike, I'll be with you in a few minutes. I want to have a word with Collins."

"*Les*, it's been a while . . . How's things?"

"As good as could be expected."

"That doesn't sound too good." Tim was fishing.

"Tim, after that polite smack on the wrist from Phillips, what do you expect? He'll be bitching to Murray and raise merry hell."

"I guess so . . . Listen, why don't I cheer you up and entice you to join me for a coffee, or something stronger, across the street at the Pen & Wig?"

"The old haunt, huh? I'm tempted . . . Let me see." Collins checked her watch. "How long?"

"Gimme fifteen. I promised Summers, I would see him before I left."

"I don't understand you, Tim. You're a damn good lawyer, and you keep representing these losers, and what for, *nickels and dimes?*"

"Maybe I enjoy giving the underdog a chance."

Lesley shook her head. "Same old Tim, a knight in shining armor. You know Murray would take you on in a minute."

"*Prosecution* . . . Nah, I don't have the killer instinct."

"*Like me?*"

"You know the old saying, Les . . . If the cap fits?"

"*You're mean* . . . So why should I have a coffee with you?"

"Because I'm handsome, intelligent, and an excellent lawyer, and you're beautiful."

"*Ha . . . Ha-ha!*" Lesley burst into laughter. "You *are a* charmer . . . Fifteen minutes then . . . *And it's against my better judgment.*" Collins flashed her special "Colgate," then turned to leave, her stilettos inflicting further damage on "the old oak tree."

* * *

Mike rubbed his wrists to return the circulation; it was a relief to get free of the steel.

"I'll be watching you, white boy." Jackson eyeballed Mike as he turned to leave.

Mike hung his suit jacket on the peg and released the knot in his tie, then flopped on top of his cot kicking off his shoes.

"All this shit to say four words . . . 'Not guilty, Your Honour.' I ask you. *What the fuck!*" Mike rubbed his forehead.

"Summers, Matheson to see you." "Ugly mug" unlocked the cell door. "Move over, Mike, and gimme a seat." "So how did it go?" Mike asked.

"With Phillips, you never can tell. But you did the right thing showing the court respect."

"What's next?"

"Jury selection, and remember, you call the shots selecting the 'valiant twelve.'"

"*What the fuck does that mean?*"

"It means *you* select the jury, and my advice is, don't make it too obvious, but stick to the men, like say ten males and two females. Remember, a woman was assaulted, and female jurors go for the jugular. Do you get the picture?"

"Yeah." Mike replied with little enthusiasm; he was lower than low. "So what's with this broad, Lesley whatever her name is?" He changed the subject.

"Lesley Collins . . . She is the top prosecutor from the DA's office. *Man,* I tell you, she is one tough lady. This is the first time we will cross swords, and believe me, I'm not looking forward to it."

"That sounds encouraging, I must say." Mike felt even more depressed.

"Be honest, Tim, where do I stand? Give it to me straight."

Tim felt uncomfortable, but there was no point in beating round the bush.

"Tim, cut to the chase." Mike was becoming impatient.

"Whichever way look at it, Mike, you're gonna do time, and my job is to make sure you do as little as possible. That's the bottom line."

"At least thanks for being honest."

"Mike, I gotta go. I have another appointment. I'll see you again tomorrow at jury selection."

"If I were you, Tim, I would be chasing that good-looking chick from the DA's office, that is, unless you are already spoken for." Tim smiled. Summers was on the nail.

"No, I'm single and unattached, but then again?" Matheson grinned. "I might just take your advice . . . *Sergeant . . .*"

*   *   *

CHAPTER 4

Bill's natural body clock awoke him. *It must be around six*, he thought as he turned to face Judy. Last night had brought the worst out in both of them, and now, in hindsight, he was having pangs of guilt; maybe he was being too dogmatic and intolerant about Judy returning to the workforce. He stretched his hand over to awaken her, and to his amazement, *the bird had flown!*

"*Of course,* Judy starts her new job today, and her mother is coming over to take care of the kids." Bill pondered, staring into the darkness. "There's something bothering me about this guy Adam Scott . . ." He paused in thought. "But that's for another day. I had best get showered and join the kids for breakfast."

*   *   *

Bill was showered and dressed in record time, slipping into his NYPD tracksuit; there was no point in dressing. His appointment with Baker was at ten.

"You're up bright and early," Bill commented as he entered the kitchen; Judy was busy preparing breakfast.

"*My first day in my new job, remember?*" June shot back, resentment in her eyes.

697

"*The hell with you!* Civility costs nothing . . . What the hell's come over you?" Bill barked.

"You should speak, the pot calling the kettle black. Now if you don't mind, I'm busy. My mother will be here any moment, and I haven't dressed yet." June was still in her robe.

The sound of the doorbell couldn't have come at a better time to avoid World War III.

"That must be Mother now. If it's not too much trouble, perhaps you can go open the door?"

Bill gave a "what's the use" shrug.

"Good morning, Martha." He gave her a reluctant peck on the cheek.

There was no love lost between these two.

"Morning, Bill." came the frosty reply.

"Judy's in the kitchen preparing breakfast." "It's all right, I can manage." Bill shrugged. *So be it.*

*   *   *

Martha, in her late sixties and tragically widowed at fifty, was a true survivor. Close to her daughter, needless to say, she was more than disappointed when Judy, in her eyes, foolishly married a police officer with as much career opportunities as a bus driver. She had her good points in that she adored her grandchildren, and it filled the gap after losing her husband, Ted. She was the traditional "mother-in-law meddler" and poisoned Judy's mind on a number of occasions, especially when it came to family matters, but what's new? Time had not been good to her, with the typical operatic bust, the waistline that never was, and looking like a perfect stand-in for Mrs. Doubtfire. Her gray hair had been attacked with numerous dying saviors in the never-ending search for her lost youth, resulting in a straw-scarecrow color with nowhere else to go. Her bagged gray eyes, crow's feet, and deep laugh lines added to the "thousand words," but then everyone has to grow old gracefully, but as for Martha? *No more said!*

*   *   *

"I'll wake the kids, honey, you go and get dressed. Bill, would you like a coffee?" Martha was being polite.

"Later. I'll join the kids at breakfast."

*   *   *

"Hi, Dad, Grandma. Where's Mom?"

"She'll be down in a few minutes; she's just getting dressed. Your grandma will be taking you and your brother to kindergarten and school today." Bill answered.

"What's wrong with Mom?" Ian asked.

"Never you mind, just eat your Captain Crunch. Where's your brother?"

"He's on his way, Dad."

"Hi, Dad." Taylor grabbed his father.

Bill ruffled his hair. "Up you go." He picked him up and sat him on the breakfast stool. "And what kept you young man, may I ask?"

"He was playing with his Spiderman, Dad." Ian butted in.

"He's just jealous, Dad."

"*All right . . . All right . . .* Eat your breakfast, and I want to see clean plates this morning."

"How about you, Bill?" Martha asked.

"Just coffee, Martha. I can pour it myself," Bill answered, his tone icy.

"You're looking nice, honey." Judy had just entered the kitchen, and Martha was pouring it on.

"Yeah, I must say!" Bill interjected. "You look as if you're going to beauty contest."

"Sarcasm is the lowest form of wit." Judy was taking no crap.

"My, we are sensitive. If I had a secretary dressed to the hilt like you, I am sure *you would* be saying something."

"*Well, you don't, do you!* Just coffee for me, Mother. Adam will be here soon."

"Adam is it now . . . *Nice* . . . Moreover, a personal chauffeur into the bargain . . . Ask a silly question: Why can't you drive your own car? I mean this guy . . . eh, Adam"—Bill was adding salt to the wound—"will have to bring you home after work . . . *Cosy, wouldn't you say?*"

"You're sick. Driving that heap, you bought me would embarrass the lowest form of life."

The sound of a car horn broke the "Mexican standoff."

"That must be Adam now. I gotta go, Mother. Bye, kids, I'll see you tonight, and be good." June finished the last of her coffee.

"I wish you luck, honey." Martha couldn't resist the parting shot. "Thanks, Mother, after so long, I'm gonna need it . . ."

*   *   *

"He seems really nice."

"Who seems really nice?" Terry was busy over the stove, swirling the scrambled eggs.

"Brent . . . *Your latest!*" Laura replied.

"That's a nice way to put it, I must say," Terry joked. "I feel like some kind of man-eater . . . Scrambled eggs coming up, with fresh toast and coffee. Now why don't you grab the morning paper and enjoy your breakfast?"

"I'm not used to this five-star service." Laura laughed. "*Hmmm . . . I never knew you are such a good cook.*"

Terry burst into laughter. "Scrambled eggs . . . *Are you serious?*"

"Whatever, it's a lot better than hospital food. Come and join me." Laura opened the *Times.*

As she read the front page, her complexion turned an ashen grey. *There it was in bold print . . .*

Summers Goes to Trial for Attempted Murder

Michael Summers pled not guilty yesterday in the central court to the attempted murder of Laura Williams, the daughter of the often-outspoken Senator Dave Williams. Trial by jury will commence on Monday, September 23, at 10:00 a.m. in District Court 3. State Judge Randall Phillips will preside. When interviewed yesterday, District Attorney Jake Murray had this to say . . .

"What is it, honey?" Terry sensed the dramatic change in Laura's behaviour from happy and carefree to attending a funeral.

Laura suddenly burst into tears and turned the front page of the *Times* to face Terry.

"Laura, calm down . . . Calm down. Let's face it, honey, we both knew this was inevitable, but look on the bright side—this time this mongrel will disappear from your life forever. Now take a sip of your coffee and count to five."

Laura reached over and affectionately squeezed Terry's hand.

"Terry, I don't know what I would do without you, but will I have to appear in court? The thought scares me to death."

"Honey, your uncle, the DA, will make sure of that. Your testament is key to the prosecution's case . . . *Don't you want your day in court?*"

Laura pondered before she answered. In her mind, she would rather just disappear from New York and start a new life somewhere as just plain Laura Williams.

Laura wiped her eyes. "There were times, Terry, I have to admit, that I thought I would be happy to see him dead after what he did to me, but time heals everything, and worst of all, this is all because of my own stupidity."

"*Honey, cut the guilt trip.* As they say, it takes two to tango. *Now* . . . are you going to waste my gastronomic experience or what?"

Laura flashed a halfhearted smile. Uncharted waters was on the horizon, but worse still, the media frenzy was about to begin . . .

*   *   *

The breakfast dishes now in the washer, it was time for R&R. In short, feet up and relax.

"TV, honey?" Terry asked.

"Anything but the news," Laura answered. She didn't want a reminder of what lay ahead.

"Then can I entice you to glass of white wine to celebrate your homecoming?"

"It's bit early in the day, but then . . ." Laura finally smiled. "How can I refuse when you put it that way?"

"Now *you're* talking. I'll be back in a jiffy."

Laura opened the refrigerator and grabbed the wine bottle and a couple of glasses.

"Get your feet up and relax. Just think of yourself as being on vacation."

"I'll drink to that . . . Cheers." They touched glasses.

"Terry, changing the subject, what do you think is going to happen at the office?"

"Well, for a start, I've already tendered my resignation, and that will cause maximum pain. Furthermore, with you on convalescent leave and what with Blakely jumping ship, I'm afraid the boat is now sailing without a rudder." "What a mess!" Laura conceded.

"Laura, I hope you don't mind me asking, but when you are finally given a clean bill of health, what are *your* plans?"

"That's the three-million-dollar question, Terry. I have to be honest in that I haven't given it much thought. But if I'm being honest with myself, I'm just running away from the problem."

"I guess I don't blame you, but don't worry, honey, there's plenty of time . . . Another refill?"

"I think I'll go easy for the moment, Terry, but changing the subject, what's going to happen to you?"

"Don't worry, I can last for a few months on my severance pay."

"But what about Blakely's offer from Hewlett-Packard?"

"You know, sometimes I get concerned about Blakely's real motives. Like is it the job, or is it me?"

"Blakely is Blakely, Terry. I've known him since I joined ABM. He plays the field as a modern-day Casanova, but when push comes to shove, he doesn't have the balls. Besides, have you met his wife? *Good looking but dangerous.*"

"I get the picture." Terry laughed.

"If I know Blakely, Terry, he'll come to the party. Just be patient." The phone rang.

"Now who can this be?" Terry rose to answer the phone.

"Who knows. It just might be Blakely?" Laura joked.

"*Yeah, that'll be right!* Terry Johnson here . . ."

"Terry, Mark Smith from personnel."

"*Mark,* I had intended to phone you this morning to inform you that I am taking my outstanding leave with immediate effect."

"That won't be necessary, Terry. Fred Morris, our new boss, has instructed accounts to settle all your outstanding entitlements, including severance pay, in lieu of notice, provided you arrive at the office this morning to collect your personal effects. A check will be raised by finance for your collection."

"Don't worry, Mark. It will give me the greatest pleasure. Inform Morris that I'll be there before twelve."

"I got the gist of that." Laura couldn't help but overhear the conversation.

"It looks like I'm gonna have to leave you, Laura, but I should be back around three depending on the traffic. There's plenty of food in the refrigerator, just help yourself."

"Don't worry about me, Terry, I can manage."

"I had better get changed. I can't go in tracksuit pants now, can I?"

As Terry was about to leave for the bedroom, the loud ring of the phone startled her.

"*What the hell this time?* This must be telethon day."

"*Yes?*" Terry gave a disgusted sigh. "Terry Johnson speaking."

"Terry, it's Jack Blakely."

"*Jack* . . . Your ears must be burning. I was just talking about you to Laura."

"*Laura Williams?*"

"Yes, she's staying at my apartment until she gets on her feet."

"I'm glad to hear she is recovering . . . A bad business . . . Give her my best. Terry, the reason for my call is that Alan Beazley, VP personnel, wishes to interview you today at HQ. What time would be suitable?"

"I have another appointment. ABM is kicking me out of the office." Terry could hear Blakely laugh.

"Deja vu."

"*You got that right!*"

"The time Terry?" Blakely cut the slack.

"Say around three?"

"Just a sec, Alan is here with me now . . . He is nodding his head. Then I will see you at three sharp. Ciao."

"What did I tell you?" Laura was highly delighted as Terry placed back the phone, a big grin on her face.

"*Well, I'll be darned!* But, Laura, it looks like I'll be gone for the whole day."

"Don't worry, Terry, I'm a big girl. Besides, I can always contact you on your cell."

"Thanks, honey, for understanding, but now I must *really* get dressed and wear something that'll knock 'em cold."

*   *   *

"I tell you, Terry, the way you look today you are a certainty to get that job." Blakely was laughing all the way to his office. "You had Beazley eating from your hand."

"*Jack!* You make me feel terrible."

Jack was still grinning as he opened the glass-panelled door, the pronounced gold lettering depicting his new title: *J. Blakely, VP Marketing.*

"So you finally made it!" Terry stood for a moment in admiration.

"Yeah, I feel pretty good." He opened the door. "But, Terry, it's not all sugar and spice, there's plenty to be done . . . Take a load off. This guy Morris has a lot to answer for. I have been having nightmares thinking about the mess I have to clean up, and, Terry, that's why I am so glad to have you on board . . . Coffee?"

"No, I'm good, Jack . . . Say, this is a nice office." Terry was taking it all in.

"A big change from ABM, huh? In addition, you will be pleased to know that Rita commences as my personal and confidential secretary on Monday first."

"That's great, Jack." The news brought a smile to Terry's face." At least that will be *one person* I know in the office . . . Jack, I know you have a lot on your plate at the moment, but have you given much thought toward the hiring of Pitt and Davis?"

"Terry, I would love to have them on board, but my budget at the moment is not in good shape, as you can imagine. We are top heavy in marketing as it is, and that means redundancies, and redundancies cost money. Give me sometime till I settle in and do some restructuring."

"I understand, it's just that I half expected . . ."

Blakely cut her short. "You have my word, Terry . . . Now, more importantly, here is your contract of employment and job description. I'll leave you for a few minutes as I have some chores in the office to attend to.

Take your time, and read it carefully before signing." Blakely passed Terry the papers.

"Thanks, Jack . . . On second thought"—Terry smiled—"that coffee wouldn't go astray . . ."

*   *   *

"Pleased?" Blakely was back in the chair.

"*Am I!* It's a lot more than I expected."

"Yes, and you have a lot more responsibility."

"As they say, Jack . . . there's no free cheese in the mouse trap." Terry grinned as she scribbled on the bottom line. "There, the deed is done."

"Welcome aboard, Terry." Blakely rose and warmly shook Terry's hand.

"*My god, that time already!*" Terry tapped the crystal on her watch. "Six thirty."

"Do you have another appointment?" Blakely asked concerned.

"Sort of," Terry pondered.

"Is there a chance you can take a rain check? There's so much I have to discuss with you, and I thought it would be opportune over dinner."

Terry was in a dilemma. She had left Laura the whole day and, to make it worse, on her first day out of hospital. And then there was Brent and their dinner date.

"*Terry?*" Blakely was becoming impatient.

"Can you gimme a sec, Jack, while I make a call?"

"Of course . . . Do you want me to leave?"

"No, not at all." Terry opened her cell phone and dialed.

"Laura . . . Terry here . . . Yes, good news, I got the job. I will tell you all about it later . . . Yes, it's about this evening. Something has come up, and I won't be home until late . . . That is the other reason I am calling . . . Please give Brent my apologies when he arrives, but what I am suggesting is that you go to dinner with him. It will be a nice evening out for you, and he is good company . . . Of course, I don't mind . . . Then it's settled . . . No, I don't know what time I'll be home . . . The spare key to the apartment is in the fruit bowl on the breakfast bar . . . Enjoy yourself . . . Ciao." "Boyfriend trouble?" Blakely begged the question.

"Just a friend, nothing serious."

"Thanks, Terry. I appreciate it, but time is running away with itself, and I think we had better make tracks. You have your own car?" "Yes," Terry answered.

"*Hmmm*, that makes it awkward. I guess it would it be easier to give you the address of the restaurant than trying to tail me through the traffic."

"Whatever, Jack."

"The restaurant is Stephanos on . . ."

"Ethel, is the boss free?"

"I'm afraid not June, he's with a client at the moment. A Mr. Niven, the CEO of Mercury Wealth Solutions . . . Do you get the picture?" Ethel made a sort of face.

"Thanks for the tip, Ethel, I'll get on to it right away."

June returned to her desk and quickly opened the Mercury file. This was her first assignment, and she had all but finished her conclusions.

* * *

"So let's get this straight. Cooper doesn't have a leg to stand on in that the contract he signed is clear and concise and the return on investment was never guaranteed and would fluctuate depending on market forces. When the market was good, Cooper was happy, but now because of the downturn, he's suing for losses in that as fund managers, we should have advised him to change the mix of his portfolio from aggressive to balanced."

"That's the gist of it, but one of my legal assistants has been reviewing the case. Why don't I call her and save some time to get her overview and recommendations?"

Phil lifted the phone. "Ethel, can you ask June to join us and fetch the Mercury file? Thanks, Ethel."

"June, the boss wants you in his office to discuss you know what."

June smiled. She had already crossed the i's and dotted the t's and just in time, thanks to Ethel.

"Thanks, Ethel, for the tip." June picked up the folder, then knocked on Phil's door.

"Come in."

"Good morning, Mr. Stevens." June was purposely keeping it formal. "June, this is Mr. David Niven, the CEO of Mercury Wealth." "Mr. Niven, nice to meet you." June cordially shook his hand.

"Likewise." David smiled, taking in the scenery.

"Grab a seat June." Phil pointed.

June opened the folder and spread the papers on Phil's desk.

"June, why don't you save us some time and walk us through your conclusions."

"Sure . . ." June flicked through her papers. "Let's start with the meeting of May 26, with Barry Leeds, the fund manager for Jason Cooper. Let me draw your attention to the minutes of that meeting . . ."

"So, Cooper, at his own insistence, demanded Leeds change the spread of his investments from passive to aggressive to pursue better returns, knowing full well the risks involved and against the advice of Leeds?"

"But it gets worse . . . Listen to this . . ."

"Thanks, June, nice job. Now perhaps you can leave me and Mr. Niven to discuss legal recourse and costs."

"It was nice to meet you, Mr. Niven." June gave her warm smile before leaving. The proud look on her face summed it up; she knew she had cooked it.

"I like her, Phil. She's smart and has the looks with it."

"I'll not disagree with you on that front, Dave . . . Now let's wrap this up. I know you are a busy man."

*   *   *

As Phil escorted Niven through the office to the elevator, David momentarily stopped at June's workstation.

"Thank you again eh . . . Mrs?"

"Miss," June smiled. "June Mathers."

"Eh, Ms. Mathers . . ." Niven smiled, again his roving eyes doing a makeover, and within minutes, Phil returned.

"June, can I see you in my office in a few minutes? I have to make an important call."

*   *   *

"The boss wants to see you now, June. He's free, just go straight in."

Phil was waiting like a tiger ready to pounce as June unsuspectingly opened the door.

"Phil, you startled me," she protested as he enveloped his arms around her, burying his mouth into the soft nape of her neck while kicking the door shut with one swipe of his foot.

"*God . . .* I miss you June." He panted, looking into her eyes for a second before bruising his lips against hers in a long, breathless kiss.

"*Darling, please!* I miss you just as much, but I get nervous in the office. I'm sure Ethel's no fool."

"June, honey, you worry too much. *So let them think!* Gimme one more kiss, and I promise I'll stop at that." "Only one, then you prom—"

June never finished as Phil smothered her lips.

"Okay, honey, I surrender." Phil threw his arms apart in protest as June pushed him away.

"Thanks, darling. *Now* can I take a seat?"

*   *   *

"Honey, you did well today." Phil had cooled off and was now sitting at his desk, facing June. "Niven was really impressed with you, and for that matter, *so was I!*"

"I'm glad, darling, I want to be an asset to the company, not just a pretty face . . . Phil, changing the subject, did you read the headlines today in the local rag?"

"About Mike's forthcoming trial?"

"Yes."

"So, what's worrying you?" Phil asked.

"I'm nervous. I know it's inevitable that I will be called to give evidence for the prosecution."

"June, you don't have to. You can refuse on the grounds that you are still legally married to Mike, and a wife in the eyes of the law can refuse to testify against her husband unless, due to mitigating circumstances, she agrees."

"What's *your* advice Phil?"

"If you wish to see justice done, I don't think you have an option. Anyhow, I'll be by your side all the way, so don't worry your pretty little head." "Thanks, darling, I knew I could depend on you."

"Lunch?"

"I thought you would never ask . . ."

*   *   *

Lesley was about to order her second drink when Tim arrived.

"*You took your time, I must say.*"

707

Was it sarcasm or just Lesley's dry humour? But Tim was Tim and, true to form, always the gentleman. He had been admiring Lesley for some time from afar, and this was his fifteen minutes in the sun, and no way was he going to screw it up.

"*Bartender.*" Les raised her hand.

"I apologize, Les. Here, let me get this."

"Vodka martini, straight up with a twist."

"Boy! That's rocket fuel, and at this time in the morning?"

"*Tim* don't be such a fuddy-duddy. You're not in court now, in front of Phillips, the hanging judge."

Tim laughed at Lesley's remark; maybe she had something.

"What'll it be?" The bartender impatiently tapped the bar top; the place was jumping, and all he needed was two "I can't make up my mind" lawyers.

"One martini straight up with a twist and one Johnny on the rocks."

"*That's more like it!* But I never would have pegged you as a scotch drinker."

"I'm no James Bond, if that's what you mean. Like, vodka martini, shaken not stirred."

"Touché." Les couldn't help but laugh at Tim's "throw back." There was another side to this guy that she had never seen.

"Cheers . . . That is, until we cross swords in mortal combat next Monday." Lesley laughed.

The Pen & Wig in the legal fraternity is synonymous with the White House, where history is made in the world of criminal justice—from the tsunami of sentencing to befit the crime or, worse still, three-strike incarceration. *Whatever,* many a deal was colluded over a drink at this very bar. This plagiarized English pub, situated only within walking distance from New York's central courts, was the haven for celebration or suicide ideation as lawyers either wept or laughed as their careers either went down the toilet or up the flagpole. The bar from the "Old Oak Tree," the heavy wood panelling, the taps of warm English ale, the dim lighting, and odor of spent cigars, not to mention the caricatures of famous departed judges lining the walls, was an ambience only lawyers would appreciate.

*　*　*

"Tim, you know you are going to lose this case, don't you?" Les took a sip of the fresh martini. "*Hmmm,* this tastes better than the first one!"

"How many times have I heard that before?" Tim laughed. "But on a more serious note, regarding the trial, Summers will be found not guilty of attempted murder. *How does that grab you?*"

"In your dreams, Tim, *get real!* Your client is staring down the throat of a minimum twenty-five years in the pen." "We'll see." Tim grinned.

Lesley drained the last of her drink.

"Tim, thanks for the drink, but I gotta get back to the office and face the music. No doubt old 'Iron Side' has been on the blower to Murray complaining about my lateness this morning."

"You never know. Phillips's bark is worse than his bite."

"I'm not holding my breath."

"Les, before you go, I have a confession to make."

"*A confession!* Tim, you're full of surprises . . . I'm waiting."

"Les, I know you are gonna think me crazy. But I have always admired you and never had the courage or opportunity to ask you out to dinner until now."

"Tim, I'm flattered." Collins was taken aback.

"Seriously, Les, *I mean it!*"

"Tim, you are full of surprises. I would be delighted, but there's only one problem. As you are the defence lawyer, and I am the lawyer for the prosecution and on the same trial. If we get too cosy and are seen in public, it could be classed as collusion to dissuade the outcome."

"You have a point there, Les, but is this a polite way of saying . . . ?"

"*Of course not,* I would love to join you for dinner, but on one condition. You get Summers off with less than a fifteen-year stretch." "Deal!" Tim was beaming.

"See you in court then on Monday . . . *And don't be late* . . . Ciao."

Before Tim knew it, Les was gone, and he smiled as he hailed the bartender.

"Another Johnny on the rocks . . ."

CHAPTER 5

There was a distinct chill in the air as Bill hung a left into the Pearl Streetcar park and parked the Pontiac in the nearest slot to the entrance. He had made good time through the morning traffic and had a least half an hour to spare before his meeting with Baker.

"*It looks like winter is coming early this year,*" Bill spoke aloud as he locked the car and briskly walked toward the entrance, his breath producing a puffs of steam and much to his surprise as he approached the elevator, he bumped into none other than Dan Brown!

"*Dan,* what are you doing here? I thought you were still on R&R!"

"*Hold the elevator, Dan.*" It was Lucas, legging it down the hallway, doing the police "fitness test."

"*Bill?*" Lucas was out of breath.

"*Don't ask . . .* I'm here at the request of Baker for a ten o'clock meeting. As for what it's about, your guess is as good as mine." Dan turned to Bert, a surprised look on his face.

"Let me guess. *Don't tell me we are all going to the same ten o'clock meeting!*"

"You got that right." Lucas hit the nail.

Bill grinned. "Then since we are early, why don't I buy you guys a coffee?"

"Yeah, *why not, Bill. After what we've been through, the NYPD should be buying us all a coffee!*"

"No such luck." Bill laughed.

The elevator chimed.

"Cafeteria, Bill?" Brown was ready to hit the button.

"First floor, Dan."

*   *   *

"Boy, this coffee hit the spot," Lucas commented after the first mouthful. "*Christ, Bert,* didn't you have any breakfast before you left this morning? The way you're wolfing that sandwich, it's like there's no tomorrow."

"Naw, I didn't have time." Bert gave a silly grin. "Jacky was lying on my shirt tail."

"You should be so lucky!" Bill commented, a smile on his face; he was enjoying the guy thing.

"*Listen to this guy, Dan.* Remember that call to that broad in Buenos Aires. *Man, that phone was smoking hot.* What do you think, Dan?"

"*Get off the street, you guys!* I owe Mona. She saved my ass, getting Tony and me out of Argentina, or I would be rotting in the dreaded Caseros Prison. But . . ." Bill had that glint in his eye. "I gotta admit, she was one piece of work."

"So, you *did you* have something going?" Lucas wouldn't die.

"Bert, stop playing detective, you're not good at it."

Dan burst into laughter. "*You got something there, Bill!*"

"So, what's this, the Boston Tea Party, or is it just that you guys can't read the time?"

Baker tapping his watch as he stood over the table; the guys hadn't noticed him in the cafeteria.

"We were just leaving, Ted," Bill answered, a half grin on his face.

"Don't sin your soul, Hayden . . . Then if that's the case, let's leave together."

* * *

Baker pointed to the empty chairs.

"Let's get started . . . Firstly, thanks for coming in this morning and breaking your leave, and to reiterate the commissioner's sentiments—nice job, even though our embassy in Sao Paulo is still cleaning up the carnage." Baker raised his eyebrows. "Unfortunately, we lost a good detective in the process." Baker opened the folder and extracted three official-looking documents.

"Oh . . . Before I continue, I forgot to mention that I have recommended each of you for commendations."

"Thanks, Captain . . . But . . ."

"But nothing!" Baker cut Brown short. "You each deserve it. That was one helluva mission. *Navy SEALs couldn't have done better!* Now . . . Detective Lucas, I'm pleased to inform you of your promotion to detective sergeant . . . Detective Brown, I am also pleased to inform of your promotion to lieutenant . . . And lastly, Sergeant Hayden, I am also pleased to inform you of your promotion to lieutenant. With immediate effect. Congratulations." Baker rose and warmly shook each of their hands.

"Take a seat, gentlemen, I'm not finished yet. Lieutenant Brown and Sergeant Lucas will still continue as partners." Brown turned and shook Lucas's hand.

"I was hoping to get rid of you, you big heel, but no such luck!" The one liner brought a simultaneous burst of laughter.

"Oh, and congratulations. Bill."

"Thanks, Dan."

"Sign these papers, and give them to Stace in the passing, for the payroll department. You can go now with the exception of Lieutenant Hayden."

"Thanks again, Captain. We'll catch up later, Bill." Brown shook Bill's hand as he left.

"Bill." Baker had that serious look. "I know how you must have felt when I mentioned the Brown and Lucas partnership."

Bill gave a big sigh. "Yeah, it did come home."

"It goes without saying we all miss Tony, but life goes on." Baker picked up the phone. "Stace, send in Detective Martin."

Bill had that puzzled look on his face; with Baker, you can never tell.

Baker studied Hayden as he began his sales pitch.

"Janice Martin has just earned her gold detective shield for outstanding work in narcotics and a commendation for brainchilding a successful sting resulting in two of the big boys being the guests of Uncle Sam for a very long time, not to mention getting fifty million dollars in uncut coke off the street."

"I'm impressed but . . ."

"*Let me finish, Bill* . . . She requested a transfer to Homicide, and Commissioner Evans has granted her request. Needless to say, it comes at an opportune time when we are a man short, and that's the other reason why I called you here today."

There was a knock on the door. Maybe it was opportune, as Bill had already put two and two together and from his facial expression, he was already spoiling for a fight.

"Come in." Baker looked toward the door; at this stage, the less said, the better.

*   *   *

Janice Martin was tall at five ten. She had that confident look which could either be bad or good. Her lean taught figure smacked of a regular gym routine and, if there is such a thing, a sensible diet. There was no doubt she was pretty, perhaps too pretty for a cop, but if she could do the job . . . *Well* . . . After all, there was "beauty and the beast." Her short-bobbed black hair gave her a sort of macho look, but her sparse makeup and slick red lips brought the female gender back with a jolt. The blue eyes, narrow face and jawline, and crow less eye bags placed her in her early thirties. Her slim-fitting blue slacks and modest heels were complemented with the short jacket to match the simple white blouse and tiny diamond ear studs. The coveted gold detective shield on black leather dangled from her neck with the holstered forty-five-calibre Browning just peeping below her jacket. The resemblance to Demi Moore was uncanny, but Bill was no Michael Douglas, and *Disclosure* was not on the cards. As yet.

*   *   *

"Grab a seat, Jan, let me introduce you to Lieutenant Bill Hayden, your new partner."

"Lieutenant." Jan offered Bill her hand, but there were no takers.

"*Hmmm,*" she commented as she sat back in her chair, a slight blush on her cheeks.

"Jan, you'll have to excuse the lieutenant. The shock of a female partner unfortunately has raised, as you have observed, a degree of hostility."

"Captain, to be absolutely blunt . . . *I'm used to it!* But as partners, we are going to be spending a lot of time together and with respect, Lieutenant . . . *You had better get used to it!*"

Baker tried unsuccessfully to mask his smile . . . *This babe has style.*

Bill was biting his tongue. "Listen, before we get too cosy, Detective, married women and kids are not my scene and have no place in detective work." Bill was ready for the Marquis of Queensbury rules.

"I hate to disappoint, Lieutenant." Jan held her left hand up, emphasizing her naked wedding finger. "Divorced, no kids. It was giving up police work or marriage. Now can we shake hands?"

Hayden grinned. He had met his match. Maybe a female partner wasn't such a bad deal after all, *especially one with looks!*

Bill smiled and offered his hand.

"Welcome aboard, Detective, and no more of the lieutenant stuff. Call me Bill . . ."

BLUEPRINT PRESS

PART 12

The Trial

CHAPTER 1

The remainder of the week had passed quickly with the newly promoted lieutenant given a clean bill of health, returning to duty just in time for the Summers trial. His new, shall we say, more-than-attractive partner, Detective Martin, caused a bit of a stir in the office, or was it envy? The sexist comments were to be expected, but in time, they would die a natural death for as sure as God made little apples, one female detective was just the tip of the iceberg. Bill was taking flak from Judy over his sexy partner, but then she had little to complain, what with Bill's promotion and the extra income, not to mention her seemingly more-than-friendly relationship with Adam Scott, and for a change, the shoe was on the other foot.

* * *

June had enrolled at NYU for the next semester to continue reading law, her divorce now in progress, and the "For Sale" sign on the house bringing more interest from the neighbours than potential buyers. The next hurdle was the forthcoming trial and the media circus. She was already searching for rental accommodation, and Steven had accepted a scholarship at Cornell University in medicine, and Sheryl was in her own private world, more interested in the opposite sex than her studies.

* * *

Laura was still on the mend, and Terry had delayed her start date with HP for one week to attend the trial. Both she and Laura had already been subpoenaed to give evidence for the prosecution, and the very thought of standing in the witness box was sending bad jibes. Brent had been a great support, taking Laura to dinner and keeping her company when Terry was bogged down with late evening meetings.

*   *   *

It was a trying time all around, worse than a three ringed circus. And as to how it will end? It's in the lap of the gods . . .

CHAPTER 2

"I'm afraid you'll be stuck in the courtroom this morning until after I take the stand."

Bill was passing a general comment to his new partner as he made his way through the morning traffic after picking her up from the Pearl Street car park on their way to the central criminal courts.

"Don't worry, Bill, an attempted murder trial is not an everyday experience. I'm sure I won't be bored."

Jan felt more comfortable with Bill since he let his guard down, and having a male partner was also a new experience for her.

"Have you had breakfast?" Bill asked. "It's just turned nine, and we have plenty of time before the court opens its doors."

"And you?"

"Naw, I was in a hurry this morning. I didn't want you hanging around the car park in the cold. Besides my wife has suddenly decided to take a secretarial job and my mother-in-law . . . Well, she's a test pilot for a broom factory. And always kept busy."

"That bad?"

"*You haven't met my mother-in-law!*"

"*You guys!*" Jan shook her head, a smile on her face. Maybe it brought back memories.

"So?"

"So?" Jan's mind was occupied somewhere else.

"So have you had breakfast?"

"*What,* a divorced cop living on her own . . . Are you serious, Bill?"

"Then it's settled. I know a diner that has the best breakfast and coffee in town, and better still, it's on our way, and the tab is on me."

"I've only known you for a couple days, and I'm beginning to like you already."

"Don't run away with yourself. I'm a real bad ass at times."

"I don't believe it!"

"Give it time, Detective . . ."

*   *   *

"*Strange . . .* I've never noticed this diner before even though I have passed here many times," Jan commented as Bill parked the car in front of Jake's Last Chance Diner.

"It's tucked in between Barry and Wythe Avenue, just off Broadway. Most beat and cruiser cops hangout here for breakfast. I guess it's because of the healthy food, huh?"

Jan burst into laughter at Bill's wisecrack. Most cops, especially cruiser cops, wouldn't have a hope in hell of passing the fitness test, but they are part of the New York facade, expected by the tourists and portrayed in every criminal movie.

*   *   *

Jake's is the typical New York diner with a cabin that could be mistaken for an oversize Greyhound bus; the exception was the bold red, white, and blue stripes painted on its highly polished aluminium exterior. As for the food? *No more said!* But the atmosphere made up for any deficiencies. For sure, Jake's is a traditional New York icon when it comes to the diner experience.

*   *   *

Two black and whites were parked side by side, after presumably the night-shift stint.

"I see what you mean about cruiser cops," Jan commented as they walked from the car.

"Well, there's one thing for sure." Mike smiled. "Jake's has the best security in town. But excuse the pun, the coffee is to die for."

That brought a smile. It just proved that everyone had another side. "Let's get out of this chill." Bill opened the door.

*   *   *

Inside was typical diner, the kitchen hatch in the background, the specials scribbled in chalk on a blackboard that bows whiter than black, and the customer orders pinned on a rotating carousel waiting for the kitchen hands.

The long-simulated wood Formica bar top stretched the full length of the diner, with its swivel barstools and starved elbow room. Famous sport celebrities such as Babe Ruth and Cassius Clay and Joe DiMaggio to name a few, adorned the walls, giving the diner the guy's thing and the place to be.

* * *

Jake, the owner, was in the front line, calling the shots and buttering the customers; at this time in the morning, the place was jumping and the eaters grumpy when the service was slow.

"I see what you mean, Bill, with the boys in blue. Maybe they are all bachelors or none of their wives can cook?"

"Maybe the scenery is better here." Bill grinned.

"*Get off the street*, you male chauvinist." Jan shook her head; Bill just laughed.

There was at least six oversize cops sitting at the bar enjoying their own conversation between mouthfuls of burgers and scrambled eggs.

"Let's try and find a couple of stools."

"Bill, *over here*." Mario raised his arm, recognizing Bill. Tony and Bill were regulars.

Bill grabbed Jan's arm. "Thanks, Mario . . . Meet my new partner, Detective Jan Martin."

A couple of beat cops turned on hearing the comment and gave a scowl; Jan was in a man's world.

"Eh . . . err, nice to meet you, Jan." Mario's face was the mask of surprise.

"Bill, about Tony . . ."

"Mario, I appreciate your condolences but . . ." Bill was lost for words, a lump in his throat.

"Say, what can I get you guys?" Mario broke the deafening silence.

"Eh . . ." Bill composed himself. "Jan?"

"Firstly, I have to try this fabulous coffee I've heard so much about. And . . ."—Jan studied the blackboard menu—"a chorizo toasted sandwich on rye."

"Good choice, and you, Bill?"

"My usual."

"Okay, that'll be . . ." Mario was frantically scribbling the order; the lions were getting restless. "Be with you in a minute . . . Let me see. . Two coffees, one toasted chorizo sandwich and scrambled eggs with crispy bacon . . . I'll go get the coffee."

"Thanks, Mario." Bill sighed and leaned on the bar top, memories of the good times filling his eyes. Maybe it was the wrong choice of diner, but it's better to face reality than hide from the truth. It was time now to shake it off. "Eh . . . So, tell me a bit about yourself." Bill swallowed, turning to Jan. It was the only conversational piece that Bill could think of to avoid ruining his good intentions over breakfast.

"I'm not gonna give you 'true confessions,' if that's what you want. We don't have the time."

Bill's facial expression changed at Jan's opener, his laugh lines now back. "So, no biographies, but I'm still interested."

"Graduated from the police academy at twenty-two. Served in the force for eleven years from beat cop and now finally to homicide detective and the coveted gold shield. Married for five years, unfortunately ending in divorce. A clash of the titans, so to speak. My ex felt his career was more important than mine and demanded I resign from the force and start a family. From there on, it was all downhill, reaching the stage where I hated him more than I ever loved him. I'm glad to say I'm now my own woman. I have my own apartment, and I'm able to concentrate full time on my career. *Ta-da* . . . How does that grab you?"

"That'll do for now." Bill took a sip of his coffee, a sly grin masking his approval. This gal had something.

"And dare I ask my boss?"

"What you see is what you get. Married with two kids, a wife that has visions of grandeur—a cop's wife not being one of them . . . The bottom line—a pretty tired marriage with the same old excuse, 'If it wasn't for the kids.' Now are you gonna finish that sandwich? Because that dog's gonna be barking soon."

"How about you?"

"I'm full, Jan, I really only wanted the coffee . . . *Mario*, the tab . . ."

*   *   *

The drive to the central criminal court in Manhattan was less than fifteen minutes from Broadway, and Bill and Jan were making good time.

"We should be there in a few minutes," Bill commented as he turned into Center Street. The tall, drab-looking building in dark-gray granite would scare the crap out of any criminal.

"Have you been here before, Jan?"

"In my previous assignment in narcotics? You gotta be kiddin'. I know the place like the back of my hand."

Bill grinned. "Ask a silly question . . . Now how the hell do we find a parking space?"

"You took the words right of my mouth."

"There's only one thing for it. We park in the no-parking zone, and I use my NYPD sticker." Bill pulled into the curb.

"Excuse me, sir." The beat cop patrolling the court entrance knocked on the window.

"*Awe . . . Awe . . .* We got company." Bill rolled down the window.

"Excuse me, sir, but this is a no-parking zone." The cop pointed to the sign. "You can't park here." Bill flashed his shield.

"Lieutenant Hayden, NYPD Homicide. I'm here to testify in a criminal case, and I'm running late."

The oversize boy in blue sighed, shaking his head and shrugging his shoulders. "I'm sorry, Lieutenant, but I'm afraid you're gonna be late for that court case because you can't park here." Jan had to stifle her laughter.

"I don't think it's funny, Jan, and neither will Baker, if I'm late . . . It's okay, Officer, you're just doing your job."

"Better still, Bill, gimme the keys." Jan opened her palm. "I won't be called to the stand, so why don't I drive around until I find a spot?"

That brought a smile. "I think we are going to make a good team. It's court 3. I'll keep a seat for you. The NYPD sticker is in the glove compartment with the yellow meter hood. Jan, try and make it before ten. I believe Phillips is on the bench, and he's a stickler for punctuality." "I'll try, Bill. You had better move it . . ."

* * *

As Bill walked down the highly polished terracotta hallway to the court section and the "Halls of Justice," he could just imagine the thoughts in the minds of both the victims and perpetrators as they walked the walk. The thought was scary, and here he was once again, about to testify for the capital offense of attempted murder.

The oversize security guard blocked Bill's path as he tried to brush past in his haste.

"Sir, can I see some ID?"

Bill flashed the gold shield, and the guard promptly nodded, stepping aside.

The courtroom was almost to full capacity, and Bill scanned the audience, searching for his colleagues.

"*Over here, Bill.*" He spotted the raised hand of Dave Adams from CSI, with Dr. Ken Brody, the police pathologist, sitting next to him.

They were seated on the right-hand side of the courtroom, directly in front of the barrier behind the prosecution's desk.

"*You're cutting it neat,*" Adams commented moving aside to create more room on the wooden bench seat.

"Parking problems," Bill replied as he looked anxiously toward the entrance, hoping to see Jan in the process.

On the other side of the courtroom sat Laura Williams, accompanied by her friend Terry Johnson and a male companion. Bill could certainly remember Terry. *Who wouldn't?* Ironically, they were seated in the second row almost immediately behind June Summers and her two teenage children, Steven and Sheryl. Their hostile expressions provided little comfort and support to their mother, who looked stressed and uneasy as her eyes met Bill's.

One can only imagine the thoughts running through their minds.

"*Well,* move over then." It was Jan.

"*Jan!* Thank God, you made it."

"So, you need my moral support, you big wuss."

Bill grinned. "Let's just say, I was worried in case you got lost."

"*Yeah . . . Yeah.*"

Bill didn't reply, having been distracted with the noise of the "valiant twelve" shuffling into the jury box.

"They look a mean bunch. I wouldn't wish to be in Summers's shoes." He turned to Jan.

Suddenly the courtroom came to life; there was a pronounced gasp as the macabre audience spotted Summers accompanied by Tim Matheson, his defence lawyer, taking their seats.

"Take a load off, Mike. I'll request these cuffs be removed when I get the opportunity."

All eyes turned to the rear of the court, the noise of the large wooden doors finally closing, the paparazzi monopolizing the back wall next to the entrance. Time is money.

But where was the prosecution? Matheson anxiously scanned the courtroom before turning to Mike.

"I don't know what's happened to Collins. *Christ,* if she's late today, Phillips will go into orbit!"

"Is that good or bad for me?" Mike asked with a chuckle.

"Mike, the only thing that matters to you now, *is the benevolence of the jury.*"

Before Tim could continue stressing his point, there was a loud knock on the courtroom door.

Tim turned at the commotion. "All bets are off to know who this is."

True to form, it was Lesley Collins talking to court security, whom, after a few seconds, let her pass.

"If I didn't know better, I would say that Les planned this. She just loves the grand entrance."

Mike was like, *So what's the big deal? Rome's burning, and Tim's more interested in a stupid broad being late.*

"Tim, I think you've got the hots for this chick, but how about staying on *my* case?"

Mike's words went over Matheson's head as Les opened the swing gates and momentarily turned to the defence, giving Tim a sexy smile before finally taking her seat.

"*Maaan* . . . Now I really know."

"Be quiet, Mike, it's almost time."

No sooner had Tim passed the comment than the door to the judge's quarters opened.

Matheson glanced at his watch and grinned. "Phillips, *right on time!*"

* * *

The judge looked exceptionally fresh as he briskly entered the court, his robe flaying behind him as he spritely took the stairs, two at a time, to the "hallowed" bench.

The bailiff's voice echoed throughout the courtroom.

"Please be upstanding for State Judge, the Right Honourable Randal Phillips."

Phillips paused for a moment to firstly scan the audience and then the jury, his stark no-nonsense stare sending a deliberate message. Then he robotically took his "throne" and scanned the papers neatly stacked on his bench, prepared prior to the commencement of the trial. He opened his spectacle case and donned his half glasses before finally turning his attention to the courtroom and slamming the gavel down hard on the bench.

"*This court is now in session.*" He took a deep breath, then continued.

"Before I commence, I wish to draw the court's attention to the fact that this is *my* court, and *I will not tolerate*, under any circumstance, unruly behaviour or outcries to the detriment of this trial. If such behaviour occurs and is persistent, I will close all proceedings and continue behind closed doors. That also applies to the media and the so-called paparazzi. Furthermore, any attempt to take photographs will be classed as contempt, with the person or persons being immediately ejected by the court security." Phillips turned his attention to the jury box.

"Ladies and gentlemen of the jury, have you accordingly and unanimously appointed a foreman?"

A tall, slim, well-dressed elderly man with white hair and rimless glasses rose to his feet.

"We have, Your Honour. I have been appointed as foreman. My name is Eric Armstrong."

"Thank you, Mr. Armstrong, be seated. Stenographer, please put on the record that the jury's foreman is a Mr. Eric Armstrong." Philips slammed the gavel again.

"The State of New York versus Michael Summers in that on the evening of August 12, 2003, at approximately 8:30 p.m., you assaulted one Laura Williams at apartment 6B, Elm Apartments on Watt Street, inflicting serious bodily harm to the detriment of her life and with criminal intent to murder. How does the accused plead?"

"I thought I pleaded not guilty earlier?"

"*Mike,* keep your fucking voice down. Philips is giving you a second chance to reconsider your plea, *now get on your feet!*"

"I plead not guilty, Your Honour."

"For the record, the defendant pleads not guilty to the charge of attempted murder. Also, for the record, Mr. Timothy Matheson is the appointed lawyer for the defence and representing the district attorney's office and the State of New York is Ms. Lesley Collins, the lawyer for the prosecution. Counsellor Collins, please begin with your opening statement." "Thank you, Your Honour."

"So, what's with this?" Mike asked.

"It's protocol in that the prosecution gets first priority, *as the state is charging you with the offense.*"

"So?"

"So, it means she's gonna try and nail your ass to the wall."

"That makes me feel better already. Thanks, Tim, for your heartfelt explanation."

Les looked really smart in her fine blue pinstriped trouser suit and modest heels. Her low-cut white blouse with a tantalizing flash of cleavage would certainly keep the male jurors occupied. Her ebony-black hair swept back in a bun was a touch of class, and the dainty diamond stud earrings and the fine gold necklace gave the prosecution the edge on the catwalk.

"I tell you, Tim, that babe's a dish."

"I heard you."

Collins slowly and deliberately walked to the centre of the floor, her expression solemn and serious as she turned to face the jury.

"Ladies and gentlemen of the jury, you are here today to perform a very special duty in the eyes of the law, and that is to determine guilty or not guilty of one Michael Summers, for the heinous crime of attempted murder . . . A vicious crime to terminate an innocent human being's life. You will be presented with witness statements, evidence from the Homicide Department, testimonials, and medical evidence of the heartless, vicious beating of a young woman, a father's daughter, resulting in the miscarriage of her unborn fetus and more so, a threat to her very own life . . . What do I see before me?"

Collins dramatically turned to face the courtroom populace for a few pregnant seconds before sharply turning back to address the jury.

"I see before me twelve upstanding citizens, honest everyday New Yorkers, the very people who have made this great country of ours what it is today. The greatest country in the world." Collins turned to face the courtroom again before the final curtain, then back to the jurors. "I know you will make the right decision . . . The only decision . . . and that is to proclaim a verdict of guilty. Ladies and gentlemen of the jury . . . I thank you. My case rests."

"Thank you, counsellor . . . Mr. Matheson for the defence."

"Thank you, Your Honour."

Matheson took to the floor and walked toward the jury box, passing a fleeting smile to Collins.

"Ladies and gentlemen of the jury. You have heard the prosecution . . . And Ms. Collins is correct, in that attempted murder *is* a heinous crime. Murder sends a shiver through each and every one of you sitting in the jury box today, and rightly so. But what does attempted murder really infer? Think about the charge one more time . . . *attempted murder*. The fact is the accused had no plan to intentionally murder Laura Williams. Therefore, the charge is purely a semantic trumped up by the prosecution and cannot be classed as attempted murder without the intent *to* murder. In fact, when you hear the circumstances leading to the event . . . *You*, the jury, will undoubtedly conclude one verdict and one verdict only—and that is aggravated assault resulting in grievous bodily harm. To send a man to prison for the rest of his life is an unenviable responsibility that rests on each of your shoulders this day, and if there is . . . I repeat. *If there is* . . . the least element of doubt in your minds, then there can be only one verdict, and that is *not guilty!* Thank you."

* * *

Phillips stared over his half glasses as Matheson returned to the defence desk. The enormity of Mike's predicament was now taking its toll, and he stared down at his shackled wrists; Collins's words still ringing in his ears. *"I know you will make the right decision . . . The only decision . . . and that is to proclaim a verdict of guilty.* He was a loser no matter what; it was just a case of how and when.

"Mike, are you feeling all right?" Tim was concerned at Mike's state of mind. He was pale and drawn. It wouldn't be the first time the accused tried to injure himself in order to delay the trial.

"Yeah, I'm okay." Mike half mumbled before turning to face June and the kids. But if he was looking for sympathy, he was short-changed. Especially from Steven, who was on a hate campaign with his "it's too late for tears" look.

June turned away. She couldn't bear to look into his eyes.

"Your Honour." Matheson was on his feet.

Philips gave a pronounced sigh. *"Yes, Counsellor?"*

"The accused is experiencing severe cramps in his wrists and in the interest of Mr. Summers's health . . ."

Before Matheson could finish Phillips gave the order.

"Security, please remove the prisoner's handcuffs until such time as he returns to the cells. *And, counsellor,* there's no need to quote the Geneva Convention, and it's too early for a plea bargain, so if it's not too much trouble, perhaps I can continue? *Bailiff . . ."*

"The prosecution calls Teresa Johnson to the stand."

"Shit . . . That's me!" Terry didn't expect to be first past the post.

As she opened the swing doors and walked to the witness box, Terry felt as if the whole world's eyes were upon her.

"Do you know this broad, Mike?" Matheson turned to Summers, begging the question.

"Never met her in my life, but Laura was always talking about Terry, her best friend."

"That adds up."

As for Terry, she was dressed to kill, so to speak, and today she crossed the line in the sand, *in fact, the whole Sahara desert!*

"Ms. Johnson, please place your left hand on the Bible, then raise your right hand and repeat after me . . . I, Teresa Johnson, do solemnly swear to tell . . ."

"Please take your seat, Ms. Johnson."

Collins was already on her feet strutting the "catwalk." She stared at Terry for a moment as if sizing her up with eye-to-eye contact before finally giving Terry a warm smile. It was the old prosecution tactic to gain the witnesses' confidence.

"Can I address you as Terry?"

"Certainly."

"Eh, Terry . . ." Collins paused. "Laura Williams . . . Would I be correct in assuming that you and Laura are best friends?"

"You could assume that."

"Terry, please answer the question with a yes or no." "Yes."

"And you both work with the same company, ABM?

"Yes."

"And am I correct in stating that Laura Williams is the marketing manager and technically your boss?"

"It's nothing to do with technically . . . *She is my boss!*" Collins's legalistic terminology had rattled Terry, like she was talking down to her, and her reply brought a burst of laughter throughout the courtroom.

"*Order . . . Order . . .*" Phillips slammed the gavel twice, inducing instant silence.

"*Ah . . . Hmmm . . .*" Collins cleared her throat. "Let's start again . . . Did Laura Williams ever confide in you about her dating life?"

"*Dating life?*"

"Let me put it another way . . . Boyfriends."

"No, Laura kept her personal life to herself."

"But she *did* confide in you about Mike Summers."

"Sure, I knew she was having an affair with a married man, some highfalutin executive . . . She never told me his name, and I never had the opportunity to meet him."

Collins was holding a sheet of A4 paper.

"I have here your signed statement to the police. And I quote: 'Laura met this guy on the rebound after a previous disastrous relationship and fell head over heels for this corporate Casanova who promised her the world and then dumps her like a roadside bomb when she tells him she's heading for the maternity clinic . . . Laura was plenty mad and threatened to call his wife and spill the beans to his company for impropriety.' Unquote."

"I can't remember the exact wording, but that's as good as it gets."

"I see . . . And when Ms. Williams informed you about her pregnancy and her boyfriend's refusal to accept that he was the father, what was your advice?"

"I advised her to convince him to have a paternity test to prove that he is the father."

"And what was her reaction?"

"She was going to blow the whistle if he didn't come to the party."

"I see, and did she confide in you that she had demanded that the accused meet her that evening?"

"No, but I was worried about her mental state and asked her to join me at my apartment for at TV dinner and do the couch potato, but she refused, and of course now I know why. I told her when she arrived home, once she settled down, to give me a call to make sure she was all right, but when eight forty-five arrived and there was still no call, I became concerned and decided to call *her* myself, and . . ." Terry shrugged and made a face. "The rest is history."

"I see . . . And can you recollect Laura Williams's exact words when she answered the phone?"

"*Eh . . . eh . . .* Something like '*Terry . . . Terry . . . Hurry . . . Hurry . . . He tried to kill me.*' Then the phone went silent."

"*Something like?*" Collins swung around to face the jury as if to stress "pay attention," then dramatically about-faced to face Terry.

"Terry, I need you to be absolutely sure. '*Something like*' is not good enough."

"Then I am absolutely sure that these were Laura's exact words."

"Thank you, Ms. Johnson."

Collins turned to face the jury once again.

"Please note the contents of Terry Johnston's call on the evening of August 12, 2003, at eight forty-five in the evening. Quote: '*Terry . . . Terry . . . Hurry . . . Hurry . . . He tried to kill me.*"

Collins turned her attention to Terry once more.

"What crossed your mind the first time you visited your best friend in hospital?"

"Crossed my mind?"

"Like how did you feel? Angry . . . distraught . . . sad?"

"I felt if I could get my hands on the jerk that did this to Laura, I would . . ."

"*You would?*"

"*Castrate the bastard!*"

There was a rumble of laughter from within the courtroom.

"*Order . . . Order.*" Phillips slammed the gavel. "*I will not tolerate these continued interruptions. Do I make myself clear?*" You could have heard a pin drop.

"But you weren't going to stop there, were you? In fact, you were determined to stop at nothing to bring the perpetrator to justice . . . Is that correct?"

"Yes."

"Then can you tell the court what crossed your mind?"

"As I was driving home from the hospital, my mind was searching over and over again as to who Laura's secret lover could be. My gut feeling told me it had to be someone she had met in her capacity as marketing manager with ABM. She had to entertain clients and subcontractors, as the company outsources contracts for advertising, product literature, and so on. Laura was always meticulous with her appointments and kept a phone book in real time." Terry stopped for a moment to catch her breath and further recollect.

"Carry on, Ms. Johnson."

"The identity of this man had to be staring me in the face, and in my opinion, the clue lay in Laura's PC. But Laura's computer was encrypted, so I had to approach my boss to convince him and get his approval for the DP manager to crack Laura's firewall."

"And what was the result?"

"There was over one hundred names with dates, companies, and so on."

"Then what happened?"

"My boss took it from there and faxed the information to Lieutenant Perino of NYPD Homicide."

Collins paused again, then turned to face the bench.

"I have no further questions, Your Honor . . . Thank you, Ms. Johnson."

"Counsellor Matheson, do you wish to cross-examine the witness?"

"I do, Your Honour."

It was Tim's turn to question Terry, but inwardly he had to admit there was no rabbit in the hat.

"Ms. Johnson, you mentioned you are Laura Williams's best friend, is that correct?"

"Yes."

"Best friends usually hang out together, like going on double dates and all that girly stuff, and I must say I find it hard to believe that you never discussed boyfriends. Yet you mentioned Laura was recovering from a bad relationship. Just how many bad relationships did Laura Williams confide?"

"Only one," Terry answered abruptly to the point of rudeness; she didn't like Matheson's insinuations.

"But she *did* have other relationships, didn't she? In fact I would go as far to say, *many other relationships . . . Isn't that true, Ms. Johnson?* And that you being her best friend are trying to protect her reputation. A woman in her late twenties desperate for a lasting relationship, searching for a mature partner, especially a married one?"

Tim was trying to rile Terry in the hope she would react and say something she would regret.

"*Objection, Your Honour*, Ms. Johnson is not on trial here, and the defense is purposely trying to taint the victim's character to convince the jury she is some sort of man-eater or loose woman."

That comment brought another burst of laughter from the courtroom, and Phillips, in his sheer frustration, brought the gavel down hard. The crack could have easily been mistaken for a gunshot.

"*Order . . . Order . . .* I will not tolerate any further interruptions of this nature . . . Don't try my benevolence. *Objection sustained.* counsellor Matheson, you will discontinue this line of questioning. The prosecution is correct. Stenographer, place this on record, with the question disregarded."

"Then I have no further questions, Your Honour."

Tim walked back to his desk, sporting a smug grin and gave Collins a sly wink in the passing. He had made his point and juries don't forget.

"Thank you, Ms. Johnson, you may step down."

Terry was more than relieved as she returned to her seat, her ordeal over for the time being.

"Bailiff, please call the next witness to the stand."

"Would Lieutenant David Adams please take the stand."

"That's me, Bill, move over and let me pass." Adams was carrying a manila folder and plastic zip bags.

"Mr. Adams, please place your left hand on the . . ."

"Be seated, Mr. Adams."

Lesley was already in front of the witness box, spoiling for the next round.

She knew she was on a winner, and she was hell-bent in humiliating Tim. "Lieutenant Adams, you are with the NYPD?"

"Yes."

"Then can you explain to the court in what capacity."

"For those of you who don't watch televised crime dramas . . ."

Adams was interrupted with a burst of laughter from the court. Philips just smiled and decided this time to ignore the outburst. He could also appreciate the humorous side.

"Please continue, Lieutenant."

"*Eh* . . . CSI is an abbreviation for 'Crime Scene Investigation.' My department consists of laboratory technicians, photographers, and fingerprint and blood spatter experts. Our job is to examine the crime scene with a fine-tooth comb for the tiniest of clues."

"Then perhaps you can elaborate on the scene that you first encountered when you arrived at Laura Williams's apartment."

"I have here my written report. White pregnant female. Mid—to late twenties. Brutally attacked. Bruising to the neck, a possible attempted strangulation. The fetus was aborted and has been taken for blood and DNA analysis. The doc's preliminary examination . . . Severe bruising to the ribs and lower abdomen from blunt-force trauma, most likely as the result of her attacker going into a frenzy and frantically kicking the victim. She is in a critical condition and unconscious, and she may not pull through. Her close friend . . ." Adams glanced at his notes again. "A Terry Johnson called 911 at approximately eight fifty-five. The paramedics were fast on the scene as the victim was unconscious and as the result of her life-threatening condition, she was rushed to the emergency hospital at Roosevelt Memorial."

"And did your people take photographs of the crime scene?"

"Yes, it's standard procedure."

"And do you have these photographs with you?"

"Yes, I do, but I must stress the scenes caught on camera are not for the squeamish."

"Your Honour, I wish to present these photographs to the jury as evidence of the sheer brutality of the assault proving intent to murder."

"Continue, Counselor."

Collins glanced at the evidence, but only for a few seconds. As she flicked through each of the images, she was aghast and visibly shocked at the horrific images of the blood-soaked foetus, its tiny premature body perfect in every detail, never to experience the gift of life as the result of a wanton act by a would-be murderer. It was just too much, and she placed her hand to her mouth and coughed.

"Counselor, are you all right?" Philips asked concerned at her paleness and a possible faint in the making.

"I'm all right, Your Honour. I appreciate your concern."

Collins handed Phillips the evidence, who briefly glanced at each frame; he had seen worse.

"You may now pass these to the jury. Stenographer, please record the pictorial evidence at the crime scene as exhibit A."

"This is not good, Mike, you just have to look at the expressions on the faces of the jurors."

"Lieutenant, what was your impression when you first arrived?"

"It appeared there had been a struggle, as the phone was still hanging from its cradle. But the remarkable thing was there were no fingerprints with exception of that of Williams's. The apartment had been methodically wiped clean. Even the vacuum cleaner was emptied. My first assumption was that whoever committed this crime was smart and made sure everything, with the exception of the victim's blood, was squeaky clean, but with one exception.

He or she overlooked this small scrap of paper found below the chair." Adams held the plastic zip bag high for the jurors to see.

"Record the scrap of paper as exhibit B. counsellor, please pass the evidence to the jurors."

"Lieutenant, what is the significance of exhibit B?"

"When we analysed the paper in our laboratory, we found it to be paper for the manufacture of check books commonly used by all major banks."

"An almost impossible task to track the bank. So what was the next step?"

"The case was transferred to Homicide, and the late Lieutenant Perino and Detective Sergeant Bill Hayden were assigned to the investigation."

"I have no further questions, Your Honour."

"Counselor Matheson, do you wish to cross-examine the witness?"

"No questions, Your Honour."

"Bailiff, please call the next witness for the prosecution."

"The court calls Dr. Kenneth Brody."

"Bill, I'm gonna have to squeeze past you again." Ken's larger-than-life frame was a replica of the late Marlon Brando.

"You'll have to cut out these greasy donuts at coffee break, Ken." "Don't tell Pauline." The big man laughed in friendly banter.

*　　*　　*

"And you are the police pathologist?"

"Forensic pathologist."

"*Eh,* forensic pathologist . . . And, Dr. Brody, did you examine the foetus at the city mortuary?"

"Yes."

"Then can you tell the court in layman's terms your medical conclusions."

"Certainly . . . Miscarriage as the result of blunt-force trauma to the lower abdomen, resulting in the victim's body aborting the fetus. The fetes was approximately twelve to thirteen weeks into pregnancy and was of male gender."

"And what further medical evidence did you uncover?"

"Firstly, I ran a make on the blood group, a significant factor in determining the father. However, DNA testing is preferred, as children have 50 percent of their mother's DNA and the remainder the father's." "And how did you finally conclude the identity of the father?"

"At the crime scene, I removed skin tissue from below the victims nails as I noticed blood deposits on her fingers, indicating she may have scratched her assailant's face as she frantically defended herself."

"And?"

"DNA matching proved that the assailant and the father of the fetus were one and the same."

"But tell the court how you finally identified the father."

"When Michael Summers, the accused, was finally taken into custody, we took a saliva swab and ran a DNA test, which proved unquestionably he was both the father and the perpetrator."

"And, Doctor, is that man here in his court today?"

"Yes."

"Can you point to this man?"

Brody pointed to Summers, causing a pronounced hush in the full-to capacity courtroom.

Collins turned to the jury box once again.

"Ladies and gentlemen of the jury, take note that Dr. Brody identified Michael Summers, the accused."

"No further questions, Your Honor." Collins gave Tim a smug smile as she walked to her desk. It looked like her bet was in the bag.

"Counselor Matheson?" Phillips stared over his glasses.

"No further questions, Your Honor."

"Bailiff, please call the next witness."

"The prosecution calls to the stand Lieutenant William Hayden."

"I like the sound of the 'lieutenant' bit." Bill smiled as he rose to his feet, only to be met with the "Hulk" Brody trying to squeeze past.

"We gotta stop meeting like this, Bill," Brody joked.

"Tell me about it!" Bill laughed, breathing in and holding his stomach. "Please raise your . . ."

*   *   *

The prosecution was holding the floor, and the jury must be asking themselves why Summers was determined to plead "not guilty." As for Mike's lawyer, Tim, he was in a hole that was getting deeper by the minute.

*   *   *

"And, Lieutenant, what struck you as being unusual about at the crime scene?"

"As Lieutenant Adams stressed, it was too clean. *In fact, scary clean.* I have here his comment from my notes. 'We found this on the floor. I'll pass it to forensic for tests. But prints? The suspect is no fool . . . *Nothing!* The place is clean. Even the vacuum cleaner was gone over.'"

"And then?"

"My partner, Tony . . ." Bill paused, a lump in his throat, the mention of Tony's name was enough. "*Eh* . . . Please excuse me, Your Honour . . . *Eh, err.* It's just that Lieutenant Perino and I were very close friends, and it brings back memories."

"I understand, Lieutenant . . . Just take a few moments." For once, Phillips was showing his other side.

"I'm good, Counselor . . . *Eh, ahem.*" Bill cleared his throat. "Do you wish me to continue with the reply, Counselor?"

"Please."

"Tony had a knack for piecing two and two together. When he was onto something, he was like a seagull on a hot fry."

There was an instant burst of laughter. Philips slammed the gavel again and again.

"*Order . . . Order!*" But even he had to smile at Hayden's comment.

"Lieutenant, please refrain from your colourful descriptions."

"My apologies, Your Honour."

"*Ahh . . . Hemmm.* Please continue, Lieutenant."

"Tony and I discussed the mystery of the cleaner-than-clean lounge, and we agreed to visit the crime scene one more time. In our second investigation, what struck us was the vacuum dust bag was gone and the one thing that CSI had missed was to search the garbage from the collection chute. It was only a hunch, but if the perpetrator had emptied the vacuum cleaner, it was highly unlikely he would take it with him. Or . . . Laura Williams was a clean freak or she had a thing for vacuum cleaners."

Bill's comment ensued another round of laughter.

"*Order . . . Order!*" Phillips brought down the gavel. "*I will not tell this court one more time . . .* Please continue, Lieutenant, and may I once again remind you, less of the *Seinfeld.*"

There was more laughter, only this time Phillips could have bitten his lip.

"Lieutenant?"

"I beg your pardon, ma'am. The assumption we arrived at was, if this were the case, then the only place to discard its contents was down the garbage chute, and Tony decided to question the apartment manager, a . . ." Mike glanced at his notes. "Eh . . . a Chris Benson. We were in luck, as the garbage was not collected until the following day. I quote Benson's statement." Bill read from his notes. "'As I told you, the garbage is not collected until tomorrow. Now the problem is, three apartments on each floor use their own chute going into one garbage collecting bin in order to avoid blockages with too much stuff coming down at the same time.' He escorted us to the basement where he identified bin numbers 4, 5, and 6 as the ones collecting garbage from level B, being the same level as the Williams apartment."

"Please continue, Lieutenant, I'm sure the Jury are intrigued with your fine detective work."

"After a lengthy search sifting through mounds of garbage, we finally uncovered a plastic bag that contained a blood-soaked face towel and a disposable paper garbage bag containing carpet dust and pieces of torn paper."

"Your Honour, I wish to present to the jury the hand towel as exhibit C and the paper scraps pieced together to form a bank check, as exhibit D." Collins raised the plastic zip bags shoulder high for the court to see.

"And what was your next step, Lieutenant?"

"It would take at least three to four days for forensics to come up with the results. Meanwhile, a potential killer was on the loose, and most crimes are solved within the first forty-eight. So we had to move fast. Our next step was to work on the list of names from Laura's phone book, as faxed by Mr. Jack Blakely, her boss at ABM, but where were we to start with over a hundred names? But Tony, as usual, had the answer. I mean you don't have to be Einstein to work out that whoever was pumping . . . *Eh . . . Err*, I mean having sex with the victim, when bearing in mind the duration of the pregnancy of around five months, he must have met her around six months ago. You don't have to be a mathematician to work that one out."

Again, laughter erupted. It was not Phillips's day. *"Order. Order . . ."*
"And?" Collins was intrigued; this was TV stuff.

"Our educated guess concluded that the dating session would have been around March or February. When I checked, I came up with three names, and after contacting their companies, one was in Canada on the date of the offense, and the other was in Europe on business. That only left us with only one name—a Mike Summers from Global Marketing. I phoned Global and spoke to Summers's secretary, who confirmed that he knew Laura Williams, but he was out of town on business and would not return until the weekend. Meanwhile forensics had pieced the Citibank check together and learned that it was made payable to Laura Williams for twenty thousand dollars. The account holder was a Michael Summers, Citibank 309 Canal Street. Our next step was to get the address of the account holder. The district attorney provided legal clearance to investigate this guy Summers's account through the Freedom of Information Act, via a warrant from Judge Donnelly."

"And the conclusion, Lieutenant?"

"The check belonged to Michael Summers, 14 River Street, East Village, and a warrant was issued for his arrest."

"And is this man here in court today?"

"Yes."

"Then can you point to him?"

"Will the jury please note that the lieutenant identified the accused, Michael Summers. I have no further questions, Your Honor."

This was an annihilation of the worst kind, but Matheson was no dummy; he had been there before.

"Counselor Matheson?"

"No further questions, Your Honour."

"The witness can step down."

Bill was more than relieved as he stepped from the witness box; it was the final curtain to a police operation that went bad and would haunt him for the rest of his life, and for what? He looked at Summers sitting at the defense desk and shook his head. Where is the justice in this world? For sure, Summers would go down, *but at least he had his life!*

*   *   *

"You did well, Bill." Janice moved aside to give him his seat.

"Thanks, Jan . . . You know, I have been in the witness box countless times during my career, but this one I will never forget."

* * *

Phillips paused and glanced at the wall clock.

"As the time is now approaching twelve noon, I am calling a recess for lunch. This trial will resume at one thirty. Please ensure punctuality. The jury will also retire for lunch, to be held in the jury quarters at the expense of the state. May I remind each member of the jury that no phone calls are allowed or any contact with the media or relatives. The court security will collect your cell phones, to be returned at the close of this trial . . . *Security*, please escort the accused to the watch house."

Phillips slammed the gavel once.

"This court is in recess until one thirty."

"Please be upstanding for the Right Honourable Judge, Randal Phillips."

* * *

Brent held Laura's hand as they rose to leave the court while waiting for the rush to peter out, the paparazzi rudely crushing through the bottleneck to get to the court halls and their precious cell phones.

"Are you all right, Laura?" Brent asked, concerned at her drawn complexion.

"Thanks, Brent. What I would give to relax over a coffee."

"Well, we can easily fix that, can't we, Terry?" Brent gave Laura a warm smile.

"I can't thank you enough, Brent, for your support." Laura warmly squeezed his hand.

Terry kind of shrugged in puzzlement. The situation was getting kind of cosy.

"Do you want to join me and your mother for lunch, darling? Of course, your friends are welcome." It was Senator Williams.

"No, I'm good, Father, I couldn't face a heavy lunch."

"Nice to see you, Terry."

"And you too, Mrs. Williams. Don't worry, Laura is in good hands."

"I'm sure." Margaret gave her daughter a kiss on the cheek. "Try not to stress yourself, darling. Remember what the doctor said." "I will try, Mother." Laura gave a "not again" sigh.

"There's a little Italian *pasteria* across from the courthouse, then of course there's the English pub, the Pen & Wig for a bar lunch and a pint of warm ale . . . So, what's it gonna be?" Brent was grinning from ear to ear, trying his best to liven up the company.

"*Hmmm . . .* On second thought, Brent, maybe I will settle for the pub. They *do* serve wine, don't they?" Terry laughed at Laura's comment.

"Then it's settled, and, Brent, I got news for you." Terry grinned. "You're on the tab."

* * *

"It looks like we are stuck here for the day." Bill turned to Jan as they stood on the court steps.

"I guess so, but it's not *all* bad . . . I don't know about you, Bill, but I could eat a horse."

Bill shook his head. "Hell, you just had breakfast at the diner!"

"So is my boss going to help a damsel or should I say, a detective in distress?"

"If you put it that way. Where did you park the car?"

"*You lazy lout!* You mean we're gonna drive, and after I busted my ass trying to find a parking spot!"

"Stop complaining, Detective. Besides, I'm paying."

"Pulling rank, huh?"

* * *

"So, where's this secret rendezvous?" Jan was teasing.

"It's a little Italian eatery on Canal that serves the best thin-crust pizzas in the whole of New York." Bill gunned the Pontiac and slipped into the lunchtime traffic.

"This is an APB." The red LED on the radio phone was flashing violently. "Robbery in progress at Asian grocery store 16 Center Street. All cars in the area, please respond. Approach with caution. The assailant is armed."

Bill turned to Jan. "Well, what are we waiting for? It's only a block away. We'll be there in five minutes . . . Open the window, Jan, and lock the magnetic light to the roof and hit *that* siren."

Bill pressed the gas, leaving a trail of rubber, the siren wailing, the lunchtime pedestrians showing little interest. This is New York, so what's new?

"Alice, Lieutenant Hayden here. Detective Martin and I are only minutes from that address, requesting backup."

"Bill, approach with caution, this guy is armed. Backup is on the way." "Thanks, Alice."

"Over there, Bill." Jan pointed. "*Pull over.*"

The beat-up old Chevy parked in front of the store, most likely the getaway car.

Bill hit the sidewalk running. "*Stay back . . . Stay back . . .* Police." He flashed his gold shield to scare off the pedestrians, but the sight of their drawn guns was enough.

"Jan, there's a narrow passage at the side of the store, most likely leading to the back entrance. I'll take the front, and you take the back."

Jan nodded and sprinted up the narrow alley while Bill cautiously approached the front door to the minimarket, his police special grasped in both hands, his arms outstretched as he kicked open the glass door, then crashed his back against the wall out of gun sight.

"*Police . . . Police.* Drop your weapon and come out with your hands above your head."

"*Are you fucking serious, copper boy!* This is my third strike, and there's no way I'm going back to the big house. I have this Chinese chick here, and this shotgun against her neck has a hair trigger . . . All I want is a safe passage to my car, then I'll turn the slant eye loose. So don't get no smart-ass ideas, or so help me, I'll blow this fucking babe's head off."

From where Bill was positioned, he had a clear view of the large, round bevelled mirror used by the cashier to get a take on customers as they entered the store, the CCTV camera directly above, actively scanning the premises. He could now clearly see his opponent standing between the heavily stocked food aisles, his face shrouded with a grey hoodie with black lettered "Michigan University" embossed on the chest. He quickly turned as if he heard something, and Bill momentarily got a "mug shot" of his black complexion. He was an ugly SOB pressing a sawn-off shotgun that resembled a pirate's musket held to the Chinese woman's neck, who was sobbing in fear for her life to the point of hysterics. This guy was a mountain, around two fifty to three hundred pounds and the shell to go with it. Bill could hear the police siren in the distance, and he had to do something fast before the black and whites spooked the "mountain."

Meanwhile Jan had arrived at the rear entrance. The door was ajar, and she cautiously pushed it open with her foot before rushing in, moving her outstretched arms from side to side, her firearm cocked, held firmly in both hands.

"This must be the fucking storeroom, and the door unlocked is just asking for trouble." She shook her head as she proceeded with caution toward the store exit, staying close to the stacked containers to provide cover.

"You can never tell. These people often work in twos." She whispered under her breath.

But where was this guy? She could hear a woman's hysterical screams. *"Please . . . Please let me go."*

Jan crouched to her knees, looking below the shelving to search for feet, but the store, as with all Asian minimarkets, with its narrow aisles and shelving stacked to the gunnels with all kinds of sauces colourful sachets, rice bags, and vacuum-packed foods, made it almost impossible to see anything.

I gotta do something and fast. Bill hit the floor on his hands and knees using the same tactic as Jan, searching below the shelves for feet.

Got em! "He can't see me, but I can see him," Bill was whispering to himself.

"I know you're there, pig. You had better listen and listen good, or I waste this chick . . . *Do you hear me?*"

"Yeah, I hear you, *whatever you name is!* Listen, don't do anything stupid. We can work this out."

The robber's voice was the "circuit breaker," pinpointing his location, and Jan made her move, crouching between the shelving. At last, she could get a bead on him.

"I'm gonna count to ten, and if you don't give me the door, you're gonna have chop suey for lunch . . . One . . ."

Bill was now directly behind him, and there was no time for debate. It was now or never, and in a flash, he made his move, catching the "no-brainer" by surprise as he pressed the muzzle of the Browning hard into the side of his neck.

"Drop it, big boy . . . *I said drop it!* Don't make me . . ."

"Okay . . . Okay."

The "mountain" hastily dropped the "musket" to the floor, the impact blasting a ball of buckshot as it discharged into the stacked food shelves, glass and food debris spraying the air with deadly shrapnel. The shock made Bill stagger back, dropping his gun as he raised his hands to protect his face from the hail of lead as he crashed to the floor. It was the break the black man was praying for, and in a split second, he grabbed Bill's gun. Now the shoe was on the other foot and a new hostage to boot as the Chinese woman ran for dear life.

"On your feet, Detective, or so help me, you'll be another cross in the police cemetery."

Crack . . . Crack . . . Crack . . . The three rounds from Jan's forty-five found their mark, shattering the robber's jaw, spraying Bill with bone and flesh fragments, the other two shots in a tight group tearing a gaping hole in the black man's neck, the fountain of blood from his severed jugular spraying the air with blood spatter. It was over for the big man as toppled like a sack of potatoes, crashing to the floor amid the debris of soy sauce and sweet and sour . . . His last Chinese stir fry.

Bill staggered to his feet, wiping the disgusting cocktail of flesh fragments and food from his sports coat.

Jan was in a semi daze as she stared hypnotically at the motionless piece of garbage. She had never discharged her firearm in anger, let alone kill a real-life villain.

"Are you wounded, Detective?" the cruiser sergeant asked, his gun drawn. "I'm good, Sergeant, it's not my blood. Do me favor and call CSI." Bill turned to his partner, glad to be alive.

"Jan, I owe you one . . ." Bill gave a wry smile. "Something tells me we are going to get along just swell . . ."

CHAPTER 3

"Bailiff, call the next witness." Philips looked fresh after his lunch break.

"The persecution calls Dr. Paul Nathan, the senior trauma surgeon at the Roosevelt Memorial Hospital."

"Christ, Tim, what am I doing here? I would be as well pleading guilty. The DA's 'captain's choice' is hitting me with everything except the kitchen sink."

"Don't worry, Mike, that's coming next." Tim was just as frustrated as Mike, and somehow, he had to prove Mike's fifteen minutes of insanity was out of character.

"*Maaan* . . . I just love your sense of humour."

"Please take the stand, Doctor, and place your left hand on the Bible, then raise your right hand and repeat after me . . ."

Collins was back on stage and loving every moment of her time in the sun.

"*Ah . . . Hmmm . . .*" Les raised her hand to her mouth, an overzealous gesture to clear her throat, a tactic to wake the jury after an overindulgent free lunch.

"Dr. Nathan, you are the senior trauma surgeon at the Roosevelt Memorial hospital, is that correct?"

"Yes."

"And were you on duty on the evening of May 12, 2003?"

"Yes."

"And do you remember Laura Williams being admitted to emergency?"

"I do."

"Then perhaps you can tell the court why you were urgently called to the emergency room."

"As a trauma surgeon, my responsibilities are to attend serious accident cases. For example, automobile, motorcycle, and potential homicides—in short, emergencies that are life threatening and require urgent surgery."

"I see . . ." Collins turned to face the jury as if to say wake up and pay attention.

"May I stress, Doctor, that my next question in no way breaks your Hippocratic oath between the patient and the doctor, as this is a legal requirement under oath."

"I understand."

"Then can you tell the court the seriousness of the victim's injuries."

"At approximately nine ten, I received an urgent call to emergency. A young woman, with life-threatening injuries as the result of an assault, was unconscious, and her blood pressure was dropping dangerously low due to excessive haemorrhaging that may require immediate surgery."

"And what was your prognosis upon examining the patient?"

"Her pulse was low, and she was in shock and required a blood transfusion, or she would die from heart failure. A check on her blood type was carried out by pathology, and a transfusion was induced. I then decided to administer intravenously the drug Mannitol, which, through a somewhat complicated chemical process, helps suck water out of the brain, thereby reducing the swelling."

"I see . . . Please continue, Doctor."

"However, her blood pressure did not respond and was still dangerously low, as with her body temperature. It was then that I decided to place the patient into a medically induced coma. An anaesthesiologist was called to initiate the process. The patient is given Pentobarbital to induce profound coma. The basic idea is to put the brain to rest by closing down as much activity as possible. The brainwave activity of the patients ECG is flat, and the patient is completely unresponsive to all external stimuli . . . pain, light, noise, etc. Laura was then rushed to radiology for MRI and CAT scans."

"And what was the end prognosis, Doctor?"

"Crushed larynx as the result of extreme pressure or attempted strangulation, two broken ribs and a punctured lung, severely damaged uterus and fallopian tubes, which required surgical removal to stop the haemorrhaging. "And Dr. Nathan, what is the state of the patient's health today?"

"She has recovered remarkably well, considering the extent of her injuries. Her voice is returning gradually but will always have a hoarseness, but on a more serious note, she will never bear children."

There was a pronounced hush in the courtroom at the doctor's final wrap.

Laura could feel the lump in her throat but was determined not to tear. Terry could sense her body language and squeezed Laura's hand supportively while taking note that Brent was also comforting her with the same gesture. *Hmmm . . . This is getting a bit more than friendly!* Terry thought to herself.

"No further questions, Your Honour."

"Counselor Matheson?"

Tim shook his head. "No questions, Your Honour."

"Then, Bailiff, please call the next witness for the prosecution."

"*Tim,* for Christ's sake, can't you do . . . *Something . . . Anything?*"

"Will Ms. Eavon Jenkins please take the stand?"

"*Oh . . . Naw.* You gotta be kidding me!"

"What do you mean Mike . . . *Oh, naw?*"

"This Collins babe is fucking muckraking."

"So you know this woman?"

"*Do I!*"

"Just a second." Tim glanced at the witness sheet. "*I don't see her name here!*"

*   *   *

The pronounced click, click of six-inch stilettos was a head turner, and the guys strained their necks to get a load of this new broad. At around five eight with shoulder-length blonde hair that had seen too many trips to the "dye chamber" and with her above-the-knee skin-tight white skirt, Eavon was in serious trouble stepping it out. Her low-cut, off-the-shoulder floral blouse was bordering on adult entertainment, exposing her buxom cleavage, in imminent danger of full exposure as her flimsy blouse valiantly struggled to maintain its cargo against the laws of physics and good taste. As she took the stand and turned to face the court, a guesstimate of her age placed her around late thirties, but she had a pleasant face and bleached teeth to go with it. Her botoxed, lineless complexion, the rouged cheeks, light-blue mascaraed eyelids, and tattooed eyebrows gave her a sort of tarty look, but whatever, she had a full house.

*   *   *

"Mrs. Jenkins, please . . ."

"Ms. Jenkins."

"*Eh . . . Ah . . .* Ms. Jenkins, please place your left han . . ."

"*Objection!*" Tim was on his feet. "There is no record of this witness on my list, and therefore her testament should be disallowed, and she be ordered to stand down. Under the power of discovery, the persecution should have notified me within twenty-four hours as to why this witness is essential to the persecution's case in order to prepare my defence.

Philips stared over his half glasses; his brow deeply furrowed.

"Will the counsellor for the prosecution please explain."

"Your Honour, this witness only came forward late yesterday evening, and there was no time to contact Mr. Matheson, and my legal opinion was that her evidence is critical to prove the prosecution's case that the accused has a history of violence against women."

Phillips shook his head then gave a pronounced sigh. "Counselor Collins, I don't need this distraction, and you are fully aware of the legality of disclosure. Both counsellors, please approach the bench . . . Now listen to me, Lesley." Phillips stared down at her. "I don't like surprises, so perhaps you can explain, *and it had belter be good!*"

"As I stressed, Your Honour, it was just too late, and I have another character witness in the court right now willing to take the stand."

"Your Honour," Tim protested. "This is typical dirty tactics by the prosecution to further defame the accused in the eyes of the jury, and I strongly object. I quote the case of Burton versus . . ."

"Tim, don't play silly buggers with me. I know the law, and in the interest of justice, I will allow this witness to testify . . . *But this time and this time only!*"

"Your Honour, does that mean . . ."

Phillips cut Collins dead in the water.

"*Don't test me, Lesley* . . . Tim, I will record your objection and my decision to overrule. Now perhaps we can continue, that's if it's not *too* much trouble?"

Eavon was standing in the witness box, her hand clamped on the Bible, her feet screaming for a seat, her six-inch heels a modern form of Chinese torture.

The bailiff looked toward Phillips.

"Bailiff, please continue."

Tim was still smarting as he returned to the defense desk. "*Bitch!*"

"Ms. Jenkins please repeat after me . . ."

Collins couldn't wait. She was way ahead on points, *but the final bell hadn't rung just yet!*

"Eh, Ms. Jenkins . . . Do you mind if I address you as Eavon?"

"No."

"Then . . . *Eh* . . . Eavon, do you know the accused?" "Yes."

"And can you tell the court how you met the accused?"

"At a business function in the Hyatt Hotel."

"Eavon, please continue at your own pleasure . . ."

"He is good-looking, charming, and suave. Of course, when he began to pay more attention to me than the other girls, I was flattered. He fetched me a drink and then another, and we began to get cozy. I suppose in hindsight, I should have recognized the usual unhappy marriage 'my wife done me wrong' song and how he praised my personality being so different from the other broads . . . *Eh,* I mean girls . . . That are just after a good time. I get lots of guys hitting on me, but Mike seemed so different . . . *Like the real deal.* He was staying in the hotel, so I was not surprised when he invited me to his room for a nightcap."

"And?"

"I soon found out what he really wanted. One-night stands are not my scene, but then this guy had it all."

"And you had sexual intercourse?"

"If you could call it that . . . A Jekyll and Hyde with a split personality.

He was kinky and rough with it, and when I refused 'round the world' . . ." There was an instant burst of laughter.

"*Ordeeeer . . . Ordeeeer!*" The gavel slammed once more, but it was becoming a lost cause, and Phillips was in frustration land, the distraction stopping Eavon in her tracks.

"*Ah . . . Hmm,* please continue, Ms. Jenkins." Phillips was now more composed.

"He became violent and started to slap me around. I lost one of my front teeth, you know, and had to get an implant. I cost me three grand." Eavon lifted her top lip for the court to see. "Not a bad job, huh?"

Needless to say, there was another outburst, and by now Phillips had all but given up.

"Ms. Jenkins, please stick to the question."

"Oh . . . I'm sorry . . . *Eh* . . . Your Honour . . . *The pun?*" "Eavon, can we go back?" Even Collins was getting frustrated.

"*Eh . . . Err . . .* Where was I? Yeah . . . I thought this sex maniac was going to kill me as he threw me to the floor. He had a crazy look in his eyes as if he was going to enjoy raping me again. Some guys get turned on at the thought."

"Eavon, *can you get to the point!*" Tim had to smile at Collins's frustration. If this continued, the jury would lose the plot.

"*Eh . . .* Of course. I don't know where I got the strength, but I raised my leg and, as hard as I could, kicked him in the nuts . . ." Even Phillips had to smile.

"He fell in a heap clutching his family jewels, and I was outta there quicker than you could sneeze."

"And did you contact security or the police?"

"What's the point? A woman can run faster with her panties down than a man with his trousers at his ankles. Besides, guys stick together. They are all tarred with the same rope."

"And is this man here in court today?'

"Yes."

"Then can you point to him?" "Yes." Eavon pointed to Summers.

"Will the jury please take note that Ms. Jenkins identified the accused . . . No further questions, Your Honour."

"Counselor Matheson, do you wish to cross-examine the witness?"

"Yes, Your Honour."

Tim turned to Mike. "*You've given me a fucking giant headache.* You should have been completely honest with me. What else is in the cupboard?"

As Tim walked to the witness box, the smirk on Collins's face made him more determined to kick ass.

"*Eh . . .* Eavon, perhaps you can explain to the court in what capacity you were invited to this so-called business function?"

Eavon looked decidedly uncomfortable at the question.

"I have a second job as a hostess. As a single parent and with the cost of living, *can you blame a gal?*"

"I'm asking the questions, Marcy . . . Ever been married?"

"No."

"Then can I ask the age of your child?"

"A boy, ten years old."

"Your first job?"

"What do you mean '*first job*'?" Eavon was showing her colours.

"You mentioned hostessing was your second job, if my memory serves me right, is that correct?"

"Yes, if you put it that way. I'm a qualified confidential secretary. In fact, I have an interview with the CEO of Target this week." There was a rumble of laughter.

"Ms. Jenkins, may I remind you that perjury is a capital offense in a jury trial and, if found guilty, carries a minimal two years' imprisonment. In fact, I will go as far to suggest that *you are a high-class prostitute* and you saw the accused as a ticket to a gravy train. And once you had turned tricks, you would demand he see you time and time again, *but at price*, or else you anonymously inform his wife and his company, ruining both his marriage and his career, and I would go as far to say that your voluptuous appearance in court today is a ploy to get your name in the press and TV interviews for fame and fortune, like another Devine Brown—the only difference is that you are a Caucasian. *Isn't that true, Ms. Jenkins?*

"Objection, Your Honour. This is a derogative and low-life outrageous attack on the witness's character, and I demand this line of questioning be struck from the records."

"Objection sustained. Counselor, you will discontinue this line of questioning."

"No further questions, Your Honour." Tim smiled inwardly, his objective to destroy the credibility of the witness was a master stroke.

"You may stand down, Ms. Jenkins. Bailiff, please call the next witness."

"I call to the stand the witness for the defence a Ms. Laura Williams."

There was a hush in the courtroom; no one had anticipated Laura taking the witness box.

"Be brave, Laura." Brent squeezed her hand.

"I'll try, darling."

Hmmm . . . Darling now is it! Terry thought to herself. *I must be blind.*

*   *   *

"Laura, how are you feeling?"

"As well as could be expected."

"I know this must be extremely stressful for you. Just take your time and answer the questions as best as you can remember. Your Honour." Tim turned to Phillips. "May I request a glass of water for the witness?"

Philips nodded. "*Bailiff.*"

"Thank you." Laura's hand were shaking as she held the glass.

"Laura, can you please tell the court how you met Mike Summers?"

Laura paused for a moment to compose herself before addressing Matheson.

"Your Honour." Her voice barely a rasp. "My larynx or voice box is still in the healing process, so at times my voice will be barely audible."

"I understand, Ms. Williams, please continue. Should you require a break if you feel fatigued, don't hesitate to inform me."

"Thank you, Your Honour."

"Laura, can you please revert to my question."

"ABM, the company I work for as marketing manager, decided to outsource the launch of our new product, the ABM 400/2000 business machines, and the contract was given to Global Marketing."

"And what is the significance?"

"Mike Summers is the vice president of Global Marketing." Laura took another sip from the glass.

"Which meant?"

"Which meant I had to work closely with him . . . Late meetings, business lunches, and so on."

"*I see* . . . Let me draw your attention to your friend Terry Johnson's statement. Quote . . . Laura met this guy on the rebound after a previous disastrous relationship and fell head over heels for this corporate Casanova. Unquote. Therefore, would I be correct in stating you were heartbroken and that you were desperately searching for a new relationship, and Mike Summers was the perfect solution. Handsome, flattering, an executive of high standing, but . . . And I quote, a married man with a family. But the fact that Mike Summers was married was no barrier to your sexual perusal and satisfaction.

"Is that correct, Ms. Williams?"

"No, *it is not* correct!" Laura grasped for the water again.

"Are you all right, Ms. Williams?" Tim was concerned at her paleness, but he had a job to do, unpopular as it was.

"Yes," Laura whispered.

"And where did you normally meet?"

"At my apartment, or on occasions when Mike was out state, I would fly and meet wherever."

"But the accused never tried to hide, shall I put it . . . on your first date, that he was married."

"No."

"Didn't your conscience bother you that you might be destroying a happy marriage?"

"No, because Mike told me his marriage was over a long time ago and his wife was now more like a companion than a lover."

"And you accepted this?"

"Affairs of the heart are blind to reality. Mike was very convincing, especially in bed, and promised me he would divorce his wife but to give him time."

"I see . . . But after your secret hideaways were fast diminishing, you suspected that your steamy relationship was in the cool-off stage, and when the accused finally cut the cord, you were devastated."

"You could say that."

"So much so . . ." Tim turned to face the jury "So much so that Laura Williams was determined to destroy Mike Summers's life by whatever means were at her disposal . . ." Tim turned to eyeball Laura again. *"Isn't that true, Ms. Williams?"*

Laura didn't answer and just stared straight ahead.

Phillips allowed a few seconds silence before responding.

"Ms. Williams, *you will* answer the question."

"Can you blame me? I found myself pregnant, and my dreams shattered when Mike refused to see me ever again and, even worse, rejected that he was the father of my unborn child. *I was humiliated, I was devastated!"*

"So, you blackmailed him?"

"Blackmailed him! Are you serious?"

"You threatened to tell all . . . To expose him, to ruin his marriage . . . His career . . . He was a desperate man . . . Blackmailed by his mistress . . . *Yes, blackmailed* . . . In fact, I would use the term *'sexual blackmail.'"* Matheson turned to face the jury box.

"Ladies and gentlemen of the jury . . . *I ask you!"*

He turned again to face Laura, who was by now almost in tears.

"Objection, Your Honour . . . The defence is insinuating the victim has in fact committed the serious crime of blackmail. This is absurd, and the defence is unduly stressing the witness, bearing in mind her medical condition."

"Objection overruled. Counselor, please get to the point."

"But, Your Honour . . ."

"Ms. Collins do not question this court. Will the defence please continue?"

"Ms. Williams, didn't you phone Mike Summers at home?"

"Yes."

"And didn't you phone him at the office and again at his home, leaving a message with Mr. Summers's wife that he must meet you at your apartment at seven thirty on the evening of August 12?"

"*Counselor,* please get to the point." Phillips was becoming more and more impatient.

"Yes, but not in the content that you are implying."

"If not, then what was your intention?"

"To try and work something out."

"You mean maybe you could convince him to get together again with sex."

"Something like that."

"But your sexual advances that evening didn't work . . . *did they?* And when he offered you a check to financially help with your pregnancy and as final payment to leave him alone, you slapped him in anger and ripped up the check and threw it in his face. *Isn't that so, Ms. Williams?*"

"Ms. Williams." Phillips peered over his glasses. "I will not tell you again . . . Please answer the question, or I will hold you in contempt."

"I can't remember everything, it happened so fast. But the last thing that *I do* remember was gouging my nails into his face to stop him from strangling me before I lost consciousness."

"Ladies and gentlemen of the jury, the fact is, the accused, in a moment of temporary insanity, struck out and wrongly assaulted Ms. Williams in a severe act of provocation. *This is not attempted murder,* but aggravated assault. No further questions, Your Honour."

"Counselor for the prosecution, do you wish to cross-examine?"

"No, Your Honour."

"Then the witness can step down. As there are no further witnesses, I request the defence and prosecution make their final address to the jury. I call Counselor Collins from the district attorney's office representing the state . . . Counselor Collins."

"Thank you, Your Honour." Les was all smiles as she glanced toward Tim. It was in the bag, or was it?

"Ladies and gentlemen of the jury, today you have heard testaments from the victim's friend, the Homicide Division, and the Forensic Pathology Department, which, I must stress, has done an excellent job in its investigations to bring *this* . . . this murderer to trial. Let me repeat . . ." The courtroom was now in deathly silence.

"Yes, you heard me right. *Murderer* . . . He may not have killed his victim, Laura Williams, although he left her for dead with horrific injuries . . . But he *did* commit murder. The murder of an innocent life . . . An unborn child . . . never to experience the joys of living as the result of a wanton act by a selfish, callous, and heartless individual whose only objective was to save his own rotten hide."

Collins turned to face the courtroom, then abruptly about-faced, a highly dramatized theatrics to stare down the faces of the jurors on a guilt trip.

"You have heard the medical evidence from a reputable trauma surgeon at the Roosevelt Memorial Hospital. Broken ribs, punctured lung, fractured larynx, severe haemorrhaging from a ruptured uterus, which required surgical removal to save the victim's life, and above all, the death of an innocent unborn child. A tragedy worse than the tragedy in Shakespeare's *Macbeth*. The end prognosis? Laura Williams will never experience the joy of motherhood. *Can you imagine?* Never to have children . . . Never to have grandchildren! And what about Eavon Jenkins, who was beaten to within an inch of her life because she refused to participate in the accused sexual fantasies!

"Ladies and gentlemen of the jury, I leave you with that thought in mind, and *I know* there can be only one verdict . . . And one verdict only . . . *And that is guilty of attempted murder.* Thank you."

Mike sat in silence; his mind now lost in a maze of assumptions.

"Counselor Matheson for the defence."

"Thank you, Your Honour."

Tim slowly and deliberately walked to the jury box and stared at the jurors for a few seconds, trying to catch each of their eyes.

"An Oscar performance by the prosecution. Don't you think?" A few of the jurors couldn't help but grin at Tim's remark.

"The accused is a normal, healthy male going through a middle-age crisis. Has none of the male jurors ever experienced the pleasure of looking at a beautiful young woman and thinking . . . *If only?* And Mike Summers is no different. The only difference was pretty young women always seemed to come his way. It was just *too* easy. A short fling, and it was all over. Was it right or was it wrong—that is a conscience decision by both the adult parties? There's no law against infidelity, but you see, Laura Williams had gone through a number of bad relationships, and at twenty-eight the market gets smaller and smaller. She was desperate to find the right man, single or married. Who cares as long as he had the credentials and looks, and Mike Summers fitted the picture to a tee? Sure, he may have made promises in the spur of the moment that he couldn't or had no intentions of keeping. But then Laura Williams is a big girl and went into this relationship with both her eyes wide open."

Tim turned to face the court, then once again the jurors.

"But when the accused decided it was time to end it, Laura was pregnant, a desperate woman willing to do desperate things, spinning a web of destruction like a spider to keep her man. Unless he kept his promise to divorce his wife, she was going to destroy him, his career, and his family . . ."

Tim paused for a moment to allow his statement to sink in.

"Blackmail was her only avenue . . . *Sexual blackmail!* Is it a criminal offense? *No.* But it has the same effect on the victim, and when Mike Summers met Laura on that fateful evening to finally call it quits, all hell was let loose, and in her desperation, she assaulted him and ripped his check into shreds and threw it in his face. What happened next is well documented, and in a moment of temporary insanity, the serious assault took place . . ." Tim paused again.

"Ladies and gentlemen of the jury, this was not a plan to murder Laura Williams, but a peace offering that went drastically wrong. *Aggravated assault* . . . *Yes!* But attempted murder, *no!* I ask each and every one of you today to consider the facts and to search your conscience for leniency. Remember, if there is the slightest element of doubt, there can only be one verdict, and that is to find the accused not guilty of attempted murder. My case rests."

Phillips slammed the gavel, most possibly relieved that it was time to call it a day.

"This court is adjourned until 10:00 a.m. tomorrow, when at such time the jury will make their deliberation."

"Please be upstanding . . ."

*   *   *

As Mike returned to his cell, the future looked grim. Matheson had made it clear that serious jail time was inevitable. This night was going to be a long one, and the last thing he needed was shit from that loudmouth Dempsey.

The noisy rattle of the tensile steel gate to his cell felt cold and scary, and even more scary was the thought that he would have to get used to it for a long time to come.

"*In!*" Jackson, the watch sergeant, shouted before giving Mike a hard dig in the ribs with his billy club, a token reminder that he had a long memory.

Mike cringed in pain and cursed, turning to eyeball the "ape," his eyes fearsome.

"So, what you gonna do, *white boy*? Call me names again, like fat man and shit face? Get in that fucking cell before I crack this club over your skull."

He gave Mike another ferocious push and raised his club once more in a threatening gesture before slamming the steel and turning the key.

"Put your wrists through the food slot while I unlock these cuffs," Jackson barked again; he was just waiting for an excuse.

But Mike . . . Well, he couldn't resist. "I won't be in the joint forever, fuck face, and when I hit the freedom trail, I'll be looking for you, fat man."

"You fucking white piece of shit, all talk and no action. I can open your cell again if you think you're up to it."

Mike ignored the balloon and sat down heavily on his cot. There's a time for everything.

"Remember, Summers, I have my contacts in the pen, and when 'the sisters' are finished with you . . . You'll think you've been fucked by a train. Now get outta my face and hit that cot, tomorrow is red-carpet day."

Jackson gave an ugly laugh before turning and walked toward the end of cell block.

"What you lookin' at, Dempsey?" Jackson growled as he passed Dempsey's cell; he was spoiling for a fight even with his own shadow.

"Nothing, Sarge . . . *Eh* . . . I mean I didn't mean you."

"You had better watch that big mouth of yours, Dempsey, or you'll be eating bananas for the rest of your life." Jackson slowly disappeared down the cell block whistling the tune "Don't Worry, Be Happy." Maybe he would hit pay dirt on the pony's tomorrow.

It would soon be time for dinner, a thought that Mike didn't relish, but then there was always Dempsey, who would demolish Mike's share.

Summers sighed as he stripped off his tie, then undid his shirt collar before hanging his jacket on the solitary brass hook before finally kicking off his shoes and stretching out on the cot.

A long night! That would be an understatement.

"Summers . . ."

"Dempsey, *put a fucking sock in it . . .*"

CHAPTER 4

Jan was waiting in the Pearl Streetcar park as Bill parked the Pontiac in the slot next to her bug.

"You're late this morning." She shook her head. "It's a good thing I'm not a brass monkey." She pulled up the collar of her topcoat as she leaned against the front fender.

Bill rolled down the window.

"*Get in* and stop complaining. I have hot coffee and a bacon on rye sandwich from the deli here . . . That is, if you haven't had breakfast?" "*Get out of it, you moron,* and unlock the door." "*Well?*" Bill asked as Jan settled in.

"*Thanks.*" She burst into laughter. "*And no, I haven't had breakfast!*" She was still smiling as she unwrapped the sandwich paper.

"So, what happened to you?" Jan asked between bites.

"The usual domestic turbulence. You don't know how lucky you are being single."

"Don't kid yourself, Bill . . . *I know, all right!*"

"We had better get a move on if we want to be in court before ten." "Aren't you going to touch base with Baker?" Jan asked.

"He phoned me at home this morning, and I informed him he would have the report on the heist at the minimarket on his desk first thing tomorrow. Internal affairs are burning his ears. *What the hell, Jan,* that's what he is being paid for, to take the heat off guys like you and me. By the way, I'm recommending you for a citation. After what you did, you deserve it."

"Thanks, Bill, but really . . ."

"But really nothing, the chapter's closed." He changed the subject. "Looks like a big day with the media with the number of reporters preying outside the court."

"I guess so, but . . ."

"Don't tell me! Where do I park the car?"

Jan held out her hand as Bill pulled into the sidewalk and cut the motor.

"The keys please. I'll see you in court."

Bill laughed. "I think I'll recommend you for another citation . . ."

*   *   *

The courtroom, as predicted, was packed to capacity, and Bill squeezed into the remaining seat next to Dave Adams.

"Dave, ask Ken to squeeze over a bit to make room for my partner, Jan. She'll be here any minute now."

Adams laughed. "That's a tall order, Bill. You know Ken, he takes up two seats, But I'll try . . . *Ken . . .*"

No sooner had Bill spoken thank, speak of the devil, Jan was squeezing into the space next Bill in the aisle seat.

"You made it, huh?"

"Yeah, but only just. Boy, this joint is packed like sardines."

"You better believe it. It's like every man and his dog."

Jan turned to scan the courtroom more so out of curiosity. The back wall was standing room only, with the paparazzi cramping the space. Senator Williams and his wife, Margaret, were prominent in the first row, as was Laura, Terry, and their new male escort. In the second row to the right was June Summers with Steven and Sheryl.

The court was abnormally noisy, like a Chinese restaurant with everyone talking over one another, and when the doors finally closed to the public, at last there was some semblance of silence.

Mike and Tim were already sitting at the defence desk, with Collins on the other side of the court, engrossed in some official paperwork.

Summers looked pale and drawn, most likely through loss of sleep and the thought of the unknown. For him, what would this day bring? *God only knows!*

The door to the judge's chambers opened punctually, with Phillips in full regalia, sprightly alighting the four steps to the bench. He looked bright and fresh, ready for the challenge.

"Please be upstanding for the Right . . ." The bailiff's voice rang out, inducing immediate silence.

"Good morning." Phillips brought down the gavel hard. "This court is now in session . . . Bailiff, please call the jury."

The pear-shaped bailiff in his dark-blue suit walked briskly to the jury entrance and knocked on the door. "Is the jury ready to deliberate?" "Yes," came the reply.

"Then please enter the court and take your places in the jury box."

The door opened, and the twelve jurors wearily stumbled to their seats, the noise like cattle entering the freight liners. They looked as if they had had a long night, and Phillips impatiently waited until they had settled down as he drummed the bench with his fingers.

"Foreman of the jury please be upstanding. Has the jury reached a unanimous verdict?"

"Yes, Your Honour."

"Then please inform the court of your verdict."

"Your Honour, we find the accused on the capital charge of attempted murder *not guilty.*"

There was pronounced hush in the courtroom in surprise and disbelief.

"However, Your Honour, the jury finds the accused guilty of aggravated assault due to mitigating circumstances and temporary insanity, causing serious bodily harm to the victim as the result of blunt-force trauma, resulting in the miscarriage and the death of the foetus."

"Thank you, foreman . . . Bailiff, collect the jury's verdict."

Phillips fumbled for his glasses, then peered over the top to read the slip of paper.

"Will the accused please stand for sentencing."

Tim grabbed Mike's arm. "You had better make this your finest hour."

"Michael Summers, before I proclaim my judgment, have you anything to say?"

"Yes, Your Honour." Mike froze for a few seconds. "Your Honour, I made a terrible mistake that will live with me every day for the rest of my life. Am I sorry? If only I could turn the clock back, *but I can't,* and I profusely apologize to Laura Williams for the grief and pain I have caused her. I look back at myself in disbelief . . . A middle-aged man going through a midlife crisis, thinking that he is God's answer to women. To that extent, I apologize to my wife and family for the embarrassment and destruction of their lives. Your Honor, I am at the mercy of the court."

"Michael Summers, the court takes note of your remorse and subsequent plea for leniency. The jury has found you guilty of aggravated assault resulting in the grievous bodily harm of one Laura Williams to the detriment of her life, and by the powers bestowed on me by the state of New York, I hereby sentence you to twelve years imprisonment with a minimum parole period of not less than nine years and six months, to be served in the New York State

Penitentiary. Court security, please escort the prisoner to the cells." Philips slammed the gavel once more, then rose to his feet.

"This trial is closed."

PART 13

The Goldfish Bowl

CHAPTER 1

March 2013

Another year older and deeper in debt. The most powerful country in the world was heading for the proverbial fiscal cliff, and Ben Bernanke, the federal reserve chairman, was printing money like it was going out of fashion. Interest rates are at zero and U.S. government bonds are not worth the paper they're written on. Europe was a basket case, and Greece could be bought for a dollar. Obama had been re-elected for another four years on promises he will never fulfill, *that is*, as long as the Senate was Republican, and Mitt Romney was still licking his wounds, declaring it was a "done deal" because of the black and Hispanic vote. The war in Afghanistan was almost over. *At least, that's what the Coalition would love to think*, and Osama bin Laden was buried at sea, *or was he?* But more importantly for Mike Summers, it was parole review time, and today was the second most important day in his life, *if you take the day he was born as his first!*

*   *   *

"*Summers.*" The burly prison guard banged on Mike's cell.

"Get ready, the parole board sits in ten minutes, and you're first on the roster. Who knows, Summers, this might be your lucky day. *Now get the fuck ready. You only got five minutes!*" English was not this meathead's forte.

Mike wearily swung his feet to floor, then walked to the stainless-steel sink and stared into the scratched metal mirror. Nine and half years had passed since he was locked up in this shit hole, and at fifty-five, the wrinkles were on the march. His minimum jail time meant that his numerous applications for parole were just a useless formality, and today would be another exercise in hypocrisy.

Get ready? he thought to himself as he rinsed his face in the cold water. *What a joke!* Mike stared down at his orange prison outfit and white sneakers, now a shade of dirty white. *Is this guy kiddin'?* He ran his fingers through his greying hair, then rinsed his mouth from the tap. Sure, he had had some altercations with the faggots and the tobacco and drug barons, but in the joint, it was not about brawn but about brains.

"Summers, are you ready?" There was a loud bang on steel.

"Keep your fucking shirt on!"

"What did you say?" The guard angrily swung open the cell door. "I said . . . *I'm ready.*"

"Then get your fucking ass out here and clip on these bracelets . . ."

*   *   *

"Take a seat, Summers. *Don't just stand there*, you're not on parade!"

The youngest of the three parole board officers pointed to the empty plastic chair.

Mike's face reflected his disgust, but in the pen, manners and respect were a thing of the past, and you had best get used to it.

*   *   *

As the "suit" glanced through the paperwork, Mike sized up the three people that would decide his fate. The guy doing the reading reminded Mike of himself before he took the twelve-year hit, nine and a half years ago. Slim, smartly dressed in his Al Italia suit, the crisp white shirt, and dark-blue polka-dot tie with the kerchief to match brought back memories. His tanned complexion, chiselled jaw line, dark brown eyes, and swept-back, middle shade black hair smacked of the mafiosi. *Who knows?* Maybe this guy was on the take; if he is, *he wouldn't be the first.* As for the other two, the oversize woman in the KJB garb was either a bodyguard or there for the free lunch, a "no-brainer" who would make dogs bark. The other guy was a black American who could be stand-in for Morgan Freeman. Whatever. There had always got to be *one* African American!

*   *   *

"Summers, are you with us?"

"Eh . . . err, yes."

"The board have reviewed your parole application and . . ."

Mike couldn't help himself; he had been through this charade five times before, and it didn't mean jack shit, and he viciously cut this guy down to size. *"Listen, sonny . . .* Am I sorry for the crime I committed? Every day of my time in the joint and for the rest of my life. I can never get back the years I lost, or I can't change the pain of my foolish act. *Am I rehabilitated?* That's just a fancy word that doesn't mean shit in here. So I'll not waste your time any longer. So go ahead, sonny, and put your little stamp on that useless piece of paper and stop wastin' *my time. I only have another two and a half years to go!*"

*   *   *

"Summers, the warden wants to see you in his office right away.

"What's this . . . Time in the hole?"

"How the fuck should I know?"

"Can't I finish my fucking chow?"

"You heard me, *move it!* I won't ask you again."

"Summers, *you've done it again!*"

"Fuck off, Red . . . *And don't touch my chow!* I'll be back." "*Summers . . .*"

"*Yeah . . . Yeah!*"

CHAPTER 2

"Can I buy you a coffee?" Bill asked.

"After that session with our new boss, *I need one!*"

"At our desk, or the cafeteria?"

"Bill, I say let's get outta here for some fresh air." Jan didn't mince her words and was pretty vocal with it.

"The Last Chance Diner?"

"Is there any other?" She laughed.

"Jan, you had better wrap up. The weather forecast says snow is on the way."

"So, when are these guys ever right?"

"There's always a first." Bill laughed as he grabbed his keys and his heavy topcoat.

It had just turned ten thirty, and after getting a confession on the Harrison murder, it was time for a breather until the next forty-eight.

"Wow . . . This *is* cold." Bill commented as he pulled up his collar while stepping it out to the car. New York in February would make hell freeze over! "*Brrrrrr . . .*" Bill shivered as he opened the door of the Dodge Dart, the latest addition to the police fleet. "Hurry and get in, Jan, or I'll be freezing my you know what's."

"Do me a favor and cut the detail." Jan slammed the door as Bill gunned the motor to kick start the heater.

There was a few flakes of virgin snow landing on the windshield as Bill drove through the midmorning traffic. For a second, they were there, then gone forever, like life itself, temporary but permanent in death.

"Bill, I never got around to asking you how you felt when you were passed over when Baker retired last month."

"*Relieved!*"

"*Are you serious*, Bill?"

"Jan, times have changed since I was promoted to lieutenant almost a decade ago. Information technology . . . smartphones . . . tablets, you name it. I started out as beat cop fresh from the police academy to save the world, but nowadays it's not what you know but who you know. Take Glen Mitchel, our new boss. A graduate in criminology . . . assistant to the commissioner . . . Head of police internal affairs, *need I continue?* And at the ripe old age of forty, he knows jack shit about homicide, but does that matter? *No*, as long as there are diehards like you and me to protect his ass. Besides I'm over fifty, and I can retire at my pleasure with a full pension and no coronaries."

"I guess you have a valid point, Bill . . . *But have you decided?*"

"Now that's the sixty-four-million-dollar question." Bill grinned. "And in case you haven't noticed, Sergeant, *we've arrived!*"

Bill drove the Dart as near to the diner entrance as possible. *Who said the snow wouldn't last?*

The detectives sprinted to the diner, Bill covering his head with the morning edition.

"Gimme your wet coat, Jan, and I'll hang it on the peg. You go grab a seat at the bar."

"Hi, Jan."

"Jake."

"Where is he?"

Jan turned and pointed. "He's hanging up the coats. You had better set up two double espressos, no sugar."

"Coming up." Jake smiled as he hurried to the coffee machine. Bill and Jan were regulars, and what better customers than cops!

"There you go, two espressos."

"Thanks, Jake." Bill took the empty barstool.

"So, what'll it be?"

"Jan?"

"I'm not that hungry, Bill. Why don't we share a toasted focaccia?"

"Sounds good. One focaccia with bruschetta baby cause and Pecaroni."

"Say, before I fetch your order, Bill, correct me if I'm wrong but weren't you one of the detectives involved in that attempted murder case . . . You remember that broad that was the senator's daughter . . . Williams, a Laura Williams?"

"Yeah . . . So?" Bill turned to look at Jan.

"I guess you haven't read the paper this morning. Well, the guy's been released on parole. It's headlines!"

Bill grabbed the *New York Times* and spread it on the bar.

"Well, I'll be darned!"

* * *

As the big gate closed behind Summers, he shivered in his crumpled lightweight Italian suit. He had been institutionalized for over nine years and had forgotten the ferocity of the New York winter. A tall guy in heavy snow boots and fur-collared parka was leaning against the fender of the dark-blue Chevy Camaro.

"*Summers,* over here before you freeze to death."

Mike didn't wait for introductions as he trudged through the layer of pristine snow; the big guy nimbly opened the car door, the motor still running.

"Get in, Mike, I'll introduce myself later."

"Boy, this *is* a cold one!" Mike commented as he slammed the car door; his nostrils were snorting steam like a brewery Clydesdale pulling a cartful of wooden beer barrels.

"I'm Bob Clark, from the Department of Corrections. *You guessed right.* Your parole officer."

Clark offered Mike his hand, and Summers reluctantly returned the gesture; he was still carrying an almighty chip on his shoulder.

"Before we move on, first things first. I gather Warden Bartley walked through the conditions of your parole?"

Mike nodded. He had heard it all before and being lectured was not his strong point.

"Yeah, I've been there!" Mike replied, his expression saying it all. "Are you a cop?"

"Used to be . . . Retired at fifty-three but luckily nailed this job. What made you ask that?"

"Well, you don't look like a lawyer."

Clark just grinned. He had already sensed that Mike was going to be difficult, but then most parolees are . . .

*   *   *

Clark was no small fry at around six two and over two hundred pounds. Maybe this job was agreeing with him, or was it too many tax-free lunches? His complexion had that fresh "light on the booze" look, but the deep laugh lines, the crow's feet, and the seriously thinning grey hair were giveaways that he was in his late fifties. The one-inch-scar separating his right eyebrow above the steely blue eyes told its own story. But whatever, Mike had better get used to it. Clark was going to be in his face for a long time to come . . .

"I have a check here for eighteen thousand dollars, your accumulated earnings for the nine and a half years you have served."

"Eighteen grand for sweating in that stamping shop making number plates?" Mike shook his head. "I feel like the fiddler on the roof . . . But I guess it's better than nothing."

"I buy into that, but then this is not the time. Now the first thing we do is bank that check so that you can withdraw cash and go buy yourself some decent winter clothing. You can drop the suit you're wearing and the rest of your gear at the Chinese laundry not far for from the halfway house. You're gonna need that stuff when you start looking for employment."

"Don't remind me."

"*Then let's go!* I'll explain about the halfway house later . . ."

*   *   *

SENATOR'S APPEAL FAILS

There it was, front page news and in bold print.

> *The flamboyant and often-outspoken Senator Dave Williams, one of the longest-serving senators in the House of Representatives has failed in the Court of Appeals to block the parole of Michael Summers.*
>
> *Summers, who was found "not guilty" of attempted murder in a trial by jury in September 2003 but guilty of aggravated assault with grievous bodily harm and was consequently sentenced to twelve years imprisonment, has been released today on parole.*

Upon interview, the senator stated, "Who are these do-gooders that make these decisions? My daughter's quality of life has suffered from the callous assault of a convicted criminal who will now walk free in society to carry on with his life and with no remorse for his cowardly attack."

Senator Williams's daughter is currently undergoing treatment at the Johns Hopkins Hospital for cancer. The senator's wife, Margaret, unfortunately passed away in 2012 from heart failure. The senator blames . . .

* * *

"So, Summers is released, huh?" Bill was shaking his head. "What do you make of it, Jan?"

"That's how it is, Bill."

"Yeah, I guess so, but, Jan, do you know what still bothers me? No one raised the case that Summers was really the cause of Tony's death."

Jan pondered for a moment; she could understand how Bill felt but a cascade of water had passed below the bridge since then, and it was long gone. It was time to move on.

"But was he really guilty, Bill? Sure, he may have been the catalyst that lead to Tony's death, which was an absolute tragedy, but does that make him guilty? No court in the world would convict Summers on that count. I'm sorry, Bill, but I'm just telling it as I see it."

Bill didn't reply; it was best to let sleeping dogs lie. He took another sip of his espresso.

"This coffee's the best, Jake." "Thanks, Bill."

The subject was dead.

CHAPTER 3

"Sheryl, keep an eye on that pressure, the patient's pulse is dropping dangerously low."

"I have it under control . . . Doctor."

"It's time to dissect the renal artery and the renal vein and coagulate to avoid trauma to the renal vessels . . . *Good!* We are just about there. Sheryl, keep an eye on that pressure . . . Dr. Summers, once I cut the renal tube, we have a window of only fifteen minutes. Make sure that the donor kidney is cleaned in saline and ready for transplant . . ."

"Nice job, team, the new kidney is a healthy shade of pink, and there are a few drops of the precious golden liquid passing from the catheter tube. Dr. Summers, I'll leave you to close. I'll check on the patient's progress once he is in intensive care. I'm bushed."

* * *

"Steven, do you think we a have time for a coffee?"

"Sure, why don't I meet you in the cafeteria say, in twenty minutes? I need to get out of this operating garb and have a shower. You did well, sis. That patient gave me a few palpitations because of his history of heart problems caused by renal failure."

"Twenty minutes then. Do you want breakfast? It's only nine thirty."

"Hang on until I arrive . . . Ciao."

Steven gave his sister a warm smile before leaving the operating room.

* * *

"Hi, sis, have you been waiting long?"

"Only a few minutes."

"Coffee?"

"I'll get this, sis, you stay put. Anything to eat?"

"A toasted sandwich or something, I'll leave it to you, Steven." Within a few minutes, Steven returned with a laden food tray.

"Cheese and tomato?"

"Yeah, that's fine. I'm trying to lose weight."

Steven had to laugh. "How many times have I heard that one?" Sheryl scowled.

"*Ouch!* Touched a nerve, huh? Changing the subject, how's Nelson?"

"We're still together, if that's what you're asking."

"He hasn't moved in yet, has he?"

"Is my big brother still playing chaperone?"

"*Well,* you are the only sister I have."

"To answer your question . . . No . . . I enjoy my own space too much. *Hmmm,* this sandwich is good . . . Right choice."

It was a polite way of telling her brother to mind his own business.

"And how's *your* love life, may I ask?" Sheryl turned the tables.

"*Sis,* you gotta be kidding! In this job, when do I have the time? I'm flat out here at the transplant centre."

"You have to take it easy, Steven."

"I know you mean well, sis, but I only wish there were more organ donors. It breaks my heart every day watching these patients on dialysis, with liver and heart failure, waiting in their futile hope for that precious call from the donor registry. They are like fish in a *goldfish bowl,* staring through the glass at the outside world in the hope of freedom, imprisoned in their own bodies, waiting for some miracle to release them in a last-minute reprieve from their ultimate death sentence."

"I feel your passion, Steven, but you can't keep beating yourself up. There's nothing you or I can do to change it."

"Or is there, sis?" Steven had a scary grin on his face.

"I don't know what you . . ."

"This is CNN with the latest news bulletins . . . Trevor McDonald reporting. Good morning. Senator Dave Williams has lost his appeal to stop Michael Summers's parole. Summers was released from prison today after serving only nine and half years of a twelve-year sentence for the aggravated assault of the senator's daughter, Laura Williams. Judge Gilbert Cummings from the appeals court had this to say . . ."

Sheryl turned to her brother, who had turned an ashen grey.

"Steven, *are my fucking ears hearing right?*"

Steven just kept staring blankly at the wall, too shocked to answer. It was the bad dream returning to haunt him.

"*Steven, do you hear me?*"

He gave a dejected sigh, then shook his head.

"Yeah, I hear you, sis, *and I still can't believe it!* After all these years!"

"Do you think Father will try and contact us?"

"*Father!* He's no father of mine. The misery he caused our family . . . Sheryl, I'll have to leave you. I have to check on Mr. Martin in intensive care." But Steven's thoughts were on other things.

"Listen, sis, are you free this evening?"

"Let me check my roster." Sheryl opened her phone. "Yep, I'm free, and you?"

"I'm on call until seven tomorrow morning. I have something I want to discuss with you."

"Why the cloak and dagger?"

"It's not the time nor place . . . Seven then?"

"I'll make it, but who's on the stove?"

"The good old pizza . . . You fetch the wine . . . Listen, Sheryl, I really have to go. Remember, seven . . ."

Sheryl placed her chin on her hand a frown on her face. *So, what's the big deal?* She shrugged before taking another sip of her coffee. *I wonder . . .*

* * *

Jan could feel the constant vibration from Bill's phone, which was obviously in silent mode, and just why he wasn't answering was anyone's guess.

"This was a good choice, Jan." Bill was wolfing down the focaccia.

"I hate to interrupt your breakfast, Bill, but aren't you going to answer that call?"

"That'll be Mitchel . . . *Let him wait!*" Bill shrugged off Jan's concern.

"I tell you, Bill, you're not doing yourself any favours." Jan was shaking her head.

Hayden could be as stubborn as a mule when he was in one of his moods.

"*Jan,* you worry too much. Finish your focaccia, and I promise I'll answer that call."

"If you say so . . ."

* * *

"Hayden here."

"Bill, it's Sergeant O'Neil from the front desk. Mitchel is going off his brain trying to contact you. He has just phoned, ordering me to keep calling until you answered. I tell you, he's in a shit of a mood."

"You can inform him you managed to contact me, and I'll phone in, in a few minutes, once I finish my coffee. Thanks, Liam."

Bill turned to Jan and gave her a cheeky smile. Whatever, he was taking his time . . .

Hayden here.

"*What hell's your game?* I've been trying to contact you for the last half hour. I have better things to do than hang on the phone trying to contact you, Hayden . . ." There was a pregnant pause. "*Are you still with me?*"

"*Yeah,* I heard you . . . So what's the tsunami? Can't a guy grab some breakfast after spending half the night getting a confession from Bronson for that bank heist and the murder of the guard?"

"So, what do you want, *a medal?* This is a 24/7 job, and if it's too hot in the kitchen, you know what to do. I'm not Baker, and I'm not gonna take your shit . . . Do I make myself clear, Hayden?"

"*Yes, Captain.*" Bill gave a big sigh, making sure Mitchel got the body language.

"Here's the deal. There's been a shooting in the Bronx. A black kid was burned. I want you and Martin to get your asses over there *like now!* Contact O'Neil at the front desk for the address." There was a loud click as Mitchel smashed the phone into its cradle; he was plenty mad.

"So, what was all that about?" Jan asked.

"We get on our bikes and get over to the Bronx. A black kid was iced, probably gang or drug related, so what's new?"

Bill dialled again. "Liam, what's the address of . . ."

CHAPTER 4

Steven took another sip of his wine to wash down the carbo feast.

"Sheryl, what's wrong with the pizza? You've hardly taken one bite."

"I'm scared, Steven . . . I . . . *I am just scared.* What if something goes wrong?"

"Sis don't get cold feet on me now. Without you, it's a no-go. Take another glass of wine and calm down."

"*Christ, Steven,* you scare me! Haven't you got a better bad idea?" Sheryl took a "breath" break. "Now just say . . . *And I'm saying just!* Where do we start?"

"*The selection of the potential candidates?* I knew you would ask that! *Simple* . . . Their crimes against society and the damage and heartbreak they have caused everyday ordinary people."

"That's easier said than done." Sheryl was being the devil's advocate.

"We search the records of prisoners who have been recently released on parole where their sentences don't befit the crime."

"And *I know* the first candidate that comes to *your* mind!"

"*Exactly!*"

"And the place and the equipment?" Sheryl wasn't going to let it go. In for a pound, in for a penny, so to speak.

"There's lots of used medical equipment for sale. It's a case of searching the Net. Hospitals are always updating. Sis, just leave that part of the equation to me . . . *As for the place?* I rent a storage facility. It's not a big deal, and I'll purchase a portable air conditioner and induction water heater with storage and disposable tanks."

"I'm amazed, Steven. You've certainly done your homework. You must have been planning this for some considerable time."

"*I have, sis,* but the news today brought it all home."

Sheryl was still borderline on listening to her brother's shocking plan, but she had to admit it had merit . . . But the risks?

* * *

"Good afternoon, Fort Knox Self-Storage Facilities, how can I help you?"

"My name is Derek Newman. I'm searching for a storage facility near my apartment, for convenience."

"And where would that be, sir?"

"Chambers Street, near Pier 21."

"The nearest facility we have to that location, sir, is 20 Bloomfield Street, leading to Pier 53 on the waterfront, about a twenty-five-minute drive if you take West Street."

"That sounds ideal. What is the largest storage facility you have available?"

"Fifteen by twenty by nine. All our units are climate controlled. Rental . . . Just one second, sir . . . two fifty-five a month, and we have only two units available, numbers 18 and 26, all ground floor, facing the car park."

"That sounds ideal."

"And for what duration, sir?"

"At least six months."

"Then I can discount that to two forty."

"You have a deal."

"If you start next week, because it's in the middle of the month, I will give you the first two weeks free."

"It gets better all the time, and your name is?"

"Darin Crombie, I'm the area manager."

"Darin, I'm a very busy man, and I wish to pay in cash. I'll cover the whole six months and send the amount to you by courier. Please provide the courier with the receipt and the key to the unit for my collection."

"That seems in order, sir. When do you intend to settle?"

"I will send the courier before twelve tomorrow morning."

"Thank you again, Mr. Newman, it was a pleasure doing business with you. Should there be any problems or if you need further clarification, don't hesitate to call me on my cell phone. The number is 0638 . . ."

"Can I make a withdrawal now?" Mike asked the pretty teller with the black shoulder-length hair and the "teacher" glasses, like a younger version of the Greek singer Nana Mouskouri. She was a dish all right, and Mike. . . *Well . . .*

"Certainly, Mr. Summers." She gave the Citibank smile, flashing the pearly whites.

"What do you think I'll need, Bob? I haven't a clue about prices."

"You'll get a shock, Mike . . ." Clark crinkled his eyes, then pouted his slips. "Say fifteen hundred. That should get you started."

Mike gave the teller his best shot. "You heard the man!" He smiled.

"Certainly, sir, and in what denominations?"

Mike poured it on. "A mixture of hundreds and fifties . . ."

*   *   *

As Mike and Clark hit the sidewalk, the snow was refusing to let up.

"Let's get to the car, Mike, you must be freezing in that lightweight suit."

"Hold it, Bob." Mike grabbed his arm and looked into the sky, admiring the natural beauty of the falling snow, then inhaled the freezing air as if it was his last. "*Man,* it's great to be alive." His breath steamed, resembling a coal locomotive leaving the station.

"Bob, after nine and a half years, can you blame me?"

"That's for another time, Mike . . . *The car.*" Clark pointed. "Before we get snowed in.

"Get in while I clear the windshield." Clark reappeared holding the large rubber scraper that he had retrieved from the trunk.

Bob turned the key, then wiped the inside of the screen with the back of his hand to clear the misting.

"First stop, Macy's . . ."

*   *   *

"At least now I feel like a New Yorker in winter!" Mike grinned as he crunched through the pristine snow-laden sidewalk. The Jeep windbreaker, the thick blue stone-washed Levi's, and the heavy winter boots painted a picture as the two men trudged to the car; Mike still carrying his precious 2003 wardrobe that hopefully the dry cleaners could rejuvenate.

"It's a saviour I bought the thermal underwear, Bob, and this Timberland heavy woollen checked shirt." Summers turned to Clark, a wide grin on his face.

Mike had that unique expression of freedom written all over, a far distance from *Les Misérables.*

"Are you hungry?" Clark inquired as he turned the key.

"I tell you what, Bob . . . I feel like a millionaire with this nine hundred bucks I have left burning a hole in my pocket. So why don't I treat you to lunch at Burger King? I've been dreaming about a big whopper for over nine years."

"*Why not!* Jaycee will kill me." Clark rubbed his overhang. "She has me on a low-carb diet."

"Your secret's safe with me, Bob, I won't tell if you don't."

Clark had to laugh. Summers wasn't such a bad dude after all. "Well, what are we waiting for, Bob?"

* * *

"Two whoppers! *Where the hell have you put it, Mike?*"

"*Remember, nine years.*"

"*Heh . . . Heh . . . Heh.*" Clark laughed, wiping his mouth with the paper napkin. "Mike, this is a good opportunity to tell you about the conditions of your parole."

"*I knew it was too good to be true!*" Mike was moving his head from side to side.

"Firstly, as you are classed as a low-security risk, there's no need for a GPS ankle bracelet."

"*Gee, thanks, Bob!*" Mike was being sarcastic "*And . . .* What's the bad news?"

"I'm taking you to a halfway house, where you must stay for no less than two months."

"And where is this hotel, may I ask?"

"On the corner of Jackson Street and Leonard in Queens. It's the only place with a vacancy at the moment. It's near the subway and the Queensway Express, so it's easy to get around if you don't have wheels." Mike didn't comment; he was taking it all in.

"Don't look so down, Mike, *it could have been the Bronx!*"

"I should be thankful for small mercies, huh?" Mike shook his head again. "Well, I guess anything's better than the pen!"

"Your housemates, of course, are all male ex-cons, and you must report to the manager every night by no later than 11:30 p.m. lights out. The local police will be keeping an eye on you as the prison system has to inform them of parolees. The first two months is at the government's expense, and thereafter, it will cost you four hundred a month until you find your own accommodation. You meet with me at my office, Tuesdays and Thursdays, no later than nine thirty in the morning. I will put you in touch with a number of companies that employ ex-cons . . . Oh, by the way, no alcohol and no drugs, or your feet won't touch the ground. Here's my card. I think I have covered everything . . . Any questions?"

"*Nah,* I've had enough depression for one day, but I would appreciate hitting the cot for a couple hours. I'm bushed."

The rooming house was pretty run down, but then if it's free and owned by the city . . . *what do you expect?*

"Sam Barrett, I'm the manager here." He scowled. looking up from his desk.

*   *   *

This guy was ugly, his ears and eyebrows showing the scars from the Marquis of Queensbury. The thinning hair, the six o'clock shadow, and the nicotine lips could easily fit a poster for the Most Wanted. He was piece of work all right and not to be messed with.

*   *   *

"Mike Summers."

"*So?* Sign here for these towels. If you lose them, it'll cost you twenty bucks . . . Shared john and shower down the passageway. Toiletries, you can buy at Priceline at the corner of the next block. Room 14." Barrett chucked the key with the blue plastic tab in front of Mike, then swung his feet onto his desk, showing the soles of his boots. "I'm busy." He scowled as he opened the news rag. "Are you hard of hearing? *Move it!* This is Heartbreak Hotel, dude. You can count to fourteen, can't you?" Barrett pointed to the hallway, then buried his nose in the sports page.

Mike walked the dim "hall of fame" searching for his room while accidently slamming into another "guest." Fourteen was a bad omen—*Would you believe, the same number as his cell in the big house?*

The unshaven guy with the tattooed neck and complementary skinhead stepped back on impact and eyeballed Mike.

"You lookin' for trouble, man?"

"*Eh . . . Err . . .* Sorry, buddy, I was just . . ."

"Shut your mouth, pussy, and stay outta my face." "Muscles" brushed Mike aside like a ragdoll, but Summers kept his cool and just shrugged. There was no point; he was used to this shit in the pen.

"*Fourteen at last!*" Mike screwed his eyes peering in the dimly lit hallway at the number on the chipped green-painted door before finally turning the key.

Not knowing what to expect, he switched on the solitary lightbulb dangling from its frayed cord, the tobacco-stained curtains refusing to acknowledge the daylight. He stood for a moment absorbing his new "cell," a rose by any other name. The grey-painted walls, the tobacco-stained ceiling now resembling the colour of a Cadbury bar, and the once proudly lacquered oak floor could be mistaken for a dung hut in Nigeria.

"*Maaan!*" Mike placed his five-cent "Samsonite" on the solitary plastic chair, then sat down heavily on the side of the cot while still staring at his new surroundings.

The door frame had been cannibalized with crude carvings by previous guests, leaving their autographed initials and vulgar comments complete with artistry that you find on public toilet walls. No TV, no stainless steel can, no sink, no mirror; as for the wooden six-drawer tallboy minus the drawer handles that had most likely been stolen for the recycle dump and the solitary clothes hook behind the door, these were all the comforts of home. Even the No Smoking sign was a joke, with the first three letters of the second word replaced by some smart-ass with "Fuc."

"*Hell,* I had it better in the pen . . . At least I had a fucking TV!" Mike was speaking aloud as he unzipped his jacket and swung his feet onto the bed.

The world that he remembered had changed forever, and what lay in front of him in his ill-gotten freedom was now another nightmare.

*   *   *

"The kid's brother confessed. Another gun tragedy, and sadly a young man dies at the age of twenty . . . *It's beyond me.*" Bill shrugged. "What's the world coming to? An argument over a half gram of coke, a trigger-happy kid, and *bam*, another cadaver for the city morgue." Bill shook his head as he placed the key in the ignition before turning to Jan. "Another murder solved in the first forty-eight, huh? I'm sure Mitchel will be happy. I'll get a statement from the shooter first thing in the morning, that is . . . unless he changes his mind once his drug-fuelled brain clears."

"So what's new?" Jan had seen and heard it all before; in New York, the gun and drug scene was a daily occurrence.

"Are you driving back to headquarters now, Bill?" Jan asked.

"Yeah, but only to drop you off and pick up your car. By the time we get there, it will be after nine, and whether Mitchel likes it or not, my report can keep until tomorrow."

Bill hit the stock switch and signalled driving slowly past the black and whites and the ambulance, the paramedics pushing the gurney with the body bag.

"Bill, have you anything on the cards for this evening?" Jan asked, changing the subject.

"Not really. I thought I might just grab a beer and sandwich at Bud's on the way home."

"Listen, a better idea. I'm meeting Chris for a drink and late supper. Why don't you join us?"

"Naw, but thanks, Jan, for the thought." Mike grinned. "I'm getting kinda tired being the third wheel."

"*Get out of it!* You know you're welcome."

Mike laughed. "Yeah, I know. So how about you and Chris?"

"Like?" Jan had a good idea what was coming, After nine years as his partner, he was like her brother, always looking out for her when it came to affairs of the heart, and it's only a matter of time before Bill demands that Chris take a lie detector test. She had to smile at the thought.

"So what's so funny?"

"Nothing, just something that crossed my mind."

"*You haven't answered my question, Sergeant.*"

"Pulling rank, huh?" Jan was laughing. "Listen, we have only been dating for three years, and besides, he hasn't popped the question . . . *Not that I want him to!* I'm happy with the way it is. Our relationship doesn't interfere with my job, and I still have my freedom. Then there's the problem with Chris's two teenage kids from his divorce. I'm not at the stage of being a stepmother just yet, and you know when it comes to the kids or me . . . *No more said!*"

Bill laughed at Jan's remark. She certainly had both feet firmly on the ground.

"How about you, Bill? You and Judy divorced years ago, aren't you lonely? Come to think of it, I've never heard you mentioning a relationship, and I know you're not gay." Jan laughed at her own joke.

"Well, you're right on the second count, but there is someone special, and here we are at the car park."

"Why, you son of a gun! *Is that it?*"

"It's enough for one day . . . Tomorrow at nine, I need your support when we meet with Mitchel. Or so help me, I'll say something that I'll live to regret. Give my best to Chris. I'll take a rain check."

"Thanks, Bill." Jan opened the car door and disappeared into the near blizzard, Bill's last words still running through her mind. "There *is* someone special." She opened the door of the beetle and quickly turned the key, her breath freezing on the windshield.

"*Come on, heater . . .* Chris, I've just finished . . . *Of course, I'll drive carefully.* Gimme fifteen . . . Ciao."

*   *   *

Mike awoke with a start, and for a fleeting moment his mind was confused. No meal calls or lights out, and the room was fucking freezing! He shivered as he swung his feet to the floor, yawned, then raised his arms above his head in a groaning stretch.

"*Brrrrrr . . . What the fuck!* At least my last room was warm." Mike was reminiscing. "Now I know why crims spend most of their lives in prison. It's just too hard once you're institutionalized. Free lodgings, laundry, food, medicine, TV, you name it . . . Everything except freedom, *and that's a fucking joke! I don't even have the fucking time . . . The bastards even stole my Rolex!*"

*   *   *

Mike pulled back the drapes and wiped the windowpane with his hand, making little difference as he peered into the night. The snow-laden streetlights resembled Christmas trees as they sparkled in the darkness, producing a sort of halo effect. Thankfully the snow had stopped and the traffic sparse. As for the few pedestrians braving the subzero temperatures, they were either sending a message or oblivious to the danger of being mugged, raped, or murdered. But then this is Brooklyn . . .

*   *   *

Summers slipped into his windbreaker and opened the door, hoping to avoid bumping into "Mr. Muscles" again. As he passed the front desk, Barrett looked up, the cigarette dangling from his lips ready to drop its ash overhang into his coffee cup . . . *Not that the slob would notice!* And whatever happened to the "No Smoking" rule! Must be for ex-cons only!

Is there no justice in this world? Mike had to laugh at his own pun.

"So, what's so fucking funny, Summers? You better remember, lights out is eleven thirty, when I throw the key away."

"*I heard you!* You must get off on this kinda stuff, huh?" As usual, Mike couldn't let it go.

"*Summers,* I'm the king here, and you're jack shit. Remember, I'm the guy who decides whether you walk the walk or end up in cell 'Shangri-La.' Do you get my drift? So button up that big fat lip of yours and get outta my face."

"Whatever turns you on . . . *Your Highness.*" Mike grinned as he slammed the front door behind him.

As Summers hit the sidewalk, the chill in the air almost took his breath away, but for Mike it spelled one thing: *freedom.* And for once in a *very long time,* he had a spring in his step as he walked toward the all-night gas station.

"Free Timex Watch With Every Five Gallons of Gas."

"*Well, I'll be darned!*" Mike was now in the world of "throwaways" and "Made in China." It was hard to imagine, but a timepiece he needed badly, and in his state of wealth, who cares what it looks like.

"Maybe I can do a deal." He grinned as he entered the gas station.

*　*　*

"Hmmm . . . Nine fifteen." Mike raised his wrist, admiring his ten-dollar windfall, its luminous dial glowing in the dark.

"*Not bad.* At least now I can tell the time, and boy, am I hungry!"

*　*　*

Leonard Street is a typical Brooklyn backstreet with rooming houses, mini supermarkets, liquor stores, and "hand car wash" franchises, complemented with an assortment of working-class bars and diners run by Koreans or Chinese and the Irish. It was all too busy for Mike to take in as he walked past the intersection of Jackson toward the elevated freeway and the below-bridge parking, where the night bums were staking their claims with cardboard beds and their few meager possessions, "brown bagging" the cheap liquor to insulate their booze-soaked bodies from the cold. The oil drum with its sparking wood fuel lit up the shadows, a scene only too familiar in the Big Apple with the onslaught of winter.

Mike stopped and stared at the ugliness for a moment, then decided to hastily move on; he was attracting too much attention for his own good.

The large, flashing green neon sign with the oversize shamrock looked the real deal. Kelly's Irish Pub . . . Guinness and pub food.

"*Hmmm . . . At least I'll get out of the cold!*" Mike's breath froze in bursts as he pried open the heavy green wood-panelled doors.

*　*　*

The pub was typical Irish blarney, the large, polished oak bar with fonts of draft Guinness, Kilkenny, and the local brews Michelob and Millers. On the counterfeit aged brick wall spanning the back of the small bar hung a full-size Irish flag, with the unmistakable stripped colours of green, white, and orange. Green representing the Catholic populace, white the symbol of peace, and orange for the Protestants. Needless to say, in keeping with Irish tradition, harps and shamrocks were in abundance, and pictures of the plaintiff himself in the popemobile driving down O'Connell Street, the most famous street in Dublin. But who could resist smiling at the sight of the man-sized leprechaun standing under the spotlight next to the small bandstand, in full Irish costume? The buckled green hat, the pantaloons, the pirate shoes. the oversize ears, and that crazy grin holding a pint of the dark brew. Irish music was constantly playing in the background, but the baby of them all was the large circular wood fire in the centre of the floor complete with chimney stack and mesh spark protector. The atmosphere was warm and cozy, and the Guinness even better, and the smell of that stew was to die for . . .

*   *   *

This is my kinda place. Mike smiled as he sat on the heavy wooden barstool while taking in the scenery. The pub was relatively empty except for the few regulars, which made it even more appealing. *Maybe Tuesday evening is Arthur Guinness's night off.*

*   *   *

"What'll it be, buddy?" The young barman finished polishing the glasses.

"Do you have a pub menu? Or better still, what's that mouth-watering aroma?"

"Irish stew, the house specialty."

"Then I'll order that and a pint of Guinness."

"*Good choice.* I'll go place your order with the kitchen. The Guinness will take a few minutes."

"No sweat."

Mike took a sip of the dark brew and leaned on the bar with both his elbows. It had been a long time coming.

I wonder how the kids are doing? he thought to himself. *And June . . . I never heard from them even once during all the time I was in prison.* Mike took another sip from the pint glass before pondered for a moment. *I guess I can't blame them . . .*

"Your food, buddy."

"Thanks, I can't wait."

The barman was about to reply when a customer called. *"Danny, another pint when your free."*

"Be with you in a minute . . . Here's your cutlery and a slice of *aran bread*. Enjoy the stew . . ."

The food long gone, and the Guinness drained, Mike felt like a new man, but time was passing, and he glanced at his expensive timepiece.

"Almost ten! *What the hell*, I'll make it . . . Danny, another pint."

"Coming up."

"Say, Danny, would you have a pay phone here and a phone book?"

"Where have you been, buddy? I haven't heard that one for a long time!"

"So?" Mike glared.

The young guy sensed that he had struck a nerve, alarmed at Mike's reaction. Trouble wasn't on his watch.

"I apologize, man . . . It's just that everyman and his dog these days have smartphones. There's a pay phone at the back next to the restrooms. The phone book is hanging on the wall."

"No big deal . . . Can you gimme some coins?"

"Quarters, okay?"

Mike nodded and slipped a ten over the bar.

*   *   *

Sheryl had just switched on the lights and closed the door of her apartment when the phone rang.

"Christ! I hope this is not Steven again, I've had enough for one night . . . Sheryl Summers here."

There was a scary silence that seemed like forever.

"Listen you, pervert, either answer the phone or fucking hang up. *Do you hear me?"*

"Eh, um," a man's voice answered in a tone of uncertainty. "I'm sorry to disturb you at this time in the evening, but I'm trying to locate my daughter, a Sheryl Summers, whom I have lost contact with for a number of years. The family previously lived in East Village. You are the sixth call I've made, and who knows, six may be my lucky number."

Sheryl immediately recognized the caller's voice; even after nine years, how could she forget?

"Are you still there?" The silence was deafening.

"Why, Father? After all this time, why you are trying to come back into our lives now?"

"*Sheryl*, I knew it was you when I heard your voice. Listen, honey, I'm still your father, whatever. Sure, I made a mistake and hurt the people I loved most, but *I've* paid my price to society. I know life for me will never be the same again, and I can only imagine the hardships you and your brother have experienced, and I pray you can find it in your heart to forgive me. I would love to catch up with you over a burger or something, if only just to see my daughter again."

"I'll have to think about it, Father. We have all moved on, and to be honest with you, this I don't need. And take my advice: don't even think about trying to contact Steven. He's never forgiven you for what you did to Mother. You broke her heart, you know. So please don't give us any more grief."

"And your mother?"

"I don't want to speak about it, Father. If you don't mind, it's getting late, and I have an early start tomorrow."

"I don't suppose there is any way I can make you change your mind?"

"Please, Father. Don't be difficult."

"Well, if you do have second thoughts, you can find me at the halfway house on the corner of Jackson and Leonard in Brooklyn . . . The number is 763 . . ."

Sheryl abruptly hung up, then dialled. She needed another drama today *like a hole in the head!*

"*Steven*, can you guess who just phoned?

* * *

Mike signed the book and entered the time. No one was at the front desk, and he could only assume that, that lazy-ass Barrett had hit the sack early or was in the cot with his slag. The corridor was eerily quiet as Mike took his last trip to the communal bathroom. Three open showers, three vanity basins, and two cans. The mirrors had seen their day, cracked and steam damaged, and Mike could only imagine the chaos in the morning. The secret was to hit the "stables" before the "coliseum and the lions." He would set his expensive timepiece to buzz at seven, but now it was time to fill the electric heater with quarters and get his head down. His first day as a free man was anything *but* what he expected! Freedom was an illusion; your life constantly governed by the rule of law. Incarceration was just another version, the difference was that you are in a goldfish bowl and given everything else free, and tomorrow Mike would inevitably face another challenge, but what was to come was beyond even *his* belief . . .

CHAPTER 5

"Bert."

"Bill . . . You're in early this morning," Lucas commented between slurps of coffee.

"Yeah, I gotta get my report on Mitchel's desk before he arrives. I'm not exactly his favourite son."

"*Heh . . . Heh,*" Lucas laughed.

"Bert, I'm going to the coffee machine. Are you okay?"

"Yeah, I'm good, Bill." From being bitter enemies years ago, after the Brazil affair, these two had become the best of friends.

Bill placed the polystyrene cup next to his laptop, booted up the computer, then positioned his notepad within easy reach.

"I can't believe this black kid's name . . . Michael Jackson. I guess they have to be proud of someone." Bill shook his head and began to type. "At approximately 9:30 p.m., on the evening of . . ."

* * *

Jan slammed the door of the beetle; she wasn't going to hang around in this cold. The snow had stopped, then thawed, then inevitably froze again, turning the slush into ice, and she was having trouble keeping her feet.

"This fucking weather!" She cursed as she slipped and slithered in her balancing act to the front entrance. "Bill will be doing his proverbial. It's nearly ten."

"And under questioning the brother finally confessed that he was the shooter. I subsequently arrested him being in possession of prohibited substances: cocaine, ice and amphetamines, and a large cache of marijuana . . . Further charging the accused with culpable homicide and in the possession of an unregistered firearm. A statement will be taken in the presence of a witness by twelve noon today at the Pearl Street HQ . . . Lieutenant W. Hayden."

Hmmm, I guess that wraps it up. "Now for a refill."

Bill was about to descend on the coffee machine when Jan interrupted.

"This one's on me."

"So, what happened to you this morning?" Bill tapped the face of his watch. "Did Chris sleep on your tail?"

"I'll ignore that remark. Black, no sugar, huh?"

"*You got it!* When you come back, I want you to go through my report just in case I've missed something . . ."

*   *   *

"That's pretty accurate . . . Bill, when you retire, you should consider a second career as an author."

"Enough jokes for one day, Jan, here's Mitchel now."

"Good morning, Lieutenant . . . Sergeant . . ." I'll see you both in my office . . . say . . . in thirty minutes." He checked his watch.

*   *   *

"Bill, I don't suppose you had a chance to read the papers this morning?"

"Read the papers! *Hell, Jan, I didn't even have time for breakfast!* Don't tell me it's more good news." Bill was being sarcastic.

"Read it for yourself." Jan slid the paper in front of him.

"Laura Williams died peacefully in the early hours of yesterday morning in the John Hopkins Hospital after a long battle with cancer. The funeral will be held today at three o'clock at Green-Wood Cemetery, Brooklyn."

"*The coincidence is inconceivable!*" Bill was shaking his head. "Christ, Jan, *I still can't believe it!* Summers gets released on parole, and his victim Laura Williams dies on the same day. I can see now why the senator was trying to repeal the parole board's decision. *I still can't get over it.*"

Jan frowned. "So why the hurry for the funeral? That's what puzzles me."

"You got me there, Jan! Maybe some religious thing, or her father just couldn't take any more and wants to lay his daughter to rest in peace with a low-key funeral without the media circus. Remember, this nightmare has been hanging over that family for almost a decade, and I guess enough is enough . . . And now this!"

"When you put it like that, Bill, I can see your point. But my question is, *do you intend to go to the funeral?*"

"Jan, that case will stay with me for the rest of my life. I lost my best friend, and this low-life Summers walks the streets a free man . . . *Do I intend to show my respects?* I'll inform Mitchel I'm taking the afternoon off. Does that answer your question?"

"Can I join you?"

"Are you sure?"

"Just try me."

"Mitchel isn't gonna be happy!"

*   *   *

Mike was showered and dressed before 7:00 a.m., his assumption correct that these lazy-assed cons would be sleeping on their tails until at least ten. After all, what have they got to look forward to? Stacking shelves in Woolworth's or washing dishes in the Delhi or, worse still, getting a lecture from their fucking parole officer . . .

"It had just turned eight." Mike was having a conversation with himself; *at least there was no disagreements!* "Which reminds me . . ." He paused. "I have to check in with Clark this morning at nine thirty at his office. Let me see . . . Now *where's that fucking card?* He searched the back pocket of his jeans. "Ah, here it is . . . 14 Oliver Street, and where the hell is that? *I wouldn't have a fucking clue.* I suppose there's no point in asking 'I'm smarter than a fifth grader' at the front desk. That is, if he's not still with the sandman."

Mike slipped into his heavy jacket and turned off the heater. Why waste quarters! As he switched off the lights and closed the door, it was a big difference from his steel-riveted cell with the small peep hatch, and suddenly his stomach gave an ugly growl. His body clock was still in prison mode, missing the daily ritual of meal breaks.

"Yeah, I hear you." Mike's brain now conjuring up the thought of a "full house" greasy breakfast at the nearest diner. *"Man,* I can't wait."

He opened his step and headed for the sidewalk, still carrying his plastic Macy's bag containing his precious business suit, shirt, and tie. It was breakfast first, then the nearest dry cleaners.

The snow was falling once again, and the flakes melting on Mike's face were refreshing and invigorating. It had been so long . . . so long, in fact, that it was hard to remember.

It was below zero, and for the few pedestrians that were brave enough to face the elements, it was heads down and no good mornings, and Mike couldn't help thinking, "What has happened to the friendly New Yorker?" He shrugged it off and carried on.

"Ah, here we are! Brook's Diner." Mike applied the brakes, his boots sliding in the fresh layer of snow.

As he opened the diner door, he was met with a blast of warm air and the aroma of sizzling bacon and scrambled eggs, and he quickly filled the empty stool at the breakfast bar. It just felt *so* good to be out of the cold.

"What'll it be, buddy?" The blonde waitress with the breast implants, the "Colgate smile" and crisp white apron asked.

At least she is friendly, Mike thought. *She may be on the wrong side of forty, but with these blue eyes and that friendly smile, she still has something.*

"*Err,* what do you suggest . . . Eh?"

"Sandy."

"Eh, Sandy."

"That depends how hungry you are!"

"Do I look as if I'm overweight?" Mike laughed.

"Nah, you could do with a good feed. I suggest the house special: bacon, scrambled eggs, chorizo, and hash browns on toasted rye."

"You've sold me."

Sandy scribbled the order on her pad, then ripped out the page and placed it through the kitchen hatch.

"One special with hash on rye." She yelled before turning again to Mike and filling a healthy-sized mug with black coffee. "Help yourself to sugar and cream. Your breakfast will take fifteen."

"*Sandy* . . ."

"I'm coming, gimme a sec."

*   *   *

Mike was stuffed, but he wasn't going to surrender as he washed down the last morsel of toast.

"You must have been hungry, mister," Sandy commented as she cleared Mike's plate. "Can I get you a refill?" She gestured with her eyes at Mike's empty coffee mug.

"*Why not!*" Mike returned the warm smile.

It was time to move on as he glanced at his watch.

"What's the damage, Sandy?"

"Coffee and the house special . . . Twelve dollars straight."

Mike extracted a twenty from his billfold. "Keep the change, Sandy.

"Thanks, *eh?*"

"Mike."

"Come again." A she turned to serve another customer; Mike interjected.

"Sandy, before I leave, as I'm new to this part of the city, perhaps you can direct me to Oliver Street."

"Sure, that's not far from here. Turn left at the intersection, and it's about two blocks . . . About a ten-to-fifteen-minute walk if you don't have wheels. Of course, you could take the subway, but if you want to burn off that breakfast, if I were you I'd leg it. You can't miss it, it's before you come to Niemeyer Square."

"Thanks, Sandy, I'm sure you'll see a lot more of me." "*Sandy* . . ."

"*Keep your shirt on, I'm coming . . .*"

*   *   *

Sandy was spot on; it was about a fifteen-minute walk, but Mike was enjoying the ear-nipping fresh air, and more so, he had unloaded his suit on the way, at a Chinese laundry. It would be ready for collection in a couple days. "Ah, here we are . . . Number 14 . . . *Again!* That number's haunting me."

Mike stood back and looked up at the four-floor office block. It was the right place, all right. *I mean who could miss the large block capitals above the glass-panelled doors: "The City of New York. Department of Corrections."*

Summers had made good time, and the brisk walk had brought the color to his cheeks.

"Can I help you, sir?" the female behind the desk inquired, her smile reflecting her boredom. She was in her late forties and big size, her face heavily lined and eye bagged. For sure, she wouldn't launch a thousand ships. *Most probably an ex-con.* Mike smiled to himself.

"Mister, can I help you?" The smile was long gone, the voice agitated.

"I'm sorry . . . I have an appointment with Mr. Clark."

"Your name?"

"Summers . . . Mike Summers."

The "Russian cement truck driver" studied her computer screen for a few seconds.

"Yeah, I have you . . . Second floor, name's on the door. Elevator's on the left."

Mike shrugged; there was no point in niceties. Who knows, maybe *she* was still on parole!

Mike knocked on Clark's glass-panelled door, the name clearly signed. *"Come in . . ."*

"Mike!" Clark greeted him, as if surprised. "Take the load off." He pointed to the empty chair in front of his desk. *"Not bad . . .* Right on time." He tapped the face of his watch.

"After nine years in prison, old habits die hard."

"I guess so." Clark didn't pursue the comment, his expression reflecting other things on his mind.

"So how did your first day on the outside go?" "Different."

"I can understand. And the accommodation?"

"Different."

It was a lost cause, and Clark changed the subject.

"Mike, this is rather delicate." Clark produced an official-looking document. "I have here a restraining order signed by Judge Gilbert Cummings, effective immediately."

"*A restraining order!* What the hell is this all about?"

"Calm down, Mike, losing your cool will get you nowhere. Just count to five and let me explain."

"*I'm waiting . . .*"

"This order was requested by Senator Williams . . ."

"*Are you fucking serious?* There's no way I'm interested in contacting him or harassing his daughter. *Man,* I've spent nine years trying to forget her."

"Mike, let me finish . . . Laura Williams sadly passed away in the early hours of yesterday morning after a long battle with cancer."

"*Christ!*" Mike sat back in his chair rubbing his chin with his hand, shocked at the news.

"*Exactly!* Now do you get the picture?"

"*No, I don't!* But maybe I'm just fucking dumb. Listen, I feel really sad about Laura, but then who wouldn't? But I still don't get it."

"It's simple, Mike. Williams doesn't want you within breathing distance of his daughter's funeral."

Mike sighed, shaking his head, trying to make sense of this whole charade.

On parole and now a fucking restraining order . . .

"Don't worry, Bob, I'm not that stupid."

"*Good.* Now, more importantly I'm still in the process of trying to find you work. You are well qualified, but it won't be easy. As the result of the GFC, unemployment stands at 9.5 percent, so you can just imagine."

"Yeah, I get the picture. Is there any other good news, Bob?" "No, you can go . . . Next week, same day, same time . . ."

*   *   *

Mike was still shell-shocked at the news of Laura's death; even though it was the dreaded big C, in some ways, he still felt guilty.

He stopped at the newsstand and purchased the *Times* and there it was in bold print on the front page: "Laura Williams died peacefully in the early hours of yesterday morning in the John Hopkins Hospital after a long battle with cancer. The funeral will be held today at three o'clock at Green-Wood Cemetery, Brooklyn."

"*Three o'clock, Green-Wood Cemetery, Brooklyn . . . Hmmm . . .* I haven't a clue where that is, but then I can easily take a cab . . ."

CHAPTER 6

"I thought that kid would never sign that confession, but thanks to your female persuasion, Jan"—Bill smiled—"he finally cracked. He'll go down for culpable homicide. The gun accidently discharged in their drug-fuelled struggle, and unfortunately Jesse kicked the oxygen habit. Michael was pretty cut up about wasting his brother but when you play the drug card, the outcome is always the same. An overdose, a suicide, or a homicide."

"You can't save the world, Bill, but hadn't we better get going? It's almost two thirty, and the snow isn't letting up."

Bill lifted the phone. "Liam, send someone up to escort this kid back to the watch house."

"Sure, Bill . . ."

* * *

Bill took his heavy topcoat from the stand. "Would you mind driving, Jan? Somehow, I feel bushed. Maybe I'm getting too old for this shit." "Don't tell me your gonna desert me?"

"*Heh . . . Heh . . .* Don't put ideas into my head. Here, let me help you with that jacket."

"The keys." Jan held out her hand.

"Brings back memories, huh? When I was trying to find a parking spot at the court for the Summers trial."

"Don't get all nostalgic on me. That was a long time ago and you were still rebelling against the thought of a female detective as your new partner."

"Yeah, I remember, but a river has passed since then." Bill pressed the elevator button.

As the detectives walked to the doorway, a blast of icy air met them as the automatic doors opened.

"*Brrrrr . . .*" Bill shivered. "*Christ!* What a day for a funeral . . . Why is it that its either raining or snowing for the big sleep?"

"Bill, let's move it, or we'll both be looking for a place at Green-Wood . . ."

* * *

As Jan drove through the slushed roads and the passing snowploughs scattering sand and salt on the roadways, she had to ask the question.

"Why are you putting yourself through this, Bill?"

"Closure, I guess . . . For me, funerals . . . like public toilets and dinners with the in-laws are to be avoided at all costs. And for the life of me, I can't fathom why I would willingly subject myself to a lethally boring reminder of my own mortality. Dying is like sex. It's definitely better with other people around. Maybe I'm just lonely. Will I ever be the same again? *I doubt it.* But that's how it is, Jan."

"Boy, now you've got *me* thinking. Changing the subject. We had better get the umbrellas from the trunk because, *mister,* unbeknown to you, we have finally arrived . . ."

*   *   *

Jan cautiously steered the car into the long winding driveway, its rear end slithering for a moment from side to side before she dropped the shift stick into low. In the distance, the small gathering of mourners looked like miniature snowmen holding cocktail umbrellas as the priest braved the weather to pay the last rites of the deceased. Strangely, no sooner had Bill and Jan stepped from the car than the snow suddenly stopped. Jan turned to Bill. *"Don't say it!"*

*   *   *

"To my adorable wife and my lovely daughter . . . I say sleep well and good night . . ."

There was another burst of sobs from the surprisingly large number of mourners, when considering the weather and the funeral at such short notice.

"There are light refreshments at the Hyatt Hotel on Fifth Avenue. You are all welcome, and I sincerely thank you for your condolences."

Dave Williams's voice was on the point of breaking, and on that note, the mourners began to slowly disperse toward the funeral cars and their waiting cabs.

"That was a touching comment from the senator," Jan commented as she and Bill trudged through the snow-covered grass toward the car. *"What a tragedy,* and for men who lose their lifelong partner and their best friend, it's almost a death sentence."

Bill cringed at the thought; having been divorced now for over eight years, he knew only too well the curse of loneliness.

"Bill, are you with me?" Jan could see that distant look in his eyes.

"Yeah, let's get outta here . . . Listen, a better suggestion . . . How about you buying me drink?"

"You cheapskate! So much for the gentleman."

"Bill Hayden, is that you?"

A woman's voice came from the midst of a small group of people deep in conversation.

"*Terry Johnson!* I didn't recognize you."

"*Mrs. Terry Donnelly* . . . This is my husband, Nick."

"Well, I'll be darned, married and all. Nice to meet you, Nick." Bill offered his hand. "Detective Lieutenant Bill Hayden, NYPD."

"Yes, and we have two lovely boys, of course staying with their grandmother today. You know, Bill, this guy pestered me every time we met in the elevator and to get him to shut up, I had to finally agree to marry him."

Mike laughed at Terry's comment; she hadn't changed one bit. But the other gentleman accompanying Terry looked familiar. He was holding a young boy's hand whose eyes were swollen and red.

"Haven't we met before?" Bill inquired, "Your face looks familiar."

"Brent Kennedy, Laura's husband. Most likely you recognized me from the trial. This is our adopted son, Desmond . . . I have to thank Terry for introducing me to Laura, who was the love of my life." His voice was cracking. "Brent, what can I say? Please accept our deepest condolences. I wish you all the best, Terry. Perhaps we can meet again under happier circumstances. Bye, nice to meet you, Nick . . ."

"Let's go, Jan, this stuff is hard to take."

"*Bill . . . Bill Hayden.*"

It was a woman's voice, and Bill turned, stopping in his tracks.

"*June Summers!*"

"Bill, I know what you are thinking, but I felt the only decent thing to do was to pay our respects. We all sat through that horrible trial together, and the scars will remain with us for the rest of our lives . . . *Eh,* this is my husband, Phil . . . Phil Stevens." Bill shook his hand.

"And . . . ?"

"This is Steven, my son, and his sister, Sheryl."

"*Wow!* All grown up."

"Steven is a surgeon and Sheryl an anaesthesiologists. Both work at the Austin. As for me, I'm proud to say I returned to NYU to complete my law degree, and I am now a partner in my husband's law firm . . . Stevens & Stevens."

"*June,* that's really great news, and I take my hat off to you and the kids after what you have gone through."

"I heard on the grapevine, Bill, that you and Judy divorced."

"Yeah, nearly eight years now . . . Ran away with a car salesman, would you believe it? But don't cry me a river, I'm well and truly over it." Bill could sense June's stare at Jan.

"Oh, I forgot to introduce you to my partner, Detective Sergeant Janice Martin . . . *As for me?* I'm still a bachelor, and it's going to stay that way. June, it was nice to meet you and the family, but we have to push on."

"Just before you go, Bill, do you ever see Rose, Tony's wife?"

"No, we've completely lost touch. After Tony died, she sold up and moved to Chicago to be near her sister, and as far as I know, she never remarried."
"It was nice to meet you again, Bill . . . Jan . . ."

"How did she know Tony's wife?" It was begging the question.

"Jan, *would you believe it!* They were next-door neighbours and good friends . . . Barbecues and all that stuff, and you can just imagine the trauma when we issued a warrant for Mike's arrest."

"That's one helluva story and a twist you only see in movies. *Brrrrr* . . . Bill, let's get the hell out of this cold."

"Hang on, Jan. That guy peering from behind the tree . . . *Am I seeing things?*"

"What guy?" Jan scanned the horizon.

Bill looked again. "He's gone. I could have sworn that was Mike Summers . . ."

*   *   *

It had been a day for Mike, what with the shock of Laura's death and the restraining order, notwithstanding the cloak-and-dagger fiasco at the cemetery, and he breathed a sigh of relief as he sat in the back of the cab.

I'm sure Hayden recognized me, but then even if he did, he was not to know." Mike convinced his inner thoughts.

"Where to, buddy?"

"Drop me off on the corner of Jackson."

Mike sat back and relaxed. The ride would only take around fifteen minutes, but it would give him plenty of slack to reflect.

Laura and the kids looked good, and as for Phil Stevens; I always knew from our college days that June had a crush on him. Well, she got him in the end, but I really miss the kids. I'm sure I can get to Sheryl. She has a soft heart, but Steven?

He's a chip off the old block and doesn't treat fools lightly, especially old fools like his father. I guess I can't blame him, and the way Sheryl spoke on the phone, I can only assume he hates me. We were always close, which makes it all the sadder . . .

"Mister, is this good enough?"

"Yeah, just pull in here . . . What's the damage?" The cabbie checked the meter.

"That'll be fourteen fifty."

Mike unfolded a twenty and shook his head.

"*Fourteen fifty,* I don't believe it!"

"Are you serious, dude . . . Where have you been all this time?"

"Keep the change. Next time I'll take the subway."

"Suit yourself, buddy, but thanks anyway."

Mike followed the cab as it slowly slipped into the traffic, the exhaust excreting freezing carbon monoxide. He stood for a moment on the sidewalk, feeling dejected and lost; his newfound freedom was not all it was cracked up to be.

Hmmm, I wonder if that blonde at the diner is still on . . .

*   *   *

"It's all right, Mother, I gave Sheryl a ride here. Besides we both have to check in at the hospital when we leave."

"Can I expect you two over for dinner this weekend?" June asked as they were about to depart.

"Can I bring Nelson along?" Sheryl asked.

"Of course, honey."

Steven was moving his eyes from left to right to attract his sister's attention. "*Ah . . . hemmm, eh, Sheryl,* have you checked your roster?"

"*Eh?*" Sheryl screwed her eyebrows, confused at her brother's question; he knew she was only "on call" this weekend.

"How about you, Steven?" Phil asked. "It would be a nice change to have the family all together. What with your busy schedule at the hospital, your mother never sees you these days?"

"Phil, I'm sorry, I'll have to take a rain check. Something very important has come up."

"That's too bad. Anyhow, should you change your mind, you know how good your mother's cooking is . . . Listen, honey, we gotta to go." Phil turned to June. "Remember, we have that dinner appointment with Collins tonight at seven thirty."

"I almost forgot . . . Sorry, kids we must go." June gave Sheryl a kiss on the cheek. "Bye, honey."

"So, what was all that about?"

"Keep your voice down, Sheryl, I'll tell you all about it when we reach the car."

*   *   *

"*So?*" Sheryl closed the car door.

"*Christ, Sheryl*, gimme a sec to start the car and get some warmth into this heap."

Steven turned the key, and the antique Fairlane roared to life.

"When are you gonna change this piece of junk?" Sheryl asked as she sat on the musty seats.

"Cars are not my priority, I have more important things on my mind, which brings me back to your question."

Steven slowly drove down the snow-covered driveway making sure he kept his distance in the funeral cortege.

"I have rented a facility at Fort Knox Self-Storage on Bloomfield Street near Pier 50, not too far from my apartment, and only ten minutes from yours."

"*Fuck, Steven!* You *are* serious."

"*Sis,* this is not a game, *I'm deadly serious.* That's why I was trying to signal you to keep your weekend free to join me and come see the storage unit."

Sheryl was more than quiet; her brother was deadly serious, and could she cut the chase and run?

"I can't disappoint Mother now after confirming I would attend dinner."

"I guess not." Steven shrugged. "Not to worry, I'll go down myself and check it out. It should be large enough at fifteen by twenty by nine, *and get this* . . . It's climate controlled!"

Sheryl was still in deep thought.

"So what do you think? And oh, I forgot to tell you it's only two forty a month . . . *Sheryl . . . Are you listening?*"

"*Eh . . . Err . . . Yeah . . . Yeah*, that should be adequate for a mini operating room, but climate controlled, that's a big question. The way I see it, whatever, you'll need a portable AC."

"I've already got that on my list, which I need your opinion on, and I thought we could grab a coffee in the hospital cafeteria, and you can give it you're blessing."

Sheryl nodded in part disbelief, "brain fuzzed," semi dazed by it all.

*   *   *

"Are you sure you don't want anything, sis?"

"No, I'm good."

Within minutes, Steven was back with the warm brew.

"Thanks, Steven." She took a sip of the latte, holding the cup in both her hands, a source of comfort. Then she nervously looked around, as if she was being watched, before unfolding theA4 and studied it for a moment before slowly running her finger down the list.

"Heart monitor, blood oxygen calibrator, blood and antigen analysis detector, endotracheal tubes, oxygen sup . . . *Hmmmm*, you've done a pretty thorough job, Steven, but then you were always a stickler for detail."

"Is that a compliment or sarcasm?" Steven could feel the tension in Sheryl's voice.

She shrugged. "You're my brother, and I love you. *Steven* don't take this the wrong way. You are a highly respected transplant surgeon and passionate toward your cause, but are you sure you want to go down this path? *A modern-day Robin Hood. A 'Latter-day Saint'?* The only difference here is you will be stealing from the healthy to heal the chronically sick."

"Sis, I know it's against the law, but I'll make thoroughly sure that we will never be caught. Sure, the first one will be most traumatic, but after that when you see the joy and happiness it brings to the patient and their immediate family, there's nothing more precious than the gift of life."

"But, Steven, *we will be criminals!*"

"Maybe in the eyes of the law, sis, but not in the eyes of humanity. I'm asking you once again, sis."

"There's no need, Steven . . . I must be out of my mind. I'll catch up with you later, as I'm running slightly late for a briefing, and you know what Morgan is like . . . Ciao."

* * *

Steven was free for the evening, and it was food for thought. He would normally spend time in his consulting suite on his laptop scanning the Net for the latest medical research papers on organ transplants. Rejection drugs had come a long way, and it was no longer deemed essential that a donor requires matching bone marrow or an organ from an immediate family member.

"I might as well call it a day," Steven spoke aloud. "Computer hard disks can be traced as evidence and easily hacked, and I'm not as stupid as that. And of course, e-mails expose the sender through their return address. So first stop, cyber cafe . . . Now where is the nearest one on my way home?" He opened his smartphone to search the Web. "Let me see. Hmmm, Soho.

I might have known."

Steven scribbled the address on a notepad . . . 125 Watts Street, Soho.

That's not too far from here. Turn right on Grand Street, and it's all the way. It's almost as if I planned it!

*   *   *

Mike was a lonely guy, at least pen the pen, the company, although not the most desirable, was better than the "Piano Man." And as for females? It was a fantasy on the starvation list, and the more he thought about that sassy blonde from the diner, the more his loins ached. *I guess what they say about a leopard is true. Life isn't like the movies, it's like the public swimming pool with flab and hair where it shouldn't be . . .*

The five-minute walk to the diner was over, and as Mike opened the door, the blast of warm air was more than welcome, and he could finally feel his ears. At six in the evening, the patronage was relatively small, the peak periods being breakfast and lunch, McDonald's and Burger King giving the traditional American icon a hard time.

Mike took a stool at the bar, searching for the blonde bombshell.

"Coffee, mac?" the young kid asked in his heavy Brooklyn accent, the white apron and the milk bar cap something else. Most probably a student, Mike thought. *But where's Sandy?*

"Black, no sugar . . . Say, kid, would you happen to know if Sandy is on tonight?"

"No, she's not." He poured the steaming coffee from the percolator. "But if it's important that you see her, she's sitting at the window table right behind you. She often comes here for dinner."

"Special discount for staff huh?" Mike grinned. The joke didn't impress.

"Whatever turns you on, mac. Here's the menu, the specials are on the board." He pointed to the chalk-smeared blackboard on the wall behind him.

"You're pretty outspoken, kid. If I were you, I would watch my mouth?"

"Thanks for the advice, *grandpa, I'm busy.*"

Mike could feel his adrenaline rise, but this kid was for another a day, and besides, when on parole, altercations are not on the menu.

Mike picked up the coffee mug. *"Sandy, is that you?"*

It was the old surprise ploy, and Sandy fell for it, hook, line, and sinker.

"Mike . . . Mike, is it?"

"I didn't think you would remember. Would it be rude of me to ask if I can join you? That is, unless you are waiting for someone?" "*No* . . . Eh, no, be my guest. I was just about to order." Mike took the seat opposite.

"You look really well." Mike smiled, the old door opener.

"Have I changed that much from this morning?"

Mike laughed out loud. "It was just a figure of speech, but you *do* look a lot different from this side of the counter."

Sandy laughed. "I'll take your word for it. So, what brought you back, was it me or the food?"

"I would be telling you a lie if I said it was the food." Mike laughed again; he was back to his old charming self.

Sandy's expression reflected Mike's flattery. In her late forties, this kind of stuff was a thing of the past, and who could blame her?

"Well, as much as I enjoy your compliments, why don't we concentrate on the food for the moment? What I would recommend, that's if you are hungry, is the . . ."

*   *   *

"So, Sandy, tell me a bit about yourself."

"Like?"

"For a start, if you are married."

"The old marriage question, huh? And how many times have I been down that road?"

"This food is good, Sandy." Mike knew when to break it.

Sandy took a sip of her coffee to wash down the remnants of the barbecue pork ribs, then sat back to relax.

"I'm bushed . . . So?"

"So?" Mike returned the question.

"How about you, Mike, are *you* married?"

"*Was* . . . Now seems a long time ago."

"Kids?"

"Two . . . A boy and girl, all grown up in their midtwenties. In fact, I haven't seen them in over nine years."

"Must be tough?"

"Let's put it this way: self-inflicted wounds."

"It's like that, huh?"

"And you, Sandy? I'm still waiting."

"Divorced . . . Didn't work out. Caught him cheating not only once, and I had enough. Sometimes I think it was my fault. When Jason was born—he's now nineteen, a freshman at NYU—he was everything I ever wanted, and I guess I neglected Des, but the indications were always there, like the song 'Lipstick on My Collar.' But enough of that, I'm happy now. Had a few relationships. Didn't work out for one reason or another. He's married again, *so I've heard*, so there's no point in keeping in touch. The candle in the wind has gone out a long time ago."

Mike felt uncomfortable; it was Deja vu by any other name.

Sandy searched in her purse.

"Let me get this." Mike raised his hand to attract the "rebel without a cause."

"Are you sure?"

"Of course, it's the least I can do to repay you for suffering my boring company."

"Oh, I wouldn't say that." Sandy gave Mike her special smile.

"Kid, the check." Mike was becoming impatient.

"Forty-three fifty."

Mike passed him two twenties and a five spot.

"Keep the change." The kid didn't reply.

Sandy could see that Mike was annoyed at the young man's attitude.

"He's just had a 'Dear John,' and I don't blame her. He's a moody one."

"You seem to know this kid well."

"I should, *he's, my son.*"

There was a fatal pause as Mike was hit by a train at the level crossing.

"Now it all makes sense, and I can't blame him for looking out for his mother . . . Changing the subject, can I chance my luck and offer to buy you a drink?"

Sandy pondered for a moment; she would have to be naive if she didn't see it coming.

"Mike, I don't want you to think that . . ."

"*Sandy.*" Mike stopped her. "I will understand if you say no. After all, we only met this morning."

"Where to?" Sandy laughed.

"Kelly's Irish Pub . . ."

*　*　*

The cyber cafe was crowded with young teens playing games and the undesirables on the porn sites. Steven stood for a moment looking like a fish out of water, amazed at this hive of activity.

"Can I help you, dude?" a young man in his late twenties in T-shirt and jeans, who had forgotten what a razor looked like, queried.

Steven turned and looked toward the counter. This must be the owner or the manager of the franchise.

"I would appreciate your help . . . *First time.*"

"It's ten bucks an hour. Do you have a computer at home?" Steven nodded.

"Then it's just the same, only you pay for renting the machine and the Internet cost."

"I'll probably need at least an hour." Steven went for his billfold.

"There's no need to pay now, you're on the clock. Your name?"

"Derek Newman."

"Computer 15, on the far left. Here's your ID. You log in as normal. If you get stuck, just holler."

"Eh . . . Thanks. Fifteen, you say?"

Steven searched the line of computers occupied by the tranced cyberholics in the dimly lit cavern until at last he found the magic number. He took his seat and booted the large desktop, then entered his pin. It wasn't that scary after all.

"Let me see . . . Medical equipment suppliers . . . *Boy,* these are some hits!"

"*At last!* This one seems interesting . . . International Medical Equipment Supplies. 'We supply new and used medical equipment in all categories . . . delivery costs apply . . . contact imes@hotmail.com or NY 1-800 . . .' I'll contact them by phone tomorrow, it's too late now." Steven signed out and walked to the front counter.

"What's the damage?"

* * *

Jan parked the Chevy on the street in front of Bud's. At this time in the evening, there are no parking restrictions.

"Watch your feet, Bill, on the iced sidewalk." Jan struggled to keep her balance as she hurriedly opened the pub door.

"Looking after the old man, huh?" Bill laughed.

"*Get out of it!* Backup, remember?" Jan was also laughing.

The bar was "old time" and cosy.

"I like this place, Bill . . . *So this is your secret hideaway?*"

"Well, let me put it this way: it's walking distance from my apartment, and the last thing I want is to be charged with DUI. Wouldn't Mitchel be ecstatic, I've been a thorn in his side since he was appointed captain . . . Grab a stool."

"Bill, what'll it be?"

"Hi, Karl, the usual."

"And the lady?"

"Jan?"

"I'll just have a Bud, I'm driving . . . Bill, why don't I take the car tonight and pick you up first thing in the morning?"

"I'm not complaining." Bill grinned as the scotch and the beer chaser was placed in front of him.

"You look down, Bill," Jan commented; after nine years as his partner, there was nothing she didn't miss.

Bill took a deep breath then gave a big sigh. "I'm at that 'go nowhere' stage in my life, Jan, and I suppose the funeral just helped to scuttle the ship. How does that song go? 'Son, can you play me a memory . . . I'm not really sure how it goes. But it's sad and it's sweet and I knew it complete . . . When I wore a younger man's clothes . . .'"

*   *   *

"Hi, Sandy, who's your friend?" the cocky barman asked in his heavy Irish brogue.

"None of your business, Shawn." Sandy returned a cheeky smile. "Shall we sit at the bar, Mike?"

"Whatever, Sandy."

"I feel better with both my elbows on wood, don't you?" She smiled.

"Yeah, I'm at home." Mike grinned. This broad had something in her character that made him feel relaxed.

"Then grab a stool." Sandy laughed.

"Looks like you are a regular here." Mike was on the prowl.

"Not really. Shawn is a regular at the diner, although I do confess, I come here now and again to chill out, but only when I have one of my *off* days. Looking after a teenager in today's climate is no joke . . ." Sandy paused for a second, then a smile crossed her face. "*Besides,* I love the Irish pub ambience, and as you can see, the staff are warm and friendly . . . *And as for that log fire . . . !*"

"Say, didn't I see you in here last night?" the middle-aged barman with the seriously thinning hair and the deep laugh lines asked.

"Yeah . . . Mike's the name."

"Any friend of Sandy is a friend of mine. Shawn O'Malley." He warmly shook Mike's hand. *"Now,* what can I get you two?" "Sandy?" Mike asked.

"Eh . . . I'll have a Bailey's on the rocks, and you, Mike?"

"I'll try a drop of the famous Jameson with a beer chaser."

"Coming up." Shawn smiled, then went about his business.

*   *   *

Jan took a sip of the Bailey's. *"Hmmm* . . . Tastes good, but I shouldn't indulge. This stuff is deadly on the inches."

"You look in pretty good shape to me!" Mike was pouring it.

"Flattery will get you nowhere, *mister."* Sandy was in good form.

"Say, changing the subject, you never told me your name." Mike was on the inquisition trail.

"Sandra Watson . . . Never liked Sandra. Sandy suites me better. And Mike what . . . may I ask?"

"Mike Summers."

"Mike Summers?" Sandy repeated the name. "Where have I heard that name before?" She screwed up her face, thinking.

The game was up; Shawn was already staring at him in a peculiar way, having overheard the name. This guy was on to him, and it was time.

"You most likely heard it on CNN," Mike let it out, somewhat relieved. *"Not the . . . !"*

"The same . . . But Sandy just let me . . ."

"Now it all makes sense . . . The directions to Green-Wood Cemetery . . . Laura Williams the Senator's daughter . . . The parole appeal . . . The new face on the block . . . The halfway house on Jackson . . . *Christ, Mike, you gotta be kiddin'!"*

"Sandy . . . Sandy . . . Hold it . . ." Mike held her arm, fearing she would turn and leave. "Just gimme a chance, that's all I ask . . . I mean what did you expect? Like 'Hi, Sandy, I'm an ex-con, and I would love your company . . .' Sandy, I made a terrible mistake, and I wish I could live that day over again, *but I can't!* I've paid my price to society, all nine and a half years of it." Sandy peeled off Mike's hand and rose to her feet.

"Sandy, I'm asking you to please stay. Besides, you don't really know me. It's not as if I'm a murderer. We all make mistakes. It's just that there are some more serious than others." Mike gave a dejected sigh. "Sandy, if you must go, I can't stop you, *but I honestly wish you wouldn't."*

Mike's plea bargain made Sandy stop in her tracks, and she briefly turned and stared for a moment into his blue eyes. What did she see? A desperate lonely man just released from prison with probably not a friend left in the world, even his own family, in total rejection. Maybe she should give it a second thought; besides, although in his fifties, he is still handsome, and there was something about him that deserved a second chance.

"Against my better judgment, I'll stay. Maybe I'm just plain crazy, but I believe you."

"Thanks, Sandy. You won't regret it. Can I get you a refill?" "An Irish coffee . . . *Shawn . . .*"

* * *

"And that's the whole story, Sandy, I haven't kept anything from you." Sandy didn't comment. *It was one helluva confession!*

"It's time I hit the road, Mike, it's nearly eleven."

"*Hell,* I had better get going as well. I have to check in by eleven thirty . . ."

CHAPTER 7

Steven arose bright and early. He was a man on a mission, with a shopping list that would make a hospital proud. Cranmer had requested him to assist in a liver transplant, planned for two thirty today, and no doubt his sis would be the anaesthesiologists. To assist the director of surgery at the Austin was a feather in Steven's cap and a mark of his surgical skills, but he had other priorities before then; the first being to phone IEMS.

He finished the last of his breakfast coffee and chased the mouthful of toast.

If my memory serves me right, I'm sure there's a pay phone on the corner of Grand, not far from the hospital . . . Hmmm.

He glanced at his watch one more time.

"Nine fifteen. They must be open by now,' he continued talking to himself.

"Fifteen-minute parking, that should be enough." Steven spoke out loud as he filled the only empty slot. "Thank God the snow has stopped!" He spoke through his chattering teeth and slipped into the phone box. *"Am I in luck . . . The coin box is still intact!"*

Now where's that bloody number? Here we are. Steven was having a conversation with himself as he placed the stack of quarters and the "laundry list" on top of the armoured pay phone and began to dial.

"Good morning, IEMS, how can I help you? Helen speaking."

"Helen, I'm phoning on behalf of a client from Russia who wishes to purchase medical equipment for a private hospital in Moscow. My company is Global Exporters, located here in New York City. My name is Derek Newman, I'm the CEO. Helen, perhaps you can connect me to the right person to walk through my list."

"I'll put you through to Mr. Stevens, our sales manager . . ."

"Stevens here . . . Dale Stevens . . ."

* * *

"Mr. Newman, I'm checking our stock right now. Just bear with me for a few more seconds."

"Tell me when . . ."

* * *

"This must be your day, Mr. Newman, we have every item in stock."

"That *is* good news . . . And the total?"

"The system has automatically calculated your potential order and . . . the bottom line is . . . Let me see . . . sixteen thousand five hundred, to be exact." "Is that the best you can do, Dale?"

"I'm afraid so."

"And if I pay in cash?"

"*In cash!*"

"Yes, Dale, *you heard correctly*! Although I have a letter of credit and an export license, my client wants to wire me the funds once I confirm the damage. Dealing with private customers from the republic is different."

"*I see* . . . And in cash? *Hmmm* . . . The best I can do is a 5 percent discount."

"*Deal!* Now the next problem is I need to pick up the goods on Saturday morning, as I have packing and shipping deadlines to meet, not to mention the dreaded customs."

"Mr. Newman, we don't normally work on a Saturday, but . . ." There was a few seconds' pause. "Well . . . I suppose as you have a deadline to meet and you are paying cash . . . I can make an exception." There was another pause. "Let me see . . . If you could make it by, say, nine, I'll make sure the goods are ready for pickup. *Oh*, Mr. Newman, before you hang up, perhaps you can give me your business phone number and company address."

"Certainly . . . Global Exports. I'm the CEO, but unfortunately, as we have just moved into our new premises today, our phones and systems are still in the process of being commissioned. In fact, I'm phoning from a client's office."

"*Eh* . . ." Stevens paused again, another roadblock in the making. This whole deal was rather unusual, but cash is cash, and there's no better security.

"I guess that should be all right . . . I look forward to seeing you on Saturday morning. Thanks again, Mr. Newman." "The pleasure is mine . . ."

Stevens hung up and sat for a moment, rubbing his chin. "*Hmmm* . . ."
The phone rang. "Yes, Helen?"

*   *   *

He still had plenty of time on his hands at only ten thirty and another four hours before the afternoon surgery. The use of a public phone booth was virtually untraceable, and he might as well make the best of it.

Steven had done his research well and listed a series of phone numbers he had put together yesterday evening. He slipped the quarters into the box and began to dial.

"Good morning, thank you for phoning Hertz. Please listen to the phone menu and press the appropriate number, or just simply wait and a customer service officer will attend to you as soon as possible. Be aware that your call may be used for training purposes . . . Press 1 for . . ."

*   *   *

"Hertz Commercial Vehicle Hire, how can I be of assistance? My name is Vivian."

"Vivian, I wish to hire the largest commercial van or truck that you have that allows me to drive on a standard driving license."

"That would be our Mercedes Sprinter van with a V6 diesel engine and five-ton payload. All our commercial vehicles are white in colour. Our special for this week only is rent for seven and get two free. The daily rental is eightyfive straight."

"That's neat. Can I pick up the van on Saturday morning? I'm sorry I can't be more specific about the time, as I'm so busy at the moment."

"I fully understand, sir, just provide me with me your name, then I can tie up all your details when you arrive to collect the vehicle."

"My name is Derek Newman."

"Derek . . . *Eh?*"

"*Newman* . . . Thank you, Vivian, for your excellent service."

Steven placed the receiver back in the yolk, a satisfied expression on his face.

"Now next on the list . . . Let me see . . . The medical equipment . . . The van . . ." He drew a line through the first two. "The coveralls and the magnetic sign . . ."

*   *   *

Mike moved aside the rag curtain and peered through the dirt-clouded window. The street was surprisingly busy at this time in the morning even though the temperature was still below zero.

I guess no matter where in the world, Mike thought, *everyone is chasing the almighty dollar, and Brooklyn is no different.*

Once again, he had escaped the onslaught in the communal bathroom, but for how long? And his thoughts now turned to his rumbling stomach and the mirage smell of bacon and eggs, his taste buds already salivating at the mere thought.

Then there was Sandy! How would she react this morning after sleeping on his "true confession"? There was only one way to find out, and that was to follow his stomach! He dropped the curtain and donned his heavy windbreaker, the brisk walk to the diner and a paper on the way was just what the doctor ordered, and suddenly freedom wasn't so bad after all . . .

*   *   *

The diner was really busy. There were cops, construction workers, and even the "suits," engrossed in the morning editions or dog-eared pulp fiction, between mouthfuls of Brook's cholesterol specials. As for finding a vacant stool . . . It was worse than the reality show *Survivor*, but Sandy came to the rescue of the "antique Casanova," just in time.

"Over here, Mike." She raised her arm high for him to spot.

"Oh, Mike, is it? Must be someone special, Sandy, *huh?*"

"Get over yourself, Joe, and enjoy your breakfast."

New York's finest just laughed. This was Sandy at her best.

"Remember, I'm not spoken for, so just gimme that special smile, and I'm all yours."

"How can you suffer that chauvinist, Jim, in that black and white every day?"

801

The sergeant almost choked on his burger at Sandy's remark. "You got *that* right, Sandy, but I guess someone has to do it." "Thanks." Mike grabbed the empty stool.

"Coffee?" Sandy winked.

"Black, thanks."

"I'll be back in a sec to take your order . . . Yeah, yeah, I'm coming . . . *Keep your shirt on!*"

*   *   *

The special was going down a treat, as for Sandy? She was over the top with orders and had no time to converse. But the body language and telepathy was a turn on, and Mike the ladies' man was back in business.

*   *   *

"So how was the food?" Sandy asked, an opener.

The dust had settled as the diners gradually dispersed to their cars or the subway, and she finally had time to breathe.

"I really enjoyed it. Not the most healthy, but a big change. You look good."

"You should see me first thing in the morning with no makeup!" "I would like that." Mike caught her eye.

"*Eh* . . ." It was getting hot and heavy, and Sandy felt a bit uncomfortable.

"Just gimme a sec, Mike, while I attend to this customer." Her face slightly bloomed.

"At last." Sandy was back pretending to wipe the bar top.

"Sandy, I wondered if you are free tonight?"

She smiled. "Is that an invitation?"

"You know what I mean? I would like to make up for last night's *Titanic*." Mike sort of raised his eyebrows.

"Pub grub?"

"Whatever, Sandy." "I have a better suggestion" "Like?" Mike was all ears.

"*Like,* some home cooking at my place! That's if you want to take a chance and your stomach is cast iron?"

"*Heh . . . Heh . . . Heh,*" Mike laughed. "It will be my pleasure . . . And the time and of course, your address?"

"I'll be free at six thirty . . . So, say, eight?"

"No sweat."

"I don't live far from here, only about fifteen minutes. It's Brook's Apartments on Jason . . . Apartment 2B."

802

"Brook's?"

"Yeah, my boss, he owns the place . . . I only rent."

"I'll be there on one condition . . . I fetch the wine." "White . . . A Pinot grigio, preferably Italian . . ."

*   *   *

"Yes, say, two yards by eighteen inches and the lettering to be bold red on a white background . . . Global Exports with the number . . . 1-800-5368 . . ."

"Thanks, Mr. Newman, these magnetic strips will be ready for pickup on Saturday."

Steven hung up and put a line through yet another item on his list.

"Now let me see . . . Custom Work Wear . . . Seven six . . ."

"Yes, two coveralls, one small and one medium size in a red-orange colour, and can I pick them up on Saturday? You say you can print my logo on the back when I come to collect, and more importantly, of course you have stock . . . Thanks again, Eran . . . Saturday around say . . . ten . . ."

*   *   *

Steven felt good; everything was going to plan and strangely without a hitch. If he can finish early today after the liver transplant, his first stop will be Fort Knox Self-Storage.

He gunned the engine of the vintage Fairlane and slipped into the traffic; he still had plenty of time before the surgery, and hopefully he could share a coffee with his sister to discuss the progress on operation "Goldfish Bowl."

*   *   *

"Mrs. Jenson, I can't imagine the trauma and grief you and your family are experiencing. To keep your husband on life support to preserve his organs, while fully understanding that he will never recover after having been diagnosed as brain dead, is not only courageous but compassionate for those unfortunate people waiting in desperation for an organ transplant. Your husband's dying wish to become an organ donor is exceptional and courageous, when considering the life-saving surgery for nine patients on the critical register for kidneys, liver, pancreas, heart, lungs, and corneas . . . You should be very proud."

Nancy Jenson burst into tears as her husband Dave was finally wheeled into the operating room for his last voyage, and she kissed him gently on the forehead.

"Goodbye, my love, after forty years of marriage, I still love you as if it were the first day we met."

Her daughter and son enveloped their arms around their mother to give her support.

"Mother, it's over now, and may Dad finally rest in peace."

Nancy's sobs could be heard as she followed her husband all the way down the corridor to the operating room and Cranmer, the director of surgery, even he had a tear in his eye.

The transplant team had kicked into high gear after receiving the call that a male person had had a serious brain haemorrhage causing a stroke and was unlikely to recover on life support. Blood samples and recipient matching required urgent interrogation of the transplant critical list in order to get the recipients prepared for immediate surgery, as each organ had a life span of only fourteen hours in ice preservation and suspended animation . . .

*   *   *

"Nice job. The liver is turning a bright pink, and blood is starting to flow through the hepatic artery and portal vein. Give it a few more minutes, Steven, then close. I'll leave you to it, I'm bushed."

Cranmer stripped off his rubber gloves as he left the operating room on his way to inform the patient's relatives the good news.

"*That's it, sis!* Nurse let's get this patient to intensive care. As usual, nice job, sis. Once I shower and freshen up, I'll call you, and when you're free, I'll meet you in the cafeteria."

"I have a few post surgeries to check, but I should be okay. How is it going?"

"I'll tell you about it later . . . Ciao."

*   *   *

"Number 14 in front of the car park . . . Eight . . . Twelve . . . Ah, here we are, and it couldn't be better placed!"

Steven parked the car only yards in front of the steel-louvered security door. He left the car, then stood for a few moments, scanning the car park and surroundings to make sure the coast was clear. The icy wind from the Hudson suddenly flared, and a dusting of snowflakes brushed against Steven's cheeks. It was going to be a cold one, and he made haste to the storage unit.

"If only sis were here." Steven commented as his breath froze in the icy wind.

He turned the key, then grunted as he heaved the heavy steel roller door.

"*Bloody hell!* Now I know why it's called Fort Knox!" Steven quickly stepped inside from the cold and switched on the strip lighting, then pulled the roller door down behind him.

"*Nice . . . And clean too!* And the size is perfect for what I need. *And climate control!* It doesn't get any better."

As Steven was admiring his newfound operating room, he suddenly turned his attention to the temperature control dial and set it to sixty-five to test it, and within minutes, the warm air was streaming through the split system. It was too good to be true, and Steven stood for a moment, admiring his good fortune.

"Sink, reasonable size with water supply and floor drainage. . . *Hmmm* . . . Two sets of double power points and plenty of lighting . . . This is a real find. I don't know why I didn't think of this sooner . . . *Won't sis be surprised when she sees this place. It's better than M*A*S*H!*"

*   *   *

Mike smiled to himself as he walked back to the halfway house. He was feeling good after that oversize breakfast, but more to the point, he had cracked it with the adorable Sandy, his mind now conjuring all sorts of sexual fantasies. It had been a long time . . . *Too long!*

He stopped on the way at the Chinese laundry to pick up his suit, shirt, and tie; he had to get back in the job market, and first impressions always tick the boxes.

"Am I too early?" Mike passed the Chinaman the ticket.

He studied the ticket for a moment, then smiled, flashing his "fried rice teeth" and with that bowling ball head, all that was missing was the hat and pigtail!

"No, all leady." He walked to the rack of plastic-bagged garments, efficiently sliding each one aside on their hangers as he checked tabs.

"Here we are." He placed Mike's suit on the counter. "Nice, good as new. That will be . . ."

*   *   *

Within minutes, Mike was opening the front door of his new abode. What he would do for the rest of the day was anyone's guess. Maybe he would just hit the cot and have forty winks.

As usual Barrett was at his desk, checking the traffic, a cigarette dangling from his tobacco-stained lips, the ash ready to crash.

"*Summers.*" Barrett barked, the original "Johnny Rude."

Mike turned and eyeballed him. He didn't like Barrett's attitude; in the pen, no one stood for that shit. You wanna play the hard card, you had better be bulletproof, or you end up in the prison hospital or, worse still, the funeral parlour.

"*You talking to me?*" Mike returned the compliment.

"I don't see anyone else." Barrett sarcastically looked from side to side. "So, it must be you, dude . . . Clark wants you to phone him."

"What's it about?" Mike was puzzled; he had just seen Clark yesterday morning.

"*How the fuck should I know!* What, am I your mother or something? You phone him, you don't phone him, *personally, I don't give a crap!* I'm only the messenger. The pay phone's in the hallway."

Barrett flicked the ash from his sodden cancer stick and returned his nose to the pony page and the LA races.

*   *   *

Mike slipped the quarters into the coin box while holding Clark's card to check the phone number.

"Clark here, Department of Correction Services."

"Bob . . . Mike Summers."

"*Good*, I was waiting for your call . . . Listen, I want you to drop by my office first thing in the morning, I have something on the job front that may be of interest."

"I hope it's not stacking shelves at Westfield's?"

"Just be here before nine." Clark abruptly hung up. When it came to excons, you take no quarter.

"*Hmmm . . .* What was that all about? Mike shrugged and hung up. He had more important things on his mind. *Like hopefully getting laid.*

Mike splashed on the cheap cologne and brushed back his full head of greying hair; the stretch in the pen had taken its toll. As he was finally about to leave, he suddenly turned for one last time to study himself in the cracked mirror, its silver backing peeling and blotched, and Mike moved his head to and fro to get a clearer painting. Naivety about his age and vanity about his looks was in his genes, and he was back to his old self and the thrill of the chase . . .

*   *   *

He still had thirty minutes slack before his "dinner date" with Sandy, but then he had to find her apartment and of course a liquor store for the all-important Pinot grigio.

As Mike stomped down the dimly lit passageway, his heavy winter boots made their mark, and Barrett turned his attention from the sports channel to make sure parolees signed the ledger, entering their names and time of departure.

"*Hold it, Summers,* don't be a hard ass. I've shit people like you. You never signed the book yesterday . . . You break the rules once more, and you're history. *Cappice?*"

Mike ignored him and turned the book, then signed.

"Remember, eleven thirty lights out."

"*Yes, mother.*"

"*Why you fucking . . .*"

Mike slammed the door hard, venting his contempt as he hit the sidewalk, the icy wind biting into his cheeks, and he stopped for a moment to pull up his collar and search for the Camel pack. He tapped a stick from the yellow and gold with its famous logo, the cigarette paper sticking to his lips.

It was a cold one, all right, the red glow warming his hands as he killed the blue flame from his twenty-cent lighter. He took a deep drag, gave a slight cough, and was on his way.

Why I ever started this filthy habit is fucking beyond me, he was thinking to himself. *I never smoked before, but in the "grey-barred hotel," to kill the time, it was either tobacco or uppers and downers, and drugs is not my scene. But I have to kick this somehow. Besides, where can you smoke these days? It's banned in almost every fucking place except the street . . . Fucking "Nanny State"!*

*   *   *

The liquor store appeared from nowhere.

Strange, Mike thought. *I haven't noticed it before, but maybe just as well, it's too tempting, and booze is sacrilege when you're on parole.*

Liquor stores for some reason are all owned by Koreans, and this one was true to form.

"Yes?" the middle-aged Korean man asked, studying Mike's face.

In this neighbourhood, it was no secret about the halfway house, and "made in Korea" kept one hand below the counter while the woman behind him, whom one can only assume was his wife, anxiously watched as backup.

"Would you happen by chance to stock Italian wine?" Mike asked.

The guy quickly relaxed and sort of signalled to the woman. The clientele that normally frequent the store wouldn't have a clue where even Italy is!

"We do, sir, but not a large range. Do you have the name?"

"Pinot grigio, does that ring a bell?"

"You are in luck, sir, can I select for you?"

"You are my saviour." Mike was relieved. He had been around, but Italian vino was not his forte.

"Ae-youne, fetch the gentleman one bottle of Dolcetto d'Alba Pinot grigio. This is excellent wine from the south of Italy,"

"Eh, make that two."

"Certainly . . . Ae-youne, give the gentleman a nice bag."

Mike smiled. "Thanks again and . . . ?"

"Sixty-two dollars including tax."

"*Wow!* It would be cheaper flying to Italy."

"I'm sorry, sir, but fully imported wines attract substantial duty to protect our American wineries."

"I'll take your word for it." Mike shook his head, giving a half-hearted smile as he placed two fifties on the counter.

What will tonight bring? *At least the wine will be good!*

* * *

Mike pressed the bell.

Sandy had just finished cooking the fettuccine alfredo, and it was perfect timing, as she spooned the last of the grated parmesan cheese into her special sauce and hastily took a taste.

"*Hmmm* . . . Perfect, even though I say it myself. *Coming . . .*"

She peeped through the glass peephole just to make sure. These days, you never can tell. It was Mike all right, his cheeks a fresh pink, pronounced against his white complexion, and she quickly undid the safety chain and the Yale.

"I must say, Mike, you're punctual."

Mike gave her a kiss on the cheek, then handed her the carrier bag containing its precious cargo.

"Buonasera, signora, ho due bottliglie di vino bianco grazie."

"Italian with it . . . *Not bad !*"

"Well, aren't you going to invite this poor traveller in from out of the cold?"

Sandy burst into laughter. "What am I thinking . . . *Come in . . . Come in . . .* Here, let me take your jacket. Grab a seat on the sofa, Mike, and make yourself at home or, better, still do me a favor and put the wine in the freezer just to quickly chill it. Dinner will be served in a couple of minutes . . ."

* * *

"Sandy, I tell you, you should open your own restaurant. I can't remember the last time I had such delicious pasta."

"They say the way to man's heart is through his stomach . . . Can I entice you to another helping?"

"Sandy, as much as I would like, I'm stacked. But I'll have another glass of that wine."

"Sorry, no dessert. I was held back at the diner.

"I'll forgive you," Mike teased.

"Why don't you take your wine and grab a seat on the sofa while I stack the dishes in the washer?"

"Are you sure I can't help?"

"Hey, this is woman's work, do as you are told!"

"Ciao, Bella." Mike laughed as he made a beeline for that comfy-looking sofa. The comforts of home only a memory, but all in all, this had the makings of a pleasant evening . . .

*   *   *

Mike couldn't help admire Sandy in her grey woollen tracksuit, although loose and comfortable, it touched all the right spots, and as for that shoulder-length blonde hair? So maybe it was slightly bottled, who cares? For a woman on the late side of forty, she was still a catch, and the more Mike studied that body, the more the signals went to below his belt. Her blue eyes, the way she smiled, the walk, and the warmness of her personality all added to the mystique of this adorable creature and the ultimate prize . . . fulfilling his sexual fantasy.

*   *   *

"*At last!*" Sandy crashed on the sofa next to him. "Comfortable, huh? *Oops,* I nearly spilt my wine." She swung both feet onto the coffee table.

"Yeah, I must admit, all the comforts of home. It certainly shades Kelly's Bar. Cheers." Mike touched Sandy's glass and nudged a bit closer.

"Mike, for some reason, I really enjoy your company."

"I hope it's a good reason." Mike grinned as he stared straight into Sandy's eyes. "*God, Sandy,* that perfume you're wearing is tantalizing . . . Soft, fresh, and feminine."

"That's a new line, I'm impressed." She smiled placing her feet on the floor and setting her wineglass on the coffee table. It was as if she was preparing for "close encounters."

Mike moved even closer, still staring into her eyes, their lips now only a few inches apart, and he could sense her warm breath, and their lips gently touched. It was a kiss searching for a reaction, and Sandy didn't disappoint him, placing both her hands behind his neck and savagely bruising his lips. The moisture from her warm her tongue almost drove him crazy, and the collateral damage was predictable as he slipped his hand below her sweatshirt and cupped her soft breast in his hand, manipulating the nipple between his fingers, and Sandy groaned in ecstasy. Then out of the blue, she suddenly pushed Mike away.

"*No, Mike, no!* I don't know what came over me . . . What must you think of me?"

"I think you're adorable." With no bookmark, Mike was desperate not to lose the place.

"Mike, as much as I like you, it's too early for the cot. *I've only just met you.*

She could see the disappointment on Mike's face, but she wasn't a one-night stand.

"Sandy, I apologize. It's just that . . ."

Suddenly there was the sound of a key turning in the lock.

"*Shit!* Excuse my French. That must be Jason. I didn't expect him home until at least ten thirty! He must have finished basketball coaching early . . . *Ah . . . Hmmm . . .*" She embarrassedly straightened her sweatshirt, guilt on her face.

"Jason, you're home early tonight!"

Jason's back was to them as he hung his green and white-sleeved NYU jacket on the stand.

"Yeah, I . . ." He froze at seeing Mike. "*I didn't know you were having company tonight!*" The hostility in his voice portraying another "James Dean."

"*Jason* . . . Don't be so rude!"

"It's all right, Sandy, it's a small thing. Let me introduce myself . . . I'm Mike Summers, a friend of your mother."

Jason ignored Mike as if he was the Invisible Man.

"Can I get you some supper, son? There's some pasta in the oven."

"I'm not hungry. I had a dog on the way home." He turned and glared at Mike. "I'm going to my room, Mother. I have an assignment for tomorrow." Jason turned and left, the "quiet man."

Sandy gave a big sigh. "I'm sorry, Mike, he was close to his father, and he still has this crazy idea that we might get back together again."

"I understand, Sandy." Mike grasped her hand to comfort her. "But I do think it's about time I made tracks." He rose to leave.

"I'm so sorry, Mike."

"Don't be. I've had a lovely dinner and great company, but all good things unfortunately must come to an end."

Sandy stood on her toes and gave Mike a light kiss on the lips.

"That's for understanding. Come, I'll see you to the door. Will I see you for breakfast tomorrow?" She held his hand as he slipped into his jacket.

"Wild horses couldn't stop me . . ."

CHAPTER 8

Steven dialled.

Sheryl gave a sort of a groan as the perpetual ring of the phone disturbed her beauty sleep. She unravelled Nelson's hand from around her naked waist and stretched to silence the ring.

"This can only be the hospital or that stupid brother of mine . . . Yes . . . Sheryl here."

"Wake up, you lazy bum, it's after eight."

"Who is it, Sheryl?" Steven could hear the sleepy voice in the background.

"Oops . . . A bad time, huh?" Steven laughed.

"Get to the point, *you moron.*"

"I thought we agreed to meet this morning around nine."

"*So* . . . It has only just turned eight. Don't get your knickers in a twist."

"That's my sister, always the lady. Do you want me to pick you up or are you coming to my place?"

"Your place. I need my car."

"Ciao and give Nelson my regards." Steven couldn't resist the shot.

"I'll say it again . . . *Moron* . . ."

Steven smiled as he hung up. "*That's my sis . . .*"

*   *   *

The doorbell rang.

"That must be her now."

Steven folded the *Times* and finished the last of his coffee as he rose to answer the door.

"Good morning, my lovely." Steven gave his sister a peck on the cheek. Come in, you look frozen . . . Take your coat off and grab a seat at the bar while I pour you a warm coffee."

"At least *your* apartment is warm!" Sheryl commented as she removed her heavy jacket. "Can you believe I've been waiting for my heating system to be repaired for the last two days . . . *Bloody apartment management!*"

"Look on the positive side, sis . . . How does it go? *You've got your love to keep you warm*," Steven sang the chorus.

"*Joker* . . . At least your coffee's good . . . So, what's the deal?"

"The plan is, firstly we have to . . ."

Steven emerged from the bedroom dressed to leave, wearing a dark-blue baseball cap, heavy windbreaker, stone-washed Levi's, and tan work boots.

"Do I look the part, sis?"

"*Jesus Christ, Steven!* What's with the moustache?"

He laid the driving license on the breakfast bar for Sheryl to see.

"*Steven, you never . . . ?* Derek Newman!"

Steven shrugged. "So, the guy passed away with kidney failure. It's not as if I'm stealing his identity, and I'm sure he wouldn't complain as it's for a good cause. He's around my height, and there is a distinct facial likeness, of course with the exception of the moustache . . . So, I wear the dark shades."

"*You should fucking audition for* Criminal Minds." "*Ha-ha,*" Steven laughed at his sister's criticism.

"And how about me?" Sheryl asked, looking at her brother's getup.

"Don't worry. I've ordered two coveralls from a work wear outlet. We'll drive there first to pick them up. They are an important part of our deception."

Sheryl shook her head. "Boy, you're something else!" "Here, take this baseball cap with you . . ."

* * *

"Sheryl, no cars today. I'm afraid it's cabs all the way. Cars have license plates, makes, and colours . . . It's too risky."

"As long as you're paying, boss," she answered sarcastically as she slipped into her jacket. "Where to first?"

"Custom Work Wear . . ."

* * *

"You look cute in that orange coverall." Steven laughed as Sheryl slipped into her baggy work suit, the company's named printed in three-inch black lettering on the back: Global Exports.

"I gotta hand it to you, Steven, you've left no stone unturned . . . And as for the company name, how did you dream that one up?"

"You'll find out as the morning progresses."

"So surprise me, what's next?"

The cab driver was running the meter with a smile on his face; this was his day.

"Where to now, boss?" He looked into the rear mirror.

"Signs Incorporated. 277 East Brooklyn Industrial Park."

"You got it." The driver smiled and hit the stock switch, signaling a left turn.

"Now you've really got me guessing," Sheryl commented staring at her brother.

"Just bear with me, sis, there's more to come."

"I'm sure, *Mission Impossible*." Sheryl was being both cheeky and humorous.

* * *

"Mr. Newman, of course. Your signs are ready, sir. It was touch and go, but we pulled out all stops. I'll go fetch them from the factory . . ."

"Nice job, Mr. Ellis."

Steven admired the large magnetic sign rolled out on the table. "The lettering is just right, and that will be?"

* * *

"Can you open the trunk, driver?"

"Sure thing, boss."

Steven placed the two rolls of magnetic plastic into the trunk while his sister watched on.

"We're not finished yet, sis, two more pickups."

"Can't wait . . ."

"Where to now, boss?"

"Hertz Car Rental, 355 Canal Street."

"Boy, we're moving around, but I'm not complaining." The cab driver was in his element, the meter encroaching the magic ton.

* * *

"Can I speak to Vivian, please?"

"I'm Vivian. Good morning and welcome to Hertz," the middle-aged brunette with the "I'm your mother" look greeted Steven. "Let me think, *of course,* you must be Mr. Newman. I recognize the voice . . . Global Exports . . . Nice outfits." She smiled.

"You have a good memory, Vivian," Steven replied with a smile.

"In this job, you need it. "Do you have your driver's license, Mr. Newman?" Steven turned to Sheryl; this was the litmus test.

Vivian glanced at the plastic, then looked Steven in the face.

"Shall I remove the shades?"

Vivian gave her "Hertz" smile. "No, that won't be necessary, Mr. Newman. Everything is in order. Now that was a Mercedes Sprinter van, V6 diesel engine, five-ton tare . . . Rental for seven days. That will be four twenty-five after discount. Do you wish full insurance or a five-hundred-dollar excess?"

"The cheaper is fine."

"And for one driver? Then that will be five fifty, including tax. How do you wish to pay, sir?"

"Cash." Steven peeled the greenbacks from his billfold.

"Give me a sec, Mr. Newman, and I'll print your receipt." She lifted the phone. "Jake, bring that Mercedes Sprinter to the front. The customer is here. Yes, right away."

"Thanks, Vivian."

"Here is all the paperwork and the keys. Return the van on time with a full tank. Have a nice weekend, Mr. Newman."

"Thanks again, Vivian."

"My pleasure."

The large Mercedes van appeared parked behind the waiting cab.

"I'll go pay the driver, sis. Here's the keys open the rear door."

"What's the damage, driver? I'm sorry, the city tour is over." "Me too." He read the meter. "That'll be one sixty-five, mister." Steven gave him an extra ten spot.

"Thanks, brother, anytime. Here's my card."

"Just a sec, the trunk."

"*Wow,* I nearly forgot . . ."

*   *   *

"I'm surprised we managed to load all that equipment into this truck, *and you paid with cash!*"

"Sheryl, credit cards can be traced, and of course, I gave him a phony company address, which reminds me."

Steven signalled and drove up a side alley.

"I have to remove the magnet sign before we offload at Fort Knox Self Storage. This will only take a few minutes, and while we are at it, let's get out of these coveralls."

Steven reversed the truck, the job complete.

"Are we driving there now?" Sheryl asked as they slipped into the mainstream traffic.

"No, I'll drop you off at my apartment and park the van. Tomorrow morning, say, around six, would be a good time to unload, but, sis, I need your help."

"*You gotta be kidding me! Come on, Steven*, I have a late procedure today, and I'm fucking bushed now, and what do I tell Nelson?"

"Make some excuse, sis, like an emergency 'call' out at the hospital."

Sheryl shook her head. "*What I do for you* . . . Give me a call to make it look the real deal, I don't want Nelson to think I'm two-timing."

"Don't worry, sis, *I will* . . ."

*   *   *

"You're late today, what kept you?" Sandy asked as she poured Mike's coffee.

"Parole officer, I forgot to mention it last night."

"*On a Saturday?*"

Mike shook his head. "This guy works 24/7. I don't know what his love life's like."

"Maybe he's in the closet, huh?" Sandy laughed, cracking a smile on Mike's face.

"So, aren't you going to tell me?"

"*Sandy, how about some service here?*"

"Keep your shirt on, I'm coming . . . Gimme a sec, Mike. Why don't I take your order first?"

"The usual, Sandy . . ."

*   *   *

"*A stacker in Westfield's distribution warehouse!*" Sandy had to laugh. "So what did you tell him?"

"*To go and take a hike.*"

"I thought as much."

"The only good thing that dropped from the meeting was his secretary typed my resume, which she will e-mail to the large executive recruitment firms, and who knows?" Mike shrugged.

"Sounds promising."

"Listen, Sandy, I gotta go. I need to go shopping. My wardrobe is limited to what I stand in, but I wish you could come with me. I would love a woman's opinion . . . We could make an afternoon of it and have a cosy lunch." "Sorry, Mike, not today. Saturday is our busy time, but I could meet you for a drink after work, unless you have other plans?" Sandy gave Mike a cheeky smile.

"I should be so lucky. No such chance. I'm afraid you're stuck with me, honey." Mike laughed.

"I've had worse," Sandy joked. "*Listen,* I'll be finished at six thirty, and I need to go home, shower, and change . . . Say, around seven thirty then?" "I'll keep the stool warm." Mike rose to leave.

"Mike, before you go, I just want to say I'm sorry about last night. Jason can be difficult, but there's no excuse for rudeness."

"It's only natural. Give me time, I'll win him round."

"In for the long haul, huh?" Sandy replied, a smile on her face.

"Something like that." Mike gave a wink, then turned to leave. "Ciao, Bella . . . Seven thirty at Kelly's . . ."

*   *   *

It was after six when Steven parked the Mercedes Sprinter about a hundred yards from the corner of Jackson. There was no parking restrictions, and he had a clear view of the halfway house. His sister had given him the address and phone number. The only problem was, was his father at his new home or hitting the downtown bars? Sure, he could use his cell phone to check the front desk, but calls can be traced. *No,* it was too dangerous! He would just have to bide his time and hold the surveillance until something breaks.

The windshield was freezing over, and Steven was forced to start the motor to get some heat into the cabin and return his circulation as the temperature had dropped to well below zero.

"*Come on* . . . *Come on,* where the hell are you?" Steven cursed under his breath. "If he doesn't appear soon, I'm gonna give up the ghost until tomorrow. What time is it anyway?" He checked the dash clock . . . Seven o'clock . . . *Boy,* does time fly!" He cut the motor; the cabin was now up to temperature. Besides, he didn't want to draw attention to the stationary white van with its motor running. He turned to look through the side window one more time before calling time out, and low and behold, the "Scarlet Pimpernel" appeared from nowhere.

"*I'll be darned!*" Steven yelled in his pent-up frustration.

It was his father, all right, dressed for the weather in what looked like a navy surplus dark-blue heavy topcoat, the collar pulled up round his neck. He was briskly stepping it out as he glanced at his watch; for sure he was meeting someone. Suddenly he stopped and pulled a pack from his inside pocket, flicked a stick to his mouth, then cupped both hands around the lighter flame, a bright red glow appearing from the cigarette as he indulged for a second before hitting the sidewalk once more.

I never knew he smoked! He must have picked up the habit in prison . . . Not the best habit for an organ donor. Smoking can damage kidneys and other vital organs, but for the patient on death row? He sighed. *It's the "Last Chance Saloon."*

Steven hung around, waiting for another five minutes before turning the key. The traffic was light, so he could easily keep his father in his sights, and he didn't have to wait long before Mike disappeared into Kelly's Irish Pub.

"So that's where he hangs out!"

Steven pulled into the curb and cut the engine.

"Smoking is illegal in restaurants and bars . . . *I wonder . . .* ?" he thought aloud.

Then he noticed the narrow alleyway at the side of the pub and the large, wheeled garbage containers lining the walls for pickup and a perfect spot for the smoker to take a break to satisfy the habit. No sooner had Steven's thoughts conjured up an idea than a bar patron appeared from the side door and lit up.

"I knew it! Perfect . . . It's just a matter of surveillance for the next few nights to establish if this is his regular watering hole. People are creatures of habit." He grinned. "It's all coming together nicely."

Steven turned the ignition; he would circle the block to see if the alley had a back entrance, and within a matter of minutes, his assumptions proved correct.

"The proof of the pudding is in the tasting, and the plan must be next week."

Steven and Sheryl were embarking on a dangerous mission, not for the faint of heart, fraught with human minefields and the unknown, but could they pull it off? *Only on the day will it tell . . .*

* * *

"Sorry I'm a bit late, Mike, but the diner got really busy, and Ken asked if I could stay back for another half hour . . . *What could I say?*" She took the vacant barstool.

"It's no big thing, honey, the point is *you made it!*" Mike leaned over and gave Sandy a kiss on the cheek. "*Wow,* your cheeks *are* cold!"

"Warm heart." Sandy turned and looked into Mike's eyes. It was one of these looks that sent messages, and Mike returned the compliment.

"*Eh . . . Err . . .* Sandy, what would you like?" For a moment, Mike lost his concentration.

"Something soft . . . Like . . . ?"

Mike couldn't contain his laughter. *Something soft!*

"Don't keep it to yourself!"

It was getting worse, and Mike just had to stop, or he would bring the house down.

"*It's just . . .*" He coughed. "Something that crossed my mind. I'll tell you about it when the time's right. Don't worry, it's not about you . . . *Now that drink?*" He had to change the subject, *and quick!*

Sandy frowned and gave Mike a look.

"Shawn, I'll have a Bailey's on the rocks."

* * *

The alcohol buzz was a high, and Mike was thoroughly enjoying Sandy's company. They had lots of laughs about various life topics from Mike's days as a freshman at NYU to Sandy's disastrous singing career, but the inevitable had to come.

Mike had disappeared to the alley for his five-minute "smoko" and like most inquisitive women, Sandy just had to approach the inevitable.

"It's cold out tonight," Mike commented as he grabbed the stool, a smile on his face. His nose was a close second to Rudolph's. "*No, don't tell me!* I know I should give up this unsociable habit, but just give me a bit more time, honey."

That was not what was on Sandy's mind, but then he had a point.

"Mike, what did you do for a living before?"

"Honey, your glass is empty . . . Another Bailey's?" Mike had a good idea what was coming, *but could he blame her?*

"An Irish coffee, Mike. I'm putting the brakes on." Mike signalled to Shawn.

"So?" Sandy wasn't going to let it go.

Mike felt uneasy, but if he wanted this relationship to flourish, it had to hang out in the washing sometime.

"I was in marketing . . . Vice president with a company named Global. It's no longer exists. I believe it went into bankruptcy after I was forcibly retired . . . *so to speak.* How did it all happen, you may well ask? It started with a foolish extramarital affair with a female executive from ABM that turned fatal. Namely, one Laura Williams. When I tried to terminate our relationship, she wouldn't take no for an answer and threatened to ruin me and my family. It was sexual blackmail by any other name, and in my frustration and in sheer desperation, I went . . ."

* * *

"And you were finally arrested and extradited from Brazil . . . That's one helluva story, Mike!" Sandy was moving her head from side to side in an "I don't believe it!" gesture.

"One I'm not proud of." Mike took a sip of his Guinness, his lips parched from talking.

Suddenly Sandy held Mike's hand and looked into his troubled eyes.

"I appreciate that wasn't easy, but thanks for putting my mind at ease. You deserve a kiss for that . . ."

* * *

"Thanks for walking me home."

"*Are you serious?* In this area, I wouldn't leave a dog by itself, let alone my date!"

"I like the sound of that . . . *My date.* I haven't been on a date for . . . Well, too long to remember. Let's get in out of the cold." Sandy grabbed Mike's hand and ragged him into the apartment lobby.

"Now for that kiss I promised."

She stood on her toes and threw her arms around Mike's neck, her lips warm and moist, the contact explosive. Mike didn't need much persuasion and crushed Sandy's body against his. The kiss seemed to last forever, and when their lips finally parted, the sensation was too much and Mike's rock-hard penis was pressing into Sandy's loins. It was a feeling that she had almost forgotten, and she wanted more.

"Mike . . . *Oh, Mike,* you don't know how much I want you and need you!"

She crushed his lips again in sexual perversion, and when their lips finally parted, Mike had already forced his hand inside her panties, the wetness of her vagina moistening his finger as he gently pushed deep inside. Sandy gave a shiver, then parted her legs wider to assist Mike to massage her jewel and fulfill her ultimate desire.

"Don't stop, Mike . . . Don't stop." Her teeth biting into Mike's neck while encircling him like a tropical vine as she reached her climax with an ecstatic moan.

It was time, and Mike reluctantly removed his hand and pulled her into the open elevator then pressed the close button.

"Mike, we can't, Jason's home."

"Who said we can't?"

For Mike, there was no turning back, he had dreamt of a woman for over nine years.

"Mike . . . No, not in the elevator," Sandy protested. But Mike had already raised her skirt, frantically pulling her panties aside.

"Hold it, darling, for one second." She reached down and removed her panties, then stuffed them into Mike's jacket pocket.

"Something to remind you . . . Now don't disappoint me." She opened her legs wider, then groaned at Mike's first thrust penetrating her, deeper than expected.

"Don't stop, darling, don't stop . . ."

CHAPTER 9

"So how did Nelson take it?"

"He wasn't too happy. Sunday morning is his thing, but your call sealed it. How far is it from here, Steven? I get scared at this time in the morning, especially in the winter, when it's so dark."

"Have you had breakfast, sis?"

"You must be kidding! *At six in the morning?"*

"Why don't I treat my little sis to Mickey D's?"

"Mmmm, I can smell these egg and bacon muffins and hash browns."

"Then it's a deal. There's a McDonald's on the next block . . ."

*   *   *

"Is *this* good!" Sheryl was tucking into her high-cholesterol breakfast, *but as for her brother,* his mind was somewhere else.

"Aren't you going to eat something, Steven? You've hardly touched your food."

"I've got so much on my mind, sis, and food isn't one of them. I forgot to tell you that I did a 'gumshoe' on Father last night."

"You are really going to go through with this, aren't you?"

"Never been surer. Listen, sis, you know I'm passionate about the donor transplant program in the United States, but the problem is we haven't got its importance through to the public. Although we have the largest donor receipts in the western world, China is way ahead, with 60 percent more donors. You may say it's because of their population being over one billion, and you would be partly correct, but why? *I'll tell you why.* A Professor Huang Jiefu heads the organ donor program, who incidentally was trained in Australia, had this bright idea. China has the largest number of criminal executions. I mean you just have to sneeze against the government, and you find yourself on death row, but what a waste of body organs from perfectly healthy prisoners! So, he approached the government to legalize the use of vital organs from executed criminals, provided they gave written consent. Can you imagine the harvest of organs with over seven hundred executions each year plus the normal response from the public! But here's the scoop . . . A slow lethal injection is used to prolong the life of the organ during the execution, so it can removed in real time with a surgical team standing by."

"So this is where you came up with the idea!" To remove organs from felons who don't deserve to be released into society because of the traumatic effect on the victims and the lives they destroyed." Sheryl was intrigued.

"You got that right, sis!"

"Yes, but the only difference is that they are not on death row, and you don't have their consent, not to mention, Steven, that it's a criminal offense."

"Don't rub it in, sis, I know what I'm doing. Nothing will go wrong. I have it planned down to the last T." Sheryl gave one of her sighs.

"I don't know what I've gotten myself in for."

"Shall we go?"

*   *   *

"Boy, this *is* spooky at this time in the morning." Sheryl gave a slight shiver as Steven drove into the empty cark park at Fort Knox Self-Storage.

"Just as I anticipated, no one here. It couldn't be better," Steven commented. "I'll back the van to almost touch the unit's roller door, just in case there are any prying eyes on our cargo."

"What's the unit number?" Sheryl asked.

"Fourteen."

"Is that a good omen or what? That's my birthday."

Steven just laughed. "Whatever! Sheryl, can you jump down and tell me when I'm close while I reverse the van."

"Christ, it's cold." Sheryl pulled up the hood of her heavy duffle, the icy wind from the Hudson biting into her cheeks. The forecast was for more snow, which felt like sooner rather than later.

* * *

"This is really neat, Steven. You've thought of everything . . . *And climate control!*

Sheryl was standing with her hands on her hips, admiring their morning's work.

"Sis, let's wrap it up, and get this van out of here before it draws attention."

"So where to now, big brother?"

"Back to my apartment. I need to walk through the next and most crucial step of the plan our *first organ donor.*"

* * *

Mike had slept like a log. Sex is a wonderful experience, but unfortunately easily forgotten, *that is, until the next opportunity!* He smiled as he swung his feet to the floor. The room was bitter cold, and clad in his underwear and T-shirt, he didn't waste any time feeding dollars into the meter.

"*Fucking dump!*" He cussed. "Now the next horrible life-threatening experience is showering in fucking cold eater."

Sunday was a lay-in day even for ex-cons who were either still high on amphetamines or brown bagging it back to their rooms. It was against their parole conditions, but the can can't be any worse than this purgatory. The only good thing that come out of it was the communal bathroom was empty and the slim possibility of a lukewarm shower.

Mike quickly dressed and switched off the heater, his stomach rumbling, but Sandy wasn't on this morning, and for a change, he would treat her to breakfast at the diner. They would meet at ten, and it was still early, but with nothing else on the cards, the morning paper and a coffee would fill the gap.

* * *

Mike filled the vacant stool at the breakfast bar and unfolded the *Times.*

"What can I get you?" the kid asked.

Mike looked up; the voice was familiar.

"*Jason!* I didn't know you worked on Sunday."

"*So?*"

"*Eh . . . ?*" Mike was taken aback; this kid was coming on heavy.

"*Your order, sir,* if it's not too much trouble, there are other customers waiting to be served."

"Jason, why can't we be friends? If nothing else, for your mother's sake."

"I'm waiting." He scowled.

"*All right . . . All right.*" Mike raised his hand, giving in. "Coffee's fine, black."

This stuff Mike didn't need, especially from this selfish, ill-mannered kid.

I suppose I should be thankful for small mercies; the thought rang through his mind as he placed his nose back into the newsprint.

"Your coffee." The tone in Jason's voice was hostile as he slammed the mug on the bar top.

"Have you been waiting long?" A sexy female voice whispered in Mike's ear.

"*Sandy!*" Mike rose to his feet to greet her with a kiss, but then changed his mind with Jason looking on.

"No, I've really just arrived. Say, why don't we grab that booth? It's more comfortable than sitting at the breakfast bar, and we can have a private conversation."

Mike sort of motioned with his eyes toward Jason.

Sandy put on a false smile and walked to the booth, Jason watching his mother's every move.

"I've been thinking about you all night." Mike looked into her eyes from across the table.

Sandy smiled. "Good thoughts, I hope."

"The kind you wouldn't want to know, but seriously, honey, I really have genuine feelings for you."

"The feeling's mutual, Mike, but I was worried you wouldn't turn up for breakfast. You know the cliche 'Will you still love me tomorrow?'"

"Honey." Mike leaned over and held her hand. "Don't say that. You make me feel as if I only have one thing on my mind."

"Can you blame me, Mike? But it's my own fault, letting my guard down."

"Honey, what we had was special and . . ."

"Can I interrupt? *Your order?*" It was Jason glowering as he stood impatiently with his order pad.

Mike took a deep breath; he would have loved to tell him to take a hike, but if he wanted to get to Sandy, he would have to get to her son first.

"*Sandy?*" Mike asked.

"I'll stick with your favourite, Mike . . . The breakfast special."

"That'll be two specials . . . Eggs sunny side up with toasted rye, and make sure the bacon's crispy."

"*Is there anything else?*" Jason gave a disgruntled sigh.

"Coffee black. Thanks, Jason," Mike answered through clenched teeth.

"Ten minutes." The expression on Jason's face was bordering on murder.

Mike sort of shrugged it off; he didn't wish to make his feelings too obvious.

"Go easy on him, Mike, he's going through a difficult patch after his breakup with his girlfriend," Sandy reacted. "I'm really worried."

"Honey, I wish I could help, but I don't know where to start. Adult kids at my age are not my forte."

"I understand, Mike, and that's what . . ."

"Your orders. Enjoy your breakfast."

It was Lucy the waitress, and Mike breathed a sigh of relief. He was looking forward to a stress-free breakfast, and he smiled as he finally tucked into his eggs.

"Honey, you were about to say?"

Sandy took a sip of her coffee; she seemed rather nervous.

"I don't want you to take this the wrong way, Mike, but I think we should cool it for a week or so."

Mike sat back and wiped his mouth the with his napkin, a shock wave on his face.

"*Why, honey?* Have I done something wrong? If I have . . ."

"It's not you, Mike, *it's Jason!* I have to give him more space to get over his father. I'm sorry, Mike, but that's the way it is."

Mike rubbed his chin, then stared into Sandy's eyes.

"Is this really what you want, honey? I know I've only known you for a couple of dates, but I thought we had something special . . . Sandy, I'm asking you, don't throw your happiness away. Give it time. Jason will come round. Kids go through phases. Just give me more time to prove it."

"I've made up my mind, Mike. I'm not saying it's forever, just be patient. Besides, you can see me every day at the diner, and who knows?"

Mike raised his hand. "Lucy, the check please."

"Mike, don't be like that, at least finish your breakfast."

"*It's just my fucking luck!* If I had a dog, it would be probably run over. I'm sorry for you, Sandy, get a life." He passed Lucy a fifty. "Keep the change, honey."

"Is there something wrong with food, sir? You've hardly eaten anything."

"Somehow I've just lost my appetite." Mike threw his napkin on the table. "Goodbye, Sandy . . . If you ever change your mind . . ."

*   *   *

The Mercedes van was parked in the same spot across from "Heartbreak Hotel" and where Steven could get a clear view of the comings and goings. He had to make sure that his father's regular watering hole was Kelly's Irish Pub. Yesterday, it was around seven in the evening when Mike "walked the walk," and if Steven's hunch was correct, he should see his father appear for his alcohol infusion any moment now, and no sooner had the thought crossed his mind than Mike appeared like clockwork.

Mike stopped just outside the front door and lit the Camel stick, taking a deep drag, then exhaling. The pub was only a ten-minute walk and Steven could easily track him. He would park the van across the street to get a rough idea of "smoko" time.

*   *   *

"Mike, all on your own tonight?" Shawn, like all barmen, needed an opening, but he was also inquisitive.

"Something like that." Mike looked really down.

"Two-pack bourbon on the rocks?" Shawn asked.

"Yeah and keep 'em coming."

Shawn iced the glass and poured the bourbon.

"You look down, Mike, do you want to unload?"

Mike shook his head. "Sandy gave me the ass today. *That bloody teenage kid of hers!*"

"When it comes to kids, Mike, you ain't gonna win. I went through the same myself. Kids spell trouble . . . Anything to eat?"

"On a night like this, there's only one choice . . . *Irish stew!*"

"Now you're talking."

"Hold it, Shawn, I'm gonna pop out for a quick drag. I'll be back in five." Mike disappeared toward the restroom and the side entrance.

*   *   *

"True to form, *I knew it!* Smokers will brave all the elements to get lung cancer and pay for it . . . *I ask you.* Now it's just a case of the hit, and the quicker the better." Steven was talking aloud before he opened his smartphone and searched the phone book.

"Sis, Steven here. I hope I'm not disturbing anything?"

"*If I said you were, would it matter?* It's my brother on the line . . . So why the call?"

"Tomorrow evening . . ."

*   *   *

"I smell alcohol from you, Summers," Barrett barked at Mike as he signed the book.

"*Oh, do you now! What was your mother? A fucking bloodhound?*" Mike growled.

"You watch your mouth, Summers. I can easily throw the book at you, so don't trust your luck, or you'll be back in that six by four, smelling your own farts."

Mike looked Barrett straight in the eyes. "And don't trust *your* luck! I've shit guys like you. Report me to Clark, and they'll be carrying your body parts out a piece at a time."

"*Who do you think you're talking to?* You jumped-up fucking con." Barrett was now on his feet, eyeballing Mike, the veins protruding from his neck in anger.

"So help me, step outta line one more time with that big mouth of yours, and it will give me the greatest pleasure."

Mike chucked the five-cent BIC back on the desk and slammed the heavy book closed.

"Go crawl up your own ass." He turned and walked to the pay phone, a "Mexican standoff."

Mike stacked the quarters up at the side of the phone, then dialled, ignoring Barrett's continuing onslaught of abuse.

"Sandy, Mike here . . . Hold it, honey, I know, but don't hang up. Thanks . . . I was hoping that you would turn up at Kelly's tonight, but I guess I read it wrong . . . I know what you said, but sometimes we say things we don't really mean in the heat of battle and end up regretting it. Anyhow, 'I just called to say I love you.'" Mike was laughing aloud. Maybe it was the bourbon, but he was in a jovial mood. "Okay . . . Okay. Honey, I apologize for phoning at this time of night, and no, I'm not drunk, if that's what you are thinking! Will you be there for breakfast tomorrow? Oh well . . . Then will you join me for a coffee? Well, at least that's something. Good night, honey, sleep tight." Mike placed back the receiver, a grin on his face. "If you don't try, you'll never know. *Besides, tomorrow is another day . . .*"

*   *   *

Sometimes the transplant team was busy, and other times . . . It's a case of supply and demand and "the long wait." Steven, as usual, was punctual and arrived at the front desk before seven thirty; however, Sheryl was a different kettle of fish, being an anaesthesiologists. She could be called upon for any surgery that demanded a general anaesthetic.

"Good morning, Jill," Steven greeted the night sister, her shift about to end.

"Dr. Summers. You're bright and early this morning." "Has my sister arrived?" Steven asked.

"Yes, she told me to tell you that she is in cafeteria."

"Thanks, Jill, have good one."

"That's a change, early for once!" Steven muttered under his breath as he legged it to the elevator. The cafeteria was at ground level, and he pressed 1.

"*Over here, Steven.*" He heard the voice, then spotted the raised arm.

"Good morning, sis."

"Would you like a coffee or some breakfast?" Sheryl rose to her feet.

"Naw, you stay put, sis, I'll fetch it myself."

Steven returned with the polystyrene cup clasped between his hands, absorbing the warmth.

"*Christ,* it's cold out this morning, and the weather bureau is forecasting snow before the day is out." Steven took the vacant chair facing his sister.

"Steven, I don't have much time. I have an operation at eight, a liver tumour. So why the 'tomorrow evening' call last night?"

"Because it's time for our very first donor."

"Can you be more explicit?"

"I've been watching Father for three nights, and he hasn't disappointed me. True to form, he leaves the halfway house at between six and seven thirty and . . ."

"So let me get this straight. He frequents this Kelly's, whatever it is, and emerges in the alley a half hour later for a drag. We will wait in the alley with the van out of sight. I dress up like a whore, wig and all, and proposition him. Once I get his undivided attention, you approach him from behind and smother his breathing holes with a chloroform-soaked cloth. I help you with the limp body into the van, then inject him with two cc's of Propofol, just enough to send him to 'Disneyland' until we arrive at Fort Knox."

'Sheryl, *I couldn't have summed it up better myself.*" "So Steven, what's your schedule today?"

"I'm free for the whole day. That is, unless someone croaks it and the relatives become benevolent with their next of kin's organs."

"Then where shall we meet and when?"

"My apartment at six . . ."

*　*　*

Mike relaxed on his cot, reflecting on his day while staring at the ceiling. He was disappointed with Sandy. He felt sure she had smoked the "peace pipe" and that she would meet him for breakfast, but sadly it was not to be. The meeting with his parole officer was just as bad, with Mike refusing to go for the interview at Westfield's as a store man. Needless to say, Clark was pissed off at Mike's attitude and didn't mince his words. Maybe once his CV hit the search engine, he might have more luck returning to the corporate scene.

"*Aw, what the hell!*" Mike spoke out loud as he glanced at his watch. "It's just turned five. I'll grab some shut-eye until six, then I'll go visit my favourite watering hole." He took a deep breath, lay on his side, and closed his eyes.

Unfortunately, when you wake up, the world hasn't changed, but unknown to Mike, tonight his world *would* change forever . . .

*　*　*

Sheryl rang the bell; she was carrying her "hold all" and the Madame Tussaud getup.

Steven peeped through the security peephole.

"Hang on, sis, while I unlatch."

"How are we for time, Steven?"

"Don't worry, we're okay. You look pale. Are you feeling all right?" Steven gave his sister a hug.

"*Honest?* I'm scared shitless!"

"The first cut's the deepest, sis. The next will be like second nature."

"Let's take it one step at a time. I had better get changed. I fetched the daggiest outfit I could find in my closet."

"*This I gotta see!*"

Fifteen minutes had passed, and Steven was getting impatient, continually glancing at his watch and pacing the floor.

"Come on, sis, we gotta get through the evening traffic." He raised his voice.

Steven had already mastered the false moustache and the goatee, beard, and the aviator shades; all that was left was the hoodie.

"So what do you think?" Sheryl was standing on the "catwalk."

"*Wow, sis!* You're wasting your time in the medical profession with that getup. I can be your pimp if you change your mind." Steven was trying to control his laughter.

"Get out of it, *you joker!*"

"So?" Sheryl did a three sixty.

"The shoulder-length red wig the eye shadow to match, and that dress! Covered in turquoise sequins, *I'm glad I'm wearing these shades.* But how are you gonna walk on these heels?"

"Just make sure you are ready to catch me . . . I'm more worried about the cold. My fanny is friggin' freezing. And as for this little fur jacket that barely cover my tits . . . *Maaaan.*" She shook her head.

"But isn't that the deal?" Steven grinned.

"Come on, let's get our asses out of here. I'm freezing my ass off, *and that's inside the apartment!*"

"Do you have all the medical stuff?"

"Everything." Sheryl patted the small leather bag. "*Then what are we waiting for?*"

*   *   *

Mike yawned and swung his feet to the floor, then stretched his arms above his head and gave a pronounced groan. An afternoon nap was not always the solution, often causing one to wake up worse than before. He walked to wall mirror, his reflection between the cracks gave him a reality check.

"Mirror . . . Mirror, on the wall. On second thought, don't answer that." Mike laughed as he ran the brush through his greying hair.

"*Wow!* It's cold in here." Mike shivered, feeling the aftermath of his catnap "*It's warmer in Kelly's!*" He slipped into his heavy boots and the "navy surplus" topcoat.

"*I'm outta here!*"

CHAPTER 10

"It's not quite seven, sis, and if everything goes to plan, he should appear any minute." Steven parked the van in the usual spot.

"Stay calm, sis, once he enters Kelly's, we drive round the block and reverse the van into the back alley. It's pitch dark at this time in the evening and shouldn't attract any attention, especially on a Monday, when the pub action isn't even in first gear."

"I'll take you word for it, Steven, I don't profess to be a barfly." Sheryl took a deep breath. *"I can't wait to get this shit over with!"*

"Easy, sis, count to five."

"I can't believe you are so calm . . ."

"Hold it, he's just appeared!"

*   *   *

Mike had just had an altercation with Barrett, and he wasn't in the best of moods. *That bastard I don't trust. He's just biding his time to pin something on me and go squealing, like the dog he is, to Clark. There is nothing that mongrel would enjoy better than to see me back in the can.*

Mike hastily opened the pub door to get out of the biting cold and hung his coat on the stand before making a beeline to the open log fire to warm his credentials.

"Hi, Mike, you're a bit late tonight," Shawn greeted him.

"It's a long story that I would rather forget . . . Shawn, the usual . . ."

Shawn gave Mike a peculiar look, moving his eyes to the left toward the other end of the bar as if he was trying to tell him something.

"I'm sorry, Shawn, I didn't catch that." He rolled his eyes again.

"A two-pack bourbon, easy on the ice, and a Bud chaser."

"Eh . . . Sure, Mike, coming up." This time Shawn flicked his head to the left.

"Shawn." A woman's voice echoed from the other end of the bar. "Why don't you just tell Mike I'm here?"

A broad grin crossed Mike's face as he recognized the familiar voice. It was his "time in the sun."

"Sandy . . . I'll be darned!"

"Well, are you gonna ask me to join you, or should I take a rain check?"

"What do you think? Shawn, whatever my date is drinking . . . *Same again.*

As for Sandy, she was looking sexy in her chunky white woollen polo, skin-tight stone-washed Levi's and knee-length suede boots. *Maaaan!* And that blonde hair and those voluptuous breasts, it's not good for the heart. Guys have had an aneurysm with less.

Mike patted the stool on the pole table next to the crackling log fire.

"It's a lot warmer over here, honey."

Sandy turned toward the bar as she joined Mike.

"Shawn, I'll have a drop . . ."

"*Of the Bailey's . . .,*" he interrupted, a big grin on his face. "Sure and be Jesus . . . And with one cube of ice." His Irish brogue added to the flavour.

"You took the words right out of my mouth . . . Hi, honey." Sandy gave Mike a warm but fleeting kiss on the lips.

"Hold It! One candy is never enough."

"*Uh-uh* . . . Not in front of the children." Sandy burst into laughter.

"*Oh . . . All right!*" Mike replied like a spoiled kid.

"We have all night, darling." Sandy affectionately squeezed Mike's hand as she perched on the high stool and crossed her legs.

"Thanks, Shawn." She took a sip from her glass, then looked into Mike's eyes. The look that launched a thousand ships. "Are you mad at me?'

"What for?"

"For not joining you this morning over coffee."

"Disappointed, yes . . . *Mad, no.* So why the change of mind?"

"I missed you, you big heel . . . *Satisfied?*"

"Sandy, just gimme five." Mike pulled the pack from his pocket.

"*Mike!*" Sandy gave him that look.

"*Honey,* I'm trying my best, believe me. Just give me a little more time, I promise. I'll go get my jacket."

"Oh no you don't, mister. If you get comfortable out there, you'll take fifteen minutes instead of five . . ."

"Do you see what I have to put up with, Shawn?" Mike laughed. "I promise, five."

Mike walked toward the restroom and the alley door, the Camel already hanging from his lips, the call of the nicotine too strong.

*   *   *

The fifteen or so minutes that Steven and Sheryl had been waiting felt like an eternity; worse still, the motor was cut and at minus four, it was reminiscent of an expedition to Everest, *only without the Sherpas!*

"If something doesn't break soon, Steven, I'll be suffering from friggin' frostbite."

"*Be quiet, Sheryl!* Speak of the devil . . . *You're on . . . Remember, no names . . .*"

Mike leaned against the brick wall and took a deep drag, the bright red glow from the cigarette giving a scary glare in the semidarkness. He gave a slight cough, then moved his shoulders in a sort of a shiver, the cold biting into his underdressed torso.

"You're not dressed for this weather, dude, are you some kind of a masochist or something?" Sheryl suddenly appeared from the shadows.

"So where did you appear from, honey? You must be my guardian angel." Mike smiled.

Sheryl now had his full attention; men were suckers for a piece of ass and a deep crevasse, and what better "Broadway" than "ladies of the night"?

"So why the secret, honey, you would do better on the sidewalk?"

"With two strikes . . . *Are you kiddin' me?* I don't take no chances unless I share the judge's bed . . . But . . ." Sheryl smiled. "That's for another day . . .

I'm fucking freezing, and by the looks of you, darling, you need my love to keep you warm."

"*Where have I heard that line before?*" Mike smiled and killed the Camel about to leave.

"Hold it, dude, as they say, the proof is in the tasting . . . I do 'round the world' for two big ones, but you pay for the motel and dinner, and I don't

mean Burger King! *I've got more class that that!*" *Come on, Sheryl, keep him talking.*

Steven had moved stealthily along the wall; in the shadows, his dark hoodie and black jeans made him almost invisible, and Sheryl could see him positioning himself from the corner of her eye. He was ready for the kill, but somehow, she must get her father to turn his back to face him.

"Naw, not tonight, honey." Mike shrugged, about to leave.

Sheryl had to think fast, but what? There was only one way, and she walked toward the sidewalk, then turned sharply to make him face her.

"*Dude,* you don't know what you are missing. Have it your own way, big boy, but maybe if I show you some of the merchandise, it might change your mind."

Sheryl began to pull her skimpy top down, exposing part of her full breasts . . . *Now* she had his full attention. After all, what man refuses a free burlesque show, and Steven didn't need a second awakening, as he sprang like a cheetah about to capture its prey, the chloroform-soaked cloth held in his right hand.

"*What the fuc . . .*"

Mike fell like a log as the chloroform clouded his brain, and he slipped into a state of unconsciousness.

"I've got him Sheryl, he's in no-man's land. Just grab his legs to get him into the back of the van . . . *Hurry . . . Hurry . . .*"

*   *   *

Steven turned the motor over and gently eased it into first, keeping the engine's noise as low as possible before turning into the deserted street now devoid of traffic. Monday night for the "gig" was the perfect choice.

"Sheryl, are you all, right?"

"Yeah, I've taped his eyes, but can you switch on the cabin light? I need to search for a vein to administer the Propofol . . . Okay, Steven, you can cut it now. He'll sleep like a baby for a couple of hours and wake with no memory of his ordeal."

"Nice job, sis. We should arrive at Fort Knox in say . . ." Steven checked his watch. "Another thirty minutes or so."

Sheryl looked at her father lying peacefully in his induced temporary sleep, pangs of guilt flashing through her mind.

"Steven, I can't believe we are doing this to our *own* father."

"Sis, think of it another way . . . It's payback time for the grief and hardship he has caused Mother and our family, not forgetting his poor victim, Laura Williams, whose life he ruined and the real reason for her ultimate demise. Now he is giving the gift of life to a deserving sick person in the jaws of death."

Sheryl went quiet; it was all too difficult to digest.

"Sis, we all have some kind of darkness, which, in one way or another, we struggle to manage, but mine is for the good of humanity, and to that extent, my conscience is clear, and I have peace of mind. These ex-cons will never pay their so-called price to society. Spending time in prison is like going to confession—it doesn't change one goddamn thing!"

*   *   *

"*Where the hell is that guy?*" Sandy was becoming anxious. "*He must be freezing his nuts off!*" She glanced at her watch.

"Do you want me to check?" Shawn offered.

"Could you?"

"No sweat, the place is quiet . . . Be back in a jiffy." He walked toward the restroom and the rear door.

The alley was almost pitch dark except from the shimmers of light from the streetlights, casting an eerie shadow from the large garbage bins.

"*Mike . . . Mike . . .* are you there?" Shawn raised his voice. "Strange . . . No one can just disappear into thin air like that!"

He could smell the tobacco smoke, and he looked down at his feet for the source, and there it was . . . *the still-smoldering cigarette stub.*

"*I'll be darned . . . Camel!* That's Mike's, all right . . ."

CHAPTER 11

"Jan, are you just about finishing that confession on the O'Malley shooting?"

"*Listen, you big oaf.* It's about time you learned to type. *Don't hassle me.*"

"I can, it's just that you are faster than me." Bill was controlling his laughter.

"*Yeah,* the one-finger stuff. Go make yourself useful and get me a coffee from the vending machine." Jan gave Bill a look.

"You mean you actually like that shit they call coffee?"

"I get the message. Here's the dollar, you friggin' scrooge." Jan shook her head.

"And how about me?" Bill was still fooling around.

"You joker . . . *Get out of it and let me finish, or we'll never get outta here!*"
"*Oh . . . Oh . . .* Here's trouble." Jan moved her eyes to the left.

"Just in time. I thought you may have called it a day." It was Mitchel on a mission.

"Christ, Jan, this is all we need."

"I didn't catch that, Hayden, you were saying?"

"I was saying to my partner, is there anything else we need. We are just finishing the O'Malley' statement."

Jan covered her mouth in case she laughed.

"It looks like your old foe Mike Summers is back in the limelight again." The name Summers now received Mike's undivided attention. "*Summers?*"

"*You heard right!* It looks like he jumped parole, or he's a victim of some kind of foul play. Whatever, the bottom line is he has disappeared from outside a bar in Brooklyn. Here's the address. I want you two to go and check it out."

"*Tonight?*" Bill raised his voice.

"*You heard me . . .* Is that a problem, Hayden?"

"It's just that . . ." Bill put on a face, then changed his mind. "Whatever you say, Cap."

Hayden studied the address, then passed it to Jan.

"So will I phone you at home, or will tomorrow morning do?" Bill was chancing his luck.

"*Hayden* don't be such a smart-ass. It'll get you into trouble one of these days. Now if there's nothing else, maybe *I* can go home!"

Mitchel turned and left, muttering obscenities under his breath.

Jan looked at Bill and shook her head. "*You'll never learn, mister,* throw me the keys . . ."

*   *   *

"*Good,* there's not a car in the park. I'll back the van as close to the shutter door as I can to make sure we aren't seen." Out of the blue, Steven grinned as if it were a game. "Kinda like the body snatchers, huh?"

"Where did that come from? *Steven?*" Sheryl shook her head. "You have a weird sense of humour." She sighed. "I give up . . . Anyhow, he's out like a light. He won't give us any trouble."

"That's good, sis, you did well. Our problem now is getting him into the storage unit. He's a deadweight and like a ton of bricks."

"*Tell me about it!* I nearly put my back out lifting him into the van."

"You're outta shape, sis." Steven grinned, his sister not believing how her brother could be so calm.

"Sheryl, just you stay put, I'll get out and open the van doors so we can reverse even closer."

Steven unlocked the padlock and pulled the shutter up, then quickly switched the lights. The van doors now wide open, he could reverse the van partly inside the storage unit. He had checked out the unit earlier and switched on the climate control, and everything was ready for the "big sleep."

"Hang on, sis, while I wheel the operating table right next to the van, then we can just slide him over . . . Are you ready? *Pull . . . Sheryl . . . Pull . .* ." "Okay, he's clear." Sheryl panted.

"*Quickly . . . Quickly . . . Sis.* Wheel the table in, and close the door while I go park the van."

*   *   *

"Nice part of town, *I must say!* Just pull in behind that black and white, Jan. What a shit of a night, it must be at least five below. If we get snow, that's all we friggin' need."

"Stop complaining, Bill, you're showing your age."

Jan pulled into the curb, only to be met by an enthusiastic cruiser sergeant flashing his torchlight directly into their faces.

"*What the hell!*" Jan hit the window switch. "Cut the light, Sergeant, or I'll end up using a white stick . . . Detective Sergeant Martin, Homicide." Jan held up the shield on the neck chain for the oversize cop to see.

"Sorry, Sergeant." He embarrassingly apologized. "It's just that . . ."

"Save it, Sarge, we *all* want to go home." Jan was a straight shooter and didn't mince her words.

Bill was already on the sidewalk, flashing his shield.

"Lieutenant Bill Hayden. So what's the take, Sergeant?"

"Some guy . . ." He glanced at his pad. "A Mike Summers, it seems he comes out for a smoke and mysteriously disappears, leaving his broad in the lurch and his personal belongings on the peg."

"So who made the call?"

"The barman . . . *Um* . . . A Shawn Jameson. After Summers failed to reappear some fifteen minutes later, he did the gentlemanly thing, doing the broad a favor, and went to the alley to search for the 'invisible man.' The broad's name is Sandra Watson. She serves at the local diner."

"You can hit the road, Sergeant, we can take it from here. Just hand in your report at the precinct."

"Thanks, Lieutenant. Let's go, Jake, it's coffee time."

The sergeant didn't need a second prompt, and the black and white slipped into the night, most likely heading for the golden arches and a cholesterol hit.

"You take the barman, Jan, and I'll take the date." Bill was already opening the door for his partner.

*   *   *

"So let's go through this again . . . You met this guy in the diner where you work, and you got cosy and he asked you out for a drink."

"You could say that."

"And did you know he was an ex-con on parole?"

"Yeah, he told me . . . So is it a crime to give a guy a second chance?"

"Lady, that's your choice . . ."

"Bill, I have something here."

"Don't go away . . . Eh?"

"Sandy."

"I'm not done with you yet . . . Yeah, what is it, Jan?"

She held up the cigarette butt that the barman had retrieved.

"Shawn reckons this belongs to Summers. It's the brand he smokes. He found it on the ground in the alley, still smouldering. I'll wrap it in a napkin and get forensics to check the DNA against the data bank."

"*That's a break at least.*" Mike turned to Sandy. "There's not much we can do at the moment. After twenty-four hours, if he hasn't turned up, as per procedure, he will be listed as a missing person." "*Is that it?*" Sandy was furious.

"What do you want me to do, honey . . . get the sheriff and round up a posse?"

"Thanks for nothing, Lieutenant! Now if it's not too much trouble, I have an early shift in the morning."

"Yeah, we're finished. Here's my card. Should anything come up, give me a call . . . Jan, I think there's nothing else we can do here. Let's call it a night. Say, can you drop me off?"

"I'll think about it." Jan gave a cheeky smile, and just as they were about to leave, a big guy in a sheepskin jacket entered the bar in a hurry.

"Can I help you?" Bill blocked his path.

"I'm Bob Clark, Mike Summers's parole officer. I just received a call from . . ."

*   *   *

Steven gave three knocks on the steel shutter door.

"Sheryl, it's me," he whispered.

Sheryl quickly unhooked the inside padlock.

"Okay, Steven, it's open."

The steel door rattled in the sidetracks, making an unearthly noise, and Steven didn't waste any time in slamming it shut.

"You're panting," Sheryl commented as her brother exhaled his freezing breath.

"Yeah, I parked the van out of sight on the other side of the car park, below that clump of trees, then broke the hundred. The place is deserted, and no one saw me . . . *Sis.*" He inhaled. "Time is not on our side, so let's get started. Firstly, I need you to check all the equipment and administer the general anaesthetic while I change and scrub up."

*   *   *

"Everything is in order, Steven . . . The blood oxygen and blood pressure monitors . . . Oxygen supply . . . Endoscope screen . . . Sterilized instruments . . . Airway tube and catheter . . . Saline and antibiotic drips . . ." Sheryl was crossing her checklist. "It's all stations go, Steven. I'll only take a couple of minutes to scrub and glove up."

"Help me to remove his shirt, sis, when you are finished, then you can put him under."

*   *   *

Sheryl was busy tapping the back of her father's hand, trying to detect a suitable vein to inject 6 mg of sodium pentothal, the powerful anaesthetic drug.

"*Ah*, here we are! Give me a sec, Steven. *Hmmm* . . . That should keep him for at least four hours. I'll enter the oropharyngeal airway, then connect the oxygen supply and heart monitor . . . *I'm good* . . . Now I'll help you to remove his shirt slacks and shoes . . . *And for god's sake, Steven,* cover him up with a surgical sheet. The less I see of my father naked, the better, and Steven, the catheter insertion *is all yours.*" Steven just grinned at his sister's remark and went efficiently about his business.

"It's all going well, sis, considering you'll also have to stand in as scrub nurse . . ." Steven gave his sister a cheeky wink. "Now help me roll him over on his right side in order to get easy access to his pelvic cavity. The left kidney is easier to remove because of the longer renal vein and the renal artery, resulting in minimal surgical detachment of the small intestine. *And oh, sis,* can you swab that area with Betadine antiseptic wash while I check out the endoscopes?"

Sheryl nodded and began to wash the area Steven had lined with a marker pen. The computer screens checked; it was now time to begin the delicate surgical procedure to remove the involuntary donor's kidney.

*   *   *

"That's it, detached, Sheryl, the renal veins and arteries clamped and most of the surrounding fatty tissue removed. But I think we have a problem, as Father's kidney is large, and even if I stretch the laparoscopic apertures to the maximum, I don't think I can extract the kidney using the Lina endo-bag . . . No, *it's just too big!* I was hoping I wouldn't need to make an abdominal incision, as it's just another complication, but I'm afraid I have no option. Sis, pass me the laser scalpel. That will eliminate any excess bleeding. A three-inch incision I think will be sufficient . . ."

*   *   *

"How's it from your side, Sheryl?"

"All the vital readings are excellent. I must say, Father is a strong individual. I guess the stretch in prison toughened him." Steven was too busy to reply.

"I'll close. Sheryl, flush the kidney with Trans End solution to wash out any clots. The solution will preserve the kidney for at least twenty-four hours. There's an Eskimo box next to the freezer. Use the simple cold storage solution. Fill the biohazard bag with solution and place the kidney in it. Then fill the Eski with ice, but be careful that you don't get ice bruising, so make sure there's plenty of Trans End in the bag, almost keeping the kidney afloat."

"Finished, Steven." Sheryl stood back, still keeping a wary eye on the monitors.

"Now seal up the Eski with that duct tape. I'm just about finished here."

*   *   *

"Let's dress him, sis. I want you to administer an intravenous antibiotic and saline drip. I need to insert a drain in the wound to avoid any blood clots. The good news is that his urine is flowing through the catheter like gold into the collection bag, although there are traces of blood, but that's normal."

"Father should come to in about an hour's time, but he will require immediate hospitalization and intensive care . . . *Steven, are you listening?*"

Steven could sense even though the operation went well that his sister was more than concerned; it was only natural, the patient being their father.

"So what next?" Her voice was anxious.

Steven didn't reply; he had too much on his mind to stop and explain his next move. Their journey had only just begun.

*   *   *

"So, what do you make of it, Bill?"

Hayden had gone unusually quiet on the drive home. Sure, it was after ten, but it was not like Mike, who could talk the hind legs off a donkey.

"We should be there in around another ten minutes, I'm bushed. Are you meeting Chris after you drop me?"

"Where did that come from? You never answered my question . . . *mister!*" Jan barked.

Bill gave a half-hearted laugh. *"And you never answered mine!"*

"Get out of it! How long have we been partners? I know Bill Hayden only too well, and there's something running through that mind of yours . . . Do you want to share it with me?"

"Jan . . . It's just that this guy Summers keeps coming back like a bad penny, and whatever way you dress it up, he was the cause of Tony's death.

Maaaan . . . It's scary. He's gonna haunt me to the death." Mike gave a big sigh. "Getting back to your question . . . *What do I think?* I really can't put a handle on it. Sure, Senator Williams would like to drive a stake through Summers's heart, *but he's not that stupid!* No, there's something strange about his disappearance . . . I mean this guy is on parole, so why would he risk going back for another stretch? Kidnapped? That's laughable. Robbery? An ex-con on parole? I think you can cross that one from the list . . . And this broad Sandra Watson seems genuinely upset . . . *No, Jan*, there's something strange going on, and for the life of me, I just can't figure it out."

"My advice? Sleep on it, Bill . . . Here we are! *What time tomorrow?*"

"Eight. I'll buy you a coffee . . . So?" "So?" Jan shrugged.

"Are you meeting Chris tonight?"

"Mind your own business . . . Eight tomorrow, and go easy on the scotch . . ."

*   *   *

"Sis, the most important thing now is to keep him warm. Wrap him up in a couple of warm blankets, it's cold out there. And make sure before we leave him that the intravenous drips are intact, and he has access to oxygen through his nasal passage. Hide the small oxygen bottle below the blanket. I've taped the Eskimo box closed and addressed it to Professor Cranmer at the Transplant Department . . . Austin Hospital . . . Marked '*Urgent!* Organ for Transplant.'"

"You have me baffled, Steven, and for the life of me I'm still trying to place the pieces of this jigsaw together."

"Just stay calm, sis, and pay attention. I've spent a horrendous amount of time in the planning, *so don't worry.* I guarantee nothing will go wrong. Your number 1 priority is to make sure Father will fully recover from the general anaesthetic and post operation shock. He must be kept warm, and don't forget to make sure he has his wallet, driver's license, and so on. Now enough of that. I must contact Professor Cranmer, as time is a luxury we don't have." Steven opened his laptop.

"For Christ's sake, Steven! You are not going to contact him by e-mail, *are you?"*

"Sis, calm down. *I'm not that stupid . . .* I changed my e-mail address to thehood@hotmail.com, so there's no way it can be traced back to me. Now let me contact the professor, and you just do the job you're trained for . . . It's late, but he'll be at home by now. When the e-mail hits his computer, it sends a 'code one' red alert to his phone and where a donor organ is concerned, he'll swing into action, *believe me.*" Steven began to punch the keyboard.

Professor Cranmer,

A male donor kidney organ for transplant will arrive at the Austin within the next hour. The donor wishes to remain anonymous. He is fifty-four years old and in excellent health. His blood group is A positive. Blood samples for pathology analysis are inside the Eskimo box. The donor's left kidney has been surgically removed by an experienced surgeon at a private clinic. The kidney has been flushed and placed in a biohazard bag with Trans End solution using the CSM method to preserve the organ for over twenty-four hours.

Please don't treat this as a hoax. There are hundreds of patients on dialysis and on death row . . . This is their gift of life . . . Don't waste it.

The Hood

* * *

Cranmer had dozed off after his "sundowner" and light supper. He had good intentions of watching the sports channel and keeping his wife, Marjorie, company, but alas, good intentions go astray when mental fatigue creeps in and the sandman takes over. Although his day at the Austin was uneventful, as professor in charge of the transplant unit, the paperwork was more taxing than surgery, and Marjorie just smiled as she studied her husband of thirty years, now deep in slumber. His greying, thinning hair, the eye bags, the long laugh lines, and the inevitable "turkey neck," but to Marjorie he was still as handsome as the first day they met, and as she glanced at herself in the lounge mirror, she had to admit time waits for no one. She had often thought of plastic surgery, just enough to get rid of the sagging neck and the slack jowls, but she was too scared. Maybe just as well, she smiled at the thought. People might think that Jimmy remarried again to a younger woman.

At sixty, Marjorie still looked well, with her regular trips to the hairdresser and yoga classes and Clarins facials. Her eyes were still a clear blue, and her complexion looked ten years younger than her age, and as a couple, they were well matched and inseparable. Their two children, James Jr. and Alex, now both in their late twenties, had embarked on careers in the banking fraternity and were rapidly climbing the corporate ladder. Both boys were now engaged, and wedding bells was now just a matter of time, and for Marjorie life was good.

* * *

"I know I shouldn't, but I think I'll go pour myself another small cognac," Marjorie was talking to herself as she rose to her feet, a contented smile crossing her face.

Then something caught the corner of her eye. The red alert light on the phone cradle was blinking feverishly. It was a "code one" signal that an organ was available for transplant, the information sent by e-mail to her husband's security address on his laptop.

"*Jimmy . . . Jimmy . . . Wake up!*" Marjorie gently shook his shoulder.

"*Ah . . . Hmmmm . . .*" Jim yawned, then rubbed his eyes. "I'm sorry, honey, I must have dozed off."

"Not to worry, darling." She smiled reassuringly. "But you have a 'code one' that's just come through, and we both know what that means."

"It always happens late in the evening or at some godforsaken time in the middle of the night," Cranmer grumbled as he slowly came to.

"It's most likely a road accident, darling. You know what young people are like, and I pray that someone has not lost their life."

"Don't worry yourself, honey, more and more people are donating organs. It's sad that you lose a life to give a life, but no more of that, I've got work to do . . ."

* * *

Cranmer studied the e-mail, his hand rubbing his chain in thought. He screwed his eyebrows once again and reread the message.

"What's wrong, darling?" Marjorie was standing behind him, always there for her husband.

"This is highly unusual, Marj, and whoever sent this e-mail knows how to reach me. What do you make of it?" Marjorie leaned over his shoulder.

"*Hmmmm . . .* What do you intend to do, Jimmy, and who's this mysterious Hood?"

She could see that her husband was wrestling with his ethics and the Hippocratic oath. If it were a false alarm, it would be catastrophic for the critically ill patient to be given hope, then shattering disappointment should it be a hoax . . . But could her husband afford to ignore it?

Jimmy turned to Marjorie with that searching look.

"*I say go for it!* You have had disappointments before, darling, but this e-mail, for some reason, seems genuine. Remember, nothing ventured nothing gained."

"Thanks, honey, I knew I could depend on you. I'll search the transplant waiting list and select the most critical patient suffering renal failure in category 8 or less, and call 911 for an ambulance for an immediate transfer to the Austin . . . Let me see . . . Here we are . . . A Jennifer Donkins . . . Address . . ."

*   *   *

The sparsely furnished apartment as usual, felt depressed and empty, devoid of all human company, the exception being the framed photo perched on the TV cabinet of Bill's two sons reflecting happier times when they were all of ten years old. Hayden gave a big sigh. *If only life stood still and never changed. In hindsight, sure, I could have done things differently, but history has proved that the result would inevitably be the same.*

Bill turned on the heating, then slipped out of his heavy topcoat and kicked off his shoes.

"*Ah,* that feels better . . . But first things first before I settle down to 'square eyes.'" Then he smiled. "The one good thing about bachelorhood is that there is no one to argue with."

Bill gave a cunning smile as he approached the small kitchen to open the refrigerator and retrieve a cold Bud. The Johnnie Blue on the breakfast bar had taken a hit, but there was still enough of the "Water of Life" to ease his loneliness, and he wasted no time pouring a "two-pack" before corking the green bottle.

"*Boy, am I looking forward to this!*" Bill sank into the "yesterday" chair and placed his swag on the miniature side table.

"*Now* it's time to relax." He sipped the scotch, then gave a groan of satisfaction before chasing Scotland's finest with a cold one.

"I wonder what's on Sky?" As he picked up the remote, the sudden ring of the phone startled him.

"*Now* who could this be? Just when I'm about to enjoy my own company!"

'Yes, Hayden here."

"Why so formal, darling, I've been waiting patiently for your call."

"I'm sorry, honey, it's been one of these days, but just to hear your voice . . ."

*   *   *

Steven's cell phone buzzed, and he motioned to his sister, putting his fingers to his lips, to keep quiet.

"*Professor Cranmer!* I'm sure this is not a social call. How can I be of assistance, sir? And you have just received this e-mail . . . *I see* . . . It certainly is unusual, but I agree with your decision . . . *My sister?* I'll try and contact her, but

I think you should contact another anaesthetist to be safe . . . Yes, Justine Kent is a good choice . . . Call me back if you have no luck, and I'll try and contact Sheryl . . . About an hour, but you can start the patient on dialysis as soon as she arrives. My opinion . . . for at least two hours before surgery to detox the blood and give the new kidney the least chance of rejection . . . I'm on my way."

Steven closed his phone, then turned to Sheryl, a huge grin on his face.

"*Yes!*" he yelled, emptying his lungs. "*I knew he would buy it!* Now here's the scoop . . ."

* * *

"How is the patient, sis?" Steven asked; he was busy with the "night getup" and the Madame Tussaud replica of the late Derek Newman, right down to the false moustache and even the mole below his right eye.

"His vital signs are all good, if that's what you're asking, but, Steven, we need to hurry, as we only have about one and a half hours before Father returns to the land of the living."

Steven had already finished dressing in his black hoodie, baseball cap, and shades and was good to go.

"*Christ, Steven,* you really look like Newman. You scare the friggin' crap out of me." Sheryl was shaking her head.

"Sis, slip into that dark tracksuit and sneakers, and don't forget the shoulder-length red wig and the aviators, just to be safe."

"Steven, let's go through this one more time . . . You take the Mercedes truck to transport Father to a park bench in Central Park as near to the main road as possible. To make sure the van can't be traced, you use double-sided tape to overlay the existing number plates with the false ones you stole from the wrecker's yard. We make Father look like a bum suffering from an overdose or too much meth. Then you phone from a public booth, dialling 911, *emergency ambulance.* We park in an inconspicuous place, out of sight until we make sure the ambulance has arrived and Father is safe."

"You're on the ball, sis, but there's one small thing you have overlooked. How to get the donor organ to the Austin . . . Here's what I plan to do . . ."

* * *

"Let me get this straight . . . *You are delivering the Eski by taxi personally?* Christ, Steven, *are you fucking serious?*"

"Let me finish, Sheryl . . . Here's the deal . . . You follow me in my car and park it out of sight. I call a cab to take me to the Austin and deliver the organ to the front desk personally. I explain to the night sister that this is a 'code one' alert transplant delivery, and that the professor is waiting for it to arrive. By the time she hangs on the phone, I'll be long gone, and that's where you come in. You pick me up in the Fairlane, and I drive you back in the Mercedes. We change the number plates, and then we switch, and you drive the van back to Fort Knox and park it out of sight, then pick up your Beamer from the car park and head for home. I arrive at the hospital about fifteen minutes later, and no one suspects. Tomorrow I return the van, and who is any the wiser . . . *Oh, there's just one more thing!* I need to find out where the nearest emergency hospital is to Central Park . . . Hang on while I dial directory inquiries."

*　*　*

"Of course, Huntington Hospital, 270 Park Avenue, emergency and 'after hours' . . . And the phone number . . . Just a sec operator, while I go get a pen and paper . . . 11743279 . . . Got it. Thanks again and have a good evening." Steven turned his sister, who was taking it all in. "You got the gist of that, sis. I forgot about Huntington, and it's less than five minutes from the park. I'll go fetch the van and then once Father is settled down, I'll drop you off to pick up for the Fairlane . . ."

*　*　*

It had just turned eleven forty-five and now almost two hours after the kidney surgery. The traffic was exceptionally light, and Steven was making good time.

"I'll reach Central Park if all goes well in another ten." Steven spoke out loud while constantly glancing in his side mirror to check on Sheryl to make sure she was keeping a safe distance behind. The drill was he would signal when he reached the perfect spot to offload. The temperature had dropped below zero, and that was a worry, but with the emergency hospital only five minutes away, hopefully there shouldn't be a problem, he subconsciously kept reassuring himself.

"This looks like the perfect spot with the park bench right on the sidewalk . . . I'll signal to sis."

He pressed the emergency triangle for only a few seconds with the flashing yellow lights, he didn't want to draw unnecessary attention and hit the indicator switch, slowly pulling into the curb while glancing into his side mirror one more time to make sure Sheryl had pulled in a good fifty yards behind.

"Sis, you are doing a great job." Steven smiled as he planked the sidewalk. "Come on, sis, hurry, hurry, I need your help." He called as he gingerly opened the rear door of the Mercedes.

"Easy, Sheryl . . . Gently . . . Okay, he's comfortable . . ."

Suddenly a car pulled up in front of them, and a young man in his midtwenties dressed in a heavy windbreaker hit the sidewalk running.

"Can I help you guys?" he called, screeching to a halt.

"It's okay, we found this poor guy lying on the sidewalk, and we placed him on the park bench. He looks in bad shape and needs urgent medical attention to get him out of the cold, or he'll suffer from hyperthermia which could be fatal . . . Say, eh?"

Something suddenly crossed Steven's mind. *Was this a problem or an opportunity?*

"Bob," the dude replied.

"*Bob,* can you be a good Samaritan and call 911? I was in such a hurry to complete a delivery for FedEx . . . I forgot my phone. We are a delivery subcontractors, and this crate has to be at JF within the hour to catch an international flight to Europe."

"No sweat, I understand. I'll call 911 right now, and you guys can be on your way. Your name is?" He turned to Steven, but before he could finish, they were both already in the van, disappearing into the night traffic. "Strange . . . Well, at least I have the license number . . ."

*   *   *

Steven was really legging it; in fact, he was almost on the verge of sprinting down the hospital driveway, but where was his sister? The snow had just started to flake, and in the street lighting, his visibility was severely clouded.

"Ah, there she is!"

He spotted Sheryl slowly driving the vintage Fairlane down the avenue, now only fifty yards away from the hospital entrance, and Steven breathed a sigh of relief as he cautiously turned and looked either way before waving her down.

"Move over, sis, I'll drive. Nice timing. Just direct me to where you parked the van, then you can be on your way."

"How did it go?" Sheryl still looked stressed.

"*Like a Swiss watch, sis . . . Like a Swiss watch,*" Steven repeated himself, a proud grin smothering his face.

"*God, Steven,* do I feel relieved! Listen, we're almost there. The van is parked just out of sight down that side street to your left. I can get out here to save you the trouble."

"*Are you serious?* No way! I'll drive you there. At this time of night, who knows, you might *lose* a kidney." Steven was laughing at his own macabre humour.

"*What kind of joke is that?*" Sheryl shook her head in disgust. "Ciao . . ." She opened the car door. "*Call me,*" she answered rudely.

"Sis, calls can be traced. We'll meet in the hospital cafeteria first thing tomorrow over a coffee. *Oh* . . . One other thing! Switch off your cell. Cranmer might be trying to contact you. Listen, sis, I'm sorry about that stupid insensitive comment. Drive carefully, and thanks again, honey, you did good, and remember, because of our so-called heinous deed, someone and their family are given the greatest gift of all . . . *A second chance at life . . .*"

*   *   *

"I'll leave you to close, Steven, I'll go clean up and inform the family of the good news."

"Sure, Jim, that's not a problem. The family can come and visit the patient in intensive care in around thirty minutes."

As Steven studied this young woman's face, her cheeks now changing from a pale yellow to a healthy pink, he knew he had done the right thing and had no regrets.

*   *   *

Cranmer, although fatigued, always got the greatest pleasure to take time out to speak personally with the recipient's family to tell them the "state of the nation," especially good news, and tonight although the circumstances unusual, it was still an adrenaline rush.

As he approached the waiting room, he could see the drawn, anxious looks on the faces of the relatives—the mother, the father, and what appeared to be the patient's husband. A small boy around three years old was fast asleep in his grandmother's arms, a scene Cranmer was more than familiar with.

"Don't rise . . . Please sit," Cramer reassured them.

The male in his mid-thirties seemed more anxious than the others and couldn't wait to beg the question.

"Doctor, I'm Jennifer's husband. I apologize but . . ."

"There's no need to apologize, Mr. Donkin's, I fully understand your anxiety . . . The good news is, everything went exceptionally well. Your wife will be transferred to intensive care shortly, then you can briefly go and visit her. The next twenty-four hours is critical, as there could be a chance of

rejection, but at this stage, I feel it's highly unlikely."

"Doctor, how can we ever thank you?" The husband was almost in tears.

"It's the donor you must thank, but unfortunately I can't give you his name, as his kidney was donated from a private clinic while stressing the donor's request for anonymity . . ."

CHAPTER 12

As the professor slowly walked to his office, he was feeling more than fatigued. At this time in the morning and after a gruelling four-hour operation, he was showing his age, and who could blame him?

"Ah! Steven. I was just heading to the intensive care unit, but you have saved me the journey."

"You look bushed, Jim," Steven commented.

"It's not a case of *looking . . . I am!* At my age and . . ." Jim glanced at his watch. "Nearly three thirty in the morning, I think it's about time I called it a night."

"A cup of coffee?" Steven smiled.

"*Aw, well,* if you put it that way." Cranmer smiled. "Come to my office, and maybe we could indulge in something a bit stronger." Cranmer gave Steven a wry smile.

* * *

"Grab a seat . . . I don't know about you, Steven, but my legs are sending me a signal."

Cranmer sat down heavily in his leather exec chair, then stooped to open the lower drawer of his desk.

"*Ah here we are!*" He placed the half-empty bottle of single malt and two glasses on the desk.

"I only partake on special occasion, and I think tonight fits the bill." He poured two small measures, then smiled again. "It's not befitting for two prominent surgeons to smell of alcohol. After all, what would the patients think, huh?" He smiled again and lifted his glass. "Cheers, to once again a successful transplant."

"Cheers." Steven touched Cranmer's glass with the familiar ringing tone of crystal.

"There's something I wanted to discuss with you, Steven, and I felt tonight, or should I say this morning, is as good a time as any."

Cranmer took another small sip of the scotch. "Hmmm . . . *Good!*" He sort of smacked his lips. "It's like this, Steven . . . I'm now sixty-three years of age, and like all good thoroughbreds"—he smiled again—"it's about time to retire and enjoy the rest of my life in green pastures. Which . . ." He took another sip. "Brings me to the point that I need to train someone to take my place. You are an excellent surgeon but also a good administrator, and it is my intention to recommend to the board your promotion to assistant director of surgery, that is . . . if you do me the honour of accepting?"

Steven was taken aback. "*Eh . . . Err* . . . I'm lost for words . . . I don't know what to say."

"So I gather that's a yes." Cranmer was grinning all over.

"But my age and there's . . ."

"Leave that to me. *Yes*, there will be ripples as you will most certainly be the youngest assistant director of surgery in the history of the Austin. But times change. The world is moving faster, and younger people are eager to embrace with open arms new technology and new challenges in the field of medicine. Research and development is at the forefront of medical science, and who knows, in less than a decade, we may see organs regrown and cloned using stem cells . . . *So?*"

"I'm honoured, Jim."

Cranmer sat back in his chair, a satisfied look on his face. "Well, Steven." Cranmer emptied his glass. "I think that's enough drama for one night. The next time I open this bottle is when I retire and you are sitting in this chair."

Cranmer opened the booze drawer and tucked the single malt away for another day.

"There's one more thing, Steven, before you go . . . *The donor kidney!* The pathology report was excellent in that the kidney was expertly removed by a highly qualified surgeon using all the latest preservatives and flushing techniques. The blood samples supplied were checked for abnormalities or disease and given a clean bill of health. It was almost too good to be true. But did I do the right thing? And this person, the Hood, is this the start of something that might get out of control, and can the hospital be held liable for not reporting the incident to the police? I intend to call an extraordinary meeting with the board tomorrow and explain the unusual circumstances."

"Jim, whatever . . . You did the right thing. If you need my support for the meeting, don't hesitate."

"Thanks, Steven, I knew I could depend on you. Get your stuff, and I'll accompany you to the car park."

"I'm gonna stay, Jim. I'll use the staff quarters for some shut eye. I want to keep an eye on our patient, bearing in mind the unusual circumstances."

"I understand. Then I'll catch you in the morning. I might be a bit late . . . Good night, Steven, or should I say good morning . . ."

* * *

"*Tutt . . . Tuttt . . . Bill, answer the bloody phone.*" Jan was pissed off as she waited patiently for Bill to answer her call, the motor running.

The loud ring of the phone made Bill cringe, and he placed the pillow over his head to kill the noise.

"*Go away . . . Go away!*" he yelled. "Aw, well then." He fumbled across the bedside table, searching for the receiver. "Fuck it!" he cussed as the phone clattered to the floor.

Jan shook her head; it was all too familiar. "And what were my last words?" she complained to herself.

"Yeah . . . Yeah . . . Who's this?"

"Jan . . . Remember me? *Your partner.*"

"*Eh* . . . Oh . . . Jan . . . I'm sorry, I must have overslept. It's that bloody alarm clock again."

"Yeah and pull the other leg."

"Jan, gimme fifteen minutes, and I'll be down."

"No way, I'm coming up."

"Are you sure you can take it?" She could hear Bill laughing.

"*That guy . . .*" She shook her head and opened the car door, the icy blast making her shiver. "*Christ, it's cold out!*" She pulled up her coat collar.

Jan impatiently pressed the security buzzer. "Come on you, moron . . . *Hurry . . . Hurry.*" She stomped her feet in the cold.

Suddenly the security latch buzzed, and the door opened.

"*At last!*" She hastened to the elevator and pressed the button.

* * *

The apartment house was low to middle class, and as Jan walked the musty, stained, carpeted hallway, she couldn't help but ask herself why Bill stayed in this dump. It wasn't as if he couldn't afford better on a lieutenant's salary, and the alimony problem was now long gone. *"I give up,"* she muttered under her breath as she pressed the doorbell.

"Coming . . ." Bill opened the door looking worse for wear, a bath towel wrapped around his waist.

"Boy, are you a sight for sore eyes! Do you know what time it is?" Jan barked.

"Don't remind me. Listen, I'll only be another ten minutes while I shave and dress. Make yourself at home, you know where the coffee is."

"I should. I've done this so many times." Jan walked to the coffee table and picked up the empty bottle of Johnnie, then dropped it in the garbage bucket accompanying the five or six empty Buds. "Musta had a helluva party last night . . . Now where's that coffee?"

*   *   *

"Come on, don't be so bad natured. I said thank you for the coffee, didn't I?" Bill was trying to lighten it up as they drove to Pearl Street.

A slight grin crossed Jan's face. Who could be upset with this joker?

"Ten o'clock, and I can just imagine Mitchel's face when we arrive." Jan shook her head.

"You worry too much, Jan. Don't worry leave it to me." "Yeah, that's exactly *what* I worry about!"

*   *   *

Sheryl nervously lifted the receiver in the public phone booth and dialed the number. 1-174-3279.

"Good morning . . . Huntington Hospital, emergency department." Sheryl slipped in the ten-cent coins.

"Eh, good morning, I wonder if you can help me. It's regarding a 911 call to attend a gentleman found lying on a park bench in Central Park late yesterday evening?"

"May I ask who is calling?"

"My father is missing, and I wondered if it is the same person."

"I'm sorry, I am no allowed to give personal information over the phone unless you can identify yourself.

"I'm asking you please." Sheryl laid on the "Elizabeth Taylor."

"All I can tell you is that a man was picked up by paramedics that fits your description. He is in intensive care and out of danger. I'm sorry, I can't give you his name, as there is a police investigation in progress. *Hello . . . Hello . . ."*

*   *   *

Mitchel was in the midst of his coffee break when "Homicide's finest" finally arrived. Stace knocked on his boss's window, then pointed. Mitchel nodded and picked up the phone.

The desk phone rang, and Jan automatically looked toward Mitchel's office; she could see him with the phone to his ear.

"You know who's on the end of *that call*, Bill, don't you?"

"Don't tell me, let me guess." Bill just laughed. Same old Bill.

"In my office now and bring Martin with you." There was a loud crash as the receiver hit the cradle.

Bill held the phone away from his ear.

"Something tells me Mitchel isn't happy . . . I wonder why?" *"Get out of it, Hayden . . . Let's face the music."*

* * *

"Sit." Mitchel pointed to the empty chairs. "At least this time you have both arrived before lunch. I suppose I should be thankful for small mercies.

Is there something funny, Hayden? If there is, then don't keep it to yourself. Let us all in on the joke."

Bill just shrugged; he was on a loser no matter what.

"Now would it be too much to ask what happened on the missing person? A one Mike Summers who mysteriously disappeared from a pub night while on parole?"

"What do you want?" Bill retaliated. "So the guy takes time out. It's nothing new with parolees. I told Clark, his parole officer, that the deal is we wait forty-eight, and if he doesn't turn up, we issue a missing person report and take it from there."

"And that's it?"

"You tell me, Glen?"

"I want decent detective work, that's what I want, and that's what the taxpayer pays you for . . . Hayden, for the life of me, I can't get a handle on you. You're a loose cannon with no respect for authority. You lost your partner nine years ago . . . *Get over it,* or so help me, one more step outta line, and I'll fire both of you, and if you don't think I can juice it . . . *Try me!*"

Bill looked deadpan at Mitchel. He was a hard nut to crack, showing no emotion.

"Now for your information, the invisible Mr. Summers has mysteriously turned up in the emergency unit at Huntington Hospital on Park Avenue and is now in intensive care, recovering from a kidney snatch. *You heard right,*

Hayden. Someone or some persons surgically removed one of his kidneys without his permission. So, I'm ordering you and Sergeant Martin to get off your asses and go over there right now and report back to me ASAP. I want to keep this under wraps from the media. If they find out, they will blow it out of all proportions like the Bay Harbor Butcher. The next thing we know, it will be the New York Kidney Snatcher. Any questions? I didn't think so . . . *Get outta my sight before I change my mind.*"

Bill took his seat at his desk, then swung around his chair to face Jan. "*Do you think Mitchel was annoyed?*"

*   *   *

"I thought I would catch you here."

"Good morning, sis. Can I get you something?" Steven looked up, his eyes dark circled from fatigue.

"Stay where you are, Steven, you look washed out. I can get my own coffee."

Sheryl was back in a heartbeat, sitting beside her brother in the hospital cafeteria, anxious to find out how the kidney transplant went.

"*God!* You look really fatigued, Steven." She took a sip of her coffee, a concerned look on her face.

"Yeah, I stayed up all night just to make sure there were no complications, and now after three years our patient, can't believe she is passing urine. I'll never forget that look on her face when I held up the urine collection bag. But I've got more good news for you . . . Would you believe Cranmer is going to recommend to the hospital board that I be promoted to assistant director of surgery?"

"*Steven* . . . That *is* fantastic! But boy, will there be few noses out of joint."

"The very point I made to Cranmer, but he just shrugged it off."

"Steven." Sheryl looked uncomfortable. "I have a confession to make . . . I phoned the hospital to check on Father to make sure he was all right."

"*You what!* Are you crazy?"

"Keep your voice down, Steven, and let me finish . . . I phoned from a public booth, *I'm not that stupid!*"

"*Hell, sis,* you had me worried there for a moment."

"Calm down . . . He's recovering well in intensive care."

"Well, that's good news, but I had no doubt about his recovery. *Now* he's finally paid his *real debt* to society!"

"Steven, you're so unremorseful. My advice to you is to go home and get some shut eye and when you wake up, hopefully you will be in a more pleasant mood. Listen, I'll give you a call later in the afternoon."

"I think I'll take your advice, sis, it's been one helluva long night!"

* * *

"*What did I tell you?* This bastard Summers is going to be the death of me. I should have wasted him when I had the chance in Argentina."

"You don't really mean that, Bill, now, do you?"

"*You stupid bastard!*" Jan yelled, thumping the horn as the BMW cut her up, the driver giving her the one finger in retaliation. "I've a good mind to pull that moron over and give him a piece of my mind . . . *Eh,* what was I was saying?"

"About Summers . . . Yeah, if I had my time over again, he would have unfortunately died from gunshot wounds resisting arrest." "*You know, I really believe you.*" Jan was taken aback.

"That dude is rotten to the core. Besides I would have saved the state the cost of his jail time."

It was a lost cause, and Jan decided to change the subject.

"We've arrived, in case you haven't noticed." She signalled and turned into the hospital car park.

The morning temperature had dropped even lower, and the snowflakes were now falling freely.

"Jan, try and park as near to the entrance as possible. Even 'brass monkeys' would complain about *this* weather."

"I'll try my best. Hell, Bill, you are behaving like an old man."

"What do you mean, *like?*"

"*Get out of it!* Lieutenant, we got work to do."

They had just entered reception when they bumped into Bob Clark, Summers's parole officer, on his way out.

"Something told me that I would bump into you guys . . . It's Summers, all right. He seems to be recovering well, when considering he woke up with only one kidney." Clark sighed, shaking his head. "*Can you believe it?*"

"Bob, in our line of work, you get to a stage where you come to believe anything."

"*Hmmm,* I guess so." Clark shrugged. "He's in good form. Bill, I would appreciate if you come up with something to bring me up to speed."

"Done deal," Bill replied. "Listen, we must go, Bob, my ears are still burning from Mitchel's roasting this morning."

"Like that, *huh?* I'll wait for your call . . . *Ciao.*"

*   *   *

As the detectives approached the front desk, the duty sister stared up from her screen, happiness not being one of her attributes. She had that "old war horse" look, like a veteran from Teddy Roosevelt's last charge at Kettle Hill. Most likely in her late fifties, and with that ridiculous "Florence Nightingale" starched cap perched on her swept-back grey hair, she spelled trouble with a capital *t*. Her penetrating blue eyes encircled with the dreaded crow's feet blended in well with her lean, wrinkled complexion and narrow orange peeled lips complemented with the yellowed ivories, she was definitely not "Leonardo's lady with the smile." But shift sisters in Emergency have to be admired; be it gunshot wounds, stabbings, overdoses, or just plain ordinary heart attacks, you just never know what's coming through that door . . .

*   *   *

"Yes?"

"I'm Detective Lieutenant Hayden, and this is Detective Sergeant Martin from NYPD Homicide."

"Lieutenant, I'm busy, get to the point."

"We are here to interview a Mr. Michael Summers who was admitted to Emergency late yesterday evening."

"Can I see your credentials?" The "war horse" barked.

"*In public?*" Bill couldn't help himself; it was too good to miss.

The look she gave Bill was a "Friday the thirteenth" job, and the message was loud and clear.

"*Sarcasm is not becoming, Detective!*"

Bill took it on the chin and just shrugged; the sister was his match, and on seeing the gold shield, she nodded in silence.

"Second floor . . . At the end of the corridor, you'll see in large capital letters on the wall, 'IC.' For the uneducated, that means 'Intensive Care.' Check with the nurse in charge. Now if there's nothing else?" She was back on the screen.

Bill turned to Jan, who was now grinning all over, with a "let's go" look.

"*Boy!* Did she put you in *your* place?"

"Okay . . . Okay . . . So, you win a few, you lose a few."

"With that broad, there's no winners." Jan couldn't contain her laughter as they walked to the elevator.

*   *   *

"Excuse me, sir." The young nurse blocked their paths to the IC unit. "Can I help you?"

"We're from NYPD Homicide, to interview Mr. Summers. Your *boss* at the front desk gave us the green light."

"Sister McGregor?" "Yeah, that name would fit." The nurse's smile said it all.

"Come with me, but you can only stay fifteen minutes. Mr. Summers is still not out of the woods as yet, and stress in his condition is not recommended."

"I understand, Nurse. We'll try our best," Bill replied, this time no more wisecracks.

*   *   *

"*Driver,* this is fine. You can drop me here."

"Sure thing, buddy. That'll be thirty-five fifty. Are you sure you want dropped off here? In this weather, *man*?"

"I like walking in the snow. Besides, I need the exercise." Steven laughed as he gave the cabbie two twenties. "Keep the change."

"Whatever turns you on, dude, but thanks for the tip." He cleared the meter, then drove into the slow-moving traffic.

It was about a mile's walk to Bloomfield Street and Pier 50, leading to Fort Knox Self-Storage. Steven had parked the Fairlane there when he returned to pick up the Mercedes Sprinter to return it to Hertz, hence the reason for the cab ride. The "hand back" went like clockwork, with no suspicions, but now he had to get out of his disguise and return to his apartment on West Street to decide the next Hood victim. As for Derek Newman, he was definitely now deceased.

Steven was looking forward to some R&R, and when he finally drove into the underground car park, he felt more than relieved. It had been a hectic two days, not to mention the strenuous drive through the falling snow and snailing traffic. He parked the car and gave a shiver, wasting no time in reaching the elevator. It had just turned four in the afternoon, and a cup of hot coffee was a dream. He pressed 6. "Come on come on." His breath was freezing in the below-zero temperature.

"At last." The elevator chimed.

*   *   *

856

The coffee went down a treat, the heating on full blast; it doesn't get any better. Steven was already in his stockinged feet, sitting in front of his laptop, enjoying turkey on rye.

"Somehow, I have to find information from the Correction Services data bank of the most recent parolee releases for 'white collar' crime now staying at halfway houses." He was frantically searching the Net while talking out loud.

"*Got it!* Now let me see . . . The parole board has to be kidding, letting this guy on the streets . . . Dennis Watters's Ponzi scheme stole millions from gullible retirees with get-rich schemes . . . Monies never recovered, and he gets sentenced to five years and is released after three for good behaviour. *Would you believe that shit?* Now where's this dog staying?"

* * *

Summers was propped in the hospital bed, an array of tubes from his nose to his wrists like a high-rise with external plumbing, but taking it all into consideration, he didn't look too bad, considering he was firing on one kidney. He was sipping a drink through a straw when the detectives approached, and he quickly stopped and placed the drink aside.

"I suppose you are here to see me?"

"You got that right, Summers! Do you remember me?" Hayden asked, venom in his voice.

"Don't gimme nightmares. I'm feeling like shit as it is."

"Cut the carnival, Mike, we are here to take a statement, and the quicker we get to it, the quicker we'll get out of your hair. This is my partner, Detective Sergeant Martin."

"There's no need for the drama, Hayden, I've been there before." Summers had just raised the bar.

Jan already had her notepad in her hand. "Shoot, Bill."

"*Don't tempt me!* So, Summers, let's hear the song."

"Nothing to sing . . . I was at Kelly's Irish Pub with a lady friend, minding my own business, when I decided to go out to the side alley for a smoke."

"So?"

"I was busy filing my lungs when this young broad approached me. Maybe she was doing tricks. Anyhow she bwas a looker. Shoulder-length red hair, a postage stamp that was supposed to resemble a skirt, tits that were desperate to see the sun, and legs that you could only imagine where they went. Anyhow she offers me round the world at a price that was too hot to ignore. The next thing I know, someone did a Dexter on me, and I wake up in intensive care with one of my filters gone." *"And that's it?"* Bill asked.

"So what do you want, a movie script?"

"Is there nothing else you can remember?"

"Yeah, there is . . . It's bad enough losing a kidney, but my pocketbook is another thing. *Can you believe it!* I get fucking robbed into the bargain. My driver's license and five big ones." "Strange." Bill turned to Jan.

"It somehow doesn't seem to fit the crime scene."

"I agree, Bill. I've taken your statement, Summers. It will be typed up and returned to you for signing."

"Aren't you going to caution me? I mean I broke my parole conditions, stepping out and consuming alcohol." Summers was being sarcastic.

"Don't be a smart-ass, Summers or I might just read you your rights. Let's go, Jan, the smell in here is getting to me." The detectives turned to leave.

"So when will I have the pleasure again?" Summers fired a parting shot. Jan grabbed Bill's arm. "Don't, he's not worth it . . ."

*   *   *

"So where do we start, Bill?" Jan asked as they stood in the elevator.

"We have very little to go on, but the petty robbery bothers me. Let's go back to our friend at the front desk to find out who the person was that called 911. I'll let you speak to her."

"Coward."

CHAPTER 13

"Robert Anderson, and his address?"

Jan checked her notes. "Nineteen Hellock Street, a rooming house in the Bronx next to Hunts Point Meat Market."

"Nice address. At least he can get a good steak," Bill joked.

"I know the location. Full of low-class rooming joints and all the problems that go with it."

"Yeah, I wish I had a ten spot for every time we've been there. Life is cheap in that dump, a hot pot for homicides, drugs, pimps, and grand theft auto. When we get to the car, Jan, I'll call in to do 'a make' on this dude. Turn the motor, Jan and get some heat into this heap. I'm gonna keep on my jacket until my circulation returns."

"I don't blame you." Jan laughed while pulling her collar up.

"Nicky, it's Bill Hayden here. Listen, I need you to 'do a make' on this guy . . . His name is Robert Anderson. Yes, Caucasian. Last known address . . . Jan, gimme that address again . . . It's 19 . . ."

"Just give me a few minutes, Bill . . . Here we are . . . You got a nice one . . . Robert Anderson, Caucasian, born 1975, convicted one count armed robbery, sentenced five to ten. Convicted grand theft auto and suspected burglary with intent of bodily harm, sentenced one to five. Released on parole six months ago."

"Thanks, Nicky, I owe you one . . . Ciao."

"Bill, that makes a bit more sense."

"Yeah, let's go and visit our friend. This should be interesting, and if my hunch is right, he'll be up to no good and on welfare . . ."

*   *   *

Jan pulled the car into the sidewalk just outside the run-down rooming house. The bums hanging around the doorways sheltering from the cold suddenly evaporated into thin air; the smell of the law does wonders.

"Jan, stay close behind me. I need backup, and make sure your weapon is locked and loaded. In this part of town, they will sell their mother if the price is right."

Bill glanced at the almost-illegible occupant's register on the graffitied lobby wall.

"Second floor, Jan."

"I'm with you, Bill." The detectives cautiously climbed the stairs in almost total darkness, the light globes long gone.

"Nineteen." Bill signalled to Jan to get ready as he cocked his police special and banged on the door.

"Police open up . . . *Open up now!*"

"For fuck's sake, Angie, gimme that that joint and the rest of the swag. I'll go flush it down the john."

"Are fucking serious? That's all we have!"

"Shut up, bitch, and go cover yourself up and let me do the talking."

Anderson pulled on his grubby jocks and rushed to the toilet, flushing it twice just to make sure.

"*For the last time, open up, or we'll smash the door down!*" Bill screamed, banging on the door with the grip of his forty-five.

Suddenly the door opened, with Bill being confronted with a half-naked man looking like shit, his bony frame in need of a decent wash and a good meal. The unshaved face, the unruly matted hair, the bloodshot eyes and tobacco-stained lips, the needle-potted arms—all clues to an interrupted dope session.

"Back off, mister." Bill pointed the loaded Browning at Mr. Universe's forehead.

"Hold it . . . Hold it, I'm not resisting, *eh, err*, Detective." Bill flashed his gold shield.

"Just stay where you are, buddy, and remain cool. Jan, search the joint for drugs and firearms. *And you lady.*" Bill pointed his semiautomatic at the broad sitting in bed holding up the sheet to cover what once used to be her precious assets, but drugs and booze had taken their toll, and they were now dead volcanoes. "Get dressed and get your ass outta here before you go down for three."

The broad didn't think twice; she was dressed and gone, leaving a vapor trail.

"Ah, what have we got here?" Jan called. "Look what the cat dragged in . . . A forty-five Smith and Wesson, which I assume is unlicensed, and a pocketbook with three one-hundred-dollar bills containing a driver's license belonging to one Michael Summers. Now unless that's your name, mister, you had better start singing like a canary."

"Cuff him, Jan."

"Listen, I can explain."

"I'm listening." Bill pointed to the empty cot. "*Sit!*"

"My name is Bob Anderson, and yesterday evening . . ."

"So you saw this poor guy lying on a park bench and called 911."

"Yeah, I mean I saved this guy's life, didn't I? He was in a bad way. At least, that's what the paramedics told me. I thought I might get a reward or some kind of recognition from the mayor. You know the kinda stuff you see in the papers and on the TV all the time. *Detective* . . . All I'm asking for is a break. I'm on parole, and I've been keeping my nose clean, but an ex-con with no job and on welfare? I mean the temptation of this guy's wallet was just too much."

"Not good enough, Anderson, you have to do better than that."

"Better than that! What the fuck do you mean?" Anderson was losing it.

"*Admit it* . . . You're in the 'organs for sale' market just like they do in India. Kidneys . . . livers . . . You name it."

"What the fuck are you talking about? *Are you fucking crazy!*"

"If I didn't know your criminal record, you're so convincing, I could almost believe you." But Bill was running out of patience. "Now listen, fuckhead, here's the deal, and it's nonnegotiable. You rat on your accomplice and spill the beans on the syndicate, and I talk a deal with your probation officer. We put you in the protection program, and you start a new life after you testify."

"Are you fucking crazy? I swear, you got the wrong guy."

"*Okay, Jan, cuff him.* Buddy, I threw you the olive branch, but doing hard time in the pen seems more attractive. Only this time they'll throw the key away. *Cappice?*"

"*Okay . . . Okay . . .* Hold it. This is the truth, so help me." Anderson held his hands above his head in protest.

"I wasn't the first to find this guy. I just made it up to be the hero. When I pulled up in front of this white van, there was this guy and a chick there already and . . ."

"And the guy?"

"I didn't get a real good look at his face. He was wearing a hoodie, but I noticed a large mole on the right side of his face below the eye, and oh, he had a moustache. It struck me as odd why the guy would wear shades at this time of night and didn't have a cell phone in his line of work because of some shit lame excuse."

"And the woman?"

"Pretty face, probably in her midtwenties, also in a hoodie, but I did notice her shoulder-length red hair."

"And the van?"

"Some model of Mercedes, but when they drove off, I felt there was something wrong, and I took the registration number . . . AYP 9976."

"Cuff him, Jan, and read him his rights."

"But you said if I cooperated . . ."

"My advice to you, Anderson, *never trust a cop . . .*"

* * *

(Back at Pearl Street HQ)

"Book him, Sarge."

"What's the charge, Bill?"

"Robbery . . . I'll sign in this wallet and its contents as evidence. Don't bother with the mug shots and printing. He has a rap sheet already and is on parole. Pete, maybe you can contact his parole officer."

"Sure thing, Bill."

"I hope your fucking dog dies, Hayden." "Get him outta my sight, Pete."

* * *

"How about we grab a cup of coffee, Jan? I need one. I don't know about you."

"Cafeteria or at our desks?" Jan grinned.

"Cafeteria . . . If Mitchel spots us, it will be into his office and another Mexican standoff."

"*I'm amazed.* This is the first time you're not behaving like 'Conan the Barbarian'."

"Is that a compliment?" Bill laughed.

"If the cap fits . . . Now who's on the coffees?"

"Grab a table, Jan, I think it's my time. Feeling hungry?" "A sandwich wouldn't go astray. You choose . . ."

* * *

"Hmmm . . . This is good." Jan was relaxing; after all it was past three in the afternoon. Detective work has no boundaries, and regular-time lunches are unfortunately one of the many luxuries you forfeit.

"I know there's something in that mind of yours. *Come on, don't keep me in suspense.*

"Don't talk with your mouth full. Didn't your mother ever tell you?"

"Okay, *Mother*, get to the point?"

"Firstly, the number plate was a 'no-no' from a Pontiac Deville that had been crushed ten years ago. *Now the Mercedes van . . .* That's a different kettle of fish! It's just a pity Anderson didn't know the model, but on the other hand there are only a few. So we check up with the manufacturer for the sales of the most popular model and colour."

"But where to from there, Bill?" Jan was puzzled.

"We get a handle on the most sales of Mercedes vans in white and in New York for the last twelve months. These vehicles are normally popular with small businesses, courier services, and rental companies. It's a hunch but a long one, and we gotta start somewhere."

"And Mitchel?"

"*He can fucking wait . . .*"

"And *I* thought 'Conan' was dead!"

*   *   *

"Sheryl, when are you free at the hospital?" Steven was on the phone to his sister. "Around five . . . Can you pop in on the way home? So buy him a pizza or something or, better still, treat him to romantic dinner on me. I'm sure I can afford it when my promotion comes through . . . What's it about? I'll tell you when we meet . . . So, I can expect you around say . . . six to six thirty, depending on the traffic . . . *Of course I'm serious about that romantic dinner!* Ciao, sis."

*   *   *

As the detectives returned to their desks fearing the worst from Mitchel, they were pleasantly surprised. For some reason, the captain had left early.

"That's a change," Bill commented as he took his chair. "Must have gone brown nosing it with the DA or some high-ranking senator to further his ill-gotten career."

"*Bill,* have you nothing good to say about our illustrious boss?" Jan was being jokingly sarcastic.

"*No.*"

"*That's it!*" Jan laughed.

"The Mercedes van, remember?"

*   *   *

"What have we got, Jan?"

"According to the Mercedes New York office, I spoke with the marketing director, a new model was launched at the beginning of this year and has been very popular. It's the Mercedes Sprinter van V6 diesel 85 with the largest sales in white going to Hertz Rental."

"That makes sense. I'll contact Hertz's New York office and explain our investigation and request their assistance." Bill lifted the phone and dialled.

"Operator, can you put me through to Hertz Rental's head office in New York City please?"

"And you rented out eleven vans in the last ten days? Thanks, Mr. Denver, I would really appreciate that . . . Our fax number. It's 97881 . . ."

"Now we are getting someplace, Jan." Bill placed back the phone, a wide grin on his face. "My real worry is, are we going down the wrong track and the van is owned by a private individual or company and we have to start all over again."

"That had also crossed my mind, Bill." Jan frowned.

"Stand by that fax machine. According to the accounts department, there are eleven customers. We'll split the number down the middle—five to me and six to you."

"*Gee, thanks*, I'll have to go back to school on that one."

"Sorry, Jan, that's one of the benefits you get with rank. You have to be able to count." Bill was laughing.

The fax machine in front of Mitchel's office rang, then started to spill out an A4 sheet.

"That's our baby."

"Puling rank again, like 'Jan, go and fetch it,' huh?"

"Now whatever gave you that idea?"

"You had better employ a food taster for your next cup of coffee." "*Now you tell me!*" Bill couldn't stop laughing at Jan's comment.

"The Mercedes van, remember?"

"*Touche!*"

*   *   *

"How's it going, Jan?"

"*Heavy!* I've only managed to get through to four, and they are all genuine rentals, three companies and one private . . . And you, Bill?"

"I've had better luck. I'm on my last call, but I'm losing hope fast. Operator, you say there's no such number or company? Can you try once more just to make sure . . . I appreciate that, but this is a police matter. I'm from NYPD Homicide, Lieutenant Hayden . . . It's really important . . . Thanks again." Bill placed back the phone. "Jan, I think we have struck pay dirt. Now I need to phone the Hertz office that rented the van."

"I'll keep my fingers crossed, Bill, and everything else."

Bill laughed again. "I'll try and work that one out later . . ." He held his hand up and pointed to the phone. "Yes, is this Hertz Rental? And you are? Vivian . . . *You are about to close!* Vivian, if you could just give me a few minutes of your time . . . Yes, I know it's late. My name is Hayden, Lieutenant Bill Hayden, NYPD Homicide, working on a case, and your information may be critical in an arrest. Thanks, Vivian, I promise I won't keep you long. It's regarding a rental transaction of a Mercedes Sprinter van to a company named Global Exports, phone number 1800-3568 . . . *That van was returned this morning!* I'll be darned. You see, we phoned that company, and there's no such number. Can you hold the van for CSI evidence like prints and so on? *It's been thoroughly cleaned and is rented out again!* I see . . . But you must have gotten a driver's license for insurance purposes . . . *You have* . . . Sure I'll give you a second to check . . . Yeah, I have it in front of me . . . A Mr. Derek Newman of 26 Dyer Avenue, Manhattan . . . A classy address, huh?" Bill could hear Vivian laugh in the background. "One more thing, Vivian, and I promise I won't keep you any longer than necessary . . . Can you describe this person? There were two people that came to collect the van, wearing orange coveralls with the company logo on the back. *Interesting* . . . Yes, carry on, Vivian, you are doing great . . . A man and woman, you say . . . About five ten, moustache, and a mole on his right cheek and wearing shades . . . And the woman? In her midtwenties. Pretty with shoulder-length red hair . . . And you say they needed the van in a hurry to pick some sort of equipment . . . *Thanks, Vivian*, you're a saviour. Have a good evening and thanks again for all your help . . . Sure, I promise I'll use Hertz." Bill laughed as he dropped the phone. "No more calls, Jan, *we've nailed it!*"

*   *   *

The bell rang. Steven checked his watch. "That must be sis." He cut the TV and went to the security peephole. It was his sis as predicted.

"Gimme a sec, Sheryl." He opened the door. "Thanks for coming. You look *really* cold." Steven gave her a kiss on the cheek. "*Come in . . . Come in.*"

"Coffee?"

"I wouldn't mind one, Steven, but I don't have much time. I'm already in the doghouse with Nelson. I made reservations at Angelo's in Little Italy for eight, and I'm already running late due to that heavy snowfall."

"Well, there's one thing, sis . . . You got style. I'll go pour the coffee. Take off your coat."

"No, Steven, I can't stay, so make it quick . . . Thanks." Sheryl took a sip.

"I have another candidate."

"*Another candidate!*" Sheryl almost choked. "*You mean . . . ?*"

"*Exactly!*"

"Steven . . . I . . ."

"Hold it, sis. Everything went without a hitch, and we can do it again, but you have to believe in what we are doing."

"Steven, however, you dress it up, we are breaking the law, and if we are caught . . . *Well* . . . It doesn't bear thinking. We lose our license to practice medicine for the rest of our lives . . . Struck from the register, not to mention a long prison stretch."

"But that's not gonna happen, sis. I plan everything so meticulously."

"Things can go wrong, Steven . . . How about the guy that stopped his car to help us?"

"That was really a godsend, sis, when you think of it. We used it to our advantage, didn't we?"

"But we might not be so lucky the next time."

"There will be no next time, *trust me.* Now, getting to the point, I have another perfect candidate. His name is Dennis Waters . . ."

* * *

"Operator, can you put me through to Derek Newman of 26 Dyer Avenue, Manhattan?"

"One moment, sir. I'm sorry, sir, that's an unlisted number, but I can put you through to the concierge at Grey's Towers. The address you gave me is for that apartment building."

"I would appreciate that, Operator . . ."

"Grey's Towers. My name is Denver, the night concierge, how can I help you, sir?"

"Can you put me through to a Mr. Derek Newman?"

"Did you say Mr. Derek Newman, sir?"

"Yes."

"Sir, I hope this is not a shock to you, but Mr. Newman passed away almost one year ago. His apartment was sold and now has a new owner."

"Are you sure, Denver?"

"I've been a concierge at Grey's now for over ten years, and I'm absolutely sure. I went to Mr. Newman's funeral."

"Then maybe you can help me, Denver. My name is Hayden, Lieutenant Hayden, NYPD Homicide, and I'm working on a case of stolen identity."

"I see. Anything I can do to help the police, Lieutenant."

"Can you describe Mr. Newman?"

"Yes, I can picture him as if he was standing in front of me right now . . . Around five ten, full head of dark brown hair, always had a neatly trimmed moustache. Pity, he had a large mole below his right eye . . . Age . . . I would say around mid-thirties."

"A young age to pass away. Do you know the reason for his death?"

"Kidney failure, I believe, Lieutenant."

"Thanks, Denver, you've been a great help."

Bill placed the phone back in its cradle, then slouched back exhaling and shrugging his shoulders.

"That bad?"

"Worse!" Bill replied. "But then all is not lost." He smiled. "The phone number was unlisted, and the address is an apartment . . . Grey's Towers, to be precise. However, I managed to speak to the concierge who has been on the front desk for over ten years and remembers all the owners, *especially the ones that go out feet first!"*

"Naw . . ."

"But get this! The description he gave me fits our man to a tee. Even down to the mole on his right cheek."

"No shit!"

"But guess how he died?"

"Don't tell me . . . Kidney failure."

"You got that one right!"

*   *   *

"What's the time, Bill?"

"Yeah, it's getting kinda late. Just turned eight thirty."

"I don't know about you, but I'm feeling peckish." Jan gestured to her empty stomach.

"If you're not spoken for, I'll treat you a burger."

"Chris is working late at the office, he called me, and if you're on the tab, what's a girl like me got to lose?"

"Then come on, let's get outta here, I'm getting sick of seeing this joint every day for the last thirty years."

"I think you are telling me it's time, Bill?"

Jan was hinting at Bill's pending retirement, but he wasn't having a bag of it.

"Oh no you don't! You're not tricking me on that one. Don't worry, Jan, I'll let you know when it's time. Now for that burger."

"The Last Chance?"

"Is there any other?" Bill chucked Jan the car keys.

"Driving again, huh?"

"Age before beauty. Besides, I'm paying. Now get your ass outta here and *stop complaining."*

*   *   *

Steven had to change his plan completely. The use of the van was now out, and the false ID was history, but on the positive side, he had all the equipment he needed for each surgery at Fort Knox. However, transport would be a problem to and fro, and renting could be tricky.

"I'll have to give that more thought." Steven was thinking aloud. "I have a 'mug shot' from the police files. I only hope he hasn't changed that much during his time in prison. And as for the halfway house where he is bunking? Under the freedom of information on parolees, I can easily get that from the data bank. My biggest problem is identifying him, then doing a stakeout to find out his movements, his contacts, and what makes him tick . . . Easier said than done. I'll check out my roster at the hospital for the next few weeks, as nighttime is the best for undercover work and surveillance. *What the hell!*" Steven checked his watch. "I might as well check out his address tonight while there is a window of opportunity."

Having made up his mind, Steven returned to his small study and opened his laptop.

"Now let me see, where do I start?"

(Austin Hospital Day 3)

It was 9:00 a.m., and Cranmer was sitting brooding at his desk, feeling more than a touch uncomfortable. He had called an extraordinary meeting of the hospital board to discuss the ethics and legalities of accepting donor organs from private hospitals gifted from unknown persons as a charitable donation to save the terminally ill. Secondly, he wished to recommend the appointment of Steven as assistant director of surgery . . . His thoughts were suddenly aborted by the loud knock on the door.

"*Come in . . . Steven*, speak of the devil! I was just thinking about you."

"Jim, I apologize that I didn't have a chance to catch up with you yesterday, as I left just after 2:00 p.m. and you hadn't arrived as yet. I was *so* tired after staying all night, I took leave of myself and went home to rest."

"That's not a problem, Steven. You deserve time off. I checked the patient this morning personally, and she is recovering exceptionally well with no sign of rejection at this stage . . . *In fact,* she is doing so well, I recommended that she be transferred from intensive care to a private room tomorrow morning. But on saying that, I'm glad you popped in, as I wanted to inform you of my decision to call an extraordinary meeting of the board, which I wish you to attend. Of course, hot on the agenda is the circumstances in which we received a donor kidney and, of course, not forgetting . . ." Cranmer smiled. "Your appointment as assistant director of surgery."

"Professor, I can't tell you how much I appreciate your faith in me, and I can guarantee my absolute dedication as your assistant."

"Steven, that goes without saying, but more to the point. You are being promoted because you are not only an exceptional surgeon, but you are also blessed with excellent communication and administration skills. In short of all the surgical staff, you are the most qualified to shoulder this additional responsibility."

"When's the meeting planned, Jim, as I have to do my rounds?"

"At 10:00 a.m." Then Cranmer smiled. "Make sure you are on time. Just because you're my assistant, don't copy my bad habits . . ."

* * *

"Well, at least you were waiting for me this morning."

"For once, Jan, I took your advice and hit the sack early and *without* a night cap." Bill closed the car door.

"There's hope for you yet." Jan grinned as she slipped the shift into drive.

The snowploughs had done a good job salting and sanding the roads, although it did nothing for your car. But the traffic was slow, with a few shunts blocking the lanes; the detectives would be lucky to reach Pearl Street before nine thirty.

"*God,* this traffic is shit house, and won't Mitchel be pleased when we stroll into the office after nine?" Jan commented.

"Hey, we gotta have our coffee and donuts first!"

"Don't push the envelope, Bill. You may be retiring soon, but don't forget, I have to live with this eccentric bastard when you're gone."

"Jan don't start this retirement thing again. Concentrate on your driving and think about that coffee and donuts, huh? Changing the subject, why didn't you ask Chris to join us last night for supper?"

"You'll meet him Bill, when the time is right, but how about changing the subject while we're stuck in this traffic and talk about our next move on the Summers case."

"It's like this. Once we clear Mitchel, we head for the city registry to get a copy of Newman's death certificate. That way, we kill two birds with one stone . . . The time and cause of death and the hospital and coroner's report. It's my hunch that someone in that hospital had access to Newman's personal effects after his death."

"But what puzzles me, Bill, is, if your hunch is right, why wait so long before stealing Newman's identity?"

"That is unless someone was planning this for a long time and Newman's death was the catalyst to kick-start the gig. It could have been anyone that ended up in the morgue that day."

"But we are back again to why Summers?"

"Yeah, that's the real curver. Every crime has a motive, and when we crack that one, Jan, the jigsaw will piece together."

"I hate to be a drag, Bill, but the five-million-dollar question has still to be answered."

"And what's that?" Bill was showing his annoyance. *"What happened to the kidney?"*

* * *

Good morning."

The members of the hospital board were already seated in the boardroom, having finished their coffee.

"I'm glad you could all attend this morning's meeting at such short notice . . . Mr. Chairman, do you mind?"

"You called the meeting, Jim, the floor's yours."

Derek Woolsey, the chairman, and Jim Cranmer had had a good relationship, having worked together for many years building the hospital's reputation as the finest transplant facility in the country. The secretary was also seated to take the minutes of the board meeting.

"Mr. Chairman, I wish the board's approval to allow Dr. Summers to attend this meeting, as his input is crucial.

"Approved . . . Seconded . . ."

"Secretary, please note the board's approval."

"Now Jim?"

"Item 1 on the agenda . . . The approval to appoint Dr. Steven Summers as assistant director of surgery, with immediate effect."

"Jim, would you wish to expand on that request for the benefit of the other members of the board?"

"Certainly . . . As you are aware, I have just turned sixty, and it's about time I planned ahead to train someone as my replacement, and that person is Steven Summers. Steven is not only the best transplant surgeon at the Austin, but he has other . . ."

"Approved . . . Seconded."

"I appreciate the board's support. Now the second item on the agenda is more complicated. A approximately 10:00 p.m. on Monday, February 11, I received this e-mail being a 'code one' alert. I have a copy for each of you to read . . ."

"The bottom line, Jim, *you* went ahead with the transplant!"

"Derek, let me explain why, and remember, I would never compromise the reputation of the hospital, let alone put a patient's life in danger . . ."

* * *

"Hmmm, these pathology results are excellent, and the patient has a 90 percent chance of full recovery . . . That makes me and the members of the board relieved . . . Jim, I can understand your ethics in saving a life and the absolute assurances and test results from pathology before you pursued with the surgery. But the question is, who was the anonymous donor, and from what private hospital and the inference of this . . . *this* Hood'? On a legal issue, the hospital has in no way broken the law, and many donors offer their organs while still alive, but the Austin is normally made aware of the donor, and on many occasions, we have surgically removed the organ or are working in conjunction with the private hospital and surgeon involved. This is a difficult decision to give approval."

Woolsey rested his chin on his hand, his elbow on the boardroom table. It was in a difficult dilemma.

"Let's put it to a vote . . . Does the board give approval to accept organs from an anonymous donor, provided all the medical checks and pathology tests are excellent before surgery proceeds?"

"Four for and four against. The chairman has the casting vote . . . For . . ."

"*The motion is carried* . . . Is there any other business? Then I proclaim the board meeting closed."

* * *

"I'll have to buy you two "Navy SEAL" surplus wristwatches." Mitchel glanced at his watch big time. "*That is unless my watch is running two hours fast!*"

"Come on, Glen . . .," Bill began to protest.

"*Captain,* to you, Hayden."

"*Eh,* Captain then." Hayden gave a disgusted look, then shrugged his shoulders before continuing.

"You *know* what the traffic was like this morning . . . *I mean?*" Mitchel rudely cut Bill off at the knees.

"*Was I late? No* . . . For your information, I was at my desk at eight sharp. You don't have to be a homicide detective when there is a heavy downfall of snow to close the case on traffic conditions. Now cut the teardrops and update me on the Summers case."

* * *

"Well, at least you have made some progress, and the death certificate of the mysterious Mr. Newman, if nothing else, will prove the guy has croaked it. *Now I'm busy.* I have a meeting with the DA and the police chief in half an hour . . . *Hold it!* Before you go, I want you to call me anytime in the next twenty-four whenever something breaks, *and Hayden . . .* That doesn't mean whenever you feel like it! Now . . ." Mitchel pointed to the door.

"Ignorant bastard," Bill muttered under his breath as they walked back to their desks. "At least you could talk to Baker when he was captain!"

"Forget it, Bill, Baker's long gone, and we're stuck with this egotistic asshole. The way to beat him is to play him at his own game."

"Maybe you got something there, Jan. As they say, 'it takes a sprat to catch a mackerel'." Bill had that devious look on his face. "Now what's on that mind of yours?" "The Summers case." Bill smiled.

"Yeah, and I don't think!"

* * *

Jan pulled into the car park of the Austin Hospital, the rows of parked cars resembling large mounds of snow as the freezing weather continued to create havoc. The weather bureau's forecast was abysmal and driving home tonight would be another *'Scott of the Antarctic'* minus the dogs and the sleds.

"Maybe Mitchel's got something on the 'Navy Seal' watches, or maybe Eskimo suits would be more useful."

"Get out of it, are you kiddin' me? Now where the hell can I find a space in this blizzard?"

* * *

"This is gonna be interesting, Bill." Jan cut the motor.

"Let's hope the sister at the front desk isn't a repeat of the last one . . ." Bill opened the car door to the icy blast. *"Come on, Jan,* don't hang around, *leg it. We should have brought our bloody snowshoes!"*

"Cut the jokes, Bill, and move your ass before I freeze to death."

The detectives stomped their feet at the entrance to reception to kick the snow from their shoes.

For a change, the night sister was pretty with a fresh complexion, probably in her mid-forties, but her warm smile said it all. She looked up, then covered her mouth to stifle her laughter as the two snowmen approached the front desk, their noses a close second to 'Coco the clown'.

"Now how I can I be of assistance with the exception of providing you both with a hot cup of coffee?" She pointed to the bubbling coffee percolator and the stack of polystyrene cups.

"You must *be* 'Florence Nightingale'," Bill joked as he poured two coffees while Jan wiped her face with her handkerchief.

"*Boy*, that's some night out! Thanks, Sister." Bill placed his card on the reception desk but not before reading the name tag.

She studied the card for a moment, then looked toward Bill, a question mark on her face.

"Donna, I wonder if you can help us or contact someone who could. You see we are in the process of investigating a case of stolen . . ."

"I see." Donna studied the death certificate. "I'm afraid I don't have the authority to discuss the details and history of a deceased patient. But as this is a police investigation, you are in luck this evening. Because of the bad weather, Professor Cranmer, the director of surgery, is still on the premises, and I'm sure he will oblige. Please bear with me, Lieutenant." She picked up the phone. "Professor, I'm sorry to disturb you, but we have in reception two . . ." She turned to Bill and Jan. "The security guard will escort you to his office."

* * *

"Take a seat, Detectives, now how can I help?" Cranmer looked rather tired; age was catching up. "You caught me at the right time. If it wasn't for this storm, I would be on my way home by now . . . Coffee?"

"No, we're good, Professor, the sister at the front desk already obliged."

"Donna, she's a gem . . . *Now* . . . ?"

Bill produced Newman's death certificate and placed it on Cranmer's desk.

"Let me explain, Professor . . ."

"I see . . . Derek Newman . . . *Hmmmm* . . ." Cranmer sat back in his chair and rubbed his chin. "I certainly remember the Newman case. It was a very sad situation. Derek had been on dialysis for almost three years and on the transplant register for just as long. He was the son of a wealthy New York entrepreneur who had passed away shortly after his mother died and left him a sizable fortune. His partner of several years . . . I'm trying to remember her name . . . *Oh, it doesn't matter*, it will come to me . . . Wanted to tie the knot even though Derek was in poor health. He felt it was unfair to her and would never agree until he found a donor. Unfortunately, his condition suddenly deteriorated, and his liver began to fail, and with only twenty-four hours to live, they finally decided to get married. We held the ceremony here in this hospital. Derek wanted to make sure Janice . . . *Now I remember her name . . . .* Would be comfortable for the rest of her life, 'willing' all of his estate to his new wife. Unfortunately, he passed away the following morning."

Jan was touched by the story. "Such a sad case."

"For every sad case, Detective, there's always a happy one. That's what keeps transplant surgeons like me going . . . It's called hope."

"Thank you for that explanation, Professor. Unfortunately, there are always criminal elements who exploit the situation, and it is our conclusion that whoever had access to Mr. Newman's personal effects was light fingered and stole his driver's license, containing his picture and ID."

"That's a long time ago, Lieutenant, and it could be anyone. Employees come and go. Orderlies, cleaners, doctors . . . I'm afraid it would be an insurmountable task to try and track down the culprit. But, Lieutenant, I have to beg the question, why?" Cranmer leaned forward, his elbows on his desk, staring at the detectives.

"You've given us your time, Professor, and we don't normally discuss criminal investigations, but I feel you deserve an explanation . . . Three nights ago an ex-con, Michael Summers, who is currently out on parole, woke up on the evening of Monday, February 11, in the emergency unit at Huntington Hospital on Park Avenue . . . *Minus one kidney!* He has no memory or recollection how he got there. Our worry is that this may be the start of a syndicate common in India and China, that offer live organs for sale. Desperate terminally ill people, especially the wealthy, will dig deep and only encourage this illicit trade."

Bill suddenly noticed the colour in Cranmer's face change.

"Did I say something that shocked you, Professor?" Bill asked.

Without another word, Cranmer placed a copy of the e-mail in front of the detectives.

"Well, I'll be darned!"

* * *

Cranmer lifted his phone. "Lieutenant, unless I'm mistaken . . . Let me make this call . . . Steven, can you spare me a moment? Yes, in my office, it's important."

Bill turned to Jan and shrugged, as if to say, *So what's next?*

There was a loud knock on the door. "Come in, Steven."

"*Bill Hayden!*" Steven stopped in his tracks upon recognizing his friend.

"*Steven Summers!* I'll say it again . . . *I'll be darned!*" Bill was completely taken aback.

"Lieutenant, it appears you two know one another. Steven is the assistant director of surgery here at the Austin and, of course, my replacement in waiting. I'll let the detectives explain . . . But you had better grab a chair, *Steven . . .*"

* * *

"*That's bizarre,* to the point of almost insane. You mean to tell me that there is every chance that *I* transplanted my father's stolen kidney?"

"*Hold it, Steven!*" Bill cut in. "Let's not jump to premature conclusions. The only way we will know for certain is through a DNA check. The professor has already confirmed that the hospital pathology department has blood samples. If the professor agrees, I'll pass these to NYPD Forensic Pathology Department for type matching against your father's data file."

Steven looked pale and drawn. His acting was so convincing, his hand and footprints in cement at the 'Chinese Theatre' was a have.

Cranmer searched in his drawer again and pulled out the ever-evaporating single malt before placing the bottle on his desk accompanied with four whisky glasses.

Cranmer grinned. "This is only the second time this year that I have had the occasion to justify the partaking of alcohol in my office."

"I'm sorry, Professor, but we are on duty." Bill quickly cut to the chase.

"*Detectives . . .*" Cranmer had a devious smile. "This is for medicinal purposes only."

Bill turned to Jan, to gauge her reaction, who just smiled and shook her head. Bill was like an open book.

'Well, if you put it that way, Professor, I never go against the doctor's orders . . .'

* * *

"Professor, if you don't mind, I'll take my leave . . . I need to urgently get in touch with my sister." Steven already had his cell phone opened.

"Of course, Steven. I'm sure you will be visiting your father tomorrow, so take the morning off."

"Thanks, Professor . . . Thanks, Bill."

* * *

"Well, at least the snow has stopped!" Bill commented as they trudged through ankle-deep snow on their way to the car.

"I suppose we will have to report to Mitchel when we get to the car?"

"You got that one right!"

"What do you make of it, Bill?" Jan asked as she unlocked the door.

"One helluva twist . . . Would make a good TV series, *huh?*"

"So, the next question . . . Where do we go from here?" Bill shrugged his shoulders. "Flip a coin."

* * *

Steven dialed. "Sis, it's me . . . Something has come up. I had a visit from the police . . . *Calm down . . . Calm down.* They don't suspect anything. Listen, I need you to be at my apartment tomorrow before eight. I'll tell you when I see you . . . Don't worry, Cranmer has given us both the morning off . . . Ciao."

CHAPTER 14

You'll be pleased to know that Mr. Summers has been moved from intensive care to an open ward and is recovering remarkably well. Your father must be popular." Dvina smiled. "You and your sister are the third visitors this morning, and its only just turned nine. *Oh,* can you please sign Mr. Summers's visitor's book? The police want to keep track."

"I understand, Sister." Steven picked up the pen, then glanced at his sister. But who are the other visitors? A Robert Clark, parole officer, and Sandra. . . It was too late . . .

"If there's nothing else, Mr. Summers, you can go straight up."

Steven pressed the elevator button. "What floor did the sister say?"

"Six." Sheryl answered as the doors opened. "Steven, I still don't think this is a good idea, and you vowed that you would never contact Father again."

"I told you we have no option, sis, unless you want the bloodhounds on our trail. Just keep calm and play the part."

"So did you notice who were Father's other visitors this morning?"

"I got one, the parole officer, but the other . . . That sister, she's no dummy. Anyhow, it doesn't really matter. It's Bill Hayden we have to worry about. We're almost there . . . Remember and pour on the 'drama queen.'" The elevator chimed.

Jan had picked up Bill, the usual morning ritual, snailing through the morning traffic.

"You weren't slow on that whisky shooter last night in Cranmer's office. *'I never go against a doctor's orders.'* Who did you think you were fooling? I mean it's not even original." Jan was laughing her ass off.

"I didn't notice that your hand was paralysed."

"*Lieutenant*, remember? I don't want to go on report for insubordination. I had no option but to obey an order." Even Bill had to laugh at that remark.

"*Heh . . . Heh . . . Heh . . .* Let's save the semantics for our meeting with Mitchel."

Jan gave a wry smile "Whatever you say, Lieutenant."

*   *   *

The hospital ward was a six-bed unit segregated with railed curtains for privacy when required. Fortunately, only half of the beds were occupied, and Steven and Sheryl had no problem in recognizing their father propped up in bed in the third cubicle to their right. He looked in remarkably good shape when considering, with the exception of the ugly intravenous antibiotic drip and the twin oxygen tubes inserted into each nostrils, he resembled a dragon about to blow flames. Mike, it seemed, was oblivious to his surroundings or even his medical condition, engrossed in a cosy conversation with a middle-aged blonde to the extent of hand holding.

Steven nudged his sister. "*So that's the other visitor!* I gotta hand it to Father, he's only been on the streets for three weeks, and he's dating already. *Maaaan!*" Steven shook his head. "Listen, sis, someone's gotta interrupt Romeo and Juliet, and I hate to tell you, but you have all the acting skills."

"*You gotta be kidding me? You coward!*" But before Sheryl could continue her protest, Mike suddenly looked to his left as if distracted by a movement catching his eye. *Was it really Steven and Sheryl?* His expression was frozen in time.

As for Sheryl? She was always daddy's girl and couldn't control her emotions, rushing to her father's side to give him a kiss on the cheek and a gentle hug.

"Sheryl, honey, are my eyes deceiving bme?"

"It's me, Father . . . It's just that I'm nine years older. But more to the point, *how is the patient feeling?*"

"*Running on one filter?* I'm surprised that I feel no different. In fact, I'm hoping to get discharged in another five days . . . *At least, that's the doc's prognosis.*"

Steven was just standing quietly in the background, absorbing the "play out" and planning his next move.

"I think it's time for me to leave, Mike, I don't want to interrupt a family reunion. I'm sure you have lots to catch up on . . . Besides, I have an afternoon shift at the diner."

"*Don't go just yet, Sandy.*" Mike firmly clasped her hand. "I want you to meet my two children . . . Sandra Watson . . . Sheryl and my oldest, Steven . . . the quiet one." The sarcasm didn't go unnoticed.

Sandra gave an "eyebrow" smile.

"*Steven*, aren't you going to say something?"

"It's a pleasure, Sandra, and, Father, I'm glad to see you are on the road to recovery." Steven gave his father a temperate handshake.

"Sandra, would you believe that my two children are both in the medical profession?"

"*Really!*"

"Steven . . ." Mike begged the return.

"My sister is a qualified and highly respected anaesthesiologists, and I have just been recently appointed to assistant director of surgery . . . We are both with the Austin Hospital."

"*Wow!* I *am* impressed," Sandy reacted. "Mike, you must be so proud."

"*I am . . . I am . . . Believe me!* Steven, do you know that Sandy was with me on the night . . .*"

"No, I didn't . . . Listen, Father, I'll let you rest. I have a surgery at ten this morning, and Sheryl and I will need to make tracks. I'll have a word with the resident doctor before I leave. It was nice to meet you, Sandra. I'll try and visit you again tomorrow, Father. Have plenty of rest and keep an eye on your fluid intake and output."

"Take care, Father, I'm sorry we couldn't stay longer." Sheryl had a tear in her eye as she gave her father a parting kiss.

"Tomorrow then . . . Sandra . . . Ciao."

"Thanks for staying, honey." Mike warmly grasped Sandy's hand as they left.

"Your son, Steven . . . What can I say? He's a strange one." She shrugged.

"Yeah." Mike sighed. "When it comes to sons, it looks like we are both in the same boat, only without a paddle . . ."

* * *

"Hayden, you're shitting me!" Mitchel sat back in his chair, with the "am I hearing right?" look.

"That's how it is, Glen . . ." Bill shrugged. "It's like we've just hit a brick wall."

"Let me get this straight . . . And now we are waiting for the pathology report to match the DNA profile with that of Summers?"

"That's the bottom line . . . But, Glen, even if the DNA matches, let's face it, we're no further forward."

"*Don't remind me.* I'm just waiting for the commissioner and the DA to breathe down my neck if this story leaks. But . . ." Mitchel rubbed his chin and furrowed his brow. "The son's a transplant surgeon and the daughter an anaesthesiologists . . . *Hmmm* . . . Something smacks about this whole deal?"

"Glen, these kids were genuinely upset, *believe me!* Especially Steven . . . I mean *can you just imagine?*"

"I know where you are coming, from, Bill, but . . ." Mitchel was hanging in there.

"Listen, Glen, we checked the visitor list at the Huntington this morning, and both Steven and Sheryl Summers were there first thing this morning to visit their father. But I take your point. In our line of work, nothing surprises me . . . But Glen, I've known these kids since they were knee-high. Besides, what would be their motive?"

Mitchel gave a big sigh. "Yeah, I guess you are right. Listen, don't let me keep you guys, I have the commissioner this morning . . ." Mitchel glanced at his watch. "In about ten minutes . . . Keep me up to speed if anything breaks . . ."

* * *

"Well, that went surprisingly well," Jan commented as she took the chair at her desk.

"Yeah, but I suppose Mitchel has a point, and I can't blame him." Hayden had that look on his face.

"*Come on*, spill the beans."

"It's only a hunch." Hayden lifted the phone. "Greg . . . Hayden here. I'm working on a case, and I want to pass something by you . . . That's great, Jan and I will be there in about fifteen minutes. We are just about to grab a coffee . . . Thanks, Greg, appreciate it."

"*Greg Ellis, the DP manager?*" Jan couldn't hold it.

"Jan, do me a favor and get two cups from the vending machine." *"Is that it?"* She gave Bill the look.

Bill just grinned. "You know what they say about curiosity . . ."

* * *

"Bill . . . Jan . . . Haven't bumped into you two guys for a while. Grab a chair. So why the honour?" Greg joked.

"Greg, I have a problem with a case we are currently investigating and not being a high-tech cop . . ." Bill smiled. "Hell, I'm still learning to send an SMS on my cell."

Ellis laughed. "Same old Bill."

"After thirty years on the force, I'll give you the benefit."

"Get out of it, Hayden! Come on, lay it on the table, and I'll see what I can suggest."

"Where to start?" Bill glanced at Jan. "I'll try and keep it as short as possible. Here's our problem. I need to . . ."

* * *

"Hmmm . . ." Ellis was listening intently to the detective's predicament and Bill's exploratory suggestion. Greg frowned, then gave a sort of cough before endeavouring to explain the so-called "mystique" of the Internet.

"Firstly, Bill, let me explain. The Internet is not like tracking a cell phone where the call or calls can be precisely pinpointed to a location in real time . . . A restaurant . . . street . . . apartment block . . . private house, you name it. Let me start by explaining the term 'IP address' or 'Internet Protocol address.'

If you are both familiar with the abbreviation, stop me." Bill turned to look at Jan, who just shrugged.

"*No?* Okay, then let's start from the beginning, and don't be embarrassed, most users give the same reaction. *Let me see* . . . An Internet Protocol address identifies your computer hardware on a network. Home or personal computers typically connect to the Internet via a router and cable or DSL connection or 'digital subscriber line.' Each piece of hardware has its own unique IP address. This could be a laptop, desktop, and/or router, but here's the spike. When you go to the Internet, be it Hotmail, Google, or whichever mail server you use, the request goes via the router then to an Internet server using a digital subscriber line . . . Or DSL . . . For example, AT&T. The local telecom company then searches for your IP address in the active directory, checking the account information, and if everything is confirmed, proceeds to a firewall, and finally to your mail server . . . Say, Hotmail or Google, giving authority to proceed and subsequently opening the account. So, let's take this person's e-mail address . . . thehood@hotmail.com. Each time he or she sends an e-mail using that address, the location of the hardware can be traced through m the IP address via the Internet server. But here's the problem. He could be using Internet cafes or just moving around, and bear in mind that only approximate locations can be determined. For instance, a high-rise apartment or multilocation in a specific part of town like Chinatown or say, Little Italy, then it's up to your good detective work to track down the user."

"*Hmmm* . . . I see." Bill was visually disappointed, thinking his brainwave was on the money. "Another suggestion . . ."

"Go ahead."

"If this person sends an e-mail again and the recipient returns the communication, keeping the connection open, would this be a solution?"

"Bill, let me put it this way. It's worth a try, but I'm afraid there's another more serious roadblock. You need special dispensation to get the Internet server's permission to provide this personal information, as it's a breach of privacy. However, all is not lost. You can request this information though two channels . . . PRISM surveillance, a secret program run by NASA to collect data from service providers, or under the Patriot Act. Whichever one you use; you will need to lean hard on the commissioner and or the DA to issue a warrant. Time frame? At least a week, if you are lucky. That's the bottom line, Bill. Listen, if you need me to explain this to Mitchel, don't hesitate to lift the phone."

"Thanks, Greg, I owe you one. Don't worry, I'll be on that blower before you can say 'Jack Robinson.' Jan, let's go and approach Mitchel as by the time the message from the tail of the dinosaur reaches the brain, let's just hope there's not another organ snatch from the Hood."

"*You guys.*" Ellis shook his head, laughing at Bill's comment. "Ciao. Bill, glad to be of help."

*   *   *

Bill puffed his lips and gave a look as they stood in the elevator.

"Not a damp squib, Jan . . . But a big disappointment."

"Come on, *get out of it* . . . This e-mail thing would have never crossed my mind, but our big challenge now is convincing Mitchel to move his ass."

"Yeah, he's our next 'firewall.'"

"Going high-tech now, are we?" Jan laughed.

"*Get out of it!* A guy's gotta sound intelligent now and again." The lift doors opened.

"Jan, grab a seat at your desk while I approach Stace."

"Yeah, what's it, Hayden?" Mitchel's PA scowled; his nose buried in a mound of paperwork. His new boss believed in less paperwork and more delegation, and Stace was the fall guy.

"Tell Mitchel I need to meet with him, *it's urgent.*"

"Captain Mitchel to you, Hayden."

"*Go fuck yourself,* just pass the fucking message . . ."

CHAPTER 15

(One Week Later)

"*You two in my office now.*"

The gust of wind from Mitchel's body displacement as he passed the detectives almost blew the papers from Bill's desk.

"What now?" Jan turned to Mike as she rose to her feet.

"So, he's in a foul mood." Bill shrugged. "*What's new?*" He crumpled his coffee cup before chucking it into the trash bucket. "So much for our coffee break, huh?"

"Good morning, Stace, I see you are gainfully employed." Bill was being sarcastic. The paperwork on the PA's desk was increasing by the day, and it couldn't happen to a better guy.

"*Go fuck yourself, Hayden.*"

"*Now, Stace,* that's no way to cuss in front of a lady." Bill gave a scornful laugh.

"I assume you are talking about yourself?" Stace sneered.

Jan couldn't help but laugh. "You asked for that, Mike."

"Listen, who's side are you on anyway?" Mike was showing his annoyance at being outsmarted.

There was a loud rap on the glass panel from Mitchel's office.

"What the hell's keeping you two? On a busman's holiday or something, are we?"

Bill nimbly opened the glass door for Jan to avoid another blast.

"*Coward.*" Jan scowled as she brushed past. *As for Bill,* as usual he could see the funny side, his face smirking with subdued laughter. Mitchel pointed to the empty chairs, a scowl on his face that would scare a grizzly.

"*Hayden*, for the life of me, I can't read you! With you, everything's a big joke. Well, maybe this will wipe the smile from your face . . . I've just had a call from Huntington Hospital's emergency room, and here's the scoop. A Dennis Waters arrived there late last night, and guess what? Yeah, you guessed right! *Minus one kidney.* But here's the line . . . Waters is an ex-con just released on parole, sentenced to five years for white-collar crimes, paroled after three . . . Am I singing from the same sheet or what? *Rings a bell, huh?* Now unless my sixth sense eludes me, Water's kidney would have arrived at the Austin and is now happily functioning in a terminally ill patient suffering from renal failure."

Mitchel took in a huge sigh, then exhaled, screwed up his face, and shrugged his shoulders.

"This is all I fucking need, *believe me!* Excuse my French, Jan."

"I've heard worse."

"*Christ,* would you believe it, Glen." Bill burst in.

Mitchel gave Hayden that look.

"*Err,* I mean, Captain. I specifically instructed Professor Cranmer to call me anytime, day or night, should he receive another e-mail from 'Broken Arrow.'"

Mitchel had to smile. Hayden had a way of using words.

"For your information, Stace is trying to contact him now. *What a frigging mess!*" Mitchel ran his fingers through his hair, showing his frustration. "Take this." Mitchel passed Hayden the slip of paper. "It's not all bad news. I was successful in getting a warrant from Judge Willkie after the DA received clearance from the attorney general to crack the Hood's Internet Protocol address under the Patriot Act. This is the number you contact at AT&T. A Ross Rossini, he's waiting for your call. Now my other problem is both the DA, and the commissioner are breathing down my neck, and I'm not looking forward to report the Hood's latest victim"

Suddenly the phone rang. "Yes, Stace? Put him through." Mitchel covered the mouthpiece with his hand. "Cranmer on the line." He motioned with his other hand for Bill and Jan to leave. "*Professor,* I've been trying to contact you for the last hour . . . I appreciate it . . . Listen, I have just received a call from the Huntington Emergency Room . . . I thought as much . . ."

* * *

"Jan, let's grab a coffee and do a recap before I phone this guy err . . . ?"

"Ross Rossini."

"Italian, huh?"

"With a name like that, he's certainly not Irish!" "You never know." Bill grinned.

"Where to? The cafeteria?"

"Yeah, at least we'll get some peace there!"

* * *

"Sheryl, go home and take some rest, you did good."

"And you, Steven?"

"I want to stay a while longer and check on the progress of the patient. The kidney was almost a perfect match, but you can never underestimate rejection. I'll call you later, sis, most likely in the afternoon. Ciao, bella."

Steven smiled, relieved. Everything had gone without a hitch, but maybe it was time to change his tactics. With Hayden on his case, he had to be extra cautious.

* * *

Bill took a sip of the brew, then turned to Jan, his brow furrowed deep in thought.

"*The motive . . . The motive?*" He repeated the words again and again.

"I agree, Bill, unless we nail the motive, we can't prevent the possibility of yet another reluctant kidney donor."

"*Hmmm . . .*" Bill rubbed his bristle. "Let's step through it a piece at a time . . . Two cons released early on parole. Both high-calibre, successful individuals, white-collar executives. Most likely in good health, both in their late forties to early fifties."

"Carry on. So far so good." Jan was taking notes.

"Summers ruined a young woman's life and that of his family, and not forgetting the murder of an unborn foetus. His victim, a vivacious, young female executive, died childless, her life cut short, the aftermath of her near-death experience from the terrible beating she took. The perpetrator?

He's back on the street after only serving nine years of his fifteen-year sentence. Has justice been done? *No!*"

"So?" Jan was struggling to follow Bill's line of thinking.

"*Now Waters,* he's a different kettle of fish. A 'watch your wallet' accountant with a get-rich Ponzi scheme, paying returns to the investors with their own money. He stole retirees life savings and investment in pensions, ruining hundreds of gullible people, losing their homes, and sending them to an early grave. He goes down for five and out in three . . . Has justice been done? *No!*"

"So you think this surgeon is some kind of vigilante, a Robin Hood robbing the rich to pay the poor?"

"No . . . More like a 'Latter-day Saint,' robbing their organs to heal the terminally sick. A Robin Hood by any other name." "It certainly hangs together," Jan commented.

"Like the use of Hood' in his e-mails . . . Yeah, I think you have something Bill." Jan was still scribbling. "So we get a list of white-collar criminals whose sentences didn't befit the crime and are up for parole."

"Something like that," Bill replied, still rather unsure. "But more importantly, Jan, prevention is better than cure. I had best phone this . . . this . . . ?"

Jan shook her head. *"Ross Rossini from AT&T, remember!"*

Bill grinned as he opened his cell phone. "Just testing." He glanced at the paper and dialled.

* * *

"Captain, your call to Commissioner Green."

"Put him through, Ken . . ."

"Glen, keep it short. I have a meeting scheduled with the mayor in around fifteen. I gather this is not social?"

"I'm afraid it's more bad news, Henry . . . Another organ snatch yesterday evening . . ."

"Fuck! Don't tell me, spare me the agony. This is all I fucking need, panic in the streets. 'The Brooklyn Organ Snatcher.' I can just picture the headlines . . . And I'm up for re-election in two weeks' time. Now you listen to me, Mitchel, if I go down, you're coming with me . . . Cappice?"

"Henry, for fuck's sake, cool it! I have my two best detectives on the case."

"I don't give a shit if you have J. Edgar Hoover on the case . . . I want results and no more of your fucking bull dust, or we'll both be an unemployed statistic . . . *Now I'm fucking busy.* The next time you call, it had better be good news!" The phone went dead.

Mitchel crashed the receiver into the cradle, so much so that the noise even made Stace turn in the outside office.

"Fucking Paddy . . ." Mitchel was fuming at the gills. "He sits on his fat ass all day kowtowing to the mayor and the DA . . . *Fucking politics . . ."*

* * *

"Sis."

"Yes, Steven." Sheryl's sleepy voice was barely audible.

"I'm sorry to break your afternoon snooze . . . Listen, is Nelson there?"

"Of course not. *He has to work, you know!*"

"Then I can talk freely . . . Sis, I have another candidate lined up, a Mario Spillane, just released on parole. Sentenced to ten for fraud with a pyramid scheme, released after six. Never recovered all the monies, leaving venerable people destitute . . . He's, our man. I want to meet with you this evening at Fort Knox to discuss our next victim."

"Steven, why don't we call it a day? You know the story of the bank robber who becomes too cocky after successfully robbing a number of banks . . . He's in jail now. Do you get my message?"

"Sis, all I'm asking is that you give me half an hour of your time to discuss it . . . Seven then?"

"*I must be out my fucking mind* . . . Seven then . . . Now, if it's not too much to ask, *let me get some fucking sleep.*"

*   *   *

"Ross Rossini?"

"Yes, how can I help you?"

"Lieutenant Bill Hayden, NYPD Homicide."

"*Bill,* I've been waiting for your call. I know you are anxious, so get right down to it. I traced the IP address from the hardware used to send the e-mail through the Hotmail server tracking the e-mail address thehood@hotmail.com, used yesterday evening. Now I can't pinpoint the exact location, but it was sent from a storage facility at Fort Knox Self-Storage, 20 Bloomfield Street, five minutes from West Street, leading to Pier 50 on the waterfront. Guys, that's the best I can do."

"*The best!*" Bill was beside himself. "Ross, that's music to my ears."

"Listen, I have that IP address on a red flag, so if it comes up again, I'll immediately get on the blower."

"Thanks, Ross, what can I say . . . Ciao . . ."

"Somebody up there likes me." Bill looked up at the ceiling and made the sign of the cross.

"I thought you weren't a practicing Catholic." Jan couldn't help but laugh at Bill's antics.

"*I am now . . .*"

*   *   *

"Well, don't keep a lady in suspense . . . What's the scoop?"

"A unit at Fort Knox Self-Storage."

"The one on Pier 50 on Bloomfield?"

"That's the one!" Bill was smiling like he had just won the lottery.

"Now the three-million-dollar question . . . *Which unit?*" Jan asked.

"By the size of that facility, I've passed there a few times, there must be at least three hundred units. But listen, it's the ideal solution for a secret *M*A*S*H* hospital."

"So where do we start?"

"This is going to be a long day, but we gotta start somewhere, and the first thing we do is to phone the manager of Fort Knox and throw ourselves at his mercy, as he may ask for a warrant to divulge personal information on his customers. People get careless when they rent things, like use their credit card or their real name. Directory inquiries please . . . Can you give me the number for . . ."

* * *

"Fort Knox Self-Storage, Crombie speaking."

"Can I speak to the manager?"

"Speaking, how can I help you?"

"I'll be as brief as I can, Mr. Crombie."

"Derek."

"Eh, Derek . . . I'll get straight to the point. My name is Bill Hayden, Lieutenant Bill Hayden, NYPD Homicide. I need a big favor, Derek. It's like this . . ."

"I really appreciate your cooperation. I'll stand by for that fax . . . Thanks again."

* * *

"That was easier than I thought. Listen, Jan, a fax is arriving any minute from Derek Crombie, the manager at Fort Knox. He's agreed to provide me with a list of current customers at the Bloomfield site. I don't know what we'll find, but a name may jump out."

Bill gulped the last of his coffee.

"Let's get outta here. Something tells me we're gonna have our work cut out tonight."

* * *

"Your estimate was correct, Bill." Jan was scanning the mound of names. "Hell, there must be at least two fifty to three hundred names here. What are we looking for?"

"Any name that sounds professional, like a surgeon or doctor, single them out. It's a long shot, and it may boil down to the old-fashioned stakeout 24/7, but it's worth a try. We'll split the list down the middle."

"Then I'd better go get some coffee for the long haul."

"Good idea, Sergeant."

"What's with this sergeant stuff . . . *Oh, I get it!* Pulling rank so I pay." "Your detective work's getting better all the time, Sergeant . . ."

* * *

"*Bingo!*" Jan yelled suddenly.

In two seconds, Bill was at her desk, staring over her shoulders at the red circled name.

"Bill, do you recognize this name?" Jan was pointing with her finger.

"*Do I!* Derek Newman, I'll be darned. That's our man's fatal mistake . . . What did I tell you, Jan? Unit number 14***." "Do we move on it now?" Jan asked.

"No, the operating room is one thing, but without the surgeon, it's a loser."

Then Bill thought for a moment.

"To be safe, here's the deal. We get our asses down there like now and stay outta sight for however long it takes until this pimpernel 'Newman' shows up . . ."

CHAPTER 16

"I hope you have brought your cologne with you." Jan cast that grin.

"What kinda dumb question is that?" Bill asked as Jan drove into the drive-through at Burger King.

"*I'm serious!* God knows how long I will be trapped with you in car. It could be days, and you're not short in the gas department."

"What's this, true confessions? After all these years . . ." Bill touched his heart, trying to hide his laughter. "I'm mortally wounded.

relationship will never be the same." He couldn't control himself any longer and burst into laughter.

"Don't you think I don't know when you roll down the fucking window in the freezing cold after passing a sneaky fart."

Bill was now cracking up and couldn't control himself.

"And don't give me that good detective work shit!"

"I tell you what. To make up for all these years of torture and the damage to your nostrils, I'll buy the burgers."

"Never mind the burgers You should recommend me for a commendation for courage above and beyond the call of duty. Now they were both in harmonious laughter.

Bill cut it. "*Hey,* let's get serious. We have a big decision to make."

"And what might that be, may I ask?" Jan asked as she pulled up at the server.

"*The burgers* . . . What else?"

* * *

"It's just after six, Jan, I think we had better make roads."

"Yeah, I'm finished, but I gotta go to the ladies' room first. The last thing I want is to get caught short in this weather in the Fort Knox car park."

"Then I'll wait for you in the car out front."

"*Christ, Bill,* are you some kind of camel? Don't you want to go?" Bill laughed. "It's easier for us guys. I can always go behind at tree." "*In this chill!* Aren't you scared of frostbite?" Jan was with the jokes.

"Mountaineers describe the sensation as a 'Frosty Johnson' or the falling off of the male organ, but at my age, the problem is finding it!"

Jan burst into laughter. "I'll put that one in my book for the stag night, but more importantly, the restroom . . ."

* * *

The car park was eerie and deserted. At six thirty in the evening in winter, it was pitch black with the exception of the scattered lights in the parking bays, casting shadows that would make an excellent backdrop for a horror movie. In fact, it was so cold with the biting wind from the Hudson, *even the seagulls were walking!*

"Where to park, Bill?" Jan had slowed to a snail's pace.

Bill pointed. "Over there, on the far corner where those trees are. It will provide some cover. Don't worry, I have a pair of night binoculars in the glove compartment . . ."

* * *

"Do you think this guy will show? It's coming up for seven," Jan asked, concerned.

Bill exhaled. "Stakeouts always seem to drag, and your guess is as good as mine . . . *Hold it!* Over there, Jan . . . *To the right.*" Bill was already focusing his binoculars. "An old heap and a black BMW SUV have just entered the car park."

"Yeah, I can just make them out."

"They certainly look suspicious, like they are doing a reconnaissance. Hold it, Jan, they are heading this way. Get your head down below the dash."

"*Are you fucking serious!*"

"Cut the comedy, this is serious. You can explain it to Chris later . . . In the line of duty, *remember.*"

The headlights of Steven's Fairlane lit up the unmarked police car as he stopped for a moment to double-check before pumping the brakes twice to signal to his sister that the coast was clear, then continued to proceed to the other end of the car park below the remaining trees.

"It's okay, Jan, they have gone now, you can come up for air." "I should be so lucky." Jan gave an "emphysema" cough.

"*Okay . . . Okay.* I get the message." Bill was busy with the night sights.

"So, what's the scene?" Jan asked anxiously.

"Two people . . . Can't tell male or female. They are both wearing black hoodies. It may just be a coincidence, like two people here at the wrong time, but I gotta admit, they are acting more than suspicious. Let's just wait and see if they take the cheese."

*   *   *

"*Bingo!* We got our man. *Unit 14.* We didn't have to wait too long after all." Bill's eyes were glued to the binoculars.

"Have they gone inside?" Jan was on edge.

"Yeah, they have entered through the side door . . . Too quick for me to get a glimpse inside."

"Is it time?" Jan asked, her adrenaline rising.

"Yeah, let's take 'em. Check your firearm. Something tells me this may not be a walk in the park."

"Locked and loaded."

"Then hit the gas. No siren, I don't want to spook them."

The screech of the tires and the smell of burning rubber sent the seagulls flying, their wings beating frantically as they fled the scene.

*   *   *

"Steven, I didn't like the look of that car at the far side of the car park." Sheryl pulled back her hood.

"It did seem unusual, but I checked it out. Sheryl, for Christ's sake, calm down." Steven was showing his annoyance.

"So, what's with the big meeting? Because I'm warning you, Steven, if it's doing another trick . . . *I'm out.* It's just too dangerous, and you are getting too cocky."

"Come on, sis, without you, I will have to close down our kidney transplant program." Steven had that silly grin on his face as if it was all a big joke.

"*Christ, Steven*, this is a game to you, *isn't it?* Like you are God with the power of life and death . . . *What was that?*" Sheryl suddenly stopped in the middle of her plea bargain.

"Sheryl, for a moment there, you scared the crap out of me. You're just imagining things . . . I didn't hear anything."

"I tell you, that sounded like a car screeching to a halt outside our unit."

You could have heard a pin drop as they both stopped the conversation and listened. The loud bang on the roller door suddenly shattered the silence.

"*Police . . . Police . . .* Open up and raise your hands above your heads . . . *Now!* Do you hear me? I'll give you one minute before we break the door down."

The detectives unholstered their semiautomatics, clasping the grips with both hands, arms rigid straight in front.

"*Steven, it's the police.* My god, what are we going to do?" Sheryl was already on the verge of hysterics.

"It's over, Sheryl, there's nothing we can do. The game is over."

Steven shrugged, his face now an ashen gray, his whole life flashing in front of him. From being the hunter, he was now the hunted, and he dejectedly began to slowly raise the roller shutter.

"Cover me, Jan!" Bill yelled as the light from inside pierced the darkness, momentarily blinding him.

"I'm right behind you, Bill. I've got a bead on them."

"Hands above your head . . . *Above your head* . . . Do you hear me?" Bill screamed. "And don't even sneeze."

The two figures were a sorry sight, standing there scared out of their minds and shaking in fear, their hands above their heads reminiscent of Vietcong prisoners of war.

Bill stood for a moment in disbelief, slowly lowering his weapon. There, in front of his eyes, was a fully equipped hospital operating room but the biggest shock of all—*lo and behold, Steven and Sheryl Summers!*

"What the fuck!" Bill couldn't control his anger. "I should have twigged. It was too obvious to be true. You and your sister, the perfect surgical team." Bill was shaking his head. "Why? I ask you why, Steven? I've known you since you were a kid."

"Bill, just give a moment to try and explain."

"*Explain!* You broke the fucking law; *how do you explain that?*"

"Bill, just gimme some slack before you cut me loose. White-collar criminals, their sentences never befit the crime. They get a slap on the wrist and are back on the streets within five to ten, supposedly paying their debt to society, and just think of the lives they have ruined. I decided I would level the playing field and for a change *rob them* to heal the terminally ill. It was *real* payback time. No one died, and two people on death row were given a second chance in life. *Is that so wrong?*"

"I can understand, Waters, but why your father?"

"After what he did to my mother, and don't forget the death of Tony. He was my first choice."

"So, a modern-day Robin Hood, huh? Rob the rich to pay the poor, only you were dealing in human organs to heal the sick. Well, you ain't no Robin Hood, and I'm not the Sheriff of Nottingham. *Are you both out of your fucking minds?* You broke the law, and you are lucky you are not facing a murder charge. A long prison sentence . . . Never to practice medicine again, and with your surgical skills, an inconceivable loss for the very patients you are trying to save."

"Shall I cuff them, Bill, and read their rights?" Jan was in limbo. Why was Bill taking so long to arrest them?

"I've been a police officer for over thirty years, and I've never broken the law, but then there is always a first time. Steven, I agree and sympathize with your sentiments and criticism of our penal system, but it's like bubble gum—the flavours nice when you are chewing it, but once you spit it out, it's forgotten. Many times, I've sent criminals down to be released on parole too early by the 'do-gooders,' only to commit another crime, another day. I have nothing but the highest respect for the work you both do, but this is a 'broken arrow,' so here's the deal, take it or leave it. You leave this place squeaky clean. No fingerprints or any clue that could lead to your arrest, and if you swear on the Bible, you will never do this again. I'll turn a blind eye . . . One more thing, leave the lights on."

"*Bill, are you serious?*" Jan couldn't believe her ears. Was she hearing things?

Bill turned to Jan. "For once in my police career, I'm letting the honest crooks go . . . Now let's get to the car.

* * *

Bill was back on the binoculars, the Pontiac now out of sight.

"I'll give them half an hour before I phone for backup."

"I hope you know what you are doing, Bill. If young Summers fucks up, this could be the end of an illustrious police career, not to mention your pension."

"Let me worry about that, Jan. Besides, I pull rank, *remember?*"

Jan sighed, shaking her head. *What's the use*, she thought? Bill, as usual, was as stubborn as a mule, and she would just be wasting her breath.

"Jan, they're shutting shop and leaving now, I'll phone in for backup." Bill picked up the radio phone.

"Lieutenant Hayden. I need two black and whites. This is a red alert."

"The address, Lieutenant?"

"Fort Knox Storage, 20 Bloom . . ."

* * *

"Glen, for Christ's sake, think positive!" Bill's hackles were up. "Yeah, I know who I'm speaking to . . . Listen, Jan and I have had a shit of a night, and we are as disappointed as you, but at least we shut down the operating room . . . Okay, so maybe we jumped the gun, but we could clearly see the lights shining from below the door, and I made the call . . . So maybe they were watching . . . How hell do I know? Yeah, forensics and CSI are here now . . . You'll have my report on your desk first thing in the morning."

* * *

Bill was more than quiet as he concentrated on his one-finger typing. So he was lying to his back teeth; whatever, he felt he had made the right decision.

"Can I speak, boss?" Jan broke the ice.

"Yeah," Bill answered, his head down, fingers punching the keyboard.

"You look as if you have more than that report on your mind. I mean the way you dressed down Mitchel last night, like you had made up your mind that you were taking no more of his shit and fuck the consequences!"

Bill shrugged. "Every dog has his day. I'm getting too old for this shit."

Bill thumped the keyboard with his forefinger one last time. *"That's it!"* He keyed the laser printer then finally looked up.

"Jan, I really appreciate how you supported me last night. I guess they broke the mould when they made you. I have something to say to Mitchel, and I want you to be there. Shall we?" He pointed to the captain's office.

Bill collected the sheets from the printer and stacked them up. He turned and grinned. "Don't look so down, Jan, this is my finest hour." Bill had an unusual spring in his step as he walked the walk.

"Hey! Where do you think you're are going?"

"Fuck off, Stace." Bill opened Mitchel's door unannounced.

"Listen, I'll call you back, Henry, something has just come up." Mitchel slammed the phone down, his eyes blazing. "What the hell do you think you are doing, Hayden, barging into my office as you feel like?"

"Close the door, Jan." Bill ignored Mitchel's outcry. "My report on yesterday evening's sting and my letter of resignation." Bill placed the papers in front of Mitchel. "Glen, I have completed over thirty years of service, and I'm calling in my retirement, on full pension, effective immediately." Mitchel was taken aback and for once lost for words.

"Eh . . . Err . . . Bill, sit down." His tone drastically changed. "Why don't you think this over? If I have given you the wrong impression that I have something against you . . . Listen, we can sort things out."

"I've nothing against you, Glen, you have a job to do . . . It's just my time."

"Bill, you are one of my finest detectives . . ."

"Don't try, Glen, I've made up my mind. At my age, there's more to life than getting calluses on my ass sitting at stakeouts. Do me a favor, Glen, and process my papers as soon as possible. Now if there's nothing else." Bill rose to leave, then suddenly about-faced. "There's one more thing . . . I'm recommending Detective Sergeant Martin to be promoted to lieutenant . . . She deserves it."

PART 14

The Final Curtain

"Speech . . . Speech . . . On your feet, Hayden."

Bill's retirement party was in full swing. He had commandeered the NYPD club in the Bronx for his "swan song," the bar and lounge theirs for the night, and when cops get together, anything goes. Bill had thrown five grand into the pot for finger food and free booze; after that it's on the tab.

"Come on, Bill." Jan gave him a more-than-gentle nudge.

Bill rose to his feet, but not before finishing the last of his scotch. He needed 'Johnnies' courage.

"*Ah . . . Hmmm . . .*" Bill's throat clearing had the effect, and the booze hyped crowd went suddenly quiet.

"Guys, what can I say but thank you for turning up at my retirement party."

"Are you serious Hayden? It's the free booze."

There was a burst of instant laughter. "That's gotta be Lucas." Bill laughed.

"After thirty years in the force, Bill, what are you gonna do now?" "Hey, I thought this was my speech, Johnson."

Bill's comment brought another burst of laughter.

"But to answer your question. Chris . . . I have a belated date with, shall I put it, a beautiful Latino in Buenos Aires."

"A man or a woman?" That literally brought the house down.

"Didn't you know I'm out of the closet?" Bill couldn't resist. "That question could only come from Menzies . . . Stick with it, Tom, and audition for the X Factor. There's always the wooden spoon." The crowd were now in stitches. "But seriously, guys, it's not an easy decision after thirty years of service . . . I was just my time. I'm heading into the second and final stage of my life, a new country and a new partner . . . And no, Chris, I hate to disappoint you, but her name is Mona."

"Why Hayden you old dog . . . After all these years." It was Brown.

"Nine years to be exact, Dan. I'm sure you remember her. I don't like long goodbyes, but I'll miss your ugly mugs, and of course, I'll never forget my ex-partner, Tony Perino."

"*Hear . . . Hear . . .*" There was a resounding cheer.

"I'm sorry, guys, but I have to call it a night. I have a plane to catch tomorrow evening, and I don't want to keep a beautiful signorina waiting. I'll send each of you an invitation to the wedding . . . Oh, and the last guy standing, please switch off the lights."

That comment brought the house down with lots of handshakes and back slapping as Bill and Jan pushed their way through an overindulged crowd . . .

* * *

"How do you feel, Bill, after all that?" Jan gunned the motor of the Pontiac.

"You didn't have to leave, you know."

"Are you serious, Bill? When these guys go over the top and there's a female cop in their company . . . Well, you can add two and two."

'So?"

"So?" Bill had an idea what was coming.

"About your budding romance with the beautiful Mona?"

"I met her during my stint in Brazil. We had something going, then after I was divorced, we kept in touch, and one thing led to another . . . You'll come and visit, won't you?"

"Wild horses couldn't stop me . . . Bill, I'm really happy for you . . . *I mean it!*"

"I know you do, Jan, but here's where I get off." Bill had reached his apartment.

"Then can I chauffeur you to the airport tomorrow?"

"No, as much as I appreciate your offer, one farewell is enough. Bye, Jan, I promise I'll keep in touch."

"I'm gonna miss you, you big heel." Jan's eyes were full. "Bye, Bill, and good luck and lots of happiness, you deserve it . . ."

* * *

Bill stood for a moment, watching the bright red taillights of the Pontiac disappear into the evening darkness. There were lots of thoughts passing through his mind, and he could just picture Mona standing there at the airport. *God, she is beautiful, and I'm so lucky and to get second chance at my age . . .* He smiled at the thought as he slipped his security card into the slot.

The lock gave a loud click as the door opened. In his captivated thoughts, Bill had failed to notice the figure of a man lurking in the shadows. Too late . . . The familiar feel of cold steel pressing into the back of his neck didn't need painting.

"Don't think about it, Hayden, and open that fucking door now, or there will be a large hole straight through to your mouth. Do you get the picture?"

"Whoever you are, you are making a big mistake. I'm a police officer."

"Do you think I fucking don't know." He pushed Hayden so hard, he almost smashed his face against the opposite wall in reception.

"Turn around nice and easy, and don't try anything stupid."

"I'm not armed." Bill held his hands above his head as he turned to face his assailant.

"Well, I'll be darned! Jake Monroe, so when did you hit the streets?"

"For your information, today. It's been a long fifteen, and I've thought about you and that partner of yours every day. Too bad about Perino, but it couldn't have happened to a better guy."

"So what's this, a revenge party, Jake?"

"Shut your big mouth, Hayden. I spent fifteen years in the can because of you and that crazy Italian, and I'm now I'm gonna take fifteen years off your life. You promised me if I blew the whistle, you could cut a deal . . . Twelve months to two years maximum. You fucking conned me, and I went down big. Can you imagine the life of a whistle-blower in the can? I've been fucked from New York to Santa Fe. I'll never have a decent crap again."

Bill could see the Browning semiautomatic wavering in Monroe's hand. He was scared, but could Bill talk him out of it?

The Browning kicked twice. The first copper nose thudded into Bill's chest cavity, the impact throwing him against the wall. The second went through his lungs, drowning Bill in his own blood as he slid to the floor and rolled onto his side.

"The debt's paid in full, Hayden. I've taken back the fifteen years you owe me." Monroe was gone in a flash.

Bill tried to move, but he was choking in his own blood. And the cold, that terrible cold . . . Suddenly his cell rang, and with the last of his ebbing strength, he pulled it from his blood-soaked pocket.

"Bill, darling, I've been waiting for your call to get your flight details. Bill, are you there, darling? Bill, do you hear me, is something wrong? Bill . . . Bill, please speak to me . . . Please, Bill, I'm scared . . . Bill . . ."

The cell phone rattled to the floor, submerged in a pool of warm blood. Bill's eyes glazed over; his breathing now stopped. For Bill, this was his final curtain.

To be the one who makes the difference, the one who dares to dream, how do we surpass our limits to find the strength we never knew we had? Sadly, we are all living in a goldfish bowl, passing time watching trains go by all of our lives.

*   *   *

*'If you want a happy ending, it depends where
you stop the story'. 'Orson Welles'.*